THE FETTERS OF FATE

THE BLADEBORN SAGA, BOOK FIVE

T. C. EDGE

COPYRIGHT

Previous book in the series:

The Song of the First Blade (Book 1)
Ghost of the Shadowfort (Book 2)
An Echo of Titans (Book 3)
The Winds of War (Book 4)

CONTENTS

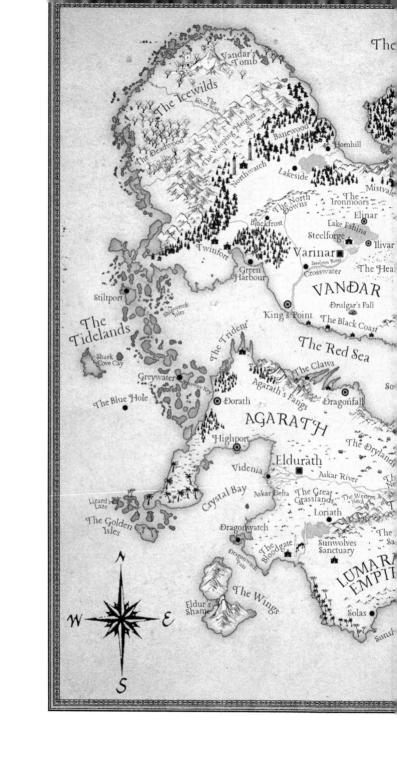

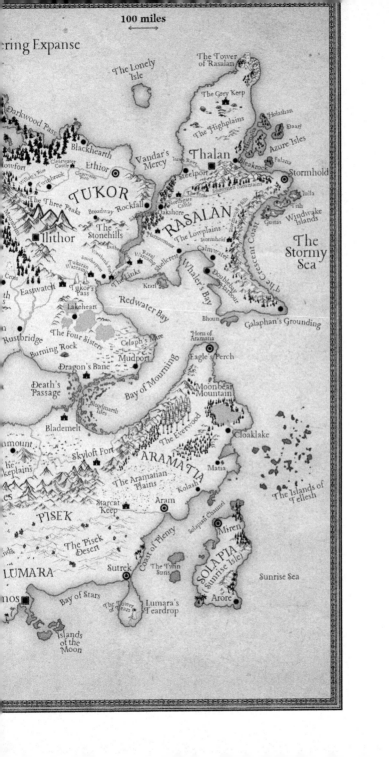

PROLOGUE

The Moon Queen of Lumara sat alone on the beach, brushing an ornate ivory comb through her long silver hair as she looked out over the bright, turquoise waters that glittered off the Bay of Stars.

It had always been silver, her hair, ever since her birth in Lumara's hands, and for that Lumo was grateful. When Ilith had aged, his golden curls had started to go to grey, and even Thala the Far-Seeing Queen's locks had lost some of their lustre.

But not mine, Lumo of the Light thought, as a warm wind passed across her luminous cheek. *I was silver-haired to start with, and I am silver-haired still.*

She was old, though, in other ways. The bitter sting of mortality had stolen some of her *light,* and there were wrinkles about her eyes and mouth, and aches between her joints. Once before, she would ride her cats and wolves and bears for long hours at a time without feeling any soreness the next day. That was no longer so. "I grow old," she said, to her pack. "Perhaps that is why she comes? To tell me how much time I have left? To tell me it's time to die."

Her pack were all around her, lounging on the sand, or further up the beach where it gave way to softer grasses. Her youngest starcat, Salania, was stretched out beside her, purring happily as she rolled onto her long black back, splaying the soft pads of her forepaws. Lumo smiled and gave her a rub on the belly, and of course that only made Manataro jealous, the great golden sunwolf loping over at once to nuzzle at the side of her neck, demanding attention.

"So *needy,* Manataro," she chuckled, giving him what he craved: a good deep scratch at his long black mane, though even that took more effort than it used to, thick as the fur was there.

The sunwolf opened his jaws and gave an enormous yawn, then slumped down beside her, causing the sand to billow and stir. Behind her, Lisillia and Tanotto and Preela were all lazing, with over a dozen other cats and wolves scattered here and there. Further off sat the twins, Gatosh and

I

Latosh, the huge white moonbears each staring out in a different direction, ever-wary of attack. In some places their vigilance might be warranted, but not here, east of Lumos, her city. *We are well guarded,* she thought to them, trying to get the twins to relax. It was, as ever, a losing cause. Moonbears were not built to relax, Mother Lumara had long ago decreed.

The morning was growing old when Lumo finally saw her, the ship emerging on the horizon, a spec at first quickly taking shape as it sailed directly her way. Queen Thala had chosen the place, and the day, and as ever she'd been right. *She has probably seen this meeting already,* Lumo knew. *She has watched it all unfold within the Eye and only needs to repeat the script.*

Her pack all watched the ship draw near, ears pricked up, eyes fixed and staring, silver and gold, bronze and black. With her own two eyes Lumo of the Light would not see half so well, but her pack gave her great vision. Through their eyes she could see, through their noses she could smell, through their ears she could hear the world around her more acutely than even Varin in his prime. Such was the benefit of bonding a large pack. Spread them far and wide, and the world was hers to sense and feel.

The ship was a galley, beautifully constructed, slim and lean with a great white swan for a figurehead, its long neck arched and wings furled back. That made the Moon Queen smile. Thala had always very much liked her swans. The ship moved as easily as any vessel had any right to, captained and crewed by the Seaborn of her blood. *My favourite,* Lumo thought. She had spent time with Varin's boastful Bladeborn and Ilith's humble Forgeborn and Eldur's fierce Fireborn in the past, but she liked none so much as Thala's Seaborn, with their easy laughter and love for song and the way they were so at one with the water.

The winds were soft and warm, filling the gold and blue sails. Lumo remained sitting, cross-legged, until she saw the ship draw close, wondering if they might drop anchor in deeper water and lower a swan-skiff to bear the queen hence. Instead she heard a call - detected by Lisillia who had the most sensitive hearing - for the oars to be manned, the sails furled, and the galley to be driven right up to the beach.

It came ashore with a scrape of wood on sand, and at once a plank stairway was lowered from its decks so Thala could step easily to the strand. The Far-Seeing Queen looked as regal and beautiful as ever, radiant in her dotage, bright with wisdom. She flowed toward her in that ethereal way, walking alone, smiling all the while.

No words were shared until the two had clasped hands, and put their lips to one another's cheeks, left and right, kissing. Then Lumo turned and led her guest along the beach, arm in arm, her pack walking attendance around them, and said, "You came, Thala," with a playful smile. "I wondered if for once you might have gotten something wrong."

"I get many things wrong, lovely Lumo," Thala replied, in that smooth and mellifluent voice of her. "But *Rasalan* does not. What I see in his Eye is truth. And I have been blessed to see your beautiful face many times these last long years."

"You are far too kind," Lumo chuckled, moving along in her robes of silver, beside the queen in sun yellow and ocean blue. "But I know what I see when I look at my reflection in the water. An old face, not a beautiful one."

"Old can still be beautiful. Has the moon lost its luminance after all these years? No. And so it is with you, its queen. You will grow more lovely until your dying day."

My dying day. "And is that why you've come, Thala? To give me a last goodbye, as you did with Ilith before his passing?"

Her pause was telling, though she only said, "I come to speak with my old friend. To share in her light, and her warmth and her glow, and see the wonders of her thriving country. There are places and people that I would like to visit. Places and people that are. And places and people that are *yet to be.*"

Lumo could not help but smile. Ever had the Far-Seeing Queen been mysterious to the rest of them, with her cryptic ways and unwieldily wisdom. *Varin's opposite,* the Moon Queen reflected. The great Steel King had not been short of wit, but when it came to talking, he preferred a plainer path. *Never did a man speak so forthrightly. And never has a woman been so infuriating,* she thought.

They talked for a time as they walked, discussing matters both past and present, reflecting and reminiscing on times long gone. Soon they came to a clutch of palm trees where Lumo had prepared refreshments; cakes and colourful fruits, sweetwines and ports, delicacies and treats found only here, in the far south, that she knew the Queen of Rasalan enjoyed. Lumo poured the wine herself - she had brought no servants with her today - and they sat in the shade beneath the fronds as the cats and wolves found snug spots to lie down, yawning and stretching and grooming themselves beneath the trees.

"I forget how beautiful they are," Thala said, observing them as she took a sip of sweetwine from the hills of Azore. "How many do you keep in your pack these days, Lumo?"

"Two dozen, since Salania came of age. Eleven starcats and eleven sunwolves and the twins, Gatosh and Latosh. Sola keeps a similar number, if you're wondering, though he favours the wolves over the cats, of course."

"Of course." Thala smiled. "And how is he? Well, I hope?"

"Brooding," Lumo told her. "As was always his way. And growing old, like I am." She tasted her wine. "But we have had peace for a while now, which is good. A transitory peace, I am sure it will be, but it's pleasant while it lasts."

The Far-Seeing Queen nodded, saying nothing. *She has probably seen a dozen wars between my people and my brother's in the coming centuries,* Lumo thought. They had broken into two lines when Lumara left them, the Lumosi and Solasi Lightborn, ever at quarrel with one another. It was the great grief of Lumo's long life to have them walking these different paths, one of vengeance and hate, the other of peace and love. That Thala could not tell her of all she'd seen made these meetings of theirs difficult. Once before it had been easier, yet over the last few decades the Queen of

Rasalan had grown more insular, more mournful, burdened by all the horrors she'd glimpsed in her master's all-seeing Eye. She still smiled, of course, and spoke in that calm and reassuring way of hers, yet behind her eyes Lumo sensed a great duty in the Far-Seeing Queen.

And is that why she has come? To give me a duty of my own?

Thala took another sip of her wine, as the big male starcat Jambo loped over to sit beside her. "Jambo, you've grown so big," the queen said, giving him a scratch beneath the chin. A purr rumbled out of him. "You were just a starkitten when I saw you last."

"You remember his name," Lumo observed. "It is remarkable that you recognise him, wise queen."

"I remember them all," Thala said, smiling down at the starcat. "Tell me, Lumo. Do your children keep packs of their own, as you and your brother do?"

"Smaller ones, yes. The light weakens down the line, Thala, I'm sure you know. My grandchildren can only bond four or five at a time before they begin to become overwhelmed. And *their* children and grandchildren even less. In time I am quite sure that my Lightborn will be blessed only by a single bond." She watched Thala's eyes, and saw that it was true.

"The world is expanding, Lumo," the Far-Seeing Queen said, in that far-reaching way. "In the growth of our populations, the bloodlines will thin, and thus will the gifts within. This is only natural. When I peek through the pupil I glimpse a world most changed from what we have now. In time the luminous animals of this land will grow wilder, and more dangerous, and any Lightborn seeking to secure the bond will need to display great courage in the act." She looked out to the twin moonbears, sitting on a rise up the beach. "The bears will become especially rare, and Moonriders rarer still. Most who attempt to bond them will perish, but each will be a noble death."

Lumo had not expected such candour from her. "Do the restraints upon you weaken, Thala? You are rarely so open as this."

"I am old, as you are. In the short time I have left, I want to prepare for a better world. Great Rasalan has instructed me, Lumo, and guided me, as ever he did. There is much I cannot tell you, of course, but…there are some things that *must* be shared, lest they will not be done."

Then this is why she's come. "What is it you need from me, wise queen?"

"Your guidance," Thala said. "And your *light*. There will come a time, millennia from now, when this world we have built together will falter, and threaten to fall. The outcome of this lies beyond my sight, Lumo. Whether Rasalan refuses to show me, or does not know himself, I cannot say. There is much I cannot say, in truth, and much I cannot know, and yet…yet…"

Lumo reached out and took her hand. "You are shivering, Thala."

"I shiver for what the world will become. For the terrible count of death that will follow. When the forces of darkness rise, those of light must come forth to meet them. So it always was, and so it will always be. Ilith, he…" She breathed out, as though wanting to say more, wanting to tell her something, but checked herself. She shook her head. "I cannot speak of this. I risk betraying the bonds of my oath and promise, and going beyond my bounds. Already I fear I risk too much, but much must be risked, Lumo, if the people of the future are to prevail."

She had never seen Thala so fearful and frank. *What has she seen? What tortures her so?* "You spoke of guidance, Thala. What wisdom can *I* give *you*?"

"Much and more, my sweet friend. Yet this guidance I speak of pertains to a journey. I wish for you to escort me to the northeast of your lands, south of the mountain where the moonbears live."

"The Everwood?" Lumo asked, confused. "You wish to see Aramatia's Twelve Trees?"

"I wish to see them, yes. And to meet the people there. They are a simple folk, is that true?"

"A holy folk," Lumo said. "Worshippers of Aramatia, raised by her to tend the trees." She paused in thought, and turned her eyes to the south, out across the sparkling sea. "I suppose you know that her eagle is gone. Calacan. He flew out across the Sunrise Sea two years ago and has not been seen since. I fear he has perished, Thala, in searching for her, and other worlds. He has never been gone this long."

Something passed the eyes of Thala, the Far-Seeing Queen. "Calacan is not yet dead, Lumo. I...have seen him, in the Eye. Seen his light, against the dark. In time the eagles of his bloodline will take up residence in the Everwood trees, drawn to them as a child is drawn to the skirts of his mother. They will find comfort there, during Calacan's absence, in these great trees of Aramatia's making. And these holy people, this simple folk... in time they and the eagles will learn to live in harmony. In time they will learn to *bond*."

A frown twisted at the Moon Queen's ageing brow. "But they are not Lightborn, these people. What bonds they build will be weak, Thala, as a man and his horse, a bond of friendship and duty, but no more. They will not share sense and sight and sound, as we do with our bonded packs."

"Lumo," Thala said, taking her hands, holding them softly. "I asked for your guidance, great queen, *and* for your *light*." A look of sadness, and need, was etched into the Sea Queen's eyes. "I am sorry, my old friend, but there is a sacrifice I must ask you to make."

1

Elyon

3,280 Years Later…

In the cold gloomy feast hall of Oakpike Castle, men spoke in lament, telling stories of the dead.

A single hearth burned low and sombre, and there were half a dozen torches clasped in iron sconces on the walls, but all the same, it was dimly lit and dreary. *A place of loss and mourning*, Elyon Daecar thought. *A place weighed heavy with defeat.*

Nearby, Sir Barnibus was telling a tale about Lancel. "I remember the time he chased a pack of wolves from the carcass of a deer," he said, as others stood around to listen, or sat at the benches clasping their horns of ale. "He was only six or seven at the time, but even then he was brave. He ran at them with a stick, shouting, and they scattered away into the trees. I remember how his father had scolded him for his recklessness, yet I just stood there, shaking my head, wishing I could be so bold." He smiled sadly, his eyes misty with tears. "He proved his courage again…out there on the battlefield. Lancel….he was never frightened of a fight, not even when the odds were against him. I hope you hear that, Steel Father," he said, turning his eyes to the vaulted oak ceiling above, half hidden amidst the swirls of pipe smoke and gloom. "I hope you were watching when he fought Malathar and Vargo Ven. He…he fought well, and with honour. He should be close to you, my lord. He's earned that, for what he did. He's earned a good place at your Table."

"Hear hear," called Sir Rikkard Amadar, banging his fist against a heavy oak table. Other men echoed the call, as Rikkard raised his drinking horn and called, "To Sir Lancel of House Greymont, who fought with courage and valour until the end. Let us honour him, so Varin might hear us. Let us sing of his glories and deeds."

Elyon did not join in the song this time, as they started into a rendition of '*He Comes, He Comes, to Sit at Varin's Table*', a popular lay at these wakes. It was a defiant and rousing number, intended to be sung as loudly as possible, to send a fallen Varin Knight on his way to the afterlife, and his Eternal Seat.

And all for nothing, Elyon thought dourly, as the voices filled the hall. *If there is such a place as Varin's Table, Lancel will get no vaunted perch.* No, those seats near the head were reserved for dragonslayers, not *attempted* dragonslayers. They were reserved for kings and First Blades and champions. *For men like me*, he knew, finding little pleasure in that fact. Elyon had slain the famed dragon Ezukar in a storm, and several others too during the Battle of the Bane, as men were calling it. There were few men in all history who could say the same.

I stand in rare company now, as a serial killer of Agarath's spawn. And when I die, the Steel Father will welcome me with open arms. He will stand and embrace me as a son before all the lords and knights gone before, and I'll sit down forever with ancient kings and heroes, among names known by every soul across the north, from fresh-faced child to old haggard crone. Elyon Daecar, dragonkiller ten times over. He huffed quietly to himself at the thought and took a good long swallow of ale.

The song went on for a time, each verse shouted out louder than the last. In all the appropriate places they added the name of Lancel Greymont for Varin to hear. It made a raucous din, enough to banish the sense of despair for a time. Though not long. As soon as the song ended, a short silence spread out on the room like a blanket, before Lord Rammas stood from his bench and went into a story about Sir Rodney Thurman, a man of the marshes, who'd died that day on the field as well.

Lancel, Elyon thought. *Sir Rodney. Sir Grant Ashby, killed by a Starrider. Sir Charles Waynewood, overwhelmed by dragonknights. Sir Otto Morley and Sir Oliver Mantor and Sir Karson Stone as well.*

All were Varin Knights who'd fallen during the battle, and all were honoured tonight as tradition did dictate. Yet they were only the tip of the iceberg. It was believed that over ten thousand northmen had fallen on the field of battle four days past. Ten thousand knights and men-at-arms and bowmen and spearmen. Ten thousand men of the marshes and lakes and rivers. Ten thousand Kanabar men and Amadar men, Rammas men and Oloran men, and Payne men too under the charge of Lady Marian. Ten thousand men who'd left behind wives and sons and daughters and mothers. Ten thousand men who'd never see home again.

And Wallis Kanabar among them. His loss was most grievous of all, the Lord of the Riverlands crushed as the fortress came down around him, its ancient magic undone by the relentless assault of dragonfire. Some clung to the faint weak hope that Lord Kanabar had somehow survived, though if he had, none had seen him since. *He'd be a captive*, Elyon thought, *and that might be even worse.* A man like Wallis Kanabar was not born to be caged. *He would sooner die and be done with it. Ascend to the Eternal Halls above and sit back to watch the show…*

Elyon took another long drink of strong brown ale, reflecting on the count of the dead. Lord Shorton was thought perished as well, the tall, long-nosed Lakeland Lord believed to have been with Lord Kanabar when the towers fell. The toadish Lord Fullerton had been within the fortress too, though had been injured by dragonflame earlier on during the night and evacuated to receive medical attention. His wounds were severe, it was said, and he remained in a critical condition. After the battle, his men had taken him back to his seat at Lakeheart, a beautiful white-stone city nestled between three of the Four Sisters further to the north. *We'll have word on the wing any day now, telling of his death,* Elyon thought miserably. These men had all sat at council with him, guided him, advised him. Now all of them were gone.

He gulped down another quarter-mug of ale, looking across the hall. *I still have Rikkard, thank the gods, and Killian as well, and Rammas.* As Lord of the Marshlands, Elton Rammas would take on the temporary title of Warden of the East until Sir Borrus should return to take up his father's mantle. *If ever he does.* Borrus Kanabar had gone off on some foolhardy quest with Elyon's Shadowknight half-brother, and Sir Mooton Blackshaw too, and there was no knowing what had happened to them. *They should have been here, fighting. They should have been defending the fortress, not trekking to the distant north to hunt shadows...*

Elyon tipped back his head and gulped until his drinking horn ran dry. The room was beginning to swim before him. *I'm getting drunk,* he realised, and that wouldn't do. They had many scouts and outriders watching the way south, yet he had to remain clear-headed. The Agarathi would not remain at the wreckage of Dragon's Bane forever, he knew. *They'll lick their wounds and regather their strength and then come again. But where?*

He pushed his horn aside and stood, needing a breath of fresh air. It had grown fuggy in the hall, the smoke thickening with the grief, and half the men were deep in their cups. He would not reprimand them for that, not tonight. Heavy drinking was common post-battle and at these wakes as well, and he had no right to stamp on that tradition. But for all that, he wanted to stay sober. *The men still look to you,* he told himself. *Be the leader they need you to be.*

He stepped through the hall, past tables laden with war-weary men, and out onto the balcony overlooking the yard. The air outside was cool and fresh, at once quenching him of his growing fatigue. Oakpike Castle stood amidst the hills south of the Four Sisters in a pretty land of lakes and valleys and forests rich with game, a stout old castle built four hundred years past following the ravages of the Twenty First Renewal. It perched atop a rugged hill like a crown, with gnarled old oak and ancient elms foresting its northern and western slopes, and high flint cliffs tumbling away to the east and south.

Further to the north, the valleys and hills bled away into blackness where the sprawling lakes of the Four Sisters stretched far, the largest of them a hundred miles across from north to south, and near the same from east to west. Elyon could see the moonlight dancing on the distant waters, see the faint shapes of towns twinkling upon the shoreline. Away to the southwest, lights were moving in a long snaking column, wending up the road from the Marshlands. Elyon squinted to better see them and took a grip of his godsteel dagger, but they were too far away for him to make out their colours and arms.

Some of Rammas's men, most likely, he guessed. Many bands of soldiers had arrived over the last couple of days, the army beginning to knit back together following the chaos of the retreat. By now there were some twenty or so thousand reassembled here at Oakpike, but that was only half of what they'd had at the Bane.

But we cannot stay here long, he knew. *No, as soon as men stop coming, we'll have little choice but to leave,* The question was where. He had spoken to Rikkard, Rammas and Killian about that, and other captains and commanders besides, but none could agree on what to do next. Rammas suggested a direct strike in retaliation for their humbling defeat. "We march back to Dragon's Bane and take them unawares," he'd declared two nights past. "They'll not expect us to be so bold. Strike hard and strike fast and see what comes of it."

Sir Killian was more circumspect. "A direct attack will lead us to catastrophe," he'd returned in his whispery voice. "We march back there and we'll only be routed a second time over. I do not disagree that we ought to be proactive, however. These are *our* lands, lands the enemy can never hope to know as well as we do. We use that to our advantage. Break up into smaller strike forces. Target their dragons with our best fighters, their dragonknights and their leaders as well. Probe, sally, sabotage. Assault their flanks and drag them into a guerrilla war. That would be my advice, young prince."

Elyon thought the idea more worthy of merit than Rammas's blusterous talk of a direct attack with all their strength, though Rikkard had another idea. "The Agarathi have come to destroy the north," he said quite plainly. "They have marched here to dig us out, root and stem, to burn our cities and end our bloodlines. Vandar is many cities, yes, but one above all. A city built to withstand dragon attack like no other. A city that will render us all but lost should she fall," He looked to the three other men. "It might be wise to march home to Varinar. Gather our strength there, and prepare to face our enemy in a final assault."

There had been much talk on all that, though in the end, they'd not been able to agree on their course. In truth, Elyon didn't much like the notion of tucking tail and running back home like a pack of beaten dogs. *What would Wallis have said to that? What would my father say, if I lost one battle and called it quits?* No, it felt too defeatist. Too meek. *We are Vandarian, Bladeborn. We do not turn our backs on a fight.*

He was standing at the rail, mulling deeply on it all when he heard a voice behind him.

"Sir Elyon."

He turned. Lady Marian Payne was standing in the archway leading into the feast hall, a shimmer of dark grey armour peeking out from beneath her long grey cloak. He shifted at once into a bow. "My lady. I wasn't aware you were here tonight."

"I'm not. Leastways not for the wake. I would not want to intrude on your traditions." She stepped out to stand beside him at the balustrade, looking down into the castle yard. It was crowded with men and tents and makeshift shelters, the stables overflowing, every tower and turret full to bursting. The rest were in camp beyond the walls, scattered among the valleys and woods in their thousands. "I'm sorry about Lancel. I know how fond you were of him."

Elyon gave a slow nod. "He was always Aleron's friend, more than mine," he told her. "Barnibus as well. The three of them would do everything together when they were young, though I would join them from time to time, as a pesky younger brother does." He smiled at the memory. He had always liked Lancel and Barnibus well enough, though only over these last months had he come to rely upon them so deeply, and see them as Aleron once had. Loyal, lighthearted, and unerringly companionable. Yes, he would miss Lancel greatly.

Marian ran her gaze over the heaving yard. Men were roasting meat below, and some were drinking, yet there was little laughter now, little mirth stirring in the cold night air. "Every man here has lost someone they care for. Fathers, sons, brothers, friends. We all must use our grief as a whetstone, to sharpen our resolve. War leaves us no other choice, Sir Elyon, but to set our jaws and move on."

Elyon had been told that Marian's host had been depleted almost by half during the battle and ensuing retreat, as she tried to hold the western flank. *She marched to join us with five thousand at her back, and now has no more than three,* he thought. No doubt she had lost men close to her as well, during the battle. He wondered if Saska's friends were among them. "I'd ask of Roark, my lady, and the others. Did they survive the night?"

Her head shook slowly in bitter regret. "No…not all of them, I am saddened to say. Quilter perished by the jaws of a sunwolf, and Braddin was sorely injured in the gut by a length of Lumaran steel. He may yet survive, we hope, though his fate remains uncertain. The others still live, Roark and Lark. Roark in particular seems quite unkillable, despite his meagre skill and lack of Bladeborn blood. He claims to have slain half a dozen stout men, one of them a dragonknight." She smiled faintly. "I do him the honour of believing it."

Elyon was glad to hear that some were alive at least. When the fighting had spread out, he feared all four of Marian's loyal men would perish, though it seemed they had more lives than most. "Did you manage to retrieve Quilter's body?" he asked her.

"Alas, no. He remains on the field, burned or rotting by now. He has plenty of company out there," she said, with a clench of the jaw.

Elyon understood her distress. It was common practice after battles to permit the dead to be gathered for burial and cremation, as their religious customs decreed, though on this occasion that had never been an option. Their retreat had taken them too far north for that, and they had no choice but to abandon them. It had left a sour feeling inside many, to leave their kith and kin behind, even if some had been retrieved, thrown onto the backs of horses, or carried on shoulders and backs when the horns rang out the retreat. Lancel was one of them. Barnibus had taken him upon Biter's back, his great strong warhorse, and ridden him north, so he might be returned to his father's castle for burial. Others had done the same, though perhaps only one in a hundred corpses had been retrieved from the field of battle that day, likely even fewer than that. The rest were destined to rot in the sun or become carrion for crows and wolves and dragons. The thought of it enraged him. *Dragons, feasting upon my fallen brothers, my countrymen.* He closed a fist and breathed out slowly. Defeat was a bitter enough tonic to swallow without having to dwell on the fate of the dead as well.

A burst of sound exploded from within the feast hall, as another rendition of *He Comes, He Comes, to Sit at Varin's Table* came bellowing out into the night. This time the name of Sir Charles Waynewood was being honoured, as Lancel had been earlier. Marian listened a moment, then said. "He slew a dragon, I'm told. Sir Charles."

"He did," Elyon confirmed. Several of the men had told their accounts of the story that night. It was a smaller dragon, such as they said, but vicious. Sir Charles had taken several fierce blows from its whipping tail before he cut through its neck in a savage cleave, opening its jugular and letting its blood wash out to redden the earth. It turned out to be his final act. No sooner had he claimed the kill than a troop of dragonknights had overwhelmed him, puncturing through the weak points in his armour with their long black dragonsteel spears. Sir Charles had been an old knight, one of the few clad in a full suit of godsteel plate, yet still it hadn't saved him. "The men say it has earned him a good placing at Varin's Table," Elyon said. "It is the sweetest desire of all Bladeborn knights to claim a dragon kill before death. Sir Charles ascends in triumph. He is one of the lucky few."

Marian gave no response but to nod in silence, listening to the song as it echoed from out of the hall with an inscrutable expression on her face. It was the first time Elyon had seen her in the days since the battle, yet he'd heard many accounts of her gallantry on the field from those who'd been there to bear witness. There was even talk that she'd slain a dragon herself. When he put that to her, her response was merely to smile and say, "Whoever told you that tale has exaggerated, I fear. I *helped* kill a dragon, would be a better way of putting it, though in truth I helped kill three. Sir Gereon and I operated well in tandem, and we had many good men in support. I could claim no individual kill, sir. Such a triumph still eludes me."

In the yard below, the pure laughter of a child trilled out into the night. Elyon looked down, as a small gaggle of girls and boys came bursting out of a tower door, weaving between the tents and shelters and darting past slumberous men. An old woman went after them, cackling at them to return to their beds. "Back, back inside," she called out. "Your lord father will have m'head. You're not s'posed to be out here. Back inside with you! Now!"

Elyon raised a faint smile as he watched. It was a comical scene, watching the crone hold up her skirts and try to give chase, as the children scampered away. After a short time, a few of the livelier soldiers were joining in, either helping the crone in her chase or elsewise protecting the children in their escape. Soon enough, the laughter of the boys and girls had spread amongst the men and the yard had taken on a more jovial air. Elyon's smile spread a shade wider. "Lord Burbridge's brood," he said, to Marian's questioning frown. Mayhew Burbridge was the Lord of Oakpike, a middling lord of the Lakelands who had willingly opened his gates when Elyon and his host had come marching from the south, with their hundreds of wounded in tow. "He has twelve children, I'm told. These will be some of the youngest."

"Twelve seems a little excessive."

"He wanted sons," Elyon explained. "The first half dozen or so were daughters, so he had little choice but to keep on trying. You see the two boys down there, about eight? They're his first sons. And twins. The gods blessed him double."

"Or cursed him double," Marian said to that. "Twins can be problematic, Elyon. Some men favour them - if one dies, they have a spare - but others worry that they will war over the right to be heir. I've heard rumours of that very thing happening in Ilithor, with Prince Raynald. It seems he has developed a taste for ruling in his twin brother's absence."

Elyon had been privy to the same talk, though Marian had a tendency to know things he did not. "Have you heard anything from Eagle's Perch, my lady?" he asked her. "If Prince Robbert should perish there, Raynald may well have his way."

"To lose a beloved twin, but gain a crown...I wonder if Raynald would consider that a welcome trade?" She shrugged. "I've not heard anything of the fate of Prince Robbert Lukar, no. Yet I have had word from my own lands. Word of a greatly troubling nature." She rested a hand on the balustrade and turned her eyes north. She had to take a moment to compose herself before speaking. Then she said, "The city of Thalan has been attacked, Sir Elyon, on the very same night as the Battle of the Bane. It is largely destroyed, I have been told. My capital city...in ruin."

Destroyed. Thalan. Elyon stared at her in mute shock. "But...Thalan is so...so far north. There's no way a southern army could have..." He stopped, realising his folly. This was done by no host of men, he knew. "Dragons," he said, and Marian nodded. "I saw a flight of them soaring northward during the battle," he remembered. "I had wondered where they might be going, but...Thalan. I hadn't expected an attack on Thalan." He had never visited the capital of Rasalan, yet had heard many tales of its beauty. The harbour around the Izzun. The palace with the mountains at its back. The city levels with their colourful plazas and temples and roofs of blue and gold. The switchback stair that led to the famed Brightwater Academy, overlooking the city below, a haven of art and music and science and magic. "My lady, I'm so sorry."

"No more than I am, Elyon." There was something deeper than grief in her eyes, though the Lady Marian would shed no tears. "Thalan is not

Ilithor or Varinar. It is not blessed with such stocks of godsteel to lace its walls and towers. We have ballistas and scorpions, yes, and Bladeborn bowmen to defend us, but our defences are scant compared to your own. If Dragon's Bane can be overwhelmed in mere hours, such a city as Thalan stood no chance at all. It is a calamity to my people, and to me, yet through my anger and grief, I must take stock and look for answers." She turned to meet his eyes, steady and stern. "Why, Sir Elyon, would Thalan be targeted? Think on that a moment, and then answer me. Why?"

He did not need to think on it long. *Even now, as we do our dance up here, he seeks to strip away your one advantage. Even now he moves against you.* Those had been the words of the Dragonlord Vargo Ven, as he circled around him atop Malathar's back when all the world fell to fire and death below them. *He*, Elyon thought. *Eldur.* He swallowed in a dry throat and answered. "Eldur led the attack, so he might blind us," he said, keeping the shiver from his voice such as he could. "It was not the city that was their target, my lady. It was the Eye, and the king who commands it."

She nodded. "I came to the same conclusion. I've spent the last two hours with Master Hortus in the rookery, writing letters and sending crows so we might ascertain the truth of all this. Yet early reports suggest Garlath the Grand was sighted at the palace, ridden by an old man dressed in a crimson cloak. It is said men quailed to even look upon him. That he had red eyes and bore a black staff, topped with a glowing orb. You know of what I speak."

"The Bondstone." Elyon felt a cold shiver crawl up his spine. "Then our worst fears are realised." *And Vargo Ven wasn't lying.* "It's how he's controlling the dragons. How he has summoned so many from the Wings." He thought again of the moment the Agarathi horde charged upon their lines. When the army at the Bane stood in formation, awaiting them. When he walked the walls of the southward barbican, listening to Lord Kanabar bellowing 'hold' as the trebuchets and catapults prepared to swing, as the bowmen waited to loose their arrows upon the onrushing host. *And the skies*, he thought. He remembered that moment most clearly of all. How the skies had swarmed, just as the Windblade had warned. How the dragons had come bursting from the darkness like sleek black shadows, raining death and doom. The Bondstone was the leash that bound them to their master. The Soul of Agarath, men called it. The soul of the dragons' divine father and creator. *But…if we could cut that leash, sever that tie…* "We need to destroy it," he said suddenly. "The Bondstone. We shatter the Soul of Agarath, my lady, and the dragons will scatter and flee."

She ran a finger down the sharp line of her angular jaw. "The same thought has crossed my mind, and more than once." Her eyes met him in a questioning stare. "What do you know of Agarathi prophecy, Sir Elyon?"

"Little and less, I regret to say."

"Feel no regret. Prophecy is often the realm of the foolish and the fanciful, yet on the rare occasion, these forecasts do yield truth. So it would seem in this case." She spoke then of an arcane Agarathi prophecy that long foretold the rise of Eldur, one that claimed the Fire Father would rise benevolent, a beacon of hope and order, intent on ending the War Eternal. "It is clear enough now that certain elements of this prophecy have been lost through time or otherwise misunderstood," she continued. "Eldur has arisen, yes, but not in the form foretold. If I recall correctly, the same teachings talk of returning the world to balance. Of extinguishing the final embers of the gods' power on this earth. A power that resides in the ancient artefacts that are the great heirlooms of our kingdoms and nations. Destroy these, or else control them, and the gods' influence upon us will wither and perish. The cycle of Renewals will end, and the seeds of a long-term peace be sown, so that future generations may reap a rich harvest of harmony and kinship."

Elyon wondered if such a thing would ever be possible. "War is written into our blood and bones," he said, looking into the hall. "Men seek quarrel to elevate themselves to a favoured perch in the afterlife. Life is ephemeral, but what comes after lasts forever. I'm not sure we'll ever have a long-term peace, Marian. That sounds too idealistic to me."

Another song was drifting out from the smoky hall, though a softer, more sombre one known as the *Ballad of the Brave*. It too could be modified to reflect the name of the man being honoured. In this case, Elyon heard the name of Sir Otto Morley spilling out into the cool of the night. Morley was a younger brother of the Lord of Mudport, a man well-liked among the marshmen. He had fallen to dragonfire, Elyon had heard, though slew several men even as he was burning. *Brave indeed.*

He listened for a short time, doing Sir Otto that honour at least. *I should go back*, he realised. He had intended on getting a breath of fresh air only, and clearing his head of the weight of the ale, yet had been gone too long. *I must stand by my brothers. I am prince to them still, and champion. I cannot be seen to be abandoning them at this time.* He turned to Marian. "I…"

"Need to rejoin them," she said. "I know."

He was grateful for her understanding. "We can talk later, my lady. This matter of Thalan calls for an urgent council. My uncle will wish to discuss it, and Sir Killian and Lord Rammas as well." All three had tried to avoid this talk of Eldur's rise, yet that could happen no longer. *We must confront it. We must confront* him. "Will you stay tonight in the castle?"

"I shall return to my camp outside the walls. I prefer to walk among my own men."

He nodded. The ale was still thick enough in his head as to slow his thinking somewhat. There was so much of what Marian had told him that needed unpacking. He had an urgent query before leaving her. "The Eye of Rasalan. Was it destroyed, do you know?" He had guessed at once at Eldur's purpose. *And most likely, Hadrin is dead too.* In that at least he felt some joy. He had little love for the Rat King of Rasalan, and all his petty cruelties.

But Marian shook her head. "I told you Eldur was spotted flying atop Garlath. This was when he arrived. Upon leaving, he is said to have borne with him another. King Hadrin, I'm told. He was taken, and the Eye with him."

Elyon frowned to hear that. The words of Vargo Ven echoed between his ears once again. *Even now, as we do our dance up here, he seeks to strip away your one advantage. Even now he moves against you.* "Our one advantage," he whispered. He caught the confused look on Marian's face and told her of what the dragonlord had said.

She listened calmly, pondering, then said, "Eldur must think that Hadrin is sighting the future within the Eye. That he is alerting us to where he may strike. This is the advantage he refers to."

"Then why not just kill Hadrin? Why take him?"

"To use him," Marian said. "To turn one of our strengths against us." She looked to the distance in a thousand-yard stare. "Or perhaps he is searching for something. You were hunted, Elyon, as were some of the other bearers. Perhaps Eldur seeks to gather the embers of the gods. Perhaps he has some purpose for them."

The word *perhaps* would not help them, not now. "We need to consult a scholar," he said. "We need certainties, Marian, not guesswork."

She smiled at that. "I asked you once if you might fly south, to Aram. Do you remember?"

He did. It was the day she arrived at camp at Dragon's Bane, marching eastwards down the coast from her post at Kirkwell Castle. "You wondered if I might seek word of Saska," he recalled. The very next day, he had tested himself upon the open plains north of the Bane, flying high and far and getting into a tangle with a certain riderless dragon in the midst of a thunderous storm. "At that point I could scarcely conceive of flying so far. But now…"

"Now it is different," she said. "You are appreciably improved in your mastery of the winds, as proven time and again. You have managed long flights before, though nothing so far as this, I'll grant. Even so, I wonder now if you might chance such a journey?"

"To find Saska?" he asked.

"To find Ranulf Shackton," she said. "You have not met the man, but Saska spoke of him to you, I know. If there is anyone who might have the answer to this riddle, it is him. Long has he studied the Relics of the Fallen."

Elyon found that he was shaking his head. "I would not know where to start."

"Ranulf sailed to Solapia, though I doubt he is there still. It may well be that he has travelled to Aram, where Saska is sure to have gone as well, in search of her grandmother. You could kill two birds with one stone, Elyon."

"It's other flying creatures that I need to kill, my lady, not birds. And I'd be sure to meet some of those on the way." *They might even seek me out, as Ezukar did*, he thought. *If I should grow weary, or need to rest…* He was shaking his head again. "The risk is too great. I must stay with my men."

"That is your choice, of course. I can only give my advice, such as it is." She looked at the Windblade, sheathed at his hip. "You have a power that no one else possesses, a power to move between continents and kingdoms as quickly as any dragon. Do not shackle yourself to this army, lest there be a good enough reason to do so. It is well commanded by seasoned men. Would you not do more good using the gifts you've been given? You alone can cross mountains and lakes and seas in mere hours, Elyon. Only you. Do not waste that."

He pondered her words for a short time, then said, "I have been thinking of flying to Varinar, I will admit. If I have a need to make a long flight, it would be there, to share in my father's counsel." There had been word of another Agarathi army at the Trident, a threat that his father would no doubt be taking seriously. "It may be that I'm needed there, even more than here." *And it may be that Rikkard is right,* he thought, *and we need to march this army back to help.*

She dipped her chin. "You must go where you think best. And I understand your need to return to your capital, and your father. I feel the same pull. With this news from Thalan, my men will no doubt urge me to march back to my uncle's lands to defend them. They will fear an invasion now. They will be worried for their families."

Elyon could ill afford to lose three thousand men. "Will you bend to them, my lady?"

"I will consider," she said. "But should my lord uncle send word asking that I return, I may have little choice. We all have our duty, Elyon. Who is mine to, if not the man who raised me? The man who put a godsteel blade in my hand and instructed me on how to use it? The man who always believed in me, when so few others did?"

Elyon had not thought her so sentimental. "Family is important," he agreed. "Yet there is a bigger picture as well."

"But are you seeing it?" she challenged. "This war may not be won by slaying dragons, Elyon Daecar. Or by rallying to the defence of a single city, even one so great as Varinar. You said it yourself that the Bondstone must be destroyed. I do not disagree. But will your father have the answers you seek? Or might you find them on the lips of another?"

She stepped in with those words and placed a palm on his cheek. "Think on what I've told you," she said. "These last days have been long, I know, and you need to restore your strength. But once you have, I would warn you not to limit yourself. Go to Varinar. Go to Aram. Go to where the world needs you most. Do not fear these long flights, but embrace them. And do not fear to leave your men behind. They can manage without you, as they have before and will again. A bird such as you should never be caged."

She leaned forward, and kissed his cheek, just above the thick black bristles of his beard. Then she turned from him and left, so he might rejoin the lament to the dead.

2

Amara

She found him in his solar, writing a letter with a grimace on his face.

"A wise man once said that wars are won with ink, as much as they are with steel," she said. "A pen can do more damage than a sword, when wielded by the right hand." She drew forth and poured herself a cup of fiery Sutreki red. "Who are you writing, Amron?"

"My father-in-law. I've not heard back about Lillia yet."

"Of course you haven't." She scowled to think of Lord Brydon Amadar and the vicious trick he'd played on her. A trick that lost her a finger and forced her to kill a false king. "That bastard will not give her up so easily, Amron. Wine?"

He shook his head. "She's *my* daughter, and should be in my keep. He has no right to keep her against my will."

She turned from the counter and took of a sip of wine to warm her. These Sutreki vintages were not for everyone, spicy as they were, but Amara Daecar liked to keep a broad palate. "He will claim the crow was killed en route," she said to her brother-in-law. "You'd be better off putting that letter into the hands of a trusted rider this time. At least then he'll have no excuses to hide behind."

"I'll do just that." Amron set the quill aside and sat back in his chair. It creaked under his great weight as he reached across and massaged the pain from his left shoulder, wincing.

"It still troubles you?" Amara had wondered if his mastery of the Frostblade might render him free of his aches and ails, but alas that didn't seem to be the case.

"The pain only goes away when I hold the Frostblade, as I've told you. My blood-bond initiates its healing effect. Otherwise my discomfort remains, yes." The dark shadows beneath his eyes suggested sleep had been difficult to come by of late, and that wasn't likely to change, not with the world falling apart at the seams. "Was there something you wanted, Amara?"

Yes. For you to take the crown and sit the throne, and become the king you were meant to be. She said none of that. A dozen times was enough and by now she was only nagging. "I wondered if you'd had any further thoughts about Vesryn," she said. "He is wasted rotting in a dungeon, Amron, with the Sword of Varinar well mastered. If *you're* not going to take it up again, then perhaps…"

"No, Amara. I'm *not* giving him back that blade."

"Then you would cut off your nose to spite your face. This is folly, Amron. The Agarathi have won the Bane. Another army threatens to cross the Red Sea. And still you let your pride dictate to you."

He gave her a frosty look, those silver-blue eyes of his showing not a glint of warmth. "My *pride*? You misplace your words, Amara. It is not pride that drives me, but justice. I cannot be seen to permit Vesryn possession of the holiest of our blades, not after all he's done. How do you imagine the Taynars would react to that after they believe he killed their king? We would have open conflict in the streets, and that we can ill afford. We've got enough bloody conflict to worry about."

There was truth in that, to be sure. Word had only just come of the fall of Dragon's Bane, news so alarming as to have set every man, woman, and child in Varinar on edge. *As if they weren't frightened enough already,* Amara thought, *knowing Dalton Taynar's army have been driven from the Trident. Now they hear that the greatest fortress in the north has fallen, and in a single night no less…*

"Vesryn never killed their king," she said belligerently. "*I* did. You should not have told them otherwise." He'd done that before she could agree, the day he'd returned to Varinar after so long away. Before Amara could do anything about it, he'd declared that Vesryn be put in chains, and marched away to tell the Taynar men gathered outside the palace that their king was dead, and that the perpetrator was taken into custody.

"If I'd told them you killed Godrik, it would be you down in the dungeons in your husband's place. *You* facing the gallows, Amara." He shook his head firmly. "No. You may plot and scheme from time to time, but you've got a good heart and I'll not see it stop beating on my brother's account. If there's a neck to be put in a noose, it'll be his."

"You don't mean that. Your own brother?"

"My own brother who knew of a plot to have me killed and said nothing. My own brother who is partly responsible for the death of my eldest son. Is that the brother you're talking about, Amara?" He let a short silence linger. "Yes, I would let that happen. Vesryn is dead to me already; seeing him swing will be nothing but a formality."

She had so much to say to that, but in the end, said nothing at all. Everything Vesryn had done had been through childish folly and vain ambition, and he'd been too damnably stupid to dig himself out of the hole he'd made for himself when he was young. *Janilah,* she thought, *my devious cousin. If there's a man to blame for all this, it's him.*

"I can see I'm wasting my breath." She gulped down her wine. When he got into one of these moods, there would be no use trying to reason with him. "And the others? Are you to give them a reprieve?"

19

"The Greycloaks?"

"Yes, them. If Vesryn is considered guilty of the crime of kingslaying, then surely they are too? All three of them stood by as Ellis Reynar was thrown from that balcony, Amron. I'll be upset enough to see my husband on the gibbet...but if he doesn't have company..."

Amron shifted in his chair. "He won't have company. I have no choice, Amara, not if I want to unite this kingdom, but to make concessions...."

"For traitors?" she broke in. "For men who stood by while their own king was murdered, your very own cousin. How can you let that go unpunished?"

"Through necessity. If I have Nathaniel Oloran executed, his lord father will never support me. Nay, he may just become my enemy, and a powerful one at that. The same goes for Lord Strand if Sir Gerald's neck is wrapped in rope, and Lord Porter as well should Sir Alyn suffer that fate. These are influential lords who must be appeased, to better secure Vandar at this time. If pardons must be given, so be it. It won't sit well on my conscience, but that's the reality of ruling. Few decisions ever do."

She snorted softly. "At least you're admitting to ruling. You're king in all but name. Just sit the godsteel throne and be done with it. And do it quick, else Dull Dalton's likely to plant his skinny arse there instead once he gets back."

That struck a nerve, she thought, seeing a flinch ripple through his rugged scarred face. "Dalton won't be king," he said, after a moment to digest the notion. "At least, no more than I will. The best compromise right now is for us to work together until the war is over. Squabbling over the right to rule is a matter too absurd to consider when there are armies marching on our doorstep. I will grant Dalton the Sword of Varinar to appease him, and a claim to rule beside me. I will permit the release of Sir Nathaniel, Sir Gerald, and Sir Alyn to satisfy their lord fathers. And I will keep Vesryn in chains to meet the same end." He judged her reaction coolly. "Now, was there anything else?"

She gave him nothing but a smile. *King in all but name*, she thought. It was much as it was when Ellis Reynar wore the crown. All through the weaselly little man's reign, the true king was Amron Daecar. *And so it is again.* "Nothing," she told him. "It's just good to see you talking with authority, whether I agree with you or not. Now, if you'll excuse me. I have a date to attend."

"A date?" He sat up a little, the leather of his jerkin scuffing on his seat. "With whom?"

"Jealous?" she teased. "Oh, so we come to the truth of why you want rid of your brother. With Vesryn gone, you'd have me all to yourself." She cocked her head alluringly. "Isn't that so?"

"Nonsense. I am only concerned for your well-being. You're hardly the most popular woman in this city right now, Amara, and least of all amongst the Taynars."

"Stuff the Taynars and their lickspittles, I have no time for them. I'm well loved among the smallfolk and that's greatly more important."

20

"So you're venturing into the outer city?" He frowned disapprovingly at the prospect. "I would say that's unwise. Much as they like you down in the Lowers, there are tens of thousands of newcomers to the city and not all of them will…"

She waved a hand to quieten him. "Sweet as I find your concern for me, I'm not heading to the Lowers, fear not. I plan to venture no further than the streets at the base of this very hill, in fact, and my date is a man you know rather well. Short, with a patchy greying beard, paunchy little belly, and bucketloads of *luck*. I think you may have heard of him."

Amron made a grunting sound. "Oh. Well…just don't get drunk, Amara. I know how you are. Both you and Walter like a drink."

She held up her hands. "Guilty as charged. We both like a good many drinks, you might say. Wines are a particular favourite of mine, as you'll know, though I would not say no to the occasional fruity cider or berry ale, especially during a warm summer's day. Oh, and there are certain whiskies and brandies and rums that I enjoy as well, and who doesn't like a good strong port or a nice sweet sherry?"

She grinned at him, though her brother-in-law did not seem especially amused. He shook his head, then passed his eyes over the scrolls and parchments upon the table as though wishing she would leave so he could return to his work. *Dull work*, she did not doubt. Ruling often was, though Amron had always taken to it just as well as he had the battlefield. *Pen and sword*, she thought. *He is equally skilled with both, though he might not like them the same.*

"Just make sure Walter is fit to travel tomorrow," he said eventually. "I plan to travel south to Crosswater to meet Sir Dalton in person. He sails up the Steelrun as we speak, Lady Brockenhurst reports, with the bulk of his remaining host."

"Oh?" Amara hadn't known about that. "You'll take the Sword of Varinar with you, I take it?"

"It's part of the reason I'm going. The sooner Dalton can learn to master it, the better."

She shifted back over to the drinks counter and poured a little more wine. *If I'm to stay a moment longer, I might as well drink a little more.* "Will you continue down to King's Point after?" she asked, sipping. The last they'd heard, the Agarathi and their allies were still amassing at the Trident, having frightened Dour Dalton away across the water, along with his tens of thousands of supposedly stout men. "If the enemy crosses the Red Sea, King's Point will be their target. Ought you not make your stand there?"

"The city is being bolstered as we speak," Amron informed her. He picked up his quill pen and tapped a spare sheet of parchment. "Wars are won with ink, as much as steel, as you say. I have written instructions for our own banners to sail east from Green Harbour and the Twinfort, to help secure King's Point against attack. Borringtons, Crawfields, Rothwells, Blunts and Brightwoods. They're keeping a careful watch on matters under Lord Randall's command, though they need to remain flexible. If the Agarathi should decide to lay assault to the western gate instead, they must be there to defend it."

Amara thought that unlikely, but had learned not to offer too loud an opinion on such matters. She was not well versed in war, as Amron and others liked to remind her, though so far as she understood it, the Agarathi were far more likely to sail to King's Point, destroy the city with their dragons, and continue sailing up the Steelrun River, with Varinar their big juicy target. But they'd have to get past Crosswater first, she knew, a great fortress castle sitting astride the Steelrun and blocking the path to their capital. She imagined that's why her brother-in-law was going there, in large part. *But if these rumours of dragon numbers are as they say...*

She thought on that a little more as she sipped her wine.

"I thought you were leaving?" Amron said, when she stood there saying nothing. "What else is on your mind?"

"Your son."

Amron's face was as a stone, hard and inscrutable. "What about him?"

"What about him? He has just lost a battle, his first, and seen death on an unimaginable scale. He is only twenty, don't forget, hardly more than a boy. I wonder how he's taking it, that's all."

"Many men see war at a younger age. Elyon can handle it. I have had letters from both Rikkard and Killian and both attest to Elyon's growing stature and strength. There is no sense in worrying about him."

"He should come home," Amara said. "All of them...they should march back to here to help defend us."

"That would be premature. They have suffered a defeat, yes, but the enemy suffered more dearly. Rikkard wrote that we lost ten thousand men. It sounds a great number, but he is of the belief that the Agarathi lost some thirty to forty thousand of their own, and more than a dozen dragons besides. Many would consider that a resounding victory."

Not me, Amara thought. *Not with scores of dragons still swarming the skies. And those other rumours too...* "Did Rikkard mention..." She could hardly bring herself to say it.

"What?" Amron pressed. He placed his pen down. "What, Amara? Spit it out."

"Eldur," she managed, after untangling her tongue. The name came out in a breathless whisper. "Did he...did he tell of the Fire Father, in his note?"

Amron's jaw tensed. "No. But Killian did. And I've heard the rumours."

"You don't believe them?"

"I do believe them," he said. "With all we've seen, it makes a deal of sense, horrifying as it may be to confront. The Fire Father rises up out of the flames, as the Blades of Vandar reemerge from the darkness to be wielded against him in war. Walter calls it fate, and providence. Over our long months away, he spoke regularly and at length about the Last Renewal. Perhaps he was right all along."

He speaks about it so calmly. "And how do you plan to defeat a demigod, Amron?"

"As I would any other enemy."

22

"But he is not any other enemy. He is the Father of Fire, who stood amidst gods and monsters through an age of eternal war. He is an entity beyond anything living."

"We cannot know what he is," Amron said bluntly. "He *was* these things. Who knows what he is now. A shell and a shadow of his former self, he might be. But even in his prime, he perished eight times. He can perish again, and this time there will be no god to revive him."

She observed the tautness around his mouth, the narrow cast to his eyes, the slow movement of his chest as it moved up and down. *This man... this man is born to save us,* she thought. *Crown or no, he will lead us through the night.* "My king cousin was trying to gather the blades," she said. "To combine them, people say. If such a thing is possible, *you* would wield that weapon, Amron."

"If it was possible it would have been done before." He waved it away. "Janilah plotted for decades and what has come of it but ruin and defeat? All the north knows him for the monster he has become." He closed a fist on the table. "Would that he'd chosen another path. There were many who long admired him, myself included, and my father. Little did any of us know the treachery he was committing all along."

"But the blades," Amara pressed. "All have returned now, as you say. You have two here in your possession. Your sons possess two others..."

"*Sons.*" He gave a deep sigh. "I had three sons, Amara. Aleron, Elyon, and the babe who died with Kessia when she brought him into this world. Jonik is of my blood and seed, but he is not my son."

She frowned at him. "You cannot blame the boy..."

"I don't blame him. But I don't know him either. If you're thinking I can just wave my hand and have every Blade of Vandar gathered here at my feet, you should think again. Each blade has a will of its own and they grow stronger during war. They are the echoes of Vandar himself, parts of his spirit split and parted. They *want* to be kept apart, Amara. Gathering them will be all but impossible."

She snorted softly. "No wonder my cousin had such trouble then."

"Indeed. And Janilah is still missing, lest we forget. Some say he sank down into the stone of Galin's Post and entombed himself for his shame."

Amara laughed at the thought of it. "He would never do such a thing. Janilah is far too prideful to die that way."

"No matter. He is missing, thought dead, and the Mistblade with him. But should he return, do you imagine he would hand the blade over willingly? Do you think Jonik would give up the Nightblade, that so defines him? That Elyon would surrender the power of flight?"

"Elyon would do as you command, as his father, lord, and king."

"I'm not king. And you do not understand. It takes a tremendous amount of willpower to untether oneself from a Blade of Vandar. I should know. I held the Sword of Varinar for twenty years before I had to give it up."

"But you did."

"With immense difficulty. I came to see that my obsession with the blade had grown too strong. Aleron's death snapped me back from that black reverie."

She remembered those days, those long dark days in Varinar when Amron had fallen to despair following his maiming, when Aleron had been slain by the Shadowknight's blade. It still pained her to think that Vesryn had a hand in it all. *But he did not know his nephew would die,* she told herself. *He thought he would lose in the final, that's all. He'd never have helped kill Aleron, never…*

She took a swallow of wine to steady her thoughts. "Vesryn gave up the Sword of Varinar too," she reminded him, half wondering whether it was wise to mention her husband's name again. "He gladly laid it at your feet, Amron."

He snorted disdainfully. "Vesryn acted through shame. It can be a powerful motivator."

"He acted to make you king. He knows your worth and value. As do the people. They have heard your story, heard of the Snowskins' prophecy, heard of how you came to bear that blade." She flicked a hand to the Frost-blade, resting against the wall by his desk. A soft glitter of kaleidoscopic mist rose from the top of its scabbard, sparkling magnificently in the fire-light. "You walked into a land of shadow and emerged even stronger for it. *Varin Reborn.* The name has always trailed you, Amron, but now it's being spoken more than ever before. The people look to you as their saviour. And now this with Eldur, Varin's mortal enemy. Who better to face him than you?"

The man who refused to be king shook his head. "It's not as simple as that. You mean well, Amara, I know, but wars are greatly more complex than one man against another, duelling for the fates of all. Now please, this is not the time. I have letters to write and preparations to make and need to rest before I leave." He looked past her, to the door. "And you have a date to attend, good sister. I will see you in the morning."

She decided to honour the request. "As you will, Amron. I'll make sure I don't get too drunk."

She swept from his solar at that, marching out into the corridor at the summit of Keep Daccar. Amron might have taken up residence in the palace, but no, he couldn't be seen to be doing that, of course, not with these determined efforts to keep that spiky steel crown off his head. Rogen Strand stood outside on guard, looking as grim as ever. He was a tall spare man, all gristle and gaunt cheeks, with dark watchful eyes that gave little away. Among the men of Northwatch he'd been known as Whitebeard, on account of the frost that clung to the bristles of his face from his regular rangings, but the name made little sense to Amara here. In truth his beard was more brown and grey, and a little ragged besides.

"Rogen," she said. "How bored are you, at this precise moment?"

He looked at her curiously. "My lady?"

She waved to Amron's door. "It is dull work, isn't it? Standing here all afternoon?"

She saw the answer in his eyes, though the man would never admit it. "I am sworn to serve Lord Daecar," he said.

"*King* Daecar," Amara corrected. "We need to start saying it more. Maybe eventually he'll come to believe it."

Rogen Strand inclined his head. "I would gladly call him king, my lady. He is greatly more worthy of the title than my uncle was."

Ah yes, your uncle Godrik, who I slew. She wasn't sure if Rogen knew that she'd been the one to drive the knife into the old man's wrinkled neck or not, but something told her he wouldn't much care if he did. "You don't like your brother, do you Rogen?" she asked him.

He frowned. "Gerald?"

"Do you have another?"

"I did. Steffon. Though he died during the war."

"Well, not that one. Though perhaps you misliked him too, who can say? Yes, I'm talking about Sir Gerald," she confirmed. "I hear he treated you poorly when you were a boy?"

The ranger nodded stiffly. "I was blamed for the death of my lady mother. She died on the birthing table."

And there were few who missed her. Lady Margery Taynar had been as miserably dour as her brother Godrik, and the rest of the family. "Death in childbirth is quite common among Bladeborn families," she said. "I'm sure you know this, but there are some who say it augurs the coming of a great Bladeborn, so long as the child survives, of course. Perhaps such is the case with you, Rogen. Amron speaks very highly of your skill, and Lord Borrington as well. '*I have never seen a finer ranger*', he wrote to me once. And here you are, guarding a door." She smiled playfully. "What a waste."

Rogen did not smile. "I do as Lord Daecar commands."

"*King* Daecar."

"Yes, my lady. King Daecar. I do as he commands, though will find myself at the heart of a fight soon, I'm certain. My lord has kindly seen fit to have me garbed in a suit of godsteel armour, from the Steelforge. I will make good use of it, when the time comes."

"I'm sure you will, though I don't much envy you. I have never looked upon a man clad in godsteel plate and thought it was kindness that put them there. Those suits look terribly stifling to me."

"They take some getting used to, I will admit. I am more accustomed to leather and fur. The only godsteel the rangers bear are the blades they carry. The wilds do not call for plate and ringmail."

Amara looked him up and down. There was a breastplate beneath his black woollen cloak, dark grey and unpolished so that it hardly caught the light. She imagined this man would never stand in a gleaming suit of silver on the battlefield, as other proud knights and lords were wont to do. Dark dull colours suited him better. *That'll be the Taynar in him,* she thought. He looked much more like his cousin Dalton than his piggish brother Gerald, to be sure. "I take it you've been training in full plate, then?" she asked him. "When you're not guarding this door, of course."

25

"I have. To grow used to its feel. Mostly at night, when my duties are done."

"Ah. So that explains the ringing in the practice yard. I did wonder."

Rogen Strand shifted on his feet. He did not seem especially comfortable in her company. *Is that because I'm a woman*, she wondered, *or because I enjoy a jest?* "I hope I haven't been keeping you awake, my lady."

"Not at all. There's nothing more soothing to a woman's ears than the sound of singing steel. It makes us feel so wonderfully safe, knowing you're out there, sharpening your skill."

He didn't get the sarcasm. "Well, I…"

"I'll leave you to your watch." She took a step away and turned back on a whim. "Oh, I should say. Amron intends to release your brother from his cell, and grant him a full pardon for his treasons." She smiled. "I'm sure that pleases you."

His eyes said no. "I had hoped to watch him hang."

"As had I. Along with Sir Nathaniel and Sir Alyn, but alas politics has intervened."

"A shame." Rogen Strand closed a leather-gloved fist, flexing.

"A very great shame," she agreed.

She left him there, wondering why she had told him. *Do I expect him to take matters into his own hands?* She knew he wouldn't. He had travelled with his older brother down the High Way, after all, and done nothing. *No, this man is loyal to Amron, that's clear, and will not circumvent his rule.* It angered her more than she could say to know that Sir Gerald and Sir Nathaniel and Sir Alyn would all walk free, when her husband would continue to rot…

And for a crime he didn't commit, she thought. *It was me who slew Godrik Taynar. Me.* If Vesryn hadn't arrived in time, she'd have lost more than a few fingernails, she did not doubt. *He saved me, and now he's to die in my place.* She wasn't sure she could live with that.

She found Walter Selleck huddled over a stack of parchments in a tavern called the Drunk Duck, scribbling by candlelight. The inn was situated down a cobblestone alley at the base of the hill atop which Keep Daecar perched, a pretty lane with lanterns hanging on tall pinewood poles and spring flowers bursting from pots on every sill. It was quiet inside, save for a few other patrons, nursing their wines and ales over whispered conversations.

Walter looked up as she joined him. "Sir Connor not with you, my lady?"

She waved to the barkeep. "Wine, Beecham. Dealer's choice." She was well known here. "We are a stone's throw from the castle gates, Walter," she said to the scruffy man. "I have no need of Sir Connor's protection tonight, and he needs all the rest he can get." Sir Connor Crawfield had suffered a wound to the gut not so long ago and was still in the latter stages of recovery. Amara had a look over Walter's notes. "What are you writing about?"

"Your beauty, what else?" He grinned through his scraggly beard. Walter was not a handsome man, but he had playful, inquisitive eyes, and a lighthearted wit she much admired. "I could fill many volumes with tales of

26

your charm, Amara. Only this afternoon I strolled the library at Keep Daecar and wondered whether there would be sufficient space within to adequately express how delightful you…"

"OK, settle down now, Walter. That's quite enough of that." She glanced over his scribblings once again, as the barkeep set down a large cup of Solapian red, from the coastal vineyards of Arore.

"Fair warning, Lady Amara," he told her, in a husky old voice that carried the rot of a lifetime spent smoking a pipe. "Our stocks aren't going to last much longer, not with trade routes shut. Best enjoy that while it lasts."

"Thank you, Beecham. I will, I'm quite sure." She took a long sip as the barkeep trundled off. "Amron told us not to get drunk," she told Walter. "Apparently you're leaving tomorrow for Crosswater."

"Yes, he rather thrust that on me earlier. I think he wants us separated, Amara, lest we get up to some mischief while he's away."

"A fair concern." She tapped her finger on the wooden table, glancing over the notes once again. There were some sketches among them. She saw a snowbear, or was it a moonbear? *Snow*, she decided. *It lacks that crystal fur.* There was a mountain as well, with a great open doorway, and a small cluster of intrepid souls, preparing to enter. *Vandar's Tomb*, she guessed. Another showed a land of rolling hills and valleys all filled with mist. From the mists came demonic shapes and ghouls, reaching up with grasping fingers. "You have a talent for drawing, Walter. I never knew."

"Neither did I, until I picked up a pen and started scratching. That was after my godly blessing. I suspected it was all just luck, but now I'm not so sure. Perhaps it was just a talent I never knew I had?"

He'd been a carpenter and furniture maker once, before his life had taken a tragic turn when his family was burnt to death by a business rival named Podrick Percival. Amara suspected the skill of carpentry and drawing had some crossover. "I doubt luck had anything to do with it," she told him. "You're a creative soul, Walter, and always were, blessing from a god or no. And quite frankly it cannot be luck, can it? You told me you think it's deserted you."

"My luck? Oh no, how can it have? I'm sitting here with you, after all. And that makes me the luckiest man in the world."

"I'm serious, Walter."

"And so am I."

He doesn't want to talk about it, she realised. That was unfortunate, because she was keenly interested to hear more about that. *Later*, she decided. *I'll fill him up with wine first and return to this later.*

So they drank, giving Beecham a good runaround as he went to and fro from the cellars to fetch Amara all her favourites. They moved on from the rich Solapian red to a fruity golden nectar out of the Golden Isles, then burned out their insides with a fierce and fiery Agarathi vintage matured in the vineyards north of Highport. After that they needed something lighter, so Amara called for a delicate berry cider from the orchards of South Lumara. A sweetwine from Rasalan came next, before finally they returned to where they'd begun, and Solapia, where the best wines were made.

"And I thought my stocks were running low *before* you came here tonight," complained Beecham the barkeep. "Goodness, my lady. You have an appetite on you this eve."

"Don't I always?" She smiled at him through lips stained red and purple. "Fetch some water, will you Beecham. My brother-in-law insists we're not to get too drunk."

"Aye. Right away, my lady."

The tavern was empty by then but for the pair of them, the final few stragglers stumbling out through the doors into the cool of the night. The fat tallow candle on the table had burned low, growing fatter still as the wax spilled over its edges to pool and gather at the bottom. Beecham returned with his water jug and poured two large mugs. "Drink freely of that, my lady," he said. "Not so likely to run out."

Amara took a modest sip and then promptly returned to her wine. It was more for Walter's benefit. Like a drink though he did, he couldn't handle it so well as she could. *And there are so few who can,* she reflected. If there was such a thing as *Wineborn,* Amara Daecar would consider herself the Varin of that order. She smiled to imagine it. "Wouldn't it be wonderful if we could just sit down with our enemies, and compete over who could drink the most," she said. "It would be so much more fun than all this ghastly warring."

"I daresay we would fare rather well," Walter quipped, grinning. "With you in our ranks…and the men of East Vandar. The rivermen especially. Gods, they love a drink. Though the men of the marshes push them a close second, oh yes."

"I had the pleasure of travelling with some such, for a time," Amara told him. "Blackshaw men, led by Sir Mooton. You might know the name. The Beast of Blackshaw, people call him."

"Rings a bell, yes. A big drinker, is he?"

"Oh yes, very much, and a bigger man. Thickest neck I ever saw. Sir Connor could not abide their company, these Blackshaws, but I found them a riot. Lillia as well. But I'm not even sure Sir Mooton would have stood against the mighty force that was Sally Scarlet."

Walter wasn't aware of the name.

"One of the Flame Manes," Amara explained. "A big woman, burly at the shoulder. She drank every man under the table at the inns along the lake when we travelled here from Ilivar. She could outdrink even me, I'd think, though we never locked horns like that. She was more interested in humiliating the men who challenged her." Amara smiled, though it was a sad smile. "She's…she's dead now, along with the rest of them. Only Carly is still alive, poor thing."

She'd kept Carly close by as often as she could, taking her as her body-guard when she walked the city streets, much to Sir Connor's vexation. It still haunted her to think of how many had died that day. Sally Scarlet. Will Red. Crowfoot and Sunset Sam. Mad Maroon Murley and Renfort of the

Rust and the rest. All had been slain outside the gates of Keep Daecar by Godrik's men, the same day Sir Connor suffered that stab wound to the gut. *And when I put that knife through Godrik's neck, it was for every one of them,* she thought. A part of her wanted the world to know that. *I did it and would do it again a dozen times over. But it's my husband who's taken the blame...*

Beecham was clearing the last of the tables and looking very much like he wanted to close up for the night. Amara called over to him. "How long do we have, Beecham?"

"As long as you should like, my lady. I'll keep myself busy till you want to leave, don't fret."

Walter was looking a little bleary-eyed by now. "I...I really ought to go, Amara. Lord Amron...he intends to leave, bright and early."

"*King* Amron. And he will. You said earlier that he wants to separate us?"

Walter took a gulp of water, then wiped his mouth with the back of his sleeve. "So we don't get into mischief," he said. "I can see why he might think that. Given this evening."

"Have you ever thought that he wants you nearby because of your luck?" It was time to return to that matter; she wouldn't get another chance.

He frowned, then shook his head. "My luck isn't what it was, as I've told you." He turned to look out through the frosted glass window into the cobbled lane outside. A cat was wandering by, cool as anything. Walter smiled. "Nine lives. Think I've used mine up, my lady."

"Though you don't know for sure," she pressed.

"Well...I suppose not. Not until such a time as I am faced with a threat of some sort. I have...I have felt my light *dimming*, certainly, though Amron seems to think that it's all in my head." He smiled a little drunkenly. "He's been terribly supportive of me, you know. Even without my luck and my light, I feel a sense of purpose at his side." He gestured to the papers of scribblings and sketches. "I'm to write his story, and the story of this war. Can there be a greater calling, for a lowly man like me?"

Yes, you can help me get my husband back, she thought. Saying it quite so plainly as that might not serve, though, and she didn't want to do anything untoward to achieve it. Sometimes she even wondered why she would bother. Vesryn had proven himself an utter fool and befouled his honour beyond repair, yet for all that, she loved him. She could not help that any more than she could the daily movement of her bowels. She would do without both if she could, but she couldn't. *I love him, and seeing him hang will destroy me.* She knew that in her heart. *My heart, which wants what it bloody wants, no matter the mess...*

"Do you want to know what I think, Walter?"

He looked up at her, nodding faithfully. "Of course. Always."

"I think Amron's right. I think it's all in your head. I think you have just as much light and luck as you ever did. You only need to *believe* you do."

He smiled faintly at the thought. "Perhaps you're right."

Amara didn't like this doubtful side of him. Walter Selleck had always been a man of conviction and faith. "The day we met, you saved my life from that falling building," she said. "I would be long dead if it wasn't for you, and how many others can say the same?" She had wondered that often. How many people were still breathing because of Walter Selleck's gift. "How many men and women have you saved, Walter? Have you ever cared to keep count?"

"I fear a count would prove impossible. My luck always did work in mysterious ways, Amara."

Mysterious ways. "But you have more control over it than you think," she said. "You can channel it, if you really put your mind to it."

He didn't seem sure about that. "I don't know if that's…"

"When that building crumbled around us, we were the only two who survived," she reminded him. She recalled it like it was yesterday. Walter had rushed in and thrown his arms around her, and as the walls fell down upon them, they'd been miraculously untouched. Yet others hadn't been so fortunate, caught and crushed in the collapse. "You channelled your powers toward saving *me* that day, Walter. Subconsciously, perhaps, but you did. And you've done the same with others before as well. You have more control over your luck than you believe. And I don't think Vandar is done with you yet."

He took up his cup of wine, sipping pensively. "I suppose it's possible. But it makes me wonder as to your intentions, I confess." He looked into her eyes. "Do you have some scheme brewing, Amara? I thought you were done with all that."

"I am. This is no scheme. Just a favour, that's all."

"A favour?" He placed down his cup, blinking at her. "What would you have of me?"

She might as well just say it. "Vesryn."

He sat back at once, throwing his head from side to side. "No. I can't collude in freeing him. Amron…after all he's done for me…"

"*You've* done more for *him*. He'd be dead but for you, he's told me so himself."

"Even so." His guard was coming up, and she could hardly blame him for that. Amara did have something of a reputation. "I'm not going to be a part of this. Use Sir Connor, if you must. Or the Carly girl, or the boy Jovyn. You have many catspaws and cutthroats who'll help you."

"I don't need catspaws and cutthroats. You mistake my intent, Walter. I don't want anyone to be harmed. I just…" She sniffed. "I just want my husband back, is all. He doesn't deserve to hang for a crime he didn't commit." She laid her hand on the table. The tips of her fingers were still red and raw from when her nails had been torn off, and her pinky was still missing. That part was unlikely to grow back. "*I* killed Godrik Taynar, Walter, but Amron won't let me say it. I can't live with seeing Vesryn die for me. You have to help me." She sniffed again. "*Please.*"

"My lady…" His voice was a choked whisper. He reached to take her hand, holding her palm delicately. "I don't know what I could do…"

"Use your luck," she urged him. "Channel it. Think of Vesryn, and imagine him a free man. Perhaps…perhaps that might be enough?" It was all she had, though it sounded absurd to say it. *Mysterious ways,* she thought. "Do you think you could do that for me, Walter? Do you think…do you think you could *try*, at least?"

"Of course." He said the words without hesitation. "I don't know if…I can't say that…" He cut himself off. *He doesn't want to tell me it won't work. He doesn't want to tell me to my face how desperate and stupid I'm being.* "I'll try," is all he told her. "I'll think of Vesryn every day. I'll…I'll pray to Vandar that he finds deliverance. It's…it's the best I can do, my lady."

And it's the best I'm going to get. She took up her cup and drank deep. *You're in Vandar's hands now, Vesryn. He'll judge whether you're worthy or not.*

3

Saska

The giant caught her with a shuddering blow that sent her careening wildly across the marble courtyard. She lost her feet and tripped, landing in a puff of ochre dust, and spun her eyes up to look at him.

"Do you yield?"

"No." She gasped the word out and surged to her feet, swinging an upcut that glanced off the misting metal of his breastplate.

"Good." He swerved backward as she came at him again, side-slashing, thrusting, hacking. Her attacks grew as ragged as her breath. Sweat streamed from her hair down her forehead and into her eyes, stinging. She slowed to wipe them clean, and her opponent saw his chance. One moment she was swinging hard and the next she was on the flat of her back, blinking up through blurred eyes, fighting for breath. The giant stood over her. "Do you yield?" he asked again.

Never, she thought, but when she tried to say the word, nought but a spluttery mess came out. Sir Ralston swung his misting greatsword around and put the tip to her neck. "You yield," he told her. "Stand up, brush yourself down, have a drink of water, and gather your breath. Then we go again."

Saska did as the Whaleheart bid her, pulling in several long breaths until the fires in her lungs were doused. Gradually her breathing returned to normal. She stood and walked wearily over to the stand where the jugs of water and clay cups were laid out, aching with every step.

"Here." Sir Ralston handed her a cup and she gulped down a full measure. It was hot today, the air still and windless, and the courtyard had grown stifling. Beyond, a short corridor gave access to a balcony overlooking the south of Aram and its bustling harbour. Saska could see the sea sparkling distantly out there, bleeding into the blue horizon. She longed for a dip in the cool coastal waters. *Soon*, she thought. Once she was done with her training, the sweet-scented gardens atop the palace awaited her, with their pools and fountains and pretty cherry trees. She'd have a good long relaxing bath then.

Sir Ralston was looking down at her, as she refilled her cup and drank another measure. "You lost form," he said. "And focus. You went down much too easily."

"It was the sweat," she complained. "It got in my eyes."

"You had already lost your form by then. Don't blame the sweat." Sir Ralston Whaleheart was eight feet of muscle and scarred flesh, beneath a full suit of godsteel armour. There was no man more formidable. *And few so lacking in praise,* Saska thought bitterly. Her gargantuan guardian was decidedly ungenerous when it came to complimenting her efforts in the sparring circle. *He is a hard taskmaster, to be sure. Perhaps it's payback for his time spent in Lord Krator's cells?*

She would forgive him for that. Sir Ralston had been savagely treated by Krator's guardsmen, and had almost died in the Red Pits a while back, suffering several serious stab wounds that would have put an end to many a lesser man. *But not my Rolly. My unkillable Wall.* A tough swordmaster he might be, but by the gods he'd earned it. *And it's what I need. I don't need anyone coddling me.* She was supposed to be a granddaughter to the last of the Varin kings, after all. *The lost heir of Varin need not be wrapped in wool.*

"Are you ready to go again?"

There didn't seem to be an option to say no, even if she wanted to. It was the Whaleheart's express duty to train her, toughen her, sharpen her until she could be sharpened no more. It seemed to Saska that fate had made her a weapon, and any good weapon needed to be honed, lest its edge grow dull. *And this man is my whetstone,* she thought. "I'm ready," she told him.

"Good. Then step back into the sparring circle. Helms on this time."

She turned to the table and put on the godsteel helm she'd been given, a scuffed dinted thing with a set of bladed crab claws reaching from its crest. It would have been worn by a Rasal knight or lord once, she knew, though how it had found its way down here she could only guess. *House Swiftwater,* she thought. Their sigil was a crab with blades for claws. *Some Swiftwater man once owned it.*

The rest of her was garbed in godsteel too, a mismatched set from a dozen different northern houses and kingdoms. The Butcher had been tasked with outfitting her as such. "I shall go out and find the pretty princess the armour she needs," the Bloody Trader captain had said. "I have many contacts whom I can call upon. Sellswords, mercenaries, merchants, yes, I know many of these who will have the parts you need. Breastplates and helms and gauntlets, these will be easy to get. Some other parts less so. But the Butcher will see it done."

He'd been good to his word. A mere two days later, he'd returned to the palace to deliver the aforementioned items along with sabatons, cuisses, greaves and gorget, vambraces, pauldrons and plackart, and several other components besides. "As ordered," the scarred sellsword had said, grinning proudly from ear to ear. "Not all will fit the pretty princess well, but it was the best I could do at short notice."

He hadn't been wrong about the fit. The breastplate was too broad in the chest, the pauldrons too wide and clunky, the sabatons too long in the toe. The gauntlets fit nicely, for which she was grateful, and so did the greaves and vambraces, but the rest was a little too loose for her build. To combat that she had to wear quilted shirts and breeches to pad herself out, and that didn't exactly help the heat. When she'd trained in Thalan, she'd never even worn proper armour, nor trained so much with godsteel blades either. *And I only had Leshie and Astrid to spar with.* The Wall was a different prospect entirely.

She stepped into the sparring circle to face her foe. "I want you to focus this time," he told her, as they took their places. "You think you were focused last time?" He shook his huge head. "You weren't. Your mind was wandering and you were looking for a cheap killing stroke. You have to earn it first. Work the opponent around until you find a good opening. Then strike. But not before."

I'm tired, she wanted to say. *I'm tired, hot, drenched in sweat, and sore down to my bones. Leave me alone.* But she said none of that. Instead she dipped her chin, pulled down her visor, and stepped forward to engage.

She did better this time. Not well. Just better. They fought for some three or four minutes, she judged, before she found herself staggering outside the circle again, tripping over her overlong sabatons as she fell to the dusty marble floor. This courtyard was not oft-visited, she had decided, from that dust. It coated the floor, and had stained the walls as well, drifting in from the desert when the gritty sandstorms blew in from the north. The palace was so staggeringly large that she imagined there were a good many places here that no one ever trod. *Perhaps I could get lost in one of them?* she wondered. *Go and hide somewhere where even the Wall will never find me...*

The Whaleheart loomed above her once again, victorious. "Stand," he boomed. "That's enough for today."

She stood to face him, craning her neck up to meet his impassive eyes. "You know, a kind word here or there wouldn't hurt. I miss my *Rolly.* This Sir Ralston the Swordmaster isn't as nice."

"My job is not to be nice. It's to train you, that's it." He turned away and walked back to the water counter.

She followed right after him. "How hard are you going on me?" she asked. "Be honest."

"You wouldn't like my answer."

"I don't care. Just tell me."

"A quarter," he said, removing his bucket-like greathelm. As with the rest of his godsteel plate, it had been retrieved from the armoury of Lord Elio Krator and returned to his gigantic person.

And it fits him like a glove, Saska thought, a shade envious. She yearned to have a set of her own tailor-made to her frame. "A quarter," she repeated. "Of..."

"Of my strength," he said. "That would be my judgment. Perhaps a third."

She took off her own helm and placed it aside on the stubby-legged reinforced table, built to bear the metal's weight. Her hair was soaked beneath, rivulets of sweat licking down the back of her neck to pool in pockets in her armour. She began removing her gauntlets as she spoke. "So you're saying you could be fighting four times as hard as you are now?"

"Three or four, yes. That would be my judgement."

She had to laugh. Sir Ralston Whaleheart had cut the head off a dragon in a single swipe, legend said, and there was an oft-told rumour that he could cleave through godsteel with a good strong heft as well. *If he wanted to, he could cut me right in half. I'm never going to be able to match him, not in strength at any rate.* "You have my vote, Rolly," she said, placing her right gauntlet next to its twin. She was wearing leather gloves underneath; those came off too, and at once she felt much cooler.

"Your vote? In what?"

"To wield the Heart of Vandar, if it's ever restored. Who could be better to bear the heart of a god than the biggest, strongest man in all the world?"

He grunted at that. "I'm Rasalanian. The Blades of Vandar are for Vandarians to bear."

"Like *me*?" she laughed. "I've never even been to Vandar." She was being facetious, of course, but it made it a great deal easier for her to treat it all flippantly.

"You're directly descended from its founder," Sir Ralston told her. "It's hard to come to terms with, I know, but your grandmother has no reason to lie to you. King Lorin was your grandfather. If Lady Safina is right, only you can bear the Heart of Vandar, Saska." He put an enormous armoured hand to her shoulder. "That's why I'm here, to support you and train you. I'll be with you until the end, this I promise." He smiled for the first time in days. "I'm your Wall now, remember. That will never change."

My Wall, she thought. Until a time comes when *I'm* the wall, against all the darkness. Her heart fluttered nervously at the thought of it. If what her grandmother said was true, they had an overwhelming amount of work yet to do. *And that gives us time, at least,* she consoled herself. She'd only learned the truth of who she was days ago, and every morning she woke up with her sheets soaked in sweat, and her head all full of nightmares. She hoped that one day soon she might wake to a dry bed and a clear head, but wasn't going to count on it.

Footsteps sounded behind her and she turned to find the Butcher climbing up the steps. His tattered cloak flapped behind him, patched and sewn in a dozen shades of red, slashed here and there like the many scars that crossed his flesh. He entered the duelling courtyard and looked around, grinning broadly. "Warm here," he noted. "This is good for training. The more you sweat when you train, the less you bleed when you fight. My brother the Baker likes to say that."

35

"You shouldn't be up here," Sir Ralston admonished. "How did you get into the palace?"

"I have leave to go where I please, Whaleheart. For all the good help I have given the pretty princess." He smiled at her. "You look pretty even in this ugly armour. How is this so?"

"You flatter me, Butcher. I suspect I look a sight."

"No, never."

The Wall took a pace toward him. "I said you shouldn't be up here," he boomed. "What do you want? Have you come to deliver some message?"

"I come to train," the sellsword told him. "I had a thought...a good thought, I think." His grin broadened. "The pretty princess trains with the giant whalehearted knight, this is true, but she should train with the Butcher as well. I can present to her a different challenge. Not the forms, no. The sellsword stances. The fluid fighting I have learned during my long years in the south."

"No," Sir Ralston told him. "We have no need of you. Go."

"The Whaleheart is cruel. The Butcher tries to help, that is all. He was a pit fighter for long years, yes, and a great champion at that. You would do well to observe me. Even you may learn a thing or two, giant."

"No, I said. Our training is done for the day, and Lady Saska must focus on her recovery."

"Tomorrow, then. I will return tomorrow."

"No."

Sir Ralston did not like the Butcher, that was plain to see. He seemed to consider sellswords an unseemly sort, and had little time for them. *The pair do look rather alike, though,* she mused. She'd thought the Butcher a big man, and he was by any fair comparison, but even large men looked small next to Sir Ralston Whaleheart. Aside from the height disparity, their gruesome scarring and bald heads gave them a similar aspect. Leshie liked to call the Butcher 'Minnowheart', or 'Small Wall', on account of that, and once Saska had heard her call him 'Parapet' as well, which she had to chuckle at, but that was just Leshie. She loved her nicknames and loved trying to undermine the Butcher even more. Unfortunately, he seemed to enjoy it equally. When Leshie had called him *parapet* he'd laughed louder than anyone.

He wasn't laughing now, though. "I come here to help, and you merely turn me away. No, this is not courteous. A knight should know better."

"So should a sellsword. I have no interest in your stances, skilled though you might be. If you wish to train, do so with your own men. You'll not come here again."

The Butcher had never looked so offended. The scars on his face tightened as he glared. "I am not a knight myself, but I am sired of one. A Buckland, from your own lands of Rasalan. That makes us brothers, of a sort. I would never treat a brother as such." He swished his patched red cloak and strode away.

"Stop," Saska said.

The Butcher swung back around before he reached the steps. "No. You need not apologise for him, pretty princess. The man is called Whaleheart, yes, but in truth his heart is cold and small. He is not a kind man, but that is not your doing." He bowed. "I will leave you."

"Fine. But come back tomorrow. Midday. We'll start then."

"What?" growled the Wall. "My lady, no. This is my training yard, not yours. You cannot invite anyone you please…"

She cut him off. "I can, actually. Within reason. So far as I see it, having the Butcher here will add some variety." *And maybe he'll actually have some praise for me*, she thought. She couldn't see a downside to it. The Butcher was clearly a gifted warrior and would offer a different challenge as he'd said. *And it'll make it more fun too.*

"He can't be trusted," Sir Ralston claimed. He gave her a firm look. "He doesn't know the *truth*, my lady."

Ah yes, the truth. Saska's true parentage was being kept secret from all but a few, owing to the risks she would face if her identity ever got out. "You will be hunted, sweet child," her grandmother had told her. "The Fire Father will seek to eliminate all threats to his hegemony, and if he should discover that the heir of Varin yet lives, he will send all his strength to destroy you."

Wonderful, she'd thought to hear that. It hadn't stopped her telling Leshie, though, who deserved to know for all she'd done, and Ranulf, though of course he'd worked it all out already. Sir Ralston had been told, so he might prepare her, and so had a few in her grandmother's confidence, but that was all. She wondered now if the Butcher ought to know as well, but that was probably inadvisable. She'd come to trust him for his faithful service over the last few weeks, but if he found out, it would be sure to reach the ears of green-eyed Merinius and Marco of the Mistwood too, and then it might come into the attention of Slack Stan as well, and after that all the world would soon find out. *That wobbly jaw of his does like to jabber. Best not get it jabbering about this.*

The Butcher looked curious, though. "What truth are we discussing, I wonder?"

"Nothing you need know about," the Wall warned.

Saska sighed internally. *Say it like that and he'll only be more interested*, she thought. "The truth is Sir Ralston had a dear friend who was slain by sellswords once," she said, thinking up the lie on the spot. "He has since harboured a firm dislike for your ilk, Captain Butcher, if that explains his discourteous conduct toward you." She caught Sir Ralston's frowning glare, though ignored it. The Butcher merely smiled. *He knows it's not the truth Rolly was referring to*, she thought. *But no matter, he's discreet enough to let it pass.*

"I see. Yes, this does explain things. We sellswords do have a habit of killing people. Who was this friend, Whaleheart?"

"No one you need know about."

"A sore matter. I will not probe further." He turned to Saska and gave a bow. "Tomorrow, then. I shall return at midday." He swished that crimson cloak, gave a customary grin, and was gone.

Sir Ralston glared at the steps long after the man had departed. Saska

37

was halfway through removing her armour when he said, "Why did you lie like that? I've had no friend slain by sellswords." The thought seemed to offend him.

"You'd have to have friends first," Saska teased. The man was not a social creature, she knew. His life had been one of duty, always. No time for friendship or lovers. "I lied because you were making him suspicious. If I say, 'don't think about dragons', what are you thinking about?"

The Wall gave no answer.

"Dragons," she answered for him. "It's the same thing when you mutter about some secret to a man and don't tell him what it is. He's only going to wonder. So you have to give him something else. And the longer you take to think of a lie, the more suspicious it'll look." She unlaced the links that bound her breastplate and pulled it off her body, laying it with a *clunk* on the table. "You do hate sellswords, though," she told the giant knight. "I wasn't lying about that bit."

"They have no honour. All they care about is coin."

"Untrue. The Butcher had every chance to give me up to Mar Malaan, but didn't. Krator would have paid him handsomely, and his men wouldn't have died either. He risked his life for me, same as you would have."

The Wall was unconvinced. "Shackton says he never stopped talking about money, the whole time you were on the road."

She couldn't deny it. "I'm not saying he doesn't care about coin. Just that there's more to him than that. He only wanted fair compensation, that's all." She pulled off her quilted jerkin, soaked with sweat, unveiling her linen undershirt. She could smell the heat pouring off her, and the stink, that too. "I'm going to go and bathe," she told him. "Coming?"

He shook his head. "Those baths are not for me. I will wash elsewhere, then come and stand guard on you."

"You needn't be so vigilant in the palace, Rolly. No harm will come to me here." It was no use telling him that, though. Sir Ralston had stood sentry over her from the start. She remembered fondly those days on the Steel Sister when he would stand on deck in his armour and cloak, saying nothing, watching the crew with his suspicious eyes. *He even watched over me at night*, she recalled. Sir Ralston didn't seem to need rest like normal men. It was those long years standing guard over King Godrin that honed that talent. *Godrin, my great uncle.* She was still getting used to that too.

"There are always threats," the Whaleheart claimed. "It is when you feel most safe that you need to be most careful."

She didn't understand the logic there but had no desire to question it. "Fine. I'll see you later, then."

The steep climb to the terrace gardens was a workout she could do without, her legs burning with every step despite unburdening herself of her sweat-soaked training garb and armour. The pyramid palace was shaped in three soaring tiers, the lowest built of bricks coated in bronze, the middle silver, the top gilded in polished gold. On every tier were many smaller levels, with balconies and terraces and huge, feather-like banners flapping on the wind. Along the stone staircases, torches burned in sconces of bronze, silver, and gold as well, each of them cast in the likeness of an eagle in some form or another. Some had grasping talons and others snapping beaks, and others still had wings outstretched as though about to take flight.

Everything in Aram was eagles, Saska had long since learned. They were seen in stone and silk, cast in marble and carved in wooden masts. Ships showed them, as did garments both functional and fine, and it was unheard of to find a town square that did not have at least one statue or fountain showing the likeness of Calacan, the Eagle of Aramatia. The city guards wore them as well, on the crests of their halfhelms, and half of the Aramatian houses had an eagle on their arms, in some shape or form.

Unsurprisingly, the high terrace gardens had several of them. The biggest was at the heart of the gardens, a great marble-cast statue facing out to sea. Saska liked the look in its eyes most of all, as it gazed toward the horizon, as though wondering what might be out there. She remembered what her maids Milla and Koya had said once, about how Calacan had flown out beyond the horizon and discovered other continents and lands across the impassable seas. She spotted her grandmother, sitting beside the pools in the shade of a cherry tree. "Do you believe there are other continents out there?" she asked, walking over.

Safina Nemati looked up from the heavy leather tome in her lap. She wore a long silver dress in the finest silk that covered her from shoulder to ankle. From its sleeves and hems poked hands and feet wrinkled and spotted with age. Her hair was a shimmer of grey going white, gathered in a black hairnet encrusted with tiny sparkling diamonds. She always dressed well, did the Grand Duchess of Aramatia. Despite the rich mix of royal blood in her veins, Saska always felt so decidedly un-royal in her presence.

"We have legends that say so," her grandmother answered. "Do I believe them? Some, yes. A curious mind always strives for more, Saska. It seems much too limiting to believe that this world of ours is restricted to the lands we know." Safina Nemati smiled to see her granddaughter so bedraggled and sweaty. "How was training? I trust you are giving your giant knight a good runaround."

"Sir Ralston never runs," Saska replied to that. "He darts occasionally, and makes good use of the sidestep and backtrack when needed, but running? No. I think he'd break the palace if ever he tried."

Her grandmother laughed musically. Though growing physically frail, she remained stout of spirit and that laugh was proof of it.

"What are you reading, Grandmother?" It still felt odd to call her that, though less so by the day. She peered at the book, spying the title for herself. *"Gods and Monsters: A Compendium of Terrors from North and South."* She raised a brow. "Not exactly light reading."

"I've never had much of an interest in light reading, child."

"It's written in the common tongue."

"Yes. The author is one Bulivar Broadhurst, known as the Sorefoot Scholar. Have you heard of him?"

Saska nodded vaguely. "I think Elyon had a book by him, when I stayed in his tent at Harrowmoor. Some history or the three northern kingdoms, or some such."

"Yes, I've read it. *One Continent, Three Kingdoms, A Hundred Kings.* The title never made much sense to me, as there have been many Rasalanian *queens* as well, but still, a good read."

Saska remembered the name. She'd even glanced through some of the book herself, during those long days when Elyon was absent during the siege. "Why was he called the *Sorefoot* Scholar?" she asked.

"You can probably guess. He liked to range far and wide in search of the truth and travelled all across the world in a career spanning six decades. His focus in this particular tome is, as you can guess from the title, the gods and monsters who have lived among us. It's an exhaustive collection." She tapped a finger on the page she was reading. "This chapter here deals with the Lumaran prophecy of the Ever-War."

Saska frowned. "I thought that was an Aramatian belief?"

"So some think. In truth it originated in Lumara, though Aramatians, Piseki, even Solapians have their own versions. It's a commonly held fore-telling of the apocalypse all across the south, and goes by many names. The Ever-War is most common of them. I thought it prudent for me to read up on what old Sorefoot writes of it."

"And?"

"And nothing I don't already know." She closed the book with a *thump.* "Bulivar Broadhurst did not espouse any theory of his own. He merely included the chapter on the Ever-War for extra context. Gods, monsters, and the Ever-War are inextricably linked, after all." She reached to a side table and took up a cup of lemon water, sipping through her rumpled lips. "Thirsty, child?"

In this heat? Always. Saska nodded and took up a cup of her own, drinking deep of the cool lemony liquid. Then she peeled off her linen undershirt and breeches and slipped into the nearest pool, enjoying the kiss of the cold water against her skin. Soaps and scrubbing brushes were set aside for her use. "Shall I call upon the maids?" her grandmother asked. She had a little bell on the table beside her. One little shake of it and a host of servants would come running.

"That's OK. I prefer to wash myself." Saska had never been completely comfortable being the lady and not the lowborn. *Though I did grow used to being attended by Yasha, Milla, and Koya,* she thought. A part of her missed that. The three maids had become fond to her during her time as Krator's captive, and she'd learned a great deal from them besides. The language, most of all. Yasha had helped deepen her understanding of Aramatian and always made sure they spoke in the local tongue while they bathed and oiled her, and made her clean for their master.

She wondered what had become of them. *I told them to run,* she remem-bered. *I told Yasha to get the others out, to come to Aram and rejoin me if the battle went ill.* At that point, a full clash between Krator and Kastor had been imminent, and Saska hadn't known what the outcome might be. Now she did. *Krator lost,* she thought, as she scrubbed at herself with a scouring brush. She'd heard that the day she arrived in Aram, less than a week ago. After many sallies and probes and skirmishes, the Tukorans and Aramatians had come together upon the plains outside Eagle's Perch, and Lord Elio Krator's army had been driven back by the northern host. Now Cedrik Kastor had taken the fort city for his own, and was surely planning to further his invasion along the coast. Saska wondered what the point would be. Forts could change hands, and cities too, and armies could clash in the field, yet in the end, in the grand tapestry of time, none of that would matter.

Unless we defeat Eldur, the Ever-War will swallow us all, she fretted, scrubbing herself pink. The world would become a battleground of terrors unimaginable, and civilisation as they knew it would collapse into chaos and darkness. Her grandmother had told her that the last remaining embers of the gods needed to be put out once and for all, if the cycle of Renewals was to end. *If not, half the monsters in that book will come crawling out of the shadows.* It might already be happening, for all she knew. She looked out beyond the gardens, to the wide open ocean, and imagined ships being pulled under by krakens and monstrous sea-beasts. *They'll come up from the depths, and they'll come down from the mountains, and they'll clamber from their caves and creep from their woods.* Saska shuddered to think of it. *But we have time*, she told herself, as she often did. *We still have time to stop it.*

The shadows were moving across the terrace gardens as the sun fell away to the west. Saska moved with them, changing from one pool to another so she might remain in the sunlight a little longer, enjoying the contrasting cool of the water with the warmth of the sun on her shoulders and back. She paddled to the front of the pool and stretched her arms out onto the warm stone that bordered it, relaxing. Birds chirped in the trees, and insects buzzed about her, and below came the faint distant sounds of the city far away. It was as idyllic a setting as she could imagine, a paradise atop the world. *If the Eternal Halls are anything like this*, she thought, *death won't be so bad.*

She wondered which hall she could go to, when that time should come. All the gods kept different halls and gardens in the afterlife, everyone knew. Varin's Table. The Hall of Green. The Ocean Halls of Rasalan. Eshina's Grove. The Great Forge. There were dozens of them, more than Saska could remember off the top of her head. Some were reserved for particular men or women; others were open to all. Varin's Table, for instance, was kept for men of his order only, though all men and women of Vandar would be able to visit Eshina's Grove. The Hall of Green was the same; only Emerald Guards could go there, yet the Great Forge was where every soul born of Tukor could wander, just as all those born of Rasalan could enter the sea god's magnificent halls.

But what of me? Where will I go when I die? Saska's father had been called Thalavar, she'd learned, the secret son of King Lorin of Vandar and Princess Atia of Rasalan, who'd been Godrin's younger sister. *Will it be Eshina's Grove, then?* she wondered, *or Rasalan's Ocean Halls? If I am truly Varin's heir, will I get access to his Table?* She doubted that as much as she doubted it even

41

existed. Saska had always been more pragmatic than pious and did not spend her time pondering the vagaries of the afterlife.

Until now, she thought. It had been more on her mind of late, that was true, but only because her true heritage had finally been unearthed, and only because death felt much more likely than ever before. Now she thought about it a lot. And not just the northern notions of the afterlife, but those of the south as well. She was half Aramatian, after all, and they held different beliefs down here. *The dead join the stars*, she thought. *They float up into the Blackness Above and join the Field of Fallen Souls. Will I join them too, one day? Will it be the Eternal Halls that call to me, or the stars? Or will my soul simply split apart when I die, to go its separate ways?*

She continued to ruminate as the sun bled lower in the west, pulling the shadows across the stone until all the pools were shaded. It had grown chilly by then, so she waded back through the pool and climbed out the other side, letting the water run off her smooth olive skin and down the lash-scars on her back, old wounds from her days under the roof of Keep Kastor. A white cotton robe had been laid out for her. She drew it over her shoulders and pulled the tie about her waist to cover herself. Then she went to sit with her grandmother.

The old woman had the book about gods and monsters open in her lap once more, though had swapped her lemon water for wine, as she was wont to do at this hour. Saska could hear the servants scurrying through the residence behind them, preparing dinner as the sun went down. The smells were wafting out and making her mouth water. She'd never eaten half so well as she had here in her grandmother's care.

The Grand Duchess filled her a cup of wine. "Have a drink, child. It will help you unwind."

Saska hesitated. "Sir Ralston won't approve. He thinks wine is damaging to my recovery."

"Your recovery involves more than just physical rest, as the Whaleheart ought to know. Your mind must also have a chance to relax, and in this, a touch of wine helps." She nudged the cup closer. "Drink. Your Grand Duchess commands it."

Saska didn't need to be told a third time. She drew a long sip, letting the liquid warm through her chest. "He thinks I'm in danger," she said, looking out toward the darkening sea. "Sir Ralston. Even here in the palace. He said that the safer you feel, the more wary you must be."

Her grandmother chuckled. "Never was there a more wary man than Sir Ralston Whaleheart. He was always the same when he stood guard on Godrin. Unsmiling, unflinching, immovable. Not a man for a banquet or ball, perhaps, but there's no one better to shadow you." She folded her hands in her lap, atop the open book. "And I daresay he's right to be cautious. The palace might be safe enough, yes, but the city beyond is another matter. Lord Krator has many supporters here still who may risk a bold play to win his grace. Lord Hasham is doing what he can to cast light upon the shadows they hide in, but this is no simple task. We may face a fight here in Aram yet, Saska. My rule is not so secure as it seems."

As if we don't have enough to worry about, Saska thought to that. She had to sit in terror at the prospect of a demigod hunting her down. Worrying that Lord Elio Krator might be out for vengeance was salt in that open wound. "Maybe we should tell them," she said, thinking out loud. "About who my father was. And who I am." *And what I'm meant to do,* she thought, with a shudder.

But her grandmother shook her head. "To expose you to the world would only bring the wrath of Eldur down upon us. No. Secrecy is our ally."

"But if Lord Krator knew, at least. He and his allies. Might they understand better what the *real* threat is? Might they not support us?"

"Some might. Others would not. We are part of a puzzle, child, that only a select few are even aware of. Men of power are naturally distrusting. They will come with their questions and their doubts and most will not believe us. They will think they are being manipulated, lied to, deceived. And this may only multiply our enemies, rather than grow our base of allies, at a time we can least afford it."

Saska felt wearier than ever all of a sudden. Secrets were treacherous things, and her grandmother wasn't wrong. *Men do not like being kept in the dark,* she thought. *Even if the secret was devised to protect them, they can rebel against the truth when they hear it.* Secrets bred lies, and lies bred resentment. *And do I resent?* she wondered, as her mind went back to King Godrin, and she thought of those scars on her back. *Do I resent being left to suffer under the roof of Lord Modrik Kastor? Do I resent that my great uncle Godrin never saved me, never told me, never prepared me for what was to come?*

She did. A part of her, at least. How could she not? She'd asked her grandmother if she'd known where she had been taken as a child, but she'd said she hadn't. But Godrin was a different matter. *He knew,* Saska had already decided. *That's why he said what he did, that day we met in the palace in Thalan.* He'd apologised for all she'd been through, as though in self-rebuke, as though he was to blame, and then he'd uttered those fateful words that had been with her all the days and nights since.

You're exactly where you're meant to be.

My crutch, she thought. *The shoulder on which I have leaned.* For long months she'd fallen back on those words, even when all felt helpless. She would whisper them to herself when she was alone, turn to them in the dark of night when she knew not where her path would take her. But now she knew. It had taken her here, to her grandmother, to Aram and the truth of her sire.

I am a piece of a puzzle. A puzzle whose parts were scattered through time by Thala, the Far Seeing Queen. That puzzle was coming together now, and yet the final picture it made remained shrouded in doubt. No one knew for certain what the future would bring. Victory or defeat. A world at peace between north and south or a battleground of eternal war, filled with gods and monsters and beasts of a bygone age. A world where all must fight for survival. A world of darkness, doom, fire and ash, with the fire god Agarath, laughing above it all.

Saska drew on her wine, a long deep sip to settle her nerves. Darkness was coming upon them now, the skies melting into a purple-pink dusk, lined with thin bands of clouds that stretched to the far horizon like long red fingers, reaching for a brighter dawn.

But before dawn comes, I'll need to sleep. She dreaded sleep now more than ever, and no wonder she needed the wine. In her sleep there were no gate-keepers to guard her against her thoughts. No Rolly. No Agarosh. No one to stand sentry against the terrors of her dreams, where she spent her sleeping hours thrashing and tossing and turning, sweating her sheets sodden as she used to, once before. She remembered a night at the academy in Thalan, when she'd been screaming in her bed, reliving the nightmare of Lord Quintan's death. Leshie and Astrid had shaken her awake, faces pale in the dim torchlight of their dorm. *They looked frightened,* she recalled, *and worried.* Yet the terrors had always hounded Saska at night. It had been the same with Master Orryn. When she first arrived at Willow's Rise after Lord Modrik Kastor's death, she'd suffered from night terrors often, Orryn had said. *He would sit outside my room sometimes,* she recalled. *He would guard the door as Rolly did on the Steel Sister, in case I should wake in the night...*

Orryn... She felt sad every time she thought of him. He had been a good man, right down to his marrow, honest and unfailingly kind. *My true father,* she thought. *As Llana was my sister and Del my brother.* They were her first real family, the first family she'd ever known. She'd met Marian and her men after, and Ranulf and Leshie and Astrid, and then Elyon and Barnibus and Lancel and Rolly, and now she had her grandmother too. But Orryn, Llana, Del. That had been a simple time. Working the fields. Hunting the woods. Cooking and cleaning in the farmhouse. She had never been so contented as she had been then. *And now they're probably dead,* she thought. *And if not yet, they will be soon...*

"I dreamt of him again last night."

The words took her grandmother by surprise. She looked over, eyes raised. "The same as before?"

Saska nodded. She didn't need to explain who 'he' was. "He burst into flame, as he always does. And the skies. I saw more dragons in the skies than ever." *And one bigger than the rest...* She turned to look down at the book in her grandmother's lap. *Gods and Monsters: A Compendium of Terrors from North and South.* "Is there a chapter on...on Drulgar the Dread in there?"

The question needn't be asked. Drulgar the Dread was the greatest of all calamities, the most feared of Agarath's followers, above even Eldur. A book of gods and monsters would not be complete without him. "Sorefoot devotes twenty pages to the Dread alone," her grandmother confirmed. "Much of what we know of him is myth, however. There is little true history of that time."

That time. The concept was so strange to Saska. *Time didn't even exist then, not as it does now.* The gods were said to have warred for thousands of years before they eventually fell. *Or left,* she thought. It was a common belief in the south that the gods had never fallen, only departed, to raise new conti-

44

nents and battlegrounds beyond the seas. Either way, their War Eternal had raged for millennia, and somewhere during that time, Agarath had raised up Drulgar the Dread from the depths of his fury and hate, conjuring his most fearsome weapon to lead his children against Vandar's hosts in war. By the time the gods had fallen or fled, most of the monsters they'd made were long gone, yet some remained, crawling away into the darkness of their woods and mountains or diving to the depths of the seas. It was those creatures that were prophesied to return by the Ever-War, bringing unutterable chaos along with them. Saska wondered if Drulgar himself might return as well, given what she'd seen in her dreams. *But he can't, can he? He is long dead, long gone, slain by Varin in his grief-stricken rage…*

A clank of armour broke Saska out of her thoughts, as Sir Ralston appeared across the high gardens, wreathed head to heel in his misting armour. The mere sight of him helped to still Saska's beating heart, helped douse the doubts within. *Rolly, my watchful protector,* Saska thought. She turned to look beyond the terrace, out past the city walls. A large camp had sprung up out there now, as the commonfolk came in from the hinterlands. *For safety,* Saska knew. *And for Agarosh.* There were markets now, and bazaars, and tens of thousands spread out in a great sprawling camp. And each day, sermons were sung and prayers were given for the great moonbear who'd returned from the mountain.

For me. To help protect me, and watch over me, just as Sir Ralston is. In that, at least, Saska took some comfort. *The Ever-War draws all monsters from the shadows,* she thought. *The wicked…and the righteous.*

4

Ranulf

The upper terrace of the *Regal Eagle* was busy with the sound of chattering men, sharing in the latest gossips and discussing prospective business opportunities. The two terraces below were more rowdy, popular among the common dockworkers and deckhands as they were, yet the top terrace portrayed a more refined air. Here the harbour officials, shipwrights, merchants and magnates liked to rub shoulders; ambitious men keen on enhancing their prospects and wealth. Ranulf Shackton was waiting on such a figure. He'd met many a man of ambition in his time, yet few so openly persistent in his desires than a certain merchant by name of Cliffario Denlatis.

"He is often late," Sallor Sanara said, as the wait went on, and another jug of wine was brought out by a server. "Cliffario likes to keep his own time. Important men often do."

Leshie looked at the small shipwright with a frown etched upon her reddish brow. "Denlatis isn't important," she scoffed. "He's just an upjumped merchant with a few ships, that's all."

"And a few short years ago he was nothing but the son of a docker, destined to a life of squalor and scraps," Sallor returned mildly. He poured the wines. "Cliffario has always played the part of an important man, even before he built his wealth. After his first major trade he invested in fine clothes and jewellery to better present that image. 'I show them what they want to see', he confided in me once. He even had training in elocution and body language, all the little things we take for granted. Oh, he came well-prepared for success, Leshie. And now he seems set to rise higher still."

Beyond his wildest dreams, Ranulf thought, taking a sip of his fine fruity wine. Cliffario Denlatis had crawled out of the mire into which he was born, refashioned himself into a man of civility and rich tastes, and won over the docks of Aram. Shipwrights like Sallor liked him, merchants favoured him with their trades, customs officials turned a blind eye to his underhanded tactics, and he'd even grown close to a good many sellsword companies and groups, not least the Bloody Traders with whom he dealt often. *He's much like another man I know, who climbed out of the gutter and accumulated the power and influence of a lord.* Ranulf had not seen Vincent Rose in long months, but in Cliffario Denlatis recognised a kindred spirit.

The sun was setting on the coastal waters, rippling red and vermillion between the ships at anchor. Ranulf ran his eyes over the bustling harbourside, trying to spot the man he'd come to meet. Built high up against the city walls a hundred metres east of the gate, the upper terrace of the Regal Eagle afforded them an excellent view. It had been built in the image of the three-tiered pyramid palace itself, with the triple terraces representing those tiers, and much like the palace, only patrons of a certain importance were permitted to the top. Yet still, the merchant was nowhere to be seen.

Leshie gave out an impatient grunt. "How long are we going to have to wait?" she complained, as was her way. The girl was either loving life or hating it; there seemed no middle ground with her. "It's getting boring now."

"A little longer, at least," Ranulf told her. Cliffario was a good hour past due, though apparently that wasn't uncommon. "Just enjoy the view, Leshie, and drink your wine. He'll be along shortly."

"The view is *much* better at the top of the palace. And there's more than enough wine there as well. Why couldn't Denlatis have come to *us*? He should be grateful for the deal he's getting, not keeping us waiting like this."

She wasn't exactly wrong, though Ranulf was hardly going to groan about a trip through the city and down to the docks. He'd begun to feel a little cooped up in the palace, and dangerous though times were, he felt safe enough with Leshie at his side, and some of the Butcher's men as well. He could see Merinius down on the docks now, strolling among the crowds outside the tavern, and knew that both Slack Stan and Marco of the Mistwood were keeping a watch on the tavern as well. They might have been invited up there, but the rules at the Regal Eagle were strict - only one bodyguard was permitted entry per patron, elsewise the place would become too crowded. Leshie was officially that person for Ranulf, and Sallor had never cared to keep security himself. Upon the upper decks there were many a keen-eyed mercenary and sellsword keeping guard upon their clients. Ranulf had little doubt that some of them would be Bladeborn too.

"Maybe he's been attacked?" Leshie was going on. "At least then he'd have an excuse. A man like that probably has lots of enemies, don't you think? One of them might have dragged him into a dark alley for a good bit of stabbing."

"I would think *you* have the more enemies here, child," Sallor Sanara said softly. "I will admit, I am quite disturbed that you have chosen to forgo your disguises. There are still many Patriots roaming the city streets, and they frequent the docks as well. After what you did at Eagle's Perch, Elio Krator will surely be hunting you."

"Let him." She grabbed a date from a bowl on the table and threw it into her mouth, chewing. "I heard he pissed his feathered breeches when he saw Cedrik Kastor on the battlefield, all decked in godsteel armour. And that sunwolf of his turned as meek as a little puppy." The girl laughed at the thought of it, untrue though it all was. "Krator's been found out, Sallor. He lost Eagle's Perch to the Tukorans, he lost this city to the Duchess, and he's lost Saska now as well." She chewed, swallowed, and gulped down a measure of wine. "The man's become irrelevant."

Sallor Sanara's seamed old face remoulded into a genial smile. "Ah, the confidence of youth. You speak with such zeal, child, yet in this I fear you have missed the mark. Lord Krator remains a danger, as do his supporters. He is one among many, I readily admit, but that does not mean he should be discounted. And this red hair of yours...and pale freckly skin. You are not so hard to spot now as you were before."

"Good. I want people to see me." She gave Ranulf a swift glance. "Hiding was never my thing. Nor was creeping around, pretending to be someone I wasn't. I'm Leshie, Bladeborn spy and bodyguard, who trained under Lady Marian Payne of Rasalan and calls a princess my best friend." Another glance came Ranulf's way, this time with a little pat on the hand for good measure. "Sorry, Ranulf, but it's true. Saska's my best friend. You've always been more of an annoying uncle to me."

"Uncle? Come, give me father figure at least."

She shrugged. "Fine. Father. I suppose I *was* playing your daughter all that time, though if I hear myself called Ersella San Sabar one more time..." Her face went so red from the rage of it she looked like she might just burst. "It's bad enough when Scarface keeps calling you Ersel, but Ersella..."

"I think Ersella is a very nice name," Sallor said. "I know two myself, as it happens. Both lovely ladies."

"Lovely isn't something I *ever* want to be called."

Fear not, Ranulf thought. *No one's ever likely to...* "I understand your concerns," he said to Sallor. "But Leshie's partly right. We're here under the protection of the Grand Duchess now and have the Bloody Traders helping to guard us, and her own city soldiers besides. Will that stop Krator or some rogue Patriots seeking vengeance? Perhaps not. But I think it's fair to say that both Leshie and I are done playing merchant and daughter."

"Damn right." Leshie pounded a small fist on the table. "Done and damn well done."

As ever, her boisterous lack of self-awareness garnered her a few sideward looks, though the girl seemed to welcome them these days. *She is known now,* Ranulf thought, *as we all are.* Their arrival in Aram a week past had made it impossible to remain incognito, and word had spread through the city like wildfire about the long-lost princess called Saska and her queer group of companions. *A Bladeborn spy, a band of mixed-blood sellswords, a renowned Rasal adventurer, and a moonbear so revered as to be worshipped as a god. We are an unlikely group to be sure.*

"Well, if you insist." Sallor Sanara wasn't quite so sure, clearly. He had always been a man of caution and clearly saw little need for this additional exposure. "Though, if I might correct one point you made, Ranulf...you have *several members* of the Bloody Traders protecting you, not the entire company itself. The Butcher is a fearsome captain, yes, but only one of many, and there is still the matter of the Surgeon to consider. I warned you before that he was hunting you, by employ of the Warrior King. How can you be so sure he has reneged on that contract?"

"Because Small Wall said so," Leshie told him. "He met with him a few days ago and cleared all that up."

Sallor Sanara cocked a brow. "Small Wall? This is another name of yours for the Butcher? You have so many nicknames, child, it can be hard to keep up."

"I like them," Leshie said proudly, "and I'm good at coming up with them too. Butcher looks like Sir Ralston, with all those scars and that big bald head. So Small Wall. Or Parapet. I have a few others as well if you'd like to hear them?"

A wrinkled hand was raised, extending from the shipwright's golden damask robe. "Another time perhaps," he chuckled. "I dread to think what cruel nicknames you have for me."

"I've a few," Leshie said with a sly grin. "Though they're all nice, I promise. You've been good to us, Sallor, so I wouldn't call you anything mean." She paused to think a moment. "You know...the Grand Duchess will reward you, if you ask her. For all the help you've given us. Maybe she'd gift you another ship or two, or a chest of gold? Without you Saska would probably still be with Krator and that Pigborn Sunrider, whatever his name was..."

"Mar Malaan," Ranulf said.

"Yeah, him. The clammy one who looks like he weighs thirty stone. You helped hide us when we came here, Sallor, and you funded our trip to rescue Saska too. That's deserving of a reward. You've done much more than Denlatis has, and yet *he's* the one who's set to become filthy rich."

"I am a man of simple needs, child, and share not in Cliffario's boundless ambition. Ships and gold I have already. Unless Her Serenity can grant me *time*, then I should not wish to trouble her."

"Time?" Leshie scrunched up her cherubic face. "What do you mean?"

"More days, months, years, to savour the fruits of my labour as I steer through my dotage." He smiled a twinkly smile. "With the ash-cloud of war sweeping down upon us, I fear this will be denied me, as it will so many others. The Ever-War is upon us, they say. A year from now, will this fine tavern still be standing? Will this city? This duchy? The things I have heard of late...they make me consider the time I have left." He looked at Ranulf. "You have never known me as a morose man, my friend, but much darkness has been reported about the docks these last days. My ears open to many rumours, some more outlandish than others, I'll grant, but even those cannot be ignored. When demigods rise from millennia-long slumber, nothing can be disregarded."

Ranulf leaned forward across the small circular table at which they sat, overlooking the bustling docks. The noise of the terrace was plenty enough to hide their conversation. "What have you heard, Sallor?"

"Much and more, and every tale more grim than the last, old friend. No fewer than three reports have reached my ears of leviathan attacks over the last week, all occurring close to land across the Coast of Plenty and Bay of Stars. Three, Ranulf. That is quite unheard of for animals that are typically placid, and speak of a great turning of the tides. The seas are raging as the skies are swarming, and we should all fear what comes next. The rise of Eldur has augured in a coming age of unprecedented chaos, and only today did I hear tell of a *krelia* prowling the Solapian channel."

Ranulf was already shaking his head. "No...that cannot be. The krelia is thought extinct."

"As Eldur was thought deceased, yet here he walks among us, arisen once more."

"What's...what's a krelia?" Leshie whispered, watching on with eyes big as saucers. "Is it like a kraken?"

"Oh no, child, the krelia is no kraken," Sallor told her darkly. "It is a creature of deeper malice, rarer and profoundly more dangerous. Men can fight krakens, and some even seek them out for their hunts, as they do leviathans and manators and the other monsters that lurk beneath the waves. But the krelia? No. It is a creature to be avoided, *never* sought out. A terror that lures men into its jaws with sweetness, only to devour them in acid and agony. When the krelia is near, all the world seems suddenly bright and joyful. Men laugh, sing, shout out in glee. They see the distant shape in the water and set their sails toward it, manning the oars and pulling with all their strength. The shape is different to all, they say. A mother or a lover or the face of a dear sweet child. It is the deepest love in the heart of a man, made manifest. So they rally to reach it, rowing and roaring in cheer, yet as they grow closer the image begins to fade. As an oasis in the desert, it flickers and blurs and yet the men do not stop. They row harder, and sail faster, hopelessly entangled in the creature's web. They cannot let it pass without seeing it. They *cannot*, else they will never know joy again, they fear. So harder they row, harder, harder, even as a part of them starts to scream out a warning, somewhere away in the back of their heads. But it's not enough. The spell is too strong for them to overcome. So they heave and pull, heave and pull, not realising the terrible truth until it's too late. Until the light turns to dark and the joy turns to dread, and suddenly, before they even know it, they are tumbling, ship and all, down into the abyss of the monster's jaws and into the hell of acid that awaits within."

He stopped, for just a moment, to judge the look of horror on Leshie's face. "When the krelia is done, the seas fill with bones, child," he told her. "This is how one knows that a krelia has been near. The skulls and bones, polished to a bright white sheen, floating on the surface of the water. No one knows how this happens. Bones are denser than water, so should sink, but not after the krelia has sucked the flesh from them. Some believe this is another part of its magic, a light side to the dark. The krelia was made by the ocean god Rasalan, they say, to be an entity of boundless fear. Yet even after it has devoured its victims, it sends their bones back up to the surface to be collected for cremation or burial in the custom of their sires." He smiled at the notion. "It is a fanciful thought, perhaps, but isn't the world so full of such riddles? And here we find ourselves again, hearing stories of floating white bones, gleaming in the sun. And an Aramatian warship, four-masted and bulky, who never made it home to port."

Despite the unseasonably humid evening, Ranulf felt a cold shiver climbing up his spine. He'd heard the stories of the krelia before, stories that were no more than myth these days. It had been over two thousand years since the last recorded sighting, long enough to consider every last one of them dead. How many there once were, no one could say. Two, three, ten? Perhaps there was only ever the one. *But one is enough*, he knew. If the tale was true, all men would take pause before sailing the Solapian Channel from now on. "Who is your source on this?" he asked his friend.

Sallor leaned back in his chair and sipped his wine. "You doubt the tale, Ranulf? Well you shouldn't. The Ever-War draws all terrors from the dark-ness, you know this as well as I. Myth and legend, my friend, are racing toward reality. A man goes to sleep one night in his bed, with his wife beside him and his children resting peacefully in the next room. But when he wakes the world is changed. The village or town he lives in is burning. He hears screams ringing out through the streets. Darkness had been drawn upon the world like a blanket of fog. Is it a dragon out there, he wonders, turning his town to embers and ash? Has a sand-drake crawled out of the dunes to lay waste to his land? Is this the work of men or monsters? He ponders it, but only for a moment, because suddenly he is thinking of his family, of the wife and children he must protect. So he wakes them, tells them to dress, and flees into the hills. He sees that others have done the same, and joins them, and before long there are many more, refugees from other towns and villages all heading in the same direction, seeking a sanc-tuary where they might be safe. Someone calls out that he knows where they must go, and seeing no better option, they trek across the plains in a great horde of lost souls, in search of salvation. The days and nights begin to pass by, and every moment they worry for what monster might come upon them, what band of terrible men might seek them out.

"But the man has other worries now too. He worries for his daughter, because he sees how some of the men are looking at her. He worries for his wife, should their foul attentions fall upon her instead. He worries his son will be snatched from him in the dead of night to be taken into bondage. And his wife worries too. She knows her husband cannot protect them all alone, so she picks up a hoe or a rake or a pitchfork, or sharpens a stick to be used as a spear, and they take it in turns to guard the children as they sleep. Food becomes scarce, the water wells dry up, the streams and rivers they pass turn to dust. The old begin to die from exhaustion and the heat and the youngest among them too. Men begin to quarrel over who gets the remaining food, over who should lead, over the slow pace they are setting. The old and the young are slowing them down, they say, and before the man knows it, the strong are grouping and taking what they want, and his fears for his family redouble. He takes his wife aside and tells her, 'We have no choice now. When they come for us, we'll have to fight. For our food. For our children. For each other. We fight, my love, for our right to survive'. Because that is what the world is now, for them and everyone else. A world fractured and broken and doomed. A world thrown into chaos by the whims of the long-dead gods, who still shape our course, even now. The Ever-War, my friends, is upon them. As it is upon us all."

He stopped, shook his head slowly from side to side, and turned his eyes to gaze over the twinkling water. For a long moment no one said anything. Then eventually Sallor gave a sigh. "I apologise, child," he said to Leshie, seeing the discomfited expression on her face. "I am not usually so sullen, as I have said, but the times have turned me such. Perhaps it will not come to that. Perhaps…perhaps there is still hope."

"There is," Leshie insisted, her voice an impassioned whisper. She reached out to grip his hand, squeezing. "There *is*, Sallor. There's a chance we can stop the darkness, end the War Eternal. This…this *Ever-War*…it doesn't *need* to happen. Together, we can stop it. Saska can…"

Ranulf kicked her gently under the table.

"Ouch," she exclaimed, turning. "What did you do that for?"

You know, he thought. *You damn well know why, Leshie.* He said that with a hard glare, though Sallor didn't seem to be paying much attention. He had turned back toward the ocean, gazing away toward the southeast with a look of trepidation etched into his eyes. "There is something else I haven't yet told you both," he said. "A rumour that adds credence to all this talk."

"What rumour?" Ranulf asked.

"One that tells of a great eruption at the Wings, as though the mountain of Eldur's Shame itself did crack open like an egg, emitting black ash and red lava and a thunder of dragons too numerous to count. The men at the docks are taking it as another omen, an indisputable sign that the Ever-War is truly here. The dragons, Ranulf. The *thousand* dragons. It has long been a part of the prophesy, though I cannot believe there could ever be so many. And…and *one*…" He paused to collect himself, though Ranulf sensed he knew what was coming. "One, they claim, was vast beyond all conceivable proportion. As a giant among children it flew out and upward in a great swirling spiral, wreathed in flame, to disappear into the dark of the skies. It has not been since seen then, that I have heard, but…" He paused again and met Ranulf's eyes. "You know of the dragon I speak."

Ranulf did not delay in his answer. "The Dread," he said. "They say Drulgar has awoken."

Sallor nodded shakily. "Yes. The men of Dragonwatch claim so, though at such a distance nothing can be certain. The Fire Father has worked to revive him using the ancient power of the Bondstone, it is said. The Soul of Agarath, Ranulf, has a power we cannot understand. Some have come to believe that Agarath himself works his will through Eldur, as Vandar works his will through his shattered heart. The gods are returning this world to the battleground they fought over for millennia, and yet in Drulgar…" He paused to swallow in a dry throat. "The Dread is a calamity beyond all reckoning, and...if true...then there is nothing and no one that can stop him..."

"Drulgar was defeated by Varin once," Ranulf replied to that, as evenly as he could. His friend was being unusually jittery and overly dramatic and it would not serve to join him. "He wounded him gravely in single combat and forced him to flee back across the Red Sea. Drulgar was never seen again. One man, Sallor. One man bested the dreaded dragon, with only the Sword of Varinar to hand."

"Man? You call Varin a man, Ranulf?" Sallor Sanara's brow creased into a deep frown. "It is folly to say so. Folly. Nor did Varin fight Drulgar alone. He had his son and daughter with him..."

"Who were both slain," Ranulf pointed out. "Elin and Iliva fought bravely, the legends say, but Drulgar slew them both before Varin faced him."

. "Yes, and did not the grief and rage of a father drive him? Did not the deaths of his children allow Varin to summon a rare power to defeat the beast? I am not of the north, but I have heard your legends told a hundred times and read your accounts as well, and in most it seems that Drulgar was weakened, wounded, and wearied by the time Varin faced him in their duel."

"Elin had the Frostblade, didn't he?" Leshie said. "And Iliva the Wind-blade." She looked at Sallor. "I heard that too. Both did damage to Drulgar before he killed them. I have always wondered if Varin would have beaten Drulgar by himself...you know, from the start, without their help."

"We can never know." Ranulf didn't see much sense in engaging in meaningless guesswork on a battle that took place thousands of years ago. "This is history merged with myth, where the details have been lost and warped and embellished over time. The statue of Drulgar at Dragonfall shows a beast unfathomable in its size, yet many people believe he was truly that large. He wasn't. He can't have been. A fearsome dragon he was, greatly larger than those we know today, but not the flying mountain some believe. This is the myth surrounding the history, the fantasy that cloaks the truth. And so it is with Varin as well. A man? No, he was much more than a man, but not so much as our myths and legends make us believe. The greatest among us today are not so far from him as you think, Sallor. The gap between Varin and a man like Amron Daecar is more a cleft than a chasm, my friend."

"So you're saying Amron Daecar could defeat the Dread?" Sallor found the idea preposterous by the tone of his voice. "Folly. I say again, folly. Lest Drulgar have risen a shadow of himself, there is no force on this earth that can stop him..."

"Ah, there you are!" broke in a voice far too jolly for their dark discussion. "I've been trying to track you down for ten minutes..." Cliffario Denlatis wore silk and satin with an extra length of golden fabric thrown across his shoulder. His left canine was gold, his right silver; both caught the nearest bloom of torchlight and glinted as he grinned.

Ranulf took a second to gather his thoughts as the merchant swanned forward in that exuberantly vainglorious gait. He'd half forgotten why they were all there in the Regal Eagle with all this talk of gods and monsters. "Late?" he said, finding his tongue. The comment irritated him, though that was likely the point. "Are you sure you haven't gotten that a bit muddled up, Cliffario?"

"Yeah…exactly," added Leshie. "We've been here over an hour waiting for you."

"Oh you have? That is a shame." Denlatis halted a moment to wave his personal bodyguard back. The man retreated to a support column to watch from a distance. "I was quite sure I said the hour of the red eagle for our meeting."

"You didn't. You said the hour of the…the…" Leshie looked at Ranulf. "What comes before the hour of the red eagle?"

"The hour of the orange eagle," he answered.

Leshie rolled her eyes. "Everything is eagles here. It's so stupid. Why not just use numbers like we do in the north?"

Ranulf could not deny that the ancient Aramatian custom of keeping time was rather confusing to newcomers. Every hour was named for the eagle, typically with a colour attached, though not always. The stroke of midnight began the hour of Calacan, for example, the great Eagle of Aramatia ushering in a brand new day.

Cliffario Denlatis moved forward to take his seat, smiling insouciantly all the while. "Northern methods of time-keeping are dull, as are many of your traditions," he said. "Why not add some *colour* to proceedings, I ask you?" Before Leshie might answer, he poured a cup of wine for himself and said, "You of all people should understand the merits of adding colour to enliven a thing, Ersella. This red hair of yours is quite enchanting. The last time I saw you, it was slick and black, and your skin was a deal darker too. The real you is *so* much prettier."

Leshie's anger melted away at once with the compliment. It was alarmingly predictable how easily the girl could be won over by a handsome man with a honey-coated tongue, filling her head with flattery. "You…you think I'm pretty?"

"Oh yes, very pretty indeed. Though you don't look much like an Ersella anymore. What is your real name, do tell."

"Leshie," she said, in half a giggle.

Astonishing, Ranulf thought. Even after all that talk of krelias and krakens, of Eldur and the Ever-War, she can giggle like a little girl.

"Leshie." Cliffario considered the name for a moment. "Yes, it suits you. Leshie…close as kin to the long-lost heir of Aramatia, so the tales tell it. How funny to think that the mute girl I met at the Red Pits all those weeks ago was really a Bladeborn warrior from Tukor, deep in a princess's trust."

"She's my best friend. Saska is. We trained together in Thalan."

"Oh, I've heard."

As was ever the case, Ranulf felt unsettled by the merchant's sly presence. *He always seems to know more than he's letting on,* he thought. The Grand Duchess had been quite explicit that no one find out who Saska really was. "They know she is my granddaughter," she had said to him. "Let them have that, and nothing more. Her true identity must be protected, Ranulf. At all costs. Do you understand?"

He did. Of course he did. But he wasn't so sure about Leshie, who might just let it slip under Denlatis's charms.

He decided to take charge. "You're an hour late, Cliffario," he said. "Play innocent all you like with your oranges and reds, but we all know your late arrival is intentional. That's fine. We can forget it. So long as we get right down to business and bypass all this small talk."

Leshie might well have hissed at him, such was the look on her face. "It's not small talk. We were having a nice conversation."

"And ten minutes ago you wanted to castrate him for keeping us waiting."

She looked aghast. "*I did not.*"

Ranulf wasn't going to argue. "Cliffario. I have spoken at length with Her Serenity about the deal we struck and she is willing to elevate you, pending certain conditions, and permit you to wed the Lady Asherah Tamaar."

The merchant smiled easily. "Wonderful. What conditions are these?"

The gall of the man, Ranulf thought. *Anyone else would show a little more gratitude.* "The death of Lord Elio Krator, for a start." He took a brief moment to savour the curdling expression on the merchant's face. *What, did he think it would go so easy?* "Naturally, Lord Krator will have an important say in whom his cousin weds, Cliffario," he elaborated. "She is his heir, after all, and the Grand Duchess is adamant he not be entirely bypassed in this process, not so long as he is alive, at least."

Denlatis sat back in his seat, fiddling with the point of his angular chin. There was a deliberateness to the man in his affectations. *This one means, 'I'm thinking',* Ranulf thought to himself. *'I'm thinking and I want to look perfectly calm while doing so'.* "I confess myself mildly confused," Denlatis said after a short time. "Lord Krator took the princess captive, did he not? He denied the Grand Duchess knowledge of her own granddaughter, concocted a plot so the world would think the girl dead, and even conspired to have Her Serenity assassinated as well." His eyes turned to the others in turn. "Oh, you haven't heard this rumour?"

"We've heard it," Ranulf said. "Without proof, however…"

"Proof. Yes, a tricky thing. Perhaps if I could find some for you? Might that simplify matters?"

Ranulf puzzled on that. There had been a failed attempt on Safina Nemati's life some months ago, before she'd returned to Aram, though the assassins had all been killed before they could be caught and questioned. What proof Cliffario could find was, therefore, highly debatable. *And trustworthy?* Ranulf wondered. *Probably not.* "As I understand it, Lord Hasham has instructed his own men to seek the truth of this failed assassination. I don't know what you could add to the investigation, Cliffario."

"I have means Lord Hasham does not. And contacts. Let me make some inquiries for you."

Ranulf's doubts remained, though there wasn't any real harm in it. "Fine. But it'll be unlikely to change things. Not unless the proof is irrefutable."

"And this about imprisoning the princess? Kidnapping her and concealing her existence. Trying to force himself upon her? All this bullying and abuse and foul leeching she had to suffer. Such a series of crimes should be plenty for Her Serenity to strip Lord Krator of his lands and titles and let them pass onto the Lady Asherah instead. Or am I wrong?"

You're right, Ranulf thought. Krator had done plenty to have sealed a more grisly fate than that, yet it wasn't so simple as the merchant was making out. "Elio Krator has too many allies to cast him out so abruptly," he told the man. "Her Serenity does not wish for any civil violence to erupt between the Aramatian sun and moonhouses."

"Of course...yes, I understand." Denlatis smiled and waved a hand out toward the ocean. "There is violence enough across our fair world to let the flames of such spread to this city. This deal we have struck, Ranulf, might not even come to pass in the months and years to come. There are a hundred ways one can die today, and there might be a hundred more tomorrow. Yet a forward-thinking man prepares to profit, just in case. That is what I am doing, in my pursuit of the Lady Asherah."

And all the wealth that comes with her name, the man didn't say. Yet his eyes said it well enough. Beautiful though the Lady Asherah was, Ranulf was quite certain it was her wealth and status that Denlatis was after, not her looks. "A worthy pursuit," he said, as a courtesy. "And one that will have to go on a little longer. Lord Krator's death will, however, expedite matters."

The merchant raised a trim black brow. "Are you asking me to... Ranulf, my good friend, surely not? I cannot partake in anything so wicked as assassinating a powerful sunlord."

"I'm not asking you to do anything of the sort."

Cliffario Denlatis rolled the tips of his fingers along the tabletop, one after another after another. "Well, his parting *would* make things simpler, this cannot be denied." His eyes shifted from Ranulf to Leshie to Sallor. "I'm sure you all fear a reprisal, for the efforts you have gone to in disrupting his plans."

"A part you had a hand in too, don't forget," Ranulf said. "You funded our escape by paying for the Butcher and his men to escort us, Cliffario. If Lord Krator is aware of this..."

"He isn't. I am always very careful to cover my tracks, Ranulf. Some creatures are prey, others are predators, but the life I have built makes me both. I have eyes in the back of my head, my friend, and more ears than I can count. So far as Krator knows, you were the one to fund your little rescue mission, not me. There is nothing to link me to that."

"He knows about your association with the Butcher and the Baker. He knows you have dealt often with the Bloody Traders."

"I deal with many sellsword captains and companies. I even gifted

Krator a strong complement of Bladeborn men for his war, who fought well for him, I'm quite certain. I offered him ships and gold and jewels, to try to win his favour. All he knows of me is that I wish to win the hand of his cousin. Do not go thinking a man like Elio Krator has even given me a second thought, since last I saw him. I am a fly to him, an annoyance, and no more." His fingertips continued to drum against the table, *tap tap tap.* "And perhaps that makes me dangerous. Some flies can spread disease, after all."

The merchant grinned like a wolf, spinning the stem of his cup between his nimble fingers. "Well, much to mull upon," he went on. "So long as we have an accord that the Lady Asherah will indeed be mine at Lord Krator's passing, I am happy. It is awfully perilous out there these days, and the sunlord is no young man. He will join the stars, sooner or later."

As might we all, Ranulf thought. There was a part of him that felt terribly unseemly even having this discussion, but it was necessary to keep the merchant off his back.

Denlatis stopped spinning the cup, drank a short measure, and placed it down upon the table. Then he stood. "Well, I have other business to attend to," he said. "Ranulf, I will see you again soon, I should think."

Never would be better. Ranulf merely smiled.

"And Leshie, a great pleasure to meet you *officially.* You shall have to come and join me in my villa one evening, so we might get better acquainted. I should dearly like to know more about the mysterious redheaded girl from Rasalan."

"Tukor, actually. I'm Tukoran."

I know, said Denlatis's eyes. He took her hand and kissed it sweetly. "Until then, my dear." Leshie looked like she could die happy at that moment. The merchant spun to Sallor Sanara. "My good friend, I will see you about the docks." Sallor seemed like he had something to say to that, though Denlatis didn't stop to hear him. Within a heartbeat he was striding away into the crowds, waving for his bodyguard to return to his side. A moment later he was gone.

Ranulf turned his eyes over the balcony edge. It did not take long for Denlatis to appear outside the Regal Eagle, marching ferociously through the crowds with his bodyguard hard on his heel. Two others were awaiting him below, brawny men in heavy cloaks with longswords at their hips. *Mixed blood Bladeborn,* Ranulf knew. Cliffario Denlatis would only pay for the best. They walked ahead of him, clearing the crowds for him to pass, shoving aside anyone who might get in the way. *Already he thinks himself a lord,* Ranulf thought bitterly. There was something inside him that would take pleasure in seeing the man's downfall. *Never forget where you come from, Cliffario. The lofty Lightborn of Aram certainly won't.*

Leshie was watching the merchant's departure too with a puzzled look on her face. "You don't think he'll actually do it, do you? Try to have Krator killed?"

Ranulf shrugged. "He might. At the least it will keep him occupied."

"A time of turmoil brings great opportunity to a ruthless man," Sallor put in. "Cliffario has many contacts within the underground world. He will weigh the risk against the reward and make his choice from there." He stood suddenly from his seat, pushing his cup aside.

Ranulf frowned at him. "You're leaving, Sallor?" He'd hoped to continue their conversation now that the merchant was gone.

"Unfortunately, yes," the old shipwright said. "I have much to arrange, and must see to my captain and his crew before I depart on the morning tide."

"Depart?" Ranulf misliked the sound of that. "Where are you going?"

"Far from here, my friend, I regret to tell you. Before too long it will become too dangerous to travel, whether by sail or saddle or sandle, and I intend to escape these walls while I can. I aim to take ship to the Telleshi Isles in a bid to wait out the coming storm."

"Sallor, I…"

The man raised a wrinkled palm. "Do not waste your breath in trying to persuade me otherwise, Ranulf. I have thought on this long and hard and know it is the right choice for me. I assure you, many others think the same." He looked out over the harbour, bustling with men and mounts, wagons and wains. "Busy as the docks appear, a good many ships have fled for distant islands these last days, where they hope the war will not touch them. It may be a vain hope, perhaps, but sometimes hope is all a man has." He smiled and looked to Ranulf and Leshie in turn. "And if there is any breath here to be wasted, let me be the one to waste it on you. For I ask you to come with me, my friends. Gather your things and meet me at the docks at sunrise. Bring your princess, bring your Whaleheart, bring others if you wish it so. Bring the people and possessions most dear to you and come too." He gave them both another look. "But I see that you will not."

"You know we won't, Sallor," Ranulf said. "We can't. We have things…"

"Things you must do. I understand." He smiled once more and pinched Leshie's freckly cheek. "A waste of breath, as I say." He shifted away from the table, straightening out his robes. "Farewell to you both, and good luck. This most of all, you will need." Then, without so much as another word, he shuffled away across the terrace, moving swiftly into the crowds.

Leshie watched him go, befuddled by the abruptness of the parting. "Sallor…what…where are you going?" She took a step to chase him down, but Ranulf seized her arm.

"Sallor has never been one for long goodbyes," he told her. "This is his way. Let him go in peace, Leshie."

"But…but he'll *die*, Ranulf. You heard him earlier. These leviathans and that krelia thing are out there. And other things too, probably. Krakens and greatsharks and other monsters. And dragons. They're everywhere now. It's much safer here, isn't it? What if…what if…"

"He knows the safe way to go." Ranulf smiled as he watched his old friend melt away into the crowds on the terrace, sharing nods and looks with men he knew, passing the occasional word of parting. He was glad for him, glad he'd taken account of the coming storm, and sought to find shelter while he could.

Because it is coming, he thought to himself, recalling the story Sallor had told. A husband and wife, fighting for their family. A world torn apart by the whims of the gods.

It is coming, and soon.

5

Jonik

A cold wind tugged at the folds of his cloak as he looked out over the walls of the fort. To the east a pale dawn was breaking, touching the high passes of the Hammersong Mountains in a soft golden glow. The mists swirled, and the winds whispered, yet for all that this was no longer the place Jonik knew. *The shadows have gone in retreat,* he thought. *The order is dead, and the darkness with it.*

Beside him, his old master stood, taking the watch alongside him. During their attack on the fort, most of the senior men of the order had been slain, yet not all. Some were merely wounded, or else knocked unconscious, and others still had escaped beyond the walls to vanish into the maze of mountains beyond. If they should band together and mount a counter, they might cause a problem. Jonik had put the gate under continual watch as a precaution.

"I spoke again with Kagnor earlier," Gerrin said, gruff-voiced and craggy-faced, wrapped tight in a heavy woollen cloak. "He isn't going to yield, Jonik, no matter what you or I or anyone else tell him. Dalbert's the same. They're old, too old to change now, and Dalbert's gone half-mad from his wound. You let them out, and they'll slip a dagger through your ribs first chance they get, or skulk off to join the others in the mountains. Best keep them caged for now. Or…well, the *other* thing. Sometimes it's just best to put a rabid dog down, rather than wait for them to bite you."

Jonik nodded silently, as he stared across the short stone bridge and down the pass that led through the mountains. He could still remember the day he'd set off down that road, with Shade at his side and the Nightblade at his hip, leaving Gerrin and the rest of the order behind. *I went off to slay my own father. I went off to change the world.* That had been the lie he'd been sold, at least, a lie repeated by Gerrin himself, over and over again. *Because he was deceived as I was. The Shadow Order itself…everything…all of it was a lie.*

"We'll keep them in chains for now," he said eventually. "You broke from the yoke, same as me. We have to give them the same opportunity."

Gerrin merely grunted at that. It was clear enough he knew just where this road would lead. *Death,* Jonik thought, *for them or me or one of my men.* It was all the senior men here knew, all they'd been groomed to be. Killers. Assassins. 'Tools sharpened for a purpose', as Hamlyn the Steward had said. *Agents of fate,* Jonik told himself. *Gardeners, tasked with pruning the tree of time, to shape it to Queen Thala's sight.*

The skies were brightening yet further, bringing focus to the valleys far below. The touch of sun upon the towers and walls was rare here, yet of late the clouds had lifted, the mists thinned, and the sun burned high above them. It looked set to be another fair day. In weather, if nothing else.

"Henrik hasn't come around yet either," Gerrin went on. "Nils, Zacarias, Hopper, Trent, they're all old enough to be lost, Jonik."

Jonik shook his head to that. "They're all young enough to break free, Gerrin." Henrik was of an age with him, a friend, if he could have called him that, during his time here at the fort. Hopper was a few years older, though Jonik had never once spoken to him, and Nils, Zacarias and Trent he knew only by sight and name, each of them a year or two younger than he was. *Young enough,* he thought. *Still teens, most of them.* "We came to liberate the younger ones," he said. "I'm not going to be so quick to give up on them."

"Their conditioning is deep."

"So was mine. Look at me now."

"No." Gerrin said the word firmly. His eyes dipped to the blade at Jonik's hip. "You had a rare incentive to break free. That blade. Your family. These boys have no such motivation."

"They don't?" Jonik couldn't understand his reasoning. "What about freedom? What about choice?"

"*Choice?*" His old master's lips broke into a mocking smile. "Have any of us ever had choice, Jonik? Aren't we all just tied up in a web of fate? Isn't that what the Steward told you?"

Not in so many words, Jonik thought, though he couldn't deny that was the gist of it. "He told me the future is shrouded in doubt from here," he said stiffly. "Queen Thala…she only saw so far. Everything the order has done has been to help guide us to this point. But from here, no future is set. Henrik and the others can still have a life, Gerrin."

"Or they can *take* one. Yours, I fear, or mine. The younger boys aren't so far gone to be turned, perhaps, but the older ones…"

"Deserve a chance," Jonik broke in belligerently. "I'm not going to keep them all locked up in their cells indefinitely. And that's the end of it, Gerrin. It's decided."

The scuff of footsteps behind them gave Jonik respite from further questioning, as the next pair to take the watch arrived atop the wall. Sansullio, it would be, alongside Harden, a pair of sellswords who could not be more dissimilar. The former was tall, dark of skin and purple of eye, as lithe as a dancer and criminally comely, much loved among the host. The latter didn't command such popularity, though that was hardly rare for a man of the Ironmoors. Grey, grim, and staunchly miserable, Harden fit the lands of his fathers well.

"Pretty sunrise," remarked the Lumaran, striding effortlessly toward them across the wall walk. His smile matched it well; a warm and radiant sight after a long cold night. "I feel I have been deceived, my lords. On our journey here, you both spoke of a place of storms and darkness, never kissed by the lips of the sun. But these last days have been still and bright. This is most confusing."

"The world has changed, Sansullio," Gerrin told him. "Our liberation of the fort has rid it of the darkness."

"A strange sort of magic. Perhaps the fortress's name should be changed too, then? *Shadow*fort no longer fits it."

It fits it well enough, Jonik thought. *For all the secrets that have been hidden here.*

Harden shuffled in, glum eyes looking over the parapet and across the bridge, to where the craggy grey mountains rose up. "Any trouble?"

"Nothing," Gerrin said. "Thought I spotted a bit of movement a couple of hours ago but was just a mountain goat. Doubt any of them will be back."

Men had been sent out to try to hunt down the escaped Shadowknights and masters, though only a few sets of tracks had been found, leading away into the mountains or the twisting path they'd taken to get here. *That* was of more concern to Jonik. Jack o' the Marsh and Captain Turner and the others were still in camp down in the foothills a week's trek from here, and if any rogue enemy should happen upon them, they'd have little means of defending themselves against a well-trained man of the shadows. To ease Jonik's concerns, Emeric Manfrey had gone down to fetch them, taking Sir Lenard Borrington and the Silent Suncoat with him, departing the very morning after they'd taken the fort. No one was expecting them back for another ten days at least. Their return couldn't come sooner, so far as Jonik was concerned. *I need my friends at my side,* he thought. *And now, more than ever.*

The remaining men of his company had been depleted during the siege. Three more of Sansullio's Sunshine Swords had perished, and one of the Blackshaw men, Crasson, had been mortally wounded when a shadow took form and pricked him through a gap in his plate, puncturing his liver. His dying had been slow and unpleasant. The other losses had been inflicted by friendly fire, Sir Corbray Walsh and the Piseki mercenary Kazil both slain by Sir Borrus Kanabar when his mind had been turned to madness. The scarred giant Big Mo had been badly wounded by the Barrel Knight too, as had the dark youth Cabel, though it was hoped that both would recover.

And all to create a distraction, Jonik thought angrily, *so the Steward could take me under his spell.* He closed a fist around the hilt of the Nightblade, feeling a spike of fury course through his veins. *He could have come to the gate. He could have met us further down the pass, to explain the truth of the order, and its purpose.* But he hadn't. Hamlyn had let the bloodshed play out, he'd let Jonik and his companions purge the order of most of its men. Those men had served their purpose now and the mage had no further need of them. Only the boys and a few spare prisoners remained now. *And all for me to manage,* Jonik thought.

He left Harden and Sansullio to the watch, moving down from the wall with Gerrin at his side. The ward below remained silent and shrouded in shade, though he could smell the first wafts of bacon drifting out from the kitchens.

Sir Torvyn, he knew, hastening down the steps. The ageing heir to House Blackshaw rose early each morning to cook breakfast for the others, favouring bacon, eggs, and thick cuts of warm buttered bread. After two long decades in Pal Palek's pits he was adamant he eat as much fatty bacon as possible before he die, and thankfully the fort was well stocked in it, with larders full of pig and chicken, mutton and lamb, beef and venison and great sacks of spuds, barley, flour, beans, turnips and a great deal else. Most of that had been reserved for the Shadowmasters, once, but seeing as Gerrin was the only one of those left, he didn't mind sharing it around.

Jonik and his former master parted ways in the yard, the older man taking to his bed. "Need to sleep," he said. "Can't take these long cold nights like I used to."

Jonik nodded and watched him go as he crossed to the Night Tower, set right across the inner ward opposite the gate. The men had all found beds in there, though during the evenings they preferred to gather in the library, a thick stone roundtower that was about the only homey place in the fortress.

The smell of bacon grew stronger as Jonik continued into the kitchens, stirring a soft rumble in his gut. Sir Torvyn was at the fire, turning long strips of the meat with a pair of tongs over a fat-stained iron grate. He was a wiry man, above average height, with sunken fidgety eyes, gaunt cheeks, and a head of brittle greying hair. It hadn't always been like that. Once before, he'd been powerfully built, but his long years in captivity had stripped him of all that. "Morning, Jonik," he said, spotting him coming. "How was the watch?"

"Uneventful." Jonik moved to a stone counter and poured himself a cup of cold water, fetched from the icy rills that ran down through the mountains. "Gerrin saw a goat, but that's about it."

Sir Torvyn smiled amiably. "A goat or a ghost? Did it have an Ilithian Steel blade, perchance?"

"It was a goat, Sir Torvyn. Gerrin is certain the missing men are long gone."

"We can but hope." The old knight continued turning the strips of bacon. Fat dripped from the grate, popping and spitting in the fire. "I worry for what will happen when we leave, however. There won't be so many of you left then, and I can only keep Borrus and Mooton on the leash for so long. Soon enough, their impatience will wear thin and they'll take flight from here whether I like it or not."

Jonik drank his water, suddenly wishing it were wine. *Or something stronger.* He unfastened his swordbelt and placed it with a *clunk* on the counter, setting the Nightblade and its scabbard aside. "Will you wait at least until Emeric returns?"

"That is what I keep telling them," Torvyn assured him. "But I cannot be certain how long they'll agree. Borrus in particular wants to see the back of this place. The longer he waits here, idle and fuming, the more likely he'll do something rash." He gave Jonik a cautious look. "You know of his resentment, and his pride, young lord. A man like Borrus Kanabar does not like to be *used*, least of all to kill his own companions, and by means of sorcery of which he has always held a distrust."

"I know." Borrus was rightly enraged by the hex the Steward had put on him, and had blustered several times about marching back to the refuge and slaying the mage himself. "Trying to kill the Steward that would be folly," Jonik told Sir Torvyn. "He is a mage and Whisperer with powers beyond our reckoning. Borrus would have scant chance against him."

"You don't have to convince *me* of that, Jonik. But you know Borrus Kanabar. He thinks very highly of his abilities."

"His abilities are not in question. No Bladeborn could beat a mage of such power, not unless he could catch him off guard. One word from the Steward and Borrus would be right back under his spell."

Torvyn inclined his head as he turned a side of bacon. "True enough, though Borrus believes otherwise. He has spoken of mustering Mooton to join him, and Sir Bulmar and Regnar and the others as well. Together, they might have a chance."

"No," Jonik said. "The Steward will see it coming. And besides, he cannot be killed. He's too important."

"Oh?" The old knight set his tongs aside, and turned to face him. "What role does the mage have to play, pray tell? We have all been wondering, and you have no great face for lying. There's something more you're not telling us, isn't there?"

Jonik turned his eyes aside. He had told them only what Hamlyn had permitted, and no more. *One secret, but not the other,* he thought. He had spoken to the men of the Book of Contracts given to Hamlyn by Thala, the Prophet Queen. He had told them that the mage had built the order by her command, its purpose to carry out those contracts, to steer the course of history toward this very moment and time. The men had taken that much as he had, in stunned bewilderment, hardly able to believe it, yet there was a second secret too that was equally if not more astounding.

Ilith, Jonik thought. *The Worldbuilder. The great Forgeborn King, lying in eternal stasis on that cold stone slab.*

Hamlyn had been explicit that no one should know of the presence of the ancient king. "The world cannot know what we are doing here, Jonik," he had told him, the night he'd led him to Ilith's bedside. "Until the other pieces of the puzzle come together, Ilith must be kept safe, he must be kept hidden, and so must his last living heir. If either of them should fall, the world will fall with them. And me, Jonik. Only I can perform the transference, when the time is right. If I die before then, all is lost. I trust this knowledge to you, and you alone. When your friends leave this place, they cannot go armed with the truth. They cannot know of Ilith, or Tyrith, nor can they know of me. The risks are too great. You must share this with no one."

"I won't," Jonik had said, though it wasn't so easy as that. *Because they deserve to know*, he thought, as he kept his gaze from Sir Torvyn's shrewd eyes. *They all know I'm hiding something. They know there are mysteries back in the refuge that I know of, and will not tell them.* A fume of resentment had begun to brew among some of the men for that already, and it would only get worse, the longer he sealed his lips. *They deserve to know*, he told himself again. *These men have crossed oceans and kingdoms and mountains for me, they've killed for me and they've died for me, and what do they have to show for it? Nothing*, he knew, *but the knowledge that they've been manipulated, lied to, deceived. And now I lie to them still. These men, who have risked it all.*

Torvyn smiled, picked up his tongs, and returned to his cooking. "Well, in your own time, then," he said, when Jonik gave him no answer. "I suppose whatever you're hiding must be important if you're refusing to tell us. Alas, I trust you, young lord, to know what is best. Or perhaps the Steward still has his claws in you? I would hate to think that this mysterious mage is somehow pulling your strings."

"He isn't," Jonik said at once. "Hamlyn, he..." He paused a second, realising his mistake. "The *Steward* means not to interfere with us anymore. I would know if he was in my head, Torvyn. I've had it happen before. I'd be aware if he was manipulating me."

"Of course. I am merely expressing my concerns, young lord. This sorcerer is clearly a being of dreaded power, and I cannot help but wonder whether he is exploiting you for some sinister end." He smiled once again, in a bid to keep things light, and turned another side of bacon.

Hamlyn, Jonik thought. *Damn it, I said his name.* It was a famed name too, not one that Torvyn Blackshaw was likely to be ignorant of. *Might he put the pieces together, somehow?* It didn't seem likely, but still... "I assure you the Steward has no control over me, Sir Torvyn. You needn't worry, not on that account."

Sir Torvyn Blackshaw began moving the cooked rashers of bacon onto worn wooden plates, before adding more meat to the grill. "I hope you're right, young lord," he said. "Now I wonder...are you going to stand there idle all morning, or lend me a hand?" He smiled. "I could do with some help."

Jonik pulled up his sleeves. "Hand me that box of eggs," he said.

He spent the next quarter hour breaking eggs in a bowl and carving trenchers from loaves of bread, a task he'd done often in his youth. It reminded him of those days, standing at the counter beneath the soot-stained roof, fearing he might make a mistake and get the back of the cook's hand for the blunder. That cook had been called Stalk, a tall skinny man who'd once been a Shadowknight, but was instructed to work the kitchens after he twisted his knee in a fall. *He died when I was fifteen or sixteen,* Jonik recalled. Hacked up by one of the younger boys if the story he heard was true. That happened occasionally; a boy cracking under the pressure of their abuse, lashing out suddenly and violently, and dying for the trouble. No such behaviour was tolerated here. If a boy fought back, they were discarded as bad blood. *Or given over to the mages,* Jonik thought darkly. Blood magic. He hadn't forgotten about all that.

Eggs mixed and trenchers carved, Jonik left Sir Torvyn to continue his cooking, pacing back out into the yard. The torches in the windows of the Night Tower were doused now, and from the doors came some of the men, stirred from their sleep by the promise of a hearty breakfast. A few of the Sunshine Swords jostled forward, along with Regnar and Norwyn and the fearsome form of Sir Mooton. "Eaten already, lad?" Mooton asked as the others passed right by without a word. The Sunshine Swords offered polite smiles, though the Blackshaw men preferred frosty nods. "Oh, don't mind them," Moot said. "They're miserable before they've broken their fast." He slapped his thick belly. "Us rivermen like to eat well."

"I'm aware," Jonik said. It wasn't hunger that soured their moods, though, he knew that well enough. "Borrus not up yet?"

Mooton shrugged his enormous shoulders. "We don't share a room. How would I know?"

"You might have seen him."

"Might have. But haven't. Actually, come to think of it, there was no loud snoring coming through his door, so I'm guessing he's awake. At Cabel's bedside, most likely. Wants to be there when the lad wakes up."

Jonik wasn't certain that was smart. The last thing Cabel saw was an engaged Borrus Kanabar trying to kill him. *Not the nicest thing to wake up to.*

"He's got a sensitive side, has Borrus," Mooton was going on. "Always did, behind all the drinking and killing and whoring. If that lad dies, it'll snap him, be sure of it. You'd best hope that doesn't happen, lad, else your precious Steward'll have a target on his back."

"Cabel won't die, Gerrin says. And I've told you about the Steward, Mooton. You try to fight your way back there, and he'll make you wish you hadn't. What he did was terrible, I won't deny it, but it's all for a greater cause."

The Beast of Blackshaw snorted like a bull, mist pouring from his nose. "So you've said. And it's bullshit, all of it. The only cause now is fighting the war." He shook his massive scabbard, rattling the godsteel greatsword within. "We need to go, Jonik, and add *these* to the defence of the realm. My blades are wasted here, same as Red Wrath, same as *that.*" He looked at the Nightblade. "It was forged to drink dragonblood, boy, and there're dozens of those out there now, killing our countrymen. We've done what we needed to do here, and paid for it too, but now it's time to go. A day, two, tops, and we're leaving." He put a massive paw on Jonik's shoulder. "And I hope that you'll come with us when we do."

I can't, Jonik thought, as Mooton passed him by, *much as I might want to.* No, he still had to think about the boys he'd come to liberate. *They need me still. I cannot abandon them yet.*

He crossed the yard to the short stubby barracks tower in which he'd once lived. Outside the door stood one of the Sunshine Swords, dressed in scalemail and golden cloak beneath a heavy mantle of undyed wool, fetched from the storehouse for the cold. "My lord," he said, as Jonik neared.

Jonik stopped before him. "Jullio. When does your watch end?" Sansullio's sellswords were polite to a man and steadfastly loyal to their captain's orders. *But will they go too?* Jonik wondered. There was money at the Shadowfort, and plenty enough to pay them, but Sansullio would likely be drawn to another adventure now that this one was complete. The thought was a sour one. *I'll be left with only Gerrin soon at this rate. Gerrin and the rats and the shadows.*

"I have another two hours, my lord," Jullio said, in that flavoursome Lumaran accent. "Manallio is scheduled to replace me."

"Two hours is a long wait. Head inside and grab yourself a trencher of bacon and eggs. I'll cover the door until you're back."

"My lord." Jullio bowed and took the offer without question, marching away across the yard in a swift smooth stride. As soon as he was gone, Jonik turned and entered the building, climbing the turnpike stair to the floor above where twenty sleeping cells were lined up on either side of a long stone corridor. Only thirteen were currently occupied by the younglings who resided here.

He paced down the middle, calling, "How are you all this morning? Hope you all slept well. Knock once on your door if you're awake. Come now, and be quick about it." He raised his voice so it penetrated the thick walls and doors, speaking in a friendly tone. From within the cells, came a series of knocks, tapping from either side of the corridor. Jonik smiled, counting thirteen clear sounds. He knew well enough that the boys were required to wake at dawn, and anyone caught sleeping longer would risk a beating from their master. "Good. Your breakfast will be brought up soon enough. You have until then to rest, sleep, do as you please. It'll be bacon, eggs, and buttered bread again. This afternoon, if things go well, you'll all be let out into the yard to enjoy the sun."

He could almost hear the thrum of anticipation behind the doors. Letting them sleep longer. Feeding them well. Permitting them time outside their cells. These were not things given freely in the Shadowfort.

That done, he returned to the yard to find Jullio crossing with a bowl of bacon and eggs to hand. "How is it?"

"Better than ever, my lord."

"Not a fan of the bread, Jullio?"

"No, it upsets my stomach. I have always had an intolerance for bread."

Jonik smiled, then continued down a covered colonnade through to the other side of the fort. *An intolerance for bread. What a curse that would be.* When he was a boy here, Jonik all but lived off the stuff, old and hard and sometimes mouldy though it was. Well, that and watery broths, with the odd bit of meat inside. It was no wonder the men of the Shadow Order grew up lean and mean. And all the while, the larders were full. *Hunger was just another tool of theirs, to bend us to their will.*

He found another of the Blackshaw men, Radcliffe, guarding the older boys' barracks. These were in their early to mid-teens; the other housed the younger boys who hadn't yet hit puberty. "Radcliffe, go fetch some breakfast," Jonik told him "I'll take the watch for a few minutes while you're gone."

"Aye." Radcliffe was heavy-bellied and bushy-bearded in the manner of the Blackshaw clan, forty if he was a day. *And more frosty with me than ever.* The man had been close with Crasson, and his friend's death had stung him some. *No doubt he blames me for that too.* The burly man trudged off wearily, leaving Jonik to enter and climb the spiral stair. The barrack was little different to the last, grim and dark. As were many of the boys inside, as was common at their age.

"How are you all this morning?" Jonik called out. "Hope you slept well. Knock once if you're awake."

The knocks came back, though it took a little longer than in the first barracks. *These older ones are more defiant,* he knew. He had reflected on how he would behave were he an apprentice here, and the fort was sieged by a former Shadowknight gone rogue. *Would I relent so quickly to my new master? Would I hate him for what he'd done?* He suspected so, and so needed to tread lightly. In time he hoped they would come around. *But enough to be set free upon the world?* It was a question he couldn't yet answer.

"Breakfast will be coming soon," he went on. "Same as yesterday. Bacon, eggs, buttered bread. The best yet, I'm told." He paused, sensing the rise in anticipation behind the doors. It was amazing the impact food had on a growing boy. *A valuable currency,* Jonik thought, *these stocks we have in the pantry.* He would be careful to spend it wisely. "Feel free to rest until then. And talk, if you like, get to know each other a little more. There is no one listening, I promise you. You'll not be punished for communicating."

The sun had begun to creep over the walls as he returned outside the barracks, painting the cobbles in a golden glow. *It's almost pretty,* Jonik mused, looking at the towers and walls, the high cliff faces, the glimmer of ice and snow melting in the glaciers. He saw things he'd never noticed before. The sight of green shrubbery, clinging to distant scarps. The peaks beyond the peaks, stretching away to the south, where some higher prominences rose up at the edge of sight. The shapes of birds of prey, circling above the valleys, spotting and swooping on their kills. *Was it like this, once before?* he wondered. *Before Hamlyn and his mages corrupted the place with their magic? Was this the place that Ilith envisioned, for his people to flee to in their time of need?*

He set back off through the fortress, making now for the dungeons. These were further to the rear, where the sun had not yet reached. In a smaller courtyard bordered by high, lichen-covered walls was a heavy iron door guarded by Sir Bulmar Brown, leal captain under Sir Mooton Blackshaw's charge. Unlike the other Blackshaw men, he was un-bearded and ungenerously-bellied, with no more than a gentle curve of gut beneath his stained leather jerkin. "Sir Bulmar," Jonik said. "I'll have the keys, if you would."

"Of course." The knight produced a ring of keys for the main door and individual cells below. "The scar-faced one was making a terrible racket before dawn, my lord. I tried to shut him up, but he wasn't having it. Ranting and raving for a good hour, he was. I don't imagine the others are best pleased."

"Dalbert," Jonik said. The man had a grim scar across his face running diagonally from temple to jaw, horribly splitting his lips. "Gerrin says he's gone half mad."

"Yes, I'd say so. Though half is selling it short. I see little purpose in holding him here myself, to be honest. Best put him out of his misery. Some men are just wrong in the head."

"Perhaps. I will judge myself. Fetch some breakfast, if you like, Sir Bulmar. I can handle it from here."

The man frowned. "Is that wise? Some of these men are feral, and like to bite your nose off if they get a…"

"I shan't be going inside the cells, Sir Bulmar. I'll only speak with them from the outside."

"I see. Well, if you're certain."

"I am." Jonik reached out and took the ring of keys from him. "Bring back breakfast for them as well, if you would. And thank you, Sir Bulmar. I don't say it often enough. Thank you…for all your help."

The man dipped his chin in courtesy. "I shall return shortly, my lord."

My lord, Jonik thought, as he shoved the key into the lock and turned. *Will I still be a lord to these men when they leave me to go fight in the war? Will I be a lord when I'm forced to give up the Nightblade?* Something unpleasant prickled inside him with that thought. A voice within was shouting freely, *I won't! I can't! I'd sooner die than give it up!*

Jonik quietened the voice, driving it back into the dark places of his mind. Often he had reflected on what Ranulf Shackton had once said, about giving up the Nightblade when the time came. Now, meeting Hamlyn, seeing Ilith, hearing of their plans and purpose…well, he understood why. But all the same, the thought was starting to keep him awake at night. *They tried to take it from me once*, he remembered, *when the Whisperer Ghalto summoned me to Russet Ridge.* The demon had died that night, his head parted from his body, along with the rest of his men. *I killed to keep it. I became death that night. Will I do the same again if they try to take it from me?*

No, he told himself firmly. *No, I was a different man then. I had no meaning in my life, no purpose. I was lost, alone, weak…*

And what purpose do you have now? asked a voice. Was it another part of him? Was it the blade itself? He couldn't be sure; they were one and the same. *You came here to liberate these boys. That was noble of you, so noble, Jonik. A righteous cause kept the whispers at bay. What cause do you have now?*

"The same," Jonik whispered, unbidden and out loud. He turned to make sure Sir Bulmar was gone. He was alone. "I have the same cause. Liberation. Freedom. For those like me."

And when that is done, what then? asked the voice. *What will your purpose be then, Jonik? Who will you be, when you set the blade aside? Who, but another Bladeborn bastard, discarded, unwanted, unloved…*

He pushed roughly through the door in a scream of rusted hinges, eager to leave the voices behind. His doubts were growing stronger, prodding and poking at him night and day. *My purpose fades,* he fretted, *and with it the blade's will grows.* It frightened him to think like that. He knew how a misjudged purpose could drive a bearer to madness. *It happened with Janilah,* he thought, *the Mad King of Tukor.* He'd heard about the massacre at Galin's Post. He knew full well what the king had become. *The Mistblade drove him to madness in pursuit of a purpose he'd never reach. The atrocities he inflicted, the things he's done...and I...I have his blood. Does the same weakness not live in me?*

He stopped at the top of the stairs, pushing his palm against the wall to steady himself. *Janilah, my grandfather. Cecilia Blakewood, my mother.* He was still reeling from that news as well, amidst all the rest. His mother, who'd come through the portal door along with the heir of Ilith. *My mother, the bastard daughter of Janilah Lukar.* Jonik had heard her called the Bastard Bitch of Blakewood. A cruel spite-filled woman who some named a witch, pulling at her father's strings. *My mother, the accursed. My mother, who bore me only to give me up...*

Grimacing, he pressed on down the stairs, plunging into the darkness. He would not give the woman a moment more of his thought. Torches burned low on sconces on the walls, set at intervals along the stairs. He snatched one from its holding and continued into the gloom of an open hall. The torchlight illuminated a dank rotting space with cells to either side. Water was dripping from somewhere, and further back he could hear rats squeaking and scurrying on the floor. A voice hissed out from his right. "Who's this now? Gerrin, that you?"

Jonik stopped at the heart of the dungeon. The cells were aligned six by six on either side, each with open iron bars through which the men could see him.

"It's Jonik." The voice was from Zacarias, a young man no older than eighteen and a newly minted Shadowknight. He had short black hair and a fuzz of bristle on his upper lip. "The turncloak."

"Aye, that he is," growled Kagnor, an old Shadowmaster of Gerrin's vintage. He sneered at Jonik through the black iron bars, then puckered his lips to spit. The saliva hit Jonik square in the chest.

"Good shot," he said. "Though odd that you should aim it at your liberator."

"Liberator? You hear that, lads? *Liberator!*" Kagnor lurched toward the bars, gripping them hard between his weathered fingers, pressing his face as far forward as he could. His eyes were manic. "I call you *conqueror,* turncloak. I call you *murderer.* All but a few of us are dead because of you!"

And good riddance, a part of him thought. He decided it better not to say that, though. Kagnor and Dalbert were past saving, Gerrin was probably right on that, but the others he wanted to turn to the light. For that he needed to guard his tongue. "All but a small number of the apprentices survived," he said, addressing the younger captives. "They are being kept safe in their rooms, and let out in groups to enjoy the sun." He turned to Henrik first, then looked at the others in turn. Hopper, Trent, Nils and

Zacarias. "All of you are welcome to join them, if you like. It is not my intention to keep you down here for long."

"Then why are you?" asked Hopper, a big lad of twenty-two or three with one leg a little shorter than the other. It gave him an awkward gait.

"You know why, Hopper."

"Trust," he said. "You don't trust us, do you?"

"Would you?"

A silence fell. Then Dalbert started cackling inanely, swiping at his bars with his flailing fingers. Jonik peered at him. The man's hands were cut and raw, fingernails chewed off, strange symbols and markings written upon the walls of his cell in his own blood. He had always been a little demented, had Dalbert, but a nasty wound during the attack had hastened his descent.

Over the noise, Jonik said, "Your cellmate is quite entertaining. I can see why you don't want to leave."

Kagnor barked loudly. "Look, the turncloak's learned humour. What, was it those chums of yours up there taught you to speak like that?"

"Yes, actually. You might want to try it."

The Shadowmaster spat again, though this time missed the mark. "We're lone wolves here, turncloak. Friendship only makes you weak."

"So you preach. I know now otherwise." Jonik scanned the faces of the young men, wrapping his fingers around the hilt of his dagger to enhance his senses. Sight, hearing, smell were all heightened. He focused on their vital signs. Heart rate. Breathing. Perspiration. Those were harder to hide than words, giving off signals they were struggling to conceal. *Zacarias wants out*, he thought. *Trent as well.* He had a sense that he could trust them. They were younger, more mild. The others would take more convincing.

Dalbert was still making a racket. "Would you shut it, Dalbert!" screamed Kagnor. "If these walls weren't here, I'd rip your tongue out. That wound of his is festering, turncloak. How about you put him in here with me, let me finish him off."

Jonik hid his distaste. He addressed the younger men. "Can you not see what he is? Is this the sort of man you want to turn into?"

None of them spoke. *They have learned to keep their mouths shut, as I did.*

Kagnor grunted loudly. "You see, lads. He's painting me as the bad guy, as I said he would. Us and them. That's what this is. You wouldn't want to become traitors like Jonik here, would you?"

"I'm not a traitor. You all know me for the man who mastered the Nightblade. Henrik, you knew me best. We spoke often enough. You know I was committed. Until I found out the truth."

"What truth?" Zacarias asked.

"No truth," roared Kagnor. "Lies!"

"Lies! Lies! Lies!" raved Dalbert.

"The truth," Jonik said calmly, "is that we are nothing but weapons, to be discarded once spent of their use. You all know this, even if you won't admit it. We keep the world in balance, they tell us. We help steer its course." Jonik had been preached those words all his life, only doubting them when he left to walk another path. Yet ironically, they were true. *And more so than I ever realised.* "There is no lie in those words," he told them. "The Steward built this order himself to carry out a book of contracts, written by the demigoddess Thala. We have done what had to be done, shouldering a duty that has turned us into shadows. I include myself in that, for the things I've been forced to do. But all that…it's over now. The order has served its purpose. There is nothing for you here."

This time even Kagnor was silent, and Dalbert too had quietened in his ravings. Eventually, the Shadowmaster grunted his disdain. "Lies. Like I said. You speak of gods and myths and fantasy, boy. I don't believe a word you've said."

"Why not?" asked Trent, who had the cell across from Kagnor. "It…it makes sense. Everything Jonik has said…" He looked at him. "I believe it."

I know you do, Jonik thought. He could tell he wasn't lying. "Then you're a wiser man than Kagnor, Trent."

"Or more gullible," the old man snarled. "If this is true, I'll hear it from the Steward. He only has to come down here and tell us himself."

He won't, Jonik thought. *He doesn't care about you anymore.* "I'll ask him."

"Yeah, you do that. Run along now. Go on, turncloak."

Henrik cleared his throat. During their attack on the fort, Jonik had made sure to knock him out, rather than kill him. He had a gash on the back of his head from that, and the right side of his face was bruised from where he'd hit the ground. "Is the Steward dead?" he asked.

Jonik turned to face him. "No, Henrik. The Steward is alive. And Fhanrir and the others as well." There were several other mages here under Hamlyn's rule. Dagnyr. Agnar. Vottur. All had long bought into his purpose. "I have no reason to lie to you."

Henrik nodded. He looked old for his years, though perhaps that was the eyes. *They were always thoughtful,* Jonik recalled, *and kinder than most.* Perhaps that's why, among all the boys he'd grown up around, Henrik had been the closest he'd had to a friend. "If the Steward and the others are alive, then Jonik must be telling the truth. Otherwise why would the Steward permit all of this? Do you have an answer for that, Kagnor?"

"I need no answer for *you,* boy. Until the Steward comes down here, or one of the others, I'll not believe a word of it. Not a word."

"Shadowmaster," Jonik said. "I feel sorry for you, truly. You have climbed to a height among the order, and yet here you are, caged and wretched, only now finding out that you've been kept in the dark all along." He stepped closer to the man's bars. "That isn't a slight on you. You are what they made you, and you were never meant to know. I don't blame you for doubting me, Kagnor. But everything I've said…it is the truth. I swear it."

"So says you. The word of a deserter means nothing. Bring one of the mages here. Bring them down, and maybe…maybe then I might believe it."

Jonik took a step back. He had thought it might come to this. "So be it," he said. "If that's what it takes."

6

Cecilia

He stood before her, misty-eyed, so very handsome and so very tall. "I always wished this day would come," he said, stepping forward suddenly and quickly to reach out and take her into his arms. "Mother. Oh mother, how I've dreamed of this moment all my life."

She squeezed back, tears streaming down her cheeks. He had the muscular chest of his father, and his height, that smoky black hair and those silver blue eyes. *He'll break hearts*, she thought, as she pushed aside a lock of hair and looked at him. *My son.* A smile burst upon her face, giddy and unrestrained, and a moment later they were laughing and hugging again, overwhelmed to meet each other at last. They went to sit side by side upon the soft cushioned sofa, with jugs of wine and trays of food on a table before them, everything they could hope for, everything they could want. "Tell me everything, mother," he said, holding her hand. "I want to know everything about your life."

"You first," she came back, giggling. She didn't giggle, she *never* giggled, but today she did. She didn't care. "I want to know it all."

She imagined a different life in the dream to the reality her son had lived. A life where he'd been happy and free, hunting and riding and training to become a knight, winning tourneys and friends wherever he did go. She smiled to listen to him, and they drank wine and ate. He was everything she hoped he would be. Charming, funny, smart and kind. The perfect son, the perfect knight, the perfect man, chivalrous and noble in a way all men should be. There was sunshine in his smile and music in his laughter, and laugh he did, loud and often, the sound echoing out through the chambers of her mind, ringing away into the depths of her cold black rotten soul...

She awoke with tears on her cheeks, to silence, utter silence.

Her son was gone and the laughter with him, and instead she saw walls of pale stone and a high carved ceiling, a door of banded oak and little more than that. She looked at that door, the door her son had walked through several days ago. Cold memory flooded her mind, washing the warmth of the fantasy away. And she remembered the truth. The truth of that first meeting.

She had been sitting on this bed then, the same as now, waiting. "I will bring him to you," the mage called Hamlyn had told her. He had left after that for a little while, during which she'd paced from side to side in nervous anticipation, occasionally sitting again, only to stand and pace once more. But she'd been sitting when the door opened, and Hamlyn led her son through. She stood at seeing him, so abruptly she almost fell. Her legs felt weak as riverbank reeds, and her heart was hammering so hard she could hear it, and she'd smiled, bright and true, to see him for the first time.

"Jonik," she had said, taking a pace toward him.

But he had not smiled back, not as he did in her dream. He did not tell her how he'd wished this day would come, or that he'd dreamed of this moment forever. He merely looked at her coldly through eyes more silver than blue and said, "I'm told you're called Cecilia."

"I am," she'd said, swallowing. "Lady Cecilia Blakewood, your...your mother."

There had been something in his eyes to suggest he'd heard the name. "King Janilah's bastard?" he asked. "The spider."

"I'm not what they say I am," she'd blurted. "Don't believe it, Jonik. Ilithor is a web of lies." She looked him over, the eyes, the hair, the height. He was leaner than she'd imagined in her dreams, tall and tough and hard of face. *He looks much alike to Elyon*, she had thought, *only narrower and slimmer and less obviously comely*. The height was the same, though, and the hair, if longer, and those eyes, the shape of them, if not the exact colour. Keen, smart, curious. *But darker*, she saw, *more troubled and cold*. She had wanted to say so many things to him, to tell him about every time she had wished she'd kept him, how much regret and pain she'd felt over letting him go, how her father had forced her to do it, made her do it, how it wasn't her fault, it wasn't, it wasn't.

But she'd had no chance. Before she might speak again, her son had turned to Hamlyn and said, "I need to return to my men. I have to see that they're all right."

The sorcerer hadn't questioned him. "If that is your desire, Jonik."

"No..." Cecilia took several sharp paces forward. "No," she'd pled, "You can't go, not yet."

"Why not?" Jonik looked at her with empty pits for eyes. It was her dream made a nightmare, her darkest dread come true. "I have two dozen men out there who have travelled halfway across the world for me. Some are dead and others are dying. *They* are important to me. *You* are not." He'd turned with that and marched away, and hadn't returned to her since.

He is out there now, she thought, sitting on her bed. *He is out there in the fortress, and yet he will not come to me, he won't come to visit his mother.* Did she expect anything different? Did she believe that pathetic fantasy would really come true? *No*, she reflected. *Deep down I knew it would be this way, if ever we met. Deep down I knew he would hate me...*

74

She stood from the bed and made dourly for the door, stepping out into the empty corridor beyond. She had been given free rein to walk the halls back here, to explore the rooms and admire the statues and sculptures, but there were many places she could not go. Locked doors barred the way down certain paths, and there were iron gates to cage her too. A large part of her had wanted to return to the portal door and escape back to Ilithor, but she had no way to reach it. "You will stay," the mage Hamlyn had told her. "You will stay here with Tyrith, to keep him comfortable and keep him calm. We must all work to protect the boy's destiny, Lady Blakewood. This has always been your true calling. This has always been your fate."

Calling. Destiny. Fate. These were words that Cecilia had never put much credence on, at least not until she'd come here. Hamlyn had spoken to her of Queen Thala's Book of Contracts, of their duty and purpose, of the intent to reunite the Five Blades. For that to happen, Tyrith was essential, the mage said. "He has come to us, as foreseen, and brought with him the Hammer of Tukor. When the time is right, we shall pass the torch from Ilith to the heir. This time is coming soon, my lady, and you will play your part. This is your duty and purpose now. Tyrith is your fate."

My fate. A boy I only recently found out existed. Though in truth he wasn't a boy at all. At five and twenty, Tyrith had left behind his boyhood years long years ago, though retained something of a childlike manner at times. A lonely life up in his divine ancestor's forge had stunted some of his development, making him emotionally fragile. Cecilia had wondered if the transference of Ilith's spirit might somehow infuse him with the demigod's wit and wisdom, but Hamlyn had only opened his hands and said, "We cannot know for sure. What lies ahead, none can say. The path that led us here, Thala did light with her gift of foresight, yet beyond there is only darkness, and doubt. We must find the light ourselves, my lady. *We* must find the way."

Tyrith had been given the bedchamber next to hers, an exact replica of it in size and features. Cecilia stopped at the door and listened. She could hear him within, mumbling in his sleep. *He suffers as I do in his dreams,* she knew. *He does not like it here any more than me.*

"Can't sleep, my lady?" She turned to find Hog moving down the corridor toward her, the big sellsword taking shape from the gloom. There was an oil-lantern hanging on the corridor wall opposite their rooms, creating a pool of light in the darkness. Much further on, another lantern burned, though between them all was shadow.

Cecilia breathed out. "You frightened me, Hog. What are you doing up at this hour?"

"What hour?" the man grunted. "There's no way of telling the time back here." He continued toward her, fingering the eight-inch godsteel dagger at his hip. "Been searching again," he said, quietly. "Looking for another way out. Can't find one, though. Every passage leads to a dead end in this cursed place, and I find myself getting lost half the time. You feel that, my lady? The *confusion?*" He looked up and down the hall, frowning. "Not sure I can stand it here much longer, nor the lad. He told me himself, he's frightened of this place. What's say I take this dagger here and cut our way back to that portal door? I remember the way there at least."

"There are doors blocking the way," Cecilia said. "And barred gates."

"Yeah, I know. That's why I said 'cut'." He shook the dagger in its sheath. "With this I'll slice right through."

I'm not so sure, Cecilia thought. There were magical protections here that none of them understood, and she sensed they were being watched as well. "We don't even know if the portal is still operational," she told him. *"They* control it, Hog. If they want to keep us here, they will."

The big man snorted, fluttering the hairs of his great moustache. "I'm not one for being caged against my will. If that portal doesn't work, I'll head on out to the fortress there, and walk on back through the mountains instead. Can't stand the lack of daylight here. It's unnatural. Sets my teeth on edge."

Haunted, was the word that came to mind. It had not been Ilith's intent when he built this great haven as a refuge for his people, but the long years since had seen much sinister work unfold. It had seeped into the stone and suffused the air with something she couldn't put her finger on. She felt disquieted here too, she had to admit. "It's just the age of the place," she said, to steady herself as much as her guard. "And the emptiness. Anything so old and vast would feel unnerving."

Hog didn't seem so sure. "The place is creepy enough, but the *people?* These mages…never knew such things still existed, I'll be honest. And that rotting one, with the stooped back and long nose." He gave a visible shudder. "That one has a cruel look to him. You don't look at a thing like that and think they're on the side of good, my lady."

Good. evil. The world wasn't so simple as that. "Sometimes there is no good, Hog, only the lesser of two evils. Other times a good man must perform a wicked deed to pave the path for something nobler." *Or a thousand wicked deeds,* she thought, as had been the case here.

Hog scratched at his moustache with the tip of his godsteel dagger. "Heard the blacksmith crying again last night," he said. "Bawling like a newborn babe he was. Think he saw something, my lady, when we went through the portal door. Something I didn't. That experience has shaken him."

"It's shaken us all."

"No, not in the same way. The lad…he doesn't have the same thick skin as we do, what with living alone up there at that forge all these years. Might just be that, I guess, but might be more." He looked to Tyrith's door. "Death, my lady. Think he saw death in there."

She had seen shapes herself when she travelled through the portal. Vague shapes that might have looked like men, though it was hard to be sure at the time. She recalled only a sense of motion, and a coldness that went deep to her bones. A world of echoing nothingness and a blurred sense of time that ended as abruptly as it began.

And then suddenly she was stumbling forward into an open stone chamber, and before her stood a man, plain and yet pleasant of face, looking like a librarian or scribe or scholar in those warm umber robes he wore. "Welcome," he had said to her. "My name is Hamlyn, the steward of these halls." He had smiled in an enigmatic way and opened out an arm. "Your friends are right through here, Lady Blakewood. Come, follow me."

She'd barely had a second to gather her bearings, before he took her through to the adjoining chamber where Tyrith and Hog were waiting beside the ancient figure of the long-dead demigod Ilith, resting on a simple stone bed. It was there that Hamlyn explained to her their duty, their purpose, their fate. And all the while, poor Tyrith had stood there staring…just staring down at the resting figure of his ancestor, a look of pale terror on his face as his destiny was unveiled.

Cecilia drew from her reverie. "Tyrith is a sensitive soul, but will grow stronger in time," she said to Hog. "He must, Hamlyn says. That's why we're both here. To look after him."

Hog looked at her with a frown. "You want to stay, then? You want to stay here with these freaks?"

"We can't leave, Hog. They won't let us, whether we want to or not."

"And you accept that?" He shook his head from side to side. "No one tells you what to do, my lady. Why would you bow to these?"

"You know why, Hog. You know what they're trying to do."

"*Trying*, aye. And failing, such as I can see. Thala, she saw only so far, they say. From here they're nought but blind men stumbling through the dark. Your son has the Nightblade, but what of the other four? They're scattered across the north, thousands of miles from here. You ask me, they'll never be reforged."

"Hamlyn says otherwise."

"*Hamlyn*." Hog spat out the name like a curse. "I don't trust much of what that one says. He looks mild enough, but he's as rotten as that other one on the inside. And you ask me, those blades are overrated. One can cut anything…another can make you fly. So what. Dragons can fly, last I checked, and normal godsteel can cut most anything too. And don't get me started on that one your son's got his grasp on. Creeping about all invisible? That's a coward's game, I've always thought. Your boy should hand it over and be done with it, get down there and fight like a man…"

She slapped him. It was a clean strike, above the protective bristles of his moustache, bringing a sharp red flush to his cheek. "My son is no coward, Hog. Remember that."

He rubbed his cheek. A shade of darkness came over his eyes. "You protecting him now? The lad who won't even come see you."

"He has his reasons."

"And you have yours. The least he can do is hear you out. You might have died going through that door for all you knew. You should tell him that. Go find him and tell him how you risked your life to meet him."

He won't care, she thought. "I can't go and find him," she said. "There's no way to reach the fortress from here. We're prisoners, Hog, if you hadn't noticed."

"Prisoners aren't often armed." He spun his dagger around between his meaty fingers. "I can cut our way through, like I said. The blacksmith wants back to his forge, and I want back to the city. You do too. What are we waiting here for?"

She was growing weary of these questions. "You're becoming as bad as Gerret. When did you stop listening to me, Hog? I said no."

"Gerret's dead," he came back at her. "Your father spilt his guts up there on the mountain, painting the snow all red. Maybe I'm picking up the slack for him."

"Well don't. I never liked Gerret. Don't make me dislike you too."

"And the boy prince? What about him? You going to let him sit on his little throne worrying where you've gone, are you?"

"Raynald will be fine."

"Will he? Some callow boy trying to rule a kingdom during wartime. You were the true ruler, my lady. *Queen*, like you always wanted."

"*Don't* tell me what I've always wanted," she snapped, her voice clapping down the corridor. "Remember your place, Hog. You're starting to drive me mad."

"More of your father in you than I thought, then."

She slapped him again, deepening the red on his cheek.

He merely smiled back, though there was something dangerous in that look. "Best watch that flailing hand of yours, *Cecilia*. I got an end to my tether, and you're near it."

Threats, she thought. *From him? To me?* The notion stirred at her anger and pride. *We may both be bastards, Hog, but I'm a daughter of kings, not some common tavern wench. I have rich royal Bladeborn blood flowing through my veins.* But she played demure to keep him onside. The man had served her well and was at his wit's end, that was plain to see. *And even loyal hounds can bite, when driven to distraction*, she knew. "You're right, Hog," she said to appease him. "I shouldn't take my frustrations out on you. I apologise."

He nodded to hear her say that. "We'd be better off fighting together on this one, my lady. I say we get your son in on it too. Might be I can break us out by myself, but be easier with him and his men. Sometimes that sneaky Nightblade comes in handy, I guess."

He really doesn't understand, does he? "Jonik won't see me, Hog. I've asked Hamlyn to pass on the message, but…"

"Ask again, till he gets it," the big sellsword cut in.

Cecilia held her anger. *The insolence. How dare he command me!* She merely smiled and nodded.

"That lad of yours will come eventually," the sellsword went on. "When he does, you enlist his help, you hear me?"

"Yes, I hear you."

"Good." He nodded, satisfied. "You know it's the right way, Cecilia. There's no point in them keeping us here." He glanced at Tyrith's door. "This duty…whatever they need of him…maybe he can come back when the time is right. But why linger till then? We're doing no good, lurking about back here."

She knew the mages would never allow it. *But will it serve to tell him so?*

Hog had a dangerous side to him, a side that Cecilia had made good use of in the past, but one he might just as easily turn on her if driven to it. *He's teetering. A few more nudges and I'll have real trouble on my hands.* That would not serve her, to be imprisoned back here with such a man.

She looked at him, making her decision. Hog had served her loyally, but his purpose now was spent. *He has become a real danger to me*, she told herself. *I need him gone, and soon.*

Amilia

She dreamed of fire. Fire and a city burning. She dreamed of a cage and a prison and a bed, and her husband, her mad king husband, squirming between her legs. She dreamed of a tower, and an Eye, and a dragon and a god. *Him.* She dreamed of him, as she did every night. His eyes, his aura, his voice. She dreamed of the end of all days.

She was drenched in sweat when Astrid awoke her, swaddled like a babe in blankets beneath the sad sunken branches of an old willow tree. It was dark still, the dead of night, and silent but for the trickling of a stream nearby. It took a moment for Amilia Lukar to remember where she was. Then it came to her in a flash. *Northwest of Thalan somewhere, long leagues from the ruin of the city.* She sat up sharply, her breath misting in the cold night air. "What is it? Has something happened?"

Astrid crouched above her in a lithe silhouette. "No, Princess. No, you were just…"

"Making noises," Amilia answered for her.

Astrid nodded shyly. "You were mumbling, at first. Then you started speaking. Then…"

"Screaming?"

"A…a little bit, yes. That's when I woke you. I feared it might draw attention."

From who? Amilia wondered. There was no one else out here but sheep and goats, and the occasional sighting of a wild horse, grazing on the distant plains. She threw the blankets off her, to let her body cool, and strode out from beneath the branches of the willow, pushing the leaves aside. Moonlight flooded down from above them and the stars were out in force, twinkling bright and silver in great abundance across the breadth of the black night sky. She scanned her eyes across the plains and saw nothing but rocks, hills, and what might have been a group of sheep, sleeping by an old broken wall.

Astrid followed her out. "What were you dreaming about, Princess?"

What do you think? "Kittens and rainbows, Astrid," she said dryly. "I've always been terrified of them."

Astrid nodded. "Stupid question," she admitted. She was a tall girl, slim and gangly, with a pinched nose and narrow face. *And my saviour,* Amilia thought. *If Astrid hadn't come and unlocked the door that night...*

She put it from her mind. Thinking of those days trapped in that bedchamber, with only Sir Jeremy Gullimer's rotting corpse for company only made her fall deeper into despair. Her only solace was that she was rid of her rat king husband. *I hope the Fire Father is torturing you, my sweet. I hope he is picking you apart, piece by piece, to feed to his ravenous dragons. I pray he's putting you through the same torment you inflicted upon me. Oh I pray it with every fibre of my being, you vile, hateful sack of festering...*

She filled her lungs with sweet clean air and banished her husband from her thoughts. She needed to think of herself, and how she might get home. *Tukor,* she thought. *Ilithor. I must get back to Raynald. I must help him rule, or at least say goodbye, before the doom arrives.* "How well do you know these lands, Astrid?"

"Not well, Princess."

"Amilia." She'd asked her to call her Amilia a hundred times already but the maid kept on forgetting. Not that she was *actually* a maid. That had just been her cover while she kept watch on the palace for the spymaster Marian Payne, though she'd been one in a former life. "Call me Amilia, Astrid, please. It's getting tiresome having to remind you."

"Yes, of course...Amilia," she said stiffly. "I'm just too used to the titles my...my lady. Is...is that OK? To call you *my lady?*"

Amilia waved it off. "Fine. If you must."

"I worked in a household before Lady Marian found me," the tall girl went on. "I told you that, I think. Didn't I? At Osworth Castle. It's the seat of..."

"Sir Dudley Reed," Amilia cut in. "I know." She'd met him a couple of times before, though had never visited Osworth. "He's a glutton and a fool, but served my grandfather loyally in the war, so he gave him the castle as reward." It had been the seat of the exiled lord Emeric Manfrey before then, a house founded by the fabled Sir Oswald. *And now that useless oaf Sir Dudley rules over it.* There was something tragic about that.

"Your grandfather?" Astrid asked. "You mean the king?"

"No. My other grandfather. Lord Modrik Kastor. He died about four years ago, you probably heard. Slipped while drunk and cracked his head on the hearth."

Astrid nodded. "I know someone who once worked at Keep Kastor. A girl I trained with called Saska. She...she used to say his name in her sleep. Lord Modrik's, that is." She looked over at the princess, frowning. "She had bad dreams too, as you do. We used to have to wake her, me and Leshie. We all trained together, the three of us, under Lady Marian."

Amilia had heard parts of this story already. "You mentioned Saska when you rescued me," she remembered. "You said she was the most skilled of you all."

"Oh she was, and I liked her a lot. She had some of the south in her. Olive skin, luscious brown hair, blue eyes. Her mother was Aramatian, Master Ranulf thought."

"And her father?"

The girl shrugged her spindly shoulders. "She didn't know. Same as me. Some northern knight most likely, or maybe a lord." She gave a sigh. "I don't know where she is now. Or Leshie. We didn't get along so well, me and Leshie. We bickered a lot...that girl was so annoying, my lady, you'd know if you ever met her. But still...I miss her too, I guess. I...I hope they're both all right. And Marian too."

Don't get melancholy now, Amilia thought. *You're all I've bloody got.* "I'm sure they're all fine, Astrid." She scanned the moonlit plains once more. "How far from the coast do you think we are?"

The gangly girl looked to the stars. "We've been heading west the last few days, and it's about a hundred miles from Thalan to the mouth of the Izzun, I remember. If we went north those first three days, then started west..." She frowned to herself, doing some vague calculation. "We can't be more than forty or fifty miles away, I would guess, at the pace we're setting. Another two or three days of hard walking and we should reach the sea, I think."

It sounded reasonable. "We can find a boat when we get there," Amilia said. "One to get us across Vandar's Mercy. If we can sail up the Clearwater Run, we'll be able to get to Ethior. My uncle Caleb is castellan there, while Lord Cedrik is away at war. He'll give us an escort to take us back to Ilithor."

"I heard he's nicer...than the others. Sir Caleb Kastor. If that's...OK to say, my lady?"

"Say whatever you want. I'm not going to pretend my mother's family are saints." She supposed that this girl Saska had told Astrid a few ugly tales of life beneath the roof of Keep Kastor, and who was Amilia to deny or defend it? Her uncle Cedrik ever appeared the gallant knight, but he had plenty of skeletons in his closet, just as his father Modrik had. *And Griffin...* Amilia had spent much time with her cousin Sir Griffin as children and saw firsthand his cruel fascination with torturing animals, a passion he'd turned on the smallfolk later on. *But he's dead now,* she thought, *killed by Elyon Daecar they say.* She had spent not a moment mourning him. She didn't imagine many had, save his father Caleb perhaps.

She turned back to her companion. "There are still a few hours until dawn, Astrid. Get some rest. It's my turn to keep watch."

"Are you sure, my lady?"

"Plenty sure, yes. I've slept enough." *And dreamed enough,* she thought.

Astrid put up no further fight, drawing back the leaves to step inside their little hideout. She reemerged a second later holding a blanket and a godsteel dagger. "Here. For the watch."

Amilia took them gratefully, then found a comfortable-looking rock to sit on for her vigil, wrapping the blanket about her shoulders to beat off the nightly chill. The blade she laid upon her lap, ready to use if she must. She stared out across the empty plains, listening to the stream trickling softly nearby, the gentle sighing of the wind as it rustled through the leaves of the willow.

It is an alien world out here, she thought. It was vast and empty, disquieting and peaceful at once. Amilia knew that herders and sheep farmers reared their animals in these parts though if they were truly here, she hadn't seen them. *Perhaps they've been drawn into the war?* she thought. It seemed that almost every man capable of wielding a weapon had been dragged into the conflict, though as far as she was concerned, they might as well go back home now and enjoy what little time they had left with their families. She shuddered in her blanket as she thought of *him* once more. Those glowing red eyes. The voice like distant thunder. The way he had tapped his staff to the ground, and sent her crashing back against the tower wall. *What chance do we have against such a foe as he? Who can possibly stand against him?*

She pulled the blanket tighter and reached down to grip the godsteel dagger. It braced her. Made her feel stronger. It even enhanced her eyesight and hearing a bit, which was useful when on watch too, she supposed. What she didn't know was how to fight, though, so her companion had been tutoring her.

As best she can, anyway, Amilia reflected. Astrid was hardly some grizzled old master-at-arms, but she'd helped her learn the basics, instructing her on the forms and how best to strike and defend. Amilia had spent her entire life watching men swat at each other in the training yard and do battle during tourneys, so assumed at least some of that had rubbed off. Well, it hadn't, not really. *It seems I never really watched, after all,* she thought. The princess had attended those tourneys because her father or grandfather commanded it, but never to observe the skills on show. *No, it was the men I was more interested in.* She'd spent her time wondering who was the most dashing beneath their armour, and waiting to see which would try to win her favour, rather than observing their mastery of the forms. She understood all that a little better now, after the regular thrashings Astrid had given her when they'd trained using sticks as swords.

I'll get better, she told herself, as she sat upon her rock, gazing across the Highplains. She turned the dagger between her fingers, lamenting the fact that they didn't have one each. *Or swords,* she thought. *Or both. That would be even better.* They might have scavenged some too, if they hadn't left the palace and the city in such haste. Amilia's memory of it all was foggy, blurred and indistinct. When the Father of Fire had thrown her off her feet with his staff, she'd smashed her head against the stone, and she'd taken a tumble as she fled down the tower stairs as well. It had left her battered and bruised, her garb filthy with ash and smoke and piss from when her bladder had emptied out from the horror of it all. The rest was just fragments, as Astrid led her on secret paths through the palace that brought them out into the hills above the city. Amilia remembered how tired she was, how broken, yet Astrid would not let her rest. "We must go north," she insisted. "We *must* keep going, my lady. You can rest soon, I promise. Just keep on walking. Come, I'll help you."

When they finally came to a stop, it was hours past dawn and the city was long leagues behind them. They sat for a while, watching the fires burning in the distance, staring in silent despair as those great thick plumes of black smoke poured up into the tarry sky. Even from so far away, Amilia thought she could hear the screaming, though those were just memories, she knew. It was a night that would live with her forever, a night that would haunt her dreams.

And so it has proven, she thought, as she clutched at her blade a little tighter.

She let Astrid sleep through sunrise, enjoying the calm burbling of the brook, the faint whispering of the wind as it blew across the plains. When the slats of sunlight began peering through the leaves of the willow, they brought the girl out of her slumber. She came out rubbing her eyes and hiding a yawn with the back of her palm. "I'm sorry, my lady. I slept too long."

"You slept as long as you needed." Amilia handed back the godsteel dagger and sheath, so Astrid might girdle it about her waist. "Your turn," she said. She'd been holding it much of the last few hours, and it had grown heavy now. Still, more time strengthening her blood-bond was only ever a good thing. "I'll carry it later this afternoon."

They set off under a bright blue sky, the air crisp and bracing, the sparse stiff grasses twinkling with morning dew. For a time they followed the stream as it trickled westward through the plains, though before too long it turned more to the south, speeding into a series of rapids that hurried and fell over sharp cliffs.

South was not where they wanted to go, though. Amilia had had few friends in Thalan and further south they were likely to meet more refugees fleeing from the wreckage of the city. She could not say how she would be received, if recognised. *I was not the queen they wanted*, she knew. *And after everything my grandfather has done…*

She put that bastard from her mind as well. He was still missing, so far as she had last heard, and she hoped he stayed missing forever. *It's your fault, Grandfather. Your fault I'm here. Your fault that I found myself tied to a bed and held down by guards as that rat king of your making pulled my legs apart.* She closed a fist as she walked, trying not to dwell on it. Her husband. Sir Jeremy. Those ancient red eyes and that unearthly voice… *Please, please just leave me be*, she beseeched. *You have me at your mercy in my dreams already. Must you haunt my waking hours as well?*

The weather turned sour during the afternoon. Blues skies grew grey and the air turned bitter cold, the winds blowing hard in their faces. Some gusts were so fierce that they had to brace their footing and drive forward as they walked, and it became so loud that they could scarcely hear one another speak. By the time the sun began wheeling away to the west, the winds had barely dropped. It was often like that out here, though, in the Highplains. *No wonder so few people live here.*

They stopped at the top of a ridge giving good vantage over the plains as the sun plunged out of sight behind the hills. "We need to find somewhere to camp," Amilia said. She was holding the dagger, squinting out across the rugged lands for somewhere suitable. "I see a tumble of boulders, down there. Do you see them, Astrid? Down in that vale?" She handed the godsteel blade over for the girl to have a look, though Astrid's eyesight was only slightly enhanced by her bond.

She gave a nod all the same. "I see, my lady. It looks like a good spot. Somewhere safe and well hidden. We should try to get there before it gets too dark." She glanced behind them, peering hard the way they'd come.

The look on her face gave Amilia pause. "What is it? Have you seen something?"

Astrid shook her head. "Nothing," she said over the wind. "Well...I thought I saw someone earlier, when I was carrying the dagger. But that was hours ago. It's nothing."

"Why didn't you say anything?" Amilia snatched the dagger right back off her and scanned south. Nothing. There was no one out there, though the fading light made it hard to be sure.

"I didn't want to frighten you. You have enough going on, my lady."

"You should have told me, Astrid. Gods, someone might be tracking us."

"Why would they? And how? We've not seen anyone for days. It's probably just a passing herder, that's all. We've seen lots of sheep, and goats. They must belong to somebody."

Amilia scanned again, slower this time, trying to spot movement. "What did he look like? Was he walking? Riding a horse? Did it look like he was wearing armour?"

"Armour? I don't know, my lady, I don't think..." She shook her head. "It was a herder, as I say. It must have been. Why would a knight come up here?"

"I didn't say a knight. I just said armour. And why? For *me*, Astrid. How much do you think I'm worth, should someone take me captive?"

"They won't." Astrid twisted her thin lips into an expression of defiance. "I won't let them, my lady. I'm sworn to protect you."

Couldn't they have sent me someone stouter? Amilia did not voice that regret. It would only upset the girl, and in truth she'd been a loyal companion thus far. "We don't have armour, Astrid," was all she said. "And one dagger between us. We have to stay away from people, as much as we can. I've told you that. When they find out I'm not among the dead, they'll come looking for me, for good and bad. It's best we stay together, just the two of us. We trust no one until we reach Tukor."

"And when we reach the coast? We'll need someone to take us across the water, my lady. And they'll ask for money, won't they? We...we don't have much to bargain with."

"We'll figure something out." Amilia hoped that they'd come upon a small fishing village full of simple honest folk who'd be more compliant and willing to help. And if not, a godsteel dagger to the throat might sway them. "We only need to cross to Tukor and sail up the Clearwater Run. We'll be safe once we reach Ethior. My uncle will protect us."

Astrid nodded. "Those boulders, then. Shall we find somewhere among them to sleep?"

Amilia felt uneasy about that now. The girl should have either told her about the man earlier, or not said anything at all. *Why now, as the world turns black? How do you expect me to sleep now, Astrid?* "We should continue," she decided. "If someone is tracking us, we'll lose them in the dark."

Astrid looked like she wished she'd kept her mouth shut. "No one is tracking us, my lady. It was a herder, I swear it."

"Even so." Amilia Lukar was not about to take that chance. "Come on, let's keep moving. I don't feel tired yet anyway."

Where the previous night had been clear and bright, this one was dark and daunting, the skies cloaked in cloud and stormy, gales blustering all about them. Amilia favoured it, though. *Try to track us in this,* she thought, driving them on. Sighting movement beneath a calm and moonlit plain was simple enough; greatly less so in these conditions. They stayed close to one another, watching their footing closely, the dagger-bearer taking the lead and the other walking behind. In some places the ground was flat and easy to cross; in others it was treacherous, scarred by many jutting rocks and endless fields of loosened scree. But they soldiered on nonetheless, stopping only occasionally to look back and listen and pray they weren't being followed.

"There's no one there, my lady, I promise," Astrid would protest. "I wish I hadn't said anything."

"It's right that you did," Amilia came back. "We'll stop at first light, for a couple of hours. Then push on through the day."

The thought did not seem to sit well with the girl, but she made no complaint. "As you say, my lady. If…if you think it best."

Amilia didn't know what to think. She was running on instinct and fear right now, desperately trying to outrun her trauma. *Another step is another step from Thalan,* she thought. *Another step from that bedchamber, and that tower, and those eyes.* She would never return to this land, not as long as she lived. She made that promise to herself as she walked, repeating it over and over. *When I step foot aboard a ship, that'll be it. The sea, then the coast of Tukor, then the river and Ethior and my uncle and home.* She could see Ilithor before her, a clear image of it in the dark as she walked, step after wearying step, through the long black blustery night. *I'll live my last days there, with Ray and my mother, awaiting the doom.* They were the only family she had left, with Robb at war and her father dead and her grandfather missing, and good riddance to that monster. *And if my grandfather ever does return, I'll kill him,* she told herself. *I'll send him down the Long Abyss to tumble through darkness forever.*

It seemed the night might just go on forever, when at last they sighted a glow of purple light breaking in the east. "Can we find somewhere to rest now, my lady?" Astrid sounded broken. Her hair was windblown and wild, eyes red and watery from the constant assault of the storm. She turned her eyes around, searching through the predawn light. "I don't see anywhere hidden."

Nor did Amilia. They were on a barren stretch, gently hilly, with some scattered rocks and shrubs and little more. She wondered if they might await the full rising of the sun to get a better look, or keep going a while, but the thought held scant appeal. *I feel as broken as Astrid looks.* "You rest," she said. "Take an hour. I'll keep watch. Then we'll swap and keep on going."

"Right here? Are you sure?"

There was little cover to speak of, but the views were good and if there was trouble, Amilia would see it coming a long way off. "Just lie by those bushes," she said, pointing to a patch of dried brush a half dozen metres away. "One hour, Astrid. I'll wake you then."

"As you say, my lady." The girl stumbled to the shrubs, laid out her blanket, and collapsed. Within moments she was snoring.

Amilia remained standing a while longer, pacing slowly from side to side as the skies erupted into a glorious sunrise. Bands of light coloured the clouds, red and vermillion, ochre and gold. The princess marvelled at the sudden and growing beauty of it, dropping wearily to a rock to gaze upon the shapes the clouds made, the play of colours and hues as they shifted and morphed. One had the form of a great castle, with towers and walls and a great bulky barbican. Another looked almost like a sword, piercing through a series of smaller clouds which burned in a deep blood red. There was a face up there too, an enormous face with a massive beard, staring down at her. In his hair she saw fins and tails and tentacles and knew at once she was looking at the sea god Rasalan, watching over his realm.

"You're doing a poor job," she whispered. "Agarath...he's winning."

She closed her eyes, but only for a second. *No. Don't shut them.* She blinked hard and looked at the clouds again, but the shapes she'd seen had all melted away. The castle was a ruin, the sword was twisted and bent, Rasalan's face was shifting as though in a great pained grimace. Other clouds had formed too. *Dragons,* she thought. *I see dragons everywhere.* They stared down at her with wild red eyes and suddenly she was looking at *him* again. The Fire Father. And she was hearing that voice, and seeing those eyes, and remembering how he sent her flying across the room to smash against the wall.

Pain ran through her lower back and sides, and her head felt suddenly foggy from the impact. She felt a warm wetness run down her legs as her bladder emptied in her terror. A voice was speaking above her...*Amilia... Princess Amilia...*just as it had that night in the tower, when Astrid shook her from her shock and led her away, down the steps. But the voice sounded deeper, somehow. It didn't sound like Astrid's, but a man's...

"Amilia...Princess Amilia...that's Amilia Lukar, that is..."

She opened her eyes and escaped the dream. Four figures stood over her, lit behind by the rising sun. It had climbed high in the east, long past dawn. It took her a second to realise what was happening. *I slept,* she thought in a panic. *I slept for hours.* She was lying beside the rock she'd sat down on. Nearby, she could hear snoring.

"What you doin' all the way up here, princess?" asked the same voice.

"She ain't a princess no more," said another, in a deeper timbre. "She's queen. Hadrin's queen."

"*Our* queen," said a woman. "Queen o' Rasalan." She spoke mockingly, and crept in closer, sniffing. "A queen who's gone and pissed herself."

"Not so queenly behaviour, that," said the first voice. They began to come into view as her eyes adjusted, a group in ragged garb, all armed and armoured in patchwork leather and broken bits of chainmail. One had a rusted sword hanging sheathless from his belt. Another bore a spear with a broken shaft and the woman had a bow slung across her back, beside a quiver with only four arrows inside. The last man held only a knife, savage and cruel.

A knife…

Amilia shifted suddenly up, looking around for her godsteel dagger. She spotted it lying half a dozen feet away, beside the rock. Before she could lunge for it, the man with the sword moved in front of her. "Best not, my queen. That won't go well for you." It was the man who had spoken first.

It might if I got hold of it, she thought. "Who are you?" she demanded.

"Your leal subjects, Your Majesty." The woman with the bow and arrows gave a cackling laugh. She sounded sixty but looked more like twenty, and half her teeth were missing. "Where you headin'?"

"Home." She decided there was no sense in trying to deceive them on that account. "Help me get there and you'll be well rewarded."

"Best open your coffers then. You're home already, m'queen."

Amilia gave a polite smile. "Well, my original home, then. My brother Prince Raynald has called upon me for counsel. I'm trying to reach the coast." She began to stand, glancing once more at her blade. "If you help me get there…"

"You'll reward us. Aye, you said." The man with the sword continued to block her way. He seemed their leader. "Gutter, help the queen to her feet. And that other one. The snoring girl. Best wake her up too."

Gutter was the man with the knife, lurking at the rear. Amilia could guess how he got the name. These were common outlaws, parasites looking for a cheap meal. *And they've stumbled upon a banquet*, she thought. It was the very thing she'd hoped to avoid. "Thank you so much," she said, with sweet grace, as Gutter took her arm and helped her up. She got a good look at his face and didn't like what she saw, all cuts and scars and dull desire as he looked down at the wet patch between her legs.

"Don't stare, Guts," the woman spat at him. "My ma has a problem with that too. Weak bladder, m'queen. But she's well past fifty, so…"

"Bad dream, was it?" the leader asked. "Aye, must have been. You came from the city, no? You saw them dragons burning it all up."

"I…I did," Amilia said.

"Why you here then? Thalan's a hundred leagues away."

"I'm making for the coast," Amilia said. "We got lost, when we fled the city."

"We? And this one is?" He drew his sword and pointed it at Astrid, who was only now beginning to stir.

"My handmaiden," Amilia said. "And loyal friend."

"She from a noble house? Who's her father?"

Amilia didn't like that question. *They're hoping to ransom her too,* she realised. She was spared answering as Astrid awoke to find the other man looming over her, the one with the spear, biggest of the group. He had a missing right ear and thick red beard. "Up," he boomed at her.

Astrid took a few moments to work out what was happening. She looked at Amilia, saw the worry in her eyes, and then in a sudden bolting rush went scrambling into the scrubby bushes. The one-eared oaf grunted and lumbered right after her, crashing around and emerging a few seconds later with the girl locked tight between his arms, squirming wildly. "Got a wriggly one here," the redbeard chuckled. "Quiet now, girl. Go better for you if you stay quiet."

"My lady, run!" Astrid managed to scream. "Run…I…I can handle them…run!"

The outlaws let out a gale of laughter. "Shut that one up, Russ," the leader said. "She's got an ugly voice. Face too."

The redbeard called Russ clamped a hand over Astrid's mouth, muting her.

"Better." The leader looked back at Amilia. He was the oldest, but not by much, no more than five and thirty. "Her father, then. Who is he?"

"Lord Delmar's daughter," Amilia told him, coming up with the name on the spot. "If you harm her…"

"Delmar? That lord over in Bleakrock?"

"Yes. Him. She's his third daughter. Harm her and you'll raise him to wroth."

"Lies," said the woman, stalking closer. "You heard her just then, Taggern. Girl ain't Rasal. Sounded Tukoran to me."

Taggern nodded. "Caught that too, Cat. North Tukor to my ear. And besides, Lord Delmar's only got two daughters. Queen of Rasalan should know that." He smiled at her. "So, she lowborn, is she? Tell it true, Your Majesty. No more fibs and falsehoods now."

"She's under my protection," Amilia could only blurt.

"Lowborn," said the ugly young woman called Cat. *For those claws,* Amilia realised. Her nails were filed and sharpened like knives, each two inches long. What remained of her teeth had been sharpened too. "And Bladeborn, most like. That's godsteel you're standing over, Tag."

"I'd noticed."

"We'd best be rid o' her. No sense in carrying dead weight." She flashed those sharpened claws and grinned. "I'll tickle her dead if you like."

"Touch her and you'll get nothing from me."

"And what is it you think we want from you, Your Majesty?" Taggern asked. He had dead eyes, heartless eyes. "Well, besides what Gutter's making clear." The foul dolt was still staring at her desirously, a spindly length of drool dangling from one corner of his mouth.

Amilia tried her best to ignore him. "Money. Wealth. That's what you want. Chests filled with gold and gemstones and jewels. Deliver me to my uncle Caleb Kastor and you'll have it."

"Or we could have both?" The leader shrugged. "Gutter, go ahead. You take her off and have your way with her. You earned it, for that deer you caught us last week. Was tasty, that deer."

Fear sliced through her like a knife. "*No.*" She pulled her arm away from the cretin. "You can't."

"Why not? Gutter's always liked you, with your pretty dresses and gems and all those naughty smiles you're known for. The Jewel of Tukor. That's what they call you, isn't it? What more wealth does a man need than what you got between your legs?" He laughed loudly as Gutter began to drag her away. Astrid was squirming and mumbling behind Russ's thick fingers. Suddenly the bearded man gave a great yelp of pain and Amilia saw a flash of red dribble down his palm. He lost his grip a moment as Astrid sprang from his grasp, bloody-mouthed, though she didn't get far. A swinging arm came around and struck her, knocking her sideward to the floor. A moment later the big outlaw was atop her, strangling at her neck with his bloody bitten hand, wild-eyed and maddened. Gutter continued to draw Amilia away; her legs were all but gone beneath her, overwhelmed by fear. "No," she was saying, but so weakly. "Stop...please...Astrid...no..."

"Changed my mind," shouted Taggern. He waved and Cat went skipping over to pry Gutter's hand from Amilia's arm. "Can't be having the queen defiled just yet. No, *I'll* take her first, I think." And he laughed. "Dumb sod, Gutter. Did you really think I'd let you..."

A length of steel exploded through the front of his head, sending gouts of blood and brain and skull flying in all directions.

Amilia's eyes bloomed in shock.

Taggern went forward, crashing dead to the ground. On the plains some way behind him a figure was running, dashing in brilliant silver armour and a dazzling golden cloak. He moved with such staggering speed that the outlaws had scant chance to react before he came upon them, drawing out a misting broadsword and swinging it right through Russ's body an inch above the navel. The man's top half slid off his bottom half, which still straddled Astrid as she struggled on the ground, trying to prise away his dismembered arms. Cat gave a wild shriek and leapt at the armoured knight, scratching. He caught her neck in his steel grip and squeezed, crushing her larynx in a bloody explosion, then tossed her lifeless body to the ground.

That left Gutter, poor dumb Gutter, who stood paralysed on the plains, pissing himself. A horrid stink filled the air and a strange imperilled squeak was ringing from his lips, and only then did Amilia realise he had no tongue. The knight stormed toward him, his face hidden in the hood of his golden cloak. Amilia recognised the tentacled shoulder clasps that held it in place. The cloak was lightly singed in places and there were some dark scorch marks and scuffs on his armour, and she knew that armour too. Gutter was still making that shrieking sound when Amilia said, "Let me, Sir Munroe."

He stopped before her and drew back his hood. "You recognised me, my queen."

"You're not a man I'm ever likely to forget."

He smiled at her enigmatically. "Let the past die," he said. "Let the future reign. I've been searching for you, Queen Amilia. You cannot imagine what a relief it is to find you."

The stranger on the plains, Amilia Lukar thought. "Give me your dagger, Sir Munroe."

"So long as you promise not to use it on me."

She would make no such promise to the man who'd led her husband's guard, the man who'd beaten Sir Jeremy Gullimer so fiercely his face had turned to pulp. "The dagger, Sir Munroe." She held out her hand.

He unsheathed it, a much finer blade than the one she and Astrid had been using, and placed it into Amilia's shaking palm. It shook no more. She spun around and without hesitation, surged forth and plunged it deep into the belly of the lackwit called Gutter, gutting him. She relished seeing the light in his eyes go out. She only wished those eyes were red. *Or better yet, my husband's.*

She turned, and tossed the bloody blade back at the knight. "You're going to take me to Tukor," she commanded, as the sun shone bright above them. "As my late husband's loyal protector, you owe me your allegiance."

He fell to a knee and placed his sword at her feet. It caught the light and gleamed, silver and red. "I am your man, my queen. I'll see you safely home to Tukor."

8

Lythian

The mists hung thick as soup, a damp grey blanket upon the roiling seas. Lythian Lindar sat hunched at the oars pulling tiredly through the choppy waters, stroke by wearying stroke. In the small hollow of the rowboat Sir Pagaloth lay sleeping beneath a frayed woollen blanket. It was long past due for the dragonknight to take over, yet Lythian continued to let him rest. *He has done enough, leading me so far,* he thought. *The least I can do is row the last stretch home.*

There was a fine mizzle in the air, falling softly from the leaden skies, the dawn gloomy and bleak, yet welcome. It had been a long hard night of rowing, dark and moonless, and the last of their long journey he hoped. How many days had it been? He had begun to lose count of them, though they'd been in this skiff for ten days at least, taking turns at the oars as they crossed the Red Sea. And before that, many more had passed as they journeyed the Drylands by saddle and sole, searching for a boat that might bear them north. *To home,* Lythian thought, giving the oars another pull. *Vandar. So close I can almost smell it.*

A seabird came down to perch upon the prow, cawing as it landed, followed by a second. Lythian smiled to see them. Large and thickset, with a white underside and black back, head, and beak, he knew them well. The razorbill was a common bird in these coastal waters between Southwatch and Death's Passage, and a good omen for a man so long from his lands. "Hello, my friends," he found himself saying. "It has been a long time since I've seen your like."

The birds paid him no mind, snapping and crying at one another before taking flight once more, beating their strong wings to the breeze. One was a little larger than the other, Lythian saw. Partners, perhaps they were. Mates. It made him think of Talasha, though of course the comparison was false. *No, these birds are one and the same,* he thought, *born to bond and breed. Talasha and I...we were never meant to be. It was a dream, and nothing more...*

He pulled once more at the oars, ignoring the ache in his lower back.

Salt spray washed across his face and distantly, he could hear the crashing of waves, breaking against rocks. *The shore.* He peered through the fogs, brightening with the rising of the sun, though could see nothing as yet. His heart thudded a rhythm of anticipation, and dread. *I have been so long away,* he thought. *What will they make of my return? What will they say, when they find out what I've done?*

Sir Pagaloth stirred from his slumber, awakened by the spray and brightening of day. He sat up, wincing, clutching at a pain in his left leg. "Cramp," he said croakily, to Lythian's questioning look. "Pass me the water skin, Captain."

Lythian took it from beneath the bench and handed it over, as Pagaloth unstoppered the top and drank deep. They'd been fortunate with the weather these ten days at sea, the skies sending them rain most days to replenish their water stores, without delivering a storm that might sink them. Their provisions of food had not yet run out and by chance no enemy had waylaid them, despite the legions of soldiers and ships crawling the plains and waters. By cover of night they had travelled on land, hiding during the heat of the day, yet here at sea there was no such cover but the weather, the fog, and the occasion thrust of land that jutted from the waters like jagged black fingers. Several times they'd sighted Agarathi war galleys on patrol and on each occasion, the winds had worked in their favour, or a thick mist had risen up, or they'd come upon a craggy island where they might vanish for a short time. *Luck walks with us, side by side,* Lythian thought. *She has helped to guide me home.*

Sir Pagaloth turned his eyes around. "No land?"

"Not yet."

"These birds. Do they range far from the coast?"

"They're not known to. Land is close, Pagaloth. Listen. There are waves breaking against rocks, forward off the bow."

The dragonknight listened over the hiss of the spray and the slosh of the waves and the cawing of the birds above them. "Might it not be another island?"

It was possible, though Lythian doubted it. The islands they'd passed were oft called Seaman's Scourge by the Vandarians, a grouping of bleak islets and rocky upthrusts spread through the heart of the eastern expanses of the Red Sea. They were commonly avoided by larger ships for the snarls of rock hidden below the surface of the water, yet a pair of men in a skiff need have no fear of them. Those islands had been left behind some days ago, however. "There are some smaller islands close to the Vandarian coast," Lythian told his companion. "But none are far from land. Either way, we're close."

"Then let me take the oars." Pagaloth stood and came to sit on the bench. "You can navigate, Captain. I have slept long enough."

Lythian reluctantly let himself be moved aside as he went to perch by the prow, squinting for a sight of land and bending his ears to the music of the sea. After a good long rest, Sir Pagaloth pulled hard at the oars, easing them smoothly and yet swiftly across the surface of the water. "I think we've passed north of Southwatch," Lythian told him. "That would put us in Rustriver Bay." By his calculation, there was nowhere else they could be. Often as they could they'd used the stars to navigate and though the skies had been veiled for two days and nights, he sensed they'd continued on the same course. "If we're lucky, we'll be near the estuary where Rustriver opens into the sea. There are many fishing villages along that stretch of coast. We ought to be able to find horses there."

Pagaloth said nothing, though Lythian did not miss the tight set of his jaw.

"You fear for how you'll be greeted?" he asked him.

"I expect a poor reception," the dragonknight said. "Your protection will only go so far, Captain. And you have been gone a long time."

Too long, Lythian knew, *and many will want me to turn right around and go back.* He knew full well that men would call him traitor for his actions, allying himself to Prince Tethian and his cult where the likes of Borrus wiped his hands of it and said no. *I stayed to keep watch,* Lythian told himself. *That is all it was meant to be. To keep watch so I might report back one day.* Yet in the end, he'd been drawn in by false promises and prophesies misread, deceived by a lie as Tethian had been, and Sotel Dar as well, and the wise masters gone before. *Eldur was meant to rise benevolent, a beacon of hope, to bring balance to the world.* Lythian in his folly had begun to trust in that too. *I trusted in it and I helped them unleash a monster. I have doomed all the world to this darkness and dread.*

"I see something," Pagaloth said. He shifted on his bench, resting in his stroke, and peered through the banners of torn grey fog. "There, Captain. The rocks, I see them."

Lythian saw them too, the fogs parting to unveil the coastline he'd longed to see. The rocks rose up in a shallow cliff, no more than eight or nine metres high, topped by a rugged overhang carved out by the toil of the sea. The waves crashed in and roared, white and frothing, to explode in great plumes of spray. "It's too dangerous to land here," Lythian called. "Turn the boat east, Pagaloth. The waters here are treacherous."

The dragonknight was strong and equal to the task. He pulled hard, turning them to row down the shoreline in search of a more suitable berth. Gradually the coast opened out before them, the mists thinning to reveal a rugged stretch of low cliffs intersected with wide pebbly strands. Many were rocky in the surf and the waves crashed violently. Lythian sighted several splintered skiffs and small vessels snagged among those rocks, and even a large old war galleon too, its guts ripped out from under it. "Keep going, Pagaloth. The beaches grow more inviting further down the coast."

Lythian knew where they were now. *Further west of the estuary than I thought.* They were somewhere midway between Southwatch and the mouth of Rustriver, each about fifty or sixty miles away. It was a quieter stretch of coast, with few villages that he knew of. He frowned, staring east in thought. There was a small muddy town that he recalled, a place called Craymire where they liked to catch crayfish at low tide. *It shouldn't be too far from here,* he thought, moving back to sit beside the dragonknight on the bench. "Come, give me that oar," he said, shifting the man down, taking the right blade. "It will be quicker with the two of us."

He kept watch as they went, staying some thirty or so metres from the shore to avoid being pulled toward the rocks. The skies brightened from a dull sickly grey to a more promising steely white, and in parts opened entirely, showing thin bands of blue beyond. The fogs dispersed as the weather warmed, though the winds continued to blow, skirling about them as they pulled and heaved. "There," Pagaloth said, after a time, gesturing to a sandy beach. "Might we be better to land here and walk?"

The seas were still churning and choppy and the going was slow, so Lythian nodded and agreed. They made for the beach, cutting past a set of slimy green rocks and over some others that scratched at the hull. For a moment it looked like they might be marooned some ten metres from shore, but they drove their oars down into the water, pushed themselves free, and slid the rest of the way until they heard the scrape of sand beneath them.

Pagaloth was first out, leaping into the ankle-high water to pull the boat ashore. Lythian followed, helping the dragonknight to draw the little boat up onto dry land, beyond the high tide line. It had served them well, that sturdy rowboat, but both were happy to abandon it. They gathered their things - weapons, rations, water - and began up along the beach. "Feels odd walking," Pagaloth noted. "I did not tell you this before, but that was my first time in a boat."

Lythian raised a brow. "*Ever?* You'd never been at sea before?"

"I am a soldier, not a sailor, Captain. I have lived all my life in Agarath until this day."

Then you are doubly brave, Lythian thought. Men who'd never been at sea often found her a frightening mistress, yet Pagaloth had not whimpered once. *And to cross a sea in nothing but a skiff...*"You row like a man born to it, Pagaloth. I'd never have known."

"Rowing is not a hard skill to master." Sir Pagaloth Kadosk strode up the beach, Lythian keeping pace as well as he could. His legs felt more wobbly than he cared to admit though he said nothing of that to the younger man. Beyond the strand, the lands spread into a broad grassland, spotted with rocks and shrubs, and the occasional patch of wood. It was a wide open country here, the soil poor for tilling though good for grazing animals. Lythian could see no sheep or cattle, however, nor farm tracks that they might follow. "We follow the coast," he said. "There is a village I know. It shouldn't be far."

It was an hour before they came upon the first sight of Craymire, a sight that was not in the least bit promising. Rising over the top of a coastal hill, they sighted a blackened ruin in the distance, fronted by a long stretch of muddy brown beach. Swirls of mist spun through the wreckage, though Lythian could see no other movement there. "This village has been razed by dragons," he said. "Come, there may yet be survivors."

There were none, leastways none who lingered among the ruin. If anyone had lived through the attack, they must have fled long ago, seeking refuge elsewhere. At the heart of the village, a small river ran into the sea, spanned by a short wooden bridge that had collapsed into a heap, forming a dam of sorts. There were a dozen corpses there, adding to the blockage, charred and rotting, dressed in scraps of charred cloth and blackened leather. Others lay strewn among the debris of the village or half hidden in the bones of the buildings, a leg poking out here, a burnt skull there, the old and young all dead. There were animals too, dogs, cats, goats, pigs, chickens. *It happened quickly,* Lythian thought. *They did not see their calamity coming, until it was too late.*

"No one has come to bury them," Pagaloth said, scanning the wreck with a frown on his dusky face. He sounded perturbed. "This village was destroyed months ago, and yet no one has come to bring these people peace."

"This entire stretch of coast has likely come under attack," Lythian pointed out. "Places like this can get forgotten." It was a foul truth, though a truth all the same. Craymire was well isolated out here, and if there had been any survivors, they weren't likely to want to come back. "We'll have to venture further inland," he decided. "There are sheep and cattle farms in the area. Be on the lookout for tracks."

They turned north, driving hard across a boggy land in search of signs of life, their boots sucking and pulling in the sticky mud. Pagaloth's dirty black hair whipped in the wind, his unbraided beard hanging heavy from his chin. He'd long since given up oiling it into prongs, though had lost some of his refinement as a consequence. *We look like heathens,* Lythian thought, *rough and dangerous.* His own face was not the same as when he'd left these lands with Borrus and Tomos at his side many moons ago. *I have aged a decade, the lustre of my skin lost.* His hair had been brown and blond and curly once, his eyes a bright keen gold, yet now in his reflection he saw nought but an old man, weary and grief-stricken and haunted by regret.

He plodded on, his worn leather scabbard knocking at his leg as he went. Within it was a dinted steel blade, castle-forged but plain, that he'd carried now for months. *Months,* he reflected. *It's been months since I've felt the touch of godsteel.* Not since he'd lost Starslayer down in Eldur's tomb, deep beneath the Wings, had he felt the bracing effects of his blood-bond. *I am half a man without it…less…a shadow of myself, a shade thinly seen…*

He drove on, pacing hard across the softened earth. "Such haste," Captain," Pagaloth noted. "Do you have an urgent engagement to meet?"

An engagement with godsteel, yes, he thought. *A renewal of a bond you cannot comprehend.* His hopes of ever retrieving Starslayer were long behind him now, yet any good godsteel blade would do. *I have others,* he thought, *stored in my room at the Steelforge.* Until he got back to Varinar, however, he would hope to get his hands on another. Rustbridge and Redhelm were both but a few days' ride from here, and would have many Bladeborn knights and soldiers guarding their walls. *Unless they've been destroyed as well…*That was a sobering thought, and a possibility, he had to admit. Last they'd heard, a great Agarathi horde had been marching across the Bloodmarshes. *Might they have breached the Bane? Might the dragons have razed the cities inland from here?* He paced onward, ignoring the fatigue in his bones. "My lands are under siege, Pagaloth. Everything must come with haste now."

They found a farm track a short while later, wending through a set of soggy fields toward a woodland of elm and ash. It looked old and rare-used, grass spouting in thick patches between the two wheel ruts, the road seeming to disappear entirely in places, before reappearing again a little further on. When they got to where it went into the woods, the trail was lost.

"Beware," Lythian warned. "Outlaws are drawn to places such as this." He held the handle of his sword as they went, though if a fight was to be had, Pagaloth would be the superior threat. He was younger, fitter, better rested, and had in his sheath a dragonsteel blade of the finest quality. After godsteel there was nothing quite like it, the black steel lined with shimmering lengths of red light from its forging, the remnants of the magic of dragonflame.

The dragonknight took a grip of his hilt, turning his sharp eyes around. "Perhaps these outlaws will have horses, Captain," he said. "Let them come, if so. They would be doing us a favour."

Lythian had to smile. *The man is not short of confidence.*

The woods grew dark and brooding the deeper they went, though much of that was due to the curdling skies above. Through the canopy Lythian sighted the gathering of lumpen clouds, dark grey to black and threatening rain. They delivered on that promise soon after, the ether opening to douse them with a heavy fall that pattered relentlessly down through the branches and leaves, soaking them both to the bone.

It was still raining when the trees thinned and they found themselves in a land of rolling hills, with a sweeping valley before them crossed with many small rills. Lythian looked out, memory stirring of a place he'd not seen in long years. "This is the floodplain of *Ashandar*," he said. "Many call it the *Valley of Tears*."

"This is a sacred place to you?" Pagaloth asked.

Lythian nodded. "Ashandar was a goddess of Vandar, one of many in his service. She was said to tend the lands, restore and replenish them once they were ravaged by war. She fell here, according to legend, creating this floodplain at her death. I've not been here in many years, not since my early days as a knight."

They descended into the valley, splashing through streams and flowering meadows, and for a short time the rains eased and clouds parted, and the sun came shining down from the skies. "Ashandar smiles upon your return, Captain Lythian," Pagaloth said. "There is a strange power here. Do you feel it, as I do?"

"A lightness," Lythian said. "Ashandar was known to lift spirits after battle, tend the ills that plagued the minds of men in the same way that she did the lands. She was a healing diety. People come here often to bathe in that restorative light."

"Yet we are alone." Pagaloth turned his eyes across the valley. "I see no one here but us."

"The war keeps people in their homes and behind their thick stone walls. Fear is stronger than faith, sometimes. And the darkness is driving away the light."

That darkness closed in once more as they rose up on the valley's northern side and left the streams and meadows behind. Lythian remembered the curious sense he'd felt the first time he came here, though he'd long since forgotten its power. "Some claim the feeling of lightness comes from the wildflowers," he recalled. "They say they have a psychedelic effect, though tests have proven inconclusive. What do you think, Pagaloth? Do you believe in the power of a long-dead deity, or are you more inclined to cynicism in this?"

"I am a man open to ideas of faith and spirituality, Captain. You know this, and saw it when we gazed together into the fire not long into our first journey across the Drylands. In the flames you saw your departed wife and son, dancing, you told me. I have sat there many times and seen my parents and uncles and brothers as well, eating about a table, or laughing at some jest."

"But was that the fire, or the *skraik*?" They had shared around a brown syrupy drink as they sat at the fire, which might have had mind-altering effects. "Have you ever sat at the flames and seen your family without it?"

Pagaloth smiled at the challenge. "No, I will admit not. It is part of the ritual to drink it."

"Then it is a man's choice to determine whether it is the substance or the setting or something more that triggers the experience," Lythian said. "Same as it is here. And other holy sites as well."

"As it should always be," Pagaloth agreed. "A matter of choice, for us all to make."

They moved beyond the Valley of Tears, to where a gloom stretched across the land. The rains regathered and the sense of lightness was stricken by a feeling of foreboding, thick in his veins. Lythian had made few choices in his life, though that was the essence of duty. *A soldier's life is not his own*, he thought. *We are but pawns on a board, to be moved here and there*. Yet of late, he'd made some choices for himself. *And look where that has gotten me. Look at what my choices have wrought...*

Sourly he walked, his boots squelching through the soft muddy earth, searching once more for a track to follow. They went in silence for a short time before Pagaloth stopped and frowned, smelling the air. "Something dead is nearby," he said. "Do you smell that foul reek, Captain?"

Once, Lythian would have detected it long before his companion, his senses heightened by godsteel, but no longer. He sniffed deep and nodded. "It is coming from beyond that hill." It was a bushy hill, covered in heath and scrub. They made their way up its shallow slope; beyond came the sound of a babbling river, winding through a spread of open woodland on its other side. Lythian sighted the source of the stench below; a bear, large and brown and brutally mangled, lay at the river's edge among the roots and rocks. They descended to inspect it. Its stomach had been slashed asunder by something savage and sharp, innards spilling out to the damp muddy earth. Its lower jaw was missing, upper right forelimb turned horrifically backward. Chunks of its flank had been bitten away, exposing the putrid flesh beneath. Flies buzzed about it in thick black clouds, feasting, and other parts had been picked at by carrion beasts too. "It cannot have been dead long," Lythian said. "The scavengers have only just started to get at it."

Pagaloth did not shield his nose from the stink. "What could have done this? A dragon, do you think?"

Lythian bent down to inspect the bite marks. "These are not consistent with dragon teeth," he said, "nor do I see any scorch marks. No, this seems the work of something else. A larger bear, perhaps." He could think of no other fiend that could do this, leastways nothing that lived in these parts. "Search for tracks, Pagaloth. They might help give us a clue."

The two men parted, Lythian moving upriver along the banks, Pagaloth stepping away through the shrubs and trees. Lythian's search yielded no reward. He found prints of the bear itself, and markings of other smaller predators, but nothing that could be their culprit. He was on his way back when he heard his friend calling to him through the woods.

"Lythian, here. I have found something." He hastened to Pagaloth's side, to find the dragonknight standing beside a deadfall where the surrounding bush had been trampled and crushed. There were some signs of prints in the mud though they were fragments only, washed away by the falling rains. "Something large came through this way," the man said. "Ought we follow it into the forest?"

Lythian was getting an uneasy feeling. "I am not sure that will serve us, Pagaloth. This creature is clearly big, powerful, and ferocious. It may well outmatch us. If I had godsteel..." He shook his head. "But I don't."

Pagaloth nodded. "My curiosity overcomes my caution, sometimes." He turned his eyes north. "We should continue this way, then."

"I think that would be wise."

They continued back toward the river, following its course northward through the open forest. The rain was still falling in a soft drizzle, the skies as grey as steel. Lythian was musing on the mystery creature. Once, these lands were inhabited by a great many large beasts, superfauna long since hunted to extinction or driven into the shadows beyond the sight of men. There were pockets in the north where ancient beasts still lurked - the Icewilds and Weeping Heights and Banewood on its border, parts of the High Hammersongs and the Darkwood, the deeper darker parts of the Mistwood and Greenwood too. He'd heard stories of creatures dwelling in the caves of the North Downs, of aquatic monsters in the Four Sisters and Lake Eshina, of the legendary fiend of Celaph's Mire and the great serpent who gave the Izzun River its name - but for the most part the north was tame, a once-wild place where man now held dominion. *And yet...*

He thought of the dead bear, its forelimb twisted back and shattered, its jaw torn off, its belly slashed open. He thought of the trampled brush and the partial prints in the mud. Some had looked broader than others. *The hindlimbs and forelimbs,* he thought. Wide rear feet for stability, with shorter blunter claws. Longer front limbs, to be used for speed when running, with savage claws for carving and cleaving during a fight. "A *drovara*," he whispered.

Pagaloth heard him. "A…?"

"Drovara. It's a creature from the olden days, shaped somewhat like a bear, though more springy and nimble. It was said to have strong hindquarters, and a lighter upper body, and would walk upright unless running. The front legs were more like arms, rangy and dextrous with retractible claws ten inches long. Those arms, Pagaloth. They'd be strong enough to snap a bear's limb and tear off its jaw, and the claws sharp enough to open its guts." He nodded. "A drovara. We would have little chance against such a beast."

His words had them moving with more urgency. Pagaloth glanced back as though they were being tracked. "This creature…when was it last seen?"

"Centuries ago. Longer, even. I heard a rumour of one that lived in the northern parts of the Mistwood, near Mistvale where I grew up. But that was just a rumour and never confirmed." He looked through the trees. "But so far south…there's not thought to be anything more dangerous than bears and wolves down here."

"It has been hibernating," Pagaloth said in a distant voice. "The spread of darkness shields all foul things from the light. This is spoken of in Agarath as the *Untar Batax'un*, the Return to the Days of Dread. To you, the Last Renewal. In the far south it is most known as the Ever-War, when all creatures crawl from the shadows, and retake the world that was once their own."

Retake the world, Lythian thought. *And I have helped open the door.* "The drovara is a territorial creature. It is nocturnal, but will soon sense us if we linger. We must leave this place at once."

They hastened on, eager to escape the trees and return to the open plains. *There must be a farm somewhere near*, Lythian thought. *We'll come upon a track soon enough.* Another thirty minutes passed by, and another followed right after, and still they had no sight of a road. The trees came and went in their clots, and the hills rose up and fell and rose again. Lythian had no great knowledge of these lands. They had been more densely populated once before, though centuries of Agarathi raids and attacks had driven the people back toward the safety of the great cities further north.

"Who controls this country?" Pagaloth asked, as they forded another stream, wading up to their waists in the slow-moving water. Beyond lay more hills and scattered woods. And no roads, as yet.

"Lord Pentar, of Redhelm. He is the Warden of the South. Sir Tomos was his son."

Pagaloth dipped his eyes and said nothing. *He still feels guilt over Tomos's death.* Pagaloth had been the one to speak of their plot to assassinate Prince Tavash, a betrayal that had led the trio of Varin Knights to their scalding dragon-maw cell, pelted at day and night by the baying crowds. Tomos had almost perished of thirst, though had managed to survive long enough to be dragged to the Pits of Kharthar to be slain by a brood of malformed drakes. Lythian still remembered the sight of his friend being eaten alive, the crunch of bone, the rending of flesh. *But he slew two first,* he thought. *He slew two, and earned his seat, higher up along Varin's Table.*

"Lord Pentar has long been charged with protecting the Black Coast," Lythian went on. "His main charge runs from King's Point to Southwatch. Lord Kanabar has jurisdiction from there, watching over the lands of East Vandar from Rustriver to Dragon's Bane at Death's Passage, and all the way up to Tukor's Pass at the border with Tukor."

Pagaloth pondered that. "Do you not find it odd that we have encountered no soldiers? An enemy could have invaded as far as we have, and no one would have been there to stop them."

"The Agarathi have invaded through this gate before," Lythian told him. "Typically their ships are spotted and an army mustered to meet them. Southwatch isn't too far, and there are always ships in the bay that can convey soldiers quickly where they're needed. Rustbridge is another large river port. And there are coastal forts further east, though we haven't seen them." He looked at his friend. "It is greatly easier to travel as a pair of men in cloaks and cowls than sneak an army through these lands, Pagaloth."

He wondered whether the war at Dragon's Bane had drawn reserve forces to the defence as well. They'd heard only rumours of the size of the Agarathi horde, but those rumours were alarming, and the count of dragons in the skies even more so. The Bane might be destroyed, the lands of East Vandar razed. So far as Lythian knew, Eldur himself might have taken claim over some great city. Might he have set his sights on Varinar, even? Might he have sent his hordes and his swarms to assail our great capital? The not knowing was a hole in his heart that he couldn't fill. *Where is this road?* he asked himself. *Where is this farm? There must be someone, somewhere, who can help us.*

He turned his eyes angrily over the misted hills. And that, by chance, was when he saw them.

Six men on horseback, too shoddily dressed to be knights or men-at-arms, were summiting a rise and riding their way. Lythian squinted, taking Pagaloth's arm to halt him. "Let them come," he said. "They have seen us already." He could feel the tension in the man's muscles, the tautness beneath his leather shirt. "Keep your hands from the hilt of your blade, Pagaloth. Let me do the talking. They will know my name."

The half dozen riders appeared more clearly now, their garb rugged, hardy, scratched and stained. Leathers they wore beneath heavy furs and pelts, with full saddlebacks affixed to their horses' flanks. Those horses were strong and large, though did not have the look of those reared to bear godsteel. All but one, at least, a snorting great beast who dwarfed all the rest. "The leader is Bladeborn," Lythian said. He knew it by instinct. "These men are not soldiers."

"Outlaws?" Pagaloth shifted his feet but did not reach for his blade. A strong Bladeborn with five stout warriors for company would be too much for the pair of them.

If only I had godsteel… "Perhaps. If a fight should start, strike hard and fast at the leader. If I can get his weapon…"

"I understand."

No more was said.

The riders thundered up the slope toward them, spreading to form a semi-circle as they neared. The man who was their leader matched his horse in size, a massive-chested barbarian with a beard of reddish brown, thickly forested and broad. His cloak was a wolf pelt, its head forming a hood. Around his neck hung a chain of many fangs and claws. "You have the look of men of the Rivers," Lythian called to them, eager to have the first word. "You are friend to us, if so. I am well known to Lord Kanabar, Warden of the East."

"Kanabar's dead," the leader rumbled. "And we're of the Downs not the Rivers."

"The *South* Downs," put in another man, ferrety faced and small, with a dead fox slung over his shoulders. "Not the North."

Lythian hardly heard him. *Lord Wallis…dead.* He would be the first of many great men slain, he feared, heavy-hearted. "The Lord of Rivers has perished, you say?" It was a most grievous loss. "How, pray tell?"

"Bane fell on top of him," the leader said. "Now who are you? You've come from the coast." His eyes went to Pagaloth, who had his hood up to shield his face. "Draw back that hood. Let me look at you," he commanded.

Lythian stepped forward. "My name is Lythian Lindar, Captain of the Varin Knights and Knight of the Vale. We need horses to convey us at once on the road to Varinar."

"Lindar?" The leader peered at him through the rain, unconvinced. "The Knight of Mists is dead. Killed in Eldurath, we heard."

"You heard wrong. I am he."

The leader studied him. "Maybe you are, maybe you aren't. You could just as well be some reaver for all I know." He looked at Pagaloth again. "*You.* Pull back that hood, like I told you. Let me see your face."

"Like he told you," echoed the ferrety man. He slid an ugly dagger from his belt. "Do it."

Lythian nodded. There was no use denying them.

Pagaloth drew back his hood, exposing his dark eyes and dusky features to join the earthy Agarathi timbre of his voice. He set his gaze upon the leader. "My name is Sir Pagaloth Kadosk, once Dragonknight of Agarath, now friend to Captain Lythian Lindar of Vandar and the Varin Knights. I am his man by oath, forsaken of my knightly vows. My life is his, now until he releases me."

That was met with a round of scoffs and a bemused snort from the big leader. "How'd you get here? You swim?"

"We rowed a skiff across the Red Sea," Lythian said. "We have been long weeks on the road, and I have an urgent need to hear tidings." *The Bane fell on him, he'd said. It fell.* "Is Dragon's Bane lost?"

"Aye, it's lost," rasped a stick-thin man with large eyes and a narrow face. He spat to the side. *"His* lot…they took it. Won the Bane in a single night."

One night. "Was our army destroyed?"

"Some. Rest fled. Made for the Lakelands, we heard, though not where." The leader kicked his heel into his horse and drove him forward a few steps. The big stallion snorted and puffed, breath misting, eyes wide and wild. "We're hunters," he said. "Heard of trouble this way, so came looking for a prize. Didn't expect to find a dragonkin, though." He drew his godsteel broadsword out, pointing it at Pagaloth's chest. Each man had a good many weapons on their belts and backs; axes, bows, blades, blunts. "Give me one good reason why I shouldn't run you you through right here."

"I have given you a reason," Sir Pagaloth said, fearless. "I am Captain Lythian's man by oath and debt of life. To kill me would be a great insult to him, and his knightly order by extension."

The lead hunter seemed to like that. His lips broadened out, showing a mouthful of lemon-brown teeth. "The world thinks the Knight of Mists is dead. Even if this is him, we could cut him up too, and no one would know."

"You could try," Pagaloth said. "Is that a risk you want to take?"

The big man didn't like that so much. He gave Lythian another look up and down, wondering. "If you're him, you're older and uglier than I thought you'd be." He gave a long sniff. "There's a stink in you that this rain hasn't washed out either. Where you been all this time?"

Unleashing the doom. Falling in love. Failing in my oaths and honour. "Travelling. It has been a long road home, and we could use your help. One horse would do. We would be happy to ride double."

"Aye, you might be. Not sure the lads'll be so happy, though." He shook his head. "We got a monster to slay, like I said. Heard a rumour that some beast's been plaguing these lands. Killed three foresters and a farmhand this last week, and savaged half a hundred sheep. Someone who saw it claimed it walked upright, slashing with long arms and claws, like some great bear crossed with a rat. Disappeared into the woods not far from here before they could get a proper look, though, so who knows." He shrugged again. "Anyhow, there's a price on its head, and I mean to win it. I give you a horse, and it'll weaken us. No, that won't do."

"We'll pay," Pagaloth said.

"With what?" The hunter scanned the pair. "You look rotten, the both of you. What could you have to barter with?"

"This blade." The dragonknight opened his cloak. "It is forged of dragonsteel, forever-sharp, and never in need of a whetstone. If you are to hunt this creature, this blade will help."

He had the man's attention with that. "Show it to me. Nice and slow."

Pagaloth drew out the blade so half of it was showing, its length rippling red even in the misty gloom. The hunters gazed at it with greedy eyes. Dragonsteel was rare in the north and worth a great deal to collectors. Some men even carried them for use, though few, given the association with the enemy. Mostly, they were bought by wealthy men to hang on walls and over hearths, fat lazy lords who would often claim to have won them in battle. Lythian misliked the custom, though there had always been a market for such. The idea of his friend's blade ending up on some oafish lord's mantel vexed him greatly. "Pagaloth, put the blade away," he said. "It is yours, and not for selling."

"Quiet now, you," said the leader. "We're negotiating."

"You're not. Slide that blade back into its sheath, Pagaloth. We will continue on foot from here."

"You won't." The leader turned his horse a full circle. The beast was growing restless, as were the men. "This man's Agarathi. Might be I'll forget that and let you get on your way…so long as I take that blade. If not, though, I'm sure to remember. We'll be taking you in chains to the nearest fort." He pointed northeast. "There's a garrison at Runnyhall, an hour or so's ride from here. Half of the men there are made up of conscripts and soldiers from the coast, men who've seen their wives and children burn. Been lots of dragon attacks here this last year, lots. They don't much like the Agarathi over at Runnyhall, oh no. One walks through the door…well, who knows what might happen to him."

"Nothing will happen to him," Lythian said. "Sir Pagaloth is under my protection, and is not to be harmed."

"Your voice isn't what it was, Lindar. Men are starting to play by their own rules now."

This is growing dangerous. Lythian took Pagaloth in at a glance, and knew at once he was ready to fight if needed. *Go for the leader. Kill him. I'll take his blade.* But it was too risky. *No, I must reach Varinar safely. I must report on what I have seen. And done.* He drew a breath to freshen his lungs. "I know what beast you're seeking. We came upon the carcass of a large bear only a short time ago. This overgrown *bear-rat* that was sighted. That is an apt description you gave. It describes the drovara well."

"A dro…drovara?" The leader shook his head. "No, can't be. Not here."

"The bear had had its gut torn out, its lower jaw ripped off, and its forelimb savagely snapped. There were chunks of flesh bitten from its body consistent with a drovara's jaws. And they are known to favour damp woods near rivers and make their lairs in caves. Search the forests south of here for hidden caves and you will find it, I assure you. Attack by daylight and you might take it unawares. I would not seek it out by night."

The big man stammered a few words. "What…you think I don't know my own business. I'm a lifelong hunter, Lindar. I know how to track a drovara."

"You'd be the first man to do so for many years. Give us a horse, and I will lead you to where we found the bear, to save you much time. You'll be able to pick up the creature's tracks from there, and follow it to its den."

Before the leader could consider it, the skinny, haunted-face man said, "We got *your* tracks to follow instead. Right back to this bear. We don't need you." He turned. "We don't need him, boss. How's about Len and I find this bear, you take the captain and his Agarathi pet to Runnyhall. Might be a prize in that as well." His lips opened into a wolfish grin. "And we'll have that blade too."

"I'll be giving the orders here, Bean, not you." The leader rummaged through his beard with thick fingers, searching for a chin to scratch. "Aye, sounds about right, though. You understand, Lindar. We can't be knowing for sure that it's you under all that hair and filth, and this man of yours might be a spy. Our duty is to the realm. We let you leave, no knowing what you might do. No." He shook his head. "You're coming with us to Runnyhall."

Lythian wanted no blood today, though the urge to seek it was tempting. He gave Pagaloth a glance, then slowly shut his eyes, relenting. The dragonknight relaxed his grip on his blade. "Fine," he said. "Take us. I hope whoever is in charge at Runnyhall is better suited to treat with me."

The leader shrugged at that and then opened out his palm. "The blade, dragonkin. Come, hand it over. Call it payment for crossing these lands."

Lythian had no fight left in him, not over this. "It is OK, Captain," Sir Pagaloth said to him. "I was never going to be allowed to keep it, not here." He ungirded his swordbelt from his waist and handed the blade over, sheath, belt, and all.

The big hunter could not have looked more pleased. "A prosperous day, and happy to do business with you. Bean, Len, go find that bear. We'll take these two to Runnyhall, and be back by last light."

9

Elyon

The storehouses in the cellars beneath Oakpike Castle made clear the lord's concerns. "We're a small castle here, my prince, too small to feed you indefinitely. I can host you for some weeks, at the edge of need, but I have to consider my own people. We've got a standing force in the hundreds only, and the wagons have stopped coming in. Unless we're resupplied by Lakeheart…well…"

"I understand," Elyon cut in. His host numbered almost thirty thousand and they'd plundered Lord Burbridge's stores enough. "We'll be moving on soon." *And me sooner*, he thought. "Take this up with Lord Rammas. He'll be in charge when I leave."

"Leave, my lord?" Burbridge had an expressive face. Big twisty eyebrows contorted to show his concern. "You're going somewhere?"

"I'll be flying west, in due course." He'd intended to leave already, but matters here in the Lakelands had proven a great distraction. The last days had seen several attacks on nearby towns and Elyon had felt compelled to lend his blade to their defence. Driving off dragons was busy business, and Vargo Ven's minions had begun to spread out through the south of Vandar in search of easy targets. It had created a great deal of debate in council. *And they'll be waiting for me there*, Elyon knew.

He turned and headed back through the cellars and up the plank stairs to the hall above. Lord Burbridge shuffled along behind him, an ageing lord who would not lift a sword in this war. *He wants us gone, and understandably so*, Elyon thought. Oakpike Castle was not a high-value target and was well hidden amidst the valleys south of the lakes. *No doubt the good lord wants to keep it that way.*

The yard beyond the great hall was as chaotic as ever, every spare nook and cranny taken by some knight or man-at-arms for his tent and privy space. Many stopped to salute him as he went, or passed on words of greeting. Elyon returned them all, walking chin held high and back straight. Appearances were important, his uncle Rikkard continued to tell him.

"Walk with strength, always," he would say. "It will rub off on them, and they'll need it."

"Feel free to join us in council, my lord," Elyon said. "You can express your grievances to the group."

Burbridge slowed and shook his head. "Ah, my thanks, but no. I am not of high enough blood to join such an esteemed assembly. I shall discuss matters with Lord Rammas, as you say." He bowed as low as his creaking back would allow, and departed.

Elyon entered the castle keep and climbed the steps toward its summit. They had taken Lord Burbridge's own solar for a council chamber, a temporary appropriation that the old man had willingly permitted. *He had been all too willing to give us everything we needed at first,* Elyon reflected. *But we've stayed too long and he's growing nervous.* He marched into the chambers to find the others already gathered. "Don't stand," he said, as Rikkard and Rammas made to rise. Sir Killian was stood at the hearth, leaning an arm on the wall and looking into the fire. Lady Marian had her place at the window, her eyes drawn to the east as ever they were. *To Rasalan, and home,* Elyon knew. *It is only a matter of time before she leaves.*

Elyon took his place at the head. "I have just been down in the cellars with Lord Burbridge. Suffice it to say, it isn't looking good. The man is worried we'll strip every morsel of meat from his bones."

"He oughtn't complain," Lord Rammas said. He had a thick square jaw, densely stubbled, and an equally thick and muscular physique. His voice matched his look, blunt and hard. "Every vassal of these lands needs to feed us for the good of the realm. We need this army strong."

He's going to love dealing with you, Elyon thought. "Even so. We can't be staying here much longer. Killian, have you devised plans to counter?"

Sir Killian Oloran turned his eyes from the fire. The light bloomed about his golden hair, swept handsomely back behind his ears. He spoke in a whispery voice as soft as a lover's kiss. "We're finalising the squads best suited to the hunt, each led by an experienced Bladeborn knight. We will harry and harass them and keep them contained. It will give us time, if nothing else, to reinforce our strength from the rivers and marshes."

A guerrilla war. That had been Killian's idea, and the one with the most merit. While the bulk of the army would remain together, to be led under Lord Rammas's charge, other parties would seek chaos. *Make them bleed,* Elyon thought. *Kill them by a thousand cuts.* "Have you decided who'll be leading the parties?"

"I will take one," Killian said. "Sir Gereon of Greyguard another, and my captain, Sir Soloman Elmtree a third. Barnibus is also eager for blood, as you might expect. He has asked to be given charge of a company of his own."

"I know." Elyon had spoken with Barnibus about that already, though wasn't certain he was in the right frame of mind for it. He sensed he might seek vengeance for Lancel's death by doing something rash. "I'd prefer Barnibus join another company, as second-in-command. What of Garrick?

He has proven his use and seems keen to spread his own legend. We might want to make use of that."

"The Grinning Knight," Rammas scoffed. It was the name the men were giving him, though Sam Garrick was no knight at all. He had had his own likeness embossed onto his faceplate, inclusive of perpetual grin. "He's skilled enough. But I'd never have him lead a team."

"No, I wasn't thinking to lead." Elyon would agree with that, though during the Battle of the Bane, when the fat knight Sir Lawrence Bollingbrook had fled, Sam Garrick had taken charge of his men and fought with great distinction. "But we can still make use of him." He noticed the expression on his uncle's face and turned to him. "Uncle, you still have your reservations?"

Rikkard mused a moment. "I wonder about the wisdom of splitting our strength."

"Only a small part of it. The bulk of the army will stay together."

"A campaign of terror will deal more damage on the enemy than a great host sitting idle in a fort," Killian said. "We'll target their outriders and scouting parties, draw what dragons we can down to duel. Blind them to our true intent, as we mount our strength and regroup."

"Yes, I understand the strategy. It is risky, is all I'm saying."

He's grown fearful, Elyon thought. *The defeat at the Bane is a shadow hanging over him.* "No more than any other strategy we might choose, Uncle." Rikkard had said again that they might consider retreating as far as Varinar, but most still rallied against that. They had strength still to oppose Vargo Ven here in the east, and a guerrilla war would greatly waylay him. *As to that...* "Have we had any further report on Ven's movements?"

Rikkard answered, shuffling some papers laid out before him. "Our scouts report his main strength remains at the Bane. It seems likely that he will turn his sights on Mudport next, to secure the harbour. Southwatch is also a likely target. It would allow them to resupply easily by ship across the Red Sea."

"Will either hold long if attacked?"

"Honestly, no, not if he sends his full strength, or even part of it. If the Bane can fall in a night, neither will stand for long."

"We'll be ready to march to their defence," Rammas put in combatively. "A siege isn't so simple when you've got an enemy army marching up your backside."

"Which is the only thing staying Ven's hand," Rikkard agreed. "Mudport and Southwatch are well defenced against dragon attack. They will fall against a large assault, but the possible cost is giving Ven pause. We slew many dragons at the Bane. They can only have so many."

Elyon did not want to get into that debate again. They'd speculated over dragon numbers enough and it was proving a futile exercise. *No, it's the dragon in the room we need to confront.* "Eldur," he said, turning his eyes around. "Has he been sighted?"

The name ushered silence into that high council chamber like an unwanted guest. Killian turned his eyes back to the fire, Rikkard inspected the set of letters laid out before him, Rammas ground his jaw. It was left to Lady Marian to answer from the window seat. "Not since Thalan. It would be safe to assume he has returned to Eldurath."

"*Assume* is the word," grunted Rammas. "We're assuming a lot here. We don't know for sure he's risen."

Marian's sharp grey eyes drove into him. "He is risen. We'll not go through this again, my lord. It will do you no good to bury your head in the sand and hope that this all goes away. It won't."

"Are you suggesting I'm a coward?" Rammas's hard voice went harder.

"No, you're no coward, Lord Rammas. Stubborn, yes, and pigheaded, for a certainty. But a coward? No. I'll say that for you at least."

Elyon raised a hand before Rammas might retort. "Squabbling will get us nowhere. Eldur is back, that is an irrefutable truth. Every word to the contrary is a word wasted, and I've no tolerance for verbal profligacy right now. You four gathered here are some of the finest warriors and military thinkers in the north. How would you seek to defeat him?"

"Through strength of arms," Rammas said. He folded his muscular arms together, the dark leather fabric of his tunic straining at the seams. "By defeating his forces in the field."

Spoken like a true Marshlander. Rammas was a man of blunt force and singular focus, useful if limited. "That could take years, and cost countless lives. We must find a way to expedite his fall."

"Save marching on Eldurath, I don't see one. And that would be folly, even for me."

Elyon pondered that. "You believe he will stay hidden in his city?"

Rammas nodded. So did Killian and Rikkard. "Eldur need not risk himself, not when he has so many pawns to do his bidding," Rikkard said. "And he may not be the being we speak of in our histories. Time has a habit of exaggerating the truth. It's possible that he is more vulnerable than we realise. If so, why come forth?"

Elyon wasn't so sure. "We've heard reports from Thalan that men quailed to even look upon him. That their hearts gave out to darkness and dread at his presence. That sounds very much like the dark demigod we teach our children about to me."

"Depends on these men," Rammas grunted. "Weak men would quail at near anything. And begging your pardon, Lady Payne, but the Rasalanians aren't so stout as we are."

The remark was ignored. "Firsthand accounts would be useful," Marian merely said. "Unfortunately, we are dealing here with word on the wing, and I know of no one who confronted Eldur directly. Someone might come forward, however. The days since the attack are still young."

"Unlikely," Rammas said. "You told us the sorcerer went straight for the Tower of the Eye, then left. The only person who got close to him was your rat-faced king."

"Perhaps. Though we cannot know for sure. Someone may come forward, as I say."

Elyon wondered if she might have heard something more, from her insider, perhaps, though she did not elaborate. Elyon did not know the insider's name, but she had assured him once that she had someone in the palace who would keep an eye on Amilia for him. As yet, there had been no word as to the Jewel of Tukor's fate. Most likely, she was killed in the carnage and this inside agent alongside her.

"I may fly up there myself, to investigate," Elyon said. "Once I return from Varinar."

"That's a lot of flying, Elyon," Rikkard warned. "Thousands of miles. Are you certain you're ready for that?"

"I have to be. Lines of communication are already starting to falter, and I need to be capable of flying long distances to share news."

"Varin Knight, Prince of Vandar, Bearer of the Windblade…carrier crow." Killian smiled at him. "Don't you think you've got enough to do already, Elyon?"

"I have no choice, Kill. The dragons are killing every crow they see, and the enemy have bowmen sticking them with arrows too. If the north goes dark, we'll be blind. I have to act as our eyes."

"Within reason." Rikkard's voice was cautious. "Don't overwork yourself. You don't yet know how your body will respond to a thousand-mile journey."

"Varinar is half that far, Thalan the same." *And Aram*, he thought, meeting Marian's eyes, though he didn't want to share that with the others. Crossing to the south would be much too dangerous, they would tell him. *And they'd be right. It's a risk too far right now.* "I can manage five hundred miles. If I need to stop, I will. There are many strong forts and castles that will lend me a bed to rest in. Once I'm well practised, I'll be able to traverse these lands at will."

"And when that happens, you might want to make Eagle's Perch a priority," Killian said. "Kastor has won the fort, but for what? Our invasion plans have long since been abandoned. He would do better sailing home to help defend the north."

"The Perch is closer than Varinar and Thalan both," added Lord Rammas. "Might be worth a flight."

They want me to fly to the Perch, Marian to Aram, Rikkard to not risk it at all. Elyon found himself torn between the lot of them, though would stick to his own plan. "I'll add it to the list, but that's for the Tukorans to figure. If they feel Lord Kastor's army is better placed defending the realm, they will call for them."

"They'll try. Whether the crows make it or not is another matter."

"I know, Lord Rammas." Elyon was regretting his speech about being the north's eyes. *They'll have me flying messages morning, noon and night.* "Varinar is my target, and my father. We could sorely do with his guidance and counsel and to better understand what is happening in the west. We have heard of his travels and latest deeds. He may yet have a notion as to how to defeat Eldur that we haven't considered."

"The Sword of Varinar," Killian offered. "It may be the only blade that can strike him down."

Elyon doubted it. "Eldur is flesh and blood. Any blade can kill him. The Bondstone, however, is another matter. We've heard rumours that the Soul of Agarath awakened the Fire Father, and that he is using it to command the dragons." He shared a look with Marian once more. "Lady Marian and I...we believe destroying the Bondstone will greatly diminish the demigod's power. If we could somehow shatter it..."

"The Bondstone is likely to be in Eldurath," Rikkard said. "There is no way of reaching it."

Not for you, Elyon thought. He chose not to voice his thoughts with them, however. If flying to Aram would be considered too risky...

Still, Rikkard read his intent. "No, Elyon. You cannot go there alone. You would have no hope of making it out alive. And even if you reached the Bondstone, you'd have no way of destroying it. The Windblade has not the power or the magic for it. You'd need to first master the Sword of Varinar. Only with it, might you stand a chance."

Elyon wholeheartedly agreed. "Once you've mastered one Blade of Vandar, the others are easier to learn," he said. "I fly to Varinar at first light, as I say. I have much to discuss with my father."

10

Jonik

"Your mother would like to see you," he said. "She has asked, multiple times."

Let her ask a thousand more. "I'm not here to see her."

The Steward sat with legs neatly folded in a well-worn mahogany armchair, a Briarwood smoking pipe clutched between his fingers. Smoke rose from its chamber in soft grey curls, reaching for the high vaulted ceiling. *He seems a normal man, sometimes,* Jonik thought. *Just a man enjoying a smoke and a read and a cup of wine in his library.* Thousands of years old though he was, Hamlyn had the face of a man in his mid-thirties. Shallow lines spread from his eyes, and there were some creases upon his forehead, yet elsewise it was an unremarkable face, pleasant and yet plain, not the sort you'd look at twice in a crowd. *The eyes, though.* Those were a different matter. Burnished brown, they carried within them the span of his years, as windows to his ancient soul. *If he has one.* Jonik understood the man's burden and task, yet for all that, the things he'd had to do to fulfil his duty…they hardly bore thinking about.

"You blame her for abandoning you as a child?" Hamlyn asked mildly.

Yes, Jonik thought. *I blame her for that and hate her for that.* He didn't want to talk about the woman who'd birthed him, though. "I came to ask if you would come with me to the fortress dungeons. The prisoners…some of them don't believe what I've told them of…"

"You shouldn't be telling them anything, Jonik. They do not need to know."

"I disagree." Jonik met the mage's eyes and didn't relent in his gaze. *I will not wilt to him, no matter who he is.* "They have served a lie all their lives. They have earned the right to know why."

The Steward smiled pleasantly, though there was something empty about that smile too. *He is like a man who has forgotten what it is to feel emotion. The long years here have made him cold.* "I can see why you might think that, but we see life very differently, Jonik. Tell me, young one. Why do you care about these men?"

"Because I was one of them, once. They deserve a chance to be free."

"They will never be free, Jonik. Not unless we fulfil our purpose here. Until that time comes the whole world will be held captive. Nothing matters, but our duty."

He cannot always have been this heartless, Jonik thought, as he studied the mage's face. There were innumerable stories and legends of Ilith the Worldbuilder, and the name Hamlyn appeared in many of them. *Hamlyn the Humble,* men had called him. He was Ilith's closest companion, his most loyal confidant, helping him create his wonders, and asking for no credit for his deeds. *He was there when Ilith broke apart the heart of a god and used it to forge the Five Blades,* Jonik thought. *He was at his side when he raised up Ilithor amidst the mountains, and erected Varinar upon its ten hills, and built Thalan astride the Izzun.* Ilith's greatest triumphs were not his triumphs alone. Others helped him, and Hamlyn most of all. Yet all the same, he never sought praise for it. *He was always a man of duty,* Jonik knew. *And here he remains, doing his duty still. No matter how unpleasant and perverse.*

"One of the others, then," Jonik said to him, seeing his cause was lost. "You don't care for these men. Fine. I do. Let another of the mages come with me."

Hamlyn considered it, quiet and methodical. He sat with hands clasped before him in his lap, neat in posture and pose, expression unreadable. He had a more genial side, Jonik had seen, yet this…this detached persona was more prominent. Eventually he nodded and said, "Fhanrir will go with you. Wait here. I will summon him."

The Steward stood and slipped past him in a billow of dark umber robes, moving through the library door and into the cavernous hall beyond. The whisper of slippers on stone soon faded into the deep silence of Ilith's refuge. Jonik watched him go, pondering his position. He had expected his return here to be more simple than this. *Kill the old ones, spare the young ones, slay the mages and strike the Shadow King from his throne.* It was an uncomplicated goal, perilous yet easily defined. No longer. *Now I have vengeful knights and disgruntled soldiers and restless sellswords to deal with,* he thought. *I have prisoners who will try to kill me if they get half a chance, and the threat of shadows lurking beyond the walls. Emeric is gone and I don't know when he's coming back. Jack, Turner, Braxton, they might be dead for all I know. What if they never return? What then? What will I do without them?*

He paced side to side through the library, trying to collect his thoughts. They had turned doubtful and anxious these last days, without his friends beside him. He had Gerrin, yes, and Harden said it like it was, and Sir Torvyn too had a quiet wisdom to his words. Yet none were Jack, poking fun at him and making him laugh. None were Turner, enthusiastic to the last. None were Emeric, who he leaned on for guidance most of all. Without them, he felt more exposed than he would like. He hated how vulnerable that made him feel.

Hamlyn's return came promptly enough, giving him welcome respite from his bitter concerns. He moved in smoothly with the shambling old creature Fhanrir at his side, second in seniority among the mages of the fort. "You want me to come talk to the prisoners, do you?" the creature asked. He had a snide way to him. An unpleasant way.

"If you would," Jonik said courteously.

Fhanrir made a grunting sound. "If it'll stop you asking again. Come on, then. Let's see this done."

They moved through the refuge together, Jonik slowing his stride for the ancient mage to keep up. He wore a frayed grey robe that looked near as old as he was, hooded to hide the grotesqueness of his face. Fhanrir was rotting, that was plain to see, his flesh accursed and bloodless, skin sloughing off his bones. His nose was long and armoured in warts, the tip curving and dangling past his nostrils. Beneath it lay a mouth of purply-black lips, broken brown teeth, and a chin clad in brittle strands of white hair. Jonik wondered, as they walked, whether he might clothe himself in some illusion to avoid appearing so twisted and foul. *Parsivor did,* he reflected. That creature had appeared as a jittery youth called Trigger before unveiling his true self the night Gerrin killed him. "Do you always look like this?" he asked Fhanrir.

The mage scowled. "Aye. What else. Not pretty enough for you, boy?"

"Do you not have skill in illusion?"

"I have skill in many things," Fhanrir said. *Fhanrir the Foul,* Jonik thought. *That'd be a good name for him.* "Illusion…that's easy enough. Pretty trick to make use of when needed. But here? Why bother. My energies are better spent elsewhere."

Blood magic, Jonik thought. *Dark rituals in the occult, to stain your soul, and rot you from the outside in.* "Hamlyn says you knew Ilith as well. You look good enough for your age, if true."

Fhanrir laughed. Though it sounded more like a cough. "I knew him, true enough. Hamlyn and I are the only ones left who did."

"There were more of you before?"

"Eight," he said. "The last of them died long before you were born."

"What about the others?" There were three other mages under Hamlyn's charge; Dagnyr, Agnar, Vottur. "Were they not born during Ilith's time?"

"After. Long time after. Vottur is my great-grandson. Agnar was grandson to another of us. Solvin, his name was. Died three centuries ago. One of the originals. Dagnyr…his father was Marthen. He was strong in the occult, that one. For a half-breed, that is. They don't live so long, though, not like us purebloods."

Purebloods. Half breeds. Jonik didn't even want to ask, but felt compelled to. "You bred with human women?"

"Who else? I tried to woo a stormhag once, but she turned me away."

Jonik disliked the sound of Fhanrir's laughter as much as he disliked the mage himself. The stormhags were the former lovers and wives of the battle god Dhatar, legend said, somewhat related to the Whisperers in their magic. At Dhatar's death, those who survived the war had crawled away into the hills and mountains, appearing during storms as beautiful maidens to lure unsuspecting men to their deaths. Jonik wished that Fhanrir had been lured as such. He had an image of the shrivelled old creature boiling in a witch's pot, screaming, and couldn't help but grin.

"What, you think I'm too ugly even for a stormhag, do you?" Fhanrir asked, taking Jonik's smile for an insult. "Well, wasn't always that way, you know. I was young and handsome once, like you."

Jonik could hardly believe it. "Did you have lots of sons?"

"Enough. All dead now."

"And daughters?"

"None. Tukor favoured men for his magic. Ilith, Hamlyn, me and all the others. Men. That wasn't a gift he gave women."

"But the stormhags…"

"Were made of Vandar." Fhanrir shuffled on down the long cold corridor. "Rasalan, though. He passed power to his womenfolk through Thala. Lots of female sea-mages there."

Jonik tried to picture life as it must have been then. Gods and demigods and great beings walking the earth. *And here I walk alongside one. A lesser one, yes, but an ancient being all the same.* "Did you ever meet the gods yourself?" He could not begin to imagine what that must be like, to meet a god. They were always depicted in such monstrous scale and splendour in their statues and paintings, far beyond the demigods they bore. *Vandar could create life,* he thought. *He could change and rearrange landmasses as he saw fit.* It was inconceivable, and seemed more myth than history, too much for a mere mortal to perceive.

"I've met many things in my time," Fhanrir said. "Gods, monsters, heroes, kings." Something wistful came upon his foul face, though it seemed only half-remembered, the shadow of a time long gone. "That was a fonder age, back then. People were brighter, stronger, more noble. The light of the gods shone down through their followers and from them to the early generations of their people. That light has dimmed now. All of this…everything…" He looked at Jonik and didn't hide his disdain. "It's just shadows of shadows, living in the shade. The world is a lesser place than what it was. And the people…even more."

They continued on down the wide stone corridor as Jonik reflected on his words. *Sons,* he thought. *He's had many sons, and grandsons, and great-grandsons too, and no doubt the other disciples did as well.* Yet all that remained of them were a few, two from the elder days and three of mixed blood, weaker in the arts of the occult. Jonik shuddered to think that Ghalto the Whisperer or Parsivor might have sprouted from Fhanrir's decrepit loins. *And the women forced to breed with them,* he thought. *Women like my mother, who were nothing but slaves too, in their way…*

He turned that thought roughly aside. *No, I'll give her no pity,* he told himself. *She chose to give me up, unlike the others. She chose it for her father's favour…*

On they went in silence, darkness brooding about Jonik's thoughts. He had a question he had to ask. He didn't want to, but he had to know for sure. Breaking the quiet between them, he said, "How did all the others die? The other disciples of Ilith…the purebloods, and their heirs?"

He got the reaction he'd anticipated, as Fhanrir stopped to peer up at him. He pointed with a skeletal finger. "You know how, boy. But best you not think about that. Won't make it any easier on you."

"The boys…" Jonik began.

"Aye, the boys," the creature cut in. "You think I *want* to look like this? You think the others wanted to die for it, to spin their spells and rot for it?" He prodded that bone of a digit into Jonik's chest. "It's no nice way to go, believe me, but we do what we must for the cause. You, me, Hamlyn, all of us. Best you start thinking the same as we do. We have never bent our backs to sentimentality here. Every death of every boy serves a purpose." He prodded with that finger again. "*Every* death. Remember that. And *don't* interfere."

Jonik stared down at him. A part of him wanted to pull the Nightblade from its sheath and drive it through the creature's heart, the future be damned. *They're boys, just boys,* he thought, clenching his jaw. *These aren't cattle reared for slaughter.* "There must be another way. Why boys? Why not…"

"Men? Would that be better on your gentle sensibilities, boy?" His finger jabbed again, once, twice, thrice, harder and harder each time. "One life means nothing, boy or man, not a dozen nor a hundred nor a thousand, commoner or king. We do what we must. What. We. Must." He moved so close Jonik could see the blackness glowing in his eyes, deep and old and dangerous. "*Don't* interfere. I warn you. *Don't.*"

Jonik didn't back down. "Why don't you just kill me then, if you're so worried?"

"Hamlyn." Fhanrir snorted through his warty ruin of a nose. "He's got a softness in him, but not me, and mayhaps he knows something I don't. If I had it my way, that black godly blade'd be back in the vaults, safely hidden and out of your grasp, and you'd be cast from here for good. You have no right to it, *none.* Never think otherwise."

Jonik's gloved fingers squeezed into a ball. He reached to pull the Nightblade, sliding it a dozen inches from its dark sheath.

Fhanrir watched, eyes gleaming. "You going to strike at me, or give it to me?"

"I don't know." Jonik growled the words out; it was an honest answer. Half of him wanted to cut the creature down, the other to give up the blade and be done with the burden for good. To walk away from the fort forever and forget he was ever here. He took several long breaths to compose himself, battling back the voices in his head. Fhanrir watched all the while. Jonik could not place the look on his rotting face, half shadow, half death. "I'll give it up, when I must," he forced himself to say at last. *I have to, don't I? When the time is right, I must.* Even so, he felt himself perspiring at the thought, a cold sweat wetting his brow. That voice was screaming inside him…*no, you can't! You can't!*…but he shoved it back into the darkness and ignored it. "I know it'll be difficult, but I will."

"I know you will, boy. One way or another, *you will.*"

They went the rest of the way in silence, passing through the vastness of the refuge. It was a cold place, silent and still. A cursed place, full of foreboding and dark corners where dark deeds had been done. Jonik felt a hate rising inside him, a resentment he could scarce control. Hate for all the lies. Hate for this creature beside him. Hate for his mother, his cruel cold mother, who'd set him on this path as a babe. But most of all, a hatred for his fate. *I'm an assassin-turned-courier*, he thought dismally, *that's all I ever was. Sent out to fulfil my long-foreseen duty, before bringing the blade back, for another more worthy to bear...*

They reached the exit several minutes later, a great black door guarded by a pair of gigantic stone knights twenty feet tall. They were etched in magnificent detail, almost ethereally lifelike, so much so that Jonik wondered if they'd in fact been alive once before. *Were they some giants made stone by magic? Set here to guard the refuge against intrusion?* He'd seen many other such statues about the chambers and halls, some in the likenesses of great gods and kings and heroes of the past, others nameless knights and warriors like these. There was a magic back here that Jonik did not know existed. *The world is more full of it than I realised*, he thought.

The wind was blowing briskly beyond the black door. It felt good on his face and singing past his ears after the suffocating silence of the refuge. Through high heavy clouds the sun shone down in shards, knifing through the mountains and valleys and bringing light to the once-shadowed fort. Fhanrir turned his beady eyes up and around, squinting against the light. *He favours the sun not,* Jonik thought. *This mage belongs in darkness.*

The old sorcerer shuffled on toward the steps leading down toward the inner ward. "How many of you are left?" he asked. "These friends of yours you came with."

Jonik had a think. "Fifteen or so."

The way the creature considered than and nodded made him uneasy. "I'm surprised there're still so many. Heard there's a war to fight." Jonik sighted an unsightly grin on those purply black lips. "These men of yours not warriors? Aren't they getting restless, waiting about up here?"

You know they are, creature. "They'll leave soon. I had wanted to ask Hamlyn about…"

"Using the portal?" Fhanrir stopped once more and frowned up at him. "Now we can't be having that, boy. People coming and going all the time. What with the secrets we're trying to keep."

Damn your secrets. Jonik had had about all he could take of all that, and Fhanrir's snide manner wasn't helping. "It would help cut down their journey by weeks. I don't see the harm in…"

"You don't see the harm in anything. You think we've stood vigil here for thousands of years just to let a few mortal knights and sellswords come walking through our halls?" He turned and carried on going, dragging along that rotting corpse of his. "Answer's no, if you didn't catch that. You go ahead and send them away down the pass. Better yet, leave the Nightblade here and go with him."

Is he doing this on purpose? Is he trying to provoke me for some gain?

The steps led down through the upper ward, bordered by a high black wall. Beyond that was another set of steps that fell away into the fortress proper. There were quads down there, and yards for training, and tight lanes squeezing between buildings. Further off, toward the front, was the outer ward where the curtain wall stood, embracing the fortress gate. Opposite the gate was the Night Tower, with the kitchens and stables, animal pens and armoury to the left of it, and the roundtower library to the right, beside the barracks for the younglings. The older boys' barracks was a little deeper into the fort, as were the dungeons, though all were visible from up here.

"What's the hold up? Enjoying the view, are we?"

Jonik answered honestly. "I was never allowed up here as an apprentice or knight. The fort looks…smaller than I used to think."

"Aye, because you've seen the world now, haven't you? Our little fortress isn't big like some others we built, but it's strong and hard to reach, that's the main thing. Ilith didn't build it to house a garrison. It was just a front for the refuge at the back. And that's big enough, don't you think?"

Boundlessly so, Jonik thought. He'd not been allowed to explore the refuge at his leisure, though Hamlyn had taken him around some of it, and still there remained a great deal to be seen. *Not that I want to.* It was empty and lifeless, wonderfully constructed and yet utterly inert. Jonik could tell it was the work of Ilith, though, even if he hadn't known. It had his signature grandeur and scale and no doubt many of the magnificent statues were carved by him as well. But not all. The long centuries before the Shadow Order had been founded gave Hamlyn and his followers ample time to carve many more. *And it shows.* There were hundreds of them, perhaps even thousands, littered throughout the countless chambers and halls.

But still, you can tell which ones Ilith made, Jonik thought. They just tended to draw the eye a little more, with a motion and vitality that the others couldn't match. For there had never been a sculptor to match him. *Nor a blacksmith nor mason nor mage.*

As they continued down the steps toward the dungeons, Jonik mused on what Ilith would have made of all this. His refuge sitting all but empty, his fortress corrupted, his good friend Hamlyn keeping him in stasis on a cold stone slab, neither living nor dead, never to rise again. Would he have condoned everything Hamlyn had done, endorsed it for the greater good? Would he have condemned Queen Thala for laying Hamlyn with this burden? He had no answers. Ilith was known as a benevolent demigod and king, and the same was true of Thala. *Yet she instructed all this. She put it into motion. She saw the future and tampered with time, no matter the amount of pain and suffering it would bring.* Jonik did not know what to think of it all. *Maybe she should have just let it all be. Maybe she should never have interfered at all…*

"How many prisoners you keeping?" Fhanrir asked as they descended. He sounded equal parts impatient and uninterested, as though wanting to get it done.

"Seven."

"Their names?"

Jonik told him.

The mage bustled on in that shuffling tread, as they reached the bottom of the steps and made for the courtyard where the dungeons were located. The yard was bathed in sunlight. Outside the dungeon door, Norwyn had charge today. He was much less diligent than Sir Bulmar had been. Sitting on a stool, he appeared asleep, his thick-bearded chin resting on his equally thick chest. "Norwyn," Jonik said loudly, to wake him.

The man stirred, angling his eyes over to the noise. He blinked drowsily. "What is it?"

"I'm here to visit the prisoners."

Norywn shrugged, then patted himself down in search of the keys. He found them on the floor beside his stool. "There, take 'em." He tossed them over, then looked at Fhanrir. "Who's this one? Mage, is it?" His hand went to the handle of his blade.

Fhanrir ignored him. "Open the door, boy. I don't have all day."

No, you've had millennia. I would have thought you'd be more patient by now. Jonik said nothing as he thrust the keys into the lock and turned. Norwyn didn't look so pleased about being ignored, but chose to express his anger with a glare and a grunt. Jonik pulled the iron door open. He stepped inside, Fhanrir following, leaving the door ajar behind them. The sun swam in and flowed down the steps. Down they went to the cells below.

Half the prisoners were sleeping, it sounded by the mumbles and snores. *There is no sense of time down here in the darkness.* Jonik knew how that felt, to be caged without sight of daylight. Often in his youth he'd been locked away in much smaller spaces, for hours and even days on end, to 'harden him up' as he was told. "Wake up," he called out. "I brought Fhanrir down to see you."

The creature moved to the middle of the dungeon, cloaked and cowled. The nostrils of his long warty nose opened and closed. "That one's going to die," he said, almost at once. He was looking toward Dalbert's cell. "His wound will kill him. Stinks of death, he does. Day or two and he's done."

"Good. Had enough of his bleating." That was Kagnor. The grizzled old Shadowmaster appeared from the dark of his cell to stand at the bars, bedraggled and reeking. He rubbed his eyes. "Goes on and on, he does. Though been quiet most of today. Who knows, maybe he's dead already."

That might explain the stench, Jonik thought. There was something more than excrement and body odour filling the air down here.

Fhanrir shook his head. "Not yet, but soon." He turned to face Jonik. "*Care.* You say you care about these men, boy. Yet here you are, letting a long-serving knight suffer and die."

"We did what we could for him."

"Aye, so you say." Fhanrir looked around the cells, sneering. "Or maybe he's not the one you're trying to save. Nor Kagnor, I'd wager. Only these young ones interest you, isn't that so?"

Jonik didn't want to have this conversation in front of them, though all the same, they knew it to be true. "Kagnor has refused to listen to me. Perhaps he'll heed you. That's why you're here."

"I'm here because Hamlyn asked me. There is much I would do for him, to make his life more simple." The old mage turned to look at Kagnor. "You have questions for me. Make them quick, and I'll be gone."

Kagnor squinted at him through the bars. "I've got me some questions, aye." He flung a hand at Jonik. "The turncloak said the Shadow Order was built on Queen Thala's command. True, is it? That this wise goodly goddess founded an order of assassins and sneaks?"

"*Demi*goddess," Fhanrir corrected. "And then mortal, after Rasalan fell."

"Yeah. Her. All this her idea, was it?"

"Her foresight lit the way." The mage bowed his head in a moment of reverence. "Her Book of Contracts has been the holy tome that has led us. The rest…that was us."

Jonik frowned. "The rest?" He'd thought every contract had been foreseen by the Far-Seeing Queen. He'd thought they all had a purpose, each a stepping stone toward the final outcome. "You mean you took on other contracts yourselves?"

"The men needed to be kept sharp. All blades need honing."

Jonik was shocked. "So you sent them to kill innocent people? For *training?*"

"We did what we had to. And I'll not answer to you."

Kagnor started laughing in his horrid mocking way of his. "You really have gone soft, turncloak. Gerrin was always weak on you. You were never so tough as the other lads here."

Jonik was tempted to rip the Nightblade from its sheath, cut through the bars and cut through the man, but refused the urge.

"So it's true?" came the heavy slow voice of Hopper, limping toward the bars. "What Jonik told us. About Thala? That's all true?"

"I've said so, haven't I?" Fhanrir looked at the young man disinterestedly. "What else? Any of you got anything more to say?" He barely gave them a moment to think, turning his eyes sharply around the cells, then aiming his eyes back at Jonik. "Then I'm done here, and not soon enough. Don't ask me to come back." He took a shuffling pace closer, lowering his voice for only Jonik to hear. "And that's all they need to know, you hear me. *No more.* You best keep the rest of our secrets to yourself if you know what's good for you." He spent a moment glaring to make sure Jonik understood, then began shambling back toward the stairs. "Come," he said. "I'll have a word with you outside."

Jonik was loathe to follow his commands though saw little choice but to go with him. He trailed the old creature up the steps, as Kagnor mocked him for a servant still. "Can hear your shackles rattling from here, turncloak," he called after him. "Can't see 'em, but I can hear 'em all right!" His laughter chased Jonik out into the sunlit yard above. Cruel cutting laughter. *And truth,* Jonik thought.

He stopped outside the door, shutting it tight and turning the lock. Norywn was gone, his stool sitting empty beside the door. *I can't have him on guard again,* he told himself. There was a risk a man like Norwyn might take it upon himself to kill the prisoners, if left unchecked, in vengeance for Crasson's death. Sir Torvyn had assured him no Blackshaw man would do such a thing, though Jonik wasn't going to count on it. *Best give the duty to men I trust,* he decided. Norwyn was no longer in that category.

"You need to kill those men," Fhanrir said.

Jonik turned to look at him.

"They're dangerous," the mage went on. "All of them. I see things you don't, and I *smell* them too. A few of them want you dead. They'll kill you for themselves, and they'll kill you for that blade. Those dungeons stink of death and desire."

Jonik's eyes went to the black iron door, narrowing. "No. None of them are strong enough to bear it."

"They don't know that."

"They do. They know, Fhanrir."

"As you say." The mage snorted through his rank rotting nose. "Kagnor. Next time you see him, he'll tell you what you want to hear. Don't believe it. That one will always want you dead."

As you do, Jonik thought. If there was someone here he couldn't trust, it was Fhanrir. *He is only trying to sow doubt in me. He's trying to make me fearful.* "I thank you for the counsel," he told him. "I'll be sure to think on it long and..." He trailed off, his ears alerted to the scuff of footsteps coming their way from down a passage. Jonik turned to find Norwyn marching back out with Borrus on his heels. *Shit.* The look on the Barrel Knight's face made him step forward at once to stand between the big man and the little mage. "Borrus, what are you doing here?"

"This him?" Borrus kept on plodding forward. "This the Steward?"

"No, it's not him, Borrus..."

The big knight met him at the centre of the yard, swinging out a paw to shift Jonik aside. "Out of the way. *Move, Jonik.*"

He's been drinking, Jonik realised. Alcohol was not commonly kept here, yet Jonik knew that some of the masters liked to keep their own stores. Gerrin did. With his whiskey. Borrus had clearly come upon a stash somewhere. "Borrus, stop. This isn't the Steward, I just said so."

"That other one, then. Fhanro, or whatever." Borrus peered past Jonik's shoulder to look at the mage. His face contorted in disgust at what he saw. "Yeah, that'll be him. Gerrin said he was a twisted little monster." He pushed Jonik to the side with a little more force and drove forward across the cobbles. "The boy says the Steward needs to live, says I can't touch him. But you? Why not you, monster?"

Fhanrir did not shrink back as the brawny knight drew upon him. He stood his ground, peering up with his beady little eyes, unafraid. "Sir Borrus Kanabar, *Lord* of the Riverlands," he said.

Borrus scoffed. "That'd be my father, mage. Lord Wallis. You've got things mixed up."

Fhanrir only smiled. "Have I?"

Borrus's brow furrowed in confusion. He seemed unsettled all of a sudden. "What are you saying?" He looked at Jonik. "What's he saying? Do you know something?"

Jonik shook his head at once. "No, nothing." His heart thumped with concern. "Fhanrir, you'd best go."

"No. I'll hear this first," Borrus commanded. "If you know something of my father…"

"Your father is dead," the little mage said. "Dragon's Bane has fallen to the Agarathi, and he's dead, along with ten thousand of your countrymen."

Borrus stared in shock. "You…you lie!" He tore Red Wrath from its sheath in a song of steel. Silver mist rose from its edge, infused with swirls of crimson. "Tell the truth, monster, or I'll run you through right here!"

"I am telling the truth, *Lord* Kanabar. You'd best run along back to your lands. They will need you there now more than ever, a man so masterful as you."

"You…this…you're lying…"

"The world is changing, my lord. You have missed much on your *long march* up here."

The vein in the side of the big knight's head grew fat with blood, pulsing. He stared hard at Fhanrir, half lost to disbelief, then turned his gaze on Jonik. "You…this is on *you.* I should never have been here. I should never have come!"

Jonik slid back half a step. "Borrus…"

"You! You and your bloody quest. You and your godsdamned life debt! Well I've paid that now, haven't I, you bastard! I killed a knight because of you. Sir Corbray…he was down in those cursed pits for how many years? How many years did he suffer, only to die for you and your precious Shadow Order. These boys…these bloody bastard boys we've died for and killed for. Who the hell are they to be worth paying so much? I should march into those barracks right now and kill every last one of them!"

"Sir Borrus, my lord…I don't think…"

"Shut it, Norwyn. Of course I won't. I'm not bloody mad!" Borrus paced to the side, then back again, as though needing to get his big legs moving. Fhanrir stood watching with a grim little look on his face. "If you were this Steward I'd strike you down, make no mistake," Borrus roared at him. "Well you keep your secrets, and you keep your fort, and you keep that refuge you're hiding in back there. I've had it with your lies, boy," he said to Jonik. "You and this creature and that Steward, you can keep each other too." He spun on the spot, shoved Red Wrath into its sheath, and stamped back out of the yard.

Norwyn hesitated a moment, then went after him, giving Fhanrir and Jonik a sour look in parting. *They see me as in league with this mage*, Jonik thought. He hated the notion, but could he deny it? *I'm keeping their secrets, I'm protecting these boys, I'm still a man of the order, whether I like it or not…*

"Let him go, Jonik," Fhanrir said. "We're best rid of him. Just let him go."

You want them gone. You want them all gone. But he couldn't let Borrus leave like this. The rest would go with him, he knew, most of them if not all. *My lies have driven a wedge between us. They deserve more than that. So much more.*

He left the mage behind, marching through the passage that led toward the outer ward. Jonik could hear Borrus bellowing out for the men to gather. "Everyone, on me," he shouted. "You up on the wall, come down. Harden, over here. Everyone! Get over here now!"

Jonik hastened out to find the company assembling from their stations. Harden had been guarding the younglings' barracks, the gate was being watched by Manallio, Sir Torvyn was busy preparing the next meal with the help of his cousin, who liked to eat half of what he cooked. "What's all this, Borrus?" the Beast of Blackshaw complained, chewing, as he and Torvyn emerged from the kitchens. Mooton had a side of ham in his fist. The other men had been enjoying the sun in the yard, or napping in their rooms, or reading in the library. Everyone came at Borrus's summons. "You've got everyone in a stir. What's happening?"

"News from the south." Borrus noticed Jonik slinking in from the rear of the fort and gave him a scowl. "More lies from this one," he growled, pointing. "Seems the Bane's been lost, and my father...my father with it." He buried his grief in anger, opening and closing a fist. "It's time to leave, *right now*. Not in the morning, not in an hour, now!" He looked around. "Torv, no more complaints from you. You're sworn to House Kanabar. If this of my father is true..." He swallowed, hardly able to say it. Jonik knew how much Borrus had loved and admired his father. *As everyone else did*, he thought. "*I'm* your lord now," Borrus went on. "And Warden of the East. So enough of this waiting for Manfrey to come back. Gather your things... we're leaving. And you sellswords, I say come too. You're fighting men and need a fight to stay warm. I'll pay you all and pay you well. Get your things. I won't give you another chance."

Jonik stood there utterly silent as Borrus wheeled around and disappeared into the Night Tower. The Blackshaw men followed at once, all but Sir Torvyn and Sir Mooton who stepped over to inquire what happened. "That the truth, lad?" Mooton asked, looking a little stricken. "That about Lord Wallis...and the Bane?"

Jonik neither nodded nor shook his head. "Fhanrir told him. I don't know for sure."

"Would he have any cause to lie?" Torvyn asked.

Jonik could think of a reason or two. But given what they'd already heard at the harbours across the north, and from that mysterious dwarf Black-Eye at the Whispering Drunk...well, it made sense. "I fear not."

"Gods." Mooton's great head swayed side to side in dismay. "Gods, the Bane...fallen? How long's it been since...and...and Lord Wallis..." He took Jonik by the shoulders. "What else did he say, this mage? Come, lad, what else!"

"Nothing." Jonik stood there, too dispirited to remove the man's massive hands. "He said nothing else, Mooton."

"Release him, Moot," Torvyn instructed gently. "Go and fetch your things, and mine. We'll find out more when we reach the foothills." Mooton gave a heavy lamenting sigh and trundled off, looking pale. Torvyn took a soft grip of Jonik's arm. "Come with us, Jonik," he urged. "Set the boys free and come too."

Jonik could hear Borrus inside the tower, shouting orders for someone to help him put on his armour. "He doesn't want me with you, Torvyn."

"He blows hot and cold, you know that. He'll calm." Jonik said nothing. Torvyn waited a moment longer, then added, "If you would only tell us the full truth, perhaps then he would understand?"

The truth, Jonik thought. *The full truth. Ilith, and the heir. The portal door, to speed their way.* He wanted to, richly he wanted to, but somehow he couldn't. He had promised Hamlyn and there was something bigger than them here, something even he didn't fully understand. "I can't," he whispered. *They'll hate me for it, and curse me for it, but I can't.* "They're not my secrets to tell, Torvyn."

"I understand." Sir Torvyn smiled a smile he would greatly miss. a reassuring smile, avuncular and kind. "It has been eye-opening, spending time in your company. I will never forget what you did for me, saving me from those pits, Jonik."

It seemed like a lifetime ago now. Everything had been more simple then.

"Is there something you would like me to tell your father, if I should see him. Or your brother?"

Jonik looked into Sir Torvyn Blackshaw's eyes. He had never spoken to him of his parentage, not directly, though the secret had slipped out long ago now. "No, Torvyn. I don't imagine either of them would want to hear from me...after what I did." This was not the time to reflect on his past, and his nightmares. All the same, he saw a flash of a golden blade, and blood soaking into a decked tent floor. He saw an edge of steel striking at a neck, again and again and again, hacking through plate and flesh and throat. *My father. My brother. My task.*

"I would think the opposite," Sir Torvyn said. "Your father was always fair-minded, and I understand this of young Elyon as well. If I should tell them of this Book of Contracts, explain to them the nature of your fate, then..."

"I would prefer you didn't. I don't want anyone excusing what I did."

Torvyn nodded in his quiet way, his eyes giving a rapid blink, mouth a quick twitch. "They'll hear of it eventually. That cannot be helped."

"Or they'll die before they do," Jonik said. "Elyon was at Dragon's Bane. He might...he might already be..." He found he didn't want to finish the thought. The idea of never seeing Elyon again, of never being able to explain, and apologise, and beg forgiveness...it was too raw to confront. He turned his eyes aside to see Sansullio striding over to join them. *He's leaving too*, he realised at once. The Sunshine Swords were heading into the Night Tower as well, to gather their things.

"My Lord Jonik" Sansullio said. "It greatly pains me, the thought of letting you down, but I feel...I feel I must..."

"You needn't explain, Sansullio. You've served me longer than you ever needed to, and paid for it in blood. I would never expect you to stay."

The sellsword gave a faithful bow. "You grace me with kind words, my lord."

"I'm no lord, and never was." Jonik felt a thick sense of grief rising up his throat. He wondered how he would manage things without them. *I'll have Gerrin,* he told himself. *Gerrin...but who else?* Big Mo and Cabel were still recovering from their wounds. Bound to their beds, they'd be no help at all. That left only Jonik and Gerrin to look after the infirm, the prisoners, the boys in their cells. *How will we feed them and guard them?* he fretted. *Who'll watch the gate when we're sleeping?* He stared out in dull despair, wondering how it had come to this. *This was not the way it was supposed to go. This was not the fate the Nightblade promised...*

Gerrin stepped over with Harden at his side. "Jonik, we'll be all right," his old master told him. There was a soft edge to his rough voice and a caring look in his eyes. "We'll make it work, I promise you. Harden is going to stay with us."

Jonik looked at him. "You...you will?"

"I'll stay," the grim sellsword told him. "Leastways for a little while. By the sounds of it, the whole world's at war down there. Got no particular desire to join in." He managed a craggy grin.

Jonik could have hugged him. "You'll be most welcome, Harden."

"Not sure there's anything welcoming about this place, but I see your meaning. I'll stay with you till Emeric gets back. After that, we'll see."

"He'll be back soon," Gerrin assured them, as confidently as he could. "Sir Torvyn, you'll likely see him on the road down. When you do, tell him to make haste. Looks like we're going to be shorthanded here for a while."

"I'll insist upon it," Torvyn said.

"You remember the way through the passes?"

"I've a good mind for mountain tracks. We'll find our way."

"I hope so. Down is easier than up, true, but there are still ways to get lost on the descent." Gerrin puzzled on that, scratching the rough grey stubble of his chin. "Snows haven't been coming down the last few days, so that should make the hidden clefts and chasms easier to spot. Just be careful, Sir Torvyn, and don't rush for the sake of saving a few days. This war's not going anywhere for a while."

Sir Torvyn gave that smile of his. "I'll be happy enough to participate in this one, having missed most of the last."

"An itch that needs scratching, I'm sure." Gerrin returned the smile. Across the yard, the men started to reappear from the Night Tower, garbed in their armour for the trek. Radcliffe and Sir Bulmar approached to ask about provisions.

"We'll need food for the journey," Sir Bulmar Brown said, with a doubtful edge to his voice. "Lord Jonik, would it be possible for you to spare..."

"Take what you need, Sir Bulmar. You'll be able to restock when you reach the villages down in the foothills."

The knight dipped his chin in courtesy and left, taking Radcliffe with him, who couldn't have looked happier to be leaving. "I shall make sure they don't unfairly deplete your larder, young lord," Torvyn told him, moving to follow. "You have many a growing boy here who'll need to be kept well fed."

Cattle for slaughter, Jonik thought. He could almost see Fhanrir's rotting face grinning, those little beady eyes, watching from afar.

Before long the provisions had been gathered and packed and the men were assembling at the front of the ward by the gate. Mooton stepped forward to heave off the lengths of black timber that barred it, setting them aside. Norwyn and Regnar pushed the gate open. Beyond, the bridge stretched across the chasm toward the stone plateau, where the high peaks bled away to the distance. Jonik had never seen such a lack of fog and mist here. Everything was clear and pristine, the views uninterrupted. *A beautiful, horrible day,* he thought.

Last to emerge from the Night Tower was Borrus, draped in steel and flush of face. He saw Jonik standing aside, paused, then stepped over. Awkwardness came with him. "Shame to end it like this, but it must be done," he said, as stiff as a wooden plank. "You'll take care of Big Mo and Cabel, see them back to strength?"

Jonik nodded. "I will."

"And once they're fit and ready, send them down to find us. I'll take them into my service, and pay them well. It's the least they deserve for what they've been through."

"I'll tell them," Jonik said.

The big man nodded. "What I said back there, calling you a bastard. I didn't mean it, Jonik. And I haven't forgotten what you did for me…back in Solas. I might not be here if it wasn't for you, so…well, I'm not good at this sort of thing, you know that already." He gave Jonik a heavy slap on the arm. "I don't hate you. And I don't blame you. But I have to go. My father…"

"I know, Borrus. I'm sorry it's come to this. And I'm sorry…for your father. If it's true."

The man nodded regretfully. "As am I." He gave him a final look, then sent his eyes beyond him to the fort. "You'll…be all right? With these mages. And that blade?"

"I'll be fine."

Borrus Kanabar nodded once more. "Well…so long as you're sure." He didn't seem to know what else to say, so decided to say nothing more. Turning, the Barrel Knight moved heavily across the cobbles and out through the gate to join the others. The farewells were done, and that was that.

Jonik stood in silence as his former company crossed the bridge, and began down the pass, armour rattling and scraping on the stone. The wind seemed to pick up as Harden and Gerrin pulled the gate shut, then heaved the wooden bars back into place, locking it tight. Above them, the clouds moved in, blocking out the sun.

Jonik felt suddenly very cold.

11

Saska

The hum in the crowd was of fear mixed with wonder, though none of them dared get near it, even in death. Moonlord Hasham led the way on his mighty horse, flanked by a host of guards in white and grey scalemail armour, their fluttering cloaks embroidered with the Hasham house sigil; two moons, side by side, one silver and one white. "Clear a path," the great moonlord was calling. "Come, move out of the way."

His men echoed the order, driving the crowds back so that the royal litter might come through. Saska sat beside her grandmother, well shielded and protected by several other guards to either side. They were Nemati soldiers in silver and black, and at their lead was Sunrider Tallar Munsoor, the Grand Duchess's loyal servant and advisor. Across from Safina and Saska sat the hulking figure of Sir Ralston Whaleheart, armoured from head to heel in his misting godsteel plate. "You should not lean your head out of the carriage," he warned, as Saska peered through the curtains. "You do not know who might be out there among the crowds. A single arrow could kill you."

Not likely, she thought, *with all these men about me.* Sir Ralston had wanted her to wear her armour as well, for added protection, though she'd insisted against it. It was far too hot and far too uncomfortable to be wearing full plate outside of her training, and besides, Joy wouldn't be strong enough to carry her then. "You worry too much. No one out here wants to hurt me."

The Whaleheart frowned at the folly of the remark. "*Many* want to hurt you," he said sternly. "Sunlord Krator and his allies most of all. Even those well-loved have enemies."

"Nice to hear you think I'm well-loved."

The giant knight bristled at her insouciance. "You do not take things seriously enough. She does not, Grand Duchess."

Safina Nemati smiled. "No, perhaps not. But one might say you take things *too* seriously, Sir Ralston. I sense my granddaughter is only trying to redress the balance."

"Too seriously? My lady…what could be more serious than what we are trying to do?"

"Nothing. Nothing ever has or ever will be. But that does not mean you must approach it without a jest and a smile. *Smile*, Sir Ralston. It will brighten your day."

The Wall grunted. "I don't smile."

"It's true," Saska said, yawning. "He doesn't. I'm not sure he knows how, Grandmother."

The old woman chuckled as the litter rolled over the gritty ground beyond the city gates, the mid-morning sun already growing hot. The crowds had turned thick as flies upon a corpse out here, raising their chaotic encampment a little way north of the towering walls. Through the gap in the curtains Saska could see the tops of the tents spreading far and wide across the plains, clothing the land to the edge of sight in a forest of cloth and canvas. "It seems so much more vast down here," she said. "How many are there now?"

"Well over a hundred thousand," Sir Ralston told her.

"There were half that only days ago." Saska had watched the camp evolve from the terraces atop the palace. Every dawn when she woke the sprawl of tents and shelters seemed to expand, and by dusk the same day it had expanded yet further. The stream of newcomers never seemed to stop. "Are they all here for Agarosh?" That was how it started, she knew, worshipers and devotees come to look upon the great moonbear. But since then…

"No," the Whaleheart said. "Most seek safety from the war. Only the faithful are here for the bear."

Saska wasn't so sure how safe it was camped *outside* the city, rather than in, but didn't voice her thoughts. The carriage was moving slowly as the people were cleared aside, hauled along by a quartet of muscular carthorses who could pull the Whaleheart's weight. Sunrider Munsoor rode up beside them upon his grey-maned sunwolf, *Amullo*, pulling back the drapes to give them an update. "Your Serenity, we will be stopping in a moment. I will have your parasol ready, to shield you from the sun. Be careful, the ground is uneven underfoot and sharp in places. I shall be at your side, to make sure you do not fall.."

"Thank you, Tallar."

The man bowed and departed, the curtain waving shut.

"He is very attentive," Saska noted. She liked what she'd seen of Tallar Munsoor, a bookish-looking man with two bushy long sideburns, brown going grey, and clean-shaven lips and chin, who seemed more a scholar than a Sunrider to Saska's eyes. But then, Mar Malaan had never seemed much of one either, fat and flowery as he was. Saska had always assumed every Sunrider and Starrider to be fierce and deadly, warriors born, but that wasn't always so. "How long has he been in your service? I've never asked."

"Too long, he would tell me," her grandmother said, smiling. "Tallar has been a leal servant of mine for over two decades, and has long since become my primary counsellor. He's been present for many seminal moments in my life, and yours as well, child."

"Mine?" Saska had spoken but rarely to the man. "What moments could he have…"

"Your birth, for one, of which he bore witness."

Saska frowned. "Witness? He was *in* the room at the time?"

"No, outside it, protecting it, as he has the secret ever since." She laid her hands in her lap, folding them one over the other. As ever the Grand Duchess was regally and impeccably dressed in flowing silk and satin in black and grey, with a triple bronze, silver, and golden circlet resting atop her head. "Finding those you can trust implicitly is a rare thing in this world. Tallar would rise to the stars before betraying my trust, and I see the same quality in you, Sir Ralston. You are an unequalled bastion of strength in arms, yet in matters of faith and service you are just as strong."

The Wall bowed his massive head. "Kind words, my lady, and appreciated." The carriage began to slow to a stop and the giant picked up the flattop greathelm set beside him on the bench, to place it over his head. "I wonder if the Butcher is considered worthy of the same praise," he said, voice echoing in that great steel bucket. "Lady Saska seems intent on including him in our training. I deem that unwise. And too great a risk."

"He's been good," Saska rallied back. "The Butcher's a skilled swordsman and knows tricks even you've never seen. He's had you on your heels once or twice, Rolly, don't deny it."

"I don't deny his skill. Only his ability to hold his tongue."

"He doesn't know anything. Stop worrying."

"Not of your true lineage, no. But he knows I'm training you. He knows you have an important purpose. He may look stupid but he's not. And people are starting to whisper."

Let them, Saska thought to herself. *Let them find out my great holy purpose, and let the enemy find out too. Maybe then someone else will take on the burden.* She said none of that. She felt like she had no agency of her own, like she was just a tool and a pawn and a servant, the same as she'd been all her life.

Only at Willow's Rise did I have a normal life, she reflected. *Why can't I go back there and live in peace?* But of course she couldn't. Willow's Rise was probably deserted or destroyed by now, and if not yet it would be soon, and everyone who lived there with it. She sighed as the carriage stopped, then smiled as Joy poked her nose through the curtains, big beautiful eyes looking right at her. *It's like she knows.* The starcat was closely attuned to her feelings and hated it when her thoughts turned dark. *My light,* Saska thought. *My heart. My joy.*

"I'm going to ride the rest of the way," she said abruptly. "I'll see you outside."

"No, I don't think that's…" Before Sir Ralston could stop her, she slipped through the drapes and into the saddle on Joy's back, to pace to the front of the lines, wind in her hair.

Lord Iziah Hasham had come to a stop a little way ahead, overlooking a shallow depression some way left of the road. The world was craggy and rugged and red out here to the north of the city, dry as dust and unwelcoming to strangers, though to Joy it was home. The starcat leapt straight up onto a boulder to take in the thing they'd come to see; a dragon, savaged and mauled, lying dead amidst the dust of the basin.

"Princess." Lord Hasham had only just noticed her. He rode a great white stallion, magnificent to behold, barded in glowing grey links of armour. Not as magnificent as the moonbear he used to ride, but still, for a horse it was beautiful. "You thought to get the first look, did you?"

"It gets stuffy in the litter, my lord. And Joy calls to me." She reached forward and scratched the starcat under the chin, enjoying the rumbling purr beneath her. "I much prefer to ride in the open air."

"I understand. I have never favoured carriages myself." The moonlord turned his stern umber eyes back to the litter, to find Sunrider Munsoor unsaddled of Amullo and helping the Grand Duchess out onto the ground. A pair of servants awaited to one side, holding aloft a broad white parasol to protect the elderly woman from the sun. Sir Ralston climbed out last, looking gigantic and angry even within his greathelm. A host of soldiers followed, the crowds now well-controlled and corralled beyond.

Further back, across the flattened plains outside the city, was the great colourful chaos of the refugee encampment, and further off still Saska could see the soaring pyramid palace that had become her home, way back beyond the walls and across the Amedda River, which wound its way westward along the border of the duchy. Much as Saska had come to love the palace, she was happy to be free of its thick stone walls for a while, and the constant watchful attention of her bodyguard, guardian, swordmaster, and whatever else Rolly might wish to call himself. *I've had my fair share of prisons,* she thought, staring toward the palace pinnacle where the beautiful, serene gardens and pooled terraces lay. *No matter how lavish and grand.*

She turned back to the dead dragon with a question on her lips. "Is this a known dragon, Lord Hasham?" There was no saddle on its back, which suggested it was wild and riderless, as so many of them now were. *A thousand,* Saska thought, shuddering at the idea. That was the number Leshie had blurted when she burst into her room some nights ago having gone with Ranulf down to the docks. Apparently, an eruption at the Wings had seen a thousand dragons spill into the skies, as the prophecy of the Ever-War had foretold. Most likely it was an exaggeration, yet still…

"No, not that I am aware," the moonlord answered. He had a deep resounding voice, loaded with authority, and the distinguished features of a grand old battle commander to match; refined grey beard, trim and neat, hard eyes that missed nothing, a mouth and lips well accustomed to calling orders, and more comfortable scowling than smiling. It wasn't much of a stretch for Saska to imagine him riding a moonbear, as he'd done for long years before its death at the Burning Rock. *Hothror,* the bear had been called. Saska had heard him named Hothror the Horror during her years living in Tukor, though she suspected now it had been no horror at all, but a wonder as Agarosh was. It was common enough for the people of north and south to give such names to the beasts they feared.

"Do you mind if I get closer?"

"The beast is dead," Hasham told her. "I am certain it can do us no harm...yet all the same, this is a question for your grandmother, my lady, and not my permit to give. We should wait."

Saska glanced back. Her grandmother was still making her way toward them, picking carefully across the rocks and loose stones. She waited atop Joy's back, feeling the tension in the starcat's body as she sniffed the air and stared down at the dead creature with narrow, curious eyes. Even in death, the starcat feared the beast. *But not Agarosh,* Saska knew. She had a sense that the great moonbear feared nothing, and certainly not this dragon that he had slain. "Did anyone witness the fight?"

Hasham gave a gesture to the vast humming crowds. "I have men asking that very question, but early word suggests the fight occurred unseen, and by night. I would think Agarosh sensed the dragon's coming and came out to hunt it."

"Is that normal? For a moonbear and a dragon to fight like that?"

"It is an uncommon occurrence in the wild, though not unheard of. Once in every while a dragon will fly toward Moonbear Mount, and incite a bear's ire, leading to a clash. There are dragon skeletons there that attest to this...in fact I saw one myself when I ventured to bond Hothror in my youth."

Saska found the notion wildly fascinating. She had the utmost respect for any Lightborn brave enough to seek such a bond, knowing the fatality rates. It was said only one in every ten who braved the bond made it out alive, and those ten were already some of the stoutest and hardiest and purest of all Lightborn souls. "Did it not make you think to turn back, my lord?" she asked, curious. "Seeing the bones of a dead dragon along the way?"

Lord Hasham gave a rugged smile. "It was a little...off-putting, I will admit. But I had to make a choice. Go on and face my fate, or turn back, and bring shame to my house. Well...that is no choice at all."

Death and honour, Saska thought. To die upon the Mount was considered a worthy and noble fall, much more appealing to an intrepid young Lightborn than the indignity that would follow a retreat. "What of the Fireborn?" she asked. "Do *ridden* dragons and bears ever clash?"

"Not since the War of Fire and Light six hundred years ago. Then, yes, Fireborn dragonriders and Moonriders would fight. It was a damaging war to the moonbear population. Before that time, there were many more, yet afterward their numbers were greatly reduced. And never recovered, I regret to say."

"How many are there now?"

"A handful only. I know of just four Moonriders in active service, two under the rule of the Lumarans, and one each of Piseki and Aramatian descent. Our own is a man by name of Risho, of House Ranaartan. He is a young man, only two and twenty, inexperienced but courageous. His father is Moonlord Rhanor Ranaartan, who has the command of Starcat Keep to the west of here. As I understand it, Moonrider Risho is currently far away to the north, working under the command of the dragonlord Vargo Ven. That was, of course, by Empress Valura's permit. Your grandmother would never have sent Aramatians to join the Agarathi in their war, if given the choice."

He spoke with a clear tone of distaste for the empress, who had bent so easily to the demands of the Patriots of Lumara and their warmongering ways. Saska had heard that Lord Hasham spoke vociferously against the Lumaran Empire joining the Agarathi cause during the warmoot several months ago, as her grandmother had as well, but all to no avail. "This is the lowest number of Moonriders I can recall," Hasham went on, "though if you wish for a lesson in history I would suggest you consult with Sunrider Munsoor." He glanced back again, as the host made their painfully slow ascent to join them. "That being said, there are sure to be a number of unbonded bears residing upon the mountain, and within its hidden caves. If one is to know, it will be Agarosh." He gave Saska a wondering look. "I understand you can commune with him?"

She nodded. "Of a sort. I can sense his thoughts…when he lets me."

Hasham stroked the thick bristles of his grey beard. "You might want to consider inquiring. I have long wondered why so few Lightborn have bonded bears in recent years. It could be a simple matter of numbers, or something else…" He did not further that thought, as the Grand Duchess finally joined them at the lip of the hill, shuffling along at Tallar Munsoor's arm. "Your Serenity," Hasham said, bowing from atop his horse.

Safina Nemati smiled at him. "So, this is what we have come to see, is it?" Her eyes went down to the dragon.

"Yes, my lady. Slain by Agarosh, we believe."

"Who else?" She tottered forward beneath the shade of her parasol. "Why is no one down there inspecting it, Lord Hasham?"

"We were awaiting your pleasure."

"This is no pleasure, believe me, seeing a butchered dragon. Get down there and check its fangs and claws for blood. I would want to know if Agarosh was wounded." She turned to Saska as Hasham bellowed for the inspection to begin. Men descended into the dusty basin at once. "I am sure he is fine, child. Agarosh leaves often on his hunts and lonely rangings and does not return for many hours. He will reappear unharmed, and soon, I know."

Somehow Saska believed it. The dragon was large, yes, but not so large as the moonbear and by the looks of it, it had been savagely slain. Deep red cleaves ran the length of its body and its neck had been horribly mauled, exposing the raw flesh of its throat. Sir Ralston was looking at Agarosh's work appreciatively. "I am glad the bear is on our side," he rumbled. "It was folly of the dragon to attack."

"Why did it?" Saska asked.

"It didn't," said Tallar Munsoor. "At least, it didn't attack Agarosh." He looked across the encampment outside the city. "The dragon was drawn to this, to the smell of goat and chicken and mule, and the promise of an easy meal. It was likely preparing to attack the camp when Agarosh intercepted it. They can leap very high, the moonbears, when need requires." He nodded. "This would be my take. Agarosh caught the dragon by the throat and landed here in this depression, where he mauled it to death." He ran his finger down a long shaggy sideburn. "I wonder if he continued the hunt to the north, into the plains. If he sensed a further threat, he may have been compelled to follow."

Sir Ralston lifted the visor of his greathelm, to peer into the rugged red hills. "A beast as large as Agarosh leaves tracks."

Tallar Munsoor understood. "I will muster a host to follow."

"Make it a strong host, should Agarosh need aiding," said Safina. She let the Sunrider see to that, as she beckoned Lord Hasham closer. The man dismounted from his horse and stepped to join them. "Iziah, this camp has grown too large, it seems to me. How many men do we have protecting it?"

"Two hundred. A mix of mine and yours, and city guards as well. I agree, they have grown insufficient."

"We should seek to bring as many into the city as possible," the Grand Duchess said. "Those who cannot be catered for should be relocated to the south where it is safer."

"Or sent back to their own lands," Hasham returned. "This rabble has grown unruly, and is another headache we do not need. If we let them into the city, they will bring but hungry mouths with them, and disease. I fear it will do more harm than good."

"Is there disease among them?" Safina Nemati looked up at the once-Moonrider with questioning eyes. "Or is that speculation, Lord Hasham?"

The man admitted the latter. "It is a fear," he said, "but a valid one. The red flux is common in camps such as this. It may already be spreading without our knowing. I have men making inquiries."

The Grand Duchess tapped her chin. "We should look to relocate them regardless, spread them, and make sure they have access to clean water and sanitation, such as we can. This will help to stave off the worst of the flux, should it threaten to spread."

Hasham nodded. "I can see to it that they're uprooted and moved south, as you suggest."

"Yet by your tone you disagree?"

"I do. These people should never have come here. The faithful make their pilgrimage to look upon Agarosh, but most are not so driven. They are sheep, following the herd, when they ought to have remained in their fields. I would have word sent out for them to return to their own lands and villages. If they still fear a northern invasion, they needn't. There is no such threat now."

"The Tukorans hold the Perch, Iziah."

"Yes, and they will soon abandon it and go home. The Tukorans lost many men during the battle with Lord Krator's host and will not be resupplied with the Agarathi marching into the north. They are isolated, alone, and will soon lack for food. When the Perch was taken, the last men standing burned the stocks of grain and slew all the animals. The provisions that might have sustained the northerners are depleted, leaving them little choice but to…"

"Attack?"

"Depart. Attack would be folly. Even should they defeat Lord Krator's army a second time, they will suffer severely for the effort and render themselves incapable of further advance." He had an unyielding way about him on this, a face and tone of voice that said, *'this is my world, I know what I'm doing'.* "This Tukoran lord, Cedrik Kastor, is arrogant and stubborn by all accounts but must know that his battle is done. I would not be surprised if he should spread his sails and haul his anchors by the waning of the moon, and flee back to Ethior, or wherever he holds his seat."

Ethior, yes, Saska thought. *And Keep Kastor, where I suffered so much.* She held her tongue.

"And if he does so, will that make us safer or more at risk?" The Grand Duchess looked wary all of a sudden. "Lord Krator has mustered many more men to his cause, Iziah. He is busy, yes, bidding to win back the Perch, yet should the Tukorans leave…"

"You believe he would come *here?* That he would…" Hasham shook his head, swaying it between his broad, feather-cloaked shoulders. "No, Krator will not seek civil war. He would not dare try take this city by force."

"We gave him an army, Iziah. And he has grown unhinged." She looked at Saska. "He might seek reparation for long imagined slights."

"Now would be a good opportunity." Everyone craned their necks to look upon the grim face of Sir Ralston, peering down at them through his upturned faceplate. "The world is in turmoil. Chaos creates opportunity for a man like Elio Krator."

"The army is *not* his," Lord Hasham said angrily. "It is an Aramatian force, with mixed loyalty to different houses and factions. If he sought to use it to overthrow you, Safina, many would revolt."

"And die for it. Do not underestimate him, Iziah. Elio knows how to use his wealth and power to manipulate and intimidate by equal degree. The army *is* his, and those few who would speak against him will suffer the worst of his iniquity should they do so. Elio Krator has it in him to be an evil man. He needs only the right motivation to follow that path into darkness."

He's followed it far enough, Saska thought. The idea of Elio Krator trying to reclaim her made her shudder as much as the idea of Cedrik Kastor doing the same. *I hoped and prayed that they'd kill each other on the field, and yet both bloody men are still standing.* She looked at her grandmother through determined eyes. "We should go north, Grandmother. We're going to have to eventually, so why not now?"

"There's more war in the north than there is here," Sir Ralston reminded her. "It's not safe to leave yet. You're too early in your training, and unready."

"Unready for *what?*" Saska felt compelled to challenge him, someone, anyone. She looked around. When no one answered, she said it straight.

"To kill a demigod? *Me?* Are none of you seeing the lunacy in that? Do you not hear how mad it sounds."

"We hear just fine." Hasham spoke bluntly, giving the servants holding the parasol a sharp look, though both were trained to be present and not seen, to hear yet not listen. "It sounds mad, yes. However you ought to trust your Grandmother, and in your friend Ranulf Shackton as well. They're not here to lead you astray."

No, just into the very fires of hell. She said nothing, seeing no merit in it, though had the sense Lord Hasham did not believe it. *And why should he? I hardly believe it myself.* This was not a matter to be discussed here in the open, though, with ears all around them to hear.

Her grandmother said as much. "Our tongues grow hot in this heat; let's cool them. Saska, come with me. We ought to return to the sanctuary of the palace."

No, she thought. *I've only just been let out.* "I'd sooner stay and have a closer look at the dragon."

"You've seen it. Why get closer?"

"To study it. I may have to fight one of these one day." *And a big one,* she thought, shuddering. "It would be valuable for me to learn of its weak points."

Her grandmother looked up at Sir Ralston, who nodded. "The idea has merit. Some things are better taught live, than in diagram."

"Go, then. I will see you back in the litter when you're done."

That bloody litter, Saska thought. She hated riding inside it when she had Joy loping along outside. If there had been one positive of the long march to Eagle's Perch with Krator it had been spending so much time with the starcat. "When do you think we'll go north?" she asked the Wall, as they made their way down the rocky slope. "It's safer here right now, yes, but won't be for long. And you've heard the rumours. Ranulf says there's only one possible route north now that's even half-safe. The rest are growing too dangerous."

The Wall gave her the answer she'd expected. "We'll go when we deem it the right time, my lady. There could be no better place for you to train than inside the palace right now."

"And if every possible route north gets shut off?" Ranulf's council had been concerning on this, with all the rumours he'd heard down at the docks. There was talk of some krelia creature prowling the Solapian Channel and krakens and the greatwhales were rising from the depths to plague the southern seas, and likely those of the north as well. The Tukorans still held Eagle's Perch, so trying to leave that way was too risky right now, and going west would be worse than folly with the dragons so wild and wanton. So far as Ranulf said it, the best way would be through the Everwood, and then across the Bay of Mourning to Mudport or another harbour in East Vandar. But that wasn't so simple either. The Everwood was a mysterious place, not easy to pass, and the Calacania people who lived there were evasive and wary of strangers. "The longer we stay, the harder it'll be to leave," Saska finished. "Why is no one seeing that?"

"We see it," Sir Ralston told her. "But it is not yet time." He marched on, trying to outrun her questions, but Joy was a great deal more swift over this ground.

They caught right up. "Then *when*? When all the world is crawling with monsters and the skies have gone dark with ash and wings? You ask me, we should cross north now, while we can. Ranulf thinks the same."

"I am aware of Ranulf Shackton's thoughts. He is entitled to them, as you are yours. But these are not our decisions to make." He pressed on until the dead dragon loomed before them, looking vastly more large and grisly up close. "Now are you done? Or can I do my job?"

Saska relented. This was a complaint to take to her grandmother, not her Wall. It wasn't fair to hack at him like this when it was the old woman who made all the decisions. "Fine. Tell me about this dragon, then."

She learned little she didn't know already, in truth, though seeing the creature up close was an experience in itself. The Wall took her around every part of it, pulling out one of his greatswords to carve and cleave as needed. He showed her the throat, and the unique tubes through which the beast breathed fire. He peeled off one of its scales for Saska to inspect, a heavy piece of plate armour that took a great deal of strength to sever. He even took a great swing to open its belly, digging through its innards to expose the source of its inner flame.

"It has a special organ," he told her, "its purpose to make fire from flammable gasses and air. It is well protected, as you can see, though not impossible to puncture. Most Bladeborn are taught to target the heart, though to pierce this organ is more simple, in practice, so long as you can get beneath the beast in battle." He hacked and slashed some more, carving the creature open, to the shock of those watching nearby. Even Lord Hasham, giving his orders atop the hill, had raised his large grey brows in surprise. "Here, the heart is protected in a basket of tightly packed ribs, and deep enough within the chests of larger dragons to be hard to reach, lest impaled by a greatsword such as this, or a long spear. In the biggest dragons, no weapon can reach the heart; there is far too much muscle and scale and bone in the way. The flame-making organ is not so fiercely defended, however, as you can see."

Saska was still getting her head around the idea of trying to get *beneath* a dragon in the first place. The stench was also quite overwhelming and Joy was liking it not at all. She had to dismount to let the starcat retreat a little. "But getting *under* the dragon…"

"Isn't easy," the Wall agreed. "This is something Bladeborn Knights are taught; how to manoeuvre a dragon into the best possible position to land a killing strike." He looked the beast over. "Other options are the neck and the eye, beyond which lies the brain. A blade driven through each will typically kill it. Though that will expose you to its teeth, and flame."

"Or you could just cut its head clean off in a single swipe?" Saska offered.

"Or that." The Wall took the comment seriously. "Few have the strength, however, and this isn't possible with larger dragons. The one I killed was only of middling size."

"So you've told me." She had another long look at the beast in its entirety; tail to teeth, all scale and horn and jutting bony spikes. "It's hard to imagine...fighting one of these things." She'd heard so many stories, but they always seemed somewhat mythologised, dressed up by the singers and bards. "I've fought and killed men, and one of Mar Malaan's Sunriders too, but this..." She shook her head, her silence enough.

The Wall understood. "You have not been raised on the glory of it. Many Bladeborn boys grow up wishing for such a duel. Even should they die, they will do so with honour..."

"And soiled breeches," Saska said.

"Sometimes, yes," the Wall allowed. "It has been known to happen."

Saska wasn't surprised. Her bowels felt a little watery just being near the thing, and this one was dead. She tried to picture it, upright and breathing and looming above her, its chest swelling with dark red flame, lips pulled back showing those rings of savage teeth. She wondered at how quickly it would move, how fierce and wild it would be as it snapped and tore at the ground, its only intent to kill her. And then she tried to imagine it being twice at large, five times as large, ten, a monstrous unstoppable calamity not of this time. She gulped at the thought and said, "How big is this one? Compared to...Vallath, say?"

"Small," Sir Ralston said. "Less than half the size, or smaller."

Saska nodded and paused for a moment. Then she just came out and said it. "And Drulgar? How big...how big would he be?"

The Wall stiffened within his enormous suit of armour, a titan of a man. *Even he fears it. Even him.* "Bigger," he could only say. "Greatly bigger, the legends say."

A shivery breath exited Saska's lungs, and her heart thundered within her. When Leshie had come to her that night telling of the eruption at the Wings, it wasn't just the swarms of dragons she'd spoken of. One dwarfed all the rest, Leshie had said. *But if Drulgar is arisen, where is he?*

"My lady, you have gone pale."

"Speak for yourself." She laughed uncomfortably. "I can see your face within that helm, Rolly. You look unwell. More than usual."

"The smell is quite overpowering," he claimed as a reason. "Draw out your sword, Saska."

She looked at him, confused. "My sword?"

"Yes, your sword, draw it out."

She did as he bid her, wrapping her fingers about the hilt and pulling, steel whispering against leather as the blade caught the light of the morning sun, gleaming. "And what do you want me to do with it?"

"How do you feel? With godsteel to grasp, how do you feel?"

Fearless, was her first thought. It wasn't quite true - there remained a haunting echo of terror inside her at the prospect of her awaiting fate - yet her fears were greatly dulled and diluted. "Braced," she told him. "Against whatever I might be forced to face."

"Good. Fear is useful. It gives us focus and clarifies our intent when properly harnessed. But it must be managed."

I know, Saska thought. *Marian taught me that.*

Sir Ralston turned to the dragon. "Strike it. Cut at its armour and flesh. See that it is but blood and bone. *Feel it,* Saska, running up your arm. This is your training this morning."

She hesitated, seeing the guards watching her from the lip of the hill. By luck she was beyond the sight of the people camped outside the city walls, yet many of Hasham's men were watching. "It's so public here, Rolly. They're looking at me. Oughtn't we…"

"Strike it," he repeated, louder. "Cleave its armour clean in two, and you will know the strength it takes. Aim for the links between the scales and strike. *To stance, soldier, and strike!*"

Saska did not hesitate further. Driven by the power of his voice, she took stance before the beast where its flank was well intact, and lifted her blade against the rising sun. It glittered bright and silver, a sparkle of dust rising off its edge. Men called those mists Vandar's soul as they called the steel his body. *The body of a god, to strike down the children of another.* And this was nought but regular godsteel. *Imagine,* she thought, *what it would be like to wield his Heart?*

"Strike!" Sir Ralston cried. "Swing down hard and strike!"

So she did, heaving with all her strength. The blade hacked at the dragon's hide, driving hard through its tough scale armour. It did not quite get through, but almost.

"Again!" The Whaleheart roared. "Again, again, again!"

Saska hauled the blade back out in a spray of rich red blood. Again she hacked, and again and again.

And then she hacked some more.

12

Ranulf

Leshie was laughing as she walked into the room. "Gods, that girl. You'll never guess what Saska's spent her morning doing, Ranulf. Go on, have a guess?"

Ranulf looked up from the book he'd been reading, setting his quill to the pot. "Um...I don't know, Leshie. Training with Sir Ralston?"

"Yes, just that. Training with the Wall like she does *every...single...day.* That's something exciting to report to you, isn't it?"

You needn't report to me at all, he thought, *or interrupt me so often. Or so early.* "Of course." He racked his weary brain but had little time for this game. "I don't know, Leshie. I've been up most of the night working. Why don't you just tell me?"

"You're boring, Ranulf. So shamefully boring."

No, I'm tired. "I'm aware," he said. "You tell me often enough." He'd never been accused of being boring before he was paired with the feisty young Bladeborn, yet since then the charge had been levelled at him more times than he could count. It might vex him if it came from someone else, but now he was quite used to it. "So, are you going to tell me or not?"

"She's been hacking up a dragon!" the girl cried, gleeful, as though it was the greatest thing she'd ever heard. "You should see her. She's covered in it, blood and gore and everything. She *stinks*, Ranulf. I mean, *really* stinks. It's hilarious. Come and see!"

Ranulf wanted a bit more information first. "Did she kill this dragon, Leshie?" he asked, quite calmly.

"Yeah, she killed it," the girl said, deadpan. "Saska, who everyone's trying to protect. Her grandmother saw a dragon coming from the top of the palace and sent her granddaughter out to face it alone. Not the Whale-heart, no, or Small Wall and his men or the Sunriders and Starriders and city guards and..."

"I get the picture." The Tukoran girl did not know when to stop sometimes. "So who killed it?"

"Agarosh," she said. "Apparently, anyway. He's gone. Killed it overnight and ran off, they're saying. Half the city's gone down to look at the dead thing." She frowned, seeming to realise she should be offended by that. "They didn't invite us. Do you think I should be pissed off?"

"No." The girl was pissed off about most things and needn't add this to the list. "You don't need to be included in everything."

"And *you* do?"

He peered at her. It was such an empty accusation. "No. Well I wasn't, was I?" He felt exasperated and she'd only been with him a minute. "I have other things to be doing. Important things. They know it's best not to bother me."

"Like what?" There was a smirk on Leshie's lips and a challenge in her voice. "You've given up that little secret you were carrying around in your head. And you've dealt with Denlatis. What else could they need you for?"

Her words stung more than she realised. Ranulf's duty these last months had been to find Safina Nemati and seek her counsel, as instructed by King Godrin in the stolen page of the Book of Thala. The very night he'd arrived at the city, after the Grand Duchess had spoken to Saska of her sire and her fate, Ranulf had been given time with Safina himself. He had spoken to her then of the secret he'd been carrying, the formula only he had known, how for months he'd been writing it out each night and burning it right after, to ensure he recalled it…but that night, finally, he could write it out and pass it on. "I will keep it safe, Ranulf," Safina had assured him, "and I too shall memorise it. We shall be the only three. Our minds, and this parchment, will tell the tale to unite the Blades. Should one or another be destroyed, there will be others, just in case."

Ranulf had breathed out a long-held sigh of relief, though in many ways he'd felt a sense of loss in that moment as well. He had been special, given an ancient task by a great wise king, but now he was but one of three with whom the secret did reside. *I could die now,* he thought, *and the world would lose nothing.* It was a sobering thought, to not be needed, after being essential for so long. *A piece of Thala's Puzzle I was, but that piece has been replicated, one-made-three, and now my duty is done.*

He snapped himself out of it. *No, there is still more for me to do. Help Saska, support her and guide her. Find us safe passage to the north. That is my purpose now.* He shuffled some papers on his desk, notes he'd been taking and compiling over the last few days. Leshie looked at the book beneath his nose. "What's that then?" she asked. "Wait, let me guess. It's a book about that Never-wood place?"

"*Everwood,*" Ranulf corrected, though he sensed she already knew that. Leshie liked to get things wrong intentionally just to annoy him. He tapped the book. "*Myths and mysteries: A History of the Calacania,*" he told her. "It's a fractured history, but this is the best compendium there is. The Calacania have always been elusive."

"So you still hope to go and speak to this mysterious tribe?" Leshie seemed confused. "I thought Big D told you no about that?"

Ranulf understood Big D to refer to the Grand Duchess. Another of

Leshie's inexhaustible list of nicknames. "It's still being decided. I only need to complete my research and get leave to take a suitable host with me." He looked at her. "I would hope you'd join as well, when the time comes."

"Me?" she snorted. "Are you serious? Don't I annoy you enough as it is?"

Yes, plenty. He wanted her where he could see her, though, and beyond the clutches of the merchant. She was useful with a blade as well, there was little use denying it. "You have your uses, Leshie. And I know how bored you get staying in one place for too long."

"Oh, so this is for *me*, is it? You're doing it for my benefit?" She saw right through him. "Whatever, Ranulf. Maybe I'll come, maybe I won't." She drew her godsteel dagger and spun it between her fingers to scratch at the side of her nose. She had a shortsword as well, sheathed on her opposite hip, and had become quite lethal with both. "Who else would go with you?"

"Sunrider Munsoor, I would hope. He helped me last time I came here, when I wanted to visit the Everwood, though in the end the expedition amounted to nothing. His involvement is one of the sticking points with Her Serenity. She likes to keep him close by for counsel."

Leshie didn't seem too interested. "Who else?"

"The Butcher, perhaps. Sir Ralston doesn't much like his interference in Saska's training, so maybe he'll come as well. I'm not sure. Some of the men under Tallar's charge, certainly. Again, these details are yet to be decided."

"Yeah, well, we *just* came from that way," Leshie said. "Didn't we pass near the border of the Everwood after we had that tangle with the Pigborn and his piglets?"

"It was some way north of us, but yes, we were close enough."

"Well you should have thought to go and visit them then, shouldn't you?" she said, with a vastly annoying tone to her voice. "Who wants to go all the way back there?" She spun her blade once more and shoved it back into its sheath. A red sheath to accompany her fine red armour. *The Red Blade*, she had taken to calling herself lately, though the blades she bore were about the only thing that *weren't* red on her person, sheath and armour and hair included, and the many freckles that spotted her forehead and cheeks. So far no one had called her the Red Blade back, though, to her great disappointment no doubt. "Well, I'll think about it. What's interesting about these Cala-people anyway?"

"*Calacania*. Or the *Calacanians*. Both are fine to use." He tapped the book. "They're derived from an ancient Lightborn line that share close bonds with the Everwood Eagles. These eagles are said to derive themselves from Calacan, the Eagle of Aramatia, hence the name. They all live together within the canopies of the great Everwood trees. These they call the *Imlania*, the *Branches to the Blackness Above*. Through their roots and trunks and branches the souls of the fallen rise into the heavens, to live among the stars. They're..."

Leshie cut him off. "I'm going to have to stop you there, Ranulf. This sounds like the start of a lecture and I want to get another look at Saska before she bathes." She paused, hand on hip. "Just tell me one thing. These trees. Are they big?"

"The biggest in all the world."

"And these eagles?" She squinted at him closely.

She's wondering if they can be ridden, he realised. "They're very large, yes, much bigger than those we get in the north."

"Huh." She chewed on her lower lip. "Do people fly them?"

There it is. "Once before, yes. Not for centuries, however, that I know of. The eagles aren't so large as they were."

Her interest withered. "Well, sounds fun enough, I guess. Keep me in mind, anyway." She turned to leave, but stopped as she reached the exit. "Oh, I should say, I'm going to visit Cliffario tonight. Take him up on that offer of dinner at his villa…"

Ranulf felt a sharp stab in his chest. "No, Leshie. You *cannot* trust that snake."

She grinned and gave a loud laughing huff. "Gods, you are *so* easy to wind up." She spun on her heels and was gone.

Ranulf puzzled on her intent for a short while as he listened to her feet whisper away down the hall. Most likely it was just to taunt him, yet he could not put it past her going through with it as well. *Maybe I should talk to the Grand Duchess about this, or Lord Hasham, and have her watched?* The notion held little appeal, though. Leshie was much keener than she made out and would know at once if she was being trailed. Her movements were already restricted as well, though Ranulf sensed she would find a way out of the palace one way or another if she wanted to, unheard and unseen. *Damn her slinky silent sneaking,* he thought. The girl could move like a bloody cat.

He stood from his leather-padded chair, setting his quill pen aside, and began striding through his private office chamber and out into the hall. The palace was so grand and vast that he'd been granted several rooms to himself, a quota far beyond his needs, yet welcome all the same. Leshie had rooms nearby and liked to make use of the proximity, interrupting him night and day and often sneaking up on him to give him a fright. *Maybe I should ask to be relocated at least,* he thought. It wouldn't matter, though. The girl would find him anyway.

He made for a set of inner steps that zigzagged upward through the palace, scaling level by lofty level until he reached the golden tier. The guards en route had grown used to his presence and waved him on without a word. As he reached the high terraces of the top tier and stepped out into the morning sun he could hear Leshie laughing still. "This is fuel for more nicknames," she was chortling. "Princess Pong. Lady Dragonguts…"

"The Long Lost Stink of Aramatia?" Ranulf offered, walking briskly toward them past cherry trees and shaded pools and pure-water fountains that gave off a serene tinkling sound. His attempt at humour received laughter that could best be described as polite. *What am I doing, competing with a child?* "Saska, I heard what happened. Leshie was insistent that I come and take a look."

The blood of Varin, Lumo, and Thala did a twirl, causing gouts of dragon blood to fly off her robes and splash upon the gleaming white pavestones. "How do I look, Ranulf? Is this what a warrior should be?"

"After a battle, I have no doubt." Ranulf smiled at her. "Was it your idea?"

"Rolly's. He thought I should learn what it's like to cut through scales." Leshie huffed. "And *I* shouldn't? Why wasn't I invited to join?" She turned to look up at the Wall, who was spattered in droplets of dragon blood himself. The man stood almost twice her height, a looming tower of scratched grey steel. "You could have told me, Big Butch."

Sir Ralston might have rolled his eyes, though he was wearing his flat-topped greathelm so it was hard to tell. "I would rather you not conflate me with that sellsword," he thundered.

"And I'd rather you include me when you go off carving up dragons. Sounds like fun."

"It wasn't his choice, Lesh." Saska laughed and began peeling off her bloodied robes, exposing a set of unspoiled undergarments beneath. At once Ranulf and Sir Ralston averted their eyes, though Saska only gave a chuckle. "I'm not going to expose myself to you fully, don't worry. And you've seen me naked before, Rolly."

"You *have*?" Leshie was fascinated by that. "But you were always so…so prudish, Sask."

"I was a lot of things," Saska said, shrugging. "We were washing in a river, out in the plains," she explained. "You should have seen him, Lesh. Never seen Rolly so uncomfortable."

"But he's *always* uncomfortable. I mean, look at him. It makes *me* uncomfortable just seeing him standing there like that in that armour all day." She turned her eyes right up. "Aren't you hot?"

The Wall thought it best to ignore her. "My lady," he said to Saska. "I shall go to the eastern sparring yard to prepare for the day's training."

She smiled. "Fine. I'll wash and come down."

"Wasn't hacking up a dragon enough work for one day?" Leshie wondered.

"No," the Wall said, then marched away.

He was replaced by the Grand Duchess, who came tottering out from the lavish lounging chamber inside with a towel and spare clothes to hand. She set them down on a table beside the nearest pool and then motioned toward the water. "Wash, child. The smell is rather foul." She turned to Leshie. "Back already, I see. And you brought your friend Ranulf with you. Good. Your coming is most opportune, Ranulf. We have matters to discuss inside. Come, the others are waiting."

They left Saska to bathe in private, venturing to the cool of the royal residence. Moonlord Hasham was present already, along with Tallar Munsoor and several others Ranulf didn't know. Leshie took one look at them and then sidled up to Ranulf's arm. "And I thought Saska smelled bad," she whispered, wrinkling her nose. "They must be from that camp outside."

Ranulf agreed. "Who are your new friends, my lady?"

"Well you know Iziah, of course," the Grand Duchess said playfully. "And Tallar. These others are fresh to the city."

"Fresh would not be the word I'd use," Leshie said, under her breath.

Ranulf hushed her. "Well met," he said to them, giving them a neat bow of greeting. "I take it you're living in the camp of the faithful?"

Most of them looked at him blankly.

"They do not all speak your northern tongue, Ranulf," Tallar Munsoor said amiably. "If we could perhaps switch to Aramatian?"

"But I don't speak Aramatian," Leshie complained.

"You will soon learn," the Grand Duchess told her. "I shall have tutors brought here to the palace to instruct you."

Leshie lowered her eyes. "Um…I am very grateful for the offer, Your Serenity," she said, finding her courtesies. "But I have tried to learn, and I just…" She shrugged and bit her lip, looking ashamed. "I'm not good with languages. I'm a soldier, not a scholar." She glanced up at Ranulf as though he might be proud of that line.

She needs validation. He laughed to give it to her. "And a fine soldier she is. I would say her efforts are best left honing those skills, which are considerable." He put a hand to her back to guide her away. "Perhaps you might rejoin Saska outside?"

The girl put up no fight. Once she was gone, Tallar Munsoor made the introductions. "This is Toshin," he said, of one of the newcomers, a tall, thin-jawed old man with a dangle of grey beard on his chin. Another he named as Penrost, younger and stronger of frame, in the ragged worn garb of a seaman. A third had a quiet wise way about him, a small man of middle years and solemn stance who held his hands together before him and kept his head politely down. His name was Kentu. The last was a woman. "Min," Tallar called her. She would be well described as scarecrow-ish, though a very old scarecrow that had long since seen its best years pass.

"Well met," Ranulf said again, this time in words they could all understand. "My name is Ranulf Shackton of Rasalan. Sailor, scholar, searcher." He smiled, wondering where all this was going. "It must be a great honour to be invited up here to the top of the palace?"

"The terrace here has the best views over the encampment," Moonlord Hasham rumbled. He didn't seem so pleased about it. "Her Serenity insisted."

"I did," the old woman said. She wore silver and black today in fine threaded fabrics, and a twisting circlet in the city shades of bronze, silver, and gold atop her head. "We have grown concerned of the camp's size, Ranulf, and its scale is best seen from up here. Min tells us that many squabbles have broken out over space, and there have been small outbreaks of the red flux that are of grave concern."

The moonlord nodded. "As I feared."

Camp representatives, Ranulf thought. *Is that what these four are?* "The red flux is a wretched malady," he agreed. "I have seen it many times in my life.

Quarantining those infected would be the best course of action, to prevent the spread." He sensed they knew just how to deal with it. *That's not why I'm here, to give medical counsel.*

"We are seeing to that now," Hasham said. "However our priority is to ensure it does not spread into the city. We must be careful. In times of war a clearer hierarchy emerges among the servants of city and state. Soldiers became citizens of the greatest worth and their lives must be protected, to be spent when needed, and not taken without cause."

He doesn't want his men dying because of this rabble. Ranulf nodded his understanding. "Do you expect the encampment to swell further?"

"Yes," Hasham grunted. "More bulbous and bloated with every dawn." He gestured to the woman Min. "Tell him."

The scarecrow shuffled forward nervously. She was stick-thin, with a shock of white hair, skin rumpled and worn and leathery as old parchment, and a milky left eye. "My village," she croaked. "I was one of the first to leave. Place up near Starcat Keep, on the river. Came down by poleboat with my family. But others…they're sure to follow. From my village and others. Be thousands more coming…"

"*Thousands,*" repeated Lord Hasham, in a blustering voice that caused the old scarecrow to flinch. "Thousands by the day. To be fed, watered, housed and given sanctuary, they hope." He looked at the Grand Duchess. "She hopes it too. That we might open the gates and let these people swarm in, to strip us clean like locusts."

"Do not be dramatic, Iziah," the old woman scolded. "It has never suited you to panic." She smiled at Ranulf. "Most bring their own rations and shelters, and what little possessions they have. They are not all expecting to be let within, though of course my instinct wishes it so. What sort of ruler would I be if I watched them starve and shrivel outside my walls, taken by hunger and heat and dehydration and dragons."

"*Dragon,*" Hasham came back. "It was one, and it is dead."

"The first one need not be the last. Min…" She faced the white-haired scarecrow. "You saw others, did you not, on your journey down the river?"

"I did, my lady. Several. Flying north."

"*North,*" said Hasham. "These dragons make for the north, Safina. They care little for us here. This one slain by Agarosh was a rogue and no more."

The Grand Duchess considered that. "Dragons are not the only perils plaguing our lands. Ranulf, you have heard rumours of this at the docks, reports you have relayed to us. Your friend the shipwright was first to tell of this eruption at the Wings, and the emergence of the Dread…"

"Unconfirmed," Hasham said at once. "This disturbance was witnessed from Dragonwatch, many long leagues from its source. Eyes can deceive even the sharpest of minds, and the men of Dragonwatch have never had the keenest wit."

"Wit is not something I look for in a watcher, Iziah. When a man sees a dragon, they know it. And when they see a dragon much larger than the rest, they know that too. It was Drulgar."

The moonlord gave a harrumph. "Then where is he? One sighting from afar, and we're all convinced. I'd sooner wait until we have word of Varinar burning. Then perhaps I might believe it."

An odd thing to wish for, thought Ranulf, though he could see his point. Drulgar the Dread had a known vendetta against Varin and by extension the city he founded. *And the bloodline he spawned...* He put that thought aside. Saska's identity was safe and hidden and they were committed to keeping it that way. "Varinar would be his likely target," he agreed. "Though dangerous as well, even for him. The city was built to withstand dragons, and the Dread most of all. The millennia since his death have not weakened it; to the contrary, the city is proud of its reputation as impenetrable and continues to bolster its defences each year."

"It's as bloated as that camp down there," Hasham said to that, swinging out a white-feathered arm. Ranulf had always found the raiment of the Aramatian highborn houses equally arresting as it was amusing. He could never quite decide which was the more prominent. "Varinar was once much smaller, Ranulf, correct me if I'm wrong?"

"Greatly so. The city being smaller, that is, not your being wrong."

"The Ten Hills," said Tallar Munsoor, standing much as the pious stranger was, with hands clasped before him, feet neatly together. "They are contained within the original inner wall. The city's expansion has spread to the many less prominent hills to the south of its early construction. These hills, as I understand it, each house tall defensive towers. And the outer wall is a vast thing, godsteel-laced and most busy with weaponry; ballistas, catapults, scorpions, trebuchets, and others as well. And many hundreds of bowmen, of course."

"Thousands," Ranulf corrected. "Though that would depend on the threat level." He liked Tallar Munsoor enormously, seeing in him a kindred spirit. He was less fond of Lord Hasham. "Your description is otherwise good, Tallar. The city is much larger in area and population than it once was in the elder days, but that by no means makes it weaker. It merely means there are more people at risk. Yet even so, its unique construction was intentionally designed to protect them. When a dragon attacks the populace, they must get close to them, either to unleash their flame or dive upon them with claw and fang. The high walls and hilltop towers make this difficult, and should any dragon look to get near the ground between the hills - districts known as the Lowers in the city - they will have to dive past many hazardous weapons, as Tallar described. It is a furious gauntlet they run, and one few dragons have ever dared. Those that have tend to die quite quickly. To win Varinar would take an enormous force."

"Or an enormous dragon," Lord Hasham shot back. "Or better yet, a great thunder of them, hundreds strong, with two hundred thousand men and mounts in support to batter at the gates below. This the Agarathi have. But that is for the Vandarians to worry about, not us. We have concerns of our own to consider." He turned to the three men standing aside. "The occasional rogue dragon may continue to come here, or it may not. We cannot know. But what we have heard of are other perils, emerging from their shadowed places. You…" He pointed at the man with the spindly grey chin-beard and narrow jaw. "What was your name again?"

Toshin, Ranulf remembered, as the man wet his lips and said it.

"Yes, you. Come forward. Tell us what you've seen."

Toshin almost stumbled as he stepped away from the others, quite unable to meet Lord Hasham's penetrating gaze. Ranulf understood. He'd spent much of his life among greatlords and royalty so was used to their ways, but this man seemed a simple herder or husbandman and looked overwhelmed to be in such surroundings. "Y…yes, yes sunlord…"

"*Moonlord,*" Hasham said, frowning so hard his eyes were almost lost beneath his brows. "I am *Lumosi* Lightborn, not Solasi." He seemed greatly offended by the blunder, though let it pass. "Go on. Speak."

The man bowed, shivering. "It was…it was a drake, a…a sand-drake, I should say, my lord. Came over from Pisek, we think, from those dunes in… in the desert out there." He swallowed, hoping that might be enough. Another hard look from Hasham demanded elaboration. "It…it killed some people I know, friends of mine. I…I have no family. Came out through the earth like it was nothing, all thrashing teeth and jaws. I fell… as…as I fled its wrath. Knocked my head on a rock and when I woke up…" He trembled in his skin, knees all but knocking. "They were dead…all… almost all of them. They're saying it's the Doomfall. That's why so many creatures are crawling out of their pits and lairs. It's why so many people have come here, to the city. Where…where it's safer."

Doomfall, Ranulf thought. It was a Solapian name for the Ever-War, he knew, though the meaning was just the same. "You did not come to praise Agarosh the One-Eye, then?" he asked the man.

The herder looked at him with less fear than he had Lord Hasham. *He can meet my gaze at least.* "No, not…not me. I came for safety. Heard the Magnificent was here, guarding the city. Knew he would protect us."

"So you *did* come for him, of a sort," Tallar put in mildly. "Not as one of the faithful, perhaps, but it was the One-Eye that drew you here."

"I…yes, I suppose so. But for protection, not…not for praise."

"Well you ought to start praising him now," Lord Hasham told him. "But for Agarosh that dragon would have brought a great deal of death to the encampment last night."

The thin man took it as a command. "I will, my lord. I will pray to him daily from now on."

"I'm sure." Hasham waved him back impatiently, feathers fluttering. "You, come forward."

The younger man stepped forth, the stouter man called Penrost in the rugged sailor's garb. "My lord."

"You sailed down the eastern coast, is this true?"

"Yes, my lord. That's true." He had an unusual accent, spiced with the flavours of Rasalan.

Ranulf had to ask. "Do you have Rasalanian heritage, or have you just spent much time there?"

"Neither," was his response, "though I have spent much time with Rasal men, aboard ships. My life has been spent by deck and salt spray, sky and sea. I am a man of the waters; the open ocean is in my soul. The land has never called to me."

"Yet here you are, cowering beneath our walls." Hasham had no more time for this one than he had the others, it seemed. He was looking at them all as though they might spread the flux themselves. "Why?"

"The seas grow treacherous. The *great blue maid* is infested, my lord."

"With what?"

"Creatures of fin and tentacle, tooth and horn. Manators, leviathans, greatsharks, krakens, krelias, and more. All rise now from the depths below, unleashed from the drowned pits of Daarl's Domain."

Lord Hasham gave a heavy sigh. "Spare us this Rasal religious talk. They've got too many gods by half."

"Now, Iziah, don't be so abrupt with our guest." The Grand Duchess smiled at the young sailor, showing a defter touch. "We have heard from Ranulf of this devilish krelia, haunting the Solapian Channel, yet you passed through unscathed, you said?"

"By luck, Your Serenity. We kept a tight line near the coast, for fear of raging whales and savage greatsharks, though not the krelia, to tell it true. We did not hear of its prowling of the Channel until we had safely passed, and come to land here at the Aram docks. We were fortunate in our course."

"I see. And your journey had taken you from Rasalan?"

"No, not so far as that. We were on a long hard voyage, fishing the deep eastern ocean for rare catch, south of the Stormy Seas. On our return we passed close enough to Eagle's Perch to see smoke rising from the city, high up on the cliffs. We sailed closer, intrigued, as seamen often are, to sight the Tukoran armada at anchor off the coast. It seemed, to mine own eyes at least, that many ships had been destroyed, my lady."

Ranulf had not expected that. "Destroyed? How?" His thoughts went to Sunlord Elio Krator. Had he mounted a response against the Tukorans upon the sea?

"The ships I saw were broken and wrecked," Penrost elaborated. "Shattered masts and shredded sails lay upon the sea. I saw no ships burning, none aflame. The men aboard ship proclaimed this the work of Bhoun, and his grey-skinned spawn. A pod of great grey leviathans had risen up in the region, we heard from a passing vessel, to smash and destroy the old enemies of Rasalan. This was a Tukoran host, who had not long ago sieged your lands. And this was Bhoun's revenge."

Ah, sailors, such a superstitious god-fearing lot. Ranulf missed this sort of talk. This man was not a trueborn Rasalanian, but he certainly spoke like one.

"Bhoun," Moonlord Hasham said, sounding irritated. "This is your god of whales, is it?"

"Not mine, my lord, oh no. I am not Rasalanian."

"You might have fooled me."

The man showed his palms. "A lifetime spent among such folk rubs off, my lord. And the men of the *Haunted Horn* are a godly flock."

"Haunted Horn?" Ranulf asked him. "This is your ship?" It sounded a rather dreary name for a fisherman's carrack, but Ranulf had heard a lot worse. He gave that some more thought. "How many of the Tukoran ships were destroyed?"

"I could not tell you. The seas were rough, the skies bleak and blustery, and with word of whales beneath the waves, we did not linger long. I got but a glimpse, yet the wood and cloth in the water told its own tale. Many ships were sunk. Bhoun is a wrathful god."

Lord Hasham fingered the stiff grey bristles of his beard. "It's as I said, then. The Tukorans will have little choice but to take what ships they have left, and sail home. They will depart, I have no doubt."

It sounded likely to Ranulf as well. *Though if the Tukorans set sail, what will Lord Krator do?* He had heard nothing from Cliffario Denlatis of late and in truth did not expect to. *He'll see too much risk in trying to kill him.* The man was ambitious, but hardly stupid. *And he likes to play both sides.* That was a more concerning thought.

"Well, let us hear from our final guest." The Grand Duchess Safina Nemati gestured for the last man to step forward. It seemed to Ranulf that he had not moved at all since he'd arrived, though when he did, his stride was neat and precise, his hands never unfolding from his navel, where they entwined in a pious embrace.

And who is this one now? Ranulf wondered. *Is he to tell another tale of gods and monsters?*

"Tell us where you're from, Kentu."

"As Her Serenity commands." His voice was warm and soft, quietly spoken and pleasantly restrained, yet clear. The antithesis of Lord Hasham, who looked down at him as though he was a strange bug to be squashed. "My name is Kentu, as you have heard, and I hail from the lands of Hollowhill, far north of the Aramatian Plains."

And not so far south of the Everwood, Ranulf thought at once, seeing the map of the region in his mind. Hope swelled within him. *This is why I'm here.*

"I am by trade a humble gardener, in the fashion of my kith and kin." Kentu showed them his hands. The tips of his fingers were calloused and brown and green, stained by his work. "Long have we tended the rare vines and plants that grow beneath the hills, a god-given service to Aramatia, she of light and life." He bowed.

Safina was smiling at him. Lord Hasham was not. "You told me you came south as a messenger?" the Grand Duchess said.

"Yes, this is true. There have been dark stirrings in the forests west of the Everwood, and the Winged Mountains beyond. I came to report on them, compelled by a sense of duty, yet I find I am too late." He smiled enigmatically. "It seems you already know."

"It would appear so." Hasham studied the man closely. "Are you willing to journey back north, in the company of this man?" He gestured to Ranulf. "Will you lead him to the heart of the Everwood, where the Calacanians dwell?"

"I will lead him to the border. If worthy, the Calacania will find us, and permit us passage to the Twelve Trees."

Hasham looked displeased. "You said you had had dealings with them before."

"I have. Or rather, *they* have had dealings with *me*. Our vines and plants have healing properties as you know, and other medicinal uses. I bring them sometimes to the forest, to foster friendly relations and goodwill with the eagle-folk. But always they find me, never the other way around."

"Such is the way," Ranulf said. "I've read how hard to find they are. It would be most useful to have a guide." He looked at Tallar Munsoor. "Will you be…

"Coming as well? Yes, it has been decided. Her Serenity can do without me for a short time."

Ranulf dipped his head into a bow. "Thank you, my lady." Tallar's presence would be important, he judged, to act as Safina's voice.

"You're to leave as soon as arrangements are made," Lord Hasham went on, eager to get this done. "Make haste for the Everwood, find these people, speak to them, and convince them of our need to pass, should we require it. They're a tetchy tribe and easily mishandled, but if needs be, remind them on whose lands they live. The Everwood is a holy site, yes, but remains under Aramatian authority, and thus they answer to its ruler." He looked at Ranulf, Tallar, and the pious man called Kentu. "Make sure they understand that, if they seek to deny you passage."

A good thing you're not coming with us, Ranulf thought. Tact had never been a great resource of the Moonriders. "We'll impress upon them our need, my lord."

"See that you do." Hasham turned to the other three newcomers. "You three, we thank you for your voices here today. You've proven informative. My men will take you back down to your camp and see you well situated as reward. Kentu, you're to remain here in the palace, where you'll be taken to private quarters. Master Shackton and Sunrider Munsoor will come to you when ready to discuss the route."

"As you command." The man of the Hollowhills bowed low once more and slid away alongside the others, leaving with the herder and the seaman and the scarecrow.

Hasham watched them go in silence. Once out of earshot he said, "Your thoughts, Ranulf?"

"My…"

"Thoughts. On Kentu. I know you have a nose for liars and charlatans. What are your first impressions of him?"

"Limited, until I spend more time in his company."

"That's why I said first impressions."

"Well…he seemed honest."

"And trustworthy?"

"Yes, I would say so. I do not see what he might gain from deceiving us."

Tallar Munsoor agreed. "The gardeners beneath the hill are a queer sort, most odd to outsiders. Life spent underground will do that to a person. They are, however, faithful above all else, and deeply religious, much as the Calacanians. They have had many interactions with them in the past and Kentu's being here is fortuitous. It is not an opportunity to waste."

"Well and good then." Hasham accepted that and looked happier for it, though not happy, *never* happy. "You'll take a strong guard with you. There are many perils on the road as we have heard, and it seems only to be getting worse." He ground his jaw.

"Something bothering you, Iziah?" the Grand Duchess asked.

"Much and more, yes." Hasham turned his umber eyes to look outside. The sound of playful frolicking could be heard among the pools. Leshie must have gotten in as well. The thought made Ranulf smile. *They are young, so young,* he thought, *and we often forget.* It was nice that they could spend time like this, being just that. Young. Hasham's mind seemed to be on the same thing. "We are trusting much in your granddaughter," he said. "She is strong, I see that, and determined as well, but it seems much to ask of her. Are we certain of her fate?"

Her fate. To reforge the Heart of Vandar and with it, help end the war. Ranulf wished it wasn't so, but Safina seemed adamant that only Saska could bear such a weapon, as Varin's direct heir. "All our fate is shrouded," the old woman said. "I have explained this to you, Iziah. The Far-Seeing Queen saw only so far. From here a fog of uncertainty lies before us, but beyond it there is light, a light we must all strive to reach. Within the mists lie many dangers, yes, and paths unseen, yet for all that, some things are known." She paused. "Saska's heritage is undeniable, as is her prophesied fate. And we all must help her fulfil it."

Her words left behind a residue of silence. Hasham tilted up his grey-bearded chin, Tallar Munsoor stood hands clasped before him, and Ranulf thought of the overwhelming task that lay ahead. *Find the blades, gather them, unite them.* All that would take place in the north, thousands of miles from here. *And much remains unknown,* he thought, *even to Safina.* By intent Queen Thala had kept apart the pieces of her puzzle, to be brought together at the time of need lest the enemy unearth it and seek to destroy it. They knew that the Hammer of Tukor must be used to reforge the Heart, but little more than that. *Secrets, lies, deceits,* Ranulf thought. The puzzle was forming, but it was not near complete, and there were pieces out there that still needed to be found.

He cleared his throat. "Securing a safe way north is an essential first step," he declared. Hasham looked relieved for the silence to be broken. *He mislikes this arcane talk,* Ranulf thought. *He remains too much a sceptic.* "No prophecy can be called true until completed and fulfilled, and most are never so. Queen Thala set the board, but we must play the game. It's up to us. Sir Ralston trains Saska in arms; this is one move, the shifting of a piece. Another is finding safe passage into Vandar. Beyond these, many others remain. But we'll keep on playing the game until it's won." *Or lost,* he didn't say. It remained a distinct possibility.

Hasham's face hardened up again. "I heard you liked the sound of your own voice, Ranulf. Saska spoke of impromptu lectures among the gardens of Brightwater Academy when she studied there with the redhead girl." He looked at him. "Yes, I understand that well now."

Ranulf could hardly deny it. "I like a captive audience, what can I say." "Nothing more, please. I have much to see to." Hasham turned to the Grand Duchess and fell into a sharp bow. "I will see the encampment spread and relocated, as you require, Sereneness, and contain these outbreaks too."

"And you look so happy at the prospect." She smiled and touched his feathery arm. "You understand now why we cannot be sending these people away, Iziah, with such dangers lurking about their lands?"

"I understand better, yes," he allowed. With that he strode away in a flutter of feathers, pristine and white.

Safina watched him go. "Ah, Iziah Hasham. The Lord of Doubt. He was never so before Hothror perished. Proud, always, and commanding, but not so complaining. Much is lost when the bond is struck." She put her hands together. "Well, you two best make your preparations. But first, Ranulf, a private word."

Tallar Munsoor bowed and slipped away to give them time alone.

When he was gone, Safina Nemati's eyes creased in sudden unease and she looked at once much older, and more tired. "I had not anticipated this," she confided, her posture slumping. She drew back to sit upon a soft cushioned chair. "I thought we would have more time."

"Time, my lady?" He followed, though did not sit.

"To prepare. To plan. To *think*, Ranulf. To take a breath and think. The perils are mounting more quickly than I ever feared, and Thala's Puzzle is horribly incomplete." A great expression of strain and defeat came upon her face. "Until now we have had a roadmap of sorts, yet this shroud, this uncertainty…"

Ranulf sat and took her hand, uninvited. She did not draw it away. "We'll get through it, my lady," he promised. "I have great faith that we will."

She looked at him. The light in her honey eyes was fading. "Do you believe that? Truly?"

"Truly." He squeezed tight. "And you do too, I know. We all…we all feel overwhelmed sometimes, Safina. Even you. Even you're allowed to feel that way."

"Feel, perhaps. But *show?*" She shook her head. "I cannot be seen to falter, Ranulf. Not by Saska. I above all must be strong for her." She looked up sharply, hearing the voices of the two girls approaching from outside. At once she pushed to her feet, wiped her eyes, straightened out her robes and set a smile to her lips. Ranulf followed, stepping away from her so the distance between them was appropriate. "Girls, girls…we could hear you in the water," the old woman called out, as she spotted them appear. "Teens will be teens, they say. But you have training to do, do you not?"

Saska had a towel about her body, using another to dry her hair. "I'm going down now, Grandmother. Rolly can wait."

"Of course. Yes of...of course he can."

Saska frowned at her as she approached. "Are you all right?" She glanced at Ranulf. "What were you all discussing in here?"

Your fate, the future, our fears. "I'm to journey north, to the Everwood," Ranulf told her, sparing Safina the need to answer. "We have a guide who lives in the Hollowhills, who will help lead us."

"One of those stinking men?" Leshie made a face, her red hair dark and dripping wet. "Better you than me. I'm *definitely* not coming then."

No...you're not. He looked at the relaxed expression on Saska's face, an expression she only had when her friend the Red Blade was around her. *You're going to stay here, Leshie,* he thought. *Because she needs you much more than I do.*

13

Amara

He held his hand up against the blaze of torchlight, ruts cutting horizontal across his rugged forehead. His cheeks were heavy with thick black stubble, offsetting the silver blue of his eyes. They squinted as she moved in closer, recognition dawning. "Amara," he whispered, into the cold gloomy silence. "What…what are you doing here?"

"Visiting my husband," she said.

He sat up. "Does Amron know? If you're doing this behind his back…"

"Then what? He'll condemn you twice over, and me as well?" She laughed that away. "Fear not, sweet husband, Amron is gone."

"Gone?" Vesryn rose from his festering bed and stepped toward the bars, bringing with him a sour unwashed smell. "What do you mean *gone*?"

"Gone," she repeated. "To Crosswater. In the defence of the realm."

He sighed loudly. "The way you said that, Amara…I thought you meant…"

"Dead? Amron Daecar?" She laughed. "Now who could kill one such as he?"

"He isn't invincible. Every great man in history is long dead, don't forget."

She smiled. "True, though I sense your brother has much work to do yet." She pressed up to the rusted iron bars. "How are you, dear husband? Are you being treated well?"

"Well enough. I am fed, and given ale. My request for fresh clothes has not yet been granted."

She chuckled musically. *Gods I missed him. So very much.* "I can tell. Why is it that every time we see one another after so long apart, you stink like some fetid bog?" She reached through the bars and cupped a palm to his black-bearded cheek. "Oh Vesryn, life has not been kind to you of late, has it?"

He drew away. "It's no more than I deserve, for the pain I've brought."

You've brought great joy too, and pleasure, she thought. "You're not so wicked as you're making out," she told him. "I have tried talking to Amron about you a dozen times, but…"

"But he remains intent on putting my head in a noose, and rightly."

"*Wrongly,*" she said. "He's doing it for politics, not hate or vengeance. To heal the realm, he tells me. The Greycloaks are to be released."

He gave that no reaction, but to nod. "He needs their fathers' support. I understand. I might do the same thing in his position. Amron always knew best what to do." He peered at her through the dim, flickering torchlight down in the quiet of that low lonely dungeon. "He still refuses to take the throne, I take it?"

"For now. But you know Amron. He doesn't need a crown to be king."

"And the Sword of Varinar? Tell me at least he bears it himself?"

She shook her head. "He plans to give it to Dalton Taynar."

Vesryn shut his eyes slowly, as a man realising some dreaded fear. "I worried he would. He wants nothing more to do with it, not after all I've done. I have sullied the noblest blade in our kingdom…for the noblest man."

Amara had had it with this lionising of her brother-in-law. "You give him too much credit. He is a warrior without equal, yes, but in nobility is outmatched by many. I might call upon your brother's difficulties with alcohol, and his weaknesses as a father. I could claim he let his own lust for glory consume him, to the detriment of his family. If I wished it, I might paint the picture of a selfish man, Vesryn, and there would be some truth in that too. Oh, Amron has his faults, sweet husband. As we all do."

Vesryn looked at her through the bars. A weak smile pulled at the corner of his mouth. "None of us are perfect. Is that what you're trying to say?"

"Trying? I think I've said it clearly enough." She grinned at him and produced a ring of keys from behind her back.

His eyes opened wide as watermelons. "Where on earth did you get *those?*"

"The gaoler is a greedy man with a sweet tooth. I fed him honeycakes and he fed me snores."

"You drugged him?"

"Oh don't make it sound so shocking." She took a step away from the bars, placing her torch into a sconce on the wall. "Do you want me to open the gate or not?"

He retreated to the rear of his filthy stone cell, melting into shadow. "I do not," he said, fearful. "I have no intention of running, Amara, not again. It is high time I faced up to my crimes, and I'll not have you embroiled in them too. No, don't tempt me."

She laughed. "Oh, silly man, I mean not to free you."

He frowned. "Then?"

Her answer was to unclasp her silver brooch, wiggle her shoulders, and let her cloak slip away to the floor, unveiling the scant silken dress she wore beneath, with high leather boots and a silver satin scarf for company. "Now, let me ask again. Do you want me to open the gate or not?"

He opened his mouth, and closed it, silent.

"I shall take that as a yes."

It had been too long since she'd felt her husband's warmth. *Too long, and I know not if I'll ever get a chance again.* She beat back her worry and grief as she turned the key in the lock, and pushed open the rusted bars. *This might be the last time I ever see him, before he's led in shackles to the gallows.* She would make it worthwhile, if so. *Every time must be like the last…*

He finally found his voice. "Amara, I…I'm filthy. You shouldn't get too near…"

She pressed her hands into his chest and drove him onto the bed, straddling him at once, filthy rags and all. Her lips shut him up from talking in a long, passionate kiss. He managed to break away, spluttering, "Amara, are you certain? *Here? Down here, in this cell?"

"I know this cell well," she told him "It was the same one I had when Godrik imprisoned me." *The same one where they cut off my finger*, she thought. She tried not to dwell on that.

"But…what if someone should come…what if…what if…"

"Shut up, Vesryn. Just…shut up."

Thankfully, he did.

Her husband did not last long, not after such a time apart, though their coupling was as impassioned as ever. "It would seem this cell excites you, my love," she teased, once they were done. She slid off his lap to lie down beside him. "That has to be a new record, even for you."

"Yes, I…it's been a while. I hadn't expected…" He fell silent, looking up to the rough-hewn ceiling, spotted with nitre and patches of lichen. She wondered for a moment if he regretted it. *Will this only make things harder, me coming to him? Would he prefer it if I just kept away?* She reached to his cheek, pulling his lips to hers, and kissed him. "What are you thinking about, sweet husband? Am I being too blithesome, with all this japery?"

"No," he said softly. "No, I would not have you any other way."

"Then what?"

He stared upward, a deep sadness swimming in his eyes. "I don't want to die, Amara," he said quietly. She hadn't expected that. Vesryn had been stoic in his acceptance of what was to come, even demanding Amron that he kill him by his own hand, for the wrongs he'd done him.

"Vesryn…" she whispered. She found she did not know what to say. *What solace can I give him? What does he want to hear?* "We don't know what the future holds," she managed. *Hope. He needs hope.* "It may not yet be your time…"

"It will be," he said, still staring up, unblinking. "It must be, and I accept that, but…" He swallowed. "I have mulled…on what will come next. I fear there will be no seat for me now, not at Varin's Table. The Steel Father will not permit me there, after everything I have done." He stared up, a hollow look in his eyes. "I fear the Long Abyss, Amara. I fear falling… forever. I fear the endless darkness of it all."

Her heart broke to hear him talk like this. "You'll *not* go to the Long Abyss, Vesryn," she promised. Tears welled in her eyes, sudden and hot.

"You're a good man, a good knight. You've been a good father to Lillia…"

"I'm not her father. Amron is. And I betrayed him." He tried to turn over to face the wall, but she held him where he was. "You shouldn't come again," he said to her, retreating into his shell. "It only makes it harder. You should go, Amara. Leave me. Forget me. The world would have been better if I'd never been born…"

"You don't mean that." She sat up and took him by the shoulders, shaking his bulk up and down on that thin, soiled mattress. "You don't!"

"I do. I mean it. Amron, Elyon, Lillia…*you*…all of you would be better off without me."

"Would I? You think I would be better off?" She slapped him hard across the cheek to knock some sense into him. "Don't presume to tell me what I would and would not be. I have loved you hard for twenty years, you stupid man. And now you're telling me they were a waste?"

"You might have loved another. A man better fit for you." The shame in him was palpable, a horrid throbbing ugly thing. "I have not been able to give you what you wanted most. I have not been able to give you children."

Tears trickled down her cheeks, grief-struck and angry. "We raised Lillia, and Elyon and Aleron in part too. That was enough for me."

But it wasn't. It never had been. She had always yearned for a child of her own flesh. He knew that too. "I cursed us, Amara, with my treacheries. I'll never forgive myself for that."

"You never cursed us," she came right back. "Women are born barren all the time. And some men as well. This has nothing to do with your past."

"It does. I know it does."

She slapped him again. "Stop saying that." *I can't let him wallow,* she told herself. *I won't leave him in this state.* "Think of the good you've done. Think of the love we've shared, and the laughter. You can curse yourself for mistakes you've made, but you cannot claim to be a bad husband to me. You have always been there for me, Vesryn. You have always loved me fiercely. And I you. Don't you dare take that away from me. Don't you dare!"

She seemed to get through to him with that. He blinked and looked at her. "Amara, I didn't mean…"

"I know what you meant. And I understand, Vesryn, I do, but you cannot let your life boil down to a few mistakes you made in your youth. It's hard in this cell, with little to do but think. Believe me, I know. When I was here I spent half my time crying. I cursed myself for my part in Rylian's death, for plotting to steal the Windblade, for getting every one of the Flame Manes but Carly killed. I've made my share of mistakes too, Vesryn, and I've wallowed in them too, as you're doing, but when I'm here with you, *I'm here.* Be here with me too, here, now, not back in your past with your demons, or in a future that has not yet come. We do not know how much time we have left, any of us, not with all that's going on in this world. I would spend whatever minutes or hours or days I have with you laughing and making love like we once did. I would spend it happy, and imagining a better world, not moping in dread and despair, worrying for something that may never come to pass..."

"Okay," he said, taking her shoulder. He sat up. "Okay, Amara. I'm sorry. It...it was a weak moment, is all. I did not intend to bring you down..." He pulled her into a hug, gripping tight at the taut muscles in her back. "I will be better, I promise. If you should come back...I'll...I'll be better."

It was all she wanted to hear. She could not bear to see him so drawn out and desperate, so wretched. "I should have brought wine," she lamented, her chin resting on his strong shoulder. "You remember, how we would make love for hours, then drink until dawn. Even on days when you needed to stand guard on King Ellis, we would make the most of the time we had."

He drew away and smiled at the memory. "I remember," he said. "Those were simpler times, back then." His eyes moved to the small chipped wooden table across the cell, half hidden in the gloom. "I have no wine, but there is ale, on the table. It's not especially good, but it should pass."

She slid off the bed and went to fetch it, taking up the small clay jug. Vesryn sat up, swinging his legs to the floor. He seemed to catch a whiff of himself as he moved. "I'm sorry...for the smell. If I had known you were coming..."

"You'd have done what? Licked yourself clean like a cat?"

He laughed gently. "I'd have done something. I hate that you have to see me like this."

"I've seen you like this for twenty years, in one state or another. You're my husband, Vesryn. Unwashed hair and dirty clothes do not change that." She returned to him with the ale, taking a gulp. The urge to spit it back up was strong. "Are you certain this is ale?" she said, recoiling. "I feel I might have accidentally picked up your chamberpot."

His laughter strengthened. "You always did know how to make me smile, Amara."

"It was always my favourite thing. Well, that and raising Lillia into the little terror she's become." She handed him the ale.

He had a sip, then wiped his mouth. "Have you heard anything from her? I hope Lord Amadar is keeping her well."

"Lord Amadar," she growled. "You mean the man who tricked me into this very cell, for my life to be used as a tool with which to bargain? That Lord Amadar?"

"The very same. You're still bitter about that?"

She held up her missing pinky finger. "Always, Vesryn, yes. Of course I bloody am. And he continues to prove a pebble in our shoe. Amron has written him about sending Lillia here, but so far we've had no response. He means to keep her to himself, the rotten bastard. Mould her into a little Kessia."

"She already is a little Kessia."

"In looks, yes, but in character, less so. She's greatly more wilful and

next. Rarely did a day go past when there wasn't some gathering or banquet or ball. She could not recall the last one, though. Nor when a king had last held court.

The air was brisk and breezy outside, a blustery mid-spring afternoon. She found Sir Connor Crawfield at the top of the palace steps, fully recovered now of the wound he'd taken the day the Flame Manes had been slaughtered. Their leader, Carly, was with him, her fiery hair whipping in the wind. They were not alone.

Amara almost fell over in shock. "*Elyon?*"

Her nephew turned. His hair was windblown and rich, chin and cheeks thickly covered in a short ink-black beard, eyes silver-blue and keen. He looked so much alike to his uncle, always had. Even more so than his father, many said, whom Aleron had shared more of a resemblance with, though the Daecar men all looked much the same. "Auntie. How are you?"

She rushed forward and hugged him. "Me? How am *I*? How are *you*, Elyon!" She pulled back, putting her palms to his face, looking him over. "You look tired." His eyes were a little bloodshot, the top of his high cheekbones above his beard turned red from the sun, his forehead too. "You flew here?" she realised. Of course he had, how else would he have come so quickly? "When did you leave from the Lakelands? You can't have made it all this way in a single day, surely?"

"I left early this morning," he said, tiredly, though with a smile. "I had to stop several times, but…I was intent on getting here by sunset."

Amara was stunned. "Oakpike must be almost a thousand miles from here."

"More like six hundred," he said. "It's the longest I've flown." He gestured to the others. "Sir Connor tells me that Father is not here. I came to talk to him, Amara. There are things we must discuss."

She could only imagine. War, dragons, the Agarathi, Eldur, and much else besides. "He sailed to Crosswater almost a fortnight past. He'll have arrived some days ago by now, I would think." She feared he would leave, seeing that look on his face. "You'll not go now, Elyon? You need to rest and eat. Have you eaten? Did you take rations with you for the journey?"

"I stopped to take some lunch at Ayrin's Cross," he told her. "They were…surprised to see me, shall we say."

"I should think," put in Carly. "Some steel god like you, descending from the skies." She looked at him lustfully through a set of sly turquoise green eyes. "You should stay, Elyon, like your auntie says. You remember the promise I made you?" She grinned at him, in that wicked way she had.

Amara knew just what that promise was. She imagined Elyon might just need it, too, after all he'd been through. She took him by the arm. "You *will* stay," she said, insisting on it. "Your father can wait, Elyon. You can fly to Crosswater tomorrow when you're recovered."

He didn't look like he needed much more convincing. *A gust of wind might just topple him,* Amara thought. He looked exhausted. "I…I suppose one night won't hurt."

"It might, if you want it to," said Carly. She gave him a wink and Elyon smiled back. "Or I can be gentle, as you prefer, my prince."

Sir Connor cleared his throat. "You ought to be careful with that, Carly," he said, terribly proper. "Lord Daecar is adamant he not be called king and thus Sir Elyon needs to remain just that. *Sir*, not prince."

She shrugged. "Sir, prince, makes no matter to me. It's the boy beneath the suit of armour that I care about."

Amara noticed that the pavestones were cracked nearby to where they stood. "Is that…is that where you landed?" she asked.

Elyon looked at the damage. "It wasn't my finest landing, I'll admit. After so long in flight, I came down a little too fast…"

"He saw me, my lady, and just couldn't help himself," Carly said. "Shot right down with a smash and a crack and gave me a big long kiss." She nudged Sir Connor. "Right, Con?"

"Well no, actually. That's entirely wrong." Sir Connor frowned at her. They were as dissimilar as two people could be, though Amara found their pairing amusing. She felt Carly needed it too, after the losses she'd suffered.

"Well, maybe that's just my fantasy then," Carly offered, shrugging. She gave a tress of radiant red hair a twirl and blew Elyon a kiss through lips of similar hue. "I like to make men's fantasies come true, too, oh yes. You said say the word, my prince, and I'll do the same for you, like I promised."

"Sir, *not* prince," Sir Connor said. He looked around as though some indignant Taynar might be lurking in the shadows, and there were plenty of those left in the city, to be sure. "We ought to retire to Keep Daecar," the head of the Household Guard said. "We'll be able to speak more freely there."

No one disagreed, so off they went.

The route was not a long one, Daecar Hill lying adjacent to the Palace Hill and just a short walk away. Sir Connor took the lead, Carly the rear. Amara walked with her nephew between them, who overtopped her greatly when wearing his full armour. His Varin cloak hung at his back, stained in places and a little singed at the edges. She noticed many scuffs and marks on his godsteel plate that had not been there before, marks that could only have been made by weapons of fierce forging, dragonsteel swords and spears and the finest blades the Lumaran Lightborn bore.

And fang and claw as well, she thought. Elyon had fought and slain his share of dragons now, she knew, and Carly wasn't half wrong. *A steel god*, the girl had said. To most, Elyon had been elevated to such, attracting many nicknames these last months. *Lord of Storms, Master of the Wind, Prince of the Skies*, Amara had heard him called. Some men were calling him the *Serial Slayer*, for his many noted dragon kills, though his father might lay claim to that title as well. Despite all that, to Amara he was still just Elyon. *My sweet nephew*, she thought, *the playful, cheerful boy I once helped to raise.*

There was little cheer about him now, though, nor the playful grins and smirking jests he once liked to make. "The city is quiet," he said, turning his steely eyes around. "Are there plans to bring the smallfolk in through the inner walls?"

"Your father did not get around to that, before leaving," Amara told him. More and more had come from the towns and villages surrounding the city, to seek shelter, yet for now they were allowed into the outer city only. "He did banish the tax, however. Godrik had imposed a charge upon every man, woman, and child entering the city. Your father put a stop to that the moment he returned."

They continued down the street toward the base of Daecar Hill. The flowers that typically lined the paths and festooned the many high terraces and balconies were not in rich bloom this year. *All the city gardeners are away,* Amara thought. *They have exchanged their forks and trowels for blades and bows.*

"It must be getting crowded down in the Lowers," Elyon mused. "Who has charge here with my father away?"

It was a good question without an easy answer. There were no great-lords present in the city, nor many middling lords of noted prestige either. Instead the likes of Sir Bomfrey Sharp and Sir Winslow Bryant and Sir Hank Rothwell oversaw city security in Amron's stead. Amara told her nephew the names.

"Sir Bomfrey...he's uncle to Sir Quinn, isn't he?"

"The Varin Knight? Yes, I believe so. A big blustery man, is Bomfrey. He has charge of the Taynar soldiers here. Sir Hank is managing the Roth-wells and Crawfields in the city, and the other Daecar banners here, though they're scant enough. Most of the Daecar men are out defending the western gate around the Twinfort and Green Harbour, under Lord Randall Borrington's command."

"Yes, I'd heard. And Sir Winslow? I recall the name, I think..." Elyon took a moment to recollect. "Of course. He was Commander of the Lake Gate under King Ellis. A Reynar man." He seemed to understand. "Father is spreading the command between the different houses," he realised. "He seeks unity between us."

"He has no choice. We must unite if we're to survive."

"I agree," Elyon said. "Though in the east, they're being much less impartial. I get called 'prince' wherever I go. I suppose Dalton and his army are doing the same with him." He kept on walking a few paces, then said. "Did Father sail to meet him? We'd heard Dalton's host was driven from the Trident."

"Driven...or tucked their tail between their legs, and ran?"

Elyon gave that a frown. "That isn't fair, Auntie. We were driven from Dragon's Bane as well, for the loss of ten thousand good men. If Dalton faced anything like what we did..." He shook his head. "You heard about Wallis, I assume?"

She nodded. "I wept for him. And Lancel, even more. He was still so young."

"He died bravely, fighting Vargo Ven and Malathar the Mighty. Few men can say they went out with such courage."

Amara was impressed by Elyon's composure. *He has grown harder, stronger, a little colder perhaps.* A war leader needed to be as such, though. *If he breaks down and weeps for every loss...*No, he couldn't do that. He had to bottle it up and thrust it aside until all this was done. How full that bottle would be by then was anyone's guess. Aleron, Rylian, Lythian, Lancel, Wallis, Melany….Elyon had lost much already.

They reached the switchback steps that wound up the hill to Keep Daecar, climbing back and forth as the city spread out beneath them. At the top of the hill, they found Sir Penrose Brightwood manning the gate. He blinked to see Elyon return. "Gods, Sir Elyon. You're back."

"For tonight only, Sir Penrose. How are you? Protecting my auntie well, I hope?"

"Of course, sir. Always." He called for the gate to be opened. "Just the one night? Where are you to go next, my lord?"

"Crosswater," Elyon said. "To visit my father. After that…well, I'm not sure." He gripped the Windblade and summoned a swirl of air about him, for the knight's benefit. "There are many places that call to me."

Amara smiled to see the wonder in Sir Penrose's bright eyes. Other guards who'd long served in the keep responded similarly as they continued on through the yard and up the entranceway steps. "They were much the same when they saw your father return with the Frostblade," Amara told her nephew. "You have to see it, Elyon. The way the mists melt so colourfully, it's quite something, really."

"I shall see it tomorrow, Auntie." He pressed on into the castle.

A dinner was hastily arranged for his return, brief though it would be. Amara called for the kitchens and cooks to prepare their best. "You needn't bother, really," Elyon told her, but she ignored him. The wine stewards and house sommelier were instructed to dig out the finest wines they had left in the cellars. Those old Azore vintages from Solapia that Amara had mentioned to Vesryn were found and decanted. Stocks were starting to run low, but Amara cared not for that. *I must make these moments count*, she thought. She'd haunted Keep Daecar alone these last weeks, and whether visiting Vesryn or spending an evening with Elyon, she would make the most of it, knowing it might be their last.

Sir Connor did not join them for dinner, nor Carly or any other member of her household. "I have a watch to attend," Sir Connor said. "I will leave you to catch up alone. Carly said something similar. "Sir, prince, my lord," she said to Elyon, once he was changed and ready to dine. She grinned as she played with the titles. "I'll let you and Lady Amara speak alone, and will see you when you're done. I'll be the one in your bed…" She leaned in and whispered something in his ear that made him smile, then turned and swaggered away, hips and hair swinging.

Thus it was that they dined alone, just the two of them, sitting opposite one another at the heart of the family feast hall. Above the hearth hung Vallath's Ruin, the Mercyblade that had once slain a great dragon and crippled a prince. Amara found herself looking at it as she sat. Amron had dealt such death with it, and Aleron might have too, were he still living. Now it was Elyon's by rights to bear, though he had a better blade, and had never wanted to wield it, even so. *And so who will take it now?* Amara

wondered, as she often did. *Or will it just hang in here forever, denied its last taste of war? Haunting this place…as I do.*

Elyon did not dress up, as he once used to. In his youth every dinner, feast, and festival called for the finest garments the city could offer. Tonight he wore a simple leather tunic and blue woollen breeches, clothes over which he could fasten his armour if needed. He seemed a little tense, unable to relax. Amara wondered for a moment if that was the stress of flying so far, a strain she could not hope to understand, yet in truth she knew better than that. "You're safe here, Elyon," she assured him. "You can rest. There are no enemies for a thousand miles."

"Six hundred," he said. "And dragons fly more quickly than I do, across long distances. They could come at any time."

"Not here," she said, trying to soothe his worry. "And we'd have good warning anyway. You can rest easy, if only for tonight.

He nodded, spooning a measure of soup into his mouth; a rich creamy broth of potatoes, onions, and hunks of pork and beef. It had been one of his favourites as a boy.

"How is it?" she asked.

"Good. I find I have to eat a lot, when I fly. It uses a great deal of energy." He seemed to relax a little with some food in him. "This is perfect, Auntie, thank you."

"Well, I only gave the order. The cooks are the ones you should thank."

"I will before I leave." He had always been so good with that, treating commoner and king alike. He reached to his goblet to warm his belly with a sip of wine. "I had hoped to see Jovyn while here. Could he not come?"

"I sent a man to the Steelforge," she said. "He told me Jovyn was on duty this evening, standing sentry on Elin's Tower." There were four towers at the corners of the Steelforge, where the Knights of Varin trained and lived and were buried at their death. South-facing was Varin's Tower, looking toward Varinar, the capital city. Facing east, across the lake to the city of Ilivar, was Iliva's Tower, named for Varin's only daughter. To north, peering toward Elinar on the distant shores, was Elin's Tower, for Varin's firstborn son. West facing was Ayrin's Tower, Varin's lastborn, who reigned long after his father's death. And embracing them all, Mother Eshina, the great lake named for Varin's noble wife and mother to his children. A lake at which festivals were held yearly, fertility festivals praising the wonders of birth. *And disappointments,* Amara thought. She took a sip of wine.

"I shall visit with him tomorrow before I leave," Elyon decided. "How is he?"

"Well," Amara said, though it was a lie. In truth Jovyn had not been the same since he'd left Lillia. "He seems to get taller by the day. And more handsome. You might want to take him with you, when you…"

"I can't," Elyon broke in.

She realised why at once. "Of course. Yes."

"I have mastered only some of the Windblade's power," he went on. "Once I'm stronger…maybe I could use the winds to transport others with me, in some way. I have read accounts of that before, from old kings and champions of the past. I'm not certain how it would work, but…well, there's much I still don't understand. When I fought Ezukar, the blade harnessed the power of the storm, pulling lightning from the skies, to fire at him. It happened much on instinct, and hasn't since." He looked aside, where the Windblade rested in its sheath by the table. "The blade remains much a mystery to me."

So say the greatest scholars, Amara thought, *even with subjects they've spent their lifetime studying.* "That is wise, Elyon," she said. "Your father always thought the same. That is why he extracts such power from the blades he bears. Never stop deepening your knowledge. You don't know what you will unearth."

He had another sip from his wine cup, then looked suddenly at her hand, as though noticing it for the first time. "I'm sorry, Auntie. I haven't asked…your hand, how…"

"It's fine. I don't even notice anymore." She wiggled the little bit of stump she had left, still bandaged at the top where the flesh was raw. In the same hand she bore her chalice. "I self-medicate often. Perhaps that's why it never hurts." It did, in truth, but it would not serve to mention that.

"Connor said you were at the palace to visit Vesryn." His jaw tightened a touch, though not as much as it had before when her husband was discussed. *Like last time,* she thought. The last conversation they'd had had been at Elmhall Hold, the Blackshaw seat, the night he'd learned of Rylian's death long months ago. It had been a tense and emotional exchange, and Elyon had ridden for Dragon's Bane at dawn the next day. *I told him of Vesryn's intent,* she remembered, *and he laughed at that, and bitterly.* To restore the glory of House Daccar and put Amron on the throne. It hadn't worked out like Vesryn had wanted. Not much had, of late.

She answered his question. "I was. He is still my husband, Elyon. And I still love him." She paused, sensing a challenge in him. "Would you condemn me for wanting to see him?"

"No," he said at once. "I've never doubted your love for one another." He thought a moment more. "I'm not sure I can ever forgive him for his betrayals, but killing Godrik Taynar…after what he did to you…" He paused again, selecting his words. "Yes, I understand why he did that. I had a mind to fly here and do the same when they sent me your finger in a box. If it wasn't for the calming counsel of the others, I might have. Some wrongs can only be answered with blood, Amara."

"I killed Godrik," she said, suddenly. The air stilled and silenced. "That was me, Elyon. I killed the king."

"He was never king." Elyon stared at her. "How did it happen? We were told that Vesryn slew him when he stormed the palace to save you."

"He killed others. So did Connor, Carly, Jovyn, Penrose. They all came for me, but too late. I stuck Godrik in the neck with a knife. That was me. And I'd do it again."

He studied her. "You feel nothing? For taking a man's life?"

"*That* man? No. Just justice, and vengeance." She took a gulp of wine, showing her missing finger. "My regret is not for Godrik's death, nor my part in it, but your uncle. Your father has burdened him with the blame, Elyon, to appease the Taynars, and shield me from their reprisals. He'll let Vesryn hang for it. And that's on me."

Elyon did not say anything for a while. There was much to ponder in that, complexities to unravel. Eventually, he rose from his seat, walked the length of the table, and circled around to her side. He came to sit beside her, taking her hand. "I'm sorry, Auntie. I know how hard all this must be for you."

She had no words. *Such a sweet boy,* was all she could think, her eyes turning misty. *So compassionate, so caring.* "It…it hasn't been easy," she admitted, when she found her voice. "With Lillia away, and…and you. And your father…he has a realm to run now, a war to fight. He tries to be understanding, but he has no time for me. And your uncle. Seeing him…down there, like that. I…I feel so alone, Elyon. Alone and…and helpless."

She felt foolish for even talking like this, when Elyon was out there fighting for them all, watching his men suffer and die and never being able to rest for fear of a fight. *Who am I to cry on his shoulder? Who am I to burden him with this?* She tried to fight the tears back, but couldn't help it. Down they came, scorching past her cheeks, and no sooner had she broken down than Elyon pulled her into a hug, and held her there, strong and comforting, until her eyes ran dry.

"You're not alone, Auntie," he told her. "I will always be here for you, no matter what. Always."

She sobbed her last, clinging tight, promising herself she'd not weaken again. *This is the last thing he needs. He's been flying all day, you stupid woman, flying to see Amron, not you. Now fix your face and drink some wine, and be happy, as you said to Vesryn. Be happy and share stories and laugh, and make the most of this time. You may not get any more of it.*

She managed to follow her own advice, putting on a stronger facade, wiping her eyes and fixing her smile and telling her nephew that she was OK, that she just needed to let it out. She poured them more wine, telling him of the vintage, if only to straighten out her thoughts and regather her composure. Elyon knew what she was doing, but let her be. "It's one of my favourites," she said, swirling the wine in the chalice, letting it breathe and open out. She took a good long sniff and went on about flavours and spices, before having a sip and doing the same once more, "Go on, you try. Perhaps you'll pick up more than I did."

He did as bidden, playing along, and soon enough they were sharing stories as she'd hoped, and reminiscing. They ate some more, drank in moderation, and even laughed a little too. "I shouldn't have *too* much," Elyon said, as his lips grew red. "I'm flying tomorrow morning, after all."

Amara laughed at that, and didn't try to convince him otherwise. The red of the wine made her think of Carly, though, and that promise. She could see Elyon growing more tired as the evening went on, and did not want to deny him the pleasure of the girl's company. "You should go, Elyon," she told him, after a while. "Don't sit here with me on my account. There's a nubile young woman awaiting you in your room. Enjoy your time together. You should seek comfort in one another, while you can."

He nodded slowly, an old interest flickering in his eyes, as a dying flame threatening to gutter out. Elyon had always had a great fondness for the charms of women, though not of late. "I've not been with anyone since Melany," he said, thinking back on that for a time. It was a bitter tale, of love and loss and betrayal. And not one he wanted to revisit. "And before then..." He looked at her, wondering. "I never told you about Saska, did I?"

She shook her head. She didn't know the name, though it rang a bell. "The girl...from your tent at Harrowmoor?" she asked. She'd overheard Lancel and Barnibus talking of her once, she remembered, before the royal wedding in Ilithor. Amara knew Elyon had helped the girl escape, and gotten ten lashes for all that trouble, though they'd never spoken about her directly. "She was taken in by Cecilia Blakewood, wasn't she?" *That horrid bitch.* "As a breeder, for my king cousin's foul programme?"

Elyon smiled distantly, nodding. *A real smile,* Amara thought. *A longing smile.* "She was no breeder, Auntie," he said. "Saska...she was there as a spy, to kill Cedrik Kastor, though I talked her out of it. She was a servant in his household once...abused by Lord Modrik. A servant. A spy. A *princess.*" He smiled again. "And more, I think. She was much more."

Amara wasn't quite understanding. "Princess? How can that be?" It made no sense to her.

"Well...it's a long story," he said. "Though, if you want to hear, I'll tell you."

"And Carly?" she asked him, thinking of the divine creature in his bed. "Shouldn't you go to her, before she falls asleep?"

Elyon refilled his wine cup, and settled in. "Let her sleep," he said.

14

Lythian

The dungeon door opened with a rusty metallic shriek, and the chamber flooded with firelight. Heavy boots met stone, stamping down the steps. Lythian counted three sets.

"Which cell is he in?" he heard a voice say.

"Here, m'lord. At the back." The gaoler appeared with a ring of rusty keys in his grasp, fiddling for the right one. Behind him stood a knight in silver breastplate, gauntlets and greaves, with a rich red cloak hanging from his shoulders and red leather boots on his feet. His cloak was fixed by a brooch showing a silver bolt piercing a red dragon, the sigil of House Pentar. With him was the standing commander of Runnyhall, an up-jumped young hedge knight called Sir Clarence Farning, who had no business at all running the operations of a fort.

"Hurry up," said the red-cloaked knight. "Find the right key, damnit."

The gaoler fumbled a little more before he got it right, twisting the key in the lock. The knight pushed past him with an oil lantern in his grasp. He held it up to douse Lythian in light. "Gods, it's really you. Captain Lythian, I can only apologise for the treatment…"

"It's OK, Sir Storos. You were not to know."

Sir Storos Pentar stood before him, the spit of his younger brother Tomos. Their father, Lord Porus Pentar, had gone through three separate wives in his time, siring five sons. Storos was the fourth, Tomos the fifth, both sired of Lord Pentar's third wife, Lady Smalling. *The comeliest of them,* Lythian knew, *and she gave him the comeliest heirs.* "Goodness, I feel as though I'm looking at a ghost. When I was told you were here, I hardly let myself believe it. Sir Clarence made your identity sound most uncertain." He looked at the man angrily.

Sir Clarence Farning shuffled on his feet. "I didn't…didn't know, my lord. I'd never met Captain Lythian before."

"But you know *of* him, yes? You know of his deeds, of his virtues, and his honour? You know he went to Agarath with my younger brother by the order of Lord Daecar. You know of this man who returned by rowboat, bearded and filthy, with an Agarathi man at his side. This man who said, quite explicitly, that he was in fact Captain Lythian Lindar. You knew all of this, Sir Clarence, and yet it *still* did not convince you?" He spoke again before the man might respond. "My father made a grave mistake in giving you the charge of this garrison. What has this world come to when men such as you are elevated so." He stared at him. "Go. Get out of my sight. And fetch the Agarathi from his cells. Captain Lythian will wish to see him."

Sir Clarence scurried off, taking the gaoler with him. It was a nice moment for Lythian. "You're the first friendly face I've seen since I returned, Sir Storos. I trust you didn't ride far?"

"From Southwatch. I've been stationed there for a time. I came at once when I heard of your plight."

"You have my thanks." Lythian stood from his bed, stretching the ache in his lower back. He had been permitted fresh clothes, at least, and a bucket with which he might wash, though all the same a sour stink still cloaked his person. A stink Sir Storos was trying to ignore, as best he could. "How does your father fare?"

"My father? Oh, not well, I'm afraid. His ails get the better of him, Lythian. My brother Alrus returned to Redhelm not long ago, to be ready, for when the time comes. We don't imagine Father has too long."

Alrus was the Lord of Redhelm's eldest son, and next in line to rule. Lythian had always liked him the least of Porus Pentar's brood. "I heard he took a wound in a training accident last year," Lythian said. "An arrow to the leg, was it?"

"Yes, a great blunder on the part of a young archer, though innocent enough. It has stripped Alrus of his ability to fight, though he was never much of a swordsman to begin with, in truth." He smiled. "Tomos had the best of my father's blood in that regard. He was the only one of us who made a Varin Knight."

"You might have, Storos, had you pursued it."

"You do me an honour, Captain, but I fear you're being too kind. Either way, Alrus is well placed to sit our father's seat, leaving the rest of us to help guard the coast. Glarus and Doros hold posts on the Black Coast, at Nightwell and Chilgrave respectively. Both have come under attack over the last weeks, though the forts hold firm for now. I do expect one day to hear that another of my brothers has been slain." He sighed and shook his head. "Tomos…we received his bones, did you know? They were sent from Dragon's Bane some weeks ago. A gift from Vargo Ven, if you'd believe it."

Lythian would believe anything, given what he'd seen and done. "I heard. The hunters who brought us here were generous enough with their tidings." *Though only once Pagaloth handed over his blade*, he thought bitterly. "More so than Sir Clarence and his men."

"*Clarence.*" Sir Storos shook his head. "I knew him from a boy and he was always a fool. These are desperate times, Lythian, if we are having to turn to such as he." He gave him a quizzical look. "What else have you heard? You know of King Amron, I hope, and Prince Elyon? You know of the blades they bear, the dragons they have slain?"

Lythian nodded. Such news was the light that had kept him company in the darkness. "I was told, yes."

Storos had an enthusiastic face, much as Tomos had, with long brown hair tinged red and a brisk way of speech. "So you have," he said, smiling. "Though I'm sure you've more to learn. And much to tell. Come, the day is yet young. Let us start on the road to Redhelm. We can share in our news by horseback."

Lythian held back. "Redhelm? Sir Storos, I must return to Varinar. I've been far too long away."

"You will. Redhelm is but a short diversion and my father would be joyed to see you." His expression turned more sober. "Tomos, Lythian. We have his remains, yet not the story of how he fell. They are…incomplete, shall we say, his bones. And there are markings on many of them that suggest a gruesome death. My father would hear the tale from you. He insists upon it, as does my brother Alrus. Come, the day is bright and good for riding. I have express orders to accompany you there."

The day was bright, that was true, and greatly more so than the grim bleak weather they'd encountered the day of their return. Great banners of white cloud rippled across the skies, blown forth by a strong southward wind. In the yard of the fort, men played at training, firing arrows at targets or duelling with blunted blades. It seemed lazy, forced, and much for Sir Storos's benefit. Lythian Lindar knew a poorly run outfit when he saw one, and Sir Clarence Farning was no leader of men. *Pray this fortress is never attacked*, he thought. *It won't last more than a minute.*

The fort commander himself was returning from another tower, walking toward them in a nervous, shifty gait. Behind him came two soldiers flanking a man in a heavy cloak, moving with a limp. "Is this him?" Sir Storos asked. "Is this our Agarathi guest?"

Sir Clarence spoke awkwardly. He had a spindly bit of yellow hair on his chin, and a pimply, angular jaw. "Yes, my…my lord. This is he."

"Why is he limping? Take that cloak off him, let me have a look."

Sir Clarence swallowed, nodded and the cloak was removed. "He tried to fight," the young knight blurted at once, as Lythian looked upon his friend. "He fought hard, my lord. The men were only trying to restrain him…"

"Silence, Farning!" Sir Storos snapped. He turned to Lythian. "Captain, I must apologise twice over for the conduct of my men. They will be duly punished for this, I assure you."

Lythian did not respond. Sir Pagaloth's clothes were torn and bloodied, his lower lip swollen and split, right cheek gashed, eyes black with bruises. There was bruising on his arms, neck, and shoulders as well, his dark hair was torn and sheared, and the long black beard that had once clad his chin had been shaven off with a knife, and harshly so, leaving many scrapes and cuts behind. Lythian's fury simmered at the sight. "I said he was not to be harmed," he said in a voice low and dangerous. He looked Sir Clarence in the eyes, though the man could not meet them. "I said that to you, several times. I *told you* he was under my protection."

"I…I did not know it was you, Captain Lythian. I feared you…might be lying. I feared you were a pair of spies, sent to deceive…"

Sir Clarence felt the back of Sir Storos Pentar's hand, a swift hard swipe that had the young knight tumbling to the dusty floor. Half the men in the yard looked up. "Back to your training!" Storos roared at them. "Be lucky I don't have every one of you whipped." He fumed a moment, then put his eyes back on Sir Clarence. "I'm going to return here on my way back to Southwatch once I've escorted Captain Lythian to Redhelm," he told him. "If I do not find the culprits with stripes upon their backs, I'll have you flogged to within an inch of your life, Farning. Do you quite understand me?"

"I…yes, yes I understand my lord. Of course." He climbed back to his feet and bowed, his cheek flush from Sir Storos's strike. "Forgive me. I'll make sure that justice is done."

"See that you do." Sir Storos waved him away. "And bring fresh clothes and a basin of water for Sir Pagaloth to wash in. *Now*, Farning. Don't make me ask again."

For a second time, the fort commander scampered away out of sight.

"Sir Pagaloth. You have my sincerest apologies for the conduct of these men. Please don't go thinking that they represent the men of South Vandar. They do not. Any friend of Captain Lythian's is a friend of mine, and of House Pentar by extension."

Pagaloth managed a polite bow, though the effort of it looked painful. "I understand their hatred," he said, with grace. "And at times of war in particular. They have suffered greatly from my people, and only sought to seek amends. I do not blame them for it."

"You are too noble, and too generous," Sir Storos said, "but we've far too many boors and heathens in these ranks." He inclined his head in respect of the dragonknight and gave him another look over. "I do hope none of these injuries is serious?"

Pagaloth stoically brushed his concerns aside, as was his custom. "Superficial cuts and bruises," he said. "And my hair and beard will grow back."

He looked different without them, younger and less fierce. His beard in particular had been greatly cherished by the man, Lythian knew, as was the case with many of his ilk. It was a grave insult to shave it, and so roughly. *And that limp…* "What of your leg, Pagaloth. Can you ride?"

"Yes. I fell awkwardly when struck by one of the men. A twisted ankle, nothing worse. They made sure not to inflict lasting damage."

"You needn't cover for them," Sir Storos said, looking angrily over the yard. "If you see any here, point them out."

Pagaloth turned his eyes across the yard as a courtesy. "I am afraid not, sir. I have never had a good eye for remembering faces."

Too noble indeed, Lythian thought. *His guilt makes him see every slight and attack against him as worthy penance for his crimes. And does mine not do the same?*

The basin was soon brought out, set out of sight of the men so Pagaloth might wash and dress in private. "He seems of high noble blood, Lythian," Sir Storos said while the dragonknight was gone. "Is there any fire in him?"

"Distantly. He had early aspirations of saddling a dragon in his youth, though his blood proved too dilute."

"I see. He carries himself well, that is for certain. Have you known him long?"

"From the very first day we set foot in Agarath," Lythian informed him. "He was charged with escorting us from Dragonfall to Eldurath, to ensure us safe passage across the Drylands."

"And he's been with you ever since?"

"For much of the last months, yes. I would not be here without him."

"Well, no wonder you count him so dear. I do hope Tomos felt the same."

"I believe so, yes." Lythian said nothing more. It was unstable ground he did not want to tread just yet. "I would ask of Borrus, Sir Storos. We parted a long time ago, in the wilds of the Western Neck. The last I knew, he was being taken to Solas to find a ship home. Pray tell, did he make it?"

"Ah, well there's a mystery. There have been rumours among the men at Southwatch that Sir Borrus returned by way of the Three Bays. He landed at Calmwater, they say, and then made for Mudport." He gave a perplexed smile. "There was even word of some great quest to fell the Shadow Order in the north. But that's all I know."

That was most unexpected. "So he didn't fight at Dragon's Bane?" Lythian would have expected Borrus to rush right back to the defence of the realm.

"No, not that I'm aware of. It seems to me that Sir Borrus is back, and yet isn't, if you understand me. His whereabouts remain uncertain, last I heard, though you'll have to take what I say with a rather large grain of salt. Lines of communication have stuttered of late, you see. And I've been rather busy, fending dragons from my walls."

Just outside the gates, a small host was mounting up, twelve men-at-arms well armoured and armed and cloaked in crimson slashed with silver. "Our escort," said Sir Storos, as Lythian spotted them. "The captain is Bladeborn, though not the rest." He gave Lythian a swift inspection. "I am in remiss, Captain. You ought to be properly outfitted for our ride. They will have armour here for you to wear. Hard strong leathers and some plate. Not godsteel, alas. Come, let's get you garbed before we leave."

Lythian chose to stay where he was. "I'm content to ride as I am, Sir Storos. Though if you'll permit me a request..." He let his eyes drift down to the scabbard at Storos's side. "Might I feel the touch of godsteel, once again? I happen to have lost my own blade long months ago. I've been cast out from the warm haven of my blood-bond ever since."

The knight looked at him sympathetically. "Of course, of course, I can quite imagine the pain of that parting, and my blood-bond pales in comparison to yours." He reached to his belt and unhitched the sheath that carried his dagger. "Here. You can carry it until we reach Redhelm, when I'll find you something better."

"My thanks, Storos." The sun seemed to shine just a little brighter, then, as Lythian's fingers wrapped about the hilt, and he felt at once the power of his bond, full and deep and radiant as the dawn. His eyes scanned beyond the fort to the far horizon, taking in a world as a blind man given the gift of sight. A smile spread across the rugged beard that clad his face. The clarity was impeccable, the details crisp. In his ears came the songs of birds unseen, the chirping of insects in the brush, the distant bleating of a goat somewhere off through the fort. He could smell the horses and their many strong scents, and the men in the yard as well, detect the sour fogging breath of a man who'd been drinking wine. It all came to him at once, the sights and smells and sounds, a fond feeling, most dear to him and most missed.

Sir Storos was smiling as he watched. "Whole and one again, Lythian," he said. "Your sword...Starslayer, I recall it was named. A great blade, of many famed deeds. Where was it that you lost it?"

In the depths of hell, where I should have had the strength to slay the darkness before it could rise. Lythian fixed the sheath to his belt, and unclasped his fingers from the hilt. "A story for another time. The wound is still too raw."

"Yes, I quite understand. Our own ancestral blade is most treasured by my father, and brothers. *Silverdoom.* I trust you know of it?"

"I know it well. Your father bore it twenty years ago at the Burning Rock. He wrought much damage on the enemy with it that day."

"Yes, as he likes to remind us." Sir Storos smiled. "Now it hangs above the mantelpiece in his solar, gathering dust. It ought to go to Glarus, now that Alrus is enfeebled, though our father refuses to part with it. 'A great blade is only great because of the deeds done with it,' he would often tell us. 'You have blades of your own. Make them great, and earn them names'." He reflected on that for a moment. "I suppose that's true, in a way, though Silverdoom was a famed blade before he bore it. I told him he was a hypocrite to his face, once. Well, you can imagine how he took it."

Not so well. Lord Porus Pentar was a proud man, not cruel but direct and sometimes harsh. A fourth son calling him hypocrite would not have gone down well.

"Alas he hoped to give the blade to Tomos, I do not doubt. He always loved him the most. Tomos, who was so much more skilled than the rest of us." Storos shook his head and turned his eyes aside. "His loss had been sorely felt by us all. And the not knowing..."

He wants me to tell the tale right now.

"Tell me, at least. Did he die well?"

Lythian placed his hand on the man's shoulder to console him. "With honour, and with courage, defiant to the last. He died well, Storos. Varin was watching."

That seemed to appease the man. He gave a silent nod, then called for his men to bring horses, as Pagaloth crossed the yard to rejoin them.

"Please, take these steeds. They're strong and quick, and they'll need to be. Travelling these lands has grown perilous."

They left Runnyhall behind, a place Lythian hoped never to see again. Before long it dwindled out of sight behind them, lost to the hills and woods that marked this part of South Vandar. Pagaloth rode beside him. "How does it feel, Captain? To have godsteel back in your grasp?"

"Invigorating," Lythian said.

The dragonknight frowned with those sharp black brows, though his face looked lonely without his beard. "That is all you're giving me? *Invigorating.*"

"I'm no bard, Pagaloth. I have not the words to describe it."

"Well, you have one."

Lythian smiled. "True. Though not one to do it justice." He thought a moment, then said, "Imagine a long cold night, wet and windy and dark. To bear godsteel again is the light, the rising of the sun in the east." He glanced over as they cantered down a worn old track. "How was that?"

"It will serve. Somewhat trite, my friend, but passable. No, you are no bard."

The men were nervous as they rode, constantly watching the skies. And watching Pagaloth too, Lythian did not fail to miss. Nor did the dragonknight. "They do not trust me, Captain," the man noted, after a short while.

"You're unarmed," Lythian pointed out. "And Sir Storos has permitted your presence here. They have no reason to fear you."

"It is not me they fear, but the dangers I may bring. These are paranoid men, Lythian, haunted by the terrors above." He glanced up. "They fear I will draw a dragon down upon them."

"Give them more credit. They're not so irrational as that."

"I see it in their eyes. They sense a demon in me."

Lythian didn't much like this talk. It made him wary, and eager to ride at the rear of the group where he could keep an eye on the men ahead. *They're good loyal men, Pentar men, chosen by Sir Storos for this charge*, he told himself. It should have been good enough, but it wasn't. War bred fear and fear bred folly, and he had to be on his guard.

After an hour, the black bones of a village emerged in the east, down in a distant valley beside a small green lake. Sir Storos trotted down the column to join them. "That was the village of Gillytarn. It was destroyed a month ago, or thereabouts. Before then Harleytown, Bogmorsham, and Highacre fell, and since then Littlehelm, Fairfront, and the entire Scarlet Valley have burned."

Lythian knew every name. *Pretty towns all of them, and some strong and sturdily defended as well.* Highacre was a walled town built atop a broad hill, with four small towers at its corners. Littlehelm too was a stout enough place, and Fairfront was once the castle seat of a famous knight called Sir Franklin the Fair, whose adventures and lovers were legend. *And yet none stood a chance,* Lythian thought, every town and village, fort and castle destroyed another dagger driven through his heart.

"The coastal villages have been sorely ravaged as well," Sir Storos was going on. "Though only more recently have the dragons begun to fly inland. The early attacks were the worst, when the people were more complacent and caught unawares. Harleytown and Highacre suffered tremendous casualties, though since then droves of men and women have been making for the cities, dragging their children and old and infirm along with them. High walls stacked with scorpions and ballistas is what they're after, though in these parts, only Redhelm and Rustriver provide what they need. Already both are full to bursting. Many are being left out in the cold, I regret to say."

They passed other ruins over the course of the next few hours, farmsteads and hamlets and old abandoned forts melted down to black mulch. One was the *Shell of Wildrock*, a once-prosperous castle that had been the jewel of House Pentar many long centuries ago, before they took stewardship of the south. It had been destroyed in an earlier Renewal, the eighteenth or nineteenth so far as Lythian could recall, so badly burned by dragonfire so as never to be restored. Lythian had ridden past it several times over the years, yet never had he seen it like this. The old bones of its great towers and walls, once crumbling and black, were reduced to heaps of misshapen tar. The gatehouse and barbican that had remained standing after the castle's fall was no more, blasted apart and destroyed. "Was Wildrock occupied?" Lythian asked Sir Storos. "Had a garrison been sent to the Shell?"

"No," Storos answered. "Some vagrants perhaps had laid claim to the place, but no true soldiers were here."

"Yet the dragons attacked it anyway?"

Sir Storos scowled at the skies. "The dragons are wilder than ever before," he said. "Most are unridden, untethered from their Fireborn, and see enemies everywhere they go. Unoccupied castles such as the Shell of Wildrock have come under attack, and it isn't the only one, believe me. I've even heard reports of them fighting one another, snapping and raging in the skies. The sentries at Southwatch have seen all sorts of frenzied behaviour, Lythian. One bowman told me he witnessed three dragons killing another. They shredded its wings until it could fly no more, pursued it to the ground, and then feasted on it living. Can you imagine? Cannibalism, amongst these foul beasts. As if they're not foul enough."

Not all, Lythian thought. He had come to find great beauty in the dragons he'd had the honour to know. Neyruu, fierce and yet tender, whose great roar of anguish at Kin'rar's death still came to him sometimes in his sleep. Garlath, so widely feared, yet like-for-like as Lord Marak was; strong, powerful, stoic, noble. These wild beasts were just that; wild, untamed, and driven by a primal urge to spread chaos and fear across these lands, at the behest of their divine master. But it did not describe their race.

He kept those thoughts to himself, however, thinking it wise to just nod and stay silent. *They will curse me for a sympathiser*, he thought, *for a lover of dragons and a traitor besides*. He would have to admit to his part in Eldur's rise

176

o late. Jaws came down upon his head and when the fellwolf
ıt, the headless man fell.

Lythian was roaring. "Back, behind the wagons!" He surged
ngage. Behind him now, Sir Storos was blaring orders and his
narging on. Lythian did not wait for them. He slid before the
took position in Strikeform stance. "Look at me, foul creature!
' he roared.

olf looked at him with round black eyes, lightless and pupil-
oty. Its face was half man, half wolf, more disturbing than
d say. *A mistake*, he thought. That's what the histories said of it.
Dhatar's creation, the battle god whom Vandar had given
te his own minions. *He had no flair for it, lest his intention be to*
erhaps it was, because this thing was a nightmare, long-limbed
d *wrong*.

ure moved oddly, cocking its head like a bird, sensing a more
llenger. Lythian waited, half an ear on the sounds of the
nen. He could hear the hooves of their horses thundering, the
r blades being drawn. He did not turn nor glance at them.
on his foe.

ounced the attack came quickly, but Lythian Lindar, Knight
ready. Ducking beneath the fellwolf's slashing claws, he
ıys slippery as fog, and swung. The godsteel dagger came
fur and skin and flesh and bone. An otherworldly shriek
the air and a long-clawed hand hit the mud.

reature was gone, blood gushing a trail from its severed limb.
aping, it fled into the gloom, howling and crashing through
it!" Sir Storos bellowed. "Sir Oswin, give chase. Do not let
ptain of the guard turned his horse to the wood and rushed
going with him. Sir Storos came abruptly to Lythian's side.
ian. Goodness, that was a fellwolf!"

he beast's front paw sat in a puddle of blood on the ground
ing to twitch even now. The claws were not so long as the
as the beast so deadly, but all the same, it was not of this
e. *All foul things come forth*, he thought. "We need to get these
Storos." Lythian turned to them. The women were holding
eath the wagons, though some had emerged now to stand
ering and looking on in horror. The men were pale and in
ns in their hands held tight, knuckles white. "You people.
aded?"

ı," said one of the men, a greybeard who must have been
He clutched a pitchfork between his weathered hands.
Scarlet Valley was dangerous to cross, but…but we had no
ı was burned five days ago. We thought…we thought
e safer."

toros said. *If you can get in through the gates*, he didn't. "We
dhelm also, friend. I am Sir Storos, fourth son of Lord
he Helm. Your saviour here is Captain Lythian Lindar,

soon, though not yet. *Amron will understand*, he told himself, *and Elyon. They
will understand why I stayed. They will understand what I was trying to do.*

Sir Storos's eyes were on him, though. "You must have seen a great deal
of the dragons during your time in the south, Lythian. How were they, up
close?"

Terrifying, beautiful, alluring, magnificent. "As you see them, Storos. They
have a grace to them, yes, but they are brutal creatures."

"Are they as smart as people say?"

"Smart? Yes. They have an intelligence of their own."

Sir Storos nodded, contemplating. "These hunters who found you south
of here. I'm told they were hunting a drovara. You came upon a dead bear,
is that so?"

"We did. The injuries and tracks we found were consistent with the
drovara, though it's possible I was wrong." He looked at Sir Storos. "Have
you had word from them?" He was interested to know if his instinct on that
had been correct.

"From them, no. Dead men do not speak, after all."

Lythian frowned. "They're dead?"

Sir Storos took a deep breath and nodded. "Yes. All of them. Sir
Clarence sent some of his own men to shadow them. 'To make sure they
were safe', he told me, though I rather think he wanted to claim the creature's carcass for himself. Many a wealthy lord would pay a princely sum to
have a drovara's head above his hearth. Well, Clarence clearly thought he
could let the hunters do the hard work, before swooping in and taking the
kill. In the end he claimed nothing but a pile of dead bodies and severed
limbs."

Lythian wasn't in the least bit surprised. Bitter though he was at the
hunters for taking Pagaloth's blade, he had not wished them such an ill fate.
And no doubt Sir Clarence has claimed that fine dragonsteel sword now. That annoyed
him tremendously. "Monster hunting is a dangerous business," he said.

"*Life* is a dangerous business these days. And the terrors aren't just
coming from the skies. A *drovara*, Lythian." Storos shook his head. "I'd
sooner fight a dragon, one of these smaller ones at least. We're bred on
that, duelling drakes, but a drovara? And that's not the only foul creature
I've heard tell of. Only a few days ago a messenger came reporting a *grulok*
roaming the high hills of the South Downs, only fifty or so miles west of
Redhelm. My brother Alrus has sent out men to find it, but still… these are
strange times, truly."

"A grulok?" Pagaloth asked, cantering quietly alongside them. "What is
this creature?"

"A brutish beast of rock and stone," Storos said. "A soldier of Vandar
during the early days of the War of the Gods. It is said that when Vandar
fell, the few gruloks who remained in his service laid down where they
stood, to fall into a deep unbroken sleep. How many there were, no one
knows. Five, ten, twenty, a hundred? Any large boulder or mound of rock
might be one. I had always thought this a myth to tell our children, a game
we would play with them when we went out on walks. 'Don't go too close to

that rock, young one, it might be a sleeping grulok,' we would say. But it seems the myth was true all along. A world of monsters is awakening."

But which side will they fight on, or will they take a side at all? Storos was not wrong about the grulok, an early form of man, though much larger and more intimately connected to the earth Vandar carved them from. In those days, long before the form of man had been perfected, there were many strange variants that took shape from the natural world. Creatures of rock and wood and sand and soil, all in different sizes and shapes. As the millennia passed, the gods improved their designs, creating beasts with teeth and claws and wings and fur, and then men came along, blessed with the ability to wield weapons, to shape the world themselves in the image of their masters. As time went by, the gods stepped back, to let their favourite sons and daughters do their bidding. Blessed with the gifts the gods had given them, the Five Followers emerged from the chaos of the War Eternal to begin the dominion of men. The beasts and monsters that had once served their masters were driven back to the shadows, hunted, forgotten. *Until now*, Lythian thought. *Until now, during this Last Renewal, as they come forth once more…*

Noon came and went, the company stopping only to water their horses at a stream and pass around some hard bread and cheese for eating. Pagaloth was given his ration grudgingly, though took what he was given with good grace. "You will have to excuse my men," Sir Storos said. "They have been on a strict ration at Southwatch, to better preserve our stores. There is a worry that hunger will become a great enemy in the coming months. Much of the farmland in these parts has been razed and the harvests lost. And that is to say nothing of the livestock. Every day we hear new reports of them being taken off by dragons, and the bears and wolves in the region have grown bold as well. There are just so few people here now to defend the herds. Many farmers have driven their cattle to the cities, in the hope of housing them closer to the defences, yet that causes problems of its own. Others have simply butchered their beasts to be salted and cured for storage, but that meat will spoil eventually. Even for those who do not fall to battle, harsh times lie ahead. *Desperate* times, Lythian. And they're sure to get more desperate still."

The man's words were well illustrated over the following hours as they rode past blackened fields that once bore wheat and barley. Across the lands crossed vast tracks of scorched earth where the dragons had belched their flame. Carrion crows settled in swarms over dead animals, picking at whatever meat they could find. The stink was overpowering, of smoke and ash and death, the air suffused with a haunting gloom through which they could not see. Visibility became so poor at times that Lythian could no longer see the front of the column.

"Stay close," Sir Storos commanded his men. "And listen for movement. The dragons may not be done." He turned to Lythian and Pagaloth. "This was the Scarlet Valley," he said. "The breadbasket of South Vandar. The soil here was always so rich it looked almost red in the right light. Now

men are coming to call it the *Black Valley*. T
again."

They continued through the ashen fog,
stink and the smoke. Wine was produced h
covering the valley slopes to the west. It
southern continent, but in the north it wa
Borrus will not be happy, he thought. Even
made him smile. *The Lord of the Riverland*
Vandar. He wondered what Borrus would
death. He wondered where he was, and
indeed that was true. *Much is amiss here, tho*
light was named Amron and Elyon Dacc
their champions. They could not have chosen bett

"Stop. Quiet. I hear something." Sir
blade. The company halted about h
Ahead." Lythian gripped the dagger l
silence came the sound of screaming, sc
"Come, quickly!" Sir Storos put his hee
into the gloom.

The screaming grew louder, sepa
Lythian heard. All were women, but
and the shrieking of young children.
deep and dreaded, rumbling through t

The fog grew less dense as they
border town in ruin, through more f
low stone wall, to right a small woo
the sky like the meatless bones of sea
that ran between them as figures an
wagons had stopped on the track
beneath them, as men fought off s
and scythes and hoes sharpened to s
dinted blade. Lythian saw that two
for their families.

He leapt from his horse, insti
with his godsteel dagger to hand
narrowing his focus on the beas
enough.

Fellwolf, he thought.

It was an older form, much
thicker fur and a more flattene
savage, cluttered fangs. Standing
its forelimbs, giving out an eerie
tearing out his throat. A woman
spear, catching the fellwolf in th
as the woman dove backward,
from its other side. The steel bi
seeping up through its long ra

free, but to
stood uprig

"Back!"
forward to
men were
creature and
Look at me!

The fell
less and em
Lythian cou
A mistake o
leave to crea
horrify. And p
and gangly a

The crea
powerful cha
approaching
scrape of the
His eyes were

When it p
of Mists, was
stepped sidew
down, cutting
ripped throug

Then the c
Twisting and l
the trees. "Afte
it flee!" The ca
forth, his men
"A fellwolf, Lyth

"I know." T
at his feet, seem
drovara's, nor w
place or this tim
people to safety,
the children ben
beside them, shiv
shock, the weapo
Where are you he

"R…Redhel
long past sixty.
"We'd heard the
choice. Our farn
Redhelm would b

"It will," Sir S
are heading to R
Porus Pentar of t

famed Knight of the Vale, returned at last from the south. We shall escort you to the city."

"My thanks…oh, my thanks…" The old man dropped to his knees. "We have lost so much…so many have fallen…"

"None more will follow," Sir Storos said. "You have our promise in that."

It was small solace, though without their arrival, the entire group would surely have died. As the children and women crawled from beneath the wagons, the sound of wailing redoubled. The two dead men were surrounded, one small child clutching at the forester's headless corpse and refusing to let go.

"Her father," the old greybeard said softly. "My…my son." The other dead man had been a father of two others, and a husband and a brother and a son as well. "We're family, all of us. Dairy farmers and foresters, from near the coast."

"Why did you not leave before?" Sir Storos asked him, as sensitively as he could. "The coast has been ravaged."

"Hope," the elder answered. "And folly, that too."

The dead men were loaded onto the wagons, Pagaloth helping despite his limp. When one of the women sighted him she screamed and pointed and backed away. "Agarathi! He's…he's a dragonkin!"

"He's with me," Lythian assured her. He raised his voice to address the group. "This man is friend to us and a guest in these lands. Do not bear him ill will for his ancestry. He is bound to me by oath."

The farmers and foresters seemed too stricken by grief and horror to give much more thought to Pagaloth's presence. Dragons had besieged them, yes, and driven them from their lands, but the fellwolf was no creature of the south. *It was made to protect these lands, once,* Lythian thought, *long before the age of man. Now it turns against us. What are the people meant to make of that?*

By the time the dead had been loaded, the horses came galloping back through the trees in a cloud of kicked-up ash. Sir Oswin Cole led them, giving a shake of the head as he dismounted. "It escaped, my lord," he told Sir Storos. "We tried to follow its tracks, but we lost it in the gloom. I decided it best we turn back, lest we lose our way. With luck it will bleed out from the stump and perish in due course."

"I see." Sir Storos did not seem entirely satisfied, though Lythian judged the course correct.

"You made the right decision, Sir Oswin," he said. "Without its right arm it will be severely weakened, even should it survive."

Sir Storos rubbed his chin. "I ought to have gone myself. I do not like the idea of a fellwolf roaming these lands, armless or no."

"It would likely have escaped evasion, even had you given chase," Lythian said to him. "The fellwolf can outrun a horse even on a straight road; over rocks and roots it is even more capable. And chasing in this ashen gloom carries risk."

"Risks that other unwary travellers will now have to face." Sir Storos

Pentar sighed. "I shall have hunters sent from Redhelm to make sure it is slain. Else we will track it ourselves on our return journey." He nodded at the decision made. "Let us get these poor people back on the road. They will slow us, but we have no choice but to accompany them."

They camped that night on a wooded plain surrounded by a ring of fire, long hours from the Scarlet Valley and the horrors they'd left behind. Sir Storos set a watch to guard them, should some foul creature come upon them in the dark. "What curse is this, that we must watch our own lands for dangers, and not only the skies?" he bemoaned. "These lands were once of peace and plenty, rich in crop and song. Now the first children of our own gods assail us, as well as those of the enemy."

The gods don't care, Lythian thought. *They were cruel and capricious and cared not for the value of life and death. War was their game, and the monsters their pawns, and only once man was made did some semblance of a soul appear.* The world they lived in now was of the demigods' making. Varin, Eldur, Ilith, Thala and Lumo; the Five Followers. They were the bridge, the turning of the tide, and from them sprouted all the goodness in the world, art and culture and love and music, great cities and kingdoms raised during times of peace. Yet always the shadow of the gods lingered, always the shadow of war.

Lythian stared out past the ring of fire, into the darkness beyond. "The gods *are* war, Storos," he said, recalling what the scholar Sotel Dar had once told him. "Ours, theirs, all of them. And never did they care about us."

soon, though not yet. *Amron will understand,* he told himself, *and Elyon. They will understand why I stayed. They will understand what I was trying to do.*

Sir Storos's eyes were on him, though. "You must have seen a great deal of the dragons during your time in the south, Lythian. How were they, up close?"

Terrifying, beautiful, alluring, magnificent. "As you see them, Storos. They have a grace to them, yes, but they are brutal creatures."

"Are they as smart as people say?"

"Smart? Yes. They have an intelligence of their own."

Sir Storos nodded, contemplating. "These hunters who found you south of here. I'm told they were hunting a drovara. You came upon a dead bear, is that so?"

"We did. The injuries and tracks we found were consistent with the drovara, though it's possible I was wrong." He looked at Sir Storos. "Have you had word from them?" He was interested to know if his instinct on that had been correct.

"From them, no. Dead men do not speak, after all."

Lythian frowned. "They're dead?"

Sir Storos took a deep breath and nodded. "Yes. All of them. Sir Clarence sent some of his own men to shadow them. 'To make sure they were safe', he told me, though I rather think he wanted to claim the creature's carcass for himself. Many a wealthy lord would pay a princely sum to have a drovara's head above his hearth. Well, Clarence clearly thought he could let the hunters do the hard work, before swooping in and taking the kill. In the end he claimed nothing but a pile of dead bodies and severed limbs."

Lythian wasn't in the least bit surprised. Bitter though he was at the hunters for taking Pagaloth's blade, he had not wished them such an ill fate. *And no doubt Sir Clarence has claimed that fine dragonsteel sword now.* That annoyed him tremendously. "Monster hunting is a dangerous business," he said.

"*Life* is a dangerous business these days. And the terrors aren't just coming from the skies. A *drovara,* Lythian." Storos shook his head. "I'd sooner fight a dragon, one of these smaller ones at least. We're bred on that, duelling drakes, but a drovara? And that's not the only foul creature I've heard tell of. Only a few days ago a messenger came reporting a *grulok* roaming the high hills of the South Downs, only fifty or so miles west of Redhelm. My brother Alrus has sent out men to find it, but still… these are strange times, truly."

"A grulok?" Pagaloth asked, cantering quietly alongside them. "What is this creature?"

"A brutish beast of rock and stone," Storos said. "A soldier of Vandar during the early days of the War of the Gods. It is said that when Vandar fell, the few gruloks who remained in his service laid down where they stood, to fall into a deep unbroken sleep. How many there were, no one knows. Five, ten, twenty, a hundred? Any large boulder or mound of rock might be one. I had always thought this a myth to tell our children, a game we would play with them when we went out on walks. 'Don't go too close to that rock, young one, it might be a sleeping grulok,' we would say. But it seems the myth was true all along. A world of monsters is awakening."

But which side will they fight on, or will they take a side at all? Storos was not wrong about the grulok, an early form of man, though much larger and more intimately connected to the earth Vandar carved them from. In those days, long before the form of man had been perfected, there were many strange variants that took shape from the natural world. Creatures of rock and wood and sand and soil, all in different sizes and shapes. As the millennia passed, the gods improved their designs, creating beasts with teeth and claws and wings and fur, and then men came along, blessed with the ability to wield weapons, to shape the world themselves in the image of their masters. As time went by, the gods stepped back, to let their favourite sons and daughters do their bidding. Blessed with the gifts the gods had given them, the Five Followers emerged from the chaos of the War Eternal to begin the dominion of men. The beasts and monsters that had once served their masters were driven back to the shadows, hunted, forgotten. *Until now,* Lythian thought. *Until now, during this Last Renewal, as they come forth once more…*

Noon came and went, the company stopping only to water their horses at a stream and pass around some hard bread and cheese for eating. Pagaloth was given his ration grudgingly, though took what he was given with good grace. "You will have to excuse my men," Sir Storos said. "They have been on a strict ration at Southwatch, to better preserve our stores. There is a worry that hunger will become a great enemy in the coming months. Much of the farmland in these parts has been razed and the harvests lost. And that is to say nothing of the livestock. Every day we hear new reports of them being taken off by dragons, and the bears and wolves in the region have grown bold as well. There are just so few people here now to defend the herds. Many farmers have driven their cattle to the cities, in the hope of housing them closer to the defences, yet that causes problems of its own. Others have simply butchered their beasts to be salted and cured for storage, but that meat will spoil eventually. Even for those who do not fall to battle, harsh times lie ahead. *Desperate* times, Lythian. And they're sure to get more desperate still."

The man's words were well illustrated over the following hours as they rode past blackened fields that once bore wheat and barley. Across the lands crossed vast tracks of scorched earth where the dragons had belched their flame. Carrion crows settled in swarms over dead animals, picking at whatever meat they could find. The stink was overpowering, of smoke and ash and death, the air suffused with a haunting gloom through which they could not see. Visibility became so poor at times that Lythian could no longer see the front of the column.

"Stay close," Sir Storos commanded his men. "And listen for movement. The dragons may not be done." He turned to Lythian and Pagaloth. "This was the Scarlet Valley," he said. "The breadbasket of South Vandar. The soil here was always so rich it looked almost red in the right light. Now men are coming to call it the *Black Valley*. These lands may never be tilled again."

They continued through the ashen fog, shielding their mouths from the stink and the smoke. Wine was produced here too, Lythian knew, vineyards covering the valley slopes to the west. It did not match the wines of the southern continent, but in the north it was the best they had. Now gone. *Borrus will not be happy*, he thought. Even thinking of his overlarge friend made him smile. *The Lord of the Riverlands, one of the most powerful men in Vandar.* He wondered what Borrus would make of this news of his father's death. He wondered where he was, and why he'd gone so far north, if indeed that was true. *Much is amiss here, though in the darkness, there is light.* That light was named Amron and Elyon Daecar. *The Five Blades come forth to choose their champions. They could not have chosen better...*

"Stop. Quiet. I hear something." Sir Storos Pentar had his hand on his blade. The company halted about him, eyes craning skyward. "No. Ahead." Lythian gripped the dagger he'd been given, and through the silence came the sound of screaming, some way distant up the valley slope. "Come, quickly!" Sir Storos put his heels into his horse and galloped away into the gloom.

The screaming grew louder, separating. One voice, two, five voices Lythian heard. All were women, but he heard the shouting of men also, and the shrieking of young children. Among all that was a growling sound, deep and dreaded, rumbling through the air. *A wolf? A bear? No, larger...*

The fog grew less dense as they rode hard up the valley slope, past a border town in ruin, through more fields of charred wheat. To left was a low stone wall, to right a small wood with spindly black trees reaching to the sky like the meatless bones of seared fingers. They charged up the road that ran between them as figures and shapes materialised ahead. A pair of wagons had stopped on the track. Children and old women huddled beneath them, as men fought off some foul shaggy fiend with pitchforks and scythes and hoes sharpened to spears. One held a wood-axe, another a dinted blade. Lythian saw that two of the defenders were women, fighting for their families.

He leapt from his horse, instinct striking forth. Taking flight on foot with his godsteel dagger to hand he surged forward past the company, narrowing his focus on the beast. A wolf fell short, though was close enough.

Fellwolf, he thought.

It was an older form, much larger than a common wolf, with longer thicker fur and a more flattened, humanoid face, large black eyes and savage, cluttered fangs. Standing on its crooked hind legs it slashed out with its forelimbs, giving out an eerie howl as it caught a man across the neck, tearing out his throat. A woman screamed and drove forward with her hoe-spear, catching the fellwolf in the flank. It howled again and slashed again as the woman dove backward, just as the man with the axe swung down from its other side. The steel bit into the meat of the monster's leg, blood seeping up through its long ragged fur. The forester tried to pull the axe free, but too late. Jaws came down upon his head and when the fellwolf stood upright, the headless man fell.

"Back!" Lythian was roaring. "Back, behind the wagons!" He surged forward to engage. Behind him now, Sir Storos was blaring orders and his men were charging on. Lythian did not wait for them. He slid before the creature and took position in Strikeform stance. "Look at me, foul creature! Look at me!" he roared.

The fellwolf looked at him with round black eyes, lightless and pupilless and empty. Its face was half man, half wolf, more disturbing than Lythian could say. *A mistake*, he thought. That's what the histories said of it. A mistake of Dhatar's creation, the battle god whom Vandar had given leave to create his own minions. *He had no flair for it, lest his intention be to horrify*. And perhaps it was, because this thing was a nightmare, long-limbed and gangly and *wrong*.

The creature moved oddly, cocking its head like a bird, sensing a more powerful challenger. Lythian waited, half an ear on the sounds of the approaching men. He could hear the hooves of their horses thundering, the scrape of their blades being drawn. He did not turn nor glance at them. His eyes were on his foe.

When it pounced the attack came quickly, but Lythian Lindar, Knight of Mists, was ready. Ducking beneath the fellwolf's slashing claws, he stepped sideways slippery as fog, and swung. The godsteel dagger came down, cutting fur and skin and flesh and bone. An otherworldly shriek ripped through the air and a long-clawed hand hit the mud.

Then the creature was gone, blood gushing a trail from its severed limb. Twisting and leaping, it fled into the gloom, howling and crashing through the trees. "After it!" Sir Storos bellowed. "Sir Oswin, give chase. Do not let it flee!" The captain of the guard turned his horse to the wood and rushed forth, his men going with him. Sir Storos came abruptly to Lythian's side. "A fellwolf, Lythian. Goodness, that was a fellwolf!"

"I know." The beast's front paw sat in a puddle of blood on the ground at his feet, seeming to twitch even now. The claws were not so long as the drovara's, nor was the beast so deadly, but all the same, it was not of this place or this time. *All foul things come forth*, he thought. "We need to get these people to safety, Storos." Lythian turned to them. The women were holding the children beneath the wagons, though some had emerged now to stand beside them, shivering and looking on in horror. The men were pale and in shock, the weapons in their hands held tight, knuckles white. "You people. Where are you headed?"

"R...Redhelm," said one of the men, a greybeard who must have been long past sixty. He clutched a pitchfork between his weathered hands. "We'd heard the Scarlet Valley was dangerous to cross, but...but we had no choice. Our farm was burned five days ago. We thought...we thought Redhelm would be safer."

"It will," Sir Storos said. *If you can get in through the gates*, he didn't. "We are heading to Redhelm also, friend. I am Sir Storos, fourth son of Lord Porus Pentar of the Helm. Your saviour here is Captain Lythian Lindar, he complained. Amron had spotted that as well. Dalton's cloak was blue, yes, but more gloomy. A Taynar cloak, held by a silver brooch wrought in the Taynar house sigil. "He *should* be wearing his Varin cloak," Botley went on, as though personally aggrieved. "Is he the First Blade of Vandar, or is he not? This is an insult to the order. An insult, I say."

"Unintentional, I'm sure." Amron had worn his Varin cloak in a bid to cast aside house allegiance, as was his aim, but it seemed Dalton Taynar hadn't got the crow.

"You say unintentional, my lord. I see leave off the 'un'. The Taynars have always been petty and peevish. He's done this on purpose, oh I'm certain of that."

"You're not meant to take sides, Lord Harrow," Amron reminded him. "Your allegiance is to the crown, not any one house." It had been decreed as such by King Haldar the Heedful ever since the castle and Vanguard were raised. The Castellans of Crosswater and Lords Protector of the Vanguard were sworn by oath to stay out of house squabbles and answer only to the king.

Lord Harrow nodded. "I'm aware, my lord. That's why I show allegiance to *you*."

Amron sighed. "I am not king, Botley. I have explained that to you already."

"And *he* is?" The Lord Protector peered across the docks at Dalton. "He of the flesh of that traitor Godrik, who won his crown through perfidy and sin? All good upstanding men of this realm know the truth of that now, my lord, and if they don't, they soon will with these Greycloak confessions. *You* are King Ellis's legal heir and ruled in his stead for twenty years. You rule still, as far as I'm concerned."

Amron shook his head. "Birds are swifter than boats, I suppose," he murmured.

Lord Botley Harrow did not get his meaning. "My lord?"

"I take it my good sister Amara has been writing you?" The woman had friends spread far and wide and the Lady Horsia Harrow was one of them. "Or your wife?"

"My wife…well, I couldn't say. I do not read her correspondence. Though it's true she favours you greatly over these Taynars. How could she not? All good upstanding men of the realm, I say. Well let me include the women in that as well, and the old and infirm and the children too, and let's throw in the hogs and hounds and horses, why not? Anyone with a shred of decency and honour knows well enough what has been going on of late." He stopped, seeing Sir Dalton and his highborn host approach. "Well, I've said my piece. I'll try to hold my tongue, my lord. I know you're not here to stir trouble."

No, to cast it out, Amron thought, *and heal this bloody kingdom.*

A bank of grey cloud rolled overhead as Amron awaited the First Blade of Vandar and his men, blotting out the mid-afternoon sun. A chill deepened in the air, the winds picking up, the sails and banners upon the castle

Amron

The fleet had a ragged weary look to it, moving ponderously upriver under sail and oar and rope pulled by horses along the banks. Some were listing and showing wounds, some had sails singed and burned, others looked like they might just sink entirely if only they should stop moving. Banners flew from their masts and poles, but even those looked listless.

Perhaps that's just the Taynar colours, Amron Daecar thought. They'd chosen blue and grey for their house raiment, the same colours of the kingdom, yet hardly the same shade. Where Vandar's banners flapped in bright silver and rich royal blue, those of the Taynars were as dull, dour and dreary as half the men of their house.

One such man stood at Amron's side, though Taynar was not in his name. "They look in need of a long rest," Rogen Strand remarked, whose lady mother had been Margery Taynar, sister of the erstwhile and short-lived king, Godrik. Lady Margery died the day Rogen was born, and the world was better for the exchange. He wore the dark grey godsteel armour that Amron had gifted him and was starting to wear it well. Though stained and scratched it suited him, overlaid with a rough black woollen cloak to beat off the spring chill. Through dark eyes he surveyed the incoming host. "I suppose that will be my cousin's flagship."

Whitebeard was looking toward the great four-masted, three-decked galleon that lumbered along at the head of the fleet. It was a heavy vessel, wide and bulky and could house several hundred men. Amron squinted, but could not see the First Blade on deck, neither to bow nor stern. Still, he knew the ship and he knew the name. "*The Iron Champion*," he said. "Yes, that's Dalton's."

Behind the Iron Champion the fleet followed, a hundred mainsails strong. *Or weak.* Much of Dalton's host had been destroyed when they were driven from the Trident, and some others had remained at King's Point to help guard the coast. The rest were retreating to the great river harbour of Crosswater for tending and restoration.

Some were massive galleons like the Iron Champion, others smaller many-oared galleys, sleek and swift. There were low-slung dromonds and tall strong carracks and many cogs with single sails. Those sails were not only in the Taynar colours. Their lesser allies were with them, as they'd been at the Trident. Cargills and Strands, Flints and Porters, Sharps and Stones, and many middling and minor houses beneath them. Lord Penrith Oloran had sent a force to fight beside Sir Dalton's host as well, though the crotchety old Lord of Elinar would never call an Oloran lesser than a Taynar. Nay, both were among the Vandarian greathouses, alongside Daecar, Amadar, Kanabar, Pentar, and Reynar, though the last of those was fading. Above them stood only the holy House of Varin, a line broken since the fall of King Lorin forty years past.

The fleet was approaching the *Vanguard*, the great fortified river gate that barred the way to the castle. It spanned the entire Steelrun River, a massive wall a dozen feet thick and a hundred feet high, with space for a thousand bowmen to stand atop it and rain arrows upon an invading fleet. The wall walk had a thick parapet and covering roof to protect the archers against dragons, and high above it at the heart of the river loomed a great statue of Varin, perched upon a rocky islet, with many interior levels and murderholes and windows through which the bowmen could fire. Upon the riverbanks to east and west were two more statue-towers; Elin and Iliva, Varin's firstborn son and daughter who fought with him against Drulgar the Dread, the Great Calamity of an age long gone.

All had been raised by King Haldar the Heedful, who had built too the fortresses of Northwatch and Eastwatch to help secure Vandar's borders a thousand years ago. History said Haldar was as close to King Bayrith of Tukor as Varin had been to Ilith. *Bayrith lent Haldar the use of his finest Forge-born*, Amron recalled, *masons and builders to work rock and stone*. They lacked much of Ilith's magic, but not his fondness for scale. Amron smiled as he gazed out from the high castle walls of Crosswater. Ever did he like to look upon the mighty Vanguard, and think of those days of old.

Across the harbour below, a great groaning gave out as the river gate was raised. Though massive itself it looked small within the Vanguard. Huge lengths of iron chain rattled as they rose from the water, green and rusted and slimy with weeds, and the steel gate lifted with them, to permit Sir Dalton and his fleet to pass.

"Should we not descend to greet them, my lord?" asked Lord Botley Harrow, the *Castellan of Crosswater* and *Lord Protector of the Vanguard*. He'd held the post for many long years, taking it from his father at his death during the war. Long had the Harrows defended Crosswater and the Vanguard. *And long may they still*, Amron thought.

He nodded and they started down.

The Frostblade rested at his hip, misting mystically as he walked. Amron Daecar had elected to wear the colours of his order and not his house today, though like the Taynars they were much the same, silver and blue though of different hues, brighter and more hopeful. Across his broad shoulders hung his Varin cloak, rich blue, with the kingdom's coat of arms

on the back. Beneath, his interlinking suit of lobstered godsteel plate misted softly, confidently, as fine a suit of armour as you could hope to find anywhere in the north, silvery gold with a band of royal blue bordering the breastplate. Hand resting on the pommel of the Frostblade, he felt complete. His ails were gone, the pain in his shoulder and thigh erased. He walked upright and tall, his stride powerful as it had always been. The men of Crosswater bowed as he passed, or closed their fists in salute. Many smiled and looked up, for Amron Daecar was a tall man at six and a half feet, with a little change. *But still…*

There was always that *but*, brewing in the back of his mind. Take his hand off the Frostblade's pommel and his blood-bond would be severed, and the blade's healing power with it. His limp would return, his shoulder would throb, and he would become that shambling creature again, looked upon with pity for the shadow he'd become.

But not yet, he told himself, as he did each day and night. *I will give it up… but not yet.*

They reached the river harbour below the high castle walls, as the ships came swarming in to dock at its many wharves, or sit at anchor further off lowering rowboats to bring the soldiers and sailors to port. Walter Selle withdrew his great book of notes and scribbles and at once started addi to its pages, documenting the day. Whitebeard moved his eyes around high walls and the skies beyond, ever wary. He had been like that for last two weeks, constantly searching the skies for threats whether they on deck or horseback or high up on the castle walls.

"Your man is vigilant," Lord Harrow noted. He was a heavy-jawed jowly man, Harrow, with a thick bull's chest and tree trunks for legs, th not tall. Much the opposite of Rogen Whitebeard, who stood almo height with Amron, spare and lean and grim. "He reminds me som of Captain Lythian, trailing you everywhere, my lord. Not in look, but in prudence and preparedness. The Knight of Mists never did rest in his search for danger."

Amron smiled to think of the man. He missed Lythian dearly. lacks Lythian's humour, though is learning," he said. "He has be lessons from Walter here."

Harrow's broad jaw broadened further. "A funny fellow indee had kept them most amused during the days they'd spent here Dalton's fleet. "He is a good man for a feast. A drinker and r always welcome at my table."

From the decks of the Iron Champion, Sir Dalton Tayna now, moving stiffly down the gangplanks in his sleek suit of si Harrow frowned as he watched him gather with his captain pions on the docks; Sir Brontus Oloran, Sir Taegon Cargi approached from great galleons of their own, and his heir an Rodmond, who had sailed with him. Amron saw Sir Quinn and Sir Ramsey Stone, and Sir Marcus Flint, all Varin Kn once served beneath him. *No longer.*

Lord Botley Harrow gave a grunt. "He isn't wearing h

15

Amron

The fleet had a ragged weary look to it, moving ponderously upriver under sail and oar and rope pulled by horses along the banks. Some were listing and showing wounds, some had sails singed and burned, others looked like they might just sink entirely if only they should stop moving. Banners flew from their masts and poles, but even those looked listless.

Perhaps that's just the Taynar colours, Amron Daecar thought. They'd chosen blue and grey for their house raiment, the same colours of the kingdom, yet hardly the same shade. Where Vandar's banners flapped in bright silver and rich royal blue, those of the Taynars were as dull, dour and dreary as half the men of their house.

One such man stood at Amron's side, though Taynar was not in his name. "They look in need of a long rest," Rogen Strand remarked, whose lady mother had been Margery Taynar, sister of the erstwhile and short-lived king, Godrik. Lady Margery died the day Rogen was born, and the world was better for the exchange. He wore the dark grey godsteel armour that Amron had gifted him and was starting to wear it well. Though stained and scratched it suited him, overlaid with a rough black woollen cloak to beat off the spring chill. Through dark eyes he surveyed the incoming host. "I suppose that will be my cousin's flagship."

Whitebeard was looking toward the great four-masted, three-decked galleon that lumbered along at the head of the fleet. It was a heavy vessel, wide and bulky and could house several hundred men. Amron squinted, but could not see the First Blade on deck, neither to bow nor stern. Still, he knew the ship and he knew the name. *"The Iron Champion,"* he said. "Yes, that's Dalton's."

Behind the Iron Champion the fleet followed, a hundred mainsails strong. *Or weak.* Much of Dalton's host had been destroyed when they were driven from the Trident, and some others had remained at King's Point to help guard the coast. The rest were retreating to the great river harbour of Crosswater for tending and restoration.

Some were massive galleons like the Iron Champion, others smaller many-oared galleys, sleek and swift. There were low-slung dromonds and tall strong carracks and many cogs with single sails. Those sails were not only in the Taynar colours. Their lesser allies were with them, as they'd been at the Trident. Cargills and Strands, Flints and Porters, Sharps and Stones, and many middling and minor houses beneath them. Lord Penrith Oloran had sent a force to fight beside Sir Dalton's host as well, though the crotchety old Lord of Elinar would never call an Oloran lesser than a Taynar. Nay, both were among the Vandarian greathouses, alongside Daecar, Amadar, Kanabar, Pentar, and Reynar, though the last of those was fading. Above them stood only the holy House of Varin, a line broken since the fall of King Lorin forty years past.

The fleet was approaching the *Vanguard*, the great fortified river gate that barred the way to the castle. It spanned the entire Steelrun River, a massive wall a dozen feet thick and a hundred feet high, with space for a thousand bowmen to stand atop it and rain arrows upon an invading fleet. The wall walk had a thick parapet and covering roof to protect the archers against dragons, and high above it at the heart of the river loomed a great statue of Varin, perched upon a rocky islet, with many interior levels and murderholes and windows through which the bowmen could fire. Upon the riverbanks to east and west were two more statue-towers; Elin and Iliva, Varin's firstborn son and daughter who fought with him against Drulgar the Dread, the Great Calamity of an age long gone.

All had been raised by King Haldar the Heedful, who had built too the fortresses of Northwatch and Eastwatch to help secure Vandar's borders a thousand years ago. History said Haldar was as close to King Bayrith of Tukor as Varin had been to Ilith. *Bayrith lent Haldar the use of his finest Forge-born,* Amron recalled, *masons and builders to work rock and stone.* They lacked much of Ilith's magic, but not his fondness for scale. Amron smiled as he gazed out from the high castle walls of Crosswater. Ever did he like to look upon the mighty Vanguard, and think of those days of old.

Across the harbour below, a great groaning gave out as the river gate was raised. Though massive itself it looked small within the Vanguard. Huge lengths of iron chain rattled as they rose from the water, green and rusted and slimy with weeds, and the steel gate lifted with them, to permit Sir Dalton and his fleet to pass.

"Should we not descend to greet them, my lord?" asked Lord Botley Harrow, the *Castellan of Crosswater* and *Lord Protector of the Vanguard*. He'd held the post for many long years, taking it from his father at his death during the war. Long had the Harrows defended Crosswater and the Vanguard. *And long may they still,* Amron thought.

He nodded and they started down.

The Frostblade rested at his hip, misting mystically as he walked. Amron Daecar had elected to wear the colours of his order and not his house today, though like the Taynars they were much the same, silver and blue though of different hues, brighter and more hopeful. Across his broad shoulders hung his Varin cloak, rich blue, with the kingdom's coat of arms on the back. Beneath, his interlinking suit of lobstered godsteel plate misted softly, confidently, as fine a suit of armour as you could hope to find anywhere in the north, silvery gold with a band of royal blue bordering the breastplate. Hand resting on the pommel of the Frostblade, he felt complete. His ails were gone, the pain in his shoulder and thigh erased. He walked upright and tall, his stride powerful as it had always been. The men of Crosswater bowed as he passed, or closed their fists in salute. Many smiled and looked up, for Amron Daecar was a tall man at six and a half feet, with a little change. *But still…*

There was always that *but*, brewing in the back of his mind. Take his hand off the Frostblade's pommel and his blood-bond would be severed, and the blade's healing power with it. His limp would return, his shoulder would throb, and he would become that shambling creature again, looked upon with pity for the shadow he'd become.

But not yet, he told himself, as he did each day and night. *I will give it up… but not yet.*

They reached the river harbour below the high castle walls, as the ships came swarming in to dock at its many wharves, or sit at anchor further off, lowering rowboats to bring the soldiers and sailors to port. Walter Selleck withdrew his great book of notes and scribbles and at once started adding to its pages, documenting the day. Whitebeard moved his eyes around the high walls and the skies beyond, ever wary. He had been like that for the last two weeks, constantly searching the skies for threats whether they were on deck or horseback or high up on the castle walls.

"Your man is vigilant," Lord Harrow noted. He was a heavy-jawed and jowly man, Harrow, with a thick bull's chest and tree trunks for legs, though not tall. Much the opposite of Rogen Whitebeard, who stood almost at a height with Amron, spare and lean and grim. "He reminds me somewhat of Captain Lythian, trailing you everywhere, my lord. Not in look, per se, but in prudence and preparedness. The Knight of Mists never did seem to rest in his search for danger."

Amron smiled to think of the man. He missed Lythian dearly. "Rogen lacks Lythian's humour, though is learning," he said. "He has been taking lessons from Walter here."

Harrow's broad jaw broadened further. "A funny fellow indeed." Walter had kept them most amused during the days they'd spent here, awaiting Dalton's fleet. "He is a good man for a feast. A drinker and raconteur is always welcome at my table."

From the decks of the Iron Champion, Sir Dalton Taynar appeared now, moving stiffly down the gangplanks in his sleek suit of silver armour. Harrow frowned as he watched him gather with his captains and champions on the docks; Sir Brontus Oloran, Sir Taegon Cargill, who both approached from great galleons of their own, and his heir and nephew, Sir Rodmond, who had sailed with him. Amron saw Sir Quinn Sharp as well, and Sir Ramsey Stone, and Sir Marcus Flint, all Varin Knights who had once served beneath him. *No longer.*

Lord Botley Harrow gave a grunt. "He isn't wearing his Varin cloak," he complained. Amron had spotted that as well. Dalton's cloak was blue, yes, but more gloomy. A Taynar cloak, held by a silver brooch wrought in the Taynar house sigil. "He *should* be wearing his Varin cloak," Botley went on, as though personally aggrieved. "Is he the First Blade of Vandar, or is he not? This is an insult to the order. An insult, I say."

"Unintentional, I'm sure." Amron had worn his Varin cloak in a bid to cast aside house allegiance, as was his aim, but it seemed Dalton Taynar hadn't got the crow.

"You say unintentional, my lord. I see leave off the 'un'. The Taynars have always been petty and peevish. He's done this on purpose, oh I'm certain of that."

"You're not meant to take sides, Lord Harrow," Amron reminded him. "Your allegiance is to the crown, not any one house." It had been decreed as such by King Haldar the Heedful ever since the castle and Vanguard were raised. The Castellans of Crosswater and Lords Protector of the Vanguard were sworn by oath to stay out of house squabbles and answer only to the king.

Lord Harrow nodded. "I'm aware, my lord. That's why I show allegiance to *you*."

Amron sighed. "I am not king, Botley. I have explained that to you already."

"And *he* is?" The Lord Protector peered across the docks at Dalton. "He of the flesh of that traitor Godrik, who won his crown through perfidy and sin? All good upstanding men of this realm know the truth of that now, my lord, and if they don't, they soon will with these Greycloak confessions. *You* are King Ellis's legal heir and ruled in his stead for twenty years. You rule still, as far as I'm concerned."

Amron shook his head. "Birds are swifter than boats, I suppose," he murmured.

Lord Botley Harrow did not get his meaning. "My lord?"

"I take it my good sister Amara has been writing you?" The woman had friends spread far and wide and the Lady Horsia Harrow was one of them. "Or your wife?"

"My wife...well, I couldn't say. I do not read her correspondence. Though it's true she favours you greatly over these Taynars. How could she not? All good upstanding men of the realm, I say. Well let me include the women in that as well, and the old and infirm and the children too, and let's throw in the hogs and hounds and horses, why not? Anyone with a shred of decency and honour knows well enough what has been going on of late." He stopped, seeing Sir Dalton and his highborn host approach. "Well, I've said my piece. I'll try to hold my tongue, my lord. I know you're not here to stir trouble."

No, to cast it out, Amron thought, *and heal this bloody kingdom.*

A bank of grey cloud rolled overhead as Amron awaited the First Blade of Vandar and his men, blotting out the mid-afternoon sun. A chill deepened in the air, the winds picking up, the sails and banners upon the castle walls flapping noisily. Men watched on from the walls and towers and docks. Through the shade Sir Dalton came marching, chin raised, skin ghostly pale, jaw set. His eyes were two blue bruises, his cheeks dark sunken pits. *He looks older than last I saw him,* Amron thought. That had been a good long while ago, back during the Song of the First Blade in Varinar. Much had happened to Dalton Taynar since then, and little of it good.

To his left walked his nephew Rodmond, the only son of his younger brother Grayson who had perished of wounds suffered in the war. To his right came Sir Brontus Oloran, the cousin of Killian and Nathaniel, and a fine gifted swordsman, one of the best in all the north. Sir Taegon Cargill, the Giant of Hammerhall, marched loudly along, armour clanking. The man was monstrously large, surpassing seven feet with ease, all brawn and little brain as most of the Cargills were known for. The other Varin Knights came behind. *And all are wearing their cloaks still,* Amron didn't fail to miss. That was promising if nothing else.

"My lords," Amron called out, claiming the first word. "I am relieved to see your fleet arrive, at last. We have been waiting for you for some days."

"The winds were against us, Lord Daecar," said Dalton Taynar. His voice sounded older too, somehow, and glummer than ever. "We had to go slow for the weak and wounded. Many of our ships are in need of attention."

"I saw. Nothing a lick of paint will not address." Amron turned to the man's nephew. "How are you, Sir Rodmond? You look well. That's good. A man can be changed after his first taste of war, for better or for worse."

It was a courtesy. The young man did not look well, though no Taynar ever did. Still, Rodmond was the best of them in cheer. *A bright spark amid the Taynar gloom.* "If I got a taste, it was but a morsel, my lord." Rodmond Taynar bowed. "We spent most of our time camped outside the fortress walls…before the retreat."

"Most of war is waiting, Sir Rodmond. You'll learn that soon enough." Amron put his attention on Sir Brontus, and frowned. He noticed he wore a pin on his breast that seemed to denote a special rank. It was a blade, gold and long, casting a sunburst. "I do not recognise this badge, Sir Brontus. What does it signify, pray tell?"

"The Sword of Varinar," Dalton Taynar came in. "I have named Sir Brontus as First Blade of Vandar in my stead. The pin shows his rank, in lieu of the blade itself."

This was unexpected. Dalton was a fine knight, but Sir Brontus was the superior swordsman, and more liked, and would be the better choice to lead the Varin Knights. *Is this to appease Lord Oloran?* Amron wondered. *Or is something else going on here?* It smelled a bit off, either way. "Were you injured, Lord Dalton, at the Trident?" he inquired. "I confess you look in good health to me."

"My health is fine, Lord Daecar."

"Then why stand down as First Blade?"

"I cannot be First Blade."

"Why not?"

"Because he's king," lumbered the great witless voice of Sir Taegon Cargill. He crashed his gauntleted fist against his breastplate with an echoing clang. "The king is dead! Long live the king!"

A few others took up the call, though it soon faded at the look of displeasure on Amron's face. This was always likely to come up, but now was neither the time nor place to correct them so publicly. "*My lords,*" he declared loudly, to silence them. "We all have grievances that must be addressed, I'm sure. Let us stay our tongues until dinner. Lord Harrow is to host us in a private feast where we shall have a chance to give voice to our complaints."

"Why not here?" blustered Cargill. "Why not *now?*"

Amron ignored him. "Lord Harrow, see Lord Taynar and his host situated in their quarters. Each of you will have privy chambers," he told them. "The soldiers will find plenty of room on the banks of the river to camp."

"*Lord* Taynar? You mean *king*. King Taynar...he's king..."

Amron turned from them and marched away, leaving Sir Taegon to pick a fight with his back. Whitebeard and Walter followed as he crossed to the portcullis gate that gave access to the castle. Some of his men were awaiting him there; Sir Torus Stoutman, Vilmar the Black, Sir Ralf of Rotting Bridge, all men from Daecar lands who'd come rushing to lend Amron their support as soon as he'd reached Varinar. All were seasoned warriors, and none were young. Amron liked it that way. He wanted older men around him he could rely on and trust, and each had brought trusted men with them too, and some sons, and even grandsons as well, in the case of Sir Ralf.

"Looked awkward," Vilmar the Black said in his monotone growl. He was neither lord nor knight, but a warrior to his bones, a famed hunter who'd been known to brave the darkest and most dangerous lands in the north. 'The blackness calls to me,' he was fond of saying, so men had started putting it into his name. He had black hair too, long and wild, and a beard to match, and black hair on his forearms and sprouting from the top of his leather vest. "He's more beast than the monsters he hunts," Walter had said of him, and he wasn't far wrong. *A loyal beast, though.*

"It was expected, Vilmar," Amron said.

"Was it?" asked Sir Torus Stoutman with a quizzical grin. "Long live the king, hey? You expected *that?*" Sir Torus was half a dwarf, a tree-stump of a man as wide as he was tall, barely passing five feet tall. "We might get a chant of that going ourselves, boys. *King Amron,* aye, to drown out that great oaf Cargill. How about that?"

"I'd rather you didn't, Torus."

"As you please." Sir Torus smiled. He rarely didn't. "We invited to this dinner you're hosting, then?"

"Lord Harrow will be hosting it."

"Ha! You can split hairs too. Thought you had enough gifts."

Amron smiled, the jagged scar that ran down the right side of his face from temple to jaw turning deep and red. "You can attend, though I don't want it to descend into slurs and accusations. We're here to make peace."

"You needn't worry about us, not in that," promised Sir Ralf, a quiet-spoken man in his late sixties who'd been raised to knighthood by Amron's grandfather Balion, and served at his father Gideon's side during the war. "It would seem that they're the more likely to seek quarrel, my lord."

"And blood," grunted Vilmar. The huntsman fingered the godsteel axe that hung at his hip, one of many weapons he kept to hand. He was an armoury all unto himself, was Vilmar.

"No, there'll be no blood spilt here tonight." Amron was adamant in that. "The air just needs to be cleared, that is all. There was always likely to be tension at our first meeting."

He continued walking past the gate and into the castle, quite aware that they remained on show. Appearances were important and the entire realm was holding its breath on this. *No one wants quarrel*, he told himself. *We have far greater threats to face, and need not be facing one another.*

His private quarters gave view over the river to the south, a warmly furnished solar reserved for greatlords and kings and men of high renown. Amron spent the next two hours alone, looking over the rushing waters of the Steelrun and watching the men upon the docks below. He ruminated, wrote letters, mused on the fate of the world, then when the allotted time approached, changed into fine leathers and a warm wool doublet, threw on his Varin cloak, and descended through the castle with Whitebeard at his flank to see this business done.

Crosswater Castle was large enough to house two feast halls, one capacious and grand and quite able to fit a thousand, the second closer to a hundred, intended for more intimate gatherings. The *small hall* would be used tonight. When Amron entered through the iron-banded doors he found that only his own people had arrived. *More games*, he thought. *No doubt they intend to keep me waiting.* The hall was already filling with smoke, mostly due to Sir Torus Stoutman who kept a large rosewood pipe on his person at all times. He sat blowing rings, legs up on a long oakenwood table, a tankard of ale in his grasp. Vilmar the Black was with him, supping on some dark mead, as was Walter Selleck, regaling them of one of his many tales. Sir Ralf stood aside with Lord Harrow, the pair engaged in a private discussion, sipping wine.

"To your seats," Amron called, as he entered. The feast was to be had on a single table at the heart of the hall. Amron took his place in the middle, Sir Ralf to his right, Lord Botley Harrow to his left. The others fanned out either side of them, while Whitebeard stood sentry behind, seeking whatever shadows he could find.

Then the wait began.

A quarter-hour later, after a great deal of grumbling and grousing from his men, the sound of footsteps began echoing from beyond the doors. They opened with a groan and a herald stepped forward, garbed in Taynar blue and grey. He took stance before them, bowed and called out, "Dalton of House Taynar, *King of Vandar*, and his heir and nephew, the Crown Prince Rodmond Taynar."

Dalton entered, dressed in a fine grey lambswool doublet and muted blue mantle. Rodmond followed behind, looking reluctant. *This one wants no part of this*, Amron thought. *Well, he'll not have to suffer the title of prince much longer.*

"Sir Brontus of House Oloran," the herald cried. "First Blade of Vandar, and heir to Eversky. And Sir Taegon of House Cargill, the Giant of Hammerhall."

Brontus strode within, golden-haired like his cousin Killian, his Varin cloak flowing resplendently behind him. The Giant of Hammerhall came behind, stamping forth like a bull looking for something to charge, all snorts and empty swagger. After that, the herald introduced Sir Quinn Sharp, Sir Marcus Flint, and Sir Ramsey Stone, all in Varin blue, as well as Lords Barrow, Kindrick, Rosetree, and Lord Gavron Grave the Ironfoot. Several more followed in, minor lords and household knights whom Amron knew but little, each wearing the colours of their houses in a motley of surcoats, cloaks, and heavy mantles clasped with pins and brooches in silver, gold, ruby and onyx.

Lord Harrow gave a quiet huff. "Do you think they brought enough men? What is this petty oneupmanship? It was supposed to be a private feast."

Amron chose not to respond. "Welcome, my lords," he called, standing from the bench. "Please, come forward and join us."

Dalton Taynar was frowning as he looked upon the seating arrangement. "I had expected an elevated table, Lord Daecar," he said, looking confused. "This is highly irregular, to sit face-to-face."

"Barriers must be broken down, my lord. Please, do sit opposite me. The rest of you may sit where you like. There is plenty of space for you all."

Glances were exchanged, and a few mutters were shared, before Sir Rodmond strode forward to sit opposite Lord Harrow. Sir Brontus Oloran took his place in front of Sir Ralf of Rotting Bridge. Sir Taegon seemed most displeased with his placing. "And who are you?" he huffed, staring at the man opposite him. "You're no knight or lord."

"Alas no. I am a humble scribe, is all." Walter Selleck had his notebook on his lap, a quill pen to hand, and a large smile on his red-cheeked face. "I am tasked with documenting events, sir. Might I ask…well, I hope this is not too impertinent, but would it be all right if I were to draw your likeness, as we feast?"

The giant looked lost. "What is this farce? Where are your *proper* lords and knights, Lord Daecar? These…these are all mutts and mongrels."

"Mutts and mongrels," laughed Sir Torus Stoutman, sitting next to Walter. "Aye, can't be denying that. Vilmar over there's more beast than man and I've got a good bit of dog in me too. You'd find that out if ever we crossed swords."

Sir Taegon peered at him, then burst out in thunderous laughter. "*You?*

I'd have to get down on my knees to strike you, dwarf. Do you have a name, half-man?"

"I do, as it so happens. Do you want me to write it down so you remember it?"

The giant scowled. "Some no-name knight, no doubt. Wouldn't be worth remembering anyway."

"Well, let's try, shall we?" The stocky little knight turned his eyes around the table. "You have the honour of meeting Sir Torus Stoutman, Knight of Steelvale. Stout and steel by name, stout and steel by nature." He blew out a whirl of pipe smoke. "I'm half your height, Cargill, but double your size." He winked and gave a gap-toothed grin. "If you catch my meaning."

Sir Taegon was as slow as a glacier, but he got there eventually. "What did you say to me, dwarf?"

"Oh, I think you heard. The blush on your cheeks suggests it's true as well. Come on, let's cross *swords*, as I say. You've got me in height, I've got you in length."

Amron swallowed his chuckle. "Sir Torus is fond of a bawdy jest, Sir Taegon," he said, in a bid to restore some control. "Ignore him."

"It's true," Sir Torus said. "I like a naughty joke or two, though most of the time, I mean no offence. Unlike with you lot, arriving late. *That* was intended, I'm sure."

"We've been long at sea," the giant grunted.

"River," came in Torus at once. "You've been long *on the river*, I think you meant to say. The sea is a very different body of water, sir. Here, I'll draw out a map for you, next to my name. You can study it later when you climb into your cot."

"Damn you!" Sir Taegon was as hot in the head as he was large. He surged to his feet, causing the entire table to rattle as it brushed his massive thighs. "You want to poke at me, imp, let's make it with steel! We'll see how sharp your tongue is then."

"My blade is sharper. And honed in giants blood." Sir Torus sat back and sucked on his pipe. "I know how to fell big trees, sir. There's an art to it, I'll show you if you like…"

Amron had heard enough, amusing though it was. "That'll do, Sir Torus. And sit down, Sir Taegon. We're not here to hurl insults at one another."

"And what are we here for, my lord?" asked Dalton Taynar. A frost at once filled the air. "To discuss the murder of my father, perhaps? By your own flesh and blood, no less. Is this feast meant to somehow give me solace, to heal so deep a wound as that?" If it was indeed a deep wound, the man showed little grief for it. He stared through eyes dark and hard, though there was nothing resembling pain within them.

"Your father's death was unfortunate," Amron started. *But earned, ten times over*, he thought best not to say. "And you have my deepest condolences for his loss. Yet what's done is done, and the culprit is in chains. We're here to discuss the future, not the past. If we continue to look behind us, with an enemy out in front, we will perish to a man. I'm here to make sure that does not happen."

"I want Vesryn brought here," Dalton returned sharply. "I want him brought here so I can kill him myself."

"No," Amron told him. The word echoed through the small hall.

"No?" Dalton glowered. "And why not? If Vesryn is to die, why not here, by my hand?"

Because he's my brother, Amron thought, *and not yours to slay.* He said nothing.

"Sir Vesryn stole the Sword of Varinar, let us not forget," Sir Brontus Oloran came in. "He stole the blade and deserted his post, a crime that calls for death in itself. I was there, Lord Daecar, the night your brother disappeared from Harrowmoor. From that moment on, his life was forfeit."

"It is more complicated than that," Amron said. He glanced aside, to see Walter whispering something to himself, hands held as though in prayer. *Again?* He'd seen him do that before…

"How?" asked Sir Quinn Sharp, broad-faced and homely, though a decent sword and man of acceptable honour. "I thought the laws on desertion were clear."

"They are. In theory, if not in practice, Sir Quinn." Amron decided not to say anything more on it. *I'd need Amara here to plead Vesryn's case. That's not for me to bother with.* "Vesryn is locked away in the palace dungeons in Varinar, that is all you need to know. His fate is not a priority at this time." He held a hand up, lest someone try to butt in. "But as to the blade he stole, it has since been recovered, and needs must be mastered by an appropriate hand. I had expected that to be you, Lord Taynar."

Dalton's dull grey eyes showed mild surprise. "You have it here? The Sword of Varinar?"

He did not know I had brought the blade. Good. "Yes. It was my express intention for you to claim it as soon as possible, so you might begin the process of mastering it. That is no easy task, and takes much practice, training, and time, of which we have little and less to spare. Whether it be you or Sir Brontus, someone must claim it, and soon. I should be happy to help instruct whomever that is, in the complexities of the bond."

"I would be honoured, Lord Daecar," said Sir Brontus at once.

Amron looked at him. "So it *will* be you, then?" He could sense the discord already.

"Yes, my lord. His Majesty cannot bear the blade, as he said at the docks." He glanced at Dalton. "He is king."

You don't believe that, Amron thought. He decided just to say it plain, and get it done; the game was growing tiresome. "No, he is not king, Sir Brontus. It is time we put this fallacy to bed."

"It's no fallacy!" thundered Sir Taegon. "His father was king, now his father is dead! Makes him king, by law."

"Well look at him, the big man understands succession," Sir Torus laughed. "Shouting louder than everyone else doesn't make it true, though."

"It is true, dwarf! Even a blind man could see it."

"A blind *corrupt* man, maybe." Sir Torus sucked on his pipe. "Though… aren't we all forgetting something." He scratched at his bushy beard, deep in thought. "Oh, yes, that's it, it's just come to me." His eyes went straight for Dalton. "Your father murdered his predecessor to gain the throne, didn't he? Rather makes your claim void, I'd say."

"Slander!" Sir Taegon thumped a huge fist into the table, cracking wood, and several of the other men flew to their feet as well, hollering. "You say that again, dwarf, and I'll put your head through this table instead of my fist!"

"I've got a hard head."

"We've heard these accusations before," called Sir Marcus Flint. "They are unproven. King Ellis *fell* from that balcony when drunk. Everyone knows it."

Enough of this, Amron thought. He did not stand to join the rabble. The power of his voice would be plenty enough. "King Ellis did not fall, but was thrown," he said, voice ringing cleanly through the hall. *And now the killing blow.* "Sir Nathaniel Oloran has since confessed as much, and so have the other two Greycloaks present that day."

A hush spread out through the small hall like a cold winter wind. Amron savoured the looks on their faces, drinking in their shock. *It tastes better than any wine,* he thought.

"My cousin…" started Sir Brontus. "He…

"Has found the righteous path and confessed of his sins," Amron said. "He told me himself how Janilah Lukar threw King Ellis from the balcony. A suspicion well shared by a great many in this kingdom has now been confirmed, beyond a doubt. And within his confession to me, he spoke too of your father, Dalton. He told me of Godrik's part in this infamy."

Amron had never seen a man look so horribly caught out. "I…no, that cannot be. It cannot. My father had no part in the king's death. Nathaniel must be lying. He…he must."

"He is not," Amron leaned forward on the table. "And you know that, don't you, Dalton? Deep inside, you know it."

"I…" The man gulped, the apple in his neck going up and down. "I don't know what to say, my lord."

"The truth would be a good start." Amron turned his eyes across the table. None could meet his gaze, and that was telling enough. "So be it," he said, when no one spoke. "Silence can be as revealing as words, and you've told me all I need to hear. Know that I have no intention of humiliating you, Dalton." To do so would only sow resentment, he knew, when it was unity, not enmity, that he wanted to reap. "Nor do I need to know how long you have known the truth, or how much of a part you played in this plot yourself, if any. I sense this was the work of your father, and the Warrior King. I sense you were nought but a pawn, as we have all been, and that your father drove you down this path. But there is no reason why you cannot step off it, and join the one upon which I walk. It is the future that concerns me, not the past. We must leave that where it belongs, and walk forward together now, side by side, as one."

Dalton looked at him through cloaked, suspicious eyes. "Side by side? You…you mean not to take the throne?"

"I have no intention of such. I sense it will only lead to further infighting. Your side will claim that Ellis Reynar changed his line of succession by his own free will. That whatever confession came from the mouths of the Greycloaks was coerced from them, and ill-gotten. I have no time for that. Right now, it is only the war that interests me; fighting it, winning it, securing this kingdom and all the north for future generations to live in. That is my sole focus, as it should be yours."

Dalton's jaw was tight as a drum skin, though Amron sensed something approaching relief in the man's eyes. *Heavy is the crown*, he thought. *The weight of command has become too much of a burden for him.* "If you are not to rule, and nor am I, then what are you proposing?"

"That we share the rule, and fight together, not against one another. I can say it no more simply than that."

"*Share* the rule?" sneered Sir Ramsey Stone, a cruel-looking little man with wicked eyes and thin lips. "But that's never happened. Ever. Vandar has always had a single king."

"Many things are happening now that have not happened before," Amron said. "We need not be afraid of change, my lords. Nay, we must embrace it."

Sir Brontus was rubbing at the light blond hair that carpeted his cheeks and chin. "I would ask what you intend to do with my cousin, Lord Daecar. Is he to hang for this?"

"No. Sir Nathaniel is to receive a full pardon, same as Sir Gerald and Sir Alyn."

"You're to release them?" Dalton sounded as shocked as he was capable of sounding. "Even after…"

"Yes. I have spoken with their fathers and agreed to pardon them in order to keep the peace. This is one concession I am willing to make. Another is keeping Vesryn in chains for his own transgressions. A third is permitting one of you to bear the Sword of Varinar, as First Blade." He looked upon the two men seated before him. "You were both beaten semi-finalists in the Song of the First Blade, and it is apt that one of you bear the sword in the wake of my son's death, and brother's betrayal. I shall leave it to you to decide upon that yourselves."

He could already see the risks in that. *Sir Brontus wants what he was promised*, he thought, *though Dalton will wish to claim it as well now.* They were muddy waters that Amron did not want to wade through. *And yet…*

"I would warn you to make your decision on this quickly. You have heard of the Agarathi victory at Dragon's Bane, I'm sure. And this force that drove you from the Trident…" He paused, seeing Dalton's eyes shift aside. "Do not question your decision to flee," he told him. "My father did so once, at Eagle's Perch, when the Moonrider Justo Nemati broke his siege.

There is no dishonour in calling a retreat when a rout is the only alternative."

"If only they'd done more than sit idle outside the walls for months on end, though," said Sir Torus, with that toothy grin.

"No need for that, Torus," Amron reprimanded. He wanted to tell him more plainly than that. *Shut up, you bloody fool,* he might have said. *We're making progress.* But then he had this won already, he sensed. *They are caught out, broken, all but bending the knee.* King in all but name, Amara had said to him. *Well, perhaps she was right.* "Those orders to starve out the Trident came from your father, did they not?" he asked Dalton.

"They did. He was concerned about a civil war between the houses and wanted me to preserve men. It was not my choice, Lord Daecar. I would have preferred a more active siege. Had we won the Trident before the enemy amassed…"

"You would only have had to abandon it anyway," Amron said. "Winning a fort is often the easy part. Holding it can be another matter. Had you fought to keep it, you may have been utterly defeated, your army destroyed, your fleet as well. So far as I see it, your retreat has served us all." He took his first sip of wine of the evening, victory assured. "All the same, the Agarathi will soon sail the Red Sea, as they marched the Bloodmarshes, and lay siege to our coastal cities here in the west. The sooner one of you learns to master the Sword of Varinar, the better we'll be able to repel them."

Brontus and Dalton shared a look. "I will take it," the latter said. "I am sorry, Brontus, but if I'm not to be king, I shall be First Blade. As Lord of House Taynar I have the better claim."

"A lordship does not improve one's claim," Sir Brontus Oloran came back at him. "Not in this. The First Blade is a contest, to be won on merit, not freely given." He hesitated a moment, then said, "I would challenge you, Lord Dalton, to a duel, to settle it. Tournament conditions, in the yard here at Crosswater. As it ought to be."

Dalton looked less than pleased with that. "A minute ago I was your king…"

"And a minute ago I was First Blade of Vandar." Sir Brontus Oloran took a grip of the pin on his left breast. "You gave this to me yourself, my lord…"

"And I can just as easily take it away. The Sword of Varinar should revert to me, in light of these…confessions."

Sir Rodmond Taynar touched his uncle's arm. "If I may, Uncle."

Dalton turned to him sharply. "Yes?"

"Forgive me, but I do not believe you have the authority to make this decision alone. We cannot forget that the Song of the First Blade is a sacred contest, despite recent desecrations. This is no course to be taken unilaterally."

Dalton looked like he could kill him, but what recourse did he have?

"Your nephew speaks wisely," Lord Harrow put in, deep voice purring through the hall. "No authority is given to a Vandarian greatlord to bestow such rank. The fairest course is to duel for the honour, as Sir Brontus suggests."

He has no choice, Amron knew, *lest he be called a coward.* Dalton was mulling on it darkly, but seemed to realise the same thing. "As you will, then," he said finally. "Lord Harrow, will you make preparations?"

"It would be my pleasure. Might I suggest we do this quickly, as Lord Daecar says? Tomorrow would be best."

Dalton liked the sound of that even less. "I have not trained much of late. The collar of command has called upon much of my time. It tugs here, it tugs there. You…you understand, Lord Amron?"

"Most intimately." Amron mused on it. "Sir Brontus, have you trained frequently of late yourself?" Amron had always known him to be most fastidious in his training. Few were so active in the Steelforge sparring yard as Sir Brontus. Only Aleron, perhaps, spent more time there than him.

"No, my lord. We have been travelling by ship for some weeks. I have trained little in that time."

Amron had another sip of wine. "Then tomorrow should suit you both," he said.

Dalton nodded sourly, then stood from the bench, pushing his wine cup aside. "Then I should train, while I can." He looked bitterly down at his fellow Varin Knight. "Sir Brontus, I shall see you in the yard on the morrow." He threw a leg across the bench and marched away, leaving his lickspittle lords and knights to ponder what they should do.

"You might want to consider doing the same," Amron said to Sir Brontus. "You would not want to be at a disadvantage."

"I am at no disadvantage, Lord Daecar." Brontus stood confidently and gave a sharp bow. "All the same, it would not be wise to drink tonight. I shall leave you to your feasting, my lords." He stepped away out of the door, Sir Marcus Flint leaving with him. A moment later, the other knights and lords took their leave, scurrying from the hall as quickly as they could.

Sir Taegon Cargill remained behind a moment, standing beside the table. He looked greatly smaller than normal, somehow, shoulders pulled in, head down, as a child caught doing something naughty. "My Lord Amron, I…I did not know of…of these treacheries," he said. "If this is true that Lord Godrik helped plan King Ellis's death…" He shook his enormous head, dark of hair and brutish of brow. His large lips glistened wetly. "I never…I'd never have said what I did. About Dalton being king. Never."

Lies, Amron thought. *You knew, Sir Taegon. Not at first, perhaps, but later, you knew.* "What's done is done," he said. "I do not blame you for showing loyalty to your lord uncle, who has long supported the Taynars. You only did what you were bidden. Now I bid you turn your eyes south, and prepare for war. We need you, Sir Taegon. I see a dragonkiller in you."

The giant bent his back in a bow. "I will not let you down, Lord Daecar." He rose again, turned, and left looking restored to size.

Last to depart was Sir Rodmond, who sat neatly in place, awaiting his chance to speak. Amron turned at him. "You have something to say, Sir Rodmond?"

"I do, my lord." He moved his eyes to the door. "I would echo what Sir Taegon said, though from my lips, you'd hear no lie." He raised a mild smile. "I know our houses have always been fierce rivals, but in Elyon I found a friend at Harrowmoor, when we both recovered from our injuries. I took an arrow to the flank," he explained, pointing, "when the parley at the gate broke out into violence. Your son was later flogged, for killing Sir Griffin Kastor, as I'm sure you've been told. We were friendly enough before then, but after…well, we confided much in one another, and I told him how I lacked any interest in being my uncle's heir. I still do, in truth. Becoming a greatlord has never interested me, less so becoming a king. I pray always that my uncle will have a son of his own, or name another before me, but today at least you have stripped me of the burden of having to worry about ever taking the throne. So…I suppose what I'm trying to say is thank you, my lord. Thank you for taking back the command that King Ellis should never have stripped from you. No matter who wins tomorrow, my uncle or Sir Brontus, it is obvious enough who steers our course. As ever was thus, Lord Daecar, it is you. And we are all the stronger for it." He stood at that, gave a low bow, then turned and stepped away.

Lord Harrow gave Amron a nudge as Rodmond left. "Smart boy. You should listen to that one."

"Smarter than his uncle, certainly," added Walter. "And greatly more approachable as well. A pity Lord Dalton did not fall at the Trident. Things would have been much easier with Sir Rodmond at the helm."

Amron didn't want to hear such talk. He stood as well. "I'll leave you to your feasting," he told his men. "Feel free to drink, but not too much. I want you clearheaded tomorrow."

"Why?" inquired Sir Torus Stoutman. "It's not like any of us are duelling for that blade."

Amron had reached his limit with Stoutman's pithy humour. "I think you've japed enough for tonight, Torus. At least in my company. Feel free to resume when I leave. I'll see you all in the morning. Walter, a word." He stepped away.

Walter seemed a little confused by the summons, though rose from the bench and pursued Amron to the other side of the hall. "Have I done something wrong, my lord?" he asked. "I hope you're not angry with me for sharing a jest with Sir Taegon? You did tell us to hold our tongues, but…"

"I'm not angry with you, Walter. If a spot of jesting raised my ire, it would be Torus here, not you."

"Yes, I suppose that's true. Well then, what is it you want?"

"I saw you whispering to yourself earlier when we spoke of Vesryn. You had your hands together and seemed to be engaged in some sort of prayer. I've seen that several times, in fact. You did the same on the ship, when Vesryn came up in conversation, and again on our first night here when we feasted with Lord Harrow. Always Vesryn. Always some whispered words on your lips, and hands together in prayer." He looked down at the scruffy little man. "What is your game?"

Walter looked up, all innocent. "Well, I don't know what you mean, Amron."

"*Lord* Amron. Or *Lord* Daecar. Or *my lord*. You'll bloody well use my noble title if you're going to lie to me, Walter."

"If I was to use your title, it would be *king*." Walter looked to the table. "They all think it, you know. As they do in the east. Rodmond thinks it too, clearly, and Sir Taegon may be a giant, but he's a diminutive little shrimp next to you, and bows to strength, that's clear enough. If Sir Brontus wins tomorrow, he'll call you king as well. Sir Killian is the Oloran heir. With him and Brontus you might have the Olorans even without Lord Penrith's support. You have the Kanabars, Pentars, Amadars already. What else do you need? You're king, Amron. Just admit it."

Amron was losing his patience. "I will accept this sort of talk from Amara, Walter, but not you. You get ahead of yourself. And don't try to change the subject. What were you whispering to yourself when Vesryn was discussed? What is it about my bloody brother that interests you so?"

Walter could be the most annoying man in all the world when he wanted to be, as well as the luckiest. He was channelling that gift right now with great relish. "He's an interesting man. Is it such a crime on my part that I find him such? And watch me a little more closely and you'll see I like to pray often, and about a great many things. It isn't just about Vesryn, you know."

"It is. I know it is." Amron almost grabbed him by the scruff of the neck, but refused the urge. "This is Amara's doing, isn't it? She's put you up to something."

"So little trust," Walter sighed, shaking his head. "Amara's scheming days are done, my lord. You should think more of her than that."

Amron ground his jaw. He had his answer. *Amara. Always Amara.* "Go on then, back to the others, draw your pictures and scribble your notes."

Walter couldn't leave quickly enough. He gave the briefest bow known to man and slipped away before he could be questioned further.

Amron marched to his rooms, far more dissatisfied than he should be given the success the evening had been. One of Sir Torus's three sons had the guard of his room tonight. All were much the same in height to their father. Darun, this one's name was, his eldest. He opened the door for Amron to enter. "My lord. How did it go this evening?"

"Well, Darun," Amron said as he passed him. And it had.

Then why was he so angry?

He knew why, really. *Vesryn. Amara. Godrik and Janilah and Hadrin, Cecilia Blakewood and my bastard born son.* All the treachery and treason, the bleakness and betrayals. The north had been torn apart by it, shredded by it, bloodied and brutalised like some beaten corpse, and then kicked about a bit more for good measure. Tonight Amron had begun to revive it, yet the darkness still festered in him, and he sensed he knew why that was too…

It was the pain he felt as soon as he took his hand off the hilt of the Frostblade. The discomfort as he changed into his bedclothes and climbed beneath the blankets. His ails seemed to be getting worse when his blood-bond was severed, keeping him awake at night, stealing him of sleep. *The longer I hold the blade, the harder it will be when I give it up,* he knew. It was like a drug, in that way, on which he feared he was growing dependent.

"But I will give it up," he told himself, as he settled down in the darkness of his room. It was his own little prayer, repeated nightly to reinforce that promise. "When the times comes, I will give it up. I *will* give it up. I *will*."

16

Robbert

"I do not like this," said the young prince, as he watched his lord uncle return from beyond the fort. "It feels like a defeat, to parley with him. My father would never have allowed it."

"Your father is dead," Sir Bernard Westermont reminded him, in his rumbling voice.

"Yes, Bernie, I know." Prince Robbert Lukar gave a slow shake of the head. "You think such a thing would slip my mind?"

"I'm just saying. No point in wondering what Prince Rylian would have done. He's not here, that's all I mean. He...he's dead, Robb."

"Again with the reminder." Robbert might have laughed if it wasn't all so painful. His father had been his idol, and now he was gone. *Slain*, he thought, *for trying to take the crown off Grandfather.* He still did not...*could* not... believe that. Much had gone amiss back home and he was much too far away to make sense of it.

"Well...mayhaps you could overrule him?" Sir Bernard offered, pointing toward Lord Cedrik Kastor as he rode proudly toward the gate of Eagle's Perch, his noble escort trotting at his back. "You're *king* now, Robb. Your brother says it so, in his letter." He was a big man, Bernie Westermont, and Robbert's second cousin through his great-grandmother's line. *A big loyal lout*, he thought. He liked Bernie a great deal, though the knight had been miserably provisioned in his grant of wit.

"I won't be king until crowned," he told the big man. "And Raynald might be wrong. My grandfather may yet be alive."

The letter had come through a long while ago and much might have changed since then. They'd had word of the slaughter at Galin's Post, the king's unveiling of the Mistblade, and his subsequent disappearance. Robbert had received scant word from his twin brother during the early weeks of the siege, and nothing since then. *Nothing for months.* He knew that his lord uncle Cedrik had been in communication with Lord Gershan and perhaps others as well, but even those crows had stopped coming of late.

We're all out of wings, he thought. *Isolated and alone.* But all the same, Robbert Lukar wanted to continue this fight. *For my father*, he told himself. *I will keep on going for him.*

A warm coastal wind was gusting fiercely, causing the banners of Lord Cedrik's host to flutter as they approached the gate. He had taken his favoured knights and lords with him to the parley; Sir Gavin Trent, his blustery battle commander; Lord Simon Swallow of Blackhearth, Lord Lewyn Huffort of Rockfall, and Lord Wilson Gullimer of Watervale; Sir Wenfrey Gershan, grandson to the Master of the Moorlands, and an Emerald Guard the same as Sir Lionel Vance and Sir Jesse Bell who were riding escort with him also.

But not me, Robbert thought bitterly. *He knows I want to stay, and fight. He knows I'll just cause trouble.*

"Well you ask me, this is all for the good," said Sir Lothar Tunney, another of Robbert's loyal guards. Men called him Sir Lothar the Looming or Tunney the Tall for his impressive height. At six feet and eleven inches was he one of the tallest men in Tukor, towering over all but a few in the north. Robbert could not think of many who outmatched him. *Sir Taegon Cargill, yes, he's a great giant brute. And the Whaleheart. Him, certainly.* Robbert Lukar had never met the King's Wall, but everyone said he was eight feet tall and shockingly muscular to go with it. Not Sir Lothar, though. He was skinny as a pole.

"What's for the good, Lank?" asked Sir Bernard, confused. He might have been called Sir Bernie the Barnyard for all that straw in his head.

"All this," Lothar answered pleasantly, waving to the approaching host with a staggeringly long arm. "They look happy enough, don't you think? Means it went well, so we're probably going home." He looked down at Robbert, who stood only at middling height, a full foot shorter than the man. "I know it's not what you want, my prince, but I think it's for the best. There's nothing for us here."

"There's blood," grunted Bernie. "Blood and victory, Lank." He looked up at him, though didn't need to crane his neck so much as Robbert did. Bernie was some six feet and four inches of brawn. He probably weighed more than Sir Lothar too. "How can a man so tall as you be so craven?" he challenged. "We don't *want* to go home. We want to smash the Aramatians, every one of them." He crushed a fist into his open palm to make his point. "And that sunlord most of all."

Krator, Robbert thought darkly. He could see him in the distance, riding away toward his vast encampment, saddled upon that monstrous sunwolf of his. For long weeks the two armies had sat facing one another across the field, prodding and probing and engaging in sallies and skirmishes, before finally they had come together in a great clash of steel and claw. Robbert recalled it fondly. He'd not been involved in those skirmishes, but the main battle was not something he was going to miss, no matter what his uncle said. *He says he wants to keep me safe from harm. He says I'm to be king. But I know different. He just wants to take all the glory for himself, that's all. He wants me sitting idle while he wins all the battles and acclaim.*

But not that one. No, Robbert Lukar wasn't going to miss *that* fight. The skirmishes he would take or leave, but he'd be damned if he'd watch from behind their defensive lines as that great tide of Sunriders and Starriders came snarling, as the huge southern camels and massive warhorses and the paladin knights atop them came charging across the plains. *Not by Ilith*, he remembered thinking. *As Tukor is my witness, I will win glory for my house today. I will make my father proud, as he watches from the Hall of Green!*

The battle had been a savage affair, as chaotic and bloody as a born warrior like Robbert Lukar could have hoped. With Big Bernie and Looming Lothar at his sides, the prince wrought great death upon the enemy host that day, killing some two dozen men, a pair of Starriders and Sunriders among them, before their foe spun about and rode headlong in retreat. It had all started not long past dawn, the skies scratched with thin red clouds, and ended at noon with the sun shining high above them, smiling down upon their victory. Robbert recalled the great cheer that spread out upon the plains as the enemy tucked their tails and ran, and the count of the dead that was conducted after had proven heavily in their favour. Almost ten thousand killed. Less than half of that lost. The only problem was, Sunlord Krator had not been among the slain.

"You should have let *me* hunt him," Robbert had said to his uncle, once the battle was done and he found him in his tent. "You should have given *me* that charge, uncle! My father would have killed him and so would I. So…why didn't *you*?"

His uncle had ignored the challenge. "Sunwolves are fast, Robbert," he had merely told him. "And sunlords can be cowards. He escaped. There is nothing else to say."

"You should go after him." *And don't talk to me like I'm a child*, he thought. *I'm eighteen, almost nineteen now. And a prince and maybe a king besides…*

"No." Cedrik Kastor poured himself a cup of wine and sighed, turning to him. "Did you not hear me? Sunwolves are *fast*, Robbert. We have men raiding the enemy rearguard as we speak, but Elio Krator is long gone. We will not catch him now."

Robbert had been furious. "The entire point was to kill him!" he'd shouted, his blood up from the battle. "You said it yourself, before the battle started. *Krator needs to die.* You made that clear, uncle, and now…" He gave his head a brisk shake. "Now he can just muster more men and march right back. All we've done is waste our own soldiers!"

He had been proven right in that as well. Less than three weeks after they'd run him off, the sunlord returned, with an even greater force at his back, spoiling for vengeance. It was the luxury of fighting on home soil. *He must have had men out there all the while, gathering his levies to reinforce him*, Robbert knew. The sight of their return had not gone down well with the men, many of whom were nursing wounds from the battle or growing sick from the spoiled water sources, hungry from the lack of food. Robbert could feel the collective tension as soon as they appeared on the horizon, restocked and resupplied and gleaming bright beneath the dazzling southern sun in their bronze and golden shirts of mail and colourful feathered cloaks. The next morning, they awoke to find Lord Krator's camp spread out anew upon the plains, only a short half mile from the fortress walls. Lord Cedrik had called a council at once and Robbert was damned if he would miss it.

"We have visitors," the Lord of Ethior had said. He poured himself a small cup of rich red wine, swirling it around the bowl. He did that sometimes, without even drinking. Robbert supposed his uncle thought it made him look elegant. "What would you have me do, my lords?"

"Go home," Lord Huffort had said, almost at once. "We have ships enough remaining to get us home to northern shores. If we don't go now, those bloody whales might come back and start smashing them up again. Then where will that leave us?"

"Stranded," said Lord Swallow, nervously. The Lord of Blackhearth was no fighter, and clearly had no taste for battle. "I see no choice but to abandon the fort, my lord. We face the threat of these grey leviathans, yes, but hunger is just as big a battle. We might last a month, perhaps two if we're careful, but no more than that. Not with the storehouses burned."

They should have anticipated it. Once the battle outside the Perch had been won, it hadn't taken them long to complete the siege, knock down the gate, and ransack the fortress. By the time they had bashed their way in, however, all the livestock had been butchered and burned, the storehouses set aflame, the granaries destroyed. In his rage, Lord Cedrik had made an example of the enemy soldiers who remained, flaying some, quartering others, using the rest for sport so his men could sate their thirst for blood and purge themselves of their anger. It had been an unpleasant affair, and not something Robbert agreed with, but to interfere would have only made him look weak, so he had stood aside and let it happen. *And I felt all the weaker for it.*

Lord Cedrik turned to his battle commander, Sir Gavin Trent, a bull-chested blustery knight who had been his right-hand man for years, all snorts and scowls and scars. "And you, Gavin? What would you recommend?"

The man thought on it a time, glowering all the while. "We might send out raiding parties to gather more provisions," he said. "Hunt the plains south of here, search for towns and villages we've not yet pillaged…"

"We've pillaged them all," Lord Lewyn Huffort said to that. He ground his stubbly lantern jaw. "We destroyed every settlement for fifty miles before the Aramatians came. And you may have noticed, Sir Gavin, but there's a rather large army blocking our way."

"I'm aware, Lord Huffort. If you'd let me finish…" He met the lord's eyes, then went on. "We'll find no salvation to the south, not with regard to restocking our food supplies, not with this army at our door. If we have need of food, it's north we'd best look. Send some ships home to gather provisions to resupply us."

Lord Huffort scoffed. "With all these wrathful whales about? We send those ships home, they might not come back. We can't take that risk. They're our only way off this bloody rock."

"I agree with Lewyn," came the calm voice of Wilson Gullimer, the handsome Lord of Watervale. He had an orchard of apples stitched onto the front of his surcoat, his house sigil. "We took this fortress in the hopes of continuing our invasion further south along the coast. Lest we attack Lord Krator's army for a second time, I do not see the point in waiting here to starve. We should go home, my lords. There will be plenty more fights to be had there."

"Fights, yes, and *answers* too." Huffort gave another heavy grunt, displaying his full repertoire of them. "I would return to Ilithor and find out what happened to my son. Your grandfather said he was killed, Sir Wenfry, during this riot at Galin's Post. Disembowelled. Was that not the word he used?"

"Yes, I...believe so, my lord," the young Moorlander said.

"*Disembowelled*," Huffort growled. "By the *mob*. I'd see them pay for this myself. Edwyn was one of Janilah's Six. His *Six!*" His eyes moved to Robbert. "I wonder what your twin brother is doing about this, my prince. Vengeance. I hope he is seeking vengeance for my son's foul murder."

You have others, Robbert thought. Sir Edwyn had been his third son, he knew. His second was here at the Perch with him, his eldest sitting his father's seat at Rockfall in his absence. "Raynald will be doing what he must," was all he said.

"He'll be doing nothing," his uncle dismissed. "Lord Gershan has made it quite plain in his letters to me that Lady Cecilia Blakewood is in charge, though she likes Raynald to think otherwise, of course."

"Because she's much cleverer than he is," said Lord Swallow. He looked at Robbert. "Begging your pardons, good prince. I'm sure you're much smarter than your twin. Firstborns usually are."

Robbert had heard that ridiculous myth before. "And if Ray had come out of the womb before me? He'd miraculously have been smarter, my lord?"

Swallow swallowed. He was an ugly man, all ticks and nervous twitches, small, spindly, and lacking in clout. A quick stare down from Robbert had him shifting his blinking eyes away.

"No one is saying Raynald is not a clever boy," his uncle said. "You are both very clever, Robbert, and even more gifted with godsteel, but no matter how clever you might be, neither of you will ever match your auntie in cunning and wit. Cecilia Blakewood is devious, crafty, and ambitious as well. Unless King Janilah should have returned to his throne by now, I have little doubt she is the true ruler of Ilithor, at this time."

"Then we're all bloody doomed," Huffort harrumphed. "A bastard and a woman, sitting the throne? Gods forbid."

"I didn't mean she was actually sitting the throne, Lewyn." Cedrik gave a sigh as though he was surrounded by utter fools. "Just that she is currently manipulating the boy."

"And the king?" asked Lord Gullimer. Robbert liked him greatly more than these others. Swallow was a true lickspittle, Huffort a moody grump, Sir Gavin a soldier with absolutely no airs and graces at all. Gullimer might have been but a middling house, but its lord was as all lords should be;

courteous, noble, and loyal, and a man who understood right from wrong. "Have we had further word on his whereabouts?"

"No," Cedrik said. "The crows have stopped coming, Lord Gullimer. And we have none left of our own to send. We are blind to news from the north, presently."

Are we? Robbert looked at his uncle suspiciously. There was no knowing for certain whether he'd received further word or not as to the king's true fate. *Perhaps my grandfather is truly perished, and he will not tell us?* If King Janilah was proven as dead, then that would make Robbert King of Tukor, beyond all doubt. *Which he doesn't want, lest I wrest control of this army from him.*

He decided his own voice needed to be heard. "My lords," he said, speaking loudly, clearly, and in a tone redolent of his father. *Show them who you are,* he thought. *Show them that you are Rylian's son and heir.* He turned his eyes from one man to the next, then said. "We should gather our strength, ride out of the gate, and smash Lord Krator's host just like we did before. We have plenty of men left, and almost all of our best." The men they had lost during the battle were mostly youngsters and conscripts who had scant experience of war. "We rout them, as we did last time, and continue straight down the coast to Cloaklake. It's a large city, and will have more than enough food to resupply us. From there, we continue onto Matia, Kolash, and then Aram. We can have the capital taken within months, and Aramatia all but conquered."

His uncle was the first to snicker, after which all the others followed, save Lord Gullimer. "Oh, to be a boy again. You have quite the imagination, Robbert." Cedrik swirled his cup. "It's an attractive prospect, I will admit, though without reinforcements from the north I fear we will be grossly outnumbered." He gave another chuckle. "Still, something to think about. I shall ponder until the morrow, when we can meet again." He put his cup down, never taking a sip. "I have heard you all, and will consider. Until tomorrow, gentlemen."

He ends the meeting as soon as I speak, Robbert had thought, raging. He'd marched right back to his own chambers to vent to Bernie and Lank, though it didn't much help. *I'll try again tomorrow,* he told himself, once he'd calmed. *I'll make them take me seriously.*

The next morning, they had gathered once again. There had been an acrid smell of smoke rising from the eastern seas, plumes billowing distantly on the morning mists. Robbert had feared the worst even before he reached the lord's chambers for their council. "More ships were destroyed last night," Sir Gavin Trent had reported dourly, standing over a table map of the region. There were some carved horses, knights, ships and siege weapons upon it, which Lord Cedrik had arrayed to display their strength, and that of Krator's as well. Sir Gavin reached to the grouping of little wooden ships that represented their fleet, and brushed several of them aside. "Our fleet is further depleted," he intoned. "Another two dozen were lost."

"*Two dozen!*" Lord Swallow's eyes widened in worry. "How? Whales again? Not those cursed whales…"

"Whales do not tend to breathe fire, or set ships alight, Lord Swallow," Lord Cedrik said coolly. "No. This must have been the work of dragons."

Sir Gavin shook his head.

"No?" asked Cedrik. "Then what, Gavin?"

"Some Aramatian fireships were reported as among the wreckage," the gruff battle commander said. "This was Krator, my lord. He must have sent them under cover of dark, to try to cripple us. He means to trap us here in the fort, starve us out, or force us to engage. With the ships we've lost, we no longer have enough to get everyone home."

The tidings were most ill, though Robbert smiled through it all. *Good. We'll be forced now to fight, as father would have wanted.*

"We could make two trips," posited Lord Gullimer. "The southern coast of Rasalan is not far. Yes, it would be best if we could sail back to Tukor, but failing that, we can cross to the coastal harbours west of Galaphan's Grounding, and march back to Tukor overland. This way, we should be able to convey our men home."

Lord Cedrik mused on that. "How many men can we take, in a single crossing?" He looked at Sir Gavin Trent.

"With our numbers, and the ships we've got left…maybe a half, or a bit more if we squash them all in. Two trips would be enough."

"We should take our best back on the first voyage," Lord Huffort said. He looked tired, like he'd had a bad night's sleep, with big black bags beneath his eyes and course stubble across his cheeks. "They need to be prioritised."

Robbert had never taken the man for a coward, but gods was he showing his true colours. "So you'd leave crofters and cobblers and bakers' boys to defend the fortress while we're gone, my lord?" He shook his head. "We'll split our strength. If we take all of our best soldiers, then Krator will just storm the fortress as soon we raise anchor and kill everyone who's left behind." They had about thirty five thousand remaining, or thereabouts. "I'm not about to leave fifteen thousand men here to die."

Lord Gullimer agreed. "Quite. We must leave sufficient men of experience here to help protect and lead the rest, if we're to choose this course."

"*We* shall choose no course," Lord Cedrik Kastor reminded him. "*I* shall choose it, Lord Gullimer." He cupped his elbow in his palm, hand to chin, and began pacing from side to side. "We must be cautious, however, of a trap. It might well be that the sunlord wishes for us to sail home, so he can target us once more at sea. With our fleet so weakened, we will be vulnerable, even on a short voyage." He walked around to the side of the table where the map depicted the eastern coast. "There are many bays to the south of here where Krator might be hiding his fleet, ready to be unleashed when we set sail. I am a knight and a warrior, not a sailor. It is not my fate to perish at sea, beneath the sails of some cursed ship."

"We can send out scouts," offered Lord Swallow. "To find out if Krator is hiding ships in these bays."

"And if he is, do you think he would just let these scouts of ours pass unmolested?" Cedrik gave him a scolding look. "Use your head, Simon.

Krator has the coastal road blocked and barred, and will be on the lookout for scouts, night and day…"

"Then we fight," said Robbert, seizing his chance. "We have not the ships to sail home, not all of us at once, and fear a trap even if we do. We are running out of food, the wells are poisoned, and clean drinking water is growing scarce. What other choice do we have, Uncle? We *have* to attack while we're still strong."

He's bending, Robbert saw, in a moment of hope. He could see the cogs turning behind his uncle's eyes, searching for their best course. Men called Cedrik Kastor a killer born, the finest sword in all of Tukor now that Robbert's father was dead. *If we sail home, men will call him craven instead.* It would be too much of a wound on his pride, Robbert knew. Whichever way they turned, there would be perils and threats. *Why not face our enemy head-on?* he thought. *If we're to die, let's do it with swords in our hands, not whales and wood beneath our feet and fireships bearing down upon us.*

"Much to consider," the Lord of Ethior finally said, refusing to come to a judgement just yet. "Let us see what the new dawn brings."

Robbert feared it would bring more dire news of burned ships and crazed grey leviathans, the wrath of the whale god Bhoun as some of the men were saying, yet in the end, all it brought them was an envoy.

He arrived alone at the city gates at first light, riding atop a golden sunwolf and holding aloft a white banner of truce, calling out that Lord Elio Krator wished to parley. Robbert had found his uncle at once and told him not to go. "What will you gain from it?" he'd said, breathless from the run. "Either we sail north or we attack. Nothing Krator says is going to change that."

His uncle had raised a hand to calm him. "Robbert, dear nephew, must you question every one of my decisions? There is no harm in talking with the man. Much of war is compromise. You'll learn that, one day." He'd patted his arm and mounted his steed, then rode right out through the gate, with his lords and knights at his back.

Now he was returning, trotting along as though in triumph as he reached the gate and passed into the yard beyond. Robbert turned and looked down from the battlements, to watch his uncle dismount. "Should we go down and find out what happened, my prince?" asked Sir Lothar Tunney.

Robbert sensed he wasn't going to like it, either way. "With me," he said to his two men, as he strode to the stone steps at the rear of the wall walk and descended the battlements to join the others in the yard. Many hundreds of soldiers cluttered the place, watching on eagerly. *Some hope to sail home, others to fight,* Robbert knew. *And what will my uncle's verdict be?*

"Uncle," he called, marching toward him. Lord Cedrik Kastor was dressed in his polished godsteel plate, black and silver and dark pine green, with an ink-black cape draped at his back. His lords and knights were resplendent in their house colours as well, proudly displaying their arms. All had brought banner-bearers to the meet, making a great show of northern nobility and strength. "How did it go, Uncle? What did Krator have to say?"

Lord Cedrik gave no swift answer. He took his time, as he always did, handing his horse to a groom, straightening out his cloak, making certain his fine godsteel broadsword was fixed perfectly at his hip. Then he walked over to Robbert with a flat expression on his face. It was a dark face, though not of skin. That skin was pale as ice and his eyes were just as cold, his hair black and wavy, neatly swept back behind his ears. *A cruel face*, people said. Robbert knew the stories of his lord uncle and his lord grandfather too. *Keep Kastor was a house of horrors*, he'd heard men say. *The things they do to southerners there…*

"It went well," the Lord of Ethior finally said. He allowed himself a smile, and put a hand on the prince's shoulder. "I think you'll be pleased, Robbert. Yes, you'll be most pleased."

"We're to attack, then?" A thrill stirred within him, the thrill of the battles to come.

His uncle merely nodded and said, "We'll not be going home, just yet."

17

Elyon

The Steelrun River had earned its name not just for the Vandarian obsession with blades, but the colour of its silvery waters. They glinted bright against the high spring sun as Elyon flew above the wide waterway, looking upon it from an angle as never before. The wind rushed through his hair; his cloak billowed and rippled behind him. There was a dull ache in his head from the wine he'd drunk last night with Amara, yet it was not so fierce as it had been when he'd awoken. *And it was worth it,* he thought. *She needed it as much as I did.*

Ahead, he could see the great castle of Crosswater perched proudly where the Steelrun met the Tanwar, a narrower, wilder watercourse that came rushing down from the North Downs to join the Steelran as it trundled away to the sea. Beyond the castle, the Vanguard loomed, with its huge statue-towers and massive gate. Elyon could see many ships in the river harbour, bobbing on the restless waters. He squinted, seeing sails and sigils of Taynars, Olorans and their allies. *They've arrived, then,* he thought.

He descended through some wisps of white cloud, reducing his speed and altitude as he approached. To either side of the river he saw tents and pavilions set up on the banks, bustling shoulder to shoulder around cookfires and pissing pits. It looked a strong enough force, perhaps fifteen or twenty thousand men, though it was impossible to be sure from up here.

Bursting past a flock of gulls, he neared the castle's north-facing gate. The soldiers there began to notice him coming and he heard shouts spreading out upon the walls. Some men were hastening toward the ballistas and scorpions at the heed of their commanders. *I'm not a dragon,* Elyon wanted to cry out to them. *Is the godsteel armour and blue Varin cloak not a good enough giveaway?*

He landed hard outside the gate before they could fire a shot, the impact of his landing sending a jolt through his head that threatened to reignite the ache in his head. He was still wincing from that when the gate commander came rushing forth to greet him. "Goodness me, well goodness…Sir Elyon? Sir Elyon Daecar?" He turned to his men. "It's Sir Elyon Daecar!" he bellowed. "Rest easy, the Master of Winds is with us!"

A cheer broke out, though that didn't much help Elyon's head. He raised a steel hand to try to calm them, but they took it for a salute and only cheered the louder. *Arg. Too much wine.* "Commander, I've come to see my father. Is he here?"

"Oh yes, Sir Elyon, yes. He's overseeing the Song of the First Blade as we speak."

The Song of the… Elyon wasn't understanding. "You're going to have to explain that, sir."

"Of course." The man turned to the gate. "The Taynar host arrived yesterday afternoon, Sir Elyon. I'm not fully acquainted with the details, but I believe there has been some contention over who should take on the mantle of First Blade. Lord Taynar and Sir Brontus Oloran are competing for the rank and blade. They were the losing semi-finalists last year, as I understand it."

They were. Elyon had watched almost every single bout. "Where is the contest taking place?"

"In the training yard. Half the castle has gathered to watch."

Elyon could hear them now, the din of a thousand voices humming in the distance. He did not know Crosswater well. "Take me," he said.

"At once, my lord."

The yard was centrally situated within the castle grounds, set outside the main keep that soared high at its southern side, overlooking the Vanguard and harbour. Some wooden stages had been erected for the spectators to watch, though many were perched wherever they could, gazing down from balconies and wall walks and the lips of tower windows. Some had climbed up onto the roof of the stables and the armoury had been clambered upon too, every spare space taken. Elyon could see that three judges sat high on one stage, and there was an announcer too, calling the contest. He had a flashback to Varinar, to the arena, to Aleron and Jonik, to blood and death and storms and rain and the changing of the world…

He pushed all that aside. "Where does my father watch from?" he asked the commander.

"I'm not sure, my lord. Somewhere with a good vantage, I would think…"

"There," Elyon said, spotting him. He was on a north-facing balcony jutting out from the keep, several floors up. There were some other men with him, though Elyon could not see who they were at a glance. "Thank you, Commander. I shall make my way from here."

He chose not to fly, for fear of causing a distraction, but instead marched behind the roaring crowds and through the broad arched doors that gave access to the keep. No one seemed to notice him, their attention on the duel. Elyon tried to hear a call from the announcer to get an idea of who might be winning, but it mattered not. *Neither are good,* he thought, marching faster. He strode quickly up the torchlit turnpike stair and came to the floor his father had been on. Through the dim stone interior he could see the bloom of daylight outside, framing his father and his men upon the balcony. He steadied his breath and marched right out to join them.

"Father," he said.

Elyon's heart was beating hard, *ba-dum, ba-dum*, as Amron Daecar turned to face him. He stared a moment, then blinked, then said, "Elyon? My gods, Elyon, what are you doing here?"

"I came to see you, Father."

The other men were looking at him as well. One was short and scruffily dressed and clutching at a notebook, another even shorter and stockily built, garbed in a patchwork of dinted godsteel plate armour and tough old leathers. Elyon knew him as Sir Torus Stoutman, as he did the beastly hunter called Vilmar the Black, and the old greybearded knight called Sir Ralf of Rotting Bridge, all leal Daecar men. The Castellan and Lord Protector of the Vanguard, Lord Harrow, stood with them also, but Elyon barely noticed them. He was looking at his father. At the man's rugged smile, at the keen light in his steel-blue eyes, at that savage scar that split the right side of his face from temple to jaw. At his great looming height and width and strength, a strength that had been stripped from him the last Elyon had seen the man, now restored.

He looked upon the great man with an unrestrained smile. For long months he'd feared his father gone. *Amron Daecar…is dead*, King Hadrin had told him. Elyon had rallied against that, trying not to believe it, yet all the same it had tortured him, that snivelling voice and ugly little smirk and those words, repeating again and again in his head. It was not until recently that he'd heard of his father's return, his uncle Rikkard telling him of that a little more than a month ago. *His return and his renewal and his revival,* Elyon thought. *He is as grand and vigorous as ever. It's just as Amara said.*

He cleared his throat. "Father, can we speak? In private?"

Amron nodded. "Of course. Yes of course, son." He strode at once from the balcony, throwing an arm around Elyon's shoulder to lead him down the hall. *His left arm,* Elyon thought, gleeful. *He could barely move it the last time I saw him, barely lift a cup of wine without it slipping through his fingers and crashing to the floor. And he would limp on his right leg too, when he wasn't using his crutch.*

It made him happier than he could say to see his father's ails gone. "Your injuries, Father. I'd heard conflicting reports. Are they healed permanently, or…"

"Temporarily. It takes the power of the Frostblade to tend them. It's only temporary, Elyon." He sounded like he didn't want to talk about it. "Come, we can speak in here." He led him into a private solar, pushing through the door. As soon as they were inside, alone and in private, Amron Daecar threw his other arm around his son and hugged him tight in a crunch of godsteel armour.

Elyon was taken aback. His father had never been a tactile man. "Father…you'll crush my armour if you hug me any harder…"

"We'll have it hammered back out." Amron tightened his embrace. "I have missed you, son. Gods, you cannot know how proud I am of what you've been doing. Of who you've become."

"I…" Elyon swallowed the lump in his throat. "I…I've only done what…what I thought you would have, Father. What Aleron would have, had he been…"

"Don't diminish your successes. They are *yours*, Elyon, no one else's." Amron released him and walked to the drinks counter. He began pouring two cups of wine.

"Father, I shouldn't. I had a little too much last night."

His father looked over his shoulder. "With whom? Where did you come from today? You can't have flown from Oakpike?"

Elyon had to laugh. "Auntie Amara said the same."

"Amara?" He grumbled something under his breath, finished pouring the cups, and walked over, handing one to his son. "One drink won't hurt. This is a moment to toast, Elyon. I'll not have Amara steal it away from me." He gave a disapproving scowl, though it melted away quickly enough. "How long were you with her?"

"Just one night. I flew yesterday morning from the Lakelands, in the hope of seeing you. She convinced me to stay for the evening."

"Yes, well I suppose I can't blame her for that. She's missed you greatly, son, as I'm sure you saw. And Oakpike to Varinar in one day? That must be terribly wearying, flying so far. I suspect you needed the rest."

Wearying was hardly the word. Elyon had scarcely felt so tired as when he finally dragged himself to bed, to find Carly Flame Mane there as promised, lying nude as a newborn with her long red hair flung haphazardly across her scarred back. *I must have been exhausted, because even the sight of her did not stir me.* The fact that Carly had been snoring like a hog didn't much help either. *She snores like Borrus Kanabar after a night in his cups,* he thought, smiling. In the end, he'd sought another bedchamber, and had left her to her dreams. *And entered my own, with the girl of silver and blue…*

"It's draining, certainly," he answered. "Nice to prove to myself that I can handle long flights, though. So long as I can stop along the way, great distances should not hinder me." He tapped his cup to his father's in toast of their reunion, then had a sip.

Amron drank and smiled. "My son, Prince of the Skies. I'm astonished at how quickly you've mastered the blade, Elyon."

"I've not mastered it yet. There is still much to learn." He looked at the white blade sheathed at his father's hip. "Might I see it? Amara spoke of the colours the mists give off, as they melt. She told me they're quite something."

Amron drew the Frostblade from its ornate white and silver scabbard, a shimmering length of icy steel, engraved along its length with mystic markings and glyphs. The pommel was formed of a thousand tiny snowflakes, linked to form an orb, the cross-guard and hilt studded with crystals uncountable, making them glitter and gleam like frozen snow. From its edge rose a soft white mist that spread upward in a haze of iridescent dust. Elyon had never seen anything quite so beautiful. He smiled and gave a shake of the head. "Mine feels rather unspectacular by comparison."

The Windblade had a lovely flowing design of its own, though had not the power to mesmerise like this. Amron waved that off. "To the contrary. There's no blade more striking in its powers than the Windblade, and that's greatly more important. I know you have always had a fondness for aesthetic appeal, but looks aren't everything, son." He gave him a teasing smile and shoved the Frostblade back into its sheath. Elyon noted how he kept his hand resting atop the pommel to maintain his blood-bond.

His aches and ails will return should he remove it, he knew. He was about to inquire further about that when a rising swell of noise exploded from out in the yard. It pulled Elyon right back to the urgency of his coming. He turned to look down the passage. "Is there any way we can stop that?" he asked.

His father seemed not to understand. "Stop it? The Song? Why should we?"

Elyon did not hesitate. "I had hoped to bear the Sword of Varinar myself, Father."

"Yourself? Is one Blade of Vandar not enough for you, Elyon?" He studied him a moment, eyes tightened in doubt. "Careful, son. The lure of the blades…"

"It isn't about that," Elyon was quick to tell him. "I don't want to keep it permanently. Only for a short time."

"I see. And why, exactly?"

"To cut the Bondstone," he said at once. "The Sword of Varinar is the only blade that can destroy it." He could already see his father would not agree to his proposal, but on he went anyway. *I have to try.* "I believe I'm the only one who can do it, Father…destroy the Bondstone, that is. I have tested myself now. I can fly far and fast and go to places no one else can reach, and in secrecy as well if I'm careful. If I am given time to learn to wield the Sword of Varinar…not even master it, just learn to wield it…then I think…I think I can destroy it. I think I can end this war, or at least sever Eldur's link to the dragons." He stopped, misliking his father's silence. "What…what do you think?"

"Elyon…"

That's a no, then. "You think it's too risky?"

"Too risky? The Bondstone's location is unknown, Elyon. Where would you even start?"

"Eldur has it," he said. "He bears is on his staff. We have witnesses who say as much, from Thalan. You…you do know about Thalan, don't you?"

"Yes, I heard."

"Eldur is using the Bondstone to control the dragons. They're everywhere, Father. We need to destroy it. It's our only chance."

"And you think you can do this alone?" Amron stepped forward, voice softening. "Son, my gods…your courage is inspiring, but you know this cannot be. You're talking about facing Eldur. About flying to gods know where, Eldurath or the Nest or even the Wings. You're talking about doing the impossible. It's suicide, my boy."

Elyon had half-expected this. *No, more than half.* "I know how it sounds, but what choice do we have? Sever the Soul of Agarath and it's over. I have to try."

Amron shook his head. "The risks are too great. If you fly there and do not return, we will lose two Blades of Vandar. That is a gamble none will agree to. And this all assumes that the Sword of Varinar can cut the Bond-stone anyway. That may not be so."

"The Sword of Varinar can cut anything," Elyon said. "That's its unique magic."

"We cannot know for sure." Amron Daecar shook his head once again, with an extra note of finality. "I am sorry, Elyon, but this I cannot permit. Nor could I even if I wished to." He waved a hand to the door. "The Sword of Varinar will go to Dalton or Brontus. To deny them that honour would risk civil war."

"So it's about politics."

"It's about a great many things. I do not doubt that destroying the Bondstone is a worthy course, and perhaps an essential one, but this is not the way." He put a strong gnarled hand on his shoulder. "You're doing plenty enough already, son. You needn't risk yourself with such folly."

Folly, Elyon thought. It sounded like folly, to be sure, but still, he wasn't seeing another way right now. He decided not to pursue it, though. *He'll not agree, no matter what I say.* It was always going to be a long shot. "I understand," he said eventually.

His father must have seen something in his face, or heard something in his voice, because he looked at him suspiciously and said, "You may not share blood with Amara, but she's passed a part of herself onto you all the same. You share her inclination to scheme, Elyon. As proven when you stole that blade…"

"I didn't *steal* it." Elyon took umbrage with the word. "You weren't there, Father. What we did was just." *And what we did led to Rylian's death.* He still felt wounded by that. It still drove him, each day, to be better.

"Call it what you will. You have a tendency to circumvent authority when you feel the cause is worthy. *Don't* do so with this, Elyon. It is not for you to interfere."

"Interfere? So you think I would try to steal the Sword of Varinar, take it without your permit?" He tried to sound indignant, but in truth the thought had crossed his mind, if briefly. *I could take it, fly off somewhere, master it in secret.* Of course, it wasn't so simple as that. The blade would be too heavy to lift at first, let alone fly with, and his father was right, it would cause great harm between the houses. *He is trying to heal Vandar, heal the north,* Elyon told himself. *Don't get in his way.* "I won't interfere," he said, to his father's hard stare. "You have my word."

"I'll have your *oath*." Amron Daecar moved his hand from the pommel of the Windblade to its hilt, and reached out with his other. "Your godsteel

214

oath, Elyon. Swear it by that shard of Vandar's shattered Heart. Swear it by the Windblade."

Elyon narrowed his eyes. "You don't trust me?"

"Don't sound so pained," Amron scolded. "I trust you, yes, of course I do, but even with your word you can be reckless. I'd sooner have your oath, so I might better sleep at night." He shoved his hand forward. "Swear it."

Elyon wilted. He had no other choice. "Fine. If it'll put your mind at ease, why not?" He gripped the Windblade and gave the oath and, in a fashion, felt all the better for it. He took a sip of wine once it was done in a bid to soothe the aching in his head, though it did little to help. Another cheer rumbled from outside. "So...who's winning, then? I couldn't hear the announcer's score, with all the noise."

His father looked to the door. "Sir Brontus, though it's been a fairly even contest, and quite cagey. He took the first bout twenty points to sixteen. The second was even when we stepped away, six apiece."

"It's best of three, same as last year?"

"The same," Amron said.

Another roar came rushing down the corridor, and Elyon listened for the announcer's call. Through the noise he heard the score bellowed out. "Eight to seven," he said, "to Dalton. "Who are the judges?"

"Three of Lord Harrow's men," his father said. "It just happens that they practice in tourney conditions here often, and his men often take turns judging bouts. They're well enough versed in it. Dalton tried to argue that we send for more experienced judges, but he was overruled."

"Why? Does he feel they'll favour Sir Brontus?"

"He wanted more time to prepare," Amron said.

"And Brontus didn't?"

"No, he's eager to see it done."

"Yes, because he's the superior sword." Elyon was not surprised that Sir Brontus Oloran was winning, not with his tourney record in the melee and knockout contests. He had not Dalton's war experience, yet in the duelling circle was the more impressive and skilled combatant, most agreed. "Who do you want to win?"

"I have no preference," his father said.

Elyon had another sip of wine and raised the corner of his mouth in a smirk. "Of course you do, Father. You'd prefer Sir Brontus, as most would."

"I'm not so sure. I had to tell Dalton that he wasn't a king last night. If he should lose the rank of First Blade as well, it might put him in a dark place."

"Good. And let him stay there." Elyon had little time for Dalton Taynar, the sour gloomy man who'd made Vesryn's life hell at Harrowmoor, and who stood by his poisonous father as they stole the throne from under Daecar noses. "If you ask me, he should be in chains, not fighting for a chance to bear the Sword of Varinar." Elyon shook his head bitterly. "Amara told me about the confessions and concessions, Father. You're to release the Greycloaks, after what those bastards did?"

His father looked weary all of a sudden. *He's had this fight before,* Elyon knew, *and not just with Amara*. He didn't want to add to his burdens, but still…

"I'm pardoning them for the good of the realm."

"But not Vesryn?"

"No. He killed a king."

"Godrik Taynar was no king. And Vesryn didn't kill him, Amara did."

Amron showed no surprise. "So she told you."

"She *loves* him, Father." Elyon wasn't so sure why he was saying this. He had been the first to learn of his uncle's betrayals, and had cursed him for it, hated him for it, yet time had weakened his ire. This wasn't about Vesryn, though, not only. It was about Amara, whom he loved. "If you hang Vesryn, it will destroy her," he said. "Are you sure you want that on your conscience?"

Amron gave a grunt. "And what's the alternative? Free him, with the others? My brother, who knew of the plot to have me killed…and by my very own son. Who helped Jonik enter the Song of the First Blade, so he could kill my firstborn boy, and gain the Sword of Varinar for himself, to give it to the Warrior King?"

I can't defend him. I don't want to, Elyon thought. But he did anyway. "Vesryn made mistakes. He was young and stupid and he made mistakes, and they have haunted him all his life. And he didn't give the Sword of Varinar to Janilah…he kept it, ran with it, and cursed himself as a turncloak in the act. He did that for you, Father, to make amends. That's all he's been trying to do." He peered at him. "And…Aleron. You don't believe Vesryn knew he would die, do you? You can't believe that. He would never have let that happen if he knew."

"It doesn't matter whether he knew or not. His actions helped it happen. He's responsible. I cannot forgive that, no more than I can forget it. If I let Vesryn go free then it'll stir the Taynars and their allies into a frenzy. Yes, Amara slew Godrik, and yes, he bloody well deserved it, but the whole world thinks it was Vesryn and we'd all do well to keep it that way. If Vesryn loves her, he will die for her. All of this…everything…we're doing it to *protect* her, Elyon."

He understood that. But even so… "The guilt will destroy her. She'd rather the truth get out, I know it. You should have seen her last night. I've never seen her break down like that before."

Amron lifted his chin, frowning. A softness came over his hard, stony face. "She broke down in front of you?"

"She's lost," Elyon said. "Without Lil and Vesryn her life has lost all meaning. I just…I feel sorry for her, Father. I hate seeing her like that. Amara was always so strong."

"And you think releasing Vesryn is the answer? He'll only march to war and die anyway. We all may, Elyon. I'm sorry, but Amara's distress is not important in the context of what we're facing. Once Lillia is back in Varinar, she'll have some purpose back in her life. It's the best I can do right now."

"But…"

"It's the best I can do right now," his father repeated, more firmly. He gave Elyon a hard stare. Outside, they heard the announcer call out a three-point hit for Sir Brontus Oloran, giving him the lead ten points to eight. The crowd gave an almighty roar that suggested, if it needed proving, that Sir Brontus was their favourite. "We should go outside," Amron said, already turning. "It will not serve for me to miss the end of the fight."

Elyon had much and more to talk about with his father still, yet understood his need to stand witness to the contest. He nodded and followed him back out into the bright sunlight, blinking through the glare as they stepped onto the grey stone balcony and the yard came into view below. The two combatants were circling one another, Dalton in Blockform and Brontus moving between the nimble forms he favoured, trying to find an opening. Elyon did a quick round of greetings with his father's men. He knew them all well enough. Sir Torus Stoutman came regularly to Blackfrost, as did Sir Ralf, though he'd not seen or heard much of Vilmar the Black for many long years. "Thought you were dead," he said to him.

The hunter scowled through his great black beard, a wondrous forest of a thing. "Still got that tongue, then." His scowl became something that might have been a smile, though it was hard to tell for sure with Vilmar. "Oh, I'll not die yet. Not when it's starting to get good."

"Good?" Elyon asked.

"Good," the man said, running the tip of his index finger along the blade of a throwing axe. "The earth is starting to *crawl*, boy, all sorts of foulness seeping from the dark. Good time to be a monster hunter like me."

Vilmar had always had an intensity about him. Elyon recalled how his uncle had gone hunting with him once to the Banewood, a story Vesryn liked to tell him when he was a boy. *Came back with a grimbear's head slung over his shoulder*, he thought. It still hung in the trophy room of Blackfrost Castle, among many other great beasts long dead. "What are you doing here then?" Elyon wanted to know. "Shouldn't you be out there, doing your thing?"

"Aye, sooner or later, I'll be gone. Once there's a beast to match me, something foul and ancient."

"Dragons are foul and ancient," Elyon pointed out.

"True enough, but they're for you knights to dance with. I deal in darker fiends."

"It sounds rather like an excuse, doesn't it?" came an affable voice behind him. Elyon turned to find the small scruffy man with the notebook standing beside him. He had a pot belly, patchy beard, red cheeks and shaggy hair. "I think Vilmar here just prefers the comforts of this castle, to the dangers of the wild."

Elyon gave the man a smile. "You must be Walter Selleck."

"I'm glad my reputation precedes me."

"Amara is very fond of you. She spoke a great deal about you last night, and the adventures you've had with my father." He took his hand and shook it briskly. "Thank you, for guiding him, Walter. Amara is certain he'd not be here today were it not for you."

"And she's right." Walter Selleck was not so humble as he looked, apparently. He grinned in a way that made Elyon like him immediately. "Though I can't take all the credit. Whitebeard was there also." He gestured to the shadows of the balcony, to a man Elyon had not noticed before. "Rogen, come meet Amron's son."

Elyon had heard of the ranger as well, of course. He fit the description Amara had given him. 'Ghostly and grim', were the words she'd used. 'A typical Taynar'. He was tall as well, his ungroomed black hair and ragged beard salted with grey, frame wreathed in dark, well-worn godsteel armour. *Not so much a ranger as a knight*, Elyon thought, *though a dark knight to be sure.* "Rogen, a pleasure." He took the man's steel wrist in his own and shook. "I'm told there's no one who knows the Icewilds better, nor the Weeping Heights."

"The tribes might disagree."

"Well, yes. I was speaking of Vandarians in particular."

"I have spent much time in those lands, yes."

"It's how you got the name Whitebeard, isn't it?"

He nodded stiffly, and glanced over the balustrade as another cheer rang out. Elyon did not sense much of a conversationalist in this Rogen Strand.

"Another score for your cousin," Walter said. "A two-pointer." It put the overall score for the second bout at ten each, all square. The small man gave Elyon a little tap. "Rogen's not so fond of his family, you'll learn, Sir Elyon. He above all wants Sir Brontus to win."

The ranger overheard. "I care not who wins," he said. "Dalton may be cousin to me by blood, but I do not know him. I met him only a handful of times in my youth before I was sent to Northwatch." He gave Elyon a swift bow and then retreated back to the shadows to keep watch.

No sooner had he left than Sir Torus replaced him, bustling up to the balcony edge. He was so short he could barely see over the top of it. "Would you like me to fetch you something to stand on?" Elyon teased. "You seem to be growing down in your dotage, Sir Torus."

The stout knight gave a bark of laughter. "I grow down any more and I'll be underground." He had a large rosewood pipe hanging from his lips, puffing smoke. "So, how's the Windblade been treating you, lad? You having some fun with it, I hope?"

Everything was fun to Sir Torus Stoutman. "There's a certain joy to flight, Sir Torus, yes."

"You'll be staying with us a while, will you?" He glanced over to where Elyon's father and Sir Ralf of Rotting Bridge were in conversation. "We could sure do with having you around. King's Point will be coming under attack any day now, we're hearing."

As will Mudport, Elyon thought, *and Rustbridge, and Southwatch as well most like.* If Thalan could be attacked so far north, few places were safe. "I'm not sure, Sir Torus. There's another Agarathi army at the Bane, I'm sure you've heard. If they strike at another city I may have to fly to help defend it."

In the yard below, Sir Brontus was pressing forward in Strikeform,

Elyon's favourite of the five. A part of him missed duelling like that. Fighting with the Windblade was wildly different and he'd had no one to teach him, adapting his own new style. *Strikeform in Flight*, he might have called it, with a certain measure of Glideform thrown in as well. *Or Flight-form*, he thought. *That might work.* Sir Brontus favoured Strikeform and Glideform as well, graceful and swift as he struck with long flowing arcs. Dalton remained in defensive Blockform, shutting him off, watching him warily. The assault came to nothing in the end. "Dalton's scarcely making any aggressive moves," Sir Torus complained. "All his points have been scored off the back of Oloran's errors."

As ever was thus, for those who favoured Blockform. It was the first form to master, the most important in both duelling and combat. 'Safety first,' his father always taught him. 'If you cannot defend yourself, you're as good as dead'. Amron Daecar's Blockform had been almost impenetrable, same as Aleron's, though Elyon had preferred the more showy stances. *I had my own tutor in Lythian*, he thought, *my own mentor and guide*. His father, of course, mastered all the stances, a feat rarely seen, yet in Strikeform Lythian was always the better. "Many men master Strikeform," his father had said to him once, "but if you want to know who *the* master is, it's Lythian Lindar, the Knight of the Vale. If you want to favour Strikeform, son, there is no man better to teach you."

A clang rang out below, and the crowd opened their mouths in a cheer. Sir Brontus had snuck through Daton's defences to score a two-point hit, taking the lead. "It'll be over soon," Lord Harrow said, joining them. "We'll be feasting and toasting to the first Oloran First Blade in two hundred years tonight. The long Taynar wait will have to go on."

And that wait had been even longer, four centuries rather than two, when the famed First Blade Sir Rufus Taynar had led the Knights of Varin through the Twenty First Renewal. He was succeeded by Sir Oswald Manfrey and then Galin Lukar, two names of similar renown, though for different reasons.

Up above them, the skies were beginning to turn grey, thickening with the promise of rain. Elyon looked west, to where heavy bands of dark cloud were marching forth like some great invading force.

"Weather's turning," said Lord Harrow. "Augurs promised as much, though not so soon."

"It won't favour Sir Brontus," Amron declared. "He likes a dry deck for his favoured forms. Blockform is much the better in the wet." He started into a lecture about the many merits of Blockform, as Elyon gave a quick roll of his eyes.

Harrow smiled at him. "Heard this speech before, have you, Sir Elyon?" he asked him quietly.

"Too many times to count." Elyon turned to face the Lord Protector. "My lord, I wonder if you've taken on a boy named Del here at Crosswater in the last few months? Tall, about sixteen, messy black hair. From North Tukor. Does that ring a bell?"

The man rubbed at his broad jowly chin. "I'd have to ask my lady wife,

Sir Elyon. She runs the household staff in the castle, though I don't recognise anyone of that description."

Elyon expected as much. Still, he liked to ask anyway whenever he arrived somewhere new, in the vain hope that Saska's adopted brother from Willow's Rise might yet be living, and somewhere in the north. If he was, it was unlikely to the point of impossibility that he would be here in southwest Vandar, yet all the same there was no harm in finding out for sure.

"This boy someone important to you?" Harrow asked.

"To someone I know. A friend, Lord Harrow. I ask by force of habit." He looked to the yard, as Dalton prodded for a two-point score, slipping right through Sir Brontus's defences with a stiff arm jap. "Sir Brontus is growing frustrated," he said. "The pressure is beginning to get to him."

"Dalton is giving him nothing," his father agreed. "The more Brontus tries to open him up, the more he'll leave himself exposed."

"A miserly Taynar," quipped Sir Torus. "Well, who woulda thought?"

Just let it be done, Elyon thought, growing impatient. He wasn't enjoying this, not one bit. It only made him think of Aleron, of Jonik, of the day one beloved brother had died and he'd sworn vengeance against another. The skies were growing darker above them by the minute, that thick swamp of gloomy cloud lumbering in from the west, and that wasn't helping either. *It rained that day too,* he remembered. *The sun went into hiding, and Vandar's Smile was blotted out. A darkness came upon the world that day, as it came upon my heart.*

Yet he did not leave. *I have been seen now,* he knew. Men were looking at him from the stands and tower windows and it would not do well for him to step away. *Father must watch, and so must I.* He put his eyes on the two combatants, circling and wheeling about one another as the rains began to come down, light at first, then harder and harder. Distantly he heard the first low rumble of thunder, rolling in from the west.

"You want to do something about this weather, lad?" Sir Torus japed. "You being Master of the Storms and all that?"

Elyon had not been near a thunderstorm since the day he'd fought Ezukar. He touched the Windblade's swirling pommel and felt something, an energy and excitement ringing through the steel. *It enjoys the storm,* he knew. Or was it something more?

He turned his eyes upward, scanning. Dragons had always been believed to mislike storms, yet of late that myth had proven false. *They embrace them,* Elyon thought. *They use the clouds to hide, to strike fast and be gone. Darkness is their ally, and fume and ash and smoke.* It made him wary. *There are three Blades of Vandar here, in this fortress, right now,* he thought.

He moved to his father's side. "It's dangerous, us gathering like this," he said to him, in a low voice. "You were hunted, *tracked,* Father, just as I was." He looked skyward as the clouds continued to swell, as the rains came down hard, as the thunder bellowed in the distance. "What if they should be drawn to us again?"

"Then they will fail again," Amron Daecar said. "I slew Zyndrar the Unnatural, just as you slew Ezukar, son. The dragon that plagued Ilithor has not been seen for a long while either. It may be dead as well. Sending lone dragons to hunt us is a strategy that has proven misjudged. All Eldur has done is sacrifice some of his most fearsome weapons. He'll not make the same mistake again."

Elyon felt the air sharpen and tense upon that grey stone balcony. *The men do not like to hear his name spoken aloud.* He sensed doubt in some of them, or perhaps it was just fear. But in his father there was no such doubt, no such fear. *He is just another enemy to him, to be defeated and slain. Varin Reborn,* he thought. *It's as Amara said.* They were all calling him that across Varinar, she had told him last night. *The dauntless and redoubtable Amron Daecar, returned from the dead, to give us all hope.*

The rain was coming down in sheets now, and half of those below had begun to seek shelter. Muddy puddles were fast appearing in the yard as the two knights danced their duel, splashing and swirling and striking. Above the roar of rain and thunder, the announcer had to shout yet louder to be heard. "If this gets any worse, the judges won't be able to see what's going on," Elyon heard Walter Selleck say. "At what point will it be called off, my lord?"

"It won't be. We need this done." Amron Daecar stood with a tense grimace on his face. The stone awning above the balcony helped protect them from the worst of the rain, yet still they were getting wet. He gave the skies a look as though they were some enemy to be destroyed. "Damn this weather. What's the latest score, anyone? I missed a couple of calls."

"Fifteen points to thirteen, to Lord Taynar," said wise old Sir Ralf. He had been born to a whore and had never known his father, yet all the same, there were few men so proper and chivalric as the Knight of Rotting Bridge. "This is slipping from Sir Brontus's grasp. It seems all but certain to go to a decider now, my lord."

He wasn't wrong. It took another ten minutes for Dalton Taynar to reach the required twenty, but reach them he did, and the contest was evened up, one bout apiece. The two competitors walked to their seats either side of the circle, where their supporters were gathered beneath the pouring rains. In Dalton's corner, Elyon saw his friend Sir Rodmond, whom he hadn't seen since Harrowmoor. Sir Ramsey Stone was there as well, as was Sir Quinn Sharp, and several other lesser lords too. The Giant of Hammerhall, Sir Taegon Cargill, stood a little aside, as though wanting to put some doubt into peoples' minds as to whom he was there to support. *As if anyone cares,* Elyon thought. On the other side, Sir Brontus had the backing of Sir Marcus Flint, another Varin Knight. Lord Mantle was there as well, and so was Sir Symon Steelheart, the pretty Knight of Nine-Hearth. The Flints, Mantles and Steelhearts were all long-time allies of the Olorans.

The two parties were in deep discussion, it looked. "What are the rules on postponement?" asked Walter Selleck.

"They're complicated," Amron answered. "In cases of extreme weather, if both parties agree to delay, they can." He scowled at the skies once more, though the rains had settled into a rhythm, and weren't getting any worse at least.

"Is that likely?"

"No. One fighter always has the upper hand and will insist they continue. Dalton will want to push his advantage now."

It seemed he was right. Elyon sensed more resolve in the Taynar camp, where the Oloran contingent were deeper in debate. *They're wondering whether to put forward a postponement plea,* Elyon thought. He studied Sir Brontus's expression, and knew he wouldn't. *He knows Dalton won't agree, so why bother? It will only show his opponent he doubts himself. Better to portray confidence and calm. Show him you won't back down.*

The announcer called out time, and the two combatants stood, donning their helms and picking up their swords. Brontus stepped forward first, and that said it all. He took position, ready to fight, moving into Blockform. Dalton seemed not to expect that. "This might go on a while," Lord Harrow said. "Brontus will tighten up now and wait for the weather to clear. He's got a strong Blockform too so far as I know."

"He does," Amron confirmed. There were some brighter patches, further west, though the rains were not yet waning. He rubbed his jaw. "It could yet go either way."

Elyon was done watching. A duel between two men in Blockform was a dreary affair, and not one he cared to witness. The rains had caused half the crowd to scamper for cover, so why not him? *I have better things to be doing…duties to attend.* His eyes went upward, ever wary of the threat lurking in the clouds. He drew the Windblade from its sheath and turned to walk down the passage. "Where are you going?" his father demanded of him.

"Hunting."

"My kinda boy," Vilmar growled, appreciatively.

Amron grabbed his arm. "Do you sense…"

"Not yet. But the dragons are often attacking from heavy cloud cover in the east. It serves to make sure, Father. I'll do a few passes and report back."

He marched straight inside, down the corridor, and into his father's solar. He had seen a balcony there earlier, on the southern side of the keep, and thought it best to take flight from there, rather than in front of the crowds. The harbour bustled below, the Vanguard standing bulkily beyond. The waters of the river were restless, churned up by the driving rain. A heavy mist had descended here, wet and grey, reducing visibility. *Good conditions for an attack,* Elyon thought. He gripped the Windblade's haft but heard no warning whispers. *Are they out there? Do you sense them?*

He had no reply, nothing to give him pause. Of late the Windblade had come to alert him preternaturally of danger, working with him, it felt, as his blood-bond to the blade strengthened. *My purpose is true,* he thought. *I am giving the blade just what it wants. The blood and death of dragons.*

Swinging the blade aloft, he summoned the winds to wreath him, pulling him from the stone balcony and up into the rain-soaked skies. He flew a pass over the castle, high enough to be ignored by those below, a spec amid the mire and no more. The bout was resuming in the yard, the knights cagily circling back and forward, prodding and probing, both in

Blockform stance. Elyon flew higher, and further west where the storm had come from. The clouds thinned for a time, then thickened anew further off, darker than ever and more dreaded. If there was to be a respite from the rain it wouldn't last. *They're tasting the appetiser only,* he thought. *The main course is yet to come.*

To the south he went, soaring above the Vanguard with its great statue-towers of Varin and Elin and Iliva. To east he flew, over the army in camp along the banks, above the woodland that bordered the river. He swung back around to the north once more, passing the castle for a second time, and still felt no threat of dragons amid the clouds. But he kept on flying, because he was enjoying himself all the same. There was something about soaring above the world in a storm that lit a joy inside him. In clear whether he could see further, and see more, yet the storm felt a friend to him. He felt more powerful in its embrace, bonded to its fearsome will. He remembered the lightning, the way the Windblade had summoned it from above him. The way he had swung on instinct and fired it upon Ezukar. The smell that followed, the burning singeing smell. The way the dragon had fallen, tumbling insensate to the earth, to perish in the fields far below.

Come for me, he thought, as he stopped to hover among the clouds. Thunder rumbled about him, and flashes of lightning lit the skies, silver and electric blue, for Vandar. *Come for me, here in my world.* He had fought many dragons now, slain many dragons, but only one had been in a storm. He wanted that again. He wanted to thrust the Windbalde aloft and feel the lightning brewing above. He wanted to see it, see the webs of light glowing, crackling, joining, erupting. He wanted to feel that energy, that thrill, that power, as the storm answered his summons. *Come for me,* he thought again, looking north and south, east and west. *Come for me. Enter my world. Come for me if you dare.*

But none came. He heard no whispers, felt no threat. *We are safe here, for now.* He decided to rejoin his father, report back as promised. Descending down past the castle, he glimpsed the bout once more, though it was only in passing. He could not make out who was on the offensive, no more than he knew who might be winning the final bout. *Let it be done. Let us raise the left hand of the winner aloft and put the Sword of Varinar in his right.* He only wished his uncle Rikkard was here, or Killian, Brontus's cousin and heir to his house, and the more experienced and gifted warrior besides. Either of those would have been better than these two, and more deserving. But they were half a world away and had never entered the Song last year. That left Dalton and Brontus. *Let it be done,* Elyon thought again. *And let it be Brontus.*

A flash of black caught his eye, something airborne flapping beneath him. His heart barely gave a flutter. *Crow,* he knew at once. He spun in flight, giving chase. The bird was strong and determined, beating hard through the rains and winds with its powerful wings. It had on its ankle a rolled scroll sealed with a blob of silver and red. *Pentar colours,* Elyon thought, *from the east.*

He kept his distance so as not to disturb it as it made for the rookery, homing in. Elyon followed, landing on the exposed steps that wound up into the crowmaster's quarters. The stone looked almost alive from all the rain dancing upon its surface. He climbed, dripping wet, and knocked on the heavy wood door. He heard shuffling beyond, then the handle turned and the door groaned open. A small man in grey robes stood beyond, frowning up at him. "You…you're…"

"Elyon Daecar. Might I come in?"

"Please, yes, my lord, get out of that rain." The old man stepped right back to give him entry into his modest chambers. It was a great deal quieter within, a cosy and cluttered space. "Are you here to watch the contest? I fear the storm has grown so loud I cannot hear it anymore. Or perhaps it has ended by now? Who won, might I ask?"

"The fight is ongoing, Master…"

"Corbitt, my lord." He closed the door behind Elyon, shutting out the sound of the storm, then rummaged around for something he might use to dry. The best he could find was an old set of robes, though Elyon refused.

"I'm only going to get soaked again when I step without," he said, pushing the Windblade into its sheath. The old man looked at it in a state of rich intrigue, a reaction Elyon had grown quite used to. "I believe you have a visitor, Master Corbitt," he said, drawing his attention.

The crowmaster looked right up at him. "Ah, yes of course. And what is it you want of me, my lord?"

"Not me," Elyon said. He gestured to the set of crooked wooden steps that led to the rookery above. "A crow just came in, bearing a letter. I'd like to know what it says."

"Oh, did it now? One for Lady Horsia, I would think. She keeps a good many pen-friends." He gave a chuckle. "I do believe your auntie is among them, Sir Elyon."

I'm not surprised. "Please check, if you would. I believe it had a Pentar seal."

"Oh? House Pentar?" The old man seemed surprised by that. "I will confess, crows have not been coming so often from the east of late. I wonder what it might be?"

Elyon was wondering the same. *A call for more men,* he thought. *A warning of an Agarathi landing in the south, perhaps, or an attack on Southwatch or one of the other great forts along the Black Coast.* All were possible. And none were likely to be good. He thought it best to find out before returning to his father, thus saving this old man a journey in the rain. He waited a moment as Master Corbitt shuffled up the steps. There was a great deal of flapping, a little bit of puffing, and then the old man returned with the scroll to hand.

He broke the seal and opened it out. "It's from a Sir Storos," he said, reading, "of House Pentar. It seems you were right, Sir Elyon. You have a good eye."

Sir Storos Pentar was a son of Lord Porus, Elyon knew. "Has there been an attack?" he asked. "On Redhelm, or…"

A little smile broke out on the old man's wrinkled lips. "No attack, my lord. Rather better news than that, I would say." He reached out to hand the letter over. "It would appear that Captain Lythian is alive, after all."

224

18

Cecilia

"I'm sorry, Hog," she said, as he woke suddenly, blinking up at her through the gloom. "But I'm not about to spend my days in darkness, living side by side with a rapist."

"R..rapist?" His hands and feet were bound in rope, though the gag had not yet been shoved into his mouth. He peered at her in deep confusion, fighting to escape his stupor. "I'm no...no rapist..."

"Oh you are, and thrice over, according to my sources." She listed the names. "The milkmaid from Dunmoat? The barkeep's wife at the Brindle Boar in Mardale? The cobbler's daughter you molested in Broadway? Do none of them ring a bell?"

"I...I don't know what you're talking about!" Panic took root in him. He tugged at the ropes tied about his wrists, struggling to wrest his hands free, to no avail. "Gerret...you're thinking of Gerret! He was the honourless one, not me! What are you doing, my lady? What...what is this?"

Your reckoning, she thought. True enough, Gerret had always been greatly worse than his larger, older companion, but that hardly made Hog a saint. He was a sellsword, after all, and those were typically a wicked sort. That about the rapes was true, she knew, and Hog had done a great deal of murdering and marauding in his time as well. *You are a loose end, Hog, and these mages need you tied, same as me.*

"It'll be quick," Cecilia assured him. She did not want him to suffer needlessly; he'd earned that much at least, for his service. "They said they'd make it quick and painless."

He stared up at her with widening eyes as the truth of his fate sank in. "You're...you're to *kill* me? No, you...you can't. My lady...you *can't*..."

"I'm afraid our hosts have twisted my arm. They cannot have you leaving this place. Not with all you know."

His eyes dashed hard about the room, as though expecting to find shadows lurking in the darkness, sharpening knives. But they were alone, for now. "You sold me out? To those…those freaks? You told them how I wanted to leave?"

"They already knew."

"What…*how?*"

"How do you think? *Magic.*" She walked to the door and opened it up to peer outside. *Where are you?* She'd been told they would know when to come. The last thing she wanted was to have this conversation. *I should have gotten the gag into his mouth sooner, before he came around.* The tonic she'd slipped him last night had worn off quicker than she'd expected, though, and she'd only just finished binding his hands and feet when he awoke. They were the priority, however. If he'd awoken gagged and yet unbound at the wrists, he'd have killed her sure as the sunrise.

"Please, my lady. *Cecilia*…please. You don't need to do this. You *can't.* I've served you loyally…I've served you well."

She turned back to him, as he tried and failed to sit up on his bed, wriggling like a worm on a hook. "Much has happened that I didn't plan for, Hog. I'm sorry, truly. But this is out of my hands. If it were up to me I would let you walk free from here, but it isn't. They believe you've grown too dangerous. They don't trust you…"

"I'll be good," he blurted. "They can trust me. Tell them…tell them they can."

But I can't. "Their minds are made up. I'm sorry."

He spluttered out a few more pleading words as he struggled against his bonds, though Cecilia ignored him. She looked out through the door, listening for footsteps. She could hear none as yet.

"You…you bitch. I can't believe you would do this to me. You hateful treacherous bitch!"

The pleading is done, then. "Yes yes, bitch, bastard, spider, witch. I've heard them all before, Hog, and a great deal worse."

"Cause they're true, every one of them!" He spat at her across the room, though the spittle fell well short. "A son-less whore, that's all you are. No wonder your boy won't come see you. Who'd want a mother like you?"

Not many, she had to admit to herself. *Not Jonik.* He had ignored her pleas to see him for days, weeks, a lifetime it felt. She did not let the doomed man see her pain, though. "Thank you for making this easier on me," was all she told him. "They say men show their true colours at the end, Hog. Go on, let it all out."

So he did, unleashing a dazzling diatribe of insults and curses that would have made the most foulmouthed of sailors blush. It was all easy enough to ignore, though…until he cut right through the meat of it, and thrust at her open wound once more. "I pity you, Blakewood," he growled at her, snarling. "You're trying to be good…you're trying to be better…but you're still just an evil callous bitch at heart, and that will never change." He mustered strength enough to spit a second time, and this time he hit his mark, striking her right on the cheek with a glob of yellowy-brown phlegm. Then he laughed. "You remember what it felt like, that portal? It lasted an instant only, aye, but you remember. The emptiness, the darkness, the *eter-*

nity of it." He looked at her as Sir Gerlon Rottlor had, the day she'd had him hanged at Galin's Post for treason, with an expression of utter and immeasurable hatred. "That'll be your fate forever, bitch. The Long Abyss. It's reserved for people like you."

She wiped the mucus from her cheek with the back of her sleeve. "Then I'll see you there," she merely said. "A rapist thrice over, and a murderer too many times to count. You booked your spot in the Abyss long ago, Hog. And you'll be visiting sooner than I."

He seemed to have other ideas. With a sudden bellow of rage, he staggered to his feet and surged toward her, swinging hard with his tied up hands. Though he took her somewhat by surprise, he was ludicrously cumbersome fettered in rope at the hands and feet and easy enough to evade. She slipped sideways as his momentum carried him forward, crashing against the wall with a sickening crunch as his face smacked into the stone. When he spat this time out came spittle and blood and broken teeth as well. She cringed at the sight of him and took a few steps back, expecting him to hop after her like some great demented rabbit.

He didn't. Instead he turned the other way, heaved forward with his weight, and smashed out through the door into the corridor, screaming through the red ruin of his mouth. "Tyrith...lad, you...you listen to me! Get out of here...*get out*! You can't trust this bitch, she's using you...she's just *using* you, lad, get out..."

No, that won't do. Cecilia sped forward, drew the dagger she'd taken off Hog from her belt, and slipped it straight through his back. A bloody cough erupted from his mouth as the godsteel pierced his heart, a spray of red spattering the nearest wall. "I didn't want it to go this way, Hog," she said behind him. "You left me no choice."

He staggered forward, and turned to her unsteadily. The knife slipped smoothly from his flesh. "B...b...*bitch*," he managed to croak, as the colour drained from his face. He blinked, fell, and died, landing in a sprawling heap at her feet. The blood leaked out beneath him, red and warm on the cold stone floor.

They arrived some ten minutes later, by which time the pool of blood had spread sticky and wide, glistening darkly beneath the lamplight. The old rotting one called Fhanrir wrinkled his long warty nose as he appeared from the gloom. "I said we'd take care of him," he admonished her. "We might have used him."

"How?" Cecilia stood by the wall outside her room, the bloody blade still in her grasp. Hog was not the first man she'd killed, but she'd known him, liked him well enough, and it felt wrong to end it like that. *I curse myself anew, but I had no choice. He'd have done something reckless. He had to die.* "How would you have used him?"

Fhanrir sneered at her. "Never you mind, woman." *Blood ritual,* was all she could think, though that didn't make sense. It was only the boys they used for that. *Young* blood, untainted. Hog was too old and grim for that. Fhanrir had another of the mages with him, one Cecilia hadn't met, though it was never easy to be sure with those cloaks and cowls they wore.

"Vottur," he said to him, in a horrid rattling rasp of a voice. "See this place cleaned up, and the body removed. *You*, woman, come with me."

Cecilia bristled and stood her ground. "You said you would come at the right time. I didn't want to have to kill him myself."

"It's done." The old creature turned his eyes uncaringly to Tyrith's door. "Did he hear anything?"

"No. I don't think so."

"Think? I'd prefer you know for sure."

"I haven't heard anything," Cecilia told him, begrudgingly. "I gave him the tonic, same as Hog, so he'd sleep through it. I'm sure he heard nothing."

The mage sniffed the air, nostrils flaring, then nodded. "Fine. Come, then." He began shuffling off down the corridor, giving a perfunctory wave for her to follow.

They walked in silence, leaving behind the stink of iron and shit from the instinctive emptying of Hog's bowels as he fell down and died. After a while the quiet grew uncomfortable, though the mage seemed not to notice. *Time isn't the same to him as it is to me.* Fhanrir had lived through the age of the Five Followers, thousands of years ago. *A five minute silence to me is a blink to him, hardly noticed.* She was not accustomed to such, though. "Where are you leading me?" she asked.

"Outside."

She frowned. "Outside?" She'd not stepped foot beyond the refuge as yet. Her weeks here had been spent cloistered in the rear, in passages dark and dreary. "Into the fort?"

"Yes. Outside. To your son."

She stopped entirely. "My…"

"Son. Name's Jonik, you might have heard." Fhanrir gave her an unpleasant grin. "The boy's been having it hard of late, what with all his friends abandoning him. There's a lot on his young shoulders, much for him to manage, and he needs more hands to help him. He thought of you. Might have used that big sellsword of yours too, but, well…you just killed him."

She wasn't understanding. *Is this some cruel trick?* "You were going to let Hog live? I thought…"

"Try not to think too much. It's up to us to do that here."

"I've asked for days to see my son. Weeks. Why now?"

"I just told you."

He needs help, she thought. *But has he asked for me?* She doubted it. Nor had she heard anything of his company abandoning him, or anything else for that matter. All her energies had been directed at trying to keep Hog in line, trying to tend young Tyrith as the Steward had asked of her. Now *this*? She felt like putting the bloody blade through the mage's neck and bloodying it further. "I want to see Hamlyn," she demanded. He was the senior authority here, she knew. He'd have the answers.

"No."

No. Cecilia hated the word. Few men told her no. *Only Father had with any regularity, and he I could still twist. But this one?* She had no power to manipulate these mages, no silk with which to spin her webs. *I hate this place. I should never have come.* It had been fear of her father that had driven her here, but he might just be dead by now, slain in his duel with the dragon atop the world. And Jonik. The thought of meeting him had drawn her to plunge into the darkness of that portal as well, but look where that had led her. *He wants nothing to do with me. He has made that clear enough.*

"I want to see Hamlyn," she said again. She folded her arms, though kept ahold of the godsteel dagger, for added effect.

Fhanrir looked at it. "Careful you don't scratch yourself. No, I said."

"Why not?"

"Hamlyn is resting. The toils of mortal life weigh heavy on him."

"*Mortal* life?" These mages were not mortal so far as she could figure. "He's lived thousands of years."

"And he's been dying every day of them. Just slowly. Our duty is to slow his dying further, keep him strong, for his task. You know this already."

She sheathed her blade. The threat was never going to stand, not with him. "Has Jonik asked for me personally?"

"Yes," he said, though she sensed falsehood in his voice. "He needs you."

Needs. It was what every mother wanted to hear of her son, though she could not trust his words. *Jonik does not need me, nor does he want me,* she told herself. It was easier to think that way. To live in hope only made it harder. "What about Tyrith? Hamlyn asked that I watch over him. That's my duty here." *My solemn duty,* she thought. *My chance to do something right.*

"Hamlyn has arranged for the old forge to be reignited," the old mage told her, "the workshop polished and prepared. Tyrith will have plenty to occupy himself, now that he has settled. There are countless books here for him to study, countless scrolls. He has spent his life in Ilith's ancient forge, yes? Well now we shall open the doors of his refuge to him. Do you think he will like that, Cecilia? To be able to read and work at his leisure?" His purply black lips peeled back into a rotted smile. "Of course he would. And Hamlyn…when he is restored to strength, he intends to spend more time with the boy as well. To instruct him in his ancestor's ways. If Tyrith is to become as Ilith was, who better to help guide him than Ilith's closest friend?"

No one, Cecilia thought. *And certainly not me.* "And what will I be to him?"

"A mother, as you have been. Tyrith still needs you too."

She could believe that part at least. Tyrith was emotionally fragile, weak and needy, and pawed at her like a puppy whenever she came around. But her true son? *No. If he needs me, it's as a servant, not a mother.* It sounded like he had been left shorthanded with the departure of his company. *He'll have me shovelling shit and scrubbing countertops and I'll smile and nod and do all that he asks of me. If this is my way in, so be it. Maidservant, mucker, I'll be whatever he needs me to be. Eventually he might call me mother.*

She walked on in silence, refusing to give in to that hope. It was like a weed in the back of her head, always growing no matter how many times she pulled it out. *Hope is treacherous,* she tried to tell herself. She was imagining Jonik smiling at her, telling her stories of his life, as they ate and drank and laughed, like they had in her deceitful dream. *Don't give in to it. Ignore the fantasy. Remember the truth. He hates you, and probably always will...*

She marched on, past grand statues and through high vaulted halls, pulling weeds, strangling hope. They were in a part of the refuge where many great rooms were linked, one after another after another, spreading in an endless series of magnificent chambers. She recognised the route; it was the same one she'd taken the day she arrived, when Hamlyn himself had led her through to the refuge's rear, deep in the mountains. She much preferred it here. It was brighter, less foreboding. There were more torches and lamps upon the walls, and in some places shafts of sunlight cut down from windows high above them, ushering in a natural glow.

A few moments later they came to the chamber that contained the portal door. It looked different, somehow. They continued closer, and then she saw it. *It isn't shimmering,* she realised. *It's just a black rock wall.* "You deactivated it."

"It's served its purpose." Fhanrir shuffled on past it. Everything about him was blunt and brief. "We can't have just anyone stumbling in."

"But...the people. If Ilithor comes under attack..."

"It will fall. Or it will rally. That is not our concern."

This place is soulless. She fell a step behind him as he tottered on, studying the cold black door, its surface inert and unmoving. The depth to it was gone, that strange enticing sense of eternity that rippled and folded into the blackness. She shuddered to recall it. This portal had been built so the people of Ilithor might flee here at their time of need. Now the very men who had helped Ilith build it had shut it off. *Soulless,* she thought again. *They say I have no heart, but these...*

She decided not to question Fhanrir on it any further. He was a prickly self-righteous old creature and would not respond well to her inquiries. *Secrecy. This is about secrecy, above all. It's about something greater.* She had to remind herself of that sometimes, that their mission had a deeper meaning to it, a more profound goal.

They are here to try to save this world, she told herself. *That is why they built the order, at Thala's command. That is why they carried out contracts.* They had made this place a house of horrors at her urging. They had accursed themselves, befouled themselves, damned themselves for that. *Perhaps we should be praising them for their sacrifice?* she wondered. *For standing vigil here so long, shackled to the evil of their unspeakable, abhorrent duty?*

She pondered that some more as Fhanrir led her on, shambling through a sequence of capacious, high-ceilinged chambers. More statues stood attendance, immaculately carved, astonishingly lifelike. One chamber, briefly glimpsed through a grand stone archway, glowed brighter than all the others. She saw within a great statue carved upon the eastern wall; Thala the Far-Seeing Queen in all her wise resplendence, extending forth above a high stone lectern topped with a leather-bound book, illuminated by a shard of light cast down from the ceiling above.

The Book of Contracts, she thought. *The source of the order's foundation, and purpose.* She slowed as they passed, her eyes drawn to its ancient authority, wondering how many men and women of high renown had perished by the content of its pages. "Are there any contracts left?" she found herself asking.

"The order's disbanded," Fhanrir said, still walking. "What do you think?"

"You told me not to think. I hoped you might give me a straight answer."

He seemed to like that, by the twist of his carious mouth. "Didn't take you for a woman who needed things spelt out for you, Cecilia. No, there're no contracts left. We've done our duty now, save one."

"The transference," Cecilia said.

"Aye. Won't be so long now. Once Hamlyn's strong enough, and had more time with the boy."

"And when it's done?"

"When it's done?" He stopped and turned to look at her.

"I asked Hamlyn what would happen to Tyrith. Whether he'd *become* Ilith once his spirit has imbued him." The blacksmith was afraid of that, she knew, terrified of losing himself to the will of another.

"Did you now? And what did Hamlyn say?"

"He said he didn't know."

A laugh rattled up Fhanrir's wrinkled neck. "And you think *I* might? Why's that? I was never near so close to Ilith as Hamlyn was, nor so gifted besides. I'm Hamlyn's servant, same as Hamlyn was Ilith's. It wasn't me Thala gave the book to, Cecilia. I do what I'm told, that's all. Always have."

Somehow Cecilia doubted it, though saw little sense in rendering such an accusation. Instead she asked of the transference, querying Fhanrir on its method.

The mage only snorted. "You'd not understand. Might as well try explaining the art of godsteel metalwork to a lackwit. You have some sense for a woman, I'll grant, but best not trouble yourself with the ancient and arcane. It'll only hurt your head."

"Try me." She stood her ground.

He gave another snort. "No. I haven't the time or patience. Now do you want to see your son or not?"

He's hiding something. "Of course I do. I've asked a hundred times."

"Then enough questions. He's waiting for you outside."

Her suspicions gave way to a flutter of nerves as they reached the great black doors and stepped without. A mid-morning sun was climbing in the east, cast above the tips of the mountains. Thin banners of sleek white cloud moved briskly on a biting wind. She pulled her cloak tight about herself and ran a hand through her hair to neaten it, straightening herself out such as she could. Her time at the rear of the refuge had stripped her of her regal dress. Her garb was plain; cotton underclothes overtopped with a dress of brown dyed wool, belted at the waist, over which she wore a heavy cloak. No jewellery glistened at her neck; there were no bangles and bracelets girdling her wrists. The make-up she wore to enhance and prettify her features was gone, left behind in Ilithor. *I have the look of a commoner,* she thought, *ageing and growing frumpy.*

She took ahold of her godsteel blade - Hog's blade - to settle herself. Unlike most Bladeborn women Lady Cecilia Blakewood was used to its touch. It was one of the benefits of being born a bastard, excluding her from the normal expectations of a highborn lady, bred to bed and wed a man of high station. She clung tight as she advanced at Fhanrir's side, drinking in the fresh mountain air. The fortress felt abandoned. The upper ward was empty, the training yards rang still as stone. There were no lights in the windows, no candles lit, no torches flickering. She heard no voices, saw no figures move in the shadows. No watchers manned the walls, no sentries stood the towers, only the wind and the scuffing of their footsteps stirred the air.

"Don't worry, he's out here," Fhanrir assured her.

Cecilia had started to get the feeling that this was some twisted trap. That there was no one here at all but shadows and ghosts. That her son had left with the rest. She was about to respond when she saw the first sign of life up ahead. There was a man emerging from a short squat tower, a tray of empty cups and bowls in his grasp. He set it down as he exited the building, pulled a ring of keys from his belt, and thrust it into the lock, turning. He was grizzled and grey, with cropped thinning hair and a rugged facade, dressed all in frosted black. Fhanrir stopped as he sighted him. "Go ahead, Cecilia. Gerrin will take care of you from here."

Gerrin. Cecilia recognised him, though vaguely. She had spotted him once or twice in Ilithor over the years, meeting her father. *Jonik's master,* she knew. *The man who fostered him here, all those years. The man who raised him.* "I... I'd rather you..." She cut herself off, realising that Fhanrir was already shambling away up the alley, leaving her alone. She had questions for him. *Am I to stay out here now, in the fort? Am I allowed to come and go? What of Tyrith? You said I was to continue to play mother to him, help guide him, keep him calm.* But the mage was gone, seeming to vanish into the morning mists. She turned back. Gerrin had spotted her and was approaching in a brisk step.

"Lady Blakewood. You came." His voice was rough and harsh, though more friendly than she might have supposed.

They are in dire straits, that's clear, she thought. *Perhaps Jonik did ask for me after all.* "Sir Gerrin. You served my father once, in his Six. I remember seeing you when I was a girl."

"That was long ago, my lady."

"I have seen you since as well. Many years later, after you'd infiltrated this order."

"At the command of your father," Gerrin pointed out. He came within five feet of her and stopped.

"Of course. We were all but pawns to him, were we not? As he was to his fate."

"It would seem so." The man's lips wore a weary smile. He glanced over Cecilia's shoulder, up through the fort. "Fhanrir brought you down?"

Cecilia nodded. "Were you aware of this Book of Contracts, Sir Gerrin?" He had been here decades, she knew. Surely he'd been privy to some of its secrets.

"No, my lady," he told her. "It was never my remit to know."

"Then you did not know of Ilith either?"

He shook his head slowly, as though struggling to believe it. "No. Jonik...your son. He told us only last night of Ilith's fate. As he did yours."

"He never told you I was here?" It shouldn't have surprised her. His bastard bitch of a mother being closeted back in the refuge wasn't information Jonik was likely to want to share. *He wants to forget I ever existed,* she thought. *Hog was right. Who would want a mother like me?*

"He didn't mention you, no. Not until last night. We have been pushed to the edge of need here, my lady." He glanced past her again, frowning. "He said you had another man with you, a sellsword in your service. We had wondered if he might come as well. Where is he?"

"Dead."

His frown deepened. "Dead?"

She nodded, though didn't want to elaborate on that just yet. "You served my father long years, Sir Gerrin. As an Emerald Guard. As a sworn sword. As a spy and shadow. I take it you knew I was Jonik's mother?"

He shook his head. "It was not my place to ask."

He knew, she thought. *He must have known.* But then...perhaps not. *My father did like to keep the pieces of his puzzle apart,* she knew. The comparison with Queen Thala was not lost on her. *She scattered her puzzle too.* "But you knew who his father was, of course?"

"Yes. Of that I was aware."

"As you were his purpose." She could not decide what to feel. She could not decide whether to trust this man or not. "You raised him so he might one day kill his own father."

The smile on his face was gone. "I raised him at your father's command. I raised him to one day wield the Nightblade." He stared at her through hard grey eyes. "I protected him. I fostered him and I named him. I have loved him as a son..."

"As I have a mother."

"You gave him up," the old knight came in. His words rang as harsh and bitter as the wind, gusting through the snowy fortress.

The accusation stung. "By my father's command, same as you. Do you think I wanted that, Gerrin? Do you think I wanted to hand over my only son, to be raised a weapon?"

He held his tongue, but his eyes showed doubt. Eventually he spoke. "Both of us have been pawns, as you said. I should not be so quick to judgement. But Jonik..."

"Hates me. I know."

"He hates all the world," Gerrin said suddenly. He turned back behind him, scanning through the lower ward that widened out toward the gate and curtain wall of the fort. A worried look came over him. "The last days

233

have been bleak, Lady Blakewood. I trust you were told what has happened here?"

"His company abandoned him."

"It's worse. Those who left are but one problem. The other is the issue of those who have not returned. We had hoped that Lord Manfrey would be back by now, but there has been no sign of him."

The exiled lord, she thought. "Why did he leave?"

"To bring several others of our company here," Gerrin explained. "They were non-Bladeborn, left behind in the lower foothills until we safely took the fort. Jonik greatly misses them. They have been critical in his growth this last year, yet without them…"

"When did Manfrey depart?" Cecilia asked.

He thought a moment. "Almost three weeks past. It's possible they have been slowed or waylaid or become lost along the way. In truth I should have gone myself, knowing the route as I do." He lowered his voice. "But there is another possibility, one I dare not speak."

"Dare it, Sir Gerrin." Though she could probably guess herself. "You fear they have been attacked on the road? Killed?"

"It's possible. A number of men of the order escaped during the attack, and there are others I know of who aren't accounted for." He glanced once more over her shoulder. "Jonik told me there are five mages in the refuge. I know of nine who have lived here in my time. Two are dead, one by Jonik's hand, one by mine. Means two are missing, out on some contract or another, or dead, perhaps, though Jonik's getting no answers on that. Makes me uneasy either way. Meknyr and Vaynor, those are their names. If they're out there…"

"You don't trust them," Cecilia said. He was making that obvious enough. "Hamlyn and these mages. You fear them."

"I fear a yoke. I fear shackles and fetters unseen."

"The order is broken, Sir Gerrin. Fhanrir told me himself they have but one duty remaining. Why should Jonik's men be at risk? Why should Lord Manfrey be a target?"

"I am not saying he is."

"It sounds like you are."

"I'm saying he might be," the gruff knight went on. "Whether by design or by chance. The men who escaped here might have crossed his path on their descent. As might a returning mage. Or they might have been sent. All ends must be considered, yet they lead to the same destination regardless, should Emeric not return." His eyes darkened. "Jonik suffers under the weight of his bond. The Nightblade has become a burden to him, and his purpose…" He drew a breath and scanned the ward once more. "He feels he has been deceived. He thought his coming here a noble deed, the start of something greater, and yet he finds himself in shadow again, little more than a thrall. I fear his spirit is darkening. And if his friends should not return…"

Is this why Fhanrir sent me out here? Cecilia wondered. *To try to bring him to the light? Keep him calm as I have with Tyrith?* If so the mage would be in for a rude awakening. "He should give it up," she said. She thought of her father, of the madness the Mistblade had wrought upon him. "He *must* give it up, Gerrin."

"I know. And he knows it too, deep down. But..."

"But?"

"But you know what I'm about to say. You know how tight that hold can become. He understands what he has to do and yet is not so trusting either." His voice sunk lower. His eyes shifted left and right and he took another pace toward her. "He suspects he will become a loose end should he hand it over, as will the rest of us. We know too much, he says. Once he gives the Nightblade up, they will kill us. He keeps it to protect us."

Frozen fingers climbed her spine. *Hog*, she thought. *A loose end, to be tied.* "The others were allowed to go..."

"They knew only a part of the truth, this of the Book of Contracts, little more. They did not know of Ilith and the heir. The Steward will not let that secret get out."

"The Steward is weakened," Cecilia said. The winds picked up suddenly, blowing hard down the passage, pulling at her cloak. She reached to her blade, gripping tight. Gerrin's eyes glimpsed it, saw the blood upon its edge.

"Whose..."

"My man's," she told him at once. "He had become a threat." *A loose end*, she thought again.

"You killed him yourself?" There was surprise in his voice, if not condemnation.

"I had no choice. Fhanrir said they would be there, but they weren't. I took matters into my own hands."

Gerrin nodded his understanding and had another look through the ward. "I would wipe that blood away, my lady. We would do well for Jonik to trust you. We would do well to stick together here."

She did as he bid her, drawing out the blade, wiping it down upon the sleeve of her cloak. The blood had dried by now, though, so it wasn't so easy to wipe off.

"Here," he said, taking it off her. He spat onto the length of the steel and cleaned it for her, before handing it back. "Keep that close. Jonik, myself, Harden...we mean you no harm. But there are others."

"Others? Who?"

"Prisoners, taken during the attack. Jonik means to..." He cut himself off as she looked past his shoulder, following her gaze. Her son was emerging now from another stone building across the ward. He stopped as he stepped out, looking over at them through the swirling white mists. "He's been cooking," Gerrin told her. "We've many mouths to feed here."

She had no reply. Her son wore black wool and shadow, his eyes bordered in darkness. One pale hand clutched at the lightless hilt of his ancient blade. He looked leaner than she had seen him several weeks ago, ghostly white and haunted. For a moment he just stared. Then in a clean hard stride, he stepped over.

Cecilia tried to still the restless stirring in her heart. Those weeds of hope were growing as she thought; *this is my chance. I can spend time with him, help him, serve him. In time he'll learn to love me.* She pulled them out as quick as she could but they kept on growing, growing, growing…

Jonik came to a halt in front of her. He looked at Gerrin. "How long have you been talking?"

"A few minutes. Fhanrir brought her out."

"Where is he?"

"Gone. Back to the refuge. You know he doesn't like it out here."

Jonik's face was emotionless. *I birthed a babe, pink and perfect, and here he is now, cold and hard as stone.* "Fhanrir told me you needed help, Jonik." Her voice was as pathetically weak as it had been the last time. *I become a wretched worm around him, longing for his love.* "He said you've become shorthanded."

Her son nodded. "Where's the other one? Your sellsword."

"Dead," Gerrin said, before she might speak. "*They* killed him."

"Why?"

"Hog was a dangerous man, not worthy of trust," Cecilia explained, sharing a glance with the old Emerald Guard. "He is not the sort to keep a secret, Jonik." That was a lie. Hog could always be counted upon for that, and had been privy to many of her recent crimes. But here? No, perhaps not. *He needed to die*, she told herself again. *I had no choice.* "I hope I will be enough," she said to her son. "What do you need of me?"

"The boys," he said. "I thought they could do with a woman's touch. And yours in particular."

"Mine?" It wasn't what she'd expected. "What exactly do you…"

"They call you a spider," Jonik cut in. "They say you have a way with words. I want you to spin a web for me."

She wasn't understanding. "What sort of web?"

"One of hope. I want these boys to understand that there is a world out there where they can be free. Maybe you can help with that. You're an outsider, and they're not used to women here. They might trust you more than they do me."

"The older ones are the bigger problem," Gerrin explained. "Their conditioning is deeper, Lady Blakewood. They see us as usurpers, not saviours. They may be more inclined to listen to you."

"Of course. I'll do what I can, but…" It wasn't all adding up to her. "These boys, I thought…well, I didn't realise they were to be set free."

"That's why we came here," her son said, stiff-jawed. "To liberate them."

"Yes, I understand. But…"

"What? If you have doubts, go ahead…speak them."

She chose her words carefully. "It's only…these boys. I was under the impression that they were still….still needed?"

"*Needed*. You're referring to the blood rituals. The occult." She hadn't expected her son to come out and say it so freely. The words were issued darkly from his lips. *Even giving voice to it disgusts him.*

236

She cleared her throat. "Hamlyn is weakened, Fhanrir told me. I took that to mean…"

"That they will need to pluck a boy or two from the cells, to restore his strength? Yes, I am aware. I have spoken with Fhanrir about this already. He has warned me not to interfere more than once."

"And you're to go against him?" She did not think that wise. "Jonik, he's right. Hamlyn needs to be strong so he can perform the transference…"

He grunted her to silence. "I know. Fate, they call it. Destiny. I know all about *that*, Cecilia. I know how important it is. It doesn't change how much it turns my stomach. But I'll not interfere, not any more than I must." He clenched his jaw. "We have come to an arrangement."

Something about the way he said that disquieted her. "You and Fhanrir?"

"Yes. He needs blood to restore Hamlyn's strength. Bladeborn blood, young blood. There are thirteen younglings here in one barracks. Another nine teenagers in another. I have accepted that not all of them are going to live. I have accepted that they were brought here to serve a purpose. I accept that not because I want to, but because I must. They will be the last, Fhanrir promises me. Two, he'll need, three at most. I have agreed to allow it." He closed a fist and opened it and closed it again. The other clung hard to the Nightblade, and he stood there quietly, staring into shadow, as though listening to a voice only he could hear, and for a moment, a terrible moment, she saw something dark and deranged glimmer behind his eyes. Something familiar. *Like Father*, she thought.

Gerrin noticed it too. He stepped forward to stir Jonik from his trance. "You have run your father's breeding program for many years, Lady Blakewood," he said to her. "You spent those years selecting the best girls for the duty. It was your talent, to choose well and choose wisely. We…" He glanced at Jonik. "We would have you use those talents again."

Cecilia Blakewood felt a sickness brewing in her gut. "You…you want me to…"

"Choose," Jonik snapped at her. "Yes, we want you to do what you're good at, and choose. Why else do you think you're here?" He spun about and showed her his back, grunting, "Show her the cells," to Gerrin as he left.

19

Amilia

"Do you see anything, Sir Munroe," she called, standing far back from the edge of the towering chalk cliff. The winds were blustering so hard across the headland she feared a fierce gust might just blow her to her doom. "Are there any signs of life down there?"

The knight peered out to the south, unaffected by the winds, his godsteel plate far too heavy for the squalls to shift. His golden cloak flapped noisily as it clapped against his legs. "There are birds, my queen. Plenty of seabirds nesting in the cliffs, gannets and terns they look like to me. I see a colony of seals as well, fur seals I think, and there are a few walruses resting upon a small islet in the bay. But people? No, not as yet." He drew back from the cliffside and turned to her. "We'll have to continue further south."

Well we're certainly not going back north, she thought. They'd come from that way, and seen little sign of life there either, save a few scant fishing villages that would not serve their purpose. Sir Munroe had explained that they were both hard to reach and unsuitable for their needs. Most were accessed only by steep stairs cut into the cliffs, and the fisherfolk there tended to fish close to the shore from creaky old skiffs that would not be sturdy enough to bear them safely across Vandar's Mercy. What they needed was a good strong cog or carrack capable of braving the seas this time of year. Those would be found further south, the disgraced Captain of the King's Guard insisted.

He continued away from the edge, gesturing down the coast from the headland. "I know of a place that will suit us," he said. "It's another day's walk from here, or thereabouts. If we make good time we should reach it by nightfall."

"What place?" Amilia asked him. She could not help but be wary of the man's intent, no matter how faithful he'd proven so far.

"A coastal town called Swanshallow."

"Swanshallow," she repeated. It wasn't a place she'd heard of. "Are there lots of swans there, Sir Munroe? Do the waters run shallow off the shore?"

He gave a laugh. "To the contrary, my lady. There are no swans there that I know of and the waters run dark and deep. As to why they call it that, who can say? I suppose it's like giving a nickname like 'giant' to a dwarf, or 'tiny' to a giant. The town founders were trying to be ironic, I would think."

"You Rasalanians have a curious humour." She looked south. The cliffs continued high above the seas far as her eyes could see. "Does this town have a harbour?"

"It does, my lady. The deep waters allow for it. Swanshallow is known for its popular fish market, and…well, brothels, of which there are many adjacent to the wharves. It tends to draw a rough crowd, but with me at your side, you needn't fear. If fortune favours us, we'll be able to find passage there."

Brothels. A rough crowd. Amilia didn't like the sound of that. "Is there another option?"

He thought on it a moment. Sir Munroe knew these lands like he knew the swerve of his sword, he'd told them. *And he should.* He'd been the captain of King Godrin's guard for long years, travelling the realm with his liege, accompanying him along with that great brute Sir Ralston Whaleheart as Godrin met with his subjects, great and small. Having knowledge of Rasalan's peoples and places was a part of his remit and duty.

And how many of those people despise him now? Amilia wondered idly. *How many would like to see his head mounted upon a spike as a traitor, mired in disgrace and dishonour?* It hadn't always been like that. Sir Munroe had been known for his chivalry throughout his years of service to his king, an upstanding knight considered one of the finest swords in Rasalan. *But that all changed when he stood by and let Hadrin cut his own father's throat,* she thought. Everyone knew about that now. His loyalty to her foul feckless husband had soured and corrupted his reputation, never to be restored.

"There are other coastal towns, my lady," Sir Munroe said after a short consideration, "though none that will suit our needs until we come upon the mouth of the Izzun. But the river mouth is many days walk from here, and will be greatly more populated as well. If it's secrecy you seek, Swanshallow will best serve us."

She *was* seeking secrecy, there was no lie there. *But so is he,* she knew. *He is a desperate man indeed, to latch himself onto me.* "Fine," she decided. "We'll make for Swanshallow. And let us hope we'll find a captain who will take us."

They returned together to their overnight camp as Astrid packed their meagre things. The coastline here atop the cliffs had a road of sorts, a worn old track that followed its route from south to north for many hundreds of miles. They had slept some two hundred metres away from it beneath the branches of a grand old maple tree, with good views across the plains, should a traveller happen by.

Astrid watched Sir Munroe through narrow eyes as they neared.

239

"Still don't trust me?" the knight asked her. He gave a haughty huff; despite rendering himself so very regretful and contrite in Amilia's presence, Sir Munroe Moore could not conceal his arrogance for long, not when it came to Astrid. He was from a highborn house of great esteem and she was…well, just a baseborn girl from the north of Tukor who'd been a maidservant most of her life. "I saved your life, girl, or have you forgotten? I know it was a week ago, but still…you can't be *that* absentminded."

"I haven't forgotten, sir." Astrid's glare only sharpened. "Nor have I forgotten the *king*."

"What king?"

"The king. Your king. Godrin. The one you betrayed."

He laughed that away. "Rumours. Wicked rumours you'd best ignore. I had no knowledge of that."

You did, Amilia thought. *And everyone knows it.* She saw no profit in saying it, though. "Water under the bridge," was all she said. Her priority was getting back to Tukor, to her uncle Caleb's care first of all. Once in Ethior she'd decide what to do with the faithless Sir Munroe Moore; until then he was proving useful and she did not want to rock that boat.

Astrid did, apparently. "You knew," she told him, refusing to stand down. "Everyone says you were there when Hadrin did it, just standing outside as the king's throat was hacked open. The maids in the palace were all talking about it, behind your backs. I was there to watch and *listen*, and I did. I know more than you realise."

"Well of course you do. You're one of Lady Payne's cheap little pets." He looked down at her in distaste. "Perhaps I should have let that big one strangle you? Would you prefer that, girl, to be dead?"

Astrid reached for her neck, grimacing at the memory. The redbearded oaf called Russet had throttled her so savagely you could still see his finger marks on her skin. "You see, my lady. You see his *true* side. He's just using you to get a pardon. If he delivers you safely to Tukor, he thinks…"

"I know what he thinks, Astrid," Amilia cut in. She didn't want to have this discussion right now, not in front of him. "We made a bargain. Sir Munroe is sworn to me now. He has earned my protection, for saving us from those men."

"And Sir Jeremy? Can you forgive him for that? He killed him, you said…"

"I *never* killed Sir Jeremy Gullimer," the knight was quick to make clear. "The poison did that. I only beat him, at my king's command; as his sworn guardian it was my duty to carry out his word, where I agreed with it not." He looked at Amilia, suddenly apologetic. "You know I had no ill feelings toward Sir Jeremy, I hope, my queen? That you sought out his bed is not for me to judge. Nay, I understood it, given what Hadrin had become. I never expected it to go that way, none of it. I hope you know I am not to blame."

I'm still deciding, she thought. Amilia had loathed Sir Munroe for what he'd done, but she understood the bonds of duty and the moral quandaries it imposed. "I have lived in a king's court all my life," she merely said. "I have seen often the blurred line between duty and honour. Now let's put this aside, and not speak of it again. Sir Munroe, lead the way."

The man bent his back into a clean sharp bow. "As you wish, *my queen.*" With a flick of his golden cloak, he strode away across the plains, returning to the road.

Astrid lingered behind, watching him like a hawk as he left. "You don't believe that, do you, my lady? He's only trying to save his own skin."

Aren't we all? "Was he lying when he said he saved your life? Or me from being raped by that mute?" Her green eyes stared impatiently. "No, Astrid, he wasn't. For that at least, he's earned my favour…"

"But…"

"But nothing," she bulled in. "And don't go telling me he was in league with those outlaws again. That is nonsense and you know it."

Astrid looked down, prodding at a stone with her foot. "I…I still think it's possible," she mumbled. "How can we know for sure he didn't set those brigands upon us? It makes sense, doesn't it? He comes in, saves the day, and uses it to get in your trust." She scowled after the man as he moved away from them. "He saved my life, sure, but not really. I was only in that situation because of him."

Gods, give me strength. "You're being ridiculous, Astrid." She'd espoused that conspiracy theory more than once already and Amilia had had her fill of it. "It was a lucky coincidence that he arrived when he did, that's all. Now enough. I don't want to hear it anymore. And why do you care so much anyway? *I'm* the one he wronged, not you. Unless you were secretly bedding Sir Jeremy as well?"

The gangly girl looked aghast. "No. Of course not. I'd never."

"How can I know for certain?" She stepped in. "Were you? Were you bedding him behind my back?"

"No!" The girl shrank away. "No, my lady, I wouldn't dream of it."

"Why not? My tryst with Jeremy was a secret between the two of us. You can't have known about it, Astrid. There was nothing to stop you from pursuing him."

"I *didn't* pursue him!" she wailed. "I promise it, my lady. And he'd *never* have gone with a girl like me. I'm like a bag of bones, all lanky and awkward, Leshie used to say. I've been called ugly all my life. A handsome knight like him wouldn't look at me twice…" Tears welled in her eyes. "Please. Please, you *have* to believe me."

Gods, I wasn't being serious. Amilia hadn't expected such a reaction but was in too deep now to unveil it as a jape. She took the girls shaking hands. "I believe you, Astrid," she assured her. "And you're not ugly, or a bag of bones. Leshie was cruel to say so."

"Others have said it too. It wasn't just her." She wiped her eyes and sniffed through her pinched nose.

"Well…none of them should have. Girls can be cruel, especially when they're young. You're very pretty, Astrid, don't let anyone tell you otherwise."

Her eyes shone out, big and glassy. "You…you think I'm pretty? Truly?"

"Truly," she said, smiling behind the white lie. She wasn't, in all truth, leastways not in any traditional sense. "Many a man would be lucky to have you." She reached out to wipe a tear from the girl's sharp cheek. "Now come. Sir Munroe sets a strong pace. We wouldn't want to get left behind."

They caught up to him a few minutes later, the road running far ahead of them, rutted by wagon wheels and fading from sight up the coast. In places it was overgrown with grass; in others the ruts were delved so deep as to become pits, treacherous for carriages and carts to pass. Sometimes it ran unnervingly close to the cliffs, no more than a few metres from the edge. In places Amilia even saw that sections of the cliff had given way, collapsing under the weight of time and decay and taking the road with it. Where that had happened the road had been retrod, wending a little inland, only to meet back up with the original path further on. Amilia moved to Sir Munroe's side. "Do people travel this way often?" she asked him.

"Not often, my queen. It's typically ridden and walked by the fisherfolk who live in the villages we've seen, for trade and such. Sometimes soldiers pass this way too, when making for the north, though rarely. The fortress stations across the Highplains have long terms of duty for the men who man them. They only change the guard once every year."

"How many are there? Fortresses that is. Up north."

"Fortresses. Not many. Though there are dozens of watchtowers along the coast. Those are usually manned by only two men at any time, who come and go from The Grey Keep, at the heart of the Highplains. It's there that the main northern garrison is stationed. Then there's the Tower of Rasalan at the northernmost tip, though that is a holy sanctuary as much as it is a fortress. Rasalanian kings and queens would often journey there for spiritual retreats and during times of strife, to seek counsel from the gods. According to legend, the tower is where Rasalan gifted Queen Thala his Eye, so she might watch over us at his passing."

Amilia had heard that legend before. "They say Tukor left his Hammer in the mountains for Ilith to find. Some say it took him a month, others a year, others even longer than that. When he finally discovered it, it's said he looked down through the valleys and knew there was no place more beautiful in all the world. So he called upon his followers and told them they would settle there, in that spot, and build the greatest city the world has ever seen. It's where Ilithor stands today."

The knight gave that a smile. "The gods are queer, are they not? One rips out his own eye and gives it as a gift. Another plays hide and seek with his hammer. Another still leaves his own body to be mined for a magic metal, and his heart to be shattered and remade into blades. Most odd, wouldn't you say?"

It was hard to argue otherwise, yet all this talk…suddenly Amilia was starting to think about *that* night again. The tower and the Eye and her husband and Eldur with those red, red dreaded eyes. She took a sharp breath, changing the subject. "A day's walk, you said, to Swanshallow." She blinked and looked down the long coastal track, appearing and disappearing among the hills. "It is along the coast the whole way."

"Yes, more or less. The road works inland a couple of times, but never for more than a mile or so, and it always comes back to the coast."

"And this town. Is it at the bottom of a cliff like the other villages we've seen?"

"It is, my queen, but the cliffs aren't so tall south of here. Fear not, I'll help you down the steps, if you need me."

I don't, she thought. The man was being too damn helpful for his own good. *My queen this, and my queen that. My queen my queen my queen…*

I'm not your bloody queen! Amilia wanted to shout at him. She did not know whether Hadrin's cousins were alive, or who would next claim the crown, but she didn't care. *They did not accept me as queen when Hadrin was here, and they won't accept me now.* And even if they did, she'd only laugh in their faces and tell them 'no' all the same. *I want off this rock and realm for good. I want to see my brother, and sleep in my own bed, and watch the world end from the White City, not here in this godsforsaken land.*

"It might be sensible for you and your maid to stay at the top of the cliffs, while I inquire at the docks," Sir Munroe was going on. "I'll go down and find passage for us, then return to you once it's done. There is no sense in you walking the streets of Swanshallow unless you must. It's a grubby town, my lady. No place for a queen like you."

I'm not a queen, she thought. *I'm not a bloody queen.* "No," she said to him. "We'll stay together."

He dipped his head and made no complaint. "As you wish. I would recommend hoods, at the least. It would go better if you're not spotted, not until we get you safe at sea."

She looked at him. "I could say the same about you, Sir Munroe. You're not well-loved among the commons anymore."

He lifted his stubbled chin high and proud. "Yes. I am aware. For these dreadful *slanders* that have been spread about me."

She looked at him in bemusement. *He'll never admit it…even to himself.* "Slander or truth, it's what people believe that matters. You're largely disliked now, Sir Munroe, and that means it's best that you're not spotted either." She looked him up and down. "What will you do about that famed golden cloak of yours? If you go down to the docks wearing that, you might struggle to find a ship captain who'll deal with you."

He gave that a disgruntled huff. "Lowborn knaves, is what we'll find down there. They will deal with me or else feel my steel."

She rolled her eyes. "I'll not have your pride getting us all killed," she told him. "You can wear one of the cloaks we took from those outlaws."

He bristled at the suggestion. "I could slaughter all of Swanshallow if I wished to, my queen. There will not be a single good knight among them to oppose me."

"Yes, I don't doubt your prowess, Sir Munroe. Even so, it would be better to avoid violence, if we can. Genocide is not the answer."

He walked on stiffly, chin held high. "Fine. I'll wear Taggern's cloak, if I must."

She frowned at him. "How did you know his name?"

"Whose name?" he asked.

"Taggern," she said.

He looked at her blankly for a moment. "You told me it," he said, after a pause. "You told me his name had been Taggern. That leader of theirs, if you can call him that. I led the king's guard for over a decade. That wretched cur only led three other mongrels. And good riddance to them all."

She looked at him in suspicion.

"What? You think I was somehow associated with that scum?"

Amilia glanced back, though Astrid was walking some way behind and didn't seem to be listening. "Astrid thinks you set that whole thing up, to get into my good graces."

He showed what he thought of that with a snorting bark of laughter. "What utter tripe. That pet of yours ought to be more thankful I saved her worthless life."

The man was confounding. "You do realise that I *like* Astrid, don't you?" she said sharply. "You realise she saved me from that chamber *you* locked me up in…"

"*I* never locked you up anywhere, my lady. That was Hadrin. I told him a hundred times not to treat you as he did, but he could not be reasoned with. The Eye…it drove him mad, what he'd seen."

"Yes, I know. I was on the receiving end of that *madness*, Sir Munroe, and Astrid saved me from it, and has continued to serve me since. Yet you insist on debasing and insulting her in my hearing at every opportunity. Why?"

His neck tightened. "Because…" he started.

She waited. "*Because?* Come, Sir Munroe, let me hear it."

"It's not her," he admitted, through a jaw clenched tight as a drum. "It's that godsawful woman she serves. Lady Payne. I have never agreed with her training these young women as spies and sneaks, my queen. It reeks of dishonour. And besides that, the woman is utterly insufferable. I have never met anyone so unbearably arrogant in my life."

Amilia Lukar had to laugh out loud at that. "I'm sorry, Sir Munroe, but to hear *you* say that is…well, it's quite comical. Have you heard the expression 'pot calling the kettle black'?"

He walked rigid as a redwood beside her. "Yes, I've heard it. But with some people arrogance is earned. With others it is not."

She had no idea how to talk to this man sometimes. "You sound bitter," was all she said. "I've heard it remarked that Lady Marian Payne is the second finest sword in all of Rasalan. Would you say there's any merit in that?"

"She's gifted," he said begrudgingly. "But second best? No. Behind me there are many who would stand in line before her."

"Behind the King's Wall," Amilia told him.

He looked over. "Sir Ralston?"

"Yes. Or is there another King's Wall I'm not aware of?" She smiled at him mockingly. "Now don't tell me you believe you're superior to the giant?"

"In skill, yes I am," he said at once. "I'm a master of two forms, my queen, and highly proficient at the rest. Sir Ralston would have me in brute strength and power, no one would doubt it, but in speed and skill I'm the better."

"Not the way I've heard it, but that's not for me to judge." Amilia was enjoying teasing him. "But these rumours, just to clarify…they place the King's Wall first and Lady Marian second in prowess. You're third at best, Sir Munroe."

He looked at her with a smile so forced it looked painful. "And who says this, exactly?"

She shrugged to vex him. "Many people. It's been all over my grandfather's court for years."

I'm wounding him, she thought. *Oh joy, he bloody hates this.*

"Well…people are entitled to their fantasies, of course. One day perhaps Lady Payne and I can settle this debate in the sparring circle, though my honour as a knight and a man would surely preclude me from such a bout. To fight a *woman,* after all, would be most indecorous."

"No indeed, the shame of a possible defeat would be rather too much for your ego to bear, I would think. Better to hide behind your honour." *Or lack thereof,* she didn't say.

She tortured him a little more as they went, though soon grew bored of his company and retreated to Astrid's side, where she spent the remainder of the day.

By the time they came upon the first sight of Swanshallow the sun was setting and dusk was near at hand. "Astrid, hand Taggern's cloak to Sir Munroe," Amilia commanded. "And be careful with his golden cape. I'm sure he wants it neatly folded and stored in your bag."

"If you'd be so kind," the knight said, detaching his commander's cloak and handing it over. He took the rotted old thing that Taggern had been wearing and smiled despite the stink. "My thanks to you, my lady."

Astrid looked confused by his sudden courtesy.

"I told him off earlier for being rude," Amilia explained. "He's going to be nice to you from now on, Astrid."

"I will. And I hope you'll forgive my boorish behaviour thus far, Lady Astrid. It was unfair and unbecoming of me. I hope we can be friends."

The gangly girl blinked at him. "I'm not a lady."

"You are to me." Sir Munroe donned the ragged cloak and arranged it so his armour was almost completely concealed. There was some blood soaked into the collar from where the knight's dagger had burst through the front of Taggern's head. He picked out a little chunk of skull - "Oh, we missed a bit," - and flicked it aside. "Well, shall we, ladies? The steps will only get more treacherous in the dark."

They descended the cliff down the carven rock stair, fit with rickety old handrails to left and right. Half the wooden pylons were wobbly and a few were missing entirely, leading the rope to dangle on the floor in places. Still, the stairs weren't so steep as Amilia had feared, nor were the cliffs so high. As they turned a corner, Swanshallow came into sight beneath them. It was bigger than Amilia Lukar had expected, though the stink was already thick in her nose and precisely what she'd feared. *Fish.* She misliked it greatly and always had. The air was always so pure in Ilithor, high up in the mountains where she'd been born and raised.

"It's so dark down there," Astrid said, from the back of the line. "Why aren't they lighting their torches and lamps? It's almost nighttime."

"The town is as lit as it's likely to be," Sir Munroe told her. "Swanshallow is a dingy place by night, though it is brighter at the docks, where the brothels are."

"Do we have to go near them?" Astrid sounded worried, as if she might be mistaken for a courtesan and dragged into some dark alley.

"Alas yes, my lady. The pillowhouses cannot be avoided here. Stay close to me and you'll be just fine." He stopped a moment as he descended. "Which of you carries the dagger?"

"I do," Amilia said, standing behind him.

Sir Munroe reached into his soiled cloak and drew out his own godsteel dagger, the one that had seen the cloak's original owner to the worms. "Here," he said. "Take this, my lady."

Astrid seemed genuinely surprised by that. "Um. Thank you, Sir Munroe. I do feel better now."

"Good." The man smiled, turned, and continued down the steps.

They passed a wooden lift as they reached the bottom, creaking and groaning as it swung gently on the wind. Amilia supposed it was used to ferry fish and other goods to the top, and vice versa. Sir Munroe confirmed as much when she asked him. "Many of these cliff-bottom towns and villages have them," he said. "Most of Rasalan's coast is lined with these sorts of cliffs. Great for defence, but elsewise troublesome when you want to build thriving coastal communities. These lifts help, though most of our major cities are in the south of the country, around Whaler's Bay where the coastline is flatter."

They found a muddy lane that led down to the docks and followed it past winesinks and alehouses and potshops, past hawkers calling their trades and merchants haggling in the shadows. Night had descended by now, and the darkness served their need for secrecy. Amilia could scarcely make out the features of anyone as they went, every man and woman and child cloaked in shadow and gloom. Only those close to the few hanging lanterns and lamps were even half recognisable, and even then most wore heavy cloaks against the bitter chill, with hoods and cowls to match.

Further down the street, they passed their first brothel, a three-storey pile of planks and nails that looked so unwieldy it might just topple down onto the street. There were balconies on the second and third floors from which scantily clad women called out to passersby. *They must be freezing,* was all Amilia could think. Some had bare breasts and others bare backsides, and one she saw stood completely nude, leaning sultrily upon a rail and sipping on a cup of wine, smiling to the men below as they gawped up at her lustfully. Where the streets were dark, however, those balconies were well-lit.

"These folk need to know what they're buying," Sir Munroe said. He glanced up at the women but little more. "This is but a taste of what Swanshallow offers. It gets a great deal worse further on."

The worst of it was the stink, though, to Amilia's sensibilities at least. Bare flesh she'd seen a thousand times before, in the raucous parties she would sneak to under her father's nose back home, in the marble bathhouses she frequented, in the hosts of knights and squires and handsome stableboys she'd taken to her bed. She batted not an eyelid as they emerged at the docks, where the crowds thickened and the whorehouses did too, lining up one after another in a great procession of firelit balconies teeming with whores of all different types from all across the world. Amilia saw tall women and short women, women from the north and women from the south, women with tattoos and women with piercings, hairless women and hirsute women, women who were slim and women who were fat; some were stunningly beautiful, others grotesque, some old, some young, and some were men. Astrid did not seem to know where to look, so decided to just stare down at her feet. Sir Munroe continued to bustle them past the throngs to where the masses thinned along the wharves. The stink was much worse here. *Can I go and wait back by the brothels?* Amilia wondered. At least there the smell of perfume hid some of the stench of fish and unwashed men. Here the reek was so appalling it made her eyes sting.

"OK, we made it." Sir Munroe sounded relieved. He glanced back to the line of brothels. "Some ship captains will no doubt be amongst that rabble, though others may be aboard their ships I hope. Why don't you two stay here while I ask around?" There was a rather less debauched venue nearby, a cart selling wine with a few chairs and tables scattered about it. "There. Get off your feet and drink some wine. I'll come find you once I'm done."

Amilia and Astrid shared a look. "Fine," the princess said. "Do you have any coin to pay with, Sir Munroe?"

"It's in my cloak," the man said. "My other cloak. Astrid, if you would."

Astrid slung her pack from her shoulder, opened it up, dug around for a while and came back clutching a coin pouch. She handed it over so the knight might pick out the necessary coppers. "Here. That will buy you all the wine you want. The rest should be plenty to give us passage." He thrust the pouch into an inner pocket, safe in his keeping.

"All three of us?" Amilia still had the feeling that the man might 'accidentally' leave Astrid behind.

"Yes, all three. And if any captain wants to haggle me down to what I cannot afford, I have this." He tapped his sword hilt, beneath his cloak. "Keep your daggers to hand, should you need them," he said in parting. "I shan't be long."

They bought a cup of wine each from the merchant and took their seats overlooking the harbour. There were many ships out there, bobbing on the waters, though in the dark of night they were hard to make out in detail. *At least one must be heading across the Mercy in the morning*, Amilia thought. She had a sip of her wine and found herself pleasantly surprised by the vintage. "Not bad. Have a taste, Astrid."

"I'm not a big drinker, my lady."

"So why did you buy a cup? Go ahead, drink it. We might be waiting a while."

Astrid drank, though slowly, as Amilia worked quickly through her portion and returned to the wine merchant to buy another. "Very nice," she said to him, handing back the wooden chalice. "I'll have one more, please, and don't skimp on the serving this time."

The man grumbled something as he poured, filling the cup near to the brim. "How's about that, girl? Better?"

"Better." Her previous serving had been a little short by comparison. She swirled, tasted, and nodded. "It's from the Scarlet Valley," she said, savouring the flavours. "There's an earthy undertone, a hint of oak."

"Aye." The wine seller peered at her face, hidden beneath her hood. "You're not from around here. Tukoran, is it? And highborn too by that accent. And the way you speak to me besides." He grunted. "What you doing in a place like this?"

"Just passing through," she said, offhand. The wine emboldened her to speak more freely. "My friends and I are looking for a ship to Tukor. Do you know of any leaving on the morning tide that can accommodate three extra passengers?"

He thought on that for a moment. "Might be I do, aye." He said no more.

"Well?" She wasn't sure what he was waiting for, and then it came to her. "Ah, I see. You expect me to pay for the information. I hoped you might be more decent than that."

"Where'd you get that idea? This seem like a decent place to you?" He looked around with a sneer. The noise from the nearby line of brothels was loud and constant, a din of shrieking voices and drunken laughter and brawling. It was chaotic and was only likely to get more depraved as the night went on. "I gotta add to my coffers wherever I can," the wine seller told her, "and you look like you can spare a coin or three. Times ain't good for a lowly wine-monger like me."

They're not good for anyone, Amilia thought. It was a strange curiosity for her to be handling coins and haggling. Everything had been handed to her on a golden platter all her life. She wasn't certain she'd ever paid for anything, in fact, until this very transaction. She shrugged. "Fine. I'll pay, if you insist on it. Let me just fetch my money."

She turned around to collect the coins she'd left on the table and saw at once that Astrid was no longer alone. There was a scraggly old man standing over her, peering so close his nose almost poked her in the eye. *He's drunk*, Amilia knew at once. He had wild grey hair, thinning on top, a horrid tufty beard, and a smile so brown and foul Amilia could almost smell the reek of his breath just to look at it.

She stepped right over. "Astrid, is this man bothering you?"

The sotted old creature looked up at her, blinking. "Botherin' her? I'm...I'm not botherin' anyone, m'lady."

Amilia looked at her friend. "Astrid?"

"I know him," the girl said, unexpectedly. "He recognised me and came over."

"You *know* him?" Amilia couldn't work out how that might be.

The drunk gave a brisk nod. "Got a good eye for faces," he declared proudly. He wore a leather jacket and seaman's garb, salt-stained and scuffed. "I took this one 'cross the sea, while back. How...how long ago was that? I forget."

"A long time," Astrid said. She looked up at Amilia. "This is a ship captain, my lady. We sailed on his boat across Vandar's Mercy, when I first left Tukor. Me and Lady Marian and the others..."

"Shackton!" the captain shouted suddenly, spittle flying from his mouth. "Aye, you were with Shackton, that scoundrel!" He gave a great bark of laughter, fogging the air with the stink of whiskey and garlic. "He was all skin and bone, and full o' stories too! And that southern girl with the blue eyes. Who could forget her? Very pretty, that one, beautiful girl, aye..." He had one hand propped up on the table for support, smiling crookedly. "No prettier than you, though," he said to Amilia, "if that's not too bold o' me to say." He gazed at her a moment, trying to get a better look under her hood. "Do I know you? You look familiar."

"We've never met," Amilia said. "I've got a good eye for faces too."

The old sea captain pondered it a little longer, then pursed his lips and shrugged. He looked at Astrid again. "Where are those others, then? Lady Marian...she train you up well, did she?" He didn't wait to hear Astrid's answer. "I bet she's been drawn into this war down south. Terrible stuff, all that. Terrible. But she'll be playin' her part, oh aye, you can be sure o' that." He smiled, reminiscing. "I remember...she had you climb my masts, clambering up them like monkeys as part o' your training. And all that swordplay you did on my decks. The lads got a good laugh outta that, though I'm sure you're better now?"

Astrid nodded. "We all got better."

The man barely seemed to hear her. "And that storm! Do you remember that storm, girl? Marian had you all on my prow in the wind and rain, masterin' your fears or some such folly. I'm still amazed none o' you went overboard, and if you had that woulda been the end o' you, no way we'd have been able to fish you out..." He frowned and studied her face. "What was your name again? Good with faces, not so much names..."

"Astrid."

"Aye, that's it. Astrid. The frightened one. You were always bickering with that wild little redhead who looked like she was about eight. The one who was throwing up her guts half the trip." He laughed again.

"Her name was Leshie," Astrid reminded him. "And I'm not frightened. Not anymore."

The old man raised a ragged grey eyebrow. "You sure about that? You still got that worried look about you, same as before."

"I *don't* have a worried look," Astrid came back at him.

"Aye you do. No shame in that, though. We can't all be heroes."

Astrid was about to respond when the wine seller stepped over, beckoning Amilia's attention. "Did you have that coin for me?" He looked at the drunk captain, and seemed eager to see the transaction done.

Amilia put the pieces together. "Let me guess, this is the captain you were going to recommend?"

The seller had no reply, but to ask for payment once more.

"For what? You haven't given me anything." She took pity on the man, though, and picked up a coin from the table. "Here, take it anyway. In fact, take it all, and bring more wine over. Our new friend here is thirsty."

The seller looked happy enough with that. He returned a few moments later with a jug of wine and an extra cup. Amilia invited the captain to sit. "Please, or you'll topple over."

"Much obliged, girl, aye, much obliged." He sat unsteadily as the seller poured him a serving, then promptly drank it down. After that he laughed. "Tastes like water after whiskey. Best way to sober up, aye. Wine after whiskey, what could be better?"

Amilia was looking at Astrid, who seemed upset to have her courage called into question. The princess had another question on her lips, though. Clearly, the seller was going to recommend this captain, Astrid already knew him, and it seemed he was to be sailing on the morning tide. *Perhaps we don't need Sir Munroe after all*, she thought. "What's your ship's name?" she asked him.

He sat back, knuckly calloused fingers curling around his empty cup. Amilia refilled it herself. "Nancy. Good caravel." He pointed out to the waters. "That's her…right there." Amilia could see a shape, with a few lanterns swaying in the mists, but little more. "We're leaving on the morrow. Lads are in town now, having their last bit o' fun before we go back across the Mercy."

"You're crossing Vandar's Mercy? Where will you make harbour?"

"Blackhearth," the captain said, drinking, then wiping his mouth. "We go back and forth a lot, ferrying goods and such, passengers too. Was where I picked this one up." He gestured to Astrid. "Her and Marian's lot. Quiet on the waters now, though, what with the war. Be our last crossing for a while, I should think." He looked at the two girls. "You hoping to get home, are you?"

"We're trying to get to Ethior," Amilia told him. "Could you be persuaded to change your course?"

"For Ethior?" He shook his head. "Not likely. You want to go there, you'd be better getting to Blackhearth and then going by horse or carriage."

Amilia pondered it for a while, sipping her wine, then promptly put her cup aside. It was not the same vintage. Some horrid watered-down swill the seller clearly reserved for the drunk and ignorant who wouldn't know any better. She gave the merchant a sharp glare to show her displeasure, then resumed her conversation. "Could you make port a little further down the coast from Blackhearth, perhaps?" Somewhere closer to Ethior? It would not require any detour on your part and would shorten our journey considerably."

"Depends on the wind and waves, but aye, maybe."

Amilia felt Astrid pinch her arm. She leaned across to share in her council. "We should go with him," the gangly girl whispered. "He's uncouth, but trustworthy. We could go to his ship right now and sleep there overnight. Sir Munroe would never find us."

It wasn't the worst thought. "You still want rid of him?"

"Of course I do. Just because he starts calling me 'lady' doesn't mean anything. He's only saying that for your benefit. I wouldn't be surprised if he threw me overboard when no one's looking and claimed I tripped."

"I'd never believe that, Astrid. He has no reason to harm you."

The girl looked at her insistently. "Even so. We should leave him. He's served his purpose now. We don't need him anymore, my lady…"

"What are you two whisperin' about?" The captain peered across the table at them. "You wondering if you got enough coin, that it? Well don't you worry. My rates are low and especially so for my friends."

"How low?" Amilia asked.

"Depends. How much you got?"

Nothing, she thought. *We just exchanged our last coin for this watery piss.* Not that it was going to be enough to secure passage anyway. "We have promises," she said. "You'll be paid well once we reach Ethior."

"Ain't goin' to Ethior, girlie, just told you that. And promises don't pay for whiskey no more than they do women. Need something more real."

"I have this." Astrid opened her cloak a few inches and showed the old captain Sir Munroe's godsteel dagger. "Get us safe across the Mercy and it's yours."

The scraggly old man leaned in to get a better look. "Fine blade. Marian give you that?"

"No. Someone else."

He continued his appraisal. "Worth a goodly sum, I'd have thought. You sure it's yours to give away?"

"It's mine," Astrid lied. "Until we reach Tukor. Then it's yours."

"I think not." Sir Munroe Moore appeared from the darkness as if from nowhere, armour clanking softly beneath the rotting bloodied rags of a dead man's cloak. "That is *my* blade, my lady, as you well know." He stepped forward with a cold smile on his lips. "And who is your friend?"

"Name's Wilkins. Captain of the caravel Nancy. Who are you?"

"Never you mind that, Captain Wilkins." Sir Munroe Moore looked at Astrid darkly, though the smile never left his face. "The dagger is an heirloom of my house, very dear to me, and not for sale. I have this, however." He placed his coin pouch on the table with a tinkle of silver and gold. "I asked around the docks and was told you were the man to see. You sail for Blackhearth at dawn, I'm told. Is that enough to secure passage for three?"

Astrid looked like the world had just kicked her in the nethers. Another few minutes and they might have slipped away.

Wilkins pulled the string to open the pouch and fumbled about inside, fingering through the coins and biting one or two to make sure they were real.

The knight looked displeased by that. "You question my integrity? We're not here to cheat you, old man."

Wilkins closed the pouch and grinned horribly. "Can't be too careful. Prefer to take that blade, though."

"It's not for sale, I said. Though I'll be more than happy to give it to your gut if you test me."

Wilkins took no heed of the threat. He had a gulp of wine to 'sober up' - which made more sense now, given it was mostly water - set his hands to the table, and pushed himself to his feet. The coin pouch vanished into his coat. "It'll do," he said. "Come. I'll show you to your cabins. We got a couple going spare."

20

Janilah

The floorboards cracked beneath his great weight as he plodded toward the bar. "Ale," he said, resting his gauntleted hands on the stained scratched wood. A dark wind blew restlessly outside, keening through the trees, rattling about the rafters. "And bread and cheese. Do you have something warm on the pot?"

The innkeep looked at him through eyes wide with fear. His voice issued out in a trembling whisper. "The wife's got a…a stew on, stranger. Onions, carrots, a bit of rabbit. Not much, but…" He swallowed. "Will that…will that serve? We don't want any trouble here."

"I'm not here for trouble." Janilah Lukar pulled a gold coin from his cloak and placed it on the bar with a *clunk*. "The stew will serve, so long as it's warm."

The man reached out carefully and took up the coin in his tremulous grasp. "My…my thanks, good sir. That's very…very generous of you." He took a step back. "I'll have the food brought over at once. Please…please, take a seat."

"I'll stay standing." These flimsy wooden seats and stools were not near strong enough to hold a man in full godsteel plate. He glanced back at the trail he'd left as he entered. "Sorry about the blood and broken floorboards. I hope the coin will pay for it."

"Oh it will. A gold sabre? Yes, that's more than enough." He smiled uneasily and glanced at the bloody footprints. "I'll have that…that blood washed out right away." The barkeep was a skinny nervous man with a balding scalp and shrewish face who looked about forty. He poured out a thick strong ale, scuttled into the kitchens to fetch the food, then set to scrubbing the floors with mop and bucket.

The inn was empty but for Janilah's custom, a quiet lonely place on the banks of a slow-moving river choked with sticks and branches and other runoff from the nearby wood. Janilah had never known of it, and likely never would have if the dragon hadn't led him here. "I saw a stable outside," he said, taking a bite of bread. Bits of crust and crumbs fell into his unkempt grey-brown beard. He brushed them aside and washed the bread down with ale. "I'll sleep there tonight. I'm sure the coin covers that too."

The innkeep stopped in his scrubbing. "We have beds upstairs if you'd prefer. The coin was generous, most generous. Feel free to take a room, any you like. We're empty otherwise. Haven't had a guest here for days."

"The stables will be fine." Janilah had another gulp of ale and glanced at the innkeep's efforts. The blood he'd trailed in was dark and thick, almost black in the dim light of the inn. "Dragon blood can be hard to get out," he said. "It would be easier to just change the boards."

"Dragon....dragon blood?" The innkeeper's voice became a squeak.

"What you're washing. My footprints. That's dragon blood."

The man looked down in horror. "Gods...gods, I thought, well I thought I'd heard something, a while earlier. A terrible screeching in the woods that shook my very bones. That was...?"

"The sound of a dragon drying," Janilah said, chewing on a mouthful of bread. He prodded his tankard forward. "More ale, if you would."

The barkeep rushed back around and filled it full from a flagon. He looked at Janilah in mute astonishment, less afeared now, more admiring. *He thought me some killer, no doubt, when he first saw me enter. He thought me some brigand come to pillage his possessions and rape his wife.* He could not blame the man for coming to that assumption if it were so. Under his heavy hooded cloak, Janilah wore a set of armour fit for a god, fashioned and reforged by the heir of Ilith himself with the Hammer of Tukor to grasp, but little of that was visible beneath that great woollen mantle he wore.

The barkeep was staring at him as he ate. "That dragon," he said, in a breathy voice. "Did you...fight it alone?"

Janilah spooned a measure of rabbit stew into his mouth. "It wasn't much of a fight," he said. "Others have proven sterner adversaries."

"*Others?*" The man's eyes were big as goose eggs. "How many dragons have you slain."

"Four."

"*Four?*"

Janilah drank down his ale and ripped off another bite of bread. "I slew one many years ago, as a younger man. The other three have been much more recent."

The man looked at him disbelievingly. "But you're so...so..."

"Old?" Janilah said.

The innkeep spluttered. "No, of course not, I would never..."

I am old, Janilah thought, *and fresh from two heart attacks besides, but I feel young, and strong, and clear of mind, my purpose never purer.* "Calm," he told the barkeep, "and fetch me another serving of stew."

Janilah Lukar picked up his ale mug and drank deep as the man hastened away, reflecting on the past few weeks, on the dragons he'd fought and vanquished. The first had been a long time coming, a battle staged atop the world at Ilith's ancient forge against a purple-black beast that had circled the city for weeks. Scarcely in his life had he felt so alive as when he stood before it in his godly plate armour, holding the Mistblade aloft, shimmering blue from head to heel as the icy winds blew about him. The dragon had been wary of the blade at first, wary of its power, and had fought cagily for a time before Janilah finally drew it forward to smite its carcass atop that icy plateau. *And now it rests there forever,* the king thought, *beyond the forge that fashioned the blade that slew it; the site of its eternal undoing.*

He'd left Ilithor that very night, ranging out into the wilds to seek the blood of Agarath's spawn. Another of the fire god's leathern brood had fallen to his blade in the lands southeast of the city ten days later, a battle that took place by moonlight upon an open meadow under a sky strewn bright with stars. The setting had been different, the result the same. Once he'd defeated his foe, the king had slept beside the beast's ruin, savouring the scent of its death, wallowing in the glory of the kill. *Come to me,* he had thought, *staring up at the starry skies. Come to me, spawn of ash and flame. Come face the wrath of Vandar, come face his holy herald.*

He had continued on his hunt south the following morning, passing fields and plains, woods and rivers, keeping to the wilds such as he could. *The Mistblade will guide me,* he told himself. They were as one now in purpose and mind and deed, as one in their intent. Several times Janilah sensed the blade thrum and whisper and knew a dragon was near, yet each time they passed high overheard before he might draw them down.

Until today, he thought. Though today he'd not needed to draw the beast down at all. He'd found it sleeping among some rocks, curled and camouflaged and warming itself in the sun beside a pile of blackened bones. What they were, he could not say. Sheep. Goats. Herders or their children. He would make it its last meal all the same.

So in he'd crept, a silent blue ghost, getting near enough to smell the beast's foul breath as a putrid smoke billowed through its sleeping maw. With a scowl and a strike, he drove the Mistblade toward its neck...yet at the last minute the beast awoke, jerked aside, and the Mistblade missed its mark, cutting into its shoulder instead. A panicked shriek had filled the air, and at once the coward scrambled back over the rocks, unfurling its wings to flee. Janilah watched it go, though knew it would not get far. His strike had all but disabled one wing, he saw. "We follow," he'd said to the Mistablde. "We track its blood. Come."

The rest had been easy, the dragon badly weakened by the time he found it in the woods not far from this inn. Drained of energy, it could muster no flame, nor strike with any strength through fang and claw. The whimpering sound it made was pathetic. "You are weak, like your master," Janilah had told the creature, as he put it out of its misery and opened its neck up to feed the soil. The gush had been a beautiful sight to behold, pouring forth in a great black fall, and Janilah Lukar had known that he was doing god's work, Vandar's work, the one true god, the god of gods, their lord and king, mightiest of them all. "I am his will and his wrath," he'd said, as he watched the dragon die. "Go with your kindred in the Eternal Flame. I shall send more to join you soon..."

The doors to the back of the tavern swung open and the innkeep reappeared, a bowl of steaming stew in his palms. He placed it down and then refilled Janilah's cup. The king withdrew from his thoughts. "You planning to stay here long?" the man asked him. "In the area, that is?"

"I'll leave at dawn," Janilah told him. "You need not awaken me, I'll be gone by the time you rise. But I would ask one thing of you."

The barkeep nodded. "Of course. Yes, anything."

"Give me what food you can spare. I have been weeks on the road and my rations are running low."

The man nodded. "Our larders are not what they were, but I will give you what we can." He put his hands together. "This is a great thing you are doing. These dragons, they have become a blight upon our lands. A group of soldiers passed this way not a week ago, speaking of swarms of them further south. There was some battle, they said, at the fortress of Dragon's Bane. One claimed there were a hundred dragons there. *A hundred,*" he repeated, shaking his head. He picked up a mug and started polishing it with a scrap of cloth. "I can scarce believe it. But now it seems these dragons are flying north, and even here on our quiet peaceful lands. We need more like you, good sir, to drive these beasts away."

There are few like me, Janilah thought. "More ale."

The innkeep put aside his mug and cloth and filled Janilah's tankard once more. "Killing dragons must give you a thirst," he said, with a squirrelly smile. "I wonder…do you have a name? There are many singers who come by here on their travels and I'd be only too honoured to share your story."

"My name is Janilah Lukar."

The man laughed. "Janilah Lukar is dead, gods rest him, so I think you're having a jest with me, good sir." He chuckled again. "Who are you, mighty stranger? I'd like to tell of the dragonkiller who stepped through my door."

"Janilah Lukar. People once called me the Warrior King, though I'm a king no more. My calling is higher." He took his mug and gulped, The man was right, killing dragons was thirsty work.

"The Warrior King?" He peered at the bearded old stranger behind the hood. "No, no, that cannot be…"

Janilah opened his cloak and let the light of the Mistblade shine out, and for a moment that dingy little tavern turned from night to day, before darkening anew. The skinny innkeep stumbled right back in shock, crashing into the bottles behind him. "You're…you're…"

"Janilah Lukar. Be calm and be quiet. I came only to eat and drink in peace."

The man was staring at him as though paralysed from heel to head. Janilah gave him time to compose himself, finishing off his food as he did so. Eventually, the innkeep stirred from his trance and said, "Your Majesty, I…I didn't mean to…I had no intention of offending…"

"I know. I've been missing for a long while, though what do I have to hide from now?" He pulled back his hood, allowing his unwashed hair to hang free. He was dirty, bloody, grubby, old and seamed of face, though had never felt so content, so utterly righteous in his task. *Two paths*, he thought. *I followed the wrong one for too long, but now...* "Perhaps I might trouble you for a bath as well. Do you have one?"

The innkeeper sped suddenly around the side of the bar, and went right down to his knees before him, genuflecting as though before a god. *And might I still become one?* He put that thought aside. "Stand," he told the man.

He did so, misty-eyed as he gawped up at him. Though dirtied from his travels, Janilah's armour gleamed resplendent in that dingy little riverside tavern. The man's face swam with wonder to look upon him. "That armour. I've never seen anything so...so..."

"The bath. Do you have one?"

The man blinked and nodded. "Oh yes...yes we do, my king. We had one brought here for the guests to use, at a price. But not you, of course. I shall instruct the wife to boil water enough to fill it."

"Tepid water will do." Lest they had a full staff back there that Janilah didn't know about, filling a bath full of piping hot water would be a near-impossible task for one woman alone. "I'll not have your wife overburden herself."

The innkeep bowed low and stepped away backward, only turning once he was through the door. Janilah heard excited whisperings to the rear, then footsteps as someone heavy rushed up the steps. A moment later the man reappeared. "My wife is preparing it for you. An honour. What an honour this is to host a king." He put his hands together once more. "We are godly folk here, Your Majesty, long-time supporters of your house. My own family was once of Vandar as well, when the Lukars ruled as Wardens of the South. I have an ancestor who fought in Lord Galin's army when he sieged Ilithor and won this kingdom. The soldiering blood has withered since then, but we've always been faithful to your rule." He made a pained face. "When we heard those monstrous slanders of what had happened at Galin's Post..."

"That was no slander," Janilah told him. "I butchered those people in my bloodlust and my madness. But those times are gone and I am a changed man now." He wrapped fingers about the hilt of the Mistblade, and his form danced a cobalt blue. "I have seen the light."

The man collapsed to his knees again, bathing in the glow of the blade. "My king, take me with you!" he wailed. "I will serve at your side, my wife as well. We will join this holy crusade!"

Janilah smiled down at him. "I would not have your deaths on my conscience. Rise. You are well suited to your life here."

The man rose, pink-cheeked and flush with fervour. "I will spread the word of you, then. I will shout of what you have done."

To who? Janilah wondered. They seemed well isolated here, on this glum little river beside this glum little wood. "Speak to those who pass, but be careful what you say, and to whom. I still have enemies, and they will not be so quick to forgive."

The bath was soon prepared, giving Janilah respite from the man's overzealous ramblings. He washed himself clean, squeezing the filth from his hair and beard to brown the water, then dressed in the cotton underclothes his hosts provided, put his padded leathers over the top, and went back downstairs to re-garb himself in his armour. He found the wife there, feverishly scrubbing at the dirt, polishing the misting godsteel to a sparkling shine. She looked up as she saw him, a squat-nosed woman with a piggish homely face, large bust, and wide hips. Her husband was near the door, still trying to get the dragonblood from his floorboards. "I hope you don't mind," the woman said. "I thought your armour could do with a spruce."

"You have my thanks," Janilah Lukar told her. He could not have hoped to happen upon a better pairing, isolated, alone, and faithful to him despite his crimes. *Perhaps there are more out there who still favour me? More who would still call me king?* It was dangerous to think like that, but those echoes of his old self could not be completely silenced. A part of him still wanted to return to Ilithor, return to his throne, continue the hunt for the blades that had eluded him…

No, he told himself. *No, that path is done. I walk a new one now. And it may yet bring me my salvation.*

When the wife was done he stepped forward to don his armour. "Must you sleep outside, great king?" she asked, standing with her husband side by side, holding hands. "Will you not stay instead in a bed? We have several, and would happily give you our own, if you should like."

"The stables will be fine. I would not deprive you of your marital chamber."

"You're certain? Are you sure we cannot persuade you…"

"Melicent, *please*," said the husband, in a low voice. "He has told us no. We *must* respect his wishes."

"You have been very kind," Janilah said, as he finished fixing his armour and swung his old cloak back over his shoulders, fastening it at the neck. He turned to the door. "If you go directly south from here, through the woods, you'll come to a clearing, about a quarter mile in. You will find the dead dragon there, which I shall butcher for you tomorrow, when I leave."

They didn't seem to understand. "Butcher, my king?" asked the husband. "Why would you…"

"To sell. The internal organs can be sold to apothecaries, healers, mages. The bones as well. They are much sought after for medicinal and magical use when ground down to a powder. Or you could sell the bones to collectors, as you can the fangs and claws and scales. The head…that is most prized of all by rich men who like to mount them on their walls. Sell that too, or else mount it in here." He looked to the hearth. "There. Hang it there, above the fire. You'll draw visitors from miles around."

Neither husband nor wife seemed to know what to say. The carcass would make them rich beyond their wildest dreams if they acted quickly and prudently and found the right buyers for its parts. Janilah doubted they would, but cared not either way. When words failed the pair, they simply fell to their knees once more, still clutching at one another's hands. "We shall never forget this, great king," the wife, Melicent, wept. "Will you return here, one day? Will you come see the head of the dragon you slew, mounted on our wall?"

I'll have forgotten you by then. "Of course. I could think of little I would like more." He stepped to the bar and picked up the satchel of rations he'd been given. "Farewell, and be safe. I hope the war does not reach you here." He strode out into the night, making for the stables.

There were no horses within, but for an old piebald gelding that looked in want of a good meal. It stood in a stall, looking at him through dull dark eyes as he entered and bolted the doors. "I'll be sharing your chambers tonight," Janilah said. "I hope that's all right?" The horse gave no answer.

The wind was gusting outside, causing the trees to rattle their branches and the stable door to clatter and creak. Janilah found a comfortable-looking heap of hay and settled down, unhitching the Mistblade from his waist to lie beside him. The stable was as draughty as expected. Through gaps in the wooden plank walls the breeze pushed in, whistling as it came. Beneath all that he could still hear the river moving languidly outside, rolling on out to sea. He tried to think of what river it was, but could find no answer. *Just some unnamed brook,* he thought, *known only to those who live near it.* Tukor was not known for its waterways, not like the Riverlands of East Vandar, or the heart of Rasalan where both the Izzun and three rushing tributaries that joined to form the Forks came crashing through. His kingdom's most famous river was in the north, the Clearwater Run that started up in the High Hammersongs and ran west to east through the kingdom to empty into Vandar's Mercy.

Vandar's Mercy, he thought. Legend said that the gods Tukor and Rasalan were always bickering like brothers, and so Vandar had come to rend apart their lands, ripping the Sibling Strait into existence and creating the great bay that bore his name. Janilah had always loved the tale. *Such power,* he thought, *such might, to alter the world at his will.* He lay beside the Mistblade, listening to the whispered echoes of Vandar's voice. *I am yours, great god,* he promised. *I know your heart's desire now, and so long as my lungs hold breath…I will see it done.*

He fell into a peaceful untroubled sleep, with a smile upon his lips.

When morning came, the wind had died and the sun was not yet risen. Janilah Lukar stood from his heap of hay and brushed himself down, hitched the Mistblade back to his hip, gave the old gelding a parting smile, and stepped out into the predawn gloom. A stillness haunted the forest, and the river seemed to run yet slower still. Into the trees he paced, crunching over twigs and roots and rocks, to butcher the dragon as promised, and set upon his way.

The scavengers had already begun to get at it, a host of wolves drawn to the promise of flesh, yet they scattered at the sight of him and he set about his task. By the time he was done, the sun was peeking over the top of the trees, showering golden light down through their branches. Janilah stepped to the severed head of the dead dragon, cut out a small fang, and added it to the others. *Three,* he thought. *Three in as many weeks.* It was not nearly enough to make a difference, not yet. He set off south under a pristine spring sky. *I must seek more powerful prey.*

It was long past noon when he first saw the man, staring out at him from the way he'd come. Janilah turned from the old traveller trail he'd been following to face him. The man was on horseback, a little beyond the latest little woodland the dragonkilling king had passed through, some three or four hundred metres back. Around him were rolling grassy hills and wooded valleys, a pretty land at the bottom of Tukor. Faintly, he could see the colossal twin statues of Tukor's Pass to the south. *The way to Vandar,* Janilah thought.

He waited, watching to see what the rider would do. *He cannot know me, not from so far away.* The king was always careful to walk with his cloak well fastened, concealing his blade, and kept his godsteel helm safely stored in his pack with his rations and the trophies he took from his kills. With his hood over his head he was just another traveller upon a trail rare used. He even wore heavy leather boots to hide his sabatons. *I'll not have a glint of godsteel giving me away.*

The rider continued to watch him. He wore a hooded cloak as well, and had a sword at his hip. Another was tied up on his horse's flank above his saddlebags. Janilah stood as still as a millpond, slowly enhancing his eyesight to take in all the detail he could. A distance of four hundred metres would render a stranger a mere spec of colour to a regular man, but to a Bladeborn blessed with acute eyesight it was different.

The details continued to form. Above the collar of his cloak, Janilah saw a flash of silver. *He's wearing armour.* His gloves were too thick, lest he have grotesquely fat fingers. *They hide gauntlets, as I hide my sabatons in these boots,* he knew. *This man is Bladeborn. He has been following my trail through the woods.* A Rasalanian, was his first thought. *An assassin sent to hunt me.* But he had enemies not just in Rasalan. He could be of Vandar too, or even Tukor. This man could be from anywhere.

The face-off seemed to last an age, yet in actual fact it was but moments before the rider continued to canter his way. Janilah scanned the woods beyond the stranger, expecting others to follow him out, but none came. *He cannot think to defeat me alone?* Only another champion would have a hope of doing that, and this was neither Amron nor Elyon Daecar, nor his grandson the Ghost. *Might it be Vesryn?* That thought gave him pause. He had heard nothing of the fate of Vesryn Daecar of late. *Has he found me? Had he come to claim his vengeance?* His hand moved into his cloak. *If he still holds the Sword of Varinar, the power of the mists will not protect me…*

The rider was nearing quickly, only a hundred metres away. Janilah remained perfectly still. *No,* he realised, *it's not him.* He was being paranoid, as he used to be. How could he be sure this stranger even knew who he was? *Unless he found the inn, and the barkeep and his wife…*

The horseman was almost upon him, quickening as he came. He opened his mouth and shouted, "My king…my king! Please say that it is finally you…"

Janilah frowned. He knew the voice and he knew it well and suddenly he saw the face behind the hood. He had never seen the man with a beard before, but still, it was him, and not who he'd expected. He pulled back his own cowl to show his own face, and Sir Owen Armdall did the same. That beard of his was a ragged straw mess and his typically immaculate hair had never looked so dishevelled.

"My king!" He leapt straight from his steed as he arrived to fall to a knee before him. "Your Majesty, I have been searching for you for months," he panted. "Ever since you went missing at Galin's Post that day, I have dedicated my life to finding you." He drew the sword from his hip and placed it on the ground before him. "I swear to you my solemn oath that…"

Janilah stopped him. "You swore me your oath long years ago, Sir Owen. You don't need to do so again. Rise."

The Oak of Armdall stood, re-sheathing his blade, looking more a vagrant than a gallant knight of his Six. Each of Janilah's sworn swords were given dual blades when they joined his private guard, their hilts and pommels fashioned in their sigils of their houses. Sir Owen's had the likenesses of oak trees, the metalwork detailed and intricate. "My king. I have spoken words of service before, I know, but I would say them again if you ask it. Never have I forsaken them, or you. I pledge myself again to your service." He bowed his unwashed head.

Janilah considered him. The Oak of Armdall had been unwavering in his service in Ilithor, that was true. *But do I need him now? Do I want him?* Sir Owen had been the one to strike down his son Rylian, though for that he could not be blamed. *No, that was me, my fault, my doing.* "How did you find me, Sir Owen?"

"By perseverance," the young knight breathed out. "And luck. Yes, there was luck involved as well." He smiled, the skin of his face stretched thin over high cheekbones chiselled of stone. "I searched for weeks after you'd gone missing, back in the city, but there was no sign of you. Then one day there was a great rumbling high up in the mountains. I had been in the palace at the time, and I thought it had come from the top of the steps, so I went through the tunnels and climbed the stair the next day and saw it. The dragon, lying dead on the plateau, the same one that had been flying above the city for weeks, seeking something…seeking *you*, people said. I knew at once that you had been the one to kill it, my king. And I sensed, sensed you were not yet done. So I left the city that very day and have been seeking you out ever since."

This is a man of faith, Janilah thought. "I was kept in a basement for a time," he said, "by a woman named Ethelda Rivers. She was there, in the square, the day the dragon first came. She told me you stepped out to challenge it to a duel, Sir Owen. I was proud when I heard that. But tell me… what of my grandson? Should you not be protecting the prince instead?"

Sir Owen made a sour face. "He did not want me, my lord. He cast me out for what happened with Prince Rylian. He blames me for the death of his father."

"You are not to blame for that," Janilah said.

"I know. I tried to tell him so, but he would not listen. He has his own Emerald Guards around him and does not make use of the Six. We are but a few, now that Sir Rees and Sir Maxwell and Sir Edwyn are all dead. It's only Sir Kevyn now, and that new one, Mallister Monsort. Sir Fredrick will be recovered soon as well, but all the same, we've been discarded."

"So you thought to find me instead?"

"Yes, my king. Your grandson is not yet ready to rule, and nor has he been doing so. The Lady Cecilia has been in charge during your absence. But now that I've found you…"

"I do not intend to return to Ilithor, Sir Owen."

"My king?"

"Must I repeat myself? You said it yourself. I am not done yet. Until the skies are cleansed of leathern wings I will not rest, Sir Owen."

The knight nodded. "Then I will not rest either."

Janilah considered it. He had grown used to life alone and had not expected company. Yet if I'm to have it, why not this knight who is conditioned to trail me? That had been his job for long years. *Let him retain it,* he thought. *Give him a purpose too.* "You can stay," he said. "It would be prudent to have another set of eyes to watch over me as I sleep."

"Another set?" Sir Owen looked confused. "Do you have some other man with your, sire?"

"The Mistblade has kept watch over me," the king explained. "It alerts me each night should someone come near."

Sir Owen nodded. "The unsleeping shard of a god's heart is a fine sentry, my lord." He presented his horse. "I have my blades, and plate armour, and extra rations as well. If it is battle with dragons we seek, I am well prepared. I will not let you down, Your Majesty."

"You never have, Sir Owen." That wasn't true. There was no one in Janilah Lukar's life who hadn't let him down at one time or another, yet the Oak had proven loyal and deserved the praise. "Tell me. Have you encountered other travellers on the road? Have you shared in their tidings of the war?"

"I've kept my ear to the ground, sire. There's talk of battles and beasts and a coming dark, the rising of monsters ancient and forgotten. Nowhere is safe anymore. I fought a grimbear myself, south of the Stonehills. It must have been hibernating there, deep underground."

"Did you fight well, Sir Owen?"

"I could not judge that, sire. All I know is that I slew the beast and suffered not a wound in the fray." He pulled a claw from his pocket. "I took a token by which to remember it. The rest I left for the wolves and the crows."

"You might have skinned it for a pelt," Janilah said. "The grimbear's coat is known to be particularly warm, and valuable as well."

"I might have done so had it been winter. As to the value, my father is rich enough." He smiled through his dirty blond beard, though briefly as he said, "I trust you have heard of Dragon's Bane, my king? About the fall of the fortress, and the many dragons swarming the south."

Janilah nodded. "I heard."

"And Thalan, sire?"

The king tensed. "No." He'd heard nothing of Thalan. "Tell me, Sir Owen. What happened?"

The sworn sword stiffened. "Well, this might just be tavern talk, but I heard that Thalan was destroyed, my lord, by a great thunder of dragons, the same night that Dragon's Bane came under siege. Though I'm sure your granddaughter is OK. It's said there are passages that lead from the palace into the mountains. King Hadrin would have retreated with her there for a certainty." He frowned. "Though…"

"Though?" Janilah loomed forward. "Speak, Sir Owen. If you know more of Amilia…"

"No, it's not that, sire. It's King Hadrin. One man at this inn…well, they were claiming he'd been taken."

"Taken?"

"Yes, sire. He and the Eye of Rasalan." He laughed, bemused. "By Eldur, if you can believe that? This madman was saying that the Fire Father has risen from his tomb, some dark chamber beneath the Wings. That he's been using the Bondstone to rally all the wild dragons to his cause. It's all folly, of course. This fool was drunk, so hardly one to trust, but…my king? My king…sire, where are you going…?"

Janilah had turned and started walking away. *So he's risen,* he thought, *the enemy prophecy fulfilled.* He could hear the Oak of Armdall jumping back into the saddle, riding after him.

"Sire…it's south, is it? We're to continue south? Not north…not no Thalan?"

The Eye of Rasalan, in Eldur's possession, and King Hadrin his slave and augur… Janilah mused on that as he walked on, wondering, wondering…

"Sire? Sire?" Sir Owen came catering up beside him. "We're near the border to Vandar, sire. There are many there who'll not welcome us. Ought we not turn back? There are dragons here as well…

"Few," Janilah said. "Too few, Sir Owen." Ilithor might be assailed one day soon, he knew, but until that time came, the action was to the south. *And so are the dragons,* he thought, as he strode on toward Tukor's Pass.

21

Jonik

He stood over the big man's bed. "Dead?" he asked, half in shock. "How?"

Harden did not seem to have an answer. "Can't say, Jonik. Found him like this just now. Guess he wasn't as strong as we thought."

"But he was recovering. He was healing."

"False dawn," the man of the Ironmoors told him. "I've seen it before. A man seems to be on the mend, then *bam*, one day he's dead. Might have bled out from inside, or burst a vessel in the brain or heart, hard to say." He paused and gave a sigh. "Shame. He was a good man, and loyal, and with Cabel..." He sighed again and shook his head, weary. "What do you want to do with him? Did he tell you his chosen funeral rites?"

Funeral rites, Jonik thought. They had enough on their plate already to be worrying about funeral rites. But still... "He never spoke of it. I don't think Mo ever thought he would die."

"He never thought he'd come up against a raging Borrus Kanabar either. Maurice was a good strong sellsword, but no match for the likes of him."

Nor was Sir Corbray, or Kazil, or Cabel either. Jonik didn't want to be reminded of that. It still stirred a fury in him every time he thought of how Hamlyn had hexed the Barrel Knight, and for what? To buy some time? A few extra moments. He flexed his hand, clinging to the Nightblade with the other.

"His mother was half Piseki, he told me," Harden was going on. "The rest of him was northern, though. Did you know where his father was from?"

"He mentioned the Tidelands once," Jonik remembered. "Think his father was from there." He couldn't recall much more of Big Mo's heritage, because he was certain the giant, scar-faced sellsword didn't know himself. "What do they do with their dead in the Tidelands, Harden?"

"Depends. Most sink them with rocks, I think, leave them for the sharks and crabs and whatnot. There's some honour in that or something. They worship a lot of Rasal gods there."

"We're short on water," Jonik pointed out. "Unless we toss him down the well, we'll have no choice but to bury or burn him."

"Burn would be better than bury. The ground is bloody hard."

"Fine." Jonik didn't imagine Big Mo would care either way; he'd never seemed a spiritual sort and burning a body was common practice in Pisek, he knew. *Though they use special scents and perfumes and throw spices and powders on the body,* he remembered, *and say ritual words I have no hope of knowing. Unless...* "There's a section in the library about religion," he said. "Customs and such, marriages, funerals. Take a look, Harden. See if you can find some Piseki verses we could use."

"Right." The man sounded less than pleased about that.

"And gather wood for a pyre. We'll burn him out in the ward this evening."

"Wood we have plenty of," Harden said. "I'll see to it." He prepared to step away.

"Have you checked him over?" Jonik asked before he could leave. "For fresh injuries?"

The grim old sellsword turned back wearily. "You think someone might have finished him off? Who, Jonik? It's only the two of us here, and Gerrin and your mother..."

"She's not my mother."

"As you say. Point is, none of us has any reason to see Mo to the Halls Above. You're being paranoid."

Paranoid. There was truth to that, but still. "You had the watch last night, didn't you?"

"You know I did, and a bloody long and cold one it was too. I was *about* to go get some rest when I checked in on him. What are you suggesting?" Harden's seamed grey eyes tightened into a glare.

"Nothing. Just that someone might have crept in without your knowing."

"Who?" Harden asked. "You think those men who escaped might have climbed the walls somehow, got back in? And for what, Jonik? To kill a man who was half dead already, and leave the rest of us alive?"

It sounded absurd when he said like that, but all the same, Jonik had to consider all ends.

"*No one* got in," the Ironmoorer went on bluntly. "I was on watch all night. I'd have seen." He looked vexed, tired, and annoyed. "And besides, I *did* check him over before you got here, so it happens. He's showing no new wounds, nothing untoward." He flung out a hand in irritation. "Check him yourself if you doubt me. Go on, take a look."

"No," Jonik said. "I trust you, Harden."

"Well good. Because I stayed here to help you while Manfrey's away, and the exile's long past due. A part of me's wishing I'd left with the others, a part getting bigger by the day. This place sits wrong in my bones."

Jonik had no response to that. Sometimes he felt so tired and lost he couldn't see through the darkness, couldn't work out friend from foe. *Paranoid*, he thought again. *I grow paranoid and distrusting, as I was before…before Turner and Jack, Brax and Devin and Sid and Grim and Emeric. Emeric, where are you? Jack…you've taken so long…*

"Look, Jonik, I'm here to help, you know I am, but there's only so much we can do. Blaming people…casting doubt…that's not going to help anyone."

"I know, Harden. I didn't mean it to come out like that." He had not slept last night, nor the night before that, nor the one before that either. He could not recall the last time he'd slept more than a couple of hours at a time. The whispers were starting to keep him awake at night, and no longer could he keep them at bay. "I'm tired, is all. Everything comes out worse when you're tired."

"We're *all* tired, lad. And I'm almost three times your age, don't forget."

"I haven't forgotten that. How could I? I mean…look at you."

The shadow of a smile cracked on the old man's lips. "Good. A bit of humour. That's what we're missing. Can't remember the last time I laughed."

"You're from the Ironmoors. You don't laugh."

"True enough. Heard someone else laugh then." A sigh blew through his grey-bristled lips. "Gods, we're a grim lot, aren't we? Me, Gerrin, you… hardly a winning trio when it comes to witty repartee. I miss those Blackshaws. And your shipmen most of all. Captain Turner…Jack o' the Marsh…wouldn't be so dour here with them around."

No, Jonik thought. *It wouldn't.* "They'll be back soon."

"Not soon enough. Yesterday would have been better, and the day before that better still."

Jonik nodded. "Do you want to leave?"

"I can't leave," Harden grunted, looking more grim and grey than ever all of a sudden. "That night you told us about Ilith was the night you condemned us to stay. They killed your mother's man for it. I'm shackled to this godsforsaken place now, same as you."

"Only for a while," Jonik tried to tell him. "Once Hamlyn's done the transference…"

"And when will that be? And why should it change anything? They're worried their precious secret will get out and all of Agarath's minions will come swarming here to kill him. That won't change until the heir's done his job and hammered those blades together, and how long will *that* take, gathering all those blades?" He looked at the Nightblade like it was some cursed weapon, shackling them all to this cheerless fate. "That blade, Jonik. When do you suppose you'll hand it over?"

"When I must." *I'll do it when I must.*

"Why not now? Why not today? It's crushing you, lad, wearing you down. You're doing no good with it here."

"I'm protecting us, Harden. If the men who escaped come back, or some other threat creeps over these walls, you'll be happy I've still got it."

"That the only reason, Jonik?"

266

Damn him. "Yes. What else?"

Harden considered his next words as Jonik's steel gaze bored into him. The old man's lips twitched, as though he was about to speak, once, twice, and then he said nothing.

But Jonik wasn't done with him. "What?" he demanded. "Speak. Come on."

"Your grandfather," the old sellsword finally said. "The Mistblade drove him mad. We're worried, is all. Worried you might…"

"Might what? Go the same way?" Jonik didn't let him speak. "My *grandfather*, if you want to call him that, was a villain, mired in treachery and deceit and murder. The Mistblade drove him to madness because his purpose was impure, ignoble, driven by ego. Can you say the same of *me*, Harden? Can you? Coming here to save these boys from a life of service and abuse? What is that if not a noble calling?"

"I'm not denying it is."

"Then what? What are you worried about?"

"You," Harden said. "I don't know what it is. Being here, where you were brought up. Those lurking bloody mages. The truth of this place. All of it maybe, I don't know, but either way, it's turned you inside out, Jonik. Your calling *was* true, yes, but it's not the same now. It's compromised. *You're* compromised."

"Compromised?" A fury was burning inside him. His fingers held the hilt of the Nightblade so tight his knuckles had gone bone white. "How, Harden? Tell me. What have I done to compromise…"

"You're going to let some of these boys die!" Harden shouted. "You're going to let that old sorcerer take them. You'll let him open their necks and drain their blood, these boys you've come to *save*."

"I have no choice!" Jonik rallied back, his anger ripping free of him. "You think I want that? If I say no, what do you think will happen? Every single one of them will die, and us as well. Sacrifice the few to save the many. What other option is there?"

"Kill them," Harden growled, gripping the handle of his own godsteel blade. "Fhanrir, the Steward, all of them. Maybe Borrus had the right of it all along. Maybe *that's* why you're so restless. Maybe *that's* why the Night-blade's getting into your head. Because it *wants* them dead…*that's* your next noble calling. Kill them all and be done with this place forever…"

"And doom the world." Jonik would not entertain this folly. "You would doom the world to eternal shadow, for the sake of a few bastard boys?"

"Yes."

"*Yes?*" Jonik was incredulous. "You'd see millions burn, kingdoms fall, the War Eternal last forever?" *He's being stubborn, that's all. He can't truly believe it. He can't.*

But still the old man nodded. "You know only what they've told you. How can we be sure the heir can't reforge those blades by himself, without this…this transference? How can we be sure he even needs to? We're following a roadmap written thousands of years ago. Use your head, Jonik. Can't you see how mad that is?"

"You haven't been back there. You haven't seen him. You haven't spoken with these mages, or seen the book. You don't know what you're talking about, Harden."

"I know enough. I know blood sacrifice is an evil stain on the soul I could never condone. And boys? Innocent boys, reared for slaughter? It's inhumane, and you know it is. Next time that rotted one comes, you should cut him down and end him."

"No. And I'll not listen to this anymore." Jonik stamped forward, pushing past the old man and out of the door before he might do something he'd regret. He needed air and away from this pestilence and away from Harden most of all. He burst out of the Night Tower and into the lower ward to find Gerrin already there.

His old master had a deep frown upon his beaten brow. "I heard shouting. What happened?"

"Big Mo's dead." Jonik kept on going. He could not deal with Gerrin right now. His mentor understood what he had to do, knew it was the only way, but still... *I don't want him trying to reassure me. I just need to be alone.*

He marched through the ward and up the steps to the top of the wall, looking down through the craggy mountain passes. For a split second he thought he saw men moving up from far below, and his heart stirred at the thought of seeing Emeric and Turner and Jack and the rest...but it was nought but a trick of the mind, a few wisps of mist shapen as men, quickly blown away on the breeze.

I'm going mad. Maybe Harden was right. He set his hands on the top of the stone parapet, crunching through the thick layer of snow, for no other reason than to feel the cold and blunt the storm raging inside his head. *Damn you, you grim old bastard. Damn you for making me confront it. I know it's inhuman, I know it's vile, but I have no choice, there's nothing I can do...*

He paced along the battlements, moving his legs, trying to outrun the whispers in his head. But they were with him more than ever now, sometimes inaudible, sometimes clear, but always there, echoing in the darkness. When he'd first struck out alone with the Nightblade, abandoning the order, they'd been much the same, urging him toward violence, but that changed when his purpose became true. *A good just purpose stills them,* he thought. *A fractured mind only makes them all the louder, insisting on a path of blood and war...*

It was a horrible truth to face. *I have grown fractured, broken...compromised, as Harden said.* There was a large part of him now that longed to give the blade up, to be free of that burden for good, but another part, more vocal, more insistent...another part that wanted him to keep it...to keep it forever...

"Jonik, are you all right?"

He drew from his thoughts and glanced back. *Her. My loving mother.* "I'm fine," he grunted at her. "I want to be alone." He turned away to look back through the mountains, hoping beyond hope she would go.

She didn't. "I understand that one of your friends died. Gerrin just told me. I'm sorry, Jonik..."

"He died overnight. I want to be alone, I said."

Still she lingered. "How is the other one faring? The younger one? Is he starting to come around?"

Blasted woman. She had been down in the fort only a handful of days and had grown greatly more persistent in seeking time with him. He sighed loudly and gave answer. "He sleeps a lot. I'm not sure if he'll ever be the same again." It was another cruel blow. Cabel had fallen into a brief coma after Borrus's attack and had been in and out of consciousness ever since he first awakened. Mostly he slept, feverish and afeared as he mumbled in his dreams, but even when awake his memory seemed scattered, and half the time he didn't even know who Jonik was. *Brain damage*, Gerrin called it. Another victim of Hamlyn's hex.

"I'm sorry to hear that, Jonik." The woman moved a step closer behind him. "I've been meaning to talk to you…about the boys."

Not now, please. It was the last thing he wanted to discuss, but he could hide from it no more than he could outrun it. "And? Have you made your selections yet?" The words were bitter on his tongue. *I have my own mother dirtying her hands for me. What sort of creature have I become?*

"One, yes. One of the older boys. He's sixteen. Is that…*too* old?"

He felt sick, disgusted, defiled. "Fhanrir prefers…younger ones."

"Yes. Gerrin mentioned that to me. He explained that Fhanrir would prefer two younglings, but if we were to select three, we'd have more flexibility in their age. One of the younglings, and two of the older ones. An early teen and a later one, perhaps. He…he suggested that might be OK."

Jonik continued to look down the passes, trying to ignore the writhing nest of snakes in his gut. How could he weigh the lives of two children against three, based on nothing but their age? "I…I'm not…I don't…"

"I think that three would be best," the woman went on. "The younger children…they are so innocent, and some of them are quite sweet, despite the lives they have led here. If we could choose just the one, perhaps that would make it a bit…easier?"

Nothing about this was easy. Nothing about it was fair. "Which boy?" he rasped. "You said you'd chosen an older one."

"Yes. A boy called Runar. He has a darkness in him, Jonik, more than the others. It's in his eyes. They're empty, and cruel. I know he's only sixteen years old, but a man is often fully formed by then. I feel if he were to be released, he'd only turn to malice. There are others like that, but none so dark as him. If choosing him and another of the younger teens allows us to spare a youngling, then…well, I suppose we ought to take it."

Jonik closed his eyes. "Fine," he whispered, so faintly, over the wind. "Runar. He can be one of them."

"Right. Good."

He did not hear her move away, did not hear the crunch of snow as her feet broke through the ice. *Just go. Please…go.*

"The other two…" she said. "I will have to take a little longer, with that choice. There are a couple of candidates, for the younger teen. But the youngling, well…" She left the rest unsaid, apparently struggling with the dilemma.

Though how can I be sure? They say this woman has no heart. "Was there anything else? If not, I'd prefer to be alone."

"Just one more thing," she said, "I'll leave you to your brooding in a moment, but.."

"*Brooding?*" He turned sharply on her, taking umbrage with the word. "You make light of this? Of *me?*"

"I speak it as it is, Jonik. You're standing looking out upon the valleys, pining for your friends, struggling with your fate. You're brooding. It's an apt description."

"Then let me brood. It's not something you do in company."

"In a moment." She stayed where she was, her cheeks stung pink by the wind, brown hair flapping and flailing behind her. There was a resolve in her eyes Jonik hadn't seen yet. *Green eyes,* he thought. *They're nothing like mine.* "I'd first ask what you intend to do with the prisoners?"

"What I do with them is no concern of yours."

"I beg to differ. Gerrin says you're considering letting them all go. Even Kagnor. Did I get that right? The old Shadowmaster who's pouring honey in your ear."

Like Fhanrir warned me, Jonik thought. He'd said that Kagnor would tell him what he wanted to hear, and put a knife in his back the first chance he got. So it had transpired, the first part at least. Every time Jonik visited the prisoners the man had greeted him with a mawkish grin, turning his scowl to sweetened smiles in a bid to win his freedom. Gerrin had been utterly clear in his thoughts on that. "You either kill Kagnor, or you leave him in there to rot," he'd warned. "Fhanrir wasn't wrong, Jonik. He'll have you dead, one way or another."

"Yes," he said to the woman who'd birthed him and betrayed him. "Kagnor. You got that right."

"I'm learning, then." She smiled. It looked real enough, curse the woman. "And the others are…" She screwed up her face in concentration and counted on her fingers. "Nils, Zacarias, Trent, Hopper, and Henrik. Henrik is the one you sort-of knew here, before you left, yes?"

"Yes." He wasn't sure what she was trying to get at. "If you have a point, spit it out. You're eating into my brooding time."

"Well, we wouldn't want that." Her smile loosened up a little more. "My point is a simple matter of concern, Jonik. For you. For the boys you've so kindly put under my charge. For all of us."

"And yourself most of all, no doubt."

She chuckled at the accusation. "Self-preservation is a necessary feature of all life, superseded by only one thing. A mother's desire to protect her son. *That* is my motivation here."

He didn't believe it, wouldn't believe it. "Go on, then, speak. What would you have me do with them? Kill them, like Gerrin says? Keep them rotting in those rat-infested cells."

"He's only trying to protect you, as I am. The man is the only father you've ever known."

He snorted to hear her say that. "You two will be getting wed next."

"He's a little old for me, I think. And hardly the comeliest, but he's got a good heart." Her eyes twinkled. *She likes this game,* Jonik thought. Words were her power. It was why he'd brought her out here in the first place, to try to help bring the boys around. Selecting the three…that was only a part of her duty, a punishment, cruel and petty though it was, and a way to ease his own burden. But the rest was to do with that silver tongue of hers. *Paint them pictures,* he'd told her. *Bring the world beyond these walls to life. Make them want to leave. Make them want to be good, and live well, and live free.*

"So," he said. "You'd kill them all, would you?"

"By no means, and nor would Sir Gerrin, as I'm sure you know. Kagnor, yes. *That one* is beyond redemption, and needs to be put down for the safety of us all." She must have caught the look in his eye. "You think me cruel for that? Heartless and unmerciful? No, just pragmatic. Kagnor is rotten to his core from what I've heard. And you know what they say about one bad apple in the basket?"

"You chuck it out so it doesn't spoil the rest. That's just what I intend to do."

"So you'll pack him a nice full bag of provisions, shove him out of the gate, and wave him on his way?"

"Something like that."

"Armed?"

"Of course not armed. He's an old man. Without a weapon what can he do? Climb back over the wall and slaughter us as we sleep?" He scoffed at the thought of it. "Even with godsteel he'd have no chance, not at his age."

"No, I don't suppose he would. The walls do look awfully sheer and icy, and that frightful wind, always blowing…" She turned her eyes over the parapet, across the bridge, and down the misty passes. "I imagine he'd give up quickly enough and just head on down the mountain, rather than starve or freeze to death out here waiting for his chance to strike." She nodded, ever so serious. "But I wonder…what about when he reaches the foothills, and beyond? A man like that is hardly likely to turn to good honest labour and find a quiet little village in which to settle. No, I rather think he'll take what he wants. Food, clothes, a horse, a woman or three. As soon as he arms himself, he'll be dangerous to everyone he nears. That man will turn outlaw, Jonik, you know that as well as I do."

She had a point, he had to admit. *Bloody woman, painting her pictures.* "There are a thousand outlaws in the north," he decided to say, giving over to belligerence. "What's one more?"

"One more is one more, Jonik. It's not a population you want to increase."

"So I kill him, then?"

"Yes, you kill him. You've made a bargain to give up three innocent boys to Fhanrir. What is Kagnor's life next to that? Kill him, and see it done. There is no predicament here."

"No, you wouldn't think so. Life is clearly expendable to you. Even that of.."

"My own son?" she came in, before he might level the attack himself. "Well of course, I must consider all life expendable if I'm willing to hand over my own infant child. Isn't that true, Jonik? You've got it all figured out, haven't you."

"There's nothing to figure out. The facts are plain. Even a blind man could see them."

"Very droll. A little trite, but droll." She smiled stiffly. "But tell me, if you would. What have *you* done in the name of duty?"

His eyes flattened out. He knew where this was going. "You know what."

"You killed your own brother," she said, as if he needed reminding, "as I gave up my own son. I did what I did for duty to my king, as you did for duty to your order. I was bred to be a breeder, as you were bred to be a blade, and both at my father's command. If there is a man to blame, it is him. We're not so different, you and I."

He sneered at that. "I'm nothing like you."

"How do you know? We've only just met."

"I've heard things…"

"As have I. Those names, oh those names people give you. Ghost of the Shadowfort. Hadrin's Horror. Death Made Flesh. Nightstalker. There are others too, aren't there? Do they fairly describe who you are?"

He didn't answer. His mind was in the past, reflecting on a sour memory, reflecting on a lie. *That is what they will call you now, but it is only one…one of a hundred names you'll have.* The Nightblade had whispered that to him once, when it promised him he'd be a leader, a champion, when it promised him something greater. *A lie,* he thought bitterly. *A sour rotten lie. You never said it would end here,* he thought, turning his eyes down to his hip. *A leader for a few months. A champion for ten turns of the moon. Names that will rise and fall as quickly as the ocean tides.* He looked at the blade in scorn, tempted to rip it from its sheath and toss it down the chasm. *I don't need you,* he told it. *I'll make my own way alone…*

His mother's voice broke the silence. "Well? Have I cut too close to the mark?"

Yes, he thought. "No," he grunted. He tore his eyes away from the black wisps of smoke and looked at her. "Those names don't describe me. They're not what I wanted to be." *But they're true, every one.*

"It's the same with me," his mother-for-a-day told him, weaving her web. "They call me spider, witch, the Bastard Bitch. There are kernels of truth in those names, I'll confess, but they're exaggerated for effect, same as yours." She studied his face for a prolonged moment. "You don't believe me," she said. "You still think I'm lying."

Yes, he thought. *Yes, I think you're lying. You gave me up for duty, perhaps, in part, but also for favour and ambition. Don't deny it.* But he kept his mouth shut. He didn't want to dig deeper into this cesspool. He didn't want to have this conversation at all.

"Fine," she said, after a time. "That's fine, Jonik. You have the right to believe what you want." She smiled uneasily and her eyes moved away. *A mask. Just a mask, like that snake Vincent Rose.* "So, the prisoners. We were talking about what you're planning to do with them."

A conversation I don't want to have either. "We were," he said. "Kill Kagnor, I heard you. What would you have me do with the others?"

"Release them," she said, unexpectedly.

He frowned at that. "You'd have me set them free?" It was the choice he was leaning toward, though Gerrin insisted they be kept locked away.

"I would have you give them a choice. They're young, like you. Killing Kagnor I understand, but them? No. I know that would not sit well with you."

He was glad to hear her say it. "I had thought about letting them out, to help us. Since Borrus and the others left…"

"A worthy idea. *If* you can trust them." She peered at him carefully. "*Can* you trust them, Jonik?"

He gritted his teeth. "Maybe. I'm not sure. I…I don't know anymore…"

"Anymore?"

"Fhanrir," he grunted. "He seems to think they all want me dead. That they might try to steal the Nightblade from me." *Those dungeons stink of death and desire,* the old mage had said. Jonik had brushed that off at first, but now…now he wasn't so certain, without Borrus and the others here, without more men about him he could rely on and trust. He was more vulnerable than ever, was the truth of it. "I doubt any of them could lift it, let alone master it, but still…"

"You can't be sure."

"No."

"And that's the reason Fhanrir wants them dead?" she asked. "Because he fears the Nightblade will be taken." The woman pondered that a while. "It makes me wonder, then…why hasn't Fhanrir killed them himself? Or had one of the other mages do it?"

"I don't know. Because of me, probably. He knows I'll oppose it."

"And rightly," she said. "But where does that leave us, Jonik? You want to free them, but you fear you cannot trust them. So…? What do you plan to do?"

She's leading me. "I'm sure you're about to tell me," he said.

Her smile returned. It was a nice smile, he could not deny it, broad and arresting, an expression that best conveyed the natural beauty of her face. He could quite understand how she could lure men into her web and bed with that smile, no less the silver tongue she bore. And damn him, damn him to hell, he found he wanted to hear her. He had been there and back again on what to do with these men, Gerrin pulling him one way, Harden another, Fhanrir another still. One counselled imprisonment, another freedom, another death. It seemed this woman was more in line with Harden's thoughts. *And my own.*

"So? What would you do?"

"Release them, as I have said. But not here within these walls. Unless you trust them you cannot take that risk. Send them away, as you might have done with Kagnor. Send them with the rest of the boys."

He had not anticipated that last part. "You'd have them *lead* the younger ones?" He looked at her suspiciously. "That's what I was thinking too."

"We are much alike, as I say."

He had no response to that this time.

"These prisoners are older," she went on, "men full grown, and most of the boys are but prepubescent children, smooth-skinned and squeaky-voiced. If you send them away alone, they'll only be preyed upon, and many will be drawn into a life of crime. They need figures of authority to show them a better path. These young Shadowknights can guide them, unshackled from the shadows of this order, now that they are."

Jonik nodded slowly, pondering that as he'd pondered it often during his long lonely nights on watch atop this wall. She was right, in all of it she was right. If he let the boys loose and sent them off down the mountain, they would only scatter. The strong would prey on the weak and many would not even make it to the foothills at all, picked off by wolves and bears and bandits along the way, or else they'd get lost in the snows and icy winds and fall foul of some hidden ravine. None of the younger ones had even made the journey down the mountain before, and there were a dozen wrong turns and routes they might take, perilous paths that would only lead them to their doom. But with Henrik, Hopper, and the others guiding them? All had ventured forth from here before and in Henrik especially Jonik saw a leader. He only wished Emeric was here to help. The exile was the most natural leader Jonik had ever known; if he was here, he might instruct Henrik on the task, and read his heart for signs of sin. *That was his gift too,* Jonik thought. Emeric had an uncanny ability to read people, divining in their souls their deepest desires and what darkness might lurk within.

But Emeric was *not* here, nor was Jack nor Turner nor the rest…nor Shade, his faithful friend, who had been with him longest of all. *They're gone, and may never come back.* He had to admit that to himself now. He had to consider the prospect of never seeing them again.

He cleared his throat. "I'll give it more thought. Perhaps…" He looked at her, his mother. "Perhaps you might speak with them? The prisoners. I heard you're good at reading people too."

"Too?" she asked.

"Emeric," he explained. "He had a gift for it. But he's not here, and I have you. So…"

"Of course." She wore another smile; softer, faithful, more reassuring. *A real smile?* he wondered. "Of course I will talk to them, Jonik."

He nodded. "Thank you." The words came out in a stiff whisper. "I have thought about giving them more comfortable accommodations, private rooms of their own in one of the towers. With a view, maybe, through the valleys. It would be better for you to be able to speak to them alone."

She nodded. " I agree. And Kagnor?"

Kagnor. "I'll deal with him myself."

"You should let Gerrin do it," she said.

He was already shaking his head. "It's my decision, my judgement. I should swing the blade."

"I don't agree. A leader should delegate, as you have with me. Gerrin and Kagnor hate one another, I'm told. Let the sworn sword challenge the Shadowmaster to a duel. Let him kill him fairly, and with honour, and let it be done."

"A duel?" Jonik hadn't considered that option. It would allow Kagnor to go out with some grace. But then… what if Gerrin should be killed, or badly wounded. He could not afford to lose him. "No. The risks are too great."

She arched an eyebrow. "Is there a chance he might lose?"

"There's always a chance. One misstep. One poorly-timed strike. There was a Blackshaw man. Crasson. One of the Shadowknights managed to slip his blade through his armour to puncture his liver. It seemed innocuous, and then he was dead. I'll not take that chance with Gerrin."

"No, nor should you. I had mistakenly thought it a mismatch."

It is a mismatch, Jonik knew. The chances of Kagnor striking Gerrin down were slim to none, but unless it was none to none he would not risk it. *My own honour be damned, I'll just throw Kagnor from the walls myself and be done with it.* He was growing weary of these dilemmas, weary of this place. How such a foul creature as Kagnor had led him through such despair was baffling. *Perhaps that makes me a good, moral man, to labour over it for so long?* He laughed that aside. *A good moral man…who intends to throw him from the wall…*

He turned around to look back into the lower ward, encircled by the black brooding buildings and looming towers of the Shadowfort. Not long ago it had begun to feel brighter here yet now it was darker and more grim than ever, a place of ghosts and whispers. *Ghosts,* he thought. *Whispers. Brooding black buildings.* An empty smile tugged at his pale frosted lips. *Perhaps I belong here, after all.*

"I'm going to help with the pyre," he told his mother. He could see Gerrin down there now, gathering wood. Across the yard, a light was moving through the windows of the library tower. *Harden,* he knew, *looking for those verses.* "Maybe you could help Harden in his search," he said. "He's trying to find out about Piseki funeral rites."

"Your man was Piseki?"

She'd never met Big Mo, nor been inside the Night Tower. Her nights were still spent in the refuge, with the heir, and her other duties. *She has more on her plate than I do,* Jonik realised. *And she does it uncomplaining…unlike me.* "Part-Piseki," he told her. "His father was from the Tidelands, I think."

She seemed to understand. "No lakes around here for a water burial," she said. "There is a well, though…"

He gave a small huff of laughter.

"Sorry," she said, reading it wrong. "Poor joke. I shouldn't be making japes when you've just lost a loyal man."

"It's fine," he told her. "I laughed because I said the same to Harden, just now." He looked at her. "Perhaps we're more alike than I thought."

"Well…I *did* tell you, Jaycob."

He frowned. "Jaycob?"

She looked suddenly sheepish, as though she'd made some appalling blunder. "Oh…sorry, it just slipped out. Jaycob was my grandfather, on my mother's side. Lord Jaycob Blakewood. A kind man, and noble. I loved him dearly as a child."

He wasn't understanding. "Then why…"

"It's silly. It just slipped out, like I said. Ignore me, Jonik." She began to move away.

He stepped after her. "No. I want to know. Why did you just call me that? Do I look like him or something?"

"A little, yes, I suppose you do. But…" Her eyes took him in, bright and misty, with an expression she could not fake. "It's just…this is the longest we've spoken so far, and…that name." She smiled uncomfortably. "Well, *I* never named you, Jonik. Sir Gerrin did that, as you know, and Jaycob…that was the name I was always intending to give my firstborn son. In honour of my beloved grandfather. I always knew that, from a child." She smiled again and shuffled her feet. "But don't worry, I'll not do it again."

Jaycob, he thought, as she turned and moved off, crunching away over the snow to help Harden with his search. He could not say if she was lying or not, yet it sounded plausible enough either way. *Jaycob*. He liked the name. It sounded nice, the sort of name a chivalric knight might have. Sir Jaycob, proud knight, hero of some famous battle. Sir Jaycob who all the woman coveted and all the men called friend. Sir Jaycob, so tall and strong and charming, as comfortable with a commoner as he was with a king. Sir Jaycob, born to a happy home, who lived a happy life.

Jonik, the Ghost of the Shadowfort, did not suit the name. *Sir Jaycob is everything I am not*, he thought. He looked down at the Nightblade, and scowled. *And you are to blame.*

22

Lythian

They came upon Redhelm at dawn on a crisp misty morning, the city emerging from the pall of night beneath skies blazed bright with crimson clouds. Sir Storos Pentar smiled broadly as his city came into sight, framed at her back by the looming hills of the South Downs. "There she is," he said, gazing out across the plains. "Home."

Not to me, Lythian thought, though it would do for now. Even from this distance, he could see that the gate was teeming, the road to the city crowded with carts and wagons and wains that stretched for over a mile from its walls. "How many of these will be given entry?" he asked, as they continued on up the road. Storos had told them that Redhelm was already full. He could not believe that these at the back would ever get in.

"Not many, I fear," Sir Storos admitted. "They live in hope, but it is fading. There was a time when you might wait half a day to get past the gates, now you might wait a week and still be here."

Lythian saw signs of that as they went. Many people were sleeping atop their wagons, or beneath them, and others had erected makeshift shelters against their sides. Some of those looked semi-permanent as though they had not moved for long days. "Would it not be better for them to move on?" he asked. "They must realise they'll not get in. It will be safer further north."

"They cling to hope, as I say. The city stewards are still trying to find more space for the people inside, though that takes time, and there isn't much left. Every day the gate guards come out here to tell them to move along, but many don't listen. They only weep, and beg, and continue to wait. Most of these have nowhere else to go."

The gates were opening as they approached the hulking barbican, and several dozen soldiers swiftly appeared to keep order in the queue. Beneath the rising sun the people stirred and woke, throwing off their blankets and sleeping rags to beg, once more, for entry. It was a wretched thing to witness. Within moments the air filled with the wailing of mothers, the babbling of infants, the desperate beseech of men pleading for sanctuary.

Amid all that, a smaller host, no more than a half dozen in number, came riding out to greet them. "Sir Storos," called out their captain. They were called the Redcapes for the colour of their lightweight cloaks, emblazoned with the city sigil; a red-coloured helm framed by a set of rocky hills. "We received your letter telling of your coming. And of your trials on the road." That letter had been sent from Fort Stalton two nights past, a stout old castle where they had camped overnight. "Please, let me escort you to your father. He is gathering to welcome you in the Blood Hall."

"As you will, Sir Heymon," said Storos. "I would first ask that you make sure our friends are let through the gates." He gestured to the passengers they'd picked up upon the slopes of the Scarlet Valley. There were eleven of them, from old men to young children, a family of farmers and foresters all huddled about their wagons. "We met these good folk on our way here," Storos explained, to the captain's querying look, "and promised them entry into the city upon arrival. I would see them hastened to the front of the queue. They have been through a great ordeal and lost several of their family members on the journey. I do not want them to suffer further."

The Redcape captain seemed unsure. "We've had people waiting here many days, seeking entry, my lord. If they should see these folk let in..."

"I understand." Sir Storos rode up to him and lowered his voice. "But you *will* see it done, Sir Heymon. Discreetly, if you must. I know you do not want to cause a riot, but I gave these people my word, and mean to keep it." He turned to Sir Oswin Cole, the captain of his guard. "Sir Oswin, I will leave you in charge, to make sure that it is done. See that our friends are safely housed and come report to me straight after."

Sir Oswin nodded. "As you command, my lord."

Sir Heymon didn't look so happy with that, though appeared in no mood to fight it either. He turned his horse, barking orders for his men to stay with Sir Oswin, before leading Storos, Lythian and Pagaloth through the gate. "You mentioned in your letter that you encountered a fellwolf upon the road, my lord," he said to Sir Storos. "And a drovara as well, is that correct?"

"The drovara, no. It remains elusive, somewhere in the woods east of the Valley of Tears. Captain Lythian lessened the fellwolf a forelimb, but it escaped thereafter. Have word sent to every hunter in the city to seek it out, Sir Heymon. It might well be dead already, but I'm taking no chances. Five gold sabres for its head."

The captain looked like he might just want to take the contract himself. It was a generous prize for an injured fellwolf, easy work for a skilled Bladeborn, armoured and armed. "I'll put the word out," the knight confirmed. He had a lazy left eye, Lythian noticed, though it did little to diminish his good looks, with those high sharp cheekbones and tousled tawny hair. "The city boards are not lacking for contracts at this time, my lord. It seems not a day goes by when some foul creature is not reported to be roaming our lands. The hunters are doing a roaring trade, and the sellswords too. Many of them have taken up the work in response to the rewards on offer."

Sir Storos nodded. "Is the grulok captured or killed yet, Sir Heymon?"

"No, not as yet. It has proven most elusive, my lord. It needs only go to sleep and appears again as a rock or boulder, almost impossible to find. The hunters have taken to prodding at every stone they see, in the hope it might awaken. It's ridiculous, if you ask me. Some even believe the grulok may fight on our side, against the enemy. There are some strange folk here, campaigning for the hunt to end. Wars stir all sorts to madness, it would seem."

"That is not madness, Sir Heymon, but desperation," Storos said. "The grulok was fashioned by Vandar himself as a soldier in his early wars. Perhaps these people are right."

Sir Heymon raised a brow at that, with a sceptical smile to go with it. "Well...we can but hope, my lord. Personally, I would prefer to rely on men, not monsters, to defend us."

They rode on through the streets of Redhelm as the sun climbed higher in the east. Light spilled in from over the red stone walls casting its glare upon the city. Lythian pulled back to ride at Pagaloth's side. The dragonknight was looking about from beneath the shade of his hood, his bruised dusky eyes deep in study. "The City of Blood," he said, in an ominous voice. "That is what we call it in Agarath. It is a feared place."

A city paved in dragon bones, painted with their gore, Lythian thought. That is what the people here like to claim, but in truth it was due to the reddish tint in the soil and rocks mined in the South Downs.

"It has a grim facade," Pagaloth went on. "It feels like I'm riding through a nightmare."

"Blame the Lukars for that," Lythian told him. "Before House Pentar became Wardens of the South, the Lukars had held the post for five hundred years. Over that time they built Redhelm into what you see today. They gave it its daunting face, Pagaloth. Before then, it had been as any other city. Tinted red, yes, and grand, but not so explicitly macabre."

House Lukar had always been like that, combative and proud, even before Lord Galin Lukar decided to uproot from Vandar, abandon his holy post of First Blade, and siege Ilithor, taking half his allies with him. But they made their mark here first, building the barbican into a great bulky thing, topped by a great stone helm crested with the coiled stone corpse of a dragon. Its walls were crenelated as such as well, half the merlons in the likeness of dead drakes too, and atop each of its many soaring towers perched a knight spearing a dragon in the neck or heart or eye, immense sculptures that were as impressive as they were provocative.

Lythian had never favoured it, in truth. He preferred the grand regal beauty of Varinar, with its high castle-topped hills and sparkling lake, the ageless elegance of Ilivar and Elinar, the broad white streets and tall statues found all over Ayrin's Cross. Those cities lifted up their heroes where Redhelm pulled down their foes. Lythian preferred to see Varin standing vigil, Sword of Varinar at his hip, than another nameless dragon screaming in death. Half the statues in Redhelm were as such. And almost all had been raised by House Lukar.

They came upon the central thoroughfare that led through the city's heart, a broad street paved in red and brown brick with stone knights standing sentry along the route. Beyond was the high red keep, built above it all. There were many soldiers bustling here, men-at-arms and knights in the colours of the houses they served, freeriders and sellswords in their cobbled suits of armour. All were part of the great garrison that Redhelm kept in times of war. Lythian inquired as to how many men there were to protect them, should the Agarathi come.

"We have some eight thousand in the city, at this time, Captain Lythian," Sir Heymon told him. "With thousands more manning defensive forts in the hinterlands, ready to march here at our need. We have worked tirelessly for long months to improve the battlements and defensive weaponry upon the walls. A strong force we can repel, but from what we've heard of Dragon's Bane…" He sighed anxiously. "Some say there were *fifty* dragons there, and a hundred and fifty thousand men, with many hundreds more Starriders and Sunriders besides. I have even heard that a Moonrider was there, laying waste to our ranks as they fell in retreat. If *that* army should march here, or even a small portion of it… well, we would have little hope against such a horde." His eyes ran over the bands of soldiers going about their work. "There is a great tension here, as you can surely feel. We expect that the Agarathi will march this way soon enough, and should they cross the river at Rustbridge, we will no doubt be next."

Sir Storos nodded thoughtfully. "My lord father will have put these soldiers on alert, to ride to the defence of Rustbridge, when the time comes. We would do well to combine our strength in this. Have you heard more from the east, Sir Heymon? How fares the army that was driven from the Bane?"

"They have regrouped at Oakpike, under the banners of the Daecar prince. A rider came but two days past, telling of hunting parties and sally forces led by Varin Knights. They seek to disrupt the enemy through raids and sorties, targeting rogue dragons as they sleep and drawing them into a shadow war. They mean to put fear into their hearts, Sir Storos. Your brother Alrus feels it will have a limited impact, however, against such a massive force. 'Pinpricks in the hide of a bovidor', I think he said."

Storos gave a huff of laughter. "My brother Alrus haswith reg always been a guarded man, most given to caution. Yes, that sounds very much like him."

They trotted on down the bloody-brown cobbles, men moving aside to let them pass. The last time Lythian had come through here, it had been commoners, not soldiers, who'd watched him ride through.

Men called out to me, he remembered, *common cobblers and costermongers, masons and minstrels, weavers and winemakers and everyone else in between. They wanted their fears of the Fireborn allayed. So I told them that all would be well, that no war would come upon them, that I was travelling with Borrus and Tomos, their favourite son, to meet with King Dulian so we might bring an end to the silence between our kingdoms.*

He had even stopped and given a speech to that effect, soothing their fears and smoothing out their ruffled feathers, telling them that the dragons that had been sighted flying in from the coast were scouts, and no more, and did not augur a larger threat. "You shan't see another dragon here again," he recalled telling them. "Not for many years." He wondered now, as he rode on through the city, if a man had ever been so catastrophically wrong.

There were few regular folk among the crowds. Lythian supposed they had been told to stay in their homes, or else ply their trades elsewhere. "Where are all the refugees being housed?" he asked Sir Heymon.

"Wherever we can fit them, Captain Lythian. It is all being carefully managed, with regard to how many we can take in. Disease and hunger are fierce concerns, so numbers must be kept in check. If everyone should be allowed through the gates, many more will starve, Sir Alrus fears."

Alrus again. Lythian found that curious. "Does Lord Pentar's health worsen?"

The Redcape nodded dourly. "Most quickly, I regret to say. He still sits his seat as lord, on occasion, but Sir Alrus has taken to holding court, and running city affairs in his stead. Redhelm has fallen under his rule now, in truth."

It was grim news. Alrus Pentar was *not* his father. *And no friend to me,* Lythian thought.

They rode on, hastening down the central thoroughfare, leading to the high red keep that loomed above the city. The path wound upward like the tail of some great serpent, leading them back and forth until finally they came to the doors to Lord Pentar's hall. Two Redcapes barred the doors with long steel spears painted scarlet. At Sir Heymon's command, they thrust the butts of their weapons into the ground with a *thud* and stood aside. The men dismounted their steeds and prepared to enter the hall by foot, but Sir Heymon turned to stop them, and said, "I am sorry, Captain Lythian. But you must relinquish your arms."

Lythian frowned at him. "Why? I have come armed to this hall many times in the past."

"As guest of Lord Porus. Sir Alrus is more wary, and has made this decree. None are to enter the Red Hall of the Helm so armed, lest they be servants of the city. You are not, alas. Please, leave your dagger with the guards."

I like this not, Lythian thought, though he did as bidden, stripping his belt of the sheath and dagger that Sir Storos had given him and handing it to the soldiers. "I told you I would find you a more suitable blade when we reached the city, Lythian," Storos reminded him, "and I will. You don't need that dagger anymore. I'll see you properly outfitted when we're done."

Lythian nodded his thanks as Sir Heymon looked at Pagaloth. Until now he had kept his eyes determinedly away from the Agarathi. "Is he armed?" he asked Sir Storos.

"He has a voice of his own," Lythian said. "Ask him yourself, Sir Heymon."

Pagaloth spared him. "I have no blade upon me, sir," he said. He opened his cloak to prove it.

No blade, only bruises, Lythian thought angrily, *and a shroud of dignity that no man can pierce.* It had not been a pleasant time in the north for Sir Pagaloth, yet he had not let it wound him. *His penance,* Lythian knew. He saw it in the beatings those louts at Runnyhall had given him, in the shearing of his hair and beard. He saw it in the cold stares of Sir Storos's men, in the way the farmers and foresters they had rescued on the road had given him a wide berth. *He sees penance in every insult and injury, fair justice for his crimes.* Lythian had told him a dozen times that he had done plenty enough now to atone for Tomos's death, but still he did not listen. It made him anxious as to what Pagaloth might say within the hall. *Just keep your mouth shut,* he thought. *Let me speak on your behalf.*

The doors to the Blood Hall were opened with a great wooden groan, and the interior came into view. Lythian had hoped to find Lord Porus Pentar alone, or else with Alrus only, but that hope was quickly shattered. The hall was crowded either side of the centre aisle, highborn and lowborn alike awaiting them within. Lythian ran his eyes upon them. *They have come to hear the tale of Sir Tomos,* he realised. *They want to know what happened to their beloved Red Knight of the Helm.*

As they entered, Sir Heymon called out their coming in a ringing voice. "Lord Pentar, I bring you Captain Lythian, the Knight of Mists, and his companion from the dark south." He gave Pagaloth a glance, but did not name him. "And your son, Sir Storos, ridden here from Southwatch to deliver them." The knight bowed and moved aside, his duties done.

Sir Storos stepped forward. "Father," he said, bowing low to the man's high seat. Lord Porus Pentar sat as a child embraced by a chair too large for him, a crumbling wreck of a thing greatly more diminished than Lythian had seen him last. Shock ran through him to see him in such a withered state. Through rheumy eyes he peered down, gout-ridden and grimacing, though cognisance was not his ally. *He hardly knows me, no more than he does his son,* Lythian thought. *He must be but days from the pyre.* "I have escorted Captain Lythian and Sir Pagaloth to you, as commanded," Storos went on. He presented them with an open arm, though Lord Pentar did not turn his eyes. "We have ridden with great haste from Runnyhall to be here at your summons, Father. Not a moment has been spared in delay upon the road."

Sir Alrus raised a hand and stood from the seat beside his father. "*Haste,* Storos?" he asked, with a mocking frown. He had not his younger brother's fair face, but one plain and homely, a little too broad at the brow and plump at the chin, with an ill-defined jawline poorly concealed by a thread-bare beard the colour of new-tilled earth. He had a crutch beside his seat, to aid him when walking. The arrow wound he had taken had left him with a limp, Storos had said, and the subsequent inactivity had made him stouter than Lythian recalled, giving him a fleshiness that his brothers did not share. "You left Runnyhall long days ago, did you not? A turtle might call that haste, but a host on horseback? No."

Laughter swept through the hall like a gale. Lythian noticed a shade of blush climbing Sir Storos's neck. "We came upon some farmers on the road, brother," he said in defence. "They slowed us greatly. I wrote as such in my letter to you. The fellwolf...I spoke of the fellwolf, Alrus."

"I know, Storos, I know. You needn't take my jests so seriously." Alrus Pentar had never been a man for jesting, lest he intended those jests to cause hurt. "Come, brother, embrace me." He turned to the high seat. "Father, look who has come visit. Storos is here, with the Knight of the Vale. He has come to tell us of Tomos's death."

Storos stepped away to greet his brother, leaving Lythian and Pagaloth alone on the aisle between the teeming commons. The Blood Hall was no less macabre than the rest of the city. Its pillars were wound about by dead stone drakes, dripping blood. Amongst its wooden rafters bowmen and spearmen had been carved, launching projectiles at the beasts. The walls swam with beastly imagery, painted by the Lukars, death duels and blood rituals and scenes of dragon torture. Lythian had seen them often, and never found them far from tasteless and unseemly. He did not like this hall, no more than he did the energy within it. The people were looking at him darkly. He did not like that either.

He stepped forward. "Lord Pentar, might I ask that we speak privily? The story of Tomos is a telling you should hear alone first. Your audience chamber would be more appropriate."

"This is the Blood Hall, Captain Lythian," Sir Alrus told him, looking down from the dais. "A place of story and song, and most appropriate for such a telling. Tomos was a Varin Knight, to be lauded and cheered at his death, so the Steel Father might hear. We have gathered such who knew him this morn to celebrate the young man they all loved. Would you deny them the chance to hear what befell him?"

Lythian was not going to be cowed by the man. "They can hear it from the singers and bards, once Tomos's life is put into song, as it should be. But a father should hear of his son's death in private."

"And why is that? Is this a tale you fear to tell?"

"Fear, no. But it is a morbid tale, and one best privily spoken." He moved his eyes from the crippled knight to the dying lord. "I ask again, Lord Pentar. For our friendship, do me this honour of a private audience. You need but open your lips and say the word and..."

"Alas you ask the impossible, Sir Lythian," came in Alrus. He bowed his head in despair. "My lord father has lost his ability to speak and thus can only listen. He would hear you now, here in this hall. He would hear of the son he loved and lost, whose bones lie before you..."

At that he waved and out came a tall armoured knight, carrying in his arms an ornate box, deep red leather, banded in silver. The knight opened the lid and Lythian looked upon the remains of Sir Tomos Pentar, the Red Knight of the Helm.

"A gift, from a dragonlord," Alrus went on. "A gift of bones and a tale untold." His voice grew rich with pain. "We all here wish to know it. Please, sir, would you deny us? Would you deny the wet nurse who suckled Tomos at her breast, the armourer who forged his fine plate, the baker who made the sweetbreads he so loved when he was a boy? What of the squires who trained with him in the yard, the girls who would chase him in want of a kiss? Would you deny them, Captain Lythian? Would you deny all those here, who have come to hear you speak of the young man we all adored?"

Lythian was sick of the man's cloying voice. He was about to open his mouth to speak when someone in the commons shouted, "We want to hear it! The Red Knight was beloved by us all. We would hear how he died. We would hear it!" Shouts of assent followed, echoing through the pillars, and suddenly the entire hall was shaking with the demands of a hundred voices.

This is a losing battle, Lythian thought. He raised his hands to call for calm, stepping several paces away from Pagaloth in the hopes he might be forgotten. *I will charm them,* he told himself. *I will tell them a tale they want to hear.*

"Friends," he began, "friends, I hear you." Slowly their voices stilled and a quiet came upon the hall. "I know Tomos was much loved and cherished by you all, as he was me. Let me put your minds to rest." He turned to his left and his right, reaching for the rafters with his voice. "I tell you now that Sir Tomos Pentar fell proud, and strong, and gallant to the very last, with the blood of dragons gleaming red on the edge of his blade. He fell fighting, defiant of the cruelties of his captors, beneath a shining banner of sunlight as Varin, the great Father of Steel, did watch from his Holy Seat."

Murmuring broke out. Many seemed relieved. Others smiled, some wept, a few put their hands to their faces or raised them to the roof in prayer. Lythian had known Tomos was well-liked here, but not that he'd touched so many lives. *Will as many weep for me, when I die?* He doubted it greatly. *Not when they find out what I've done…*

"What about the bones?" a woman shouted over the noise. She pointed to the box. "The bones are all bitten, some o' them chewed. You're sayin' that were dragons what did it?"

"I am, good lady," Lythian answered, turning to where the voice had come from. He spotted her, a crone of sixty in a moth-eaten dress with great sagging breasts. He wondered for a moment if this was the wet nurse that Alrus had spoken of. "Tomos died fighting in the Pits of Kharthar, sentenced to death for…"

"For what *you* did," a big man bellowed. "*You* murdered King Dulian. You started this war and you killed Tomos too!"

"No, that is not true," called out Sir Storos, striding to Lythian's side. "That rumour has long ago been dispelled, Mathen, as well you know." The big man called Mathen nodded dumbly, as though he'd forgotten all that. "Captain Lythian was imprisoned upon his arrival in Eldurath, along with my brother and Sir Borrus Kanabar," Storos went on. "This was the doing of Prince Tavash Taan who has since crowned himself king. *He* was responsible for his uncle Dulian's death as he was much else, including

284

Tomos's execution. Now I beg you all to heed your tongues and show calm. This is Sir Lythian Lindar, Captain of the Varin Knights, famed for his devotion to his knightly honour. Long has he battled to return here, through sun and sand and strife. Give him the courtesy of listening to him."

"Yes, give him that courtesy," agreed Sir Alrus, though with a devious look in his eye. "None here can deny that the Knight of Mists has suffered greatly. One needs only look at him to know that. New scars I see, and a face aged a decade in a year. Such is the case during terms of confinement, in which he has clearly seen torment and abuse. As Tomos did, I am quite sure." He stopped and the air went still. A flick of the eyes and he was looking at Sir Pagaloth. "Tell us, Captain Lythian, of your silent companion. We would all dearly like to know more of this Agarathi stranger who broods so darkly in our midst."

Lythian had never liked Sir Alrus. At this point he hated him. He unclenched his jaw and said, "You have the honour to know Sir Pagaloth Kadosk, Dragonknight of Agarath. He was guide to us as we crossed the Drylands, and has since become a friend, as he was to Tomos as well." He closed his lips and said no more.

Sir Alrus smiled. "Honour? An *honour* to meet him? Perhaps, or perhaps not. You do know that many dragonknights are killing our countrymen, do you not? Estimates say that ten thousand Vandarians were killed at the Battle of the Bane, Sir Lythian. Many by dragonknights such as this, I am sure."

The crowd stirred. "Why is he here?" someone spat. "Why would you bring *him* here?"

"He is sworn to Captain Lythian by oath," Sir Storos answered.

"Why? Why would some Agarathi swear an oath to a Varin Knight?" A small man with the biggest eyebrows Lythian had ever seen was using them to good effect, twisting them in a frown. "And in wartime? Makes no sense. No sense at all!"

"We *shall* make sense of it, fear not," exclaimed Sir Alrus Pentar. His lord father watched on, though looked confused by much of what was happening. *He would not be enjoying this farce, not in his right mind,* Lythian knew. "So let me ask you, Captain, what reason did this dragonknight have to swear you his allegiance?"

Lythian misliked where this was leading. "There came a day, during my time in the south, where Sir Pagaloth's fate was put into my hands," he said, remembering the morning that the dragonknight had been found wandering the wilds of the Western Neck. When they had gathered upon the hill above the woods for his trial, and Prince Tethian had let Lythian decide what was to be done with him. "I chose to spare him the death that others were asking for. He took it for a life debt and swore me his sword. He has been in my service since then, disavowed of his commitment to Agarath, and his oaths as dragonknight of the realm."

Sir Alrus was fingering the flesh beneath his chin. "Curious. A most curious tale. And where were you, at this time?"

"In the Western Neck."

"The Western Neck? Truly? And you went there after you escaped your captivity in Eldurath, is this so?"

"Yes."

"How did you escape?" a man called out. "Tomos never did. But you and Kanabar…"

"We heard rumours of Fireborn helping you," shouted another. "Is that true, Captain Lythian? Did you join with them, these rogues?"

Lythian spoke wearily now. "We were rescued by the Dragonlord Ulrik Marak, and a Skymaster named Kin'rar Kroll…"

Mention of Lord Marak had the crowd at once in full voice, the hall erupting into a chaos of shouts and calls. A hundred questions seemed to be screamed at him, but once again Sir Alrus silenced them with a raised palm. In a high thin voice he called, "So it is true, that the Fireborn saved you? Oh, this tale gets more curious by the moment, Captain Lythian. Now I ask you *why*? Why would a man such as Ulrik Marak, a feared Fireborn rider and a killer of kings, wish to help a Varin Knight like you?"

"For the sake of honour," Lythian told him. "And a promise kept."

Memory began to flood through his mind, as he stood lonely at the heart of the hall. Some sour, others hopeful. Memories of love, loss, murder and betrayal. He thought of the days in the wilderness of the Western Neck. He thought of the Wings. He thought of the depths beneath the mountain of Eldur's Shame, and the heat down there in the Fire Father's tomb, and the great stone mount of Drulgar at his back, and the weeks he'd spent in fever thereafter, fighting for his life. He thought of the parley and perishing of Tethian and the awakening of a god. He remembered Kin'rar's death, and Neyruu's scream, and the battle in the ruins under the rain, with Ashun Klo and Rackar and Kartheck and the days that had followed, the long days in the wilds, as Mirella had fallen to a fever of her own, and Lythian, in his folly and regret, and put his hands to the poor girl's mouth and nose…and shut her eyes forever.

He remembered it all in one long flashing sequence, as he stood there in that hall. The trek to the Nest with the beleaguered remnants of their camp, the discovery of Marak there atop the world, wounded and in the care of Skymaster Sa'har Nakaan. The long cold days they'd lingered in the blackened husk of that great high fortress, in darkness and doubt, before *he* came again, *Eldur* came, with his dragons and his staff and the Bondstone and his *voice*.

And Talasha. He remembered her most keenly of all. The way she looked at him, smiled at him, the way she kissed him and touched him and loved him, the way she showed him what it was like to feel that way again, so long after the death of his wife and newborn son. *I loved her, and love her still*, he thought, racked by guilt and loss and shame. He could feel their eyes boring into him, the eyes of the hall, but cared not. In silence he stood there, dwelling upon it all. Dwelling upon the day that Talasha had left him, bewitched by the father and the founder of her kingdom, by the divine being that started her bloodline, all those millennia ago.

He had been travelling ever since that day, by sandal and saddle and sail. The trek down from the Nest had been long, and the ride across the Drylands yet longer. They had left Cevi there, not daring to take her with them. "Return to your family," Lythian had told the handmaiden. "Go back to your father and your sisters and your brothers, Cevi. Where we're going it will not be safe."

The girl had wept fierce tears, and told him once, twice, thrice how she wanted to come too. It was for Pagaloth, he knew. "Take me with you," she begged. The handmaid had fallen in love with him, and could not see beyond the pain of their parting.

Lythian had taken her hands in his and held them tightly together. "I will keep him safe, I promise you, Cevi," he had told her. "I will not let him come to harm. You will see him again, one day."

Empty promises, he thought now, as he stood before the dais, enclosed by glaring, unsympathetic eyes. He had promised himself that he would protect Cevi, after what he'd done to Mirella. He had promised himself he would not let Talasha come to hurt or harm, and had broken that vow as well the day he let the Fire Father take her, impotent to act. *I have failed them all,* he knew. *I have made many promises, to myself and to others…but I have broken them, every one.*

"Nothing more to say, Captain Lythian?" Alrus Pentar was looking down upon him pitilessly. "You have been quiet for several long moments. Would you not share the rest of your story with us?" He looked to his audience and heard them call out in assent. "You spoke of honour, and a promise kept. Was this promise of Lord Marak's just to you, and Borrus Kanabar? I wonder why it did not extend toward Tomos, my dear beloved brother. I wonder why he was slain and you were not. I wonder a great many things, as we all do, and yet we are hearing few answers from you." He stopped and rubbed his fleshy chin. "Perhaps we might bring your companion forward instead. Sir Pagaloth, come forth. Let us hear your side of this tale."

Lythian turned at once to Pagaloth, and shook his head. Sir Alrus noticed. "Something to hide, Lythian? Why should this man not speak before us today?"

Lythian spun back. "Is this a trial, Alrus?" he asked sharply. "Do you have us here before you to answer for some crime?"

"I made no mention of a crime," the man said, innocently. "We seek only honesty, and truth. Much is amiss here, and this dragonknight has played his part. So tell me, Sir Pagaloth Kadosk…why have you wedded your life to this man? Why was it that others called for your death, when Lythian here sought to save you?"

Say nothing, Lythian wanted to tell him. *Say nothing, Pagaloth. Be silent.* He tried to shout that with his eyes, but Pagaloth was not looking at him. He stepped forward in a proud gait, and lifted his chin, shorn of hair and slashed with a dozen cuts, his face badly bruised. *No,* Lythian thought, even as the dragonknight opened his lips and said, "They wanted me dead for my betrayal, my lord. They sought vengeance for this act."

"Betrayal?" asked Sir Alrus. "And who did you betray, pray tell?"

"Men I admired. Men who sought to stop a war by plotting murder."
He stared forward. "It was I who spoke of the plot to have Prince Tavash
killed," he told them. "Lord Marak, Skymaster Kin'rar...both spoke to me
in trust, yet I betrayed them, as I did the Varin Knights. Had I kept my
faith, Tavash would have been slain in Dulian's place, Sir Tomos would still
be alive, and war may have been averted. I caused the death of your
brother, my lord." He lowed his head. "And for this my life is forfeit. Do
with me as you please."

Penance. Lythian thought. *Curse you and your need for penance, Pagaloth. Curse
you and your probity and pride.* He felt cold all of a sudden, as he saw the look
in Sir Alrus Pentar's eyes. "As I please, you say?" He took a pause and went
on in a low voice. "Your death would please me, I think."

"No," Lythian said loudly. He stepped forward. "*No.*" Dark mutters
were beginning to spread through the hall. He could all but hear the sound
of daggers being drawn, knives sharpened. "Sir Pagaloth acted by
command of his oaths as a dragonknight of his realm. He was following
orders only, and has lived in a torment of guilt since that day. I vouch for
him, with all the power of my station. If you would curse him for this
crime, Sir Alrus, you would curse me too. His fate and mine will be
shared."

"You *threaten*, Lythian? You threaten *me*, who will soon be Lord of
Redhelm and Warden of the South. You, of a middling house?" He looked
at him with a disdainful frown. "You are a knight and a soldier, but no lord.
Do not presume to threaten me in my own hall, or talk to me of your
station. The Knights of Varin are a broken shield, and you a broken man."

Lythian bristled at the insult. *A broken man. Is that what I am?* "This is not
your hall, Alrus," he came back. "It is your father's, whose shadow you will
never escape." Lythian stared at Lord Porus, hoping he might stir, but the
old man was lost. *He cannot help me. He is a shell now, a shade, slipping into
darkness.*

Dread was grasping at him with cold black fingers, as the hall grew loud
with calls for Sir Pagaloth's head. *And mine,* Lythian thought. Some were
brazen enough to bellow for the Knight of Mists to join him. "Traitor!" he
heard someone say. And another was bellowing out, "Turncloak! He's
turned his cloak for the dragons. He's soft on them, *soft!*" Others shouted
words to similar effect, and over the tumult, Sir Storos was trying to seize
back calm. "Alrus, no," he was shouting. "Lythian cannot be harmed, lest
you incur Lord Daecar's wrath. Hang the dragonknight if you must, but..."

"Be quiet, Storos! Know your place and be quiet!" Alrus Pentar shot his
eyes left and right and two soldiers bellowed out for silence, smashing their
heavy spears into the ground. "You think I would truly harm the Knight of
the Vale? Fool! You have always been a fool!" He snapped his eyes down to
his father, and bent his back to whisper something in his ear. Lord Pentar
stared blankly forward, seeming not to hear. A moment later, Alrus turned
his ear to his father's lips, as though to listen to him speak. *A show,* he knew.
This is all a show. Madness has seized this hall.

The heir of Redhelm stood straight once more, raised his hands for quiet, and shouted, "My father has listened, and he has spoken! For his betrayals and his crimes, the dragonknight must die! The Lord of Redhelm decrees it so!"

"LORD PENTAR!" Lythian roared. He was done with this charade. Done. "My lord, listen to me! You *must* listen to me!" He strode forward several steps but found his way blocked by several guards as he neared the stage. His attempts to shove past them were futile. "Porus, hear me! For our friendship, hear me!"

"He can hear you, Captain Lythian," sneered his eldest son. "And he has given his decree." He raised his arms aloft once more. "Take him outside! Shout out the call! Let the streets ring loud with the news! Sir Tomos's killer has been found!"

Killer? This was lunacy. Before Lythian even knew what was happening, Pagaloth was being bundled toward the doors. He made to give chase, but the soldiers held him back as the doors were kicked open and a warm wash of daylight poured in. The crowds followed, hectoring and shouting at Pagaloth as they went. Lythian searched for Sir Storos and found him by the dais, looking pale. "Storos, you must stop this!" he yelled. "You must see that Pagaloth isn't to blame!"

The man looked lost. "There's…there's nothing I can do, Lythian. This is out of my hands. And perhaps…perhaps it is just."

"*Just?*" He could not believe what he was hearing. "Just, to kill a man without a trial, to let him be condemned by this jester's court?"

"He is Agarathi, Lythian. The…the enemy. My brother seeks to make a show of him, I think. I'm sorry…I cannot help you." He turned his back to him and strode out into the light.

"Storos! Storos, listen to me! You gave us safe passage, you gave us your word!" When he got no answer, he turned his eyes around in search of another to plead to and found Sir Heymon nearby. "I knew your father, Sir Heymon," he said, desperate. "He was a good man. He'd not have let this happen."

The knight chose not to hear him.

There was no one else, no friends here, only foes. Two large soldiers came forth and grabbed Lythian by the arms, marching him out into the brisk morning air. He squinted against the bright harsh sunlight as he stepped beyond the hall. Outside, a gallows loomed to the right of the high steps, erected upon a wooden stage. Several dead men were already hanging from the gibbet on lengths of hempen rope, their faces pale as curdled milk, arms limp at their sides. One had an eye pecked out by crows. Another had seen his innards removed before execution, for what crime Lythian couldn't say. The crows had gotten to him too. Others stood upon the wooden scaffold, awaiting their next meal. They watched Pagaloth eagerly as he was led up the steps, cawing.

Lythian was trying to think as he was bundled along. *What can I do? Who can I turn to?* The baying of the mob about him was vile; it reminded him of Eldurath, as he and Borrus and Tomos were dragged along to the Pits of Kharthar, beaten and starved and wreathed in rags. The irony did not escape him. *It is happening again, and here in Vandar.* He had been a fool to think it would have gone any different. *Why did you have to say anything, Pagaloth? Why didn't you just keep your mouth shut?*

People were spreading the word as they went. "We have Sir Tomos's killer," they called. "We have the man to blame! Come watch, come watch, come see him hang!" The soldiers below were pouring up the winding road in their colours of red and scarlet and purple and pink. Armour clanked and clattered as they came, and the air bustled loudly as the news was shared. "He is caught! Come see him hang! We'll have our vengeance for the Red Knight of the Helm!"

Lythian was brought to the edge of the stage where Sir Alrus Pentar awaited him, leaning on his crutch. "I am sorry for this, Captain Lythian," he said, as magnanimously as he could, even as Pagaloth was bound hand and foot and hoisted atop a stool. "I see you care for him, and this life debt is clearly important to you, but facts are facts, and my father *has* spoken. For want of King Tavash himself, this man is the next best thing." He turned, and commanded, "Rope his neck," then turned back. "I do hope you understand."

Words are wasted on this man, Lythian knew. *No plea or petition will turn him.* Instead he made an attempt to reach across and grab a soldier's godsteel blade, but his efforts were spotted and swatted away. "Now come," said Sir Alrus, tutting. "None of that. Unless you want to join him?" He gestured to the gibbet, and his eyes said, *just give me an excuse.* "I have always admired you, Lythian, as has all the realm, but this is how it must be. Do not take this as a personal offence. It is justice, and no more."

Justice. Lythian turned to look at Pagaloth, who stared out across the city with a look of calm on his face. *Justice,* he thought again. *Penance, for his crimes.*

"You do this, Alrus, and you will come to regret it," Lythian warned him. "I swear as Varin is my witness, I will not forgive, and I will not forget."

The heir of Redhelm merely smiled, turned, and addressed the crowd, calling out in a high ringing voice of his brother Tomos and his many virtues, praising the man they had all loved and lost. He flung a hand to his side and told them of the culprit, standing upon the stool before them. "This man is to blame," he shouted. "This dragonknight, who betrayed our fair Tom. This creature was in league with King Tavash, the enemy. I would have him flayed, and tortured, I'd have him drawn and quartered… yet his own confession has earned him clemency. He came here willingly to admit to his crime, and by this I give him mercy. *Mercy!*" he bellowed, louder, as the people called for a harsher end. "We will not become as the savages from the south. Leave them to their wicked ways, here in Redhelm we deal with justice differently. But justice we shall have, and vengeance! Soon the dragon king will fall and his kingdom will fall with him, but until then, we have this dragonknight instead!"

The crowd roared approval, a bloodlusted din filling all the air. Lythian gazed at Pagaloth, who stood still and serene, accepting his end with grace.

I am sorry, Lythian could only think. His eyes grew wet with grief and anger. *I am sorry, I have failed you.*

Sir Alrus Pentar turned to face the condemned. He met eyes with the executioner standing beside the stool.

A flash of silver glinted in the skies overhead…

…and the heir of Redhelm shouted, "Now!"

23

ᗷalasha

The hall was black as night but for the light of the Bondstone, shining from the top of his staff. No torches filled the sconces on the walls, no lamps or lanterns swayed. *He likes to control the light*, she thought. *He likes to control it all.*

"Father." She went down to one knee eight paces before his dragon-skull throne. "You called upon me."

"Rise." His whispered voice filled the room, and she rose at once to her feet to stand before him. In its embrace he sat, white-haired and ancient and ageless at once, wrapped in a simple maroon robe that hid all but his hands and head. One of those hands clutched his black wood staff; the other rested along the jaw of the dragon, stroking at one of its savage sharp teeth. "Tagathon," he said. "Tell me of him."

Talasha bowed her head. "He was a great dragon, my lord. Your descendent Queen Melliana rode him during the War of Wrath, which was the Tenth Renewal of the War Eternal. She was our first queen, following a thousand years of kings. After they were slain during the Battle of the Drums, both were lionised and honoured; she with a great temple, seen at the heart of the city, Tagathon by being used forever as a vessel from which future kings and queens might sit and rule."

He looked at her with gleaming red eyes. "A vessel?"

"Yes, Father. It has long been custom here to mine the bodies of our fallen dragons, as the Vandarians mine the body of their fallen god. The Children of Agarath watch over us, even after death. Their scales are used for armour and shields, their teeth for spear and axe heads. When alive the magic of their breath forges dragonsteel. Tagathon was afforded a place in all remembrance, by carrying forth the royal line."

Eldur the Eternal did not speak for a long moment. *He knows this*, the princess thought. *Sotel Dar has taught him our history, the history he did start.* She could not help but gawp in wonder to look upon him. Here was the seed of her kingdom and her people. It still felt like she was walking through a dream.

"This throne has borne your brother," the Fire Father said. Darkness enrobed the space about him, so thick that Talasha could not see the walls. Even the ground at her feet was scarcely visible. The room felt mystical in the Father's presence. *All he touches feels so,* she thought. *Even me. I am more when I'm near him.*

"He became king after our uncle," she replied. "King Dulian, who was son of Tellion, my grandfather, and direct descendent of the Line of Lori, pureborn of your own royal blood, my lord."

"Lori," he said, so softly. The stiff pale skin at the corner of his mouth wrinkled. "My son."

"He was a great king, my lord. After the Battle of Ashmount, he sought vengeance for you, and for Karagar. He and Dor...they slew the Father of Steel for all the blood he had shed. Varin's son Ayrin followed him in rule. A milder man, they say, less quarrelsome. He reigned for two centuries before his death, a prosperous and peaceful time between our kingdoms. Then his son Amron took the throne. He bestirred bloodshed, as his grandfather Varin had. It was the Second Renewal, after the War of Fire and Steel."

She did not know why she was telling him all this. *Sotel has told him,* she thought again. She had even spoken to the old scholar of it, yet all the same the words came flowing forth. As ever it was in his divine ethereal company. *I want to please him, serve him, I want our great Father to love me...*

"Dulian," he whispered, thinking. "Tell me, child...was he a good king as well?"

She remembered Dulian as a peaceful man, a kind man, a beloved uncle. Memory of her childhood flooded her mind, her days hawking and hunting on the delta, her trips to the river gardens at Videnia, her favourite place in all the world. Dulian's crippling had stripped him of his legs, but he'd become a better man for it, many said, a wiser man. *Until the madness set in. Until my brother got his claws into him...*

"He was a good king, my lord," she said. "I miss him dearly."

"How did he die?"

She hesitated. His eyes were on her, searching. "They say a Knight of Varin killed him. A man who came here under guise of peace and parley." Somewhere in the back of her mind she remembered him, this knight. *Lythian,* something in her whispered. *Sweet captain.* She felt a strange stirring in her heart, though it felt numb somehow, muted, *dangerous...*

"That is not the truth," the Father told her. "Tell me the truth, child. You need not protect him."

She swallowed. The truth. She sifted through her memory, yet could not divine the truth from the dreams, separate the reality from the fantasy. Much of her recent life felt strange to her, a shadow at her back unseen. *The light is before me,* she knew. *He is the light. The Father and the Founder. He who will wash away the sins of the world, he who will spread Agarath's Eternal Flame. All else is shadows and ghosts.*

Her lips broke open and she said, "My brother had him killed, my lord. Tavash. He killed Dulian so he might take the throne."

"As he killed your mother?"

She nodded. "Yes, Father. He threw her from a balcony by his very own hand. Tavash always craved power." *My brother*, she thought. Suddenly she realised she did not know where he was. He had been king, she remembered, yet…where was he? "I have not seen him since I returned," she found herself saying, with a frown.

But…returned from where? She'd had a dream that she was at the Nest, living among its blackened ruins, but that was just a dream, wasn't it? Her mind felt so muddled up here at the top of the palace. Every day seemed to bleed one into the next until all sense of time was lost to her. She thought hard, trying to pull together her fractured memories, but the Father's voice drew her back.

"Your brother is no longer with us, child," he said. "He has joined the Eternal Flame."

She looked up into his pupil-less eyes. She found she felt nothing, no grief at her brother's loss. "How did he die?"

"Fire." The word echoed through the black hall. "Your brother was a kinslayer, child, who slew his uncle and his mother. This is a grievous sin, yet in the Eternal Flame he shall be absolved and washed clean. My master welcomes him home."

Your master. Agarath. She felt herself trembling, but not from the cold. "Will he rise as well, my lord, as you have?"

"He *is* risen." Eldur tapped his staff against the stone floor and all the world seemed to quake and rumble. A light bloomed, harsh and red, spreading to all corners of the room, and in the shadow the Father made she saw him. *Agarath. Laughing.* Then the light drew back, receding like a sudden tide, and darkness and silence fell anew. "I carry with me my master's *Soul*. With it, I enact his will."

To spread his Eternal Flame, the princess thought, *to swallow all the lands in fire and ash and bring about the Untar Batax'un, the Return to the Days of Dread.* A dull terror awoke with her, but only for a moment, then it was gone. Sotel Dar and her dear cousin Tethian had preached benevolence in the Father, and peace. They spoke of Varin's heir, and the Heart of Vandar. They spoke of balance, of controlling the last embers of the gods. *And they were wrong*, she now knew, as Sotel Dar did as well. *Eldur is Father to us all, yet even he has a master, and his name is Agarath, the All-Father of Fire, whose will is law and truth…*

"Child." The whisper filled her mind. She found that she had been gazing into the Bondstone, the Soul of Agarath, staring at the swirls of colour and the shapes they made, mesmerised. It was the essence of a god, the spirit that forged the world. *These lands were his to make and break as he pleased.* She drew her eyes from the glowing orb and looked upon her beloved Father once more. "Tell me of the sea king, Thala's last scion. What has he seen in the Eye?"

She cleared her throat. "Little, Father," she told him. "It is said this king is weak in his foresight, unlike his father and forebears. His control of the Eye of Rasalan is unpredictable." She paused and then said, "Death. He sees much death, my lord. He need not even tell me that for me to know. It is in his eyes. They are haunted."

The Eternal ran a finger over the teeth of Tagathon, musing. "The scholar has spoken to me of Varin's heir. I must have him found, child, and destroyed."

"Yes, Father." She lowered her head; she could feel his anger. "He is trying to locate him. All day he stands before the Eye, searching, yet in vain. He cannot control what he sees, he tells me. The Eye is a window; he knows not what will pass by…"

"The heir must be found. Or what use is this prophet king?"

She nodded at her toes. The air in that dark chamber seemed to fizz and simmer. "I will impress upon him your need, my lord." She recalled fractured memories, discussions once had before the Father had awoken, of this heir of Varin and who he might be. *Sotel never knew,* she recalled. *He said the last Varin king died forty years ago, childless. And the knight…the sweet captain… he…he said the same.*

Lythian, she thought once more. A memory flashed before her. Of a woodland and a campfire and a rocky overhang protecting them from the rain. Of bodies wet with sweat and writhing, and the joyous bliss of love-making. She gulped air and thrust the memory aside. *A dream. It was just a dream. If he should know. If he should see…*

The Father was looking at her. "Death," he said. "Whose death does the scion see?"

She took a moment to compose herself, ridding her mind of her sordid dreams. "Men, Father, women, children. Of north and south. Of all lands, near and far." Up here at the summit of the palace all was quiet and calm, yet beyond the walls of Eldurath the world was falling to chaos. "He sees bloodshed, and carnage, and violence across the world. He sees beasts of a bygone age rising, yet in glimpses only. Nothing is clear."

A pale finger ran over a jagged dragon's tooth. "Has he seen more children fall?"

Children. Dragons. "Yes, my lord. Some."

The air fell to silence, and there was a sudden fear and darkness in her heart. The news had come in not long ago. Zyndrar the Unnatural had been slain by the Champion of Frost, Ezukar by the Champion of Wind. A *nameless one* had been sent to seek the Mist, a beauty in purple and black and blue, yet nothing had been heard from him. *Our Father fears him dead as well,* she knew, *he feels it deep within him.* Eldur the Eternal had long fostered the children of his master, raising them, leading them, loving them, and now they were dying. The fortress of Dragon's Bane had been won, but at what cost? And still others were falling, nameless ones too young and inno-cent to know the deadly perils the northerners bore. *Every death is a knife to his heart, a cut at his master's ambition.* It made the Father wroth, and yet more…it made him fearful.

She turned from that thought. *No, he knows not fear,* she told herself. *I project it upon him only, that is all. It is my fear, my weakness, not his.*

The princess wet her lips and drew a shaky breath. "The Rasal king," she said. "He did speak of one vision, more clear than others. A blue blade, and the bodies of dragons, bloodied and butchered. It is a herald of the Dark God Vandar, a herald of woe. A murderer, Father, who seeks to slay all of Agarath's Children."

A crease twisted at the Fire Father's mouth. "Who is this man?"

"The scion does not know. All is blurred about him. Yet his revelry is clear. He taunts the Children before he slays them, and his savagery knows no bounds. He takes joy in these murders, Father. They give him pleasure."

A pale hand closed into a fist. "Find him," he whispered, in a voice low and deep and dangerous.

Talasha Taan nodded. "I will have the scion search again for this vision. It will clear, in time." She paused, then ventured, "And what of *him*, Father? The Lord of the Children?" She looked at the blood-red fire that burned deep within Eldur's eyes. "Drulgar. Is he…awakened, as they say?"

"He rests, and he waits, upon the nest that was once his. From there he once brooded, watching over the world, and so he broods again. When the time is right, he will stir." A thin smile marked his face. "I shall go to him soon."

She remembered the mountain of rock in the shape of the Calamity, she remembered the Fire Father resting against it. The scale had been unfathomable, a creature to dwarf even Garlath the Grand. *He will destroy them all*, she thought. *He will bring terror to all the world.* Something cold coiled inside her, a foul feeling in the pit of her stomach. A feeling that this was all wrong, the will of darkness and dread and an evil beyond imagining, yet so swift as it came so it faded, as she looked into the face of her Father once more, and felt soothed.

He smiled at her, and the light of the Bondstone was reaching out to bring a warmer glow to the room. "You have served me well, child," he said. "You, last of my line. By your hand was I awoken; by your efforts the Eternal Flame shall spread, to bathe all the world in its embrace. For this you require reward, daughter of my blood. It has come to me that you are incomplete." He stood, stepping down from the dais within a pool of soft red light. "Follow me outside, child. I would see you made whole."

She followed without question, keeping two steps behind him as he drifted through the hall in his loose-fitted crimson robe. The palace at the heart of Eldurath had become a lonely place. Below, the city teemed with fire-followers and zealots and ever-growing crowds of worshippers, yet up here few souls were seen. Guards stood sentry upon the lower steps, and dragons flew through the mists outside, yet the throne room and halls of residence itself were empty save a few.

They came to a high balcony jutting from the king's quarters, wide and broad, with flowering plants and vines edging their way up the sandstone walls. At the balcony edge stood a parapet with a thick balustrade and pillars beneath, each shaped and carved into the likeness of a king or queen long dead. Beyond, the city spread, a hundred floors below, half-hidden within the smog of dust and smoke that blanketed Eldurath like a shroud. Lights twinkled far beneath them, more than Talasha had ever seen. *Fire,* she knew. They burned everywhere now, in iron basins upon roofs and across the many city plazas and held in the hands of the faithful, who bore their torches day and night. They shone out in numbers uncountable, tens of thousands of them dotting the city like stars, red and orange and deep dusky gold.

"My children," the Father said, looking down upon them. "Never was the city so populous during my reign. The world has expanded, in my time away."

Talasha was getting that cold feeling again. "How many of them will die, Father?" she asked.

He stared down. "Many. And joyous they will be, to feel the warmth of the Eternal Flame. It is a place without suffering, without hate. A place where all are equal." He turned to her. "Do you wish to go there, child? To join your mother and uncle and brother, as an ember of the fallen?"

No, she thought, afraid. *Reward. Incomplete. I will make you whole.* The Father's words rushed through her mind. *Is he to send me to the Eternal Flame, for my service? Send me to my family?* She wanted to draw back from him, but stood her ground. "The unknown…it frightens me," she admitted.

"Fear is not weakness, child," he told her. "Even during my immortal millennia I knew it, when I would face a savage foe, fear the pain and suffering I would endure. It comes in many forms. Fear of pain, fear of hardship, fear of loss, fear of death. All such fear is melted away when the Eternal Flame washes over us. Death need not bring dread, my daughter. Beyond this world of darkness, there is light."

He's going to kill me, she realised then. *He prepares me for my reward, the gift of death and flame undying.* She tried to drive her fears away, but couldn't. *I don't want to die*, she thought. She wanted to believe him, wanted to, but a part of her couldn't. "Father, please…"

He put a white hand on her cheek. It felt rough and yet smooth, tender yet harsh, youthful and ancient at once. His face was the same. Affection she saw in his scarlet gaze, then darkness. His mouth shifted, at once kind and then cruel, and his skin was cold stone, unaltered by time, yet a moment later looked paper-thin and ghastly. And she knew it again. *He's going to kill me.*

His eyes moved away, searching the shrouded skies. And those ageless lips broke open in a whisper. "I hear her come," he said. "Your gift."

Talasha followed his eyes and saw in the distance a shape take form, a dragon flying down from the dark of the night against a high red moon. *Death by fire*, she thought. *I suffer the same fate as my brother.* The dragon was going to burn her alive.

She stared immobile as it drew nearer, regarding the width of the wings, the slender body, the graceful neck. It flew swift and smooth, as fluid in flight as any dragon the princess had seen. *I know her*, she realised. *I know her well.* Those beautiful grey scales, that lithesome form, the flash of colour, red and blue and gold and green, as her armour caught the light. *Neyruu.*

Memory stirred once more, as silt kicked up from a murky riverbed. She had flashes of Kin'rar Kroll, Neyruu's wise and kindly rider, and his death under a rain-soaked sky. She could hear in her head the soul-tearing scream that Neyruu gave out at his death, recall how the dragon had landed among those old rotten ruins in the Western Neck and burned Ashun Klo alive in vengeance. She remembered how Neyruu had lingered in their company even after Kin'rar's fall, how she had trailed them for a time, staying near, as though watching over them, protecting them, as Kin'rar would have wanted.

Cevi, she thought. *Mirella. Sir Pagaloth the dragonknight and…and Lythian.*

She blinked, seeing him clearly before her all of a sudden. She could feel his hands on her, taste his lips, hear his warm world-weary voice as he tried to fight the love that had grown between them. *A love I embraced, and cherished*, she thought, *even as he fought against it. My captain, sweet captain, where are you now?* He had been at the Nest, she remembered, when he'd left her. *The Father took me away, and Marak too, and Sa'har and Sotel, and the rest were left behind. Lythian, did you flee before the Dread came down? Cevi, Sir Pagaloth, are you safe?*

It all rushed through her mind in a blur, clear and stark and real. *It was no dream*, she now knew. *It was real, it happened.* She tried to hang onto that thought, cling to it, hold it dear, yet even as she did so it began to fade, like smoke slipping through her fingers, impossible to grasp.

"Child."

She snapped out of it and turned to him, Father to them all.

"Go to her," he said.

Talasha watched as Neyruu opened her sleek grey wings and came to land on the balcony before her. She stepped forward, wondering at the cruelty of having Neyruu of all dragons be the one to kill her. Yet all the same, she reached out with a palm to touch her snout. *I don't blame you*, she thought. *This is not your fault.* The dragon rumbled, a warm sound of kinship, as a soft billow of smoke rose from her nostrils to coil into the turbid sky.

"She was friend to you," the Father said.

She turned to face him. "Yes. I knew her well."

"Now you will know her better." The Bondstone throbbed and glowed bright, and the patterns in the stone shifted and moved. "I tether you, Child of Agarath and Child of Eldur, from this day forth until death. By Great Agarath's might you shall be bonded. By the light of his Soul, you are one."

One? Talasha thought. *He means to…*

Light flashed from the Father's staff, and the princess felt a strange sudden rending inside her. She sensed a part of her torn away, another part given, and in that moment, perceived another presence inside her head. *Neyruu*, she thought. *I am hers and she is mine. We are one. Until death parts us.*

She met eyes with the dragon and looked beyond them into her soul. And there, down in the dark, she sensed another. A remnant of a beloved Fireborn, the part of his soul that still lingered. *Kin'rar*, she thought.

He was sounding out a warning.

24

Saska

She turned the dagger between her fingers, the curved steel a radiant blue, handle and pommel of pristine silver. "Does it actually have any special powers, or is it just a regular blade?"

"It's significance lies in the line who have held it," her grandmother said idly, turning a page in her book. "We've talked about this already, Saska, several times. This is the blade of the House of Varin, handed down from father to son…"

"And daughter, in my case."

"For the first time, yes."

From a father I never met, who never even knew who he was. Saska looked over the symbols and markings on the hilt and pommel as she had a hundred times before. They were written in an old language, long fallen into disuse, some divine tongue that Varin and his contemporaries once favoured. The words formed a simple maxim - *Steel, Service, Honour, Light, against the Hordes of Fire we Fight* - that Varin had been said to like. "Words to live by," her grandmother had told her. "Words handed down through his line for them to live by too."

Saska wondered now if she'd lived by them herself. She was new to steel, though had always served, that was true. *And honour?* She considered herself of noble heart, yes, and had *light* in her veins as well from her mother's side, though was sure that wasn't what Varin meant. *I have not spent my life fighting the hordes of fire either,* she thought, though that was about to change. Her grandmother had said that the old Varin kings used to wear this dagger at their hip when they went to battle, to remind them of their duty. When Saska had asked, "What duty?" the old woman had merely pointed at the blade and said, "To fight the fire, child, as they were born to do. Just the same as you."

Born to fight the fire. Saska spun the blade once more, wondering why it had become her burden to carry, not her sire's. *Why couldn't my father have taken on that duty instead?* Her father Thalavar had been born in secret and

299

raised in secret, never knowing who he really was. *The Lonely Isle*, she thought. She'd passed near to it when she'd sailed across Vandar's Mercy, and heard that it was a cursed place, afeared by sailors and avoided at all costs. *Was that ever really true?* Perhaps those rumours had been spread to stop people ever going there? Perhaps they were another part of this puzzle to hide my father from the world?

She thought back to what Ranulf had told her about the Book of Thala. "I came upon some intriguing passages," he'd said to her one night in his study. "One was written by King Astan, Godrin's father and your great grandfather, I suppose he would be." He'd smiled in that avuncular way of his. "He'd written into the book of his daughter Atia, and how he'd foreseen her death in the Eye of Rasalan. Let me see if can remember the passage…" He paused and thought a moment, then told her the words he'd cast to memory. "*My daughter will die,*" he recited. "*She will die by the last month of this year by a child of great consequence. My sweet Atia. I have seen your death, but I can do nothing to change it. By Varin's blood you'll sire a boy. And this boy, I see, must be hidden.*"

A child of great consequence, Saska had thought. She had struggled to get her head around that. "Something must have gone wrong," she'd decided, shaking her head. "This duty was supposed to be my father's burden, not mine. A child of great consequence, Ranulf. It should be him sitting here, not me."

Ranulf had given her a searching look. "Do you blame your grandmother? For not doing more to protect him?"

She'd not been able to deny it. "She took him in as a servant, to watch over him as King Godrin asked. And then she let Elio Krator snatch him away and have him beaten to death. She should never have let that happen."

"Her priority was you, Saska. Your father's part was done."

"His part? What, to fall in love with my mother? To sire *me*?"

"Yes," Ranulf had said. "Thalavar's fate was never to wield the heart of a god, Saska. Godrin knew this, and so did your grandmother. His fate, his *consequence*, was to make sure *you* were safely brought into this world."

"*Me*." She'd laughed at that, a laugh full of scorn and mocking. "You don't think he would have been better suited to the role? A tall strong northman with curly black hair and bright blue eyes, ready to lead his people to victory." She felt a pale shadow compared to that image, a frightened lost little girl. Even his name was godly - Thalavar, a mix of Thala and Varin. Hers was just some common name given to her by one of Lord Caldlow's scullery maids, she'd been told. "He'd be about forty now, wouldn't he? A seasoned warrior, master of the forms. We wouldn't have to worry about any of this. Training me. Hiding me. Protecting me. He'd already be in the north, gathering the Blades of Vandar, reforging them. He'd probably already have killed Eldur and destroyed the Bondstone and won the war all by himself. And instead…instead you're stuck with *me*, the slave girl from north Tukor."

Ranulf had placed his cup of wine aside, put his hands to her shoulders, and said, "No, Saska, we're not *stuck* with you...we're damn well blessed to have you. Your father was a mix of steel and water, yes, but you've got the *light* in you as well, and who better to fight the darkness? The blood of Varin and Thala and Lumo all run thickly through your veins. Never has there been anyone with such a mix. There is *no one else like you*."

No, she thought now, as she sat at the breakfast table, fiddling with her trinkets. *There's no one like me.* And that was part of the problem. She didn't fit a mould, didn't make any sense. *When we go north, we're going to have to gather those blades. How am I ever going to convince the others to give them up? With my father it would have been easy, but with me...*

She shoved all that aside. As ever, it was best not to think too far ahead lest she become overwhelmed and agitated and consider taking flight with Joy to the hills. *I'll have support, lots of support,* she told herself. *No one expects me to do this alone...*

She reached to the table and picked up the necklace of shells little Billy Bowen had made for her, all of different shapes and patterns and colours. A smile touched her lips to think of the boy. Sometimes she wished she could take him up on his offer to wed her and sail the seas with him, venturing forth to places unknown. *Maybe I will, one day,* she thought. *Once I finally strike these fetters from my ankles and wrists...*

"Why don't you ever wear that?" Her grandmother turned another page of the great tome in her lap. She had a cup of sweet lemon tea held light between her spotted fingers; her favourite breakfast drink. She looked up. "It's pretty. You should wear it sometimes. I think it would suit you."

"It's clunky," Saska said. It was pretty as well, and meant a great deal to her, but the shells were all different sizes and many of them scraped and scratched against her neck when she put it on. "It hurts to wear."

"I could have it refashioned for you if you like? There are a *lot* of shells, Saska. If you take a few out, you might be able to actually, oh, I don't know, *lace* it about your *neck*."

"Oh ha ha. Very clever." Saska didn't like the idea of tampering with Billy's craftsmanship. But still... "Maybe you're right. Billy did make it for me to wear, after all, and not just look at."

"I'm glad you think so. Everything must fit a *purpose*, child."

"I know." Her voice was dull. It was one of those mornings, following yet another broken, haunted sleep. She feared another lecture from the old woman. "I'm not in the mood, Grandmother. Please, not now."

"Not in the mood for what? I didn't say anything."

"You didn't have to."

The woman smiled, trying to keep the tone as light as possible. "And that one? You could add that other one to the necklace as well." She was looking at the piece of coral that had called to Saska on the reef, that grey pitted stone that was as unremarkable to everyone else as it was remarkable to her. "Or maybe it's too big? It might be better off alone, as a pendant. I could have it placed within a golden housing and put on a length of sliver chain instead. How does that sound?"

"Awful. Not everything has to be gold and silver and bronze. I know you love those colours here, but it's all a bit garish to me." She placed the necklace beside the coral on the table. She liked to keep her trinkets here, where she had her morning breakfast atop the palace. "Sorry. That came out wrong. I'm being grumpy, I know."

Her grandmother looked at her sympathetically. "Did you not sleep well again last night? More nightmares?"

"A few." Saska didn't want to talk about it now. She had a small bite of lemon cake and rose to her feet.

"Leaving already?"

"Sir Ralston hates it when I'm late." Saska looked at the ancient blade of her grandfather's house. "Do you think I should take the dagger? Sir Ralston's taking me on a field trip today, did you know?"

"He told me, yes."

"You mean he had to clear it with you first?"

"You think so little of me, child."

"I think you're trying to protect me." Safina Nemati had not been particularly keen on letting Saska out of the palace over the last few weeks, though did appear to be loosening up a bit in that regard, so long as she had a strong protective guard with her. "I get that you want to keep me safe, I do, but I can't be caged here forever. I need to test myself against something *real*."

The old woman gave her an enigmatic look. "You may well get your wish today, child. Your Whaleheart has persuaded me of the same."

"What? *Really?*"

"Really. Your training has reached a juncture, he says, and you need real-world experience." She waved her over. "Come, give me a kiss before you go. I might never see you again."

"Gods. That bad? What's Rolly got planned?"

Her grandmother didn't answer, though looked a little worried all of a sudden. Saska stepped over and pecked her on her wrinkly right cheek.

"So, the dagger? Should I take it with me, or…?"

"Why not? Perhaps it will give you luck?" She smiled at her. "You may need it, child. Come see me as soon as you get back. I'll want to hear all about it."

This was a mystery to be sure, and one Saska was eager to unravel. Sir Ralston had told her they would be training outside of the palace today, though she knew no more than that. She rushed down through the palace levels with Joy at her side to find Sir Ralston at the front gate, which opened into a grand entrance hall. Beyond, the city of Aram swelled and spread in all its vast possibilities. The Whaleheart looked at the starcat as she found a nice pool of sunlight to bathe in, purring and stretching and licking a long tongue down her paw. "The cat doesn't need to come today. You won't be riding her."

Saska frowned. "Why not?"

"You'll be armoured and too heavy." He gestured to a table set up to one side, where her armour had been brought down from their usual sparring yard and laid out. Saska always hoped she might find a new set awaiting her, yet it remained the same mismatched suit that the Butcher had procured for her long weeks ago. Apparently he was still on the hunt for better-fitting pieces, but thus far none of that had materialised.

"*So*. Doesn't mean Joy can't come anyway. I don't have to ride her, she can just run beside the carriage." She glared up at him. "I thought we were past this, Rolly. I thought you liked Joy now."

"I like that she makes you happy. And yes, as a starcat, she is nice."

"That's it? Nice. That's all you're going to say about her?"

He ignored the attempt to provoke him. "The cat and you share a special bond. If she sees that you are in danger, she will only try to help, and may put herself in peril as a result. You will be armoured. She will not. Do you want to take that risk?"

Saska peered up at him. "What danger am I going to be in?"

"You'll see. I will be there as well, as will some others. The sellsword insists he come, with some of his men. And the redhead child as well."

"*Leshie*. You know her name. And she's turned eighteen now, she's not a child."

"She likes her nicknames," the Wall boomed. "So I will give her one of her own."

It was so feeble Saska had to laugh. "And 'the redhead child' is the best you could come up with? Really?"

"It's a work in progress." The giant turned stiffly, presenting her armour. "Get ready. The others are awaiting us outside the city walls."

"Outside? We're *leaving* the city?" Saska had thought they'd be off to the Red Pits or something. She beamed. "Where are we going?"

"Into the plains. Now put your armour on. This is an opportunity that may not come again."

So little of this was making sense, but at least they were leaving the city. The rest of it didn't seem to matter so much right now. Saska quickly fixed her armour in place and threw on the shining silver cloak that helped reflect the sunlight and keep her cool. Joy was still laid out on the floor, enjoying the sun. "I'm sorry, girl, but you'd best stay here today," Saska told her. "I think Rolly's getting jealous of our bond."

"I heard that."

"I know. That's why I said it." She gave Joy a kiss on her furry forehead and stood, stepping over to join Sir Ralston by the open doors. Some Nemati soldiers were milling about beyond, preparing a carriage in their black and silver garb. "Can we not ride horses instead?"

"There are none here bred to bear a Bladeborn in full plate."

"The Butcher rides a horse. And his men. They have armour."

"*Some* armour. Breastplates, gauntlets. Not full plate."

"Then can't we remove some of ours as well? How necessary is it anyway?"

"Very necessary. And your grandmother insisted upon it, as a condition of your release. Without it you will likely die."

Die. That took her off guard. Suddenly she was nervous. "Tell me what we're doing out there, Ralston. Come on. Enough of all this cloak and dagger. Just tell…"

"We're hunting a dragon, Saska," he broke in. "One has been spotted, nesting in the hills not far from here. If we get there in time we may catch it before it leaves to claim new territory."

"But…" Saska was as confused as she was nervous and excited. "What about Agarosh? Isn't that his job, to keep the monsters from the door?" The great moonbear had returned the day it slew that other dragon a while back, and had been patrolling the lands around the city since, keeping all other beasts away. Aram and its surroundings had become a haven under his watchful care. *But this?*

"Agarosh will be close," Sir Ralston told her. "If he must engage, he will."

Saska was getting a bad feeling about this. "So, who…"

"You, Saska," the Whaleheart boomed. "You're going to fight this dragon alone."

25

Elyon

The old man was taking his last breaths, it looked, rattling harshly down his throat. "How long will he live?" Elyon Daecar asked.

The lord's personal physician gave a ponderous sigh. "A day or two, perhaps. He is strong, my lord. Most in his state would have given in long ago, yet he clings to life like a barnacle on a boat." He smiled sadly and dabbed at the old man's brow with a cloth. "I will do what I can to make him comfortable, and tell you when the time draws near."

I'll not be here, Elyon thought. He did not plan to stay in the city past the turning of the hour. "My thanks," was all he said, as he stepped away from the bedside of Porus Pentar, Lord of Redhelm and Warden of the South, and out into the corridor beyond. He had met the lord but once before and that was long years ago. *Even then he seemed ready for the grave.* Porus Pentar had always seemed older than his years, people said. When he was twenty, he looked thirty, and when he got to thirty, he looked forty. By fifty he looked a man well into his sixties. Now he'd reached the ripe old age of sixty-eight and looked dead. It made sense.

Outside the lord's high chambers he found his fourth son Sir Storos awaiting him. Storos was much alike to his younger brother Tomos in appearance, though Elyon hadn't known either of them well. *Tomos,* he thought, *whose death caused all this bother.* "Is your brother awaiting me, Sir Storos?" Elyon asked him.

The knight was over ten years his senior, yet felt younger somehow. *Men defer to me now,* Elyon knew. *When they see the blade I carry, when they hear the wind, when they think of what I've done, they bow.* He didn't even need to lean upon his title of Prince of Vandar, which he was still being called in these parts, nor heir to House Daecar, which was a grand enough title in itself. No, Prince of the Skies and Lord of Storms and Master of the Winds were grander still.

"He is in his private audience chamber, my lord," Sir Storos informed him.

"*His* audience chamber? Or his father's?"

"Our father's, yes. Until…well, you can see how close he is, to his passing. It will not be so long now."

Elyon nodded. "You have my condolences, Sir Storos. I did not know your father well, but he was always a close ally to my own. He will be missed."

He began down the corridor, Sir Storos pacing at his heel. The red keep stood high at the city's rear, giving a ranging view across it and beyond the walls as well. Elyon glanced through the windows as they passed. He saw dragons everywhere, though none were living. At the Bane, there had been dragon skulls mounted atop the towers, but there were no skulls or bones or skeletons to be seen here at the Helm. Just sculptures in great abundance, all in varying states of death and dying. Many were gothic and macabre to look upon, twisted and grotesque. *Lukar work,* Elyon knew from the histories.

They found Sir Alrus Pentar sitting in his father's seat within the lord's audience chamber. Elyon marched in loudly, steel sabatons crashing against the stone. Some others were present, armoured Pentar knights and guards in their silver armour and crimson cloaks, here to accompany their new lord. *It seems old Porus has been dead and buried a while.* "Would you care to explain to me, Sir Alrus, exactly what was happening when I arrived?"

The man did not share his younger brother's diffidence. There was a pride in his eyes, and something arrogant as well. "We were executing an Agarathi dragonknight," he said curtly. "A man responsible for the death of my brother Tomos. I thought that was clear when you flew down and interfered."

"I interfered on behalf of my mentor, the very man I had come here to see." Elyon had flown from Crosswater soon after receiving word of Lythian's return. He was exhausted, in truth. Over the last few days he'd spent more hours in flight than he cared to count, crossing the kingdom like some great carrier crow. "Sir Pagaloth was a guest under Captain Lythian's protection, sworn to his service. You had no right to hang him on a whim."

"I disagree."

I thought you might.

"Sir Tomos was my brother," Sir Alrus went on, "and the dragonknight condemned him to death by his betrayal. I sought only to balance that scale. But you would not allow it, would you?" He sat stiff in his seat, a crutch leaning against its carved wooden arm. Alrus Pentar was no comely man. Round in the belly, doughy in the arms, with slightly bandy legs and a broad and ordinary face, it was hard to see how he was brother to Sir Storos. *Different mothers,* Elyon remembered. Lord Pentar was known to have had several wives, all of them long dead. "It was *you,* Sir Elyon, who had no right to get involved," he complained. "The dragonknight admitted to his betrayal. I was only carrying out justice as given to me by law. But no. Down you came, to muddy up the waters. And now here we are, at an impasse."

"We're at no impasse," Elyon informed him, edging his voice with anger. "The people of this city call me prince, do they not?"

306

The man looked like he'd prefer not to answer. He did, though begrudgingly. "My father has always favoured House Daecar," was his cold response.

But not you, after this, Elyon realised. His father would not approve of what he was doing here, driving a wedge between them and one of their strongest allies. *He has healed the rift with the Taynars, and here I am, tearing another one open.* It wasn't going to stop him, though. *Release the Greycloaks and keep Vesryn in chains all you like, Father. You play your games of politics, just don't expect me to do the same.*

"Good," Elyon said. "And as Prince of Vandar, I retain command over you, Sir Alrus. I will thus be leaving here at once, and taking the dragonknight with me."

"Oh you will?"

"Yes I will. You'll give us horses and provisions and send us on our way, and we'll forget all about this unseemly affair." *I want to see the back of this city already, and it's only been an hour.* "Follow us, or try to have Sir Pagaloth killed on the road, and you'll be met with the full power I have at my disposal." He tapped the Windblade to clarify his point. "I have lost all my taste for treachery, Sir Alrus. Don't deny me this, or seek to pursue it beyond this hall. For Vandar's sake, man, we have a war to fight."

"I am aware. Have you not seen our soldiers? Have you not seen our battlements and walls? You must have, as you came soaring in so splendidly from those skies you like to ride. I have worked hard to fortify this city for months. I know all about the war, Sir Elyon."

"*Prince* Elyon." Amron Daecar had never been afraid to assert his dominance, so why should he?

Alrus Pentar submitted, smiling icily. "Yes, *Prince* Elyon. I would, of course, *never* wish to insult you or your mighty father. But you must understand…my control here only stretches so far. Some will not bend the knee to me until my father perishes, and I am named lord by official law. These people are of the understanding that my father gave the order for the dragonknight to die. It was *his* word that put the man upon the gibbet, with a noose about his neck. *His*, not mine. And those who follow him and love him still will not take kindly to the dragonknight leaving here alive."

Elyon doubted all that very much. *It was your order,* he knew. *Your father would never have made that decision so rashly.* Lythian had told him as much, before he'd been taken off for medical treatment for a slash he'd taken to the shoulder. During the chaos of Elyon's arrival, his mentor had managed to snatch a blade from a soldier's belt and rushed up onto the stage to free Sir Pagaloth, wounding the executioner and several other guards as they tried to stop him. The distraction had proven enough and Pagaloth was still wriggling on the end of his rope when Elyon landed. "Elyon!" Lythian had shouted, seeing him. "Cut him loose, Elyon, cut him loose!" And he had, slicing the dragonknight free before his breath gave out, then bellowing out for order to be restored.

And they listened, They all put down their blades and bent the knee at once. There was a great deal of power in shooting down from the skies like some bolt of silver lightning, landing amidst a great swirling vortex of wind. *A steel god,* he thought, remembering the name Carly had given him. It had been enough to halt any further bloodshed, yet he wasn't going to count on it lasting forever. *We need to leave this city at once,* he knew.

"You will take control of these dissenters, I'm sure, as soon as your father passes on," Elyon told the crippled heir. "I am told he may die as soon as this evening. Should your focus not be on that, Sir Alrus? Lord Porus was a great man and lived a storied life. You should be spending what moments he has left at his side, not handing out pitchforks to the mob."

"That was no mob, but a crowd of good Redhelmers seeking justice for their fallen son. And I might add that the dragonknight sought the same. That was clear by the look on his face."

Elyon wasn't understanding. "Meaning?"

"Meaning Sir Pagaloth wanted to die. Meaning he knew what he had done. Meaning he longed for the sweet release of death. You denied him that, good prince. You denied him his absolution."

"Death is no absolution," Elyon came back. "He must right whatever wrongs he has committed through action. And it is evident that Lythian feels he has already done so."

"Ah yes, *noble* Captain Lythian, the *honourable* Knight of the Vale." Sir Alrus had an unpleasant smile, and an ugly habit of fondling the folds of his fleshy chin. "I see in him a man of shame as well. A man who walks under the weight of regret. There remains much a mystery about where he has been, and what he has been doing. You ask me, there was a stink of treason coming off him." His mouth twisted in a way Elyon didn't like.

"You would question his honour?"

"His honour? No. I am sure that whatever the Knight of Mists has done has been driven by *honour*, first and foremost. But honour can be restrictive, and tunnel a good man into a dark place from which he cannot escape. Such it is with Sir Lythian Lindar, I feel. He lives in shadow now."

Elyon would hear no more of this. *I'm done listening to this wretched fool.* "I'll hear the tale from him, without your personal filter, Sir Alrus. I suspect it is loaded with bias. Please have those horses and provisions prepared at once. I intend to ride out of the gates within the hour." He turned and left the audience chamber as promptly and loudly as he'd entered.

Sir Storos followed at his heel once more, hurrying to join him as he marched down the corridor. Torchlight flickered along the walls, glistening redly on the stone. "That was well done, Prince Elyon, most well done," he said.

He wants my favour. He sensed Storos didn't much like his older brother, and could quite understand why. "Will he do as I asked of him?"

"Oh yes, he'll not deny you. Alrus is a bully, always was. There has been no one to tell him 'no' since my father lost his wits, but when a stronger man stands up to him, he is quick enough to submit."

Elyon nodded as they reached the steps leading down to the central hall. Some men-at-arms in Pentar colours were waiting below, with a Bladeborn knight at their head. He stepped over as they descended. "My lord. I have seen the farmers safely situated, as you commanded," he said to Sir Storos.

"Thank you, Sir Oswin." Storos turned to Elyon. "Let me introduce Sir Oswin Cole, the captain of my guard. He was with us on the journey from Runnyhall."

"Well met, Sir Oswin," Elyon said.

The knight bowed low. "Your Highness. There is a great deal of discussion going on outside about you. I understand there was some trouble with Sir Pagaloth?"

Sir Storos gave answer. "My brother attempted to have him hanged within scarce minutes of our arrival. An ugly affair, Oswin. You did well to miss it." He gestured to Elyon. "The prince descended to put a stop to the madness, and just in time as well. For a moment I feared that Captain Lythian would himself be slain."

"He would have taken a dozen men with him," Elyon said. It was quite the reunion for him and his old mentor. *I thought to find him in counsel with old Lord Porus, not upon a gibbet defending the life of a dragonknight of all people.* But such were the times. Little surprised him now. "Come, Sir Storos. I'm eager to speak with him."

"Of course." Sir Storos turned to his captain. "Remain here, Sir Oswin. I shan't be long."

They continued through the hall, and down a passageway to the bedchamber to which Lythian had been taken. When they entered they found him under the attentions of a nursemaid, undressed down to his breeches, his shoulder sewn and strapped up in white bandaging. The nursemaid was trying to get him to drink some strong fortified wine. "It'll help, with the pain," she insisted. "Come now, drink up. Don't be shy."

"I've heard that roseweed oil is good for pain," Elyon said, as he stepped within. "Better than wine, certainly. Though not so tasty."

That got a laugh from the nursemaid, a buxom woman of middle years with her hair tied up in a net, and blood upon her white cotton shift. Lythian only grunted. "The pain is mild," he said. "I have no need for roseweed or wine or anything else." He looked at Elyon and Sir Storos. "How is Pagaloth? His neck…"

"Is badly bruised," Sir Storos told him, "and his voice is hoarse from his strangulation, but he will live."

"He's under guard?"

"In a cell," Storos confirmed.

Lythian didn't seem too comfortable with that, though Elyon put his concerns to rest. "I have instructed Sir Alrus to provide us with provisions," he said. "We'll be leaving once they're ready. *All* of us, Lyth." He turned to the nursemaid, seeking privacy. "You may leave us," he told her. "Thank you for your help in patching him up."

"Oh, it was my pleasure." The woman ran her eyes over Lythian's frame, purring, then sauntered from the room.

Lythian shook his head as she left. "You came at the right time, Elyon. Again. The blasted woman seemed intent on checking me for injuries elsewhere." He glanced down. "She was insistent I remove my breeches to make sure I hadn't suffered some mishap below the waist."

Elyon chuckled. "And she thought the wine might loosen you up?"

"Yes, probably." Lythian gave a laugh, though a weak one. He looked older than before, harder and yet sadder, and there were many cuts and scars upon his body that weren't there when he left. *He is leaner too, less muscled.* The Knight of Mists had never been so well-built as others, but he was not a sleight man either. *He must have lost a quarter of his bodyweight.*

Elyon turned to Sir Storos. "Check on Sir Pagaloth if you would, sir. Make certain nothing untoward has happened to him, and then bring him to the front hall to be ready for departure."

"Of course, my lord." Sir Storos hesitated. "Will…will you be wanting us to come with you?"

"Yes," Elyon said at once. "You travelled with Lythian and Pagaloth from Runnyhall, you said? You can travel with them still. Make preparations, Sir Storos. See the horses readied and provisions packed, and make sure that Captain Lythian is outfitted with armour and weapons." He thought a moment, then added, "And Sir Pagaloth as well. He is not a prisoner here, but a guest, and has the right to be able to defend himself. He cannot be Lythian's sworn sword if he has no sword to carry. See that rectified."

Storos seemed more hesitant about that, though did not deny his order. "As you command, my lord." He rubbed his chin. "Might I ask…which way will we be going? I had expected to escort Lythian here, and then return to my posting at Southwatch. But…he has spoken commonly of going to Varinar which…well, begging your royal pardons, my prince, but that will take us a great distance from the coast."

Elyon understood the knight's misgivings. He was clearly a man of duty and did not want to be spending weeks or even months on the road, far from his lands. He pondered it then looked at Lythian. "Why Varinar?"

"Your father. I must speak with him urgently. And I have a need to visit the Steelforge as well, to collect my armour and blades." He took a brief pause. "I lost Starslayer, Elyon, some months ago. I do not imagine I will ever get it back."

"Oh. I'm sorry, Lyth." Elyon knew what the blade meant to him. Starslayer had passed down through many generations of his house, a famed sword of many great deeds. "I can have word sent, for your armour and blades to be transferred by barge down the Steelrun," he told him. That clearly needed more explanation. "Father is not in Varinar, Lythian. He is currently in Crosswater, though is likely to continue to King's Point soon. We expect the city to come under siege any day now."

Lythian mused on that a moment. "The coastal road, then?"

Elyon nodded. "That was my thinking." He looked at Sir Storos. "Would that suit you, sir?"

The man considered it but briefly, then nodded. "My father's charge as Warden of the South has always been to defend the Black Coast. And that of his sons as well. So long as I remain on the coast, I will be within the bounds of my sworn duty."

"Then you'll provide escort all the way to King's Point?"

"Yes, my lord."

Elyon gave him a grateful nod. "My thanks, Sir Storos. You'll want to say goodbye to your father before we leave?"

"He will not know me anymore, I fear. But yes, I shall take a moment at his bedside." He retreated to the door. "I'll see to preparations, my lord. If I might make one final suggestion?"

"Go ahead."

"It might be worth ushering Sir Pagaloth out through the postern gate, behind the keep. We have a path that leads north into the Downs, after which we can circle around and continue south, unseen. I feel it would be better to avoid riding through the city, and the many soldiers in camp there, if we can."

Elyon nodded assent. "Agreed, Sir Storos. Thank you for your counsel. You've proven a great help."

"I live to serve, my prince." The knight bowed and took his leave.

Once Sir Storos was off seeing to that, Elyon took up the jug of wine the nursemaid had been wielding and poured two cups of red. He handed one to Lythian, kept one for himself.

His old mentor was looking at him with a small half-smile. "So how does it feel, Elyon, being a prince? When I left you were but a second son. Now look at you. Prince of Vandar. Lord of Storms and Master of Winds and…have I left anything out? I'm sure you've got some other names as well."

"One or two," Elyon said modestly. "But they all amount to the same thing." He tapped the Windblade. "This."

Lythian smiled to see him bearing it. "It was always your favourite, as a boy. Do you remember? Your eyes would always take on a special sparkle when we spoke of the Windblade. Now here you are, its bearer and champion. You've come a long way, Elyon."

"So have you, Lythian. I was told you went as far as the Western Neck."

The man's smile faded. "Yes, I was there. But I'd rather talk about you. About the man you've become in my absence. We have so much to talk about. The dragons you've killed. The battles you've fought. The people… that you've lost." His voice softened. "*Aleron*. I am sorry for what happened to him, Elyon. I only wish I could have been here to help you through it."

It wouldn't have helped, Elyon thought. He appreciated the sentiment, but he didn't want to dwell on the dead right now. Aleron. Rylian. Lord Kanabar. Lancel. Even Melany, whom he'd loved for a time, Melany who had been yet another pawn of Janilah Lukar. They would have ample time to talk of their griefs and losses later, but for now there were more pertinent matters to discuss.

He took a sip of wine then said, "You told me you had an urgent need to see my father. Why? Is there something you need to tell him?"

"I've been gone a long time," the Knight of Mists said. "Your father is my lord, and now my king. I must report to him on...my time away."

He's seen things, Elyon knew at once. It was clear in his tone of voice, in the shift in his haunted eyes as they moved away to the window, to look out onto the streets. "You can speak to him when you see him," he said. "But be careful, Lythian, not to call him king. He doesn't like that."

"Trouble with the houses, I'd heard." Lythian continued looking out of the window. "You seem happy enough to be called prince, though."

"It has its uses," Elyon said. "So...the Western Neck? I was told you were taken there after you were rescued from Eldurath. You and Borrus. He arrived back in the north a long time ago, Lyth. What's your excuse?" He grinned to try to keep things light, though knew at once his old mentor was not in the mood. He wondered if he ever would be again. *Sir Alrus was not wrong,* he thought. *There is a shadow about him now.*

"Borrus wanted to leave," he said quietly. "We were both given the option, but I chose to stay."

"Stay where? In the mountains?" Elyon couldn't figure out why he'd want that. *Why stay in Agarath when he could have come home?*

"I felt compelled to remain, Elyon, to keep watch." He looked at him. "You've heard who rescued us?"

"Lord Marak," Elyon said. *The man who killed my grandfather at the Battle of Burning Rock.* "And another Skymaster. I forget his name."

"Kin'rar Kroll. A good man, and noble. He perished, some months ago. And Lord Marak...he is turned against us now, though not...not of his own free will." He gave a heavy sigh and shook his head. "I can tell I'm not making much sense. Forgive me. It's hard to put words to all of this, and I...well I'm ashamed of my part in it. Deeply ashamed," he said.

Elyon could tell that much just to look at him. "What happened, Lythian?" he asked softly. "What could you possibly have done to..."

"I helped unleash the darkness, Elyon. Eldur...I helped awaken him."

"You..." Elyon made a sound, not a snort nor a sigh but something in between. He needed a second to process that. "You...did *what*, Lythian?"

"I helped raise Eldur from his tomb beneath the Wings. That's where I lost Starslayer. In hell," he whispered.

Elyon still wasn't understanding. "You went to kill him," he said. It was all he could figure. "Or...to observe, and report." Yes, that sounded like something Lythian would do. Borrus would have wanted no part in it, but Lythian....*He would have seen it as his duty to remain. But with who?* "Was this Marak?" he asked. "Did he make you do it? For saving you from the pits? Was this...was this your way of repaying a debt? Did he make you swear him some oath?"

"It was not Marak, but Tethian, Prince of Agarath."

Elyon frowned. "Dulian's son?" He had thought the young prince dead, leastways that was the rumour.

Lythian nodded. "He led a cult of worshippers and rogues who were committed to fulfilling the Agarathi prophecy of Eldur's rise." He met his eyes. "Have you heard of this prophecy, Elyon?"

He nodded. "Lady Marian Payne told me. After the...the battle at Dragon's Bane." His mind was racing from one thought to the next, though through the morass of blame and bleak confusion he saw a spark of light. "You've seen him," he said, as though realising that, truly realising it, for the first time. "Eldur. You've seen him up close."

"I have. More than once."

More than once. Elyon's heart was hammering. He had planned to fly northeast to Thalan, to find anyone among the ruin of the city who might have witnessed Eldur's coming. But now... He marched forward and took his old master by the arms, holding him hard in his steel grip. He knew that Lythian felt shame for his part in this, whatever it was, but he didn't care about that now. A man's honour can tunnel him into a dark place, Sir Alrus had said. *Well, he wasn't wrong there either.*

Elyon pushed all that aside, met his mentor's eyes, and said, "Tell me everything, Lythian. *Everything.* And don't leave anything out."

26

ℜobbert

The battle had been short, so short you could hardly call it a battle.

More like a slaughter, Prince Robbert Lukar thought, liking this not one bit. They'd swarmed off their ships at the Port of Matia so suddenly and unexpectedly that the defending soldiers had been given scant time to prepare. Some bells had started ringing out through the misty gloom and from the watchtowers and keeps the garrison had issued forth, but it was a small force, far too weak to offer any challenge.

The first men had been cut down easily. The prince himself had been in the thick of it, drawn to the thrill of battle despite his misgivings. In truth he hadn't wanted to miss out. *My uncle would only call me a coward behind my back, maybe even a traitor, and try to undermine me.* He would not have that, no way in hell, so he'd rushed right to the front with Sir Bernie and Sir Lothar and sent a half dozen more men to the stars.

And that was that. By the time he'd stopped swinging and slashing, several hundred enemy soldiers were lying dead and dying about him, and the rest were laying down their arms. His lord uncle had come up to him after, savouring the taste of victory. "Krator said it would go as such," he said, as the last of the dying men were noisily run through. "The first to attack will be those loyal to the Duchess. The rest will bend their knees and join us." He patted the prince's shoulder. "You should be proud, Robbert, for helping us secure this city. But this is just a taste. The real battles are yet to come."

They set camp that night in the hills overlooking the harbour, darkness falling to hide the blood that stained the streets. Robbert had Bernie and Lothar help him out of his armour before giving the godsteel a wash himself. *I can wipe the blood away, but there's something darker here that stains my soul.*

Sir Lothar the Looming was sensing his displeasure. "Maybe we should leave, Robb?" he said, pacing at the pavilion door. He pulled open a flap and looked out into the night, making sure no one was lurking outside. It was loud and chaotic out there, the men drinking to their triumph, if you could call it that. Lothar let the flap fall back into place and turned. "I've been talking, with some of the others. Not everyone's happy about this, Robb. Sir Tunsen's been grumbling about it in his cups, I've heard, and Sir Clive Fanning and Happy Harys have expressed their unease as well."

"Sir Tunsen and Sir Clive have a few dozen men-at-arms between them," Robbert said to that. "And Happy Harys? He's here with just one man, Lank. *Himself.* Happy's little more than a sellsword. No one's going to care what any of them have to say."

"And Sir Alistair Suffolk? Apparently he's been openly proclaiming it as treason, Robb."

Robbert looked up from his armour. The others were easily ignored, but not so much Sir Alistair the Abiding. "Really? He's been saying that?"

The absurdly tall knight nodded. "I heard it from some of his men while the camp was being set up. Sir Alistair intends to challenge your uncle on it directly, they're saying. The Suffolks are sticklers for their honour, as you know. And there's nothing honourable about this, Alistair says."

He's not wrong, Robbert thought. The Suffolks were an old house, not especially powerful anymore but utterly staunch in matters of chivalry and virtue. Their lord, Marston Suffolk, known as Marston the Moral, had grown infirm in his dotage and had not made the trip. Instead he'd sent his eldest son and heir Sir Alistair at the head of five hundred men to join the fleet when Lord Cedrik's northern army sailed south. Sir Alistair was known to share in his father's firm application of right and wrong. *Well, they don't called him 'the Abiding' for nothing.* "Does he have his men with him on this?"

"Most, I should think. My father always told me that a good lord nurtures men who act in his image. If it's so with these Suffolks, they'll be right behind him"

"Doubt it," rumbled big Sir Bernie Westermont, crouched to one side on a trunk running a whetstone up the length of his sword. "Be folly to challenge your uncle. It'll only get them all killed."

Robbert Lukar shook his head. "I wouldn't allow it."

Bernie and Lank shared a look.

"What? You don't think I have any say here? I'm a prince. A king, even, if my grandfather's truly dead. You say it yourselves all the time."

"Saying it doesn't make it true, Robb." Bernie set his whetstone aside and took up his oilcloth. "Your uncle's calling all the shots, and you know he won't suffer any dissent."

"He does have a point," Lothar agreed, rubbing his long chin. Everything was long about Lothar the Looming, who liked to make the claim that all his parts were in proportion. A claim Robbert could corroborate, having seen him in the bathhouses back home. "That's why I think we should just leave instead. I could talk to Sir Alistair, get him to agree to say nothing to your uncle. We take his ships and his men and sail home. We leave your uncle to his war."

Robbert Lukar didn't like the word 'leave'. Everyone had been using it in council and he'd been the only one to rally against it, it felt. *I wish we had, though, now that my uncle's made a deal with the devil.* "We can't leave, Lank. That would be desertion. You know what the penalty for desertion is, don't you?"

"For regular men. Not princes and heirs. Treason needs to be called out, Robb."

Treason. "So you're in agreement with Sir Alistair? You think this is treason, what my uncle is doing?"

"It's nothing good or noble, I'm sure about that."

"We've just won another Aramatian city, for the loss of only a few dozen men. Soon enough we might have another, and another. That's what I was arguing for in council…"

"But not like this. Not with *him*. We've become nothing but a bunch of sellswords and mercenaries, working for a southern sunlord. And when we win him the eagle chair, what do you think he'll do? Just let us stay? No, he'll slaughter us all in our sleep and laugh until he's hoarse." Sir Lothar Tunney stared the prince in the eyes and repeated, "We should *leave*, Robb. Tonight. We gather our allies and go and deal with the consequences when we get home."

Sir Bernie stood and lumbered to the table to pour a cup of ale. He poured three, in fact, then stomped over to hand one to Sir Lothar, reaching up, and one to Prince Robbert, reaching down. "Drink. You both need it." He downed his own as though to show them what to do, then smacked his lips and returned for a refill. By the time he'd done that, the others had taken a gulp as well and the air had settled.

Robbert put his mug aside. "I wanted this," he said quietly. "I wanted to continue this fight. It was me in council banging that drum."

"Yes, but to *attack* Lord Krator, not *join* him," Sir Lothar stressed. "Robb, listen to me…"

"No, Lank, *you* listen. My uncle made a choice. Was it honourable? No. Do I like it right now? Not really. But he made it as commander of this army and we have little option but to live with that."

"Or die with it," said Lothar.

"Maybe," Robbert admitted. "But would it have been any different if we'd sailed home? We all feared that if we fled back north, we'd be attacked at sea and destroyed. By leviathans. By Krator's fire ships and the rest of his fleet. We'd have likely lost thousands of men, maybe even tens of thousands, before we even reached land. Who knows, maybe every single one of us would be dead already, burned or drowned or thrashed to pieces by one of those whales. But this way…"

"We should have taken our chances," Sir Lothar broke in. "We should have, Robb, and you know it."

"I don't know it. I don't know how any of this is going to turn out yet. And if we turn our back on it now, then what?"

"Then we retain our honour," Sir Lothar Tunney said. "I'd sooner die at sea than fight for that sunlord."

"We're not fighting *for* him. We're fighting *with* him. And only for now. There's a difference, Lothar."

The towering knight shook his head and paced long-legged from side to side. Robbert watched him, wondering why he was defending his uncle so much. *Because he's my blood, my mother's younger brother, and I have to trust him.* Robbert may have been a prince, but he was young, just eighteen winters worn, and this was *not* his army, no matter how much he wanted it to be. It had never been his decision to make.

"This deal my uncle made with the sunlord will serve our purposes if we play it right," the prince said. "We help Krator in his coup, and he'll give us passage north through the mountains. We take Skyloft Fort and then march on Blademelt from the rear. We sharpen our swords, polish our shields, and turn them on the *real* enemy. Not these star-worshippers and their cats and wolves. The *real* enemy, Lank. *Agarath.* It's the dragonfolk we should be fighting."

The looming knight gave that a slow assenting nod. "Maybe," he managed to say. "But if we're to lose men fighting for that feather-cloaked fool, he needs to lose men fighting for *us.* Is that part of the bargain as well? Is the sunlord going to give us a legion of his Sunriders when we cross those mountains, and attack the Agarathi? I doubt it, Robb. Krator's smart. He isn't going to want to make an enemy of Agarath, and risk their fiery wrath. Not a chance."

Robbert Lukar opened his mouth to speak. Before he could respond a soldier pushed through the flaps uninvited. Sir Lothar was quick to put his blade to the man's throat. "*Never* walk in here announced," he told him. "This is the prince's pavilion. Didn't you see the banners outside?"

"I saw them, Sir Lothar. That's why I'm here. To see the prince."

"Smart mouth. What do you want?"

"Your blade off my throat for a start."

Robbert laughed. "It's all right, Lank, stand down. I take it my uncle wishes to see me?"

"He's called a council, Prince Robbert," the soldier said. "There are matters to discuss with the sunlord."

Krator. "Fine." Robbert turned to Bernie. "Stay here, Bern. Lank, with me."

The night was muggy and warm, the air still, and no breeze was coming in from the bay. Below them, the Port of Matia spread in a lake of twinkling lights, glowing gold beneath a moonless sky. *It's almost pretty,* Robbert thought, *when you can't see all the dead bodies, or hear the screaming of the women and the children.* In the harbour beyond, their fleet was assembled, a mix of Tukoran and Aramatian ships, all shadows in the gloom. *And more of the latter,* Robbert knew. They'd lost so many of their own ships to fire and fin that they could only transport a little over half of their army themselves. The rest had been granted use of some of Lord Krator's vessels, and not his best if the grumbling reports were to be believed.

He slights us at every turn, Robbert thought, as he walked through their overnight camp. It was clear to all who had eyes that Lord Elio Krator did not want to ally with his uncle Cedrik any more than his uncle Cedrik wanted to ally with the sunlord. He was merely using them, as they were using him, though it seemed obvious to Robbert that Krator had the better of the bargain.

"That's their camp over there," Sir Lothar said, thrusting his chin to the northwest as they went.

Robbert peered that way. "Not everyone's as tall as a tree, Lothar. I can't see anything past the tents." A moment later he could though, as a gap opened up and he saw the Aramatian army under Krator's command spread out upon a nearby hill. It was neater than their own, that was obvious enough at a glance. *Neat like their lord.* He'd heard Krator was a fastidious sort, obsessive with the little details, and would flog his soldiers if they pitched their pavilions poorly.

The two camps were spaced apart to avoid the risk of violence breaking out between them. The Tukorans had unfurled themselves haphazardly over one hill and the Aramatians neatly over another. The smell of ale and roasting meat was thick in the air, and cookfires burned everywhere, sending up plumes of greasy grey smoke. All that meat had come from Krator, Robbert knew, a 'gift' of friendship to seal their pact. He half wondered if it had been somehow poisoned, and they'd all awaken in the morning ill and dying, to be cut down by Krator's men. *A trick,* he thought. *Perhaps this is all some foul deception?*

Two men tumbled out before them as they passed down a muddy lane between tents, cursing and screaming and drawing draggers. One was bare-chested; the other wore no boots. What the altercation was about Robbert did not know. He looked at Lank and gave a nod and the giant knight stepped in to break them up. "Spill the blood of a brother and you'll hang," he said, wrenching them apart. "What's the fuss?"

The bare-chested man pointed his dagger at the other. "He stole my woman! Went for a piss and she was gone from my tent." He tried to lunge forward but Lothar got in the way. "I want her back, Grevon. Prettiest girl I ever saw. I want her back!"

"You ain't having her," the bootless man called Grevon said, smirking. He had a flock of birds against a starless sky on his chest. The Swallow sigil. "She's mine."

"Yours? You give her back, else I'll cut off your cock and feed it to you!"

"With that dagger?" Grevon grinned like a drunken wolf. "You'd need a greatsword for that, you dumb bloody whoreson."

"Whoreson? You calling my mother a whore now?"

"Aye. And your father n'all."

The bare-chested man roared and rushed at him, though Lothar was quick to block him once more. Robbert stepped forward. "Who is this girl?" he demanded.

"Who cares?" spat the half naked soldier, breathless and red-faced with rage. "Some bitch from…"

Sir Lothar struck him hard across the face with a long swinging arm, sending the man toppling to the mud. "You're talking to Robbert of House

Lukar, the Crown Prince of Tukor." He marched forward and hauled the man to his feet by the scruff of his neck. "Address him properly or I'll take your tongue for insolence."

The strike had broken the soldier's jaw. Blood dribbled from the side of his mouth as he spluttered out an apology. "I didn't…didn't know it was…it was you, my prince."

Lothar threw him aside. "The girl. You got her from the city?" He looked to the bootless man.

"Aye, suppose he must've, my lord. I can't be sure, though. Just took her from his tent when he was pissing, as he says."

"Take her back right now," Robbert said to the one with the broken jaw.

"My…my prince?" he slobbered.

"You heard me. Take her back where you found her." He looked to the other one. "You can help."

"Me? Why me?"

Robbert looked at Lothar. "Hit him."

The looming knight swung and the other man went down. Both were now sprawled in the filth, bloodied and broken. "Take her back," Robbert said, a final time. "If I hear you've disobeyed me I'll have Sir Lothar break more than your jaws." He let the threat settle then continued on walking. "Krator won't like this," he said to Sir Lothar. "I thought we put out word that the common folk were not to be harmed."

"We did. Not to say every man in camp's going to listen, though. After all this time away, they need the release."

"I hope you're not trying to justify this behaviour, Lank."

"No, just explaining it. These men have been sieging and holding a fort for months. You let a dog off the leash and it's going to run, Robb. And your uncle's dogs aren't so well trained."

Rabid, Robbert thought. It had been the same at Harrowmoor, before the Vandarians arrived, and Elyon Daecar took it upon himself to make sure the captive girls were not to be mistreated. *I favoured him for that*, Robbert thought. He liked Sir Elyon a great deal, even after he killed his own cousin Sir Griffin. *Blood be damned, it wasn't hard to pick a side on that account.* The noble son of the great Amron Daecar, or his snotty vile cousin who liked to torture animals as a child? In the end, Elyon had got ten licks and lashes for the affray and Sir Griffin had got a pyre. *Silly Cousin Griffin, picking a fight with a Daecar. You should have known better.*

The council meeting was to take place in a special pavilion set up between the two camps. At the borders of each, men were standing on guard, and poles and stakes had been driven into the earth to make clear their boundaries. On the Tukoran side armoured Bladeborn stood sentinel; opposite, two hundred metres away, great golden sunwolves prowled left and right, some with riders, others without, and there were many slinky starcats there too, watching with their glowing eyes.

Evidently, both Krator and Kastor were taking no chances. *Our alliance hangs by a thread*, Robbert knew. *One spark and we'll have a blaze on our hands…*

The pavilion had been set up by the sunlord's men earlier, so bore his silken drapes and colours and had feathery banners hanging on poles outside. The messenger led Prince Robbert and Sir Lothar forward. Outside the tent, Cedrik's Kastor's guards were standing to the right and Elio Krator's to the left, glaring at one another. "Ease up, gentlemen," Prince Robbert said breezily. "We're meant to be friends, aren't we?"

Sir Wenfry Gershan, Sir Jesse Bell, and Sir Lionel Vance were there on the Tukoran side, his uncle's three favoured guardsmen. What he saw in Gershan he couldn't say. The man was in the mould of his lord grandfather, a weaselly little creature who showed little prowess in battle. It was a political posting more than everything. The others were greatly more stout. Sir Lionel was a masterful proponent of Glideform and Sir Jesse a good honest knight who would not let anyone down. All of them gave the prince a bow as he neared.

Robbert turned to Sir Lothar. "Stay outside with these lot," he told him quietly. "Keep an eye and an ear out for me, Lank."

"Always."

Robbert Lukar entered the tent.

The men within stood in similar fashion to those without, standing apart with a pinewood table between them. Some were drinking wine, others were not. Fire baskets hung down from the support beams, crackling softly, but the furnishings were elsewise sparse. This pavilion had been set here for a single purpose - this meeting - and had no other function.

"Nephew, come in." Lord Cedrik Kastor was not dressed in his armour, but wore a slim-fitting brocade doublet in silver, black, and green thread, with emeralds sewn into the front to form the sigil of his house. "We've been waiting for you."

I'm sure, Robbert thought. He suspected his invite had been more of an afterthought, likely suggested by Lord Gullimer who was by far the best of his uncle's lickspittles. *They probably still fear I'll try to stir violence with the sunlord and his men.* "Uncle. My lords." He turned to his own countrymen; Lords Gullimer, Huffort, and Swallow, and Sir Gavin Trent, his uncle's battle commander. Then he looked across the table. "Sunlord Krator." He gave the mildest dip of the head.

The sunlord did the same. "Prince Robbert. Be welcome. I'm glad you could join us."

I'm sure, Robbert thought again. The sunlord did not seem like a man who could use the word 'glad' in any honest context. He was in his mid-forties, though looked younger, as fit as one could hope to be at that age, lusty and slim. From his gold feathery cloak extended vascular forearms tight with strands of muscle. When his lips took the shape of a smile, his eyes did not follow.

This man is cold, Robbert thought. "I'm glad to be here, my lord."

At Krator's side was a fat flowery man who was almost his exact opposite. "You've not yet met my leal Sunrider," the sunlord said. "Mar of House Malaan."

The Sunrider bowed low in courtesy. A heavy smell of cloying perfume wafted off his flesh. "Your Royal Highness. A great pleasure to meet you."

"And you, Sunrider Malaan." Robbert smiled back, following the formal courtesies. "So what are we discussing?"

"War. What else?" That was from grumpy old Lord Huffort, he of the stubbly lantern jaw and stern impatient eyes. "Everything's war these days, isn't it?"

"Too true, my lord." Robbert could have chewed right through the tension in the tent. *There is so much hate here I can taste it.* "Is this the sum of your council, Sunlord Krator?" The man seemed only to have brought along this simpering whale of his.

"I need none to advise me," Krator said haughtily. "Mar is here only to listen and relay what we discuss to my lords and riders. They will carry out my instructions without question or complaint."

Lord Cedrik gave a huff, taking it for a slight. "A wise man shares in the council of others," he declared. "Only a fool fails to heed advice."

Krator smiled emptily. "When I must stand judgement upon a matter of which I am unfamiliar, I will of course seek councillors to consult me. But this is a war council. I have no need of consultation in war, my lords."

More like a coup council, Robbert thought. He held his tongue on that, wondering how his uncle might respond.

He did so with a smile as empty as the sunlord's. *These two are more alike than they might care to admit.* "A war council, yes. And who better to know how to win your own city than you, my lord."

"My city, and my duchy, and my empire, one day soon." Krator took a neat sip of his wine and placed it precisely upon the table, where maps and siege plans were laid out. The sunlord gestured to a map of Aramatia, well-detailed and colourfully illustrated. "Kolash stands next in line to fall to me, however. It is a hundred-mile march down the Capital Road from here, no more than a four-day ride."

"Ride?" Lord Huffort said with a furrowed brow. "Why not sail? It'd be quicker."

Krator looked irritated by that comment. He glanced lazily at Mar Malaan, who gave answer. "My lord, if you would refer your gaze to the map, you'll have your answer." The blubbery Sunrider's cheeks grew fatter as he smiled. "As you can see, the coastal route will take us eastward first, out of the bay, then down the coast and through the Solapian Channel, after which we must turn north to reach Kolash. In all the journey by sea would likely take longer than that by land."

"And be more perilous as well," Krator added, tapping a finger on the map. "There are rumours that a krelia prowls the Channel. It would be unwise to pass that way."

"A krelia is a mythical beast," Lord Huffort harrumphed. "It'll be a kraken…"

"It's a krelia," Krator told him, dismissively. "Krakens do not leave hollow bones floating upon the water, my lord. We shall not be passing that way."

Lord Gullimer agreed. "The journey will be quicker by land. I've heard the Capital Road is smoothly shod and well maintainèd, easy to travel in haste."

"Very much so, my lord," said Malaan. "Smooth as glass, we like to say here."

"There are perils by land as well," Huffort barrelled on. "It's not just krakens and krelias that'll plague us. There are dragons too, and other creatures we've been hearing. All these foul southern beasts of yours seem to be…"

Lord Krator cut him off. "We'll be travelling by the coastal road. I shall lead my army first; you will follow behind, as you did here."

Lord Lewyn Huffort was a large man with broad shoulders and a thick red neck. He stared across the table at the smaller sunlord, bristling. "I've got another idea, *Krator*. Maybe I'll take my eight thousand men and put them back on my ships. Leave you to your unseemly coup."

"Feel free," Krator said at once, waving the man's threat away. "And die upon the seas."

"I'd sooner die on deck than die for the likes of *you*."

Lord Elio Krator's lips broke into a laugh. "How quickly you forget our bargain, Lord Huffort. Or were you never in assent of it?" He turned his eyes on Robbert's uncle. "I was under the impression that you had control over your vassals, Lord Kastor?"

"I do. No one will be leaving." Lord Cedrik Kastor gave Huffort a look that could curdle milk. "I am sure Lord Huffort did not mean what he said. We are all committed to this alliance, and the fruits it will bear us. Please, Lord Krator, go on."

The sunlord turned his attention back to the map. "Kolash will put up more resistance than we faced here. The city does not hold a large garrison, however, and will open its gates to me *if* I arrive first. But for this to happen, we must move quickly. If word should get out of what happened here, we will have a siege on our hands, which will only delay us."

Sir Gavin Trent looked at the map. "You've got men stopping that from happening, I hope?"

"I have set a net upon these lands, unfurled before your arrival. Anyone attempting to get through it will be caught and killed." He gestured to Mar Malaan.

"The fibres of this net are tightly woven, my lords," the primped Sunrider said, with a little titter that wobbled his chins. "None shall pass through."

"And if they do?" Gavin Trent went on. "None of us want to be stuck in a long siege of a subordinate city."

"We won't be," Krator promised. "Kolash will fall quickly. After which we will march upon Aram. I have men loyal to me inside the city, and have already sent word ahead to them to prepare for our coming. If only one of the gates is opened from within, we'll swarm the streets and win my throne within a day."

"We?" asked Lord Simon Swallow. "You mean to aid us this time, then, my lord? In winning the city." He glanced over at Lord Cedrik. "We lost several dozen men this evening, taking the port for you. I do hope you're not expecting the same to happen in Aram."

"No, Lord Swallow. My own men will be in support."

Robbert Lukar shook his head. "Your men will *lead*, my lord. *Ours* will be in support. We are acting only as a supplementary force, not a spear-head. Your men will make up the van."

Cedrik Kastor placed a hand upon Robbert's shoulder, giving him a light squeeze. "My nephew speaks truly, Lord Krator. This is *your* insurrection, not ours, and you must thus carry the risk. The Port of Matia was a simple victory for us, as you had said it would be, but Aram will be different. You shall bear the brunt, as per our agreement."

"I recall our agreement, Lord Kastor."

"Good." Cedrik swirled his wine, then wet his lips, as though he'd won a little victory in their game. "When the battle is concluded, I shall have my men take inventory of our dead as well. For every Bladeborn man fallen in service to your cause I will expect you to supply a Lightborn of similar prowess for mine, Sunriders and Starriders well seasoned in battle. Regular soldiers can be paid in kind, with swordsmen and spearmen from your ranks." He swirled his wine again, then placed it on the table. "As per our agreement."

Robbert had not been aware of this detail. It covered one of Lank's complaints, at least.

"That is only fair," Lord Elio Krator allowed. "But if things go to plan, I do not anticipate heavy losses on either your side or mine. You will have a full army when you march north into Agarath, my lord."

The short exchange seemed enough to satisfy both sides, yet all the same, the underlying tension was not to be entirely dispersed. Lord Krator outlined more details of his plan, allowing Mar Malaan to step in where needed to add garnish to his report. They were quite a pairing. Krator, tight of mouth and unblinking of eye, standing rigid and straight as a spear in his feathered robes; Malaan, a wobbling flan of a man dressed in colourful silk and satin who was as mirthful as Krator was miserable.

And he *was* miserable, this sunlord, Robbert could see. They had heard a rumour that he had lost someone dear to him; a woman, if they had heard it true, who'd jilted him and run back to Aram on the eve of their battle outside the Perch. Some even said that was why Krator had fought so feebly that day, that his mind was not in the fight. Others said his whole motivation for taking the throne was to impress this woman. "She said she'd only wed him if he took the eagle chair," Bernie had reported some days ago. "That's why he's doing it. All for some girl."

She must be beautiful, Robbert had thought to that. *Beautiful and brave and daring too, to run from him.* It was probably all nonsense, though. And what should they care? Krator's motives were irrelevant to them. Whether for a woman or himself or anyone else, their part in it was just the same. *Kill his countrymen, win him his crown, and turn our eyes upon the real enemy.*

Robbert Lukar nodded to himself. *We'll be conquerors,* he told himself, *marching from city to city with the heads of our enemies held aloft. We'll win fortresses and slay Fireborn and scour all of Agarath clean, then march upon Eldurath, drenched in dragon blood.* The thought made him almost giddy, and desperate to get this business with Krator done. He imagined his father, looking down upon him, urging him on with a closed fist and a beaming smile. *I'll do what he'd have done,* he thought. *If this deal with Krator gets us through Agarath's back door, so be it, it'll all be worth it. We'll be heroes, every one of us. We'll help win this war for the north.*

So deep in thought was Robbert Lukar, that he barely even seemed to notice when the council came to an end. Mar Malaan was rolling up the parchment maps and the lords were setting aside their wine cups. "My lords," said Elio Krator. "One last thing, before you leave."

The Tukorans stopped and waited to listen.

"A word of advice and caution," the sunlord told them, straightening out the feathers of his cloak. "I have sensed unease here today at what we are doing, and doubts in this alliance as well. That is natural. Tukor and Aramatia have rarely worked as one, and only recently we were facing off against one another across the field. Here, together, we can discuss our differences and put animosity aside for a greater cause, yet out there it is different." He looked to the exit. "The common soldier is not made as we are. He cannot comprehend the complexities of warfare, and when he begins to whisper of his doubts, that is the seed of dissent." He looked at them, man by man, slow and deliberate. "Prevention, in this case, is better than cure. I bid you deal with this quickly, my lords."

"Deal with what, exactly?" grumbled Huffort. "If your men are threatening mutiny, that's on you. It's got nothing to do with us."

Lord Gullimer spoke more mildly. "There is no dissent in our ranks, Lord Krator. Not everyone is happy about this alliance, but our men follow the word of their lords and commanders. They understand that this course benefits us both."

"Are you certain of that, my lord?"

"As certain as when I last spoke to my men about it, yes." Gullimer answered with great poise, as ever. "Unless something might have changed since then."

"It may have," Krator said. "Or it may *yet.* This is not something that can be ignored. You must keep atop of it, as I have. *Prevention,* my lords, not cure. Pull these weeds before they're allowed to grow."

"How can you know a weed is there if it hasn't yet spouted from the soil?" Huffort challenged, growing increasingly annoyed.

"You put your ear to the ground…and listen," the sunlord answered. "I have many spies among my own ranks listening for these growing weeds. When they hear anything, they tell me, and I order these weeds pulled." He looked them over with eyes as black as death. "Come, let me show you."

They followed him out of the pavilion into the muggy gloom between the camps. Beyond the Aramatian encampment, a host of prisoners had been gathered, three or four score in sum, their hands tied behind their backs, all dressed in ragged underclothes. Soldiers corralled them out onto

324
.

the plains at the points of their long spears, forcing them down onto their knees as sunwolves snapped about them, and starcats slinked darkly nearby with those silver-spotted coats as black as jet. All the air was filled with the unpleasant din of wailing and weeping and the desperate beseech of doomed men.

"You might have gagged them first," came Lord Swallow's jittery voice, cringing. "All this noise…"

"Is necessary," said Krator bluntly. "I *want* them to be loud. I want every soldier in my camp to hear what happens to those who defy me."

Robbert watched as the first men were run through, spears punching through guts and hearts and necks. Others were disembowelled or decapitated with swords. Some were left for the biggest meanest wolves, tearing at their throats with fangs as long as daggers, slashing their insides out with razor-sharp claws. One starcat pounced and mauled a man to death. Another prisoner was being eaten alive by several sunwolves, Robbert saw, the beasts snapping and growing as they fought to get at the choicest organs. It was carnage, bloody carnage. A wild crazed chorus of snarling and roaring and screaming that went right through Robbert Lukar's body and into his very bones.

He shivered to hear it. *These are his own men,* he thought. *His own soldiers.* His uncle Cedrik had treated the prisoners at Eagle's Perch savagely, but they were at least his enemy. *But this?* What did these men do to earn such a foul end, except whisper by night of their doubts, express their fears?

He sensed the looming shape of Sir Lothar move in beside him. "These men," the knight said in a low voice. "They're those loyal to the Duchess, I assume?"

Robbert gave a nod. "Dissenters. Krator just gave us a speech about pulling weeds." He stared out at the horror of it. "Have you spoken with Sir Alistair yet?"

The tall knight shook his head. "No, Robb. I've been out here, remember? You told me to stay outside the tent."

Robbert looked at his uncle, who stood observing the slaughter with a little smile upon his lips. *He's enjoying this,* he realised. That look worried him. "You'd best go now, Lank. Talk to Sir Alistair, and talk to Sir Tunsen and Sir Clive and Happy Harys too, and anyone else who's been complaining in their cups."

"And say what?"

He looked at his uncle again, and saw that cold callous glint in his eye. "*Nothing,*" he said. "Tell them to *say nothing.*"

27

Saska

It was dusk when Sir Ralston returned to them, the sun setting rich and red in the west over hills of shimmering gold. He strode up to the fire bedecked head to heel in his godsteel plate, greathelm clutched in the crook of his arm, dual greatswords bobbing at his hips. "I told you not to start a fire," he admonished. "Whose idea was this?"

"All of ours." The Butcher was languishing upon a shapely rock with a cup of fine wine in his grasp. "It gets chilly here by night. Not quite as chilly as you, Coldheart, but chilly all the same." The Butcher's face was a horrific lattice of savage scars and jagged rents, though his smile was so full of life that all of that was easily forgotten.

Leshie gave a giggle. "*Coldheart*. Not bad, Parapet. Haven't heard that one yet."

"It was just for you, little red. I know how fond you are of silly nicknames."

Saska stood up from her stone seat. "So? Did you find it?" Rolly had left well over an hour ago in search of this dragon nest, taking a couple of the Nemati trackers with him. He'd returned alone, though. "Where are the others?"

"They remain out there on watch. We found the nest, but the dragon was not present. I suspect it is hunting and will return overnight to sleep. The others will alert us." He looked at the fire again, grinding his teeth. "This fire…it may draw it here. Or some other creature. There's a reason I told you not to light one."

"And there's a reason we ignored you." The Butcher had a bite of cheese from the platter he'd laid out beside him. He had curiously refined tastes for a sellsword and former pit fighter. On his back was draped his tattered cloak, hanging from his shoulders in strips of crimson, scarlet, ruby, rose, and two dozen other shades of red. "If the light draws the dragon here, all's the better. It will save us the effort of climbing up to its nest."

Sir Ralston marched in angrily and kicked the fire to death with his enormous armoured feet. Ash and bits of charred wood went flying, causing several of the sellswords to duck away. Only cinders remained thereafter, reaching to tickle at the belly of the sky with their smoky grey fingers.

The Butcher watched on nonchalantly. "You have an anger problem, Coldheart. You could have just asked."

"I shouldn't *have* to ask, *sellsword*," the giant knight thundered at him. "You should do as ordered. I am in command here, not you."

"Wrong." The Butcher waved at Saska. "She is. Our pretty princess rules this roost, and she made no complaint about lighting a fire."

Sir Ralston turned on her. "Is that true?"

She shrugged. "Not exactly. I wasn't even here when it was lit."

"Where were you?"

"There." She pointed off behind some rocks.

"*Why*? I told you all to stay together. You shouldn't go wandering off alone."

"I was taking some privy time, Rolly. *Gods.*" Sir Ralston's strict rules could be overbearing sometimes. She could see Marco of the Mistwood rolling his eyes, and Slack Stan and Merinius and Garth the Glutton looked bored of it as well. "Unless you want me to squat right here in front of everyone? How about that? Let's all watch the princess take a…"

"Shhhhh," came a hiss, from one of the Nemati guardsmen nearby.

A hush fell at once. Saska gripped her godsteel blade and listened, though knew instantly it was nothing to fear. "It's just Agarosh," she said, relaxing. She could hear him approaching from a clump of nearby hills, his enormous weight sending soft shockwaves through the earth. A few moments later, the hulking moonbear appeared over the lip of a craggy hummock, crystal fur sparkling by the last light of day. He was dragging along some large carcass in his jaws, it looked. As Saska was trying to work out what, Marco of the Mistwood chuckled and quipped, "Oh, look, the One-Eye has killed our dragon."

"It's not a dragon," Sir Ralston said. "The dragon is much bigger."

"Then what is it?" The Butcher sat up. "Some other Ever-War monstrosity came crawling from its lair?"

"It's just a camel," Saska said, hand clasping her ancient godsteel dagger. "One of those massive ones you get in Pisek."

"I rode one of those once," Leshie grinned. "Never had anything so big between my legs."

The sellswords laughed. Sir Ralston shook his head, turned, and stamped away to speak to the Nemati guardsmen, who stood about them in a wide watchful ring, long silver spears to hand. The Bloody Traders returned to their banter and drinking as the corpulent figure of Garth the Glutton stood upon his stocky legs and waddled forward to relight the fire with flint and blade.

"No," the Butcher told him. "Enough games now, Garth. I like to play with the giant, but he's right, the command is his. No fire. Sit down and have a drink, you great ugly pig."

Saska appreciated that. Amusing as it was to see the two scarred men lock horns, this wasn't the time or place. She gave the captain a nod and continued away from the dying embers of the fire, out past the ring of guards and horse-drawn carriages and up into the nearby hills. Sir Ralston watched her, narrow-eyed, but seemed to realise she was heading toward Agarosh, so let it pass.

A couple of minutes later she was approaching the moonbear, who had taken that hilltop as his dining table, feasting ferociously upon his prey. Saska had been told that the moonbears of the mount did not need to eat a great deal to sustain themselves, despite their enormous size. They would hibernate a lot, and bathe by night in the Light of Lumo, shining down from her silver moon, just as the dragons at the depths of the Wings were said to be sustained by the fiery Breath of Agarath, burning beneath them. When the dragons left their islands and the Moonbears left their mountain it was different, though. They needed to hunt.

"How does it taste?" she asked, approaching slowly. "I'll admit, I've never tried camel before."

The bear lifted his gigantic head from the bloody carcass and looked at her through a set of expressive blue eyes. They held a light of their own, those eyes, more pure and radiant than any Saska had known, cobalt stars in a snow-white face. His fur had softened from its hard crystal form by now, flowing from his flesh in thick white waves. A rumble echoed from the great chambers inside his chest. She still felt in awe when she drew up so close to him, at his scale and strength and ethereal air, that divine shimmering shroud that seemed to cloak him.

"Do you mind if I sit?" Saska had quickly learned that it paid to be polite with a moonbear. A rumble told her yes, so she smiled and sat down on a rock, as Agarosh took pause in his feasting, sitting back on his massive muscular haunches. Saska's nostrils opened and closed. The iron scent of blood was thick and ripe in the air, and would be greatly more pungent for the beasts that prowled these lands. "Will that not attract the dragon?" she asked.

Agarosh's answer was to rumble. A rumble that said 'let it come'.

Saska gave that a laugh. *If only I had his courage.* "If it does, can you let me fight it first?" she asked, with a shrug of the shoulders. "Apparently that's why we're here."

The bear already knew of their purpose. He rumbled 'yes' and began licking his paw, running an enormous pink tongue along bloody claws like scimitar swords, curved and long.

Saska turned her gaze away toward the northeast, where the shadows had deepened into a blanket of darkness beneath a sky now clouded and cloaked. Rugged hilly plains spread off that way for hundreds of miles before they finally reached the holy Everwood, and further to the north of that, Moonbear Mountain, where the last of the unbonded moonbears dwelled.

It made her think of Ranulf, and how far he might have gotten on his quest. *Halfway, perhaps? Less than that? More?* She thought more was more likely than less, given how long he'd been gone, though could not say for sure. Maybe they'd come upon some devilry, another of these monsters belched up from the dark places of the earth? Reports were still coming in day after day of the perils crawling the lands and haunting the seas, and it seemed likely something might cross their path. *Sunrider Munsoor will protect him*, she told herself. They had a strong guard in the company, enough to withstand most threats, Sunriders and Starriders and some armoured paladin knights as well. *But still...*

She looked up at Agarosh, wondering if she might have asked him to go too. *I'd be happier knowing you were with him,* she thought. Agarosh had left the sanctuary of his mountain to protect her, yes, but did she really need him right now? Before today, she'd spent almost all her time behind the palace's thick stone walls, protected by hundreds of guardsman, and even out here she had a fearsome cohort about her.

"Do you miss it?" she found herself asking. "The mountain, where you lived?"

The moonbear stopped in his grooming and gazed north, a hulking white boulder beside her. She listened to that soft thrumming rumble that so few could perceive, and understood.

He does not like it here, around all these people. He is a creature of solitude now. But one of duty as well. "I'm sorry," she said to him. "I know what it's like to miss home as well. I don't even know what's happened to my family. Not my blood family. My adopted family. From North Tukor." She sighed deeply, thinking of Master Orryn and Llana and Del. "I haven't seen any of them since the day I ran. I don't even know if they're dead or alive." She felt understanding in the bear, and even sympathy, in the way his chest vibrated as he breathed, the way those jewelled eyes shimmered and shifted. "What about you, Agarosh? Are there other bears that still live on the mountain?"

She listened closely. Lord Hasham had asked her if she might talk to Agarosh about this, and she'd not had an opportunity until now. The One-Eye's rumbles were soft and mournful and told her that his own noble bloodline had long since been broken, though there remained some other moonbears there still, lingering in the caves of the high cliffs and passes, prowling the pinewood forests that clothed the mountain's slopes.

"Do you know how many?" Saska asked. "How many wild ones are left." *Wild*, she thought. It sounded too rough a word for such magnificent, sensitive, light-filled creatures. "*Free* ones, I mean. Like you."

For a long while Agarosh made not a sound as he stared solemnly away to the north. Their interactions were often like this, filled with long sombre silences in which they would communicate little. But in the little they had spoken, she had sensed a deeply mournful soul, eternally wounded by the loss of her great uncle Justo during the war twenty years before. To this day he continued to rise early for the dawn and watch the sun summit the eastern horizon, always finding some high place where he could enjoy an unburdened view in peace, a ritual that he had shared with Justo Nemati during their many long years as one.

The silence lingered on. *Perhaps he doesn't want to talk about this at all. I should leave him*, she decided, *try another time.* She rose from the rock she was sitting on. "I'll let you eat in peace," she said. "I know how annoying it is when someone interrupts your meal."

But as she stepped away, she heard a soft rumble, and turned back. The giant moonbear was looking down at her with those big blue thoughtful eyes.

"Four?" she whispered. "There are only four, other than you?"

Four, she thought, sadly, as he rumbled 'yes'. *Just four more ranging free.* Lord Hasham had not been wrong when he'd spoken of their falling numbers. *Their fate is linked to this war,* Saska knew. *If the darkness should prevail, they'll never recover, not these creatures birthed and bred by the light.*

"The others…" she asked. "Might they…join you, if you summoned them? Would they fight alongside you?" *Alongside us.* "Against the darkness?"

The bear seemed to have no answer to that, though as he looked out longingly to the north, Saska sensed a defiance in him, and a pride, a determination that this would not be their end. It was the closest to a yes she could have hoped for.

She took leave of the lordly bear at that, descending the craggy hillock to find the overnight camp being set up in the rugged red vale. All about them, stumpy hills in assorted shapes rose up black and menacing, silhouetted against the night sky, and across the valley boulders and hunks of broken rock were strewn among the patchy grasses and brittle dry bushes that took root across these lands. Saska saw that the carriage in which she and Sir Ralston had ridden that day was at the heart of a ring of tents, one for each of the sellswords and soldiers. Further off, the Nemati guardsmen stood sentry on their watch, while the Butcher and his men lingered by the carcass of the fire, drinking and laughing.

The Wall walked over as he spotted her reappear. "The camp is prepared," he informed her. "You and Leshie can take the carriage to sleep in. It will be well protected within the ring."

"Does that mean I can take off my armour to sleep?"

"It would be best if you stay in your armour until we return to the safety of the palace."

"Fine." She had no interest in fighting the man on this, and once inside the carriage, she could do as she pleased. *I could sleep nude as a newborn and he'd never even know.*

"I heard rumbling coming from the hilltop," the Whaleheart said, looking to the hills. "Care to share what you were discussing?"

"His homeland," Saska said. "Lord Hasham asked me a while ago if I might ask him how many free moonbears are left."

"And?"

"Four," she said. "Besides him. I wondered if he might go and ask them to fight for us."

"And will he?"

"I don't know. If I ask him properly, maybe, though that makes me uncomfortable. Who am *I* to command *him*?"

Sir Ralston frowned down at her. "Do I have to remind you?"

"Please don't."

"Then you know who you are." He looked at the One-Eye's vast silhouette. "Agarosh has proven a powerful protector of these lands. Another four can only be a boon to these people, but that is all he will ever be. I hope you know that."

She wasn't understanding. "Meaning?"

"Meaning the bear will not journey with us when we go north. Assuming Shackton wins us passage through the Everwood, we'll still need to sail across the Bay of Mourning before we reach northern shores. That isn't a journey an animal of such a size can make, let alone five, and our mission will remain one of secrecy. Having a moonbear with us will only provoke the wrath of the very people you are trying to engage." He took pause, then said, "And if you want my full advice…"

"*No*. Don't even say it."

He did. "I think you should leave the cat here as well."

"I said don't say it!" She pushed him hard in the chest, though it was like pushing at a mountain. He budged not a hair's breadth. "How could you even suggest that?"

He looked down at her with those hard iron eyes. "Do you love the cat?"

"Her name is Joy."

"Joy. Do you love her?"

"Yes. No. It's *more* than that." She was growing agitated at the very thought of it. It frightened her, perhaps more than anything ever had. "We're *bonded*, Rolly. I know you can't understand that, but *try*. I could *never* leave her behind."

"You have to. For her sake. And yours."

"No." She wouldn't even entertain it. She'd been gone from Joy for but a single day and already longed to see her again. *Perhaps that's why he made sure she didn't come. As a test…* "No, I can't." She shook her head firmly. "And *don't* ask me again."

"I'll ask you until you realise the truth."

"What truth? *What truth*, Rolly?"

"That the cat holds you back. That she is more a burden than a boon to you, Saska."

She swung at him, though even at full stretch he was too tall for her to strike.

The Whaleheart did not flinch. "You know it's true. The cat cannot bear you in your armour, and you will be wearing it all the time. You are far too important to be left unprotected in leathers and mail with nothing but a godsteel dagger at your hip. That is all the cat can manage."

"Joy! She's called Joy!"

"I know her name. And I know it was a mistake you ever bonding her. I knew it would cause this conflict in you. Love and duty do not mix. You must choose one or the other."

"Like you have?" she snarled.

"Yes. Duty is my life."

"Duty is your *wife*," she spat. "Does she kiss you tenderly, sir? Does she make you happy?"

He stiffened, mouth hardening. "Happiness is not important. Until your task is done, you must make sacrifices. Joy is among them."

She tried to slap him again, though this time Sir Ralston caught her wrist. She tried with the other hand and he caught that one too. The Wall held her tight. "It's difficult to face, I know," he said. "But when you go north, you will not be welcomed as you need to be welcomed if you have a starcat at your side. Think about that, Saska. *Think*." And he shook her. "Think about what will happen should she die. Think about how lost you'll be then."

She couldn't think about that. She wouldn't.

"If she dies, you'll lose all hope. How then will you meet your fate? These are questions you have to ask yourself. These are realities you must confront."

No, she thought, *no, I can't*, but she forced herself to say, "I know. You don't think I don't know that by now?"

"Then act like it." He released her and marched away, melting into the darkness.

Seething, she spun and marched the opposite way.

The air was stuffy and still in the carriage, suffused with a faint acrid undertone of perfume. It was the perfume her grandmother wore, grown old and off, sinking into the upholstery. Easily ignored when the carriage was on the move but not so much when static. She couldn't stand it.

I'm leaving, she thought. *Damn him, I'll sleep outside*. She checked through the heavy drape curtains to make sure that the Wall was not looking, then climbed down the wooden steps and made for the darkness beyond the camp.

She would not go far, but needed to be away. *I'm armoured, armed, safe. I want to be alone*. About fifty metres from the campsite she found a bundle of rocks, and sat with her back against them, facing east, hidden from sight from the rest.

There she slept, or tried to. Dwelling on her cruel monstrous fate.

28

Amron

It should have been Sir Brontus, he thought, as he circled the First Blade of Vandar, imparting his long years of wisdom.

"Free your mind of what ails you, my lord. Unburden yourself of your troubles and focus only on the blade and the bond." He walked a wide ring around him, feet crunching on grit as he went. "Feel its power and its age, feel the wisdom of all the men who have borne it. You must first secure that connection before its weight lessens. Only then will the bond begin to form."

Lord Dalton Taynar looked over at him, the Sword of Varinar held hard in his steel grip. He could only just manage to haul the tip a few inches from the floor. Swinging it, let alone sparring with it, was currently impossible. "I understand how to bond a godsteel blade, Amron," he said in a prickly voice. "I learned everything you're telling me when I was a child." It was no warm morning, yet the Lord of the Ironmoors was perspiring, his hand trembling violently from the effort.

"The Sword of Varinar is not a regular godsteel blade," Amron replied, still circling. "It requires more patience to bond, more time, and more power. It is not a process you can force."

He's struggling, Amron thought. It was ill news, though not unheard of. The Blades of Vandar were handed out to champions by tradition, who were by very definition the finest knights and swordsmen in the realm, yet even then not all could master them. Even those who had been victorious in the Song did not always bond to the Sword of Varinar as they hoped. Sometimes it just took time, sometimes it required a special moment of clarity to inspire them, and sometimes…*Well, sometimes it just isn't meant to be,* Amron thought, as he watched the dour lord struggle.

He stopped in his pacing and turned to face him. "Perhaps you would prefer to train alone, Dalton? I feel my presence here may be more hindrance than help right now."

The First Blade was still trying to heave the golden sword a little higher off the ground, as though it was a simple matter of strength. Far from it. As the bond strengthened, so the weight of the blade would lessen. It was just the same as regular godsteel in that way.

"Lord Taynar," Amron said, getting his attention. "Don't force it. The process must be natural."

"I know." Dalton's face had gone bright red, which was remarkable, because it was usually pale as bone. Eventually the effort became too much, and he spat out a great exhale of air and let the blade slip from his grasp. It hit the ground with a resounding thump. "It's only been a few days," the man grunted. "It's common for it to take much longer for the bond to form."

Amron nodded. "It can take weeks, you're right, but weeks we don't have. And sometimes it never happens at all." He paused and studied the man as Dalton caught his breath. "You know what happens when a newly chosen First Blade cannot bond to the sword, I trust?"

His answer squeezed through gritted teeth. "He must give it up, to the losing finalist." The thought of that did not sit well with his pride, nor should it. "I know the rules, Amron. A new First Blade is permitted a month to prove he can bear it. It's only been days, as I say."

"And yet you've made little progress in that time." He did not want to have to walk this path, yet blunt words needed to be said. "In times of war, the permitted month must be reduced. The First Blade of Vandar's first and most important remit is to protect this realm from our enemies. He must be a source of inspiration for our allies as much as he is a figure to fear for our foes."

"I know that."

"Then you know too that you cannot spend much more time like this. I'll grant you a week, my lord. If you haven't made any progress by then, we will have to let Sir Brontus have a try."

"I *have* made progress," Dalton came back, horrified at the prospect.

"Lifting it three inches from the ground is not progress. You've had four days. After seven, I want to see you bearing it single-handed, outstretched before you. I want you to hold that pose for a full minute before letting the blade fall back down."

The man looked at Amron as though he was asking the impossible. But he was backed into a corner and knew he had no choice. "Fine. Seven days. Seven days from now…I'll do as you ask."

"Three days from now."

His black brows twisted. "You said a week."

"I did. And you've had four days. That leaves three." He had no patience for this charade anymore. *King in all but name,* he thought. *Gods know everyone's saying it.* "We're leaving for King's Point in the morning, Dalton, and I need a First Blade who can actually bear his blade. You're the first for a reason. Not the second or the third, but the first. And for that you bear our most famous sword. But you *must* bear it, or it will go to another. We have no time for coddling now. The enemy is at our door."

The man looked utterly wretched to have his incompetence laid bare.

Thankfully they were alone, else his humiliation would be complete. "Our need is urgent, Lord Daecar, I'm aware of that, but you must understand…"

"I understand," Amron broke in. "And I know three days does not sound like much. But it is. It takes but one moment, Dalton, for you to see the light. Train tonight, and tomorrow before we leave. Train every moment you can spare. Hold the blade in your grasp, day and night. Lie with it as you sleep and never take your fingers from the hilt. If through all that you do not feel your connection kindle, then you have to face up to the fact that it likely never will. There is no shame in that. A dozen First Blades have suffered the same fate across the years."

"The same disgrace."

"This isn't about *you*, Dalton. You are a servant of this realm, and if you cannot serve, you must make way for someone who can."

"Then *you* take it up," Dalton Taynar said suddenly. "If it can't be me, let it be you." *And not Sir Brontus*, his eyes said. His pride could not handle that.

But Amron shook his head. "I can't."

"Why not?"

Aleron, he thought. Amron Daecar had put aside the Sword of the Varinar the night of his firstborn's death, swearing he'd never take it up again. That hadn't changed, nor would it. "I have the Frostblade now," he said. "My guardianship of the Sword of Varinar is long since ended, Dalton. If it won't be you, it will be Sir Brontus, and if he cannot learn to bear it quickly, it will have to go to someone who can, but know this…" He stepped forward and took the Lord of the Ironmoors by the arm. "I hope and pray each hour of the day that you find the spark to ignite your bond. You're a skilled swordsman, and have courage in you, I know. I saw that when you were but a boy and you fought to defend these lands twenty years ago. I remember watching you and Rikkard bicker over how many men you had slain." He smiled at the memory; it had only just come to him. "You were just a teenager, Dalton, yet you fought like a seasoned knight. I want only the best for you, and yet…"

Dalton Taynar was nodding. He looked suddenly younger, less grim, the boy Amron remembered. "…and yet your duty is to the realm," he said for him. "I know, my lord." He set his jaw and steeled his eyes. "Three days," he said. "By the time we reach King's Point, I'll show you the progress you want to see."

Amron met Rogen Whitebeard in the dim corridor that led off from the courtyard, leaving Lord Dalton Taynar to continue his hunt for the light. He stamped right past him in a clank of steel as Rogen turned to join him in his step. "That sounded intense," the man rasped, dark godsteel armour hidden beneath his black cloak.

"You weren't supposed to be listening."

"Couldn't help it. Sounded like you finally got through to him at the end there, though."

"I can but hope." They were in a part of Crosswater Castle rare visited, accessed through a series of dusty passages and tunnels that opened into some forgotten place in the fort. Dalton had insisted as much, preferring to train beyond the sight of his men and Amron understood. He'd done the same when mastering the Frostblade, but time was running short.

"And if he doesn't do as you asked? Then what? It'll go to Oloran?"

"Yes."

"And if he doesn't fare any better?"

"He can't exactly fare much worse." They walked down a long tunnel with old sets of castle-forged armour along the walls, many of them spotted with rust and badly scratched and scuffed from battles long ago. The iron sconces were similarly ancient. Only one in ten held a flame. Amron was done discussing the First Blade's failures. He wanted to hear some better news.

He found it in the stout shape of Lord Botley Harrow, shouting orders in the lower bailey. The main square within the castle's northern gatehouse was busy with knights, men-at-arms, spearmen, bowmen, shieldmen and freeriders all bustling about and making preparations for the morning's ride. As soon as Lord Harrow spotted him, he cut himself off mid-order and came marching Amron's way. "My lord. How was training? Is our gallant First Blade proving his worth?"

Amron avoided the question, as he had for the last few days. He did not want any rumours circulating of Dalton's struggles. "I came to see about Wolfsbane," he said. "Is he shod and ready to ride, Botley?"

"I've had the grooms working with him all morning, my lord. A great destrier like that requires a lot of personal attention, though for all the fearsome stories told about him, he's a bit of a softy really."

"He has his shy side," Amron said, smiling. "Is his barding polished and prepared?"

"They're working on it now." The jowly, barrel-chested Lord of Crosswater gave him a quizzical look. "You sure you want to ride down the river road? Might be quicker if you sail."

"Might," agreed Amron, "though I've spoken to a few of the ship captains and they tell me that the river currents and winds are unpredictable right now. Riding is more certain. King's Point is a three day canter by the river road, four if we go slow."

And just the one if I gallop all day, he thought. Wolfsbane was a truly remarkable horse. Even with Amron wearing full plate armour, he would be able to cover a hundred miles in a single day without falling to exhaustion if he pushed himself. But that was rare, and there were few horses who could ever hope to match him. In a long army column, Amron would have to keep pace.

There were some men training at one side of the yard, dressed in padded leathers, gauntlets, gorgets and halfhelms, and swinging at one another with blunted swords. Amron was not at all surprised to see that Sir Torus Stoutman was among them, easily identified by his dwarfish height, lest a child have stolen into the yard, dressed himself as a knight, and added two feet to his girth. He marched over.

Stoutman saw him, and at once the fighting ceased. "My lord. What's this now? You come down to have a play?"

Amron observed two men doubled over nearby, writhing in pain. Another had blood streaming from his nose and mouth and was probably wishing he had worn a full helm rather than half of one. "I'm sure none of these men would call this play," he said. "Try not to cripple every one of Lord Harrow's men, Torus. They will be needed when this fortress is sieged."

The stumpy knight gave a shrug. "Just trying to teach them a few lessons, is all." He pointed at the one with the broken nose and split lip. "You. What did you learn today?"

"To…to keep my guard up, my lord," he said, wiping blood from his face. "And use my shield more."

Stoutman clapped his hands together. "See. I'm always happy to share my wisdom."

Not everyone else looked quite so happy about it. "Where are your sons, Torus?"

"Here and there. Darun's knocking out a few kinks in my armour, Elmid's sorting the horses, and Hoddin's having a kip. He was on watch all last night, though he's lazy too, that one."

Amron smiled. Sir Torus's sons were all men grown, and Darun, his eldest, even had a couple of young children of his own, yet he still treated them all like his squires.

Lord Harrow was smiling too, broadening that heavy jaw of his. "And by horses you mean ponies, Sir Torus?"

The knight gave a bark of laughter. "Strongest ponies you ever did see, my lord." He squinted at him and pulled a pipe from his belt. "You coming with us to the coast, are you?"

"Me? No. My place is here. The Harrows never leave Crosswater."

"Sounds dull. I'm getting bored of this place already." He lit the pipe more quickly than anyone Amron had ever known, then took a puff. "You Harrows…you were from Rasalan once, weren't you? Old Sir Ralf told me that your forebears built that great fortress of Harrowmoor, down in the Lowplains. True, is it?"

"Every word of it." Lord Botley puffed his thick chest out like a peacock. "We're a storied house, us Harrows. We were originally of Vandar, before we went over to Rasalan and built that fort. Lord Humphrey Harrow did that. Big man. Huge appetites. Wine, women, war, you name it. You can see that in Harrowmoor, if you ever set eyes upon its towers and walls. Huge fortress, that one, all granite. Guess it's why we Harrows ended up here, protecting Crosswater and the Vanguard. Big is beautiful, we like to say…"

"Aye, we know. We've all seen your wife."

It seemed more people were listening than Amron had realised, given the gale of laughter Sir Torus's jape provoked. Lord Botley took it all in good humour, though. His lady wife Horsia was a handsome woman, though hardly of dainty build.

The laughter died when Sir Brontus Oloran appeared from the keep, striding swift and sharp across the bailey in their direction. "Here comes trouble," said Sir Torus, seeing him. "I think I'll get back to beating up these lads." He thrust his pipe back into his belt, still smoking, and went on the hunt for prey.

"Lord Daecar." Sir Brontus fell into a bow as he stopped before him, dressed in his plate armour and Varin cloak. His brooch was a steel fist, holding his cloak in place. Amron had always liked the strong simplicity of the Oloran sigil. "I wanted to talk to you about Lord Dalton…"

Again? Amron thought. He cut him off. "We've discussed this already, Sir Brontus. I have told you already that the fight was a fair contest."

"But it wasn't, my lord. The rain…"

"Is a natural feature of the world, and something we all must fight in occasionally. Not every battle is hosted under the sun, sir. Snow, wind, rain, sleet, we must face them all. As it is in war, so it is in the Song. Lord Taynar gained no special advantage."

"But sire…"

"I am not king, Sir Brontus."

"My lord," he corrected. "It was not just the weather. I've had reports that there was bribery involved as well."

Amron was loathe to even listen to this, but give the knight his due. "Go on."

Sir Brontus had brought along Sir Symon Steelheart as well, known as the Knight of Nine-Hearth, his closest friend. "Sir Symon says that he overheard some men talking in a tavern yestereve, in the castle town. They were discussing a matter of money and promises, my lord, made by Dalton's lickspittles to the…"

"*Lord* Dalton, Sir Brontus. Please, give him his proper title."

"Yes, of course, my lord. *Lord* Dalton, I meant to say. His men…they were involved in rigging the contest, bribing the judges, Symon heard. I know how that sounds, and typically I'd never dream of making such an accusation, but it makes sense. There were many clean hits of mine that were not awarded. If this judge had not been bought, I'd have won for a certainty, rain or no."

"One or more?" asked Lord Harrow.

Sir Brontus wasn't understanding. "My lord?"

"One judge or two? Or were all three of them bought, Sir Brontus, according to this whispered conversation Sir Symon overheard?"

He doesn't believe it, Amron knew at once.

"Um…just the one, my lord," said Brontus, glancing at Sir Symon.

"Which one?"

"I…well that I don't know for sure. No names were ever mentioned. I hoped….well I hoped you might be able to help, Lord Harrow. These were your men, after all, these judges…"

"Yes, they were." Lord Botley Harrow did not look impressed. "And they were chosen specifically for their probity, Sir Brontus. Now think very carefully about what you're saying. If you should declare evidence against this mystery man, you had better make it good. You may be a Varin Knight of high birth, but that will not protect you from reprisal should you get this wrong."

Sir Brontus Oloran suddenly seemed unsure. He turned to Sir Symon. "Symon, tell them…"

The Knight of Nine-Hearth was tall, willowy, handsome, and young, with a deep dimple in his chin and cheeks so clean and perfectly shaven that Amron wondered if they had ever sprouted hair. Golden locks twisted in tight ringlets from his head. He brushed one aside and said, "I would have to make further inquiries, before being sure."

"Further enquiries," said Lord Harrow. "Meaning what?"

"Well, I could try to track down these same soldiers from last night, perhaps…"

"Were they soldiers of mine, Sir Symon? Harrow men. Which house colours did they wear?"

"I'm not sure, my lord. It was quite dark, in the alehouse, and smoky, and they were wearing cloaks over their colours."

"Did you see any of their faces, then? Would you be able to recognise them if you were to see them again?"

Sir Brontus was giving his friend an urging look. "I…well I suppose I…" the Knight of Nine-Hearth stammered.

"A simple yes or no will do, sir."

"Well…" He glanced at Brontus. "Honestly…no, Lord Harrow. I was a way across the room from them and they were rather deep in their cups. And laughing a lot as well, I recall. It's possible…" His eyes flashed upon his friend once again. "It's possible they were merely jesting."

"*Symon*," Sir Brontus hissed at that. "You *told* me they were telling the truth. You said you saw them, that you'd recognise them if…"

Lord Harrow cut in. "I think we can put this matter to bed," he dismissed. "If we followed up on every whisper and rumour of wrongdoing then half the men in every city and fortress in the north would be in the stockade for one reason or another. You have no evidence, that is clear. It would be better if you just accepted that you lost to Lord Taynar fairly, and move on."

"I didn't," Sir Brontus said, in a voice so cracked and desperate it sounded like he might break down and weep right there at the heart of the bailey. Amron was vastly disappointed to see him reduced to this. It was unbecoming and unseemly. "I *know* the fight was rigged, I just know it was…"

"Well know it somewhere else," Lord Botley Harrow told him firmly. "Go, both of you, before I lose my patience. And do not mention this in my hearing again."

The two young knights went away bickering, Sir Brontus looking forlorn, Sir Symon desperately trying to appease him. Amron was worried something like this might happen. *He is falling to obsession,* he thought. *He's not even laid a hand upon the Sword of Varinar before and yet already it's got its teeth into him…*

A soft chuckle sounded behind him. "Lover's tiff, was it?"

Gods. What now? Amron turned around. Walter Selleck was directly behind him, as smiley and scruffy as ever, his great book of notes and sketches cradled in his arms. "How long have you been standing there?"

"Long enough. I'm documenting the preparations, my lord. I managed to get a nice sketch of Sir Brontus's face as his heart was broken. Would you like to see?"

"No." Amron knew the rumours about Sir Brontus and the Knight of Nine-Hearth, though had no interest in discussing or spreading them. "I grow increasingly concerned about your ability to sneak up on me, Walter. You have grown very light on your feet of late."

"Oh, it's just loud here, is all." Walter slammed his book shut, wedging it beneath his arm. His pencil found a nice snug nook by his ear. "I heard that a grulok's been spotted nearby. Apparently Vilmar's going to go and seek it out when we ride tomorrow."

Amron nodded. "It was sighted somewhere southeast of here, in the Wandering Wood. He'll ride with us most of the day, then strike out on its trail."

Harrow made a snorting sound. "A grulok. Do we actually believe those things still exist? Someone probably just got spooked by a play of shadows on a boulder, and thought it was moving. Half of these rumours we're hearing are probably just that. Shadows and dreams and overactive imaginations."

"Once I might have agreed with you, Botley, but that man died when I went out into the Icewilds and found this." Amron shook the hilt of the Frostblade, stirring a mist of kaleidoscopic dust.

"Yes…but a *grulok*, Amron? A stone sentinel of Vandar? Grimbears and fellwolves I'd accept, but that? I'm not so sure."

"You always were a man given to doubt." Amron clapped him on the shoulder. "Seeing is believing, isn't that what you like to say?"

"It's one of my preferred phrases yes."

"Well I've seen things I'd never have believed, so I tend to think differently now. Eldur is arisen, Lord Harrow. Why not a grulok or two?"

"Well…don't get me started on…on *him*, Amron. And since when were we talking about two gruloks? Isn't one enough?"

"Since Sir Storos Pentar sent his letter, informing us of Lythian's return. Perhaps I didn't tell you. He mentioned in his note that a grulok had been sighted in the South Downs, a few dozen miles from Redhelm. That makes two, Botley. It won't be long before we hear of a third, and a fourth, and perhaps many more."

"I bloody well hope not."

"They rise to fight the darkness," Walter Selleck said in a pious voice. He put his hands together. "The stone sentinels were Vandar's soldiers, once. So they shall be again. Agarath spreads fear and fire through his scaly servants. Vandar summons his own soldiers to balance the scales." He smiled. "Why not? We must all fight together for a bright new dawn."

Lord Botley Harrow stared down at him, flat-eyed. "Together? With

mindless monsters? Does he not get annoying, Amron, with all this talk?"
He turned to Whitebeard. "What of you, Strand? Don't you just want to
put your fist through his face sometimes?"

"All the time," the ranger said.

Harrow let out a harrumph. "Good. Nice to see one of you has
retained his wits."

Sir Torus Stoutman came waddling back over on those tree-stump legs
of his. A few other men had been left spreadeagled in his wake, twisting
and groaning on the cobbles. "Think I'll go with him," he announced. "Vilmar, I mean, when he leaves on this hunt. I've seen dragons before,
sunwolves, starcats, a moonbear as well, lions, a mammoth, a snowbear or
three, a leviathan and even a kraken, though only spotted that one at a
distance, thankfully. But a grulok…oh, that'd top them all. Seems an opportunity too good to miss."

Amron was astonished at how well Sir Torus could spar with an opponent, and eavesdrop on a conversation at the same time. "You'll miss it,
Torus," he had to tell him. "Vilmar the Black likes to hunt alone. You know
that."

The dwarf shrugged. "Shame. Suppose I'll have to make do with
fighting dragons, then."

"Speaking of which." Lord Harrow ruffled around in an inner coat
pocket and withdrew a few scraps and scrolls. "Master Corbitt brought me
word this morning of a few more kills," he said, consulting his notes. "One
got too close to Greyguard, this one says. A biggish one, unridden and
unnamed of course, like most of them are. Took a ballista bolt through the
eye and fell down into the sea." He unrolled another scroll. "A second was
riddled with quarrels at Chilgrave, a small female Lord Heward writes.
Landed inside the castle ground and they strung her up on the outer walls
as a warning."

"Unridden again?" asked Amron. It seemed that for every ridden
dragon there were twoscore more unbonded and unsaddled.

Harrow nodded, as he checked another scrap of parchment. "There
was a third as well, found out near Ilithor in the fields to the east of the city.
Killed by the blade, that one."

"By who?" Amron asked.

"Well that's the odd thing. No one seems to know. Usually when a
man kills a dragon, they want everyone to know about it, but whoever
took this one down just went on his merry way and left it there for the
wolves."

Walter gave a smile. "A wandering hero, shunning the light of fame.
There is a nobility in that."

And money, Amron thought. A dragon was worth a fortune when
butchered. "Was the dragon left intact?"

Lord Harrow shrugged. "Doesn't say."

"Well let's hope this mystery hero keeps on doing Vandar's holy work,"
said Walter, going all pious again. "We could use many more of him." He
gave a solemn bow.

Amron looked over the scraps of parchment in Lord Harrow's grasp. "How did these letters reach Master Corbitt? Rider or wing?"

"Riders from Greyguard and Chilgrave. Crow from Tukor. It's become a lottery sending the birds out now, Corbitt says, but some still get through, like that note from Sir Storos. The poor old man's grown most concerned about the populace of his beloved rookery, Amron. Soon enough we'll have no birds left."

Amron nodded darkly. *We are not quite blind as yet,* he thought, *but the enemy has poked out one of our eyes, and the better-seeing one at that.* Riders were slow in delivering news; crows much the quicker, yet the latter were being killed at every turn by riderless dragons that seemed to have been hexed with some explicit instruction to see their entire population extinct. He didn't like it, not one bit. The expedient sharing of information was critical during wartime, and that exchange had slowed to a crawl.

He decided to take his leave of them with that, bidding his men to return to their duties as he climbed the tower steps to his private chambers with Rogen Whitebeard as ever at his heel. Half the time Amron forgot he was there, which was about the highest possible praise he could give the man. Not once did he have to worry that some threat was approaching that he didn't see. Rogen was his eyes and his ears. And few men had such acute senses as the ranger.

He busied himself with some final preparations, writing letters and poring over maps. Those letters would be delivered by horse and rider to the lords and commanders further to the west, those stationed at Green Harbour and the Twinfort, where Lord Randall Borrington had command of the bulk of the Daecar levies. According to Lord Randall's scouts, Agarathi forces had been sighted crossing the land bridges of the Tidelands, sacking towns and communities along the way, plundering them for coin and catch alike. Though it was possible these were no more than rogue groups of deserters, broken men and bandits who'd run from their masters' whips, Lord Randall seemed certain it heralded a larger invasion. The last letter Amron had received from him had been explicit in that.

'We'll have tens of thousands of them swarming upon us soon,' he had written. 'You fear the hammer will fall hardest at King's Point, Amron. Well, I fear it will be here. With the tides going out, they can cross without ever wetting their feet. Half the scouts I send out never come back, and the few who do report a heavy mist descending across the Tidelands as well. It's some dark device of the enemy, they say. Some foul magic of the *risen.* I fear a coming horde, Amron. And I fear we've not the men to repel it."

The risen, Amron thought, as he looked over Lord Randall's words once more. Even in writing, the stoutest of his lords could not give name to Eldur. *Though the rest…*It was concerning, to be sure, and not short of likely either. The tides were said to be at their lowest in living memory, another sign of the Last Renewal, Walter had claimed. It opened many large land bridges between the islands and made a crossing possible by foot, giving the enemy a straight march to the Twinfort. *And if they should besiege it…*

He was pondering that matter when the door knocked and Rogen admitted the form of Sir Ralf of Rotting Bridge. The old knight stepped forth in his usual deliberate stride and simple garb; a leather jerkin over godsteel mail, with a well-worn surcoat on top, showing the broken bridge that he had taken for his sigil when raised to knighthood by Amron's grandfather almost five decades ago. Once upon a time Sir Ralf had been one of the finest swordsmen in the realm, though age had long defeated him. His role was more advisor and councillor now, his wisdom always welcome. "My lord," he said, bowing. "You asked to see me?"

"I did, Sir Ralf. Come in. Have a cup of wine." Amron served the man himself, then invited him to sit. The old knight took a perch upon the window seat, his seamed leathery eyes scanning the harbour below. Lord Dalton's battered fleet had been restored by now, masts fixed, sails stitched, the cracks and breaches in hulls filled in. All were river worthy and many would be sailing back down to add muscle to the defence of King's Point. Amron could see Dalton's flagship, the Iron Champion, being readied and loaded with supplies. He gestured toward it. "Do you know why it was so named, Sir Ralf?"

The old knight nodded. "*Iron* is a reference to the Ironmoors, *Champion* to a long-held expectation that a Taynar would become champion of Vandar once again, and rise to the post of First Blade. It is a prophecy, in a fashion, one Lord Dalton has now fulfilled for his house." He had a neat sip of wine. "Why do you ask, my lord?"

"Because that prophecy may be short-lived," Amron confided. "Dalton struggles, Sir Ralf. He has made little progress these last days and I fear I must take the Sword of Varinar off him, and give it to another."

"Sir Brontus," Ralf of Rotting Bridge said, nodding. "I have not missed the tension between the two. Nor the men who swear them fealty. Taking the blade from one to give to another is not likely to help, however. I trust you have given Lord Taynar a deadline, by which you expect to see improvement?"

Amron had to smile. The old man was nothing if not perceptive. "Three days. Though already I'm regretting it." He looked out of the window at the bustling harbour, shaking his head. "Sir Brontus came to me earlier, complaining of bribery and corruption. He seems to think Dalton had one of the judges paid off. It was indecorous, Ralf, and highly unlike him to act in such poor taste. To spend several days whining about the weather, and then approach me in the lower bailey with this slander, as the men make preparations to leave? Oh, I hope our conversation went unheard, but I doubt it. Already the whispers will be spreading that Dalton cheated to win."

"Do you think he knew what he was doing?" the old knight asked him. "Getting the rumour mill going?"

Amron sighed. "Possibly, yes, though I'll have to give Brontus the benefit of the doubt. Either way, this bickering over the blade has proven a problem I could do without, and not one with a simple solution. It is causing division, the very thing I have been trying to eradicate, and I can see blood being shed off the back of it. If Dalton fails to show progress, and

I have to take the blade off him and give it to Brontus, what then? If Dalton's struggles begin to wane, he may still have to deal with these scandals and slanders and such things can darken the mind of a man. So, Sir Ralf, what would you counsel I do?"

The old man did not waste a moment in answering. "Separate them," he said. He rose from his perch by the window and looked over the letters and maps scattered across Amron's desk. "If you fear bloodshed, pry these two men apart so they're too distant from one another to strike. Send Sir Brontus and his men to the Twinfort, to bolster Lord Borrington's forces, as he's been asking."

Amron nodded. He had spoken with Sir Ralf of this already, though still couldn't decide where best to allocate his strength. "And if Dalton fails to improve?"

"Then swap them, my lord. Give the Sword of Varinar to Sir Brontus and send Lord Taynar west instead."

Amron shook his head. "Brontus commands only thousands. Dalton's host is much bigger, and that is a strength I cannot afford to lose. I would be forced to split them, which would be sure to cause problems of its own… and may not even be possible. They are Taynar men, sworn to him, not me. I have no true authority to command them as the Lord of House Daecar."

"You would as king," Sir Ralf of Rotting Bridge said.

Amron looked at him. "No. If I name myself king, and strip Dalton of the rank of First Blade…" He didn't even want to consider it. All his good work would be swiftly undone and the threat of civil conflict return. "I'd send Dalton off to the Twinfort, and find that he's gone to Varinar instead to plant himself upon the godsteel throne. There is a slow madness festering here, Ralf, in Dalton and Brontus both. Dalton struggles with the blade and it haunts him. Brontus feels he's been cheated and that gets inside his head, stabbing until he can no longer think clearly. In the end it darkens them both."

Old Ralf puzzled on that. "Then it seems to me the best result would be for Lord Dalton to figure a way through his troubles, and for Sir Brontus to be sent away, with the several thousand under his charge."

"Yes," Amron said, in a grunt. "It would be the simplest course, that is certain. But it hinges on Dalton learning to wield the blade."

"A hinge that can still turn in our favour."

"How? And don't say put my hands together and pray."

The skin around the old man's eyes creased into a thousand little lines as he smiled. His had always been a pleasant face, once handsome, now kindly, and never less than wise. "Not prayer, no, but *faith*."

Amron snorted. "I don't have much faith in him, that's the problem."

"No, my lord, I'm not speaking of your faith in him, but his faith in himself. Dalton is directly descended of Rufus Taynar, who has cast a pall upon his line for almost four hundred years. You say the man is haunted? Yes, I do believe he is. By the ghost of Lord Rufus, whom the Taynars have longed to see emulated. Now here comes Dalton, who hopes to raise the blade up upon his first try. When he doesn't, he grows nervous, and when he tries again and again and makes no progress, the pressure begins to mount." He paused, then said. "And now you give him a deadline, else he'll lose the blade, and be mocked as a failure forever. That is a pressure he does not need, my lord. You should give him more time."

"We don't have more time. It is a three-day ride to King's Point, four if we take it slow. After that, a decision must be made."

"A three-day *ride*, yes. There is no reason why he cannot take longer under sail."

Amron frowned. "I had expected him to ride with me," he said. "We have matters to discuss by night, war councils to be held."

"I'm sure he can miss a few." Ralf had a sip of wine. "Under sail he'll be able to spend his days training, on deck or in his own privy cabin, away from the eyes of the herd. I've heard the tides and winds have become rather temperamental of late. It might just be that the Iron Champion arrives at the coast a day or two after the rest of us. Or *more*, perhaps, if needed."

A slow smile rose upon Amron's lips. *Wise and cunning both.* He considered it, though did not expect to get much pushback from Dalton Taynar were he to suggest it. *No, he'll bite my hand off. And it will help unburden him of the pressure too, there's a certain truth to that.* He went over to the counter and poured a cup of wine, taking a sip, thinking. Then he turned and said, "You were at my father's side when he first took up the Sword of Varinar, were you not?"

The old knight nodded. "I was there, my lord, yes. I stood witness to his suffering."

"Suffering?"

"Oh yes. Gideon Daecar did not master the blade in a day as everyone seems to think. No, he took his time and had his struggles as well, as Lord Dalton is."

Amron thought on that, then nodded. "Good," he said. "You can tell him that when you set sail."

The old man frowned. "Set sail, my lord?"

"Yes, on a triple-decked, four-masted monster, Sir Ralf. I want you on the Iron Champion with him when we leave. If there's anyone who can help Dalton through his struggles, it isn't me...it's you."

29

Saska

A heavy boot kicked her awake. "Up, up, get up, Saska! What on earth are you doing out here?"

She shifted against the rocks, stiff as a corpse in armour. The eastern horizon was a blaze of light and colour. She could hear lots of noise nearby, shouting and thrashing and some wild shrieking too. That she hadn't been stirred from her sleep by that was a mystery. "What's going on? Is...is the dragon here?" Her voice was a croak. She began pushing herself to her feet, head heavy.

The Wall reached down and helped her. "Yes. Well...no. It's not the same one. Much smaller."

She wasn't understanding. "There's more than one out here?"

"They move around quickly." He got her standing and looked her over. "Where's your helm? *Hurry*, where is it?"

She fumbled about, trying to think. She'd brought it out with her when she came to sleep out here last night, she recalled. *There.* She saw it wedged between a pair of jagged rocks and bent to pick it up, almost toppling over. The sleep still felt thick in her veins. "Smaller, you said?" She stood back upright. "How small?"

"Put your helm on and find out."

She did so quickly, jamming the helm with the bladed crab claws on the crest over her head, leaving the faceplate turned up for now. The Wall led her around the side of the rocks and she took in a view of the camp. The dragon was even smaller than she'd expected. "It's hardly any bigger than a horse." The sellswords and soldiers had it ringed off. "Why won't it fly away? It's clearly outmatched?"

"The Butcher injured it, cut its wing." He give her a nudge in the back. "Come, let's get you in there."

She stumbled forward over the rocks, still trying to catch up. "Where's the other one?" Her eyes went to the skies; to the west it remained gloomy though everywhere else the world was quickly awakening. "The one we were looking for?"

"Not yet returned. We'll hunt it later. You can limber up with this one."

Saska was getting an unpleasant feeling in the pit of her stomach. The juvenile dragon was screaming as it spun left and right, coughing up the occasional gout of fire to try to fend off the men about it. That fire withered quickly enough, though, and mostly it just came out as smoke. She could see blood dripping off its right wing, and a tear there in the thick flappy skin. There was something about its wide blaring eyes and frantic movements that made her stop. "I'm not fighting that, Rolly," she said. "It's just...just a child."

"A *child*? No, it's a *dragon*. A small one, yes, but they grow quickly, and not long from now it'll be much bigger." He took her arm and began pulling her along.

She let herself be dragged. Within a few moments they were nearing the action. Almost everyone was up and awake, though not all. Saska could see the bloated figure of Garth the Glutton crawling sleepy-eyed from his tent, hirsute belly wobbling beneath him. A pair of Nemati spearmen were quickly pulling on their scalemail shirts as well.

Saska halted again, ten metres from the ring. She watched as Leshie danced about in the dust, darting forward with her shortsword to prick at the dragon's scaly skin. The beast hissed and spun and snapped at her, but she was already skipping from its reach, her face flush with excitement. *She's made for this more than I am,* Saska thought.

"Ah, the pretty princess is here!" roared the Butcher, cavorting left and right. He wasn't wearing his breastplate, she realised, only his tattered red cloak, which whipped about him as he moved. Beneath was a body shredded with scars, some from the fighting pits, others from various battles he'd fought, many more self-inflicted for all the people he'd slain; a running tally of the dead. He flung his cloak open and showed her a rare patch of clean flesh upon his chest. "Here, my lady, I have saved this space for a dragon. Let me kill it in your honour and add a scar upon my breast!"

"No," Sir Ralston bellowed at him. "We did not come here for *you*, sellsword."

The Butcher grinned as he continued dancing around with the rest, prodding and poking with swords and spears to keep the young dragon from making an escape. Saska felt uncomfortable watching it.

"Just let him, Rolly," she said. "It's hardly what we came for, is it?"

"It's still a dragon."

Leshie came dashing over, panting from the thrill. "Where were you?" she asked Saska. "You never slept in the carriage last night."

Nor did you, Saska knew at once. If she had, she'd have discovered that Saska was absent some hours ago and reported it, or at least gone out looking for her. That she hadn't spoke volumes. *No, she found another tent to sleep in.* Green-eyed Merinius, maybe. He was a handsome man. Or could the Butcher have finally worn her down...

"I found her resting by some rocks," the Wall said, over the sound of

347

the scuffing and thrashing and shrieking. He gave Leshie a look up and down. "You should not get too close to it, girl. Your armour is leather and offers scant protection against a dragon…"

"A dragon? *Where!*" Leshie looked to the skies, feigning fear, then gave a mocking snort. "Oh, that cute little lizard over there? I've seen puppies more fearsome. It's no threat to me."

"Even a small dragon can kill a person without proper plate armour. Never underestimate them."

Leshie shrugged. "Whatever. It would have to get near me first, and I'm much too quick." She turned to Saska. "So, are you going to fight it then?"

Saska had made her decision while they spoke. She didn't like how the beast was being treated, all this baiting and taunting. "I always thought you should treat your enemies with respect," she said, disapproving. "And dragons are intelligent creatures. This is cruel."

Sir Ralston grunted out something in response, though she didn't hear him. She stepped away, calling. "Butcher, go ahead. Put the poor thing out of its misery. And make it quick."

The sellsword needed no second invitation. With a dart and a dodge and a swing of his misting broadsword, he cut the dragon's head clean off, sending it bouncing away across the stones. The body slumped and dropped, wriggling unpleasantly on the ground as a spray of thick reddish brown blood came squirting and pumping from the severed neck. "Reminds me of Marush Moonface," the Butcher laughed. "His head toppled away just the same." He turned to face Sir Ralston. "Coldheart, we have even more in common now. The size and scars we share, yes. Now we are the only two men living to have cleaved the head of a dragon clean off, and all in a single swipe!" He bellowed out another echoing bark of laughter, and a moment later, he was clutching the juvenile's head by one of its horns and holding it aloft, as his men cried out their praise.

"It was *just* a baby," Leshie said, stamping over angrily. "You kill its mother and maybe you might impress…"

An ear-splitting shriek filled all the air.

The laughter stopped at once.

Saska's eyes shot up.

From the north she sighted a great winged shadow, swooping their way over hills kissed by the rising sun. Light spilled forth from the east, red and dusky gold, and through the wakening skies came their foe.

My foe.

"Dragon!" someone roared.

And suddenly all hell broke loose.

The Butcher was running for his tent to fetch his breastplate, calling for Merinius to help him. Garth the Glutton had not yet dressed; belly hanging free, gobble wobbling below his chin, he stared up at the dragon in mute horror as the wine he'd drunk last night emptied down his leg. Leshie stood with Slack Stan and Marco of the Mistwood, blades at the ready, crouched and poised to flee or fight, whatever might come first. The Nemati soldiers were a mix. Most stood stoutly, spears brandished, shouting orders at one another; several others had moved closer to whatever rocks or cover they could find and one was crawling beneath the carriage in fear. Another had fainted.

The Wall stood utterly still, though. "Good," he said, watching the beast come as though it was a pony trotting toward them in a field. "Are you ready to engage, Saska?"

His composure gave her strength, though she wished her body knew it. Her heart was making a concerted effort to punch right through her chest and breastplate both, and her bowels had gone to water. *I'll piss myself like Garth if I'm not careful. Or worse.* A good grasp of godsteel would help see to that. She wrapped her fingers around the hilt of her sword and the worst of her terror vanished like a leg of lamb down a lion's throat. "I'm ready."

The Wall smiled at her. *My gods, that's rare.* "You remember what I taught you?"

He'd taught her a lot, though she supposed he was referring to the art of dragon-duelling. And there was a great deal to that too. "I remember." *I hope.*

"Good." The dragon was nearing quickly, and growing bigger every second. "It's larger than I thought," Sir Ralston observed. He sounded only mildly concerned, though tried to make a positive out of it. "That serves us. The challenge will be more acute, though I'll be near, and Agarosh…" He craned his neck toward the hilltop, and frowned. The moonbear was not on the perch he'd assumed last night. He was nowhere to be seen, in fact. "He must have gone off to watch the sunrise," the Wall said. "Well, no matter. I'm here. And the others as well." He put a hand on her shoulder and shook her so that her armour rattled, perhaps making sure everything was tightly fixed and fitted. "Are you ready?"

"You've already asked me that."

He nodded, looked around, and then gestured to a large rocky outcrop a few dozen metres away, surrounded on all sides by open rugged ground. "Up there. Go get its attention, like I taught you."

Saska ran. She had no time to think now, no time to doubt it or ask questions. The outcrop was some five or six metres high, shaped almost like a mini pyramid. Saska clambered up the tiers like she did every day in the palace and reached the flattened stone summit. The dragon was closing quickly now, the great grey sheets of skin that webbed its wings rippling as it turned in an arc. She could sense it scanning its foes below and looking at the Wall most of all.

No, look at me. She thrust her blade skyward and bellowed, "You, dragon, I call a duel! Fight me, spawn of Agarath! Fight me to the death!"

It twisted its slender neck to glance at her…then in a sudden dive came crashing down to earth, widening its wings and swinging its legs to land loudly beside the juvenile's corpse in a cloud of dust and grit. The weight of the impact caused Saska to stumble and lose her footing on the uneven ground…and before she knew it she was tripping sideward, legs all a-scramble, her sword slipping from her grasp as she tumbled back down the face of the outcrop shaving juts of rock off its surface along the way.

When she hit the floor at the base of the rock, her bearings were all askew. She scrambled right back to her feet, looking around. *My sword! Where is it! Where!* It was not a good start. Panicking, she saw it lodged halfway up the boulder, caught in a cleft. *It's behind me,* she thought. *It's coming, closing in…*

But when she glanced back she saw that it wasn't. The dragon stood instead by the dead juvenile, sniffing and nudging its body as though to try to make it wake. It was a tender moment, almost tragic. A soft snorting sound was coming from the beast's snout. It sounded almost like weeping.

Its parent, Saska realised, shocked. *Its mother.*

She felt a deep pang of pity for the creature twisting in her gut. Perhaps she just wanted to live free, raise her offspring in peace? This dragon did not seem to be a part of the war, not under the command or control of the Fire Father. For a moment she hesitated, wondering what to do, before she heard the voice of Sir Ralston Whaleheart bellowing in the back of her head. *Never show pity,* he had warned her. *Never show weakness. You do that and you're as good as dead.*

The voice stirred her. *Mother or not, free or not, this dragon will slaughter us all unless I stop it.* She made her decision and spun, climbing straight back up the outcrop to retrieve her blade, then turned at once and without giving it a second thought, thrust the godsteel blade skyward and roared, "You! Spawn of Agarath! Fight me! Fight me to the death!"

Those words didn't sound nearly so bold or valiant this time, though they got the reaction she wanted. The dragon looked up from the corpse of its headless offspring and turned to face her, legs splayed wide, wings slowly furling, lips pulled back and menacing. It was almost entirely grey in colour, with a few patches of faded blue spotting its shoulders and veins of red twisting down its back between spiny studs as sharp as spearheads. Its snout was squat and broad, with curved horns sprouting out the sides. A whipping tail lashed left and right behind it, looking like some long bendy serrated knife, tipped with a double-sided axe.

And those eyes. Fierce and hateful, they bored into her very soul. *It takes me for the killer of its child,* she thought. *So be it.* "Come at me!" she roared.

The dragon did not disappoint. With a trumpeting screech, it charged, crashing straight into the boulder atop which she stood as Saska dashed backward and dropped to the ground, taking cover behind it. The impact was so violent that half the rock came shattering free, splintering and spinning away across the plains in a shower of fragments and shards.

Dust and smoke filled the air. Saska dashed away at once, finding herself in open space away from the camp, carpeted in bits of loose pebbly stone and the occasional tuft of dried brown sedge. She could see the Butcher now in his breastplate, watching with Merinius at his side. Stan and Marco were there as well, and some of her grandmother's men too, though Garth the Glutton was nowhere to be seen. *Changing his breeches, no doubt.* She saw the Wall standing with dual greatswords drawn, waiting should he need to engage. But all that was seen in a glimpse. The dragon had spotted her and was prowling forward again and she needed to give it her full focus. Somewhere, away with the others, she could hear the sound of Leshie cheering her on.

The next few minutes were a frantic blur, the tension of the duel threatening to overwhelm her senses. Rolly had told her how to fight against all sorts of dragons. Small light ones, big heavy ones, skinny ones and brawny ones, long ones and short ones, dragons who favoured their long lashing tails and those who liked to blow fire and those who preferred to use their weight and power to crush a man dead between their jaws.

"Half the world thinks every dragon fights the same, that they're all just wild and frenzied, but that isn't true," her guardian had taught her. "Each is like a Bladeborn knight, favouring the forms they're best at. Some Bladeborn fight always in Blockform, others prefer Strikeform. A big confident knight might spend an entire bout in Powerform, though only if the opponent is right. Dragons are the same, Saska. They have many weapons to choose from, but commonly favour one or the other depending on their foe. But beware. As the best knights will move between the forms, so the best dragons will move between their weapons. Tails, claws, fangs, fire. Be ready for them all."

She was trying to remember all that now, though it wasn't easy. She'd read somewhere that over half of the men who ever fought a dragon recalled almost nothing of the bout afterward. *Dragon duels are only as good as those stood watching*, she recalled reading in a book once. Or something to that effect. It seemed to be the case with her, as she kept her distance, darting back every time the dragon drew near.

Focus, she thought. *Focus, Saska.* She needed to learn how the beast liked to fight, as Rolly had taught her, so she might turn that to her advantage. She could hardly do that if she couldn't even remember the beast's last move. *Focus, watch…and remember,* she thought. Rolly had been explicit in that. Dragon-duelling was like a game of chess, moving pieces on a board. Not all the time, no. Sometimes they'd be a chaotic rush of attacks and strikes and little more, especially when one or the other was significantly more deadly than their opponent, but in an even fight, with knight and dragon well matched, they involved more strategy than people thought.

Saska was learning that firsthand now. *Wait*, she told herself, over and over again. *Wait, watch, remember.* She scrambled and dodged, ducked and danced and kept her distance as Rolly taught her. *A dragon is inherently violent,* she thought. *Some are rageful, others chaotic, others more mild, but violence underpins them all. Wait. Always wait, and watch. Eventually they will show their hand.*

She kept her footing wide, her blade held two-handed before her, side-stepping, backtracking, never running or showing her back lest she must. *Always keep your eye on it. Always keep a strong grip of your sword.* If she lost that, she was as good as gone. *Frustrate it, make it lose patience. Your armour will help protect you,* she thought. *Never give it an easy target. Keep moving, left and right and backward. Judge its speed when it surges and keep the appropriate gap. And watch that tail. Look for the signs that it will spin. A long tail means a longer gap. If it favours the tail, time the strike and try to cut the tip. Many dragons have weapons there, but be careful, it may be a feint…*

It all ran through her mind, on and on and on. She tried to sift through it, but was seeing no patterns emerge. Her foe seemed to sense her doubt. It was prowling about her, stalking, waiting. At first it had been attacking more often, but now…

And then she heard it.

It was like she'd been underwater, and suddenly come up for breath, and on breaking the surface heard the sound of the sea, the creaking of the ships, the ringings of the bells in the harbour.

My gods, there's another one.

She could hear it behind her, raging through the camp. She could hear the men shouting and screaming.

Don't turn, she thought. *Don't turn… don't…*

She turned.

She couldn't help herself.

Glancing back she glimpsed fire, smoke, blood, saw movement. One man was aflame, running aimlessly away into the hills, arms flailing. Another was now just legs and a lower torso, the top half missing entirely, pink entrails spread across the rocks. She saw a whizzing red form moving through the smoke, and a massive silver one too, and another with a crimson cloak billowing at his back.

But mostly she saw the dragon. And it was much bigger than hers.

She heard a whoosh of air, the sound of something moving fast. She tried to turn back, but too late. Something hard hit her in the right flank, knocking her aside with the force of a ram. It sent her tumbling, barreling end over end across the rocky terrain, her bones juddering and rattling in her armour.

A roar shook the world. Heavy footsteps were drawing near. She blinked and breathed and managed to stand on shaky legs. She felt something sticky and warm at her side. *Blood*, her dazed mind thought. She felt no pain, though, nothing. Only weakness as she stood and peered through the visor of her faceplate and saw the blurred form of a dragon draw near.

No, she thought, *this…this can't be it.*

She tried to steel herself, gather her breath, but the assault had rendered her muddled and confused. Her right arm went up to defend herself, only to find that her sword was no longer there. Her steel gauntlets closed around air, her legs were unsteady, the dragon had stopped before her and yet there was still a loud pounding through the earth.

But who? The other dragon?

She blinked and looked up and saw a huge maw opening, ringed with lines of savage white teeth. *It's going to crush me, eat me*, she thought. Then she saw the orange-red glow sizzling and burning at the back of the dragon's throat, and knew it would cook her alive instead.

She blinked again. Everything seemed to be going in slow motion. It felt almost like a dream, a nightmare. She searched at her feet for her sword, but it wasn't there. Then she saw it, a glint of slender silver thirty metres away, and realised the dragon had knocked her that far.

It was the tail, she thought. She could feel the warm blood oozing out of her side now, see it dripping down her silver armour to feed the rugged red earth. *That tail-axe. Or maybe a spike or horn. It pierced through my plate, cut my flesh. I'm going to have to ask the Butcher to get me better armour...*

Her thoughts were inane, the mental babbling of the doomed. She made a weak effort to dash for her blade but her head was still foggy and her legs did not seem to work. She hit the ground again, and worked up to her knees.

They'll have to find someone else now, was her final thought, as she saw that great maw glowing bright with hot flame. *Amron Daecar, he can do it. The heir of Varin...it was only ever symbolic anyway...*

She felt heat, and a great roaring, and then a tremendous sudden cold.

Two great beasts went to battle above her, as the darkness pulled her down.

30

Amara

"I'm leaving," she said, as she poured the wine. "Only for a week or two, I hope. I'll be back before you know it." She turned and handed him a cup, then took a long relaxing gulp. Wine never tasted so good as it did after laying with a man, Amara had always thought. And more specifically her husband, seeing as he was the only man she'd ever lain with.

"Where?" Vesryn asked her.

She drank in the sight of him, lying propped on his elbow upon that bed. The bed was filthy, yes, the mattress soiled and thin, yet her husband remained a fine figure of meat and muscle and perfectly positioned black body hair, plenty to make a woman swoon. "Please, Vesryn, I'm trying to concentrate. You've had your wicked way with me…now put on some clothes." She flung him a robe.

He stood and threw it over his shoulders. "Stop trying to avoid the question. Where are you going, Amara?"

"Ilivar," she told him.

He gave a sigh. "Let me guess. This has to do with Lillia?"

"Who else would it have to do with? Your brother sent his good-father several letters asking him to return her, and he hasn't. I've since taken up the challenge myself and a challenge it is, because I've had no reply either. So I'm going." She drank down her wine. "And don't try to talk me out of it. You'd just be…"

"Wasting my breath, I know. Though down here I've got plenty of breath going spare. You're the only one who comes and visits me, you know. And not so often either."

"I have other things to do. My life does not revolve around my poor doomed husband, you know. In fact, Lady Bradbury is of the opinion that I shouldn't be coming at all. She's even offered to set me up with some handsome suitors, so I can move on from you once and for all."

Vesryn sat back down on his narrow bed and put his broad back against the dark stone wall. "She's not wrong, Amara," he said in a limp voice.

354

"You're still young enough to live a life when I'm gone, and remarry. Maybe even have a child. I don't think being a widow will suit you."

Then break out, she wanted to say. *Snap the gaoler's neck the next time he comes to feed you, take a godsteel sword off one of the guards above, and escape.* She did not make the suggestion, of course. Amara Daecar had promised herself she would not interfere, and would keep to that promise no matter what. And besides, she'd come to rather like the gaoler. She'd prefer not to see Vesryn snap the poor man's neck.

Amara stepped back over to the desk and sat down, crossing her legs. She plucked a grape from the bowl she'd brought him and popped it into her mouth. "I've other news," she said. "Some good, some bad. What would you like to hear first?"

"The bad, I suppose."

"Dalton Taynar is First Blade."

Vesryn did not look surprised. "You told me that already. You said Amron was taking the Sword of Varinar to Crosswater, to give to him."

She thought back. "Oh yes, I suppose I did. It was a little more complicated than that in the end, though."

"How so?"

"Well, according to Lady Horsia Harrow, Sir Brontus Oloran challenged Dalton for the right to be First Blade. They fought, she wrote me, in the castle yard. An epic battle by all accounts under sun at first, and then heavy rains, before Dalton came out the victor. The weather helped him, Horsia says. Before the rain came down, Brontus was strolling to victory."

Her husband drew on his wine, pondering that. "Are they to stay at Crosswater?"

"Some, yes," she told him. "Amron is taking a large force to bolster the defence of the coast, as I understand it, though others will remain to hold the Vanguard, should King's Point be breached. I had a letter from Cousin Gereth as well. He said that Lord Borrington has been asking for more men, though Gereth has none to give him. Apparently there's some fear that the Agarathi will cross the Tidelands."

"It's the way I'd go," Vesryn said. "Those land bridges give direct access to the Twinfort. Destroy it, and they'd be able to march right around the Greenwood until they reach the High Way, then follow it all the way here. The river route is more stoutly defended. The Vanguard in particular is monstrously strong."

He comes alive when talking of war and battle. Curse that he's not involved. "I saw Elyon, you know," she said, changing the subject. "The last time I came here. When I left he was waiting outside the palace. He'd flown all the way from the Lakelands in a single day."

"A single day?" The look of pride on Vesryn's face made Amara smile.

"Well, so he said. He might have been fibbing, though. You know Elyon." She grinned and had another grape. "He stayed the night to recover, and we ate together in Keep Daecar. Just the two of us. We spoke about you, Vesryn."

"I'm sure he had nothing good to say."

"To the contrary, I think he's starting to come around. He's a sympathetic boy, always was. Elyon only ever needs time, and he's had plenty of that now to think things over. He may never truly forgive you, but he's starting to understand you. He may even put in a good word, with his father. All this business…perhaps it may yet go away."

Her husband's eyes were mirthless. "It won't go away, Amara, and it'll do you no good to think like that. You said it yourself. Your poor *doomed* husband."

"Poor, certainly," she said, not wanting to dwell on it. "You do take joy in pitying yourself."

"I'm a pitiful creature. It only makes sense."

She smiled at that and had another taste of wine. It was the Azore vintage that she'd promised him the last time. She found herself suddenly annoyed that he'd made no mention of it. "You've not thanked me for the wine, or complimented its taste."

He tipped the cup back and drank. "It's very nice, Amara, thank you."

"Better than that piss you were drinking. I spoke to our friend the gaoler, and he admitted to me that he liked to relieve himself in your jug."

"The man must work in a brewery in his spare time then. His piss tastes awfully like ale to me. And you drank it too, don't forget."

She laughed at that. "Your sense of humour returns, sweet husband. Do try to retain it while I'm gone."

Her husband shifted a leg up onto the bed and leaned back again. "You shouldn't be going," he chided. "It's too dangerous to be travelling right now. You're safe here in Varinar. Lillia's safe in Ilivar. Can't you just let that be?"

"No. Sir Connor will be with me, and Sir Penrose and Carly too, and Jovyn has been given special leave from the Steelforge as well. I spoke to him last night. You should have seen his face when I mentioned I was intending to go back and get her. He tried to hide it, of course, but there was no hiding it from me. He loves her. It's adorable, really."

"He's only a boy."

"A boy of fifteen, and Lillia's turned fourteen now as well. It's perfectly normal to know love at that age."

Vesryn frowned in thought. "Yes, I suppose Lillia would have had her birthday by now." He studied her face. "Are you angry that you missed it? You've always loved celebrating Lillia's birthday with her."

I'm furious, she thought. *Raging and wrathful.* "She'll have more," she only said. "That sour old bastard Brydon might steal her away from me for one birthday, but he certainly won't for two. I will make sure of that, Vesryn, believe me."

He was looking at her in that way of his, judging her, showing his disapproval.

"What?" she demanded. "You don't think he'll give her up? You think Lord Bastard will deny me from even seeing her."

"He certainly will if you call him Lord Bastard. If you go in there screaming and ranting at him, he's hardly likely to hand her over, Amara.

And I'm not sure two knights, a squire, and a teenage sellsword are going to be enough to win her back by force."

Then come too, she thought, but didn't say. "I have a letter of Amron's to take with me," she told him instead. "Written with an explicit instruction to hand her over, as her lord and father…"

"And king?"

"No. He still refuses the title. But those other two should be enough."

"They won't be."

"Why not?"

"Because he's been ignoring you all along. Why should that change now?"

She didn't want to confront that question. "If he doesn't, we'll find another way."

"You'll break her out?" The question was full of rebuke.

Oh how well you know me. "I'm *going*, Vesryn," she said, avoiding the question. "And I asked you *not* to try to talk me out of it. I've had enough of rattling around Keep Daecar like a ghost in chains, doing nothing. I'm going, OK? I'm bloody well going."

"Fine." Vesryn stood and stepped over to her chair, looked down at her a moment, and then lifted her to her feet. "Dance with me," he said.

"What?" She was taken aback. *Did I mishear?* "No, what are you talking about?" She tried to pull her hands away but he had them in his grasp. "Vesryn, I'm not going to dance with you in this cell. Have you lost your wits? There's not even any music playing."

"Then I'll sing." He smiled and went through with his threat, humming out a tune as he swayed.

She looked at him in stark disbelief. "But you're…you're a terrible singer. You always were, Vesryn. Get off."

"No."

He stepped her out of the cell and into the hall of the dungeon, twirling her around as their shadows played across the floor. Against her better judgement she went with it, her robes fluttering. And then all of a sudden she was laughing, the sound echoing off the dull stone walls. "This is ridiculous," she chuckled. *Ridiculous and just what I needed, as he knew.* "I doubt anyone's ever danced down here before."

"I doubt anyone's made love here either." He spun her around and pulled her to his chest and kissed her. "Do you have time for a different type of dance?"

"*Again?* Gods, what's gotten into you?" She swooned at the rugged smile on his bearded face.

"If you're to be gone a while, I would make our time count. I'm not sure you've ever looked so beautiful…I'm not sure anyone ever has…"

She did not need any further convincing. Lies though they were, she drove him back through the door of his cell and climbed atop him on the bed. A moment later their robes were off and they were youths again, vigorous and insatiable, rolling about as they had when they first wed. It was the threat of impending doom, she knew, the endless *tick tick ticking* of the clock. That thought made everything more intense. *And we must make every moment count.*

They ate afterward, and drank down the rest of the wine, feeding one another, laughing, casting their worries aside. It was what she wanted when she was here, what she'd asked of him the last time. *When I'm here with you, I'm here*, she had said. *Be here with me too, here, now, not back in your past with your demons, or in a future that has not yet come.* And so the seconds turned to minutes and the minutes to hours and before too long, it was time for her to go. It was the part she dreaded the most, leaving him. She dressed and gathered up the cups and jugs and plates, and put them all on the pewter tray she'd brought down.

Vesryn sat in silence all the while. "Must you go?"

Don't, she thought. *My heart cannot take it.* "Will it make a difference if I stay longer? I have to go at some point, Vesryn."

Her husband nodded and firmed himself. He seemed annoyed at the lapse in strength. "I know. I only fear for you on the road, Amara. Your company is capable, but should a dragon attack you, you'll not stand a chance."

"That would depend on the dragon, Vesryn. And I'm quite certain Sir Connor would disagree with you. He fancies himself a dragonkiller, you know."

Vesryn saw right through the lie. "Sir Connor Crawfield would never make such a claim. He's far too modest."

"Fine. It was Carly who said it," she admitted. *And who knows, perhaps she could?*

Vesryn picked up the tray and carried it out of the cell for her, placing it on the steps. For a moment he looked up the winding stairway as it bled into darkness, wondering. Then he spun back and marched into his cell. "Lock the door, before I do something stupid."

She turned the key and pulled it out, then gave him a kiss through the bars. "We'll come to no harm, I promise. A week, perhaps a little more, and you'll see me striding down these stairs again, with Lillia at my side."

A shadow passed over his face. "She may not want to come, Amara. When she finds out the things I've done…"

"Perhaps she doesn't need to know. Or perhaps she'll forgive you anyway. Let's just get her safely home first, shall we? We can trouble ourselves with the *what ifs* later."

He nodded, fingers clinging to the rusted iron bars and he watched her make for the steps. Her legs felt wobbly, weak as grass. *I hate this. I hate leaving him.* She had no choice, though. She was about to bend down and pick up the tray when Vesryn said, "You never told me the good news."

She turned around. "Oh? Did I not?"

"No. Unless that about Elyon was it? This dubious notion that he might speak up for me to his father."

Amara shook her head. "It's about Sunsilver."

"*Sunsilver?* What? What is it?"

She smiled. *Gods he loves that horse.* "He's back, Vesryn. I suppose he must have slipped away from that merchant you sold him to in Rasalan, and found his way back here He was spotted outside the city gates by one of the watchmen who recognised him as your horse. I've had him brought to the stables at Keep Daecar."

Her husband's eyes glistened. "He…he came back? All this way. For…for me?"

She smiled. Vesryn had sold Sunsilver to gain passage across the Sibling Strait after he went on the run from Harrowmoor. It had wounded him to part with his magnificent chestnut stallion, yet at the time he had no choice. "For you, yes," she said. "He crossed the whole north for you. Your bond… it's as the Fireborn with their dragons, the Lightborn with their cats and wolves and bears. It was always special, Vesryn. Sunsilver doesn't care what you've done."

He did not seem able to summon words. All he could do was smile, and think, and blink the tears from his eyes. Never had a man and horse been so tightly bonded as the pair. There was a beauty in his reaction that made her want to cry too.

Eventually, he cleared his throat. "Thank you, Amara, for telling me. It makes me happier…knowing he's near, and safe. But…would you do something for me?"

"Of course. Anything."

"Don't let him go to a lesser man. When I'm gone, choose someone noble to ride him, someone good. Someone worthy of him, Amara. Choose…choose a better man than me."

She nodded, wordless, and picked up the tray. *There is no better man*, she thought, *leastways not to me.* She gave her husband one last smile, then turned and fled up the steps, before he might see her tears.

31

Amilia

Amilia was watching the dwarf again. "What did you say his name was?"

"He's got a few," Captain Wilkins answered. "The Pipe Prophet, the Smoking Seer. Those smokes of his show the future, some say, and places far from here." He shrugged. "What his real name is, I've never known. Most just call him Black-Eye."

Amilia didn't need to ask why. Even from a distance, it was clear enough that one of his eyes was black and the other blue. "Why not Blue-Eye?" she wondered.

The scruffy old captain showed a brown smile. "Mayhaps they call him that someplace else. He's lingered around Blackhearth for some years now…maybe that has something to do with it."

"Has he sailed with you before?"

"Aye, a few times." The captain had a swig of whiskey. His other hand clutched lazily at the wheel as the caravel Nancy rolled upon the waves. To the west, the shore of North Tukor worked away into the distance, with the occasional fishing village or coastal town wedged among the rocks or laid out behind some wild shingly strand. "Black-Eye likes to hop the Mercy a couple o' times a year," the man went on. "Bring those gifts of his to Swanshallow and such. People pay good coin to seek his council. If your gallant knight has any left, you might want to use it. He'll tell you your future."

I know my future, Amilia thought. *I know everyone's future. Darkness and death and doom.* She said nothing.

Captain Wilkins had another gulp of whiskey, then hung the skin from a hook on his salt-stained leather belt. "It's Sir Munroe, isn't it?" he said, out of the blue. "Your knight. Sir Munroe Moore, of the King's Guard."

Amilia looked over at him with a frown. "How long have you known?"

"All along," he said proudly. "Well, as close as makes no matter, anyhow. Thought I recognised him when I met you at the Swanshallow docks. But I was drunk, and it was dark, so couldn't be certain. When I saw him in the light of the morning, though, I knew it was him."

360

"You've seen him before?" It was the only thing that made sense to her. Knowing a name was one thing, knowing a face was something else. "Where?"

"Oakshore," he said. "I was ferrying goods down the Sibling Strait some years back, and saw him with King Godrin. The king was doing one of his circuits of the realm, meeting with the smallfolk, hearing of their trials and troubles, all that. He was always a man of the people, Godrin. Only once he got old did he keep to the palace."

"It must have been a while ago then," the princess said. Godrin had been deep into his nineties when her foul husband hacked his throat open to steal his throne. She understood that his travelling days were long behind him by then.

"Aye, a decade or so," the captain answered. "But I'm good with faces, as I told you." He gave her a knowing smile.

She sighed. "So I'm guessing you know who I am as well?" She might as well just come out and confess it. By now she was largely safe from harm, and the captain had proven faithful during their short voyage, as Astrid had said he would.

"Aye, my queen, I know who you are."

"I'm not a queen." She looked to the shoreline of her homeland, wishing she could leap off the boat and swim. "It was a mistake, me ever leaving Tukor. I'm just a princess again now, captain."

"Queen, princess, jewel, I'll call you any title you please, m'lady."

"That last will do just fine." She turned her eyes up the coastline once more, her eyes ever drawn to the lands of her birth. The crossing from Swanshallow had been easy enough, barring a couple of days of rough weather when a storm had come blowing up from the south to push them off their course. It hadn't lasted long, though, and when the winds waned and skies cleared, the captain had steered them safely to the sanctuary of the coast, avoiding the perils that lay to the north. Even at this time of year, ice floes were common, and larger icebergs too, and the waves up there could get as tall as the main mast, the captain had told her, enough to tip a ship over and send her down to Daarl's Domain.

And there's the Lonely Isle too, the princess thought, with a shudder. It was cloaked all year round in storms and fog and thunderous waves, with sharp rocks and savage reefs lingering beneath the waters to snare any ship that dared get near. The captain had regaled her of the tale of the *settlers and the madman*, when they'd sat on deck one night under a black and moonless sky.

"Hundreds of years ago, it was," he'd said, in a low and sinister voice. "Forty settlers took ship from Rasalan, seeking out some new place to make a home, families bound and bonded by blood. There were greybeards among them for their wisdom, and children for the laughter they would bring. Men to build and women to weave. Through the harsh storms they made it to the island, and by some stroke of luck, they found a pebbly beach on which to land. Beyond lay a harsh world of rock and cliffs, but it didn't stop them, oh no. Two men set off to find a route inland, and when they returned, they did so smiling. 'There are woods there,' one called out.

'Woods and rivers and fertile fields.' 'And game,' said the other, 'we saw rabbit and deer and wild hog, all drinking at the steams. And fruiting trees and root vegetables too, so abundant we could not count them.' The rest of the settlers had cheered and wept and praised the gods for this gift. It was all they had been searching for, a paradise o' boon and bounty. Yet they did not know of the malice that lurked there. For the Lonely Isle…it is cursed.

"It started well enough, though. They built their log cabins and cleared their fields to grow wheat, and hunted the woods for meat. They had brought livestock with them too, some goats and sheep and chickens, so they were not in want of cheese or milk or eggs, and in the steams and little lakes they found fish as well, and crabs and cockles too. For a year or so they lived like this, working by day and feasting by night, enjoying the fruits of their toil. The children grew, and their parents coupled, and soon many of the women were with child. Then one day the strongest man among them stood up and said, 'We have lived here happy for a year, yet the shadow o' doubt still lingers in my mind o' what lurks beyond these lands.' He had pointed north, where the island rose up into hills and mountains, all clothed in pine and spruce and grand old sentinels. 'I will leave on the morrow, to make certain these lands are clear o' perils and dangers unseen. If there are terrors to the north, I will find them, and slay them. I will make certain we are safe.'

"So at dawn the next day he left, with another of their stoutest hunters at his side - his own brother, some of the legends say, though others just say he was a friend. Either way, the pair went off on their way. For a month they were gone, and by then the worries and whispers began to spread that maybe they would never return. But then, on one bright summer's afternoon, a figure was spotted walking toward them from the hills. He had his axe slung across his shoulder, and his hair and beard were long and wild, yet they knew at once it was the head hunter…though where his companion was, they could not say. He gathered them around and told them. 'I return, yet alone. Our brother did perish on the mountain slopes, slipping on a treacherous path. I could not save him, though I did try. Yet the rest o' us can now rest easy…for what perils I found I did slay, as I said… and now…we are safe.'

"He had smiled, then, in a sort o' strange and unsettling way, and a ripple o' nerves went through the villagers. This man was different, they sensed, not the same as when he'd left. Something had happened t'him in those hills, something dark, something he would not say or speak of no matter how many times he was asked. For a few days, they began to wonder if he'd killed his brother himself, yet none had the courage to ask him or accuse him of being a kinslayer. All the same, they got worried by the way he looked at them, the way he smiled and spoke. And just then…well, that's when all the murders started happening. The first was only a few nights after, when they heard a bloodcurdling scream ring out through the night, and found a woman in her bed, savaged at the gut and hacked open at the neck. Two nights after that, an old greybeard was found burned to death after falling into the campfire, and the next morning they found a huntsman hanging upside down from a tree, his insides dangling all the way to the ground as the crows pecked out his eyes."

Amilia had felt compelled to break in at that point in the tale. She had enough darkness in her own life and didn't need to hear some horror story to disrupt her sleep yet further. "So he went mad and killed everyone?" she'd said. "If that's how this story ends, I'll have you spare me all the gory detail."

The captain had looked a bit disappointed. "But the gory detail's the best part, m'lady. I've not even told you o' the babies he carved from their mother's wombs or the children he hacked to pieces or the…"

"Enough," she broke in. "I don't want to hear it, captain. Just tell me how the story ends."

"Well…needless to say, as these murders all happen, the rest o' the settlers know it's him. By the time they all gather the courage to confront him, he's done with all his tricks and he just lays into them all with his wood axe, cutting them into ribbons. The story goes he was inhabited by some nameless malice when he went off into those hills, some corrupted spirit o' a forgotten time that he stirred from its long dark slumber. They say this man is still there, walking the Lonely Isle in search o' death. Every bird and beast has fallen to his axe now. It's why no one goes there. They fear the madman's wrath."

Amilia rolled her eyes. "Nonsense. More likely the island is used as some pirate's den, and they spread this story around so that they could operate undisturbed. That's all it is, captain. I'm sure there never was a madman at all."

All the same, she'd lost sleep that night thinking about it, and supposed that was the whole point. *I never want to go near that godforsaken place as long as I live,* she had thought, and no doubt most others thought the same. Nonsense or no, it seemed unwise to take the chance, and there were still the snags and rocks and waves to consider, and the thick haunting fogs besides. By the time the captain had steered them back into sight of the Tukoran coast, she'd breathed a sigh of relief that this fearful island had not drawn them into its snare. That had been only yesterday, and since then she'd spent her every waking hour staring out at the coastline, aching to feel the sand and stone of Tukor beneath her feet.

She turned to face the captain again as he swallowed a measure of whiskey from his skin. "Do you always sail drunk?"

He let out a bark of laughter. "Need more than a few swigs of whiskey to get me drunk, my lady. No, this skin o' mine is just to keep me sharp. I don't get drunk when I'm aboard my Nancy." He smiled that brown and broken smile of his as he gave the wheel a salacious stroke. "I'll wait till we get to Blackhearth for that."

Blackhearth. It was still another day or so sail along the coastline, waves and weather depending, and Amilia would sooner stop here if she could. *Every mile takes us further from Ethior,* she thought, *further from my uncle and his escort and Ilithor and my brother Ray.* She looked westward along the coast and spotted a few fishing boats in the distance, gathered within the broad embrace of a sandy bay. Beyond lay a cluster of hovels and shacks built of wood and mortared in mud. It looked a simple place, but she thought she might as well ask anyway. "How about that village there? Might it be possible to disembark and make for Ethior from here?"

"Aye, if you like. You'll find no horses, though."

Thought as much. "Further on, then?" Amilia knew this coastline but barely, having spent most of her life safe in the bosom of Ilithor and its surrounding lands, the mountains and valleys and pretty silver streams, the fields and meadows that opened to the east with their old woods and lively market towns and rustic traveller inns. North Tukor was almost as alien to her as the Highplains of Rasalan had been. *I do not know my own country*, she reflected. Besides an occasional trip to Ethior, she had never even crossed north of the Clearwater Run. And Blackhearth was just as foreign to her too. "Is there nowhere between here and Blackhearth we can make port?" she finished.

The grey-haired captain gave a nod. "Make port, aye. We can do that at any one of these villages, m'lady. Waters are shallow, and there are treacherous sandbanks and hidden shoals everywhere, but no reason why I can't drop anchor in deeper water and row you in on a skiff."

She couldn't tell if he was being sarcastic or not. "Then..?"

"Then you'd be stranded," he said, "and would have to make your way on foot. Horses you might find, aye, but one that can carry a man like Sir Munroe Moore?" He shook his shaggy head. "Well, I'd say you'd have a better chance o' turning this whiskey o' mine into water and convincing me it's wine. No, it'd take a big strong purpose-bred destrier to bear that man, lest he cast aside his armour and blades and ride in nought but leather and fur...and something tells me he won't be doing that."

"He won't," Amilia agreed. She felt stupid for pestering him about these horses. It was so obvious they'd need a special breed for Sir Munroe to ride.

The old captain gave her a wondering look. "There might be another way, though." His eyes glanced fore to the main deck, as if to see if they were being overheard. Other than the old dwarf Black-Eye, who was lounging atop a pile of nets, smoking on his pipe, and several deckhands and sailors seeing to their sundry duties, the main deck and forecastle were both quiet. The quarterdeck, meanwhile, hosted only Amilia and the old man.

"We're alone," she told him, as if he needed it said. "What are you suggesting, captain?"

He leaned in, forcing her to endure the unpleasant reek of his breath. "I got some herbs, m'lady, tucked away in my cabin. You know, the sort a man might take when they're having trouble sleepin'..."

"Like *nightleaf?*" she ventured.

"Aye, just that. Powerful stuff, in ample dosage, and tasteless too." He gave her another suggestive look, though left the rest unsaid. It didn't take much for Amilia to puzzle out his meaning.

"Are you suggesting we drug Sir Munroe, Captain Wilkins? To what end, exactly?"

"That'd be down to you. If you and Astrid wanted to go on your way without him, I wouldn't mind lending a hand in that. Slip him a bit of nightleaf and he'd be out for hours. Plenty o' time for us to make port somewhere and find you some horses."

She shook her head. Helpful as the captain was trying to be, she'd not risk putting him or his men in danger. "If Sir Munroe awoke to find us gone, he'd be raised to wroth and might kill you. I'll not have you die to save me a few days in the saddle."

The captain shrugged. "How about we throw him overboard instead? Drug him, tie him, and toss him. I know what he did, m'lady. Half the realm knows. That man's a traitor and deserves everything that's coming to him." He spat to the side.

Amilia was growing uneasy at this line of conversation. "I'll not condone murder, captain," she said, making that perfectly clear. "Sir Munroe's judgement will come when we reach Ethior. Once in my uncle's keep, I'll decide what is to be done with him."

He bobbed those bony shoulders, snatched his whiskey skin from his belt, and took a swig. "As you wish, m'lady."

The waters were growing choppy, the winds stirring the sea. Nancy cut through them all the same, energetically hopping from wave to wave. Amilia had a strong enough stomach for the sea for the most part, though had experienced a couple of queasy mornings aboard the caravel that had seen her retching over the railings with Astrid stroking at her back. Sir Munroe had had it a great deal worse, though. He spent much of his time in his cabin, trying to hide the fact that he was 'no true Rasalanian' as the captain liked to say. "Every trueborn man o' Rasalan relishes the churn o' the sea," Wilkins had said. "A Rasal with a weak stomach has something to hide, we like to say. It's the guilt in there, prodding and poking. There's a man with demons in his guts."

And half the world knew what those demons were.

Amilia took her leave of the scruffy old seafarer, stepping over to the port-side gunwale to watch the coast as it passed. There wasn't much to look at really, though she still smiled to see it. Gusts of wind rifled through her hair and she drank in the salty smell of the sea. Before long they were passing the bay where the little fishing boats were arrayed. Simple men stood upon them, throwing nets in the bustling waters. Further off, the princess could see women moving along the sandbanks, digging for crabs. They all had wicker baskets at their hips, writhing with their treasure, as children ran among their skirts and played games of hide and seek among the sedge and grasses that grew along the beach.

She got a better look at the men in the boats as they drew nearer. *Grey-beards and cripples*, she thought. *Those left untouched by my grandfather's cruel muster.* She saw stooped backs and withered arms, grey hair and spotted scalps and tired, drawn-out faces, seamed and wrinkled by the passing of the years. Some of the old men were struggling to pull in their nets. Others could barely throw them more than a few feet from the skiff, frail as they were. She even saw a man with his left arm missing at the elbow, and another who stood propped on a wooden crutch, his right leg gone entirely. Those two were younger men, it looked, crippled in some accident or born that way from birth she couldn't know. *I'm surprised my grandfather did not march them off to war all the same,* she thought sourly. "If you can fish, you can fight," she could almost hear him say.

Bastard.

As she looked out at those boats, a drift of smoke came cavorting past her eyes, swirling into the shape of a man flying through a shroud of fog, or so it seemed to her eyes. She blinked and looked again and the vision was gone, the smoke just smoke, dispersing on the breeze. She turned her eyes sharply to her right and saw the dwarf called Black-Eye grinning at her from atop his pile of nets. *Ignore him,* she thought, *he's just playing his games…* though her curiosity quickly got the better of her. She marched straight down the steps to stand over him. "What was that?" she demanded.

"Smoke," he said, with a grin. He had a long grey beard that spanned the entire length of his body, the weight of it adding a hunch to his back. Age had something to do with that too, the princess suspected. *There are mountain ranges younger than this dwarf,* she thought to herself, as she looked at him sitting on those nets, with his beard draped over him like a blanket to ward off the cold.

"Smoke?" she said. "Yes, I know it was smoke. But I saw something in it…"

"What did you see?"

She frowned. "I don't know. A man in flight, it seemed to me." She did not know many men who could fly, save Elyon Daecar. "What does it mean?"

His eyes crinkled with amusement. "I just blow the smokes, Your Highness. Not down to me to divine meaning from them."

Your Highness. "So you know who I am as well then?" Her eyes glanced around on instinct, though none of the other men were listening. "Did the captain tell you?"

He grinned playfully. "Smokes told me. And your face, that too. There are none so pretty as the Jewel of Tukor, they say." He had another suck on his pipe then let a billow of smoke scatter to the breeze. Amilia watched it blow off as though expecting to see some other wonder, yet was left disappointed on this occasion.

"You're very puckish for a man your age," she observed.

"Age is just a number," he said to that.

"And what's yours?"

"One hundred and eighty, if you'd believe it."

"I don't. Men don't live that long anymore."

"Suppose I'm more than a man, then." He drew on his pipe and blew, and the smokes fluttered off like a flock of birds. Amilia supposed that was his way of proving he was 'more' than a man. Then he said, "Be one hundred and eighty-one in few weeks' time, you know. Maybe you want to come celebrate with old Black-Eye? I'll be hosting a roistering ol' shindig at the Whispering Drunk. All my friends are welcome, high and low."

More low than high, she thought, to hear that name. *Some back alley tavern most like.* "Drunks never whisper in my experience," she said. The Tukorans were famous for being loud at feasts, shouting and singing and brawling until the sun came up, and sometimes long into the next day as well, so long as the ale kept flowing, and there was music to be heard.

The imp chuckled. "Not often, no, but some do. Those sharing secrets and such, they like to whisper, don't you think? And ofttimes a man only shares a secret when he's drunk, Your Highness, and brave enough to give it voice."

She peered at him in sudden suspicion. "Do you have some secret you want to share with me?" The question was tinged with distrust. "I've seen you looking at me, dwarf. And always with that mischievous little look in your eye."

"Aye, I do like my *little* looks. Though everything about me is little, isn't it?"

"Not your age," she pointed out. "You must have mage-blood in you if you're telling that true. And these smokes of yours. The captain said you're a prophet. That's mage work."

He nodded, causing that great length of beard to stir. "My mother was a washerwoman, born back in the days of King Tarrin Lukar. He'd be your great-grandfather's great-great-grandfather, something like that. I'm supposin' you know more about him than I do, seeing as he's your blood, though who knows? Mayhaps he's nought but a name in a history tome to you, Your Highness?"

"I know my family history well," she said. Her grandfather had been insistent on that, bleating on as he always did about legacy and the greatness of the Lukar line. In truth most of that history had fled her head now, though the broad strokes of it still stuck. "King Tarrin fought during the Twenty-Third Renewal," she recalled. "He was a strong warrior, redoubtable on the battlefield, though his courage killed him in the end. He led from the front in every fight, the history books say, whether a skirmish or sally or full-blown siege. 'Fires that burn the hottest burn the fastest', my father used to say. Guess that was true of King Tarrin, when he finally bit off more than he could chew."

"Wasn't King Tarrin that did the biting, my lady, but those dragons that chomped him to bits." The old man's lips were mostly hidden between his moustache and beard, but she did not need to see them to know that he was smiling. *No, his eyes do all the smiling he needs. Even the black one.*

"It was one battle too far," Amilia agreed. "You need to temper that fire sometimes, or else it will consume you."

"Wisely said." The imp inclined his head. "Would you like to sit, my lady? I feel awkward having you standing there above me. Should be me standing by all rights, not you. I'm just a lowly little dwarf after all, not some famed princess like you. Or queen. Would you prefer I call you queen, Your Majesty?"

367

"No. I left that title behind when I watched my husband stolen away by a demigod." It clearly wasn't news to him, judging by his lack of reaction. She moved to perch on a crate next to the heap of nets that he'd taken for a day bed. "You knew about that already?"

"Aye."

"From your pipe smoke?"

"From Penny Barlowe," he said. "She's a madam in Swanshallow, and a trader in secrets. Her girls like to lift them from the men they take to bed, and feed them back to Penny for an extra bit o' coin."

"The selling of women and whispers," Amilia mused. "This Penny seems to have combined two timeless trades into one."

"Aye, and she makes a pretty penny from it besides." He chuckled to himself. The penny was an old unit of currency, long since gone into disuse. *Though he probably once used it, old as he is.* "Not to say Penny's pretty, though. Not anymore, at least. Some sotted oaf took umbrage with her tricks when she was young and knocked half her teeth out, crushed her nose, and bashed her right eye up so bad he blinded her. She always likes to say it was the best day of her life."

Amilia frowned. "And why's that?"

"Because no man wanted to bed her after her face had been mangled, so she became a madam instead. Built power and wealth and influence off the back of it, and now everyone knows not to touch her girls. They do that, and they'll get the same treatment as the oaf who made her." His blue eye twinkled. "Oh, Penny got her vengeance, to be sure. Made that oaf wish he'd never been born."

"Good." Amilia was thinking of her beautiful brave knight, Sir Jeremy Gullimer, and how his face had looked when Sir Munroe turned it into a red ruin, all shattered teeth and jutting jaw and eyes so horribly bruised and swollen she could not see what lay beyond them. Suddenly she wanted to take up the captain's offer to drug him, tie him, and toss him overboard. *He says he was just following Hadrin's orders, but still...*

She couldn't get the image out of her mind, no more than she could the rest of it. The tower and the voice and those red, red eyes. How her rat king husband had been quivering and quaking and pleading for his worthless life as the Fire Father loomed before him, an ancient demon risen and reborn. "Is he dead?" she found herself asking. She looked into Black-Eye's black eye. "My husband. Is he dead? Can you see that in your smokes?"

"Let me see." The dwarf shut his eyes, the black one and the blue, and fell into what looked to be a trance. Amilia saw his mouth mumble soundlessly, saw his eyelids flicker, then he opened them up, thrust his pipe between his lips, sucked, and blew. The smoke swirled out and took form, though what they showed she could not make out. A tower? A podium? Was that a man standing before it? Was that an orb she saw? It all lasted but a moment before the winds took the smokes away. The dwarf looked somewhat apologetic. "Never works so well in the open, my lady, and especially not so when we're in motion. I need still air for my smokes. Best come see me down in the Whispering Drunk when we reach Blackhearth."

368

"I'm not going to some sordid sailor tavern," she came right in. It angered her that he would even suggest it.

"Aye, you're right, you're right. When highborn folk like you seek my counsel, I make the effort to come to them, where I can. I'd not want to subject a princess to the uncivilised denizens of the Whispering Drunk, of course."

"No, I should hope not." It didn't matter either way; she'd not be lingering in Blackhearth once they arrived, and she had little interest in prophets and prognosticators anyway, most of whom were no more than tricksters and frauds swindling the ignorant and impressionable of their hard-earned coin. Still, the little man was intriguing enough to keep her company for now, even if he fell into that category. "Have you met many princes and kings, Black-Eye?" she wanted to know.

He smiled, as though sensing her doubts. "Oh aye, many in my time; kings and queens, princes and princesses, lord and ladies of wealth and renown, First Blades and champions all. They seek out old Black-Eye for his counsel and his smokes. Only months ago, in fact, I had the pleasure of meeting a ghost."

"A ghost?" Now she knew he was japing.

"Aye. A *famous* ghost. The Ghost of the Shadowfort. You may have heard of him."

She stared at him in cold shock. "Where…where was this?"

"The Whispering Drunk, where else? He came slinking in all shadowy-like with the Beast o' Blackshaw and a few others at his side, seeking word of far-off lands. Seemed a nice lad to me. Nothing like the monster some make him out to be." He had another suck on his pipe, squinting at her all the while. "Curious. You remind me of him, a little. Something about the nose, maybe, or shape of the mouth."

Amilia didn't want this old dwarf considering the shape of her mouth, no more than having it compared to that foul killer. "The Shadowknight killed my Aleron," she said bitterly. "I had to sit and watch as he hacked through his armour and neck." She had fainted amid the horror of it, overwhelmed by the screaming and shouting and shock among the crowd. "Don't tell me he was a 'nice lad', dwarf. *Never* in my hearing, do you understand?"

The little man gave a solemn nod to that. "Aye, you're right. 'Twas insensitive of me to say as such; I forgot you lost your betrothed to him. Hard to see the truth through your grief sometimes."

"The truth? And what truth is that?"

"That the lad was a pawn, a blade sharpened and honed, to be swung at his master's will. When a man murders another man, it's not the dagger that they throw in the dungeons, my lady."

She could do without the lecture. Amilia Lukar knew all about being a pawn in a grander design. "A dagger doesn't have free will. A man does." She didn't want to talk about this, she knew at once. It only darkened her thoughts and they were dark enough as it was. "You were telling me about your mother. She was a washerwoman, you said. What of your father?"

The dwarf drew his pipe from his lips and laid his hands across his lap. "Never knew much of him, but for what my mother told me. She was a beautiful woman, my mother. Not like you, no…more a simple beauty, a lowborn beauty, you might call it. Either way, she turned a few heads where I grew up, not the sort of woman who's ever short of attention. Anyway, one sunny spring day, some tall knight comes riding through the village, with a fine lambswool cloak on his back and a fancy godsteel blade at his hip. He sees my mother sitting outside her hut, washing basin between her legs, churning at some dirty clothes. Gives her a smile, so the story goes, and comes over to introduce himself. Well, as you can imagine, she goes all swoony for him. He's got these bright kind eyes and tousled brown hair and a jaw that's crafted of stone. She invites him in for a horn of ale, and one thing leads to another. Next morning, this handsome knight's gone off again and nine months later, I squirm my way out through her legs."

Amilia didn't much like the image. "And that's all true, is it?" She knew otherwise, of course. It was a fairytale his mother told him, to hide some fouler truth. That was obvious just to look at him.

"You're wondering how such a union made a monster like me," he said, with that twinkle of mischief in his eyes. "Some village beauty and a tall handsome Bladeborn knight. Aye, I see the holes in that little tale too, my lady."

"Well…you're not Bladeborn, for a start." She frowned. "Are you?"

"Me? No. Not a drop of Varin's blood in me, though mage-blood… that's a different matter."

"So this gallant knight wasn't a gallant knight at all…is that what you're saying? He was a mage instead, and put your mother under some spell to seduce her?"

"Aye, just so. It was some hex, I figure, or else he was strong in the art of illusion. A Shadowcloak, maybe. Clothed himself in the guise of a gallant knight so he might win her heart for a night. How he actually looked…well, that's anyone's guess. Less a handsome knight and more a stunted little thing like me, I would think." He chuckled away to himself, though for her part Amilia found the notion appalling.

"He tricked her, deceived her and allured her with magic. That's as bad as forcing himself upon her. It was rape."

The dwarf shrugged. "Some might say so, but my mother never seemed to have any regrets. To her mind he was a tall handsome knight who gave her an evening she'd never forget, and a beloved son besides. She was happy with the bargain."

"And your father. This wandering mage. Did you ever find out who he was?"

"Alas no. Searched him out for a while, but in the end I saw little profit in it. I've heard many tales o' mages up in the mountains, driven into the shadows by fear o' the commonfolk. Most people hate mages, you'll find, fearing what they don't understand. I've heard that some o' them work among the Shadow Order, to give their lives some purpose." He rubbed his long beard. "Always wondered if I'm sired by one o' those. Some shadow mage come down on a contract, who sought out a bit o' pleasure along the way."

Amilia clenched her jaw to hear him talk about that. "That order should be destroyed. They bring only death and darkness."

"Aye, many think so, the Ghost among them."

She looked at him, unsure.

"That's why he was going back there, with this host o' knights and warriors he'd assembled. To destroy them, my lady, rid the world o' their wickedness." He smiled at the expression of surprise on her face. "See, not such a bad lad after all, when left to his own devices."

"No…perhaps not." She turned her eyes across the deck, staring into the open sea, wondering about all that. *If I'd been left to my own devices, perhaps I'd have walked a different path too,* she thought. *I might have married Sir Jeremy. I might have married someone lower born, much lower born, if they would make me happy.* But she was not born for that, no more than the Shadowknight had been born to live free. *My duty was to marry a king or a prince or a greatlord, to further the greatness of House Lukar. I'm a tool, same as that Shadowknight, honed for a particular purpose.* He had broken free, though, and she'd done the same. *Maybe we're not so different.*

Amilia shifted back on her crate and folded her legs beneath her, adopting a most unprincess-like pose. She wore linen and wool, scuffed and stained, and had dirt beneath her fingernails that had been there for long days. She remembered back to a trip in her youth when she'd gone to visit the lands of House Westermont to the east of Ilithor with her parents and brothers. Lord Marc had been alive then, the first cousin, once removed, of her grandfather, and he had told his third son Bernie to take Robb and Ray out hunting. *But not me,* Amilia recalled. No, she'd been told explicitly to stay in the castle by her lady mother, even though she was several years older than her twin brothers. "You're a lady, and you're not to go out and get dirty like the boys," she'd been told.

So she'd done exactly that. She'd followed them out and gotten as dirty as she could, in defiance of her mother's rules, and returned as filthy as a little princess could hope to be. Her mother had almost fainted when she saw her, though her father had only laughed. "She's a child, Clarris," Amilia remembered him saying. "Not yet a teen. Let her play with the boys every once in a while. She'll become the lady you want her to be soon enough."

But her mother wouldn't have it. She'd grabbed her by the arm and dragged her upstairs to be stripped and scrubbed clean. Amilia could still remember how scalding hot the water was, how her fair skin had gone red all over from the savage scouring her mother inflicted upon her. It had taken ages to get the dirt out from underneath her nails, and her mother's warning still rang in her ears. "If you ever get that much dirt beneath your nails again, I'll have them ripped off to better clean them, do you hear me, young lady?"

Oh, I heard you, mother. I still hear you long years later. Amilia Lukar looked down at her dirty fingernails now, and smiled. *I'm not the perfect little lady you made me anymore, Mother. I'm free now to do as I please, for the short time I have left.*

She turned back to the dwarf. "Have you seen the end of the world?" she asked him.

He met her eyes with a quizzical look on his crinkled face. "The end, my lady?"

"The end," she repeated. "It drove Hadrin mad, seeing it in the Eye. Have you seen it in your smokes? The shadow that will cover the earth?"

"My smokes aren't so far-seeing as the Eye o' Rasalan," he told her. "Nor are they so clear. I've seen some darkness, aye, but there's no foresight in that. It's happening already, clear for all to see. It's why we got heroes, fighting back. And you won't like to hear this, but men like…"

"The Ghost of the Shadowfort," she said for him.

He nodded. "Aye. Him and others, scattered here and there, all doing their part to drive the shadows away. When darkness spreads, there's always light to meet it. It's the clash that will determine the victor, but as to who that'll be…well, that's not for me to say. My smokes are but humble windows to what is or what might be." He gave a chuckle. "And half the time they're wrong."

Then what use are you? She wondered about asking him of her own future, but why bother when she knew it already? *Doom and death and darkness*, she thought. *The shadow will envelop us all.* She stood from her crate. "It's been enlightening, Black-Eye. Thank you for your counsel." *If you can call it that.*

"A pleasure." He stood up from his nest of nets, soaring a full four feet from the ground, as his beard draped down to tickle at his toes. An unseemly smile spread upon his face as he opened out his wrinkled palm and looked up at her.

"Money? You expect me to pay you? You haven't even told me anything of value."

"I told you about the Ghost, how he was headed back home. I told you the pair o' you look sorta alike."

"Yes, you did. And that is utterly useless to me." *He must be joking*, she realised all of a sudden. *This is a misjudged jest, is all.* "And I have no coin to give you, anyway. I'm a princess, not some grubby little trader."

His fingers snapped shut and his hand vanished into his robes. It all happened astonishingly fast. "Aye, you're right. It was most indecorous o' me to even ask. I thought it might make you laugh, my lady, but alas no, I misread the tone."

"So you *were* joking?"

"Course." His eyes gleamed, black and blue. "No, I only ask for coin when a client seeks me out. We were just talking, your ladyship. If you wanted to know your future, you'd have brought along a silver a two."

There was something about the way he said that, something that made her ask - "*Do* you know my future, Black-Eye?" - despite her best intentions not to.

He didn't give an immediate answer, and she sensed this was just a part of his routine. *Make them doubt*, she thought. *Make them doubt and they'll pay.*

Then he looked her up and down, up and down, his eyes slowing, frowning, as they passed her belly. He reached to his pipe, sucked, and blew, and his smokes swirled between them, rising in the shape of a figure lying on a bed...no, two figures, side by side...with shadows standing about them. As before, the vision was but a glimpse, gone in the blink of an eye. Amilia watched the smokes as they spread and dispersed, grey against the blue of the sky.

When she looked down again, there was a troubled look in the dwarf's mismatched eyes. "What did that mean?" she demanded. "Do you know? Or do I need to pay you first?"

He shook his head. "I don't know, my lady. I can't say for certain what you saw. The smokes...sometimes they appear different to one person as they do to another, as clouds do when you gaze at them long enough. You might see a fox and I might see a wolf, or something vastly different."

"And what *did* you see?" She glared at him, but his eyes did not meet hers. Instead they shifted across the ship, to where the stairs led down into the darkness of the decks below.

And from his lips issued a whisper and a warning. "Beware the silver man," he said. "One day...he's going to change."

32

Jonik

He does not know it yet, Jonik thought, as he watched Gerrin lead the doomed man across the yard. *He truly thinks he's to be set free. He thinks I'm to serve him mercy.*

"My lord, a fine day, a fine day it is," called out Kagnor, smiling that gurning smile of his. His hands were tied behind his back and he was dressed in filthy rags, yet all that was soon to pass, he hoped. Those fetters would be cut and they'd give him fresh clothes to wear, and a bag of provisions as well to send him on his way. *A hope as doomed as he is,* Jonik thought. *Just see it done. Get it over with and move on.*

"Are you certain this is what you want?" Harden stood at Jonik's side, his grim voice reduced to a low whisper. "Maybe he's been telling the truth all along. Maybe it's just peace he wants."

Peace, Jonik thought. Kagnor had claimed as such every time Jonik had visited him in his cell, smiling that mawkish smile of his and telling him everything he wanted to hear. When set loose from the fortress, he would be good, he had promised. He'd live an honest life of noble deeds and acts of kindness, and would remain law-abiding to his last day on this earth. He was an old done man, too tired to fight anymore, too worn by all the winters he'd seen to cause trouble in the world below. It was honest labour he sought, and a quite place to live out the rest of his days. The long weeks in his cell had given him time to see the truth of what he'd been, the truth of the order. "I want silence and solitude, that is all," he'd said the last time Jonik visited him, two days ago. "It's in your power to grant me, my lord. Won't you give an old man this last wish?"

Jonik watched that old man stepping toward him, thinking on his words. *I could. I could have rations gathered, fresh clothes fetched. I could send him away down the mountain. I could let him live.*

"Jonik? If you're not certain…"

"I'm certain, Harden," he said. It was what he'd decided, and he could not go back on that now. "Gerrin thinks he's being duplicitous and Cecilia does as well. I trust their judgement. We let him walk free and he'll not seek peace as he says. He'll seek blood and gain, and care not how he gets it. I can't allow that. He has to die."

The man of the Ironmoors did not respond. *He grows distant,* Jonik knew. *Few decisions I make sit well with him now.*

Kagnor continued his approach, Gerrin following a step behind. They passed the heart of the yard where Big Mo had been cremated, the scattered remains of his pyre lying blackened and burnt across the stone. The Shadowmaster gave it a glance. "Been having a bonfire, have we? Aye, can't blame you. It's bitter cold for this time of year."

"It's always cold here," Gerrin grunted. "There's no summer, no spring, only winter. Endless bloody winter."

Kagnor nodded briskly. "Aye. I fancy a nice taste of spring, though. First thing I'll do is find a pretty flowery meadow beside a stream, and sit back and listen to the birds. Always did love the sound of birdsong, and that tinkling a stream makes when it flows. Aye, be nice to hear that again. Haven't been down the mountain in long years now."

Gerrin gave no response, nor did Jonik speak, nor Harden. The winds blew through the fort, stirring the ashes of Big Mo's pyre, and as Kagnor passed them by so some of those ashes swirled about him, clinging to his legs. *Death,* Jonik thought. *The winds know it, even if he doesn't.*

Gerrin gave Kagnor a sharp push to get him moving. "Hurry up. We don't have all day."

"In a rush? Seems to me you've got nothing but time up here." The first signs of doubt were creasing at the corners of Kagnor's black eyes. *Black like his heart,* Jonik told himself. *The order made him so, true, but he's relished it. He was always cruel by nature.* "I hoped a mage or two might come see me off. Momentous occasion, this. Not often a man gets unshackled from the order, is it." He glanced back. "I'm following your lead, Gerrin. And you, my lord," he said to Jonik. "You've both shown me the light."

"Shut up, Kagnor. And face your fate like a man. You know we're not letting you go."

The old Shadowmaster stopped and did a half-turn. "You what, Gerrin?"

"You heard me." Gerrin stepped in and pushed him again, harder this time, so that he stumbled forward, all but losing his footing. "Up." Gerrin pulled him back up straight and guided him the rest of the way until he came face to face with the Ghost of the Shadowfort.

"What is this?" Kagnor had a horrid look on his face. Some sort of twisted betrayal, as though to tug at Jonik's heart. *My black heart,* he thought. *I'm just as bad as he is.* "What am I doing out here if not to be let free?"

Jonik did not want to drag this out. Executions did not happen often at the Shadowfort, but when they did, men did not die by axe or rope, but by rock and wind and the deep darkness below. "Take him to the top of the wall, Gerrin. You know where."

"What? *What!* You're to kill me?"

"Gerrin. Take him."

Jonik turned away, listening to the scuff and struggle as Gerrin hauled the other Shadowmaster up the steps. He ignored the shouts and slurs and curses. Harden remained at his side, shaking his head. "This isn't right. That man was forged at the anvil of this order. You can't blame him for what he is."

Jonik appreciated Harden's voice in this, he appreciated his just and moral heart. Much of the time his own thoughts were the same, and his instincts too, yet if he followed Harden's council, it would only lead them to doom. "Leaders have to make hard choices," was all he said.

Harden grunted. "Like handing over three children to be sacrificed by blood ritual? That sort of choice, Jonik?"

Jonik did not respond. There was no use in reigniting that debate; they'd had it often enough already and had both chosen their sides. *He does not see the bigger picture. His vision is too narrow.* He turned on his heels, to see that Gerrin had drawn Kagnor into place. *It's time,* he thought. "I do not ask you to come as well, Harden. You don't agree with this. I understand. There's no sense in you bearing witness."

Harden only grunted and followed him up the steps.

Jonik remembered the last time he'd seen a man thrown from the wall. A Shadowknight had made a grievous error while away on a long contract and fallen in love with a maidservant, losing all taste for the shadow and the cold. When he tried to flee with the woman, he'd been caught and cornered and forced to watch as she was killed right there before his eyes, then dragged back to the mountains to be slain before his brothers in black. Jonik recalled how crowded the walls and towers had been, how every man and boy of the order had come out to watch. He remembered how the Shadowknight had wept and begged and bleated, how all the men had sneered their scorn. He recalled the hate he had felt for the man, for abandoning his holy duty. *We detested him for being human,* he reflected. *Because inhuman is what they make us, and inhuman the things we do...*

He strode up to stand before Kagnor, who stood looking at him with murderous black eyes. The place of execution was a small semicircular balcony that extended over the windy abyss, its parapet wall cut with an opening through which the doomed were thrown. This man had not fallen in love with a maidservant, nor abandoned his holy order. He'd been loyal to its creed for five decades, and ironically, that was why he had to die. "Do you have any last words?" Jonik asked him.

The old man only snarled. "Just do it, and curse yourself anew, turn-cloak," he spat. "You've made your mind up. I'll not grovel to the likes of you."

"As you wish." Jonik stepped forward. "To the edge, Shadowmaster. Would you prefer to be pushed or to jump by yourself?"

"I'd prefer you take the leap with me, *boy*. You and Gerrin both. You're touched by the darkness just the same as I am. All three of us have dwelled in these shadows."

Jonik nodded slowly. "Push, or jump?"

"I'll not give you the pleasure." The old man spat in his face, then turned and stepped forward. The open air took him, and the endless abyss below. He made not a sound as he fell.

Silence cloaked the three men who remained. It lingered, on and on, until Harden gave a sharp nod. "He died bravely."

"We're bred brave here," Gerrin said.

"How long is the fall?" There it was, the disapproval in Harden's voice, edging his every word. "Execution should be quick, not drawn out."

"Depends on the crime," Gerrin countered. "Vile deeds ought to be punished by a slow end."

"His only crime was being loyal to this order." Harden looked over the edge and asked again, "How long?"

"No one knows," Gerrin told him. The two grey, grizzled men looked at one another. "Some say the fall opens out to the bottom of the earth, to take a man into the Long Abyss. Others have claimed to have seen rocks at the bottom on clear days when the mists are thin. I'm thinking they're more right than the rest. It's been long enough now. He'll be dead, Harden."

"As you say." Harden did not enjoy their company anymore. He had a final look over the edge, then turned and walked away across the snowy wall walk.

Gerrin watched him go. "He's struggling, Jonik," he said once the sell-sword was out of earshot.

"I know." It took not a dust mote of insight to work that out. "Keep an eye on him. Make sure he doesn't do anything reckless."

"Harden is not a reckless man. But we all have our limits. I fear he's going to leave."

Try to leave, you mean, Jonik thought. "The mages won't let him. And Harden's too damn belligerent to abandon us now. He disagrees with half of what I do, yes, but he's stood by me until now and I think he'll stand by me still. He cares, Gerrin. He'll not desert us just yet."

"So long as you're sure."

"As sure as I can be." He turned to look away through the high frosted valleys. Distantly, he could make out a part of the trail that led down to the foothills, the rugged perilous path that they took to come and go from the fort.

Still nothing, he thought. *They're never coming back.* He had no choice now but to try to make his peace with that. His friends were gone, dead or forsaken of him or lost, he could not say, and speculating over their fate would not serve him. His mother had spoken to him of that, tried to help sure up his mind. She told him that the empty spaces inside his head were best not filled with wretched thought and doubt. "Either cling to hope," she'd told him, "or do not think of it at all. Dwelling on the darkness will only lead you further astray."

It was wise counsel, counsel with which Gerrin agreed, though that was not surprising as they agreed on much and more. And while Harden stood in opposition to many of Jonik's decisions, he was in agreement with them on one thing too. *They all think I should give it up, hand it over, be done with it once and for all.* Half the time Jonik thought the same. Half the time he wanted to throw the Nightblade down where he stood and wait for one more worthy to bear it. But the other half…

No, do not give space for it to thrive. Do not listen to the voice, the whispers. They are only trying to lead you ill.

He turned from them, hating them, needing them, wanting rid of them, confused. His every waking hour was a battle that in sleep he could not fight. By day he could stand firm, yet when darkness fell and the fingers of slumber sank their claws into him, he was powerless to resist. In his dreams he saw a version of himself, a vision of a man cloaked and powerful, wreathed in mist and shadow, leading hordes of others through a desolate land of ash and fire and smoke. It was the Shadow Order reborn, and he was their king, an order without home or duty or purpose but to wander the earth protecting the lost and the lonely, the men and women drifting through a world of menace and monsters and ancient evil things.

In this vision Jonik was not dark of heart, but dreaded to the darkness itself, dreaded to the evil that had risen to win the world. He was the last remaining champion, a leader of the leaderless, the last dim light of hope in a world ravaged and burned. The Nightblade would whisper of that vision by day as well, tempting him, teasing him, yet waking he could resist. At night it was different, the vision a wonder, a reality, so true he could touch it. Sometimes he woke gasping, forgetting that the world was not yet lost, that they still had a chance to pass through the shadow and look upon the bright new dawn, beyond the War Eternal. *I will give it up, once our task here is done*, he would tell himself. *I'll give it up once we're safe, and leave it for another.*

Yet always in the back of his mind, the whisper of disappointment would ring. That he was *not* the last champion…that he was *not* the light… that he was *not* the leader the Nightblade promised he would be…

"Dark promises," he muttered to himself, as he stood at the precipice. "Dark deceptions, that's all they are." He knew the Nightblade's purpose, he knew its mind. *It does not want to merge with its kin. It does not want to lose itself to the will of the other four shards, to the shattered spirit that lies within. It wants to be free, independent, as it has been for millennia. It wants to keep me as its slave, nothing but a thrall.*

He drew his eyes from the mountains and found that Gerrin was looking at him with that worried look on his face. "You were talking to yourself again," his old master said.

Jonik nodded; he did that often, he knew, though half the time he quickly forgot what he'd said. "What did I say?"

"Dark promises. Dark deceptions, that's all they are." His old master studied him. "You should share more, Jonik. This internal struggle…you don't have to fight it alone."

"No one can fight it for me, Gerrin."

"We can support you."

"And you are. You, Cecilia, Harden, you're all helping. But we're nearing the end now. Soon enough I'll be able to lay it down for good and all. Soon enough, Gerrin, I'll be free of it." He gave his old master a faithful nod and left him there at the wall.

The fort was as silent and still and lonely as ever. Jonik made for the kitchens, unbelting his waist of the Nightblade and setting it aside on the chipped wooded counter. He had taken to doing much of the cooking himself, chopping, frying, boiling, buttering and preparing the food for the boys. He liked the kitchens, the smells and sounds and crackle of the fire. In a kitchen a man could be anywhere, any keep or castle across the north. He liked to imagine that he was far away, in the kitchen that he imagined the knight Sir Jaycob might have had. Sir Jaycob, the light to his shadow. Sir Jaycob, who might have lived a happy, heroic life. It was a fantasy he liked to get lost in when awake, a counter to the visions that enslaved him in his sleep. Jaycob the Good, he would call himself, or Jaycob the Fair. *Jaycob, who I might have been, had fate set me on another path.*

An hour or so later, he heard voices outside, and footsteps, as Gerrin and Harden appeared. The talking stopped as they entered to take the trays of food Jonik had prepared, topped with bowls and mugs for each of the boys. Harden saw to the younglings today; Gerrin the older boys. Jonik would take the food for the prisoners himself. He picked up his own tray and set off into the fort.

The prisoners had been separated now, so that his mother could speak to each of them in private. All had been given rooms in the Watchmen's Tower, a tall black spear of a building that overlooked the valleys to the east. Hopper and Henrik were being kept at the top of the building, for their seniority, with Trent, Nils, and Zacarias on the floors below. All had ranging views through the sweeping valleys and mountains to the east.

Jonik started at the top, with the big hobbling Shadowknight who was the oldest of the five. He found him lounging on his bed, throwing a pebble from hand to hand as he stared up at the grey stone ceiling. The room was spacious, if lightly furnished, and much nicer than the dank little cell he'd occupied in the dungeons. Now he had a chamberpot, and privacy, and a thick stone window through which he could gaze out across the world and ponder its possibilities.

"Food," Jonik said, setting the tray on a table and unloading it of a bowl and mug. He filled the latter with water from a jug. "How's the chest?"

"Getting better." Hopper threw his pebble from his left hand to his right, then sat up, swinging his legs over the side of the bed. He was a big man, a stout fighter. *A good man to protect the other boys*, Jonik thought. That was his hope for him. Hopper to act as a sergeant of sorts, Henrik, though younger, to lead, and the other three to act in support. "Slept well enough last night at least. Coughing didn't wake me so often."

"That's good." Jonik watched the man carefully as he stepped over to fetch his food. He had no bars to guard him from them anymore, and if they had an intent to attack him, there would be nothing but air to stop them. He had suffered no such assault, however, nor had his mother during her visits. *They're coming around*, he knew. *They look out and taste their freedom. She is painting her pictures, as I asked her.*

Hopper took his bowl and mug back to his bed, and sat down, shoulders hunched forward as he spooned the broth of potatoes, leeks, and bacon into his mouth. There was bread as well, which he dunked and soaked and munched hungrily. "Heard shouting earlier," he said, between mouthfuls. "You finally killed him, did you?"

Jonik didn't want to get into this, but it couldn't be avoided. Kagnor had been the only one left in the cells, and the others were smart enough to know Jonik would never let him go. "I had no choice. He would only have turned outlaw. You know that as well as I do, Hopper."

The big man nodded. "He was rotten, can't deny it. How'd you do it?"

"Wind and rock."

He ripped off a bite of bread, chewing. "Shame. I'd have liked to see that one bleed. I was scared of him as a boy, you know. He used to mock my uneven legs. Said he'd chop the other one down a bit so I didn't have to hobble. Thought he'd really do it, too. I was only seven."

Can you tell Harden that story? Jonik thought. That was cruelty beyond what the order required. That was Kagnor, him alone. "Are you willing to do as I asked you, Hopper?" He watched the man consider it as he ate. Only yesterday he'd given each of the prisoners a choice. *I'm going to set you all free,* he had said to them. *You can either go alone, or do something noble, and take care of the boys. It's up to you.*

Hopper set his bowl aside and wiped his mouth. "I almost died here once, when I was a lad. See this scar." He pointed at a cut along the left side of his neck, half hidden by his short ragged beard. "Shadowmaster Stregor gave me this when I was thirteen. He was kicking one of the younger boys, had him doubled over on the floor and was just kicking him hard in his guts until blood came out his mouth. A few others stood by watching, but me…no, something cracked. I ran at him, shouting to leave the kid alone, and tried to tackle him to the floor. He saw me coming, though, and turned me aside. Beat me so hard I thought I was going to die. This scar was from his knife. He was about to cut my throat open when my own master stopped him." He ran a finger along the line of the scar, up and down, smiling. "Best I've ever felt here, standing up for that boy. Think that's who I am, under all the layers of shit they pile on us." He looked Jonik in the eye, and there was no deception there, no lie. "I'll do it, Jonik. I'll protect whatever boys want protecting. Just know that not all of them will."

"I know." Jonik did not delude himself into thinking every boy would want to remain as part of the herd. Some would go their own way, and that was their choice, but the younglings…those would stay together, he hoped. And now with Hopper at least to guide them, protect them…he felt a weight lifting off his shoulders, just a little, but enough that he could breathe. "Thank you, Hopper. You're…a good man."

"We'll see." He had another drink of water. "But aye, I hope so."

Jonik went to Henrik next, who occupied the room next door. He unlocked the door and entered, setting the tray on the table. The room was identical to Hopper's. "Food," he said. "Stew. Bacon, potatoes, leeks."

Henrik was at the window, staring out. Rarely did Jonik find him otherwise. "Are they around today? The eagles?"

"They were, a bit earlier. Hunting down in the lower passes. They're gone now, though." Henrik turned. He liked watching his eagles. "Kagnor's dead, isn't he?"

Jonik nodded. "Wind and rock."

"Thought as much. Who's next, Jonik?"

"No one. He was the last." He poured Henrik a cup of water and took his bowl off the tray, then stepped back so the man could take it. The young Shadowknight stayed where he was. "Not hungry?"

"You spoke with Hopper. I heard you, through the window. He's agreed to protect the boys?"

"He wants to help," Jonik said.

Henrik studied him in that way of his, always looking for the truth behind a man's eyes. It had always made him seem much older than the others of Jonik's age, though never cold or calculating... more curious, even kind. "Hopper seems that way," he said eventually. "Do you think he'll be happy being second-in-command? I'm younger, less experienced. He may resent being subordinate."

You're smarter, wiser, Jonik thought. *Age means nothing.* "He's not a leader, Henrik. But you have that in you. You can find a haven where these boys can be safe."

The young man nodded, pensive, and turned back to look out of the window. He stood still for a long moment, the wind stirring his wavy brown hair. "I've been thinking where we might go, studying those maps you gave me." He glanced to the table beside his bed, where the maps were stacked, along with several books Jonik had fetched from the library. "We need somewhere where we can live apart from others at first, yet be close enough that we can integrate eventually. It's all well and good thinking we can live in isolation all our lives, but that won't be possible. The younger boys will grow and when they do, they'll seek the company of women. They'll want wives and children of their own. I'd like to nurture that in them. Lady Cecilia....she has helped instruct me on how I might do this. The steps I would need to take. The difficulties I will face."

There will be many of those, Jonik knew. Though finding a woman and siring sons and daughters was not something that Henrik, Hopper, and the other three had to consider, nor some of the older boys. All had been gelded so as not to suffer such temptation, as was the case with most of the men. Only a few were spared that fate, those with stronger blood who might one day be required to furnish the order with their own offspring. How often that had happened, Jonik didn't know. It was mired in mystery, much like everything here.

Henrik stepped from the window and moved to his bedside table. "I'm torn on where to take them," he said, picking up one sheepskin map, unfolding it onto the bed. "The wilds of North Tukor might offer us what we need. - fresh water, wood for building huts, plenty of game, proximity to other settlements, even - yet I fear it might be too close to the mountains.

The boys will only look upon them and feel that darkness stir in their hearts. Not the youngest ones, perhaps; they may grow to forget this place ever existed. But the older ones…"

Jonik stepped closer. "You would travel further afield? Where?"

Henrik traced a finger along the map, moving it through the mountains and to the west, into Vandar. "Another realm might best serve us," he said. "Somewhere where the air smells different, and the people speak in a different style. There is a route, I know, that will lead us over the Hammer-songs and down the other side, and through the northern part of the Mist-wood. We could carve out a home for ourselves there, near the town of Mistvale. I have read it to be a welcoming place, not grand but rustic, and yet…"

"Yet the mountains will still loom," Jonik said. Mistvale still sat in sight of the Hammersongs, he knew, shadowed by distance and cloaked in mist, yet visible all the same.

"Yes. I would rid us of them entirely if I could, yet the longer the journey, the greater the risk." His finger continued west. "The Ironmoors are broad and bleak and the lords there take a hard line on vagrants. If caught by some Taynar men I fear a fresh yolk. Some will be put in the mines and others the fields, but in truth most will never let it get that far. Our training will take over, and the wildness within us all. It will be blood if we're caught, Jonik."

Blood, he thought. There might be no escaping that, no matter where they went. Not with the war. Yet he had to hope elsewise for these boys. It was the one last branch of virtue that he clung to, helping them find a new life. *And if I can do that, there's hope for me as well.*

"One of my men is from the Ironmoors," he said, casting his doubt aside. "He's a sellsword, much the same as us in many ways, and even claims to have been sired of noble blood. He might be able to advise you best on which route to take, if you wish to cross further to the west."

"That would be useful." Henrik took a pause to think. "I wonder… could you spare him? He would make a useful guide, if only to help us cross those lands."

Jonik wished it could be so. "Harden is not permitted to leave."

Henrik nodded and did not push the issue further. "The other option is east. If we range toward Blackhearth, the mountains will soon fade from sight. The Banewood is haunted, men say, but we know the truth of that. We would be untroubled there, and with Blackhearth near to hand…"

"Blackhearth is a dangerous city," Jonik warned him. "Its outer districts are scarred by poverty and crime is rife. Any boy who goes there will be swallowed up into the underworld. I would not recommend it."

"Rasalan, then."

Rasalan. Jonik had a memory of a warcamp, and a dark cold night, and a flash of gold and black, father and son, light and dark. It vanished as quickly as it came.

"The people of Rasalan are kinder," Henrik said. "There are places there where we might find what we need." He pointed out a few, focusing on the great expanse of the Lowplains, and some of the larger cities around Whaler's Bay, where they might find a home in the hinterlands somewhere. They would have to cross a body of water for that, though, Vandar's Mercy or the Siblings Strait, and such an interaction would be risky.

But there are risks everywhere, Jonik knew, *and you'll not be there to help them.* He thought again of his vision, and the shadows who trailed in his wake. *Perhaps it starts with them, these boys?* he thought. *Perhaps I'm not meant to give up the Nightblade at all, but do as Harden urged and slay Fhanrir and Hamlyn and all the rest of them, let their duty die here and now, let the world fall to darkness and doom...*

He snapped out of it, pushing the vision aside once more, as he did many times a day. *Dark promises,* he thought to himself. *Dark deceptions. Don't listen.*

When he looked up he found Henrik studying him. His eyes were curious, cautious. *Gerrin's eyes,* Jonik knew. *Harden's eyes, and my mother's. They all look at me the same.* "That blade's got its claws into you, Jonik," the young Shadowknight said. He took in the black wisps of smoke, puffing and breathing through the top of his black scabbard, ghostly fingers trying to grasp for him. "Never seen the Nightblade behave like that. The way the mists move. They look....alive."

They are alive. The blade is part of me. A part of me I need to kill, if we're to survive. Jonik did not respond.

"What will you do after?" Henrik was still looking at the Nightblade, his frown deepening. "Once you let us go? Will you head south, fight in the war?"

Jonik dipped his neck in a stiff nod. "I hope so, yes."

"With that?"

Yes, said the whispers. "No," said Jonik, forcing the word out. "I intend to leave it here. It was never mine, Henrik."

The young man nodded, seeming relieved. "That'd be for the best, I think. I've read terrible tales of those who have fallen to a Blade of Vandar. That's not a burden I'd ever want to bear."

"It requires a noble purpose," Jonik said. "A sound mind, driven by a just duty."

"I've read that too." Henrik stared at it as though it was an evil thing, to be avoided and feared. "Why do you still wear it?"

"Protection."

"From who? Us?"

"Others. Some men escaped, when we took the fort. I need to protect my men." *My men,* he thought bitterly. Gerrin and Harden, and that was it. *Cabel was still abed, and fading. He is dead already, lost,* Jonik knew. *He needs no protection from me.*

"Those men are no match for you, Jonik. Nightblade or no, you've nothing to fear from them." Henrik had a look on his face, a worried look, like Gerrin got, and Harden and his mother. "You can't give it up, can you? You won't."

"I will." Jonik could sense his anger rising. "I have to."

"Why?"

He could not answer that question. That secret was a length of chain and fetters, shackling all who knew it to this place.

"It's served its purpose," was all he could say. "Fhanrir told you of the Book of Contracts. My contract took me into Tukor, Rasalan, Vandar. It took me into the tent of my father, and the arena in Varinar, where I killed my brother. It took me south, through the Tidelands, past Agarath and the Golden Isles. It won me friends and companions, saw me liberate long-lost men. I sailed halfway around the world, Henrik, past Lumara and Pisek and Aramatia and Solapia, past the Islands of Tellesh and across the Three Bays, up the Siblings Strait and through the Mercy. And all to return here, as per my contract, and my fate. All to bring back this blade, and end the order that bred me."

"Then you've lived," Henrik said, reassuringly. "And you've done good, Jonik. You're human."

"Human? They don't make us human here. They make us slaves. They make us tools."

"Then why are you still helping them?"

"For you. And the boys."

"No. It's more." The other man stepped forward. "Tell me what's back there, Jonik. Tell me what you've seen."

Jonik drew away. "No. You cannot know, Henrik. Keep the maps, keep the books. Keep thinking where you'll go. That's your duty. You want no part of mine."

He turned and left, snatching up the tray of food on the way out. His hand was shivering, the Nightblade in his grasp. Dark whispers filled his mind. He untangled his fingers, one by one by one, and ripped his hand away. *Be stronger,* he thought to himself. *Think of your father. Think of him.*

It was one of his weapons against the whispers, a memory that still felt like yesterday. His father, sitting in his bedchamber atop Keep Daecar, newly crippled and drunk and lost to a dark melancholy. Jonik remembered how he had the Sword of Varinar across his lap. How he caressed it like a lover. He'd held that blade for twenty years and there, in that moment, Jonik saw the man's obsession. *Yet all the same, he gave it up. Despite his pain and deep despair, he gave it up.*

And so will I, he told himself.

33

Elyon

The dragon was a speedy bastard, almost as quick as he was in a straight line and equally as acrobatic besides. Elyon burst through a fat wet cloud in pursuit, changing angle in a sharp descent as the lithesome beast ducked into a dive in a bid to outmanoeuvre him.

No chance, he thought. *I'll have you eventually, crow-killer.*

The dragon sped low, leading him toward a wooded valley. Trees and bushes swept past them in a green-brown blur as prey and hunter weaved between stands of elm and ash. Before Elyon knew it, the woodland dispersed and a lake opened out before them, bordered by thickets on every side. Elyon spotted a small fishing village on the eastern shore, and some little boats moored along a jetty. It looked abandoned at a glance. *The people will have made for Redhelm*, he thought. Whether they managed to get through the gate or not was another matter.

The lake was a deep calm grey, shining like beaten metal under the mid-morning sun. As they passed over the shoreline, some ducks and geese took flight and the serene scene was quickly disturbed. The dragon kept low, the furled claws on its rear legs trailing the surface of the water as Elyon sought to close the space. He dare not get so near himself, however. Water was no friend to armoured knights.

The lake was not large, nothing like those that sprawled majestically across the Lakelands to the east. Within a short half minute the far edge was nearing and the dragon was making again for the trees. Elyon kept pace, flying a half dozen metres above it. Into the trees they went once more, though it was nought but a short copse, opening quickly out into a wide plain beyond. *I have you now*, Elyon Daecar thought.

The hunt did not last much longer after that. A minute or two of cat and mouse ensued before Elyon managed to get close enough to slice at the beast's wing, sending it plummeting to the ground in a spiralling tangle of limbs, blood spraying in its wake. The prince followed in pursuit until the beast hit the grassy earth, then proceeded to complete the kill with a good firm hack at the back of its neck, severing its hissing head. Its eyes went dim and its tongue went limp, lolling out of the side of its mouth.

"Good chase," Elyon said, giving the young dragon its due. He inclined his head, feeling scant joy in the kill. All the same, these crow-killers needed killing. They had to eat, after all, and the occasional crow would not sustain them long. Livestock had become common prey, as were wild fauna such as hogs and deer, yet the smallfolk were also on the menu, smaller women and children in particular. Elyon would not have that. "I'll kill them, every one," he'd told Sir Storos Pentar when he'd asked if he would give chase to every little dragon they saw. "If each kill saves just one child, it'll be worth it."

It was tiring work, though. Long flights at a stable speed was one thing; all this twisting and turning and ducking and dodging - not to mention swinging the Windblade when in flight, which took a great deal out of him - was quite another. He took a moment to gather his breath as he stood beside the beast's beheaded corpse. "How many of you are there, anyway?" he asked the dead creature. It was one of the smallest he'd killed, hardly much bigger than a pack horse. Deadly to most, but no threat to him. "And where are all your big brothers?"

When he got no answer from the headless dragon, he swung the Wind-blade skyward and took once more to the skies. It was a warm bright day, the winds calm, a few grumpy rainclouds lumbering along here and there. Away to the south, he could see his friends trotting down the old farm track that wended toward the coast. It looked like they had found a stream and were stopping to water the horses. Elyon put the winds to work and flew at once to rejoin them.

He landed beside Lythian in a swirling dismount.

The Knight of the Vale looked over. "Success?"

Elyon nodded, sliding the Windblade into its shining silver scabbard. "He gave me a good runaround, though I got him in the end. Who's Storos talking to?" Elyon had noticed another man had joined their party, some rider dressed in Pentar silver and red. "Is he from Nightwell?"

Lythian nodded. "He found us on the road a few minutes after you'd left. Sir Glarus sent him. It seems that we're being denied entry into the fortress, Elyon."

Elyon didn't know what to make of that. "Why? I thought Storos and Glarus got on well?" Storos had been saying as such for the entire trip, telling them that both Glarus and Doros, the second and third sons of Lord Porus Pentar, and younger brothers to the loathsome Alrus, were close with him and always had been.

"They do," Lythian confirmed. "But Sir Glarus Pentar is a man of duty first and foremost, and is not one to deny a direct order from his lord."

"His lord? This came from his father?"

"No, his brother."

Elyon understood at once. "Lord Porus is finally dead?"

Lythian gave a sigh. "Regrettably, yes. Making Alrus the Lord of Redhelm and Warden of the South by official decree. He must have sent a crow ahead of us, informing Sir Glarus of their father's death. And issuing the order to deny us entry at the same time."

Elyon gave a snort. "Of all the bloody crows to reach their destination…" His eyes turned to Sir Storos, standing a little further downstream with his captain Sir Oswin Cole and the messenger in question. "How's he taking the news?"

"Well enough. He knows it was only a matter of time. That Alrus has commanded the gates of Nightwell remain shut to us has stirred in him a rage, however. Storos would like to spend this evening in mourning, at Glarus's side, sharing stories of their father and toasting his memory. But Alrus, in all his petty vengeance, has seen fit to deny him that."

"Alrus has denied him nothing. I overruled him in Redhelm when demanding Pagaloth's safe release and I'll do the same here." Elyon would not let that weasel of a man come between two brothers mourning their father. "I'll talk to him." Before Lythian might call him back, he marched downstream to where Sir Storos stood and said, "I hear we're being denied entry to Nightwell. Fear not, Sir Storos. Let me fly ahead and clear this up with your brother. I'll have the gates opened for your arrival."

The man smiled his thanks. "That is kind of you, my prince."

"It is well earned, for your loyal support. Your father was a good man, and long defended this stretch of coast. I am sorry for your loss, Storos." He thought about flying off right now, though after his dance with the dragon he thought it best to rest a while, should he encounter another along the way. "How far is Nightwell from here?"

"Another half day's ride, or thereabouts. Though in flight, I couldn't say."

"It won't take me long," Elyon told him. "I'll ride with you for a while longer and fly when I'm better rested." He returned to Lythian to find that Sir Pagaloth had rejoined him. "Where were you?" Elyon asked the dragonknight.

"I think you would rather not know, my lord. The food here…"

Elyon smiled. "Say no more, Sir Pagaloth. Would you ride with me, for a little while?"

"I thought you were flying to Nightwell," Lythian said.

"Shortly. I feel a bit of time in the saddle is needed first. Pagaloth, please accompany me at the rear of the column. There are some things I'd like to discuss with you."

Lythian gave the young prince a questioning look, though said nothing as he climbed into the saddle of his handsome courser to ride at the head of the column with Storos and Oswin Cole. Elyon had been given use of a piebald stallion when he wasn't in flight, a good strong horse, young and swift, a little wild of temperament but well capable of bearing Elyon when armoured and armed for long hours on the road. Pagaloth rode a stallion as well, dark and lean, a good match for him. With his dragon hunts and sky patrols, Elyon had spent scant time with the dragonknight alone on their journey from Redhelm. He felt it was time that was rectified.

"Lythian tells me you bested Borrus Kanabar in a duel once," he said, as they set off into a canter, staying a little behind the dozen men-at-arms who served in Sir Storos's company.

The man nodded. "The Barrel Knight was without godsteel, my lord. But yes, I drew first blood."

"Impressive. Godsteel or no, Borrus is a master swordsman. Where did you learn your skill with blade and spear, Sir Pagaloth? Was it Eldurath, pray tell?"

"For a time. My family lands were south of the capital, near the shores of the Crystal Bay. There I learned from my father, uncles, and older brothers as a boy. It was my uncle Sir Lendroth who took me on as a squire, during a time when he served in Eldurath. I spent many years there, before my uncle rode off to war."

Elyon knew the rest of that story, a tale of tragedy he'd heard from Lythian during their first night on the road. Sir Pagaloth's entire family had been destroyed during the War of the Continents, his father, uncles and brothers all falling to northern steel, one or two of them slain by Borrus himself if the tale was to be believed. After the war, Pagaloth's mother was so stricken by her grief that she took her own life; a sin so foul it condemned her to a dark and dreaded afterlife, many believed. Elyon couldn't hope to understand what it must have been like for the drag-onknight, to live through all of that.

He let a few moments pass before saying, "Then you'll have a good knowledge of the city? And the palace as well? I understand there are often fogs that hang over the streets. Dust storms and such, blown south from the Drylands. They can make visibility poor, I'm told."

"It is common, yes. Some call Eldurath the *Bronze City*, for the colour of the dust that often coats the streets, and for the hue of the sandstone build-ings. Sandstorms are frequent, and the mornings are often heavy with fog as well."

Good. Storms were friend to Elyon Daecar, whether of cloud or dust it mattered not. What he wanted was concealment from prying eyes, should he seek to pay a visit.

They continued along the old farm track until the coast bloomed into sight before them, a rugged stretch, wild and windswept that gazed out across the restless waters of the Red Sea. "Do you know the name we use for this coastline, Sir Pagaloth?" Elyon asked.

"The Black Coast. For all the times the dragons have razed it."

Almost, Elyon thought. There was one dragon above all that had earned the coast its name. "It's heavily fortified against invasion," he said. "Every thirty to fifty miles there's a bulky fort with a strong garrison and in between those there are smaller strongholds and castles too. I suppose it is much the same for you, on the other side of the sea? You have many fortresses of your own guarding against a northern attack, do you not?"

"There are several of note, yes. The Trident stands to the west, and there are strongholds and watchtowers built upon the Claws as well."

"And Dragonfall," Elyon said. "Lythian said you were stationed there when you met."

"I had been there for two years, yes. I was charged with helping defend the city against attack."

"I've always wanted to visit. The carving of Drulgar in the cliffs is said to be a wonder." Elyon paused to check the dragonknight's reaction. "Lythian seems to believe the Dread has arisen, Sir Pagaloth. Tell me…do you share in that belief?"

Sir Pagaloth steered his horse around a deep rut in the road, then said, "I could not say, my lord. Captain Lythian was the one to descend into the depths of Eldur's Shame, not me. I did not bear witness to what he saw."

"But you heard of it. From him, and others as well. What did Lord Marak say of this? Or the princess?" Lythian had told Elyon everything, as he asked him. *Everything*, Elyon thought. *And more than I could ever have imagined.* Somehow he could believe that Eldur had returned to wreak havoc upon the world more easily than he could Lythian falling in love with an exotic Agarathi princess. His mentor had not said it in quite so simple terms, but Elyon had seen it in his eyes. It was the pain of heartbreak, clear as crystal. *Mingled with his shame.*

"They did not talk of it very much, my lord," the dragonknight said. "They mentioned only a stone formation in the likeness of the dragon. Sotel Dar was insistent that the old prophecies did not mention Drulgar's rise, only that of Eldur. The scholar and the prince were in agreement that the coming of the Calamity would spell doom for all, that this was in opposition to what the wise masters had foreseen."

"Foreseen," Elyon repeated, "and *wrongly*. I was told about this ancient prophecy, Sir Pagaloth. Eldur has not risen benevolent, but evil, in the image of his master. Lythian thinks Agarath himself is using Eldur as some sort of puppet, working his will through him. What do you think?"

Pagaloth pondered, then nodded. "It could be so, yes. The god Agarath was always intent on anarchy. Fire is such, wild and dangerous, consuming all. It was Eldur who sought to distance himself from his master's destructive impulses when the gods fell. He named his kingdom in honour of him, yes, but otherwise it was peace he sought. And so it was, for many years."

"Until Drulgar stirred to sever it," Elyon said. "Until he made this coastline what it was. The Black Coast, Pagaloth, was first coined after Drulgar came. He burned and blackened every fortress, and then turned his eyes on Varinar."

Elyon did not need to tell Pagaloth the tale. There were few in the world who hadn't already heard it in one retelling or another. To some it was myth, to others history, but to most it was a blend of both. Elyon did not doubt that it had been subjected to exaggeration as well. Drulgar was not as large as a flying mountain, as some liked to say, nor could he topple entire forests with a single beat of his boundless black wings. Claims that he could melt godsteel down to its molten form in one blast of his fiery breath were over embellishments as well, he deemed. If that were so, Varin and his children would never have been able to stand against him so long, let alone defeat him.

"Drulgar's coming changed the world," Pagaloth agreed, in his thick

Agarathi timbre. "In Agarath he is revered as a god to some, and feared as a demon by others, a mistake of his master's making. Into Drulgar the fire god poured all his malice, all his hate, all his destructive power. Yet Eldur is not so. The Fire Father could be wrathful at times, yes, but he was also wise, rational, and peaceable too, where Drulgar sought only chaos. Lythian may be right, my lord. I do not think Eldur would have raised Drulgar in his right mind. If he has done this, then it is through the will of Agarath. It is through his Soul."

The Bondstone, Elyon thought. "Do you believe it can be destroyed?"

"The prophecy said it needed to be controlled," Pagaloth said.

By the heir of Varin, Elyon thought, *whomever that might be.* All knew King Lorin fell without an heir. If there was some secret son, where had he been all these years? "The prophecy has been proven false," Elyon returned. "The Bondstone is not to be controlled, but destroyed. I had thought the Sword of Varinar might accomplish this, but Lythian thinks otherwise. He says only the Heart can destroy the Soul. That the blades must be united."

"Sotel Dar and Prince Tethian preached the same."

Elyon did not care for what this wayward prince or old scholar had preached. "Could it be stolen instead?" he wondered. "Drowned?" *I could fly the Bondstone out to sea and sink it to the ocean depths. Or cast it into some fiery chasm to bury it in lava.* Elyon had considered all such options at length, his mind fixed on the Soul of a god. *Destroy it. Sever the tie. Weaken the demigod and he'll be vulnerable.*

But Pagaloth shook his head. "You cannot hold the Bondstone, Sir Elyon. Only those with the blood of Eldur can do so. The Fireborn."

"You're Fireborn," Elyon said. "Lythian told me so. From your mother's line."

"My blood is weak. Diluted, you might say. The Bondstone answers only to those of pure blood, just as the Heart of Vandar may only be wielded by the direct blood of Varin's line."

"So say your scholar and prince," Elyon said to that. "I'm inclined to think otherwise, Sir Pagaloth. If there's a man in this kingdom worthy enough to wield the Heart Remade it's my father."

"Or you?" the dragonknight offered.

"No, not me. None compare to Amron Daecar."

"As none in Agarath compare to Lord Ulrik Marak," Pagaloth said, "and yet he could not himself touch the Bondstone, even when he was Lord of the Nest. For many long years he held that post, marshalling and nursing the Fireborn recruits and overseeing the bonding process, yet not once did he place a hand upon the Soul."

"It was never moved?" Elyon asked him.

"No. The Bondstone had sat in place on its holy plinth ever since the fortress was raised, before the Fire Father claimed it. Now he bears it upon his black staff, as a sorcerer of dreaded power."

Elyon watched him for a moment through the corner of his eye, as they cantered slowly along the coastal road. He could only imagine how he would feel if he laid eyes upon Varin, the wonder it would inspire to look upon the father of his kingdom. He could not help but think Sir Pagaloth would have felt something similar. "How did it feel, being in his presence?" he asked, after a few moments. "Lythian spoke of a queer paralysis. He told me it happened first in the depths of the mountain, and again at the Nest, both times in the presence of your Fire Father. He told me he'd never felt such profound dread and fear, yet for you it was different, wasn't it?"

"Of course. I am Agarathi. He is our father and our founder, the greatest figure in all our history."

"Yet still you chose not to join him?"

"Chose? No, there was no choice. Marak, Sa'har, Sotel, Talasha, none of them had a choice. Eldur compelled them to join him."

"His *voice*," Elyon said. Lythian had spoken of the power of Eldur's voice. "How long do you think these coercions might last? Could Eldur's grip on them begin to weaken, in time?"

Pagaloth jutted his jaw skyward, heavy with course black stubble and scabby cuts from where his beard had been hacked off. "How much rain is in that raincloud, Sir Elyon? How long is a dragon's tail? These are questions without answers."

"So you don't know?"

"I am a humble soldier and know nothing of such sorcery. Perhaps the charm will weaken over time. Or perhaps by distance from the source. I do not know. It might last forever."

"Or someone could work to unbind themselves, through sheer will," Elyon offered. "A stronger mind, perhaps. Or one driven by something deeper."

The dragonknight frowned at him. "Deeper?"

Elyon smiled. "Tell me of Talasha Taan," he said. "You were witness to her relationship with Lythian. Was it real?"

"So far as I saw, yes. They loved one another."

Elyon still found it hard to believe. The Knight of the Vale was the model of chastity, his only concern his duty to the realm. Elyon had always thought it unhealthy, in truth, though his father had been much the same since the death of his lady mother Kessia. With Lythian it was different, though. His wife Talia had died young and in childbirth and he'd never sired an heir. Elyon had often asked him of that, whether he would take a new wife who might give him a son so that his line did not end with him, but the Knight of the Vale was wont to avoid the topic. After a while, Elyon had stopped bringing it up, yet always he harboured hope. *Not with an Agarathi princess, though,* he had to admit.

"What did the others think of it?" the prince went on. "This union between Bladeborn captain and Fireborn princess? Did they disapprove?"

"It was not overt," Pagaloth told him. "Princess Talasha…she was the more wanton of the two, and greatly more free-spirited. I do not think Captain Lythian would have courted her were it not for her advances. She did not care to hide it so much as him."

"So *she* made it happen?" He wasn't surprised by that in the least.

"It was much her doing, yes," the dragonknight answered. "They would go hunting in the woods together, so they might be alone, and often would steal away when no one was looking. The others knew, of course, yet they kept it as quiet as possible. The princess was insistent, and unconcerned of any reprisal. Many times she asked Lythian to run away with her, and after their descent into the mountain, when he fell into his deep fever, she kept to his side almost constantly, nursing him back to health."

Elyon thought on that for a time, as they continued along the track. *Something deeper,* he thought. *Perhaps there is some destiny in this union.* He looked at the dragonknight, and asked, "Have you ever been in love, Sir Pagaloth?"

The man did not seem to expect the question. "Once, yes, when I was younger."

"Then you'll understand its power. A power that nothing else on this earth can overcome, some say. I've heard it said that love is a spell, Pagaloth; powerful, all-consuming, capable of passing between the planes of the living and the dead. How else do we love those who are gone, if not by some magic? If the princess did indeed love Lythian as you say, she may be able to use it to break free, overcome the Fire Father's controls."

Pagaloth looked at him through those dark brooding eyes of his. "Something deeper," he said.

Elyon smiled. "Exactly." With that, he swung his legs over the saddle of his stallion. "Take the reins, sir, if you would. I have a promise to Sir Storos to keep."

The flight to Nightwell was as short as Elyon had hoped, a brisk twenty-mile dash along the coast. He kept an eye out for dragons as he went, though the only one he saw was a dead one, lying down on some beach not far from the walls of a minor fort. Most likely it had been shot down by the men there and butchered for parts, judging by the spread of blood and gore upon the sand.

He paid it little more than a passing glance as the high black walls of Nightwell appeared. Of all the forts along the Black Coast, Nightwell was the darkest and most gloomy, outwardly at least. Inside it was pleasantly furnished, with a great hall filled with candles and tapestries, and rooms of the same to accommodate what highborn men might pass through. According to Sir Storos, the garrison numbered five thousand here, and the outer defences were deadly.

Elyon decided to land upon the wall walk atop the northern barbican, rather than outside the gate, landing so swiftly that he gave a poor watchman the fright of his life. "Easy there, you don't want to go toppling over the edge," he said, as the man shifted backward so suddenly it looked like he might go slipping between the merlons. He grabbed his arm to steady him. "I'm here to talk with Sir Glarus Pentar. Send for him, if you would."

"No need," said a man behind him.

Elyon turned and came face to face with his quarry. He'd met Sir Glarus just once before, though his face was still familiar. Not as fair as Sir Storos, or as foul as Lord Alrus, but somewhere in between, plain but pleasant, with a roundish red nose, squarish, if a little flabby jawline, and cropped brown hair that was thinning at the temples and crown. Glarus Pentar was forty years old, a knight of passable skill, though a good battle commander. He'd held Nightwell stoutly so far, the reports said, and his men had brought down several smaller dragons of their own. "Sir Glarus, that was quick," Elyon said to him. "You must have heard I was coming."

"I *saw* you coming, Sir Elyon." The man stood almost at a height with him, bigger than his brothers, and thicker at the shoulder. "It just so happened I was expecting you. My lord brother suggested you might fly ahead."

Elyon squinted at him, searching for signs of treachery. "A good read on his part. I was told by your brother Storos that Lord Alrus has denied him entry."

"He has denied all of you entry, my lord."

"You know why, I suppose?"

The second son of Porus Pentar nodded. "You come with a dragonknight who was complicit in young Tomos's death. Or so Alrus says."

He isn't wrong, Elyon thought, though it wasn't so simple as all that, and Elyon had no intention of discussing it. *Let Lythian explain it all when he arrives. He'll do a better job than I will.* "I understand you to be a man of duty, sir. You abide by the commands of your lord, yes?"

"Of course."

"And when a command comes from a higher authority?"

"Only the king has higher authority."

"Not a crown prince?"

The Commander of Nightwell frowned. "I was of the understanding that your father and Lord Taynar were to share the rule. There is no king at this time."

It was getting confusing, all this. Elyon did not agree with his father's humble need to keep the crown off his head, and had decided to call himself prince to all and sundry. *Maybe eventually Father will get the message and just sit that bloody throne.* "My father is king," he said, with conviction. "In all but name. Come, Sir Glarus. Your dear brother is fast approaching and he would seek to grieve with you." He put his head into a sympathetic bow. "I'm most sorry for your loss. Your father was a great man, all agree." *Unlike your worthless older brother.*

"Thank you for saying that, Sir Elyon."

Prince Elyon, he thought, though he decided it would be churlish to say, at this time.

"However," Glarus went on. "I would prefer not to grant entry all the same." When Elyon frowned, Glarus stepped in. "I fear my older brother has had word spread through the ranks of my men, Sir Elyon," he said, under his breath. "If the dragonknight passes these walls, he will be in peril."

Elyon crunched a fist. "I told him not to pursue this," he said, through clenched teeth. "Need I fly back to Redhelm and remind him?"

"You told him when he was but a knight and heir. He is Lord of

Redhlem now, and Warden of the South. Alrus feels it within his rights to hunt the dragonknight so long as he remains on his lands."

"These are the king's lands. My father's lands."

"Be that as it may. Alrus will see the dragonknight dead, if he can, and claim innocence thereafter. I'm sure he would be safe with the likes of Captain Lythian and my brother to watch over him, but alas it is not worth the risk. However, I will not miss this opportunity to mourn my father with Storos; who can say when...or if...we will ever see one another again with the realm and world in such disarray. I shall, therefore, have a pavilion erected outside the walls instead, where we might raise our cups in toast. My brother and his men may stay there. Captain Lythian and the dragonknight as well. And you, of course, though..."

Elyon didn't like the sound of that '*though*'. "What is it, Sir Glarus? Has something happened?"

The man nodded dourly. "The crows have come in at a heady rate today, Sir Elyon. Many are being hunted as I'm sure you know, but today I've had two fly into my rookery. One from Redhelm and another...well, dark tidings from the east. Though hardly unexpected." He withdrew a scroll from the inner pocket of his maroon cloak, worn over a suit of mixed godsteel plate and mail. "Mudport has come under attack, Sir Elyon. Lord Morley got word out calling for aid as he saw the Agarathi coming, though as to whether anyone will get there in time..."

They won't, Elyon thought at once. *Not unless Rammas and Killian march their army south to meet them.* There was only one way of finding out for sure.

He turned to Sir Glarus Pentar. "Tell Captain Lythian I've been called away when he arrives," he said. "And for them to continue on without me come morning. I will return to them when I can."

He did not wait for the man to confirm. Stepping back, Elyon Daecar summoned the winds to his will...and made with all haste to the east.

34

Robbert

The sunwolf was monstrous and mean. Black was its mane, bloody its maw, its shoulders thick with muscle and long shaggy fur. Robbert Lukar had never seen such an ugly old brute. He stood before it in Blockform stance with a smile shining behind his faceplate. "Here, pup, come and taste my steel."

The wolf charged. Robbert ducked, rolled, and slashed. Steel bit flesh and bone and its left hind leg went spinning, the stump gushing blood. The sunwolf roared, tumbled, and scrambled back to its three remaining feet. When it ran at him again, it did so with a grotesque limp, leaving a trail of red upon the pavestones, but come at him it still did. *Brave creature,* Robbert thought. He'd give the beast that at least.

He slew it with a sideward slash that took off the wolf's lower jaw and opened its neck, ending their bout. Around him a hundred others were raging. Leaving his foe in the filth he spun and drove his blade through the back of a man in a scalemail shirt, hoping it wasn't one of Krator's. That was unlikely; Lord Cedrik and Lord Krator had made sure to separate their forces and attack different parts of the city, but still, the fighting had been going on for a while and anything was possible.

Robbert pulled out his blade and kicked the body over to make sure. All of Elio Krator's men had been given white feathers to pin to their breasts, so there would be no confusion as to their allegiance. This man wore a white feather. *Oh.*

"Bernie!" he shouted.

The big man hacked a Kolashi bowman in half with his misting bastard sword and came rushing over. "What, Robb? You hurt or something?"

Robbert gestured to the dead man at his feet. "White feather," he said. "What do you think I should do?"

Bernie had a quick and simple solution. He bent down, ripped the white feather away, and crushed it in his steel fist. "There. Done. He shouldn't have been here anyway…fool must have gotten himself lost."

"They're meant to be our allies," Robbert said. "Maybe he was a messenger?"

"Accidents happen." Sir Bernie Westermont shrugged, then flew back into the action, bellowing and swinging.

The city square in which they fought would probably be a pleasant place on any normal day. There was a fountain in the centre with a statue of a soaring eagle as its heart, some pretty glass-fronted shops bordering the square's western edge, a line of taverns on the east with tables and chairs set up outside. The cobbles were colourful, gold and silver and bronze, or had been at least before being covered in bodies and blood. The rest of it was ruined too. Those tavern tables were shattered and broken, the pretty shops all had their windows smashed in, and the water in the fountain that usually ran clear was now stained with the ichor of the dead and the dying.

It's war, Robbert told himself. *It's just war. This is normal.*

He didn't like it, though. When they'd fought against Lord Krator's army outside of Eagle's Perch, the thrill had filled him all the way up, but this was a more bitter tonic to swallow. That was army against army, an even fight upon the field. This was slaughter, savage rotten slaughter, and on a much bigger scale than they'd inflicted at the Port of Matia.

A man screamed and came at him from the right. Robbert turned his spear aside with a flick and sent his head flying away across the square. When it landed in the fountain with a wet red splash, he heard Bernie roar out, "Shot, Robb! Did you mean to do that?"

Robbert Lukar didn't answer.

More men came pouring from an alley, screaming in their foreign tongue. Robbert supposed there must have been another small garrison that way, though couldn't recall much of the maps Mar Malaan had shown them. The fat Sunrider was much more pleasant to be around than Elio Krator - minus the cloying stink of his perfume, of course - and perhaps the sunlord had recognised that, because over the last couple of days, it had been the scented whale who'd taught them about the city. It had all gone out of Robbert's head now, though.

Are we in the left part of Kolash, or the right? Is this one of the market squares that Malaan told us about or that one where they like to put on shows? He knew they were close to the docks, at least, given the stink of fish and salt in the air. *Maybe I should do what Lank suggested after all,* he thought. *Go and find a ship and sail back home, terrors of the depths be damned.*

The thought held no appeal. He continued the killing instead.

The men spilling out of the alleyway numbered forty or so, though Robb and his men were good to the task. The prince ducked away as a spear came for his face, spun to the side, took another man in the belly with his broadsword, and pulled his dagger to slash open the spearman's throat. Another spear prodded forward, brandished by a skilful youth no older than he was. It missed his visor by a mere inch or so, the tip scratching along his faceplate as Robbert twisted away. His heart almost skipped a beat and that was rare. He thanked the boy by killing him quickly and sending him on his way to the stars.

The rest were dealt with by his men, who quickly overwhelmed them in a raging bloody charge. Robbert had command of a host of two hundred today - mostly those he didn't know, common soldiers with little or no Bladeborn blood - and was intent on two things; making sure as few of them as possible died, and making sure as many of them as possible got their first kill. It wasn't for reasons of hate for his enemy or anything so sour as that, but power. *There is power in that first kill*, his father had taught him. *A man knows then if they have what it takes. And if they do, it gives them the strength to fight on.*

Robbert watched as the last of the city soldiers were slain, before turning his eyes around the square. On the far side, a pair of Kolashi pikemen were being hacked up by six of his own. Another sunwolf had appeared as well, from where he could not say. It was a young one, no larger than the direwolves you got in parts of the north, its mane barely grown in. All the same it had killed two of his men, judging by the savaged bodies lying nearby to it. Robbert didn't want any others dying on the wolf's account. "Bernie, if you don't mind."

"Pleasure." Bernie Westermond charged away, armour smashing stone, screaming at the men to clear a path as he went. The wolf saw him coming, snarled, then seemed to think better of the challenge and went scampering away down an alley. "Coward! Come back you blasted cur!" Bernie would have gone after him if Robbert hadn't called him back

"Bernie! Let it go!" he bellowed. "The square is ours. Let it go!" Bernie stopped, though begrudgingly, and looked around to see that the fighting in the square was done. "Form up," Robbert roared. "On me, men!"

The soldiers under Robbert's charge gathered before him, as he leapt up onto the lip of the fountain to get a better view of them. *Green Company*, he might have called them. Many were young, recruits who'd never felt a woman's warmth or grown hair on their chins, stableboys and farmhands and cobbler's sons from all across North Tukor. *My uncle wants them blooded*, Robbert knew. *He wants his army strong for when we march north, and the real war begins.*

"Men," he shouted. "We've cleared another square. For Tukor!"

"For Tukor," came the return call. "Tukor! Tukor!"

"You've fought well, every one of you! Who killed their first man here in this square?" he asked them. "Shout out your names and let them be heard!"

The calls came back. "Martyn," a young man shouted, and, "Briggs" and "Percy" called a pair more. An older voice bellowed, "Ben Butters," and another shouted "Theo the Bold!"

"Theo the Bold? Theo the *Bald* more like!" The jape came from somewhere in their midst, provoking howls of laughter from some of the seasoned men, of which there were few in the troop.

Robbert waited until the laughter was done. "Five more," he then said. "Five more who have given out the gift of death! We honour you, we are proud of you, but do not despair if you are yet to send a man to the stars… your chance will come soon enough." He pointed with his bloody sword in the direction of the loudest fighting, still ringing out through other parts of the city. "We go on, men! We don't stop until the city of Kolash is ours!"

A few more calls of 'For Tukor' spread through the throng as Robbert hopped down from the fountain and went over to Sir Lothar Tunney. "How many have we lost, Lank?" he asked. As ever, the tall knight had been doing a count as Robbert gave his address.

"Overall? Twenty-nine."

Robbert nodded. It wasn't quite zero, but wasn't too bad, given the inexperience of the company.

"You sure we should keep fighting?" Looming Lothar went on. "We've done our part. More than enough. No one else here needs to die."

"Everyone dies, Lank. Whether here or someplace else, what does it matter?" He patted the giant on the arm and called the order. "Follow me, men! For the north! For Tukor!"

Robbert Lukar led the way, with Lank and Bernie at his sides. All three were armoured from head to heel in godsteel plate and near enough invulnerable against an enemy of this sort. It wasn't so for the rest. He had a few old Bladeborn knights and soldiers in his company who had breastplates, gauntlets, helms and the essentials, but most were not so lucky. Some had castle-forged plate in varying states of use. Others wore coats of mail underneath their jerkins and surcoats. The least fortunate wore only leather, scuffed and stiff, with dinted halfhelms on their heads. It would not surprise Robbert at all to learn that of those twenty-nine dead, most were poorly outfitted.

"Where are we headed, Robb?" Bernie wanted to know as they went.

Robbert Lukar had no answer for him. "Don't know. Wherever the fighting is." They moved in some semblance of a formation down a narrow stone alley, the cobbles loosely fitted underfoot, curved and slippery. The fighting ahead grew louder and fiercer until they turned a twisty corner and saw battle raging before them, spreading out across the docks, hosts of ships bobbing on the waters beyond. Robbert remembered there had been a few barrack towers here according to Mar Malaan's maps, and a thick old roundtower that housed a garrison of several hundred near the fishmarket. He could see it now, further down the harbour, see the soldiers boiling out of it like angry ants, see the bolts and arrows flying from the windows and ramparts and roof.

Robbert called the order for them to join the fight, and went charging into the thick of it. "White feathers!" he yelled, over the din of battle, the steel song and the screaming. "Watch for white feathers! Remember who we're fighting!"

He had an inkling that Krator mightn't care anyway. *He's saving his best men as well,* he knew, *keeping them for whatever battle he deems more worthy.* There weren't so many Sunriders and Starriders in Krator's host tonight, not many strong armoured paladins in their plate and scalemail and fine feathered cloaks. Most were just regular rank-and-file soldiers, expendable and easily replaced.

And we'll have their like fighting alongside us when we march on Agarath, Robbert thought, as he swung his blade through a man's right arm, then took his legs from under him, then stabbed another through the neck and opened a third at the belly. That had been the agreement between Kastor and Krator. *Like for like.* For every green boy who died under Robbert's command, they'd get a green boy from Aramatia in return. He was starting to wonder if there was any point. *They're just bodies on the battlefield,* he thought, as he killed a couple more, *untrained and unskilled. Most of them will just get in the way.*

An arrow pinged off his pauldron, drawing his eyes up to the top of the roundtower where a small battalion of archers and crossbowmen fired down on them from the roof.

"Lank, with me."

The prince drove forward, bursting through the tower doors. There was fighting going on in there already, a crash and clamour echoing out around them as men fought in the main entrance hall. Robbert went right for the turnpike stair, spiralling around and around until he came to an open chamber at the top. There were windows cut into the thick stone walls here, through which archers were firing. Robbert Lukar and Sir Lothar Tunney slew them to a man, then looked to the wooden door in the ceiling above them.

"Must have pulled the ladder up after they climbed through," Sir Lothar noted.

Robbert nodded. "Lank, get up there."

"I'm not that tall," the knight protested.

"Just do it. Jump."

Lothar grumbled something under his breath, stepped underneath the door, crouched down, and launched himself upward in an explosive leap. He crashed right through the trapdoor, smashing the wood to splinters, and landed on the roof above. Robbert heard panicked screaming ring out through the night as he followed, jumping deftly through the opening and onto the tower's stone summit. Sir Lothar was already at work killing the archers and crossbowmen, who turned and tried to fire at him as he dashed and swung. It was all in vain. Arrows and quarrels went bouncing harmlessly off his armour without even making a mark. *They have nothing with which to hurt us.*

Robbert let his countryman do the work, as he moved to the parapet that overlooked the harbour, watching the fighting below. *No Sunriders,* he thought. *No Starriders.* If the city of Kolash had any such men or women here, they must have been fighting elsewhere, because he hadn't seen them. A few wolves, yes, but they were neither armoured nor saddled and had likely been let out of whatever stable or pen they were being kept in to help in the city's defence when the fighting broke out. Against regular soldiers they were savage adversaries, but against a man dressed in the Body of Vandar from head to heel, no.

I need a proper challenge. Give me a few Sunriders, with the finest Aramatian steel to grasp, wolves with claws that can cleave through my armour. Let me face a foe that can actually hurt me. Give me a challenge. Give me a moonbear…

"Robb, it's done." Lothar came striding over to join him, sounding listless. Blood dripped from his silver armour, rich and red as it caught the pale moonlight.

Robbert understood the man's lack of enthusiasm. Sir Lothar was not a cruel man who took pleasure in wanton killing, no more than he was. *He wants a challenge, a fair fight.* Both had spent their lives duelling other Bladeborn, sparring with them, training with them, contesting in the lists and tourneys. "This isn't what we trained for," he said, staring down at the fighting. "If this is all we're going to face in Aram, I'm not interested. Let my uncle bloody his blade instead."

"So you'll tell him no, will you? That you won't fight?"

Robbert wasn't sure what he'd tell his uncle in all truth. *I'm just venting,* he knew. *When it comes to it…* "I don't know. Maybe," is all he said. "He's becoming just as bad as Krator, getting us to do his dirty work. I don't like it, I'll tell you that much. I don't like how similar they are. They'd never admit it, but it's true. Those two are cut from the same cloth."

"A black cloth," Sir Lothar agreed. "Dark as death and stained in blood. All monsters are cut from it, Robb."

Monsters, Robbert thought. *Is my uncle truly that bad?* "Krator's worse," he told the tall man. "This coup…my uncle would never stoop so low as to bring civil war to Tukor. He'd never massacre his own people as the sunlord is doing."

The towering knight gave him a look.

"What? You think he would?"

Lothar shrugged to a clank of armour. "Maybe, if it would win him the throne. When I look at your uncle, you know what I see? I see a man who wants to be king, a man who acts like he already is. He's dangerous, Robb, I hope you know that."

"Meaning?"

"Meaning you need to watch yourself around him. It's my job to look out for you, Robb, same as Bernie's. And we both think it."

"Think what? Come on, Lothar, spell it out for me. Are you saying you think my uncle, the younger brother of my mother, whom he loves most dearly, is going to try to have me killed? Is that it? And Raynald too? Because he'd need to sail home and kill Ray as well, of course, if he's to take the throne. You are aware of that, I hope."

"That you've got a more skilled, gifted, and handsome brother called Raynald? Yes, I am aware. Oh, and he's more charming too. And funnier than you as well. And from what I've heard, he has a much bigger…"

"OK, that's enough."

"I'm just saying, Robb…"

"I know what you're saying, Lothar. You're doing your job, and warning me of my uncle. Fine, I agree with you, in part. He's ambitious, dangerous, and if I were to die by some natural means, or in battle, I doubt he'd shed a tear. But killing me and killing Raynald? No, he'd never cross that line."

Lothar only shrugged once more. "Just know that if it came to that, I'd kill him in vengeance for you, Robb. Or Bernie would, if not me."

It might take you both, Robbert thought. Fearsome warriors though his two protectors were, there was no one more deadly than Cedrik Kastor, or so he liked to claim.

Below, Sir Bernie Westermont was completing the rout, and further off the sounds of fighting had quietened too. Robbert made his way back down to the company and gathered them around once again. He found an empty crate to stand on and went into his usual speech, calling for the names of those who'd killed their first man. A few came back, though he barely heard them. 'For Tukor', went up the cries, and 'for the North', and even a few cheers for the prince himself. *You should be cheering Big Bernie*, he thought. *He's the one doing all the killing for you…*

He went to Lothar again right after. "How many?"

"In total? Thirty-six."

"So we lost another seven."

"You always were smart, Robb. Less so than Raynald, of course, but sharp enough all the same."

"Enough with the lip, else I'll have yours cut off."

"You'd have to reach them first, short-arse."

Robbert scowled, showed the tall man his back, and called for his men to follow him to the main gate.

They encountered a few more pockets of fighting along the way, steel clanging out down darkened passages and through the many small quads and courtyards they passed. After a while Robbert forgot the route so had Lothar lead in his stead, the tall knight guiding them through a warren of narrow alleys and lanes in which a man could easily get lost. Robbert tried to ignore the *other* sounds he heard as he went, though he couldn't ignore it all. The butchery was one thing, the abuse another. When he sighted a young Kolashi girl bundled into a dark corner by a clutch of Swallow men, he had them stripped naked and lined up along a wall.

"You were told not to touch the women," he shouted at them, as the four men stared down at their toes. One was already weeping, knowing what the punishment would be for rape. "Did you not hear that? Were you not told?"

"We weren't, Your…Your Highness," one stammered. "Lord Swallow, he never said…"

Robbert put a steel fist through the man's jaw, shattering bone. "Lie to me again and I'll have your tongue torn out as well as those soft little stones you carry between your legs." He turned. "You other men. Did you know?"

The other three stared down. The one who was weeping only wept the louder, though none of them had anything to say. Their silence was enough.

"Take them away," Prince Robbert commanded. He waved for one of his senior men to take charge of them. "Sir Krelyn, have them bound at the wrists and joined at the ankles to make sure they don't try to flee. As Swallow men, I'll let Lord Swallow deal with them." He turned to the grizzled Bladeborn knight. "Oh, and get their names, to make sure. I'll want to check in later and see that it's done."

Robbert did not trust the likes of Lord Simon Swallow to geld his own men. His father had always called the man weak. "A man too weak to levy the proper punishment will always see dissent and dishonour in his ranks," he'd taught his son. "Be strong, but fair, and you'll cultivate both honour and respect in your men." It did not mean you would not get bad apples, but better a rotten one or two than a whole tree gone foul.

By the time they reached the city's eastern gate, a further five men had been added to the train of prisoners. Two had been wearing Swallow colours, the other three of House Huffort, though now all of them just wore their skin. Their arrival brought a great deal of mocking laughter as they entered the bustling square. There were thousands assembled, the many smaller companies returning from their charges, sweat-stained and spattered in blood. To one side, a field hospital of sorts had been set up; Robbert ordered for his wounded to seek attention there, and off they went in a shamble of limping, groaning men. Elsewhere, tables were laden full of jugs of ale and wine and great plates of food; roasted duck and chicken, charred fish, braised lamb, pots of potatoes mashed and boiled, with breads, hunks of cheese, and local fruits as well of many different shapes and varieties.

"Go, feed yourselves," Robbert ordered. "You've earned it."

As *Green Company* went to the tables to feast, the prince spotted Sir Alistair the Abiding in disgruntled discussion with several others, Sir Clive Fanning and Happy Harys among them. It looked a heated debate, as the men attempted to appease Sir Alistair of some wroth. Robbert could quite guess what it was about. "Lothar, go see what that trouble is with Sir Alistair. He might be teetering."

"He told me he'd cause no problem," Lothar returned.

"Things change. After a night like this…" Robbert noticed Lord Gullimer approaching through the crowds. "Go, Lank, I'll come over in a moment. Try to settle him down if you can."

The handsome Lord of Watervale arrived a few seconds later. "Your Highness," he said, inclining his head, his hair as neatly groomed as ever. "It seems you've been busy hunting rapists and malefactors. I commend you." He gestured to the prisoners as they were led away by Sir Krelyn, to taunts and slurs and fistfuls of thrown food. "Whose are they, pray tell? Not any of mine, I hope?"

"Swallows mostly, with a few Hufforts in for good measure."

Lord Gullimer's bright blue eyes showed scant surprise. His own men were fewer in number and greatly more virtuous than the hordes under Houses Huffort and Swallow. "Not all men are able to resist the spoils of war, I regret to say," the lord told him. "The thrill of battle stirs a beast within them, one they're unable to control, no matter the risk. I daresay many of them think the punishment a bluff, and who could blame them? We have all heard the rumours of Keep Kastor, after all."

Robbert raised his eyes. He hadn't expected the man to speak so frankly about that. "My uncle would not take kindly to hearing you say that, Lord Gullimer."

402

"I'm not speaking to your uncle, my prince. I'm speaking to you."

Is this a test? Is he spying for him? No. Lord Gullimer was too noble a man to act sneak. This was coming from the heart. *He falters, as others do, under my uncle's charge. He mislikes what he is seeing here.*

"Such wickedness cannot be permitted, of course," the square-jawed lord went on. "I have sent soldiers of my own out into the city to make sure the women of Kolash are not being mistreated. I suspect more men will be marched through naked in due course, however." He tapped the cleft in his chin. "I only wonder what will happen when a senior man is caught in such disgrace? One of your uncle's commanders or knights, perhaps. Do you imagine Lord Cedrik will have them gelded, my prince, as he might a common soldier?"

No, Robbert thought at once. *He'll give them a pat on the back and ask for details.* Cedrik Kastor would care not if half of Kolash was raped and molested, that was the truth. It would not serve to say that so openly, however. If this was Lord Gullimer's way of declaring to Robbert his allegiance, the prince was keen to keep it subtle. "I suppose this charge was not given by my uncle then?" he merely asked.

"Hunting rapists and abusers? Oh no, that is a task I have taken on myself. Your uncle did bid that I come here and take inventory of the dead, however. All commanders were asked to keep a count, as you know. What is yours, Prince Robbert?"

"Thirty-six. We were forced to leave them where they fell."

"They will be retrieved overnight, now that the city is won." Lord Gullimer had no blood on him, not a spec of red staining that fine maroon and green surcoat he wore over his godsteel plate. Gullimer was one such man whom Lord Cedrik would save for a later fight. He was a fine swordsman, athletic and youthful for his age, and had a son among the Emerald Guards. *Sir Jeremy,* Robbert remembered. He had been part of his sister's protective guard when she sailed with her rat king husband to Thalan. Robbert thought of Amilia rarely, though when he did he missed her greatly. *She'll be safe, at least, from horrors such as these,* he told himself. *Thalan is much too far north to be under threat of attack.*

At the gate, the sound of horns began blowing, accompanied by a deep thumping of drums. *He comes,* Robbert thought, closing a steel fist, as he spotted the banners and barded horses approach, saw his uncle waving out to his host as he rode in through the gate upon his jet black destrier bedecked in his black-green steel and inky cloak. *He arrives a conquering hero,* he grumbled to himself. A killer born, they called Cedrik Kastor. Robbert hadn't seen much evidence of that of late.

Lord Huffort rode behind him at his right, Lord Swallow to his left. Lords Crabby and Craven, Robbert had heard them called around camp, Huffort for his perpetual foul mood, Swallow for his well-known cowardice. Robbert did not fail to note the look of mild displeasure on Lord Gullimer's face as he observed their arrival, nor the fury with which Sir Alistair Suffolk was glaring at the Lord of Ethior. Something about that look made Robbert nervous. Sir Clive looked worried as well, and Happy Harys didn't look so happy. Lothar loomed above all of them, looking Robbert's way. His face was strained and screaming out a warning.

Shit…gods…he's going to say something, Robbert realised.

He paced away at once, hoping to get there first, but by the time he'd gone but a half dozen paces, Sir Alistair was marching hard across the square in the direction of Lord Cedrik. Lothar moved at once to stop him, but the Abiding only swatted him back. Over the din of the thousands assembled, all the scuffing of boots and scratching of sabatons, the feasting and laughing and drinking, the neighing of horses and wails of the wounded and those horns and banging drums…over all that, Robbert could not hear what Sir Alistair was saying, but whatever it was, Lord Cedrik did not like it.

He arrived only to hear his uncle say, "….bondage? You call this bondage, Sir Alistair, to my face?"

"Bondage, yes. Thraldom, servitude, call it what you will." Sir Alistair Suffolk thrust a finger in the direction of the city. Already people were starting to hush and watch, and those horns and drums had died away. "We have lost hundreds of men tonight for that sunlord, hundreds for this misbegotten coup. Do you know anything of the man with which you're treating, Lord Kastor? Do you know of his past? Do you know of the woman he is trying to depose? If not, let me spell it out for you. One is reviled, the other revered. You bend your knee to the former, my lord. It is injustice, what we're doing, acting sellsword to that man. It is dishonour and disgrace. And I want no further part in it."

The look on Cedrik Kastor's face was so cold he might have been chiselled of ice. "Please, Sir Alistair, do speak your mind." He made himself smile, and of course Swallow smiled as well, and the rest of his lickspittles too, and many hundreds more who were gathered around to watch.

But not everyone, Robbert saw. Many were not smiling.

Sir Alistair the Abiding was one of them.

"I have tried to hold my tongue," he said. "The gods know I have tried. But tonight saw the end to that charade, and I will hold my tongue no more. My lord, let me say this quite plainly. Your army is rotten from the top down. Half of your Greenbelts are savages, given to butchery in battle, ill-disciplined and cruel. I have seen them torturing men tonight. Not even soldiers. Men, just regular men of Kolash, trying to flee the fighting. I have seen them abusing women, assaulting children. *Children*, my lord. Did you hear that correctly? I have been forced tonight to execute several of them by my own hand for such deviance. Several dozen others have been fettered for punishment, yet I have to ask myself whether you will give them their due. I had my doubts at Eagle's Perch when I saw how you treated the prisoners. Then I heard of this alliance and it only got worse. Now tonight…"

He shook his head, as though accepting what his words would bring. "My father Lord Marston the Moral would not be able to look me in the eye should I return to him and tell of what has happened here. Should I tell him I did nothing, said nothing, of this sickness." He lifted a hand and pointed it right into Lord Cedrik Kastor's cruel comely face. "*You*, my lord, are the source of this pestilence. It plagues your men, and has seen us joined in league with a man just as foul as you are. I will not stand by any longer as my honour, and the honour of my men, is stripped away like meat off the bone. I will not be left here a skeleton of shame, dishonour, and regret. No!" And he shook his head. "I would sooner die than serve another minute under your command." He ripped off his right gauntlet and threw it to the ground at the hooves of Lord Cedrik's horse. "I challenge you to a duel to the death."

Shocked murmurs hummed out across the throng and Robbert felt the hairs go up on the back of his neck. The Lord of Ethior was staring at Sir Alistair as though forged of stone, eyes deep and dark as pits. Robbert saw the left one twitch, saw his nostrils flare, but that was it, elsewise he did not move. His jaw looked so tightly clamped shut he might just shatter his own teeth.

The square went deathly silent. *Do it*, Robbert thought. *Do it, and die.* He had not expected that thought to come, but it did, and he stood behind it. *I want my uncle gone. Sir Alistair's right, the rot in this army starts with him.*

But another part of him called a warning. Sir Alistair Suffolk was known as a disciplined and skilled combatant and had won acclaim at tourneys across Tukor, a specialist in the duel and the melee. *If he defeats my uncle, I will have to take charge*, Robbert knew. As appealing as that was in theory, in practice it would put him right between a rock and a hard place. Continue this alliance with Krator, and then march on Agarath, or risk obliteration by land or sea. They were five hundred miles from Eagle's Perch now, closed in by Aramatian cities and strongholds on all sides. *They'll have us surrounded*, Robbert fretted. *There will be no way out, lest we take ship.* And that came with its own dangers too.

The thoughts tumbled through Robbert's head in a sudden flow. Most likely his uncle would win, but all the same, if he didn't… *I'm not ready to rule*, he realised. *I'd have no choice but to keep this alliance intact, wouldn't I? And they'd hate me for it, wouldn't they? No*, he told himself. *No, I cannot let that happen.*

"Sir Alistair," he called, his voice ringing out over the silent square. Men turned at once to face him. "As your prince, I bid you withdraw your challenge. You are overwrought from battle and the horrors you have seen. Please, think calmly and let us retire to my uncle's tent where we might…"

Lord Cedrik Kastor dismounted from his horse, his crow-black cloak flapping at his back as he landed on the hard stone cobbles. Robbert's voice was cut off as the crowd broke out in hushed whispers. Slowly, deliberately, the Lord of Ethior stepped forward until he stood but a few feet away from Sir Alistair Suffolk. He opened his mouth to speak and silence fell anew.

"*You* challenge *me* to a duel?" he asked.

"Yes," Sir Alistair said loudly. He glanced at Robbert. "I'm sorry, Prince Robbert, but I can no longer abide…"

It happened so quickly. So quickly Robbert almost missed it. One second Sir Alistair Suffolk was speaking, and the next his mouth was full of blood and he had Lord Cedrik's dagger lodged in his throat.

"You would be no challenge," Robbert heard his uncle whisper, as he

405

twisted the knife, and held the man close so he might see the light leave his eyes. "You are beneath me, Sir Alistair the Abiding. And when I return home, I'll send your father to join you."

Sir Alistair's eyes had time to flare in fear, before Lord Cedrik drew out his knife and shoved him to the ground, where he lay down on the cobbles, choking on his blood.

35

Cecilia

The workshop was warm and sweaty, loud with the sound of hammer on metal. Orange light filled the air, shimmering above the fires of the forge. In a sweat-stained vest and with the Hammer of Tukor to grasp Tyrith worked upon his wonders, pounding, shaping, casting blades and axes, spears and shields, suits of armour bright and gold.

Cecilia had only just arrived. She wore a nightgown and a frown. "It's very hot in here, Tyrith," she called over his hammering. "And *loud*. You do realise how late it is, don't you? You know my room is just down the hall?"

He only just then seemed to notice her. With one last pound, he brought the Hammer of Tukor down upon his latest creation, then set it aside with a thud. He raised the iron mask he wore when he worked, showing a face flush and pink and shining. "My lady. Sorry…did you say something?"

The harsh ringing was still in her ears. "It's late, Tyrith," she said, cringing. "And you're being very loud. I'm trying to get some sleep."

"Oh? I hadn't realised the time."

Why would you? You've not stepped foot outside once since we arrived here. "Please just stop. Read a book or something if you're not tired. You've got hundreds."

Fhanrir had not been lying about that when he'd told her Tyrith would not lack for reading material. The dark days at the rear of the refuge were long gone now and the blacksmith was all the happier for it. It was enough at least to keep the shadow of fear from his mind. The fear of the unknown. The fear of having another's spirit consume him. He nodded. "Yes. You're right. Of course. I had thought it much earlier, my lady. Fhanrir only came to me a short time ago, so I took that to mean it was daytime."

"Oh? And what did he want?"

"He spoke to me of…the Steward. He says he will come and speak to me soon. About…about my ancestor, and the…the…"

"Transference," Cecilia said for him. "All will be well, Tyrith. I have a strong conviction that *you* will remain *you*, once the spirit of Ilith imbues you." *That should serve,* she thought, *for now at least.* She had no energy to coddle him tonight. "Tell me, did Fhanrir say when Hamlyn would come?"

"He gave no day or time, no. He just said *soon.*"

And that can mean anything with these mages. Soon to her was a few hours, maybe a day or two. To them it could mean half a lifetime.

"Why do you ask, my lady?"

"Curiosity," she simply said. The truth was much more sinister and nothing she wanted to talk about with him. *Boys and blood and sacrifice.* She turned from the thought, lest he see the disquiet in her eyes. She shaped her lips into a smile and had a cursory look over the weapons and armour he was making. "Is it all godsteel?" she asked.

"Yes, my lady. Every piece. They have great stocks of it here. And Fhanrir permitted me to melt down other blades from the armoury and reforge them to my own designs. I'm learning a lot, from Ilith's notes. I thought what he'd left at his forge above Ilithor was all there was, but no. There is a great deal here as well, new techniques I'd not read of before." He smiled, lost to his passion. "Would you like to see?"

"Another time, Tyrith. It's terribly late…"

"Yes, of course, of course. Say no more. Another time." He smiled and pulled off his mask, letting his sodden blond hair tumble about his forehead. "I'll just get some reading in, then, before I retire to bed. It helps me sleep." His face went suddenly thoughtful. "Have you heard from Hog yet?"

She was about to step away. *Gods, this again.* "No, Tyrith. I told you he went away."

"Right. Yes." He gave that enthusiastic nod of his. "Through the portal, you said."

"Yes. The portal. He returned to Ilithor to help protect my nephew Raynald, as I asked him. I've explained this to you."

"I know, but…" He brushed aside a few strands of wet hair. "Well, Fhanrir told me the portal is deactivated. He said it's been like that for a while. Since before Hog left."

I'm too tired for this. I should have told him the bloody man was dead. It was like nursing a child, all this censoring of the truth. "Fhanrir seems happy to volunteer much information to you, Tyrith," she said, avoiding the question. "It is never so with me."

"Well…no, I don't think he's got anything to hide from us, my lady. We are all just spokes on a wheel, in a fashion, each of us with our duty. Together, we roll forward. We progress. There need be no secrecy between us."

Some secrets are useful, she thought, *when they protect you from something you'd rather not confront.* "What else has Fhanrir been telling you?" She edged her voice in accusation and got the desired response. Tyrith was always desperate to please her, as he had been her father, and would soon forget about this matter with Hog. "I don't like that you two whisper behind my back, Tyrith. If we're in this together as you say, you'll share with me what he tells you."

"And I would, my lady. You know I would. I keep nothing from you."

"Then?"

He looked at her like a lost lamb bleating for its mother. She didn't feel especially good about twisting him about like this, but if it put a stop to a few awkward questions, so be it. "Then nothing, my lady. He hasn't said anything you don't know."

"Yes, I'm sure." She gave him a suspicious look to drive in the knife. "Your hammering. Are you not worried it will keep them awake?

"They don't hear it, my lady. The mages all have bedchambers a good distance from here, so I understand it. It's only the one at the door who might hear, but he's awake anyway, and it's still quite far. This place is very large, my lady. It's as big as a city, really. I don't think I disturb anyone. If I did, I'm sure they'd tell me."

She processed the information, nodding pensively. Lady Cecilia had spent much time in the Shadowfort library trying to find illustrations and diagrams to show the layout of the refuge, but had found nothing on that account. Instead she'd listened, watched, and learned, wandering the halls and corridors and chambers that remained open to her. She was testing them, seeing how far she could go, working out if they were truly watching. This place was cloaked in mystery. She was trying to draw back the veil.

She turned her eyes to the Hammer of Tukor, resting upon the anvil. "It is the most powerful magical artefact ever devised," she said. "It *feels* the power is has wrought, you once told me."

"It does, my lady. Like the portal. It was how I discovered its location in the first place."

She did not want to talk about the portal. "Can it sense other magic, Tyrith? Illusion? Deception? Trickery?"

"If commanded to do so, yes. There is no magic or mystic art that can outwit me when I hold the Hammer, my lady."

"Are we being watched?" she asked bluntly.

He frowned at that. "Watched, my lady?"

"The door. You just said there is one at the door. One mage?"

"Yes. There is always one at the door, I sense. He guards the way."

As I thought. Cecilia felt the hairs stiffen on the back of her neck, cold fingers crawl up her spine. She had passed the doors that led from the refuge to the fortress many times now and had never *seen* anyone there. Yet of late she'd sensed a presence, felt a stir in the air, heard breathing. Once she'd even spotted the faintest shift of a figure, camouflaged in the darkness, watching. It had made her wonder…

"Do their cloaks hold magical properties, Tyrith?" she asked the heir. "Do they shield them from eyes that are not permitted to see?"

"No." He gave a shake of the head. "No, I don't believe so, my lady. I have sensed no magic weaved into the garments they wear. They are regular cloaks, I believe."

409

"Then how? How do I pass through the doors without seeing the watcher?"

"Shadow," he said. "They enhance its properties, cloak themselves in shade and gloom. Wherever there is darkness, they can hide."

She nodded. The shift of movement she had seen had come from a shadowy portion of the hall, away to one side where the light of day could not disturb them. "How do you know this?"

"I know," he said. "By instinct, and by study."

Instinct. She wondered for a moment if the transference was somehow happening already. Was it a slow process? Was that the real reason Hamlyn had been absent so long? Ilith was no longer lying in stasis on his slab either, bathed by the shard of light cast from above. He had been moved, but to where Cecilia did not know. Could it be that Ilith's spirit was imbuing Tyrith even now? And his knowledge, his skill?

"You seem concerned, my lady," the blacksmith noted. "You needn't be. These mages may look foul, but their hearts are fair, and their duty sacred. They assign a watcher to the door only to protect against attack from the fortress beyond. The hearts of men are fickle, Fhanrir says. And fearful. There is never knowing if one of the men outside will come here with an intent to bring blood. The watcher makes sure this is not so."

"How?" Cecilia asked. "What powers do these mages possess, Tyrith? Does the Hammer show you?"

He nodded as he said, "Yes, if I should focus on such a thing. I haven't, however, nor do I often see them. Even their names I forget."

"Agnar, Dagnyr, Vottur," she said. "Vottur is Fhanrir's great-grandson." Jonik had told her that, though a part of her wished he hadn't. It only made her think of Fhanrir abed with a woman and the thought of that was most abhorrent. "They're all mixed blood, man and mage. I assume their powers are limited."

"Suggestion and illusion," Tyrith said. "Whisperers and Shadowcloaks."

"Shadowcloaks?" The term rang a bell somewhere.

"I read it in Ilith's writings. It was a name given to men able to cloak themselves in illusion. They would weave and wear shadow, my lady. At a basic level it would permit them to conceal themselves in gloomy corners. When mastered, men could appear as another person entirely."

"The one watching the door. You're saying he's one of them? A Shadowcloak?"

"I would think they all have that power, to some degree. Not true illusion, perhaps, but the ability to hide in shadow is not difficult to learn."

"And Fhanrir? Could he have mastered this art of illusion?" *A Shadowcloak,* she thought. Gerrin and Jonik had spoken of a mage called Parsivor, who could clothe men in deception and disguise. "Could he appear as someone else? Someone we already know?"

Tyrith seemed confused as to why she would ask that. "I don't know, my lady. Such sorcery would require an extraordinary depth of mastery, to be convincing. Taking on the guise of a stranger is one thing, but someone you know…" He shook his head. "Every detail would have to be correct, every shadow in place. Men see what they want to see, what they expect to see, so in many cases an imperfect version might convince, yet not if you were *looking* for faults and imperfections." He wiped a hand through his sweaty hair. "I'm not sure why you're saying this, my lady. There is nothing untoward occurring here. The killing is done, Fhanrir assures me. None in the fort or refuge will suffer any further."

We're suffering just being here. Cecilia was not going to cast aside her concerns, no matter what Tyrith said, and his eagerness to repeat what Fhanrir had told him was making her wary as well. "I trust you not to mention any of this to anyone," she said. "Our conversations are to be private, Tyrith, and confidential."

"Of course, my lady. Though there truly is no need."

"Humour me. My son is here, as I have told you. As his mother it is my duty to protect him, and as your guardian my purpose is the same. I only want to see you both safe."

He smiled at her fondly. "We are safe, my lady. I would sense if there was anything sinister at play, and your son…he bears the Nightblade. There are few so mighty as he. He of all people ought to have nothing to fear."

Even the mightiest can be cast down by the demons within, Cecilia thought. Power could be self-consuming, a gift and a curse, two sides of the same coin. *I saw it with my father and I'm seeing it with my son.* It terrified her, in truth. The way he would mutter to himself, and gaze down at the Nightblade for long moments, sometimes scowling, sometimes smiling, lost to some conversation or vision she had no hope of knowing. Every time she tried to probe he would remind her who she was to him. "You gave me up," he would say in a bitter voice. "You have no right to ask me or lecture me, Cecilia. Go back to the refuge. I've seen enough of you for today."

Yet at other times he was kinder and would thank her for her help with the younglings and the boys and the prisoners as well, and they would even sit and talk and share stories, as she had imagined in her dreams. It was never quite so perfect as that, of course, but it was something. He would confide in her the truth of his burden, yet in the same breath, would grow angry and agitated should she suggest he give it up. It was the same for Gerrin, and Harden, she knew, who she would talk to when Jonik was sleeping or taking his watch upon the wall.

Only two nights ago the three had gathered in the roundtower library, to whisper of their concerns while Jonik slept. When Cecilia had asked them straight what they would do, Harden had said, "Leave," almost at once. He was a grim-faced man, all grunts and snorts, grey all over from his hair to his stubble to his garb. A typical Ironmoorer, hard and mirthless. "We tie Jonik up when he's sleeping. Drug him so he's out for hours. And we go. Carry him down the mountain, all the way if we have to, and leave that bloody blade behind."

Gerrin had disagreed. "We cannot go. The mages won't permit it. And what about the others? Cabel? The boys? The prisoners? You'd leave them?"

"Course I wouldn't leave them. Jonik's going to set them all free, isn't he? Well then, they can come with us or go their separate ways, whatever they please. Leave these mages to do their foul duty, and see the back of this place for good."

"And Cabel? He's too weak to travel, Harden. We carry him too?"

"Yes, we carry him. Most likely the lad won't make it, but we'd have to give him that chance. I'd never leave him here for those mages and their experiments."

Experiments? Cecilia hadn't been sure what he meant by that. "What do you mean?" she'd asked.

"With the boys," Harden had answered with a grunt. "This blood magic. Gerrin's let slip all sorts of stories to me, Cecilia. The boys…sure, we know all about *that*. But seems some of the men have been taken into the refuge before as well, never to be seen again. And prisoners too, brought from down below. Isn't that right, Gerrin?"

"Sometimes, yes," the former Emerald Guard confirmed. "Captives would be brought here, bound and hooded, and taken into the refuge. I never knew who they were."

Cecilia frowned. "To what end?"

"Experiments, as I say," Harden grunted. "My best guess? They've been experimenting on this transference business, how to make it work. Who knows how many men have died for it over the years. They might have been running these experiments for centuries."

"Or they might not have been running any experiments at all," Gerrin had come back. "You're only speculating."

"Aye, I am, but is it so hard to believe?" He'd hunched forward in his chair, elbows to knees. "You might want to have a look at that Book of Contracts, Cecilia. You're the only one of us who comes and goes freely. You take a look at the last page of that book, see if there's not some final surprise awaiting us in there."

Gerrin waved that idea away. "She wouldn't be able to translate it. Jonik said so himself. It's written in some old tongue no one speaks anymore."

Harden was still looking at Cecilia. "How's your memory, my lady? Good, is it?"

"It's serviceable," she'd said. "Why do you ask?"

"Well, let's say you take a look at that book, and you read a passage you can't translate. Mayhaps you can try to remember the words instead, or even scribble them down on a scrap of parchment?" He'd turned his eyes around the library. "There are plenty of books on language in here. I'm sure we can figure it out."

The fact that Gerrin didn't dismiss the idea out of hand suggested he was pondering it. He gave Cecilia a querying look. "Do you think you could do that, without being spotted?"

She had no idea. "Maybe, maybe not. There's much amiss in that refuge. I don't know if I'm being watched or not."

"Shadows and parlour tricks, is all it is," Harden said. "These mages have their sorceries, I'll admit that much, but there's no all-seeing eye watching us all. Only the gods have such a gift, and these creatures are no such thing. You just wait until the dead of night when everyone's sleeping, my lady. Pay a little visit to this Book of Contracts then."

It's dead of night now, Cecilia thought, as she stood in the workshop with Tyrith. *Dead of night and there could be no better time.* If they were watching the book, so be it, she could claim curiosity got the better of her and scuttle back off to her bed. But if not...

She left Tyrith with a smile and "sleep well," slipping through the silent refuge as the shadows lurked about her. *Shadowcloaks,* she thought again. She'd be careful to keep a closer eye on dark corners and gloomy rooms from now on, searching for signs of movement and subtle shifts in the air. The stillness unsettled her, she was not too proud to admit. Cecilia Blakewood thrived in busy places and this endless refuge with its countless rooms was about the most uncomfortable place she'd ever been. *I'd sooner be in a warcamp or a city under siege. I'd sooner live in mud and squalor than in this pristine lifeless place.*

Her footsteps pattered gently on the stone as she walked, moving down empty corridors and grand unfurnished chambers. In places torches burned, but those were few, and tonight the skies were dark and heavy and scant moonlight poured down through the shafts and windows cut high into the ceilings and walls. Cecilia clutched at her godsteel dagger to enhance her sight and senses. The fact that she was still allowed to bear it ought to have comforted her, but somehow it didn't. *There is no comfort to be found here,* she thought. *Even if it's as Tyrith says, and there's nothing sinister or untoward going on, this place is no less oppressive.*

She worked her way through the maze of chambers and halls and corridors, past statues great and small, beneath ceilings sculpted and splendid. She still spent time every day marvelling at them, and could spend a hundred more between these walls without ever having a chance to study them all. Many of the statues and sculptures she could recognise on sight, famed kings and queens and heroes of the past who she'd seen depicted in stone and ink and paint a thousand times before. Littered among the regal were those more humble but no less renowned; adventurers and voyagers who had sailed the seas and uncovered places until then unfound; historians and chroniclers who'd scribed famed works and artists who'd conjured beauty from brush and chisel; hunters who'd ranged the fearsome wilds and won acclaim by land and sea; singers, mummers, poets and bards who'd written songs and plays still performed to this day.

The refuge was a monument to all the realms of the north and those who'd shaped it, magnificent and mournful at once, a museum and a mausoleum where all the men and women she passed were long centuries dead. Yet all the same, it remained unfinished, cold and inert and barren like the womb of a crone, a place that might once have harboured life, but instead turned dry and dead. *Ilith would never have wanted this,* she thought. *For this place to be made his tomb.*

When she approached the chamber that contained the Book of Contracts, she slowed. Her eyes moved restlessly about her, wondering, and something told her she should turn back. *What can I hope to learn?* she asked herself. Knowledge could be dangerous and some secrets were better left unsaid. But Cecilia Blakewood had never taken a step back in her life and wasn't about to start now. She stepped inside.

The statue of Queen Thala loomed high above her as it thrust forward from the wall, eternally illuminated by a soft glow of light that seemed to hang in the air about her. Her hair was a flow of watery stone, her eyes wise and far-seeing, her lips in a kind knowing smile. Cecilia wondered if she ever smiled in real life.

How could she, knowing what she knew, seeing what she saw? It seemed to her a dreaded life the founder of Rasalan had lived, burdened with the weight of the future and all its wars and slaughter. *Ilith built the world,* Cecilia thought, *but Thala built the future, paving a road that has led us here....a road cobbled in blood and bone...*

She climbed the steps that led up to the plinth beneath Thala's watchful eye. The Book of Contracts lay before her, the book that was that road, each page and each contract another cobble. *Blood, bone, death,* she thought. Curiosity swelled within her. She wondered how many kings were mentioned within, how many queens, how many princes, princesses, champions, heroes, lords and ladies and lowborn too, all dead because Thala had foreseen their fall, all slain by the order to prune the tree of time and guide them to this end. She wondered how many southerners had fallen to shadows too. *It can't have only been us,* she thought. The southern side of that tree needed to be cut and trimmed as well. All lay within, every name and every place and every time, moving chronologically from the first page until the last.

She reached to open the book, spreading its pages before her. It opened randomly, somewhere in the middle, and her eyes scanned greedily for a name she knew. The words made no sense to her, and the script was hard to read as well, a beautiful flowing hand with wide curving arcs and perfect balance. *The hand of a goddess,* she thought. *But not a tongue I know.*

Cecilia Blakewood turned another page, and another, and another. Soon clumps of them were being flipped through at once and still no names leapt out to her. *Curious.* Those must have been written in another tongue too, she supposed, or else hidden in some sort of code that only the mages could discern. There might well be trickery here as well, so far as she knew, an old magic written into the ink and pages. *Perhaps only the mages can read the words,* she wondered. *Perhaps only Hamlyn.*

She turned to the last page, the final contract, to the reason she had come. She had no parchment or quill pen with which to write, so her memory would have to serve. *Though probably I'll find nothing,* she told herself. Most likely the last contract had already been completed months ago. *Maybe it was even Jonik's?* His failed attempt to slay his father had set all these events into motion. It seemed only fitting it would be the last.

The contracts seemed to be separated one per page, though sometimes they were long enough to bleed into a second as well. This last one was just the same, many paragraphs long across a double-page spread at the very end of the book. Included within would be places, she guessed, times, dates, names, and much else besides, a specific set of instructions as to how the contract should be carried out. She gave out a sigh of frustration. *I'll never remember it all.* It would take all night to try to memorise even a portion of this passage, and that was not time she had.

I should go, she thought. *What am I even doing here?*

All the same, she lingered there a while longer, trying to search for words she might recognise, if only in part. If this was indeed Queen Thala's hand, then it would be an old Rasal dialect, the first and founding language of her kingdom. It was said that the common tongue of the north had evolved mostly from ancient Vandarian, but there were influences from Tukor and Rasalan in there as well. She scanned, word by word.

The letters are the same as least, she thought. *Mostly, anyway.* Some appeared backward to her, or upside down, and there were some symbols she didn't recognise at all. *Gods, this is hopeless. You're wasting your bloody time.*

She closed the book and turned…

…to find a cloaked figure standing behind her.

A sudden gasp escaped her lips, and she stumbled at the top of the platform, tripping over her legs to tumble down the steps, landing upon the hard stone floor below in a sprawl of battered limbs. She heaved and pulled a breath of air into her lungs, coughed, and scrambled up to her knees, reaching for her dagger.

"No," said the cloaked figure. "Put it away, Cecilia. We are friends. Are we not friends?"

Hamlyn, she realised, though she could not make out his face in the gloom of the doorway. His voice sounded older, brittle and broken. "I thought you were abed," she wheezed, trying to catch her breath.

"And you took your chance to snoop?" An empty chuckle moved through his lips. "What killed the cat, Cecilia? Tell me that."

She rose to her feet, wincing at a pain in her side. Another breath rasped down her throat, burning. She exhaled and breathed again and said, "Curiosity."

"Just so. Curiosity. It can be dangerous, child." He took a step forward and into the soft light of the chamber, illuminating his face.

Cecilia took a sharp breath. The mage was a ruin, skeletal and grey, what flesh he still had all but sloughing off his bones. One of his eyes drooped horribly, his neck was pebbly and wattled, and his rich brown hair had gone chalk-white and wispy to dangle off his spotted skull.

"Does my appearance bother you, my lady?"

She steeled herself and swallowed. "I've seen Fhanrir a dozen times before."

"So you have. Though I daresay I look worse." He gazed at her through his one good eye, looking like the great great grandfather of the Steward, or his rotting corpse brought back to life, and not the Steward himself. "I can age rapidly," he explained to her. "It is a strange thing, how quickly it can happen. I may stay young for many long years before the decay begins. When it does, the descent from youth to decrepitude usually takes several months, though this time only weeks have passed. It is a sign that the end is near, Cecilia. A sign that my duty is soon to be done."

"But not yet," she whispered, trying to still her heart.

The man smiled, showing the grotesquery of the brown and broken teeth that lay beyond his torn grey lips. "No, not yet. But soon, child. Soon." He looked past her, up the stair. "What drew you to come here, pray tell? I am quite certain Fhanrir told you the book was forbidden for you to read."

He did, she thought. "Curiosity," she said.

He chuckled again. "Quite so. That dreaded dangerous thing. Which part were you reading?"

"No part in particular. I was just flicking through."

"Carefully I hope. The pages are brittle." He smiled once more. "I suppose it's only natural that you would come here. I sense you expect there is something we're not sharing with you. Do I have that right, child? You fear that there is some last contract involving you or your son?"

He's reading me, she thought. If so, what would be the use in lying? "I'm his mother. I have a duty to protect him."

"Of course you do. Can there be anything more fierce than a mother protecting her child? But in this case, you need to protect him from himself. The boy has begun to lose himself to the Nightblade, Cecilia. Oh, I know the terrible power that resides in that blade. I was there when it was forged, after all. You would never believe what it took to achieve, the depth of sorcery Ilith had to mine in order to shatter the heart of a god, fashion from the fragments those five wondrous swords. When Varin brought us the heart, he told us Vandar had given it over willingly, as he had his body as well, yet there were times when Ilith and I doubted it. The heart *resisted*, Cecilia. It was stubborn, strong, sentient. It did not want to be fragmented, and yet what choice did we have? Varin was adamant, and who could say no to *him*?"

He shook his head, sighing. "The magic Ilith wrought to shatter the heart, divide it, bind it into its separate parts…well, there was a darkness to it, to the process he devised. Few hearts wish to be broken, Cecilia, and those that are only wish to be remade. Such it was for a time. Varin spoke of how the blades were drawn to one another, yearning to be reunited. He asked Ilith for the secret to their binding a hundred times, yet Ilith feared how the king would use them. So he kept the secret from him, and over time, the blades grew apart, learning to think for themselves, live for themselves, be free. Now they exist in an opposite state to when they were first born. They rebel against the binding. They do not want to be reforged."

Cecilia had to remind herself that this was no story, no retelling thousands of years after the event. Hamlyn had lived through it all, been there at the forging and the founding, witnessed the birth of the world as they knew it. She steadied her breath. "My son…" she said, in a whisper. "It's as you say. I fear the Nightblade is trying to get him to leave, and take it with him. It fears what will happen if it stays."

"It must stay, Cecilia. As the others must come."

"Then take it from him."

He frowned at her. "Is that what you would have of me? To leave your son in darkness?" He shook his head. "No. Jonik must do this himself, lest he be lost forever to its will. I told you before that Thala saw only so far, did I not? She left us the Book of Contracts to follow, a map to guide and lead us here. But that map is at its end, the path ahead unknown. Jonik may yet have a role to play, child. I cannot interfere in that."

She nodded her understanding. "It's not your duty," she said.

"No, it is not. What Jonik does now is down to him alone, as it is with the other bearers. Thala never saw the blades being reforged, at least not that she ever told me. Her work was to create the conditions for that to take place, yet what happens now, none can know. In time the future will take shape. But alas I shall not be there to see it."

She saw a deep look of weariness on his face, a fatigue millennia in the making, and knew he had earned his rest. "It's time for me to bring you the boys, isn't it?" she asked him.

He nodded sadly and seemed to age yet further, shrinking and slumping in his cloak. "Alas yes, it is," croaked his brittle broken voice. "The boys," he whispered. "One last time."

36

Amron

The waters of the Red Sea were wild and raging, stirred up into a frenzy by the coming of the storm. From the high balcony of the Spear, Amron Daecar gazed out, praying the enemy armada was out there. *Let the seas swallow them whole*, he thought. *Let Rasalan drag them all down to his watery halls, to be jesters and fools in his court.*

His blue Varin cloak was whipping in the wind, though the rain had not yet started to fall. Spring was a stormy season in the south of Vandar, and the seas were prone to churn like this, though rarely did the storms last long. He had consulted his augurs that morning and been told this one would be no different. *A petulant rant*, they had called it. *Turbulent and angry, yet short.* Amron had hoped for a longer, more bitter tempest to take root, though apparently it was not to be. But then who could really say? The augurs had been known to get it wrong as oft as they got it right.

"When did you last have word from your sea scouts, Lady Brockenhurst?"

The Pointed Lady stood at his side, furled in a thick orange fox fur cloak with a massive high-backed collar, black and stiff and tall enough that it reached above the height of her narrow head. Her dark hair was pulled back and tightly bound in a knot, making that long nose of hers particularly prominent as it thrust forth from a face thin and vulpine. She was a slender woman, raw-boned and angular, though not old, born of Tukor though now a Vandarian by marriage. Her late husband Lord Farys Brockenhurst had died at sea some five years ago, giving her control of his seat at King's Point until their young son Florian came of age.

"Too long," she answered, in a shrill voice. "The last of them went out a week ago and have not been heard from since. I've given up sending them, Amron. They're all just being killed by dragons as soon as they're spotted."

Then we're blind, Amron thought. *The enemy could appear on the horizon at any moment.* "Lord Randall Borrington has said the same. His scouts are no longer coming back from the Tidelands. He fears the Agarathi are marching across the land bridges to batter through the western gate."

"They just might. With the Lumarans in support, the dragonfolk have more than enough men to attack through a half dozen gates if they please. Ships have been sailing up from the Crystal Bay for months; galleys, galleons, cogs, caravels, a number beyond count. The last scout who laid eyes upon the Trident said there were over a thousand sails there, maybe two. And those sails were not all red, black and gold; many bore the colours of the southern empire as well." A fierce gust of wind assailed them, causing the silver and black banners flying above the Spear to billow and crack. Lady Brockenhurst squinted out to sea. "Even if they sail in this weather, the bulk of them will still get through. And that's not even to mention their main weapon. The dragons, Amron. How many of them are there?"

"We do not know for sure, my lady. Our latest estimates run into the hundreds."

"*Hundreds*. No fortress or city in the north could withstand an attack by hundreds. Not even Varinar."

Amron nodded. "That may be so. But each dragon killed strengthens us, and many have already fallen. Their numbers sound overwhelming, yes, but they're not inexhaustible. My son told me that over a dozen dragons were killed during the Battle of the Bane, and many more have since been slain. If the enemy must suffer such a cost to win every city and every fort in the north, they'll soon find that their wings are clipped."

The Lady of the Point gave that a derisive laugh. "How many dragons did we have to face in the last war? A few dozen? Against hundreds there can be no hope. When they attack us here we will be obliterated and the Vanguard, Crosswater, and Varinar will soon follow."

Such doom and gloom, Amron thought. He put a comforting hand on her shoulder. "Anne. These are unprecedented times, but do not lose hope. We faced but dozens in the last war, yes, but all were trained and bonded to Fireborn, almost all of them large, fierce, and experienced in battle. Most of these hundreds we now face are unridden, wild, reckless, and commonly smaller than the named dragons we know. There are not a hundred Garlaths and Malathars out there, my lady, far from it."

"Oh good. You've made me feel so much better." She slipped away from him as another gust of wind came hurtling through, and turned to retreat into the safety of her chambers. Amron followed her in to find Walter sitting with young Lord Florian, a boy of eight, pudgy cheeked and freckly, with a bowl haircut that only made his round face look even rounder. "Florian, come here now," his mother said. "It's time for your bath. Leave poor Walter alone."

The young Lord of King's Point made a face. "But I want to stay with *Lucky*. He's telling me his stories. Of the Icewilds. There was a snowbear, Mother, a *big* one." The boy grinned from ear to ear, and his face took on the shape of an oval. "Lucky says that ranger killed it in one blow. The one standing outside. *One* blow, Mother. Did you hear that!"

"And a fine blow it was." Walter Selleck sat lounging in an armchair as if he owned the place. "He put his blade right through the top of the bear's skull. Do you remember, my lord?"

"Yes, Walter, I remember. It was only months ago."

"I want to hear more stories," Florian shouted. "I'm not having a bath, not today. I'm clean already. I want to hear more *stories*, Mother!"

"You can hear them later, sweety. Now come, Florian, stand up. Walter has other important things to be doing." When the child did not move, she marched in and pulled him to his feet, then turned him to the door. "Come on now, Florian, come on. If you don't settle down, I'll have the maids scrub you pink as a lobster."

The boy tried to fight, but was a weedy sort and had no strength to repel her. He was led off kicking and screaming. Walter remained in his chair, grinning. As ever, he had his book in his lap and a pencil behind his ear. "He always was an excitable boy," he said.

Amron moved to fill himself a cup of water. Outside, the winds were blowing so fiercely it felt like the roof of the tower might come ripping off its fastenings. "I wasn't aware you had spent time with him before. His mother, yes, but not him."

"A mother and son often come as a pair, I find." Walter reached to take his own wine cup from the table beside him, sipping. He looked rather too settled for Amron's liking. "Delicious. Anne always did keep the best vintages here."

Anne. Gods be good. "I hope you're not intending to stay here, Walter. We're not here to rekindle old romances, you know." He still struggled to get his head around the fact that Walter had charmed Lady Brockenhurst into bed not once, or even twice, but a good many times in the past. All since the death of her lord husband, of course, but still, they made an odd pairing: Walter, short and scruffy and lowborn; the Pointed Lady of rich ancient stock, tall and thin, not exactly comely, but hardly unpleasant to look upon either.

Walter swirled the wine in his cup. "My dear Amron, I'm quite aware of why we're here. Fear not, I mean only to share in Anne's wine and not in her bed on this occasion." He had another sip. "Though of course, if she should *order* me…well, who am I to deny her? This is *her* city after all." His grin was most unpleasant.

Amron gave no response.

The Spear was the official castle residence of the Lord of King's Point, built near the harbour upon a hill overlooking the sea. Much about the Point was pointy, not least the lady and her nose, and much about it was kingly besides, the city grand and rich and stately, a splendid monument to the greatness of Vandar. It had been built and named for Amron's own namesake; King Amron, son of Ayrin, grandson to Varin, a warrior king who'd broken the long peace his father had fostered with Agarath when he sought vengeance for his grandfather's murder at the parley of Death's Passage by the sons of Eldur, Lori and Dor. *Amron the Bold*, men called him, though perhaps *Amron the Bitter* would have been better. It was said he quarrelled with his father a thousand times over his peaceable stance, unable to accept that Eldur's sons would not answer for his grandfather's death.

Well, he had his chance in the end, Amron Daecar reflected, *when Ayrin finally died.* By the time Amron became king, Eldur's second son Dor was long dead and his eldest, King Lori, was dying, yet he still mustered his legions to seek their vengeance all the same. It was during that time that King's Point was raised at the mouth of the Steelrun River, a great city of steel and strength that was to become the jewel in Amron the Bold's kingdom. *He even moved from Varinar to rule from this very tower,* Amron thought, *where he might watch the seas night and day and plot his next attack.*

He looked out across the tempestuous sea, all white caps and high black waves. *And now here I stand in his stead, over three thousand years on...and still we do this dance, still we play this game of war.*

He had a final drink of water and put his cup aside. Outside, the skies were roiling, and the rains were beginning to come down, lashing hard and sudden against the grand stone balcony. He turned and made for the door. "Come, Walter, they'll be waiting."

They descended the spiral staircase that coiled through the tower's interior, Whitebeard stepping from his place by the door to join them. "I heard a boy screaming," the ranger said. "You should not let children look at Selleck, my lord. It will only give them nightmares."

Walter's laughter echoed down the stairs. "You're one to talk. You have the countenance of a corpse, Rogen, but I appreciate the jape."

"It was no jape."

"Then I suppose you're just naturally funny. Though past history rather proves otherwise. Take the compliment, Rogen, you don't get many. Would a starving man wave off a morsel of food?"

"If rotten, yes."

The repartee went on for the full descent and Amron had to admit, Rogen Strand was growing more skilled in the verbal spar. When they reached the broad stone entrance hall that opened out onto the castle courtyard, he told them to be quiet, however. Much as he enjoyed their bickering in private, it was not for public consumption.

They passed the doors to the courtyard, bordered by a pillared colonnade on all sides. It protected them from the rain as they moved around to the feast hall at the right of the keep, stepping inside and climbing a set of steps to the smaller audience chamber above, a stately room in which King Amron the Bold would hold his councils. Amron Daecar decided to stick with tradition and gather his lords and knights there.

"My lords, gentlemen, thank you for coming." Amron stepped in with Whitebeard and Walter. The former took position at the door, a sentinel in black and grey. The latter roamed freely to record events as per his duty. "I see you're already into the wine," Amron observed. "Good, just make sure you don't get drunk. We must all be fit and ready to fight at a moment's notice."

Sir Torus Stoutman was not drinking wine, but ale. He raised his horn and said, "The storm's to last all night, we're told, and maybe more than that. The Agarathi won't dare cross in this and if they're already on the way, all's the better. Let them sink and founder, aye!" A few other men assented with calls and raised cups.

Amron shook his head. "Dragons fear not the storm, Sir Torus. That myth has been duly put to bed. And *those* can come at any time."

The men were arranged as they pleased; some sat at the large elmwood table that dominated the heart of the room; others were leaning against carved pillars or pacing gently from side to side. Amron was happy to see that none had climbed the stage where his namesake had once had his throne. The throne was no longer there, of course - it had been moved to the palace in Varinar when Armon the Bold's own son Athran took the crown - though there were lesser thrones in place to be sat in by the lord and lady of the Spear.

Amron took the lord's seat, unfastening the Frostblade to rest at his side. As soon as he took his fingers from the pommel his pain stirred, aching deep in his bones, yet he did not let them see him wince. "Lord Warton," he said. "Has there been news since this morning?"

Lord Stanley Warton, the Castellan of the Spear, was seated at the table nursing a cup of hippocras. He was a small old man with a quiet voice and chronic cough, the shy and retiring sort, and not fond of big councils. He stood at Amron's summons. "Word from the east, my lord, yes. We had a crow…come from….from Sir Glarus Pentar at Nightwell," he said, between coughs. "Grim tidings, my lord, most grim. The estimable Lord Porus is dead."

The room did not erupt in surprise, though the news was still unwelcome. Lord Porus Pentar had suffered through many ailments this last decade and his health had receded swiftly these last months, since the onset of war. "Sad news indeed," Amron said solemnly. Porus had been a good friend to him and his family for long years. "A toast to his memory. Walter, a cup."

Walter Selleck filled him a cup of ale, then retreated to the shadows to observe and record. Tankards, horns and mugs were raised, ale and wine and hippocras drunk. Amron gave a brief eulogy, speaking of Lord Porus's stout heart, his cool head, and his honour. "He was never a man to back down from a fight, though never a man to start one either," he finished. "His loss will be keenly felt by the people of Redhelm and the South Downs."

"Hear hear," roared Sir Torus Stoutman.

The men echoed him in subdued cheer.

Once the clamour had died down, Sir Quinn Sharp said, "Lord Pentar's eldest will become lord now. Sir Alrus. Not a particularly pleasant man, but he's got a decent head for command, I've heard. Is he already in Redhelm, do we know? The city will need its new lord when it comes under attack…"

"He's there," Amron confirmed. He'd had that from Alrus's younger brother Storos, in the letter he sent to Crosswater. Sir Glarus was another of Porus Pentar's brood, his second son and commander at Nightwell. He took a look at Lord Warton and saw that the castellan had more to say. "What else did Sir Glarus write?"

The old man cleared the tickle from his throat. "The Agarathi, my lord. They are moving, Sir Glarus says, from the Bane. On Mudport. The city is under siege."

A murmur broke out, though Sir Torus looked confused. "Thought Mudport was already destroyed."

"It is, probably." Sir Symon Steelheart yawned loudly. "Dragon's Bane was taken in a night. Why would a city built of sticks and mud hold out any longer?"

Sir Brontus gave his friend a narrow glare. "Don't be stupid, Symon. Only peasants and fools believe that myth. Mudport's a strong city, well defenced against dragons. Everyone knows it."

"Everyone with a shred of wit, anyway," sneered Sir Ramsey Stone.

The Knight of Nine-Hearth ignored the sally. "All the same, it's no Dragon's Bane. When did this crow come flapping in, Lord Warton?"

The castellan put a hand to his mouth. "Less than an hour..." he coughed, "before this meeting."

"And Nightwell's what...four hundred miles from here? Five?"

"More like two," said Lord Mantle, who honoured his house by always wearing one. Even in hot weather, the man was to be seen in his heavy wool cloak. *Their sigil might as well be a mantle as well,* Amron thought. Instead it was a black bat with wings outstretched, its fangs and claws of silver steel, on a background of light stone grey. "Not a long flight for a crow."

"Nor a dragon," Steelheart said, pushing a hand through the twisting coils of his shiny golden hair. He did not seem to be taking this seriously, though to him Mudport was a world away, full of queer Marshlanders and mire-dwellers. "Mudport's ash now, let's be honest. Shall we change the name to Ashport, or is it too soon?"

Amron was looking forward to seeing the back of this boy. *Let Randall Borrington listen to your japes instead. You'll find he has less patience than I do.* "Hold your tongue, Sir Symon," he admonished. "This is not the time for joking." *Though he's not wrong,* he thought. If Vargo Ven sent but a portion of his strength against Mudport it would not hold out for long. He looked at Lord Warton. "Does Sir Glarus say anything else?"

The castellan was still standing and coughing. "Yes my...my lord. He mentioned that your son had visited him, but briefly. Sir Glarus told him of...of the attack on Mudport and he...he flew away at once to help."

Of course he did, Amron thought, pushing his fears for his son aside. *Elyon will fight the whole world if he can.* "Was he with anyone?"

"No, my lord, though...the Knight of the Vale was following. He came that very evening to Nightwell, in the company of...of Sir Storos. They drank to Lord Pentar's passing, the brothers. And there was another with Sir Lythian. A dragonknight, in his service." Lord Warton fumbled into his pocket and extracted the scroll. "Perhaps you ought to read it yourself." He shuffled forward to hand it to him.

Amron took the scroll and gave it a quick read. The men in the hall were muttering confusion. Dragonknights did not tend to enter into the service of Knights of Varin, after all.

"What does it say, my lord?" asked Sir Rodmond Taynar. The young man had decided to ride with the column, rather than sail downriver on his uncle's flagship. Life on the Iron Champion was not for him, he'd confided. "Ever do I prefer a saddle between my legs," he'd told Amron, though more likely, he just wanted to be away from Lord Dalton for a few days.

Amron rolled up the parchment and tucked it into a pocket. "It says that Captain Lythian is currently on his way here, Sir Rodmond." He made no mention of the dragonknight and his alleged complicity in Sir Tomos Pentar's death. *I'll wait for Lythian to hear that tale in full,* he thought. "As ever, we're dealing in scraps and fragments. We must await more news from the east, yet until that time, we focus on ourselves." He looked at Sir Adam Thorley, the head of the Pointed Watch, responsible for keeping order in the city. The pointed helm and shoulder caps he wore marked him as their captain. "What do you intend to do with the people here, Sir Adam? I have just come from Lady Brockenhurst's chambers and was alarmed to see that she was still in residence there. Ought she not be more safely situated, with her son? The city could come under attack at any time and these high towers make attractive targets for our winged foes."

"That they do, my lord," said Sir Adam, a man of youth and vigour, much the antithesis of old Lord Warton. "Yet we have the skies under watch at all times and rest assured, Lady Brockenhurst and the young lord will be swiftly escorted to the vaults, where they'll be safe."

But for how long? "And the people?"

"King's Point is well furnished with underground sanctums, my lord. Many are privately owned by the city elite, yet those have opened their doors to the commonfolk, at Lady Brockenhurst's request. There are other strongholds built beneath us where thousands more can be sequestered, when the time comes. Drills have been run, and the criers have been walking the streets, warning all of the coming peril. We are well prepared, my lord."

I like this man, Amron thought. *Why can't everyone be more like him?* He'd sooner take a hundred Adam Thorleys than have to deal with Sir Symon's smirks and Sir Brontus's sullen broods, the petty bickers and battles that were still going on between the loyalists of the Olorans and Taynars. A part of him could not wait for the Agarathi to come so it drowned out all this squabbling. *Give us all an enemy to fight and they'll put their grievances aside.*

Well, Amron Daecar was hoping to take that into his own hands by shipping Sir Brontus and his allies away. But first he needed Lord Dalton back, and the First Blade was soon to arrive, he knew. Only this morning he'd despatched a rider to gallop upriver and report as to the whereabouts of the Iron Champion, and he'd returned shortly thereafter with news they were fast approaching. *And how has Lord Dalton fared these last long days,* he wondered? It was a question that was soon to be answered.

The rains were beating on the roof, hard and heavy, and distantly he heard a bellow of thunder in the air. He could almost feel the hope in the room. Hope that the Agarathi were already at sea, hope that they'd be caught in the storm and have to turn back, or arrive at the shores of Vandar crippled and broken. A dragon was worth a thousand men, but that did not mean men were useless. Without them, the enemy could never occupy a city or spread the grasping fingers of their conquest across the north. Dragons were merely weapons, and weapons had their limits. *And the sea gods side with us.*

Sir Ramsey Stone shifted from the pillar he'd been leaning on to stir the coals in a brazier. The storm had brought with it a chill, and premature darkness, so several iron braziers had been lit and there were torches burning along the walls as well. Stone was a cold man himself, thin-lipped and cruel-eyed, the sort who looked like treachery. You only had to glance at him to know he'd be willing to gut his own grandmother if it meant some sort of gain. He gave Sir Brontus a sour look. "How's about this storm, Oloran?" he said, in a voice loaded with malice. "You going to blame this one for robbing you of something too?"

Sir Brontus Oloran glared from his bench. "I *was* robbed, Stone," he said in a low voice. "Any fool could see it."

Sir Ramsey laughed at him. "You're the only fool here. A fool and a failure, mewling day and night of how hard-done-by you've been. It's pathetic."

Brontus shifted as though to stand, though Sir Symon took his arm before he could. "Ignore him, Bron," he said, chuckling. "The man's a craven, everyone knows."

Ramsey Stone's eyes darkened. "*Craven?*" There were few fouler things to say to a knight. "Say that again and I'll geld you, boy. If you haven't been snipped already."

The Knight of Nine-Hearth did not rise to the bait. He was effeminate and wore it proudly. "Craven," he merely said, twisting a curl of hair around a finger. He grinned, then stood, drawing his sword. "Prove me wrong, sir."

Sir Ramsey's eyes shifted to Amron's high seat. *He hopes I'll intervene,* Amron realised. He might have done so, yet decided to let it all play out. Ramsey Stone was a craven and a bully to boot, there was no lie there. There was a certain satisfaction to seeing him called out.

The man's pause was enough to make Sir Symon laugh all the louder. "Is this your way of proving me wrong, Sir Craven? Quivering in your little black boots? It's like a whore trying to prove she's chaste by taking yet another man between her legs." He laughed again.

"If there's a whore here it's *you*, eunuch." Stone gave Sir Symon and Sir Brontus a disgusted look. "The pair of you sicken men, the things you get up to. Don't think we don't all know it."

The fury in the eyes of Sir Brontus Oloran was bright and baleful. He thrust suddenly to his feet and forward, storming around the side of the table in Sir Ramsey's direction, ripping his blade from its sheath as he went. Several men leapt to block his path, but he pushed them all aside. Cups and horns went flying, and a jug of ale was knocked over to Sir

Torus Stoutman's great dismay. Sir Ramsey Stone slinked backward in fear…

…and was replaced by the tall grey figure of Rogen Strand.

"Move, ranger!" Sir Brontus roared at him. "The man called my honour into question! Move, let me cut him through!"

Whitebeard's only answer was to turn his head to Amron and say, "My lord?"

Amron was half tempted to let the men duel right here in this audience chamber. *My royal namesake would have,* he thought, though that was no reason to permit it. Some men revered Amron the Bold for restarting the war, but Amron Daecar was not one of them. He was more of the Lord Porus Pentar camp. *I'll finish a fight, but not start one. And I'll not let blood be shed in the Spear.*

"Enough," he said. "Sir Brontus, sit down. Sir Ramsey, one more word and I'll have you escorted to your room." *Act like children, and I'll treat you like children,* those words said.

Sir Symon and Sir Marcus Flint were the two to draw Brontus back, still seething as he retook his seat. Whitebeard remained where he was until Amron gave him a nod, then returned to his place by the door. Sir Ramsey slinked back to the shadows to lean against his pillar.

"Good, now let us resume," Amron said.

The council session continued, though would not last much longer. They rarely did, lest some important tidings be shared, and those were scant enough. Though the crows still managed to move freely enough between the forts along the Black Coast, few came from further afield. The east of Vandar was dark, Tukor and Rasalan yet darker, the south as black as tar, a lightless void from which no tidings ever came. Most news they received was of troop movements, the shifting of a lord and his levies from one fort to another, city security, dead dragons, and tales of ancient beasts, rising from the wounds of the earth.

This council meeting was proving as meagre in tidings as the rest, save this news of Mudport. Which was foul enough, if not unexpected. Winning the city would give the Agarathi control of the Bay of Mourning, allowing them to sail up through Redwater Bay to Tukor, or else cross over and invade Rasalan. Amron wondered if that might be their intent. They had destroyed Thalan already, some early reports had said. If they could rout the coastal cities around Whaler's Bay, the Lowplains would follow swiftly. It would give them a stronger platform by which to assault Tukor, and then Vandar.

But when he brought the suggestion to council, Sir Torus Stoutman merely snorted and said, "The Agarathi don't give two hoots about Rasalan. They destroyed Thalan, aye, but that was for an Eye and a king, Elyon said. What's the rest of the kingdom got to offer them?"

"Land," said Lord Mantle. "Lord Daecar is right. They could have control over the entire kingdom within two turns of the moon. No man likes to fight an enemy when he knows there's another one right behind him. By controlling Rasalan they'll be able to advance their invasion without that concern."

"Aye, but at what cost? They lost over thirty thousand men taking the Bane. And how many dragons? They'll probably lose a few more winning that muddy port besides, and then what? Doublebay. Calmwater. Shellcrest. Harrowmoor. And that's just the start of it. Our Rasal friends may be kraken-obsessed crab-lovers, but that doesn't mean they don't have men to fight. Merrymarsh, Swiftwater, Browlan, Maynard, Buckland, Payne, Paramor, all greathouses, all powerful, all stocked with Bladeborn knights. The dragonfolk could take Rasalan, aye, but they'll take a wound or two while doing it, and no one wants to fight Vandar when wounded. And what do you think we'll all be doing while they march from city to city? Sitting here scratching our collective arse? Lord Rammas's army will march north to the Links. The princeling who sits the Ilithoran throne will do the same. Every sword, spear, axe and bow in the west will descend upon the enemy if they corner themselves over there." He had a swig of ale. "I hope they bloody do, but I reckon Ven's too clever for that."

Most seemed in agreement with Stoutman's dismissal, though not all. Sir Quinn Sharp put it forth that the enemy were cornered already at the Bane, and if they tried to march west, would be even more so. "If they head west, they'll have to cross the Riverlands at Rustbridge, and Lord Rammas will come in behind them anyway and cut off their retreat. We'll have them trapped and make them bleed. If you want to know what I think, winning Rasalan first is the sensible option."

"Good thing no one wants to know what you think, then," Sir Torus told him.

The debate over the enemy strategy in the east went on a while longer, until they started going in circles. It was all speculation in the end. Amron cleared his throat and the room quietened. "We can all agree that the enemy's main target is Varinar," he declared. "The armada gathered at the Trident has been assembled for that very purpose, and I have told you of Lord Borrington's reports from the Twinfort, of enemy troop movements across the Tidelands. They may well be planning to attack by two fronts, up the Steelrun and down the High Way."

"Then they'll fail on two fronts," said Sir Marcus Flint, defiantly. "No force is sufficient to overcome Varinar. Not in all history has it fallen."

"Everything in all history hasn't happened until it happens," Stoutman said to that. His pipe had appeared in his grasp and he'd begun to make good use of it, puffing happily. "There had never been a Sir Torus Stoutman before yours truly was born, not in all history. In all history there was never a man so big and dumb as Sir Taegon before his poor mother pushed the monster past her thighs. There might never have been a knight in all history who wore golden ringlets in his hair before Sir Symon the Smirker came along. And aye, there was a King Amron once, and a bold one too, but not so bold as ours. Not in all history."

"We get the point, Torus," Amron said. "There's a first time for everything, you could have just said."

427

"Aye, I could. But where's the fun in that?"

Not everything is about fun, Amron thought. It was no use telling Sir Torus that, though. Life was a game to him, to be played with gusto until he died. "Varinar has never fallen, that's true, Sir Marcus, but never have the enemy amassed against us in such numbers. I had thought that the army that won the Bane would close in on us as well, but this siege of Mudport makes me doubt it. If Varinar was their goal, why not march at once on Rustbridge? Why bother sieging Mudport at all?"

"For the harbour," suggested Sir Quinn. "To be able to resupply by ship."

"Conquest," offered Sir Adam. "Death by a thousand cuts. Not all duels end in a stab to the heart. They aim to slash at us, one city and fort at a time. They want to destroy us, my lord, and don't care how long it takes."

The room murmured agreement. And then Walter Selleck spoke up. "Are we not forgetting the most important detail?" he asked, stepping forward from the shadows. He placed his tome upon the table with a *thump*. Men looked at him as though wondering why this lowborn scribe was free to talk. "This is no normal war for land and power, no war of conquest and spoils. It is not Vargo Ven who commands from the Bane, nor Tavash Taan from Eldurath. We all know who rules them all and if you'll not say it, I will." He paused and looked around at the doubtful fearful faces, and said, "Eldur," in a whisper, then louder, "Eldur the Eternal has arisen. And it is not land he seeks, nor conquest, but fire and ash and blood and bodies, for shadow and a war unending. So when you consider your enemy, consider this....you're not fighting *soldiers*, you're fighting *slaves*, men and beasts in thrall to his will. Because when Eldur has his way, all the world will burn, north and south it makes no matter, us *and* them, all of us. This isn't a war anymore, my lords. This is a fight for *survival*."

Silence followed his words. Even the storm seemed to stop in its thundering, the rain grow quiet as it lashed at the roof. Somewhere in the hall, a man coughed, and Amron heard the sound a wooden cup makes when it *clacks* against a table. The fire crackled and spat in the braziers, the wind wailed and whistled through the door. And still the silence lingered.

Eventually, Sir Symon Steelheart gave a bemused chuckle. "This funny little man is so odd, don't you think?" he said to no one in particular. "Eldur died three and a half thousand years ago, friend, or must someone take you aside and remind you of your histories?" He turned. "I thought this scribe of yours was a learned man, Lord Daecar, not some wild-haired crackpot hollering of Eldur and the war never-ending."

"Your lack of faith will not save you, sir," Walter said to him, in a subdued voice.

"This is fear, not faith." Sir Symon pointed a finger at him. "And this sort of talk doesn't help."

Amron was inclined to agree with him. Whether Eldur had returned or not didn't matter. It made no difference to their preparations and only ripened in a man a sense of dread they could do without. Amron had heard reports of panic in the squares, riots, doomsaying and a great deal more.

"When men know the end of the world is coming," Sir Ralf had said to him back at Crosswater, "they let the shackles come off."

Amron knew what he meant. *A man uninhibited is a man to fear. Strip away the veil of law and order and he can become a beast, unchained and dangerous.* Amara had told him of the problems going on down in the Lowers of Varinar as more and more people poured in from the countryside, and the same would be happening at every city in the north. Rape, theft, murder, all would become a plague as cities starved and sat awaiting their doom. And the more men heard the name Eldur, the worse it would become.

He sensed it was time to draw this council to a close lest Sir Symon and the other doubters descend upon Walter like a pack of wolves. He rather liked the scruffy little man as he was, and not torn to pieces. "My lords," he said. "Let's leave it there for today. With luck tomorrow will bring more reliable news and we'll…"

His voice was cut off as the door to the hall swung open and the blusterous song of the storm surged in. All turned at once to find Lord Dalton Taynar striding forth, soaked to the bone in his Varin cloak and armour. The lords who'd sailed upon the Iron Champion came with him. Amron saw Kindrick, Rosetree, and Barrow, lesser lords all, and Lord Gavron Grave the Ironfoot. His left leg had been removed from below the knee after he'd snapped it savagely during a hunting trip, so the story went. When he'd asked his surgeons if he would ever walk again without a limp, they'd not been able to tell him yes. His response was legend. "Well then what the hell do I need it for?" he'd bellowed at them. "Chop it off and gives it to the dogs. I'll have a godsteel one clamped on instead." Amron had wondered why people didn't call him Gavron Grave the Godsteelfoot for that, but supposed Ironfoot had a better ring to it.

Others followed the lords into the hall, knights and captains marching forward in a show of strength. Amron didn't miss old Sir Ralf of Rotting Bridge either, who he'd asked accompany Dalton on his voyage.

Did it go well, Ralf? he wondered, as he met eyes with him. The old man had a small smile on his face to suggest yes, but more so was the manner in which Dalton Taynar moved. Strongly he strode, and with purpose, the Sword of Varinar gleaming resplendent at his hip. It shone out bright and golden as he moved past men and braziers, past tables and benches, past pillars and stools, past Sir Brontus, who eyed in hatefully, past them all. Only when he came before the stage did he stop and bend his back in a bow before Amron's high chair. "Lord Daecar, I'm sorry we took so long on the river. The winds have been against us for days."

"You need not apologise for the weather of the world," Amron said. He looked at him, hopeful. "Did you do as I asked, Lord Taynar?"

The man's response was to draw the Sword of Varinar from its sheath in a swift single movement and hold it aloft before him. Golden light branched out like a sunburst, sudden and brilliant. "I did, my lord."

Amron studied him. There was no visible strain in Lord Dalton's eyes, no sweat on his brow, no tremble to his arm. He had asked that he hold the blade before him for a full minute to show his progress, but no, after a short ten seconds he'd seen enough. "Good," he said. "I'm glad."

Dalton nodded and thrust the blade back into its ancient scabbard. There was a look of great pride on his face, and he appeared almost ten years younger and half so dour as he'd been the last time Amron saw him. "Tidings have been slim on the river, Lord Daecar." Even his voice rang out cleaner and richer than usual, more confident. "I see you've been holding council. Is there anything that I've missed?"

"Nothing that can't wait. Lord Warton," Amron said, and the small castellan hurried forward.

"Yes, my lord?"

"Have rooms prepared in the Spear for the First Blade and his lords."

"Right away, my lord." He turned and shuffled away.

Amron had another look at Dalton. "I shall visit you when you're settled, Lord Taynar." He gave him a faithful nod, and even allowed a smile. This would make matters a great deal more simple. To the assembled men, he called, "Our session is ended. Those of you who have a thirst and a hunger, retire to the feast hall below. Lady Brockenhurst is to put on a fine spread, I'm told. Sir Brontus, please stay. I have a matter to discuss with you."

The men began filing out, though Lord Dalton lingered a moment. "Anything I should be aware of, Amron?" he asked, in a quiet voice.

"I shall come and tell you later."

Dalton Taynar bowed, turned, and stepped away.

After a few more moments the room was empty but for Amron and Sir Brontus Oloran, still seated at the table. And Whitebeard, who remained at the door. Brontus looked over at him. "Does this shadow of yours *ever* talk?"

"Rarely," Amron admitted.

"He ought to think himself lucky he is under your protection. I did not like how he stepped before me earlier, Lord Daecar."

"Rogen Strand is the second living son of Lord Styron the Strong, Sir Brontus. He does not need my protection." The man might have been sent away to become a ranger as a boy, but that did not change the strength of his blood and birth. "You may be an Oloran, but you're of a lesser branch, and not in line to become lord of your house. Should Sir Gerald perish, Rogen will become his father's heir. He is just as highborn as you are."

Sir Brontus made a petulant scoffing sound, as though unwilling to face that fact. "All the same. When a man steps in my way, they must be willing to face the consequences."

"And what consequences are those?" Amron challenged. "You would try to kill him, for preventing bloodshed in this holy chamber?"

"It was Sir Ramsey's blood I wanted, not the ranger's."

"Why? For uttering a baseless slur? Sir Ramsey Stone is a Knight of Varin, same as you. You should *never* cross swords lest it be in the training yard."

"I ought *not* be just a common Varin Knight. I *should* be First Blade, my lord. Everyone knows it."

"You and the Knight of Nine-Hearth are not everyone, Sir Brontus. And there is no such thing as a *common* Varin Knight. Do not lose respect for the order."

The man submitted with a nod. "No, my lord, I spoke in haste. But Sir Ramsey..."

"I know. He has a curt tongue and likes to stir trouble. A man of temperance understands that such men need to be ignored. They gain power from the *reaction*, Sir Brontus. Do not rise to them and they are powerless."

"Yes, my lord. I understand that, yet sometimes..." He trailed off for a moment. "I know what they say about me and Symon. We grew up together, and were always the closest of friends. That is all it is, I assure you, and yet people come out with these slanders and calumnies and I..."

"You needn't explain," Amron cut in. "I am not here to judge you, Brontus. I am here to tell you that you're to leave on the morrow and sail west for the Twinfort. Lord Borrington has called for aid in light of these reports of Agarathi legions crossing the Tidelands. He needs thousands of swords, and a strong man to lead them. I thought of you."

The knight took a few moments to process that. "You're sending me away," he said. "Or is Dalton? He wants me away from the blade, doesn't he?"

Yes, and so do I, Amron thought. The longer Brontus Oloran lurked near it, the more likely he would do something stupid. "You're one of the finest swordsmen in Vandar, Sir Brontus, and you have command of over five thousand men from your lord uncle and his underlords. We are well stocked here, and have a large garrison still at Crosswater as well. The Twinfort is more weakly provisioned. I would see it bolstered."

Sir Brontus stood from his bench. "My lord, I would request that you grant me a chance to prove my worth," he exclaimed.

Amron did not understand. "I am giving you that chance, Sir Brontus. The Twinfort will soon see fighting, I assure you, and if not..."

"No, not fighting. But *a fight*. I request that you grant me a second duel with Lord Dalton, for the right to lead the Knights of Varin and bear the Sword of..."

"No. You had your chance and were bested." Amron was at his wit's end. "I have told you not to bring this up with me again, Brontus. You have complained of the weather, and brought scandalous accusations of bribery and corruption to me as well, and in the yard no less, with all the men to hear." Rumour had spread of that as Amron had feared, and men had begun to mutter of Dalton's struggles. Some even claimed Amron was showing favouritism.

Sir Brontus had the gall to suggest the same right now. "You have given him more time than you would another," he said. "I know why Dalton sailed downriver, rather than ride with the rest of us. I know why you sent your sworn man Sir Ralf with him. You want *him* as your First Blade, not *me*. Even though you know I'm better suited to the post...and the better sword besides...you want him, because he's weak and servile and..."

"And I'll hear no more of this," Amron bellowed. He surged to his feet. "Weak is the man who cannot accept his flaws and failures, Sir Brontus, and I have given you ample warning. *Do not* mention this to me again. Tomorrow, I want to see you and your five thousand men assembled at the docks. You will be shipped to the Twinfort, under the assumption that the weather has cleared. If not, we shall wait until the storm has passed, but you *will* go, Sir Brontus, make no mistake in that." He looked past the knight to Whitebeard, gave a nod, and the ranger opened the doors. "Go," he said. "And think clearly on the man you want to be, the man you *were*. The one you're becoming is a shadow of him." He gave him a final glare. "Go."

He watched the man stamp angrily from the hall, armour rattling, pushing past Whitebeard as he went. The ranger's eyes went dark. "He should not talk to you like that," Rogen growled, once the knight was gone. "Such accusations come close to treason."

"Do you want me to behead him, Rogen? Execute every man who says something indelicate in the heat of the moment? If I do that I might have no one left to command." He walked down the steps of the stage. "He'll cool off overnight and cause no further trouble, worry not. And once at the Twinfort, all thoughts of the Sword of Varinar will be long behind him."

The ranger grunted. "As you say, my lord."

As I say, Amron thought, *even if I don't believe it.* Sir Brontus Oloran had been touched by an obsession he could not control, and something told Amron that he'd not heard the last of this yet.

37

Ꝉalasha

"Blackness," the king whispered, shuddering in his tattered rags. "Blackness…blackness…I see blackness. I see the end." Pale fleshless hands trembled as they clutched at the stone sides of the podium. His eyes were big and dark and empty, reflecting the doom he saw in the Eye. "The end…" his voice quailed. "I see the end…soon…soon…it's coming *soon*…"

Talasha stood nearby, watching silently. She felt cold, though the maids had brought in several braziers to burn and crackle around them. The king's chains rattled as he shifted and shook and suddenly he was weeping, pulling his hands to his eyes and shying away. He tried to crouch but the iron fetters held him back. "The end," he cried out. "I see the end!"

"Calm, kind king. Be calm." Talasha stepped forward and placed a hand on his shivering arm, holding him softly. "Look into my eyes, and tell me what you saw."

He swallowed, the apple in his quill-thin neck going up and down. What chin he had quivered feebly and a froth of white foam bubbled in the corners of his mouth. His eyes were wide and staring. "I saw…I saw…" He blinked, just the once, and those staring eyes reappeared. For a moment he said nothing, then he blinked again. "I saw…"

He doesn't remember, the princess realised. *Or he won't tell me.* "Think. Try to think, sweet king." She smiled at him and stroked his arm, a bone wrapped in greying skin. They brought him food and water daily, yet rarely did he eat or drink. Terror had wasted him down to a skeleton in rags, chained to a plinth, his wrists so thin he could probably slip his fetters if he wished it. By night they would release him and let him lie down to sleep, but by day Lord Marak insisted they keep him chained. "The Father needs the heir of Varin found," he had told her. "And this man out there, this savage brute murdering dragons, *defiling* them. He wants him too. Once Thala's scion finds them, he will be unfettered, but not before."

When the shackled king gave no answer, the princess moved to the side of the room and poured a cup of water from a jug. His prison was a large chamber at the summit of the palace, windowless like the throne room, dark and dreary and unwelcoming. The plinth and prisoner were fastened at its heart; to one wall there was a table, with food, water, even wine, to another a simple pallet bed. Braziers burned about them, coughing up their smokey warmth, but somehow the gloom remained and the cold as well. Talasha returned to King Hadrin and put the cup to his lips. "Drink," she urged.

He drew back, like a child being given their medicine, and turned his head away, sending water spilling down his lips and into the ragged wisps of his beard.

"It's water, just water, sweet king. Drink. Yes, good, drink it down." She coaxed him with softness and kindness and the use of comforting words. *Kind king*, she called him often, and *sweet king*, and *handsome king*, all of them lies, for he was not sweet nor kind nor handsome, but petty and cruel, the rumours said, and foul to look upon, she saw with her own two eyes. But it was her duty to nurse him, tend him, comfort him. *The Father must unearth his enemies*, she thought. *I must do this for him. I must...I must...*

She had dreamt last night of a blaze, an inferno washing over all the world. It came at her like a wave as she slept, preceded by a great black cloud of smoke and ash webbed in flashes of wild red lightning. From the top of the palace she had awakened to watch as it rolled toward the city, consuming all before it as ten thousand fiery tongues licked forth and a maw of dreaded darkness bellowed out in rapture.

Men and women and children burst into flame at the sight of it, and from the skies rained molten rocks to explode upon the streets and squares. Talasha remembered how she had screamed soundlessly, how her throat had burned and her skin blistered, how her hair had caught on fire. The tears that rolled down her cheeks hissed and fizzed and dried in a flash, and her eyes began to melt as her flesh cracked open in great black pustulous rents...

And then she'd awoken, gasping, her heart punching through the silk of her sodden nightdress. She'd leapt right from her bed and rushed out onto the balcony and below, saw the city and its countless fires burning peacefully in the fog. *It was a dream*, she realised. *Just a dream.* But now she wondered as she looked at the king if it was a vision instead, some portent of the doom to come.

She gripped his arm more forcefully. "Sweet king, you must remember. Darkness, you said. The end. Was it the Eternal Flame you saw? Have you seen the face of Agarath himself? Tell me, gentle king. Please, *try* to remember."

The withered old wraith stared at her stupidly and babbled some more and she knew she would get nothing from him right now. When he got like this it was best to leave him alone and let him calm, give him time away from the Eye and all the death and dread he saw.

"I'll return soon," she told him. "Try to rest, if you can. I will have you released so you can sleep." She smiled sympathetically, placed the cup of water on the plinth next to the Eye, and left him in his chains.

Ulrik Marak was waiting for her outside the door. "Anything?" His voice was blunt.

She shook her head. "He won't eat. He hardly drinks. One day we'll come here and he'll be dead, Ulrik. The Father may not get what he wants from him."

"He must. The heir of Varin must be found."

She looked up into his craggy face. *Do you have your doubt as I do, Ulrik?* she wanted to ask him. *Do you fear the flame? Do you fear what the Father has become?* Her memories continued to rise and awaken, only to weaken and wither again, light one moment, dark the next, yet that cold coiling in her gut was not going away. *And Neyruu,* she thought. *She fears it too.* The dragon had always been sensitive, and somewhere inside her Talasha continued to perceive a fragment of Kin'rar left behind, a presence sounding out a warning for her to remember herself, remember the past, to act now before it was too late.

She swallowed in a dry throat. *Act how?* she wondered. *Do what?* She didn't understand what he meant, or whether it was all just a dream. The glow of the Father was a wondrous warm thing, and yet sometimes in his presence she could feel cold and dark and full of dread. *He'll see it,* she would fret. *He will see that I waver, and send me to the Eternal Flame.* Half the time that fear roiled inside her like a storm, and the other half she felt content, almost serene, her duty and her life and her everything to serve him, please him, make him love her and cherish her as all fathers should their daughters.

Marak was looking down at her from his towering height, broad-shouldered and grim. About his body was enrobed a maroon cloak, beneath which he wore no armour. *Soon,* she knew. *Soon he will.* "You must do better," he told her. "The Father needs an answer. Or I will have to take over." His dark eyes stared, mirthless, rimmed in red. Through the right cut a savage scar he'd won in his youth, when first he bonded Garlath the Grand.

The princess shook her head. "The scion will not respond to you," she said. "He needs softness. Not strength."

"Softness is not working."

"Nor are your chains. He has to be able to step away when he's frightened, when he sees something he dreads. He can't do that with iron about his ankles and wrists."

"If I unchain him he will find a corner to huddle in, a balcony to jump off. He might try to kill himself. I can't take that risk." His jaw was as hard as the scaly armour he once wore, densely bristled, his hair cropped short, more grey now than black. "What does the scion dread?"

"The end," she said. "He bleats of darkness and the end."

"*The* end or *his* end?"

She frowned at that, wondering. "I don't know. You think he saw his own death?"

"I am no scholar of the Eye of Rasalan. I will consult with Sotel Dar."

"Sotel Dar is no scholar of it either. No one is. The Eye is mysterious."

435

"Mysteries are made to be unravelled. We must unravel this one, lest we displease him."

A shudder went through her. She chanced a question. "You fear him?"

"All men should fear their father." His chin was broad and tight. "This world must be cleansed, Talasha, and started anew. Who are we to question that? It is the will of Eldur."

Do you believe it? she wondered. *Do you truly, Ulrik?* She thought of her dream again, the fire and ash and smoke, the burning children, the melting eyes. *Is that what you saw, Hadrin? Did you see the doom of this land? Are we to bathe in the flame as well? Are we all of us to die?*

"You doubt it," Marak said. "You doubt the Father."

She could not lie to him; he'd seen it in her face. "Sometimes," she admitted. "It is not only the north that will burn, Ulrik, when the dragons are unleashed. All lands will be of wreck and ruin, as they were once before. The world Eldur himself helped build will fall. This is not his will, but that of Agarath."

Marak's mouth twisted. "And you would question him? A god? *Our* god."

He is not the only god, she thought. "I fear for my people."

"They are *his* people, not yours. He is the Father and the Founder. Your blood."

"My blood," she agreed. "And perhaps I know his heart best." She stepped in, and her voice went to a whisper. "Ulrik, do you remember the Western Neck? Do you remember my cousin Tethian, your prince? Do you remember what he preached?"

The dragonlord frowned, a heavy brow tumbling over his eyes. Talasha could see the memory stirring. "Tethian," he said, in a voice deep and low. "He spoke of the Fire Father rising benevolent. He spoke of balance. And..." He looked to the side. "Peace."

Yes, she thought, taking his arm. "Is this peace, Ulrik? Is this the Eldur Tethian preached of?"

He drew away, unwilling to confront it. "Tethian was a student to Sotel Dar, and the scholar says as I do, princess. The world must be cleansed. It is Eldur's will."

"It is *Agarath's* will," she said. "The Father told me so himself. He told me he still served him. His *Soul* guides him, he said."

"Then it must be so. Agarath gave life to the Father as the Father gave life to us. He made the world. It is his to destroy."

He's lost, she thought. It alarmed her to think she was like this too, half the time. Perhaps Marak had moments of clarity as well, but if he did he was hiding them well. It was not so with Sa'har Nakaan. The Skymaster spoke rarely, still grieving the loss of Ezukar, his long-bonded dragon, yet sometimes in his eyes she could detect his doubt.

"The gods had their chance," she found herself saying. "Sotel Dar spoke of them *being* war. He spoke of embers being put out, so we might end the cycle of Renewals." She was remembering it all suddenly, as though a torch had been lit in the dark, illuminating the truth around her.

"Do you not remember that, Ulrik? Eldur was meant to be our salvation, not our downfall. He was meant to save us, not condemn us all to die."

"Death is a gift," Marak came back. "The Eternal Flame is a place of freedom and…"

"We have to *save* him," she stressed. "This is not what the Father truly wants. He is not himself, Ulrik…"

"And you know what he wants more than he does?" His voice was thick with contempt. "You're beginning to talk treason, Talasha."

"Treason? For trying to save him? Ulrik, listen to me…"

"No. I've listened and heard enough. Another word and I will have to report what you've said. Don't make me, Talasha. Please, do not." He gave her a hard cold look and then turned and marched away.

All sound left with him, leaving her in silence. For a long moment she just stood, heart pumping, until she stirred herself to step away, slippered feet whispering on stone as she moved swiftly through the quiet lonely corridors. When she came to her private residence she paced out onto the balcony, and looked upon the city below. Fires blazed upon the rooftops and filled the squares in their thousands, all lit for Eldur, for the Father and the Founder who had awakened from his long slumber to win the war.

Is that what they believe? she wondered. *Do they know of his true intent?*

She had no way of knowing from all the way up here. The only time she'd left the top of the palace was when she flew upon Neyruu's back, but those flights were never long and nor did they take her far. She'd taken to the dragon's saddle only a handful of times thus far, though even from the first nothing had ever felt so natural.

That night the Father had tethered them as one, she'd flown off over the Askar Delta, seen the great spreading web of waterways sparkle under the moonlight, watched the storks and cranes and river birds burst away in clouds of wings as they passed, even sighted the distant glow of Videnia upon the far shores. Never had she felt such unutterable joy…until she felt that presence lurking in the depths, heard the quiet whispered warning of Kin'rar Kroll echoing out from a place unseen.

She shuddered as she looked over the city. Neyruu was nowhere to be seen, out hunting perhaps, or perched in some high place near the palace. Sa'har Nakaan had told the princess that in time she'd have a better sense of Neyruu's whereabouts, and be able to commune with her across greater distances, yet thus far that was not the case. She was near, she knew that much, but not where. *Might I call to her, reach out? Might I fly away from this place, never to return?*

The fires were shimmering down below, some blinking to life as others died out, yet never did fewer than ten thousand of them burn, and perhaps many times that number. Talasha wondered how long it would take to count them all. She wondered how many torches were held by men, how many by women, how many by children too young to even know what was happening. Some of the fires were much larger than others, great hot blazes burning in the squares, feasting on wood and coal and sending up great plumes of smoke. Much smaller lights twinkled about them, and sometimes

437

they moved in rhythm to suggest some formal prayer or dance was taking place.

The biggest gatherings were at the temples, though, where hundreds or even thousands of worshippers would assemble to hear the priests in prayer. From this side of the palace, Talasha could see the Temple of Melliana, the Skytemple, the Temple of Fire and several others raised up for one god or another.

The Temple of Fire was the largest of them, a huge square structure built of several tiers, its walls painted in reds and crimsons and bright fiery oranges. Atop its high flat roof was an enormous iron basin in which a fire was always lit, though now it was joined by many thousands of others; torches and lamps and lanterns held aloft by the worshippers, shifting and moving with the men and women who bore them.

What do the sermons say? What do the preachers preach? Talasha Taan feared she knew the answer. Sometimes men were permitted access to the top of the palace, holy men of great esteem granted private audiences with the Father and the Founder, to spread his word below. Other audiences were given to those of high birth, men and women with rich Fireborn blood who had never bonded dragons. Some had visited the Nest in their youth, Talasha knew, only to fail in their ambitions and come away dragon-less; others had never shown such an intent, preferring to focus their attentions elsewhere. Yet all came to see him when summoned, bathing in the light of the Father, the glow of the Soul. Talasha had asked Sotel Dar what the Father's intention was.

"To pair them," the old scholar had merely said. "A wild dragon is a reckless dragon. Those that are bonded to riders are better behaved."

"He means to tether them?"

"As he did you and Neyruu, yes. He paired you because you are alike; beautiful, sensitive, smart, even impulsive at times. The best pairings are as such, kindred souls entwining to create a more harmonious bond. Marak and Garlath. Vargo Ven and Malathar. Sa'har was much alike to Ezukar in spirit, and yes, Kin'rar was well matched with Neyruu too before his death. He was a good kind soul as you are, my lady. The Father knows that dragons and Fireborn are but two halves of the same whole. The Children of Agarath and the Children of Eldur were made to be bonded, Talasha." He'd looked at her with that wise old gaze, his eyes glittering with a play of red light. "Have you ever felt as *complete* as you do now, my lady?"

"No," had been her honest answer, yet she'd never felt such dread either. More and more she was seeing the city fall beneath the Father's spell, and more and more she was realising that this was not the Father at all, but a puppet on a string, dancing to the All-Father's beat.

Dusk was soon to fall upon the city of Eldurath, when the fires would twinkle in their greatest abundance and the preachers would preach the loudest. Talasha Taan had a want to see them up close, to walk the streets and look upon the people, to hear what the sermons were saying. She turned from the balcony and dressed in cloak and cowl, pulled high croc-skin boots over her feet and stepped back out. The guards on the stairs would likely deny her passage down, she feared, else demand they accompany her to make sure she was safe. She would not take that risk. She scanned the skies and cleared her mind, and through the silence called out, *Neyruu…*

The dragon was just within range of her, her presence felt dimly somewhere off to the west. Talasha waited. Gradually, the tether that bound them as one was drawn together, and the dragon's presence swelled, stronger and stronger, before suddenly she came swooping around the side of the palace to land upon the terrace. "Took you long enough," the princess said, smiling. She climbed up into the saddle as Neyruu lowered a wing. "Down. Find somewhere quiet to land outside the palace. Ideally where no guards will spot us."

Neyruu flapped her lithe grey wings and obeyed.

The palace of Eldurath had eight sides and eight grand staircases leading down to the streets. Between the walls and steps was a massive courtyard that girded the building, replete with soldiers on their watch. Landing there would not be advisable if the princess wished to remain unseen. Thankfully Neyruu was slim and sleek and light for her size, capable of taking off without a running start as most of the bulkier dragons had to do. A side street or alley was too small a space for her, but a path of more moderate width would serve. *An empty courtyard would do even better,* she thought, sighting one between a clutch of tight twisting lanes, some way from the palace walls.

There, she thought, and the dragon did the rest.

The princess did not delude herself into thinking her landing would not be spotted, but better by commoners than guards, she knew, and seeing dragons and dragonriders in Eldurath was about as rare as seeing water around Rasalan. The little courtyard was not quite as empty as it had appeared from a distance; there was a cobbler working on a pair of shoes outside his shop, an old man sitting on a doorstep drinking a cup of wine, and across the tops of the buildings a little gang of roof raiders were on the prowl. All stopped to watch as the dragon came down and the princess slid off her wing to dash away into the nearest alley, cowled and quick as a cat. The roof raiders followed for a time, leaping from roof to roof as they liked to do, but before too long she'd passed a much broader street that they couldn't cross, and they returned to their roof raiding around the alleys.

Stay close, she thought to Neyruu. *Find a perch and keep watch.*

She looked back the way she'd come and saw the dragon flap skyward, making for an empty roof or strong stone balcony somewhere. Talasha left her to it as she wended her way through a warren of lanes and came upon the Street of Serpents, a long winding road that twisted its way through the northern districts of the city. Snake charmers were common here, so too snake-sellers offering them living and dead. In this part of the city, snakes were kept as pets by some, who would wear them coiled about their necks and shoulders as they went about their business. Others would wear them dead, their scaly skin made into boots and cloaks and gloves, and their venom was popular too, employed in a good many uses from sleeping agents to painkillers and even aphrodisiacs, Talasha had heard it tell.

Mostly, the snake just made good meat, though. As she made her way down the street, she saw hundreds of them hanging for sale on stalls, many as thick as a man's arm and several times as long. Others were being chopped and cooked and thrown in with roasted nuts and spices to make a popular dish. *Life feels normal enough here,* the princess reflected. Not that she'd ever spent much time on the Street of Serpents, but still…

She continued past the snakemongers and charmers, crossing a square cut through by one of the city's many canals. Some children were playing in the water, whipping at each other with long green reeds torn from the banks. A poleboat passed by and one of the boys jumped on, only to be kicked back into the water by the driver and slapped on the backside with his pole for good measure. The other children laughed loudly at that, before returning to their game.

Across the narrow bridge that spanned the canal, a small crowd had gathered to listen to a man preach. Talasha hastened forth to listen, though found that this was no holy man, but a common peasant from the Askar Delta, complaining of animal attacks across his lands. "I came here a week ago and still no one will listen to me," she heard him say. "We need soldiers to protect us against these river ghouls and tigerfrogs. They're coming up from the mud and snatching people as they fish, and what's being done about it? Nothing. No one cares."

He was right about that, to judge by the shrugs and empty eyes of those standing nearby. The crowd soon gave up on his pleas and dispersed, leaving him to rant at the cobbles instead.

Talasha moved on as well, turning off the Street of Serpents where it met the Poleman's Path, a long canal, broad and straight, that branched off into many others along its route. To either side was a paved road, one intended for men afoot, the others for horses, though as time went on that custom had been lost and now both men and mounts used both.

Talasha walked on the path on the left of the canal, where the streets were more open. There were jugglers here, and knife-throwers, and more fire-breathers than she'd ever seen before. Old women sat with baskets of wriggling eels for sale, and others sold frogs and toads, water rats and regular rats and winged rats, crickets and locusts coated in honey, and a dozen other types of crunchy critter besides.

Talasha waved away every offer from the pedlars and kept her hood low over her eyes. Soon enough the crowds were beginning to grow thicker as they neared the Temple of Fire. She joined the flow, like one of a thousand leaves floating on a slow-moving river, until eventually the great plaza opened out before her. Thousands stood with their torches raised, men born high and low alike, women as well, and children beyond her counting clutching at their mother's hands or scuttling between their skirts.

The great iron basin on the temple roof looked massive from down here, a huge black bowl filled with a raging orange-red flame. Acolytes stood about it, tiny against the blaze, their job to keep it fed, throwing in wood and pitch and barrels of oil as needed.

At the hour of dusk, the fires were at their greatest height, roaring and reaching fifty feet into the air, gorging on all they were given. Talasha knew that the acolytes were Fireborn, oft of weaker blood, cast-offs who hadn't made it as dragonriders, yet who were well able to handle the great heat of the blaze. Their holy master was the same, a small man in swirling robes of crimson and ochre and fiery orange, cut and slashed so as to appear as flames. He stood on a high balcony below the basin, calling out his prayers with arms outstretched.

"…come to bring us our deliverance," he was proclaiming as Talasha got close enough to hear. Thousands squashed in, eager to get a glimpse of him. The High Priest of the Temple of Fire had always been a figure of vaunted status in Eldurath, Eldur's voice on earth after the Fire Father's death. "I have met with the Eternal myself, the Father to us all, and felt his ethereal glow," the man cried. "It is a warmth unbound and everlasting, a warmth that reached deep inside me, to hold my essence tight. All my life I have spoken with his voice, as the High Priests did before me, and I do it still. His voice, his will, his *power* is in me. Hear me, good people of Eldurath. Hear me and join me in prayer."

Talasha had heard his prayers countless times before. There were many festivals in Eldurath when the people would gather in the plaza, as they would for royal weddings and funerals and coronations too. When her brother Tavash had become king, the High Priest had anointed him upon these very steps, proclaiming him Eldur's chosen hand to lead the kingdom in war. He was to remain the Fire Father's voice, he had called to the people, but a new champion had been chosen to guide them in conflict against the barbarous northerners.

He made mention of Tavash again now, calling, "Our noble King Tavash has perished in the war, battling the men of the north. The Father proclaims him part of the Eternal Flame, warm in the embrace of Agarath the All-Father, Creator of the World. Let us pray for him, in silence. Let this plaza fall quiet as we remember a great man and king, taken before his time."

A great man? Talasha thought scornfully. *A wicked man, more like, who did not fall in the war, but for his own foul treachery and sin.* She had loved her brother, in her own way, though feared him terribly as well. *He killed our mother as he killed our uncle, and had I not escaped, he'd have killed me too. I'm glad the Fire Father burned him.*

The square went quiet for several long minutes, quieter than Talasha could have believed given the huge heaving numbers in attendance. Only once the High Priest was satisfied did he raise his hands in a flutter of fiery robes and call for the prayers to continue, praising the courage of the warriors half a world away, calling for all assembled to think of them nightly, to light fires for them at their bedsides to give them strength in the battles to come.

Battles, Talasha thought. *Or slaughters?* She knew how easily Dragon's

Bane had fallen and Thalan too, and others were soon to follow, if they hadn't already. Only Varinar and Ilithor gave Ulrik Marak pause as he made his grand preparations. He shared with her little of his plans, though, and consulted directly with the Fire Father over how he would proceed.

I'm being kept in the dark, she had come to see. *The Father does not trust me.*

The prayers went on. Talasha joined the throng as they went to their knees and hummed, as they called out in unison at the required moments, as they went silent as the grave to honour the High Priest's requests. Somehow she felt herself drawn into it, her mind clouding once more, and she wondered if the man was no longer a fraud, as he'd been all his life, but truly possessing of the Voice of Eldur. *The Father gifted him with power,* she thought. *Power to control, as he does.*

"All praise the Father," the High Priest cried, and across the plaza, thousands of voices echoed him. "All praise Eldur the Eternal, who was fated to rise again." Talasha repeated the words with the rest. "All praise the Founder, who raised this city from sand and stone, to rest beside the delta." The words were said once more by those assembled. "All praise he who lived before, who died before, and lived again. Eight times did he fall and rise so we all might walk this earth."

As the rest hummed in repeat, Talasha thought, *But he never died an eighth time. I found him there, down in his tomb, still living. His eighth death was a lie.* But all the same, none would question it, or trouble to worry about such trivial things when the Fire Father was back among them, ready to lead them in their glorious triumph.

And so the High Priest went on, and so Talasha listened, and fought to free her mind to think for herself. And soon enough it became clear to her that everything the man said was a lie. He spoke of the war, of conquest, of victory, of fate. A fate to defeat the legions of Vandar and Tukor and Rasalan for a last and final time, to rid the world of their evil for good and all, and leave behind a world of peace, plenty, and prosperity.

Lies, Talasha thought. She heard no mention of the spreading of the Eternal Flame, no mention of the fated coming of the Untar Batax'un, the Return to the Days of Dread. *Lies. All lies. He means to keep them locked away in the dark, unknowing of his will.*

She looked around at the doomed hapless faces, believing every word they were told. A part of her wanted to rush up to some high place and rip off her hood to reveal herself. To call out in a ringing voice that the flames of war were to cover all the land, north and south, east and west, that the Days of Dread were returning, that monsters and madness would soon rule all. She thought of the man from the Delta, complaining of attacks across his lands, and wondered how many others like him were making the same sorts of pleas. Something told her such men were being silenced as quickly as they could speak. *Tyranny,* she thought. *We're living under the cloak of tyranny. That man is probably dead already, or in chains, the truth forever locked behind his lips...*

A sense of deepening unease was filling her. She backed away, moving through the crowds, as the prayers went on. Worshippers looked at her sourly as she interrupted them, pushing past and through that heaving sea of bodies, all humming and chanting and repeating the High Priest's invocations. The princess ignored the grunts and curses, hurdled what children got in her way, slipped through a group of strong sweaty men, and found herself near the back, where the crush was less intense.

She breathed out, her heart racing. Somewhere she could sense Neyruu's unease as well, a reflection of her own, and knew she was perched somewhere near. When she continued away from the square, the High Priest's voice soon began to wane, though on he was going, on and on, spreading the Fire Father's spell.

She turned her eyes around, searching for her bonded dragon. *I've been gone too long. If Marak should find me absent…* The dragonlord's threat still rang in her ears. She needed to get back to Neyruu, back to the palace, and hope her disappearance had gone unnoticed.

Eyes scanning the skies, she rushed on past a pair of large labourers in their sweaty vests, and bumped straight into a woman passing the other way. "Apologies," she murmured. "I'm in a bit of a rush." She kept her hood down and bustled on, but before she could step away a hand reached out to grab her wrist. "I don't want trouble," the princess said. She tugged, but the woman held on, and so she turned to her and said it again. "I don't want trouble. Please, just let me…" She trailed off, eyes widening, as she saw the woman's face. *Gods.* "Cevi? Cevi, is that you?"

Her handmaid wore a cloak and cowl as she did, casting shadows down as far as her nose. But the princess saw through them all the same. "Princess." Tears welled in the girl's soft eyes, shining in the dark of her hood. "I thought it was you…in…in the crowd."

"You were following me?"

"I saw you, on…on Poleman's Path, and I hoped…I hoped it was you…" Something uncomfortable came upon her face, a look of pained betrayal. "You…you *left* me, my lady. You left me there…in the fortress… you left us all there to die."

There. The Nest. "No, I didn't…Cevi, that wasn't my intention…" She pulled her into a hug, squeezing tight. This was not the time or the place to be having this discussion. "I'm sorry, Cevi. I never meant for that to happen. You have to believe me. You do believe me, don't you?"

"I…I have always trusted you, my lady."

"Good." She wiped a tear from the girl's eye, took her hand, and drew her aside, further from the throng. She looked around, making sure no one was listening, then turned back to her. "How did you get here? Did you walk all the way from the mountains?" Seeing her handmaid was bringing it all back once more. Memories flooded through her mind, one after another after another, from the Western Neck to the wilds beyond, from the death of Mirella and the trek to the Nest and the long cold days spent there in shadow. *And Lythian. My sweet captain.* Try as she might to push him aside, he always stirred anew, his voice, his smile, his gentle touch, and the forbidden love they shared.

The handmaid's eyes gleamed tearily under her hood. Her cloak was frayed at the hem, stained and dirtied, ripped and torn and patched in places too. "I took a mule and…and went on foot after he died. I tried to get to my father's home, but…but the lands…the creatures…they're everywhere, my lady. I don't even know how I got here without…without…" Tears ran down her cheeks. She sobbed, sniffed, and went on, "The captain, and Pagaloth…they…they left me behind as well. They told me to go back to my father, and I tried. I *tried*, but the monsters…the things I saw…" Tears crawled from her eyes. "They *left* me, my lady. Just as you did. And Mirella. Everyone I care about leaves me."

The princess took her into her arms. Her own eyes were welling to see her handmaid in such distress. "I'm not going to leave you, Cevi. Not again. *Never*. Do you understand?"

The girl nodded, smiling wanly. She rubbed her eyes, sniffing. "Am I to…to enter your service again? I miss it, being your…your handmaid."

Talasha shook her head at once. "*No*, Cevi. No." She glanced around. Her voice was low. "It's too dangerous in the palace right now, and there's no one there we can trust."

"I don't understand, my lady. The Fire Father…they say he is good, as we hoped. As Sotel said, and Prince Tethian. The High Priest, I heard him. Lord Eldur is to lead us to glory." She looked into Talasha's eyes, frowning. "Is that…is that wrong?"

More than you can know, the princess thought. "The palace is changed, as is the city," she merely told her. "Come, I know somewhere where you'll be safe. We can speak more there." Clutching the girl about her waist, she led her away, to a place she'd not be found.

38

Amilia

The old man was staring at them as they rattled down the road. He wore a roughspun cloak of undyed wool and held in his hand a stick to help him walk, wonky and wooden, the sort that looked like it had been fetched from under a tree. On his back was a patched linen sack sagging with goods that appeared far too heavy for a man his age. Even from a distance, Amilia Lukar could see the hopeful look on his face. He raised his spare hand to wave them down, and Sir Munroe Moore gave a groan.

"Ignore him," he told the driver. "We can't waste time picking up waifs and strays."

"It won't be a waste of time," Kegs returned. "He's an old man. We ought to help him if we can."

Kegs was a kind soul, Amilia had learned, the sort who liked to look out for the downtrodden and unfortunate. He was called Kegs for the size of his stomach, which could aptly be described as enormous. "Was just plain old Keg once," he'd told them when they first met, with a big gap-toothed grin, "but that was twenty years ago. I'm twice as big as I was back then, so my friends have taken to calling me Kegs instead." He'd laughed and given his great belly a thunderous slap.

One keg or two, it made no matter to Amilia Lukar. She was just happy to be on dry land again and making her way south, though the journey from Blackhearth to Ethior wasn't proving to be as quick as she'd hoped. Upon arrival at the Blackhearth docks, Sir Munroe had gone straight off on a hunt for horses, though finding strong Bladeborn-bearing destriers had proven a challenge too far. "They're all away at war," he'd told them, when he returned to the wharf where Nancy was moored. "I can't find any for sale, but apparently Sir Rupert Swallow has some in his private stables. Might you not go to him, my lady? He may be willing to treat with you."

Amilia remembered Sir Rupert Swallow as a sour old man who'd once been a close friend to her grandfather Modrik, but knew little more of him than that. "I don't know Sir Rupert," she replied. "And he won't know me.

445

Any girl might come to his door claiming to be the Jewel of Tukor, Sir Munroe. It doesn't mean a man has to believe it, especially when it means surrendering his best horses."

Sir Munroe hadn't been convinced, and had argued that her face was famous and Sir Rupert would know it, even if he hadn't seen her since she was a little girl. Amilia ignored his pleas. Though back on Tukoran soil, she preferred to remain unrecognised until she reached her uncle Caleb at Keep Kastor. "We'll have to find another way," she decided. "Captain Wilkins, might you know of someone who can help us?"

To no one's surprise, the sotted old ship captain was well acquainted with the working men of Blackhearth, and had told them of a man named Kegs who had a strong sturdy wagon that would probably bear their weight. "Even with you on it," he'd said to Sir Munroe, "in all that heavy armour o' yours. Kegs is a big man and employs the use of big oxen too. The going will be slow, but you'll get where you need to go. Wait here. I'll go see if he's somewhere hereabouts."

During that wait for the captain's return, the dwarf Black-Eye had given his goodbyes to the crew before waddling away into the muddle of dark wooden buildings that clustered shoulder-to-shoulder at the edge of the docks. "Been a pleasure, my lady," he'd said to Amilia in parting. "If you plan to stay here a little while, you'll find me down the Whispering Drunk, as I told you. My smokes work better down there."

"Yes, you said. I hope to be leaving at first light, Black-Eye. I think this is farewell."

"Aye, so it is then. And farewell to you too, my lady. Be safe now. And *beware*." He'd bowed, turned, and waddled away with that, his long white beard trailing the ground at his feet.

Amilia was happy to see the back of him. Him and his stupid magic pipe-smoke. *Beware the silver man*, he'd said. *One day, he's going to change.* Right after uttering those worrisome words that very morning, he'd left her to go back down to his cabin, and hadn't come back up for air until they pulled in at the docks.

It's just a con to get me to seek his counsel some more, she had decided. She reckoned he did it with all of his clients. Give them a few pieces of the puzzle, but never the complete set. Make them come back so you can charge them for the full picture.

Good riddance, she thought, as he vanished into the dockside gloom. *Beware the silver man? Beware the fraudster dwarf more like, with one eye black and the other blue.*

The captain had taken an hour to return, though when he did, the size-able figure of Kegs was seen to be lumbering alongside him. They'd entered into a brief negotiation as Wilkins brought up the rum, drinking on deck as the bells of the boats tinkled around them. "I'm headed for Clear-water Castle on the morrow, as it happens," the big wagon-driver had declared happily. "Got some strong brown ale that needs delivering, but no reason I can't deliver you too."

446

"We're not making for Clearwater," Astrid said. "We have to get to Ethior."

"Ethior?" The big man scratched at his fat hairless chin. "Well, Clearwater's on the way. Sort of, anyhow. The lands are much rougher from here to Ethior as the crow flies, so most heavy caravans head to Clearwater first - the road there's much flatter - and then continue on east down the river road, or else load their goods on a ship or barge and let the water do the work." He looked them over. "I take it you have no horses of your own?"

"Of course we don't," Sir Munroe said, annoyed. "Else why would we be talking to you?"

The big man bobbed his round fleshy shoulders, hidden under thick rappings of fur that made him look even bigger. "Just making sure. With horses you could ride over the hills to Ethior, but without, the road to Clearwater's best." He'd had a big gulp of rum and then rubbed his meaty hands together, to warm them against the bitter cold. "Anyhow, you're free to come with me, if you like. Won't charge you neither. The road can be dull and I'd be happy for the company. Just so long as my oxen can take your weight, that is." He peered past Sir Munroe's cloak. "Godsteel, is it?"

The knight gave a stiff nod.

"All of it?"

Another nod.

Kegs fingered his chin. "Well, we can try. Mayhaps I'll shift a few barrels of beer out to make room for you. If you've got a bit of coin to cover the loss, I'd appreciate it."

Amilia had known then that this man was honest and decent down to his overlarge bones. She'd told him that they'd pay him gladly, and the deal was struck right there. After a night sleeping down in their cabins in Nancy's reeking guts, they set out south of the city under a cold grey sky, the wagon creaking and groaning with every turn of the wheels. A mile or so outside of Blackhearth, Kegs called the massive oxen to a stop, heaved himself out of his seat, and had a look over his wagon. After a short appraisal he gave a nod. "She's strong, is Marigold. I know the groaning sounds bad, but even the strongest women tend to make such noises when they get old. Doesn't mean she's going to fall apart just yet, though."

"How old is she?" asked Astrid, as Kegs climbed back into his padded seat and took the reins. He gave them a swish and the oxen lumbered on.

"Old enough to have travelled this road a thousand times. Most other wagons would've fallen apart by now, but Marigold's made of different stuff."

"Oak," scoffed Sir Munroe. "She's made of common oak."

Kegs shook his head. "Not common oak, sir. But oak from the Darkwood. It's stronger than the normal sort, but lighter too, and hard as teak besides." He gave the wagon a rap with his knuckles.

"Why do you call her Marigold?" Amilia wanted to know, as she sat upon a cask of ale watching the world awaken around her, misty and mysterious. "Wilkins named his caravel for a woman he'd lain with once, he told me. Did you do the same?"

His look of affront said otherwise. "Marigold was my mother. Best woman I ever knew, strong as a bull and full of laughter. She worked from the age of five right up until the day a tree fell on her during a storm and killed her. Never took a day off, did my mother. I named this old wagon in her honour."

It turned out that Kegs named his oxen as well, both of which were bigger than any Amilia had ever seen. Massive at the shoulder, with broad backs and thick stocky legs, they trundled along, hour after hour, tireless and uncomplaining. "The one on the left's called Ralston," Kegs said. "That on the right's Big Ben."

Astrid had been first to ask. "Ralston? Like Sir Ralston, the King's Wall?"

"Is there another Ralston you know of?" Kegs had presented that gap-toothed smile he favoured, set in a big round homely face, beardless and pink. "No man bigger in all the world than Sir Ralston Whaleheart, so I hear it, nor stronger. Name seemed to fit."

Amilia looked at Sir Munroe, whose upper lip was twitching. Once before he and Sir Ralston had served closely together when guarding King Godrin. Now both were disgraced. Sir Munroe for letting his king be slain and the Wall for not being there to stop him. Some said the king had sent his wall away, though who could say if that were true? Amilia had never cared enough to ask Hadrin about all that. *May the bastard burn forever.*

She listened back in to hear Astrid ask, "What about Big Ben. That's not a name I know. Was he a famous knight as well?"

"A knight? Oh no. Ben was my father, though we called him Big Ben for his size. You think *I'm* big? Ha!" He laughed loudly, interrupting the calm of the cold misty morning. "My father was bigger. A lowborn Whaleheart, you might call him. He had no Bladeborn blood, but was monstrous strong all the same. When he was only twelve years old he wrestled a bear dead with his bare hands, and by twenty he was fighting broadbacks. If he were still alive he'd be wrestling dragons, I've no doubt." Another big laugh heaved from his chest.

"And who told you all that?" Sir Munroe asked, mockingly. "Your grandmother, was it? Sounds like the sort of tall tale a grandmother would conjure up."

"No tall tale, sir. You'd know if you'd ever had the honour of meeting him."

"How'd he die?" Astrid asked. The girl was always full of questions these days.

"Tree fell on him during a storm," Kegs said. "They were inseparable, my parents, even in how they died."

Amilia wondered how big this tree must have been to crush a pair of giants, but decided not to ask. The wagon rolled on, the mists cleared as the sun rose, and on they went to Clearwater.

That was four long days ago now, and ever since then the going had been so painfully slow they would probably move faster if they got out and walked. Sir Munroe had complained that a baby could crawl quicker, and

448

Astrid had responded to tell him that if he wanted them to pick up the pace, maybe he should unburden them of his weight.

"We'll go faster if you walk beside us, is all I'm saying," she'd said, when Sir Munroe gave her an indignant scowl. "I'm not saying you should leave *entirely*, Sir Munroe. No, I'd *never* say that."

"I know a Sir Munroe," Kegs exclaimed in a cheerful voice. "They sing about him around here. Sir Munroe the Mongrel, who runs along at Hadrin's heels. Here, let me see if I can remember the lyrics…"

"Best not," Amilia said. *Beware the silver man. One day, he's going to change…*

"Fair enough," Kegs agreed. He had a smile on his broad face. Amilia wondered if he knew that the Sir Munroe riding in his wagon was the very same one the peasants were singing of. He was a brave man if so, to risk the knight's wrath. *Or a stupid one,* she thought. "I've not got the best voice," the wagon-driver went on, "though it serves well enough to pass the time. And that tune…it's no Echo of Titans or Rylian the Brave, I'll admit. How about I sing one of those instead? A song for our fallen prince?" He cleared his lungs and started, "*Once before in the land of Tukor was born a man most noble and true…*"

Astrid stopped him. "Not that one." She glanced over at Amilia. "Something more jolly, maybe? Do you know any jolly songs?"

"I know a hundred."

As Kegs set into a more jaunty tune, Astrid shifted over to sit beside the princess. "I hope I got that right, my lady. Rylian the Brave. That's about your father, isn't it? I thought it might make you upset."

It would, Amilia was certain of that. "You got it right, Astrid. Thank you." She listened to Kegs singing for a time and found that his voice was more than passable. It had a good fun bounce to it, and his range was better than she'd expected as well. "You sell yourself short, Kegs," she told him. "You sing very nicely."

"Truly? Very kind of you to say. Do you sing, my lady?"

I used to, she thought. There hadn't been much to sing about lately, though. Still, hearing the big man's cheerful warbling had stirred something in her. "Do you know *The Lady of the Stonehills*? Or *The Fair Maiden of the Bay*? I always liked those ones."

"I know them," Kegs said. He didn't sound like he liked them much, though. A little too soppy, perhaps, but they suited Amilia's voice. "Shall we, then? The Fair Maiden of the Bay's a duet. I think I can remember the words."

They had spent a great deal of time singing after that, wiling away the hours as they bobbled along the road. Sometimes Astrid joined in, though her voice was plain and out of tune half the time, and once or twice Amilia had convinced Sir Munroe to sing as well. He had a wonderful baritone it turned out, rich and full, though rarely did he put it to use. Mostly it was just Kegs crooning along on his own by day, though by night Amilia liked to sing her lays and soft mournful melodies too. They didn't really suit the daytime, with all the noise of the wagon, the rattle and clatter of the barrels and wheels as they rolled over ruts and bumps and stones. But when the sun

449

fell and the moon rose, she would often sweeten the air with one of her favourites. She'd even made Astrid cry once, and Kegs a handful of times, though never Sir Munroe. *His heart is made of stone*, she thought, as he sat brooding day and night. *Beware the silver man. One day, he's going to change…*

It wasn't until the third day that Amilia sidled up to Kegs in his driver's seat, and asked him about the dwarf. "Black-Eye?" the man said. "Course I know him. He's as famous as the Crippler around these parts."

"Have you ever paid for his smokes?"

"Me? No. I got no interest in that sort of thing, but I know friends who have."

Sir Munroe had been walking solemnly ahead of them by that point, taking Astrid's advice, though it made little difference to their speed along those rutted roads. The princess glanced fore to make sure the knight wasn't listening. "The things the dwarf says. Are they true, in your experience?"

"People seem to think so. If you can figure out the riddles, anyhow." He shrugged. "That's how I understand it. Not much is clear with those smokes of his."

The princess nodded. "It's vexing," she muttered. "So you don't think he's a fraud?"

"Doubt it. The old imp's been doing it far too long for that. If he was a fraud people would stop coming to him, but they don't. He's counselled kings, you know? And other great men. They say he's over two hundred years old."

"One hundred and eighty," Amilia corrected him. "He'll be one hundred and eight one in a few weeks' time. He told me he's planning to have a celebration at the Whispering Drunk. You should go if you're back by then."

The man liked the sound of that, clearly. "Suppose we'll see. When we get to Clearwater Castle, I'll see you onto a barge to take you down the river. Be quicker than old Marigold here. Most likely I'll turn around and head straight back. Kegs isn't one to miss a party."

Amilia smiled. "I'm sure of it."

The castle was still some days away, though, at the pace they were setting. Clearly, that was on Sir Munroe's mind when he saw the old man in the road, waving for them to stop. "Just ride on by," he said, trying to convince Kegs to keep going. "Another wagon will come past soon enough. The old man can hitch a ride on that."

Kegs wasn't having it, though. "Where's your sense of charity, sir? I see a bent-backed old man struggling by the roadside, and I help him. That's just me. And so long as you're aboard my Marigold, you'll do the same." He turned from the knight. "Ahoy, stranger," he called forward. "Where are you headed this fine spring day?"

The wagon soon rolled up close enough so the old man could be heard. "Notting's Cross, if it please you."

"It does. We happen to be going the same way." Kegs gave him a warm smile.

The old man smiled back, causing the corners of his eyes to crinkle into webs of fine lines. He had lines spreading from his mouth as well, and covering his lips, and his forehead was well-rutted and sunworn. From his chin fell a ragged silver beard, and what remained of his hair was silver as well, with a big spotted bald patch at the top of his head. Beneath the heavy linen sack on his back was a spine bent by age and long years of hard toil. "Truly? Is there space for an old man to ride with you?"

"No," Sir Munroe said. "We have barrels of beer and are overloaded already. And that bag of yours looks heavy."

"Ignore him." Kegs heaved himself down from his seat and helped the bag off the man's back. "*Tukor's Hammer*, what are you carrying in here!" He marched the bag over, laughing, and reached to set it among the barrels and casks. "You a traveller, friend? A salesman?"

"Both." The old man tottered toward the rear of the wagon with his walking stick. Kegs helped him up. With a sigh of relief, he set himself down on a barrel at the back and began rubbing at his old legs. "I go from place to place, selling my wares. The bag's heavy, aye, but I got no choice in that. Need to take my food with me where I go, and my goods to hawk as well."

"You could use a mule," Astrid suggested. "Or maybe a small cart of your own?"

"Now there's a thought. You'd think an old man like me would have considered that." He worked a knot from his thigh with short knuckly fingers, sprouting with tufts of grey hair. "In truth I had one. Or both, so it happens. The cart got stuck in a bog, though, and I had no strength to wrestle it out. Nor did Lady Mary. That was my mule. Loaded her up with all my worldly possessions, but then we ran into a pair of robbers and they stole her. Been on my own ever since."

Sir Munroe offered him no sympathy. "Why does everyone have to name their animals?" he complained. "A horse I understand, but mules and oxen?"

"A mule can be just as good a friend as a horse to a lonely old man." The traveller moved his fingers to his other thigh, rubbing and working the thin tight muscle, hidden beneath old stained breeches the colour of dun. "Been without her for half a year now, though I try to make do. Not easy at my age. I don't move as fast as I used to."

"Well you can rest easy now," Kegs said, as he settled back into his seat, to get them moving again. "We'll get you safe to Notting's Cross."

Amilia didn't know the name. She assumed it was some town along the way, but felt compelled to ask, lest Sir Munroe complain again. "Is Notting's Cross near Clearwater?"

"Near enough," Kegs said, twisting his thick pink neck to look back at her. "It's a short detour, but nothing to quibble over. Might add a few hours to our journey, is all. Should make it by tomorrow night."

Amilia did not have to look at Sir Munroe Moore's face to know that he was unhappy about that. She wasn't so happy herself, but saw no alternative now that the old traveller was perched on that cask of beer.

"That a problem, my lady?"

She shook her head. "No problem." She smiled at the old man as Kegs got the oxen going. "Do you have a name?"

"At my age, I've had a few." Something twinkled in his eye. "My mother named me Talbert, though. A name for her mother's father. He was a knight. Sir Talbert the Traveller. You may have heard of him."

Amilia had heard the names of a thousand knights, but no Talbert the Traveller. It seemed only Kegs knew of him. "He was a hedge knight," the big man said from the front. "Used to range all over North Tukor, hunting for contracts."

Old Talbert gave a smile. "Aye, that he did."

Marigold struggled on, and too slowly for Sir Munroe's tastes. He had no savour for the conversation either, or the company of the old man, so climbed back out of the wagon and let them roll down the road without him. Once he was gone, Talbert said, "Your friend doesn't seem to like me. Ought I be offended?"

"No," Amilia assured him. "He doesn't like anyone."

"Oh good. I can rest easy then." He smiled at her strangely. She wasn't sure what was strange about the smile, but it was. It just felt off somehow. "Some men just hate for no reason, I find."

"He has his reasons," Astrid said. "I used to be the same. I would dislike people because I was afraid they wouldn't like me. So I'd dislike them first, if you know what I mean, to make it easier." She looked on as Sir Munroe marched up the road ahead of them. "Well...no one likes him anymore, and he knows it, so he just hates everyone first. I guess it makes him feel better."

"Did it with you?" the old traveller inquired, kneading his thigh like a cat.

Astrid shrugged her bony shoulders. "I tried to tell myself it did. But I prefer who I am now. I prefer being more open."

Talbert stopped massaging his leg and smiled at her. "That's good. Seems you've done some growing, girl. Now.... you have my name. So how about I have yours? That's how it's supposed to work, anyway."

After they'd exchanged names - a false one, on Amilia's part, who'd taken to calling herself Bethany for this trip - the old traveller started to tell them stories. Astrid listened intently, as she liked to do, and asked lots of questions, which she liked as well. The old man answered some, but not others. Amilia listened, but only idly. The stories were dull for the most part, and there was something about the man that seemed false. She put it down to restlessness on her part. *This is taking too long,* she thought. She would have expected to be in Ethior by now, and yet she hadn't even reached Clearwater, and that was almost two hundred miles from her uncle's city.

It will be quicker by barge, she told herself. She had enjoyed Kegs's company, and his singing too, but would be happy to forgo all that if it meant a quicker journey down the river. *Four, five days, that's all it will take, even less if things go well. I can hold out that long, can't I? Another week, tens days at most, and I'll be with Uncle Caleb, sharing a jug of wine with him in the Hall of Hearths and eating roasted duck greasy with fat.*

The thought sustained her, though a week or so still felt an age. She looked past Kegs in the driver's seat, past the oxen Ralston and Big Ben, past the ruts and stones that littered the road, to the knight walking in his dead man's cloak.

Beware the silver man. One day, he's going to change.

Amilia could not get the riddle from her head. She went to sleep with it, woke with it, had it circling through her mind as she went off to make her water in the trees. She wondered if it sounded worse than it was. Change could mean anything. *Maybe he'll become nicer? Maybe the change is that he's going to die?* That was a change, wasn't it, from living to dead? *Perhaps I've already decided that I'm going to have my uncle kill him. Maybe that's what Black-Eye meant by 'beware'. It's not Sir Munroe I ought to worry about, but myself, condemning him to death.* But no, that made no sense. He'd earned it for what he'd done. He was a traitor to his king, and had all but beaten Sir Jeremy to death as well. Amilia could not forgive that. *He deserves to die,* she decided. *When I reach my uncle's keep, I'll tell him so, and let him hang.*

She put the issue aside as she settled down into a nook to try to sleep. The nights were rough still, and her dreams as foul as ever. They still assaulted her as often as they could, the tower and the voice and those haunting red eyes. So far as Amilia Lukar was concerned, the world was soon to end, so when she put it all in that context, nothing really mattered. Her priority was getting back to Ilithor so she had a good view of it. *I'll stand with Ray on the highest balcony we can find and watch as the world burns. Maybe we'll make a day of it. Get some wine and food and settle in.*

The thought didn't frighten her half so much as it should, not after all she'd been through. Death was not the end, she'd always been taught, but just another door to pass. *I hope those doors are big enough. Because we'll all be coming soon.*

She bunched the hood of her cloak so that it made a pillow, and leaned it against a barrel of ale. She could hear the liquid sloshing inside, feel every knock and rattle as the wagon lumbered along. Sometimes it made her feel queasy, and she'd even had to throw up once or twice, just as she had when at sea.

Amilia Lukar wasn't made for travelling, she'd come to realise. *I should never have left Ilithor. I should have told my grandfather no. I wish he'd died in place of my father.* The gods were cruel to take Prince Rylian so early when that mean old king was still lingering in his hubris. *But we'll come join you soon enough, Father. All of us. We'll be together again, you and me and Robb and Ray, and Mother. I suppose she can join us too.*

Her thoughts drifted. The wagon found itself upon a flatter road, less bumpy, and the gentle motion threatened to lure her off to sleep. Each time she was about to nod off, however, some wretched rut or rock came along, and the lurch of the wagon broke the spell. *It's all for the better,* she decided. All Amilia ever dreamed of was death.

The day was crisp and clear, and growing warmer as they went south.

Spring flowers blossomed in the meadows they passed and there were many trickling rills that dribbled across the road. In some places planks had been laid down for carts and carriages to cross, but at the bigger streams there were bridges. Some were wooden and rickety, others made of stone. Kegs had a name for every one of them. "Rattle Wood Pass," he would say, as they rolled along one clanky old crossing that felt like it would collapse beneath their weight. "The Twins," he called another; two short plank bridges that spanned a pair of shallow brooks, one after the other. A larger stone bridge he named, "The Little Links", in honour of the mighty bridge that Ilith had built, linking Tukor and Rasalan at the very south of the Siblings Strait. He had names for other things too. A well they passed he called, "The Longish Abyss," and there was a big old chestnut tree standing alone in a field that he'd given the name, "The Sentinel."

"You familiar with any of those?" he asked old Talbert. "Some of them are mine, but not all. Everyone around here knows about the Sentinel. And the Little Links. I didn't come up with that one either."

"Aye, I heard them," the old traveller said. "I got my own names too. We vagrants like to keep our minds busy as we wander. Thinking up what to call a thing is a good way of doing that, I feel." He didn't elaborate with any names of his own, much to Amilia's relief.

The day went on, and still Sir Munroe kept resolutely out of the wagon, walking thirty metres ahead of them along the side of the road. Amilia noticed the old man watching him, studying him it almost seemed by that determined squint in his eye.

He recognises him, she thought. She couldn't figure out what else it could be, and perhaps that's what had Sir Munroe's breeks all in a twist. He was a prideful man, and honourable he still claimed despite his crimes, and the last thing he wanted was some outspoken old packman berating him on his past. Kegs had the good grace to spare him, but that wasn't to say that old Talbert would do the same. *He'll walk all the way to Notting's Cross at this rate*, Amilia thought.

She spent the next hour studying Keg's map to get a better understanding of where the town was, in relation to Clearwater. Astrid sat with her - the girl had a liking for maps - while Talbert shuffled up the wagon to sit beside Kegs at the front. The map showed them that Notting's Cross was west of the road they were on, half a dozen miles down an old track largely closed in by woods. "The road looks narrower," Astrid pointed out. "See. It's got that dotted line. Means it's less used."

Amilia had seen that too. "Kegs wouldn't agree to take the old man if he didn't think we could get there," she said, understanding Astrid's concern. She studied the road they were on as it wended past lakes and woods and fields to Clearwater Castle. The road was not a straight one, far from it, though it looked no worse from here than it had been so far. "We just passed that bridge, look." She pointed. Kegs had scribbled his own names on there. This one was called Hillview Hop. "Means we're well over halfway now. It shouldn't take more than a few more days to get there."

Astrid didn't seem to mind about the wait either way. She'd enjoyed her time clutched in old Marigold's oaken arms so far as Amilia could tell, certainly more than she had their lonely ranging across the Rasal High-plains and voyage across Vandar's Mercy. She wasn't much of a rider either, she'd told the princess, so relaxing in the rear of a wagon wasn't so bad, especially since the sun had been out most days and they'd had no trouble on the road.

So far, Amilia thought. Trouble could come at any time, she knew, and for that at least she was grateful for Sir Munroe's presence. She wondered if she might tell Astrid what that creepy old dwarf had said to her, but decided against it. It would only frighten the lanky girl and reinforce her claim that they couldn't trust Sir Munroe as far as they could throw him, and with all that godsteel plate he wore, that wasn't far at all. Rarely a day went past when Astrid didn't whisper into Amilia's ear about leaving the man behind to fend for himself. Lately, she'd been suggesting that they leave him when they reached Clearwater.

"We can find a boat and go without him," she would say. "Kegs will help us. I'm certain he knows who Sir Munroe is, my lady, even if he won't say it outright. You heard that song. Sir Munroe the Mongrel. It's not just in Rasalan that people hate him, but here as well. Kegs would be only too happy to see him in chains."

Amilia still said 'no', though. There seemed no sense in rocking that boat, and if the man was to be put in chains, it would be her uncle Caleb's fetters about his wrists, not old Lord Mortimer of Clearwater Castle.

Before too long, a purple dusk was colouring the western skies and Kegs found one of his roadside havens to park up and rest for the night. Over the last few evenings they'd slept in a clearing in a wood of elm and ash, an abandoned thatched barn empty but for a resident owl called Hoot, beneath the shadow of a craggy flint cliff, and next to a tumbledown stone wall that bordered a field wild with high spring grass.

Tonight, it was at the edge of a pretty pond attended by sulking willow trees where Kegs pulled up, some two hundred metres off the road down a bumpy sidetrack.

"Fine spot," remarked Talbert, looking around at the glimmering water. There were many lily pads floating on that water, where frogs sat croaking softly. On the far bank Amilia saw a family of ducks waddling along, the little yellow ducklings hurrying to keep up.

"Got a hundred just as fine in here." Kegs tapped the huge boulder he called a head, covered with a moss of fuzzy brown hair. "Every few miles there's a hidden treasure just off the road. It's a pretty country, this."

Amilia agreed, though pretty as the setting was, the fall of darkness always brought something of a tension to the group, and Sir Munroe's constant mutters of rogues and outlaws didn't much help. Amilia was more inclined to listen to Kegs about that, though, seeing as he was the one who knew the lands well, not the Rasal knight who'd never once stepped foot here before.

"There're bandits about these parts, there's no lie there, but most of them know me well enough," their driver had said early on. "I've been going up and down this road for two decades, don't forget. A cask of ale here, a bottle of whiskey there, and everyone's happy."

"You bribe them?" Sir Munroe had said, not caring to hide his disapproval.

"You could call it that. The Bear-Claw Brotherhood run these parts, and most others know to stay away. You're only allowed to join once you've killed a bear and taken a claw to wear about your neck. Makes them a *grizzly* sort." He'd chortled at his own joke. "Anyhow, I know them well enough. They charge a toll for using the road, though not always. Sometimes they miss me passing on through, or are busy with some other hunt or scheme or whatever else these outlaws get up to. Haven't seen so much of them of late. There are worse things crawling about up here than bears and bandits, make no mistake."

He'd gone on to tell them stories of old forgotten creatures creeping from the Darkwood, fell beasts of a bygone age that had made Astrid's eyes go big with worry. After that, they kept a watch not for bandits so much as for beasts, though thus far they'd been lucky enough to remain unmolested and ignored by both.

That night was the same, as it turned out, though Amilia still had to suffer the darkness of her dreams before she was awoken by a warm pink dawn slashed with golden clouds. "Did I make any noises last night?" she asked Astrid, as she did every morning.

The gangly girl shook her head. "Not that I heard."

She asked the same of Sir Munroe, who had been on watch before dawn. "You twitched a bit, but you do that every night. And there was a bit of mumbling. What do you dream of, my lady?"

Sir Jeremy's ruined face, she thought. *And you, squirming on a length of rope.* "The doom," she merely said, before climbing onto the wagon to resume their ponderous ride.

That day was much the same as the last. Life upon the wagon was repetitive, Amilia had found, though today the scenery did change a bit at least. To the north and west they sighted the rise of soggy grey-green hills that spread out into the moorlands of North Tukor, those ruled over by the loathsome Lord Emmit Gershan. Some said he'd sired a hundred bastards and killed several of his mistresses with his bare hands, though that must have been long decades ago because the old recreant Amilia knew scarcely had the strength to strangle a weed let alone a full-grown woman.

"Is the Master of the Moorlands still in Ilithor, do you know?" the princess asked Kegs. Gershan had been lurking about the palace when she left and she hoped most fervently that he'd be gone by the time she got back. *If not, I might have to rectify that.* Amilia couldn't stand that leering old man.

"As I understand it," the big man answered. "Left his son Sir Wilfred to rule from Lallymoor in his stead."

And he's little better than his sire, the princess thought. She knew that Sir Wilfred's own son, Sir Wenfrey, was currently in the south with her uncle Cedrik and brother Robbert. They were an unpleasant brood, those ghoulish Gershans, best left up here in these grim wet moors than allowed at court with those of richer breeding.

They passed by a lake soon after, a large still lake that shimmered silver beneath the sun. Amilia saw little fishing boats on the water, and a town on its banks. A part of her wished it was Notting's Cross even if she knew it wasn't. She had nothing in particular against the old man, but better to rid themselves of him here than have to suffer that hours-long detour. "Why are you heading to Notting's Cross anyway?" she asked him. "To trade, I presume?" She looked down the slope. "Can't you peddle your wares down there?"

He met her eyes. "Looks like pretty Bethany wants rid of me as much as that knight does."

"I mean no offence," she was quick to tell him. "I'm just curious, is all."

"Curiosity can get pretty girls in trouble." He grinned at her to help lighten the mood, though that look only sent a shiver up her spine. "Got a specific task to see to in Notting's Cross," he told her. "Bit of unpleasant business that I'll not trouble you with, Bethany."

"Do you have family there?"

"Family? No. My family are further to the west, though most of them are dead."

We'll all be joining them soon. "I'm sorry to hear it," she said. "I've lost people too."

"There's blood on the road," Astrid said suddenly, pointing over the side of old Marigold. It was further ahead, Amilia saw, and long dry, spread across the white chalk of the track. "Did someone die here?"

Kegs gave a sorrowful nod of the head. "*Many* died here," he told them. "Was a skirmish on the road some months back. Involved quite a few famous men, it did. The Barrel Knight. The exiled lord. Some monstrous man called the Beast of Blackshaw. They were all part of some group on a holy quest, people say, heading off to siege the Shadowfort. Word is that Ghost was leading them."

"Ghost? You mean the one with the Nightblade?" Astrid's eyes were big again.

"The very same. His lot clashed with a host under the charge of Sir Boleman of the Bells, famous old knight up here. Didn't go well for poor Boleman, gods rest him. Kanabar slew him himself, I go, stopped that bell from ever ringing again, and the rest of his men fared little better. Few dozen were killed, I remember." He hastened Ralston and Big Ben past the blood as quickly as he could. "Northmen killing northmen, and for what? This world of ours has gone mad."

Amilia Lukar did not disagree. Nor did she want to dwell on Aleron's killer, no matter how holy his quest.

They continued south past the lake, and before long the moors were nowhere to be seen and the lands were growing greener. Open plains turned to fields, fields to scattered woods, and by late afternoon the trees had closed in and they found themselves moving through a dense forest, thick with elm and ash. "Fear not," Kegs said in his cheerful voice.

"Seems dark and daunting in here, but we'll be out the other side in no time."

The big man turned out to be right yet again. Before they knew it, the trees were behind them, and a more welcome land lay ahead, with meadows and thickets and streams all in perfect balance. Sir Munroe slowed so that they might catch up. He pointed ahead when they reached him. "That track there, heading west. Does that lead to this town of yours, old man?"

"So happens it does. You'll be rid of me soon."

Good, the knight's snort said. "Come on then, let's get this done. It's starting to get dark already."

By the time they reached the junction where the roads diverged a heavy dusk was upon them, and the skies were clogged with cloud.

"Going to be a dark one tonight," Kegs said, as he turned the oxen onto the sidetrack. "Let's make this as quick as possible. I'd sooner be back on the main road by the time we stop to make camp."

He put Ralston and Big Ben to work, coaxing them with a whipping stick and calling out words to get them moving. The first few miles went easy enough, though after that the road became boggy and matted in mud, thick and brown and sticky. To either side were trees, tall and intimidating, so they had no hope of going off-road.

"Sir," Kegs said. "You mind checking ahead down the road, seeing if this mud dries up?"

Sir Munroe's report was not promising. "Gets worse, if anything," he said, once he'd returned. "How far is it to this town?"

"Not so far," Talbert said. "It's OK. You've done plenty enough for me." He stood from his barrel. "I can walk the rest of the way from here."

"*Now?*" Astrid seemed concerned for him. "But it's so dark. You could lose your way, or…"

"It's a straight road," Sir Munroe said. "He's not going to lose his way."

"Fall, then. In the mud. Or get attacked." She looked around, shoulders tight. "I'll bet there are wolves in these woods. And worse. Someone should go with him."

"No need." The old man was already climbing out of the wagon, gingerly lowering himself to the ground. His feet landed with a soft squelch in the mud. "I can manage."

Astrid looked at Amilia in appeal, and Amilia looked over at Sir Munroe Moore. She did not need to say anything for the knight to understand. He gave a grunt. "Fine. I'll take the old man up the bloody road. If it'll save your soft hearts, so be it." He marched over and pulled Talbert's bag from between the barrels, then swung it over his shoulder. "You got your stick?"

Talbert presented it. He had a funny little smile on his face. "Don't go anywhere without it."

"Then come on. And try not to slow me down."

Amilia watched as the darkness swallowed them, feeling uneasy. She couldn't say why.

"Right, let's get old Marigold turned around," Kegs said loudly, as a brisk wind blew suddenly down the road the way the two men had gone. The path was tight, the trees close, but apparently this sort of thing happened a lot and Kegs knew what to do. His solution was simply to back the animals up until he found space to turn, during which Amilia kept her eyes on the road, awaiting the knight's return.

"What's the matter?" Astrid asked her, as another bitter gust of wind came blowing, causing the trees to rattle and sway. "Do you think we should try to leave him, my lady? Now might be a good time."

It wouldn't be, and Amilia was fed up of telling her so. "Do you have any idea how quickly he'd catch us up? We're *not* leaving him, Astrid."

The girl yielded. "Then what is it?

"I don't know. I just have a weird feeling. Like he might do something."

"Who? Sir Munroe? You don't think he'd kill him, do you? Why would he?"

Amilia had no answer. *It's dark,* she told herself. *Windy. And this road feels awfully sinister. That's all it is. He'll be back soon.*

"Maybe *he'll* leave *us,*" Astrid was saying, as Keg's torch flickered wildly in the wind. The play of fire and shadow threw strange shapes across the trees, swaying and bending and groaning as the gale wrestled them back. It felt like some nightmare. Amilia shuddered in her cloak. "You heard what Kegs said about those outlaws. Maybe Sir Munroe will go and kill a bear and get a claw of his own. Join the Brotherhood. Bet they won't care that he's a traitor. He must realise that you're going to have him killed anyway when we get to Ethior and...."

Amilia silenced her with a sharp *shhh.*

From down the track she could see a figure reemerging from the gloom, cloaked and broad, marching out of the darkness. She felt strangely relieved to see him again, though Astrid watched him with wary eyes.

As Sir Munroe Moore neared, a sudden gust of wind sent the firelight waving in his direction, lighting up his face. Maybe it was the play of light and shadow, maybe it was something else, but to Amilia Lukar, something about his expression looked odd.

"Princess," he said, stopping before her.

She smiled uncomfortably. "Did you get him back safely, Sir Munroe?"

"Talbert? Oh yes, he's perfectly safe. Now come, shall we get moving?" He smiled at her, then looked down the track. "We still have a long way to go."

39

Elyon

"Well bugger me bloody, it's Elyon Daecar!" shouted the burly Marshlander, as he pulled his axe from the head of a foe with a crunch of blood and bone. "Thought you'd gone out west, young prince. What're you doing about these parts?"

"The war takes me everywhere." Elyon was covered in mud, blood, guts and gore and the innards of dragons and dragonknights alike. His skin was slick with sweat beneath his armour and his hair soaked down to his scalp. *Gods, what I wouldn't do for a nice long bath.* "Tell me of the battle."

The knight wore godsteel mail over heavy, padded leathers, with a surcoat on the top, just as soaked in filth as he was. He was so badly soiled that Elyon could not make out his house colours or arms. "*This* battle, my lord? The one you just fought in?"

"I only caught the end of it. What's your name, soldier?"

"Sir Halron, my prince, of House Clayton. We're a small knightly house under Rammas rule. They call me Hal the Hammer."

Elyon didn't need to ask why. The man was fearsomely large and had a warhammer in his grasp, to go along with that great battle-axe. There were several dead foes about him, hacked and bludgeoned, and many dozens more lying in twisted bloody heaps among the marshy wetlands on which the battle had been fought. "Are you in charge here?"

"After Sir Godmer died," the knight told him, nodding. "A Starrider got him, a few days ago. I took charge after."

Elyon looked around. He'd been flying northwest when he sighted the skirmish and felt compelled to join in. Such was his life now. The Marshlands in the far eastern corner of Vandar were afire with countless battles and he'd lost count of the number he'd fought in. "How many men are under your charge?"

"No more than fifty, my lord. Less now, probably." He looked over to another man nearby, busy thrusting his spear through the heart of an enemy soldier. "Cage, come over here." The soldier pulled out his spear with a burst of blood and hurried to join them. "Find out about our losses. The prince wants to know." While he was seeing to that, Sir Halron wiped his axe dry on his surcoat and said, "We heard Mudport was under attack, my lord. We were trying to make it back when…" He saw Elyon shaking his head. "That bad, huh?"

Worse, Elyon thought. Mudport was a blackened ruin, and overrun. The city had all but fallen by the time he arrived from Nightwell, and by then there was little he could do but watch in horror as every man, woman, and child was put to the sword, every tower felled, every ship in the harbour destroyed. It was wanton destruction, a cull of northerners and nothing more. Elyon had wondered if they might keep the city intact, or take the ships for their own use, but no, they had no interest in that. *Slaughter*, he thought. *They went there only for slaughter.*

"Mudport is fallen," he could only say. He pulled off his helm, to let the heat escape from the top of his head. His hair was soaked beneath, black as jet. Flying in spring was a sweaty business. "I've spent the last gods-know-how-many hours fighting in smaller skirmishes like this one. If you have some food to spare…"

"We've plenty, my lord. Come, we'll get you refuelled."

The food was passable fare, but how it tasted did not matter. Hard sweaty cheese and hunks of chewy salted beef were munched down greedily, alongside a good helping of nuts and dried fruit. Elyon found that sugar and fat were best when trying to replenish his energy stores quickly. As he ate he asked Sir Halron of the latest tidings, while his men saw to finishing off what enemy remained in the area, running off among the stands of trees that grew on the little islands throughout these bogs.

"Not much to report, aside from the fighting," the brawny Marshlander told him. "Been a lot of that. This has got to be our sixth or seventh battle over the last month."

"Any dragons?" Elyon asked.

"No, against those we tend to run, unless it's a small one. Leave them for more able men. We're not equipped for that, my lord. But when we see a group of enemy soldiers numbered up fairly against us…well, that's not a challenge we shirk. We've been taking out enemy patrols, mostly. They're growing fewer, though."

Elyon nodded. He'd heard that from others as well. "Have you come across Sir Killian Oloran? Or Sir Barnibus Warryn? Any other Varin Knights?"

"Afraid not. But when we got wind of Oloran's guerrilla war, Lord Morley sent us to join in. We'd have been in Mudport elsewise, so I suppose we can be thankful for that." He scratched his bulbous nose, thick with thin red veins. "Fallen, you say? To what extent, my prince?"

"Completely." Elyon didn't want to dress it up to be anything it wasn't. "The city is completely destroyed, Sir Halron."

The big knight nodded uneasily and looked out to his men, scattered through the bogs. "Most of us had family there. Not me. I'm lucky, I guess. No kids. Parents are dead. Never had any siblings. But these others…"

Having no family didn't sound so lucky to Elyon Daecar, though in this instance he supposed it was. "Would you like me to break it to them myself?" he asked.

"No, er….Sir Godmer would have done it himself, so best I do so as well." He took a deep breath. "Maybe some got out, before the enemy came. They had warning. Some might have escaped."

"It's possible," Elyon agreed. "It was dark when I got there, so I couldn't say for sure, but yes, it's likely some fled before the siege."

That gave the knight some solace. It was a branch to cling to in a raging river at least, a lifeline to hand his men. *Hope*, Elyon thought. *Give a man hope to hang onto.*

"Did come across Sir Gereon of Greyguard, I should probably tell you," Sir Hal the Hammer went on. "Him and his kill squad. He told us they'd killed a dragon just the day before we met them, good size one too by the sounds of it. And each had a dozen southern kills to their name besides, dragonknights, Sunriders, you name it. Been causing havoc, so I heard it."

Elyon was glad to hear that. Sir Gereon had taken several dozen skilled fighters from Oakpike, the same as Killian and his captain Sir Solomon Elmtree who led two other squads. Barny had gone with Elmtree, though Elyon had heard nothing of his friend as yet from the squads and groups of soldiers he'd passed. It worried him, though he had to put that side. *Don't die yet, Barny, that's an order. I know Aleron and Lancel are waiting for you up there, but not yet, you hear me, not yet.*

He turned back to Hal the Hammer. "Had Sir Gereon lost many of his men?"

"Only four, he said, though that was days ago, so might be different now. We stayed with them for a night, before they set off hunting again. I shared a couple of ales with that sellsword Sam Garrick. The Grinning Knight, they were calling him, and rightly I should say. He told me he'd killed that dragon mostly by himself. Seemed an arrogant sort, so was inclined to take that for an empty boast, but when I asked the others they said the same."

His legend continues to grow, Elyon thought. "Good for him. Who else have you encountered?"

The knight spoke of a few other bands of roving swords like their own, those inspired by Killian's shadow war and sent out from this fort or that to add their blades and bows to the fray. From what Elyon had gleaned from other men like Sir Halron over the last couple of days, the Agarathi patrols in the area were beginning to thin, on account of Killian's attacks, and instead the enemy had started sending out larger forces to attack the local towns and forts in much greater numbers, sometimes up to a thousand men or more. Those were not so easy to counter, and oft as not they were supported by dragons, sometimes several of them.

Utter destruction is their purpose now, Elyon knew. *They're locusts, spreading through a field of wheat, leaving death and ruin in their wake.*

"We plan to gather up in force and fight these smaller armies head-on,"

Sir Hal said with typical Marshlander pugnacity. "We've been scattered to deal with these smaller patrols, but seeing as they're grouping, it's time we do the same. Unless you've got some other order for us, my lord?"

Elyon shook his head. "Keep doing what you're doing. It seems you're well suited to it, Sir Hal."

"I'm a man of the marshes. Course I am."

Elyon smiled and stood from the rotting log he'd been sitting on, and placed his helm back over his head, visor up. "I'd best be off. Thank you for the food and the tidings, Sir Halron. And good luck." *You'll need it*, he thought.

He continued northwest, flying low beneath the clouds. The lands here were wet, boggy, green and brown, a great endless expanse of wooded islands and plank roads that reminded him of the Bloodmarshes, though without the thick reddish fogs.

There were two main roads that travellers used when passing through the Marshlands. The Lakeland Way went north along the coast, circling around the Four Sisters where it broke into two branches, one going south to Lakeheart, the other north to Tukor's Pass, where the road became known as the Border Road as it crossed into the Kingdom of Tukor. The second road was the Mudway, which linked Mudport and Lakeheart from the south. When travelling eastward through the marshes, it was the only road that permitted any sort of haste.

If Rammas and Rikkard are coming this way, that'll be the road they'll use, Elyon thought.

It did not take him long to find it. The Mudway was made of sturdy oakenwood planking in sections and hard-packed dirt in others, and there were some cobbled stone parts too where the ground was firm enough to host it. It was also terribly exposed in some segments, and were an army to come under attack upon it they would have nowhere to run but into the thick bogs to left and right of the road and that exposed them to other dangers. In places the mire was deep enough to devour a man in one greedy gulp, it was said, sticky enough to suck him down and never let go, and the marsh serpents and bog lizards were deadly. There was no threat of an Agarathi army accosting them afoot here, but dragons? Well, that was another matter.

Elyon hoped Lord Rammas would be too wise to take thirty thousand men this way. He hoped his uncle's presence at the Lord of the Marshes' side would be enough to urge caution.

In both cases, his hope was vain.

A mere quarter-hour after finding the Mudway, he sighted banners, horses, soldiers afoot in their thousands, a great unending column of men and mounts marching eastward along the road. The standards of several dozen lords whipped proudly in the wind, and men in silver armour gleamed resplendently as the sun broke through the clouds.

Elyon clenched his jaw and rushed to meet them, firing himself to the ground at the front of the van with all the haste he could muster. His landing caused the closest horses to buck and neigh, though thankfully no one was thrown from the saddle. To little surprise, Lord Rammas himself was leading, and his uncle Rikkard was with him too, seated atop their great, barded steeds.

Good. It'll save me having to hunt them down.

"You have to turn around," Elyon said at once, not caring to waste a single word in civil greeting. "You're riding for a ruin, Lord Rammas. Mudport is destroyed."

Lord Elton Rammas gave a grunt. "Feared it might be." He swung a thick armoured leg over his saddle, landing heavily. They were on an earthen section of road, with shallow bogland to either side. The cover was meagre; a few bushy islands sat lonely here and there and there was a section of thicker woodland too, though a good quarter mile off the road. "How bad is it?"

"As bad as your imagination can conjure." Lord Rammas didn't have a very good imagination, so Elyon spelt it out for him. "The entire city is a ruin. Everyone there is dead. All the ships in the harbour are burnt or sunk. I don't know who or if anyone got out. It was too dark to see when I arrived."

"And when was that?" Sir Rikkard Amadar dismounted, strode over, and pulled Elyon into a hug in a crunch of armour. "It's good to see you, Elyon."

"And you, Uncle. Two nights ago. I'd just arrived at Nightwell when Sir Glarus Pentar told me of Lord Morley's call for aid. By the time I reached the city, it was too late."

Rikkard nodded. "We had word as well, though not from Morley. A scout of ours reported that a large host was being unleashed from the Bane, though he had to ride all the way to Oakpike to tell us. We struck the camp and marched at once, but the enemy had too much of a head start on us. We'd hoped Mudport might hold out a little longer, so we might come in behind them, but…well, seems we were too late."

Much too late, Elyon thought. Dragon's Bane had fallen in a single night. It felt like folly to believe that Mudport would last longer against such an onslaught. "You must have been riding nonstop for days," he said.

"We've ridden with some haste, yes, and taken few breaks to sleep." It showed on his uncle's face as it did the others behind him. To a man the mounted knights and men-at-arms looked tired and drawn out, with dark shadows beneath their eyes. Many were sitting slouched in the saddle, half asleep. It wouldn't do. A man could rouse himself if called to battle, but it was better if he was well-rested when the song of steel was sung.

"How many men did you bring?"

"All of them," Rammas said. "The entire army."

Elyon wasn't liking this. "You have to turn around," he said again, with more urgency. He would not put it past Vargo Ven to have laid this as a trap, attack Mudport only to draw the army out of hiding. "You're too exposed on this road. You should never have marched this way."

"It was the quickest way to Mudport from where we came from," Rammas came back. "You would let the city fall without a fight?"

464

"The city *did* fall without a fight," Elyon told the Lord of the Marshes. "You were never going to make it in time, and even if you had, you'd have arrived too tired to fight. You have no cover, Lord Rammas. Turn the men around at once. I'll do what I can to watch the skies and give warning should the enemy spring an attack."

Lord Rammas was not enjoying Elyon's blunt tone, by that hard look on his square face. "Turn around, and go where? Back to Oakpike? Burbridge won't like that."

Like you care what a petty Lakeland lord like Burbridge thinks. "Rustbridge," Elyon said. "The Marshlands have fallen, or soon will. Dragon's Bane is lost, and now Mudport is as well. I've heard that Fort Bleakmire is destroyed, so too Winslow Point and Castle Crag. We have no choice now but to help draw back to Rustbridge and defend the way west from there."

Rammas's eyes burned like two hot coals. "The Crag has fallen?" It was his own house seat, Elyon knew, a strong old castle that sat on the coast north of Mudport, looking out over the Bay of Mourning. He took a moment to process it, the muscles on his jaw bulging. "We never had word. My uncle…"

"He may have gotten out," Rikkard said. "If he had word…"

"No." Rammas was not a man who wanted or needed empty words of reassurance. "No, my uncle was no coward. He would have stayed until the bitter end." He looked at Elyon. "Did you see it yourself?"

Elyon told him no. "I never went that far, Lord Rammas."

The Lord of the Marshlands looked like he wanted to put his fist through someone's face. He had the fist for it too, a great thick ham of a thing. "So it's fallen," he said bluntly. "Same as Mudport. Same as the Marshlands, of which I am sworn to protect. *My* lands…razed and ruined."

Yes, and all lands will follow, lest we stop them, Elyon Daecar thought. He did not want to give Lord Rammas time to dwell on all that. "What survivors there are will flee west and north," he said. "Their fate is now their own, sad to say, and we cannot stay to protect them. We must turn west at once. We make our stand at Rustbridge."

Our next stand, he might have said. Elyon Daecar was sure it would not be the last.

Rikkard stroked his chin. "If we march west we'll leave Lakeheart completely undefended, and the way into Tukor as well."

"The border to Tukor is for the Tukorans to protect, not us, Uncle. And Lakeheart has a large garrison of its own. Long may they defend the city should it come under assault. But Rustbridge is a crucial crossing, and pivotal if they're to cross into the heart of the kingdom. We've lost a limb out here, but a limb only. We have to protect our vital organs now. The sooner we leave the marshes, the better."

Lord Rammas stared east down the road, wishful and rageful at once, though offered no word of disagreement. "Fine. As you say." He turned to one of his captains and bellowed the order, and before Elyon knew it word was spreading down the lines. *It's going to take a while*, the Prince of the Skies

465

knew. "Do you have your baggage train with you?" he asked his uncle as Rammas rode off to oversee command.

"We needed to bring food and fodder with us, Elyon, and other provisions. We can get the men moving back west while they're being turned around. The baggage train is a long way behind us."

I like this less and less. Turning horse-drawn wagons and oxcarts around on a narrow road was a recipe for disaster. "They'll clog the road. Gods, Rikkard, this is a perfect time for Ven to attack us." He looked skyward, squinting away to the south. Even if the dragonlord hadn't anticipated this, it would take but a single scout to spot them and report the opportunity. "We have to get them moving, and quickly."

"I know. Rammas is not a man to dally. He'll get them moving as quickly as he can."

It was the best Elyon would get. "Who has the rearguard?"

"Lady Payne and her men."

Elyon was surprised by that. He'd strongly expected Marian to have gone home by now. "She didn't go back to Rasalan? I thought her uncle would have commanded her to return to Stormwall."

"He commanded the opposite, in fact. Lord Tandrick understands that the war is here in Vandar. He ordered that his niece continue to fight with us on his behalf."

Elyon smiled. He liked the sound of this Lord Tandrick Payne the more he heard about him. "I'm glad to hear it." Marian Payne only had three thousand men remaining after the Battle of the Bane, but they were good strong soldiers, well-trained and brave, and her own presence was worth a deal in itself. *For her sword and counsel both,* Elyon thought. He had a quick scan of the skies again as the horses turned west, banners fluttering and snapping in the wind. Some clogging was inevitable, he knew, but there seemed to be an urgency about them at least.

"How's your father, Elyon?" Rikkard asked him. "We've heard next to nothing from the west."

"He was at Crosswater last I saw him. By now he'll be at King's Point, most likely."

"Has the war reached him yet?"

"Not that I know of, but it's imminent. Did you hear about Lythian?"

The man's frown said no. "What of him? Has he returned? Say he has, Nephew. Gods, we need some good news."

"I'll fill you in later. But in short, yes. I travelled with him from Redhelm to Nightwell. He's had an interesting journey, Rikkard. He's seen some interesting things."

His uncle's eyes were suddenly bright. "Tell me."

"Later."

"Elyon. You would leave me in suspense?"

"The world is in suspense, Uncle. Everyone's holding their breath, just waiting to see what's going to happen next." He smiled enigmatically and said, "He's seen Eldur, several times. He's come face-to-face with him, Rikkard. Can you believe it?"

"No. Not if he's still alive. Why would Eldur not kill him?"

"It's complicated."

"I'm sure. Tell me."

Elyon shook his head. "Later. Now isn't the time." He looked past him; already the vanguard was moving back the way they'd come down the Mudway, though Elyon supposed they'd become the rearguard now, with Lady Marian assuming the van instead. "Go with the men," he told his uncle. "I'll watch the skies and give warning if any dragons come. We can talk later."

He wasn't sure when later would be. Rustbridge was still hundreds of miles from here, and they would be vulnerable almost every step of the way. It could take another ten days to get there. *Damn Lord Rammas and his belligerence*, he thought. If he'd taken Rikkard's counsel, they'd have reached the city by now. Instead they faced a long march across the entirety of East Vandar.

And what am I to do now? Fly all day and night, warding off dragons? For ten whole days? Elyon had a pressing need to go back west and find out what was happening at King's Point. *And the rest*, he knew. He still harboured a strong intent to endure a much longer flight, deep into enemy territory. *And now this. Flying escort for an army, because Rammas could not see that Mudport was doomed, no matter what he did.*

The day was still young. Elyon took his frustration out on the skies, flying swift and hard in a defensive line south of the road. An army thirty thousand strong was not easy to watch over, the prince quickly discovered. They stretched for many miles along the road, sometimes with great gaps between them. Those seemed to be broken up by the banners under which the men were marching, a dozen disparate armies chained together like a necklace of pearls. Elyon had to fly at least ten miles by his reckoning before he finally found the baggage train, a great host of carts and wagons trundling along at the rear. When he arrived, he found that they were still travelling east. It was no great surprise. The call to turn back could only travel so quickly by horseback, and Elyon had reached them long before any messenger could.

He decided it best to inform them himself, flying a slow glide over the top and calling out at the top of his lungs for them to turn around and go back the way they'd come. "Mudport is fallen," he shouted. "The Marshlands are overrun. Turn your carts and wagons around. We make for the city of Rustbridge."

When he spotted Lady Marian Payne he swept down to tell her personally what was happening. She wore her sleek-fitted plate armour and silver cape, riding her beautiful grey palfrey Stormwind. Her lips showed a faint smile to see him, but no more. Elsewise she was as stoic and inexpressive as ever.

"I see," she merely said, when he gave her explanation. "I cannot say I am surprised, Sir Elyon. I told Lord Rammas that we should withdraw to Rustbridge as soon as we got word of this attack, same as your uncle, but he wouldn't have it. He was intent on defending his lands. A noble calling, if driven by a certain lack of foresight and wisdom. Alas it has left us all exposed."

"And yet you still decided to march with him? Why?"

"Why? Well, because my uncle commanded me so. A noble calling, as I say. Rammas wished to defend his country. I wished to obey my lord uncle. Aren't we all just fools for honour, Sir Elyon?"

Elyon smiled. "It'll get the lot of us killed."

Lady Marian waved a hand and her man Roark rode forward. "Roark, send word out to my captains that we need the baggage train turned around at once. Lark, go with him. Quickly now, there's no time to waste." The men galloped off, bellowing out Lady Marian's orders.

Elyon watched them go. "Did Braddin recover?" he asked. He knew that Quilter had perished during the Battle of the Bane, and Braddin had taken a serious wound to the gut as well. When he left his fate remained uncertain. All four of them had been dear to Saska.

"The man refuses to die," was the lady's answer. She gestured to a sturdy wagon nearby, fitted with a canvas canopy. "He is unable to ride, so simply relaxes all day on the wagon. I am starting to wonder if he is faking the wound to get preferential treatment."

Elyon laughed, and it was much needed. "I'm glad he's on the mend."

"So am I. Did you fly south yet, Sir Elyon? I understand Aram is very nice this time of year."

His smile remained. "No, not as yet." In truth the idea of flying to Aram was not on his agenda. *If I'm to fly south it will be Eldurath*, he thought. He wondered if he would share tidings with her, about Lythian and Eldur and all he'd learned, but knew that now was not the time. "I will try to find you later, my lady. I'd best keep watch on the skies."

The next hours were spent as such, flying back and forward up the road, watching the movement of the men and mounts as they trickled along the Mudway. They looked so slow from up here, as though they were moving through treacle. *I have a new appreciation of speed*, he thought. Elyon could be at Rustbridge by nightfall if he left now. At this pace it would take the army well over a week.

He fell into a pattern, stopping only to take a short rest and eat. When he did that, he took the chance to hear of the latest tidings that had reached the army at Oakpike. It seemed that some crows were still coming from Tukor this far to the east, and they'd had news that Prince Raynald was mustering an army to march down and help them defeat the Agarathi and their allies here in Vandar.

"That's the rumour, anyway," his uncle told him. "The prince is only eighteen and ruling by proxy for his brother, so who can say for certain? His lords might overrule him."

What lords? Elyon wondered. So far as he knew, every Tukoran greatlord was either in the south with Lord Cedrik Kastor and Prince Robbert, or else protecting their own city seat and lands. "His auntie will, you mean," was his reply. "Cecilia Blakewood's the one ruling Ilithor, not Raynald. She's been in charge ever since Janilah went missing."

"Another rumour," Rikkard said. His tone suggested it was likely to be true, though. "As to Janilah, we've had word of some rogue dragonkiller up there, a little north of Tukor's Pass. Several dragons have been found butchered and mutilated, often horrifically, and no one can figure out who's doing it."

"And you think it's Janilah Lukar?"

"I think it's possible, yes. The king's been missing for months now, Elyon. And let's not forget what blade he carries. Your father's out there killing the likes of Zyndrar the Unnatural and you've felled how many now?" He paused, then said, "No, don't tell me. I'm envious enough as it is knowing you're going to sit for all eternity as Varin's favourite son. I don't need to hear of your latest heroics too." He gave his nephew a grin. "Point is, you and your father are having great success killing dragons. Why not Janilah? The Mistblade is extremely well suited to the task, you know. Perhaps more than any other."

Elyon thought on that during his next circuit up the road. If Janilah was truly killing dragons, that could only be a good thing, he supposed. *Let him get on with it,* he thought, as he raced along beneath the clouds. *He'll face the gallows once he's helped us win the war.*

The fact that the king was acting alone and beneath a cloak of mystery was more troubling, however. On the surface it looked noble enough, but who knew if he had other motives. *I'd not put it past him,* Elyon Daecar thought. *And not for one minute will I trust that man.*

He put all that from his mind. *Watch the skies. Look out for dragons.* He flew to the westernmost front of the army, where Marian was protecting the baggage train. Lord Rammas had taken up ahead of her now, ordering his best and bravest to fan out and watch their southern flank. Rikkard remained in the rear to do the same, and by mutual agreement, they had decided it was best to keep the army well spread out to avoid bunching. Elyon thought it prudent. There was nothing a dragon liked more than raining fire on a great host of men all squashed together. Keeping them spread would reduce that risk.

When dusk began to fall, the prince flew down to seek counsel with the Lord of the Marshes. "When do you intend to make camp?" he asked him.

"Tomorrow," Rammas answered at once. "I've already given instructions to ride through the night. We are vulnerable on his stretch of road, as you rightly pointed out. By tomorrow we'll have more cover."

Elyon agreed. He'd flown ahead earlier just to make sure and had found that the section of the Mudway they were on just happened to be the most open and exposed.

He turned his eyes skyward. "It'll be a dark night, with this cloud cover. The stars should be few and the moon is on the wane. Do you think you can ride without torches? Without firelight we'll be much harder to spot."

"I've given that instruction as well," Rammas told him. "Horses have excellent night vision, and the road is mostly straight. Some men will likely be taken by bog lizards and marsh serpents, but that cannot be avoided. I've told the men to stay wary and remain close to the centre of the road where they can, to watch for ripples in the water. There are creatures here that can strike without warning, Prince Elyon. You hear a scream, a sudden splash, and the man marching beside you is gone. I've seen it before."

Elyon shuddered at the thought of it. He knew it was unwise to travel the Mudway by night, without fire to ward off the ghoulish creatures that lurked in the swamp, but in this case they had little choice. "I'll report to my uncle," he said. "Have him spread word through his own men."

He flew back to the rear, feeling more like a carrier crow than ever. *Maybe we should start breeding Bladeborn crows,* he mused idly, as he shot swiftly down the lines, over the great rustling horde of weary steeds and soldiers. *We could hammer out little suits of armour for them so they're not so easy to kill.* He was smiling wryly to that when he landed beside his uncle in a swirl of wind and slid the Windblade into its sheath.

"Something funny, Nephew?"

"The skies are lonely, Uncle. I like to entertain myself by thinking of silly jests."

"Care to share?"

"Another time. The order from Rammas is we're to ride through the night, without torches. Send word among the men to watch for ripples in the water and stay at the heart of the road where possible. The creatures here have no fondness for the light, but without it…"

He need say no more. His uncle passed the command onto one of his captains, who did the rest. Elyon could almost sense the tension thicken as word was spread. Men shifted at once away from the edge of the road, glancing with trepidation at the black pools of water that sat still and turbid to left and right, cloaking the terrors that lurked within.

"This will help keep them alert at least," Rikkard pointed out. "Many of these men are close to exhaustion, and the same can be said for the horses. Rammas has pushed them all too hard over the last few days. And you, Elyon. You're pushing yourself too hard as well. You can't watch the skies forever."

"One night is not forever."

"And when this one night is done? We're going to be marching for a week at least. Do you plan to stay with us that entire time?"

"No," Elyon said. "There's better cover up the road, as you know. I'll stay until I feel you're safer." There were wet jungly forests just off the Mudway further on, and after that wooded hills and cliffs and crags that would provide much better concealment should a dragon come sniffing by.

"If you're sure." His uncle looked at him for a long while as they went, then said, "You need to get off your feet, Elyon, rest for a little while. When you're not flying, you're walking. When do you ever get to stop?"

"I'm fine, Uncle. Don't fuss."

"I could have Snowmane brought down here," Rikkard said, choosing not to hear him. "Sir Isaac Hemshore has been taking care of him since you left Oakpike, but I know he'd like to see you."

And I him, Elyon thought. But the sky was his steed now, and there was

470

no sense in depriving Sir Isaac of Snowname's company needlessly. "I'll be leaving soon, as I say."

His uncle continued to peer at him. "This blood," he said, looking him up and down. "I've been meaning to ask. Were you in some battle before you found us?"

"Several."

His uncle sighed. "How many, Elyon?"

"I don't know. Three, this morning. And others yesterday as well. There are lots of skirmishes to south and east of here."

"And you thought to join every one of them, did you?" There was a tone of reprimand to his voice. "I know it's hard, Elyon, but you've got to learn to pick your battles more prudently. If you'd found us yesterday, you would have saved us several days of hard marching. You must have suspected we'd be coming this way?"

I did, Elyon thought. *And I could do without this lecture right now.* "So you expect me to just smile down and wave as I watch my countrymen dying, do you? I'd like to see you do that, Rikkard. You'd throw yourself into every fight just the same as me."

"Probably, yes. But that doesn't mean it's right, Elyon. I understand the urge, I do, but sometimes it takes an outsider to give guidance and see the wood from the trees. I'm just saying…"

"I know what you're saying. And you're right. I should have come straight here the night I saw Mudport burning. I know what I *should* have done, but that doesn't make it any easier. I'm meant to be a champion to these people, Rikkard. What sort of champion would I be if I just turned my head and flew on by?"

He didn't want to talk about this now. He let out a heavy sigh and trudged on, armour clanking, wondering whether he should take up his uncle's offer to have Snowmane brought after all. The idea of resting in a saddle, even catching a bit of sleep…

No, he told himself, not giving in to that craving. *If I stop, I'll drown.* He'd heard that about some species of shark that needed to keep on swimming lest they suffocate. *Perhaps I'm the same? Just some sky-swimming shark that needs to keep on fighting, on and on and on, else I'll die.*

The march went on, the darkness deepening. The air was filled with the shuffling of men and clopping of horse hooves and the croaking of frogs in the swamp. Few men spoke but in wary mutters and there was no laughter to be heard, no marching songs, no mirth. The skies above had donned a heavy black mantle, the moon blotted, stars hidden beyond the pale.

After a while, Rikkard said, "Well, if you're going to walk, so will I." He dismounted his purply black destrier Twilight to march beside Elyon on the road, leaving the horse to navigate by himself. Their armour clinked softly, feet plugging and sucking at the mud with each step. "So, are you going to tell me about Lythian, then? I feel you've kept me guessing long enough, Elyon."

"That's a conversation to have in private, Uncle." It was too sensitive a topic to speak about openly, Elyon knew, surrounded by soldiers, and

Lythian would not favour him for spreading word of his part in Eldur's revival. In an army like this, it would soon be on everyone's tongue and the truth of it would likely be warped.

"You want privacy? Fine." Rikkard slowed in his step until every mounted knight and man afoot had passed them, leaving them at the very rear of the column, with nothing behind them but open bogland and fetid air, and the haunting pall of night. "There. We're alone. Now enough excuses, Elyon. I'll hear this story in full."

"Fine. If you insist."

When Elyon was done with Lythian's sorry tale, Rikkard went silent for a long moment. Then he frowned and shook his head. "Well, that's a lot to unpack, I'll admit."

"You're telling me."

"I don't know what's more shocking. That Lythian helped raise Eldur from the dead or that he fell in love with an Agarathi princess."

"I thought the same," Elyon told him. "He's greatly troubled by them both, Rikkard. Guilt trails his every step."

"Yes, well I'm not surprised. I'd not condemn him for any of that myself, but others…" He ran a hand through his chestnut hair, his helm clutched in the crook of his arm. "Not all men are quite so understanding, or forgiving, as we are, nor know Lythian half so well. You haven't spoken to your father about this, I take it?"

"I haven't seen him since I flew to Redhelm."

"And Lythian is making for King's Point, did you say?"

Elyon nodded, as they strolled behind the column, some twenty metres back from the nearest men. The pace was slow, the horses walking at a gentle trot, the men keeping to a sluggish, weary trudge. "He should be there soon enough, things going well. I sent word for his armour and weapons to be brought down from the Steelforge by barge. There's no knowing if that got through, though."

"We must hope. Lythian's return ought to be celebrated as a boon. Armoured and armed, there are few better, even without Starslayer in his grasp." He shook his head, still trying to get his head around all he'd heard. "The paralysis he spoke of, this dread in Eldur's presence. That is of grave concern, Elyon, for a man such as he to wilt like that. I wonder how we're supposed to fight this ancient sorcerer if his mere will and voice can subdue us."

"I'm not sure *we* are supposed to fight him, Rikkard. Only a select few will ever have that power."

"You?" his uncle said, in half a challenge. "Yes, I suppose with the Windblade in your grasp, you'd have some defence against his aura. Though even more if Vandar's Heart should be reforged. Only the Heart can destroy the Soul, you said. And this heir of Varin? Who he is?"

Elyon gave a soft laugh. "Your scepticism is pungent, Uncle. I can smell the stink of it from here, even over this reeking bog."

"Well, can you blame me? It seems this Agarathi prophecy has been proven false if they believed Eldur would rise as some force for good.

Perhaps they were wrong about this heir of Varin as well, and much else besides. I prefer to fight what is in front of me, rather than wait for some mysterious saviour to appear. Wars are never won by a single blade or duel, Elyon. It takes a hundred battles and ten thousand fights to pave the way to peace."

Elyon smiled at that. "You sound like my father."

"I should hope so. You know how much I admire him."

"I wish the same could be said for your own father, Rikkard. He still refuses to give Lillia up, Amara says, despite regular calls from Father to do so."

The heir of House Amadar sighed in vexation. "My father has much to answer for. This about Amara..." He didn't further that thought, perhaps realising they had no time to get into it now. Instead he looked at Elyon's hip and said, "I had half expected you to return with two Blades of Vandar, not just the one. That's why you flew west in the first place, isn't it? To ask your father to lend you the Sword of Varinar?"

Elyon shrugged. "It was always a long shot. And there would be no point anyway. Only the Heart can destroy the Soul, all that."

"And yet you still harbour a desire to fly south. I can see it in your eyes, Elyon. Why? Not to fight Eldur alone, surely. You're impulsive at times, Elyon, even reckless, but you were never stupid."

"Thanks, Uncle. Very kind of you to say."

"Elyon. Don't sidestep this. I want to know. What would possibly possess you to want to fly south, knowing all that you do?"

"Hadrin," Elyon said, at once.

"Hadrin?" Rikkard repeated, confused. "I was under the impression the rat king was dead."

"Marian doubts it, and so do I. I never told you what Vargo Ven said to me that night, did I, during the Battle of the Bane?" When Rikkard frowned and shook his head, Elyon said, "'*Even now, as we do our dance up here, he seeks to strip away your one advantage. Even now he moves against you*'. He was talking about the Eye of Rasalan, Rikkard, about stealing it, and the king as well. Hadrin's the only one who can glimpse the future in the orb. If Eldur's using him to steer the course of this war, to manipulate it somehow, I have to try to stop him."

"How?"

"You know how."

Rikkard was shaking his head already. "I've told you, Elyon. You cannot fly so far south alone. And I'm sure your father said the same. It's folly."

"He said the same," Elyon confirmed. "Folly. That was the word he used." *And I don't care what anyone says*, he thought. *The Bondstone is beyond my power to destroy, but a man of flesh and blood...*

"Elyon, I don't like that look."

"Then turn away, Uncle."

As Rikkard was framing a reply to that, a faint glow of orange light appeared ahead, far up the road. Both men turned to peer past the great marching column of men and mounts, frowning.

"Dammit," Rikkard said, "I thought Rammas gave explicit orders *not* to light any torches tonight."

"He did," Elyon told him, squinting through the gloom. He took a grip of the Windblade, and knew it at once. "They're not torches, Uncle." The fire was at least a mile up the road, too far away and too bright to be a simple torch. Distantly, he could hear the shrill sound of screaming in the air, a sound he'd come to know well. Men, aflame. The pain and terror of being burned alive. "Tell your men to be prepared, Rikkard. The shield-bearers and bowmen especially. This could be a long night." His voice was calm.

His uncle withdrew his blade, understanding. "Ven?" he asked.

Elyon unsheathed the Windblade. "I don't know. It might just be one rogue dragon. Or it might be more." He raised the blade aloft, summoning a swirl of wind to embrace him. *Vandar, give me strength,* he thought, as he soared away into the darkness. He sensed he was going to need it.

40

Saska

She woke with a start, escaping the dungeon of her dreams.

A dungeon of fire and fang and claw, monsters and gods, a cell of fate and fear, doubt and darkness that overwhelmed her almost every night. Sweat dappled her feverish brow, her silken nightdress damp and clammy, sticking to her skin. She gasped out as though she'd been holding her breath for long minutes, panting as she sat up, sudden and afraid.

Marienna came rushing over. "My lady, are you all right? Would you like me to fetch you some water?"

Water. Yes, water. Saska nodded. Her throat was tight, like there was a noose around her neck. She drew several long full breaths as the nursemaid fetched the water and returned, then drank deep.

Marienna was looking at her with those big brown eyes, wide and worrisome. "Was it another bad dream, my lady?"

Life is a bad dream, Saska thought, calming. "Nothing I've not had to face already." *A thousand times before.* She drank the cup dry and asked for another, then drank that one too. Dreaming was thirsty business for Saska, granddaughter to kings. *I must sweat out half my body weight every night.*

She placed the cup aside, feeling a sharp dart of pain throb through her flank.

"How are you feeling?" the nursemaid asked, seeing the discomfort flash upon the princess's face. "Do you need something for the pain, my lady?"

Saska shook her head. "I'm fine." She needed to embrace the pain, Sir Ralston had told her, learn to master it as she would her fear. There were many distractions in battle that a warrior needed to overcome, the Whaleheart said, fear and panic and pain all foes that must be defeated and dominated, lest you lose all hope of victory.

I suppose I need to defeat being useless too, Saska thought bitterly, as she moved her legs over the edge of the bed and placed her feet on the cool stone floor. "I need to get back to my training, Marienna," she said. "Go and find a guard. Tell them to fetch Sir Ralston for me."

"My lady? But your wound…it is not yet healed."

It's healed enough. "I'm sure the Whaleheart will adjust my training accordingly." Saska had had enough of feeling like an invalid, enough of this bedchamber and the cold counsel of her thoughts. *My first dragon,* she thought. *And I couldn't even wound it.* If Agarosh hadn't come and saved her, she'd be dead. *Me, the supposed heir of Varin.* Her smile was full of scorn.

The nursemaid was still looking at her. "My lady, I really don't think you should be pushing yourself just yet. If you tear open the wound again it will only take longer to heal. The sutures are still fresh."

I must sound like a lunatic. The nurse knew nothing of Saska's true nature, and likely wondered why she needed to train at all, least of all a mere week after suffering such a nasty gash. *The wound to my pride is worse, though,* Saska thought. Her doubts had mounted, one atop another, and lying here wasn't helping. She needed to hear the song of steel again. She needed to move, train, fight. *Or run,* she thought. *That would probably be better for everyone. To take Joy and run for the hills and never ever turn back…*

But she merely said, "Find a guard. Tell them to bring Sir Ralston here. That is a command, Marienna."

The girl submitted and gave a bow. "As you wish, my lady."

While the nursemaid was gone, Saska stripped out of her sweat-wet nightgown and washed herself clean in a basin of cool water, careful to avoid the bandaging that wrapped about her midsection. The wound was healing well, hastened by the ointments and balms they had applied to speed the process, though she would not be back at full health for some time yet. All the same, she could not stay here forever.

I can do some light sparring at least, she told herself. *Or work on my endurance, that's important too.* The biggest killer in battle wasn't steel or iron, arrow or claw, Rolly had taught her, but fatigue. Even the strongest warriors would succumb to it eventually, and when they did, they were defenceless.

She was pulling on her padded leather training breeches when the door opened and Leshie strode in, wreathed in red from heel to neck. The girl took one look at her, frowned, and said, "And just what do you think are you doing?"

"Getting dressed, Leshie. What does it look like?"

"Like you're getting ready to go training."

"Well observed. I asked Marienna to fetch Sir Ralston. He should be here any minute."

The Red Blade shook her head. "He won't be. He's in council with your grandmother and some others. And you're being stupid if you think you're ready to train. It's much too early. You need another week at least."

Saska continued dressing. "I need to get better. Stronger. Fitter. People died because of me."

Leshie's red eyebrows twisted into a frown. "What? No they didn't. Don't tell me you're blaming yourself for that, Saska? You've got enough to be worrying about without carrying the weight of the dead."

476

Saska wouldn't hear it. "I should have done better against that dragon. If I hadn't lost focus and been injured, Agarosh wouldn't have had to come and save me, and he could have killed that other dragon instead. He could have saved them."

Them, she thought. *Garth the Glutton. Marco of the Mistwood. Slack Stan*. All three Bloody Traders had perished during the fight, as had almost all of the Nemati guardsmen, burned to death or eviscerated or slain in some other unspeakable way. Only Merinius, the Butcher, Leshie, Sir Ralston, and three other soldiers survived, working together to fend off the beast before Agarosh could charge over and add his boundless fury to the fray.

The dragon had been overcome after that, outnumbered and outmuscled by the great one-eyed moonbear, savaging it was claw and fang, and the Whaleheart, swinging and hacking with those massive misting greatswords of his. The Butcher had played his part as well, raised to wroth by the death of his men, and even Leshie had helped distract and divert the dragon's attention as the others cut it down.

And all the while, where was I? Saska thought sourly. *Just lying there in the dirt…unconscious and utterly useless…*

Leshie had an angry look on her face. "I'm not going to listen to this talk," she said. "Not a chance. I don't like self-pity, Saska, and it doesn't fit you well. Remember when I told you about how I spent all those weeks down in Pal Palek's pits? How I lived down there in the darkness, betrayed by Vincent Rose, worrying every day that I would be raped or murdered by some guard. I had to bite my own nails to points just so I had something to defend myself with. And after, when that Shadowboy rescued us, do you know what I did?" She looked at her fiercely.

"No. What did you do, Leshie?"

"I got back on my feet and kept on going. I didn't let that hold me back from being *me*. And you, Saska, are not the sort of girl to wallow and weep. So you didn't kill a dragon on your first go. Boo hoo. So what. No one does. You're mad if you think it would have gone any better than that. I was watching, before that other dragon came along. I was watching you, and you were doing *well*. I could see you working out its attack patterns. You were being patient and looked calm and confident. Honestly, Sask. We all thought so."

I didn't feel calm, Saska thought. *Or confident*. It had all been a blur, to tell it true, and every bit of Sir Ralston's advice had seemed suddenly to vanish from her mind, stolen off by some sneaky little thief. "Thanks for saying so, Lesh. But…"

"No buts. You did your best, and that's all you can do. You'll do better next time. This whole experience…you should look at the positives. Take it as a chance to learn, and move on."

"That's what I'm trying to do. Move on. By training and not lying in bed all day, dwelling on it. We don't have time for me to convalesce like this."

"OK, for a start, I don't know what convalesce means. If you're talking about healing, then you have to take all the time you need. You can't rush

477

these things. And the sort of training you're doing with Coldheart requires that you're at peak health. What are you planning to do, exactly? Practice how to wince and grimace? Cause that's about all you're good for right now. You look like a strong wind would blow you over."

Saska smiled at that. "I can still train, so long as I'm armoured. I'll just take it slow. And I can work on my stamina."

"You can take it up with the Whale. I'm just telling you, he's *not* going to say yes. And even if he wanted to, there's no way your grandmother would allow it. After what happened…"

"I know." Saska was quite aware of how displeased her grandmother had been with how their misbegotten adventure had turned out. She'd had her arm twisted about letting Saska out of the city to fight this dragon, with the absolute assurance that no harm would come to her. Well, that hadn't turned out so well. Another few seconds and the last of Varin's direct line would have been cooked alive right there on that rugged red plain. And that was to say nothing of the guardsmen she'd lost, some of whom had served her loyally for years.

It was a losing battle, whichever way Saska looked at it. When she began removing her padded leathers, defeated, Leshie gave out a relieved sigh. "Good. Seems that dragon didn't knock all the wit out of you after all, Sask."

No, it just gave me a concussion. "You said Rolly's in council with my grand-mother? Do you know what they're discussing?"

Leshie snorted. "Like anyone would tell me."

"Shall we go and find out? Might be interesting."

"Or might not. Hasham's probably just droning on about the great unwashed again. There are more coming too. From the east. I saw them as I came here."

"More refugees? How many?"

Leshie shrugged. "I don't know. Lots. You can take a look yourself from the terrace."

The terrace gardens were as quiet and tranquil as ever. The fountains tinkled, the birds chirped in the trees, the insects buzzed and far below, the city hummed. Beyond the high strong walls, Saska could see the great camp of refugees and worshippers, segregated and separated now into smaller encampments to help reduce the spread of the flux. Their efforts to contain the illness had been largely unsuccessful, she'd heard, with up to a hundred men, women, and children dying of the disease every day. *As if they don't have enough to fear,* the princess lamented. *Are dragons and bygone beasts not bad enough?*

She looked east, across the great span of the Amedda River, with its many bulky bridges with their shops and inns and whorehouses built right there above the waters. The city was larger on that side of the river. In the north were the hills where the highborn had their estates. In the south was the great bustling port and harbour gate, with its many piers and markets and hectic sailor taverns. Between the harbour and hills lay the great sprawl of the city proper, spreading out to the eastern walls.

Saska squinted that way, over the walls and the plains beyond. "That's what you were talking about?" she asked Leshie. "The refugees?"

"Yeah. I said there were lots of them."

"It's a camp, it looks like." Saska had expected to see men and mounts and wagons rattling along the road, not a full-blown camp. She looked again. "Or...are there *two* of them?"

The Red Blade frowned, peering forward. "Yeah, I guess...it does look like two, doesn't it?" She pursed her lips. "Maybe they separated them to contain the spread?"

Something wasn't adding up. "Why are they so far away, though?" The two camps were about half a mile from the city walls and hard to make out through the dust and heat haze that shimmered above the coastal plains. Saska narrowed her vision, clutching at the dagger Varin himself once bore. Slowly the details cleared, the colours separating. "Leshie...I don't think that's a refugee camp. It looks more like..."

"A warcamp." The Red Blade looked over at her. "You don't think...?"

Suddenly it became obvious why the council had been assembled.

Krator, Saska thought, nostrils flaring.

"Leshie. With me," she said.

41

Amara

Sir Connor Crawfield returned to them on horseback, shaking his head as he pulled sharply at the reins. "Gates are shut, my lady. Apparently all newcomers are barred entry, and those leaving are being warned they won't be let back in if they choose to go. Only those operating under the official seal of Lord Amadar have leave to pass."

We'll see about that, Amara thought. "Who did you talk to?"

"Sir Gorton some-such. He had command of the Storm Gate. I don't know him, my lady."

"I do. Sir Gorton Gullberry. He's as stupid as his name sounds. His father Sir Lorton was raised to knighthood by Lord Amadar decades ago and he's had his nose up his arse ever since. That unseemly trait was passed down to his son."

Carly Flame Mane gave a mocking laugh. "Sir Lorton and his son Sir Gorton. What are the rest of them called? Morton, Dorton, and Horton?"

Amara unleashed a much-needed chuckle. She could always count on the fiery redhead to issue a tart little jape or two. "If Sir Lorton had any other sons, I'm sure those names would have been high on his list. Most likely he's reserving them for his grandsons now, though the idea of Sir Gorton Gullberry ever procreating…" She shivered in her skin, despite the warm spring weather. "Well, you'll see what I mean when you meet him. Come." She kicked her spurs and set off at a strong canter.

The city was already visible several miles down the coast, its grand grey walls and tall defensive towers standing sentinel in their eternal vigil. It did not surprise her at all that Brydon Amadar had shut his gates to the commons. Few men were so damnably pragmatic, and he'd have been worried about having too many mouths to feed should all the peasants from the nearby towns and villages come storming in.

He probably had his soldiers stationed outside from the start, she thought, *warding off the poor frightened hordes who tried to seek sanctuary behind his walls.* Those same people would have simply turned their eyes west and made for Varinar instead, most likely, which was precisely what he'd have wanted.

Bastard, she thought. *Always pushing his own problems onto other people. You're a foul rotten bastard, Brydon Amadar, and your mother was a harlot and a whore.*

That last part wasn't even true, not in the slightest, but it served for Amara to get her insults out early, lest she actually say them to his face. *Only once I've got Lillia back can I tell him what I think of him.* She'd thrust her missing pinky into that big old nose of his, and tell him she was the one who killed Godrik as well. "Look what your scheming did," she'd say to him, with twisted laughter. "You've got king's blood on your hands now, Lord Bastard." He wouldn't much like that, she knew. It would prickle at that mountain of pride of his.

She smiled as she rode on, savouring the feel of the wind as it rifled through her greying blonde hair, enjoying the view of the lake that sparkled to the north with its many boats and islands. It could not have been a clearer day, the sun high, the sky a glorious cerulean blue, not a cloud to be seen from horizon to horizon. *One might be forgiven for forgetting the world is at war,* she thought.

She would not forget it, though. During their ride from Varinar, the signs of it had never been far away. In the Heartlands south of Lake Eshina, they'd spied the distant scorched ruins of farms and villages, passed travellers telling of brigands and fell beasts upon the road, and even spotted a dragon or two, flying high and distant, cloaked among the clouds and hunting for carrier crows.

Jovyn cantered at her side as they clip-clopped along the Lakeland Pass, looking altogether more steely and handsome by the day. *He'll be needing to upgrade this rouncey to a proper war-horse soon,* Amara thought. The boy had continued to grow taller with each passing turn on the moon and now stood close to six feet, and was broadening at the shoulder as well. *Put the lad in a full suit of godsteel armour and he'll look a proper knight.*

He turned to her, a crease between his eyes. "My lady, do you actually believe Lord Amadar will let us pass?"

You don't, she thought. His tone made that obvious. "We have to hope, Jovyn. I have the note from Amron, don't forget. Brydon may have ignored his demands thus far, but when I hand him the letter myself, perhaps he'll change his mind."

"He won't," Sir Connor said, glumly. "I've said it all along, my lady. This is a wasted trip."

"Ever the optimist, Connor."

"I prefer *realist*, my lady. I think you're the only one here who thinks Lord Amadar will actually listen. And even then…well, you'll forgive me for saying it, but we're here more in hope than expectation. He isn't going to hand Lillia over."

Amara was already getting angry at the thought. "That's why I brought Carly along, Sir Connor. As plan B. One way or another, we're getting Lillia back."

The Storm Gate loomed before them shortly after, flanked to left and right by a series of surging bastions built into the thick city walls, their tops crawling with archers and bowmen and dozens upon dozens of mounted scorpions and ballistas, meaty catapults and towering trebuchets and every dragon-killing instrument Amara could imagine.

Ilivar had been founded by Varin's only daughter more than three thousand years ago, and had taken on the traits of the blade she favoured…the very same blade that Amara's nephew now used to soar the skies. The defensive towers were slender and spiralled, coiling at the top as though to mimic the shape of tornadoes and whirlwinds, and the battlements were similar in the breezy flow of their design. The twin towers that surged skyward from the barbican had been built to resemble the look of the Windblade too; silver they rose, high and tall, with streamers flying from their outer walls, each thin and wispy enough to be caught even in a light breeze to mimic the swirls of mist that rose from the Windblade's edge.

The Windy City, Amara thought. Many called it such, and its ancient features and landmarks had taken on similar names as well. The Storm Gate was one such, its doors thick and silver and plated in godsteel, so heavy that only Bladeborn men could hope to open it. Beyond lay the Hill of Hail and the Tempest Temple atop it, the Street of Silence, Windswept Square and Hurricane Harbour.

A dozen other famous streets and sites in Ilivar had been named for the wind and weather, some better than others it had to be said. Lord Amadar's private keep was known as Keep Quiet, for not all weather was loud and blustery, and at times silence did reign. Iliva herself was known to favour the tranquillity the skies granted her, high above the world where only she could soar. She would hover for hours, legend said, in silent prayer and thought, and when the grand citadel that was later built to house the ruler of Ilivar was raised, it had been named Keep Quiet in her honour.

It suits him too, Amara reflected. Lord Brydon Amadar favoured quiet, strength, and time spent in rumination. Rarely did he like to leave Ilivar lest he must, for the outside world was too loud and unsavoury to him. *And now he's shut the world away as he hides behind his thick tall walls. Gods, he must be loving this.*

A shout echoed out from the ramparts as they neared, issued by some watchman, and a moment later the postern door beside the Storm Gate opened, and the awkward form of Sir Gorton Gullberry plodded forth with a unit of six soldiers at his back, dressed in Amadar pink and pale blue.

The knight was an appallingly unappealing man to look upon, with skinny reeds for legs, a disproportionately wide midsection, and shoulders that narrowed so dramatically it made his top half look something like a triangle. The head was little better. Sir Gorton's ears were large and oddly shaped, protruding off the sides of his head like wings, though his nose was small and piggish, his eyes pale and watery and unnaturally close-set, and he had no chin to speak of. Instead he just had a neck that miraculously merged into the flesh of his face without visible border or boundary. Never had a man been so in want of a beard, yet in all their cruelty, the gods had denied him even that.

"Gods be good," Carly exclaimed when she set eyes upon him. "I understand now why there's no one knocking at the gate. Just send out Sir Gorton and they all go running for the hills."

Amara held her smile as she rode to meet him. "Sir Gorton, a pleasure to see you again," she called out.

"And you, Lady Amara." His voice wasn't so bad, that could be said for him at least, and he knew how to handle courtesy. "To what do we owe this surprise?"

"It is no surprise, as you well know. My man Sir Connor was here only a short time ago. Surely he told you I was coming?"

"I had thought you would turn around and return to Varinar, Lady Amara."

Goodness, you're even more stupid than I remember. "No, I decided instead to ride the last few miles, to confirm what Sir Connor told me." She looked around at the empty land outside the gate. It was so odd to see; on any other day there would be carts and wagons rolling in, travellers coming and going, peasants passing through and knights as well, trotting upon fine bred horses. Now all of that was gone. It was deserted, silent. "I understand I'm to be denied entry into the city?"

"All are being denied entry, my lady, save those under the signed seal of Brydon Amadar, Lord of Ilivar."

"Yes, I've heard the name." Amara looked past the knight and saw that the six guards he had in his escort had their spears crossed before the postern door, three pairs in a row blocking entry. "Isn't that a bit much? We've not come here to bring blood, Sir Gorton."

"It is standard protocol, my lady. None are to enter, save by the official grant of…"

"Brydon Amadar, Lord of Ilivar, I know. I would, however, prefer to hear this from him. He is family to me, after all."

"Only by marriage. Not by blood."

"Again, thank you for educating me about my own family tree, sir. Perhaps you'd like to tell me about my childhood in Ilithor as well? Or inform me what my favourite vintage of wine is?"

"I would not know, Lady Amara. You're said to enjoy a few."

That was worth a chuckle, she'd give him that. She dismounted from Glitter, her fine spotted palfrey, and stepped forward, drawing Amron's signed letter from her silver cloak. "I have here a sealed note from Lord Amron Daecar, whom you may have heard of, to be delivered by hand to Brydon Amadar, Lord of Ilivar, which just so happens to be this rather large city right behind you." She smiled, then drew the letter back when he groped forward to take it. "By *my* hand, Sir Gorton, not yours. Are you to deny the express command of your king?"

He frowned. "I was not aware that Lord Daecar had been crowned."

"A crown does not make a king. Amron is currently fighting to defend this realm so it might exist beyond the end of this year. He has the fealty of most of the greatlords in this kingdom and the majority of the lesser lords as well. He need but call himself king for it to be so, and by his word am I given leave to pass these gates with or without Lord Amadar's grant."

Her words stupefied the poor befuddled man. He spluttered for a response for a full five seconds before suddenly blurting, "Lord Amadar is not present in the city, right now. He's gone, my lady."

She frowned. "Gone?" That did not sound like Lord Brydon Amadar at all. "Where, pray tell?"

"I'm...I'm not sure." Sweat was appearing among the folds of his forehead.

"So you're to tell me that Brydon Amadar, the Lord of Ilivar, has left his city at a time of great peril and war and *not* told the commander of his gate where? The same Brydon Amadar who fights so hard to *never* have to step foot beyond his walls?"

"The...the very same, my lady."

Sir Connor dismounted to join her. "It is unbecoming to lie to a high-born lady, Sir Gorton. You owe her truth, not deception. Now tell us where Lord Amadar is."

Silence. The gate commander said nothing.

A proposal came from behind them. "East," offered Carly, sitting up in the saddle of her russet mare. "Maybe he called his levies and went east to fight in the war. His son and heir Sir Rikkard's out there, isn't he? Lord Amadar might have gotten a letter calling for aid."

Amara would be most surprised if Brydon Amadar had led such a force himself, if so. Once before he was formidable but he'd not swung a sword in anger in many long years. The notion of sending men was not so hard to accept, however. She looked into Sir Gorton's small pale eyes. "So? Did Lord Amadar receive such a call from his son?"

The man swallowed and wiped his brow. "I am not at liberty to say, my lady. Lord Amadar told me so himself."

Then he's hiding something. She thought about it some more and wondered if she could make this work for them. With Brydon gone, wherever that might be, getting Lillia out could become a good deal easier. "I would speak to Lady Lucetia then," she said. "She is a dear friend of mine, and I have tidings I must share with her."

"The Lady Lucetia is not to be disturbed."

Damn you, you ugly bloody fool. For a heartbeat or two she considered just bulling right past him and his guards and making for the door, but the sight of those archers on the battlements above made her think better of it. *There's a tension here,* she thought. *Rash action might lead to rash response.* She was not going to put her men in danger, not after all she'd done.

"Fine. Then I will have you summon down Sir Daryl Blunt, a sworn knight of House Daecar." Amara had left Sir Daryl here to watch over Lillia when Lord Bastard had stolen the girl away. *He can deny me audience with Brydon and Lucetia, but my own man? No.* "Have him sent for, Sir Gorton. If you're not permitting me entry, I shall be happy to speak with him out here."

The sweat was glistening on his rumpled brow again. "I...I don't know what you're talking about, my lady. I am not aware of any Sir Daryl Blunt."

Careful, she thought. *Careful now, don't get angry.* She smiled at him as sweetly as she could. "Sir Daryl Blunt is a senior household knight in the service of House Daecar," she said, ever so slowly and clearly. "He has been stationed here in Ilithor for the last few months, tasked with watching over and protecting the Lady Lillia Daecar, who is granddaughter to your lord, as I'm sure you know. He is a man of ample girth at the belly, though slim in the arm and leg, with a laugh that could awaken a storm." It was a wondrous, thunderous, rolling thing, that laugh, the best Amara had ever heard. "His hair is short and thick, with a light wave to it, the colour of oak. He has rather large cheeks that are often red from smiling, a circular face and double chin, and no beard to cover it, lest he have grown one since I last saw him." She paused. "Now, does that ring a bell, Sir Gorton, or would you like me to describe him further? His eye colour, perhaps, might be the detail you need to recall him. Or maybe you would remember him if I told you his exact height, or the particular length and rhythm of his stride, or the tone of his voice?" She smiled, thinking that plenty enough sarcasm for now. "So? Has that stirred the man to mind, Sir Gorton?"

But even after all that, he simply wet his lips and shook his head and said, "I don't know him, my lady. If he had been here to look after Lady Lillia, then he'd have been spending his time in Keep Quiet mostly. I don't go there often..."

"What do you mean 'had been'?" asked Jovyn Colborn.

The knight searched the company and found him. He blinked. "I'm not following, boy."

"You said 'had been'. That Sir Daryl 'had been' here. Why not 'is'. Unless he's gone away somewhere too?"

Amara had missed that, though the look on Gorton's formless and gormless face told her Jovyn was onto something. "No, he's here. Sir Daryl, that is."

"I thought you didn't know Sir Daryl?" Sir Connor said dryly.

Everyone was glaring at him now as his stack of lies came falling down. "He...yes, I do know him. I recall him now. Sir Daryl. It's just come to me. With the round face and red cheeks. Yes." He chuckled awkwardly.

Sir Connor wasn't laughing. "Then send for him," he said.

"I can't, no." Gorton glanced around and smiled. "The boy, um... he's...he's right. Sir Daryl is not here."

Amara was getting a bad feeling in the pit of her stomach. "Where is he?" she demanded. "Did he leave with Lord Amadar? Did Brydon take Lillia somewhere away from the city?" *Would he? Would he have done that? Hidden her somewhere beyond our reach, or beyond the threat of war perhaps?* "Speak, sir, and *don't* make me ask you again."

Sir Gorton shifted backward, looking like he was about to turn and flee through the door, but Amara moved right forward to take a grip of his arm. "*Tell me*. Now. Where is Sir Daryl? Where is *Lillia*?"

"I...I don't...,"

"*Tell me*," Amara snapped. She was done with the charade. "Right now, Sir Gorton. Where is she!"

"Gone," the knight blurted. "She's…she's gone, my lady." He breathed out. "She left…three nights past."

Amara's eyes flared open. "Left? What do you mean, left?"

"She ran away. Slipped off after dark, so I heard it. But that's all I know. Lord Amadar told me not to say anything, but…but…"

"He's gone out to find her," Sir Connor came in, already scanning the lands beyond the city. He looked back at the blabbering knight. "Is that the truth of it?"

"Yes." Sir Gorton's head flew up and down. "He mustered men to search for her and has even led them himself. The lord is very fond of his granddaughter, he loves her dearly. He has put aside everything to make sure she is brought safely back, even with these dangers about…"

"She is a girl of fourteen. *Fourteen*, Sir Gorton." Amara stared at him, eyes white-hot. "If there are risks to be had, it will be Lillia who faces them, not Brydon and his bloody men!" Her lungs were pumping, fingers crunching into fists. "Which way did she go? If you know something, anything, you'll tell me. Now!"

The game was up and the man knew it. "I would tell you, my lady, truly I would, *if* I knew. But no one seems to know which direction she went. Into the hills of the Heartlands, maybe, or away toward the Mistwood. She might have travelled up the coast, or westward, back to Varinar. Lord Amadar has sent men out in all directions to track her, and bring her home."

"Home?" Amara repeated. "Ilivar is *not* her home, sir. Varinar is."

And was she trying to get back there? she wondered. Had Lillia grown weary of her grandfather's tyrannical rules? Was that why she ran? She nodded to herself; it made sense. *She missed Jovyn,* she thought, *missed her training, missed Keep Daecar, maybe she even missed me. She ran away to try to get back to us. But which way?* The Lakeland Pass would be the most obvious and quickest route. The road circled all the way around the shore of Lake Eshina, linking its towns and cities, but then…

"We did not pass her," she said, thinking out loud. "If she was trying to get back to Varinar, she'd have taken the Lakeland Pass. We would have seen her. Or *she'd* have seen *us*."

"Not if she was trying to go *un*seen," said Sir Connor. "She would have wanted to evade her grandfather's men, to avoid being taken back. She's a smart girl…she'll have kept off the beaten track."

Gods. Gods, she could be dead. The thought was almost too much for Amara to take. *No. She's smart,* as Connor says, *smart and cunning and strong. She'd have stolen a blade before leaving. She'll be armed with godsteel and have provisions as well.*

"We passed those soldiers yesterday," Sir Penrose Brightwood put in, the last of Amara's small company. "Pink and blue cloaks. Amadar men. I'll bet they were searching for her."

Yes, that made sense.

"They're searching in all directions," Sir Gorton said. "Like I told you.

But she'll be safe, my lady, you needn't fear. Lord Amadar will not rest until she's found."

He won't rest? Him? What about me? Amara's heart was fighting to break through her chest. *Gods, what if she should be taken by bandits. The things they might do to her. Or some other peril, some other threat.* The lands were crawling with dangers and godsteel blade or no, Lillia would not be safe for long. She turned to Sir Connor. "Connor, which way would you go? If you were in her shoes....which way?"

The stoic knight considered it. She could see he had an answer in his eyes, though he did not want to utter it in Sir Gorton's hearing. He took her arm instead and drew her aside, then leaned in and said. "The lake, my lady. If she could get a boat, she might think that the best way. There are hundreds of small islands where she might hide if spotted and it would be safer than travelling to Varinar by road."

Safer, perhaps, but not safe. The lake could still get stormy, and some of the islands were thought to harbour nests of pirates. And there were the perils beneath the waters as well, ancient creatures bubbling up from the depths. It was an impossible decision to make. *Which way? Which way?*

"She likes the water," Sir Connor Crawfield was going on. "She's grown up on the lake, my lady, and knows it well, and Ilivar has no gate at the docks. Slipping out that way would be much easier. There would be a hundred sailboats and skiffs to choose from."

"She'd never get far alone," Amara came back. "She's too young to row far by herself and…" She had a sudden thought and turned. Ten brisk paces and she was face to face with Sir Gorton again. She lowered her voice and asked, "Did Sir Daryl go with her? Tell me the truth, Sir Gorton. There is no sense in hiding it from me now."

"I…" He gave a reluctant sigh. "As I understand it, Sir Daryl Blunt has not been seen since that night as well. The night Lady Lillia went missing. I will let you draw your own conclusions from that, my lady."

"Thank you, Sir Gorton." *And thank the gods as well,* she thought. Sir Daryl Blunt was a good stout knight and excellent company besides. *And a good waterman too,* she knew. There had been many an occasion where Sir Daryl had taken her out on the lake and shown skill with both oar and sail.

That settled it in her mind. Amara Daecar spun on her heels and marched right back to Glitter to climb up into the saddle. Sir Gorton watched her go with a befuddled look on his face, perhaps expecting her to demand entry once more. She wouldn't. Sir Connor was right; Lillia and Daryl would make for the lake and try to lose their pursuers there. If caught and brought back by Amadar's men, so be it, the girl's safety was her paramount concern and this tug-of-war over her custody felt suddenly meaningless now.

All the same, Amara would be damned in Lord Bastard pulled her in first.

She tugged the reins and turned Glitter to the west. The rest fell in behind her, hooves clacking hard against the road. Over the noise Sir

Connor called, "Would we not have been wise to make enquiries at the docks, my lady? Sir Gorton might have let us in if…"

"We'll find a boat further to the west of here," Amara cut in. "We'll have to stable the horses as well and fetch them on our return. It is a race now, Sir Connor. And for Lillia's sake, we're going to damn well win it."

42

Saska

Two guardsmen were standing sentry outside the council chambers, dressed in Nemati silver and black, their spears crossed to bar entry. "My lady," one said, seeing Saska and Leshie advance. "You're out of your bed."

Well spotted. "Open the doors. I need to speak with my grandmother."

"But we have orders not to disturb her, while in session."

"Open the doors, I said."

The two men chose not to die upon this particular hill, and parted their spears. Saska could already hear voices within. They grew louder as the doors were pushed open with a groan. Inside she saw her grandmother, Lord Hasham, the Wall, the head of the Aram City Guard, known as the Strong Eagle, and the seniormost religious figure in the city, known as the Wise Eagle. For a reason Saska couldn't fathom, the Butcher was there as well. All were gathered in the cool sanctum in which the Grand Duchess held her councils, a stone room without adornment but for a heavy marble table at its heart, light grey and veined in black. A large sheepskin map of the city and its surrounds had been rolled out, held down at the corners by small polished stones.

"Lady Saska." Lord Iziah Hasham was the first to notice her. The moonlord wore his great cloak of feathers, silver and white and magnificent. "You're up."

You as well? "I felt like stretching my legs, my lord." She took in the energy in the room. *Strained* would be putting it mildly. The Wise Eagle was wringing his old withered hands and the Strong Eagle's red face was redder than Saska had ever seen it. Sir Ralston's craggy facade was twisted in displeasure, and her grandmother's eyes showed a great abundant sadness, as though some horrible wrong had been personally inflicted upon her. Even the Butcher looked vexed, and that was saying a lot. *That man is always smiling.* "I saw the camp," she said. "Is it him? Krator?"

Lord Hasham growled like a bear. "It's him."

She breathed out. *Stay calm.* "As a foe? It looked like a siege camp. Does he plan to…" She could barely even say it. "Has he come to steal your throne, Grandmother?"

The old woman's eyes were low and listless. Hasham spoke for her. "It would appear so, yes. But that isn't the worst of it." He paused for breath. "Lord Krator is not alone, Lady Saska. It seems that he has made an alliance…with Cedrik Kastor."

Confusion blew through her like a cold wind, fierce and biting. Her stomach churned suddenly, as though she might just bring up her breakfast. *Two camps*, she thought. *There were two camps.* "But…but I thought…" She could scarcely summon words. "They…they *hate* one another. They're *enemies*. You couldn't find two men more different…"

"To the contrary, I think they are far more similar than we realise." The Wise Eagle fit the name. He was a small spare man, birdlike of face, with a long thin aquiline nose, searching amber eyes, and a chin so sharp it could cut glass. Upon his head lay a soft cover of long white hair, flowing plentifully past his temples and down toward the razor line of his jaw. "Both are ruthless, merciless, and ungodly in their work, it would appear. I will declare this very night that Lord Elio Krator has not the support of our good goddess Aramatia, or Calacan, who watches over us still. I shall gather all to my eyrie at the Temple of the Moon and denounce him for the world to hear. This dark crusade of his has not the backing of the Holy Eagles of Aram, I assure you."

Crusade, Saska thought. *Dark crusade.* "But…the Tukorans…I thought they would sail home? You said that, Lord Hasham. They had no food, you said, and half their ships were destroyed…"

"By Bhoun in his vengeance," said the Wise Eagle, in a high disdainful voice. "This false god of Rasalan sent his whales to shatter them, it is claimed." He shook his head, hair swaying. "No, this is a lie. Bhoun in no true god."

Lord Hasham cared not for such talk. "Let's not reduce this to gods and guesswork. I'm sure the Rasalanians claim Calacan was no true god either, but a mere eagle blown out of all proportion." He ignored the look of shock on the Wise Eagle's face and returned his attention to Saska. "We heard several weeks ago that some ships were sunk by whales, yes. It has since reached us that others were destroyed by Lord Krator himself, when he sent fire ships to burn them at anchor. This was a ploy, one designed to leave the Tukorans stranded, with no choice but to enter into an alliance with him." He slammed an open palm onto the marble table with a great echoing slap. "Krator knew he had not the numbers to win the city alone. So he's won himself another army through trickery and disgrace. Matia… Kolash…both have already been sacked. Thousands of good honest Aramatians…dead. And all for that ravening, power-crazed snake!"

Saska's heart was trying to shatter her own ribs. *Stay calm*, she thought. *This is just a hiccup. Stay calm. They're not going to win the city.* "How…how many men do they have?

"More than enough to crush us if they batter through our gates or smash through our walls."

490

Sir Ralston was more specific. "At least seventy thousand combined."

Saska swallowed. *This can't be happening.* "And us?"

"A third of that," said Hasham. "Less. And no Bladeborn, except for you here in this room, and a handful of other sellswords. I've already sent word to Lord Ranaartan at Starcat Keep to send reinforcements, but who knows if my plea will get through. If Krator's smart he'll have sent outriders ahead to ring the city and cut off communications. And even if not, there's no guarantee Ranaartan will march. He's shrewd, that one, and won't want to join the losing side."

"We shan't be the losing side, my lord," said the Wise Eagle, with palms touching.

"And how do you know that?" demanded Hasham, turning on him. "Does Calacan caw in your ear, my lord? Do you commune with the gods as you say?" He snorted so loudly that the Wise Eagle's answer went unheard. "Let us not forget that you said nothing against Elio Krator when he opened the Red Pits during Safina's absence. When he held court here in this very palace, passing his cruel judgements as entertainment for the mob. You say you are loyal to Her Serenity, but who knows if that is true? Perhaps it is just the perks of your station you enjoy? Long have I taken you as a fawning lickspittle. You bow to whoever sits the Eagle Chair, no matter their methods and politics."

The avian man looked utterly appalled to have his piety called into question. "How dare you…"

"Dare? *Dare?*" Hasham's eyes were bright with anger. "I take it as no dare to call you what you are, *Pellion*. Oh yes, I dare call you by your *true* name as well. Curse me if you wish, I care not. My duty is to defend this city, to defend this duchy, to defend she who rules it. Go whisper to your birds and gather your foolish followers beneath your roost. Your voice is empty here."

The Wise Eagle was evidently lost for words. He turned to the Grand Duchess, opening his mouth, closing it again, opening it once more to say, "You…you would let this man speak to me…in this way, Sereneness? Here in this sacred palace atop which Calacan himself did dwell…"

"So you say," dismissed Hasham. "If all you're going to do is spout and splutter of myth and religious relics, you're wasting our time. We have a war to fight. A war requires soldiers, men of battle, commanders. I see some in this room. You are not one, Pellion. Unless you've got something useful to contribute, close your beak and let the rest of us talk." He turned to the Butcher, leaving the Wise Eagle to stand in silence, blinking. "You were saying you could try to reach your brother, before Lady Saska arrived. How many men does he have?"

The Butcher thought a moment. "That is hard to say. The Baker and I had many dozens under our charge, a good count of them sired of strong Bladeborn stock. I took less than ten with me to escort the pretty princess home, and we had some others working for men in Krator's service, mostly Sunriders. If the good sunlord has sniffed out our part in the pretty princess's escape, I fear my brother may already be dead. And his men as well. But I can try to find out for you."

"Do. And the other captains in your company?"

"There are many captains in the Bloody Traders. We are a force two thousand strong in total, but rarely do we come together. Right now we are scattered. The only other captain who is here in Aram is the Surgeon, I think."

"And where does his allegiance lie?"

"To coin, and to victory." The Butcher's savagely scarred face twisted into a smile. "Pete Brown does not take risks. He is meticulous, most careful in choosing his contracts. It will not matter how much you pay him. If he thinks Krator will overcome us, he will already have left the city to seek employment beneath his fluttery feathers. Or else found some other place to observe and stay clear of the fighting, until it is done."

"He sounds like a coward," grunted Sir Ralston Whaleheart.

"No. He is a businessman. All the best sellsword captains are."

"How many men does this Surgeon have?" the Strong Eagle wanted to know. He was a bald man with a heavy stubbled jaw and stout belly, dressed in a shirt of interlinking rings in copper, silver and gold beneath a feathered cloak of the same. His helm showed a soaring eagle with wings outstretched, beak open, screeching, a cumbersome thing that he would not wear in battle, Saska hoped. It seemed more ceremonial. The helm was placed on the table beside him.

The Butcher shrugged. "Fifty. A hundred. I could not say. But that is not what you are asking, is it? You want to know how many *Bladeborn* he has. And to that, I do not know either. If he is still here, I will find out for you."

"The gates have been closed and barred," the Strong Eagle informed him. "It has been so ever since the refugees came swarming from the wastes, bringing the read death with them. There is no way in or out of the city, save by my permission."

"So you like to think. A clever man knows ways you do not."

The commander took umbrage with that, his thick neck reddening. "I've captained the Aram City Guard for more than a decade. You think you know my walls better than I do, sellsword?"

"There are ways that men like you do not see. The ways of sneaks and sellswords and spies."

Lord Hasham did not hide his disdain for that. "Sneaks, sellswords, spies. A sort we should never seek to rely on. I put my trust in soldiers, bred for battle and raised to protect this city with their lives. In the good honest riders of sun and star who have served long and true beneath the wing of Houses Nemati and Hasham. I only wish Hothror was alive to see this day. I would ride out with him and deal with both Krator and Kastor myself."

No. I want them. Saska's fear and shock were melting away into anger now. Somewhere the gods were laughing at their sick little joke, placing the two lords together. In a world gone mad, it was one of the maddest things she'd heard. *You sent me to kill Cedrik Kastor once, Lady Marian*, she thought. *Well, maybe this is my chance...*

"What about Agarosh? Hothror may be dead, but Agarosh isn't." The council turned to Leshie, who'd posed the question. They'd been speaking in the common tongue of the north thus far, most likely for Sir Ralston's benefit, whose grasp of Aramatian was best described as passable. When no one gave answer, the girl frowned and said, "What? Did I get that wrong?"

"Agarosh left, Leshie," Saska told her. "Three days ago. I thought I told you?"

"No. Why? I thought he was protecting the people."

"He was. And he will again, I hope. But...I told you how I spoke with him? About how many moonbears there are left?"

"Four, you said. Other than him." Leshie frowned. "So he went? To recruit them?"

In truth Saska didn't know for sure. It was part guesswork, part deduction, and part hope. "I think so," she could only say. "I had that sense from him, anyway. And he was seen leaving in that direction as well."

"Well that's even better, isn't it?" Leshie said, beaming. "When the bears get back, they'll make short work of that sunlord and his Pigborn pet. A few moonbears would tear that army up. I've seen what they can do."

Saska shook her head. "Agarosh wouldn't do that. Most of that army is made up of common soldiers...regular men who have no choice in who they fight for. It's fear that drives them, not fervour. It's their commanders we need to kill."

"I agree," the Butcher said. "And do you know the best way to kill commanders?" He looked around. "Assassins. Slick and sneaky assassins, silken in their step." He smiled and looked over at Leshie with a grin. "The Red Blade. This is a task for you, I think."

Leshie nodded without hesitation, stepping forward. "I'll do it..."

"No, Leshie."

"*Yes*, Saska. I can do it. I know I can."

"You can't. Elio would see you coming a mile off."

"He didn't when I saved you from that leecher. I sneaked right under the sunlord's nose to get you out. No reason why I can't sneak in there and put a bit of steel in his neck."

There's every reason, Saska thought. She wasn't going to entertain it. "He knows you now. He'll expect it. You'll get caught, Leshie. *No*."

Before the Red Blade could respond, the Grand Duchess finally spoke. *About time*, Saska thought, releasing a breath. She did not like how her grandmother sat there, silent and sombre, as though already defeated. "My granddaughter is right," the old woman said, in a tired voice. "You are so very brave, child, to even consider this, but alas I fear your efforts would be in vain. Elio Krator is not a man to be fooled twice. We must think of another way."

Sir Ralston nodded his scarred boulder of a head. "Assassination is an unseemly business. This threat must be dealt with more directly." He gripped the handle of one of his misting greatswords. "I will see it done."

Hasham raised a bushy grey eyebrow. "How?"

"By direct challenge."

"A death duel?" The moonlord seemed to have hoped for something better than that. "It will not work, Whaleheart. Krator will not take the bait."

"I was not referring to Lord Krator."

"Kastor?"

"Yes. He is Bladeborn, born to kill. There is no man more gifted with the blade in all of Tukor, so people say, since the death of Rylian Lukar. To turn aside my challenge would paint him as a coward before his men. His pride will not accept this."

"You don't know him," Saska came in. "I do. He won't fight you, Rolly."

"Is he a coward then, this lord?"

"He's a lot of things, few of them good. A bully. A braggart. An abuser…"

"Is he a *coward*, my lady?"

"No. Not that I ever heard. But when facing *you*?" She shook her head. "What would he have to gain from taking the risk, except to serve his ego and save his pride?"

"The city," Sir Ralston said, without hesitation. He turned to the Grand Duchess, sitting dourly in her chair. "Permit me to act as your champion, my lady. Should I lose, the rule of the city will be handed over freely to the sunlord…"

The Strong Eagle gave a loud harrumph. "You cannot allow this, Sereneness. To stake your rule on the swing of a sword."

"I will not lose," the Whaleheart said. "I have no fear of Cedrik Kastor."

"And why should this Cedrik Kastor, a greatlord of Tukor, wager his own life so that a sunlord can claim command of this city?" The Wise Eagle clasped his hands together, having sulked long enough. "What are the Tukorans even gaining from this alliance?"

"Passage north, and men to fight for them," Hasham told him bluntly. "They are helping Krator win the duchy. Krator will in turn help them march upon Agarath."

"And he'll give them men? Riders of sun and star?" The tone of the Wise Eagle's voice made his doubts abundantly clear. "Lord Elio Krator will not risk the wrath of Agarath. He must have another plan."

"What other plan? Please, do tell us, Wise Eagle."

"I would have to…I don't know, as yet, my lord. If you give me time to think, then…"

Leshie was chewing her lip. "Maybe he hopes to destroy the Tukorans?" she came in. "This could be a trap. Lead them here, surround them, and then attack."

Hasham didn't think much of that by the look on his face. "You're suggesting he's doing this for the good of Aramatia? In service to Her Serenity? No, girl. Krator has always longed to sit the Eagle Chair."

494

"He is self-serving," agreed the Strong Eagle. "When Lord Krator took charge here during your absence, Sereneness, he tried several times to win my loyalty through riches and reward. I see now that he was hoping to control the gates. That I might allow him passage in exchange for power, if the time should come."

"Your loyalty has always given me great succour," Safina Nemati told him softly.

"Yes, *yours*," agreed Hasham. "I might say different for some of the men under your command, however. It would take but one gate commander to be bought, and the tides of this foul alliance will come rushing in, to sweep us to our doom."

The Strong Eagle nodded. "I shall review my procedures, and my men. Only those of proven loyalty will be allowed within a hundred paces of the gates."

Hasham grunted approval, as he looked down at the map, considering it for a moment. Then he gave a growl of displeasure and said, "Enemies beyond our walls, enemies within. Krator still has many allies in this city who will be only too willing to help him. Try as I might to drag them from their nests, they are too numerous, too evasive, and too deeply embedded into the stone of this city. We must be extra vigilant. I will have additional guards posted at the palace steps, should they stage an attack upon us here. Sir Ralston, your charge is to protect those within. Stand bastion here as you did for King Godrin. Be our wall."

The giant nodded.

"And the refugees?" asked Saska. "You have soldiers out there, protecting them. Hundreds. Do you not think Krator might…"

"Kill them?" The moonlord laughed scornfully. "I'd put nothing past that man. I'll have them brought back into the city, to help man the battlements."

"You'd leave the people defenceless?" Saska said. "Those soldiers are out there keeping order. If you command that they come back…"

Hasham cut her off. "Then the hordes will have to fend for themselves. Tents and shelters are as simple to take down as they are to put up. They have legs. They can move. Return to their own lands, as I've been saying all along."

This man is ruthless. Saska supposed that was needed when defending a city, but still… "Their lands are overrun with perils, Lord Hasham. And many of them are sick. They came here for sanctuary. We cannot just abandon them now."

"We have no choice. We must look to the people within this city, not those who huddle without. Sometimes a wound is so grievous that you have no option but to cut off a limb, lest the entire body falls to infection and death. Such is the case here."

"But…"

"No," Hasham said, not listening to her. "You will not convince me of another course, Lady Saska. Save your breath." He turned sharply to the Wise Eagle, sensing he had something to say. "Yes, Pellion? What is it?"

The holy man cleared his throat, as he looked down his long hooked nose at the map. "Many times have I visited these poor wretched souls who take shelter outside our walls," he began. "I bring them food, and prayer, and hope, and yet still many are dying of this dreaded pestilence. I regret that I am even about to suggest this, but…"

"Go on." Hasham was looking at him with those piercing eyes of his. "Say what you were going to say, Pellion."

"I mean only to suggest that…if the red flux were to somehow find its way into Lord Krator's warcamp, then…" He glanced at the Grand Duchess, saw her disapproval, then at once lowered his eyes. "Forgive me, Sereneness. A thought born of fear only, and desperation. I shall purge myself tonight in penitence."

Hasham snorted. "You call yourself a man of the gods, a holy man, and yet you would unleash the red death into an army of your kinsmen? You shame yourself, Pellion."

"Yes…you're right, moonlord." The man's head sunk low, dangling down off a skeletal neck. Saska could see the bones of his spine straining at his skin. "A most terrible notion. I apologise."

Before Hasham might berate the man further, the Grand Duchess raised a wrinkled palm and said, "You are forgiven, Wise Eagle. Fear drives us all, sometimes, to say words we quickly regret." She spoke weakly, wearily, as though it was the middle of the night and she needed her bed, and not the morning, bright and warm, the sun yet young. *The light in her eyes is fading*, Saska thought. *This treachery has wounded her gravely.* "We must hope to resolve this without unnecessary loss of life, if we can." She turned to Lord Hasham. "Iziah, please see fit to send Lord Krator's herald back with a message that I would like to meet with him in parley. Perhaps…well, call it an old woman's folly, but perhaps I can get through to him. Elio was much a son to me, for a time. Maybe there is a compromise to be found."

"*Compromise?*" Lord Hasham did not like the word. "You would not consider acceding to that man, Safina. I pray that is not what you mean."

"We have other matters…more *important* matters…" The old woman met Saska's eyes, deciding not to further that thought. So far as Saska knew, the Strong Eagle and Wise Eagle were not privy to the truth of her sire, and nor was the Butcher. Her grandmother gave a shallow sigh. "I should have seen this coming," she said. "We let Elio off his leash and did not keep an eye on him as well as we should have. That is on me. But I will not see the people of this city die for my mistakes. Send word, Iziah. Tell him I would like to meet."

Hasham's nod was stiff. "Fine. If that is your command."

The old woman gave another forlorn nod, then stood from her stone seat, looking more frail and feeble than ever. She raised a hand to the door. "I think that is enough for now. You have our own war council, Iziah. Please, make use of it. Gather what captains and commanders you need and plan your defence, should it come to that. The rest of you, thank you for your wise counsel. Saska, please stay."

The others filed out to leave them alone, Leshie stopping to tell Saska

496

that she'd be out on the terraces when she was done. When the doors were shut, silence swallowed them whole. It lingered for a time until Saska's feet scuffed against the stone floor as she moved around the table. "Is there any point in me asking if I can come to this parley too?" she asked.

"It would not be wise, given all that has happened. And Lord Kastor may be there as well. He will recognise you, if so. It is an unnecessary risk."

A risk. Or an opportunity? But for who, she couldn't say. "Be careful of him, Grandmother," she warned. "Cedrik Kastor brought blood to the parley at Harrowmoor. He won't hesitate to do so again if he thinks it will win the city."

The old woman shook her head. "I do not think Elio would allow it, child, but this…all of this…it is not for you to worry about. Your attention *must* stay solely on your task. Do not let this distract you."

My task. She'd heard enough about her godsforsaken task. "My enemies are camped outside our door, Grandmother. How can I not let that distract me?"

"Elio is not your enemy, nor Cedrik Kastor."

"They *are*. Of course they are!" The comment irritated her more than she could say. "Elio Krator *killed* my father, unless you've forgotten. If he hadn't done that, I wouldn't be in this mess. I wouldn't have this *task* to fulfil at all. My father would be the heir of Varin and the world would be better for it. So yes, I count Elio as my enemy for that, and that's even no mention everything else he put me through. And Cedrik…" She blew out a breath. "The things he did to the girls beneath his roof…the things he watched his father do to *me*. The beatings. The whippings. The starvings. Do you want me to show you the lash scars on my back again? Should I tell you stories I heard of what went on there, down in the darkness of those cells? I've wanted to kill Cedrik Kastor ever since I've known him, same as I did his father. So don't tell me they're not my enemy, Safina. Don't you dare try to take that away from me."

The old woman gave a slow nod. "The *real* enemy, I meant. These men…they are beneath you. You mustn't spend your attention on them…"

"Don't tell me what I must and mustn't do. I can think for myself." She paced away and back again, then placed her hands on the surface of the table, breathing out. "I said we should have gone north weeks ago. Now look at us. Stuck. I should have gone with Ranulf."

"We have not heard from Ranulf. We do not yet know if the Calacania will permit our passing."

"Then we take a ship and sail…"

"The krelia still prowls the Channel. Many ships have been lost to it, and more monsters surge from the deep by the day. The sea is too treacherous."

"And if Ranulf doesn't return? I *need* to go north, Grandmother, for this *task* of mine. You've told me that often enough. How else are we to get there?"

The old woman had no answer, and that was the problem. *She's spent her life guided by prophecy, and yet now there is only shadow and doubt and darkness before her, through which she cannot see. She doesn't know which way to turn.*

"We should leave now," Saska said suddenly. "If Krator wins this city… what then? What will happen to me, to you, to all of us? We follow Ranulf to the Everwood, and hope he's made contact by the time we arrive."

"The risks…" the old woman shook her head. "No. You almost died a week ago, Saska. You are not strong enough yet."

"It was a scratch. I didn't almost die. You're being dramatic."

"You *did*," the woman said, more fiercely. "You lost so much blood that it was thought you might never awaken. If Agarosh hadn't carried you back to the city, you may not have made it. You could have died, and all of our hopes with you."

"*No*," Saska said, firmly. "*Don't* put that on me. I am not the hope of the world, Grandmother. I'm just a mutt, a servant and a slave…"

"You are royalty," her grandmother broke in. "Your blood is more rich and ancient than any man or woman living. You are born of light and steel and sea. There is no one like you."

"Then stop treating me like a child. Stop trying to control me. You hold on so tight I can barely breathe. How do you expect me to fight when I've got fetters about my feet?" Saska was done dancing to the woman's tune. It had been a fine melody once; now it was tuneless, harsh on the ears. *She doesn't know what to do, no more than anyone else does.*

"I took those fetters off, and look what happened…" The Grand Duchess looked at Saska's side. A thin frown creased her eyes. "You're bleeding."

"Yes, you said. I almost bled to death. But I'll do better next time. My training isn't complete, I know that, but Rolly can keep training me on the road. Out there…with all the dangers…maybe that's where I need to be? Maybe that's the best training I'll get? Fighting. Killing. Beasts and men both. I'm Bladeborn, a weapon, and a sword needs honing. There's only so much more I can learn from sparring with Rolly and the Butcher. I need to feel the fear of the battle…like with that dragon. I need to make mistakes if I'm to…" She paused. "What? Why are you looking at me like that? Why aren't you saying anything?"

"You're bleeding, child."

Saska looked down. Her pacing and ranting had opened her stitches, and a thin patch of red was soaking through her shirt. "It's fine. One stitch. I'll have it sewn back up. It doesn't change anything."

"It will delay your healing. You cannot leave until you're stronger."

"So you agree? You agree that we need to go?" Saska found herself torn on it, even as she spoke the words. A large part of her wanted to stay, to fight, to defend the city and the people she'd come to call hers. Thoughts of vengeance boiled in the back of her mind as well, thoughts so enticing she could taste them. But what was more important? Her vengeance or her fate. *Can't I have both?* she wondered. *Is that so much to ask?*

The Grand Duchess closed her eyes, and a great sigh emptied from her lungs, filled with doubt and despair. "I know that you need to go, Saska. I have known that all along. But it doesn't make it any easier. I lost my daughter too young, and now you...dragged away by this...this cursed fate." Lines spread out from her eyes as they coiled in distress. "I have been selfish, child, in trying to keep you here. I just wanted more time with you. I thought...I thought we'd have more time together, before...before..."

Saska stepped in and went to a knee before the old woman's stone seat, ignoring the pain in her side, the sticky warmth of the blood. She took her hands. They were cold, wrinkled, pale, shivering. "We'll have time *after*, Grandmother. Once it's over. We'll have time then." She smiled, trying to reassure her. "And it'll take how long to gather the blades? And...and all the rest. We'll have time then, together. Me and you. I know it's not the same, and it'll be dangerous out there, but..."

"Oh child. Sweet, sweet child." Her grandmother reached out with a crinkled palm and placed it on her cheek. "There is a great journey ahead, through shadow and darkness and doubt. But... you must see, Saska? It is for *you* to walk, not me. I'm sorry, child, but my place is here. I was born here, and I will die here too." A tear fell over the rim of her eye, wending down a wrinkle in her cheek. "When you leave this city...I will not be coming with you. You'll have to complete Thala's puzzle without me."

43

Janilah

"For you, Vandar, god of all gods," he said, as the dragon screeched and descended toward him. "I do this for you, as your herald, and your champion. I live now only to serve."

His words of prayer were issued out in a whisper as the beast bore down upon him. On an open hill the king waited, dowsed in the final glow of the sun as it sunk down into the west. Between the shallow heights and valleys wended rivers and rills aplenty, and here and there were wooded thickets green and wet. Down near one of those thickets, Sir Owen Armdall stood observing beside his horse, his armour shining silver as it caught the last light of day. He had removed his cloak and gloves and boots to enter the fight if needed. He would not be called upon this time, the king knew. *As he hadn't the last, or the one before that.*

"For Vandar," the king said, louder, as the dragon drew near. "For Vandar, I slay thee! Go back to the fiery abyss!"

The beast opened its great maw as it closed on him, to engulf the king whole, armour and all. Janilah Lukar stood perfectly still. It was another wild dragon, unnamed and unridden.

Another fool, the king thought, as the jaws swallowed him, and he plunged straight *through* the beast's body, his own form shimmering and shifting as a gentle blue haze, incorporeal and invulnerable, matter passing through matter like smoke passing through air. When he reached the cavernous cavity where the beast's heart lay, he let his arm and sword take physical form - a flash only, an instant of corporeality - and at once he heard it, *felt* it; the shuddering pain, the crippling shock, as the Mistblade cut through that great sack of red flesh like scalding water through snow, killing the dragon instantly.

Janilah smiled, re-materialising, as the beast's lifeless body tumbled past him, gouging great ruts into the earth as it landed in a twisted heap upon the hilltop.

"For Vandar," the king murmured, glancing skyward in a moment of piety. He walked over to its corpse, blood and gore flooding down his arm. "I rid the world of another of Agarath's children, another of his slaves. For *you*, my lord Vandar. Soon, *he* will see. Soon I will have his attention…."

"My king…" Sir Owen Armdall came hurrying up the hill, armour rustling against the now-silent spring evening air. "Is it dead, my king?"

"I should think so, Sir Owen." Janilah Lukar wiped the Mistblade on his cloak, then slid it back into its ancient scabbard, releasing his grip on the hilt. He knelt beside the dragon's head, to cut out his prize with his dagger, and stashed the tooth with the others. *Not enough,* he thought. *Never enough.*

"You weren't dragged along inside it this time, my lord. You passed straight through."

The king stood. "Every new technique takes time to hone, Sir Owen."

He'd attempted the 'phasing-through' approach on the last dragon he had duelled, if only to add an extra weapon to his dragon-killing arsenal. *And a powerful one at that.* When taking form *inside* another creature or object, there was a natural fight for space, with the stronger and more durable substance triumphing over the weaker. It had occurred to the king that a dragon's internal organs, its meat and muscle would all be greatly less dense than the godly godsteel armour he wore, to say nothing of the blade he bore. If he could phase past the beast's scaly armour and take physical form *inside* it, his foe would find itself defenceless. In theory, he would not even need to cut at his enemy's internal organs with his blade. No, his armour would be enough to rip and rend it apart from within.

But he had to be quick to make it work. "It requires perfect timing," he said to the knight. "To materialise my sword arm at the right moment, before retaking my spectral form. The last time I was not quick enough, and got caught."

"A most unpleasant experience, I should imagine," Sir Owen said. He tried to make light of it with a smile.

"Quite. And a dangerous one as well. If I should take form inside the creature, and then lose my grip on the Mistblade, I would be stuck. I do not imagine that would be a pleasant way to die, Owen. I intend to use the technique sparingly." And any dragon with an ounce of wit, he suspected, would soon learn to steer clear of him.

"That is wise, sire, though of course I would be there to carve you out, should such a thing ever occur." Sir Owen gave a faithful bow. "I am here to help, in any way I can."

Help, the king thought. The Oak of Armdall had offered to help him fight his foes many times since they'd come together, though so far Janilah had fought each of the dragons they had encountered by himself. He had come to favour Sir Owen's company and was grateful for his loyal service, though would not see him killed unnecessarily. "When we find a more challenging beast, I may call upon you, Owen. But for now, help me butcher this one."

The knight drew one of his godsteel blades. "As you command, my lord."

The sun was fully set by the time they were done, the dragon's carcass unrecognisable from what it had been. The head was detached, the body opened and excavated of its treasures, organs and precious parts set aside upon the bloody hilltop in a fine red arrangement. They descended the hill after and washed in a nearby brook, cleaning their armour of the gore. The Oak of Armdall seemed unusually quiet as the waters of the river turned red.

"Do you have something to say, Sir Owen? Speak freely. I would hear it."

"My king. I only wonder…what purpose does the butchery serve? You have not yet told me. Is it for the people? Those who might pass by and collect the treasure?"

Janilah smiled at him. "I butcher the beasts for Vandar, Sir Owen," he said. "They are sacrifices to his divine might, and by opening them, debasing them, and unveiling them for what they are, he will honour me." If someone happened to come by and make use of the treasure, that was only for the better, but Janilah Lukar's intent was not to make strangers rich. The couple at the inn had earned it, but he had no compulsion to help anyone else. No, his actions had a deeper meaning. "It was custom, long ago," he explained, to Sir Owen's questioning look. "When my ancestors were Wardens of the South, they would mutilate and dismember the dragons they slew, and mount their carcasses for Vandar's pleasure. In the city of Redhelm, there are many monuments to this practice. I wish to uphold it, as Vandar's herald and champion."

And I hope he will see, the king thought. *My true enemy. He will see…and he will come…*

Sir Owen mused on that. "Is that where we're headed, my king? Redhelm?"

"We will go where Vandar's will takes us, Sir Owen. We serve him now and him alone. It is the righteous way."

"As you say, my king." Sir Owen smiled faithfully. "Perhaps he will reward you, for your service. Maybe…"

Janilah raised a hand to silence him. He did not want to give voice to that hope, nor let it overcome him, as it had for so long. Yet still…he could not deny its allure. *I walked the wrong path too long,* he thought. *But I have found my way. It may yet lead me to where I long to go. A Table of my own…*

They made their camp that night among a huddle of rocks beside the stream, listening to the willows whisper as their leaves blew on the breeze, the gentle tinkling trickle of the water as it flowed down from the southern-most ranges of the Hammersongs, far to the north. Janilah Lukar had not crossed the Riverlands of Vandar for many a long year, though once before that had not been the case. He would pass through often on his way to Varinar, or when visiting the great cities of South Vandar, fostering better relations between the kingdoms of Vandar and Tukor, both of which held a special place to him. Though a king of the latter, Janilah Lukar had always considered himself Vandarian in his heart. *Tukor was always the lesser god,* he knew, *and the lesser kingdom.*

When dawn broke, the king awakened to find Sir Owen Armdall

completing his watch. He sat on a rock, looking toward the hillside where the ruin of the dragon's carcass lay, peering through the soft pink glow of daybreak. "There was a disturbance as you slept, my king," the knight told him. "The smell of the blood…it drew several beasts, I heard. One…" He had a tense look on his face. "It sounded large, and fearsome. I was going to wake you, but…"

"I am awake now, Sir Owen." Janilah rose, still garbed in his armour. "Come."

He led the Oak up the hillside, to where they had left the carcass. About it were many tracks, and great tracts of churned soil, and most of the edible parts of the dragon had been claimed. But it was the rest that was confusing. The bones had been shattered, the corpse pulverised, the skull crushed down to dust. Parts of it had been ripped apart savagely and thrown aside. The king could see the scaly tail lying thirty metres away, a talon torn off the bone and thrown yet further. One of its wings has been twisted and snapped backward, the webbing ripped apart.

Sir Owen was looking upon the massacre in horror. "What could have done this?" he breathed, gripping tight at the handle of his blade.

"Several different animals had their share," the king said, calm. "Wolves. A bear. Smaller scavengers and carrion creatures have been here, it looks. They ate the organs, and some of the flesh, but the rest…" He shook his head. "I could not say, Owen. Something more rageful, and powerful. A creature full of hate."

"Hate, yes, I should say so," Sir Owen nodded briskly. "For dragons, it looks. The *savagery*…" He turned his eyes around. "Those tracks…they look almost hoof-like, circular even. But larger. Much larger. I don't know of any cattle that get that big except the bovidor." He thought for a time. "Do you think it could be that, sire? A broadback? They are famously short-tempered, and powerful enough to tear a dragon limb from limb as well."

Janilah disagreed. "This dragon has been brutalised by something with *arms*, I would think, something more dextrous. The bovidor's horn would not be capable of doing this. This was no broadback, Sir Owen."

"Then what, sire?"

The king had no answer. Once before, scores of giant creatures had roamed freely across these lands, and many of them had been sighted over the last weeks and months, rumour said. Some were primitive, foul versions of the beasts that still lurked today, larger and uglier and more volatile than their kin. Fellwolves, grimbears, strongboars, darkcats, all had been seen of late. Oft as not these creatures were hybrids and aberrations, horrifying to look upon, but there were stranger and stronger more dangerous monsters crawling forth from times more ancient still.

What had dismembered and destroyed this dead dragon, however, the king could not say for sure. "When did you hear the commotion, Sir Owen?" he asked. "It would appear this larger creature drove off the others, judging by the tracks. Was it recent?"

"An hour, perhaps, before dawn," the knight said. He frowned, mulling on something. "The sound it made…it was most odd, my king. Very unlike the growl or snarl of a regular beast. More…unnatural. It sounded almost like a rockfall or a landslide. Boulders smashing and rumbling against one another. It sent a knife right through me, I'm not too proud to admit. For a moment I thought I must have fallen asleep and away into some nightmare, but…" He laughed a little awkwardly. "Well, I would not do that, of course, not when on watch. I'm surprised it didn't wake you, sire."

"I feel safe with you watching over me, Sir Owen."

"But the Mistblade. Would it not alert you to this danger? It was only a few hundred metres away."

"Only if it deemed it a danger," the king said. "The Mistblade is a shard of Vandar's Heart, don't forget. And many of the creatures that have reemerged from their slumber were shaped by the hands of Vandar himself. It is possible the Mistblade sensed some sort of kinship with this creature, some fondness." He thought some more, searching for tracks leading away from the hill. "It seems to have come and gone from that way," he said, pointing southward, where the spring grasses had been tramped and disturbed. "Let's see where the tracks lead."

"My lord? Are you…sure?"

Janilah smiled at the worry in his voice. "We are going in that direction anyway, Sir Owen." He clutched the ancient haft of the Mistblade. "Vandar wills it. Come."

The tracks led them down the gentle slope, past a grove of wild apple trees, through a pretty wetland of ponds and water holes that shimmered rose and gold beneath the rising sun. The tracks grew harder to follow as they went, the ground soft and wet from the recent rains. There must have been a hundred little streams cutting through this land, some barely as wide as a man's arm, others broad and shallow with beds of colourful pebbles smoothed and rounded over time. They waded through them all, the waters never reaching up higher than their knees, until they came upon a lake that looked much too deep to pass. Thick green reeds swayed and sagged about its banks, and on its far shore the king sighted a small village built of mud and thatch, half hidden by the surrounding grasses. The tracks ended at the water's edge. "It went in here," the king said.

"A water-dwelling creature, do you suppose?" Sir Owen asked.

Janilah didn't think so. "It may have just passed through. We should look for tracks on the other side."

"Yes, my king."

The knight was clearly unsure of the point of it but made no move to complain, despite his obvious reluctance. The sun climbed higher to send a shower of light upon the water, sparkling pleasantly beneath its buttery glow. Nesting birds came chirping from the trees to swoop and drink and hunt for fish, and ducks quacked happily as they paddled and groomed their feathers, attended by a flock of large white geese and a handful of graceful swans.

They continued along the banks, listening to the sing-song of the birds, the occasional croak of a frog. "It's very peaceful here," Sir Owen observed, after a short while. "You would not think there is much of a war going on, would you? Nor some dreaded monster lurking beneath the water."

"One man's monster is another man's mate. Dragons are such, Sir Owen. Friend to the Fireborn, foe to us. The same may be true here."

"You think this creature an ally, sire?"

"We do not yet know what we're dealing with, Owen. Until we do, withhold your judgements. We walk in Vandar's light, you and I. And I feel some purpose here."

That seemed to put the knight at ease, as their circuit of the lake continued. For the most part, the banks were accessible, though in sections the woods and bushes encroached upon the water's edge, forcing them to divert their course. Much of the shore was boggy as well, and thick muddy bogs were no friend to Bladeborn men garbed in heavy godsteel. They kept to harder ground, testing the earth as they went with sticks and pokes of their blades. Sir Owen made a joke that this vale was like the Riverlands, Lakelands, and Marshlands all rolled into one. "This is East Vandar in a microcosm, sire," he said. "Only without the blusterous men."

That made the king smile. The men of East Vandar were a loud and boisterous sort, that was true, many of them more barbarian than man. The Tukor that had been nurtured under the rule of House Lukar had, admittedly, taken on a certain fondness for drinking and brawling as well, though not to the same extent.

It took them the best part of an hour to reach the opposite side of the lake, where the waters trickled out into several wide shallow streams that wended away into the waterplains further south. Between those streams the earth was soggy and stony, covered in rocks and pebbles and larger boulders with moss growing about their sides. Finding tracks around the banks had proven a failure and the search seemed futile here as well.

"Ought we continue around the lake, sire?" Sir Owen asked. "Or go south? What does Vandar will?"

The king considered it, as he gazed down the shoreline. The mudhuts and thatch-roof shelters of the village were only a short walk away, and he had spotted movement there earlier, as they passed along the other side. "The villagers may have seen something, Sir Owen. Come, let us talk with them before we go south. At the least, they may have tidings to share."

The village was a meagre thing, two dozen huts built of mud and straw and dried river reeds lined up either side of a central path that led to a plank pontoon. Moored there were a pair of old rowboats, tied up on posts and bobbing on the water. At the end of the pier sat a ragged elderly man, staring out upon the lake with a fishing rod clutched in his hands. Elsewhere, two naked children were peering out from inside one of the huts, and outside another a heavy-bosomed matriarch sat perched upon a stool, weaving reeds to make a basket.

"Got nothing to give you," she said, not even raising her eyes to look at them. Her fingers kept on fiddling with those reeds, twisting and turning and folding them about. "The last men who came through here took everything we got. Turn around and go back the way you came. Else you'll both get a frog arrow through the eye. Be happy to give you *that*."

Janilah sighted a pair of men concealed among the reeds, with blow-pipes to hand, right ahead of them. "We mean no harm, my lady. We're here only for information."

"Well here's some for you. I ain't no lady, just a riverwoman and weaver, wife and mother and grandmother too." She folded her reeds, over and over, with fat nimble fingers. "It's what they all say. 'We just want directions'. 'We only want to know where this lord or that lord is marching'. 'We're here to ask how many dragons you've seen'. Starts like that, ends with them carrying off our food and furs and whatever else they wish to take. Even our women sometimes as well. Aye, one of my own daughters was taken by some man who came asking for *information*. Don't know where she is now. Dead, most likely. But not before she had her maidenhood stolen too." She snarled and spat to the side, and still did not look up. "So off with you, go. You've seen Rattle and Snore in the reeds, I'll bet, but not the others. We got a hundred arrows and darts on you. Go, else we'll make the both of you into hedgehogs and roast you up for dinner."

Janilah found that most unlikely, judging by the number of huts. "We've been following the tracks of a large creature, through the wetlands to the north of here. I believe it passed through your lake. Did you see, by any chance?"

"No. Saw nothing. Hedgehogs, remember? I thought I told you to go?"

"Mind your tongue, woman," Sir Owen came in. "If you knew who you were talking to…"

Finally, she looked up. It was a glance only, then she promptly returned to her weaving. "An old man and a younger one. Both bearded and ugly, with armour under those cloaks. So what? You think that frightens me? Go ahead, draw those swords of yours and kill us all. Whole world's ending anyway, what does it matter?" She folded another reed.

"We have no intention of hurting you," Janilah said. "If you didn't see the creature…"

"I didn't. I told you that already. If anyone saw anything out there on the lake, it'll be Codger." She flicked a hand. "That's him there on the pier. He likes to sit there, does Codger." She looked up again, with eyes that hated the world. "Just don't expect to get much out of him. He came wandering through here a decade ago, from where he didn't say. Didn't say his name either, or didn't remember it more like, then one of the boys called him an old codger, and the name stuck. He's a strange sweet man, and harmless. Ask your questions and be gone." As they stepped away, she added. "And remember them arrows and darts. We've been making hedge-hogs here for weeks, since that beast stole away my Stefany. Take a swim and you might meet them. There's a hundred just like you, rotting in that late."

Sir Owen's face had soured as they stepped toward the jetty. "Mon-strous old wench," he growled. "Sounds like she's working with this crea-ture, sire. Feeding it, with the men she kills."

"She's lying, Owen. The riverfolk are full of bluster, highborn and lowborn alike. They take after their lord."

"*Dead* lord," the Oak said, with a wicked smile.

"I would caution you to show the man his due respect, Sir Owen. Lord Wallis Kanabar was an uncivilised boor, but he was a fine warrior in his day as well. Do not let my personal animosity toward him shape your feelings. He was a servant to Vandar for many long decades, above all. We should honour him, not mock him, for that."

He marched to the edge of the wooden pier where the planking met the bank, though did not step any further, else the pontoon shatter beneath his weight. "Friend," the king said. "I'm told you like to sit and look out at the river. Did you see a creature enter, on the far side? At dawn, or a little after?"

The old codger sat with his back to them, dressed in cotton rags that might once have been white. Now they were a dozen colours, all of them filthy, torn in places, patched in others with strips and scraps in brown and green. The fingers that clutched at his fishing rod were scabbed and callused, his forearms spindly as grass. Sparse grey hair covered the back of his head, though the top was mostly liver spot and dead skin, shedding off his scalp. "Aye," he croaked, in a broken, brittle voice.

Sir Owen frowned. He hadn't expected that. "You saw it? This monster?"

"Aye," the man repeated, sounding somewhat like a frog.

"And?" Sir Owen pressed. "Come, man, describe it. Did it walk on all fours. Upright? Does it live here in your lake? Did it come out the other side?"

The old man's neck creaked up and down. "Aye."

"Aye? Aye to what? I asked you conflicting questions you old fool."

"Come now, Owen, be patient with our new friend." Janilah took up the questioning. "It left the lake, you say? Did it go off toward the south, through those wide steams over there?"

The man nodded. "Aye."

"Aye. Aye again." The Oak of Armdall's lips twisted. "You say that one more time, and I'll…"

"Aye."

Janilah reached out a calming hand, placing it on Sir Owen's shoulder. The knight had a fierce temper on him, especially when he felt he was being tricked or ridiculed in some way. "Take a breath, Owen. The woman did say we would struggle to get much from him."

"I know, sire, but still…" He drew a long deep breath to freshen his lungs and purify his head, casting out his anger. Then he asked in a milder voice. "Codger, if you would be kind enough to *describe* the creature you saw, it would be greatly appreciated." He waited. When the old man gave no response - not even an aye - Sir Owen closed a fist. "Well then. It is clear we're dealing with an empty vessel here. The man has lost his wits, sire. There's no point in…"

"Rock," said Codger. He moved his eyes away to the series of shallow streams that ran out of the lake to the south. Then he nodded. "*There.* Rock."

The Oak of Armdall frowned and gave a snort. "A rock?" he said. "There are lots of rocks over the." He turned to Janilah. "Is he toying with us, do you think, or just mad?" The Oak turned back, as if to find the frumpy riverwoman and her brood standing behind them, laughing, but the village was much as they'd found it when they arrived, the woman at her weaving, the children running naked from hut to hut, men lurking among the reeds, waiting until they were gone.

And it's time, the king thought. He wasn't likely to get much more from these people; clearly they were not of the sharing sort. *No, I have what I need.* Rock might not mean much to Sir Owen Armdall, but it was another piece of the puzzle to the king. He had a good sense of what they were dealing with now.

"Come, Sir Owen. Let us continue on our way."

"*Gladly*, sire." The Oak could not turn and leave the muddy little village quickly enough, calling for the wench to mind her manners the next time someone came by. "Maybe that's why your daughter was carried off," he told her. "You stoked the ire of the wrong man, woman. Be thankful we're in a good mood, else another one of your bitches might go missing."

She lurched to her feet at that, calling Rattle and Snore to her sides. The two men rushed from the reeds in their river rags with blowpipes primed at their lips. Sir Owen only laughed. "Gods, woman, if only you knew. You might as well send out a couple of shrews to nip at our toes. You are vermin to us, you silly old crone."

A few darts bit into their cloaks as they left, pinging against their armour. The rest flew right past. The woman's raving voice followed them for longer, though, screaming obscenities from the lakeside as they continued away from the water. Sir Owen's chuckles were as arrogant as ever.

An ugly thing, Janilah thought. "Do you have children of your own, Sir Owen?" the king asked him.

The man didn't seem to understand the question. "You know I don't, sire. That woman…she's as mad as the old man…"

"She isn't mad, she's grieving. The woman is churlish, yes, but has seen her daughter taken from her. You cannot know of her pain. A knight should be more courteous, Owen."

The Oak stared at him, close to gaping. "My king, but…"

"Yes, I know. Who am *I* to say that to you, after all I've done."

"No, sire, I didn't mean…"

"You did. And you're right. But I walk a new path now, and so do you. We must both put our pasts behind us, Owen. Petty insults to a grieving woman do nothing but service your own ego. It is beneath you."

Sometimes Janilah Lukar could hear the hypocrisy in his words, yet all the same, they needed to be said. He had been driven by his own ego and vanity for too long, but those days were done, done and dead, and thus it must be for Sir Owen Armdall too.

They continued southward where the Riverlands and Lakelands merged in a spread of great wet watery plains. From what they had heard, the fighting across the southern swathes of East Vandar remained intense, the Marshlands in particular succumbing to the hordes from the south. On occasion, they had their tidings from travellers upon the road, though mostly it was at inns and roadside taverns that they overheard such talk.

That talk had been grim of late. It was said that Mudport had been utterly destroyed, that Castle Crag, the seat of Elton Rammas, Lord of the Marshes, was burned to cinders, that Winslow Point and Fort Bleakmire and the stilt-city of Timbertown had all been lost. The count of the dead must have been catastrophic, with survivors now making for the north and west in the hopes of finding sanctuary, or else braving the waters of the Three Bays in a bid to reach Rasalan. But there were dangers there as well. The terrors that had begun to crawl out upon the lands had come up from the depths too, it was said. "Skies, seas, soil, stone, it makes no matter," an old inebriate had opined at a traveller tavern south of Tukor's Pass some days ago. "Ain't nowhere safe no more. We're all of us gonna die, one way or another."

Janilah Lukar would not have it that way. Thousands would die, tens of thousands, hundreds even, but when the dust settled upon the dead, there would be enough still living to pick up their hoes and their chisels and their hammers to till the soils and rebuild the cities and remake the world they had lost. *It is Vandar's will,* he knew. *And I am his herald, to deliver that message in blood.*

They went slowly that day, ambling through a country wet and wild and windy. The morning brought rain, gushing in a heavy spring downpour, sweet as the sunshine that followed. By afternoon, however, the weather had turned again, a great grey curtain of cloud drawn across the skies to cover all the land in shadow. Then the drizzle started, a constant unchanging drizzle that did not abate until dusk, where it lightened only enough to give them hope before returning with greater gusto, incessant and unyielding.

Sodden and footsore, the going was slow, though the king did not go about his work in a rush. The path took him where it may, the Mistblade steering his course. His hurts and pains were of little consequence to him; nay, they felt like penance for his former life, and thus he welcomed them. Only occasionally did he take to the horse's saddle to rest. Mostly he went by foot, slow and steady, watching the skies, waiting.

The land became less waterlogged as the day passed, more hilly and rugged. Down in the vales between the heights were lakes and tarns, still-watered and silver, and above them stood watchtowers from days long past, ruined and broken and abandoned.

To the east rose loftier summits, a range of mountains that ran north to south along the western border of the Four Sisters, the great lakes of this land. *The Hooded Hills.* They weren't much to look at compared to the Hammersongs or Weeping Heights or the other grand ranges to the south, but were pretty in their way, and easily walkable, with fine views over the Lakelands and the city of Lakeheart, far below.

Janilah had hiked through those hills once before, as a boy, taken there by his lady mother Lizzie Westermont and her sister Lady Luane. His younger brother Jaylor had been there as well, and Myra, his sweet little sister, her most of all. *It was her last wish,* he remembered, *to see the lakes from up in those hills.* His sister Myra had perished of a slow sickness when she was just twelve, though she had time enough at least to visit the mountains first. Janilah remembered how happy it had made her, even as her body wasted away. *The men had to carry her most of the time, They made a chair for her, a little princess throne, with poles and handles, and carried her along the tops.*

Janilah gazed out at those mountains as the dark of night closed in. He'd lost Myra first, then Jaylor only five years later, murdered on his first mission to Agarath. His father King Jeerah Lukar had followed soon after, tumbling down a set of icy stone steps to his doom, as Janilah stood behind him, a young man of twenty-two. *He deserved it,* he had always told himself. *He was weak, and sought no vengeance for Jaylor's death. Tukor needed a stronger king. I did what I had to do.*

It had cursed him, though, he saw that now. Kingkillers were cursed, and kinkillers even more so, and he'd become both that day his path had darkened. Then his mother had followed not long later, ruined in her grief. Losing her only daughter and youngest son had sent her into an inescapable melancholy. Losing her husband had been the last straw, leading to a bout of ill health from which she could not break free, nor wish to.

I killed her too, Janilah reflected. *And my wife, Arelia, who never truly loved me.* She had tried for years to find affection in her king, but Janilah had never loved her either. *She gave me Rylian, that is all. Rylian, my boy…whose blood still stains my hands…*

The rain washed down through his wild grey hair and past his face, a cold dark drizzle that might as well have been tears. *The tears of all the people I have killed. My family, my kin, my countrymen, and how many more?*

He would take all night to name them, to list out the lives he had robbed, the families he'd destroyed. He had thought he was doing Vandar's will then. He had thought he was fulfilling King Galin's promise. *I have held the torch. I have lit the way.* But that torch had been put out now, blown dead and dark by all his treacheries.

It only ever led me into ruin and defeat, he knew. *But I have a new one now, a new light, a new path. One pure and bright and true. Vandar has seen fit to give me a second chance. And this time, I will not fail him.*

They camped that night among the ruins of an ancient fort, what remained of its walls and towers little more than the tips of stone fingers poking out of the earth. *Time defeats us all,* Janilah thought, as he looked over the broken, buried stone.

"Do you know who this castle once belonged to?" Sir Owen asked him.

An old lord, long dead. "I could not say," the king answered. "The rule of

510

·these lands changed hands many times in the past. They have seen much dispute over the centuries, Owen. This castle fell long ago."

Sir Owen tied his horse's bridle rope around a sapling. Trees had spouted up in the main yard, and the brambles were thick and plentiful, clinging to whatever stone they could. "There's some shelter there, by the walls of that old roundtower. Ought I try to get a fire going, sire?"

"You may struggle to find dry wood in this weather, Owen. But go ahead, if you wish."

The knight went off for a short while, returning with a shrug and shake of the head. "You're right, my lord. It's all sodden, and poor for kindling besides. Are these lands always this wet?"

"We're between the Riverlands and the Lakelands, with the Marshlands further to the south. I will let you make up your own mind."

The night was dark and sinister sleeping amongst the bones of that fort, though the tumbled old remains of the roundtower gave them some respite from the rain. Despite his appeals to take the first watch, the king told the Oak to rest. "Sleep, Sir Owen. I will wake you in a few hours."

Once the knight had drifted away, the king rose to his feet and stepped back out into the rains. He stopped at the spine of stone where the curtain wall had once stood, found a suitable rock to sit on, and turned his eyes back the way they had come, across the darkened hills, waiting.

Time passed, an hour, perhaps more. The rain did not cease, the light did not improve. Janilah remained alert, watching, waiting. *Come*, he thought. *I know you're out there. Come.*

It was then that he saw it, a big black shadow lumbering slowly his way. The king stayed perfectly still, squinting through the rain, huddled beneath his cloak and cowl. Nearby, the horse was chewing at a tuft of grass. Janilah saw its ears prick up, then it raised its head to look.

"It's all right, boy," the king whispered. "Stay calm, and make no sound. We are friends, he and I."

The king watched the creature approach through the darkness. *Rock*, the old man at the village had said, and he had not been wrong. This was a creation of rock and rage, heavy-legged and stocky-armed, with a boulder for a belly and a pillar of granite for a chest. He recalled what Sir Owen had spoken of its roar. *Like boulders smashing together. Like a rockfall or a landslide. Natural and yet unnatural at once.* It was an elemental being of an ancient age. A being forged only to protect, and serve.

A grulok, Janilah Lukar thought.

He stood, unclasping his cloak to let it fall to the floor in a heavy sodden heap. Light shone out from his armour, green and gold; the body of a god. *My god, and his.* He took a step forward, as the grulok drew near. Through the earth he could feel its great weight pounding, *boom boom*, step by step.

The horse was beginning to pull at its rope and whinny. Janilah raised a hand to the side. "Calm. There is nothing for you to fear."

The shadow loomed before him, closing, ice-blue eyes in a grey rock face. There was a suggestion of features; a blunt curve of nose, a craggy narrow mouth, a general shape of a bumpy jaw, but little else. The grulok was one of Vandar's earliest experiments in creating life, a primitive and simple form long since lost to myth. Yet here one stood, fifteen feet tall, a stone head upon a stumpy neck above a body six feet thick. The legs were shorter than the arms, which hung by its side, widening as they reached a set of three-fingered stone hands, for gripping and crushing. Its feet were broad and annular, with small protrusions of rock acting as toes. It looked otherworldly, like nothing he had ever seen, a mountain of living rock and stone. *And beautiful,* Janilah Lukar thought.

He drew the Mistblade. "You've been following me."

The grulok stood beneath the weeping skies, rain pattering upon its massive granite shoulders. Those icy blue eyes were small within its skull, shining like lights on a distant hilltop, emotionless. *But they see,* Janilah thought. *They see this. They know.* He moved the Mistblade from side to side and saw those eyes move with it. "You know what this is."

The monster's head dipped.

It understands me. "I am his champion, his herald. It is my duty to win his war." King Janilah Lukar peered into those small primordial eyes. "Has he sent you to serve?"

The grulok stared, unreacting. Then it turned its enormous head to the right, rock grinding on rock as its neck twisted upon its shoulders, and Janilah turned as well. There was a rumbling nearby, a rending of soil. Shadows rose from the earth, the ruins coming alive. A slow smile climbed onto the Warrior King's lips.

More, he thought.

44

Robbert

"Your uncle is indisposed," Sir Wenfry Gershan said, standing outside Cedrik Kastor's tall spiky pavilion at the heart of the Kastor warcamp. "He has…company, Prince Robbert. He's not to be disturbed."

I can hear. The muffled screams were clear enough, and sounded more like pain than pleasure. "Tell him to send her away. I need to speak with him urgently."

"About what?"

Robbert Lukar looked at the spindly knight through eyes that could cut diamonds. "You forget yourself, Gershan. Don't presume to ask that of me. It is for my uncle's ears only. Now move."

"But Lord Cedrik, he told me…"

"Move, I said." Robbert grabbed the man by the shoulder and yanked him out of the way with enough force to send the Emerald Guard stumbling forward into the dirt. A few men laughed from nearby, drinking and roasting meat around a fire. Others were trundling past, drunk, Greenbelts close in his uncle's favour.

A wild lot, and depraved, Robbert thought. 'A sickness', the late Sir Alistair the Abiding had called it. 'A sickness that starts with you'. He'd been referring to Robbert's uncle, and he wasn't far wrong. *A dangerous sickness*, the prince knew, as he stepped inside the tent.

The pavilion was dimly lit, though warmly furnished, with rugs and drapes and carved wooden furniture. His uncle's desk was heaped with books, beside which a fat tallow candle burned, and there was a larger table too for councils and meetings, and a separate section at the rear, closed off by a heavy felt curtain, where Lord Cedrik had his bedchamber. The noises were coming from in there.

"Uncle, I have to speak with you," the prince called. The sounds did not stop at once. Robbert could see shadows shifting beyond the drapes, hear muted yelps of pain and the crack of a lash on flesh, and cruel laughter to go with it. His jaw clenched tight. "Uncle," Robbert called, louder. "Uncle, leave that girl alone and come speak with me."

The lash sang its leather song a final time, and one last whimper of pain sprung from the poor girl's lips. Then the noises stopped, Robbert heard his uncle mutter a few words, and a moment later the girl came bursting naked from around the curtain, her eyes red with tears, cheeks flush, bruises and whip marks all over her body. She snatched a robe hanging from a support post and made to dash for the exit.

Robbert grabbed her arm. "What is your name?" he asked her.

She looked at him, terrified.

"Your name? I'm *not* going to hurt you, girl."

"She can't understand you, Robbert. The girl doesn't speak our tongue." Cedrik Kastor came striding into view, dressed in a silken black gown. His brow twinkled with sweat, eyes with malice, dark hair swept back and gleaming. "Release her. I have no further need of the wench."

Robbert clung tight to the girl's shivering arm, even as she struggled to escape him. *She thinks I'm as bad as he is.* The thought infuriated him. Beyond the heavy drapes that partitioned off the bedchamber, the prince could see flogs and belts, fetters and canes and other instruments of his uncle's vile tortures. He snarled at the sight of them. "What were you doing to her in there?"

Cedrik Kastor made a confused face. "Does her sweet little body not tell the tale, Robbert? I was punishing her, isn't that clear?"

"Punishing her? For what?"

"Oh, all sorts of things." He gave no other answer than that. "Go ahead, let her run along. I think it's only fair that the men have their turn."

The prince could have stabbed him right there and then. "She isn't some property to be passed around," he growled.

Cedrik Kastor only laughed. "Actually, that's *exactly* what she is. Whores are property for rent, Robbert. Perhaps you never knew that. Have you ever had a whore before?"

"No. I don't need to pay."

"Need? And you think *I* need to? Come, boy, don't play the fool. When coin is involved it becomes a transaction. It makes the whole affair so much more simple." He smiled and poured himself a cup of purple wine, so dark it looked almost black. "Feel free to take her yourself, if you wish. I'm sure you'd treat her more sweetly than I did, such a sweet boy as you."

Anger simmered in Robbert Lukar. "When Krator finds out…"

"Krator? Oh, let him. That sunlord has much and more to answer for."

Robbert's intrigue was piqued by that. Enough to steal away some of his anger. The girl slipped his grip as he loosened, vanishing into the night before he could stop her.

Lord Cedrik gave a laugh. "Go on, after her, *quick*. Your fair maid is getting away, Robbert."

The prince closed a fist, opened it again. *Calm. Don't rise to his goading.* "Krator," he merely said, voice tight. "I heard he parleyed earlier this afternoon with the Grand Duchess." *Much and more to answer for, he'd said.* "You already knew?"

"Yes, I knew." His uncle took a seat on a comfortable chair, folding one leg over the other, neat and elegant.

Robbert was perplexed. He didn't seem overly put out by it. "He went behind our back, Uncle. He met with her in secret."

"It was hardly a secret. These plains are very open and I saw him ride toward the walls of Aram myself."

"And that doesn't bother you? We should have been there. What if…"

"What if…*what*? He's plotting some trap behind our back?"

"Yes. Why else would he want to meet with her without our knowing? I can't believe you trust him."

"Trust him? Oh no, Nephew, don't go thinking I trust that feathery sunlord."

"Then why aren't you…"

"Angry? Perhaps I am. I just don't wear my emotions on my sleeve so much as you do. You need to learn self-control." He swirled his cup. "Now come, have a drink of wine. You think the sunlord may be laying some trap for us. Enlighten me. What is it you fear?"

The prince took perch on a hard camp stool, ignoring the invitation to drink. "We're surrounded," he said, with a strong note of caution in his voice. "Krator can tell us the Grand Duchess is his enemy all he wants, but what if that's not true? What if they're planning to work together to destroy us? All of this…what if it's been one big ruse?"

His uncle considered that with an amused little smile on his face. "Sunlord Krator has killed thousands of his own countrymen, and many hundreds of his own soldiers, often barbarically, as we have seen. Do you really think these are things that the Grand Duchess can forgive, Robbert? Or this famous moonlord we've been hearing about? Iziah Hasham was a Moon*rider* once, you know. They are the bravest of all Lightborn, most uncompromising in matters of probity and justice. Unless you believe these atrocities are all part of this…what did you call it? *Ruse?*" He snickered.

Robbert could not believe the irony of his uncle's words. *You've performed atrocities too, Cedrik,* he thought. *And Tukor is not going to forget it.*

He merely said, "Make mock of me all you like, Uncle. Something is amiss here."

"Yes, you're quite correct. *Much* is amiss, Robbert. Not least the fact that we are in league with this sunlord at all. You and your whispering little allies seem to think I enjoy fighting alongside him, as though this was somehow my preference. Quite the opposite. What I have done here is swallow my pride to prevent our entire army from being obliterated. I have *saved* us, Robbert, and won us passage north into Agarath. Do you not think I deserve a little credit for that?"

A part of Robbert agreed. A part could not deny it. But only a part. The rest refused to believe a word that slithered through his uncle's cruel lips. "It's the way you've gone about it. It's the hypocrisy. The dishonour…"

"Dishonour?" Lord Cedrik said sharply. "Is that what you call it?"

"What would you call it? Allying with the enemy? Joining this shameful rebellion?"

"I call it leadership, Robbert. I call it *longsightedness*. You are entitled to think whatever you like about Krator's claim and coup. But to me it is irrelevant. The man is a means to an end, a stepping stone and nothing more. We are *using* him, as he is using us. I struggle to see how you do not appreciate that, boy. It disappoints me, I will admit, that you are unable to see the grander vision."

"I see it, Uncle. I know what you're doing, and I understand that choice."

"Then what is your complaint?"

"The men," the prince said at once. He drew a breath and considered his words. This was dangerous ground to tread, ice thin and treacherous. "The men you have *killed* because they disagreed with you. I don't like how you murdered Sir Alistair, Uncle. He threw down his gauntlet and challenged you to a duel. What you did was murder. It lacked honour."

Lord Cedrik's eyes turned dark as a raven's wing. "The challenge itself lacked honour, Robbert. I would not wager my life on another man's resentments. The things Sir Alistair said to me…the accusations, the slurs…do you truly believe I would grant him a death duel after that? It was not *murder*, Robbert. I put the man to death for treason, as I did the rest who opposed me. Dissent is a disease. Neglect it at your peril. One day, if ever you should rule, you will come to understand that."

I will rule, Robbert Lukar thought. *I'll rule all of Tukor, and when I do, you'll pay for your crimes.*

Sir Alistair's death had only been the beginning. That same night, several dozen of the Abiding's bravest and most loyal men had marched upon Lord Cedrik's pavilion to question him on the death of their lord. Their questions had been answered with steel and hempen rope, half of them falling to the blades of Lord Cedrik's guardsmen, the rest gathered up to be hanged at the border of their camp.

After that, the rest of Sir Alistair's five hundred men had made for the docks at Kolash to requisition ships and sail home to Tukor, joined by Happy Harys and Sir Tunsen and Sir Clive Fanning, all fleeing in fear. Robbert had awoken on a damp misty morning to the news that there had been a savage battle down at the port, with most of the renegades slaughtered before they could escape.

But not all, the prince knew. Sir Clive had not been among the dead, and at least seventy other men were also unaccounted for. Most likely they would perish at sea, but Robbert harboured hope that Sir Clive would lead them home and make it back to Ilithor. *Tell my brother Ray what has happened here*, he thought. *Prepare him for what my uncle has become, should I not return.*

He was dwelling on all of that when his uncle stood suddenly from his chair, placing his cup of wine aside. "Wait outside, Robbert," he said, "I need to change."

Robbert frowned, tensing. "We're going somewhere?"

"Krator sent a man before you arrived. He's called a council between the camps. You want to ask him about this parley, Robbert? Well, here's your chance." He flicked a hand toward the tent flaps, then marched away behind the curtain to his bedchamber.

Robbert left the pavilion, passing a disgruntled Sir Wenfry Gershan as he stepped out into the night. He spotted Sir Lothar loitering nearby, listening in on the latest gossips as he liked to do. "Learn anything?" Robbert asked him.

"Yes. I have discovered that everyone around here is drunk, Robb. And that you have made an enemy of Sir Wenfry Gershan. He's been sulking ever since you threw him into the dirt."

"Let him. Gershan is a bug."

"Bugs can still bite. Some of them are even venomous."

"Most aren't, and are easily squashed."

Sir Lothar smiled. "Well, back to your pavilion, is it?"

Robbert shook his head. "Krator's called a council. My uncle's just getting changed."

Sir Lothar studied him. "You're tense. What happened?"

"Nothing. We just…I challenged him on everything. I let…well, not all of it, but some of it out. I called him a murderer for what he did to Sir Alistair."

Sir Lothar made a whistling sound. "Brave man. How did he react?"

"Better than I thought he would, actually. He didn't put a knife in my neck at least." He laughed uneasily.

"He may yet," the tall knight warned.

The air was filled with raucous noise, men laughing, boasting, brawling as only Tukorans did. Once before Robbert would have loved life in this camp, but no longer. Its savour had soured to him now, like a sweet wine left to go bad.

Would it be any different if I was in charge? he wondered. *Would I be able to instil more discipline in these men?* His father would, he knew that much. *He'd raise all the good strong men into posts of authority, let them whip the rest into shape.* He'd have us all marching to the same tune, and there would be no Sir Alistairs, calling out his faults. *Because he had none*, Robbert thought, with a sudden deep pang of sadness. *If Father were still alive, this wouldn't be happening. Gods, I miss him…*

"Look lively, Robb," Sir Lothar said, drawing his attention. "Here he comes."

Lord Cedrik was emerging from his pavilion and marching toward them, waving for Gershan to follow, wreathed now in doublet, breeches, high leather boots, and his fine black cape printed with the bear paw of his house. "At my nephew's side as ever, Sir Lothar," he said as he joined them. "You're like the King's Wall, only a foot shorter and a third as wide. Then again, you are *only* watching over a prince."

"Not the way I see it," Sir Lothar Tunney said. It was hard to intimidate a man seven foot tall, dressed all in gleaming godsteel. "And your nephew has Sir Bernie Westermont as well, my lord. Put me and him together, and I think we make a strong enough wall."

"Formidable, yes." Cedrik's smile was sly. "And where is Sir Bernard the Buffoon? I don't see him at your side so often these days, Robbert."

Is it any wonder, when you call him names like that? "Bernie has other things to be doing, Uncle," was all he said.

"Oh? And what could be more important than protecting the Crown Prince of Tukor?"

"Bernie has taken it upon himself to train the boys," Robbert told him. "He hopes he'll give them a better chance of surviving the battles to come."

Lord Cedrik's chuckle said everything. "Well, why not? There isn't much else to be doing until we charge the gate, is there? Just tell big Sir Bernard not to get too attached, Robbert. Most of those boys will likely be dead by the end of the week."

Try telling Bernie that, the prince thought, as he turned to follow his uncle through the camp. There were several in particular he'd taken under his wing, a troop of lowborn boys and young men swept up in his king grandfather's muster. Bernie was teaching them to fight with sword and spear and giving them the instruction they'd never had back home. Marytn, Percy, and Willem had all killed their first men during the sack of Kolash, joining the ranks of the blooded, though the others were yet to take a life. Yosh, Frog, Derrick, Del, Pimply Paul, Seb the Scorpion. All would kill or be killed soon enough, and Big Bernie was adamant it be the former.

"These lads have come here with almost no training," the big knight had complained angrily one night. "Same as hundreds of others, thousands even. They never had masters-at-arms like us, Robb, or training sergeants, not even a father or brother to show them how. They're all farmhands and fishermen's sons. So I'll have to do it instead."

Some were showing promise - Paul was proving himself a capable spearman, and Del had some experience with the bow - but all the same, Robbert's uncle wasn't wrong. *Half of them will probably die when we take the city, and the rest won't last a second against the dragons.* That was just the way it was, though. Robbert had never truly appreciated how fortunate he was to be Bladeborn until he'd ridden to war. Only then did he see how vulnerable the common man was, when the horror of battle consumed him.

They wended north through tents and pavilions, assaulted on all sides by noise. The camp was hectic, unruly, and poorly arranged, straddling a spread of rugged red terrain a few hundred metres to the south of Lord Krator's more orderly army. Between the camps lay a broad stretch of no man's land, inhabited by a single pavilion, for their combined councils. It sat lonely in the gloom, lit by torches blazing on poles outside. Robbert could see that Krator's guardsmen had already arrived. *When is that not the case?* The sunlord was fastidious in his timekeeping, methodical to a fault.

They continued out past the northern border of their camp, plunging into darkness. Beyond the shroud of torches and fire pits and cookfires, the skies opened out above them, filled with stars in silver and pale perfect blue.

A pink moon was riding upon a cloud, its light shining down upon the city of Aram, with its great towering walls surging skyward in the west. Kolash it was not. *This is an altogether more formidable city,* Robbert thought.

When they reached the pavilion, Robbert turned to his uncle. "Are the others not coming? Huffort and Swallow and…"

"No," Lord Cedrik told him. "All they ever do is waste time. I will relay to them what we discuss and decide. This should be nothing but a formality now, Robbert."

Lord Elio Krator was awaiting them within in the company of his perfumed whale of a Sunrider Mar Malaan. There were maps on the table, a few candles burning low and lazy. At their arrival, the sunlord looked up. "You're late," he said.

Lord Cedrik gave no swift response. He took his time removing his cape, hanging it on a post, then gave the room a good long scan. Robbert followed his eyes and saw that another man was present as well, a tall slim man standing patiently to one side. He wore robes in the colours of Aramatia; bronze, silver and gold, with an additional length of golden silk thrown over his right shoulder. Cedrik's eyes passed over him without mention. "Late?" he said, at last. "I am not so late as I was to the parley you had earlier, Krator. I was so late to that it seems I missed it."

Robbert almost smiled at that. He watched the sunlord closely, though there was rarely much to see. His face was as remote as an island in the ocean, as hard to read as a book written in invisible ink. Over a taut rigid body he wore his feathered cloak, a style of dress that Robbert Lukar could never take seriously, no matter how hard he tried.

"I'd like you to meet an associate of mine," Elio Krator said, in that cold measured voice of his. He gestured to the man standing to the side. "This is…"

"Later," interrupted Lord Cedrik. "I'll hear of this parley first."

Krator paused. "There is nothing to say."

"Nothing? Now I'm sure that isn't the case. I've heard that Safina Nemati is a very interesting woman. You're to tell me she had nothing interesting to say to you? Nothing at all, my lord?"

"What is of interest to one man is not of interest to another, Lord Kastor. Safina's voice was once sweet to me. Now it is a ghastly croak, full of malice, mistruth and deceit. I went only to look into her eyes and tell her to her face that her time is done. And that I will take back what she has taken from me. That I will right those wrongs with blood."

Cedrik looked at him with a quizzical frown. "You have a history, that's clear enough. I hope that does not impair your judgement, Krator."

"It won't."

"Are you certain of that?"

"Yes. I am certain."

"I do hope so. My nephew seems to think you have some trickery up your feathery sleeve. He is most vexed by your behaviour, I daresay. Sneaking off for this secret little parley…"

Ah, so this is why you wanted me here, Robbert thought. He'd wondered why he had been brought along when the likes of Huffort and Swallow and Gullimer were absent. *He'll project his doubts onto me instead and see how the sunlord responds.*

For all that, he wasn't wrong. "It seemed a little clandestine," Robbert agreed.

Krator looked at him. "I understand, Prince Robbert. We are allies, and I went behind your backs to meet with our enemy. I hope you will forgive me. My intention was merely to talk with Safina in private, as I say. I wanted to tell her directly that I will bend to no compromise."

"And did she offer one?" Lord Cedrik demanded.

Lord Elio nodded. "She would have me raised as her heir, to become Grand Duke of Aramatia at her passing. Which is near, I sense. The woman has grown weak and frail, burdened by a great many ailments and physical troubles. She wishes to avoid unnecessary bloodshed, she claims. A man of lesser conviction might have agreed to this bargain, but not me."

Cedrik Kastor's voice was blunt when he asked, "And why not? Is this not what you want, Krator?"

"No. It is an offer only to dissuade me from taking the action Safina knows I must take. It is a trick, that is all. And I suspect that Lord Hasham would never allow it. Safina Nemati may be the sitting ruler of Aramatia, but the city of Aram is under the protective charge of the moonlord, to defend from all enemies, foreign and civil. He will never trust me, even if Safina might. Hasham understands the full breadth of my ambition, I fear. To be Grand Duke is but an appetiser in the feast of triumph that lies before me. One day soon I will overthrow Empress Valura, and become emperor in her place, to rule every nation under the banner of the Lumaran Empire. Though of course, when this happens, I shall rename it. Long has each iteration of this empire, each new restoration of it through the millennia, been named for Lumara. As a proud Aramatian, I will see this changed. The Aramatian Empire, it shall be, with Aram, not Lumos, as its capital."

Lord Cedrik looked perilously bored by all that. "We wish you well in your endeavours," he merely said, with a strong note of mockery, as though none of that would come to pass.

If Lord Elio Krator took note of it, he made no sign.

"I wanted to ask about this refugee camp, Krator," Cedrik Kastor went on. "There is a rumour that the red flux is rampant within it. Will that pose us a problem?"

"No," the sunlord dismissed. "I have men watching our borders, firing arrows upon anyone who might get too close. Some have tried. Their bodies will deter others from doing the same."

Robbert felt a shiver move up his spine. "These are your own countrymen."

"No. A man feared to harbour the red death is a potential plague, not a man. If one should get into our camp, hundreds will die, perhaps thousands."

"Robbert is young, and his heart has not yet hardened to the realities of warfare. Do forgive him this softness. It comes from a good place, I'm sure." His uncle smiled. "These refugees. I heard they came in worship of Agarosh, the One-Eye. Is that true, Krator? Are we going to have to deal with a moonbear?"

"My scouts report no," Krator said. "Agarosh has not been seen for some days."

"He could return."

"He is a moonbear. He goes where he wills it. A being of such light can never be entirely controlled."

"All beasts can be controlled."

Krator smiled, thin-lipped. "You northmen have a different notion to us as to what constitutes a beast. This is not a discussion to have here, now, or ever. Else tempers will flare." He ignored the snide look on Cedrik's face as he turned his eyes to the side. "Now, let me introduce you to my guest. Denlatis, come forward."

The man approached, lithe of limb and smooth of gait, slinking forward like a cat. He had a gold tooth on one side of his grin and a silver one opposite, both glinting as they caught the firelight. "My lords." He swept into a bow so low his chin all but grazed the ground. "My name is Cliffario Denlatis. A humble merchant of these lands. It is a great honour to meet you both."

"And you, Denlatis," Robbert said.

His uncle didn't extend the same courtesy. "A humble merchant? Why is he here, Krator?"

"To help, of course," Denlatis said.

"To profit," Lord Cedrik returned, disdainful. "That's all a merchant ever wants."

"Guilty as charged." The man chuckled and showed his palms. "But in all the best trades, both parties profit, my lord. So it shall be in this one, I hope."

"Denlatis has hounded me for months over the hand of my cousin," Lord Krator informed them, looking none too pleased about that. "She is my heir, and a beautiful woman besides, not short on suitors. Denlatis has forced himself forward as one of them, despite his low birth. There is something about a man of determination that I admire, though he has crossed the line into impertinence once or twice. He will be the first to admit that."

The merchant inclined his head in deference. "It is a habit I have struggled to shrug off, I confess it."

"Fascinating," said Lord Cedrik, disinterested. "Can we get to why he's here?"

"He is here with a proposal," Lord Elio said. "One that finally has merit."

"And that is?"

"A way into Aram," said the sunlord.

The Lord of Ethior could not have looked more unimpressed. "That is hardly news, Krator. You've been saying for weeks that your allies will have the gates open for us." He looked at Cliffario Denlatis, not caring to hide his disdain. "You're to tell us this…*merchant*, is the ally you were referring to?"

"No. Denlatis's appearance here is unexpected."

"Then these allies…"

"Are inside the city, and uncontactable, without help."

"Uncontactable?" Robbert could sense his uncle growing irate. "You said you sent men forward to enter the city before our arrival? You said you would command your allies to open the gates."

"I did not consider these refugees," Elio Krator said. His voice remained entirely unemotional. "Lord Hasham locked the gates at their coming, to prevent the red death from entering the city. It has made contacting my allies difficult."

Cedrik Kastor gave a sneering laugh. "And now this merchant magically appears to save the day, is that it?"

"I would not put it in those terms, but yes, in a fashion. Denlatis assures me that he knows certain ways in and out of the city that Lord Hasham does not. He will be able to see the gates open, and…"

"And in return you'll give this upstart your cousin's hand?" Lord Cedrik's lips twisted in amusement. "You would let your line be polluted by such as him? To hand over the rule of House Krator to a *merchant*."

"When I am Grand Duke, I will be elevated above and beyond my current station. And greatly more so when I am Emperor."

He's avoiding the question, Robbert thought. He had a good enough sense of Elio Krator by now to know he wouldn't hand over the reins of his house to a merchant for so little as this. *No, more likely he'll simply kill him once his use is spent, and give his cousin's hand to one more worthy.* He kept those thoughts to himself for now. If the merchant was clever, and he certainly had that look about him, he might be wondering the same thing.

Cedrik Kastor walked slowly over to a table and filled himself a cup of wine, to give himself time to think. "So tell me, Lord Krator…how am *I* to profit from this trade, exactly? You get your gates opened, the merchant gets a marriage…and us? Me and my dear nephew? What is our personal yield?"

The sunlord seemed not to understand the question. "Your personal yield will simply be upholding your side of the bargain, my lord. Thereafter, you can turn your attention north, as you please."

Lord Cedrik gave an indifferent shrug. "That doesn't excite me. You've been talking for weeks about opening these gates from within. Why should I care that it is some merchant who sees it done, rather than another of your puppets?"

"I did not ask for you to care. I am just informing you of our plans."

"I am happy to sweeten the deal, of course, if Lord Kastor feels he is being sold short?" Denlatis's smile had not moved since they'd arrived. It was a sleazy smile, beneath a thin nose nestled among high cheekbones and a refined jaw. Waves of dark hair rolled back from a hairline as straight as a bowstring, over eyes that twinkled with mischief. "Perhaps I could help furnish your forces, Lord Kastor? I have ties to many sellsword companies and have riches aplenty to hire them."

"Riches aplenty?" Cedrik Kastor laughed. "The entirety of your wealth could go missing from my coffers and I wouldn't even notice the difference."

The merchant seemed to enjoy that. "You are the Lord of Ethior and House Kastor, the richest man in all of Tukor, I've heard it said. I am but a humble merchant, making my way in the world. I would never deny that your riches far exceed my own...but all the same, my wealth is *here*, and yours is not." He gave a silky bow. "I have already taken the liberty of hiring a captain of the Bloody Traders and his men, to enter your service. A gift to you, my lord, for the forthcoming battle."

"The Bloody Traders," Robbert said, raising a brow. He'd heard of them before. "Some of them are Bladeborn."

"Just so, young prince. This captain I have hired is Bladeborn himself. They call him the Surgeon, for his lethal efficiency. And I believe his mother was a healer as well." His gold tooth sparkled in the firelight. "Lord Krator once received a similar gift from me, he will tell you. I brought him a strong host of Bladeborn sellswords at his warcamp outside Eagle's Perch. Men who, I am quite sure, fought with distinction when you clashed."

Lord Cedrik's eyes sharpened. "Is this true, Krator? You used *Bladeborn* men against us?"

"Men of mixed blood," the sunlord said. "From north and south. Mutts and mongrels really, but they played their part."

"They killed my men."

"They kill whatever men they are hired to kill. Do not let this unman you, Cedrik. It is the way of the world, the way of war. Surely you understand?"

"Do *not* patronise me, Krator. You need us more than we need you. Remember that."

Elio Krator gave a smug smile. "Look around you, my lord. What do you see? Red plains. A sandstone city. Rock and rugged desert and a sparkling blue shore. This is Aramatia, and you're far from home. No, my northern friend, you need me more than I need you, let me make that quite clear."

"You patronise me, now you threaten me? Robbert, draw your sword."

"Uncle?"

"Unsheathe your blade, boy. *Now!*"

Robbert did as bidden, and suddenly his broadsword was brandished before him, gleaming, misting silver and green. Elio Krator did not move. "Bravo. The boy prince can draw a blade. What are you trying to prove, Lord Kastor?"

"How easily he could kill you all," Cedrik said, quite calmly. "You southerners...you forget yourselves. *We* are born of a higher station, blessed and loved by Vandar, the God King. We carry with us his body, and his will." He paused and narrowed his eyes on Elio Krator. "Do *not* threaten me again."

Elio Krator gave an empty smile. "Threats go both ways, it would seem. Now, perhaps the prince might sheathe his blade, so we can go on? I'm sure neither of you would like it if Braccaro and Taro were prowling around in here with us. We do not bring our sunwolves to these councils, and you should not bring your steel. Please, put it away, young prince."

Robbert agreed with the sentiment. "I shouldn't have drawn it, Lord Krator. I apologise." He slid the blade away.

"You were only following your uncle's command." He turned to look at the merchant. "Now, Denlatis, tell us of this way into the city."

The merchant dipped his pointed chin. "With pleasure, sunlord."

Denlatis did not speak for long. Apparently, there were secret sellsword and smuggler passages that he had used often in the past, those known only to him and his own allies, that would see them safely and securely into the city. Denlatis had, he claimed, used one such passage himself to reach them, and in ushering the Surgeon and his men out of the city as well, under cover of dark the previous night. Getting back in would not be problematic, he promised, and once inside, contacting Elio Krator's allies and forging with them a plan to open the gates, thus permitting the main force of their army to enter the city, would be equally simple. Everything seemed easy to Cliffario Denlatis.

"It will be a rout," he told them, with a final flashing smile. "Your forces outnumber those inside the city greatly. Lord Hasham has even recalled his soldiers from the refugee camps, to help bolster his numbers. Is that not proof of a desperate man, my lords?"

He gave a few other tidbits of information before Lord Krator waved his hand and dismissed him, saying, "That will do for now, Denlatis. Go, so we may talk in private."

The merchant swept into another of his outrageous bows and departed to leave them alone. Once gone, Lord Cedrik gave a sneer. "How do we know that Hasham is not aware of these secret ways as well? How do we know we can trust this merchant? He has a duplicitous look to him."

Krator plucked an errant feather from the plumage of his cloak, and let it fall to the floor. "He is sly, I'll grant, though men like him often are. Denlatis was born in squalor, whelped by some shipyard slattern. His father was a docker, a simple man of low wit and even lower ambition. His son cannot be accused of the same. This ambition makes him unseemly to men like us, Lord Kastor, but he still has his uses."

The Lord of Ethior snorted contemptuously. "A vulgar little sneak is not what I had in mind."

"If I may?" Mar Malaan stepped forward, with a waft of that cloying perfume he wore. Robbert liked the simpering Sunrider much more than he did his lord, though that aroma was foul, applied to cover some bodily reek he did not doubt. He opened his lips in a faithful smile. "The method, and the outcome, are two very different things, Lord Kastor. Cliffario Denlatis is not the key we had envisaged, but he is a key nonetheless, and that is all he needs to be. He will bring this message to our allies, help unlock the door, and once he has done so, you will not need to concern yourself with him any longer."

Lord Cedrik grunted. "Good. I just want that gate open, so we can get this business done. I quickly grow weary of life in camp, sitting idle on these ugly red plains. There are only so many things that keep me amused."

"We know well enough what keeps you amused," Lord Elio said, mirthlessly.

Cedrik smiled at that. "My reputation precedes me, it would seem. Does that *unman* you, my lord? These things I like to do?"

"No. Your business is your own. I care little for your perversions, so long as they are kept from my sight."

"Perversions. A cute word. I understand you have some perversions of your own, Lord Krator. I've heard tell of many tales that discuss your treatment of northern men, and women. These Patriots of Lumara that you so proudly lead are, let us be quite honest, a despicable and loathsome lot."

Elio Krator did not agree. "They are patriots, my lord. It is in the name. Now come, we ought not let this descend into petty slurs. You are fretful, I know, and anxious on the eve of battle. Sometimes a man gets cold feet before his wedding. That is all this is. "

Cedrik didn't like that, to note the jerk of his upper lip. "You think I grow nervous? Me?" Laughter poured from his throat, an ugly sound, and mocking. "I am born to kill, Krator. Isn't that why you ran from me outside the Perch in the first place? Who in Aram could possibly give me cause to lose sleep?"

"The King's Wall, Sir Ralston Whaleheart."

Silence fell upon them like a shroud, black and heavy.

Robbert looked at his uncle, frowning. Cedrik Kastor seemed to have lost the use of his tongue.

For the first time, there was true joy glittering in Elio Krator's cold black eyes. "You didn't know?"

"No." The word was a whisper, quiet as a kiss. Cedrik's gaze fell in thought, ruminating on a memory. "There was blood…blood and battle at the docks in Shellcrest," he murmured. "One of Lord Huffort's knights… Sir Cleon Marsh…he perished by the giant's blade, he and all of his men. I had sent him in pursuit of a girl." He met Elio Krator's eyes. "This girl was involved in the death of my nephew, Sir Griffin. They left together, it was said, the giant, and this girl. A southern girl. An *Aramatian*. Would you know anything about that, Lord Krator?"

"It is news to me." Elio Krator answered. There was much that wasn't being said.

"And how do you know that the King's Wall is here?"

"Denlatis told me. I had thought him dead, in all truth. Some months ago I sentenced the giant to death in the Red Pits. That was before I left, to march to Eagle's Perch. It seems he has recovered from his wounds."

Robbert's chest was going up and down, steady. So little of this was making sense to him. "Will the giant fight us? Why would he? This isn't his city, his land."

"Why indeed." Mar Malaan smiled at him, hiding a great deal behind those blubbery eyes. "We have no answers, I say with great regret, young prince. The coming of the King's Wall to Aram was most unanticipated, and the giant was not forthcoming with his reasons."

He's lying. "And this girl? Was she with him?"

"We know nothing of this girl," Mar Malaan said in rehearsed response. He smiled again. "But alas, I fear the good sunlord has other matters to attend to." He turned. "My lord. Your captains will be waiting. They are eager to hear their orders so they might make their preparations."

Krator nodded. "I must apologise, my lords. Other duties call to me, other councils. If the King's Wall does indeed fight, however, I do not imagine that will prove a problem. You are born to kill, after all, Lord Kastor. Surely you can defeat him?"

Cedrik Kastor's jaw was clenched as tight as a drumskin. "He is big, slow, ponderous. He'll prove no hurdle to me."

A flicker of a smile played about Lord Krator's lips. "Yes. As you say. Big and slow." He inclined his head to each in turn. "Now, if you'll excuse me…"

"Wait."

He had already begun toward the door. He stopped, turned. "Yes, my lord?"

"You'll fight with me."

"I'll…I'm sorry, I'm not understanding."

"When the gates are opened," Cedrik said. "Your merchant tells us there are tens of thousands of soldiers in Aram, united in their aversion to you. We may get the gates opened cheaply, but there will still be much to do once we pass the walls. I would have you fight with me, Krator, side-by-side. You are yet to bloody your blade, and for this, your own coup." Cedrik Kastor shook his head. "I can permit this no longer. If you want this city, you are going to have to bleed for it, and kill for it, and risk dying for it. And if that oafish giant should come lumbering down some alleyway, well, perhaps I'll let *you* fight him first. You can finish what you started in these Red Pits of yours. Mount his armour in your home and put his head above your hearth. It will be your crowning glory as a warrior, Sunlord Krator, to vanquish the monstrous Bladeborn knight."

It'll be your death and humiliation, more like, Robbert thought. The prince could see no world where this feathery wolf-rider could best a man like Sir Ralston Whaleheart, bedecked head and heel in godsteel with a great misting greatsword clutched in each fist.

The sunlord surely knew it too. "We shall see," is all he said, not rising to the taunt. And that was that. He strode from the tent, Malaan wobbling in his wake.

Cedrik threw his head back and laughed once he was gone, a full laugh, most unpleasant. "Did you see his face, Robbert? The man was terrified. Gods, that was satisfying. I do so love watching a craven's veil slip."

Robbert was in no mood for such japing. *He's frightened too*, he thought. *My uncle always talks more when he's afraid.* "This girl," he merely said. "She's the same one from Harrowmoor."

The laughter stopped. "Yes, she is. The spy."

"Spy?" Robbert wasn't aware of that detail. "I thought she was a breeder. One of Auntie Cecilia's?"

Cedrik Kastor shook his head. "Your cousin Griffin received a letter at Harrowmoor, informing him that this girl was indeed a spy, one of Lady Payne's little pets. It was the reason he went to Elyon Daecar's tent that night. To bring her to me. He and that lout Griffin kept around. I forget his name."

"Borgin."

"Yes, that's it. Borgin. An unpleasant boor, that one, but useful in his way. Griffin took him along to teach the girl a lesson or two. A lesson she clearly had no intention of learning." He met his nephew's eyes. "I have always suspected that the girl was the one to kill Griffin that night, not Daecar. That's why I sent Sir Cleon after her. Until the Wall got in the way."

Robbert remembered a rumour he'd heard. "People said King Godrin sent his Wall away for a reason. He didn't just abandon his king before his death. He'd never do that, not Sir Ralston. No, he was sent away to perform some duty. To protect this girl, do you think?"

"It would seem likely, yes."

And there was *another* rumour too, whispered by their Aramatian allies, one Robbert gave voice to now. "They say that the heir of Aramatia has returned, Uncle. Safina Nemati's granddaughter. This girl…this spy…she'd be about the right age."

"Just about right, yes," his uncle agreed. He drew his knife, turning it in the firelight, tapping a finger against ist deadly, misting point, menacing. "Krator has not been entirely honest with us, Robbert. This girl is clearly of great interest to him. To kill, perhaps. Or wed. Elio Krator was once to marry Safina's daughter, after all, to secure his line and take his throne. Why not the granddaughter instead? She really was very beautiful…for a southern girl." Dark malice glittered in his eyes.

So much of it wasn't adding up to Prince Robbert Lukar, however, so much wasn't making sense. A hundred questions circled in his mind. One sprung forth from his lips. "But why would this long lost heir be in Rasalan?" he asked. "Why would she be a spy there at all, so far north?"

"Questions we can ask her ourselves, Robbert. Once the city is secured."

The prince saw something different in his uncle's eyes at that moment. "Once the city is secured," he repeated, quietly. "For Krator, or…"

Cedrik Kastor put a finger to his lips. "Shhhhh, Robbert. This is not the place, nor the time. We would do better to discuss this in our own camp, I think."

Robbert Lukar nodded, and stepped a little closer. He lowered his voice to a restrained whisper and asked, "Was this *ever* about Agarath, Uncle? Or was Aram always your goal?"

His uncle smiled a wicked, self-satisfied smile. "All roads lead to Agarath *eventually*, Robbert. But that is not to say there aren't prizes to be won along the way." He resheathed his dagger and turned toward the door. "Come. Let's go gather the others. There is much we need to discuss."

45

Elyon

He waited along upon the open field, scanning the skies for his quarry.

A white flag flapped noisily beside him, planted to meet the terms of the parley. To his right stood the landmark where the meeting was to take place; a scorched granite rock, fifty feet high, sitting craggy and incongruous amidst the open, rain-soaked plains.

The Burning Rock, Elyon Daecar thought. *Where the greatest battle of our time took place.* The rock itself wasn't much to look at, remarkable only for the simple fact that it looked so out of place out here. There were no others scarring the otherwise green land, no cliffs of crags or mountains. It was a land of fields and plains and gentle rolling hills, with the occasional little wood or lake spotted here and there.

A land of death, Elyon reflected. *A land where two hundred and fifty thousand men, mounts and monsters clashed to end the War of the Continents. Where my grandfather Gideon and King Storris Reynar were slain by Ulrik Marak and Garlath the Grand. Where my father fought his most famous battle, killing Vallath and crippling a prince.*

Once before, Elyon Daecar would live the battle in his sleep, daydreaming it through the long boring days he spent at study as a boy. He would talk to his friends about it with excited smiles, reenact it in the sparring yard, and seek out those who'd been there, to tell him what it was like. Lythian had been grilled so often on the battle that he soon stopped talking to Elyon about it entirely. Others were the same. Vesryn, Borrus, Rikkard among them. His father had never much liked to talk about it at all, Elyon learned when he was young. "Your father is not a man to laud his own triumphs," Elyon remembered his uncle Vesryn telling him once. "It's the same with many heroes, you'll find. However heroic a deed may seem from the outside, they're never the same to the hero himself."

Elyon understood that now. Even after all he'd done, he didn't feel half a hero yet.

A light rain was starting to come down again, a typical fall of spring drizzle. Elyon looked up, searching once more, but could see no wings on the horizon, no shadow in the skies. He turned once more to look at the Burning Rock, glistening as the rain pattered against its hulking black facade.

It had been known as *Winnow's Rock* once before, the prince knew, for the tragic story of Winnow the Weeping, a famously beautiful maiden who'd been jilted by her lover, Sir Franklin the Fair, on the night of their secret wedding. Sir Franklin was a storied knight himself, famed for his triumphs in battle and the bed both, though was something of a scoundrel too. He'd never turned up to wed Winnow, the story went, so she rode for his castle of Fairfront and found him abed with not one, not two, but three women, even triplets if one version of the tellings was to be believed. In her despair, Winnow had come to this rock, climbed to the very top, and thrown herself off to her death. Ever since then, it had been a popular site for jilted lovers to come and whisper their curses, to weep of their heartache and vengeance.

That tradition still held to this day for some, though for most it was the Burning Rock now. Before the war, it had been grey and dappled brown, people said, though during the battle so much dragonfire had been belched upon it that the rock had been scorched jet black.

The lands too, Elyon thought. By now these open plains had been long since restored to health, but back then they were black and burned as far as the eye could see, a smoking ruin of blackened fields and charred woods and a hundred thousand corpses.

The Master of Winds knew something about that. *I have my own Battle of Burning Rock now,* he thought, reflecting on the Battle of the Bane. The numbers there hadn't been too dissimilar. Almost two hundred thousand, all told, though less than half the count of dead. Elyon did not delude himself into thinking greater battles didn't yet lie ahead. *In the east and in the west, they will batter at our gates. And if they smash through, Varinar will be next.*

A shape appeared in the open skies. Big. Black. Alone. *Good,* Elyon thought, squinting into the distance. *He came alone, as the messenger said.* That messenger had been found by outriders some miles south of the Mudway and brought to Lord Rammas at the head of the army the day before, bearing a white flag and a sealed scroll.

"For the eyes of Prince Daecar," the Agarathi envoy had told them. Elyon had opened the letter to find an invite inside. 'Tomorrow. Midday. The Burning Rock,' it had read. 'I would like to see you again, Prince of these Vandarian Skies. To talk. Bring a white banner, and plant it by the rock. I will come alone.' It had not been signed with a name, though Elyon hadn't needed to ask. The arrogance of the dragonlord Vargo Ven was as obvious in ink as it was in person.

He watched the man come now, watched the form of Malathar the Mighty grow and swell as he drew near. *I half forgot how big he is.* Elyon had battled many dragons now, but most of them were much smaller. Malathar was a rare breed; bulky, thick-winged, stubby-nosed, black all over with sparkling plates of gold, slashed with a hundred scars. It was a wonder he could fly at all with those muscular proportions, though agility was not his ally. Elyon had learned that when they fought in the skies above the Bane. *I'm better now too*, he thought to himself. *Stronger, faster, fitter.* Back then he'd flown no further than a few dozen miles. *Now I can do hundreds in a single sitting and still have enough energy to fight.*

All the same, his body tensed to see the massive dragon descend, opening out its powerful wings and swinging its savage grasping talons to the ground to land with a heavy tremor. Atop the beast in a saddle of fine leather sat Vargo Ven, wreathed in his black dragonscale armour and with his rich black and gold cape at his back, clasped at the shoulders by gilded dragon claws. At a gesture, Malathar leaned and lowered his body so that the dragonlord could slip safely to the ground. He landed on the soft earth, bearing a short pole and white flag in his hand. As he walked to Elyon, he slowed to study the Burning Rock.

"So, this is the famous rock," he said, in that rich, elegant Agarathi timbre. "I never did see it on the battlefield that day. Standing here now, that makes sense. I had expected something bigger."

He continued forward, leaving Malathar some fifty metres back, rumbling menacingly as he stared at Elyon through eyes burning red with hate. There was no such malice to Vargo Ven, however, only that accustomed arrogance as he sauntered forward, thrust the pole into the ground five metres from Elyon's, and said, "There. We have our parley. Funny, isn't it? How a little white flag can be such an effective shield. Without it, you would kill me for a certainty. Malathar would never reach me in time before you put that windy blue blade of yours through my gut."

"What makes you think I'd go for the gut?" Elyon queried. "Cutting your head off would shut you up quicker."

The Fireborn smiled, lean and darkly handsome. "I do imagine it would, yes. Though the gut would be a slower and greatly more painful end."

"You have the wrong idea of me, my lord. I'm not a cruel man."

"No? Then who is it who's been butchering all these dragons, I wonder? The scion has seen it from his fine palace quarters. Much horrific mutilation of Agarath's noble children. The Fire Father is most vexed by this. I told him it might be you."

"I don't butcher the dragons I kill. I just kill them." *Janilah*, Elyon thought. Rikkard had spoken of these butchered dragons, with their bodies opened and entrails pulled out, heads hacked off as though in ritual. He suggested the Warrior King might be behind it. "You have the wrong man."

"So I do. I shall be sure to tell the Fire Father so. Perhaps he will be lenient on you."

"I don't fear him, Ven."

"No, of course you don't. You are a boy champion, too young and foolish to know fear." He smiled that smile of his, ever in control. "Your father. Now there is a man who *truly* knows no fear. The indomitable

Amron Daecar, peerless and fearless in battle. I do not imagine he even fears death. Well…not *his* death, anyway. Yours…"

"He's lost loved ones before. His eldest son, and youngest. His wife. He doesn't fear to lose me."

"Your sister, then."

Elyon's eyes sharpened. *Don't rise to it. He's trying to goad you.* "Is well protected," he said. "My father has no time to spend fearing for those he loves. Nor do I. Those we have loved and lost await us in the Eternal Halls. When we die, we shall see them again. Death holds no fear for the men of the north."

Vargo Ven ran a finger down the dimple in his dark stubbled jaw, and let out a light little chuckle. "How brave. Those halls of yours will be most overcrowded soon, I should think. I hope they are big, boy champion. We have already sent many thousands through their gates."

Elyon ignored that barb as well. "Our halls are boundless," he merely said. "The same as Agarath's Eternal Flame. And how many of your own will be greeted by that fire, my lord? How many of your kin and countrymen is your mad master going to kill?"

Something darkened on the dragon lord's face. "The Eternal Flame is a heaven beyond anything you can know…"

Elyon laughed to cut him off. "Keep telling yourself that. As you keep telling yourself this is the Fire Father's will. It isn't. Your master has a master of his own. It's the Fire *God*, not the Father, who wants to bathe our world in flame."

The dragonlord's thin top lip flicked into a scowl. "And who are you to question the will of a god, Daecar? Who am I?'

"So it *is* Agarath." Elyon mused on that. "I thought as much. Eldur is nothing but a thrall to him. As you're a thrall to Eldur. Are you happy with that, Ven? Being a slave?"

I'm getting to him, Elyon thought, as he watched the man's lip twitch once more. "We are all slaves to the will of the gods, boy champion. Me to mine, you to yours." His eyes went to the Windblade. "Vandar is with you, even now. He works his chaos through you. *He* has brought this war to us all. Lord Eldur only means to end it."

Elyon sighed. "No, my lord Vargo, the only ones trying to end this war are those opposed to your master. So long as he submits to the Fire God's will he is a plague upon this world that must be destroyed. As must those who blindly follow him, deaf and dumb to his true intent."

"Destroyed? By who? *You*? And your father? Or is there another you pin your hopes on?" His smile returned. "Who is the heir of Varin, boy champion? Where is this fabled hero who will wield the Heart Remade?"

Elyon spoke inexpressively. "There is no heir of Varin."

"A lie," Ven said. "You know who he is."

"Varin's last heir was King Lorin. He died without children. There is no heir."

"You seek to hide and protect him, I understand."

Elyon snorted. "Our best and bravest fight at the heart of every battle. If there was an heir, you'd know about it."

"As you say. Though forgive me if I do not believe you. You are not a trustworthy source." He turned his eyes to the Burning Rock, giving up on the questioning. "So, are you not going to ask me why I invited you here this morning? Are you not intrigued by my summons, boy champion?"

Summons. Everything the man said was barbed with some snide insult. Elyon gave no response, waiting.

The man took his time before saying. "A ceasefire." Then he watched for Elyon's reaction, but the prince would give him nothing. Disappointment glittered. "A temporary one, I should add, until you drag that bedraggled corpse of an army of yours to Rustbridge. I will grant you this clemency, and let you pass from here unmolested. Call it a gift, young prince. I am fond of giving gifts, as you know."

Sir Tomos's bones, Elyon thought. *The bones that almost got Lythian killed.* He wondered if Ven had known their return would cause such discord. *He hoped for it, at least.* That was no gift of kindness, Elyon knew that much, no more than this one was.

"You've lost five dragons to us over the last few nights," the prince said. "And you fear to lose more should you continue to pursue us. Don't cower behind false clemency, Lord Ven. Just admit that your flock is thinning, and your master is most displeased."

He had hit to the heart of it, he saw at once.

"It is your army that is thinning, boy," the dragonlord snarled back. "How many have been killed on your long muddy march? Several thousand more? What a paltry thing it must be. And your food, your fodder, your supplies…" He laughed, ragged and wild. "Half of you will probably starve before you even reach the city."

Elyon crunched a fist, thinking back.

The first night of the attacks had been the worst, starting not long after dark and lasting all through the night. Elyon had been walking at the very back of the column with his uncle Rikkard when they first saw the fire. *I knew it would be a long night then, and so it turned out.*

The dragons were like ghosts that night, appearing from the black misty skies as if from some dark unutterable void, blowing their flame and vanishing all at once, leaving dozens dead in their wake. Sometimes they would drag their talons across the road as well, gouging ruts and ripping men from their saddles, crushing them or tossing them away into the bogs to be devoured by the mire and the many monsters that lurked within. Occasionally, the men would see them coming quickly enough and beat them back with bows and spears, but that was rare. Mostly they killed at least a few on each pass, sending panic and dread down the lines.

Elyon had been in the skies throughout, doing what he could to protect them. Knowing where the next dragon would come from had proven almost impossible, even with the Windblade whispering their whereabouts and sensing their presence. Its range only went so far and the army had been widely stretched along the Mudway. Mostly Elyon spent the night chasing shadows and growing ever more weary all the while. By the time the light of dawn purpled the skies and the mists began to lift on a brand new morning, the count of the dead had been disastrous. Almost three thousand men, with hundreds more horses and mules and oxen had been burned to death, crushed, or scattered to the bogs, never to be returned.

The nights to follow had not been so bad. There was more cover by then, the Mudway leaving the worst of the open marshes behind to wend through hills and woods, past cliffs and crags where shelter was more readily found. Men and mounts had been lost all the same, at least two thousand more in sum, each night bringing more casualties as the dragons continued to harry and harass them. If Elyon had any desire to leave and return west, those were quashed with each new pass. "I have to stay," he told his uncle. "I have to stay here and help protect you."

He helped but little. Another dragon had fallen to his blade, but the other four were taken down by quarrel and arrow, the bowmen taking the spoils. On the second night the baggage train had come under assault, a dozen dragons swooping down as the Mudway crossed through an open plain. Lady Marian had been there protecting it, though there was nothing she or her men could do. The devastation had been catastrophic, nine out of every ten wagons, wains, and oxcarts burned to cinders, almost all of their food and fodder with them. It left them with scarcely enough to get the men and horses to Rustbridge, without half of them collapsing from hunger and exhaustion or abandoning their duty to vanish into the hills. Rarely did they stop, little did they sleep, and now they had to suffer a fraction of their rations. *A bite of bread and a thimble of cheese*, Elyon thought. With many long days left to go before they reached the city, he wondered how many might just desert and strike out alone, driven to distraction by fear and fatigue.

And all for the loss of five dragons, Elyon thought. Most of the men who had died were regular foot soldiers, spearmen and shieldmen and pikemen without a drip of Bladeborn blood. Few knights had fallen, Bladeborn or no. A cold-hearted commander might say it was worth it, but Elyon was not such a man. *They were men, all of them. They had wives, parents, children, lives. None of them deserved to die like that, ambushed on the road.*

He put it all aside, looked the dragonlord in the eyes. "Tell me, Ven. Was it all a ploy, the attack on Mudport. Did you only do it to draw Rammas from his den?"

Vargo Ven moved aside a lock of smoky hair, to put it neatly back in place. "The prince gives me too much credit. I only hoped for such. And so it turned out. Does the prince condemn me for this trick?"

"There's no honour in killing men on the march," Elyon told him sharply. "Nor razing peaceful cities to the ground. I was there, the night you destroyed Mudport. I saw the people burning. I heard the children crying as they died."

"Such does happen when cities burn. But I am nothing but a slave, as you have said. A slave to the Fire Father's will, who himself acts in thrall to

Agarath the All-Father. Would that I could deny his orders, but I cannot. So I'm afraid the children must burn, Elyon Daecar."

"You could deny him," Elyon said, half in hope. "You *must* see the madness in this, Ven. Killing children by the thousand. *Innocents*. Is that war to you? Is that how you would serve?" He saw a flicker of doubt in his eyes, and latched on. "You didn't come here today to speak of a ceasefire, did you? What would be the point? You'd only need to call your dragons back and the result would be the same. No, you came for something else."

The man snorted. "And what is that, pray tell?"

"You don't believe in what you're doing. You know this isn't right. You came here today to talk about deposing him. You want Eldur dead, I can see it in your eyes."

Vargo Ven gave a haughty laugh, tipping his head back to chuckle to the skies. "It seems you have me figured out, boy champion. Yes, that's it. I'm seeking you out as an ally, to plot to murder the Father and the Founder. Together we shall overthrow him and rule the world!" His mirth was as false as his manner, as false as the laughter spilling from his lips.

Elyon watched him, flat-eyed. "You're afraid of him. Terrified. But you don't need to be. We can help each other, Vargo. Why not?"

Anger flashed across the dragonlord's face. "Why not? *Why not?* You think I would betray him…for *you?* You think you can win me around with words?" A sneer pulled back his top lip. "You have no tongue for deception, Daecar. Whatever this is…whatever you are trying to do…it will not work. Your world will fall."

"It doesn't need to be this way, Vargo." Elyon took a step toward him. Over the dragonlord's shoulder he saw Malathar shift at once, moving forward. "We can save this world, you and I. You followed Tavash, not Tethian. You don't believe in this cause."

"Don't tell me what I believe in. You have no idea what's coming."

"Your hordes don't concern us," Elyon said to that. "Nor your dragons. You've lost too many already, and for what? A city or two, a couple of forts? You've driven us out of the Marshlands, but at what cost? You're bleeding, Vargo, and cannot staunch the wound. Eventually you'll bleed out. You know it as well as I do."

A smile curled on Vargo Ven's lips. "Fool," he whispered. "Oh, what a fool you are. Elyon Daecar, *Prince of Fools*." And he laughed, loud and true. "You say you know no fear, you claim you fear not death. But you will, good prince, oh yes, soon you will. When he comes and blackens the skies with his wings, when he blots out the sun and the stars, you'll know fear. When he opens his jaws and the very Breath of Agarath gushes out, to melt you in your armour, you'll know fear. When he roars, and the world trembles, and all the towers tumble about you, you'll know fear. Act brave before me all you please. When you look upon the Lord of Dragons, then *you will know fear*."

Elyon Daecar stared at him, short-bearded jaw as stiff as stone. He was not going to cower to words. "Gross embellishments will not unsettle me, my lord. If Drulgar has stirred from his slumber, so be it. We'll have to kill him as well."

"You'll try, I have no doubt. *Briefly.*" Vargo Ven twisted his neck and gestured to Malathar. "The Mighty could have killed you that night at the Bane, and he is but a child beside the Dread. You cannot truly know until you have seen him, and I have. We flew above him at the Nest and saw the vastness of his bulk, sprawled upon the ruins. Even I felt fear to look upon him. Even *me*, Daecar. Even me." He smiled and inclined his head. "I shall honour the offer I gave you, and let your army limp back to Rustbridge. Call it a final mercy. Drink with your companions, make love to a woman, enjoy what time you have left. It will be meagre, I assure you." He reached to pull the white flag from the ground. "This parley is over. I shall see you in the skies."

"Wait." Elyon stepped forward. "If you allow this to happen…"

"*Allow?*" the dragonlord snapped. "How could I hope to stop it? There is no defying the Fire Father, Daecar, no defeating the Dread. Together they will bring this world of yours to its knees…"

"And yours." Elyon took a grip of the Windblade as he saw Malathar the Mighty taking a powerful step forward, menacing, prowling, eyes burning atop a blunted snout. Tendrils of dark smoke swirled from the beast's nostrils. "Your world will burn as well, Vargo. All the world will burn, and you'll have done nothing to stop it." Malathar took another pace. Elyon drew the Windblade out, showing six inches of godly steel. "Someone has to stand up to him. Someone who can get close enough to slip a dagger through his ribs. Why not you?"

"Why not? Why not? I have told you why not! *Malathar!*" The dragonlord spun, threw aside his flag, and ran, black and golden cape flapping at his back. His hulking steed thundered toward him, lowering his wing, as the dragonlord scrambled straight up and into his saddle, scaling the beast's horned side like a mountain goat does a cliff.

Elyon ripped the rest of the Windblade from its scabbard. *I think I made him angry.* He summoned the winds to wreathe him. "We have parley, Ven!" he shouted. "You would break it?"

"The parley is over! *Over*, Daecar!"

Then let it be blood. Elyon thrust his helm down over his head and soared skyward. Below, Malathar was charging into a running take-off, thumping those great muscular wings as his claws ripped out great chunks of earth from the soggy ground, flinging them thirty metres aside. He heaved his bulk into the air, swinging around in an arcing circle. Elyon hovered above the Burning Rock, waiting. *I can kill him*, he thought. *Right here. I can kill them both.*

He could see the rage on Vargo Ven's face as he perched in his high saddle, cape waving at his back. The rain was still falling in a fine drizzle, though the skies were open, grey and blue, the sun blurred and burning in the east as it continued its morning ascent. The grasses twinkled with moisture, the hills shining as they rolled away into the distance. Malathar gave out a deafening roar, a screeching trumpeting roar unlike anything Elyon had yet heard. *Help*, his instinct told him. *He is bellowing for others to come help.*

"Daecar! The end is coming, Daecar!" Ven drew his own blade, standing up in his saddle, brandishing the black dragonsteel aloft. Red lines rippled down its length, the fire of dragons from its forging. "You cannot hope to stop it! There is no hope, not against him!"

Elyon braced as Malathar neared, embraced by a spinning vortex. The beast turned his shoulder and flashed right by, bringing a blast of hot wind with him. Elyon followed with his eyes as Malathar came around for another pass, his chest lit orange and red. He saw Vargo Ven's eyes dart over his shoulder to the distance. *Others*, Elyon thought. He glanced back. Shapes were appearing in the skies. One, two, three. *Wingriders.*

Fury simmered within him. "You planned for this!" he called out. "You call this a parley! It's nothing but a trap!"

Malathar opens his jaws, slashed with dozens of scars from the many battles he'd fought. Borrus Kanabar had given him some of those, two decades ago. *The Lord of the Riverlands and Warden of the East. Where are you, Borrus? We could do with your blade right now.*

He put it from his mind. The beast was nearing, and Vargo Ven was laughing, just as he had that night above the Bane, manic and mocking. "Half of war is traps and tricks, Daecar! The boy champion needs to know this! This good sweet boy who plays by the rules!" His laughter filled the air.

And then it was fire, sudden and fierce and scorching, gushing from Malathar's mighty maw. Elyon whipped the Windbalde from right to left in a swish, blowing the worst of the blaze aside. What was left engulfed him, but it was a weakened feeble thing, gone in an instant. His armour could protect against it. Only a sustained assault of molten breath could cook through his godsteel plate.

The Dread, he thought. *Drulgar.* 'When he opens his jaws and the very Breath of Agarath gushes out, to melt you in your armour, you'll know fear.'. Could the Calamity do such a thing? Melt godsteel with his breath? Topple towers with his roar. Blot out the sun and stars with the vastness of his bulk? *It was an exaggeration*, Elyon told himself. *It has to be. Drulgar is no world killer, but a dragon, flesh and blood and bone and killable.*

He had to believe that. Until he saw the monster with his own two eyes, he would not wilt. *But will others, when I tell them?* Vargo Ven had not been shy in confirming the rise of Eldur, months ago. The man was a posturer, pompous and preening, but he did not seem to be a liar, not in this. *And he isn't lying now*, Elyon knew. *Drulgar rests upon the Nest, as he once did. I need to tell my uncle…tell my father…tell them all…*

He turned. Malathar was swinging about again, his ugly stunted snout pulled back in a snarl. *I could kill him*, Elyon thought. *Or I could die in the attempt.* Beyond the beast Ven's wingriders were nearing. They must have been hiding just beyond sight, waiting for their summons. "Coward," Elyon said, in a low voice. Then louder. "Coward! You're a coward, Ven!"

537

The answer he got was laughter. "Tricks and traps, Daecar! These rules of yours...they strangle you!"

Not today. Much as he wanted to cut that smirk from the dragonlord's face, it wasn't worth the risk. He was a bearer, a champion, and too important. *Traps and tricks,* he thought. *And I'll not be lured into yours.*

He swung about, Varin cloak whipping, and fired himself away to the north. Over the rush of wind he could hear the dragonlord laughing, mocking him for a craven. "Coward! Me? And you call *me* a coward..."

Elyon clenched his jaw as he cut through the drizzly wet skies. *Next time, Ven,* he thought. *I'll see you for round three.*

46

Amilia

The lands were growing wilder.

Hills climbed high about them, their slopes forested with tall sleek pines and old stately sentinels. The winds were restless, blowing and gusting day and night and the sun had gone away. For long days the clouds had been thick and grey and sometimes they bellowed thunder.

Tukor's pain, Amilia Lukar thought. It was said that the wild thunder heard in North Tukor was the great god's dying breath, echoing and repeating through time.

"How much further can it be?" Astrid was saying, as Marigold rattled relentlessly along the hard dirt road, hauled by the oxen Ralston and Big Ben. "We're lost, Kegs, just admit it. We should have reached the river days ago by now."

The big wagon-driver's brow was heavily furrowed. He looked around at the high rugged lands with a cast of confusion on his broad hairless face. "It's just down the road here, I'm sure of it. We got turned around a bit, you remember? I took us down that wrong path a while and we lost time, but now I've set us straight."

"Are you *sure*, Kegs?" Astrid was looking at him in appeal. "You're certain we're going the right way?" Clearly, she wasn't by the tone of her voice, and Amilia had begun to grow wary too. The fields and meadows and pretty little brooks were gone. This was a much wilder land, high and cold and grim.

"We've gone too far west," Astrid went on, as Kegs stammered for an answer. "We need to turn south. The Clearwater Run flows across the entire breadth of Tukor and we haven't seen it once. Not *once*. That means we *must* be going west, Kegs. We need to find a road to take us south. Or else turn around and go back. We can't keep going on like this."

"We…the river, it's close. We'll see it soon, I'm sure….just over that rise there…"

"No," Astrid said firmly, almost hysterically. "I recognise these lands from when I worked at Osworth Castle. We're in the north*west*, near the heathlands, and *we're going the wrong way*." She turned. "My lady, tell him. We have to go back or go south. We *have* to find the river."

Amilia nodded. There was much about all this that felt amiss. "She's right, Kegs. We've given you ample chance to lead us the right way, and you've failed. Sir Munroe," she called out. The knight was walking ahead, as always, stiff and silent. "Come back here and help us turn this wagon around. We're turning back."

Sir Munroe stopped, paused, then turned and walked back toward them. Kegs brought the wagon to a stop. "Why?" the knight asked. "I'm not sure that's a good idea, my lady."

Amilia frowned. "I don't care what you think. Astrid's right. We should have reached Clearwater Castle days ago…"

"And we would have if Kegs hadn't taken that wrong route," Sir Munroe said calmly. "We lost over a day going that way, and the same going back…"

"But we never went back," Astrid said.

Amilia looked over at her. "Did we not?" she asked. "I could have sworn…"

"We did," said Sir Munroe Moore.

"No, we didn't," Astrid insisted. There was a look on her face, like she was only just realising that. "I remember now. We never turned back. We just kept going." Her face went suddenly white with fear. "What's happening here? Why can't we remember properly?"

"You're just being paranoid," Sir Munroe told her. "We did turn back. I remember it clearly." He turned to look up the hard earthen road, bordered by wild stiff tufts of brown grass. To their left the lands were windswept and rugged; to right rose a sea of flinty hills clotted with stands of pine. "Over that rise there, as Kegs says. We'll see the river soon." He gave the wagon a tap with his steel palm. "We keep going."

Kegs obeyed him without question, calling Ralston and Big Ben to trundle on. Marigold lurched into motion. Astrid looked utterly bewildered. "We can't…no…we *can't* go that way. It's the *wrong* way. My lady, tell them. You're in command here, not *him*."

"We'll give it another hour or two," Kegs assured her, as Sir Munroe strode ahead. He had to speak up to be heard; the winds were gusting loudly once more, causing all the grasses and trees to bend and sway. "It'll be night soon enough. If we haven't found the river by then…" He nodded. "Tomorrow. We'll turn back tomorrow."

"No," Astrid said. Her voice wasn't much more than a whisper now, stricken and defeated. "Something's happening. *What's* happening to us?" She sank down against the barrel she'd been sitting on, shaking her head, shivering.

Amilia moved to comfort her. "It'll all be fine, Astrid, don't worry. We're just lost, that's all, but we'll see the river soon, and when we do we'll know where we are. It's just a delay. There's nothing to fear."

The gangly girl glanced up at her with eyes misty with tears. "You sound like they do," she said, in a choked voice. "Why is no one listening to me? We've been going the wrong way for days. Since we left old Talbert. Ever since then...it's all gone wrong since then." She turned her shoulder and tucked her chin into her chest, pulling her cloak up to cover herself against the cold, sobbing.

The wagon rolled on, rattling over pebbles and bumps. Amilia sat on a barrel of ale and watched Sir Munroe Moore as he walked ahead of them. *Beware the silver man.*

Is he leading us somewhere? she wondered. She tried to figure out where that could be, and why. *He wants my pardon, my protection. Why would he try to mess with that?* The knight would never be accepted in Rasalan again, he knew, so he'd latched onto Amilia Lukar instead. It made no sense that he would lead them astray, unless...

Does he know I plan to put him in chains? Has he worked out I intend to hang him when we reach my uncle's care?

But that didn't make sense either. These were Kegs's lands, not his, and the big-bellied wagon-driver was their guide. If anyone had been leading them the wrong way it was Kegs, and why should he wish to do a thing like that? *Unless he's in league with the knight somehow?* But that made even less sense to her. The big man was much too kindhearted to be so duplicitous, and even if this was all some big ruse, Captain Wilkins had been the one to vouch for the driver, and he was definitely trustworthy, the princess knew.

The wind was tugging at her hair, causing it to whip and snap against her face, so she tied it into a bun and shoved it inside her hood. The day was bitter cold and growing colder, gloomy beneath that thick pall of cloud. Amilia had heaped an extra cloak about her shoulders to stay warm, but all the same the winds were knifing through her and setting a shiver in her bones. She could hear Astrid weeping by the barrel, gripped by a sudden woe, wrapped up like a babe in swaddling as she hunkered down against the side of the wagon. *It'll be fine*, she wanted to say. *It's all going to be fine, Astrid.*

But something inside her was starting to sense that was a lie. *We didn't turn back*, she thought. *When we went off on that wrong route...no, we never turned around. Astrid was right.*

She stood and marched up the wagon and prodded at Kegs' massive shoulder. "Turn around. We're going the wrong way."

He twisted his neck to look at her and there was something odd in his eyes. They looked glazed, almost, a strange milky white. Then he blinked and the soft kind eyes she knew reappeared. "Come again? You say something, my lady?"

She swallowed. "Stop the wagon, Kegs." Her voice was tight. "Or find somewhere to turn. We're going back."

"But..."

"No buts. Are you under my service or aren't you?"

"Well...I'm under no one's service, not really. No one but my own. You never paid for passage."

True, she thought. "No matter about that. You were headed for Clearwater Castle and we're going the wrong way. For your own sake, stop the wagon and turn around."

"I will…later. It'll be dark soon, as I say. We'll stop somewhere shortly and try to figure this all out then."

"There's nothing to figure out. We're going the wrong way and have been for days. We need to turn back."

"Tomorrow," the big man said. "If you're right, we'll go back tomorrow, my lady. But I still have hope that we'll see the river soon. Just over that rise there. It's just over that rise."

You said that already, she thought, suddenly afraid. *You've said that a dozen times.* "You said we'd see it over the last rise."

"Oh, did I? Must have got that wrong, I suppose. The next one. We'll see the river over the next one, down the slope. I'm sure of it, my lady. The next one."

She backed away from him. Astrid was still sobbing into her cloak. Sir Munroe was walking ahead, step by relentless step, leading them on. *Something is wrong here. Badly wrong.* How had she not noticed it before? *It's like I've been dreaming,* she thought, *only to wake into a living nightmare.* She reached to take hold of her godsteel dagger to feel the bracing effects of her blood-bond, but found the sheath was not at her hip. She frowned. *But I thought…*

She rushed over to Astrid, hidden beneath wool and fur. "Astrid, do you have the dagger with you?"

The girl's answer was to sob.

"*Astrid!*" The princess bent down and pulled the cloak away. "Do you have the dagger?"

Astrid shook her head, wiping her eyes. "I thought…I thought you had it," she sniffed.

"I don't." Panic shot through her like a quarrel from a crossbow, punching into her gut. "Who had it last? You or me?"

"I don't…" The girl screwed up her pinched face. "I don't remember, my lady…"

Neither do I. Amilia scrambled about to search for it but saw it nowhere among the barrels and casks. "Did we leave it overnight somewhere?" she asked. It made no sense to her. That dagger had been such a comfort to them both ever since they'd escaped Thalan. There was no way they would be so forgetful. One or the other, maybe at a stretch, but both? The chances were vanishingly small.

"I don't know, Amilia." Astrid was beginning to sob again, and loudly. "I don't know. I don't know what's happening…"

Amilia went back to Kegs. "We can't find our dagger."

The man blinked. "Oh? Have you checked everywhere, my lady?"

"Yes. I've checked everywhere. We don't have it, Kegs. It's lost!" She stamped back and jumped over the side of the wagon to land on the hard dirt track. Ralston and Big Ben were lumbering tirelessly up the road, but it took nothing but a brisk walk for her to outrun them. She paced determinedly up to Sir Munroe, keeping his usual thirty to fifty strides ahead. "Do you have our dagger?"

542

He turned his eyes to look down at her. They were as cold as the bitter wind, inexpressive. "No." He opened his cloak and showed her. "I have only *my* dagger, my lady. I know nothing of yours."

He's lying. "What did you do with it?"

"I don't know what you're talking about." He stopped on the road and turned directly to face her. "Calm," he said, in a quiet voice. "Calm now, princess." He touched her on the shoulder, smiled, and looked back up the road. "Walk with me, if you like. It's nicer, being on your feet."

Nicer. Yes, that was true. "Are you sure you don't know…"

"You don't need the dagger anymore. You never really did, Amilia."

I never really did. She walked alongside him down the middle of the road, moving at a languid pace, calm. She could hear the wagon rattling behind her, hear Kegs singing, hear the wind whistling past her ears. Strangely, Sir Munroe's armour did not seem to clank so much as she remembered. The cloak he wore, that dead man's cloak he'd taken off the outlaw looked slightly different too. She remembered it being more stained and scuffed than that, and there was one specific rip she recalled that didn't seem to be there at all. She only remembered it because it looked sort of like a smile, the way the fabric had torn and twisted up at the corners, and she'd found that amusing. But now it wasn't there.

Curious, she thought. *How very curious.*

She walked on.

The next thing she knew, it was dark, and she was waking from beneath a bundle of furs by the roadside. The winds had calmed, and the skies had opened to show a horned moon, silver and shining, sailing behind thin fingers of cloud. Her mouth was dry, her throat parched. She looked around for Astrid and the others, but there was no one else there.

I'm dreaming, she thought.

She stood up, confused. The road was just ahead of her, and beyond lay the rugged windswept land they'd been passing by that day. Behind her were some trees, which might have been a full forest, though in the dark of night she couldn't say. "Hello?" Her voice was afraid, weak and withdrawn. She tried to call louder. "Hello, is anyone there?"

She could not see the wagon on the road. She could not see Kegs or Astrid or Sir Munroe Moore. *I'm dreaming,* she thought again. *I must be.* But everything felt so feel. She stepped away from the trees and onto the road, looking left and right as it wended through the wilderness. "Hello," she called again. Her voice echoed out, *hello, hello, hello,* growing smaller with each repetition. "Hello, is anyone there?"

"I'm here, my lady."

She spun on her heels. The voice was right behind her. When she saw Sir Munroe Moore she stumbled back, tripping into the cold hard dirt. "You…"

"No," he said. "Not me."

She sucked a sharp breath. She didn't understand. *This is no dream.* "Where are the others?" she blurted. "What have you done with them!"

543

"They left. The girl...she convinced Kegs that we were going the wrong way, and so they left."

"You're lying." Her heart was pushing against her chest. "Tell me the truth, Munroe! What did you do to them? They would never have left me behind. Never!"

"They did, princess. I let them go freely. Neither of them have any part in this. But alas, you do."

"Part in what? What are you talking about!" She scrambled to her feet, wondering which would be the best way to run. The road was open, and the plains beyond as well, but the trees...*I could lose him in the trees.* But when she looked that way, she saw that Sir Munroe Moore was not alone. Shadows lurked among trunks and boles and beneath a canopy of heavy branches, the shapes of men, cloaked and cowled. Fear cut through her like a knife, savage and sharp. "Who...who..."

"Who are they?" Sir Munroe finished for her. He didn't give answer to that, but stepped closer, and let his cloak slip away from his shoulders. "Who am *I*, would be a better question."

Amilia Lukar watched in horror as the knight's armour dissolved into shadow and smoke, *breathing* off his body. The shroud that had cloaked him dispersed to reveal a small old man, bearded and grey, with a wonky wooden walking stick clutched in his spotted palm. He looked at her with eyes ancient and empty. "Come along now, princess," old Talbert said. "We still have a long way to go."

Amilia did not run. She did not scream. She just stood there, shivering, as the shadows closed in about her.

Beware the silver man, she thought. *One day, he's going to change.*

47

Jonik

A cold frosty wind was blowing over them as they huddled at the gate, waiting. *Twelve younglings,* Jonik thought. *Seven boys no older than sixteen. And five young men to lead them.*

That was the hope, anyway. Gerrin remained convinced a good many of the boys would scatter and go their own way, but there was nothing Jonik could do about that. *I've done my part here, letting them go.* Save going with them, there was little more he could do.

"You remember the way down?" he asked. "I know it's been a while since you left."

"I remember," Henrik said. The young man wore his black leathers and wools, overtopped with a wolf pelt for a cloak. It was a fine mantle, unearthed by Gerrin from the vaults here at the fort, and a gift to Henrik to send him on his way. *The Wolf, they will call him. The Alpha. Leader of the pack.*

"And you're sure about where you're going?"

"Sure enough for now. East, until we see the mountains dwindle. After that…we'll see."

Jonik nodded. They had spoken at length about the route the pack would take, considering each on its merits. As promised, Jonik had sent Harden up to talk to Henrik about the possible way through the Ironmoors, though the old sellsword had concurred with the young man's concerns. *Too dangerous,* was the agreed summation. If the group was caught - and that was likely on those open moors - it would be blood or chains and little in between. Instead, the plan was to head eastward through the wilds of North Tukor and, if their course should allow it, hop the Mercy over to Rasalan or even take ship to the Isles of Tellesh if they wanted to risk a longer voyage.

A haven for lost souls and vagrants, Jonik thought. *For wanderers looking to leave their old lives behind.* Getting there, though…

Hopper reached out and clapped Jonik on the shoulder. "We'll be fine, Jonik," the big man assured him. "You don't need to worry about us.

I'll take care of them, like I told you." Where Henrik had been given a wolf pelt, Hopper had one from a grizzly bear, a great thick shaggy thing that made the young Shadowknight look even larger. *The Bear*, Jonik thought. *The champion and protector.* "This'll help." Hopper gave his scabbard a shake, rattling the godsteel blade within. "We appreciate you arming us, Henrik and me. Be the difference between life and death down there."

Jonik had come to the same conclusion, having laboured on that decision for days. In the end he could see no option but to arm them, and arm them well, lest they be vulnerable to men and monsters both.

Harden gave them both a searching squint. "You use them wisely," he said, looking from man to man. "To defend, *never* attack. Don't turn outlaw, and don't turn sellsword. It's a harsh world, believe me. The tales will tell you there's adventure in the life of a sellsword, same as they will with some bandits too, but that's rare. Most are as miserable as I am, so you find another way, y'hear me? Search out somewhere safe to settle. Become herders, farmers, wed some crofter's daughter. *Sweat*, don't bleed. Work hard and honest and true, and you'll find your way."

Jonik nodded agreement. It was good counsel.

Henrik thought so too. "Thank you, Harden," he said. "We'll try our best."

"Our best would be better with a few more blades," Hopper put in, shrugging. "I appreciate you giving us this godsteel, like I say, but the others. Nils, Zac, Trent…" He glanced over at them, as they stood with the rest of the boys, barely more than boys themselves at eighteen and nineteen years old. "Why not arm them as well?"

"They are armed," Jonik said.

"Aye, with regular steel."

"Good castle-forged steel," Jonik came back, "and it'll have to do. If I arm you all with godsteel, where does it end?" He could not allow everyone to bear such a weapon, whether sword or dagger, axe or spear. Nils had been given a good strong battle-axe, Trent a longsword, and Zac a bastard sword, with all three of them armed with daggers as well.

None of them looked pleased about it, though. Even less so the older boys who hadn't been armed at all. *They resent me for it,* Jonik knew. That was fine, so long as they didn't turn their resentment on Henrik and Hopper instead.

"Here," Jonik said, withdrawing a pouch of coins from his cloak. He handed it to Henrik. "You can use that to buy food if you run out. And weapons as well, *when* you deem it right. I trust your judgement, Henrik. Arm the older boys once they have proven their loyalty, else they'll start to grow bitter. And be on your guard at all times. There are dangerous animals out there, and men as well, people who'll want to take advantage of you. When you stop for the night, always set a watch, and group your tents close together. There are some caves that will provide shelter on the way down, but be careful of whatever else might be using them." He looked over at the older boys again, heaped in their wools and furs. "It's important that one of you or Hopper are always awake. *Never* be asleep at the same time."

"I know, Jonik. We're well prepared."

"And watch the older boys closely," Jonik went on. "Endre has been looking at you sourly, and Jorn as well. They might try to take that godsteel I just gave you and strike out alone. Or worse. Keep an eye on them."

"I will." Henrik put a hand on Jonik's arm. "You don't need to worry. Let go, Jonik. We're not your burden to bear anymore."

Gerrin agreed with the sentiment. "You've done what you can, Jonik. We all have. Henrik knows what he's doing, Hopper too. There's nothing else to be said." He gave Hopper a nod. "Come help me with the gate."

The big man hobbled after the former Shadowmaster, as they went to lift the heavy wooden bars from the door. A light snow had started to fall, swirling down on the breeze in soft white flakes. Jonik pulled his cloak a little tighter as the wind knifed through his furs. He had a look over the boys once more, all warmly garbed with packs on their backs, filled with food and supplies for their trip. *Twelve younglings*, he thought again. *Seven boys no older than sixteen. And five young men to lead them.*

A few days ago, there were *thirteen* younglings, and *nine* boys no older than sixteen, before his mother's chosen three had been sent away to die. *Runar. Morris. Lucas*, he thought. Three names etched into his mind forever, never to be forgotten. *Runar. Morris, Lucas...*

Runar, Morris...

...Lucas...

Something coiled in Jonik's gut to even think of them, the last in particular. Runar had been six and ten, Morris three years younger, but Lucas only nine. Choosing from the younglings had proven so difficult that his mother had decided to do so at random. "The choice is too hard," she had said. "I just...they're all so young, Jonik. Choosing one above another...I don't think I can do it." So they'd put the names of the boys into a basket, and picked one out instead. Lucas's name had come up. *Nine*, Jonik thought. *A nine-year-old boy, who I sent away to die...*

He turned from the thought, driving it into the cold dark places in his mind to join the rest of his monstrous crimes, and looked toward the gate. He could see Cecilia there now, standing among the youngest of the children, giving them a final few words of wisdom and encouragement, telling them a final tale.

Some of the boys looked excited, others scared, others wary. A few had taken to Lady Cecilia as if she were their own mother, the younger children especially. Theo was the youngest, a boy of just five. He was the smallest too, and shy, with a mop of black hair and a mousy face. *And tears in his eyes,* Jonik saw. He could see them glistening as he stood there among the taller boys, staring up at her as she told her story. When Cecilia noticed, she broke right off and knelt to hug him, telling him everything would be all right, stroking a hand through his long black hair. Jonik watched in silence, lamenting a childhood stolen from him. And wondering...wondering... *maybe she wouldn't have been so bad a mother after all?*

The first wooden bar was heaved and set aside with a thud, the second following. A great gust of icy wind came blowing in as Gerrin and Hopper drove the gates open, pushing aside the snowdrifts that had accumulated outside. The boys turned and stared at a world they did not know. Most had never left the fort. *They were brought here as toddlers and babes, same as me. These walls are all they've known.*

Jonik could sense their trepidation. His mother could as well. "The bridge is only short," she said, to calm them. "You'll be across before you know it." To either side, the abyss fell into blackness, its bottom unseen. Beyond was the stony plateau, heaped with snow, with a wall of mountain ahead striking high into the leaden skies. To the left the path wended away beside the craggy cliffs, half lost to the snowy mists. "There. You see the path there," Cecilia was saying. "That's the start of your journey. And do you know where it will take you? Anywhere you want." She smiled for the younglings. "To a new, happy life."

The older boys didn't much care for her coddling. Already they were trundling off past her, wading through the snow with their furs and packs and scowls. *Not so much as a thank you or goodbye,* Jonik thought. Nils and Zacarias went with them, guiding the two garrons he had given them across the bridge, heavily laded with saddlebags and supplies. Trent followed, and soon some of the younglings were breaking from the herd and going as well, taking their first intrepid steps beyond the gate and out across the yawning chasm.

Jonik was reminded of the day his men had left. Borrus, Mooton, Torvyn, Sansullio and all the others. It felt like years ago, but what had it been? Months? Less, even. Time ran differently here, in the cold and the dark. *The days merge,* he thought, *one into another.* He felt a deep yearning to leave as well, to go with these boys, guide them, lead them, protect them. To find out what was happening in the world below. To learn of Emeric, and Jack, and what had befallen his friends. *And Shade,* he thought. *To ride Shade again. To gallop the plains and feel the wind in my hair. A warm spring wind. Not this one, icy cold.*

But he just stood there, watching, as the boys began their march. He could not go, he could not leave. And his friends were dead, of that he was sure.

"I'll see you again, Jonik," Henrik said, in final parting. "I'm not going to forget this, what you've done for us. What you've all done for us." He reached out and took Jonik by the forearm, shaking, then did the same with Harden.

"You be good, lad," the old sellsword told him. "And remember… there's a war going on down there. Stay out of it. No sense in you getting involved."

No, but the war might find them, one way or another. Jonik did not voice that thought. He only smiled a weak smile, as Henrik turned and stepped away.

The gates were shut and barred soon after, Henrik and Hopper leading the last of the younglings across the bridge. Gerrin did the honours, calling for Harden to help. Cecilia watched for a moment as Theo and the little

548

boys were ushered out by Hopper, smiling as the children turned back. "You be brave," she said. "Hopper and Henrik will protect you. Be strong for them. Be good for them, OK?"

Once the men and boys were lost from sight, and the gates barred shut, Cecilia turned and crossed the yard to join Jonik. She blinked away the mist from her eyes as she approached. "That was harder than I thought," she said, sniffing. "Little Theo…he was so upset."

"I saw."

She glanced over her shoulder. "Do you think they'll be all right?"

"Does it matter what I think? Their fate is in their own hands now. We've done our part."

"A *good* part, Jonik. This is a good thing, to set them free. It helps, don't you think? To…balance the scales."

The boys, he thought. *The chosen three. Runar, Morris, Lucas.* "It's a start," he said. *A start with no finish. A journey with no end. My soul is stained forever.* He said none of that.

Cecilia Blakewood nodded. "And now?" He saw her eyes flash on the Nightblade, resting and whispering and hissing at his hip. "Might you…set it aside now, Jonik?"

"I already have," he told her in a blunt voice. He could not help it. Mention the Nightblade, even look at it, glance at it, and something stirred within him, something angry and resentful and… "I do not wear it all the time anymore. I am *trying*, Cecilia. It isn't as easy as you think."

"I know that. I do. Hamlyn told me himself how strongly the blades want to remain apart. Once, no. A broken heart only wants to be remade, he said. At first they only wanted to come together again, yearned for it, but over time…"

"I know, you told me." She had spoken of her interaction with the Steward days ago. How old and rotted he was, even more so than Fhanrir, how he'd told her that only Jonik himself could give up the Nightblade. That he would not try to take it, or interfere with a fate he did not know. *Their roadmap is finished,* Jonik thought. *Now they just observe.* It had made him feel less wary of them, yet a certain disquiet still remained. "What are you trying to say?" he asked the woman. "That I leave the Nightblade here, hand it over willingly? Yes, I know that. And I will. I leave it often in my bedchamber. I don't carry it with me unless I feel there is a need…"

"Like now? You're wearing it now, Jonik."

"Because of the men. Because we were going to arm them. Because we were going to open the gates and who knows what might have come rushing through." He could feel his hackles rising. "I only wear it when I feel I must protect us. But already I can feel its grip on me weakening. I'm stronger than you think, Cecilia. I am my father's son."

"But not your mother's? Do you see me as weak, Jonik?"

"That isn't what I meant." His eyes bored into her. "Have you borne a Blade of Vandar before? Have you held one for twenty years, and then given it up? My father has. You'll tell me it wasn't wartime then. You'll tell me he had lost his post as First Blade and had no choice. I don't care about that. I saw him when he was at his lowest. I saw the grip the Sword of Varinar had on him, and yet even after all that, even…even after *I killed his eldest son*, he gave it up. He was crippled, bereaved, lost. At his weakest moment, he found strength. Why can't I do the same?"

"You can," she told him. "I know you can, Jonik."

"And you're wondering why not now?" he challenged. "Why not *here*, in this snowy square? Right here where we burned Big Mo. Where Borrus left me, and Emeric, and everyone. Why not right here?" He snorted loudly and then threw his cloak open on a whim. "Fine, have it your way." His fingers worked quickly to unbuckle his belt, then he threw it hard to the ground. The Nightblade rattled in its plain black scabbard, giving out a deep thrumming *thud* as it cracked against the stone. Whispers and shrieks filled his mind and grasping black fingers curled up at him in appeal. *No*, he thought. *No, I'll not help you. We're done.* Across the square, Harden and Gerrin were watching in silence. "Is this what you wanted?" Jonik called out to them. "A shard of Vandar's Heart, buried in snow?"

He turned back to his mother, breathing hard. There was a look on her face. "Don't say it," he growled.

She frowned. "What?"

"That you're proud of me. I can see it on your lips. I need no such comfort from you."

"I am proud of you. But not for this." She looked at the gate. "For that. For what you've done for those boys. *That* was your calling, and what role did the Nightblade play in it? That was *all* you, Jonik. It isn't that blade that defines you anymore. All it does is hold you back."

No longer, Jonik thought, storming away from it, needing to be gone. His feet felt heavy, the air thick, as though there were hidden fetters and lengths of chain tethering him to its boundless weight. He wanted to turn, wanted to run back to it, grasp it, feel its power, *disappear*, but he didn't.

You're stronger than that, he told himself. *Be like your father. Be Jaycob, the noble knight, who might have been Amron's Daecar's son in another life. Turn from the night. Turn from the dark. Turn from the Ghost…it's haunted you enough.*

He found sanctuary in the kitchens, washing, cutting, cooking, but for who? Before he knew it he'd made a stew fit for a score, a great pot on the boil with leeks and onions and chewy bits of pork, steam rising from the cauldron in thick fragrant waves.

Harden was the first to enter, drawn by the smell. He frowned at the stewpot. "We expecting company, Jonik?"

"Not now, Harden."

"Funny thing. There's a strange black blade lying out there in the yard, gathering snow. You know anything about that?"

"I said not now."

The old sellsword didn't heed his warning. He stepped in, took up a dinted pewter spoon, and had a taste of the stew. "Needs more salt, I'd say. And a bit more time to thicken." He found a jar, took a big pinch, and sprinkled salt into the broth, then began stirring.

Jonik said nothing, did nothing. He only stood there, his right fist opening and closing, glancing down at his hip. He could hear the Nightblade outside, calling for him, pleading like some lost child desperate for his mother. *I'm cold. I'm alone. I'm afraid. Help me, help me...*

He was halfway to the door when Gerrin barged in. "What are we having, then? Stew again?" He smacked his lips, and his old seamed eyes turned to Jonik as though only just spotting him. "Oh. Heading somewhere, are you?"

"There's a funny old blade outside, Gerrin," Harden called over from the pot. "Maybe he wants to take a look at it."

Jonik glared at the gloomy old sellsword. "You would try to make light of this? You would mock me, Harden?"

"Yes." Harden put down the stirring spoon and turned from the fire. "Mockery is like an axe. It can crash through a man's shield and show who they are beneath. We're testing you, Jonik. We want this to be real."

"Real? Meaning?"

"We fear we'll only wake up tomorrow to find the Nightblade back at your hip," Gerrin said.

"Or earlier," added Harden.

"You've set it aside before, Jonik," Gerrin went on. "But always it finds its way back to you. We want this to be done. For *good*, this time. We want you back, the way you were."

His ire was rising again. *Why can't they just leave me alone?* "It takes time," he grunted at them. "The bond takes time to build, and it takes time to break. Mocking me isn't going to help. It's just..."

"Making you angry. Yes, we can tell." Gerrin paused, softened his voice. "I could move it for you, if you like. Somewhere you won't find it. Just say the word, and..."

"No." It was the only word that came to mind. "I don't want you to interfere. Or touch it. We cannot know how it will affect you."

Gerrin frowned at him. "You think I want to keep it?"

"No. I don't...I don't know, Gerrin. Just leave it there. If you take it... hide it from me...I don't know what..." *I might kill you*, he thought. *Fly into a rage and kill you all.* It terrified him that he even thought that. He swallowed, knowing they knew. "Just...leave it. And stop with the japing, Harden. You're trying to help, I know. But it's not what I need right now."

He turned and put his shoulder into the door, stepping back out into the yard. The snow was falling heavily now, covering the stone in a soft white blanket. He could see the Nightblade where he'd left it, already half-covered. He slowed, stopped, stared at it, feeling a desperate urge to hitch it back to his hip. *No, I can't. I can't or I'll never let it go.*

He wrenched his eyes away, continuing across the yard in a hard stamping step, feet crunching, breath misting. When he reached the round-tower library, he pushed in through the doors to find his mother at the table, reading by candlelight. The winds blew in behind him, stirring the flames and fluttering the pages of the books and scrolls laid out before her. Jonik slammed the door shut. The air settled. "What would you have of me?" he demanded.

She turned to him with a frown. "Have of you?"

"Now. After all this. Hamlyn's got his strength back. He's spending time with the heir. Soon enough he'll do the transference. And after that…after that maybe we can go."

She put aside her quill pen. "I'm not hearing a question there, Jonik. Are you asking me what you should do when you're allowed to leave?"

"Yes, that's what I'm asking you. You say the Nightblade doesn't define me. Fine. Then what does? Who am I without it? *What* am I, but another bastard boy, without land or title or worth."

"A warrior. A leader. My…"

"No," he cut in. "I'm not your son. You birthed me, but that's it. I'm not your son, Cecilia." He breathed out; a hard hot blast of air. The wind was picking up outside, rattling at the hinges. Smoke swirled up into the rafters where the candlelight gave out to gloom. The shelves loomed like cliffs all around them, stacked high with books and scrolls and maps and dust. "I'm sorry," he said, after a few moments. "You've helped me, and done everything I wanted. But…"

"You don't need to explain. I never expected you to love me. I only…I only want to help. I want you to be happy."

"I'm never going to be happy, Cecilia. Happiness has never mattered to me."

"Then what does?"

"Purpose. Duty. *Identity*," he said at once. "That's what I was raised on. The next contract. The next task. I was an apprentice, and then a Shadowknight. *We keep the world in balance. We help steer its course.* That's what they always taught us, and they were right all along. But now what? They've hammered me into a sword and now there's no one left to swing me."

"Then swing yourself. Choose your own course, as you've been doing since you left."

"I did. It led me back here." He snorted to himself. *No, that was just fate and lies*, he thought. *A path already seen. I had no true choice in that.* "I've finished my last contract," he said. "I've done what I had to do. But now….what do I do *now*?"

"Help. Lend your aid to the grander purpose." She pointed to the door. "You know what's happening here, you alone among all of the bearers. Go to them, find them, tell them what must be done. Help them understand that they have to give up their blades. If Tyrith is to unite the Heart…"

Jonik cut her off with bitter laughter. "And you think they'd listen to me? My father, who I crippled. My brother, who I…"

"This is bigger than that," she came in. "When they learn the true scale of what has been happening, they'll understand."

"And when they find out that I let a nine-year-old boy be slaughtered like a pig, what then?"

"They'll understand that too," Cecilia told him, quite plainly. "But only if you tell them. There is no reason why that ever needs to come up. There's no reason for anyone to know."

"You'd lie?"

"I'd choose not to tell them. There's a difference between telling a lie and withholding information. This has been *our* duty to bear. No one else has any right to know. *No one*."

Her voice was hard, bitter-edged. She stood from her chair and stepped over to a trestle table near the door, set beneath a frosted window that looked out over the ward. What wine and whiskey they had found in the fort had been stashed there, for when they came together to talk or gather for their councils. *The Shadow Council*, they might have called it. *Just four baseborn bastards,* Jonik thought, *discussing the fate of the world.*

"Wine?" Cecilia poured two cups without waiting for an answer, then returned to her chair. She placed one down across the table, then took a sip from her own. "Sit, Jonik. You've had a long hard day and need to try to relax."

"You don't know me very well if you think that will happen." All the same, he took her advice and sat, stiff-backed in the chair opposite her. His eyes ran over the books and scrolls laid out on the table. "You're wasting your time with that, you know. You're never going to figure it out."

"It keeps me busy," was her response. The books were old language tomes, the scrolls the same, her quest to translate the few things she recalled from the last page in the Book of Contracts. She had been spending her evenings here ever since that night, trying to unravel the riddle, though her efforts thus far had yielded little, Jonik knew. She tapped a finger on an open page of one of the books. "There's a word here that I remember from the last contract. *Thrun.* It was repeated several times that I can recall. Do you know what it means?"

"You know I don't."

"*Blood*," she said. "The last contract mentioned blood several times, Jonik." She raised her brow. "Do you think that should concern us?"

He shrugged. "One word doesn't mean much. You said you thought the last contract was mine. The blood might refer to my father's. He bled a lot that night, in his tent."

She nodded, musing. "There's another word I've found as well. It was mentioned twice, that I saw. *Hrunthen.* It means 'royal'. And on both occasions it was in the same sentence as *thrun*."

Jonik frowned. "Royal blood?" He thought about that. Out of context, a few words meant little. "My father is of royal blood. So was Aleron…"

"So are you," she said.

He looked at her.

"And me." She gave a wry smile, though he could see the shadow of concern behind her eyes. "It's nothing, I'm sure. I found other words that were repeated at least once. One of them translates to 'divine', another to 'son'. And all of this from the first couple of paragraphs, which I focussed on trying to commit to memory. I only wish I had done better. Only these few words seem to have stuck."

"Divine royal blood," Jonik said. "Or…son of divine royal blood?" He reached to take a drink of wine, suddenly needing it. "That wouldn't make sense if it was my contract. There's some royal blood in my family, but no divine blood."

"Well, that depends on what one means by divine. Any Bladeborn blood could be considered in part divine, with Varin as the source. The same goes for Seaborn, Forgeborn, and so on. All derive from the demigods."

"Then 'son of divine royal blood' could have referred to Aleron?" Jonik suggested. "If that was the translation."

"Yes, it's possible. I'm half-tempted to have another look, though I doubt that would go down well. Hamlyn was quite explicit that I shouldn't be so curious. He asked me what killed the cat. A poorly veiled threat, delivered quite offhand." She sipped her wine. "There's something more sinister about a threat like that, I've always thought. The less direct ones are often the more believable."

"You think he'd kill you? For snooping?"

She chuckled. "No. When Hamlyn said he would not interfere, I believed him. He may be cold and detached sometimes, but we have to remember who he was, and the things he did. Hamlyn the Humble was a great man, a brilliant mage, widely revered. He will only observe from now."

"And Fhanrir? The other three? Do you trust them as well?"

Her delay was telling. "There is no reason not to," she said, as though to hide her concerns from him. "This business…" She gestured to the notes and books and scrolls. "It's just to distract me, really, help pass the time, as I say. Tyrith is convinced that we are all safe. The Hammer of Tukor shows him, he says. And I trust him in that. We have nothing to fear from the mages."

Is that the truth, Cecilia? Jonik wanted to ask. *Or are you saying this all to protect me?* She was worried he'd retrieve the Nightblade if he sensed they were in danger, that was evident. It angered him how weak they all thought he was. Lip drawn back in indignation, he said, "I'm not going to take it up again, so you can put that worry aside. And speak plainly. Do you trust these mages or not?"

A smile lifted and left her lips, awkward. "Tyrith…"

"Is a boy in a man's skin. He trusted Janilah, you told me, even as he kept him prisoner up at that forge, isolated and alone." A monstrous crime, it was, to treat the heir of Ilith as such. One of many his grandfather committed. "Tyrith cannot be relied upon to judge a man's fidelity. But you…" He eyed her sternly. "Tell me honestly, Mother. Do you think Fhanrir might act against us, in some way?"

She smiled, a flash of a thing, quickly withdrew. "Um…well, I don't know for sure, Jonik. I do wonder if there's one last…last contract." She tapped her notes, her smile returning, broadening on her lips. Rising like the sun, bright and true. "But it's all conjecture, as I say. I hope it's nothing. Most likely…it's nothing." She turned her eyes aside, trying to pull her smile down, failing.

Jonik knew why. "It just slipped out," he said. "I don't want you to think…"

"No, of course not. Of course." She picked up her cup, sipping, hiding behind the rim. "It's just…to hear you even say it. *Mother*." She smiled again. "You cannot know what that means to me."

He nodded. He'd said it and would not take it back. *I'll not rob her of this moment. She's earned it, for what she's done.* "You've been helpful, since coming here. With the boys. And Henrik, Hopper, the others. They all liked you, Cecilia. And earlier…with Theo. I suppose I saw what you might have been. A good mother. If given the chance, perhaps you'd have been a good mother." He had said too much already, he realised at once, and so stopped, then stood from his chair. "I should go. It's my turn on watch."

"Oh. You're leaving?"

"Someone needs to watch the gate." He turned and made his way to the door, stopping as he gripped the handle. It rattled in his grasp, the winds fighting to batter their way in. "Has he said when it's going to happen? Hamlyn. The transference."

She shook her head. "Not yet. I get the impression that they're still waiting for something." She looked at the books and papers spread out on the table before her. "But…soon, I'm sure. And maybe then…once it's done…" She trailed off, not finishing her thought.

Jonik felt compelled to hear it. "What? Tell me."

"Well…I wondered if…if I might come with you, when you leave? I could help, Jonik. I don't know how, but…"

He shook his head. "Tyrith will need you."

"He may," she agreed. "Or may not. After the transference he may not be Tyrith at all."

"Even so. I don't think…"

"Say no more." She smiled, then chuckled. "I know. I'd only slow you down, and get in the way. I'm better suited here, or returning to Ilithor. I'm sure Raynald misses me."

He nodded, saying nothing. The wind rattled at the door, as though knowing they needed the distraction. Eventually, he turned the handle. "We can talk more later." His eyes flashed over the books and scrolls. "Let me know if you find anything else."

It was still snowing heavily outside, the coverlets atop the stone turning to thicker quilts, piling here and there. The Nightblade was completely covered now, whimpering and whispering feebly in its icy prison. Jonik ignored it, feeling stronger, marching right past and up the stairs to the top of the wall. The air was thick with snow and mist, though through the squalls he could see the distant sight of movement down the passes. For a moment his heart lifted at the thought that it was Jack and Emeric and the others returning, but he quickly realised it was the pack.

Twelve younglings. Seven boys no older than sixteen. And five young men to lead them. If only there were six, a part of Jonik thought. *If only I'd gone as well.*

But another part of him didn't want that. Another part knew his mother was right. *I cannot let this define me. This place. That blade. I can still do good without it. Or else what did they all die for? Runar, Morris, Lucas...*

He stared across the mountains, fuelled by a new sense of purpose. Once or twice Jonik turned back to pass his eyes over the yard, looking to the spot where the Nightblade lay hidden beneath the snow. But even now he could feel the fetters of fate loosening, the chains being drawn away, rattling and ringing on the stone. His ankles were free now of their iron, to take him where he pleased. *I can choose my own way,* he thought, in a moment of hope, sweet as birdsong. *I can still make a difference, as my mother says...*

He took a grip of the godsteel dagger he kept at his hip, feeling the warmth of his blood-bond flow through him. The Body of Vandar, but not his Heart. *It's all I need,* he told himself. *It's enough and always was.*

And standing there on the precipice, he swore a godsteel oath. By the lives of the boys who'd died here, he'd bear the Nightblade no more. No matter what happened, he, would not take it back up.

48

Talasha

They knelt before his throne, heads bowed in meek obedience. Shadows filled the room. And tension, thick as mud.

"Amron Daecar," said the Father of Fire, in his rolling resounding whisper. "This is the man we seek?"

Sotel Dar put his hands together, wincing at the pain in his knees. When the old scholar spoke his voice echoed softly through the chamber, dimly lit by dragon-claw sconces bearing torches along the walls, their fires burning low and sombre. "The north has no one greater than he, my lord. I have told you of this man. He was the one to cripple King Dulian when he was but a prince. And slay his dragon Vallath, who was the greatest of the age. Many have compared him to Varin for this triumph."

A chuckle drifted through the Fire Father's pale lips. "No man living can match Varin. I fought him many times over many centuries. He was a force of monumental power, but that power now has dwindled. This Amron Daecar is a shadow of him, nothing more."

"As you say, my lord." Sotel Dar went silent.

Lord Marak cleared his throat. "He is the best they have, master. The prophecy speaks of an heir of Varin, yet our efforts to unearth this figure have all failed. The scion cannot find him. Our books and scrolls make no mention of any sons by King Lorin's loins." He turned his eyes to Sa'har Nakaan, genuflecting beside him. "We have come to believe that this heir may be figurative, not literal. The Vandarians select their First Blade through ritual fighting. It is power they follow, and strength. They follow Amron Daecar."

A white finger rubbed at one of Tagathon's teeth; the black skull throne in which the Eternal sat. "You slew his father, Ulrik. Is that true?"

The dragonlord nodded his broad stubbled jaw. "At the Battle of Burning Rock, or so they call it. Gideon Daecar fell defending his king, Storris Reynar. He was the First Blade of Vandar at the time. His son assumed the role at his death."

The Fire Father was bathed in shadow, though Talasha could see his mouth, and his eyes, like twin stars burning in a lightless sky, red as blood. His lips moved into a reminiscing smile, thinking of a time long since passed.

"I remember when Varin first raised his order of knights. *The Knights of Varin.* We were all so vain, back then. Naming our cities after ourselves, aggrandising the things we had achieved." He made a soft dismissive sound. "But what were these achievements, exactly? Peace? Plenty? Kingdoms and cultures raised in our image? Was this truly the will of Agarath? I did not see then what I see so clearly now. I let my own ego drive me. I invited Ilith to help me build this very city, this very palace, to raise it up in my honour. I let Varin and Thala convince me to set aside our quarrels and bring forth a new age of peace, and order. I went against the will of my master and in my arrogance, my hubris, the All-Father saw fit to humble me."

He paused in reflection, and a silence filled the room. For long moments it endured. Not a sound stirred; even the flames seemed to settle and grow still. Then the Fire Father opened his lips and went on. "When Varin defeated me at the Ashmount, I was left a broken man. This was punishment, for my disloyalty, my lack of faith. Agarath was displeased with me, wroth at what I had become. Peace. Plenty. Kingdoms. Cultures. *This* was never his will."

He turned his eyes to the Bondstone, clasped atop his tall black staff, and a sorrow filled his eyes. "After my defeat, I sought sanctuary deep in the mountain, drawn to the warm embrace of Agarath's Breath. There I slept, with Drulgar at my back, festering upon my failures as the millennia passed me by. And when at last I did awaken, it was to a cold and bitter truth. That this world that was raised in my absence is not real. It is a mirage, a deception, a bright veneer that blinds us to its true nature. One of war, not peace, of chaos, not law, a world where the weak wither and the strong rise, where the battle for survival is the sweetest gift of all. *This* is the world that Agarath created. And by his will, we shall see it restored."

He turned his red eyes upon them, waiting, and Talasha bowed her head low, murmuring, "Yes, Father," with all the rest. Many had gathered within the hall, all of them kneeling and bowing and humming their words of prayer. Some were the Fireborn the Father and Founder had bonded to his dragons. *The nameless ones have been given names*, the princess thought. *The wild dragons are wild no more.* But others were here too: fervent followers of high esteem and birth; religious figures; men of power and land and influence; lords and dragonknights who would lead the Fire Father's hordes into battle. Some had been at the great fortress of the Trident, Talasha had heard, only to be flown here on dragonback for this council. Others had come from the east, from the great army that had taken Dragon's Bane. *He gathers anyone with influence to his side. He brings them here to ensnare them, and bind them to his will.*

The princess kept such thoughts to herself. *I am alone,* she thought. *I am an island of sanity in a sea of slaves*. For long weeks she had worked to rid

558

herself of such tethers, grounding herself through Neyruu and Cevi, through the warning voice of Kin'rar Kroll that echoed inside the dragon, from the memories of her sweet captain that continued to awaken within her. If ever she felt herself drawn beneath the Fire Father's wing, they would pull her back, yet the freer she felt, the more frightened she grew.

They cannot see it, she fretted silently, feeling the press of thralls at her back. *They bow to him without question or complaint.* A part of her wished she could just smile and nod like the rest of them. *Would it not be better to be a sheep under the guidance of a shepherd?* she wondered. Right now she was out there alone, a lost little lamb bleating in the hills...and there were lions about.

She quietened her thoughts as the Fire Father spoke. "Who will deal with this Amron Daecar?" he asked.

At once the hall broke out in voices. "I will," called a man from the back.

"Me," said another voice she did not know.

A woman with the accents of Loriath proclaimed, "I am descended of the Skylady herself, Misha the Magnificent. Let it be me, Fire Father. Greatness runs in my blood."

"*Fire* runs in mine," boomed another man, off to one side. Talasha recognised the voice of the brawny Fireborn rider Axallio Axar, who'd been one of her brother Tavash's loyal men. "These riders are newly saddled, all but a few," he proclaimed. "I have ridden upon the scales of Angaralax for a dozen years. Give me this great honour, Lord Father. I will slay the Crippler where all others have failed."

Talasha heard a laugh almost directly behind her. She knew that arrogant laugh. *Vargo Ven.* "You're no dragonlord, Axar," the man dismissed. "This honour should go to one such. *I* will do it."

"No, you will not." Lord Ulrik Marak stood, and he alone among the host. His dark maroon robes fell from his fame, making him look like some sort of holy man or priest and not the great warrior he was. *Soon,* the princess knew. *He will marshall the Father's armies soon.* He fell into a bow, bending his thick muscular back, then stood again and said, "*I* will see it done, Father. Lord Ven must return to the east to lead your forces there, and Axallio will only fall, and Angaralax with him, should he be drawn to duel Daecar. Zyndrar was defeated by him, and Vallath before that, two dragons of much greater renown. But the Crippler has not faced *me*. As I killed the father, so I will kill the son."

A murmuring broke out, voices humming in the gloom. A smile creased the Fire Father's lips. "You would need Garlath for that, Ulrik. You would need the Fireblade. And the Body of Karagar, this too. These three I have claimed. You would have me give them up?"

"My lord..."

Eldur raised a hand to silence him. "You shall have them," he said. "I have no need of Garlath now, and nor would I wear such armour. I would think Karagar's *father* might take offence. That would be...unwise."

Drulgar, Talasha thought, a shiver moving up her spine. *Even the Fire Father fears him.*

Lord Marak bowed his head. "My lord. I will not let you down."

The shadows shifted across the Fire Father's face, the soft glowing light of the Bondstone throbbing and swirling within the orb. His red eyes moved slowly, scanning the host laid out before him. They passed over Talasha and met the man kneeling at her side. "Sa'har. You have something to say?"

Talasha tensed, as Sa'har Nakaan looked up. She could hear the simmering displeasure in the Father's voice. The skymaster had grown withered and withdrawn of late, the hairs of his long chin beard turning white and brittle, his hollow cheeks sinking further into his skull. There was a haunted look in his once-wise eyes. *He is half a man*, Talasha thought. *Half his soul died with Ezukar.* "No, my lord. Nothing," he croaked.

The red eyes stared at him, pupil-less, unblinking. "You have your doubts, Sa'har. You do not believe in the will of Agarath. Or mine."

"I do, my lord," the skymaster said nervously. "I would never dare question your word."

"Question? There are many ways to question, child. With our words, with our actions, with our *eyes*. I have seen your eyes, Sa'har. I see what lies beyond them. You portray a lack of faith."

Talasha's heart was thumping. *Keep your eyes down*, she told herself. *Keep them down or he will see…*

"I…I have struggled, I will admit, my lord. Since…since Ezukar's death. That is all it is, Lord Father. I find myself unable to escape this well of grief. I…I…"

"I have given you another dragon, Sa'har. Is that not enough?"

Sa'har Nakaan drew a shaky breath as he cowered beneath the Father's gaze. Talasha wanted to reach across to take his hand, to squeeze and comfort him, but dare not. Of late Eldur had grown increasingly unstable, and the city below had followed. *Burnings*, she thought. *There are mass burnings in the squares.* She could see them from her balcony every night, smell the dry acrid reek of charred flesh as it wafted up from below. When she flew down in secret to visit with Cevi, the handmaid would tell her that those who did not yield to the Fire Father's will were being given to the Eternal Flame.

"His acolytes go about the streets, demanding that people speak words of faith," the girl had said. "Those who do not are dragged to the squares to be burned by the High Priest and the other holy men. They call it a gift, my lady, but…I am not sure."

Talasha was. She was sure it was nothing but a lie. "Stay hidden, Cevi," was all she said. "And if they come, tell them whatever they want to hear. Do you understand?"

"Yes, my lady." She had clutched the princess's hands. "I'm frightened."

So am I, Talasha thought. She kissed the girl on the cheek. "I'll be back when I can."

Sa'har Nakaan gave answer to the Fire Father's challenge. "My lord…

forgive me, but…another dragon…it is not the same. Ezukar…we were bonded for many years. The ritual process, at the Nest. The selection and the choosing and the pairing. We were made for one another. It was harmony, true harmony. Bagrahar is…he is not Ezukar, my lord."

"*True* harmony?" Eldur the Eternal's voice hardened; a crack of thunder through the room. His fingers were thin and knobbly, chalk-white, clutching at his black wood staff. He gave it a tap on the ground, and the Bondstone swirled in its chaos of shifting colours. It seemed angry, somehow, restless. "Are you suggesting the newly bonded riders are somehow lesser, Sa'har? That my choice of pairings is wrong?"

"No, my lord. *Never*. I would never. I only mean…" His voice was thin and filled with fear. "Ezukar…he flew from the Wings of his own accord. He chose me, my lord, and I him. We were joined in the Bondsquare by a ritual that had lasted for thousands of years. He was my…my soul-mate, Father. There can be only one. Bagrahar is…"

"Not good enough for you?" Lord Eldur asked him.

"No, my lord. That is not what I meant. I only mean to say…"

"I know what you mean to say, Sa'har. And I know that you blame me, for Ezukar's death."

The skymaster's eyes blazed wide with fear. "No! My lord, no, I place no blame upon you…"

"You do. For taking Ezukar from you. For sending him to kill the boy. You blame me for his death, Sa'har."

The skymaster was breathing hard now. *He fears he will be killed right here,* Talasha knew. It took everything she had not to reach out to him, or stand and speak up. *No, you cannot. He will only kill you too.* "My lord, Ezukar was yours…yours to command as you saw fit. I do not blame you, I promise it. Never."

"Who, then? The boy?"

"I…no, I…" Nakaan panted, struggling to find the right words. "I am not a man of vengeance, Lord Father. Ezukar sought out the boy, and…"

"Was sent to the Eternal Flame. Was destroyed. By this boy."

"Father? He was not just a boy. He bears a shard of Vandar's Heart. The winds…"

"Ezukar failed," Lord Eldur interrupted. "He failed. And Zyndrar failed. And Hagralax failed. How many failures must I tolerate? The Children of Agarath are dying and their lord master is growing displeased. I have sensed Drulgar's growing rage. He feels their every death, as does their father." The Soul of Agarath roiled at his words. Talasha could feel the wrath pulsing out of it, and from Eldur as well, as he sat embraced in Tagathon's jaws. "Tell me, my children…have we underestimated Vandar's hosts?"

His question was not answered at once. That seemed to displease him yet more. Then a voice from behind the princess said, "The Blades of Vandar are powerful, my lord." It was Vargo Ven again. "With just one of them, even our strongest dragons are at risk. I have fought this boy cham-

561

pion myself. I have seen this Windblade in use. Alone, it is a formidable weapon. But if they should be combined…"

"The Heart *cannot* be remade, Vargo. It *cannot*." The burning red lights of Eldur's eyes shone out bright with anger. *And fear,* Talasha thought. *He fears the power of the Steel God's heart, as he fears the man who might wield it.*

"Yes, Lord Father," said Ven. "We will not let that happen."

A murmur of assent rippled through the hall, as though to appease the tyrant who sat before them. *A tyrant,* Talasha thought, *and a puppet. We have to get the Bondstone away from him, somehow. We must free him from its grip…*

If only she had someone to tell that to. She'd tried with Marak and he'd called her out for treason, and Sa'har…well, he was much too lost and afraid to take action. Vargo Ven would take pleasure in dragging her before the Fire Father should she say anything to him, she didn't doubt, and Sotel Dar was rarely alone. *The Father keeps him at his side, for counsel,* she knew. He seemed to hold the old scholar in high esteem for his deep insightful knowledge of the long history he had missed.

The scholar spoke up now. "If I may, my lord." At Eldur's nod, the old man went on. "It is said the Five Shards are sentient. Each has a will of its own, a will that grows stronger during war. These shards do not want to be cast back together. Even now, they will work against the will of their bearers to achieve this. Blood they may seek, that of the Children of Agarath in particular, but…"

"The blades are just as dangerous apart," another voice interrupted. This one Talasha knew as belonging to Lord Lharador, the keg-chested Commander of the Trident and Lord Master of the Western Seas. He was of scant Fireborn blood, and no dragonrider, but at sea he had no equal. As with many of the other captains and commanders, he'd been flown from the Trident where their armada was at anchor, summoned to this session of council. *And put in thrall to this madness,* the princess thought. "Amron Daecar is at King's Point, we have heard," the sea lord said in his sonorous voice, the sort that was accustomed to bellowing orders over the roar of wind and wave. "His banners have been seen by our scouts, billowing above the city walls, and the *Sword that Struck Drulgar* is there as well, we believe. We should attack now, while we can. Kill the bearers and scatter the blades."

"And lose more dragons?" asked the High Priest of Fire. He was near Talasha, in a place of prominence close to the throne, wreathed in his robes of flaming colours. "You heard the Fire Father, Lord Lharador. Ezukar, Zyndrar. Hagralax. These were some of our most fearsome dragons, and all were killed, by wind and frost and mist."

"Wind and frost," corrected Lord Marak. "The boy prince slew Ezukar and his father Zyndrar, bearing the blades once borne by the children of Varin. We cannot know for certain how Hagralax died."

"We know, Lord Marak," the High Priest came back. He was a small man with a strong voice, used to shouting out his sermons. *And burning innocents,* Talasha thought, squeezing a fist. His hair was long and dyed in hues of red and orange to match his robes, the same as the long beard that twisted from his chin in a great flaming prong, oiled and gleaming.

"Hagralax was sent in pursuit of the Master of Mists. The Warrior King. Who else could have slain him?"

"Many," Marak said. "Dragons are flesh and blood, and can be killed by simple steel. Never think otherwise."

The High Priest laughed, his voice ringing through the gloomy black hall. "Simple steel? I think not. Only the flesh of the dark god Vandar can pierce a dragon's hide."

Marak had never liked this High Priest, the princess knew, no more than he had the ones who came before. He gave him a dismissive look and said, "You are not a soldier, my lord, but a man of faith. Faith cannot be relied upon in war. War requires warriors. Men who understand that even an arrow, well-aimed, can pierce a dragon's eye and strike his brain. The same can be said of quarrels and spears, of which the Tukorans in particular are well trained. Yes, simple steel can kill a dragon."

"A small one. I'll grant you that. But these dragons we discuss were not slain by such. *Vandar* slew them, in his dark fury. His heart is a dreaded thing and must be feared. These Five Shards…"

"Are not of your concern," Marak told him. He turned to face Eldur. "My lord, Lord Lharador is right. We must lay assault to King's Point while the weather holds. The storms that have ravaged the Red Sea have calmed, but they will stir again soon. And our allies are growing restless. Already some of the Lumaran ships have raised their sails and gone south. There are rumours spreading among the ranks. Of our holy duty, of the will of Agarath. These southerners are not our kith and kin. They do not understand."

Talasha felt something stir in her heart to hear that. *His power does not extend to them. He cannot bend others to his will.* As soon as Empress Valura learned of this folly she would have no choice but to switch allegiance and launch her power upon Agarath instead. *Together with the northerners, they'll overwhelm us,* she thought. *They'll put this madness to an end.*

She could but hope. In truth she did not know if it would matter, not once Drulgar stretched his mighty wings and darkened the world beneath his shadow. *The Sword that Struck Drulgar,* she thought. In the north they called it the Sword of Varinar, the blade that Varin bore when he defeated the Dread in single combat. Ever since then the blade had been feared, and more than the other four shards. Some even said that Drulgar himself feared it, that he would tremble at the sight of it, glinting golden in the sun. But Talasha didn't think so. *It was the bearer, not the blade, he feared,* she knew. *And Varin is long dead.*

The Fire Father finally spoke. "The will of Agarath cannot be challenged by that of lesser gods. Lumara was always so, and her children. Aramatia, Pisek, Solapia, all were limited in their power. Only Vandar can stand in the All-Father's way."

"The dark god," hissed the High Priest. "We must not let his heart be remade."

"Rasalan is with him," blustered Lord Lharador, "The seas are stormy as Lord Marak said. This is common during springtime, but to this extent?

563

No. My men fear Rasalan rises against us. The Red Sea boils with perils of his making. Krakens, whales, manators, and creatures fouler than these."

Eldur smiled at that, a smile that sent an icy shiver up Talasha's spine. "They rise to claim what is theirs," he said, so softly. "These are creatures I know well. Creatures of my time. They laid claim to this world before you did, my children. So they shall again."

Something stiffened in the room. Talasha did not dare look behind her, but sensed a growing doubt among the host. *They glimpse through his spell,* she thought, *they see the glint of light through the clouds.* Many of those gathered here had families, children of their own. *They are thinking of them. They are picturing them dying, in a hundred horrific ways.*

"My lord, pardons," said Lord Lharador, speaking up. Talasha had always liked the man. He was firm but fair, a man of the people. "These monsters…they are a great risk to us. If we should meet such beasts, many of our ships are sure to founder crossing the water."

"Such is the will of Agarath," Eldur told him. "The world he made is no one's by right. A man's place must be earned, as must a monster's. This is the natural order of things. Peace. Plenty. Kingdoms. Cultures. All must be stripped away, to return the world to what it was."

More murmuring. More doubt. There was no assenting prayer of 'yes, father' this time. *He is stretching himself too far, and too thin,* the princess thought, in desperate hope. She glanced up, and saw a little crease between Lord Marak's eyes, and wondered if he was doubting him too. *Please, say you are, Ulrik.*

The Father seemed to realise it too. He lifted his staff just an inch from the ground, to tap it against the stone. A resounding thump echoed through the hall and a wash of warmth came over them, accompanied by a sudden flowing sheet of light, soft and gold. "Whom do you serve?" the Fire Father asked them. His voice filled every part of the room, every crack and crevice, every heart and every mind, delving deep into them, one and all.

"You, my lord," they said, in unison. "We serve the will of Agarath."

Eldur gestured to the High Priest. Without a word, the man in the flaming robes stood and moved to stand before them. He opened out his hands, and in the voice of Eldur, led them in their prayers.

Talasha Taan repeated the words that required repeating. She murmured with all the rest. She chanted the incantations and opened out her arms and bathed in the All-Father's light. But all the while, she retreated to a fortress in her mind. And there she thought of Lythian, and Cevi, and Neyruu, and her dreams. She thought of Kin'rar and his fractured soul, and Tethian who had died when the Fire Father rose. She remembered every fragment of her memory that had been pieced back together, forming a whole, a picture of doom. *This is wrong,* she thought, *all wrong. The All-Father of Fire will destroy us all.*

When the prayers were done, a golden warmth filled the room. The High Priest bowed to the Fire Father in his throne, and all others spread their hands forward to the floor in deep genuflection. Talasha did the same. With her eyes staring down at the stone, she heard the Fire Father rise to his feet. "I have heard your council, my children, and see that the time has come. Raise your sails, hone your swords, fix your saddles tight. Let the tides of war flow through Vandar. Crush them, as the All-Father decrees."

"We will, my lord," they said together.

"Rise. And bring glory to the creator. Rise, my children, to spread his flame."

Talasha climbed to her feet along with the rest of the gathered slaves. At the rear of the throne room the doors were opened with a groan, and a wash of natural light flooded in from without. Lord Lharador did not waste time in leaving, marching off to marshal his fleet, his lesser captains in attendance. Axallio Axar followed with several other Fireborn riders, to bear the sea lord and his men back to the Trident. After that, the rest began to file out in a processing of shuffling feet and scratching armour. Talasha stepped to Sa'har Nakaan's side, to walk with him from the hall.

"No. Not you."

She turned. "Me, Father?"

"And you, Sotel. Stay."

"Of course, my lord."

"Sa'har."

The skymaster met the Fire Father's eyes, seeming less afeared now, after the prayers and incantations. "My lord."

"You were Lord Marak's wingrider once before, and so you shall be again. Go to Bagrahar, and do not part with him until you feel the coils of your bond grow tight. I will not see this melancholy endure."

"Yes, my lord."

The Fire Father turned his neck. His long hair framed his head, white as bone. "Ulrik. Bring me the head of this Amron Daecar."

Lord Marak gave a hard bow - "I will, Lord Father," - then led Sa'har Nakaan from the hall, giving the princess a passing glance as he strode powerfully toward the doors. *He doesn't trust me,* she thought. They had spoken but little since their altercation outside the scion's chambers, and Talasha could not discount the fear that Ulrik had spoken of her treason. *Is that why I am here?* she wondered, trying to stay calm. *If he senses that Sa'har has doubts, what of me? Do my eyes reveal as much?*

"Father," she said, submitting with a bow. She painted a smile onto her full red lips. "What would you have of me, my lord?"

Even in the harsh light of day, Eldur the Eternal remained somewhat in shadow. *The light is his to command. He wears it like a cloak.* "I am told you have been seen leaving the palace, child," he said. "Where is it that you go?"

She swallowed. "The poor, my lord. I like to visit the poor, and lend them my succour. These are hard times for everyone. I have always tried to spread my warmth to those who have none. A warmth I get from you, from the little blood we share." It was a rehearsed response, should she be cornered with such a question.

And he knows, she saw. "Aren't you sweet, child. A *sweet captain* of the poor."

Her heart missed a beat. *Sweet captain.* "I…I have always championed

565

their cause, my lord." His white skin looked cracked and papery in this light, though not wrinkled like an old man. *Like aged stone*, she thought, *and growing more ancient still.* "Father…"

"You do not have to explain, child."

That made her pause. "Explain, my lord?"

"I know about the Varin Knight, the one you had me spare at the Nest. I was not fully awakened then, but now that is not so." He gestured to the scholar, in his threadbare robes. "I have spoken at length with Sotel about it, this time you shared with him in the mountains. Sweet child, do you think I would condemn you for it? For craving the wants of the flesh, even with a man of Varin's blood? Your chastity is of no interest to me. No, it is your wavering allegiance that is of graver concern."

"My…no, Father, I do not waver." She imagined the flames engulfing her, licking at her skin, blackening and cracking and rupturing. "I am yours, Father, now and forever."

"Words, Talasha. Actions. *Eyes*. Yours are much as Sa'har's. I fear I cannot trust you."

"You *can*, Father. I am your blood. The last of your true blood. You can trust me. I would never betray you." Even as she spoke the words, she found she meant them, every last one. "It's true," she said with growing fervour. "I promise it. You can trust me, Father, you can!" Tears were welling in her eyes, sudden as rain. Her heart raced, thumping in her chest. "My lord, I only want to serve you…" She fell to her knees before him, sprawling upon the cold stone floor. "Please, you *must* believe me."

He looked down at her, hard and merciless. "You are frightened. I understand. It is a plague that infects all mortalkind, this fear of the unknown, this fear of death. But you needn't fear anymore. Rise, and come with me."

She did so without question, following behind him as he drifted from the hall. His crimson robes caressed the stone at his passing, the heel of his staff tapping the ground as he walked. The dragonlord Vargo Ven awaited them outside, wearing his black dragonscale armour and gold-black cape. "Father," he said to Eldur, bowing low. He inclined his head to the princess and ignored Sotel Dar. "I wanted to speak with you in private. Of my report, from the northeast."

"Come, Vargo."

On they went, through the high halls of the palace, until they came to the scion's door. Eldur gestured for Vargo to open it. Within was the Rasal king, chained to his plinth, a wretch in rags, staring into the Eye as it moved in cloudy colours of gold and blue. A stink festered about the man's person, wafting from the room. Vargo Ven wrinkled his nose. "The scion," he said.

He hasn't seen him yet, Talasha knew. It had been her charge to take care of Hadrin, but how long would that last? Eldur had grown increasingly displeased at the king's lack of clairvoyance and it seemed only a matter of time before he would give him to the flames.

"Vargo. Tell me. Could this Amron Daecar be Varin's heir?"

The dragonlord considered it. "Yes," he said. "If it is figurative, as Lord

Marak says. The boy champion…he is strong, my lord. When I asked him of the heir, he seemed…defensive. I wondered if he might be hiding something. Or protecting someone."

"His father."

"Yes, my lord. I thought so."

Eldur stepped into the room, his feet giving out no sound as they slid across the stone. The others followed. It was the first time the Fire Father had come to visit Hadrin himself since he'd been brought here. *He's going to kill him,* Talasha thought. Something about that made her say, "Father, he is weak. I have asked Ulrik many times to treat him with kindness, but…"

He silenced her with a raised hand, stopping her in her step. He looked at the scion. "Hadrin." The name was whispered, a whisper that reached all through the room. At once the creature turned to look at him, eyes bulging and bloodshot. The bones of his face moved beneath his skin as he cringed and cowered and backed away, chains rattling. "You…you…" A stink of urine filled the air, a dark patch spreading through his rotting breeches. "Please, please…don't hurt me. Please…please…" he whimpered.

Vargo Ven snorted. "Pitiful."

The Fire Father softened his voice, withdrawing his power. Suddenly he appeared a normal man, old and kindly, with a red twinkle in his eye. "Varin's heir," he said to the shackled king. "Who is he?"

"I…I…I don't…I don't…"

"*Who?* I have wanted to know for so long and yet still you will not tell me." A throb of rage pulsed from him, quickly withdrawn. "Who? *Tell me.*"

"I…my lord, please…I have glimpsed…I have only seen…"

"What have you seen?"

"I…I cannot say."

"Cannot? Or *will* not? Are you trying to hide this man from me?"

"No! If I knew…I would say….I promise, I…"

"He doesn't know, my lord," said Talasha.

"Silence." Eldur tapped his staff. A shockwave of hot air rushed for her, knocking her back. She stumbled several paces, right into the arms of Vargo Ven. "Careful," he said to her, darkly. "You wouldn't want to fall. Like your mother did." She tugged away from him, heard him chuckle behind her.

The Fire Father looked down at the fettered festering king. "The heir," he said. "Could it be Amron Daecar?"

Hadrin's spindly neck bobbed up and down. Long grey hair waved about his temples, unwashed and reeking. "Y…yes, my lord. Yes…Amron Daecar. The glimpses. They…they showed him, I think. Scars. I saw scars. And he has one, on his face. There can be no one else. It must be him."

The Father studied him coldly. "You have a past with him. This Amron Daecar." His mouth tightened. "You would seek to use me for your vengeance?"

"No! No, I would never! I beg you!" The king collapsed into a heap of rags and bones and rattling chains, whimpering like a beaten dog. His eyes squeezed shut, as though praying all of this was nothing but a bad dream from which he might still awaken. Talasha knew different. *It is a nightmare, and we're all in the same one.*

The Fire Father held his chin high, eyes down, disdainful of the wretch at his feet. He seemed to be weighing up whether to kill him. Eventually, he moved his eyes away. "Vargo. Come forward."

The dragonlord brushed past the princess to kneel before him. "My lord."

"Did you ask the boy of this dragon butcher, as I commanded?"

"I did, my lord."

"Tell me."

Lord Ven stood. "He knew, I think, though would not say. It could be the boy himself, though he denied it when I asked him. He told me he doesn't butcher the dragons he kills. He only kills them. An arrogant boy."

"A boy you have failed to kill. As Ezukar did before you. The dragons of this age are a shadow of their forebears, as are the men."

A muscle in Vargo Ven's jaw tensed. "Yes, Lord Father. I will get the boy next time. Each time we duel he turns craven and escapes…"

"I don't need to hear your excuses, Vargo. I asked that you find out about this heir, and this butcher, and kill the boy, and what have you done? Nothing. You bring me nothing." He turned away from him, eyes simmering. "You. Tell me who the dragon butcher is. Give me a name and I may spare you."

Hadrin stopped in his mewling and looked up. His eyes were red and raw, lips cracked and broken. Talasha felt sorry for him, pitiful though he was. "The…the butcher, yes. I…I saw him again, my lord. I am sure it was him."

"What did you see?"

"Teeth, spread atop an open field. A blue blade, shimmering. Fragments, my lord, I…I see only fragments. In another there was a great shadow. A vast shadow that filled the…the skies. The man stood below, waiting, with the blue blade. He was…he was laughing, my lord."

"A madman," scoffed Vargo Ven. "This shadow, Lord Father. It must be a dragon."

The scion swallowed. The lump moved up and down in his throat, horridly oversized, like a python digesting a deer. "A dragon, yes. A dragon of…of monstrous scale, with a rider on…on his back."

Vargo Ven put the pieces together. "They say the Mistblade is blue. It is Janilah Lukar, my lord. The Warrior King."

Hadrin nodded in his rags. "He…he thinks himself a god, like…like you, my lord. He is Vandar's herald…his champion. He mocks you. I have seen it. He *mocks* you for a coward…"

Vargo Ven struck the man across the face, splitting his lower lip in two. Hadrin yelped like a mutt and retreated, covering his face with his spindly hands, weeping. The dragonlord tilted his chin. "My lord, I will take care of this for you. This dragon the scion speaks of it. It is Malathar. It is foreseen that I must go."

"No." Eldur the Eternal looked at the Eye of Rasalan for a long moment. From his red sleeve came a wizened white hand, ancient fingers reaching to touch it. The colours and shapes seemed to shift away from his grasp as though in fear, bunching on one side of the orb. He smiled. "You always did fear us, Rasalan," he whispered. Then he turned to look at Vargo Ven and said, "It was Drulgar, not Malathar, the scion saw."

"Drulgar, my lord?" Something caught in his throat. "Then…?"

"Then it is time." The Father turned, silent, and walked back toward the door, Sotel Dar shuffling in his wake, Vargo Ven moving behind them. Talasha stood where she was, as though her feet were fixed to the stone. She felt an overwhelming fear and desolation fill her heart, as she remembered her nightmares, the burning, the destruction.

Something forced her to say, "Please, Father, this…this cannot be the way." She gave a sniff. "Drulgar…you *cannot* unleash him."

Vargo Ven turned to scowl at her. "She has no faith, Lord Father. That Varin Knight of hers has made her soft."

Eldur stopped as he reached the door.

"What should we do with her?" Vargo Ven asked. "She could go the same way as her mother, my lord…I know the balcony she fell off. Or her brother. Send her to join him in the Eternal Flame. Though I am not so sure she deserves it, for this treason…"

Eldur raised a hand to silence him. A moment passed, then another, then another. Finally, the Fire Father said, "She will stay here, with the scion, for now. If this vision of the butcher is true, the Eye may yet prove advantageous." He turned to look at her with those dark red eyes. "Comfort him, coddle him, as you did your *sweet captain*. Find the heir of Varin for me, should this Amron Daecar prove false. *That* is your only charge, Talasha. Do this for me, and you may yet prove your faith."

She thought of Neyruu. She thought of Cevi. *What will they do without me?* But she could only dip her eyes and submit - "Yes, Father," - as the doors were shut and barred.

49

Elyon

He walked along the southern battlements of Varinar's towering walls, Sir Bomfrey Sharp and Sir Hank Rothwell marching at his heels.

"Did I hear that right, Sir Elyon?" asked Sir Hank, in an awkward, nervous laugh. "Drulgar the...the Dread? Did you not mean..."

"I meant Drulgar." Elyon scanned the defences as he walked, counting out the archers he saw, the crossbowmen, checking the siege weapons to make sure each had a full and proper complement of men to operate them. Some required more than others, to be sure, though half were sitting idle. "Why aren't these weapons manned?" he demanded.

"Why should they be?" asked Sir Bomfrey. He was a thickset man, big in the belly and chest, and no sufferer of fools. He looked more like a Riverlander than an Ironmoorer, with those stocky legs and beet-red cheeks. "We can't have every weapon manned day and night, Sir Elyon. When would the men ever sleep?"

Sleep. Elyon had half forgotten what sleep felt like. "Drulgar could come at any moment. We need every weapon manned and ready for when he does."

The two knights shared a look. *They doubt me,* Elyon knew at once. Both were household knights, Sir Bomfrey a loyal Taynar man, Sir Hank Rothwell in service to House Daecar. Along with Sir Winslow Bryant, an old commander of the Lake Gate under King Ellis, and a dutiful Reynar loyalist, they had the run of the city defences. *We could do worse,* Elyon thought. *Godrik Taynar could still be alive.*

Sir Hank wet his lips. "Um, my lord. Perhaps you ought to rest? Drulgar? You're really quite certain that..."

"I'm certain, Sir Hank." *As certain as I can be, anyway.* Vargo Ven was as slippery as an eel, but he'd been right about the Fire Father, and he was right about this, Elyon was sure. "Or do you doubt that Eldur has awoken as well?"

"Well..."

Steel Father, give me strength.

"It's hard to accept, is what Hank's trying to say," came in Sir Bomfrey. "It's been busy here, Sir Elyon, what with all the peasants down in the Lowers. We've got tens of thousands of extra mouths to feed, and crime is rife. It's a lot to keep an eye on, but that's just civil problems. The war hasn't hit us yet. So this talk of Eldur…"

"Believe it," Elyon said. He had no patience for trying to convince the non-believers today. "You say you've got tens of thousands more mouths to feed? Well in the east we've got tens of thousands of bodies to bury. Do you have any idea of what's going on out there, either of you? The Marshlands are overrun. We've got dragons swarming like flies. A dozen major cities and forts have fallen and we're pulling back to Rustbridge as we speak to defend the crossing at the river. So I could do without your doubts. And where's Sir Winslow? He needs to hear this too."

"He's in the north of the city, my lord, overseeing the defences there," Sir Hank told him. He was a tall, sinewy man, with a soft almost womanly voice, well into his fifth decade. His skin had gone a little pale. "The Marshlands, you say? They're…"

"Overrun, yes." Elyon looked along the battlements. "Have you run drills?"

"Drills?" asked Sir Bomfrey.

"Timing drills," Elyon said, coming close to losing his patience. "When the bells toll and horns blow, how long will it take for these weapons to be readied and manned?"

The men shared a look again.

"Gods. What have you been doing here!"

"A few minutes," Sir Bomfrey said, jaw stiffening. "Or do you want it down to the exact second, my lord?"

"I want you to do your jobs." He'd flown over some of the towers when he arrived - those built along the walls, and those that summited the many hills of the outer city - and had not been happy with what he'd seen. *This is too lax,* he thought. *They're not ready.* "I want you to run a drill this evening, after dark," he commanded. "No warning. See how the men react. Do the same tomorrow morning, at dawn. And again the next day until every single ballista, scorpion, catapult and trebuchet is manned and ready in two minutes sharp."

Sir Bomfrey's jaw clenched tighter. "As you say, my lord."

Elyon looked at the man's scowl, his reddening cheeks, the narrow cut to his eyes. "Old habits die hard, don't they Sir Bomfrey."

The knight looked lost. "I don't get your meaning."

"I'm no prince to you. You're a Taynar knight, and no man of mine. You don't like taking orders from me."

"I don't like my competence being called into question," Sir Bomfrey came back. "You'll forgive me for asking, but how old are you, Sir Elyon?"

"Twenty," Elyon said, without thinking, before realising his birthday had passed some time ago now and he'd long since turned twenty-one. "Twenty-one, I mean."

Sir Hank smiled. "I forgot my birthday too."

"Well, I've seen three and fifty winters and am old enough to be your grandsire. I've been a knight for three decades. I know how to defend these walls."

Elyon nodded. It was all he wanted to hear. "Good. Then see it done." He looked at Sir Hank. "Have you seen my auntie lately?" The two knew each other well enough, he knew, from feasts and celebrations held at Blackfrost and Snowhold, the castle seat of Lord Ronley Rothwell, Hank's cousin. Sir Hank had run the castle's defences for many long years, so had plenty of experience walking the walls. *Not that Snowhold is much to look at*, the prince thought. It was a cold grim castle, with meagre grounds and a small population of smallfolk huddled within its walls. *You could fit a hundred of them inside this city.*

"Not for a while, my lord," the knight said in answer. "Not since she left the city."

"Left?" Elyon didn't like the sound of that. Now was no time to be leaving Varinar unless there was good reason. "Where did she go?"

"I couldn't tell you, Sir Elyon. I had it from the soldiers at the eastern gate. She rode out with Sir Connor and Sir Penrose, as I understand it, as well as your old squire and that redhead girl…"

"Carly. The *eastern* gate, you said?"

"I did."

"Then it would be safe to assume she is heading in that direction." Elyon could imagine where. "My sister isn't back in the city yet, is she?"

"Not that I know of. Your uncle will likely know more than I do, however. Lady Amara has been known to visit him, on occasion."

Sir Bomfrey scowled at that. "Shouldn't be allowed. Your uncle killed my king. He should be left in his cell to rot."

There was plenty wrong with that, though Elyon had no strength to argue with or educate the man. *He isn't going to like what I do next*, he thought. "What of the Greycloaks? Have they been released yet?"

"Word came from your father a while ago," Sir Hank informed him. "He gave orders for them to ride south to King's Point. Wants every blade he can get down there, it sounds like. They're expecting some big attack."

Good, Elyon thought. If the Greycloaks had been released - much as it grated on him - the precedent was set for what he was about to do.

He looked south beyond the towering walls, where the Steelrun River rushed mightily along its course below a sky bruised by the coming of dusk. Even with the rush of the river, the noise of the men marching between their stations, the clank and clatter of armour, the distant hum of the city behind him…even with all that, it felt calm here, almost subdued, after everything he'd faced of late. All the same, his respite would be short. *One night*, he thought. *I'll stay one night and leave in the morning.*

He turned back to the two old knights. "I'd best go," he told them. "If I've been a little brusque, Sir Bomfrey, I apologise. I don't mean to under-mine you. I haven't slept much of late."

"I can tell." Sir Bomfrey gave him a look up and down, then twisted his lips into a reluctant smile. "You might consider flying over to the Steelforge to fetch a fresh Varin cloak before you leave. Yours looks beyond saving."

Elyon gave a weary laugh. His cloak was a disgrace, quite frankly. Filthy, bloodied, frayed, scorched, it was hard to identify it as the rich resplendent garment it had once been. "Fair enough, Sir Bomfrey. I fear any new cloak will only suffer the same fate, but yes, I ought to take the opportunity to get a replacement while I'm here." His armour could do with some attention as well. "I'll come and see you again on the morrow before I leave. I hope to see the walls fully stocked when I do."

"We'll see it done, my lord," Sir Hank told him, bowing. Sir Bomfrey merely grunted and inclined his head. Elyon took to the skies.

The Steelforge was built upon a thrust of land off the shore of Lake Eshina, linked to the city by a wide stone bridge half a mile in length. A single oxcart was rattling along it, delivering a fresh provision of firewood to keep the hearths burning. Elyon flew the length of the bridge to land outside the yawning archway that gave entrance into the fortress, passing the guardsmen who stood watch outside. The entrance hall beyond was tiled in hues of grey and silver and blue. Statues stood attendance about the walls, etched in the likenesses of the famed First Blades of the past. Elyon looked at the towering stone form of his father, carved with the head of Vallath beneath his foot, and the blade that struck the dragon down clasped proudly between his fingers.

As he was admiring it, he heard a voice call out, "We'll need to carve a few more of those, I'm thinking." Elyon turned to find the small stout figure of Forgemaster Merilore approach from across the hall, dressed in dun robes over a leather blacksmith's vest, worn-out breeches, and sturdy boots. "One of you, Sir Elyon, how about that?"

"I'm not First Blade, Forgemaster," Elyon said. All the statues here were of First Blades only.

Merilore waved that away with a knuckly callused hand. "You're more, so we've been hearing." He thought for a moment. "So, how about this - Windblade brandished forward, in flight, with a dragon chasing behind you? How do you like the sound of that, lad? That dragon you killed in the storm, maybe. Which one was that again?"

"Ezukar."

"Aye, that one. You tell me what he looked like, and I'll do the rest. Be my pleasure to immortalise you, young Elyon. The Dance in the Storm. Isn't that what people are calling it?"

"It's one name." Others had taken to calling it the Duel Above the Lakes, or more mockingly, the Battle of Soaking Rock. But mostly no one was talking about it at all anymore. Too much had happened since then and his fight with Ezukar was yesterday's news. "How are you, Forgemaster?"

"Me? Bored. How are *you*, is the question? Was told you came by this way a while ago. I was annoyed to have missed you."

Elyon nodded. "I came to see Jovyn." It had been the morning after his last visit here to Varinar, when he'd spent the night at Keep Daecar and gotten a little drunk with Amara. His time with Jovyn had been brief - no more than a quick catch-up - before he'd flown straight on to Crosswater to see his father. "It was very quiet, Meri. That doesn't seem to have changed."

"Quiet as a morgue, aye." The forgemaster had a red beard, red hair, red eyebrows, and red tufts of chest hair sprouting from the top of his vest. There were three forgemasters here at the Steelforge who mended, repaired, and worked godsteel into the armour and blades the Knights of Varin wore. Each was Forgeborn, blessed with the blood of Ilith in ample measure. Beneath them worked many other apprentices and lesser Forgeborn. Besides them and a fewscore scribes, squires, soldiers and serving men, the Steelforge was empty. "All your lot are at war, Sir Elyon," the armourer said. "You're the first fully-fledged Varin Knight I've seen in a while, though suppose it's easy enough for you to get around these days, with that blade of yours." He smiled. "How you handling it? Well, so I hear. Ezukar isn't the only dragon you've slain, isn't that right?"

Merilore had always been a talker. "I've killed a few." That was putting it mildly. Elyon Daecar was fast becoming one of the most prolific dragonslayers in all history, though few of them were of particular renown. It was a significant caveat, like a famous bear hunter killing a bunch of cubs and claiming themselves the bane of all bears. *I'm killing cubs and dragonlings, that's all.* And even Ezukar had been slain largely by luck. "I wondered if you might knock out a few dents in my armour, Meri? That's if you have time?"

"Time? Oh, I have all the time in the world." He grinned and waved a hand. "Come on then, let's see."

Elyon removed his Varin cloak, to show off the many little wounds his armour had taken over the last month or two. "The breastplate has taken some damage," he said, gesturing. "And the left pauldron, in particular."

Forgemaster Merilore's bushy red eyebrows twisted into a frown. "Well now, there's some work needs doing here, Sir Elyon. Come, let's get you unwrapped. How long do you intend to stay in the city?"

"One night."

The armourer gave a sigh. "Well, I suppose I'll be working till dawn, then. No matter. I'll have it all done for the morning. Wouldn't want you fighting dragons with creaky joints and whatnot. Come on. This way."

The forges were found on the western side of the fortress, a place of steamy corridors and walls that wept with condensation. Elyon followed the armourer to his workshop, removed his plate, and laid it out along a scratched wooden counter, each component lined up from smallest to largest. As a Forgeborn with the blood of Ilith, Merilore had the power to lift godsteel and rework the metal, though would gain no other gift from wielding it. Enhanced senses, strength and speed were granted only to the Bladeborn of Varin's bloodline.

The man gave each item a brief inspection, then began preparing his tools. As he did that, Elyon asked, "Did you receive a letter from me a while ago, Meri? I sent a crow from Redhelm, asking that Captain Lythian's armour and weapons be sent down the Steelrun."

Merilore was already nodding. "We got your crow, aye. Wonderful news, this of Lythian's return. I always did like him very much. There are few so courteous as the Knight of the Vale." He picked up Elyon's breastplate, moving it to a separate worktop with a heavy thump, and took up a hammer. "As I understand it, his things were put on a barge, as you asked, and shipped down to King's Point. I imagine they should have arrived by now."

That was promising news, though whether Lythian had arrived there himself was another question, and one Elyon Daecar was keen to answer. He hadn't seen his old mentor since he'd left him on the road to Nightwell, and that was how long ago now? Eight, nine days? Ten? Even thinking about it made him weary. *Over a week of near-constant fighting and defending and patrolling*, he thought. *Gods, I need a long sleep.*

But he still had work to do. His featherbed would have to wait.

"Do you have any spare Varin cloaks around here," Elyon asked, as the forgemaster began his hammering. "Mine has seen better days, as you can tell. I need to borrow one."

Melifore gestured to a trunk. "Should be several in there. Take your pick."

Elyon spent a few minutes finding one to fit him, then threw the cloak over his leathers and bid the old armourer goodbye, telling him he'd return in the morning.

"I'll have it gleaming like a mirror for you, lad," the red-bearded blacksmith said. "Who knows, maybe I'll even strengthen it up a bit too. Wats and Wain are both as bored as I am, so mayhaps I'll get them to help me. We'll make a night of it. Bit of hammering, bit of drinking. What could be better? You know how Wats works best when he's half drunk."

Elyon smiled. Wats was Forgemaster Watling, a big blacksmith in his mid-thirties with fists the size of hams and the thickest forearms Elyon had ever seen. The last was Wainwood, the oldest and grumpiest of the three, though most knowledgeable. When the trio got together, they could work wonders. "That would be much appreciated," Elyon said. Usually it was the First Blade who gave the forgemasters their orders, though lately they had free reign to do as they pleased. Getting all three of them to work together on a single project was rare, and not an opportunity to be missed. "I'll leave it with you, Meri. Add a coat of fireproof oil too, if you can. I need every bit of help I can get."

"You'll have it."

Elyon returned to the bridge beyond the fortress, stepping out into the dark of night. Half a mile away, the lights were coming on in the city, winking awake as the stars did the same in the skies above him. Elyon pulled the Windblade from its sheath, threw it aloft, and soared. After spending so long flying in the steel embrace of his brilliant plate armour, doing so in nought but linen and leather made him feel strangely vulnerable, and cold besides.

By the time he came down to land outside the palace steps, he looked utterly dishevelled and a chill had bitten down into his bones. The prince

575

took a moment to straighten out his garments and comb his fingers through his hair, before climbing the steps to the doors. There were a pair of guards on duty there. Both bowed, and one said, "Sir Elyon. What a pleasure. Is there something we can do for you?"

"You can open the doors and let me pass. I'm here to see my uncle."

The man seemed unsure. "But your father said…"

"My father isn't here. Open the doors, please."

The doors were opened.

The palace interior was like a mausoleum. Silence filled the high splendid chambers and ghosts haunted the halls. The only sound was that of Elyon's footsteps as he passed through the empty rooms and corridors. He met not a single soul until he came to the steps leading down to the dungeons. Two more guards were there, barring his way. One was a Daecar man from House Crawfield, the other a Taynar in drab grey and moody blue.

"I'm here to see Sir Vesryn Daecar," the prince said. "Let me through."

The young Crawfield soldier bowed and stepped aside. "At once, my lord."

The Taynar man stood his ground. He was sour-faced and saturnine, a typical Ironmoorer. "Our orders are to let no one pass."

"I know what your orders are. And I'm here to tell you that you have new orders."

The old soldier frowned. "From who?"

"My father. And Lord Dalton. They are running the kingdom together, as I'm sure you have heard, and have decided that you are no longer needed here. Please, report to Sir Bomfrey Marsh and Sir Hank Rothwell at the southern gate. We need all of the men we can get there. Can either of you fire a bow?"

"I'm a good archer," the Crawfield man said, enthusiastically. "Can shoot a hare from horseback from a hundred yards. Did that once, back home."

The other soldier grunted at that. "Once? And how many times did you fail? A thousand? Aye, I know an empty boast when I hear one." He looked back at Elyon, confused. "Who's to watch the traitor if we go?"

"That's not for you to worry about. Just report to the gate, and you'll get your new orders. If you stay here, you'll only be guarding the spiders and the rats."

Neither man understood, and that was just fine by him. *They will soon.* He stepped right past and down the steps, descending into darkness. The air grew colder as he went, stale and inert. Mostly it was still, though in places draughts came whispering in through old gaps in the stone. He met a gaoler halfway down, sitting in his little alcove beside a table topped with a stack of books, a pair of tallow candles and a plate of half-eaten food. The man wore a stained leather vest, buttons bulging to contain his girth, and smelled as bad as he looked. *Why are all gaolers and turnkeys always so filthy?*

The man stood suddenly from his stool when he saw him, gaping.

Elyon smiled and continued right past him.

576

At the next alcove, he found a torch burning on an old iron sconce. He plucked it from its holding, strode down the final set of steps, and entered the murky, dripping tunnel where the deepest and darkest cells were found.

A hoarse voice whispered from the shadows. "Amara? Is…is that you?"

Elyon swung the light over to his left, illuminating the figure of Vesryn Daecar, sitting up on his rotting wood bed. He held his hand up against the light, standing, moving to the bars. Elyon took a moment to gather his composure. He hadn't seen his uncle since Harrowmoor, since that night he'd confessed his crimes in his pavilion, then vanished without a trace. The prince cleared his throat. "Amara prefers her silks and sables, I've heard," he said. "Dirty leathers aren't really her thing."

His uncle squinted past the harsh glare of firelight. Recognition dawned. "*El…Elyon?*"

"Uncle." Elyon sniffed the air, nostrils flaring. "You look awful. And you smell as bad as Borrus Kanabar's chamberpot after a feast."

The man's face was drawn out, skin lined and pale, cheeks and chin forested in a salt and pepper beard. His hair was the same, tangling and curling to his neck in great unwashed waves. "You may not be Amara, but you've got her tongue." He managed a weak smile. "It's good to see you."

Elyon didn't return the courtesy. Vesryn's betrayals were still too raw for him to let himself smile in his presence. A smile would quickly turn to laughter, he didn't doubt, and then what? *We'll be happy families again?* He wouldn't allow it. "Are you strong?" he simply asked. "Have they been feeding you well?"

"Well enough. The fare is bland but ample."

Elyon moved the light, to get a better look at him. "You look thinner."

His uncle nodded. "Lack of training will do that. I don't get much exercise in this cell."

"I'm sure Amara tried to correct that." The woman had strong appetites, Elyon knew, though he wished he didn't. Unfortunately, there was no helping it, living with her in Keep Daecar. *She never did care to keep their lovemaking quiet.*

Vesryn looked at him through the rusted iron bars, the firelight catching in his silvery blue eyes. "Did she send you? Amara?"

"Rikkard sent me."

His uncle's black eyebrows descended into a frown. "Rikkard?" He didn't understand, that was plain.

"The Greycloaks have been released," Elyon told him. "More blades for the war, I'm told. Hank Rothwell just informed me they're riding for King's Point at my father's command. Sir Gerald. Sir Alyn. Sir Nathaniel. Traitors all. But even traitors get a stay of execution during wartime, it seems. Rikkard said that one night, and I found myself agreeing. So…why not you? You're twice the swordsman Nathaniel is and don't get me started on the others. We could use you, Vesryn. I'm here to set you free."

If the man was happy to hear that, he hid it well. "You don't have that power, Elyon. If the Greycloaks have been let out, and I haven't, doesn't that tell you something? Your father won't allow it."

"My father's too damn stubborn. Rikkard told me that as well, though we all knew it already. You're one of the best fighters we have, and I'll not have you rotting in this cell when you could be out there helping. And to hell with my father. He's been so worried about trying to patch up relations with the houses that he's half-forgotten there's a war to fight. Well I haven't. While he sits at King's Point waiting for dragons, I've been fighting them. If the Greycloaks can ride to the coast, so can you. I want you saddled and ready to leave at first light."

His uncle didn't react, except to raise one eyebrow and half a smile and say, "You've changed, Elyon. Amara was right. You're a leader now."

"I'm a killer. A warrior. A soldier. I'm whatever I need to be. And right now, maybe that's a traitor. So be it." He withdrew his godsteel dagger, stepped forward, and cut through the lock on the door. It opened with a high-pitched whine. "Well come on, what are you waiting for?"

His uncle stepped back into the shadows. "I can't, Elyon. I promised myself I wouldn't try to escape. I can't sully my honour any further."

"Escape? This isn't escape, Vesryn. Nor is it a pardon. You're still a prisoner, and if Father wants to take your head when you reach King's Point, that's on him. Or maybe he'll throw you into the dungeons beneath the Spear and I'll have wasted all of our time. Either way, it's worth a shot. Instinct tells me that Amron Daecar isn't going to cast aside a skilled sword when he sees enemy sails on the horizon and dragon wings in the skies." He stepped back. "Now come on. I cannot express to you how bloody tired I am. I'd hoped to dine with Amara tonight, but it seems she isn't here, so you'll have to serve. Come." He turned and marched up the steps.

He was halfway back to the gaoler's little lair when he stopped, waited, and listened for the sound of his uncle following. It took a while, though eventually the man roused himself from his cell and climbed the steps behind him. Elyon let out a breath. "Good. I thought for a moment you'd grown too fond of your shadows."

Vesryn shielded his eyes from the light. "Won't the guards try to stop us? Or the gaoler?"

"The gaoler?" Elyon laughed. "No one's going to stop us. As far as the guards know, I've come with orders from my father and Lord Dalton. Stop fretting."

They suffered little resistance along the way. The gaoler might as well have been an oversized slug for all the authority he possessed and when they reached the top of the stairs, Elyon was glad to find that the two guards had already gone. It wasn't overly surprising. Standing sentry on the dungeons was a dull and dreary charge, and the battlements would be more exciting.

Vesryn walked stiffly, as though his bones were half frozen and required a good long thawing. "I'm not doing this for you," Elyon felt obliged to tell him, as they went. "I want you to know that. This is about Vandar. About defending the kingdom, and the north. That's all."

"I know," Vesryn said. "I won't ask for your forgiveness."

"Good. Because you won't get it." He felt better to have gotten that out of the way. "So, where did Amara go? Ilivar, I'm guessing?"

Vesryn nodded. "Your lord grandfather has refused to give up Lillia. Amara took it upon herself to go and demand her back."

Elyon sighed. "I thought she might do something like that. How long ago was it?"

He frowned, thinking. "Hard to say for certain. Time runs differently in the darkness."

"Darkness? Weren't they lighting the torches in the lower cells?"

"Sometimes. But not always. That gaoler has creaky knees, he insists. Doesn't like going up and down the steps unless he can avoid it, so...well, he chose to leave me in darkness half the time. It's been worse since Amara last visited. I'd expect her back soon enough, though."

Maybe I'll fly over the Lakeland Pass, Elyon thought. If they were on the way back, he might well spot them.

He mulled on that for a little while and then put it promptly aside. That was Elyon Daecar thinking, not the Master of Winds. The boy who wanted to make sure his auntie and little sister and squire were safe, not the prince and champion who needed to lend his blade to the war. For all he knew, Vargo Ven had played another cruel trick on him and was sending a great thunder of dragons to assault his eastern army even now. Or else King's Point was coming under attack, or an Agarathi horde was marching across the Tidelands to lay siege to the Twinfort, as his father feared.

I can't waste time scouting some road, he told himself. If every soldier went rushing off to make sure their loved ones were safe, they'd have no men left to fight.

Their footsteps echoed softly as they walked, passing a lonely maid dusting a table. She gasped as she saw Vesryn and slapped a hand over her mouth, then spun in retreat, vanishing down a corridor. Vesryn sighed. "People fear me," he said. "They think I'm a kingkiller. They think I'm mad."

"You're neither," Elyon told him. "You're just a traitor to your family, that's all."

His uncle nodded. "That's fair. Though in truth it was only your father I betrayed. Everything else that happened..."

"Everything else? You mean Aleron's death?"

"I never intended for him to..."

"Die? Whether you intended for that to happen or not, your actions paved the way for it. You knew who Ludlum was. You knew he was my brother..."

"I didn't know he was going to kill him. I told you this at Harrowmoor. Jonik was only meant to win the Song, not kill him. He must have been given new orders..."

Elyon realised he didn't want to get into this. He raised a hand to stop him. "It's done," was all he said. "I'm too tired for this right now." He marched on to the doors, where the palace guards were stationed at their posts. Elyon advised his uncle to pull his hood up to better conceal himself, though of course they spotted him anyway.

"Sir Elyon? I thought you said you were only visiting him. We can't allow…"

"You can. My father himself has ordered Sir Vesryn's release."

The guards looked befuddled. "But…last he was here, he said…"

"I know what he said. Lord Dalton Taynar is at King's Point now as well, and he wants the prisoner moved to the dungeons beneath the Spear. He…"

Vesryn interrupted him. "How is your wife, Brent?" he asked one of them, in an affable voice. "And your daughter? She must be almost three by now."

Brent blinked at him. "She…just had her birthday, my lord. You… remember that?"

"Of course I do. You told me on these very steps, if I recall. As you told me of your brother's ailing health, Kerwin. How is he faring?"

The other guard nodded and smiled. "Well, my lord. He's doing much better now, thank the gods."

Vesryn smiled. "I'm glad to hear it. Give him my best, when you see him next. And you as well, Brent. Tell your family I wish them well." He dipped his chin and continued down the steps.

Elyon moved to his side, glancing over at him as they descended to the quiet city streets below. His uncle had always possessed a likeable manner and natural way with his men, damn him. *He is hard to hate*, the prince lamented. "Do you remember the names of all the men who served under you here?"

"I ran the king's guard for many years, Elyon. It was my charge to know these men." He drew a breath of clean spring air, as a man does after a long term of captivity. "You lie more easily than you used to. Your father won't like that you manipulated the guards into letting me go."

"We've been through that. He can do with you as he pleases when you reach King's Point. If I were you, I would put my hands together and pray that you find Dalton Taynar in a good mood. He still thinks you killed his father, Vesryn. Most likely he'll demand your death anyway. I'm probably just speeding up your execution."

"If that is my path, I accept it."

"You accept it? To die for a crime you didn't commit?"

"To protect Amara, yes. And when a man stands upon the gibbet, he can decide in his own head what he's dying for. I will do so for my crimes. Against your father, and this family. I have long since accepted that my days are numbered, Elyon."

"All our days are numbered," the prince came back at him. *And I'll be damned*, he thought, *if you die by a hangman's rope, when you could die duelling a dragon instead.*

They dined an hour later in the family feast hall of Keep Daecar, after Elyon had had a chance to scrub himself clean, change into fresh garb, and cut away the lengthening tangles of his beard. Neatened, trimmed, and washed, he arrived to find Vesryn already seated at the table, dressed in wool breeches and a simple jerkin emblazoned with the family crest; a knight on horseback, with a misting blade held aloft. "I'm not sure you're allowed to bear that sigil anymore," Elyon said, as he sat opposite him.

Vesryn filled him a cup of wine. "I'm still a Daecar, no matter what I've done." There was a bite to his voice. He had cut away his beard as well, leaving himself with cheeks of coarse stubble, and trimmed his hair back. He looked a decade younger all of a sudden. "If you want to chastise me, go ahead and get it over with. I tried to talk about it earlier with you, Elyon. You said you didn't want to hear it. So which is it?"

I'm still too tired for this, Elyon thought. He wasn't even sure why he had invited his uncle to have this dinner in the first place. *Because this might be the last time you spend time with him,* he thought. For all his uncle had done, he had always loved him, always counted on him, always sought out his advice, his guidance, his friendship. Rikkard was the young, fun uncle, Lythian had been his mentor and his guide, but Vesryn was always his rock. *He was a father to me as much as my real father was.* It was hard to just let all that go, no matter what he'd done.

He took a sip of wine. "It's done," he said, repeating what he'd told him earlier. "And you're right. You're still a Daecar. I'll not try to take that away from you." He picked up a spoon and had a taste of his soup, hastily prepared by the castle cooks. "It's good. Beats what you've been eating, I'm sure. Go ahead, eat up. We need you strong if you're going to…"

"Hang? Have my head chopped off by a headsman's axe?"

"Fight," Elyon said, ignoring his uncle's jape. "Here's what I want from you, Vesryn." He put down his spoon. "Kill a dragon. A big one, preferably. Join the pantheon of dragonkillers and perhaps you'll earn back some of that honour you're so desperate to restore. Who knows. Varin might even permit you a place at his Table." He checked his uncle's eyes. "I know that's been bothering you. The fear of what comes next."

The man would not deny it. "Amara told you?"

"Last time I was here," Elyon confirmed. "She didn't like seeing you so stricken and wretched. It's tearing her up, the thought that you'll die for what she did. But falling in battle? Restoring your name? That's something she could live with."

He nodded slowly. "It's a shame she isn't here. I'd have liked a chance to say goodbye."

"Who says you won't get one?"

"You do, Elyon. The fact that you're here, against your own father's commands, freeing me. That says a lot." He studied his face a moment. "How bad is it out there?"

"Bad," Elyon said, spooning more soup into his mouth. "The Marshlands have fallen, and the whole of East Vandar is sure to follow. We've lost almost twenty thousand soldiers there, and I couldn't even tell you how many civilians. We're bending, but haven't yet broken. I ordered our forces to pull back to Rustbridge to defend the river. We've got a strong army there. But how long they'll hold…well, that I can't say."

"Might it not be best for me to ride east, then?" his uncle asked. The thought seemed to enthuse him more. *He doesn't want to confront Father,* the prince realised. "I might be more use there."

Elyon didn't think so. "It's too far. And we're expecting an assault from the south, at any time." For all he knew, it might already be happening. "I want you at King's Point, Vesryn. If the Greycloaks have been allowed to ride there, the precedent is set for you to do so as well. And if you stay here…" No, that wouldn't work. Varinar was crawling with Taynar men and they could quite easily take justice on Vesryn themselves. "Just ride for the coast," he said, meeting his eyes. "And don't try to flee."

His uncle didn't like the insinuation. "Accuse me of whatever you please, but I've never been a coward. I'll face my fate with my head held high, whatever that might be. I'm not going to try to flee, Elyon."

"Good." The Prince of the Skies drank more of his wine, ate more of his soup, chewed on some meat and cheese and bread. As his stomach filled his exhaustion strengthened yet further. An awkwardness hung in the air between them. Nothing came naturally anymore, everything was strained. "I miss the old days," Elyon muttered, after a while. "We used to talk for hours, you and me. This is probably the last time we'll ever dine together, and look at us. We've barely got anything to say."

"I've got plenty to say, though I'm sure you wouldn't want to hear it." His uncle sighed. "That's on me, Elyon. I've soured every relationship I held dear…"

"No. Amara still loves you." Elyon didn't want his uncle to suffer needlessly, no matter what he'd done. "Hold onto that, if nothing else. She loves you. Always has and always will."

The prince pushed his food aside, refilled his wine cup, and drank deep. It would help him sleep, he hoped. Sometimes, despite his unutterable exhaustion, sleep came slow to him, and sometimes not at all. When he closed his eyes he would hear the wind rushing past his ears, the shriek of dragons rattling through his bones. He would replay his latest battles, the sights and sounds and smells. And oft as not, even when he did sleep, he would wake in the night, suddenly and often, expecting to be roused once more to some battle. So he drank instead, while he could, and thought of the soft pull of his featherbed, awaiting him.

When his cup was empty, he placed it down with a clunk. "I should try to get some rest. You can stay if you like. Drink, eat, enjoy your freedom while you have it. I'll see about getting you a horse in the morning. You'll need a quick one, and strong, to get you down to the coast."

"I have one," his uncle said. "Sunsilver returned to the city."

The prince was shocked. "I thought…Amara said you had sold him to a merchant, over in Rasalan. To buy passage across the Sibling Strait."

"I did. He must have escaped, followed me back here." The thought moved him deeply, Elyon could tell. His uncle blinked, lest his eyes grow misty, and drew on his wine. "He's stabled here in the keep. I might go and see him, before I sleep. Or even…" He paused to think. "Well…why wait until morning to ride, Elyon? I've had enough rest to last a dozen lifetimes in that cell. I can leave tonight."

For some reason Elyon had hoped to see Vesryn again at dawn. Maybe break his fast with him, and speak of fonder times once he had a chance to rest. But perhaps this was the better course. "Are you sure?"

"I'm sure." Vesryn Daecar stood from the table, not willing to consider it further. "I'll don my armour, and ride out at once. There's no sense in wasting time, Elyon. Though getting through the gate might prove problematic."

"I'll take you," Elyon said. His eyes went over Vesryn's shoulder, to the greatsword hanging above the fireplace. For a moment he wondered if he might give it to his uncle to bear, but the thought came but briefly, before souring in his mind. Aleron had last wielded Vallath's Ruin when he died upon the sands. He could not in all good conscience let his uncle take it. *No, if Father should see him with the Mercyblade at his hip, he'll be sure to cut him down on the spot...* "Get ready," was all he said. "I'll meet you at the gate."

Not long later, Elyon Daecar escorted his uncle through the city of Varinar, walking at his side as he led Sunsilver by the bridle. There were few horses so beautiful; big, strong, yet sleek all the same, he could run like few others, and rarely did he tire. "Take the river road," Elyon told him. "And ride hard. Sleep in the saddle if you can. Battle may be upon us by the time you arrive."

"Us?" his uncle asked. There was hope in his voice. "Will we fight together, you and I?"

"I don't know," Elyon said, and that was the truth. "I'll fly to the coast tomorrow to talk to Father, but after...I'm not sure." *South*, came that thought again, as ever it did. It was a constant thorn in his mind, prodding and poking. *Traps and tricks*, Vargo Ven had said. *These rules of yours...they strangle you.* He wasn't wrong. And Elyon Daecar was done playing by the rules.

They met Sir Hank at the south gate, busy with bowmen and men-at-arms and the landed knights they served. Elyon was glad to see that his commands had been taken to heart; the wall walks looked busier already, the battlements bustling.

"My lord Elyon," Sir Hank called, spotting him, hurrying over. "We performed the drill as you said, and quite successfully I might say. We can do better, I'm sure, but..." He trailed off, squinting as he peered past Vesryn's shadowy cowl. "Oh. So this...*this* is why you returned, my lord? For your uncle."

"It was one reason, yes. My father has ordered his release." Lies did come more easily to him now, that was true.

"Truly? You never said."

"It slipped my mind." Elyon looked around. Most of these men would be Taynar levies and it was only a matter of time before they had an angry mob on their hands. He looked at Hank Rothwell. "Where is Sir Bomfrey?"

"Taking his dinner, my lord. His second dinner, I should say." He chuckled. "The man is fond of his food."

Good, Elyon thought. Sir Bomfrey would only kick up a fuss and question him on Vesryn's leaving. "Open the gate, Sir Hank. My uncle has a long ride ahead of him."

Sir Hank Rothwell, a loyal Daecar man, assented without a word.

The gates were opened with an echoing groan, the massive twin doors parting at the centre only wide enough so that the pair could pass through. Elyon walked with Vesryn and Sunsilver out into the pale moonlight beyond the city. The rush of the river roared nearby. Above, upon the battlements, the bowmen and soldiers were gazing down, and no doubt the rumours were already starting.

Let them whisper, Elyon told himself. He was long past caring what other people thought.

He turned to face his uncle, as he climbed up into the saddle. He wore his plate armour, and a cloak of House Daecar hung down proudly at his back. Elyon had no complaint this time when he saw the Daecar sigil. "Fight for the honour of our house," he told him, as he felt a stirring in his heart. "Ride hard, and unresting. Ride for war, Uncle…and redemption."

Vesryn Daecar nodded, steeling his eyes. And putting his heels into his horse, he rode south like the wind beneath a starry black sky.

50

Lythian

"Name?" asked the soldier at the gate.

"Sir Storos Pentar, fourth son of the late Lord Porus Pentar and brother to his successor and eldest son Alrus, the new Lord of Redhelm and Warden of the South."

The guard looked decidedly unimpressed, even bored. "Didn't ask for your life story, milord. And these others?"

Sir Storos introduced his companions. "My captain, Sir Oswin Cole, and his men. And this is the famed Knight of the Vale, Sir Lythian Lindar, Captain of the Varin Knights, and his sworn sword Sir Pagaloth Kadosk, former Dragonknight of Agarath."

"An *Agarathi?*" The guard gaped, trying to get a better look past Sir Pagaloth's hood. Naturally, it was wise to keep him well covered here, until such a time as his presence could be explained.

"Most dragonknights are," Sir Storos said, with an amiable smile. "We have come to swear our swords to Lord Daecar. Would you inform him that we have arrived? He should be expecting us."

The gate guard looked at Lythian, though peered would be a better word, the way he leaned forward and squinted. "The Knight of Mists," he said, nodding, as though trusting only the judgement of his own eyes, and not the word of Sir Storos. "Had heard you were back." He turned and waved for a man, who came rushing forward. "Take a message to the Spear. Tell Lord Daecar that Captain Lythian has arrived."

"At once, m'lord." The man hurried off.

The gate was positively teeming with soldiers coming and going, men bearing a hundred different sigils and colours, spearmen and shieldmen and axmen, men with swords and men with bows, men getting ready for war. Here on the eastern side of King's Point, the gate opened onto a wide tract of grassy coastland that ended at the Steelrun River, a mile or so away, where it emptied into the Red Sea. Markets were often hosted out here, in summer in particular, yet now there were only tents and pavilions and shelters erected beside wagons, horse lines and latrines, a warcamp raised up to accommodate the bulk of the army beyond the confines of the city.

Inside the gate, it was no less hectic. Wagons and oxcarts trundled in and out down a central thoroughfare, ferrying supplies. To the right of the square, at least a hundred horses stood in the stalls of a large muddy stable, attended by grooms and stableboys. Knights came and went, trailed by their men-at-arms in shirts of mail and surcoats embroidered with their house arms and colours. Lythian saw a crowd of soldiers gathered around one petty lord, who stood upon a crate, giving a rousing speech.

"Lord Waymore," the guard told them, as they went. "He's in charge of the city finances but fancies himself a bit of a rabble-rouser too. Been going around trying to gee up the men for weeks. Thinks it'll make them fight harder, I guess."

He led them over to the stables where they handed their horses over to the grooms, then continued to take them on foot through the city.

"Been busy here ever since Lord Daecar arrived," the soldier went on, over the clamour. "He's got us all believing again, and better than Waymore ever will. I've seen him myself, several times, walking about with that Frostblade at his hip, inspiring the men. Gods, if that man's not Varin reborn, I don't know who is."

Lythian smiled to hear it. "What's the latest word on the invasion?"

"Crickets," the gate guard said. "The men say it'll happen soon, though, now that the storms have passed. The augurs thought they'd last only a day or so, those storms, but went on much longer in the end. Suppose you had some sense of that, did you? Where'd you come from, anyway? Down the coast, was it?" Before anyone had a chance to answer, the guard turned and shouted, "Ah, *milord*!" as he spotted a man marching through the crowds dressed in the silver and black banded cloak of the Pointed Watch. The sharpened shoulder caps and helm he wore told Lythian that this was their young captain, Sir Adam Thorley, whom he'd met on previous visits.

"Yes?" Sir Adam stopped before them, red-faced from his march. He was probably run off his feet from his duties, with the city so overcrowded. "What is it, Jayson? I'm busy, can't you see? And why aren't you at your post? You're meant to be manning the River Gate. Gods, do I have to put out every little fire myself?"

"Aye, milord, I was there, just now. Until I ran into these."

"These? Who?" Sir Adam turned his green eyes over the host. When he saw Lythian his face changed at once. "Goodness, Captain Lythian! I'm sorry, I didn't see you with all this traffic about."

"That's quite all right, Sir Adam."

"We've been expecting you," Thorley went on. "For some days now. There was a crow sent from…"

"Nightwell," came in Sir Storos. He stepped forward. "Sir Storos Pentar. Well met, sir." The pair shook wrists. "That crow was from my brother Glarus. I'm happy that it managed to reach you. Word on the wing has grown most unreliable, we know."

Sir Adam gave a breathy laugh. "Quite so, Sir Storos, yes. It aggravates Lord Daecar greatly. He says it cripples us, not knowing what's going on in the east. And we've had no word from Tukor or Rasalan for weeks." He looked at the guard called Jayson. "Go, back to your post. I'll take them from here."

"Milord. I sent a man already, to the Spear. To tell Lord Daecar that they've arrived."

"Then he'll have wasted his time. Lord Daecar is in an emergency session with his council." He turned back the way he had come, gesturing for the others to follow.

Lythian stepped to his side as they pushed on through the crowds. "Is there some problem, Sir Adam?" He had not known Amron to hold emergency councils lest there was a valid reason. *News of the invasion perhaps?*

"Ah, well it has to do with Lord Taynar, as I understand it. An incident, late last night. Though…well, perhaps it would be best if you talk to him yourself. I would not want to speak out of turn."

Intriguing, Lythian thought. He put it aside as they continued toward the south of the city where the Spear cut skyward in a great silver lance. The castle was built upon a rise, with ranging views over the harbour and sea, enclosed by a curtain wall and gate. Sir Adam Thorley led them through into the open courtyard, bordered by slim-pillared colonnades. Ahead was the keep itself, soaring high into the hard blue skies. To their left stood the castle feast hall and audience chamber where another Amron had once held his councils. *Amron the Bold*, Lythian thought. *The king who restarted the war…*

As soon as they entered the hall, they could hear the bellowing voice of Amron Daecar ringing out from above them. Sir Adam led them up the creaking wooden staircase to where the door to the audience chamber stood shut. He rapped his knuckles hard against the wood. The voice within trailed off and the oaken door was pulled open.

The man who appeared before them was tall, lean, dark-eyed, long-faced, and ghostly pale. He wore scratched grey armour, dark and worn, beneath a sooty black cloak. His hair was black as well, and his beard, though both showed some streaks of grey. *Whitebeard*, Lythian thought. He'd heard of this gloomy ranger from Elyon. His true name was Rogen Strand, the third son of Styron the Strong, though looked absolutely nothing like him at first glance. *That'll be the Taynar in him…*

A shout bellowed from inside the room, "Who is it, Rogen? I said no interruptions."

The ranger turned. "It's Sir Adam, my lord," he said in a dreary rasp.

"Sir Adam? Well come in, what is it?"

Sir Adam Thorley stepped inside as Whitebeard moved to make way. The others trailed in a few steps behind. Lythian scanned as he went. The room was well stocked with knights and petty lords, most of them of North Vandar, underlings of House Taynar. They stood and sat here and there, faces strained and stricken. A thick tension hung in the smoky air as braziers burned softly to either side, coughing grey smoke.

Sir Adam bowed. "My lord, I have the pleasure to present…"

"*Lythian?*" A smile tugged at Amron's black-bearded lips. "My friend… you're finally here."

Lythian dipped his head, maintaining utter propriety. "Returned from the south, at last, my lord. With a long overdue report."

A moment passed in silence. Lythian had hoped for all the world to speak with Amron alone upon arriving here; it seemed Amron was of the same mind. "Well, I'd best hear that report in private, I think," he said. "The rest of you, leave us. We can pick this up later." He gestured to the door.

The knights and lords made their way out without question, complaint or delay, passing by in a solemn procession. Lythian recognised them to a man. The seasoned Varin Knights Sir Quinn Sharp, Sir Ramsey Stone, Sir Taegon Cargill, and young Sir Rodmond Taynar were in attendance, as were the Taynar underlords Kindrick, Rosetree, Barrow and Grave, the Ironfoot. Sir Torus Stoutman passed with a grin and a wink, and Sir Ralf of Rotting Bridge put himself into a courteous bow, before the pair moved down the steps together. The castellan of the Spear, Lord Warton, shuffled past coughing and covering his mouth with a square of white cloth, dotted with red gouts of blood. The cough sounded more rabid and malignant than Lythian had last heard it, some eighteen months prior. Most surprising of the assemblage were the disgraced Greycloaks Sir Nathaniel, Sir Gerald, and Sir Alyn. All three looked haggard and hangdog as they glanced at him and plodded by. *And no surprise,* Lythian thought. Men outed publicly for treason often fell into unrecoverable states of dourness, he knew. *They're lucky to get a second chance.*

Once all of them had passed through the doors, Sir Storos Pentar stepped forward and went to a knee, posture precise. "Lord Daecar," he said in a ringing voice. "I swear to you my sword, if you will have it. And those of these men as well." He gestured to Sir Oswin and the others, arrayed beside the door. At once they fell to their knees as well. "We are yours to command, my lord, until this war is done and won."

Amron observed Sir Storos with gratitude, appreciative of the knight's observance of courtesy. "Your presence here is welcome, Sir Storos. But do you not have a post at Southwatch to fill?"

"My lord, perhaps you haven't heard? Southwatch came under attack not three days ago. We received word when we stayed overnight at Chilgrave, in the company of Lord Heward. The fortress was overwhelmed by an assault of dragons. It is destroyed, my lord."

Amron Daecar closed his eyes, breathed out, opened them again. He took a moment to himself, reflecting on the news. *It is yet another wound,* Lythian thought. *Another cut at a realm already bleeding.* Eventually, he recovered himself and said, "Sir Adam, see that Sir Storos and his men are given accommodations inside the castle, if you can find them space. Walter, please accompany them to the feast hall below while they wait."

The man called Walter walked over clutching a large book to his breast, appearing as if from nowhere. Lythian had heard of him as well. The luckiest man in the world, or so Elyon had said it. The scruffiest might be putting it more aptly to look at him. He smiled at them in good faith and led them below. Lythian ordered for Sir Pagaloth to go with them. That left only the ranger at the door.

"Rogen, wait outside," Amron said.

And then they were alone.

Amron Daecar rose from his seat, descending the short set of steps to the bottom of the stage. His face was coiled with a thousand concerns. *And pain*, Lythian saw. He had the same face of a hundred men he'd known, men who'd suffered grievous wounds in war that had never truly healed, men who lived with that agony day and night. He filled two cups of wine from the table. "A toast to your return. Come over here, Lythian. Let me get a proper look at you."

Lythian Lindar stepped through the hall to join him, footsteps echoing softly on stone. Below, a light hum of noise began to filter up from the feast hall, offsetting the quiet. "You're going to say I look older, Amron. Let me spare you having to bother; I know it full well." He took the cup offered to him, smiling. "You look older too."

"I am older. I only wish I was wiser to go with it." The former First Blade gave a craggy grin. "To your return, old friend." They clacked cups and drank deep. The wine was warm and spicy, reaching down Lythian's throat with long tangy tendrils. "Good, isn't it?" Amron said, seeing the look of satisfaction on Lythian's face. "Lady Brockenhurst keeps a fine cellar here." He refilled Lythian's cup, then his own, setting the jug aside. "So tell me, Lyth, are you well? Sir Glarus made no mention of your health in his letter, but you look strong to me. That's good. I had feared you would be bedevilled by injuries from your time in the south, but you look in fine fettle, my friend. And all ready for battle, I hope?"

The Knight of the Vale nodded dutifully, falling at once into the man's service, as was his place. "I have a few new scars, though nothing worse than that." *Not that you can see, anyway*, he thought to himself, preferring to spare the man his self-pity.

"Well, good. You're a little thinner, certainly, but still hearty enough." Amron grabbed his shoulder and gave him a shake, towering a half foot above him. It was what passed for a hug, the closest they were likely to get. "Gods, Lythian, it's good to see you. There was never a man to counsel me half so well as you, and share in my woe as well. What a bloody fool I was, sending you away." He sighed heavily, shaking his head. "I owe you an apology for that, Lyth. The harm it caused…"

"Water under the bridge," Lythian assured him. "A wise man once said that sometimes you have to pass through darkness to reach the light. So it has been with the two of us, Amron." He looked at the Frostblade, misting colourfully, majestically, at his hip. For a moment he admired it, as it deserved to be admired, this blade long lost and long forgotten, returned to the world at last. "Your journey led you to that, Amron. And mine…"

"To torture and humiliation," Amron came in, voice thick with self-rebuke. "It was reckless of me to send you to Agarath like that, with only Borrus and Tomos for company. I was a fool, Lythian, and my folly saw you suffer. Now Borrus is missing and Tomos is dead. And you…" He studied him. "I suppose you've heard all about what's been happening here?"

"Storos has kept me well abreast of the news, yes. And Elyon, while he was with me."

"Enough to fill a good few weeks on the road, I'm sure. Elyon's tale alone is quite something."

"And yours, Amron. The *Icewilds*? I was staggered when I heard you'd gone there."

"Driven by desperation, I assure you."

"And Amara." Lythian teased a smile. "It was her idea, Elyon told me."

"Isn't everything her idea? She whispered into Elyon's ear about stealing the Windblade too, I'm sure he said. Gods, that woman. If her tongue was a lance she'd be lethal." He gave a scoffing laugh, then had another swallow of wine. "So you know my story, Elyon's, all of ours. What of yours, Lyth? Come, let me hear it."

Lythian nodded, taken by a certain discomfiture. "My story? Well, I'm sure you've heard some."

"Rumours, little more. I'd hoped Elyon would have returned by now to sit me down and fill me in, but that boy seems intent on winning this war alone." He swung a leg over the bench and sat, the wood creaking under his great weight. "So, speak. Let's hear the truth of it from your lips."

The truth, Lythian thought. *The foul, rotten truth.* He took a seat beside his friend, and confessed to him his sins.

He spoke for some ten minutes without break, Amron venturing forth with only the occasional comment. Mostly he just sat, listening, nodding, looking out across the hall, pondering what he heard. When Lythian was done, Amron set aside his cup, steadied himself, and looked his friend deep in the eye. His voice was soft, reassuring and understanding, when he said, "Don't blame yourself for being human, Lythian. You only did what you felt was right."

Lythian felt a weight lift from his shoulders, as though the opinion of Amron Daecar on the matter was all that counted in the world. All the same, he would not let himself be assuaged of his guilt so easily. So he shook his head and said, "I should have done more, Amron. I *should* have been stronger. Borrus urged me to kill Eldur if we found him, and yet…"

"Yet you couldn't. Nor would Borrus have been able to. Nor anyone else. If you had tried to kill Eldur you'd have only died, and who would that have served?" He shook his head, waving the notion away. "I have never been a man to hang my helm on fate and destiny, but lately I've come to see that certain things are happening for a reason, Lythian. This," - he shook his snow-white scabbard - "did not come to me by chance. It was placed where I found it for me to find. Me, Lythian, and me alone. There was even a prophecy, you may have heard." He paused, remembering the words, then said, "*A lord of steel will come and drive the curse away. One great quest will fail, but one greater will light the way. Steel and snow will meet as enemies, but part as allies and friends. In this the frost shall be taken, and the lands grow clear to tend."*

Lythian hadn't heard those words before. "Elyon said something about a fateful finding of that blade, but…" He reflected on them. "One great quest will fail," he murmured. "That was your journey to Vandar's Tomb? To commune with his spirit? To seek deliverance."

"Yes. And it failed, quite miserably, and ended up leading me to this." He tapped the scabbard once more. "A *greater* quest. Something more important than me. Stegra Snowfist said that the prophecy had been passed down through his ancestors for two hundred years, that some sea-king came and put a curse upon those lands. I saw that curse with my own two eyes. It was a blight, some mist infused with magic. It drew me into a trance, and… and I saw things, Lythian. I *felt* things. And when I awoke, there it was. The Frostblade, driven into a boulder on the beach. Placed there by this sea-king, so I might return it here at the right time. And now, with what you've just told me of this heir of Varin…" He mused on that for a moment. "I've always known I was but a guardian of the blade, that I would have to give it up eventually. Well, now I know to whom. This heir. We have to find him."

Lythian was more hesitant. "The prophecy also said Eldur would rise as a force of good, Amron. There may be no heir."

"Or there may." Amron stood from the bench and moved over to stir the coals in the brazier. There was a chill between these thick stone walls that the warmth of spring didn't penetrate. "Elyon told you Thalan was destroyed, I trust?"

Lythian nodded. "He told me everything. Eldur stole the Eye of Rasalan, and the king who commands it."

"Weakly," Amron said. He poked at the coals. "You say Eldur knows of this heir?"

"Sotel Dar will have told him, yes."

"Then he'll be hunting him, we can be sure of it. No doubt that was why he kidnapped the king in the first place. He may hope he can find him before we do." He rubbed his chin, "Or perhaps Hadrin knows already. The Rasals have always kept their secrets from us, Lythian. And King Lorin was in Thalan before he died. Is it not possible that Lorin sired a son while there? And this son was raised in secret, trained in secret, to keep him hidden from the enemy?"

It sounded plausible, Lythian had to admit. "I have wondered the same. If so, King Godrin would have known, I'm certain of it."

"Probably. Though that hardly helps us, seeing as Hadrin cut a red smile into his father's neck. That sort of smile doesn't speak, Lythian." Amron prodded at the coals again, then limped back over to the table and sat. "Perhaps another might know. Someone who was close in Godrin's counsel. A favoured lord or knight."

"Sir Ralston," Lythian said. "Elyon told me he boarded a ship, heading south. Lancel and Barnibus were there. They had helped this girl your son had in his tent at Harrowmoor. She went with the Whaleheart. Saska, he said her name was."

Amron grumbled in displeasure. "Elyon never did share that sort of thing with me. I've heard bits and pieces about this girl, but not her name. Do you think she has something to do with it?"

Lythian pondered a moment. "Elyon spoke of a dream he had when he first met her. How she faded into a light of silver and blue. They say our dreams keep secrets from our waking minds, Amron. That there is magic in dreams. Perhaps he sensed something important in this girl. As Godrin must have, if he sent the Whaleheart to protect her."

The former First Blade mused on that, rubbing the thick bristles of his beard with a fist the size of a ham. Lythian had half forgotten how large Amron Daecar was. "Does he know where she is?"

"She went to Aram, he thinks, to find her grandmother. He told you about *that*, I take it? That this girl was an Aramatian princess, or so he was told."

"Yes, he mentioned that." Amron continued to muse on it. "There is a mystery here to be sure. This girl…we would do well to find her."

"I agree. Though her being in Aram does pose something of a problem."

"Tell that to my son. The last time I saw him, do you know what he asked me? If I would let him have the Sword of Varinar, so he might fly south and destroy the Bondstone, all by himself. He has grown fearless with that blade, Lythian. There is a passion in him, to help win this war, that makes me very proud. And wary, I will admit."

"He's changed, that is for certain. I saw it at once, when he arrived in Redhelm. The way he landed and brought order so quickly. He exudes a power that reminds me of someone I used to know." Lythian looked at his old friend, the shadow of a smile on his face.

Amron only grunted. "I wish it wasn't necessary. I'd sooner have Elyon safely back in Varinar, but that's me speaking as a father. As a commander I know he's our greatest asset. I'm just not sure I'm the right person to deploy him. I don't know if I can be impartial."

"You don't need to be. Elyon has as good a grasp on this war as anyone, and there is no one more informed. He sees the world from a new angle, Amron, quite literally, one that even you cannot. I care for him too, you know that, but my advice for you would be simple. *Trust him.* What he does may seem reckless at times, but you know he's thought it through. Trust him to make the right decisions. They may bear fruit in the end."

Amron bobbed his head in an accepting nod, acknowledging the point. "Yes, well speaking of my reckless wind-riding son, he had your armour sent down from the Steelforge for you. All polished to a brand new shine. And your blades as well, broadsword and dagger. They arrived only yesterday."

Lythian felt a sense of strength saturate his blood, just to think of wearing his armour again. There was nothing like donning your own godsteel plate, the interlinking segments, lobstered and overlapping to protect the joints and seams. He may not have Starslayer anymore, but his replacement broadsword would be just as lethal. "I was there when he sent the letter," he said. "We feared it would not have made it, but..." He smiled. "I shall be proud to wear it again, and fight once more at your side."

"No more than I will, Lythian. Just like old times, hey?"

Below them, the feast hall was beginning to grow louder with a muffled din. Lythian could hear the unmistakable sound of laughter down there, which was no surprise with Sir Torus Stoutman in attendance. The man was unashamedly jolly and had the exhausting habit of inserting a jape into every other thing he said. It was nice to hear, in truth. Laughter had been absent from Lythian's life for too long now and he missed it, the sound of it, the way it lightened the darkness in his heart. He turned to Amron with a question on his lips. It had not, after all, been particularly jolly in here when he arrived.

"Sir Adam mentioned there had been some incident last night. With Dalton Taynar." Who had been absent from proceedings, he had not failed to miss. "I take it all the shouting we heard when we arrived had something to do with it?"

The cheer leeched right out of Amron's face. "An incident? Yes, I should say so. Dalton was attacked last night in his bedchamber, a few hours before dawn. Someone managed to slip into his room while he was sleeping and stick a dagger in his gut..."

"What?" Shock blew through the Knight of the Vale like a brisk winter wind. "He's *dead?*"

"Dead. No. Just wounded. By the grace of the gods, Dalton woke up at the last moment and stopped the intruder from driving the dagger too deep. The physicians haven't told me yet how long he'll take to recover, though Dalton remains convinced he can fight. If so, it won't be well. This is a bloody tragedy, Lythian. You cannot know the trouble that blasted blade has caused."

"Blade? You're talking about the Sword of Varinar?"

"What else? Elyon must have told you about that. Dalton, Brontus, the Song of the First Blade. It's led to no end of conflict. Sir Brontus was unable to accept his loss in the contest and resorted to unseemly complaints and accusations to try to sway me into giving him another chance. He even accused me of favouritism, Lythian. The gall of the man. He'd have dragged all of our names through the mud if I hadn't sent him away, and even that didn't seem to stop him."

Lythian Lindar raised both of his eyebrows. "You're saying this was Brontus Oloran? *He* was the intruder?"

"Him? No. But someone under his employ, or another of his men? Oh yes, I'm certain of it."

"And this assassin? What happened to him?"

"Got away. Managed to kill the two men stationed outside Dalton's door, both of them household knights, both Bladeborn. I'd say he's skilled, whoever he is. Killed them quick and silent and crept right up to Dalton's bedside before he stirred from his sleep. And just in time as well. Another second and Dalton would be joining his father in the Eternal Halls."

Lythian could not understand how this attacker could get in and out without anyone seeing him. He supposed that was the thrust of Amron's ire; that the First Blade's men had been so damnably lax in securing his chambers. "So no one else saw this intruder come or go?"

"No one. There were some reports of a figure, cloaked and cowled, rushing through the castle, but at that time no one thought to try to stop him, or knew that anything untoward had occurred. By the time the alarm was raised the assailant was gone."

Lythian stood, pacing in thought. "Where did you send Sir Brontus?"

"To the Twinfort, to bolster Randall Borrington's forces. He had charge of five thousand men here, his uncle's mostly, though some Mantle men as well and others from lesser lords. I feared he'd have done something stupid had he stayed, so shipped him off. Well, more fool me. Seems the man has a longer reach than I thought."

"If it *was* him," Lythian said, with a note of caution. "Without evidence…"

"Yes, I know. There's nothing I can do, lest this would-be assassin comes to me to confess. Rather unlikely, wouldn't you say?"

"Or you could find him," Lythian proposed. He paced through the heart of the hall, circled a brazier, and returned. "Was he wounded, during the altercation? This assassin."

"Altercation?" Amron scoffed. "An altercation paints a picture of a couple of drunken men quarrelling outside a tavern. This was attempted murder, Lythian, of a greatlord and First Blade; a vile act of treachery. I've just welcomed the Greycloaks here, you probably saw. The Treasonous Trio, people are calling them. Well, I might as well march them back in here and ask if they had something to do with it." He scoffed again, and loudly. "Elsewise no, we have no leads."

He was being facetious, that was plain. *I get the mocking end of the stick*, Lythian thought. *The others just get his fury.* "So no wounds, then?"

Amron's large shoulders went up and down. "Dalton was unarmed. He said he managed to grab the assailant's wrists, to wrestle him away. I don't know. Maybe the attacker has some bruising there, on the wrists. It's nothing to go on, really. A needle in a bloody haystack and frankly we've got enough to worry about." He frowned, his thoughts suddenly wandering down another lane. "That about Southwatch. What Storos said earlier…?"

Lythian gave a reluctant nod. "Destroyed, yes, or so we heard. I assume a crow must have been sent here as well, though clearly it didn't make it. You know of Mudport, I trust?"

"Yes." Amron sighed heavily. "Dragon's Bane. Mudport. Now Southwatch. It sounds like the whole of the east is falling." He ran his left hand through the bristles of his beard, wincing in discomfort, rolling and stretching his shoulder. "How was Redhelm, when you were there?"

"Tense," Lythian said, darkly. "Alrus Pentar is no wartime commander. The trial we suffered was a farce. If that's how he means to rule, the city will not stand a chance."

"He always was a shadow of his father," Amron agreed. "Porus's death is most untimely, though there are still men of clarity and command in the east. We must put our faith in them, my friend." Another jerk of pain tore across his face as he pressed a set of strong fingers into his right thigh, kneading.

Lythian had observed the turmoil he was under, ever since he'd arrived. "The pain," he said, feeling obliged to ask. "How bad is it?"

"Manageable sometimes. Unbearable at others." Amron Daecar drove his finger down the muscle, up again, down again, up and down. He wore no mask in Lythian's presence, though with others that would not be so. "The Frostblade takes the pain away, but it's only temporary. In truth it's getting worse. These Blades of Vandar…they give with one hand and take away with the other. We will all have a fight on our hands when it comes time to give them up."

Lythian sensed a profound conflict within the man, an uneasy sense that even the great Amron Daecar might struggle to hand over his own crutch if and when the time should come. *How can he? To give up the Frostblade will be to condemn himself to life as a cripple, plagued by a chronic, unceasing agony. What sort of life would that be, to be reduced to that?*

Amron seemed to know what was going through his head. "You doubt I'll be able to set it aside?" He gave an uneasy smile, as though to hide his own inner troubles. "You needn't. I have a mantra I speak nightly. One I must have recited ten thousand times by now. Oh, I understand the value of sacrifice for a greater cause. If I should be condemned to live the rest of my days lame and in perpetual discomfort, so be it. It is one outcome that may come to pass, but hardly the most likely. A good soldier marches to war knowing they're already dead, Lythian. It frees him from fear, from the fetters that bind other men to act upon their terror, to run and hide and wilt in the heat of battle. We are dead men, Lythian, you and I. What comes after is not of relevance to men like us. Until we see the sky brighten beneath that brand-new dawn, we accept that it is still the dark of night. And in that darkness, my friend, we fight. As dead men, we fight."

He sat, teeth crushed together in a fixed expression of defiance, and just then, a commotion erupted below, voices calling out in what sounded like sudden greeting. There was a clatter of noise, a heavy stamp of footfall up the steps, then a voice called out an order, and Whitebeard opened the door.

Elyon Daecar stepped in.

51

Saska

"The threat has been dealt with, Your Serenity," Sir Ralston said, as he came to a sharp stop ahead of them in the high terrace gardens, his face spotted with droplets of sweat and blood, covering his cheeks like freckles. "Starrider Antapar has been killed, along with Sunrider Konollio and their followers. Prisoners have been taken for questioning. Lord Hasham's interrogators are sharpening their tongues and their instruments as we speak."

Safina Nemati digested that in what had become customary; with a look of deep sadness on her face that it had all come to this. "That is good to hear, Sir Ralston," she said, in a soft, solemn voice. "Antapar has always been one of Elio Krator's fiercest advocates and allies. We can have little doubt he would have been working to help him, from inside the city."

"Lord Hasham is of that belief," the Wall agreed. "We found in their hideout plans to storm the gates, with the intent to open them from the inside for Lord Krator's host to pass through. It was just as the informant said."

The informant, Saska thought. She had heard whispered talk of this mysterious figure over the last couple of days, though it appeared Lord Iziah Hasham was not at liberty to disclose his identity. *Nor his plans.* There was much going on behind the curtain that Saska was not privy to, nor her grandmother as it turned out. The wound of Elio Krator's betrayal had enervated and enfeebled her, and she no longer took an active part in any war councils. "I trust you, Iziah," she had merely said. "I trust you to know what you are doing."

"Do you know who the informant is?" Saska found herself asking, directing the question at the Wall in a voice that brooked no interest in being deceived.

Sir Ralston Whaleheart turned to look at her, his flat-topped greathelm held in the crook of his arm. He was otherwise armoured from neck and toe, his plate spattered with gouts of blood and little patches of dirt as well, from the fighting. "No. I have not been told. Lord Hasham and the Strong Eagle keep their council close on this matter."

"So you don't know what his plan is? Hasham's?"

"My principal function is to protect you, my lady," the Wall said, somewhat sidestepping the question. "That remains my primary focus."

"Yet you fought today, when you didn't have to. You risked yourself, Rolly. Who would protect me had you died?"

"The raid on Sunrider Antapar's hideout was no risk, my lady. Lord Hasham had detailed information about their numbers, where they were running their operations from, the manner of their security, and so forth. The greater risk would have been for me to stand aside, and by doing so, allow their plot to unfold as planned. I protect you by killing the enemy within these walls. I was compelled to go, by that alone."

Saska had no complaints about that, only questions. "How many of Lord Hasham's host were killed?"

"Forty-two."

"And how many did Sunrider Antapar have?"

"Over two hundred. Two hundred and thirteen, I believe. Almost all were slain, though some eighteen were taken captive, and a similar number got away. They are being hunted as we speak. Some may seek out other allies of Lord Krator's, but I suspect most will slink into the shadows and disappear. Make no mistake, my lady, this is a significant victory. It will take Krator's allies time to regroup, and even then they may have lost all taste for his treacheries. If the city is secured from within, a large part of the battle is won."

There remained something he wasn't telling her, she sensed. Some knowledge of Hasham's grander designs that he didn't agree with, perhaps, or was choosing not to relay to her in order to better protect her.

"And what about that, Rolly?" she asked, pointing over the parapet wall that bordered the terrace gardens at the top of the palace. At that precise moment, a distant thud was heard to sound as a boulder crashed into the city's eastern walls. Over the course of their short conversation, several other such thuds had rumbled through the muggy afternoon air, in fact. The bombardment had been going on for two days now, a constant and brutal fusillade that sent trembles through the city from dawn until dusk, and all the way through to dawn again. "The walls may be fifteen feet thick, and several times as high, but Krator will breach them eventually. And when he does…"

"Eventually is not a definitive scale of time," the Wall broke in. "It could, and will likely, take months, and a good many of them, for the wall to be breached. The city defences have a range superior to Elio Krator's catapults, and that means he must rely on the few trebuchets he has with range enough to assault us. And should one section of wall begin to weaken, it can be hastily nurtured from inside, fortified and rebuilt."

"Rams, then," Saska said. "A big ram will be able to knock through the gates."

"They have no battering rams," the Wall said, with certainty.

597

"They can build one. Ladders and siege towers as well. They have the numbers to overwhelm us. As soon as Cedrik Kastor's Bladeborn get past the walls, the city will stand no chance. He'll have hundreds of them, both weak-blooded and strong. Who knows, maybe even thousands. Regular men will not be able to stand up to that. Hasham's soldiers...your soldiers, Grandmother," she said, glancing to the old woman in her chair, "will be slaughtered within a day."

"That is a possible outcome," the Wall agreed. "But not for you to worry about, if we leave."

"I don't want to leave. I can't. Not like this..."

The Whaleheart went right on. "I have been discussing possible ways out of the city, that will take us past Lord Krator's siege lines without alerting him to our presence. It is critical that we pass without his knowledge, else he will hunt and harry us along the way. There are ways this can be accomplished." His eyes fell to Safina Nemati, sitting with a blanket across her lap, despite the afternoon heat. "You only need to give the order, Your Serenity, and..."

"My granddaughter will give the order, Sir Ralston," the old woman broke in, softly. "This is her life, her decision. My part in this is done."

A look of faint disapproval passed over the face of Sir Ralston Whaleheart. "My lady, if I may?"

"Of course."

"Aram is your city, the heart of your duchy, and yours to defend. Yet for this last week, you have been..." He paused, considered his words, then went on. "You have been distant, even disinterested, ever since you took parley with Sunlord Krator. It seems to me that you have given up."

Her answer did not come at once, but after a few moments of quiet, extended reflection. "There comes a time, Sir Ralston," she said eventually, and without rebuke, "when we all give up, or so it may seem to others. It may be only a temporary lapse, a temporary despair, or something more profound. In my case it is the latter. You see me as having given up, yet this isn't the truth. I have merely come to a realisation of worth, Sir Ralston, and value. In this fight, you see, I have none. I am an old done woman, not long for the stars, who would spend the last of her days here in the palace with her beloved granddaughter, before she leaves to pursue her destiny. The question of when that will be is not one I can answer, nor is it one I will attempt to influence or impede. Saska has made it plain to me that I have clung to her too hard, and I can see now that that is true. She does not need to be coddled and swaddled, but unfettered and set free, and given the authority to make her own decisions, her own mistakes, to win for herself her own triumphs. Only then can she truly grow into who she needs to be. So that is what you see, my dear Sir Ralston, a woman who has stepped back into the shade, so that others can flourish in the light."

The Wall gave that a thoughtful nod, considering it at some length. He did not show any particular emotion on his face at the woman's plight, but that was his way. It seemed to simplify matters for him, in fact. No longer would he need to consider the Grand Duchess of Aramatia in the bargain; only the word of Saska, heir of Varin, daughter of kings, was to count.

So he turned to her, looking down from his towering height, and rumbled, "And what is your decision, my lady? If you wish it, I could make arrangements to leave the city this very night. I would, in fact, strongly advise this course, before..." He paused, not giving voice to whatever he was about to say. After a moment he went on. "It is going to be a dark night, I am told, with heavy cloud cover. A small party would be best to slip the net. You, me, the redhead girl..."

"Leshie."

"Leshie, yes. And if you insist on bringing the sellswords as well, I will have to accept it. The Butcher and the other one. With the green eyes."

"Merinius."

Sir Ralston Whaleheart nodded. He seemed to make a point of forgetting their names on purpose. "A small party, as I say. All Bladeborn, I think that would be best."

"The Butcher doesn't want to leave yet," Saska told him. "His brother is among Krator's forces. The Baker. He is eager to find out what has become of him, Leshie told me."

"Yes, I am aware. A brotherly tie that can easily be severed by sufficient riches, I would think. Or else we simply go alone, you me and the redhead..."

"*Leshie.*"

"Leshie," the giant said, noting Saska's annoyance. "She has proven herself skilled, and courageous, and loyal as well, there can be no doubt. The three of us may suffice."

Saska disagreed entirely. "No. We need more. And you know we do, with all the terrors out there. And anyway, I've decided..." She firmed herself for the inevitable rebuke. "I'm not leaving Joy behind..."

"My lady..."

"It's decided, I said," she almost snapped, with fresh authority. "When Krator and Kastor set camp outside our walls, *everything* changed, Rolly, and you know it. You think I would leave Joy here, with the city under siege? Knowing what Elio would do to her should he find her?"

"You are willing to leave your grandmother behind, why not the cat?" That was low, and Sir Ralston knew it even as he said it. A look of contrition showed upon his face and at once he set into an apology. "My lady, forgive me. That was rashly said, and uncouth. I know much of this is being forced upon you."

It's all being forced upon me, Saska thought. She was done complaining about that, though, done whining of her function and her fate. If this was her lot, so be it. "It's fine. I know you only want what's best for me, but I'm *not* leaving Joy here, and that's final." Another heavy thud echoed out from the east, almost to put a full stop on that particular part of the conversation. *How kind of you, Elio. Much obliged.* The Wall had nothing further to say.

Saska turned to her grandmother, deciding to leave the topic there, to run before harder questions might be asked. "I'll be back a little later, so we can talk and dine together, Grandmother." she told her." I want to hear the rest of that tale, the one you were telling me last night. That first love of yours. The boy with the dark curly hair and chestnut eyes."

"Tamario. Oh, such a handsome boy he was too. I shall refresh my memory and regale it to you later, and in full if you like?"

"I'd like that very much."

Safina Nemati's lips shaped themselves into a soft yet mournful smile. She had come to live for their time together of late, time spent getting to know one other properly, as grandmother and granddaughter, without falling into their usual discourse of fate and destiny and war. Nay, those subjects had been outlawed by her since the day she had told Saska she would not be going with her when she left, that her place was here, in Aram, where she was born, and so would die. Instead they spoke of simple things, simple joys, of family and friends, telling stories of those they had loved and lost. They played games, whispered like children, giggled like girls, and savoured the time they had left.

Saska sensed the deep sadness in her grandmother all the while, as though this was merely the front of the stage and behind, behind the curtain, lay all the hidden turmoil within, yet she never had cause to mention it. That would only suck them down into those *other* topics again. The fate and destiny and war, and their inevitable and impending parting which would, in all likeliness, be the last time they would ever see one another. Saska would be a long time away and even if Krator and Kastor were beaten back and defeated, the Grand Duchess would not live long.

She was ill, it had become clear, ailed by some wretched malady that she'd been battling for some time. One that had been lying as though dormant, kept at bay by the old woman's strength of heart and strength of soul until such a time as her job was done. But now that volcano had been stirred to life, the lava rising, the banks broken by the betrayal of Elio Krator, who had sped her withering, sped her dying, stolen her strength of heart and strength of soul to send her wasting away more rapidly. It seemed to Saska that her departure would be the death of the old woman, the final bell to toll on her long and distinguished life. That Safina Nemati was only clinging on for the time they spent together, for those few hours a day where they whispered and gamed and giggled, and were as it should be, finally, just a grandmother and her granddaughter, lazing the days away. That when they finally parted, she would uncurl her fingers, loosen her grip, and let herself slip off her mortal coil.

And how can I leave, knowing that? Saska wondered, grief-struck. *Or is my fate more important than family, the only family I have left in the world?*

She could not think about that now. It was another forbidden topic, a 'dreary topic' her grandmother had said - this illness of hers - that they needn't discuss. "Later, then," Saska merely said, firming her voice for fear it might falter, giving her grandmother a kiss on her rumpled, paling, fore-head. "I'll hear all about handsome Tamario later."

"I'll look forward to it, darling." The old woman reached and took her hand, kissing it tenderly. Everything she did was tender now. And that only made it all the harder.

She absented herself from their company, passing through the terrace gardens. The birds chirruped and chirped in the trees, the insects buzzed and clicked, and far off now, away in the east, came the thud and rumble of the siege. Saska wondered why the city had even been subjected to this brutal bombardment if Elio Krator expected his allies to open the gates. *A distraction? A diversion? Is he trying to sow fear?* It could be that the bombardment was merely a contingency, should their initial plans fail, which it seemed they had. That news should have made Saska buoyant, though something wasn't sitting right with her. Rolly knew more than he was willing to say, that was clear, and Saska felt vexed by Lord Hasham's secrecy as well. Thankfully, she had some assets of her own to deploy. And one, in particular, who had an almost compulsive need to tell the truth.

She found her in her bedchamber, down on the lower levels, pacing from wall to well-decorated wall. As soon as Saska slipped inside, Leshie stopped in her pacing and said, "What took you so long?"

"Rolly was giving a report." Saska turned and shut the door. Her voice descended into a clandestine whisper when she asked, "So? Did you discover anything, Lesh?"

The Red Blade was not wearing her leather armour today, rather the garb of a commoner; wrappings of scuffed linen that crossed her body in a diagonal style. Her hair was tied up into a headdress and she'd even gone to the lengths of applying some facial cream, of the sort they learned to make while studying at the Brightwater Academy in Thalan, to temporarily darken her skin tone. It was easily applied and washed away, leaving no traces, and had no permanent effect, unlike others that were less ephemeral. Leshie had, over the preceding weeks, made many friends among the palace guard and, in line with her sometimes reckless need for adventure, had gone out frequently at night to sample the city's pleasures. Each time she did so, she dressed as such. By now some of the guards had learned to turn a blind eye to her comings and goings, though most of the time, she insisted, she slipped past them without them seeing her.

It was not pleasure, however, that Saska had asked her to seek today, but information. "So?" she pressed. "Come on, Lesh, don't keep me in suspense."

"Oh, but it's so fun to see you squirm." The girl grinned that wicked grin of hers, unwrapped her head of the cloth that bundled her hair, and tossed it aside. Red locks fell down like autumn leaves. Then she stepped over to a water basin, picked up a scrubbing cloth, and began to wipe her face, neck, and hands clean, exposing her pale freckly northern skin.

It seemed the girl had only just returned, or else was waiting for Saska to arrive before changing, for what reason the princess couldn't fathom. Leshie was like that; a simple enigma. Half the time she seemed the most honest, straight-talking girl in all the world, and then she'd suddenly do something terribly mysterious. She seemed to enjoy the contrast and the state of being unpredictable.

As she washed her face, she said, "The east is being evacuated. Or *has been* evacuated, I should say. Some districts, anyway, near the gate. I went there a few days ago and already people were being cleared out. When I went earlier today it was deserted, except for soldiers. There were lots of carts around as well, though I couldn't tell what they were hauling, seeing as they were covered. Barrels or something, I think. Tried to get closer, but a soldier saw me and shooed me away. Well, I think he was doing that anyway. He made that gesture with his hand, you know, like flicking it, the way you do when you want someone to clear off. He was probably saying that too - "Clear off, vermin, we don't want the likes of you around here," - but I don't speak Aramatian, so I don't know." She finished wiping her face and stood up straight. "It's not easy, with the language barrier thing. I wish I wasn't such an idiot sometimes. I mean, look at you. Babbling on in Aramatian all the time. Do you speak that with your grandmother? Aramatian? Or do you chat in the common tongue?"

"Both," Saska said. "Mainly the common tongue, though. My Aramatian is still pretty rubbish, Lesh."

"Yeah, well I wouldn't know. You sound pretty fluent to me."

"So the east is being cleared?" Saska said. "Which districts?"

"Ones near the gate." Leshie picked up a towel and continued her cleansing routine, drying her face and rubbing away the last of the cream. "The east gate. They call it the Cherry Gate, I think. There are some cherry trees there. Or used to be. I don't know."

"And they're evacuating all the civilians from nearby?"

"Yeah, right down that central thoroughfare, and either side as well. Guess it's a precaution, in case Krator bashes through that way. That Sunrider Antapar guy...that was the gate he was planning to open. Two nights from now, the plan was. I saw Hasham earlier, walking about bellowing commands...you know how he likes to do that. Anyway, he was with the Wall and said something about the plan being for two nights from now. I was hiding at the time, being all sneaky up on some rooftop...you know what I'm like...and managed to eavesdrop. Hasham was saying something about that gate...the Cherry Gate...and seemed to be asking the Wall for something. I didn't get it all, obviously...they were quite far away...but Coldheart seemed unsure. Think I heard him say something about it being too dangerous, and Hasham said something like 'there is no victory without risk'. Anyway, it was all a bit confusing, so I thought I'd go and see Butcher about it."

Saska was leaning forward. "And?"

"And this is the best part," Leshie said excitedly. "You know that informant we were talking about?"

"I do."

"Well, I know who he is. Butch didn't want to let it out - he's in on it as well, all this plotting and planning and stuff - but I have ways of making him talk...things I'll not trouble you with, Saska. Not you, sweet, sweet innocent Saska," she said, in a sort of 'baby' voice, as she reached out to ruffle her hair.

Saska pulled back, swatting her hand away. "No more games, Leshie. Tell me who the informant is."

The Red Blade did not prevaricate on this occasion. "Tall, dark, handsome, and a bloody scoundrel who's *not* to be trusted." Then she grinned, widely, like a wolf, and added, "And he's got a golden tooth."

52

Amron

A cloak had been drawn across the skies, a pall of cloud thick and grey. Amron Daecar moved his eyes from left to right, slowly, scanning, squinting, searching for his son. Pain throbbed dully in his right thigh, and his left shoulder had succumbed to an unspeakable bout of sudden, spasm-like twists and jerks. Every one of them made him grimace, twisting his features into expressions of agony, yet he refused to give in to his vast temptations, refused to touch the Frostblade until he must.

"My lord, you seem in some discomfort," Sir Ralf of Rotting Bridge observed, breaking off from their discussion. The old man stood beside him upon the high balcony of his private quarters, at the summit of the Spear, looking out over the sea. The conversation had been tense. "Would it not be better to relieve your pain when it gets this bad? Surely it becomes difficult to think straight?"

He was correct, of course, though in many ways the pain was a useful distraction for his concern, given what they'd been discussing. "The pain will pass soon, Sir Ralf," he merely said. "It is a particularly violent bout, is all. And something I must get used to."

There were few men who were privy to the realities of Amron Daecar's suffering. And fewer still - perhaps none at all - who grasped the true depths of that torment. It was a malignant, ever-expanding and ever-increasing thing, a cancer of pain that seemed to grow fiercer and more widespread with each passing week. In the company of men he could not entirely trust - and that included almost everyone - he would conceal his pain by touching the Frostblade occasionally, even curling his fingers about its hilt or pommel for extended periods of time to drive that pain away. When he walked the streets he would do the same. When he addressed crowds of soldiers, spoke with their captains, showed his face in public in any capacity at all, he would cling to the Frostblade all the while.

To show strength, he told himself. *To inspire. They want to see the commander, not the cripple, the warrior, not the wretch.* To many men he was almost mythical, and mythical could be motivating. "We're led by a demigod," they would say to one other. "By Varin Reborn, the Steel Father come again." If such a thought allowed a man to fight with more conviction, was it not worth it to play that part? Amara had always made that claim, and gods damn the woman, she was right. So in public, Amron Daecar played the part. And in private, they got the truth…they got the cripple.

A clank of armour behind him heralded the arrival of Rogen Strand. His armour had a distinctive rustle, and the man himself had a distinctive gait. Amron recognised it without turning. "Yes, Rogen?"

"Lady Brockenhurst is without, my lord. She requests an audience."

Amron sighed, reached to touch the Frostblade, and rested a single finger upon the pommel, initiating his blood-bond, sending a flood of warmth and comfort through him. At once his aches, ails, and pains were dissolved and replaced by a feeling of profound and total strength. Lady Brockenhurst was one such unaware of his torment, and it would not serve to express to her the truth. "Thank you, Rogen. Send her in."

The Pointed Lady wore her typical attire: orange fox fur coat, complete with high stiff collar, black satin gloves, brocade dress beneath. Her son Florian came with her, though as she passed through Amron's chambers, the boy searched, spotted Walter Selleck sitting in his chair, writing, and pounced, demanding brand new stories from the man he called '*Lucky*' in a squeaky-voiced, almost frantic, tirade. Walter looked a shade embattled, but closed his book, put it aside, smiled and did his duty. Young Lord Florian could be a tyrant when he didn't get his stories, and Walter was the only one who could assuage him.

His mother laughed as she joined them on the balcony. "Poor Walter. He'll run out of tales soon, I fear."

"He has a good imagination, my lady," Amron said. "I'm sure he can make some up." His tone of voice was courteous, though he had absolutely no interest in discussing the fancies of an eight-year-old boy. "What can I do for you, Anne?"

"You can tell me what's going on, Amron. There have been all sorts of comings and goings from the city of late - *my* city, I should add - and I always seem to be the last to know." She folded her long, spindly arms, most displeased. "My castellan told me that Lythian Lindar has arrived. That he interrupted your council meeting earlier. Is that correct?"

"He arrived a short time ago, yes."

"Then where is he, exactly? He has an Agarathi with him, I'm told. A *dragonknight*. I would very much like to meet this man and give him an inter-rogation of my own."

Amron had as little time for Lady Brockenhurst's meddling as he did her son's tantrums. "Sir Pagaloth is Sir Lythian's sworn man. There will be no interrogations, my lady, not from you, me, or anyone else."

"I think you rather forget yourself, Amron. This is my city, not…"

"This is not your city, Lady Brockenhurst," he felt compelled to remind her. "You are guardian to your son, yes, until he comes of age, but even when Florian does so, it will not be his city either. King's Point, as with every city in this kingdom, is under the dominion of the crown."

A smile arranged itself upon her lips, painted orange to match the colour of her cloak. "Oh. Finally admitting it, are you?"

"Admitting what?"

"That you're king."

Amron did not answer that. "My lady, I have no intention of insulting you. Nor would I wish to undermine your authority. I only mean to say that it is wartime, and you are a civilian. If I do not come to you quickly with tidings pertaining to the war, know that it is not out of spite or a lack of respect, but merely due to seniority and chain of command from a military perspective. Moreover, I have invited you to attend our council sessions several times already, yet on each occasion you have chosen not to take part."

"Well...Florian takes up a great deal of my time, and there are other matters...most important matters, to a lady...that I have a duty to perform. And take part, you say? How would I? All those lords and knights who trail you around would only look at me and wonder why I'm there." She shook her head resolutely. "No, I'd only be getting in the way."

She has no interest, Amron knew, as he'd known all along. The dry formalities of his war councils were terribly stale to her, he did not doubt. It was clear that her interest had merely been piqued by the return of Lythian Lindar, so long away, and the mysterious dragonknight in particular. Amron had no intention of pandering to her, however. He went silent, waiting to see if she had anything else, anything of merit, to say.

Eventually, she shuffled her feet, turned her eyes over the sea, and said, "So...you're out here waiting for your son, are you?" Her tone of voice was ever-so-slightly peevish, as though his silence had somehow wounded her. "Oh yes, I heard about that as well. He arrived a little after Sir Lythian did, I am told. You spoke a while and then off you came up here. There's a rumour going around that he's flown off to search for the enemy armada. See if it's encroaching upon our shores. Do I have that right, my lord?"

"Yes, that's true," Amron said. In this subject he was more than happy to talk with her. She had, after all, been sending out sea scouts for months to give warning of the position of the enemy fleet, so had every right to know. "He left well over an hour ago. Sir Ralf believes that's a good thing."

"Oh?" The Lady of the Point pointed her pointed nose at him. "How so, sir?"

Sir Ralf spoke with impeccable courtesy, as ever. "My lady, if Sir Elyon should have returned sooner, that would suggest the armada was very close, set to arrive here to siege us even by this very night. The longer he is away, however, the more likely it is that the enemy remains at anchor at the Trident."

"Yes, I understand the logic, Sir Ralf. Though of course there are other reasons he may have been delayed." She looked at Amron. "How much faith do you have in your son, my lord?"

"A very great deal," Amron Daecar answered.

The woman smiled. "Then he'll be fine, I'm sure. Sir Elyon is a master dragonslayer, so should be able to outrun them easily enough, if spotted. Or out*fly*, rather," she said, with a chuckle. "He may even lead a few of them here, drawing them from the herd, so to speak. There is talk among the tables that he did just that at Dragon's Bane. And with some success, I have heard."

Success was not a word Amron would use to describe the events that unfolded at Dragon's Bane. "Elyon will return shortly," he said, in a firm voice, as though it had been his order, his idea, to send him off scouting in the first place. To the contrary, Amron's first instinct when Elyon suggested it was to command him otherwise, until he remembered Lythian's advice, given only minutes before his son's sudden arrival: that Elyon saw things from a new perspective, a rarified perspective, that he had a grasp on the war as strong as anyone's and, consequently, was capable of making his own decisions.

And he's right, Amron knew. Elyon was untethered now from the rule of regular command, and not constrained by the limits of other men. So when his son had stood there before him in the audience chamber, in his recently polished and reinforced plate armour, gleaming with a fresh coat of fire-proof oil, a fine, richly woven and brand new Varin cloak draped at his back, and the Windblade at his hip, and said he was going to fly south, "to scout for the enemy armada," what could Amron say? He had no recourse to deny him, nor had he. He had merely dipped his chin, saying, "If you think that best, son," and told him he would be awaiting his return upon the balcony of his private chambers.

And so here he was now. Watching. And waiting.

The Pointed Lady began prattling on about dragon numbers again, as Amron gave the skies another scan. She seemed fixated on this point that there were hundreds of them, and quite convinced that they were utterly doomed, if that were indeed true. It was not the sort of rhetoric that Amron needed to hear, and one of the reasons he rarely sought her company. Anne Brockenhurst was an unashamed worrier, given to exaggeration, speculation, and a certain penchant for doomsaying. As ever, it quickly wore thin.

"My lady, perhaps you have other matters to attend to," Amron interrupted, as she went on and on in his ear. "I'm sure the ladies of King's Point could do with your leadership and support, at this difficult time. Sir Adam informs me they're all safely below, in the underground sanctuaries. It might be time for you to take little Florian there as well."

She shook her head. "I'll take Florian down when - and only when - we see wings in the skies, and sails on the water. Have you visited those sanctuaries yourself, Amron? Oh, they're finely appointed, there's no lie there, very pleasantly furnished, but they're dark, cramped, and dreary for all that, and full of weeping women. No, I shall go there only when I must."

Amron gave a curt nod. "As you wish. If you intend to stay here, however, and wait until Elyon returns, perhaps you might prefer to do so inside? Sit, relax, drink some wine. I will call you as soon as I see him."

"I'm boring you," she said, in a moment of self-awareness.

"No, that isn't…"

"You don't need to spare me, Amron," she cut in. "If you want rid of me, just say so. I shan't take offence."

Something told him that was patently untrue. "Your company is always welcome, my lady. All the same, I was engaged in an important discussion with Sir Ralf, before you arrived. I would like to see it concluded…and in private, if I may?"

"Of course. Say no more." With a certain measure of pride, she spun on her heels, and retreated inside.

Amron gave out an audible groan of relief at her departure. "Remind me to tell Rogen that I'm engaged next time, Ralf. Gods, that woman does like to go on."

Sir Ralf gave a sombre nod. "She is of tremulous character, my lord, particularly on the subject of dragons. An understandable malady, I would say."

"Understandable, yes, but not something I need to hear every time I see her. Her manner exhausts me. And if this of Drulgar should reach her ears…"

The old knight nodded, as Amron directed them back to their erstwhile discussion. Prior to Lady Brockenhurst's arrival, he had updated Sir Ralf on everything Elyon had told him and Lythian during their short reunion in the audience chamber, earlier that day. The Marshlands were overrun, he had said, and the rest of East Vandar was soon to follow. "Rammas and Rikkard are pulling back to Rustbridge," Elyon told them, before giving a brief summary of the days they'd spent being assaulted by Vargo Ven's dragons on the road. Then there was this meeting with the dragonlord himself, briefly recounted, and the unspeakable news that Drulgar the Dread, the Great Calamity, had, Ven claimed, risen up from the deep dark places of the earth and taken up his old sentry post at the Nest, resting upon the ruins of the ancient fortress, brooding and basking in his boundless, unutterable hate.

A shiver went up the spine of Amron Daecar just to think of it. *He is out there, even now,* he thought, gazing across the sea. *A weapon of total and calamitous destruction, just waiting to be unleashed.*

He turned to Sir Ralf. "These tidings of Drulgar," he said, in a slightly choked voice. His throat felt terribly dry all of a sudden, as though something was lodged in there. He coughed to clear it. "You would have it shared, would you? You would risk inducing panic?"

The old knight nodded pensively. "There can be no helping that, my lord. I understand what you're saying, about the fear it will impose on the men, but I'm of the opinion that they need to be prepared."

"There is nothing a man can do to prepare against this, Ralf. Why trouble them with it? Many - most, even - will not even believe it. As they continue to deny that Eldur has returned."

"Denial is the refuge of the fearful, my lord. But it is not to be mistaken for disbelief. A man may laugh and say they do not believe a thing, but often that is merely the mentality of the herd, a protective mechanism that provides shelter from the truth, a truth they fear to confront. But that is not to say they do not believe it, deep down, when engaged in private, honest reflection. Most, I feel, have come to accept that Eldur is alive. And if they can believe that, they can believe this."

"And do what with the knowledge? Lose sleep? Fall into despair? Abandon their posts? I tell you, Ralf, we will have a panic on our hands if this news gets out."

"It *has* gotten out, my lord," Sir Ralf of Rotting Bridge said, quite plainly. "Your son has already spoken of it to Sir Hank Rothwell and Sir Bomfrey Marsh. Soon all of Varinar will know of it, and it will not take long for word to reach us here."

It was worse than that, in fact. Elyon had also stopped at Crosswater on the way from Varinar that morning, to warn Lord Botley Harrow of the news, and had spoken with Lord Rammas, Sir Rikkard, Lady Payne and others in the east as well, shortly after his parley with Vargo Ven. Amron should not have been surprised. Elyon's style of command was much opposed to his own in certain respects, though that wasn't to say he was wrong. Only less cautious, not so given to circumspection. *Younger*, in a word.

And there was something else, something Elyon *hadn't* said. Amron had sensed it, that his son had some confession to make, before he'd lost his nerve and flown away.

Well, I'll hear of it later, when he's back. He gave the skies yet another long study. *Now where the bloody hell are you, son?*

The wait went on, the minutes ticking by, the tension mounting. The two men continued their conference as the winds picked up, talking over and between the gusts. The foul fate of the east was considered; the many fortresses, castles, and cities that had been lost. They spoke too of Dalton Taynar, who lay abed in his chambers, attended by a small army of physicians and nurses, applying drakeshell powder by the hour to hasten his healing, feeding him roseweed oil for the pain.

On his way up here, Amron had briefly stopped to talk to one of the healers. The prognosis was plain; Lord Dalton Taynar, the First Blade of Vandar, was in no position to fight with anything approaching his full strength.

"How long?" Amron had demanded.

"Until…?"

"Until he can fight, damnit."

The physician had quavered beneath his gaze. "I cannot say for sure, my…my lord. Weeks…"

"*Weeks?*" Amron roared.

"Y-yes, my lord. At least until he's back to…to full strength. The wound…it's clean, and hit no major organs, praise Ashandar, and the drakeshell powder should speed his healing significantly, but all the same, he…he…"

"I want him ready to fight in days," Amron bulled in. "Hours would be better."

The man blinked at him. He had rather googly, protruding eyes, as though they had attempted to escape his head, and only managed to make it half the way out. "Hours? No, my lord, no…that won't be possible."

"Damn it, man, I wasn't being serious. Days. Fine, I'll give you days. Strap him up, wrap him in his armour, and wheel him out if you have to. I need my First Blade. I need the sword he carries. I need him there to inspire the men."

The physician did not seem to know what to say. A droplet of sweat was beading on his forehead. He wiped it away. "Yes, my lord, of…of course. Days. We can work with days."

"Hours would be better," Amron Daecar grunted once more, leaving him.

Sir Ralf had been with him at the time, standing aside, so heard it all. He seemed to be of the opinion that the arrival of Sir Lythian Lindar, noble Captain of the Varin Knights, was most opportune, even fateful, given the circumstances. "Did you ever let him carry it when you were First Blade, my lord?" he inquired. "The Sword of…"

"I know which sword you're talking about, Ralf," Amron cut in. "And no, is the answer. The Sword of Varinar is for the First Blade only, and not to be passed around on a whim." Amron knew exactly what he was getting at. "Lythian cannot be raised to First Blade of Vandar, Sir Ralf, if that is what's on your mind. There are official channels we must observe."

"In such times as these, concessions *could* be made. Perhaps if Lord Taynar would permit Captain Lythian to train with the Sword of Varinar, so that he might…temporarily, of course…bear it in his stead, while he recovers."

Amron wished that could be so. But it couldn't. "Dalton will not allow it."

"I could speak with him," Sir Ralf of Rotting Bridge offered. "I spent much time with Lord Taynar on the Iron Champion, my lord, when we sailed down the river. I sense we came to some accord during our time together, such that he might trust me to…"

"This isn't about trust, Sir Ralf, but obsession, addiction, and jealousy. Such are the dangers of the Blades of Vandar. And Lythian would have no time to master the Sword of Varinar anyway. There is no one here who can wield it, beside Dalton Taynar, and myself."

Sir Ralf gave him a long searching look. "Did I ever tell you that I lifted the Sword of Varinar once myself?"

Amron was taken aback. "No, you never said."

"Well, there never was a cause to, my lord. A trifling thing, really, a bit of fun after a feast at Elmhall Hold. You were just a boy then, thirteen or fourteen, I'd say. There had been a duel in the yard, I recall. A three-way duel between you, Borrus Kanabar, and Torvyn Blackshaw. Perhaps you remember?"

Amron smiled, reminiscing. He had always enjoyed those visits to

Elmhall with his father, and the most humble and grateful manner in which Lord Devyn Blackshaw would host them. "We fought often outside the keep, Borrus and Torvyn and I," he said. "It's where we honed our skills as young men, as much as at the Steelforge." There was one particular bout that stuck out to him, when Amron had been bested - a rare thing, he was not too modest to admit - by Torvyn Blackshaw. So seldom did Amron lose that he'd sat with Torvyn all night during the feast, picking his brains and trying to work out what had gone wrong. *Perhaps it was the very same night?*

Sir Ralf went on. "After you and the boys went to bed, your father would, on a very rare occasion, challenge the remaining men to raise the Sword of Varinar off the ground. A silly game, driven by an excess of ale and wine, but rather fun as well it must be said, and all done in good faith, of course. Few men could move it, though me...well, to my great surprise I was able to lift it right up to my waist, and hold it there for some ten seconds, before the weight became too much."

"On your first go?" Amron asked, brows upturned.

"My very first, yes."

Amron Daecar was decidedly impressed. "You always were one of the finest knights in the kingdom, Sir Ralf. In another life, you might have made a good First Blade yourself."

"You are too kind, my lord." The old knight inclined his head into a neat and tidy bow.

Amron considered what he had said, trying to find his way to the old man's point. Rarely did he tell a story for the sake of it. "So, can I assume from this tale that you're meaning to say Lythian will master the Sword of Varinar quickly, should he be given the chance?"

"I would think he would do just that, yes," Sir Ralf said.

"I agree. But that won't happen, for reasons we've already discussed."

The old man smiled. "The last Taynar to bear the Sword of Varinar... a certain Rufus Taynar, most famed and revered...did the same as your father Gideon. He played this game as well, though more often, and with greater rewards. Sir Percival Mantor was given the hand of one of Lord Rufus's nieces, for one such victory, when he bore the blade for longer than all the rest. Others were granted lands, and wealth, even titles it's been said. There is even a tale where Rufus Taynar permitted one such victor to bear the Sword of Varinar in *battle*, my lord. Perhaps you know the name of this favoured knight? I daresay it escapes me." His wry little smile said otherwise.

"Sir Antony Buckle, "Amron said. "Yes, I've heard that story." He looked at the old man. "You're trying to prove precedent?"

"Quite so, yes I am. Just something to think about anyway."

As if I don't have enough on my mind. Amron put it to one side, refusing to so much as dwell on it. Even if Dalton had the strength of character to allow Lythian - a man he had never much liked, mostly because everyone else did - to take the Sword of Varinar into battle, temporarily and in his stead, that didn't change the fact that there simply was no time. *Unless we have weeks until the enemy attack, or a good few days at the very least, what good will any of this do?* A man could learn to bear the Sword of Varinar quickly, but wielding it for any prolonged period was another matter. *Time,* Amron thought again. He'd given Dalton time, and the man had been making acceptable progress until now, growing stronger daily, deepening his bond. It had paid off, such as it was, and now *this.* More treachery. More trouble.

Amron Daecar crunched his fingers into a fist, scrutinising the skies once more. It was a cursory thing, done a hundred times already, though this time, for the first time, something silver flashed among the clouds. He narrowed his vision, squinting, as the sunlight caught the armour once more, and then nodded, smiling. "He's back," he said.

He watched for just a moment to see that his son was flying straight and steady, unwounded and unharmed, without a thunder of dragons in his wake. Satisfied of that, he raised a finger and pointed. "There, Ralf, do you see? Right there."

Sir Ralf's eyesight was not what it was, though the Master of Winds was approaching quickly and easily identified against a thin patch of rare blue sky, a scar upon the otherwise unbroken clouds. "I see, my lord. Yes, there he is. And coming from the southwest. That is very much in the direction of the Trident, if I'm not mistaken."

Amron nodded, having identified that as well. "Ralf, if you would be so kind as to inform Lady Brockenhurst that Elyon is returning." He would rather greet his son without her, though had made a promise and would keep it.

Sir Ralf turned. Peering back into the room, he said, "Ah, it seems Sir Lythian has returned as well. He is just stepping through the doors, as we speak."

Amron looked back, just as Lythian entered his chambers. His absence had been short, during which he had gone off to make sure that Sir Pagaloth, Sir Storos, and the rest of his men were well situated, before being taken to inspect his armour. He was garbed in it now, armour long-unworn, a fine set in silver with subtle colourings of soft pine green that marked the borders of his breastplate, pauldrons, and gauntlets as well. The green dye was homage to the place of his birth - Mistvale, tucked up among the pinewood forest of the Mistwood - infused into the armour by the forgemasters and their apprentices at the Steelforge. He wore his Varin cloak as well, clasped at the neck with a brooch Amron had once given him, long ago, to denote his rank as captain.

The one and only, Amron thought. There was only one Captain of the Varin Knights, acting beneath the authority of the First Blade, and above the rest. Seeing him, Amron returned for a moment to his conversation with Sir Ralf. *He* would *look rather good with a golden blade at his hip,* he thought. *Ah, one day, perhaps...*

He smiled as his friend walked out to join him, looking younger, fiercer, than when he'd greeted him earlier in the audience chamber. Resplendent and restored, the Knight of Mists carried a renewed air of authority. There was a cast to his face, defiant and deadly serious, that said he was ready to right the wrongs, imagined or no, that he had perpetrated during his long days in the south. Amron Daecar could not have been happier to have him back. "My friend," he said. "You scrub up well."

A handsome smile touched the lips of Lythian Lindar, though one restrained. He was about to reply when Lady Brockenhurst ambushed him.

"Well now, here he is, Captain Lythian of the Varin Knights. How are you, sir? How are you?"

He turned to face her. "Very well, my lady."

"Better now that you're enrobed in your armour, I'm sure."

"Yes. Most certainly."

"Good. Good. Yes, very good." She reached to take his armoured arm. "I would like to talk with you, sir, of your time away. You have many adventures to share, I am sure, and I know you to be a fine raconteur as well." She gestured inside. Walter Selleck was in the animated throes of a tale, and had even taken young Lord Florian onto his knee as he spoke. The boy was beaming in his chubby-cheeked way, listening with great intent. "Perhaps you have some stories for my Florian, to keep him entertained? He is most fascinated by dragons, as all boys are, though of course he doesn't truly understand that they're to be feared and despised at his age. And Florian is something of an idiot as well, short on wit, but he does love his stories. Might you paint him a picture or two? You must have seen dragons up close, and many times I would think? There is word that you went to Eldurath as well? Is that correct?" She glanced at Amron; they had spoken of this already. "And you were in a cell there? Condemned to die, is that right, for murder? You and Borrus Kanabar and another…Sir Tomos, was it? The son of Porus Pentar?"

Lythian's face was as rigid as rock when he said, "I fear I will not have time, my lady, to spend with Lord Florian. I have my duties to attend to, as captain."

Amron came in at that, to spare him further assaults. Frankly, it was insulting that Lythian be accosted with these requests to 'entertain' the boy with so much else at stake. "Anne, my son is returning." He spoke tersely, and referenced the sky. It looked like Elyon had spotted them and was no more than a few hundred metres away, approaching fast.

The lady squinted. "Oh. Yes, I see him. Goodness, how magnificent he is up there…the way the winds swirl behind him, and the clouds part. Oh my. If only I were ten years younger." She gave an unseemly giggle, and all of a sudden seemed to forget about Lythian entirely. "How long has he been gone? Two hours, is that about right?"

It was roughly correct. "A little less," Sir Ralf told her.

The Pointed Lady was doing a calculation, her long thin face scrunching up like an autumn leaf. "How fast can he fly? In two hours, well…he can't have made it to the Trident and back, surely? No, not by a long shot. It's almost two hundred miles away, as the crow flies." Her calculation came to fruition, and her eyes opened out in alarm. "They're coming, they must be! He must have seen them at sea, seen the sails, seen the fleet. Two hours…there and back…and perhaps with some searching…" A tremulous quality had returned to her voice. "Gods, they might only be days away. Less, even. Even less!"

Amron saw no profit in this panicky speculation when his son was but moments away. "My lady, remain calm. Elyon will explain everything in just a moment. Please, be patient."

She didn't heed him, bleating on in a blind panic. Only when Elyon sharpened into view, the winds spinning in a ferocious vortex around him, and lowered himself down onto the stone terrace, did she fall silent, mouth agape, strands of loose hair whipping chaotically against the back of her high stiff collar. Her black eyes shone in wonder as Sir Elyon Daecar flicked the winds away, shoved the Windblade into its sheath, and addressed them. "Father, Lythian, Sir Ralf." He saw Lady Brockenhurst. "My lady. How are you?"

"Panicking," Amron said, for her. He didn't want to waste a moment with these courtesies. "What did you see, son? Is the enemy fleet at sea?"

Elyon swivelled at the waist, breathing a little heavily, and pointed out the way he'd come. Only now did Amron see the strain in his eyes. "They're coming, yes. A monstrous armada, a thousand sails strong. And dragons, Father. I saw…" He glanced at Lady Brockenhurst, wondering if he should go on.

"You saw?" Amron prompted, regretting her presence even more. "Speak plainly, Elyon. What did you see?"

"Yes, what?" Lady Anne asked, shivering, reaching to him in desperate beseech. "Dragons? How many? How many are there out there? Hundreds? Are there hundreds, sir?"

"My lady, I cannot answer that. The dragons come and go between the clouds and can be hard to see in the fogs. I kept myself hidden, such as I could, flying only so close as I dared. Yet what I saw…" He looked at his father again. "The dragons were not *riderless*, Father. Most that I saw were saddled, bearing Fireborn in coloured capes to match the scales of their steeds. That makes them altogether more canny, and dangerous."

"*Dangerous?*" the woman wailed. "All dragons are dangerous! All of them, ridden or riderless it matters not! How many were there? Oh gods, we're going to die!"

Amron was done with the woman's hysterics. "Sir Ralf, please escort Lady Anne back into my chambers."

"No, I'll not go!" the woman cried. "I need to hear this! I need to!"

"You'll hear of it later." Amron stepped away from her across the terrace, Elyon and Lythian following, until they came to the stone balustrade where the edge of the keep plunged precipitously down into the castle's southern training yard. Men were sparring down there, battering at one another with blunted blades, the song of steel ringing up from below. Behind him Amron could hear Sir Ralf murmuring gently for the Pointed Lady to go with him inside.

"Let them speak, my lady, please. A cup of wine will help, and the comfort of your son. Lord Daecar will bring you the details soon enough, I promise." He coaxed her with such words, and blessedly the woman relented.

Once alone, Amron turned to Lythian. "How many Fireborn riders were you aware of, when you were in Agarath?" His voice was calm.

The Knight of the Vale had to think a moment. "Never more than a dozen," he said, "or thereabouts."

"And how many did you see, Elyon? Ridden dragons. More or less than a dozen?"

"More," his son said at once. "I would think many more than a dozen had riders on their backs."

"Then something is amiss," Amron Daecar said. "That is too many to have been bonded naturally."

Lythian agreed. "You think this is Eldur's doing?"

A nod said yes. "He has been working to tether his children to those of his master, using the Bondstone. It would explain, in part, why they have taken so long to assail us here." He turned to look out to sea. "How far away are they, Elyon?"

"Close," his son said. "At their present speed and course, they'll be here within two days, maybe less."

Two days, Amron thought. He turned it all over in his mind, gave a nod, and then came to a defiant conclusion. "Good," he said, in a grunt. "I'm done bloody waiting for them. We're well prepared and a few more days isn't going to make a difference. Let them come."

The only benefit that he could perceive would be to give Dalton Taynar more time to heal. Could he fight in two days? Not well, no, but so long as he could step out into the field of battle, and inspire his men, he would be fulfilling a large part of his duty. Just seeing that great golden blade held aloft would do much to mobilise the hearts of his men, stir in them that extra little bit of courage and resolution. It would have to be enough.

From his chambers, Sir Ralf of Rotting Bridge stepped back out, Lady Anne safely deposited inside. "I have calmed her, my lord, such as I can. She is sitting with her son, and Master Selleck."

"Thank you, Ralf," Amron said. "But I would have you return to her at once, and inform her in no uncertain terms that this will be her last day atop the Spear. The enemy armada is but two days away, and it is possible that the dragons will assault us even sooner, to clear a path for the fleet. Have word spread that every civilian is to seek shelter in the catacombs and bunkers. Express to Lady Anne this urgency. Tell her that her duty now is to keep the people calm. I want the streets cleared of all but those who carry arms. And summon the captains and commanders of the warcamp, as well as my own privy council. Have them gathered at once in the audience chamber. I would like to address them within the hour."

"I will see it done, my lord." Sir Ralf bowed and stepped away.

Amron turned to his son. "Dragon's Bane fell in a single night," he went on. "You were there, Elyon, and you alone among us. I want you to talk to the war council, tell them what to expect. What you faced at Dragon's Bane that night was unprecedented, but it is possible the dragon numbers here will be even greater. If King's Point is to be reduced to a ruin, I would make the enemy suffer before she falls. For every five hundred dead men I want to see one dead dragon staining the earth." He put a hand on his son's shoulder. "Elyon, can you do that for me? Will you speak of your experiences at council?"

The young man nodded. "Of course, Father."

Amron smiled.

"And the people?" Lythian asked. "Ought they not be evacuated upriver? To Crosswater or Varinar?"

"Many have been," Amron informed him. "We have had ships sailing north for the last week, and many others have gone by saddle, sole, and carriage. Others have chosen to stay. This is their city, these their homes. They hope and pray we will protect them."

"We will, Father," Elyon said, fervently. His eyes flashed out to sea with some sudden craving. Amron sensed the seed of some plan in the boy.

"What is it?" he asked.

For a moment Elyon hesitated, but only for a moment. Then he came out and said it. "Eldurath, Father. It may be emptied out, undefended, the dragons gone. I *know* I can get there unseen. There are fogs that hang over the city. Lythian told me so himself, and Sir Pagaloth as well. They can be thick, reducing visibility. If I can get there..."

Amron felt a familiar throb of uncertainty in his chest as his son spoke, a familiar desire to stamp down at once upon the embers of Elyon's proposal. To tell him 'no, it's too dangerous, too reckless, it's folly'. But he caught Lythian's gaze and once more recalled his friend's advice. So where before his lips might have opened in denial, this time they stayed shut. And he listened.

When Elyon was done, Amron Daecar gave another nod. "So be it. Come with me to council, Elyon, then rest, and leave on the morrow. Take as few risks as possible, and at the first sign of peril, the first sign of *him*, turn back."

Elyon looked surprised. "You mean, you consent to this? I thought..."

"You know what you're doing." Amron's eyes flashed on Lythian once again, who seemed in agreement. "If you truly believe this is the right course of action, take it. Go. And come back as quickly as you can."

"Yes, Father." Elyon's expression shone with a fixity of purpose. "I have no intention of dying out there."

"You better not." Amron smiled, to drive away the tension, then turned toward his chambers. "Now come. Council awaits."

And gripping the Frostblade in his fist, he marched inside, without a limp, without a shamble; strong, powerful, as the commander, not the cripple...as the warrior, not the wretch.

In the days to come he would wear his public face.

He would play the part of Varin Reborn.

53

Robbert

"Better," Robbert Lukar said, as he turned aside the blow. "That was better, Frog, well done. Now come at me *properly*. Come on, come at me!"

The boy with the heavily pockmarked face grinned, showing a line of small, yellowing teeth, then surged. He wore bits of old steel and mail and bore in his grasp a dinted training broadsword. His attacks were energetic, if erratic, though under the tutelage of Sir Bernie Westermont, the hoppy little lad called Frog was making progress.

Enough to save him when battle comes? Robbert thought it unlikely, though a fighting chance was better than no chance at all, and Bernie had fashioned a few capable swordsmen from these boys.

He slapped Frog's attacks away beneath the dying light of day, stepping sideways, swerving, backtracking and parrying as needed. After a while an easy opportunity presented itself and Robbert, sensing he'd humoured the youth long enough, ended the bout with a forward dash, a trip, and a blade to the throat.

He smiled down at the defeated boy as he lay sprawled in the dust, wheezing. "Good effort, Frog, but not quite good enough." Extending a hand, he reached down, pulled him to his feet, and called forth the next challenger.

Willem was next to step forward, joining his prince in the sparring circle, accompanied by a round of cheers.

He is well-liked, this one, Robbert thought, as he observed the young man's approach.

Solidly built, and nineteen winters worn, Willem had worked as a stableboy in the moorlands of North Tukor before being recruited for the war. All that brushing and grooming and horse-handling had given him a set of powerful arms and shoulders to add to his strong, naturally muscular frame.

"Well, Willem, let's see what you've got." Robbert Lukar placed the tip of his sword to the earth, cutting a line in the sand, and stepped back to make space.

The big stableboy parted his lips in a large, confident grin. "Enough to lay steel on you, my prince." The comment earned him a roar of approval from his peers. "I'm gonna win a place at your side, you'll see."

I think not. Robbert inclined his head and smiled. "Whenever you're ready, Willem."

The young man's bravado, it turned out, was not backed up by sound technique. Oh, he had strength and power, that was true, but precision was not his ally, and after a somewhat wild and frenzied assault, Robbert spun around behind him, prodded his blunted blade into his back for the kill-shot, and ended the stableboy's challenge.

"Good show, Willem, but power will only get you so far. Against a savvy opponent, you have to be smarter. Conserve your energy, wait for the right opportunity, and then strike. Now, back to the others."

Willem, unhappily, lumbered away. The cheers that had greeted his arrival in the circle did not resound at his departure.

"Well, then, who's next?" Robbert shouted, over the noise of the encampment. Theirs was not the only group engaged in sparring, nay hundreds of other men were busy with the same and everywhere the song of steel was ringing out, fighting to be heard above the hundred other sounds that filled the air: the thrum of bowstrings, the crack of arrows on wood, bellowing laughter and shouts of command. Robert could hear men singing in a nearby pavilion, and others were spending their unused energies brawling and competing in bouts of wrestling. Along the front of the lines, wagons rolled to and fro, delivering rocks and stones for the siege, and the clip-clopping of horse hooves was ever-present as well.

Under all that was the constant grind and groan of the trebuchets being loaded and fired, followed by the heavy distant rumble of thunder, far off, as the thick stone walls of Aram were struck. Beneath the warm dusk, pink and gold, the prince could see the boulders flying away into the gloomy skies, peppering the city in a ceaseless assault that had lasted the last several days. Elio Krator had said it would serve to weaken the resolve of the defenders, and help keep them awake at night. "When the gates are opened, they will be lacking for sleep and exhausted," he had declared.

If *the gates are opened, more like,* Robbert had only thought to that. It had been almost a week now, a long week that had started to test their patience, and Denlatis still hadn't come through.

Robbert breathed out, purging his frustrations with combat, as a boy of short stature and flaxen hair called Yosh entered the duelling circle. His face showed a complete lack of faith that he would ever hope to compete with the prince, though Sir Bernie Westermont was of course on hand to offer the required encouragements.

"Go on, lad," the big knight bellowed at him. "He'll tire eventually, our noble prince. And when he does, he'll be there for the taking. Now do you want that prize or not, Yosh?"

"I want it," Yosh said, so quietly he could barely be heard.

"What? I didn't hear you. I said do you want it, boy? Do you want it or not!"

"Yes!" Yosh said, a great deal louder. "I want it, m'lord! I do. I want it!"

"Good. Then go and bloody well get it!"

Unlikely, Robbert thought. He put Yosh's prospects at about a one-in-a-hundred chance, if that, of landing a strike on his armour and thus winning himself the prize in question, which just so happened to be a place at Prince Robbert Lukar's side, as his squire.

A foolish offer, the prince had reflected, almost immediately after tending it to the young charges. He had no real desire to take on a squire and though the chances were slim to none of any of them landing a blow, there was always the risk of some terrible mishap befalling him.

Boredom, that's what it is. Just boredom. Camp life could be achingly dull sometimes, and these foolish, ill-thought challenges were common enough among the men. *I blame that damnable merchant for this. If he doesn't come through tonight, I might just kill him myself…*

The prince dealt with Yosh's challenge swiftly, though as ever let the bout go on just long enough so as not to destroy the young man's confidence. He sulked off all the same to join the rest of the vanquished. Robbert studied the rest of the challengers.

The smarter ones will wait, he thought to himself. *They'll wait in the hope that I'll tire, as Bernie said, and try to catch me out.*

He could see that Willem, cockily putting himself forward so early, was now regretting that decision, and asking Sir Bernard for another chance. The request was, of course, laughed off. Others seemed to have noted the benefits of waiting and stood by, hoping a few more might step up first.

A couple did, trying their luck early for all the good it would do. Derrick came next, a skinny creature of twenty or twenty-one with a badly receding chin and almost non-existent jawline, hidden behind a rather pathetic, wispy beard. He reminded Robbert somewhat of King Hadrin, with that famously verminous face of his. Derrick was, quite naturally, defeated almost at once. Robbert had always hated King Hadrin.

After Derrick's rather poor effort, Seb the Scorpion scuttled forth. Apparently he'd earned the name for the simple reason that, during their early days in Aramatia, a scorpion had pricked him in the backside one night, a deadly scorpion by all accounts, but somehow, after falling ill for a time, Seb had pulled through and recovered. Strong as his powers of recovery were, however, he could not match them with the blade.

That was it for the willing volunteers. The remainder waited, glancing at one another with urging looks. When no one stepped up, Sir Bernie took account of matters and began picking them out for himself. "You, get your pimply arse in there, Paul," he bellowed, pointing at one of his trainees. "Go on now, that's a bloody command!"

Pimply Paul, a boy of only fifteen wretchedly afflicted with acne across the entirety of his face, neck, shoulders and even back, grumbled something under his breath, though did as ordered. As he entered the duelling circle, however, he had a sudden thought, turned back to Sir Bernard and said, "I want a spear. I mean, can I have one, milord? I'm better with a spear, you know that. Milord."

Bernie considered it. "True enough, Paul," he said, after a while. "You all right with that, Robb? Paul here using a spear?"

The prince could hardly deny the offer, lest he out himself as concerned. "Of course. Yes, whatever you like, Paul."

The pimply boy looked very pleased with that. "My father was a spearmen in Lord Huffort's army," he said. "Died outside the walls of Harrowmoor, he did. Taught me a few things when I was younger, though. Much prefer a spear, milord. Not half bad with one neither."

"Well...let's find out, shall we?" Robbert said.

The boy seemed to grow a good few inches in height with his preferred weapon to hand. When Sir Bernie called the bout to a start, he made sure to keep his distance, prodding, poking, trying to work an opening through the prince's defences.

Not on your bloody life, Robbert thought, carefully evading his every move. The fear of one of those ripe, swollen pustules bursting into Robbert's stew was of grave concern, and as his squire, serving his meals would be a primary duty. *That and washing my smallclothes,* he reflected. These boys were not Bladeborn, after all, so had no hope whatsoever of handling his godsteel armour and weapons. *Gods, this was a bad idea. Just what the hell was I thinking?*

The spear was long, some eight feet from butt to tip, and to be fair to the spotty youth, he wielded it with some skill. Robbert watched closely, sliding left and right, vigilant. He wore regular plate armour, and bore a regular steel blade, a blunted training sword of the type often used in sparring. To wield godsteel would have made the contest grossly unfair, so the prince had decreed that he fight these boys on equal terms. A part of him was regretting that now.

In a sudden rush, Pimply Paul made his move, darting forward two swift paces and thrusting in a long arm jab. It was a fine move, though Robbert was good to the task. A long lunge drew him to the left of the thrust and down came his blunted blade, hacking through the shaft with a loud woody *crack.* The spear tip went flying, leaving Paul holding only a length of splintered wood. He turned at once. "Another spear! Throw me another spear!"

"No," shouted Sir Bernie. "Use what you've got. We don't get second chances in battle!"

The boy had a sword at his hip as well. Out it came with a rusty scrape, though much too late. Robbert Lukar was upon him, whacking at his breastplate with a heavy dull *ring.* The youth went stumbling backward, tripped, and fell arse-first in the dirt. A gale of laughter greeted his end.

"Fool. You bloody fool." Bernie stamped in, yanked the boy to his feet, and dragged him out of the circle, reprimanding him all the while with, "*Never* let down your guard, Paul! If you'd taken out your sword straight away you might have fended him off. What, do you have pimples in your ears as well to block your hearing? Have you listened to nothing I've been teaching you! Godsdamnit!" He threw the youth aside and turned to another. "Percy, you're up. Get in there and show us how it's done!"

Percy had killed his first opponent at Kolash, and moved like a man who knew it, with the defiant stride of a soldier blooded and honed who understood what it was to take a life. "I'll have a spear as well," he declared, and one was brought forward. Clearly he'd decided that his chances would be better with such a weapon. "Are you ready, my prince?" He spoke politely, in a less common drawl than the rest. Percy had served in the household of Lord Chesterforth, a wealthy Ilithoran lord, before being drawn into the king's muster. Robbert had dined in Chesterforth's residence not so long ago, some grand city manor built into a place of prominence among the Marble Steps, Ilithor's richest and loftiest level, and could have sworn he recognised Percy when first he set eyes upon him. It turned out he had. The young man had been working as a footman that very evening and had been the one to greet Robbert on his arrival, and serve him at table as well.

If I'm to take on a squire, he wouldn't be the worst option, the prince thought now. *He'll do a good job of washing my clothes and serving my meals at least...*

The thought was fleeting. As soon as the bout began, Robbert's warrior instincts were once more inflamed and after some watchful early exchanges, the Prince of Tukor carved out an opening and sent Percy back to join the rest. Sir Bernie bellowed angrily at his defeat, as though his pupils were doing a pathetic job of representing him. "Not a single hit from one of you! He's not even using godsteel, damn you all."

"Come on, Bernie, leave off," Robbert said. "I've been trained from the cradle, godsteel or no. You can't expect them to compete with me."

"Compete? I'm not expecting them to compete, Robb. I'm just asking for one blow, one measly little kiss of steel on steel! Now who's left?" He looked around, snorting like a broadback, and swung a heavy arm over in Robb's direction. "Martyn, go on. He's the best of these lads, Robb. If he can't catch you out, no one can."

Martyn was another of the blooded boys, eighteen or so, lithe and lean and quick as a cat. He decided to go without a spear, though asked if he could wield two swords instead of just one, testing the limits of the rules.

"Use whatever weapon you like, Martyn," Bernie bellowed at him.

"*Any* weapon?" asked another voice, a more timid voice, from behind the big knight.

Bernie craned his neck over, spotted the tall, black-haired boy called Del, and nodded. "Sure, why not. Anything, Del. Any bloody weapon you like." He turned his eyes back on the action. Robbert had not yet fought this Del, though sensed something canny brewing on the lad's long, slightly horsey face. He had little time to consider it, however. Martyn, the current challenger, was approaching with a shortsword in one hand and a broadsword in the other, spinning them about in some flamboyant fashion.

Pretty, Robbert Lukar thought, *but useless*. Martyn had, if memory served, been a woodchopper's son and had willingly joined the muster of North Tukor, in place of his father, who had been rendered lame after a terrible axe-based accident. "For the honour of his family," Robbert recalled Bernie telling him. As part of the early mobilisation of the north, the young man had been subjected to some eighteen months of training.

It shows, Robbert thought, as the bout began. He was nimble, quick on his feet, watchful and wary, and had clearly been observing the other bouts with great interest and attention. A minute passed, then a second, then a third, as Robbert kept the man at bay, not so much as prolonging the bout for the sake of it, as actually finding a proper competitor with which to duel.

He's good, he told himself. *This one might have made an Emerald Guard if he had any Bladeborn blood in him.* When Robbert worked an opening on his left flank, and drove forward in a sudden thrust, Marytn even had the presence of mind to turn the blow aside. It was the first proper kill-strike the prince had administered that had been duly avoided. Those watching awarded the defensive move with a murmur and almost awed applause, and Bernie Westermont, if he had in fact been seated on a chair, would have wriggled his ample arse to the very edge of it by now.

"Go on, Marty, that's good lad! He's tiring you see, tiring, like I said!"

It was an exaggeration. Robbert could quite capably duel like this for a great deal longer, if required, though without godsteel to grasp his powers of endurance were admittedly lessened.

Another minute of cageyness went by. Martyn's eyes lit up, once, twice, as he plunged forward on the attack, though on each occasion Robbert languidly tapped his blade aside. A few more of these instances occurred and, as expected, his opponent began to grow impatient. Abandoning his early heedfulness, he began to take more risks, swinging harder, puffing through his lips. Beads of sweat were rolling down his forehead and stinging his eyes, and his stance began to grow unstable, loosening.

It's only a matter of time, Robbert knew. As he circled around his opponent, however, he spotted the impossible-to-ignore figure of Sir Lothar Tunney striding determinedly through the camp in their direction. The sight of the stupidly tall knight's advance threatened to throw him off his stride, though he was quick enough to turn aside Martyn's latest assault.

He's got news, Robbert thought. Good news or bad, it mattered not. It was news, and they'd had little of that for days.

He decided it was time to end the bout. Casting aside all pretences, he surged into a vicious series of strikes that sent poor Martyn reeling. The man was utterly thunderstruck, stumbling, slipping, falling. Robbert Lukar secured victory with a gentle little tap of his blade on Martyn's breastplate. "That was good, Martyn, damn good," he told him. "Bernie wasn't wrong. You're the best of them by far."

He helped him to his feet, then turned to the others. "Well done, all of you. Stay together when the fighting begins and you may stand a chance. Bernie's taught you well."

"Not well enough," the big knight lamented.

Robbert turned from the circle, sighting the head of Sir Lothar bobbing above a crowd of soldiers, gathering about some brawl. He was about to step toward him when Bernie shouted, "Wait. Del hasn't had his turn yet. You can't go rushing off without giving him a go, Robb."

Robbert paused, turning. "No," he agreed. "No, of course not." He could spare another minute or so, he supposed. "Right, where is he?"

He looked around. From behind the brawny form of Sir Bernie Westermont came the gangly farmhand, loping forward with a slightly awkward and slightly sheepish expression on his face, as though he had done something terribly naughty and was about to be caught out.

Sir Bernie at once gave out a great thunderous laugh. "Well, I did say *any* weapon, I suppose! Good on you, Del, thinking outside the box!"

Robbert Lukar was rather less amused. "A bow?" he said, seeing the ranged weapon in the boy's grasp. "No one duels with a *bow*. Come on."

Del had taken his place in the duelling circle, and even had the temerity to nock an arrow to the string, and draw it halfway back in preparation to fire.

"Bernie, you can't allow this, surely?" Robb began.

The big knight grinned. "I said any weapon, Robb."

"Yeah, but..."

Del was looking over at Bernie, who had the duty of calling each bout to start. Another laugh exploded from the knight's lips. "Well, why not?" he guffawed. "Why bloody not! Begin!" he shouted out, loudly over the din. "Just don't shoot him in the face, Del! He has no bloody faceplate!"

The farmhand from North Tukor turned his body and took aim at Robbert's chest, pulling the bowstring taut. He stood only some twenty or so feet away. An impossible shot to miss at this distance, and without godsteel, an almost impossible shot for the prince to avoid. Lanky Lothar was still striding his way, and even waving for Robbert's attention. The prince found himself caught in two minds. Turning his gaze back on Del, he saw something glimmer in those big, shy eyes of his, and in a sudden motion, launched himself sideways. Del jerked the bow, following, and released the bowstring. A *thrum* sounded, and an arrow flashed, pinging straight into the prince's plackart, a little to the right of his navel. Bernie Westermont gave out a massive, resounding cheer.

"Well Robb, that's that!" he guffawed. "He beat you fair and square! Well done, Del, bloody well done!"

Robbert Lukar was entirely nonplussed. "Fair and square? How exactly was that fair and square, Bernie?" He bent down and picked up the arrow that had fallen at his feet, waving it around. "Steel on steel, you said. This is an arrow, not a damn blade."

"A *steel*-tipped arrow," Bernie said to that, grinning enormously. "And I think we all saw it hit your armour, Robb. Steel on steel, just like you said." He marched forward, laughing, and swung a heavy paw over Del's shoulder. "Bravo, lad, you really tricked him good, didn't you?"

"I didn't mean to...to offend you, Your Highness," Del mumbled, with a meekness that quickly dissolved Robbert's anger. "I don't really want to be your squire. I was only trying to...to..."

"Impress the other lads," Bernie came in. "He was trying to be clever and impress the other lads, Robb. Don't hate him for that."

"I don't hate him. I don't hate you, Del." Robbert repeated. "And I guess that *was* pretty smart, given the rules. I suppose it's only right I admit that much."

The faintest smile rose on the farmhand's face. "I used to hunt, sometimes, near my village. I was only support, really…mostly Saska did the firing, she was always better, but I…"

"That your girlfriend, is it?" Bernie broke in, looking at him with an indecent grin. Del was tall, a good six feet one or even two, but Bernie a few inches taller. "Didn't think you had it in you, lad. You're such a shy one."

Del flushed. "She *wasn't* my girlfriend."

"Whoa now, lad, whoa, I meant no offence. Who was she then? Just a friend?"

"Sister. Adopted sister…I…I guess."

"Ah, well that explains it. She must have been a fine archer, too, because you're not half bad yourself." And he slapped him on the back, hard enough to rattle his teeth.

"It was a good shot," Robbert admitted. "I was moving fast, but you followed me well enough. How come you're not among one of the archer units?"

"I had no choice, my lord. I wanted to be, when I was mustered. Saska said I would, but…but they gave me a sword instead, and now…"

"And now you'll be my squire," Robbert told him.

Bernie's eyes widened. "What? You sure, Robb? All this…it's only a bit of fun, isn't it? A way to get the lads pushing themselves, you know, testing them, all that. I didn't think you were serious. You've always hated squires."

The comment was preposterous. "I don't hate squires, Bernard. I just haven't had one before. But there's a first time for everything, and I gave my word. I'll not have it be said that Robbert Lukar is a liar." He gave Del the smile he'd earned. *Cheeky bastard*, he thought, *but fair's fair, he found a loophole and shot right through it.* "Come on, then. You can start by cleaning my chamberpot, how about that?"

"Your…I don't…Your Highness, I didn't really think…"

"Don't lie to me, Del. You knew what you were doing."

"I…my lord…no, I…"

"Does he always mumble like this?"

Bernie nodded. "Only when he's nervous. He's a shy lad, as I say. But there's a strength in him too. He'll not let you down, Robb."

"Then I expect to see my reflection in my chamberpot by morning." Robbert sensed he was wearing the whole 'chamberpot' gag a little thin by now, but persisted. It was all in jest, of course, though Del didn't seem to have worked that out. He seemed a nice boy, and about Robbert's own age if a year to two younger. *But vastly different in temperament*, the prince reflected. Robbert was raised on war, hearing about it, reading about it, knowing he would partake in it often in his lifetime, but that would not be so for a farmhand from North Tukor. *He's probably traumatised by everything he's seen, like half the other boys in camp.*

By that stage Sir Lothar had joined them, covering the ground more quickly than mere mortals with that silly, long-legged stride of his. He loomed above them all, even Bernie, at once rearranging the height-based balance of power. Robbert was at the bottom rung of that particular ladder, a few inches shorter than Del, and very much used to craning his neck to converse with his two gigantic companions.

Lank seemed confused as to why their esteemed company had been joined by the boy. "And who's this? One of yours, Bern?"

"You know he is, you lanky fool. I've been training these lads for weeks."

Sir Lothar shrugged those absurdly square shoulders of his. "You've got a lot of ducklings quacking about. I can't keep track of them all."

"This one's called Del," Prince Robbert said. "He's going to be doing a few squire-y duties for me, Lothar. Mostly chamberpot-based work, I would think." He sent another grin Del's way, indulging in one final chamberpot jape. This time, he saw a little smile on Del's face, as though he had finally cottoned on to the fact that the prince wasn't serious. Not entirely, anyway. "So, what's the news, Lank? Your face says there's news."

Sir Lothar gave Del a passing glance, then proceeded to ignore his presence, as a lion does a fly. "The merchant is back," he said. "Apparently with glad tidings. I came to fetch you to a meeting."

Gods be good. Finally. "Where?"

"Where do you think? Between the camps, as usual."

"Right." Robbert turned. "Bernie, stay here. Del, you can head to my pavilion, get started on scrubbing my chamberpot." *Gods, what's wrong with me today?* "I'm joking. Just go there and get acquainted with the place. If you're to serve me, I suppose we ought to get to know one another a bit. I can hear about this sister of yours, and the rest of your family, how about that?"

The tall boy nodded, saying nothing.

"I'll be back shortly," Robbert finished. And with that, he strode away.

Dusk was quickly turning to darkness now, the shadow of Aram vanishing into the deepening gloom. The trebuchets swung at the front of the lines, discharging their loads, attended by engineers and operators in great quantity. Behind them, soldiers swarmed, marching on their patrols with torches to hand, or sitting about their firepits roasting meat.

At the edge of the training grounds, Robbert and Sir Lothar passed the Bloody Traders, completing their nightly training ritual under the hard gaze of the Surgeon, their captain and humourless taskmaster. They were a skilled group, many of them Bladeborn, and even had several women among their number. Lord Cedrik had, of course, considered that equal parts disgraceful and amusing when he found out.

"I'll let you handle that lot," he had said to his nephew, preferring not to sully himself by taking any sort of account of the sellswords. "Deploy them as you see fit, Robbert. Just make sure you keep them away from *me*."

The Surgeon watched as they passed. He was a man of modest proportions and plain, forgettable face, more lightly tanned than swarthy, with brown hair, neatly barbered, and an acute precision in almost everything he did. But there was something soulless about him too, and those eyes in particular, something Robbert didn't like. At his side stood his chief lieutenant, an extremely tall and unexpectedly beautiful woman of about thirty, it looked, who was, Lothar had claimed, their best fighter, even above their captain.

"Don't be fooled by her looks, Robb," Lank had said to him several days ago, once Robbert had given him the duty of housing, observing, and attending to the Surgeon and his company. "She's a killer, that one. Her face may be untouched, but apparently she's got a hundred scars under that armour she wears."

They were from all the battles she'd fought, he'd gone on to say. The woman was called the Tigress, as fierce as she was beautiful, with two dozen stripes on her back, sides, and even breasts from a savage lashing that had almost killed her once. Apparently she'd slain over five hundred men - an absurd claim, Robbert had thought - and there was even some foul rumour that she liked to drink the blood of her victims sometimes as well, to stay young. "She may look thirty, but she's actually almost seventy," Lothar had finished. "It's the Bladeborn blood that does it. That's the only blood she drinks."

Robbert, of course, ignored most of that. "Those are just sellsword stories, that's all," he'd said. "So long as they can fight, that's good enough for me."

All the same, he didn't much like the way the Surgeon looked at him as they passed, nor the Tigress, nor the rest of them. "They don't seem to like us much, Lank," he observed, as they walked by.

"So what? They're bought and paid for by that merchant of yours. Put them on the front lines, and most of them will probably die. Isn't that what your uncle suggested?"

Robbert nodded. "He said 'why waste good Tukorans when we can use up this southern sellsword scum instead?' Those were his exact words."

Lothar nodded. "Yeah, that sounds like him."

The space between the camps had grown somewhat blurred, at the front at least, on account of the trebuchets, and the constant flow of wagons and carts and men going between them. Further back from the siege lines, the broad expanse of no man's land was still being preserved, however, populated only by the single pavilion in which they assembled for their councils.

As ever, Robbert commanded Lothar to remain outside with his uncle's personal guards, who were already there. Robbert did not miss the hateful look that Sir Wenfry Gershan gave him, as he passed. *Still bitter for throwing you into the dirt, I see.*

He stepped within, drawing the flaps aside, to find Lords Krator and Kastor already engaged in discussion with the merchant in question; Cliffario Denlatis, he of the gold tooth and the perpetual, sly grin.

The other senior lords were not present, Robbert noticed at once - Huffort, Swallow, Gullimer, nor Sir Gavin Trent, Lord Cedrik's trusty battle commander. Of late Cedrik Kastor had chosen only to confer with them on the Tukoran side of the camp, where they could discuss the subject of betraying Elio Krator in private, and at length.

Over the last week, Cedrik Kastor had expounded and expanded upon his plan to help the sunlord win the city, before turning their own blades upon him, and taking it for themselves. He had been working on this plan for a while, he claimed, and had even drawn up a list of Krator's fiercest warriors and senior commanders, to be killed as quickly as possible once he gave the order to attack. If it worked, he had declared, with great imperiousness, they would have conquered all of Aramatia. "As King Janilah commanded us. We'll win it for Tukor."

Robbert was not so sure. His uncle claimed this was his plan all along, ever since he made the alliance with Elio Krator, though if so, why had he not spoken of it until now? Why had he let dissent brew within the ranks unnecessarily? Why had he killed Sir Alistair the Abiding like that, with such dishonour, and slaughtered so many of his men?

No, this was *reactionary*, the prince knew. The dissent had deepened to the point of mutiny in certain quarters, and Cedrik Kastor had sensed it. Robbert had to give him that, at least. His uncle had to find something to unite them, and he had. Even Lord Gullimer, who had made many overtures now to Robbert, declaring him his allegiance should there be a break between uncle and nephew, was sold. "Aram would be a good base from which to rest and recover," the handsome Lord of Watervale had said, "before we strike out upon Agarath. *If* it should come to that, anyway…"

And there it was, the doubt, a doubt now shared by many. *If.* With all the stories they'd heard about these fell monsters rising from the deep dark places of the earth across land and sea, the notion that they could march north from here to Agarath, across hundreds of miles of rugged plains and high bleak mountains, and do anything other than get slaughtered to a man, had begun to grow and disseminate among the men. There was talk that the Ever-War, a popular southern prophesy and belief, had begun. *The War Eternal*, Robbert thought, *and its Last Renewal.* A thousand dragons had swarmed from the Wings, some said, and Robbert had even heard one man bleating in his cups that Eldur had arisen, and even Drulgar the Dread as well.

The prince was not sure of all that, of course, though there was no lie in the risks of marching north from here. All along he had ranted about attacking Agarath from the south, but even his faith in that had been tested. If there were even a hundred dragons out there, their army would be obliterated on foot.

How will we win Skyloft Fort, let alone Blademelt? he fretted. Getting there would be perilous enough, let alone sieging, and winning, two of the greatest forts in Agarath. *We might lose thousands on the way, and then what? Could we really batter down the walls of Blademelt with less than thirty thousand men?*

He'd reflected on all of this over the past week. And in doing so

Robbert had divined the truth of his uncle's plan. It was not so much about winning Aramatia for King Janilah Lukar or Tukor, or using Aram as a base from which to strike out upon Agarath. No. His intention was rather more circumspect and long-term than that…

To win the city, win the great impenetrable pyramid palace at its heart, and *hide*. To wait out the next few months, even years, and see how the war unfolded. *Like an army of feckless cravens*, Robbert thought, disgusted. Much as he understood the reasons, even sympathised with them, he would not allow himself to remain in Aram long. *If the north is under siege*, he told himself, *then north I shall go. The men of House Lukar do…not…hide.*

He withdrew from all those thoughts, and turned his eyes across the pavilion. His sudden arrival had halted the conversation, it seemed. Elio Krator was looking at him in that cold detached manner of his. His uncle had a smug expression on his face, as was typical, and Denlatis, of course, merely grinned and put himself into one of those ridiculous, sweeping bows he liked. "Your Highness," he said. "A great pleasure to see you again."

"And you, Denlatis." Robbert continued into the room, noting that Mar Malaan was not present on this occasion. *I might have known. There's no stink of that sickly perfume.* "We feared you had gone and abandoned us, Cliffario."

"Me? Oh, never, never. I could never abandon one so noble as you, young prince."

Yes, I'm sure. "I hear you have brought tidings."

"I have. Tidings most glad, handsome prince, and my short absence these last days can be easily explained, I assure you. You see, I have been working with Starrider Antapar and Sunrider Konollio, as requested by the good sunlord, to form a foolproof plan to open the gates. The *Cherry Gate*, is how you would call it in your common tongue. This is the easternmost gate of the city, closest to our dual encampment. With meticulous planning, we have come to a decision to strike at the gates tomorrow evening. Starrider Antapar and Sunrider Konollio will see it done. They have over two hundred men, many of them Lightborn riders as they are, and will easily overwhelm Lord Hasham's forces there. Oh, I have seen to it." His gold tooth glinted in the firelight. "And from that point on, the city will be yours to storm and swarm. Tomorrow night, my handsome young prince, will be a day of glory for us all."

Robbert looked at his uncle, then at Elio Krator. "So these men. Antapar and Konollio, was it? They're your trusted allies, my lord?"

"Most trusted," Lord Krator confirmed, unemotionally. "Tomorrow night is to be dark, and will grant us good cover to approach the city unseen. When the gates are opened, the rest will unfold as we have planned. Sunrider Antapar's assault on the forces at the Cherry Gate will draw in many others. We shall overwhelm them, then attack the garrisons Mar Malaan has outlined to you. Our numbers are vastly superior; this will not prove an issue. I will lead a large contingent myself to the palace, along with Lord Kastor and his chosen men. We will fight together, as he has requested."

"Quite so," agreed Cedrik Kastor, smiling. A glance passed Robbert's way. They had discussed this with their own lords in great detail. It would be the perfect time to destroy Elio Krator and his best men, upon the palace steps, before advancing inside to take it for themselves.

And find this girl as well that Krator is so keen on, Robbert thought. His uncle had been clear that he wanted her taken alive.

There seemed little else to say. Though as ever, Robbert Lukar studied the sly merchant Cliffario Denlatis with a note of caution. He could not decide if he could be fully trusted or not, though surely the coming night would demonstrate his faith one way or another.

We will gather close to the gates, he thought. *If they are opened, as Denlatis says, and Krator's allies awaiting us, then his loyalty will be proven.* If not, they could simply withdraw, try to form some other plan, or continue to batter the walls with their trebuchets. Eventually they would succumb, though that was far from the ideal course.

Tomorrow, Robbert thought again, with an excitement building in his chest. *Tomorrow, we'll know, one way or another.*

54

Elyon

The lands beneath him were brown and barren, an expanse of crop-less, grassless earth stretching in all directions as far as the eye could see. He could see rugged hills of black rock, the occasional copse of small leafless trees, and what looked like a road of sorts, stretching away from north to south as straight and thin as a spear.

Maybe it leads to Eldurath, he thought, as he flew beneath the clouds, his newly reinforced armour concealed beneath a thin cloak of dull, greyish-brown wool, to better blend him into the turbid skies. A single flash of sunlight on his armour might alert someone to his presence, and that was a risk he would prefer to avoid. *Not that there's anyone here to see*, he thought. He'd never seen a land so utterly inert and empty.

He continued to consider the road. It was hardly a main road, and he had not seen its source, but it was going the right way, he suspected, if his sense of direction was any great judge. Elyon Daecar had learned to navigate when in flight by using the sun, the moon, the stars, and other landmarks as well. In Vandar that was easy enough, being the place of his birth and upbringing, but here in Agarath, in the dusty red south, it was different. He knew it only from maps and stories, and frankly, there were no landmarks out here.

Only that road, and those black hills. The latter were some way off, a little east if he had it right, though weren't large enough to have a well-known name. They were more a series of hillocks and ugly stumpy outcrops really, known to the local people, perhaps, but hardly to the wider world. It didn't matter. The road, he sensed, was indeed going in the right direction, and sooner or later, as Lythian had told him, the world would change, going from brown to green, from barren to verdant, as the Drylands gave way to the much lusher lands that saturated and softened the earth north of the Askar Delta.

He flew a little lower, daring a short dive to get a better look at that road. It was not paved, but a dirt road, he saw, hard-packed and covered in bits of loose rock and stone, and rutted here and there from ten thousand turns of a wagon's wheel. Those ruts were shallow, carved over tens, even hundreds of years he would guess. Elyon doubted it rained much out there, if ever, and the ground looked hard as stone. But the furrows were unmistakable, and that was a good sign. *If wagons and oxcarts pass this way, they're obviously heading somewhere.*

He decided to stop for a moment, landing on the road where it crested a shallow rise. The flight was a long one, he'd been going for hours, and with no one around and no dragons in the skies, he took the opportunity to take a short rest.

It was eerily quiet, not a breath of wind in the air. He turned a full circle, gazing out at the never-ending plains, and found in them a strange beauty. *A beauty of nothingness, and silence,* he thought. Vandar had no such lands like this. It was green, wet, full of woods and lakes and mountains. A typical beauty, perhaps, but a beauty Elyon Daecar was used to. This was a foreign maid to him, the air hot and dry, the lands hard and cruel. There was life here, only he couldn't see it. Insects would be scuttling about, he knew, and lizards and other critters besides, and birds would circle and hunt, and at night in particular the land would awaken with nocturnal beasts, crawling from their burrows and dens.

I should like to see that, one day. To see these plains at night, the skies cast with stars uncountable upon the great open ether, bustling in their bright abundance. Lythian had told him how beautiful it was by night, one of the few things that made the crossing bearable, but perhaps stargazing was not the best use of his time right now. Only earlier, he'd glimpsed the enemy armada once again, as he'd flown across the Red Sea, and had been concerned to see how much progress they'd made overnight since his initial sighting the previous day. He had thought it would take them two days to reach the city, but with the winds driving them on and the seas doing nothing to hinder them, it might be even less.

Tonight, he thought. *They may arrive by tonight.* It would not surprise him if the dragons, in particular, began their assault by the dark of night, surging down from the blackness of the skies to set King's Point alight, just as they'd done at the Bane. Elyon had spoken of that night at council, by his father's request, and wondered, when he was done, whether it was the right thing or not. "They all just looked terrified, Father," he'd said after. "All I've done is given them a sleepless night."

"You've given them the truth, Elyon, that's all. It's up to them, now, to find their courage. That is a private struggle that we all must face."

The truth, Elyon thought. *The truth...but not all of it.* By his father's request, he'd said nothing of Drulgar the Dread, and could only imagine how terrified they would be if he had. "I fear it may breed panic, and desertion," his father had told him, "and we can ill-afford that on the eve of battle." Elyon sensed afterward that he might just have been right, given their reaction to what he'd experienced at the Battle of the Bane. It made him wonder how wise he'd been in spreading the news of Drulgar elsewhere, to Sir Bomfrey Marsh and Sir Hank Rothwell in Varinar, and Lord

Harrow at Crosswater, and even his uncle and Lord Rammas in the east as well.

Have I incited panic all across Vandar? Have I only made it worse?

He swung his small provisions satchel from his back, drew out a water-skin, and drank deep. *They have to know*, he told himself. *We can't all just bury our heads in the sand forever.* He had brought some sustenance as well; sugared nuts and fruits and some sweetbread to help fuel him. He wolfed it down hungrily, glancing across the plains and up into the skies all the while, searching for enemies. He saw nothing, not even a bird. *Nothing but heat*, he thought, as the world blurred and shimmered just above the horizon. Elyon Daecar had never witnessed that phenomenon before.

He finished his food, stoppered his waterskin with a cork, and returned it to his leather satchel. The air was much hotter down here, and he had no wind to cool him. Sweat glittered on his forehead, grouping to droplets, wending down his brow. He wore his full plate armour, faceplate raised, and with that cloak and hood it was stifling. *I'll bake to death if I linger here much longer.*

The short rest would have to suffice. He swung his satchel bag back into position over his shoulders, tightening the straps so it didn't fly free or get tangled in his arms in flight, and had another look around, slowly scanning the skies for threats. It was a hazy day, and the world was wearing a cloak of light grey clouds. Elyon had been flying just beneath them for the most part, ready to dash up and disappear if needed, but thus far hadn't been required to. It was promising. It might mean, as he'd hoped, that the lands of Agarath were not being watched, that the dragons were away at war.

Let's hope it's the same further south, he thought, resuming his journey.

He followed the line of the road, keeping that thin brown scar in sight as it speared straight through the plains. After a short while it dawned on him that it might, in fact, be leading to Highport instead of Eldurath. It was a major Agarathi city on the northern coast of the Crystal Bay, a city of scholars and philosophy and music, he'd heard, with many fountains and gardens and places of learning. *And wine*, he recalled. *They like their wine in Highport. Some of those fountains flow with it.* Borrus Kanabar had said that once, though probably just in jest.

If it's leading to Highport, so be it, he told himself. *At least I'll know where I am.* It *would* add time to his journey, though. The scholar's city was some two hundred miles from Eldurath, if memory served, a not inconsiderable distance, and a detour he could do without. It would only deplete his energy stores and make the flight back even harder. *And when I get home again, what will I find?*

Battle, he suspected. There would be no respite for Elyon Daecar.

He tried not to dwell on it, maintaining a sharp focus on watching the skies, vigilantly scanning in search of threats. Should a dragon spot him and engage, it would ruin his whole day. His plan was based upon secrecy. *Sneak in, sneak out, and get the bloody hell out of here.* As far as Elyon Daecar could figure, this entire war might just hinge on it.

Another thirty minutes passed. Thinly before him he began to make out signs of change, of the colours shifting, brightening, beneath the haze of burning air that coated this oppressive realm. Vaguely, to the southwest, the shape of a coastline began to show itself. The craggy world was waning, giving way to grassy plains, stands of cypress and acacia and, further off, soft buttery beaches along a sparkling blue shore.

The Crystal Bay. Highport would be further west along the coast, Eldurath a little way to the southeast, amidst the Askar Delta. The road he'd been following, it turned out, was heading to both of them. Below him now Elyon could see it splitting into two separate paths, one wending away through the coastal hills to the west, the other continuing on its way south. He flew above the latter, centring himself over the road as the coastline dwindled behind him. An expanse of mottled brown and green lay ahead, an open, slightly hilly savannah dappled with patches of sedge and a high quantity of small desiccated bushes. Elyon caught sight of some settlements here, simple places, cattle farms most likely, though of cattle he saw scant few. As he passed over he realised that some of the buildings were in ruin, farms abandoned, entire villages destroyed. *Did the dragons do this? Something else?* The fire god Agarath had devised all sorts of foul monstrosities, and if ancient and unholy things were returning to the north, no doubt the same was true here.

And one above all, he thought, his eyes going out to the east. *Out there, he's out there somewhere.* That's what Vargo Ven had said. That Drulgar was resting and brooding upon his Nest, awaiting his time to strike. *Might he be there now? Might he be sleeping…vulnerable?*

A part of the prince wanted to fly there, to see him, to confirm these rumours to be true. *Perhaps he's not as Ven says. Perhaps he's merely an overlarge dragon, fat in his dotage, little bigger than Malathar and Garlath. Perhaps I can kill him myself? Catch him sleeping and…and…*

And he cut himself off from thinking on it any further. It was folly, mad folly and nothing more. The Nest was hundreds of miles from here, and he was not going to fly there because of some sudden capricious whim.

He put it from his mind. *Eldurath,* he thought again, refocusing. *The palace. Your mission.* His conversation with Vargo Ven had proven profitable in several ways, not least what he'd let slip about a certain Rasalanian king. *The scion has seen it from his fine palace quarters,* he'd said, when they'd met in parley beside the Burning Rock. He was discussing this dragon butchery that was going on, but that was not of interest to Elyon Daecar. No, it was his location that mattered. *His fine palace quarters,* he thought. *Thank you, Lord Vargo, for telling me where to go.*

And now, there on the far horizon, emerging from the veil at the edge of his vision, he saw it. Eldurath, no more than a small shadow, blurred by distance and by dust, awaiting the arrival of the Master of Winds.

I'd best not keep them waiting. Get in, find him, take it, and get out, he thought. *Take back the advantage he stole…*

Beneath him the lands were growing lush now, rich with waterways, teeming with life, but he barely noticed. His eyes were on his target, the city growing, spreading as he neared. High walls sprung up from the earth, and beyond sprawled a city of reds and oranges and dark burnished golds, a sandstone city infused by the magic of dragonfire, grand and magnificent, with an enormous, soaring eight-sided palace at its heart, rising high into the hazy skies.

Elyon slowed, climbing, cladding himself in cloud. His eyes surveyed the skies, wary; there were dragons, he saw, but few. One was flying in a wide circling arc, high up near the palace, a greenish dragon of reasonable size with purple spinal plates. *Wait*, Elyon Daecar thought. *Wait, watch, learn its patterns. It may leave.*

Another he sighted much further off, flying away near the southern walls, and a third was perched against the palace exterior, a little further down, clinging like a gargoyle to the stone. It was a smaller dragon, grey, sleek, much like many others he'd slain in the north. But all the same, being spotted would not serve. *I'll fly around*, he told himself. *Enter another way.*

He checked the other sides of the palace to make sure no other dragons lurked. But he could see only those three, and if there were more of them, they were too far away to worry about. The city beneath was wreathed in a low ochre fog, though it was faint, not so dense as it might have been. Fires burned in their thousands, all throughout the city, and he sensed below him great mass gatherings of people in prayer, humming in the plazas and squares.

He continued to hover, watching, waiting, as a minute passed, and another, and another. He wondered if the Fire Father was in there, even now, sitting on his dragonskull throne, awaiting him. He wondered if his coming had been foreseen. *Is this a trap? Am I flying into a trap?* It didn't matter, either way, and he could not let it unnerve him. *I can't go back*, he told himself. *Trap or not, I have no choice. I've come too far to give up now.*

There was nothing for it. *Be bold*, he thought. *Be brave. Be daring.* Hovering high, he studied the green dragon's flight pattern, waiting for his chance, waiting, waiting. And when finally it came, he did not delay.

Elyon Daecar descended.

55

Talasha

The king was moaning again, babbling on and on about the darkness that lay ahead, the end that was soon to come. He sat curled at the foot of the plinth, his twig legs twisted beneath him, dangerously thin, head in his hands, sobbing. "The end...it's coming...I see the end...the end..."

Be calm, sweet king, be quiet, handsome lord, she might have said to comfort him. *Let me fetch you some water, let me rub balm on those sores. You should eat, you must eat, to keep up your strength. Have some wine, a bit of wine will help. Please, noble king, be quiet, and be calm, stop sobbing, please...you must stop sobbing...*

But she said nothing. Not a single word. *Why waste my breath, when he doesn't ever listen?* The scion was prone to these bouts of delirium and when they struck, she could do little but let them pass.

She stood from her little pallet bed and paced the large empty chamber that was her cell, striding slowly from wall to wall, ignoring the man's plaintive bleating. It had gotten progressively worse during her days here with him, locked away at the Fire Father's command. "Find the heir of Varin for me," he'd said. "That is your only charge." If she did that, he might just let her live. *But for how long?* she wondered. *And to what end? All the world is burning anyway.*

She reached the southern wall, touched it with her right palm, *tap,* and turned back to stride the other way. When she reached the opposite end of the room, she tapped again, *tap tap,* two laps done. More pacing and tapping followed, until she reached ten. Then she tapped with her *left* palm, just the once, *tap,* and spun around to walk across the room. Reaching the wall again, she tapped once with her left, and then once with her right. *Eleven,* she thought. The king was still moaning. "The end...I see the end..."

On she went, back and forth, tapping all the while, playing her game. When she'd done twenty laps, she tapped twice with her left, *tap tap.* Twenty-five was two taps on the left and five on the right, *tap tap...tap tap tap tap tap.* If and when she got up to a hundred, she would press both of her palms against the stone, a double tap, to signal a century. Her highest count so far had been five hundred and eighty-six, a veritable marathon that had taken her several hours before she'd begun to lose count and stopped. She could not say what she would do if she ever reached a thousand. *Perhaps I'll just smash my skull against the stone and be done with it*, she thought.

It was the way she passed the time here, this pacing and tapping and counting, trying to see how long she could go before her legs gave way beneath her. By now both of her palms were red and raw, the right one in particular, but she cared not a jot about that. Pain was *something*, at least. Something to feel. Something to think about. It hadn't even been that long since she'd been locked away here, but already the man was driving her mad. *I'll be as mad as he is when the Fire Father comes again*, she thought. She smiled at her own little joke, and did another lap.

Her marching was interrupted by the sound of the bars being removed from the door. She stopped, turning to face it as it groaned open and the maids came in. They came thrice daily, to bring her her meals, refill the water and wine jugs laid out upon the table, and take away her chamber-pot, replacing it with another. Princess Talasha Taan, in her cruel and unholy fate, was forced now to relieve herself in the presence of the wretched king. The maids had brought in a partition, behind which she could secure some small measure of privacy, but it hardly made it better.

Hadrin was worse, though. He'd forgone even the luxuries of a chamberpot now.

"He soiled himself again last night," Talasha told the maids, as they entered. By the wrinkling of their noses, they had worked that out already. "You will have to clean him. I'm not living with this stink."

"You've earned it," said one of the guards, grunting from the doorway. Talasha did not catch which one said it. It might have been any one of them, in truth; she was hardly popular here anymore. All her guards were dragonknights, clad in their strong dragonscale armour and rich red cloaks, bearing the long black dragonsteel spears common among their order. There were never fewer than three or four of them watching over her, which she found curious because just one of them would do. *Do they think me some fearsome Bladeborn knight or something? How could I possibly get past them all?*

She ignored the remark, turning her attention back on the maids. "Oh good. You've come prepared." One of them was holding a pail of water, another a heap of cloths and sponges, as though knowing the king would need a clean. A third bore fresh clothes, though they were hardly more than rags in truth, roughspun and undyed. "He has been moaning for over an hour this morning," Talasha went on. "I do not expect he will put up much of a struggle, but be gentle with him, he is very weak."

The maids did not like her any more than the guards did. They gave her little more than a perfunctory sign of comprehension, before crowding toward the king and unceremoniously stripping him of his current rags. It was a degrading spectacle. The scion wailed, thrashing, chains clanking. One of the maids unlocked them so the man's breeches might be removed. Soon enough he was naked, watery filth leaking out between his legs. With flannels to hand they descended like a pack of wolves, scrubbing, scouring, wiping him clean, dipping their hands in the bucket all the while to a chorus of sloshing sounds. Some of these maids were strong and brawny, and greatly more so than the prisoner, who had by now been reduced to little more than an emaciated ruin. The fight went out of him quickly enough and before long he just lay there, being tugged about, humiliated and debased.

Talasha did not care to watch. No matter what this man had done, it was distressing to see him being so shamefully degraded. The guards thought rather different. All the while, they were grinning, laughing, pointing, sharing little jests about the 'weak northern king' and his 'tiny little manhood'. Only one of them appeared to show any compassion for the wretch, Talasha noticed, by the pitying cast of his eyes.

"I know you," she realised, giving him a good look for the first time. "Sir Vendroth, is that right?"

"Yes, my lady. That is correct." He was an old dragonknight, and not a face she'd seen in years.

"Have you been away somewhere, Sir Vendroth? I confess I have not seen you among my lovely sentries as yet."

"I have only recently returned from Loriath, my lady, to take up a new position in the palace. I will admit, I had not expected my first posting to be guarding *you*."

"Much has changed," Talasha said, bitterly. "Tell me, Sir Vendroth. Has the Fire Father left the city yet?"

The man hesitated, then nodded. "Yesterday," he told her. "He flew east, I believe."

To the Nest, she thought. She had felt the shadow lifting, and had taken that to mean he was gone. *To hunt the dragon butcher. To set Drulgar free at last.* She shuddered in her skin and said, "Thank you for telling me, Sir Vendroth. These others aren't so generous with their tidings." She'd been asking for news for the last several days, though each time her questions had been summarily ignored.

"We're not supposed to talk to her, Vendroth," one of them said. A young knight with a cruel mouth and lazy left eye. "We just watch she doesn't try to run, that's all."

Sir Vendroth nodded, giving the scion another long curious look. By now the maids were shoving him into those new roughspun rags they'd brought, fixing his ankles back into the chains. "Ought it not be better if he was free of those fetters?" he asked.

You've missed a lot. "He has grown too fond of them," Talasha told the old knight. "In the same way that a beast can grow too fond of its cage, and refuse to leave, King Hadrin only howls when he is set free. He will die upon that plinth, I fear."

And me with him, the princess thought.

The maids completed their work, gathering up their things and passing back through the doors without so much as giving the princess a second glance. *Drones*, she thought. *Mindless drones.* The guards withdrew as well, though Sir Vendroth lingered just a moment longer. Talasha took a gamble. "I wonder if you might let me return to my own chambers, for just a short while," she said to him, in a hushed and hurried voice. "I could very much do with a change of clothes and a bath, sir. A proper bath…"

A voice cut in from outside the doorway. "Don't listen to her, Vendroth. She's tried that one before."

"She'll only try to escape," another said. He stepped back in, a thickset knight with a crooked nose and beetled brow. One of Vargo Ven's barbarians. "You want to wash? How about you use that bucket? Filthy water for a filthy whore." And he spat at her.

Sir Vendroth looked aghast. "She's a princess. How dare you…"

"*Was* a princess. That was before she opened her legs for that Varin Knight. Now she's just a filthy whore." He spat again, this time to the side, and vanished in a whirl of red cloth.

The doors were shut and barred a moment later, and Talasha knew with some conviction that that was the last she'd see of Sir Vendroth. No one with any sympathy for her plight would be permitted to watch over her, lest they try to support a rescue attempt. *Farewell, Sir Vendroth*, she thought. *Enjoy your next posting.*

She sighed and went to the table to pick at the food the serving girls had brought. Her breakfast was a plate of bread, fluffy and warm from the oven, with salted butter on the side, thin cuts of cured meat and quail eggs. Good fare, considering. For Hadrin it was the usual watery stew, with small chunks of chicken, carrot and onion floating within. Rarely did the king eat, but Talasha had long since learned that she could get some broth down his neck with a little coaxing. She did that now, finding the creature pliant and broken after the assault of the maids. Most of the broth spilled out and over his lips, but enough of it got through to keep the man alive.

"I'm sorry for that," she said, as she fed him. "They don't have to be so rough with you."

She held his chin up, managed to get a bit more broth down his throat, then went back to the table and placed the bowl aside. If she hoped to find the man at least somewhat lucid and conversational, she was left disappointed. By the time she'd filled a cup of water and turned, he was curling up in that way he did, chin tucked into his stomach, hands clasped about him, shivering and moaning.

Later, she thought. *Maybe he'll be more talkative later.*

It was unlikely. She'd been in charge of watching over the man for months, and he was only getting worse. Even when he wasn't in the throes of some bout of mania, he was still almost entirely incoherent, sitting there rocking back and forth or mumbling quietly to himself. Talasha had scarcely slept since she'd been locked away in here. Every night his ranting and raving would wake her, and she would sit up suddenly from her little pallet bed and look over to find him there, at the plinth bound up in his beloved chains, babbling inanely. Sometimes his eyes would be wide open and staring, leaking tears, but at others he would appear as asleep, gripped by a terrible nightmare.

Once when that happened, she stepped over to shake him awake, wondering if he might have seen something. "Hadrin," she'd whispered, pressing at his fleshless shoulder. "Hadrin, wake up."

He'd stirred, blinking through the darkness, and looked at her with a strange tearful smile. "Amilia?" he'd croaked. "Amilia...is that you?"

His wife, she had thought. *The granddaughter of Janilah Lukar.* She was about to tell him, 'no, it's me, Talasha', when she thought better of it and took a chance. "Yes, yes it's me, my king," she'd said, in her best approximation of a highborn Tukoran accent. "Is there something you want to tell me, Hadrin? Is there something important you need to say?"

She had hoped that he might share with her some secret...perhaps something that might help her get out of this godsawful place, so she could rush to find Neyruu, fly down and fetch Cevi, and then leave this cursed land forever...but no, he'd only stared at her, blinking, face twisting in sudden grief, and begun wailing, "my wife...my queen...my child...my *son*...no...no, please...*nooooo*..." in a desperate, fearful voice.

Talasha did not know what to make of it. The pain in his voice was unlike anything she'd yet heard, haunting to her ears, ringing out in stricken grief. She'd tried to coax some more out of him, but he'd only repeated the same things over and over and over again, plunging his head into his skeletal fingers and convulsing in a terrible fit of sobs. And when she'd asked him of it the next morning, he'd only looked at her in that blank way of his, never remembering a thing.

The other nights had been just as bad, the king waking her regularly with his wailing and his thrashing, causing his chains to crash loudly against the stone floor. The chamber in which they lived was windowless, large and open, with scant furniture, so all that noise gave out a fearsome echo. The maids always came to douse the braziers at night as well, the fires flickering softly only, throwing distorted shadows across the room. Those shadows did not help in giving the princess the sweet sleep she craved. She would watch them as she drowsed, and her mind would conjure horrors from the twisted shapes they made, horrors that only followed her down into her dreams. Sometimes Talasha awoke by herself, her nightmares becoming too fearful to bear, and she would find herself shivering and sweating in her small-clothes, heart hammering against her ribs.

Once, when that had happened, she'd found Hadrin staring over at her, his big eyes bulging in the darkness. "You see it too," he had murmured, in a strange and eerie voice. "You see the shadow spreading...and the darkness...and the flames. The north...the beating heart of the north will burn. Soon," he had told her. "It will happen soon..."

It was a rare moment of lucidity, his voice clear, cold, steady. Yet before she could press him on that, ask what he meant or what he'd seen in the Eye, he'd shut his bulging eyes and settled, falling into a deep and sudden sleep.

There were other things he'd mumbled too, things that without context made little sense to her. A black joyful cat stalking toward a kneeling man. A boy in armour being bitten and blinded by a snake. A sky dark with arrows and an island on a burning lake. A dragon with a stone spear in its jaws, a great bright light in the shape of an eagle descending through a canopy of trees. Sometimes Talasha only half-heard such things as she stirred from her sleep. At other times she'd been awake already, and had pounced upon him, trying to get him to say more, but he would always close up like a clam and lose his train of thought.

It seemed the only times he was truly granted any sort of clairvoyance was during those manic episodes. When lucid he became withdrawn, forgetful, and would only claim to know nothing of what he'd said. "I don't know...I don't know....please...I don't remember..."

By now Talasha was at her wit's end. Perhaps the Eye of Rasalan was as powerful as people said, but a tool was only as good as its bearer, and this king was no true prophet. *There must be someone else out there who can master it,* she thought. The king had cousins, she knew. If any of them were still drawing breath among the ruins of Thalan, perhaps one of them could be found and brought here instead. *One who doesn't soil himself at night, perhaps...*

She paced, back and forth, mulling on that. She'd heard it said that future events glimpsed through the Eye could only be seen by the direct descendent of Thala's line, a line of primogeniture unbroken for thousands of years. If that were so, the cousins would not count, no matter that they were royal as well. *But maybe it's not so,* she thought. So far as she knew, no one had ever troubled to find out. The Eye of Rasalan had passed down from queen to king and king to queen for over three millennia, always going to the firstborn child. No secondborn or thirdborn, let alone cousins and uncles and aunts, had ever had their turn to try to master it.

It didn't matter either way, the princess decided. The great Eye was closing, that was clear, ending its long and weary watch. Talasha did not know whether to take comfort from that or not. *Is the sea god closing his eye to the darkness that will come? Does he not want to witness the collapse of this world?* Or perhaps it was something else. *Perhaps his job is done,* she thought, *the pieces set in place already for the forces of light to prevail.* It was a rather more cheery notion.

It was all she had, in the end. Notions and thoughts and speculations and all the things that tumbled through her mind as she paced from wall to wall. She had asked several times to see Sotel Dar, if only to get some reading material from the scholar, but not once had he come. She had no books to read, no blank scrolls on which to write, no paints and brushes to help pass the time. Talasha had liked to paint, once before. She had liked to hunt as well, and sing, and dance, to drink wine and laugh and make love. But that was another time, another life, before the world had changed.

She reached the wall, performed her sequence of taps, turned, then paused at once. King Hadrin was standing at the plinth, she saw, though how he had uncurled himself from that fetal position he favoured, and stood without her hearing his chains, she couldn't say. *I suppose I was just distracted.*

"Hadrin," she said, peering at him. "Are you all right?"

His eyes were as crazed as she had ever seen them. They bulged grotesquely from his skull, the shape of the bones in his jaw and chin and cheeks visible beneath a layer of parchment-thin skin, sallow and unsightly. From the sides of his head, long brittle strands of white hair fell down, split by a scalp spotted and grey.

He looks ancient, Talasha thought, as though realising that for the first time. She knew it already, of course, but he'd appeared to have aged a further decade during his slumber. *He'd be mistaken for his father if the Wise King was still alive.* Godrin had been deep into his nineties when his son cut his throat, the princess was told, and Hadrin looked every bit as old. *Older, even*, she thought. *He could die this very night…*

The man was shivering, his lips moving soundlessly. Those protruding eyes were shot with red lines, yellowish and horrific to behold. She stepped closer, fearful. "Hadrin…what are you seeing?" she whispered. "Please… please tell me what you see."

Lips as creased and wrinkled as two strips of old parchment moved, trembling, but from between them came no words, only an unintelligible mumbling sound. The fetters about his ankles were stained with blood from the welts and abrasions cut into his skin, the flesh beneath rubbed raw. *It's a wonder he can even stand*, she thought, looking at those quill-thin legs poking out from beneath his rags, the arms that clutched the edge of the stone plinth equally wasted to the bone. He stared at the orb in a blank, wide-eyed gawp, lost to the power within.

She stepped closer. "Hadrin. Hadrin, can you hear me? *Hadrin!*" Her last repeat of his name was almost shouted, and it seemed to have an effect.

He blinked, just once, leaned back, and then screamed. "The end! The end! He's coming! The end!"

Talasha's heart all but exploded in her chest. "*Who?*" she asked him. "Who is *he?*"

There was no time to listen for an answer. From outside her cell she detected a sudden rush of movement and noise, the crash of footsteps clanking through the corridors. Men were shouting, it sounded like, rallying. She turned, staring at the door in alarm. There was a rumble, somewhere at the extremities of the palace, then more shouting, much closer. She heard the bars go on the door, then it swung open, and a dragonknight appeared. "My lady, stay here," he said in a rushing voice. "There's nothing to worry about. We have it under control."

She baulked at him in bemusement. *Stay here? Where am I going to go?* She did not know the knight. He was another of the dozens who seemed to rotate on watch up here, and in an instant he was turning to leave. "Wait," she called after him. "What is happening out there?"

He didn't tell her. The door was slammed shut and barred. She caught sight of bodies rushing past before her sight was shut off. Then more shouts and calls of alarm, and sounds of crashing. It was getting closer, closer every moment.

She whirled about. "Who is coming?" she demanded of the king. "Who is it, Hadrin? If you know something…"

"The end," he said, his voice quieter now, still staring in that wide, bug-eyed stare. Tears were rolling down his cheeks, the skin of his face pulled back in a look of strain so fierce she felt it might just rip suddenly from his skull. "He's coming…it's the end…"

"Who? *Who*, damnit!" She even rushed up to him, throwing her hand across his cheek. "Who? Is he returned? Eldur? Is the Fire Father come to kill us?"

No answer was yielded, only sobs, pathetic sobs. The colours within the Eye of Rasalan were shifting, swirling, a striking nebula of gold and blue. Talasha stared a moment. The movement made no sense to her, but she found herself transfixed all the same. A thousand times had she looked upon this relic and never had it appeared like this. *It's like it's alive*, she thought.

Another crash snapped her out of it. She turned again to the door. *It isn't Eldur*, she realised, all of a sudden. *Of course it isn't. Why would he fight his own guards?* It made no sense. More rumbles shook the summit of the palace, a particularly loud one causing the very floor to tremble. Then it came to her in an instant. *Marak! It must be Marak! He has broken free of the Father's spell, and come here to save me.* The dragonlord had been charged with leading the assault on King's Point, and slaying Amron Daecar, but had been away now for days. Away from *him*, and his controls. *The Father's spell on him has weakened*, she thought, exulting. *He has come back for me, come back to save his princess.*

Her heart was thrashing in her chest. She stared at the door, expectant, waiting for it to burst open and the great dragonlord to appear, clad in his Body of Karagar amour and with the Fireblade blazing in his grasp. Vaguely, she could sense Neyruu nearby, outside beyond the palace. Her bonded grey dragon would come and go, often hunting the delta for long hours at a time, but always she would return. *She is anxious, excited,* Talasha thought, concentrating. It was difficult from in here, behind these thick stone walls, but all the same the dragon's state of emotion was detectable to her. *What do you see, girl? Is it Garlath out there? Is Ulrik truly coming for me?*

Hadrin was still sobbing behind her. She glanced back, found him looking now at the door, eyes twisted into a hideous expression of fear. His lips moved. Words came out. "He's coming…he's coming…he's coming for me…"

"I won't let him harm you," Talasha promised the man. "You have nothing to fear of Lord Marak, I assure you, nor does he have any reason to…."

A sudden shriek cut her off. It came from outside, right outside the door, the sound of a man dying, and not well. Loud shouts and bellows followed, the clang of steel, more death. A heavy crash rattled suddenly against the door, as though a body had been thrown at it, and from beneath the wood came a whoosh of air, causing the flames of the braziers to stir, trembling. *It isn't him*, Talasha thought. She backed away. Something felt wrong.

The door swung open with a violent *crack*, the wood splintering beneath an armoured boot. A man stood beyond, clad in a cloak, steel beneath.

Misting steel, she saw. *Godsteel.*

At his side was a long silver blade, its length embraced by a swirling vortex of air. Behind him lay carnage and death, bodies scattering the hall. Blood dappled his cloak from thigh to neck in a thousand splashes and gouts.

He stepped inside the chamber, reaching up to draw back his hood. He wore a helm beneath, his visor down, face hidden behind the metal. That he flipped up also, showing himself. A black beard, short and trim. A young face, square and handsome. A pair of silvery-blue eyes, intense, focused, that stared right at the Eye of Rasalan. *I know him,* Talasha thought.

The man let out a breath. It sounded like relief. "It's here…it's…it's really here…" The words were whispered, as though to himself, and with them came a smile, quickening on his lips. For a moment he appeared transfixed, as Talasha had been, by the motion of the colours, pulsing and moving within the orb. It was almost as though the Eye itself was relieved as well, it seemed to her. But then suddenly the man snapped from his trance and strode forward, right for the plinth.

Talasha stirred as well, moving to block him. "Stop. You can go no further."

"I have no quarrel with you, maid." He brushed her aside without ceremony, approaching the shivering king. Hadrin's shrieks had been swallowed up by an utter and absolute terror. He could not speak. He could not move. Paralysed he stood, soiling his brand-new breeches. The intruder looked down at him coldly. Nothing resembling pity passed his eyes.

He's here to kill him, the princess thought. It was so obvious now. Hadrin had seen his own end, been tortured by it, tormented by the darkness that was coming. *The Long Abyss.* It was a northern version of hell, the foulest of them all, an empty black void through which the worst sinners would fall, starving and screaming, for all eternity. *That is the darkness he has seen. He had seen his own death, and even beyond it.*

"Hadrin," the knight said. He made the name sound like a curse, uttering it with disdain. "You've aged."

The king blubbered through his lips, still staring, bug-eyed. His ability to speak had abandoned him.

The knight studied the king for a long moment, shaking his head, then turned to her. "What has happened to him? What have you done?"

"The Eye has done it. His visions. The things he has seen."

"What has he told you? What has he told your master? Is he here? Is Eldur *here?*" The air that spun about his blade quickened, causing Talasha's long brown hair to billow.

"He isn't here," she said, steeling herself. "He has gone."

"Where? Where is he? Tell me!" A blast of wind burst off him, pulsing through the room. One of the braziers went out. "Tell me!"

Talasha found herself cowering from that blade. She knew what it was. She could feel its ancient power, feel the dreaded hate of the god whose heart had been shattered for its forging. She turned her eyes upon its bearer. "You're Elyon Daecar," she said. "His squire."

His eyes changed at once, narrowing. "Lythian...what do you know of Lythian?"

Much and more and not enough, she thought. "I spent time with him, in the Western Neck. We became close, very close."

Then his eyes opened. "Princess *Talasha*? Talasha Taan? But why..." He glanced around in astonishment. "Why are you..."

"Here? Locked away in this chamber? Dressed in such as these." She flicked her skirts, dirty with sweat, hardly the sort of thing a princess would wear. "I could tell you but we have no time. Not now. Later. *Later*. Right now we must go."

He looked at her, bewildered. "You're a *prisoner* here? I thought..."

"There is no time, no time, Elyon Daecar. Why have you come? Tell me, why? Is it for him? Have you come to kill him?"

"I've come to take the Eye. To blind him. Your master."

She shook her head. "I have no master but peace, Sir Elyon. It is a want of peace to whom I bow and serve. Eldur is not himself, not truly. He is seized by the power of the Bondstone, by the will inherent in Agarath's Soul. This will is death and chaos, and the ruin of the very world."

The man nodded, as though he already knew, or had come to suspect that very thing. "The north crawls, Your Highness, with terrors uncountable."

"The *world* crawls, sir. He mumbles and screams of it nightly," she said, gesturing at the king. "But all he says is incoherent. Snippets I have heard only. Fragments of things yet to come that will not make sense to me until such a time as they unfold. Only then will I understand. But we can talk of this later...later...now we must go."

The man was clearly taking a moment to catch up. "I have no means to carry you. Not so far. Vandar is hundreds of miles from here. A short journey, perhaps, but..."

"I have a dragon," she said. "She will bear me, and the king as well."

His eyes wrinkled in doubt. "He will not survive the journey. And I have no need of him."

"No need of him? Forgive me, but he may be the only man capable of helping you."

"No. There are others. Relatives. I need only find them."

She was shaking her head. "That is folly," she declared.

"I hear that a lot. Half of what I do seems like folly." Something twitched on his black-bearded lips. A knowing smile of sorts. "So Captain Lythian did tell me. He always spoke very fondly of you and your reckless ways. But that is a conversation to be had at another time. More men will come, and soon. We must go. *All* of us."

Elyon Daecar gave a snort, but made no complaint. "Fine. This dragon of yours. Is it near? I saw one, on the side of the palace. A grey one, quite small..."

Talasha nodded. "That is she. When I reach my chambers I will be able to summon her to the terrace." She drew a breath, thinking suddenly of Cevi. She was down there now, in the safehouse where Talasha had placed her. *Can I leave her? Leave her here, with the fire priests and the zealots? With their fires and burnings and sacrifices?* "I have a close friend, down in the city. I must go and collect her before I leave."

His doubt was clear. "My lady, will you not be stopped? If you're a prisoner here...and with this traitor with you as well..."

"I must try," she said, firmly. "Neyruu can carry the three of us."

"Neyruu?" He'd heard the name by the way he said it. "I thought..."

"Think later, Elyon Daecar. *Later.* Now come, help me with these chains."

Hadrin had entered an unresponsive stupor. He stood beside the plinth, just staring at the broken door, entirely catatonic. A thin line of drool dangled from the side of his mouth, and his large, watery eyes had seemed to lose all sense of sight. Talasha gave him a shake, but he just stood there, swaying, staring at the door. *This will be harder than I thought.*

"You'll need to cut him free, Sir Elyon. I do not have a key for his fetters."

The knight saw to it with his dagger, kneeling to slice right through the lengths of metal that bound the wretch's feet. Then he stood and swung a satchel bag from his back, stepping forward, reaching out to touch the Eye of Rasalan and deposit it inside. His fingers hesitated, an inch from the orb, as though wondering if he'd be able to bear it, move it, as a man of Varin's blood and not Thala's. Talasha wondered the same. But no, it gave no complaint, complying to his touch. Carefully, he rolled it along the top of the stone platform, dropping it into the bag, tightening the top. He breathed out, even smiled. "I had feared it would not yield to me."

Talasha was still trying to get Hadrin to wake up, to no avail, as Elyon drew the satchel bag over his shoulders. He took a moment making sure the straps were suitably tight. By then Talasha could hear the sound of shouting again, echoing distantly from down the corridors.

"More guards are on the way," she said.

"I know," he told her, perfectly calm. "I've been listening to them come for a while." He nodded to the king. "Get him moving, and stay behind me. I'll clear the way." He marched to the door, the Eye of Rasalan on his back, a shard of Vandar's Heart misting in his grasp. Talasha wondered if such a thing had ever happened before.

She turned to Hadrin, trying not to panic. "Come now, sweet king, It is time for us to go." She wrapped an arm around his wasted body, clinging to the man's ribs. He would not move. She could hear the guards getting closer. "Please, Hadrin, we *have* to go." She gave a tug, but he felt rooted to the floor, tensing all over, refusing to budge.

"What's the hold-up?" Elyon called back.

"He won't move."

"Try harder. How heavy can he be?"

She tried again, this time with more force, putting her back into it and driving him forward from the plinth. The effort won her a couple of feet, but he was fighting her, struggling to get back to his chains, staring at the door all the while, and murmuring again, "The end…the end…I see the end…"

"They're coming," the knight called out. "Hold here. Let me deal with them." He sped out through the doorway into the open antechamber. From down the corridor Talasha could see the black armour glistening, the red cloaks swishing, the spears bobbing as they ran. Three separate passages converged here. Men seemed to be coming from all of them.

"For Vandar!" she heard Elyon Daecar roar. There was a great sweep of his blade, from left to right, and a wall of wind crossed the hall, smashing half a dozen dragonknights to the stone. Several clattered and fell down with broken bones. One had his left leg twisted back at the knee, a savage break, and was howling in agony. A couple were merely dazed, rising unsteadily to join their allies as more men poured in from down the corridors.

Elyon Daecar beat them back, sending the wind to knock them away, or slaying them with his blade. More men came, two seeming to sprout up for every one that was killed. Where they were all coming from she couldn't possibly say, but nor could she stand there and watch. She turned back to the scion. He was gazing at the exit, seeing nothing. His eyes had all but rolled over into his skull, as though he was dead already.

"Hadrin. Hadrin, listen to me!" She shook him, violently, causing that long white hair to wave. "If you do not move, you are going to *die*. Do you understand? When the corridor is cleared, we go, OK? We have to run. Run to my chambers. Neyruu will be waiting. She'll be there, I know it."

And then she heard shouting, entering the room, as the men spilled in from outside. She turned at once, echoes filling the chamber. "Traitor!" a man bellowed at her. Talasha barely had time to realise who it was - one of her guards, yes, that big one who'd spat at her earlier, one of Vargo Ven's men - before he surged upon her, thrusting out to skewer her with his spear.

She twisted away, yelping. The spear surged past her. From her side came a low *cough*, and she spun to see that the spear had skewered Hadrin instead, driven right through his chest below the heart, piercing his liver. Blood and bile boiled forth from the wound, red and black, seeping out past the shaft of the lance. The knight let go, stumbled back. "I didn't mean…I wasn't trying to…" He looked around in a panic and then, suddenly, whirled and ran.

Elyon Daecar was there to meet him. He swung with his blade, cleaving the knight open at the belly with a savagely powerful cut. Talasha's eyes widened as the gore gushed out, emptying to the ground in a splash of hot entrails. The hall outside was a horror, full of groaning dying men. Some were dragging themselves away, trailing blood from stump legs, others cradling their severed arms. Broken bones were in abundance as well, though most were lying still, dead or insensate she couldn't say.

Hadrin stood with the spear stuck through him, somehow still standing even as he died. Blood issued freely from his mouth, cascading over his bottom lip and down the dangle of beard on his chin, turning it white to red. There was a look in his eye, she saw, of horror slowly evolving into one of almost peace, as though glad it was finally over, his torments done. He seemed to be staring at Elyon Daecar, his killer, or so he had thought.

He saw wrong, Talasha knew. *He never was much of a prophet.*

There were several more dragonknights in the room. One roared and rushed, lunging with his spear, but the attack was fended away with a flick of the Windblade. Another came behind, prodding hard. Elyon stepped sideways, the spear grazed his armour, and he whirled with a whip of wind, throwing the knight back against the wall, to crash into the table, sending plates and pewter jugs flying. Before the man could rise he was upon him, driving his blade into his neck, twisting.

Two remained. A moment later there was only one, and then a split second after that, none at all as first one of the knights, and then the other, dashed headlong from the room in retreat. The second tripped in his haste, slipping in a pool of blood, and rose red all over, stumbling off through the hall.

"Lucky it isn't his blood," Elyon observed, his voice flush from the fight. He looked around at the bloodshed he'd wrought. "These men…they have made me a monster. I had no intention of killing anyone today."

Talasha did not have time to hear these laments. She wanted gone from this chamber at once, gone from the bodies and the blood, from the palace and the city and the kingdom too. She had a final look at Hadrin, who had fallen now, forward onto his knees, still staring with those bulging eyes. *As in life, so in death,* she thought. *Be at peace, sweet king. May the sea god save your soul.*

Elyon was waiting for her at the door. "This friend of yours. Are you sure…"

"I'm sure. Do not wait for me, Elyon Daecar. Go, take the Eye and go. There is nothing for you here."

He hesitated.

"Go," she repeated, even pushing him. "I will follow."

Still he hesitated, but only for a moment. Then he gave her a look, gave her a nod, spun and dashed away.

The princess followed a moment later, passing the bodies in the hall. One of them was Sir Vendroth, she saw. His neck had been twisted violently sideways, a shard of bone ripping through his flesh, white against the ruin of his neck. "I'm sorry," she said, as if she was somehow to blame. He was a good man, a long-serving knight, and had not deserved to die.

Like thousands upon thousands of others, she thought, as she turned to rush off away to her chambers, to save Cevi from the same foul fate.

56

Janilah

He perched upon the hilltop, before the scattered ruins, waiting for his foe.

His heart was calm, beating steadily, strongly, in his chest. *This is my destiny,* Janilah Lukar thought. *This is my redemption.*

Sir Owen did not wait with him. He would not have the man spoil this moment or interfere. "This foe is beyond you, Sir Owen," he had told him. "It is a clash of gods, and you are but a man."

Janilah Lukar had removed his cloak in preparation, removed the old leather boots he wore over his armour, and the gloves that concealed his gauntlets, to leave him all in misting steel. At his feet a line of dragon's teeth had been arrayed, trinkets from his kills, a final insult and challenge. His long months on the road and in the wild, hunting dragons, butchering them, had brought him here. For days now he had waited, somehow knowing he would come.

He has seen it, the herald of Vandar thought. *The king to whom I gave my granddaughter. He has seen it in the Eye. And told him so. He'll come.*

Behind him, further back upon the hill, lay the ruins of the old fort that had become their temporary home. They had been here for days, this forgotten place amidst the wet and windy plains where the River and Lakelands met. Those days had driven a restlessness into the bones of Sir Owen Armdall, but Janilah did not heed him when he urged them to move on. "He will come, Sir Owen," he would say. "We need only wait, and have faith, and be patient. He will come."

The skies were as they had been for the majority of their stay. The rain fell in a soft damp mist, rarely waning, occasionally thickening when the clouds rolled in, grumpy and grey, to unleash a strong spring downpour. The weather did not help Sir Owen's mood, and sometimes he would raise a fist to curse whichever god had subjected them to this torment. It was unwise to curse the gods, Janilah had told him one night. "Have you not been paying attention, Owen?" the king said. "The gods still shape our path, even now. Do not bring their wrath down upon us."

The handsome knight of House Armdall was back there now, in the little shelter he'd erected among the wreckage of the old roundtower, prodding at the fire to try to keep it lit. Much of his time was spent on that fire, gathering wood, feeding the flames so they would stay warm by night, cooking the game he caught. Sometimes Sir Owen would be gone for hours, hunting wildfowl and deer in the nearest woods or seeking out travellers on the road to hear the latest tidings, but Janilah would not leave his post. No, he *could* not leave. *This is where we shall meet*, he knew. *We shall clash here on this hill.*

He waited in silence, perched upon the stump of an old tree, the Mistblade fogging softly at his hip. For months he had been guided by the blade, taken where its essence urged him, but no longer. *It wishes to stay*, the king knew. *And so do they.* He glanced to his left and to his right where there lay great boulders of craggy rock, still and silent, some a little larger than others, but all of a similar size and shape. *Sir Owen could learn patience from these creatures*, the old king thought. From the day the first of them had come lumbering from the darkness, calling up the rest of them to rise, they had gathered here, upon this wide open hill, and settled down to wait.

It all told Janilah that this was the place. "I need only wait," he told himself again. "One of these days, he will come."

But today was not that day.

For long hours the king maintained his lonely vigil beneath the weeping skies, but no, nothing stirred the Mistblade, nothing stirred the gruloks from their rest. When dusk came, and the lands were swallowed by a slow encroaching darkness, Janilah turned and retreated to the ruins. Sir Owen awaited him in the roundtower, a weatherworn cloak heaped over his shoulders. He had skinned and skewered a hare to roast, turning the spit over the fire. Drops of fat fell from the carcass, fizzling as they kissed the coals.

The man looked up, a ragged blond beard, like a bundle of dirty straw, poking from the bottom of his hood. "Nothing, sire? No sign?"

You would know if it were otherwise, the king thought. He only shook his head and took his cloak from a rusted iron hook on the broken stone wall, covered in moss and creeping vines, to throw about his shoulders. Sir Owen had raised a turf roof of sorts above them - grass and leaves laid upon a framework of sticks and branches - to help shield them from the rain. Janilah took a seat upon a block of chipped grey stone, removing his gauntlets, stretching his fingers. The hare smelled good, the promise of greasy meat causing his stomach to churn; he had not eaten a morsel since morning.

"It will be ready soon, sire," the knight was quick to say.

"No rush." Janilah Lukar took off his helm and set it aside, to let his unwashed hair, long and brown with many streaks of grey, flow out. The beard of a barbarian came with it, large and thickly tangled, a common facial accoutrement in these parts. *I have become a Riverlander*, he thought wryly. *If only Lord Wallis could see me now.*

He did not remove the rest of his armour, only the helm and those gauntlets, both of which could be easily reset in their proper place at a moment's notice. His swordbelt he unbuckled to place beside him, never straying more than an inch or two from his hip. He needed it close. He needed the whispered warnings. At some point Janilah Lukar had to give up his vigil and sleep, and he could not rely upon Sir Owen Armdall alone to give ample warning of his enemy. *The Mistblade will sense him,* he told himself. *It will wake me if he comes.*

The sworn sword gave the spit another turn, the hare crackling over the flames. "I met a traveller this afternoon, sire, further west along the road. He had some interesting tidings to share."

"Go on."

"News of your grandson, sire. Prince Raynald, that is, not Robbert. It seems he has grown restive waiting for the war to reach him in Ilithor, and mustered an army to march south. He is close to here, the traveller told me, only a two or three day march away or so he claimed. Apparently he rides at the head of a force almost thirty thousand strong."

Janilah Lukar flexed his fingers again, warming them over the fire. Darkness enshrouded them, and silence, but for the crackle of the flames, the patter of the rain on the makeshift roof. "It was unwise for him to have left Ilithor," he intoned, solemnly. "He may find himself exposed on the road. As the Vandarians have been."

"Yes, sire, I wondered the same. I even put that to the traveller, but he seemed of the mind that the army had not yet come under assault, not like Lord Rammas's forces."

They may yet. Sir Owen had found out of Lord Rammas's folly some two days ago, learning of the trials they had faced during their westward march along the Mudway from another wandering vagrant, fleeing north to escape the war. Over several long nights of attacks they had lost several thousand men, this vagrant had said, most falling to fire and fang, but many hundreds of others had been swallowed up by the marshes too, drowned in mud as they tried to rush from the road or dragged away into the bogs by one ghoulish mire-dweller or another. Apparently Elyon Daecar had been there as well, doing what he could to protect them from the skies, but to little impact. Defending several miles of road from sudden and unpredictable airborne attacks was a challenge beyond a single man. *All he is doing is chasing shadows,* the king reflected. It was better to hunt the demon who cast them. *As I am,* he thought.

"Did this traveller tell you where my grandson is leading this army, Sir Owen?" the king asked.

"He did, sire. Rustbridge, he claimed. He is marching straight down the Rustriver Road."

"Then he's exposed," Janilah declared. "There is little cover along that road." Its benefit was speed, as was the case with any road, stone-paved and well-maintained, but along the river there was little in the way of natural shelter, should some dragons come sniffing. That they had thus far gone unmolested did not mean that this leniency and luck would last. "Three days march from here, you say?"

"Yes, sire. Three days, or even two at a good pace." There was something very eager in the voice of Sir Owen Armdall. "It is thought that the Agarathi hordes will assault the crossing at Rustbridge soon, my lord. Your grandson may be looking to come down and strike at them from the north." He turned the spit again, shuffling his feet. "They could win, sire. The Pentars already have tens of thousands of men gathered at the crossing and the Helm, and with Lord Rammas soon to arrive and Prince Raynald in support as well, they might have the numbers to claim victory."

The rain was still falling gently, dripping down from the edges of their shelter. When Janilah gave no response, Sir Owen gave the spit another turn, shifted his feet once more, and said, "My king," in something of a beseeching voice. "Ought we not consider…well, with this of your grandson….should we not consider going to join him? I do not want to speak out of turn, but he is not yet fit to command such a force. He is too young, too inexperienced. And headstrong as well. I feel it would be better if you…"

"No, Sir Owen. We are not leaving. Not yet."

The man nodded, expecting those very words. "Yes, sire, but… these creatures…these gruloks…if they are truly here to serve you, then…well forgive me, sire, but would they not be more valuable fighting against the Agarathi in battle? If Rustbridge falls, the whole of East Vandar will have been conquered, and these creatures, and *you*, sire…it could make all the difference."

"All the difference." Janilah Lukar repeated, slowly, in a deep voice. "The difference will be made when their master is struck down, Sir Owen. I have told you this a hundred times. *That* is why we are here."

The knight nodded once again, remaining silent for a moment. *He doesn't believe it,* Janilah thought. *He does not share my faith.* "Yes, sire. I only think that…I only wonder…even if he does come, how will you…I beg your pardon, my lord, but how do you expect to defeat him?"

That was not a question Janilah Lukar could yet answer. *I will discover that when the time comes,* he thought. All he knew was that Vandar had gathered them here for a reason, to enact his will and his purpose. He had to believe he had a chance, even against such an ancient demon as this.

He looked at the sworn sword who had served him faithfully for so long and said, "Be patient, just a little longer, Sir Owen. In time you will have your answers." He kept his eyes on the knight, to make sure he understood, then moved them back to the fire. "Now pass me some of that hare. It looks about done."

They ate with their hands, hungrily chewing the stringy meat, licking the greasy fat from their fingers between bites. Nothing had ever tasted so good as the roasted meat Owen Armdall cooked out here. Faith in his purpose and path was not enough to sustain the king; he needed food as well, and his companion had provided it. He sucked the bones clean when he was done, flicking them away into the dark.

After that, he rose, placing the Mistblade down upon the bed of grass and bundled clothes Sir Owen had fashioned for him, close enough to the fire to feel its warmth, but not so near as to be disturbed by the flickering flames. "Wake me if there is trouble," he told the knight, as he lay down, looking out through the fortress ruins, through the vines and bushes and sapling trees that had taken dominion here, and away across the hill.

Sleep came easy, his dreams untroubled, the night passing in a flash. *Another day,* he thought, rising to a fresh and golden dawn, the air sweet with the scents of spring, the grasses twinkling in their cloaks of dew. He could hear birdsong in the nearest woods, westward down the slope, and away to the east the Hooded Hills were emerging from the mists, soft and sloping.

Janilah drew his gauntlets on, girding his waist with his swordbelt, removing his hooded cloak. His helm he kept to hand, to put on later, as needed. "Sleep, Sir Owen," he said. "Your watch is over." *And mine begins.* He strode out across the wide and open hilltop, to continue his silent vigil.

The day went the same as the last, and the one before that, and the one before that as well. The sunny bright morning did not last. Soon the clouds crept in, sneaky as a thief, and before he knew it the rains were falling, the skies curdling to their misty grey. *Today is the day,* Janilah thought. He examined the stone sentinels of Vandar, the early creations of rock and rage, turning his eyes over each of them in turn. All were as they had been the day before, and the one before that, and the one before that as well. There were no new prints, no churned brown earth to suggest that any of them had moved. *Change is slow for these creatures. They do not see time as we do.*

His back was straight, his eyes keen, his sword hand ever-ready. The dragon teeth before him lay in their places, lined up chronically, from his first kill to his last. *No,* he thought. *No, that isn't true.* Janilah Lukar had slain a dragon as a much younger man, though never claimed his prize back then. *I am lacking one tooth,* he mused, looking over them. *But still, they are far too few.*

After standing for an hour he sat, only to stand again an hour later. This was his way. He watched the sun move, a blurred shape beyond the wet grey veil, inching east to west in its slow and daily arc. Sir Owen awoke some time around midday and set off to check his snares. Janilah Lukar wondered if this might be the day that his loyal knight left him, fed up with all this waiting. *Perhaps he will ride off and swear his sword to my grandson instead?* Janilah put that notion from his mind. *No, he did that already, and Raynald refused.*

He sat down on his stump again, another hour passing by. The waiting could be wearying, enough to sap the spirit of a lesser man, but this man who had been known as the Warrior King would not let it defeat him. He had armoured his mind in a suit of plate stronger even than godsteel, fending off his fears, fostering his patience. During these long lonely hours alone with his thoughts, imagining the battle yet to come, not once did he yield to dread.

Let him come, he only thought. *Show your face, demon.*

The rains weakened, strengthened, weakened again. Janilah stood from his stump, and sat down again an hour later, only to stand once more once another hour had passed. Soon enough the sun was plunging away into the west, appearing briefly beneath a low cloak of cloud before seeking refuge beyond the plains. Colours of red and russet soaked the world, lighting up the belly of the sky. Janilah sat down for the final hour of his vigil, as ever, watching the colours darken and change and merge, listening to the birds twitter and chirp their evenfall songs. His eyes moved slowly, east to west and west to east and back again, several times, searching for his foe.

Not today, he decided at last, as he stood and retired to the ruins.

Dinner that night was duck. Sir Owen had found a hare in one of his snares again, he said, but had also put an arrow through the eye of a large male mallard and thought they could do with the change. "It will be pheasant tomorrow, my king," he said, smiling as they ate. The duck was even more delicious than the hare had been, paired with some root vegetables the knight had foraged and boiled up in a stew. "I sighted a couple in the woods today, but wasn't able to get a shot at them. If not, we have the hare at least."

Janilah tipped his wooden bowl to his lips, gulping down the last of his broth. He wiped his bearded mouth with the back of his sleeve and put the bowl aside. "Any sightings today, Owen?"

The man knew what he meant. "Nothing, sire, though I did see some strange tracks. Large, three-toed, almost birdlike. It might just be a giant chicken," he said, with half a smile on his face. "I will hunt it tomorrow, my lord. It would keep us fed for weeks, I would think."

So would a deer, the king thought, though those had grown scarce according to Sir Owen's reports. Wildfowl remained common enough, but larger game was harder to come by now that all manner of beasts were crawling the lands in search of prey. And that was to say nothing of the dragons. *They'll have stripped these lands clean within a year,* Janilah brooded. As if it wasn't bad enough that their crops and farms were being razed to the ground, that fertile breadbaskets all across the north had been utterly destroyed, and livestock poached by the thousand…now they were hunting wild game as well. If they did not stop them soon, nine out of every ten people in the north would starve by the end of next year.

Janilah slept fitfully that night, his typically peaceful slumber interrupted by a growing sense of urgency. When he woke he did so from a series of dark dreams, poorly rested and weary, his eyes heavy with black bags. "Perhaps you should try to sleep some more, my king," Sir Owen offered, having observed his restless slumber. "You were tossing and turning a lot. I am happy to remain on watch a little longer if…"

"No." Janilah rose. "I must return to my post."

The day went the same as the last, and the one before that, and the one before that as well. The morning was bright and sunny, but soon the rains came washing down. Janilah stood and sat and stood again. The sun moved from east to west, drawn along its unceasing path, never faltering, never deviating, performing its duty day by day as every good servant does.

I am a good servant, Janilah told himself, as he stood scrutinising the skies. *A servant to Vandar, the God King. His herald, and his will.* He would not let a poor night's sleep deviate him from his duty, or render him open to even the slimmest of doubts. *He will come,* he thought. *One day, he will come.*

But today was not that day.

653

Dinner was pheasant, as promised. "Well done, Owen," Janilah said, sitting wearily on his stone seat, removing his gauntlets and helm. "I like a man who follows through."

"It gave me a good runaround, but I got it in the end."

"And this giant chicken of yours?"

The knight shook his head. He had of course been japing on that account, and did not seem in the mood for jesting tonight. "I followed its tracks for a short while, but soon lost them in the woods. Other creatures lurk there now, my king. It has grown increasingly dangerous in these valleys."

It has grown increasingly dangerous everywhere, the old King of Tukor might have said.

The rains fell hard that evening, as they had during parts of the day. As they ate their roasted pheasant, a part of the shelter Sir Owen had raised fell through beneath the assault of the deluge, causing a great waterfall of rain to come lashing down upon them. The knight gave out a curse as the water splashed across the fire, putting out the flames, plunging them into darkness. Thunder roared, and lightning struck, and the woodpile Sir Owen had amassed was soaked through as well, making the creation of a new fire impossible. Further curses ensued from the lips of the Oak of Armdall, but Janilah Lukar just sat, silent, musing on the morrow.

His sleep was interrupted by the storm, though ample enough despite it, and when he woke the skies had cleared and Sir Owen had managed to patch up the hole in the roof. "I'll fetch new firewood today," he told his king, looking weary. He gave his pile a peevish kick, to suggest it was badly soaked through and would take time to dry. "There are places in the forest where the canopy is thick, sire. I'll find some dry wood there."

Janilah nodded as he drew on his gauntlets. "Be careful, Sir Owen. And stay vigilant. The storm augurs the coming of dreaded things, it is said." He strode out to begin his vigil, wondering if that might be so.

The night of heavy rain had splashed mud across the dragon's teeth, so Janilah Lukar took out a rag to wipe them clean, and set them back in place. He scanned the skies, sitting on his tree stump, neck swivelling slowly left to right, right to left, left to right and back again. On most days during their long pilgrimage the pair had seen dragons in the skies. Sometimes they would be no more than a mile or so away, sometimes ten or even twenty, flying low or flying high, scouting or hunting or simply gliding from one place to another, for what reason the king couldn't know. Even during their first days here, Janilah had sighted dragons from his stump, and Sir Owen would return from his rangings to say he had seen wings in the skies as well. But no longer. Now long days had passed without a single sighting at all. *The skies grow quiet here,* Janilah thought. *The dragons are being summoned for a larger assault.*

He could feel a change in the air, some strange tang that told him that chaos was afoot. Was Vargo Ven mounting an assault on Rustbridge? Was there trouble further to the west? Rumour had said that King's Point was set to come under attack, though they had heard nothing of that for weeks.

Is it happening today? the king wondered. *Are they to unleash their full power upon us?*

His eyes narrowed, and stayed narrow as he stood, and sat, and stood again. The sun wheeled by, brighter today than usual, the clouds thinner, wisps of white and grey, the rains falling only seldom and in short showers of sweet spring drizzle.

Today, he thought, with more conviction than ever. Somehow he knew it, from that tang in the air, from the utter silence that had fallen, an eerie silence. "The storm augurs the coming of dreaded things," he whispered. "He will come today."

He watched, waiting, standing, sitting, scanning the skies all the while. Another hour passed. Nothing. Another hour. Still nothing.

He stood, scanning, narrow-eyed, nothing.

He sat, scanning, narrow-eyed, nothing.

Noon came and went. As did mid-afternoon. Soon the sun was beginning to wane in the west. He could hear Sir Owen back in their little camp, chopping up the firewood he'd gathered, relighting the fire, preparing dinner for his king. *Show your face*, he thought. *I know you're out there. I know it...*

Movement caught his attention, drawing his eyes to the right. He frowned. One of the gruloks was shifting, just slightly, as it slept. *Odd.* That hadn't happened before. He looked forward once more, scanning slowly from right to left and left to right and right to left and...

There.

His eyes sharpened upon a shape, dark and distant, high up in the skies. *Dragon*, the king knew at once. The shadow moved neither left nor right, and that said it was flying toward him, though from this distance perceiving any detail was impossible, size the same. It was a shape only, a blot of black ink on parchment, blurred and formless, but a dragon, sure as day. Of that the king always knew. Some men mistook birds for the beasts, ravens and crows especially, but these men were not Janilah Lukar, Vandar's herald and his champion, butcher of Agarath's spawn. *I know a dragon when I see one.*

The skies were clearer than they'd been in a week, only a few loose clouds scattered here and there. It seemed to Janilah Lukar as if those clouds were all moving away in different directions, spreading away to the east and to the west and leaving before him an empty field of open sky. And into it the dragon was flying, many miles away, but approaching fast. There was a slight quickening in the king's chest, the slow, steady, sombre beat of his heart pacing forth with more alacrity, sending a flood of blood through his veins.

He's coming, he thought.

Janilah Lukar wrapped his fingers around the Mistblade's long and elegant hilt, fixing the bond between blade and blood. He could perceive within the steel an excitement, and a tension that bordered on alarm. He drew it from its sheath, holding it to his side. The mists rose from its edge, rippling and swirling in a frantic new pattern, a visual manifestation of its state. Light shone, a wondrous cobalt blue, brighter still in the coming twilight, reflecting off his armour. Green and gold that armour was, armour worn by the great kings of his line, by Galin Lukar himself and all those who had followed him. When King Galin clad himself within it, it was a fine set he wore. Now it was better; strengthened and reinforced by the Hammer of Tukor.

Armour fit for a god, Janilah Lukar thought. *And to fight a god, that too.*

The dragon was still far off, though that blot of black ink was beginning to spread into a recognisable shape. Colours cleared. *Black.* He knew that already. *And red,* he realised now. That gave him pause, drawing a line between his brow. Hadrin had once bleated of a red and black terror he'd seen in the Eye of Rasalan, bringing death on an unimaginable scale. In his folly the king had ignored him, waved him off as raving and wrong, but now that recollection was returning to haunt him. He squinted forward, wondering…

The pace of his heart was quickening yet further. Distantly, the king could hear Sir Owen Armdall behind him in their camp, no longer chopping now, but shouting, "….my king…my king, is it he? Has he come?"

Janilah ignored him. He had told him not to interfere, lest he be in dire need of help. He only raised a hand and closed a fist, as if to say, 'all is well'.

But Sir Owen didn't heed him. "Sire…sire…the dragon…sire, it…that isn't a *normal* dragon…" His voice was growing louder as he spoke, panting. He was running closer. "Sire!" his voice came, clearer now. "We must run! That dragon…that is *not* Garlath, my lord. It isn't Garlath, as we thought…."

He was still running toward him. Janilah Lukar kept his eyes facing south, facing his foe. They had heard the rumours from Thalan; that Eldur, the Father of Fire, had arrived upon a great dragon, the greatest of those still living. Garlath the Grand, the survivors who saw him were saying, or so they'd heard at the inns and taverns they'd passed where the business of whispers and rumours was still doing a decent trade. It was said that Eldur could command any dragon he wished and, of course, he'd chosen the biggest.

But Sir Owen was right. This dragon was not Garlath. Garlath was a dragon of blue and grey, not red and black, and even now, from so far away, Janilah could perceive the monster's size…a size given scale by the shape of a tiny figure upon the beast's back, perched amidst a sea of savage horns that rose up between its shoulder blades. He saw a glimpse of red robes, fluttering, white hair whipping, a staff and glowing orb atop it, casting a great bright light, orange and red, upon the craggy summit of the beast. But all of that was lost within an enormity of spikes and scales, an ant upon the back of an elephant, a spec upon a mountain. Stretching out from east to west were a pair of black and red-veined leathern wings seven hundred feet from tip to tip.

No, Janilah thought, in slow horror. *More. Even more.* The king almost stepped back, but held his ground. *I will not yield. I will not yield to dread.*

"Sire...my king..." Sir Owen came rushing up behind him, breathless. "My lord...that isn't Garlath. It can only be...only be..."

"Drulgar," the king said, drawing into his lungs a long and steadying breath. The mists were in utter frenzy now, the Mistblade humming and fizzing in his grip. "The Dread."

Sir Owen would not repeat the name. He grabbed the king's arm. "Sire...my lord...we cannot hope to fight them alone! We must go. We must!"

"Then go, Sir Owen. And I am not alone." Janilah Lukar felt a stirring to left and right, boulders rousing from their sleep. Through the Mistblade, the echoing voice of the God King sang out in rapture. The king nodded, he even smiled. "This is where I'm meant to be."

The sworn sword of House Armdall was descending into a desperate panic now. "My lord! My lord, I'm sworn to protect you! How can I leave you now? How can I? *No!*" He shouted, almost screaming the word out at the top of his lungs, as though to stir something inside himself, some strength to stay and fight. "No, I'll not leave you, my king. If you're to die here today, so will I. That is the oath I made." He drew his misting longsword.

This is a man of faith, Janilah thought, as he had that day Sir Owen had tracked him down in the wilds of Tukor. *A man of faith and courage and valour.* But all the same he shook his head, never taking his eyes off his foe. "Find cover, Sir Owen. Your blade is no use here."

He heard the knight give out some further bleating, but no longer was he listening. The king stepped away from him, across the soft spring grass that carpeted the wide open hilltop. Ahead, the lands were cast beneath a vast winged shadow, blotting out woods and forests and lakes as it moved across the world. The trees bent and swayed at his passing, and some were seen to snap and flatten by the furnace wind that followed in his wake. About the beast the air fizzed, burning, sparks and flashes of fire seeming to combust in a thousand red swirls. *A dragon god,* Janilah Lukar thought. *Ridden by a demigod demon.*

The wind reached him long before the titan, softly at first, then sudden and violent, a gale of burning air driven forth by the great bulk of the beast. Janilah stood with his long tangled hair and beard straining against the rush, the weight of his armour holding his footing there on the hill where others might just be blown away. He could hear Sir Owen calling out in desperate plea behind him but his voice was soon swallowed by the storm. In the crook of his arm the king held his helm, crested with the five miniature blades that Tyrith had added in adornment, a flourish Janilah had never liked.

I was never meant to gather the five, he thought. *But it matters not. I need only one.*

His heart was beating steadily in his chest. "I am Vandar's herald," he began whispering to himself, as the sky ahead filled with black and red. Slowly he placed the helm over his head, faceplate raised, completing his suit of armour. "Vandar's will works through me, his servant and his champion. For you, Lord of Gods. All I do now is for you."

He repeated the words in sequence, giving him strength as the dragon god loomed. The Great Calamity beat his wings, and thunder seemed to bellow, booming out across the world. Lightning wreathed him, red and wild, flashing and snapping and zipping from his scales. A long serpentine neck stretched forth from its shoulders, forty metres in length alone, ending in a head as large as a carrack. *He could swallow a broadback whole*, he thought, trying not to submit to terror. Slowly his heart rate was creeping up again, as the maw opened wide. Teeth as long as spears surged down from the roof of its mouth, their count innumerable, a forest of fangs. Beyond was crimson fire, filling its jaws, a flame hot enough to melt godsteel, the singers liked to say.

Let's find out, thought Janilah Lukar. He set his mind and steeled his eyes. *For you, Vandar, King of Gods. I stand against this titan of an ancient time…for you, and you alone.*

The king drove the Mistblade aloft, its cobalt light cast from the steel like a sunburst, bright and brilliant and divine, a challenge of one god to another. In response the Dread widened its maw and uttered an impossibly deafening roar, a trumpeting, overlapping, never-ending sound that caused his very plate armour to rattle against his frame. But Janilah did not turn away; Janilah did not yield.

Atop the beast's back, the spec of man that was Eldur the Eternal lifted his black staff to the skies, and from the Soul of Agarath a second response was given, the orb throbbing and pulsing, sending waves of light to wash upon the world, and in that light Janilah Lukar felt the ageless terror of the Fire God, saw reflected in its glow his flame imperishable, his unutterable chaos and cruelty, heard the screams of every soul consumed by the devil's wrath.

The soul of one god. The fragment of another's heart. *We meet again*, they seemed to say.

And Janilah did not yield.

The dragon gave his wings another beat; more thunder exploded, louder than before, closer, and the trees that lay beneath him waved and shuddered and cracked and fell flat. Even from a hundred metres away, the dragon was monstrous, seeming to loom right before his very nose, filling his vision. Some of the horns on its back stood tall as trebuchets, great curving crimson things that ended in savage tips, their edges serrated. The claws of its taloned feet and wingtips were long enough to tear a tower in two. Girding its neck protruded a thousand bony spikes, many as long as swords, others spears, some even like the masts of ships, and twice as thick besides. Behind it all whipped a snaking tail many hundreds of feet in length. *That tail alone could fell an army*, the king thought. *This titan could destroy us all.*

But Janilah did not yield.

When the dragon landed, the very earth seemed to shatter, the ground rending and ripping apart as the world quaked beneath its weight. Janilah

Lukar held his ground as the air began to boil around him, lifting a hand to lower his faceplate lest his skin be scorched and burned. A hundred metres away, Drulgar the Dread loomed, a towering mountain of fury and wrath. The grasses about him were afire, all nearby shrubs and bushes and trees bursting into a red combustion, the soils turned over and destroyed, all he touched reduced to ruin.

"Heed me," Janilah Lukar whispered in prayer, turning to his master, his god, his faith. "Heed me, oh King of the Gods. I stand here for you, Vandar. For you and you alone."

"You are the butcher king," came a voice, almost like a hissing whisper, snakelike. It seemed to spread eerily upon the air, as though spoken into his very ear, as though circling around him, everywhere. "You have been killing *his* children."

Janilah refused to quaver. He set his feet and raised his chin and said, "I am Vandar's herald," in a loud, clear voice. "His herald and his champion. I am…"

"A man," broke in the whisper. "Just a man in armour."

Janilah peered through the smoke, the ash, the swirling fume that was already fogging the hilltop. "Show yourself, demon," he demanded. "I have waited long for your coming."

"Long for your death."

The mountain moved before him, lowering its head, and along the long thick ridge of neck beyond, Janilah saw his foe. He stood there, upon the highest peak on the titan's back, a cloak of crimson swaying in the wind, a long black staff held in his grasp. From beneath his hood stared a pair of pupil-less red eyes, demon eyes, eyes of eternal malice and hate nestled within a bone-white face, cold like stone and soulless. There was something lizard-like about that visage, something reptilian. *Demon*, Janilah thought.

He took a pace forward, and another, and another. *I walk in Vandar's tread. I come bearing his Heart and his will. I am his avatar on earth. His vessel of vengeance and woe.*

A smile appeared on the lips of the demon demigod. "A brave one," he said, in that horrible hissing whisper. "The Warrior King, I have heard you called. A man who thinks himself my equal."

"I *am* your equal," Janilah said. "You were divine once, but no longer. You are but a man, the same as me." *And one day, I'll be more. One day I'll have a Table of my own.*

The thought came unbidden, but come it still did. That part of Janilah Lukar had not entirely died. He looked at the Father of Fire, and knew this was the way. *Vandar will reward me. He will raise me as divine for this.* Of the Dread he had not anticipated, however. Garlath he might have slain, but Drulgar…

He stopped, a mere eighty metres now from the titan. It perched upon the hill with the tips of its wings gouged into the furrowed earth, spread so wide that Janilah Lukar needed to turn his neck to see them. His mind cycled through the stories, the tales, the myths. *He is as they always said,* he thought. *A calamity of total chaos.*

But Janilah did not yield.

The demon demigod was watching him with those peculiar red eyes. He had his head turned, just slightly, in a strange way, toward the orb atop his staff. *He has a master of his own,* Janilah knew. *The Soul commands him. The Soul controls him.*

"What does your god tell you, *demon?*" the king called out. "You see, *you* are a herald, as I am. We are equals, you and I."

Something glowered in the Eternal's eyes, something dark and dangerous. *Good,* Janilah thought. *Good. Come closer.*

"Do you dare face me alone, demon? Is your Fire God urging caution?" He paused; the Fire Father did not react. "This is your last life, *Eldur,*" he said, saying his name and saying it loudly, without a tremble to his tone. "Is that not why you ran, and hid, when Varin defeated you at the Ashmount? You feared your final death. You crept into the dark like a craven…you, and this titan *dog* of yours."

The world rumbled as the Dread drew up in fury, pressing higher upon his colossal bulk, widening his wings to blot out the setting sun. Janilah craned his neck as the wall of monster loomed, hundreds of feet above him. Then he heard a calming voice. "Settle, my lord, settle," it whispered, and within it Janilah heard fear. *Never could he control the beast,* he thought. *Only the soul of his maker can do that.*

Drulgar settled, lowering once more. The earth gave way with every movement, every shift of its bulk, rending and ripping beneath its weight. How much that weight was Janilah couldn't hope to say. *Enough to crush any fortress in the north,* he knew. Yet all the same, he was not invulnerable. *He has eyes,* the king thought, *and a brain somewhere behind them.* He squinted through his visor, through the smoke and fume and ash and fire, past the horns and spikes and scales, beyond the head, the neck, and into the great cavity that was his chest, larger than any feast hall in the world. *And somewhere in there, a heart,* he knew. *A heart of flesh and blood.*

The demon was still looking at him, peering down from on high. "The Champion of Mists," he murmured. "Do you think I am blind to your intent?"

Janilah stared right back, unyielding. He saw no need to lie. "My intent is to kill you," he said.

The demon laughed, putting foul thunder into his voice, and from the nostrils of the titan great plumes of burning black smoke swirled up to blanket the skies, flashing with darts of red lighting as it rose. The sun was all but gone now, hurrying away as though in fright to plunge them all in darkness. The hill that had been pretty and green was now blackened, burning, coated in ash. *A desolation,* the king thought. *He will make all the north the same.*

"You have no power to kill me, infant," the demon demigod said, still laughing. "You are a shadow of what has come before, and this world of yours is weak. In the wreckage that will come, all will fight to stay afloat, as is the natural order of things. I shall bring the flood, Janilah Lukar, a flood of fire and fume. This is as the world was and so it shall be again. Agarath the All-Father wills it so."

He raised his staff high above his head and from it pulsed a light, so bright and violent and sudden that Janilah was forced to shield his eyes. A great cackle of laughter filled the air, as though from the voice of Agarath himself, and there was a sound of grinding, of a great maw widening, air rushing, burning, igniting. The king drew his gauntlet away, opened his eyes and saw the flame, a gushing river, wild and red and, surging and roiling toward him.

"Now!" he roared, as he saw it come, and at once Janilah Lukar drew upon the powers of the Mistblade, and his form faded, rippling, turning translucent and incorporeal. The fire enveloped him a moment later, passing over and past and *through* him, but even then, even so, he could feel the heat, the impossible heat, feel the ground melting and bubbling and burning at his feet. No other beast could emit fire so hot. *Perhaps the singers were right...*

Movement caught his eye. To his sides, to left and right, he saw them, the great lumbering shadows rising from their slumber, driving forth against the tide of flame.

Five, he thought, *eight, ten...*

Under the cover of the inferno they battled forward, resistant to its heat. One went ahead of them, their leader, the one Janilah had first met, or so it looked. Telling them apart wasn't easy, though this one appeared a little larger than the rest. He charged, roaring in that rumbling rockslide of a voice, and the others joined him, and all of a sudden the fire was washing past and waning, the air clearing, and Janilah Lukar saw them, the gruloks, rushing and laying assault to the Dread, hacking at his scales with arms of sharpened stone, thrusting with rocky spears.

A terrible bellow filled the air, and at once the titan was rearing up, beating its wings in a ferocious storm, dashing several of the stone sentinels aside. Huge rock bodies more than twenty feet tall went flying, end over end, to scatter down the hill. Others were still on him, climbing, stabbing at the titan's neck, his shoulders, his jaws. From the cuts and cleaves burning lava flowed out, the titan's blood of living flame, melting through the hillside.

The monster smashed down again, causing a chasm to open in the earth, tearing right through the world. The violence of the tremor had the king stumbling as the earth opened up beneath him. He threw himself aside and scrambled back to his feet, as his trinkets, the fangs of the dragons he'd slain, tumbled down into the widening darkness. There was a great rending rumbling sound; the very lands themselves seemed to be disintegrating beneath him. Smoke gushed and swirled about in great black unnatural swarms. Janilah cast his eyes about but suddenly it was hard to see much of anything through the smoke. *It was supposed to be Garlath*, he thought, despairing. *Garlath! How am I to fight this foe?*

He surged forward all the same, leaping between the ridges opened up in this broken world, a blue spectre trailing mist as he went. *I must get closer. I must get inside. The heart,* he thought. *The heart.* It was the only way.

Through the black swirling smoke he could see beams of crimson light shooting down from above, hear Eldur cackling wildly as he fired upon the gruloks. In that light the king could hear the screams of the fallen souls, a woeful clamour so terrible as to cast a man's heart in darkness. He pressed on through the battleground, as one of those screaming lances of light struck a grulok in the chest as he hacked at the neck of the Dread, blasting him away into the void. Another great cackle resounded. There was something joyous in it, something utterly maddened and unearthly, a sound from another time, a sound from another world.

Gods and monsters, the king thought, as more beams shot from the skies, as the demigod cackled, as the dragon god roared. *Vandar…protect me! Give me the strength to fight!*

Suddenly, from on high surged the titan's enormous head, descending like a falling tower, clad in smoke and lighting, his great jaws opened wide. Janilah stopped, staring up, as the jaws snapped down upon one of the gruloks, lifting it from its feet, crushing, shattering it in a single savage bite as shards of rock went spraying across the ground. The boulder-like head of the grulok landed and rolled to Janilah's feet, its ice-eyes thawing, darkening, going out.

Janilah shuddered. For a moment he felt paralysed, unable to do anything but watch as the titan lifted its head once more, swinging its bulk in a mighty twist, throwing several more of the clinging gruloks from its scales. A hurricane flowed out across the hillside, a gale so fierce it knocked Janilah back a step. And another, and another…

…and all of a sudden his rear foot was giving away beneath him, slipping, and he turned, twisting, reaching out to take hold of something, but there was nothing to grab. A chasm yawned before him, greedy and wide, ending in blackness. Janilah's weight took him into it. The cleft gobbled him up. He fell, tumbling, passing root and rock and dirt.

Panic soared in him, stealing his focus…and in his loss of focus the power of the Mistblade abandoned him. His body took form, re-materialising from the mists…and just as it did so he struck against the jutting edge of the chasm wall, a ledge of rock smashing hard against his pauldron… and by the shuddering impact his sword hand faltered, fingers opening, the Mistblade slipping…slipping…tumbling from his grasp…

No…no…nooooo….

He snatched out to try to grab it again, but it was gone, spinning away into smoke and shadow. The world sped past in a blur, a second passing, two, three…then suddenly the bottom of the rift rushed up to meet him, and he crashed down hard against the solid rock floor, the weight of his armour causing the stone to crack and shatter. His head jerked and rattled within his helm, fogging. There was a *clanging* sound, heard through the roar of battle above…a sound of metal bouncing against rock, lower, somewhere lower, away into the very depths of the world. *No….*

He tried to struggle to his feet, fell again, stood, stumbled and looked up. A roar shook the world above him, thunderous. Everything moved, the entire rift shifting violently from left to right and right to left, as though the very world was breaking. Janilah Lukar could only stare upward in horror as the chasm folded in and crumbled, the walls of the rift collapsing. Light vanished, giving way to darkness as the world caved in atop him. *They'll never find me*, was his only thought.

As the rock came down and down and down…

57

Saska

Darkness filled the air, a darkness of shifting shadows and whispered voices. Over two hundred men wore the cloaks of the dead. Hasham men, Nemati men, disguised beneath the colours of Antapar and Konollio, killed by Rolly and the rest only the day before. The ruse would last only so long, though in the maddened heat and confusion of it all, mere moments would be enough.

Sir Ralston Whaleheart made a sound of displeasure. "You should not be here, my lady. It is folly to risk you like this."

"The world is full of risk, Rolly. Now stop complaining, and accept it. I've made my decision and am staying."

Saska was not going to miss this, not for all the godsteel in the world. She had the option of waiting at the top of the palace with her grandmother, pacing from side to side, wondering how it was all going below. Men would come to her often, she had been promised, with messages and updates, but that wasn't good enough. *No, I have to be here. I need to be here when they come.*

They were out there now, she knew, creeping forward, a great host of men and mounts tens of thousands strong. Lords Krator and Kastor at their head; highborn, handsome, smug and cruel. She curled her fingers around the hilt of her ancient dagger, the very dagger Varin himself used to bear. Strength saturated her, a strength, it seemed, of all the great men, the great kings, who'd borne this blade before.

Steel, Service, Honour, Light, against the Hordes of Fire we Fight. The words graven into the hilt and pommel, glowing in a divine, long-forgotten tongue that Saska did not know. The maxim distilled into words the immutable clash between Vandar and Agarath, Varin and Eldur, Bladeborn and Fireborn that had lasted for time immemorial. The words did not fit *this* night, or *this* fight, but all the same, they filled Saska with resolve.

Krator, Kastor, she thought, tightening her fingers on the grip. Her grandmother had told her that these men were not her enemy, that they were not even worthy of her worry and her thought, but she was wrong. Saska thought about them often. They came to her in her dreams. Not always was her sleep haunted by the fate that awaited her, by the cloaked shadow, bursting into flame, by Eldur, by the Heart of Vandar glowing bright. Those were nightmares of things yet to come, yet often, too, she dreamed of things gone before.

The whip, the darkness, the hunger and torture and pain. The screams that rang out through the cold damp cells beneath Keep Kastor...

Vengeance was petty, the scholars said, even base, a desire driven by ill emotion above which the wise should rise. *But I'm not wise*, Saska told herself. *I'm just a girl, not long turned nineteen. No one is wise at nineteen.*

The dagger was not her only weapon. On her opposite hip, she wore her sword, less fabled but no less deadly, and every inch of her was wreathed in armour, lobstered godsteel, misting softly. Leshie, too, had now been garbed as such, if not entirely enrobed as Saska was. Complementing the red leather armour she favoured was a slim-fitting breastplate, gorget, gauntlets, plackart, and helm. All had been procured by the Butcher, who had managed to upgrade several of the more ill-fitting elements of Saska's armour as well. *With the help of a certain merchant*, she thought. *Upon whom this entire plan has been built.*

The Red Blade was with them now, peering down the long straight boulevard that ended at the Cherry Gate, a quarter-mile away. It was hard to see much of what was going on there, given the thick gloom that had gathered in the skies above. It was a windless, still and muggy night, unstirred by a breath of air, the stars and moon all blotted by a thick black pall of cloud. On such a night, knowing friend from foe would be difficult.

But soon we'll have light, Saska knew. *Light, heat, and death.*

"They're all in their positions," Leshie said, in a voice reduced to a whisper. There was no need to be so quiet all the way back here, but somehow talking any louder felt wrong. Around them, and down every street and alley, hidden and concealed, many thousands lay in wait. The eastern expanses of the city had been evacuated of all civilians, only to fill this very night with soldiers instead. Swords waited in sheathes, clutched by sweaty palms. Archers huddled in their hiding places atop buildings, bows nocked and ready. A thousand starcats and sunwolves lurked, unseen, with their riders. But down that central boulevard, all was silent, all was still. Only the soldiers in their dead-men's cloaks were there, at the gate, preparing to open it and spring the trap.

Let this work, Saska thought in prayer. *Let it end tonight.*

Her heart was pounding in her chest, battering hard at her ribcage like a ram. At her side, Joy was glaring east with those gleaming silver eyes of hers, a low and dangerous rumble thrumming from her throat, sensing Saska's agitation. The option had been there to leave the starcat in some safe place too, but no, that would not serve.

If I'm to take her north, we must face every peril together, Saska told herself. She had said that to the Wall as well, and with enough conviction that her guardian had merely nodded, and accepted it. "Fine," he'd told her. "The

665

cat first came to you to protect you, that night out on the plains. Let her continue in that role."

My protectors, Saska thought. *Joy, Rolly, Leshie.* Agarosh had not yet returned from his journey to the mountain, and she was not certain of what the Butcher would do. With luck he would join them on their quest, should he live through the night, he and perhaps others as well. *The Baker,* Saska thought. *The Surgeon...* Three bands of Bloody Traders, three captains...

...and three heroes, she had to hope, *should they play their parts well tonight.*

The board was set. Havoc was the goal. The two camps of Krator and Kastor were known to despise one another, and on that simple premise they sought to take advantage. *Throw a blade between two brawling men and there is sure to be blood.* The Baker and the Surgeon were that blade. And their plan was simple: chaos.

"It's happening," Leshie hissed. "They're doing it. It's starting right now!"

Her voice pitched higher in excitement. Saska's eyes narrowed through the gloom, searching down the thoroughfare. Distantly, she could hear the noise of fighting at the gate, though *acting* would be a better word, as men smashed their swords against one another, shouting, screaming out as though in the throes of battle.

From so far away, it was seen only faintly as the bodies and shapes moved about near the gate. The two hundred or so men dressed in the colours and cloaks of Starrider Antapar and Sunrider Konollio roared and yelled, and the gate guards from House Hasham pretended to die. There, around the gate, bodies were quickly hauled out and thrown down, the true bodies of the men of Antapar and Konollio, slain only the day before. Around their dead shoulders were already wrapped the cloaks of House Hasham, white and silver, and many were dressed in the garb of the Aram City Guard as well.

They won't know the difference when they come rushing through, Saska thought, the adrenaline coursing through her veins. *They're going to charge straight past, and straight into the net. It'll happen just as Denlatis said...*

The ruse was taking place atop the walls as well, to either side of the Cherry Gate. The archers there, many dozens of them, turned to face the false attackers as they rushed up the steps, firing at them with blunt-tipped arrows that struck and pinged harmlessly away. Some men fell all the same as the arrows bounced and ricocheted off them, playing their parts, feigning death. Others surged forth and pretended to cut the bowmen down, screaming, shouting, acting out their charade.

Beyond the walls, out there in the darkness, the lurking hordes of Krator and Kastor would never know the difference. Tens of thousands of pairs of eyes would watch and be deceived. Tens of thousands of pairs of ears would listen to the distant din of battle and know their plan was working...that the gate was about to open...that the time was nigh and the call would come to charge, to pour forth and swarm through the city like locusts across a field of wheat.

I wish I could see, Saska thought. *I wish I was an eagle, so I could fly over and*

666

see them now, Krator and Kastor, Elio and Cedrik, with their smug, self-satisfied faces. The fools. The arrogant fools. They do not know what awaits them...

Yet the same awaited others.

Tens of thousands of others.

For a moment Saska thought of the countless scores of good men out there, the proud Tukorans and gods-fearing Aramatians who had been dragged into this foul alliance against their will. Legions would die for the vanity and greed of their masters. Legions of men from the land in which she'd grown up, legions from the land of her birth.

How many of them want this, truly? she wondered. *How many of them want to be here? How many of them were mustered against their will, like Del was, so long ago? How many boys are out there now, shivering and afraid, poorly shod and poorly armoured, poorly trained and unprepared?*

The thoughts ran unbidden, one after another, a cascade of laments and regrets. They sharpened her anger, sharpened her hate. She gripped her dagger tightly between her fingers, and pictured the faces of the two men responsible.

Her hate erupted, her thirst for vengeance grew boundless. *If the fire doesn't kill them,* she thought, *I'll do it myself.*

With that, the gates groaned open.

58

‾‾‾‾‾

Robbert

"Have faith, Del," Robbert said to him, as they waited amidst the sprawling throng. "You may have only been my squire for a single day, but I've a duty to you now, and will do what I can to protect you. There will be times when I'll be right in the thick of the fighting. On no account should you try to join me. Stay with the others. Help one another, and watch one another's backs, just as you did in Kolash. Do that and you'll be fine."

The gangly farmhand with the messy black hair gave a shivery nod, causing his loose-fitting armour to rattle. "I…I'll try to…to kill a man tonight, my lord. My first man. I never did in Kolash, not like some of the others. But tonight, tonight I will…"

"I'd sooner see you live through the night," Robbert told him. If his uncle had his way, this would be their last battle in some time. *Win the city, win the palace, win a long and relaxing rest.* What happened after that was not worth considering right now. "Just keep your wits about you, Del. Be vigilant, and be brave. If everything goes to plan, the city will surrender within hours. *Hours*, Del. You only need to last the next few hours, and you'll see a bright new dawn. I promise."

Thousands teemed around them, as they waited upon the plains. *Thousands of shapes and shadows*, Robbert thought, *faceless men impossible to discern.* Rarely had he ever witnessed such a night as this, black as pitch and impenetrable to the mortal eye. Even with godsteel to grasp his nocturnal vision struggled.

There's going to be a lot of friendly fire tonight, he thought. *We won't know who we're killing.*

Sir Lothar stood beside him, looming tall above the rest. Robbert looked around, fretting on a matter he hadn't yet voiced. They'd been waiting on the plains for some twenty or so minutes now, and for the life of him, he couldn't see the Bloody Traders. Several times he'd moved between the men and boys of Green Company, and the many other companies around them, searching for the Surgeon and his sellswords, but thus far hadn't been able to find them. He put that to Lothar now.

The tall knight shrugged. "Hard to know who's who out here, Robb. They'll be about somewhere. Maybe they got shoved a bit further to the back?"

"But I saw them earlier. At camp. I *ordered* the Surgeon specifically to join us at the front of the lines. I wanted them in the van, for when we charge."

"Maybe he had other ideas," Sir Lothar offered. "I've known a few sellswords in my time. Once they get paid, they can lose all interest in dying. It's best to pay sellswords half before, and half after the battle, I've heard it said."

Your time, Robbert thought. Sir Lothar Tunney was only twenty-four years old, though made it sound like he was an old man sometimes, as long in the tooth as he was everywhere else. "Take a look for me, would you? See if you can spot them."

Lothar the Looming turned a slow, full circle, peering across the hordes spread out upon the plains. Not a single man in the entire army came close to matching his height, though the Tigress was not so far off. *Six feet and five inches,* Robbert thought. Lothar had said she was a half foot shorter than he was, and being six feet eleven, Robbert had quickly done the math. It was a quite astonishing height for a woman. *The Unseen Isles,* he told himself. The people of the Unseen Isles - an isolated and mysterious island group far to the south of the Sunrise Sea - were said to be extremely tall on average. *She probably comes from there.*

Lothar concluded his scan and shook his head. "Not seeing them, Robb," he said. "Could take a walk, but might get lost. Everyone out here looks the same to me, and I wouldn't want to lose you. Not tonight. Hard to even see the house colours in this dark."

Their conversation was taking place beneath the din of the waiting masses, a dense murmuring of coughs, sniffs, mutters and grunts, shifting feet and scraping armour. Some soldiers were mumbling prayers to themselves, beseeching the great god Tukor to look out for them this night. Others prayed to lesser gods, and many would be praying to Vandar too, the God King, the Bladeborn especially.

Robbert made no such prayer of his own. Vandar was with him always. *I wear his body as armour, and bear his body as a blade.* The Bladeborn warrior, one fully garbed in godsteel, was as Vandar's soldier on earth, his chosen and his blessed, sprung from the blood of his favourite son. Robbert might have been born of Tukor, but the Lukars were from Vandar once, the same as every Bladeborn house since the time of Varin, thousands of years ago. *It's him we fight for, most of all. This War Eternal is his to win.*

He turned to his squire, putting this business of the Bloody Traders aside. "Are you religious, Del?"

The farmhand wore armour and mail, the best Robbert could procure for him at short notice; all castle-forged, barely dinted, with a longsword at his hip - castle-forged too, and good strong steel - and a fine yew bow in his

669

grasp. *The perks of that trick he pulled*, Robbert thought, though in truth he'd done what he could to garb the rest of Green Company, and Bernie's charges in particular, in better armour as well.

"Um…a bit," was the lanky boy's answer. "Master Orryn was. He would light a candle by his bed, for Tukor, every night. We heard him often, in the north. Tukor. His dying voice."

Thunder, Robbert thought. The North Tukorans could be a strange and superstitious lot, even to him. To them storms were the echoes of Tukor's dying breath, rain his tears, thunder his voice. "Did you light a candle as well?"

"Sometimes, but only when I heard him."

Only when there were storms, Robbert read into that. "Did he bellow often where you lived? A village in the northwest, was it?"

"Willow's Rise," Del told him. "A small place, my lord. Mostly farms."

Willow's Rise. Robbert had heard that name before, he recalled. *Did he mention it last night, when we talked?* After the council meeting with Denlatis, Robbert had been drawn into battle preparations, and had only managed to speak with Del for a short time. Even then his mind was racing with other, more pressing matters. But that village. That name. It ran a bell. *Some scandal*, he remembered, *not so long ago, involving a murdered lord…*

Del was going on. "There were storms there often, my lord," he said. "But not so much in the village. Mostly in the north, up in the wilds, and over the Hammersongs especially. It was always dark and stormy up there in the mountains. We could see it from the village, in the distance. *The black storm that never ends*, we called it."

Robbert Lukar nodded. It was another of these North Tukoran legends. "I've heard the name. Some say that *the black storm that never ends* is even older than the gods. That it's the manifestation of a dark spirit the gods trapped up in those mountains, always raging to be set free."

"People used to say that in the village," Del agreed.

"Did they say anything else?"

"Some did."

"And what did they say?"

"That it was because of the formation of the mountains there…and the high clouds and winds. That the weather was just natural. Master Orryn used to say that. But maybe….maybe he just said it so as not to scare me, when I was younger."

"He sounds a kind man."

"He is. Or…or was. I don't know what happened to him, after I was taken. Or any of them. I stayed that night with the other recruits, and left in the morning, but…but overnight there was some trouble."

"Trouble?" Robbert asked. His mind switched straight back to this faint memory of a murder. "Was someone killed, Del? I seem to remember that a noble lord was murdered there."

If Del was about to answer that, Robbert Lukar did not hear him. Ahead, through the gloom that souped between the army and the city, a figure was approaching quickly, dashing as only a Bladeborn could.

Robbert saw at once that it was Sir Lionel Vance, one of his uncle's favoured Emerald Guards, who had been given the charge, along with several others, of waiting some way ahead for signs that the fighting had begun. His appearance suggested it had.

"Lothar, with me."

Robbert stepped forward to the very front of the lines. Many of their stoutest warriors had been arrayed here, Bladeborn knights and men-at-arms, brawny seasoned soldiers all eager for blood and battle. To the right, Robbert could see his uncle, utterly pristine in his fabulous armour, flanked by Sir Jesse Vance and Sir Wenfry Gershan and Sir Gavin Trent, his battle commander. Lords Huffort and Gullimer stood beside them in the company of loyal guardsmen of their houses. To little surprise, the feeble form of Lord Simon Swallow was not to be seen. *He is no fighter, that one,* Robbert thought.

Lord Elio Krator was with them, as agreed. He sat atop his regal sunwolf Braccaro with Mar Malaan at his side, riding Taro, the poor beast who had to bear him. Lothar had japed that Taro must be 'the strongest sunwolf in all the south' to carry around such a leviathan, let alone run and fight with him, and he can't have been far wrong. That said, the wolf was no bigger than many others Robb had seen, and Braccaro, certainly, was at least a half foot taller at the shoulder and thicker and more muscular besides.

Others formed up around them: Sunriders on their snarling, snapping, wolves; Starriders, saddled upon their slinky cats; paladin knights, not Lightborn, but often some of the best fighters in all Aramatia with sword, scimitar, and spear, sat proudly atop their enormous camels. There were many wide, straight streets in the great city of Aram, and those huge armoured camels would be used to ride the enemy down, Robbert had heard.

Thousands more were assembled behind, tens of thousand, stretching eastward into the gloom. They sprawled in such numbers that those at the rear were still in camp, lit by the lights that burned at their boundaries. The vast bulk of these were common soldiers, grizzled old men and boys young enough to be their grandsons and everyone else in between. Friends stood together, comrades, relations, even multigenerational families dragged far from home; grandfathers, fathers, brothers, sons, standing with swords to hand, and spears and shields, ready to fight and die as one. Thinking of that made Robbert wish Raynald was here with him, and his father even more. Instead he had Lank and Bernie. *And they're like family to me too...*

He hurried over to where the leaders were assembled, the tip of that great mighty spear. Lothar came with him, as commanded; Bernie stayed back, with the boys. Sir Lionel Vance had reached Lord Cedrik and an update was spilling from his lips. "...it's begun, my lord," he was saying, breathless. "The attack...it's begun."

"Are you certain, Lionel?"

"I am, my lord. We saw...we saw fighting on the walls. And there's a lot of shouting behind the gate, and the ringing of swords." He looked at Elio

Krator, sitting above them atop Braccaro. "Your allies have come through, Sunlord Krator. The gates will be opened any minute."

The sunlord nodded, and said something to Mar Malaan. At once word was passed through the crowds of soldiers to prepare to rush for the gate. They would start with a slow walk, moving closer, creeping forward, it had been agreed, then rush when the gates were opened. The order had last night been disseminated through the men. They knew their roles.

And we know ours, Robbert thought. He shared a decisive look with his uncle. They had spent the day finalising plans, giving orders, assigning targets. A tension thickened in Robbert's throat to think of the butchery to come, a butchery he did not entirely agree with, yet was necessary all the same. His uncle had convinced him that betraying Elio Krator and his men was critical, should they survive. "If we do not make a move, *he* will, Robbert. You know that as well as I do. We have no choice but to eliminate him. The north will be safer for it."

How could Robbert Lukar disagree with that? *A coup within a coup*, he thought. *Oh, what a tangled web of treachery we have weaved. Grandfather would be so proud...*

"Get them moving," Cedrik Kastor snapped. He waved irritably to several of his captains who swept back to relay the command to their troops.

The army shifted, moving forward in their ragged columns.

Robbert fell into step next to Lord Wilson Gullimer. "Are you ready, my lord?"

"Is it too much of a cliche to say I was born ready, young prince?" Gullimer's white teeth shone in the darkness. As ever, with so many armoured Bladeborn in close attendance, a general fog of divine mist filled the air as they went, rising, swirling, eddying in eager patterns at the promise of what was to come.

Vandar walks with us, Robbert thought. *He surrounds us and protects us and guides us.* "I'm excited to see you fight, my lord. I have heard tales of your battle prowess."

"Inflated tales, I'm sure. My men do like to overstate things." Gullimer had a charming modesty that almost felt immodest, at times, Robbert had found. There came a point where a man became so humble that he appeared disingenuous. "The same cannot be said of you, however, Prince Robbert. Your recent triumphs here in Aramatia are beyond doubt. I should be honoured to fight beside you tonight, if the chance arises."

"The honour would be mine, my lord."

Sir Lionel Vance had dashed ahead once more, to rejoin the other scouts. They were not needed. By now Robbert could hear the ringing of steel, the cries of battle away in the distance beyond the gate. Gradually, the walls of Aram took shape from the shroud, a towering facade of stone, fifteen feet thick and many times as tall. There was some movement atop them, the prince saw, shapes shifting in the gloom. That would be the soldiers of Starrider Antapar killing the archers and sentries. It looked as though most of the fighting was done. A man was waving, and another, Robbert realised.

"You see that?" he heard Lord Lewyn Huffort call, in his bellowing voice. "They're waving at us. That means it's over. They've killed all the guards."

It was pointing out the obvious, a particular skill of the Lord of Rockfall. "We know," Cedrik said to him, retaining his earlier irritability. "And keep your voice down, Huffort, or they'll hear you from the palace."

Their slow march continued, another ten seconds, twenty. *Any moment now,* Robbert thought. He could no longer hear any fighting beyond the gate, though a few shouts still sounded, ringing through the night.

"What's the delay?" someone complained.

"Something's wrong. Why aren't the gates opening?" carped another.

"Silence," Elio Krator hissed at them. "Ready on my command. We charge as soon as we see them break."

By *break* Robbert assumed him to mean 'break open in the middle'. The gates were fashioned of two enormous bronze doors, to open outward from the centre, operated by a system of counterweights, chains, pulleys and winches. This was done in the gatehouse. *They must be fighting there still, inside,* the prince thought. *That's why we can't hear them anymore.*

The men were still waving atop the walls, as though urging them to come. "Hold," Elio Krator said. His eyes were fixed at the centre of the gate, waiting for that seam to open. "Hold…"

Robbert looked back. The massive formless shadow of the army was following, breaking up. He thought he sighted the outline of Sir Bernie Westermont there, not far away, but couldn't be sure. Some figures stood out, taller than the rest around them. *Is the Tigress one of them?* Something about the disappearance of the Bloody Traders tickled at his doubt. Something felt wrong.

"They're opening!" he heard a man say.

Robbert spun. A thin break had appeared between the two giant doors.

"We charge!" came a shout. Several others echoed him.

Yet no one moved until Elio Krator gave the command. A moment passed, another, another. The opening between the doors widened, inch by inch. Robbert's heart hammered as he spied the long boulevard beyond, stretching away, straight as an arrow, through the heart of Aram. There were shapes on the ground, men, some lying prostrate, others supine, many more collapsed in bundled heaps, limbs twisted this way and that. *Dead,* Robbert knew at once. Others were on their feet, waving them forward. Some Starriders and Sunriders prowled among them.

"Antapar and Konollio," a voice called out. "It is they! They have come through for us!"

The tide could no longer be held back. Men began shifting forward, even before Elio Krator's order. Sunriders, Starriders, paladin knights started moving. Robbert's uncle was not interested in waiting for Krator's word either. He drew his godsteel blade, thrust it aloft, and roared, "On me, men! Aram is ours! *Ours!* For Tukor!"

The banks broke with those words. A thunder of mounts and men charged. Robbert joined it, glancing only to make certain that Elio Krator was among them. He was, though a little further back, Mar Malaan wobbling at his side. The Bladeborn kept pace with the beasts, cracking at the hard dry earth with their heavy godsteel plate. Noise filled the air, shouting, roaring, the sound of blades being torn from sheathes, battlecries from north and south. "For Tukor!" a hundred men bellowed. "For the North," bellowed a hundred more. Calls rang out for the king, even now, and their lord, Cedrik Kastor, and for Prince Robbert Lukar as well. In their foreign tongue, Robbert did not know exactly what the Aramatians were saying. But he heard 'Aramatia' and 'Krator' and 'Calacan' too, the giant eagle god they so revered.

And then they were at the gates, closing tighter as they funnelled in. The walls were so thick it felt like passing through a tunnel. Murder holes peered down from overhead, and for a split second Robbert thought he saw eyes glaring through them, but then they were through, spreading out into the open square that lay beyond, branching left and right into streets, lanes, alleys. Blackness ruled, a heavy suffocating darkness. There was no light, no light at all. Ahead, the wide thoroughfare bled into shadow, over a mile in length, entirely empty that Robbert could see.

Something's wrong, was his first thought. It was too quiet. Too empty. Too dark. *Something's not right.*

Krator's allies were waiting ahead, waving them forward, but for some reason they had retreated further down the street. Robbert heard them shouting in Aramatian, beckoning them to follow. Bodies lay to left and right of the gate. Some wore shirts of copper scalemail, with feathered cloaks and eagle halfhelms, others raiment in silver and white. City Guards. Hasham colours. Some of Antapar and Konollio's men had died as well during the fighting.

"On me! On me!" Cedrik Kastor was howling. "Krator! Lord Krator! With me! You'll fight with me!"

Elio Krator had just arrived. He passed by Robbert, the giant wolf Braccaro all but knocking him aside. The prince caught a glimpse of the look on Krator's face. The confusion. The caution. He shouted out something in Aramatian, to the men ahead. Robbert recognised 'Antapar' and 'Konollio' but understood nothing else of what he said. Calls came back from them. The men were at least forty or fifty metres away, and looked ready to run. Some were waving still, urging them forward. Robbert's nostrils opened and closed. There was something in the air. A low scent, undetectable to a normal man, hidden beneath a hundred other smells. From the skies above, the softest glow of moonlight broke through the clouds for just a moment, and in that moment Robbert saw something glistening across the pavestones, something wet. Had it been raining? He had spent much of the day in his uncle's pavilion, in preparation. *Maybe it rained while I was inside?*

More men were pouring in through the gates, pushing from behind, wondering why they had stopped. The square was filling, filling with thousands. Some had begun to surge up the road to make room. Others were already spreading off down the alleys, lanes, side streets. A chaos of confusion had engulfed them. Lord Cedrik was still calling for Krator to join him. Krator was still calling forward, to Antapar and Konollio, and their men, who stood their ground, some distance away, shrouded in shadow. And even some...some were beginning to retreat, creeping back, further back and away from them.

Robbert's heart was pounding. *A trap*, he thought suddenly. *It's a trap...a trap!*

He was about to bellow those words when, in a sudden burst of movement, the men ahead rushed off, fleeing left and right down side lanes, vanishing. Krator was shouting something in Aramatian, panicked. Mar Malaan was screaming too, translating for the sake of their northern allies. "Imposters!" he screamed. "Imposters! They're imposters! Turn back! Turn back!"

But they couldn't. Hundreds more were still driving forward, thousands, blocking the way, clotting the route. Half of the men at the front had not heard, and were spreading forward, down the boulevard. Robbert saw his uncle there, some way ahead. He'd stopped, turned, confused by all the commotion. His eyes were on the gate, staring out beyond it. Under all the shouting, the shoving, the din of disorder and indecision, Robbert could hear it. *Fighting.* Way back outside the gate, where the bulk of the army was still rushing. High-pitched wails reached through the shroud of noise to his ears. Screams of panic. Screams of battle. The song of the dead and the dying...

"Robb! Robb! ROBB!"

Robbert turned. Through all that he'd lost Sir Lothar momentarily, but his towering protector was back. "Lothar! There's fighting...fighting back there!"

"I know. Someone must have started early."

"They wouldn't! Why would they?" And then it came to him. "*Them.* The sellswords. The Surgeon. It was *them!*"

Lothar took him by the arm with long grasping fingers. "Robb, we need to get out of here. We're fish in a bloody barrel, Robb! This whole place is gonna blow."

Robbert wasn't understanding. "Blow...?"

"Can't you see it, Robb? *Smell* it? That's oil. Unscented, but not to *us*. We have to go! We have to go right now!"

Sir Lothar Tunney's mind was turned to a single duty and he cared not who got in the way. With a sudden and explosive burst of power he closed his fingers around Robbert Lukar's forearm like a vise and surged through the men around them, battering them aside as he ran. Robbert tried to keep pace, stumbling, charging for the nearest alley, but they had no time to make it...no time at all...

A light glowed suddenly in the skies. The first light, and only light, a glowing orb of softened gold moving swiftly up through the shroud. "Fire!" someone shouted. "Fire arrow! Fire!"

The arrow seemed to hover, for just a minute, before diving as it reached its apex. In a fierce and precipitous plunge, it descended to the cobbles, glimmering under the light of the flame, covered in a sheen of oil, everywhere, it was *everywhere*...

For a moment, as it landed, it seemed like nothing was going to happen. But only a moment. Then the oil caught light, bright and brilliant.

Then the inferno spread.

59

Cecilia

A hand shook her awake, dragging her from the darkness of her dreams. She sat up with a gasp, her heart thrashing inside her chest. A fat tallow candle burned low on the table, what light it gave illuminating the grave face of Sir Gerrin, worry-worn and haggard. His black woollen breeches were armoured in snow from the thighs down and he'd left a trail of it from the door, already melting.

"My lady, you were having a bad dream."

She swallowed, drawing a breath, wiping her eyes. She'd been crying. "My dreams are never sweet, Sir Gerrin. Not here."

"What torments you, my lady?"

Falling, she thought. *Darkness. Screaming. A place reserved for people like me.* Hog had told her that, the day she killed him. She didn't give answer, but glanced to the window. "It's still dark," she saw. "What time is it?"

"Not yet dawn, my lady. I noticed the light burning though the window. You've been here all night?"

She nodded, stretching a crick in her neck. Her arms ached awfully from where she'd been lying on them, and her left shoulder had gone hard as stone. *I grow old here*, she thought. *Old and dowdy.* "I didn't feel like battling back to the refuge through the blizzard," she said, glancing to the window. The world outside was white on black, the air thick with falling snow. "The storm hasn't yet passed."

"It's easing," Gerrin told her. "The winds have calmed a little, at least."

"Are they common this time of year? These snowstorms?"

"Not especially during spring, no. Though the seasons have already been strange here." He had a look in his eye. "My lady, there is something you should see."

The tone of his voice sharpened her senses up at once. "What? Is something wrong? Something with Jonik?" Her thoughts always went to her son. He had grown less burdened and embattled since he'd set down the Nightblade, though ever the shadow lingered over him.

But the man shook his head. "This isn't about him. He is sleeping, so far as I know." He walked to the wall and took her heavy fur cloak off a hook. "Wrap up warm, my lady. It's particularly cold this morning."

The sting of the frozen air assaulted her as soon as she left the sanctuary of the library, reddening her cheeks as she pulled her cloak in tight. The snows had deepened considerably in the yard, filling in the lanes they had shovelled between the Night Tower, kitchens, storerooms, roundtower library, and the wall walk so the men could take their turns on watch. Behind, the rest of the fort sat abandoned, hidden in the snows. Cecilia was the only one to go between the fortress and the refuge, and for that she followed a single path through the twisting alleys and courtyards that took her to the high steps that led into the mountain. *I'll have to shovel a new path after this*, she thought. It had snowed often and sometimes heavily of late, though never so badly as this.

The snow was still coming down, fat white flakes drifting incessantly from the hard black skies, stirred by the occasional gust of wind that came howling like a wolf through the ward. Sir Gerrin took her along the path they'd cleared toward the wall, feet crunching on new-fallen snow. Before long they were in a white wilderness, no building visible to either side, but a moment later the gate and curtain wall rose up before them. "Watch your footing on the steps, my lady. They're icy beneath the snow."

Gerrin offered a hand to steady her, but she refused, following in his tread as he led her up the battlements. The snow was just as thick up here, the parapet heaped and covered with a dense white blanket, filling in the gaps between the crenels. Beyond the gate lay the narrow bridge that spanned the abyss, plunging on either side into nothingness. Cecilia shuddered. Falling was her nightmare, her one true crippling fear. *Falling forever*, she thought. *Tumbling through darkness, starving and screaming, with all the other evil souls.*

Gerrin was at her side. "Do you see anything, my lady?"

White. A world of white and black. There wasn't much else to see in truth. The plateau to which the bridge led was only faintly glimpsed, and the mountains and peaks that rose up further off were entirely enshrouded by the storm. Even the bridge was barely visible, appearing and disappearing behind the squalls as the snows thickened and waned and thickened again. "Am I supposed to, Sir Gerrin?"

He gestured with a gloved hand, pointing right down to where the bridge ended, leading toward the gate. "There. At the centre."

She squinted through the snow and then saw them. "Footprints," she said, on a breath. They were faint, almost entirely filled in already, though it seemed to her that a trail had been made across the bridge and away to the left of the gate. She pushed a heap of snow from the top of the parapet and leaned over to get a better look down. "They go right to the postern door…"

Sir Gerrin nodded beneath his heavy black hood. A thin layer of snow had already begun to accumulate atop it. "And pass through," he said, leading her closer to get a better look. "The tracks are hard to see, but they're there. They seem to go up toward the refuge, as far as I can tell."

Cecilia was not liking this. "You told me the postern door was sealed. Locked by a magical protection."

"It was. Someone must have opened it."

"Who? Only a mage could do that. The prints. Are they coming or going?"

"Hard to say for certain. But coming, I think. There are two mages unaccounted for out there, my lady. I have spoken of them to you before. Meknyr and Vaynor. It is possible one of them has returned. Or both, even."

She shivered in her furs, and not from the cold. "Who was on watch?"

"Harden. At least, he was *meant* to be." Ice flakes were beginning to cling to the stiff bristles of his hoary beard. "I was supposed to relieve him at dawn, but when I came out there was no sign. It's possible he abandoned his post, given the conditions. Wouldn't blame him. He doesn't want to be here anymore, we all know that."

None of us want to be here, she thought. "Have you checked his room?"

"Not yet. I came to you first."

"Go," she said. "Something might have happened to him. If he's there, bring him here. And be quiet about it. It would be better not to wake my son."

"I understand," Sir Gerrin said. He turned and left her, fading into the falling snow.

Cecilia remained atop the wall, studying the path taken through the postern door. It led rearward through the fort, so far as she could tell, and appeared to have been made by more than one person. How many, she couldn't say. Two? Ten? Twenty? Numbers were impossible to count when men moved in single file, and by now the trail had all but vanished.

Whoever it was must have passed this way a couple of hours ago, she thought. It would take that long for the deeper prints to be filled in, and it was possible they were trying to cover their tracks as well, shifting snow as they went to hide their movements. *But why? And who?* Cecilia Blakewood had no answers on that account, though a few possibilities sprung to mind, and none of them were good. She continued to muse as she waited, anxious, pacing to stay warm, until she heard a low muttering in the air, and turned to find two shapes trudging down the icy trench through the yard, arguing at one another in hushed voices. A moment later they climbed the steps to join her.

"My lady." Harden's voice was hoarse, the skin beneath his eyes dark and distended. He looked exhausted, older and more miserable than ever, gaunt-cheeked and grim and about as cold as a man could be. *Like someone who's been standing sentry all night,* Cecilia thought. "What's all this trouble then?"

"Gerrin says you were on watch last night. Is that right?"

"Aye, I was up here. Until he relieved me." He nodded at the other man.

"You relieved him?" Cecilia looked at Sir Gerrin in surprise. "You never said…"

"I never said because it never happened. I didn't relieve him, my lady."

"You *did*," Harden insisted. "Couple of hours ago. Said you couldn't sleep and I was to get some rest. Thought it was mighty kind of you to take over early. And now this. Accusing me of some such. Just what is your bloody game, Gerrin?"

"No game. Just the truth. I woke up only fifteen minutes ago, to take over the watch at dawn as agreed. But when I came out here you were nowhere to be seen."

The Ironmoorer gave him a bitter look. "You're saying I imagined it all, then? Or lying? Is that it? You think I'm lying to you, Gerrin?"

"Someone is."

"Aye, someone. *You*. You've got form in that regard, let's not forget. You played that old man Benjy once, remember. You and those other two, hiding behind some foul trickery, sneaking into Jonik's service. If there's a liar here it's *you*, Gerrin. So I ask again, what's your game?"

"I don't play games, Harden. And I've got no cause to lie."

"What…and I do?"

"No." Cecilia stepped in to placate the man. "No, Harden, we don't think you've got cause to lie, and we don't think you imagined it either. This is something else."

His eyes swung over to her. "Go on then, Cecilia. Enlighten me. My head's about as foggy as this weather, so spell it out nice and clear. What have I missed?"

Much and more, she thought, sharing a look with the old Emerald Guard. It appeared to her that Gerrin had suddenly come to the same realisation, to judge by the look in his eyes. Whether this mention of Benjy had done it, or he'd realised it already she couldn't say. But that didn't matter. "*Shadow-cloak*," she merely said, in a slightly choked voice. "This…this was mage work."

Harden's face hardened, nostrils flaring and puffing steam. "Shapeshifter? One of these rotten old mages *mimicked* Gerrin, is that what you're saying?"

"Yes, that's what I'm saying," she confirmed.

"Same as in Sutrek," Gerrin put in, darkly. "Parsivor cloaked me as Benjy, as he cloaked himself as Trigger and Valtho as Mugs. Cecilia's right. One of the mages here has imitated me."

The implications of that were more unnerving than she could say. Cecilia found herself looking at the two men with a sudden suspicion, wondering if one of them was a mage even now. *No*, she thought. *No, it's them*. Tyrith had explained to her that it was easy to mimic someone you didn't know, but the deception was much harder when you were well acquainted with that person. Only very gifted Shadowcloaks could do that, and even then, there were likely to be subtle abnormalities in their facial features or the clothes they wore.

But clearly Harden had been deceived. She looked at him and asked, "Did you notice anything unusual about Gerrin when he came to you?"

The sellsword shrugged. "Only that he came earlier than expected. Didn't expect *that*, but otherwise, no. It was dark, snowing hard, windy. But Gerrin, so far as I could tell."

"Easy to deceive in those conditions," Gerrin said.

Cecilia nodded.

"Aye. But why?" Harden asked them." What scheme are these monsters cooking up now?"

Evidently, Gerrin hadn't told him about the tracks yet. He did that now, leading him over to the parapet wall and showing him the faded prints leading across the bridge and through the postern door. Harden gave a snarl and reached to the hilt of his godsteel sword, the leather of his glove straining as he squeezed. "Bastards," he growled. "They're up to something, I've always said it. Told Jonik a dozen times that we need to go back there and kill the lot of them." He spat to the side, the warm spittle cutting into a heap of snow. "Those monsters need to die for everything they've done."

It wasn't a debate that needed returning to. Harden had made it clear to anyone who might listen what he thought of these mages and their sacred, abhorrent duty, bemoaning it with particular vitriol whenever he got into the whiskey. *He is a simple man*, Cecilia had long since decided. *A good man, but a simple one, who fails to see the bigger picture.* The rest of them did, thankfully. If they'd had it Harden's way, and marched in force to the refuge to 'kill them all' as the Ironmoorer urged, it would not go well for them, Cecilia suspected.

"We've been through this," she said. "These mages have an important function to serve, however much we dislike it."

"So we just bend over and let them have their way with us, is that it?" Harden grumbled. "I'd sooner die with steel to hand than wait for some creep wearing Gerrin's face to come cut my throat in the night."

"That won't happen," the Emerald Guard told him. "If they wanted us dead, they'd have killed us already."

Harden gave a snort in response. "You're too trusting, Gerrin, that's your problem. Why all this cloak and dagger if they're not up to something sinister? Whoever came here last night didn't want to be seen. Hardly gives you a warm feeling inside, does it?" He looked over the passes. "We should go, all of us, right now. Wake the lad up and go. There's nothing keeping us here anymore, not since the boys left."

"The snows are too thick. The passes will be closed."

"We have godsteel. It's good enough to cut through metal and rock, Gerrin. Bit of snow shouldn't trouble us."

"You don't know these mountains, Harden. A heavy icefall could sweep us all to our deaths."

"In godsteel armour? It's too heavy. It'd anchor us to the ground."

There was some truth in that, Cecilia knew, but she was loathe to speak against Gerrin in this matter. *He lived here for almost twenty years. If anyone knows the perils of these mountains, it's him.*

Harden didn't seem to care, though. "We should *go*," he repeated. "We wrap up warm, armour up and go. The snows won't be so bad further down the mountains. A day or two and we'll be free of it."

Gerrin gave a sigh, breath misting in the frigid air. "Cabel isn't strong enough yet…"

"Strong enough? He's never going to be strong enough. The lad's a vegetable, sad as it is to say. There's no life ahead of him now, just dreams and darkness. It'd be better if he just let go and died. But until he does, I guess we take him with us. Load him onto a garron with the rest of our provisions and see if he's still breathing by the time we reach the foothills."

"And if he is? What would you propose we do with him?"

"We cross that bridge when we come to it. Most likely he'll die on the way."

"And you think Jonik will agree to this? As soon as he learns that men have entered the fortress…"

Cecilia cut him right off. "He can't. We can't tell him."

Breath puffed from Harden's mouth, though she didn't let him speak.

"We *can't*," she repeated, more firmly. "If he thinks something dark is going on, he'll only take the Nightblade back up. It'll consume him, and everything he's fought against will be for nought…" She shook her head. Her son had slept better of late, *been* better. The mood swings were becoming less intense and he wasn't muttering to himself anymore. Sometimes she saw him staring across the yard or out from a window at where the Nightblade was buried, but mostly he ignored it now. Yet for all that, she feared for him. She feared he only wanted a reason to take it back up, to feel its embrace and give in to the whimpering whispers. *We can't give him one*, she told herself. *I won't risk it.* She steeled her eyes and said to the men, "We keep this from him," in a voice that brooked no argument. "For the time being, anyway. Let me go back into the refuge, find out what's happening. If I sense anything untoward going on…"

"They might kill you," Harden said, his gaunt face twisted in bitterness. "Those monsters…if they find you prying again…"

"Perhaps I should come with you?" Gerrin offered. "I can protect you, my lady, if…"

She put a hand on his arm. "It would be better if I go on my own."

"My lady, I'm really not sure…"

"I come and go from the mountain all the time. If nothing else, I will simply visit with Tyrith and see what he knows. The Hammer speaks to him. Perhaps he has sensed something."

"Malice," muttered Harden. "There's something evil going on in there. I can taste it."

Cecilia thought of the snippets she'd seen of the last contract, the mystery of those words. *Blood. Royal. Divine.* Was it all related? Was whoever had come last night involved? *All of this has been foreseen*, she thought. *All of it. I have to go. I have to know…*

Something was compelling her, despite her fears, to act.

She looked at the two older men once more. "Both of you, stay here, act normal. Say nothing of this to Jonik. I'll come back soon."

She left them, passing down the steps to the yard, marching between the icy lanes piled high with snow to either side. The Night Tower loomed opposite the gate, wearing a hood of snow, icicles as long as dirks and daggers hanging down from its windowsills. Cecilia could see a light burning behind one of the windows, though knew that to be Cabel's room. The young sellsword had fallen back into a coma again, and it seemed inevitable now that he would die. *And he must,* she thought. *For his own sake, and my son's as well. It would be best for him to just let go.* Harden had not been wrong about that.

She hastened on, reaching into her cloak to touch her godsteel dagger. The effect was bracing, driving some of the chill from her bones, dispersing the worst of her fears, strengthening her legs as she ploughed on through the snow. The effort was taxing, the drifts coming up almost as high as her waist in places. When she reached one of the inner courtyards, she saw faint signs of prints once more, moving up a set of steps to a higher part of the fortress. *They came this way.*

She followed, putting her shoulder to the wind, lowering her hood against the sting of swirling flakes. Eventually she reached the stair that rose up to the refuge, and the white veil drew back to show the way into the mountain.

The great black doors lay open, snow pushed to either side. A thin film had gathered within the stone atrium beyond, drawn in on the wind. The prints were clearer here. She saw several sets as they fanned out. Most were broad and large, but one…one set of tracks looked much smaller. *A woman,* Cecilia's instinct told her. *Or even a child…*

The light of dawn was spreading now in the east, the snow easing, the storm passing. *It'll be a bright day,* she thought. *A beautiful day.* She steeled herself and stepped inside, never once breaking her stride.

One is always on guard, she knew, as she passed through the great empty entrance hall. *A silent sentry, cloaked in shadow.* Tyrith had told her that, and taught her what to look out for too. Sometimes she saw the watcher - a stir of shadowy movement, a fog of breath, the sound of a man shifting his stance - but today was not one of those days. *Odd,* she thought. In this freezing cold, the sentry's breath should be visible, but there was nothing to be seen. Just stillness and silence. *Perhaps there is no one here?*

She wondered why that might be. Wondered why others had come. It did not take long for her to divine some reason. *They're gathering for a purpose,* she thought. *All are drawn to it, as I am being. A fly in a spider's web, and the eyes are staring, creeping, nearing…*

The sound of the wind was replaced by the soft patter of her footsteps, echoing in the darkness. A gentle glow of predawn light filtered down through the high mountain shafts, flakes of snow glittering as they drifted quiet as death, melting and fading, never settling on the floor. There was something eerie about it, and something beautiful as well. *The same as every-*

thing here. The carved ceilings and statues and great arched doorways. *A beautiful mausoleum, grand and cold and inert.*

I was the spider once, Cecilia Blakewood thought, as her legs took her on, on and on, inexorably on. Light flickered occasionally from a flaming torch on the wall, casting shadows on the stone, dancing and twisting, set along a specific path as though guiding her to a specific place. *The spider in Ilithor, weaving her web, catching flies and other insects for fun.* Here she was not the spider, though, but the fly. *And the eyes are always watching.*

The words of Hog rang through her head as she went, the last words the sellsword had uttered before she'd put a blade in his back. "You remember what it felt like, that portal?" he'd sneered at her, lying bound in rope on his bed. "The emptiness, the darkness, the *eternity* of it. That'll be your fate forever, bitch. *The Long Abyss.* It's reserved for people like *you.*"

She had not forgotten those words. Nay, she'd spent long nights dwelling on them, on her crimes, on her past. *Have I won some absolution?* she wondered. *Have I done enough to avoid that fate?* She wasn't even sure if the Long Abyss was real, but her days here, with these mages and mysteries, had made her realise there was much more to this world than she knew. The idea of falling forever, starving and screaming…if there was even a chance it was true, she owed it to herself to be better.

And I have been, she told herself again, marching hard now for Tyrith's forge. *I've done everything I was asked to do. With Tyrith. With Jonik. With the boys. Is that not enough to make up for what I've done? Do I not deserve deliverance for that?*

Her thoughts whirled as she went. Before she knew it she was nearing the forge, rounding a corner, hearing voices. She turned onto the passage, saw the air steaming out from within, warm and red from the furnaces. She steadied herself, took two long deep breaths to purge her lungs, and walked inside.

Tyrith stood at his workbench, in conversation with Hamlyn the Humble, the Steward of these halls. There was a glitter in the eyes of the blacksmith. *Excitement,* she thought. *And nerves.* He blinked and turned to look at her as she arrived, lips moving into a brisk smile. "My lady, you've come. I was terrified I would have missed you."

"I got marooned down in the fortress last night, Tyrith. There's a terrible blizzard out there, you may not know."

"Oh, truly? No, I was not aware. But you're here now, and just in time." A nervy smile simmered on his lips. "It's…it's happening, my lady. Today. Right now. It's happening right now."

The transference, she thought. *They came for the transference.* It was just as she'd suspected. Her eyes went to Hamlyn, who stood opposite the blacksmith in his simple brown robes, hands entwined before him in a posture of piety. The decrepit creature he'd been not long ago had been restored to a man of youthful vigour by the blood of the three Bladeborn boys, plain and yet pleasant of face, the visage of one no older than forty. "Is this true?" she asked him. "The day has finally arrived?"

He gave her a slow bow of the head. "Yes, child. Final preparations are being made as we speak." He studied her eyes in that searching way of his. "You have come at the right time."

Something about that unnerved her. "There are footprints…outside," she said. "Leading through the fort. I wondered…well, I wondered…"

"Yes," he said. "They have come for the ritual."

She kept her external facade perfectly even. Inside, her heart was speeding like a galloping horse. "Does that mean…" She glanced at Tyrith. "Once it's done, Lord Hamlyn. Are we permitted to leave, as you have promised? My son. I would like to take my son away from here. He has given up the Nightblade now, as you know. But…"

"He remains vulnerable to its lure," the mage said. "I know. He will leave shortly, child. Your son may yet have a role to play in events to come, as I have told you. But that is not for me to know. My duty will soon be done. And my life of service with it."

A terrible life, Cecilia thought. *A terrible burden.* "I would hope to go with him, when he leaves. Perhaps even today, if the weather allows."

The mage looked at her through a pair of burnished brown eyes, deep and cold as a winter lake, their surface as though frozen, hiding an immeasurable body of knowledge and experience beneath. "That is a possible path. Depending on the choice you make."

She frowned. "Choice? What choice are you referring to?"

"You will find out shortly." He turned and began walking from the room. "Tyrith, come along. Cecilia, you as well."

She held her ground a moment. "I'm to…to be there, during…"

He stopped, turned to her. "Are you not *curious*, child? Do you not want to fit the last piece of the puzzle into place, see the picture it makes?"

She neither shook her head nor nodded. A part of her did, of course. Yet another…

"A choice lies before you, child," Hamlyn said." A choice foreseen, though an outcome unknown. I have no capacity to deny this to you. Now come. And prepare yourself. I take no pleasure in this."

Nervously, she followed, wondering what he meant. A part of her wanted to whirl and run, to bolt for the exit, flee into the frozen dawn, but she couldn't. *A choice foreseen, an outcome unknown. There is no swimming against this tide,* she knew.

"I'm glad you're here, my lady," Tyrith whispered to her, as their feet rustled softly against the stone. "I shall still be me, in part, when this is over. Me, but *more.* I shall never forget what you have done for me."

"I have been honoured to serve you, Tyrith."

"Serve? No, you haven't served. You have been as a companion to me, my lady. A…a mother, even. Is that OK to say? That you've been the closest thing to a mother that I have ever known."

I never was much of a mother, she thought. *Perhaps, in another life…* "An even greater honour then," was all she said.

The blacksmith smiled. "But you have a real son now, of course. A son of your own flesh and blood. I should like to meet him, before you leave. I consider him a brother, of sorts. Do you think he might come to my forge?"

"I will ask him, Tyrith. I'm sure he'd like to meet you as well."

"I hope so. There's a set of armour, my lady, I've been working on. Black armour, very slim and sleek. I got his exact dimensions from Fhanrir, so it would fit him perfectly. I thought…well, I thought he might like that."

"He will, Tyrith. Very much."

He beamed at that. "It's the finest suit I've ever made, I think. Well, perhaps along with your father's, though that I only reinforced and altered, rather than forging from scratch, so to speak." She said nothing for a moment, and he bumbled right on. "I…I hope you're not angry, my lady. That I would forge him a suit, ahead of you. I just thought…well, I thought with him being a warrior and you being a lady, that…"

But she wasn't listening anymore, her mind preoccupied by a growing fear. *Choice*, she thought. *Fate. Destiny. My being here was foreseen.*

They came to a passage that ended in an arched doorway, its lintel carved with a pair of men, standing back to back, each raising a single arm above them, merging to hold the Hammer of Tukor. Beyond Cecilia saw light filtering down from above, that same ethereal glow that seemed to hang in certain other chambers here.

The creature Fhanrir blocked the door, that long warty nose of his poking out from his hood, its tip no more than a dangle of loose, leathery skin. He craned his wattled neck to look up at her. The face behind the hood was more grotesque than ever, though Cecilia was used to it by now. A new hole seemed to have appeared in the hollow of his cheek, the flesh so badly decayed that she could see into the brown bone of his jaw. From his gums poked up three lonely teeth, no more than cracked brown stumps, and the skin beneath his eyes sagged right down to his purple, blistered lips. "She's got godsteel on her," the creature sneered. "What if she tries to use it?"

"She won't," Hamlyn said.

Fhanrir glared at her with those beady black eyes of his. "This is it, woman, the day it's all been leading to. Thousands of years in the making. You understand? If you dare try to interfere…"

"She isn't here to interfere, Fhanrir. She is here to make a choice."

Fhanrir made an ugly snorting sound, his breathing ragged and rusty, little more than a wheeze. *He will die soon*, she thought. The last blood ritual he'd performed to restore Hamlyn to health had clearly taken its toll. *Dark magic scars the soul, rots the man from the inside out.* A necessary evil, she knew, but an evil all the same.

And I've sullied my soul as well, she thought. The boys. Hog. The workers in the cavern. Sir Gerlon Rottlor, who she'd had executed for the riots at Galin's Post, when in truth they were of her own making. Hundreds had died that day, hundreds of men and women and children, children as young as two or three, toddlers in their mother's arms crushed in the rush to flee or butchered by the blade. *My father's blade*, she thought. *He killed them, not me…it was him…him…it was him, not me…*

But that was a lie. A lie she tried to tell herself time and time again. *I arranged those riots. I lit the chaos. I am to blame.* She'd wanted her father to die,

686

wanted rid of him before he might kill her himself, but not once had she considered the collateral damage. *Their blood is on my hands, every one of them. Every man and woman and child. I killed them, not him. As I killed Rylian, my very own brother….that…that was my doing too…*

"My lady, why are you crying?"

She drew from her mournful reverie. Tyrith was there before her, his eyes soft with compassion. She sniffed, wiping the tears from her eyes. "I…I just…"

She could not find the words. The mages were staring at her, Fhanrir glaring up, Hamlyn down, neither with any warmth in their eyes. *They know what I've done,* she thought. *They know what I am.* These mages had slain a thousand boys as part of their duty, but that's all it ever was, a duty, never a choice, a dark and dreaded duty that none of them had ever asked for. *But I've made choices. I've ruined lives. I killed more people than these mages ever have. I'm the real monster here.*

Tears ran from her eyes, a sudden and heavy flow. "My lady, please…it will be all right. I'll be OK, I know I will. This is all meant to be. All of it. It's only fate. You needn't be upset."

"Those tears aren't for you, boy," Fhanrir said, looking at her with immeasurable hatred. *Just as Sir Gerlon did when I hanged him on the gibbet. And Hog, when I betrayed him.* "No. This woman doesn't have the capacity to shed tears for anyone but herself."

"Fhanrir," Hamlyn said, gently. "There is no need for that. Everyone deserves a chance at redemption."

The smaller creature grunted. "So you say, Hamlyn. Just don't expect me to give her any pity. The way she's looked at me these past months…as if *I'm* some soulless monster. If only she knew the torments we've faced. None of us…none of us ever wanted *this*…"

"I…I do know that," she found herself croaking. "I always knew that…"

"Save it. You come here and agonise over choosing a boy or two. Imagine being the ones to blood them, watch them die, curse yourself over and over and over again. All the others…all the other originals are dead, but the two of us. And you haven't had to do what I have, Hamlyn. No… not even you can understand. I've been doing this for thousands of years. And look at me. You look at what it's done." He drew back his hood and unveiled the true horror of what he was.

Cecilia flinched away; Tyrith drew back, gasping. The skull was visible through a yellow, peeling scalp, both ears were missing, as though chewed off by a dog, leaving unsightly humps of mangled flesh to either side of his head. The meat of his neck opened on one side in a foul, reeking abscess, crusted with blood and pus, strands of red sinew glistening beyond.

"No, you look!" the creature growled. "You look at me, woman! Look!"

"*Enough,*" Hamlyn said. "This is not the time, Fhanrir. Draw your hood."

The mage snorted but did as bidden, pulling the hood back over his head. Cecilia could not meet his seething black eyes. She lowered her chin,

687

looking through the doorway. In the chamber beyond, shadowed figures circled a trio of stone beds, much like the one she'd first seen Ilith lying on. But this was a different part of the fortress, a deeper part. *Prepared for this special purpose*, she knew.

Ilith was there now, she saw, lying in stasis on one of the slabs, the left one, illuminated by a shaft of light, dust motes dancing in the glow, as though celebrating his imminent rise. The bed on the right was glowing as well, and empty, to be occupied by Tyrith she presumed. In the middle was another, shrouded in darkness, hard to discern at a glance. She peered at it. There was a figure lying atop it, she realised. And a man standing beside it, a small stoop-backed old man in a hooded cloak holding a crooked walking stick in his grasp.

"Who...who is that?" she asked, her voice shivering. "That girl...on the bed?" She could tell it was a girl by the tumble of hair splayed out behind her. *And the frame. The slim dainty frame.* Her eyes adjusted to the darkness. It was hard to be sure from here, but there was something about the girl she recognised. "Who is it?" she asked again.

Fhanrir's hateful stare was unrelenting. "Like you care, woman. Like you care about anything but yourself."

She didn't understand. "Who is it?" she asked again, looking at Hamlyn and Hamlyn alone.

He didn't answer her. "Take Tyrith inside," he said to Fhanrir. "Prepare him."

The blacksmith hesitated. "I...can I not have a...a moment longer. With Cecilia. I feel like I need..."

"It's time, Tyrith. Take him, Fhanrir."

The little mage grunted and reached up with a hand of fleshless, bony fingers and took Tyrith by the wrist, drawing him into the chamber. "Come on, boy, no more questions. We've only been waiting three thousand years."

Tyrith resisted. "But...I'm not sure...I don't know if..."

"It's *time*, Tyrith," Hamlyn repeated, with greater authority. His voice reached out to echo through the hall. "All will be well, I promise."

It was enough, just enough, for the young man to relent. "I'll...I'll see you after, my lady. I'll have some of Ilith's memories, Hamlyn says. A lot of them, maybe...maybe all of them, who knows? I'll be *him*, and *me*, and... well...I'll have such stories to tell. Such stories to share with you, my lady."

Fhanrir gave a low snort again, as though the boy was spouting nonsense, then dragged him away. At once several other cloaked men descended, flocking upon Tyrith like crows on a kill and settling him down onto the empty stone slab. Cecilia's heart was thrashing inside her. It looked like Tyrith was already unconscious, put under by some smell. *Goodbye, sweet boy*, she thought. Then she turned to Hamlyn again, who stood with her still. "The girl..."

"Is fated to be here. Her coming was foreseen by Queen Thala."

"But you said...you said there were no more contracts. You said that to me, Hamlyn."

"I said it to a woman who was prying, against orders. I said it to try to stop that curiosity of yours from leading you astray. But in the end, Cecilia, you were *meant* to be there. You were *meant* to translate those words. As you are *meant* to be here now. It is all fated, child, all of it. So go, because you must. Go...and look upon her."

Her legs were weak as reeds, threatening to fold beneath her weight as she walked. She crossed the threshold and into the chamber, moving between the beds of Ilith and the heir to the one in darkness, the one in the middle. The old man with the walking stick observed her interestedly as she came.

"Lady Cecilia Blakewood," he said, smiling crookedly. "Name's Meknyr, though I go by a few others as well. Talbert, most recently. Been spending some quality time with your lovely young niece here."

My niece? she thought. And then she saw her.

Amilia Lukar lay face up, pretty and pale, dressed in a simple white shift that seemed to billow gently at the edges. Cecilia rushed forward, reaching to touch her, wake her. "Amilia," she whispered, then louder, "Amilia!" She shook at her shoulder, but the girl didn't stir. She shook again, harder, and harder. And nothing.

"Won't make a difference," the mage Meknyr said, giving his walking stick a little tap on the stone floor. "She's out, believe me. And a good thing too. What comes next isn't going to be pleasant."

Cecilia spun around. "No! You can't do this!" Hamlyn was standing behind her, a few paces away. "You can't. She's my niece. My brother's daughter. You can't do this. *Please*! It's monstrous!"

Hamlyn was unmoved. "And what of the three boys? Runar. Morris. Lucas. He was only *nine*, Cecilia. A boy of nine. Was that not monstrous too."

"It's all monstrous," she blurted. "All of it."

"But necessary. As you know. We have followed every contract that Thala wrote in the book, followed her every instruction ever since the founding of this order and before. You think we would stop now, at this time? Because this girl is your relation?"

She had no answer. "Please," she could only say, feebly. "Please, you can't."

"We must. And you know we must. Think, Cecilia. Think of the words."

She thought of them. *Blood. Royal. Divine.*

"Yes," Hamlyn said, seeing them in her mind. "I sent Meknyr away long ago to complete this final contract. To bring her here, for this purpose. The magic needed to transfer Ilith's spirit into the body of Tyrith is complex, and requires at its core a great sacrifice. This core resides in Amilia. A child of divine and royal blood."

It made no sense. "But Amilia is *not* of divine blood," she said. "She is only royal, she..." And then it dawned on her, the foul and terrible truth. "She's...she's with child?" She turned and looked at the princess on the slab. There was no visible bump, no suggestion of a pregnancy. She whirled

689

again. "Hadrin's? Thala's own…her own blood?" A fist twisted in her stomach, turning her intestines. "She…she foresaw…"

"She foresaw a great sacrifice. A *personal* sacrifice. The child that grows in Amilia's womb is the last of Thala's direct bloodline. This is its purpose. To raise Ilith. So he might help herald the dawn beyond the darkness."

"No…no…" She drew her godsteel dagger, springing away, eyes darting left and right. Shadows stirred at once. Hamlyn raised a hand. "I won't let you do it. She's to be a mother. I won't let you…"

"It will happen, Cecilia. It has been foreseen by the Far-Seeing Queen herself. She who dwelt in dread, watching horrors in the Eye. Imagine the suffering she endured. Suffering she has passed to us." The mages were looking at her with their dark gleaming eyes. All had gone calm and still and utterly silent inside the chamber.

"Too late to grow a conscience now," Fhanrir rasped, nearby. He moved away from the others who remained by Tyrith's bed. "I told you not to draw that blade, woman. I told you not to interfere."

"She will not interfere," Hamlyn said, calmly. "She is frightened, that is all."

Tears misted her eyes. She blinked to try to clear them. One of the shadows shifted closer. She glimpsed godsteel within his cloak.

"No," Hamlyn said to the man. "She does not yet understand."

"Understand…" she started.

"This child is *unwanted*, Cecilia," the Steward said. "And *unknown* to Amilia, even now. Mekynr has told me himself that the princess has spent the last months in the company of her husband killing his seed with tonics. She will not mourn the loss of the child, Cecilia. She need not even know of it."

"But…but…I don't understand. You…you're not going to kill her?"

"I told you you had a choice," Hamlyn went on. "I said we all deserve a chance at redemption. Here is yours, Cecilia Blakewood. Your own life, for hers. That is the choice I give you. That is the choice foreseen."

Her blood froze in her veins. "But…but why? The child…if you only need the child…"

"The child can be safely extracted. It is the core of the sorcery; a child in its first stages of infancy, a child of divine royal blood, to die for Ilith to live. Yet it is only the core, a skeleton to be wreathed in meat and muscle. For this strong blood is needed. Royal, if not divine."

Hers…or mine… She swallowed. Words failed her.

"Your son," Hamlyn said. "We kept him here as part of the choice. His blood is royal as well, like yours, but *you* came, and he did not. This is your fate, your opportunity, and your sacrifice. Your life, for hers, Cecilia. Save your niece. Save your son. Earn your absolution."

My absolution. Tears ran down her cheeks. Her body shuddered, sword hand weakening. She felt the dagger slip, felt it slip and did not restore her grip. *My life…for hers.* The godsteel left her grasp to land upon the stone floor with a clang, echoing through the hall.

Silence settled. Hamlyn stepped up to her. He took her shivering hand in his. "We all must die, Cecilia. There is no nobler path through the veil than in saving another's life. In doing this, you may save them all. Your niece. Your son. All of them."

Her breath trembled through her nostrils; her bowels had turned to water. She thought of her nightmares, the falling, the screaming. "Will… will I…" She could barely say the words, barely give voice to the terror that had stolen into her dreams, the fear of the Long Abyss. "Will it…be enough?" she whispered, like a child, her voice so small and fragile, her very body seeming to shrink before him as she spoke. "Enough, to…to…"

"It will be enough," he told her, squeezing her hand.

She took a sharp, shuddery intake of breath. Emotion poured from her like a flood, loud in the quiet of the chamber.

"Come, child. Let me guide you."

Hamlyn began leading her toward the stone slab where Amilia lay in slumber. Her thoughts tumbled. One sprung from her lips. "Jonik…no harm will come to him here. Do you promise me that, Hamlyn? Do you promise?"

"On my very life."

"And you'll tell him. You'll tell him what…"

"I will tell him," he whispered. "I will tell him what you have done."

She swallowed, nodding, trying not to think. The cloaked men were closing in from their shadowed places. *The eyes,* she thought. *The spider on its web. And I'm the fly.* "How will it…will it be…"

"There will be no pain, Cecilia. Only joy, great boundless joy." He reached up, putting his palm to her cheek. "Brave child, you will see your son again, in the next life, do not fear. This I solemnly promise you. A second chance…with Jaycob by your side…"

Jaycob…

He lifted his finger from her cheek to her forehead, pressing lightly against the damp skin. And at his touch, the world melted away into shadow and darkness, and through that darkness, pierced a sudden light, a light that grew and widened and brightened. And within it, she saw him. Black of hair, strong of jaw, tall, broad-shouldered, smiling as he strode toward her. "Mother," he was saying, "Mother, I've so much to tell you."

She reached out with desperate grasping fingers and took him into her embrace, hugging him fiercely. "Jaycob…Jaycob, is it really you?" Tears flooded from her eyes. She pulled back, looking up at him, holding his cheeks in her palms.

"Yes, Mother. It's me. It's really me," he laughed. His eyes were light, his voice was a song, wonder shone in his dashing smile. He led her to sit in a room filled with scented candles, before a table of wine and sumptuous food, and there was music playing in the air, sweet music, heavenly music, as though all her favourite pieces had blended and merged together into the finest harmony she'd ever heard. "There's everything here we could ever need, Mother." Jaycob said. "Isn't it wonderful? Food and wine and music and each other. What else is there? What else?"

"Nothing," she said. "Nothing but you, Jaycob. My son. My beautiful son." She felt her cloak slip away from her, and her ugly woollen garments too, leaving her in lighter clothes more suited to the lush spring warmth.

He kissed her cheek. "My beautiful mother. Isn't the temperature perfect here? Spring. A perfect spring day."

She smiled. "My favourite season." There were windows along the wall, opening to stunning mountain vistas. The air was fresh and pure, birds chirping in the trees outside, the sound of the wind brushing through the leaves, and rushing water, further off, as though a great waterfall was crashing distantly down through the valleys.

"We'll go for a walk later," her son said. "A nice long walk, to take in the views. We can talk then, Mother. About anything and everything you want. But first, we should have a nap. I'm tired. Aren't you? Aren't you tired, Mother?"

"I am tired, Jaycob. Yes, you're right."

"Then lie down here. Right here on the sofa. I'll sing you to sleep if you like?"

"I'd like that very much."

"Good. I'm glad. Then lie down here. Right here, that's it."

And so she lay down her head, and closed her eyes, and listened to him sing her to slumber. Slowly, surely, she drifted away, surrendering to the song of her son, the angel, and into an eternal sleep.

60

Saska

Her eyes widened, reflecting firelight.

"*Gods,*" escaped her lips, in a whisper, as the inferno grew, spreading, swelling into a wild, ravening thing, unquenchable and unstoppable, devouring all before it. Down the streets it ran and roared, and down the alleys and the lanes, chasing men, hunting mounts, feasting upon them as they fled. By the raging bright bloom of that infernal fire, Saska could see them; the thousands of men, wolves, cats, and camels in the square and on the streets. They had appeared suddenly from the gloom as the oil caught light, so suddenly her breath had caught in her throat. And then the blaze had consumed them.

Then she heard the screaming.

"My lady, remain here," Sir Ralston Whaleheart said, drawing one of his greatswords. "Many will have survived, and in their panic they will be vulnerable. Stay here, and out of sight." He looked at Leshie. "Stay with her."

The Wall strode straight down the centre of the boulevard, toward the flames, utterly unafraid.

Neither of the girls spoke as they watched him go. They could only stare at the mayhem unfolding ahead, listen to the chaos ringing out. The screams were hardly of this world, a terrible, unutterable cacophony to curdle the blood in a person's veins. Saska had to take her fingers from her blade, sever her blood-bond, to weaken her hearing. But even then, she could hear it. *Everyone in Aram can hear this,* she thought.

Many others around them were standing, rushing forward, drawing their weapons and roaring as they went. Thousands more would be doing the same from the branching streets, chopping down the survivors as they rushed from the flames. Before the inferno had spread, before that arrow had struck, Saska had seen hundreds of men speeding away down the alleys and lanes but most would not have gotten far. They had been blocked off and barricaded to prevent such a retreat, piled high with overturned carts and wagons, barrels and casks, broken chairs and bits of furniture to pen the invaders in. Hasham's soldiers were waiting there with bows, crossbows, spears, and lances to fire and throw down upon the desperate fleeing men, and from the rooftops as well they would fire, and the windows and balconies too.

A kill zone, Saska thought, shuddering. The east of Aram had become a hell on earth.

Leshie was cringing as she listened, watching on through troubled eyes. "Maybe…maybe we shouldn't be here after all," she said quietly. It was her people dying out there, Tukorans. Northerners. *Hers and mine*, Saska thought. *They're all my people, aren't they? All of them.* "I didn't think it would be like this. The *sounds*, Saska…the…the *smell*."

Saska remembered Rasalan. The Lowplains. The villages she'd passed with Marian and her men. The smell of charred bodies was not something a person ever got used to, and Saska had seen many hundreds of them during those weeks. But all the same, she shook her head. "I want to stay, Leshie." *I have to stay*, she thought.

Leshie looked at her closely. "Why? If we're not going to fight, then…"

"We might have to," Saska told her. "Fight, I mean. If anyone comes this way…"

"I'm not sure I can kill Tukorans, Sask. What if it was someone I knew, from back home? I knew loads of people who were mustered for the war, good friends some of them. They might be out there now. Fighting and… and burning."

She winced, perhaps hearing some distinct and distressing wail pierce through the fog of noise. The blaze had lit the world, but with it had come smoke, puffing and boiling forth, swirling in a toxic black fume. Through it Saska could see only glimpses of movement. It looked like some fighting had already begun, swords flashing between eddies, wolves rushing, cats leaping, camels charging around aflame with burning men atop their backs.

The sight enraged her as much as it horrified her. *It's their fault*, she thought. *Their fault.* "There are some Tukorans I *will* kill, Leshie," she said. And with that, she drew her sword.

Leshie did the same, pulling her godsteel shortsword from its sheath. She gave a sigh. It was not like Leshie to show such restraint, though Saska understood it. "I'll kill Aramatians," she said, though with a tone of reluctance. "Not ours, obviously, but theirs. Krator's men. And that Pigborn and his piglets especially. If we smell bacon, we'll know where to find him."

Saska nodded. "Watch for cloaks and colours. Avoid silver and white, and men with eagle helms. And silver and black as well. Those are Nemati men. The rest…"

"I can see Coldheart." Leshie blurted suddenly. She peered forward, past the wagon they were standing behind. "He's there, right there, do you see? He just killed a knight in armour. Godsteel, I think. Might have been an Emerald Guard."

Saska was trying to see as well, though struggling to get a good look through the billows of smoke. "One of Cedrik Kastor's guardsmen, maybe," she said, almost to herself. "He might be close…"

"He might be dead," Leshie came in, hearing her. "I swear I saw him, before the fire started. The arrow, it hit the ground close to him, didn't you see? He was caught in it, Saska. He's *dead*, I'm sure of it."

Saska wasn't nearly so certain. Leshie was likely just saying that to make sure she didn't go and do something stupid. What a change it was. *Usually I'm the one trying to hold her back. She's the reckless one, not me…* She shook her head and said. "Full plate armour protects even from dragonfire, Leshie, and regular fire doesn't burn nearly so hot. Any man in plate could easily have survived."

The fires burned on in patches, sending great plumes of black smoke spiralling into the turbid skies, but between those patches bodies pulsed and rushed, burning men running headlong here and there, others, miraculously unharmed, fleeing for the gate or away down the side streets and lanes. Heaps of charred flesh scarred the pavestones, tripping soldiers as they ran, to be cut down as they tried to get back to their feet.

It was hard to watch, even from back here. The smoke had started to reach them, drawn upon some languid breeze, causing their eyes to water and sting. Saska gave a cough, looked again, and saw that the fighting was inching closer, that some of the enemy had begun to break through and were advancing their way, chased down by the city soldiers. "What if the plan doesn't work?" Saska said, fretting. "What if they just keep on coming?"

Red Blade shook her head. "It's working, Saska. The plan's working."

"How do you know? I can't see that far."

"I can hear it. Can't you hear it? There's battle outside the gate, I'm sure of it. The Bloody Traders have done their job and sparked chaos out there. Soon enough they'll call the retreat. They'll have no choice, with all their leaders dead…"

"But what if they're not?"

"Not what?"

"Not dead. So long as Krator draws breath, and Kastor…"

"They're *dead*," Leshie said again, utterly convinced of it, or pretending to be. "They're dead, Saska, and if not the Whaleheart will hunt them down and kill them."

The Whaleheart. Rolly. Her eyes swung through the writhing sea of smoke and bodies that filled the wide central street. "I can't see him. Do you see him, Lesh?"

The girl looked again, searching, then shook her head. "Not anymore. He's probably cut his way into the thick of it by now, you know what he's like. He'll have this battle won by himself within the hour, you'll see. And Butch is with him, and Green Gaze too." It was her nickname for Merinius, he of the pretty green eyes. "I'm sure I saw them just now."

Saska was getting a bad feeling about all this. However much Leshie lionised her colossal guardian, he wasn't invulnerable, and could still be slain the same as any other man. Saska simply could not lose him. He had become her rock, her one and single constant since she'd left the shores of Rasalan. She was suddenly desperately afraid that he would fall out there tonight. On no account, no account whatsoever, could she stand by back here and let that happen.

I'm going, she thought, and suddenly she was moving, stepping around the wagon, advancing down the street.

Leshie started. "What are you doing? Closer? You're going *closer*, Saska?"

"Rolly might be in trouble."

"What? No, how? Coldheart's never in trouble."

"He could die, Leshie. I won't let him die."

She felt her arm grabbed, as Leshie tried to spin her around. Saska ripped herself free and kept on walking.

"Saska, he said *not* to go anywhere. You're too important. The plan's working. It's working. You don't need to…"

But she wasn't listening anymore, wasn't going to stop and hear sense. Her worry for Rolly was but part of it, her thirst for vengeance another. Every violation she'd ever suffered, every torment and abuse was circling through her mind, round and round, like the spokes of a wheel, repeating, repeating. Her hate had blinded her, consumed her. *They're out there*, she knew. Somehow she knew it. *They're still alive. Both of them are…*

"Stop! Just stop, Saska! If you don't stop I'm going to have to make you!"

Saska kept driving forward. They were nearing the fighting now, though the flames were still some way off. Ahead, Aramatians were killing Aramatians, sunwolves and starcats snarling and snapping and slashing at one another with vicious, elongated claws. Some were dead already, mauled open at the belly or lying with their tongues lolling out of the sides of their mouths, their throats ripped apart, blood pulsing and spurting to the floor. The sight gave Saska pause. She turned to Joy, prowling at her side. The cat looked fearfully enraged, reflecting her emotions, a lather all but frothing at the corners of her mouth. *Can I risk her? Can I? In there?*

Leshie caught up with her again. She saw the look Saska was giving the starcat and pounced upon it. "If you go in there, Joy will be in danger. She might *die*, Saska. And where would that leave us?"

A ripple of anguish shot through her, but she ignored it. "Every man and woman who bonds a beast must face that risk," she found herself saying, driving her concerns down to the ground, pushing her heel upon them and choking them to silence. *I cannot hide from them. I've been hiding long enough.* "Every Starrider, every Sunrider, every Moonrider, every Fireborn. They *all* risk it, Leshie. I'm not special."

"But you are. Your blood, Saska…your fate…"

She'd heard enough about her fate. "I'm going, Leshie. And Joy is too. Now are you coming with me or not?"

The Red Blade scrunched her face up in defeat, groaning. "Fine. But I'm *not* fighting Tukorans. Unless they're *bad* ones. Then…well, maybe.

And if I die out there, well damn it, Saska, I'm going to haunt the shit out of you and make your life a bloody misery. Do you hear me?"

"Loud and clear." Saska turned and plunged forth.

The smoke swallowed them, and the killing, and the chaos. Suddenly, just like that it seemed, men were there, fighting right ahead of them with swords and shields and spears, their armour and surcoats scorched and stained. Some wore burns on their faces, the skin red and rent, others were limping, bleeding, dying even as they battled on. There was screaming everywhere, of men and cats and wolves and camels, a din so loud it was deafening. It felt like the world was ending. And tonight it was, for so many it was…

Saska spotted a squad of Kastor soldiers ahead, led by a large burly knight in godsteel plate and mail, engaged in battle with a host of Nemati men. *Greenbelts*, she thought, tensing. She'd suffered from their sort for long years, suffered their taunts and abuses, their leering eyes and threats, the sting of their palms, their fondling fingers. She remembered Sir Griffin, Cedrik's vile nephew, whom she'd slain with such satisfaction in Elyon's tent. She remembered his men, the same men who'd marched around the Rasal Lowplains, reaving and raping and torturing boys. *Mattius*, she thought, remembering one such boy. *They tied him to a tree to fire arrows at for sport.* Those were the Greenbelts she knew. Men bred beneath the banners of House Kastor.

She took a good long look at the burly knight and realised that she knew him. A horrid face, broad and homely, with eyes peeping out through folds of fat, and large wet glistening lips. *He always licked them when I passed, and muttered some filthy remark. I was just a child. A child.* His name lurched into her memory, a household knight called Sir Baldrin Bunt who'd long stomped the halls of Keep Kastor. *He'd been there at Harrowmoor too,* she recalled, *among Cedrik's host of mutts and mongrels.*

Leshie saw the look on her face. "Are these bad Tukorans, Saska?" she asked.

She could not be sure, not with all of them. There might be one or two honest men among them, but all the same she gave a nod. "I know the knight," she said, staring at him through the smoke, waving and hollering as his men churned about him in battle. "I think I'm going to kill him, Leshie."

"You…what? No, I don't think…"

"I need the practice. And he's got it coming." She rushed, sudden as a quarrel from a crossbow, darting forward with Joy at her side and into the midst of the fighting. Leshie shouted something and made to chase her, but Saska was gone, calling out, "Baldrin! Baldrin! Baldrin you bastard!" as she went.

The burly knight swung about to face her, bearing a broadsword in his grasp, dripping blood. He frowned, stared, and then yelled, "And who the bloody hell are you?"

Saska answered with a swing of godsteel, a diagonal chop aimed straight for those piggish little eyes. Bunt swung up, parrying the blow aside,

697

spraying blood from the edge of his blade to spatter against her faceplate. The ring of steel sang out. Saska swung again, down, then sideways, searching for an opening. Bunt was good to it, knocking her blows away, rocking back on his heels.

"Filthy sellsword," Saska heard him say, as he pulsed forward, hacking down upon her. She sidestepped the blow, swung her blade and whacked his sword aside, firmly and violently, knocking him off balance. The clang reverberated. By the time Sir Baldrin righted himself and wheeled around, she was dropping her height and swinging for his knees. He managed to hook his right leg back and lift his left, her blade clanging against his greaves. The assault left a dent in the armour but little more. Sir Baldrin Bunt's voice heaved out in laughter. "Pathetic! Pathetic bloody sellsword!" He whooshed backward, more quickly than should be allowed at his girth, belly straining against his armour. "Pathetic," he roared again, preparing to lay siege.

Saska sighted a flash of red slip in behind him. "No," she began. "Leshie, no, he's…."

The Red Blade punched the man in the small of his back with the full length of her deadly shortsword, puncturing mail, plate, bone and belly all. A few inches of godsteel burst through his gut, giving Saska's faceplate another spray of blood. Two piggish eyes widened in sudden confusion, then horror; a realisation that was that, his wretched days were done. Leshie pulled out her blade and kicked him in the back in the same motion, driving him to the floor, dead.

"He was yours to kill, I know," she said, over the din of battle. "Save it, Saska. I see you in trouble and I'm going to step in to help."

"I wasn't in trouble. I had him, Leshie."

"It just takes one strike. You think I'd take that risk? Damn it, what else am I here for if not to fight with you? We're much better working together."

"Fine." She was right, of course, and Sir Baldrin Bunt was hardly worth getting upset over. "Come on, then. Joy! On me!" The starcat was currently leaping from Greenbelt to Greenbelt, eviscerating them one and all. By now Saska could communicate with the cat on an almost subconscious level, sensing her presence and state of emotion - which happened to reflect her own, most of the time - though a vocal order was often better. "Leave them! You've done enough! On me!"

Joy finished savaging a soldier's midriff and sprung away, deft as anything, her entire maw and muzzle sopping red. The starcat knew how to pick her targets and would only go for those she knew she could kill. Bladeborn knights clad in heavy godsteel were not for her to fight, lest she expose herself to unnecessary risk. Saska had expressed this to her sternly. "Good girl," she said.

It got worse as they went on, further down the road. The boulevard was wide, its edges unseen in the fog of smoke, though occasionally the wind stirred the shroud and opened a pocket and they saw down a side street or alley, saw the bodies heaped high. Everywhere men were on their knees, or

698

doubled over, coughing up tar and blood. More were dead. Many more. Burned, scorched, blackened, cleaved, they lay silent and still and uncountable, drifting to the stars or the Eternal Halls Above, their torments over, their souls at peace.

"Do you see him, Leshie?" Saska called as they went. "Call out if you see him."

"See who? Coldheart? If I see Cedrik Kastor I'm keeping my mouth *shut*, just so you know. The sunlord we could probably kill, but not *him*."

"If we work together…"

"Then we'll die together. I'm happy to die at your side, Saska, but more like thirty or forty years from now. I *hadn't* planned on it being tonight."

The stink was starting to get overpowering, and the smoke grew thicker as well. Fires burned everywhere, some small and already petering out, others insatiable and blazing so hot you could barely get within ten metres of them. Several buildings to left and right of the boulevard had caught flame, structures of stone and timber erupting into heaving billowing blazes, pulled this way and that by the winds that seemed, suddenly, to have picked up out of nowhere.

The fighting was maddened, blurred by the swirling smokes, a hundred battles raging. The smell, noise, heat of it was almost overwhelming. Saska's eyes searched about her, seeking her Wall, looking out for a giant shadow in those mists. "Do you see him, Lesh?" she bellowed once more. "Can you hear him?"

"There's too much noise. I can't…I can barely focus, Saska."

They were passing by a roaring blaze as one of the buildings took light. Illuminated beneath it, a knot of men were hacking and slashing at one another, and Saska saw a clutch of paladin knights wheeling about on their gigantic steeds, swinging their massive kopesh swords or flailing morning stars. The spine-tingling hisses and snarls of starcats issued out from the gloom, and the growling and howling of sunwolves, in combat and in pain and in the throes of death, echoed all about them.

Maybe we should go back, Saska thought, suddenly. The manic horror of it was wrestling at her resolve, dragging it to the ground, trying to force her to submit. But she shook her head and told herself, *No! This is nothing compared to what I'll have to face later. Like nothing I'll see in the north.* It was a world of gods and monsters out there and Saska, for better or worse, had her part to play in it. *I cannot be crippled and enfeebled by such as this. A bit of fire and burning and battle.* "Embrace it," she even shouted to herself, out loud, as if she was half mad. "Embrace it! There's no hiding anymore!"

Leshie looked over at her, disconcerted. "Were you talking to me?"

"Doesn't matter. Where's Rolly? I want to fight *with* him. All of us, together. We're to go north together, so should fight together too."

"Battle fever," Leshie said, staring at her in concern.

"What? I didn't hear you."

"You've got battle fever, or…or something. Your eyes, Sask. They're… they're wild."

Good. The world has gone wild. Maybe I need to as well. "Follow me," was all she said.

They were closing in on the heart of it now, where the boulevard opened into the square within the gate. A part of Saska welcomed the smoke for the concealment it provided, sparing her the better part of the carnage laid out across the cobbles, befouled by flame, singed and scorched. Some thousands must have perished here, and many of their finest. *But not all*, she knew. The best of the Bladeborn would have survived, she felt, their armour protecting them from the fires. *Did they escape back out of the gates? Are they in the midst of battle out there?*

She could hear it, now, beneath it all, the wild crazed cacophony of noise outside. It seemed the plan had worked, as Leshie said, to spark violence between the camps. Thousands would be dying out there, thousands more fleeing, all sense of order utterly lost. It tore at Saska's heart to think of all the innocent boys and good honest men being butchered for their masters' folly, but what could she do? It was war, brutal and boundlessly unfair, but just war. *This is the world they made for us*, she thought. *The gods. This is all just a part of their game.*

"Saska, I think I saw him!"

She stopped, spun, and met Leshie's eyes. "Where? *Where*, Leshie?"

The Red Blade thrust her shortsword away down an alley. "I saw a shadow. A tall one. Rushing in that direction."

"On me," Saska shouted, and ran.

They hurdled bodies as they went, parrying and fending off any attacks that came their way. Within moments they were being gobbled up by the mouth of the alleyway, plunging down a tight lane no more than two metres wide, twisting and turning like a snake. Men had been cut down here as well. One sat against the wall, cradling his intestines and weeping for his mother. Another was scrambling around on the ground on all floors, as though looking for something, before Saska realised he'd been blinded by the fires, his face a twisted mess of disfigured, blackened flesh.

We should put them out of their misery, came a thought, but there was no time, and where would it end? A thousand men were the same, dying slowly and horrifically and in pain. So on they rushed, chasing shadows, through the grey choking cloak of fog, before they came to a smaller inner court-yard where more lanes branched out in different directions, bending and winding away.

"Which way?" Saska shouted, coming to a stop. "Which way, Leshie?"

"I don't know. How could I possibly know that, Saska? You're in the lead, not me!"

There had been fighting here too. Down one of the roads Saska saw a barricade of wagons and wood piled high. Men huddled at its base, unmoving, all of them riddled with bolts and arrows and spears. There must have been a dozen of them, all slaughtered as they tried to escape.

Saska caught movement and looked up. She could see figures on the roofs, firing down at unseen enemies. A balcony jutted out from a building and there, too, a pair of bowmen were nocking, aiming, firing, reloading.

One spotted them, swung their aim right over, and let loose without thinking. The arrow pinged straight off Leshie's left pauldron, grazing her face as it glanced against the godsteel and rebounded away.

She slapped her gauntleted hand to her cheek, then spun. "Hey, we're *friends!*" she shrieked, enraged. "Friends! Can't you see! We're on the same side you shit!"

Saska shouted out in Aramatian, translating - or thereabouts; she omitted the 'you shit' - and the bowman understood.

"I am sorry," he returned. "I did not know. It is hard to see from here."

The graze had left only a scratch and it was Leshie's fault anyway, for having her visor raised. "We're looking for the Whaleheart?" Saska called up to him. "He came down here, we think. Did you see which way he went?"

The man nodded and pointed down one of the lanes, "I saw a large metal man go that way, with another, a smaller one. It may have been him."

"What are you talking about," Leshie asked, indignant, in the northern tongue. "Is he apologising for my face? He's ruined it, Saska. Ruined it!"

"It's a scratch, Leshie. If you had your faceplate down the arrow wouldn't have hit you."

"I don't like the faceplate. I can barely see anything through it."

"You'll learn." Saska had trained often with Rolly with her visor down, so had grown accustomed to looking through eyeholes. She turned to look down the alley the bowman had referenced. "The Wall went this way, the archer said. He was with someone else."

"Who?"

"I don't know. The Butcher maybe, or Merinius. You said you saw them together earlier."

"I did. I think I did, anyway." She rubbed the blood from her face. "Guess one of them is dead, then. Otherwise there would be three."

"We don't know that. Come on. We can't be far behind." And off they went at a sprint.

They had been going for some twenty or thirty seconds more when they heard voices around a corner ahead, northern voices, Tukoran voices, calling out to one another in an animated exchange.

"....this way," a young man was saying, briskly, breathless from the heat of battle. "They went this way, I'm sure of it...I saw them, Lank. Come on!"

A second voice urged caution. "Robb, just...just be careful. The giant might be lurking somewhere around here. I saw him earlier....hunting Bladeborn knights. Butchering them. If he finds us..."

The other man ignored him. "Bernie!" he shouted out. "Bernie, where are you? Percy, Martyn, Del, can you hear me?"

The last name made Saska jolt, causing her to stumble as she ran. *Del? No...it couldn't be...*

She sped straight out into another branching courtyard, Leshie at her heels. The two men were standing ahead, looking down the different paths, trying to figure out which way to go. One was excessively tall, though not the Wall, that was clear at a glance. He was much too narrow, and not nearly so grand.

"You there!" she found herself shouting out, demanding their attention.

The two men swung about at once, brandishing bloody blades, shifting into stance. The tall one took on a Blockform pose, the smaller one assuming a nimble Strikeform, ready to launch himself forward in attack if needed. "Who are you?" he shouted, the smaller one. "You sound northern. Tukoran. Your accent…"

"Sellswords," said the taller one, snarling the word out. "Look at their armour, Robb. It's all mismatched, like *theirs*."

"Bloody Traders," the one called Robb said. "Are you with them? Tell me, right now! Are you with those *traitors*!"

"We're *not* sellswords," Saska said, Leshie at her side. Joy had taken position somewhere in the shadows, out of sight, at her command. "You said a name. Right then. I heard it. You said Del."

The two men shared a look.

"His squire," the tall one then said, confused. He must have been seven feet, a soaring pole of a man. Both were entirely clad in godsteel armour, masterfully made it looked by what she could see of it beneath the blood and dirt and soot. *Emerald Guards*, she thought. Highborn, there was no doubt. She could hear it in the refined accents of their voices.

"Who are you," the one called Robb demanded again. A breath of wind passed through, drawing off the smoke, and Saska saw him. He had his faceplate up; behind it lay a young face, late teens, most handsome, with dark hair matted to his forehead over eyes that glittered in brown and green.

I know him, she realised. *Not by sight, no, but…* "You're…you're Robbert Lukar. The Prince of Tukor."

"Yes I am. And who are you?" The young prince's eyes bored into her, narrow and intense. There were scorch marks on his plate, but he seemed unhurt. The tall one was the same. "If not a sellsword who are you? We have no women in the army."

"They're with *them*, Robb," the tall knight said. "They're not ours. They're Hasham's."

"Is that true? Are you among the city defenders?"

"We're our *own* defenders," Leshie snapped out, fiercely. "We shouldn't even be here anymore." She jutted her chin at Saska. "We were waiting for her to heal before leaving. Then you lot came and encircled the city, bastards!"

"You lot? Bastards? You're talking to a *prince*, girl," the pole of a knight admonished her. "Show the proper respect."

"Yeah, well you're talking to something much more than that. A prince?"And Leshie laughed. "Try a princess and a duchess and a *queen*, how about that!"

The two men looked utterly befuddled by that. Saska took control of matters lest Leshie say something out of turn. "We have no quarrel with you, Your Highness," she said to Robbert Lukar, with the utmost courtesy and reverence. By what means she managed to control her emotions at that time, she couldn't say. Necessity, it might have been. She knew just how gifted the young Prince of Tukor was, and no doubt this looming body-guard of his was similarly deadly. Their chances of defeating them would be minimal, she sensed. But more than that, she'd spoken truly; she had no hate for Robbert Lukar, nay, everyone seemed to agree that he was a good and honourable young man, the spit of his great father Rylian, and much loved throughout Tukor. *No, it's his uncle I want.* "I only wish to know about this squire of yours," she went on. "Del, you said. Describe him, please."

"Tall," Prince Robbert said, after a short pause, frowning at her all the while. "Not like Lank here, but tall enough. Kind of gangly, and awkward, with black hair and, um…he's sixteen I think. From North Tukor. A village called…"

"Willow's Rise," she breathed.

"Yes. What, do you…you know him?"

She swallowed. "*Where is he?*" Everything had changed, at once and in an utter instant and forever, in that moment. "*Where?* I need to find him. Please. Where did he go? Where is he!"

Even the tall one seemed taken aback by all that. "We don't…we don't know. We've been looking for our men. Sir Bernie Westermont and his company. Robb's company, really. Some of them are dead - we saw them in the main square, burned by that evil bloody trick you pulled…"

"Lothar," Robbert said, noting the man's rising ire. He took the story up himself. "We saw some of their bodies. Just youngsters, like Del. But *not* him," he said, quickly, to reassure her. "We were told Sir Bernard had rushed this way with some of the survivors, and it's possible Del's with him. That's all we know. I'm sorry."

Saska was close to panicking now. The shock of it was attempting to buckle her knees, but she righted herself, fortified herself, and said, "We're coming with you. I *need* to find him. He's my brother…"

"Your brother?" The speed at which the prince said that made it clear that Del had spoken of her. "Saska. Is that your name?"

She would prefer not to answer, but nodded; there was no space for subterfuge here. It seemed as though the young prince knew more, and had more to say, but time would not allow it.

"Robb, I'm not sure…" Sir Lothar started.

"I am." The prince waved them forward, and even went so far as to sheathe his blade, if only temporarily; no doubt he would withdraw it as soon as the need returned. But as a gesture it was powerful. "Come on," he told them, "you can join us if you want. Lothar, with me. I'll lead the way."

61

Robbert

Robbert Lukar's throat was so dry it had become a chore to swallow.

It builds a thirst, he thought, desperately parched. *Fighting through this damnable smog. Being devoured by infernal flame.*

"I need water, Lank," he coughed, as they went, stalking down the smoke-filled alleyways. "Find out if either of those girls have any, would you?"

The inferno had engulfed them both when it mushroomed and exploded from that arrow, swirling around them in a roaring vortex, all but roasting them alive in their armour. Amid that unspeakable tempest Robbert had thought, for the first true time in his life, that that was it, he was going to die. All about him, men were combusting, their cloaks and surcoats bursting alight, leather melting against their bodies, tongues of fiery orange and red licking and slathering to blacken and burn their skin. Camels had caught afire, honking out some hideous moaning sound as they charged amok, blasting burning men out of the way. He'd seen sunwolves howling, manes like bonfires, throwing the riders from their backs as they twisted and threw themselves about in agony. And starcats too, leaping and scrambling for higher ground, clawing over whatever they could find, over the dead and the dying alike.

It was utterly and indescribably horrific, and all the while Robbert had stood there, watching through the holes in his visor, powerless to do anything to help them, wondering how long the blaze would last and if, in fact, it would burn on forever.

Yet even as that thought flitted through his head, as he sweated and cooked in his Ilithian Steel plate, the fires had suddenly and just like that weakened and withered, drawing back, burning on only in pockets and patches as the world was enshrouded in filthy black smoke. And through those smokes, they had come, the city defenders roaring, charging forth to drive their foes away.

Since then, both he and Lothar had been in the thick of it, fending off the sudden flow of soldiers pouring from the streets. Outside, he could hear the raging battle, as though a fell madness had gripped at them all. "We should go, Lothar," he'd bellowed at one point. "Go, try to restore calm out there!"

He wondered if his uncle might be doing just that, but had not seen him since the inferno, nor Elio Krator either. Lord Huffort he had, though only briefly, as the Lord of Rockfall lumbered away down some lane with several of his guardsmen in tow, to vanish into the gloom. Sir Gavin Trent, too, had been glimpsed, roaring like a bellows in that enormous battle-hardened voice of his, trying to issue some command to his men, to stir the survivors back to the fight. But even that had been but a fleeting thing. One moment Robbert had spotted him and the next the tide of soldiers had come rushing down a lane to sweep across and swallow him whole.

It was at that moment that Lothar had responded, shouting, "We won't be able to restore anything, Robb. There are tens of thousands of men out there. How would we even *start* to regain control?"

"We have to try," Robbert had merely said, before he'd begun leading Lothar back to the gate, through the chaos in the square, past the raging fires and burning bodies, and that's when they'd seen Sir Krelyn. He was one of Robbert's only veteran knights, one of the captains of his company, and was lying dead at the south of the square, only a half dozen metres from the gate.

Gods, Robbert had thought, in horror. *They must have come through just before the inferno spread. My entire company might have been here...*

A quick scrambling search had unearthed the corpses of others too, some of them Bernie's charges. Pimply Paul, Frog and Derrick had all been struck down by the flames, their bodies barely recognisable. Willem, the burly stableboy, they found a little further off, his skull opened up by the hack of an axe. Yosh, too, was soon uncovered. Some beast had gotten him, a sunwolf or starcat it was hard to say, though he was badly burned as well. By beast or burning it mattered not. The boy was dead, and that was that.

Of Sir Bernie Westermont, however, there had been no sign, nor the rest of the boys. "We have to find him," Lothar had urged, frantic. "Find him and get the hell out of here. We *can't* leave him behind, Robb."

It was then, if not before, that Robbert Lukar realised how fatally their plan had failed. *Find him and get the hell out of here,* he thought. There was no notion in Sir Lothar's head of trying to win the city now. That was done, over, burned to a bloody crisp. The merchant Denlatis had betrayed them, set them up, and with it his uncle's plot to betray Elio Krator had failed as well. *A coup within a coup,* he had thought. All this dreaded treachery had won them was total and utter disaster.

So he'd nodded to Lothar and said, "Fine, let's go. We find Bernie, get out, and regroup from there. Follow me!"

And that's how they found themselves here, now, with these two girls, running in search of Sir Bernie, and Del.

Sir Lothar came back to join him, as they wended down a tight alley, smothered in smog, some way to the south of the Cherry Gate now, though exactly where the prince could not say. In this fog it was impossible to make out one street from another, and the alleys here twisted and turned in some terrible, confusing pattern, half of them blocked off by barricades or clotted with fighting men. Robbert had the sense of a starcat prowling nearby to them as well, leaping from roof to roof, watching, but made no mention of it just yet. He suspected this cat was with the Saska girl, bonded to her even. *Another piece of the puzzle,* he thought.

"They've got none," Sir Lothar Tunney said, rushing back to his side. "There are drinking wells and fountains around these streets, though, the smaller girl said. We might be able to find water there."

Robbert nodded. It was not a high priority just yet, though if they passed one by, he would not say no.

"I don't know why you said they could join us, Robb," Lank went on, under his breath. "We have no time to be picking up waifs and strays."

"*We're* not waifs and strays," the smaller of the two girls hissed from behind, overhearing them. "We're *allowed* to be here in the city, unlike *you*. *You're* the invaders, not us. *You're* the waifs and strays."

Lank thought it best to ignore her. She seemed a wild and feisty thing, dressed in some odd configuration of studded red leather armour and misting, fitted godsteel plate. The other girl, Saska, wore a full suit of her own, mismatched and by no means consistent, but good godsteel nonetheless, bedecking her from head to heel. Both had blades as well, and the girl Saska, especially, bore a fine dagger at her hip, sheathed in a striking ornamental scabbard and with a series of strange glyphs and markings glowing on the pommel and hilt.

Robbert had spotted all of that during their short conversation, puzzling out the details of the girl's identity. By now he felt he had a pretty good idea of just who this Saska was. And she wasn't just Del's adopted sister, either.

"Lank, take the lead. Watch out for threats. There are bowmen above us. And keep calling out for Bernie as well. We'll find him eventually, I'm sure of it." Robbert pulled back with that, so that he was right beside the girl. "I know who you are," he said to her.

She had her faceplate down, every inch of her concealed and protected. The helm she wore was Rasalanian, clearly, with two bladed crab claws surging from its crest. Other parts bore Tukoran details, or Vandarian, he saw. It was very much the sort of suit a sellsword would wear, with components scavenged from here and there.

After a telling pause she said, "Go ahead, enlighten me."

There wasn't much time for a long preamble, Robbert decided. So he just smiled, despite it all - and perhaps to put her at ease - and went right into it. "You're that spy from Harrowmoor, aren't you? The girl who Elyon Daecar had in his tent. The one who escaped at Shellcrest, with the King's Wall." He laughed from the bizarre coincidence of it, though it was a restrained laugh, more of a *huff* of incredulity really, given the situation. "I only took Del on as my squire yesterday, if you'd believe it, and by complete chance as well. Now I find out that this sister of his, this adopted sister, is in fact the long lost Aramatian princess that Elio Krator's been after. And my uncle too…"

"Is your uncle dead?" she asked, bitterly, and so suddenly it took him off guard. He could see a pair of bright blue eyes burning behind the eyeholes in her visor, like sapphire stars in the dark of night. "Did you see him burn?"

"No, I…I didn't see him, but…I doubt he would have burned. His armour is even finer than my own. He'll be out there now, somewhere. Doing what he does best."

"Raping women? Abusing girls? Whipping them and torturing them and starving them in his cells?"

Robbert Lukar was dumbstruck. "Did he…do you…"

"I don't want to speak about him. I just want to find Del."

She kept on going, pace by quick and steady pace, at his side, staring forward. A few metres ahead, clad in smoke and gloom, Lank and the red-armoured girl were striding side by side. She had to speed her legs at twice the pace to keep up, and seemed to be interrogating him with a series of questions, asking them just who they thought they were for doing all this, for besieging this peaceful city, for bringing such shame to Tukor, and the north. "That prince of yours," Robbert heard her say. "Why is he allowing this? I heard he was good. A good man, a noble prince…"

"He is, girl. The very best…"

"Then why is he letting this happen?" She turned her eyes back to look right at him. "Why, Prince Robbert? *Why* are you letting this happen."

"It isn't his decision to make," Lank told her. "He isn't the commander of our army."

"And why not? You're a prince, aren't you? The son of Rylian Lukar. He's a hero, even to people like me. *You* should be leading your army, not that vile Lord Kastor guy."

Robbert opened his mouth to respond. "Yes, well it's not quite as simple as…"

"I agree with her," Saska said, in a low voice. "Cedrik Kastor isn't fit to lead an army of good honest men. I know he's your uncle, but he's as bad as his father was. Maybe even worse."

"You knew my grandfather, Lord Modrik?"

"I knew him," she said, and nothing more.

"So you worked for him?" the prince pressed. "You were at Keep Kastor, in Ethior? And that's why…" He stopped. It all made so much sense. She'd *been* there, one of the southern staff they kept. Robbert thought of the poor naked girl who'd come bursting from his uncle's bedchamber in his pavilion, only a week or so ago, fleeing from his despicable tortures.

She must have suffered the same, once before, he thought. *She was just a slave, before all this. A slave who became a spy who became a princess. A Bladeborn and Light-born both…*

The girl did not seem interested in answering or discussing it. A few moments of silence passed as Robbert tried to digest it all, glancing over at her as they rushed down a tight winding alley. He caught a glimpse of that dagger again, glowing softly at her side in silver and blue, somehow brighter than regular godsteel, more dazzling and magnificent. There was something about it he recognised. *I'm sure I've seen it before…*

He was about to ask when a shadow passed overhead, sleek and slinky. Robbert's gaze shifted up just in time to see a tail vanish into the gloom, long and black and spotted silver.

"Don't worry," Saska said. "She's with me."

The starcat. "Are you…are you *bonded* to her? That's extremely rare, you know. To be able to bond godsteel *and* an animal…"

"She isn't *just* an animal." The comment seemed to agitate her. For the first time she turned to him, reaching up to lift her faceplate. The face behind it was one of astonishing beauty, refined, elegant, yet fierce, no older than he was. He had seen this girl, this spy, at Harrowmoor, but she'd looked different then. *A disguise,* Robbert knew. *Otherwise my uncle would have known her.* "I don't want to talk about Joy," she told him. "I don't want to talk at all. I just want to find Del." She turned forward again, slamming her faceplate back down, quickening her pace.

The others were still clattering along ahead, turning occasionally as they hit a blockade, calling out as they went. They passed several smaller skirmishes, some involving a dozen or so men, others battles of single combat. The fighting had spread and dispersed widely now from the boulevard, it seemed, though none turned out to be Bernie or his men. The bodies were in strong evidence too, and frequently Saska would rush off and check them, seeking a mop of black hair or gangly build, fearing the worst.

"Robb, there's fighting nearby, and a lot of it," Lank shouted from up the lane.

Robbert Lukar focused. He could hear it, the blur of a hundred blades clashing. Some sounded particularly *heavy*, the sort of ringing clang you got when large men came together. *Bernie*, he thought. "Lank, lead on."

The tall knight sped away, clanking down the alley and turning onto another, sabatons smashing against the stone cobbles at their feet. The red-armoured girl followed right behind with Saska at her heels, Robbert bringing up the rear a few paces back.

They'd gone but a dozen or so strides when he heard a voice, calling behind him, thinly and at the edge of his hearing, competing to be heard amidst the clangour of battle ringing out through the east of Aram.

"My lord," the voice was saying, slightly panicked. "My lord, Prince Robbert… my lord, say it's you…"

Robbert slowed, turning, peering back down the lane. A shape was hurrying his way through the smog, the form of a man, armoured in essentials, with a torn green cloak flowing at his back.

Gershan?

"Lank, hold," the prince said, though glancing back he realised that the others had already moved off around a bend. *Damnit.* "Gershan," he called down the lane. "Gershan, is that you?"

"Yes, my lord, yes, it's me." The Emerald Guard hurried up to him, panting, his green cloak scorched and singed and shredded down one side. Robbert hadn't seen him since the inferno had begun. "Oh thank the gods I found you, my prince. The gods are good after all!"

"Why aren't you with my uncle, Sir Wenfry?" Robbert took a quick glance behind him once more, keeping an ear out for the others. No doubt they would notice his absence in a moment and return. Losing Lank was not on the prince's agenda. *And certainly not for the sake of this weaselly little cretin.* "Speak, Gershan. I don't have much time."

"Yes, my…my lord, of course. Your uncle. I was with him, at the start, but we were separated in the fire and the fighting. I've been trying to find him, but…"

"It's easy to get lost around here," Robbert agreed. He thrust his jaw down the alley, over Gershan's shoulder. "The central boulevard is back that way, I think. You'll find my uncle there, I'm sure."

"I don't think so, my lord. I was told by Sir Jesse Bell that Lord Cedrik had come this way. Perhaps not this particular lane, but somewhere in this direction, certainly. He said that he still intends to win the city, Prince Robbert. That we're to…to find and kill our…our *targets*."

Robbert frowned at him through his raised visor. "No. That's folly, Gershan. The city is lost. We've no choice now but to retreat and regroup outside and hope we still have an army left to take home."

"Home, my lord?"

"Yes, home. To Tukor. Gods, man, what other option is there? If we remain in Aramatia we'll be slaughtered. Do you not know what's happening outside the walls, Sir Wenfry? It's chaos, bloody chaos. We're like two heads of a snake, devouring one other. My uncle, Krator, they've led us to disaster."

But Gershan hardly seemed to be listening. His hand was hovering beside the handle of his dagger, trembling it looked, his eyes turned away to one side.

Battle shock, Robbert thought. *The craven's got battle shock.*

"Godsdamnit, Sir Wenfry, would you grasp your wits!" he shouted at him. "You said my uncle is around here somewhere? South of the main boulevard? Are you sure?"

The other man nodded, somewhat absentmindedly. He glanced up, down, and away again, struggling with something, some inner turmoil. "Yes, my lord. I was told by…by…"

"Sir Jessie," Robbert came in, trying to speed the man up. "*He* should be with my uncle as well. You're his guardsmen, damnit. What about Sir Lionel?"

"I don't know, my lord. Dead, I…I think."

"What? It can't be both, Gershan. Either you know he's dead or you don't."

"It was too hard to see, my lord. I saw the…the King's Wall. He was hacking men apart, and Sir Lionel flew toward him. I am jumping to a conclusion, perhaps, but a sound one." His eyes moved behind the prince, searching down the lane. "He's out there somewhere," his voice quivered. "The giant. If we're to take the city, he has to die."

"We're *not* going to take the city, Gershan!" Robbert roared at him, losing his patience. "Would you get that through your thick bloody skull! Now go, back that way." He flicked a hand. "If you find my uncle, tell him to call the retreat. On no account is anyone to try to find their targets now. Do you understand me? None at all."

The Emerald Guard said nothing. His eyes were down, blinking, as though deep in thought, fortifying himself for something. His chest moved up and down in a heavy, slow breath.

"Are you all right, Sir Wenfry?" The man looked like he was about to have some sort of panic attack. His lower lip was trembling, mumbling something incoherent as he stared at the ground. "Wenfry, listen to me," Robbert said, reaching forward, placing a hand on the man's shoulder. "You have to focus now, OK? You have to be strong. Turn around, go back down this lane, and try to find my uncle. It is absolutely imperative that we call the retreat and try to save as many men as possible. Yes, Wenfry? Do you understand? I need to hear you say it."

The man looked up, slowly. There were *tears* in his weasel eyes, for some reason. "I'm sorry," he whispered, in a voice so low that Robbert didn't hear him at first. He had to lean in a little further to catch the words.

"What was that? What did you say?"

"I'm…sorry, my lord. I didn't want to…I never asked to…"

"To what? What don't you want to do, Sir Wenfry? What in the blazes are you talking about?"

And then he saw it.

The dagger, withdrawn.

62

Saska

They burst out into a large open market square enshrouded in darkness and smoke.

The din of battle had led them here, and of that there was plenty. Shadows shifted through the fogs, steel flashing, claws slashing. Several hundred men and mounts, at least, were in the throes of screaming combat.

"I know this square!" Leshie called out, as they came to a sudden halt. "We're not far from the main boulevard. We must have circled back around or something."

"That would explain all the fighting," Sir Lothar responded. The smokes were as thick here as anywhere, and the darkness too remained utterly unrelenting, the skies refusing to permit even the faintest hint of moonlight through the clouds. "Damn these cursed fogs. I can barely see anything." Lothar turned his eyes around, searching through the many shadowed skirmishes unfolding across the cobbles. "Bernie!" he called out. "Bernie, are you out there? Gods, this is a *nightmare*. Robb, what do you want to…"

He cut himself off, his eyes fixing suddenly to a blur of movement swishing by.

Saska had seen it too. A pair of swordsmen, hard to make out for certain in the gloom, but partly identifiable by their shape and size. One was very large, it looked, bearing what appeared to be a bastard sword in his meaty grasp, long and lethal. The other was utterly monstrous, with a greatsword in his hand, swinging fiercely. Their passing had occurred in no more than a flash, but against the other figures battling in the square, it was immediately obvious who they were.

Rolly, Saska thought. And then she shouted it. "Rolly!"

At the very same moment, Lothar bellowed, "Bernie! Bernie, I'm coming, Bernie!" He ripped his sword from its sheath with a metallic rasp, shouting - "For Tukor! For Tukor!" - and rushed straight into the fray.

"No, stop!" Saska screamed at him, drawing her own blade. "We're friends. We're friends! Stop!" But Lothar was already gone, and Sir Bernard and the Wall as well, spinning back away into the gloom. "Prince Robbert," Saska yelled, turning. "You have to stop this. You have to..." She cut herself off.

He wasn't there.

The mouth of the alley was empty.

She drew up her faceplate as though that might help, squinting back the way they'd come. "Where is he? He was right behind us."

"He was right behind *you*," Leshie said, in correction. "When did you last see him?"

"I don't know. Not long. When we heard the battle here, and came running..."

"We turned about a half dozen corners since then, Saska." Leshie thought for a moment. "I know the way. I'll go back for him."

"No, wait..."

"What?"

"Del," Saska said. "We *have* to find Del."

"And Coldheart? We came for *him*, Saska. I know you love Del and everything, but who's more important?"

Saska couldn't possibly answer that. She couldn't believe Leshie would even ask it. "Rolly can handle himself."

"I know, but a prince doesn't have just anyone guarding him. They're fearsome warriors too, both of them. Together they could kill him, Saska."

I know, I know, she thought. *Godsdamnit, I know!* All the same, she turned about and screamed out at the top of her lungs, "Del! Del! in desperate hope. "Del, are you out there? Del, do you hear me?"

"You're *not* going to find him, Saska," Leshie insisted. "It's too loud, there are too many people, and this square is *massive*. He could be anywhere. You're not going to..."

"Saska?" a voice said.

She whirled, and so quickly she almost fell. A figure was approaching, creeping out from behind an overturned wagon, clanking along in ill-fitting steel armour. He had a sword at his hip, a bow in his grasp. Long untamed hair poked out from a halfhelm.

"Del? Del!" Saska exclaimed, astonished.

"You *have* to be kidding me," Leshie guffawed.

Saska surged forward, rushing at him, grabbing him, looking into his eyes. "My gods, it's really you! It's you!" She looked him over, up and down, as if to make absolutely utterly sure, then took his hand and whisked him aside, right back to the wagon where he'd been hiding. "Are you hurt? Are you injured? Are you OK?" she blurted.

His big brown eyes stared down at her, wide as watermelons, glistening in the darkness. "You're...you're wearing godsteel," he mumbled. "That's *godsteel*, Saska. How..."

He doesn't know, she realised. *He knows nothing, absolutely nothing.*

"How are you *here*?" he went on. "I don't...I don't understand. Are you a...are you a soldier now?" He looked wretchedly confused, and wretchedly afraid, but it was him, the same boy she'd left behind at the farm, the same shy quiet boy, only older, longer in the face, grimmer perhaps and an inch or two taller besides. *My brother.* He even had a beard, or some semblance of one, wisps of black fuzz sprouting in patches from his cheeks and chin.

"Now isn't the time, Del," she told him, in a rush. "We have to get you to safety."

"But your…your armour? You look like a sellsword. Like one of those Bloody Traders…"

"We know the Bloody Traders," Saska said. "They're helping us."

"*Us?* What do you mean? Sir Bernard said that they *betrayed* us. It was a trick, he said. All that…all that *fire*…" his voice shuddered.

"Saska," Leshie said, pointedly, stepping in. "We *don't* have time for this."

Saska nodded, reaching out, putting both of her hands on his broad armoured shoulders. "You have to be brave now, Del. I'm going to take you away, all right? I'm going to get you to safety."

He shook his head at once, standing taller, straightening the slouch in his back. He looked almost a proper knight in that armour. "No. I can't go. I have to stay here, in case the others come back. Percy and Martyn, they rushed off fighting, but I'm better with the bow, so I…I stayed here, like Sir Bernard said. I just…I don't know who to shoot at. Everyone looks the same…"

Saska reached to grab his arm. "That's noble, Del, very noble, but I'm *not* going to leave you here."

He tugged back. "I'm not leaving, Saska. I'm not."

"You are. You're coming with me. Leshie, what's the safest way out of here? I'm going to take Del back to the palace."

"The palace?" Del said, bewildered. "I'm not going to the *palace*. I'm staying here. Right here. I'm staying with the others."

"The others are probably dead," Saska said to him, more bluntly than she'd expected. But there was no time to coddle him here, and perhaps he didn't need that anymore. She could sense that he'd grown harder during their long parting. Though his eyes were still shadowed in fear, he was not letting it overwhelm him. "If you stay here someone will come past eventually and kill you. There are sunwolves out there, don't you hear them? And starcats. And knights who've been fighting twice as long as you've lived. This is no place for you, Del."

"And you? It's a place for *you?* You're just a housemaid, Saska, a farmhand. How are you here? Tell me what's happening!"

"No," she said. "Now isn't the time."

He swung his bow up, drawing an arrow from a half-empty quiver, and nocked. Then he turned his eyes out into the dark of the square, squinting, searching for someone to fire at, as though to prove a point and say, *I'm not leaving. I'm a soldier now. And I'm staying here to fight.*

I could overpower him, Saska thought. That would be easy enough in her godsteel plate. She could knock him out and carry him if needed, but to where? She had no idea where she was and there was still the matter of Sir

Ralston, doing battle with the two Emerald Guards. She turned to Leshie. "Do you know the way back to the palace?"

"Of course. I know every nook and cranny around here."

"Then take Del back for me. I'll go in there and try to break Rolly and the others apart."

"I'm *not* leaving," Del repeated, adamant, turning again and lowering his bow. "I was ordered to stay here by Sir Bernard. You can't overrule that, Saska. You have no authority."

"If only you knew." Leshie's lips twisted into a wry smile. Del looked as bewildered by that comment as everything else, but explanations would have to wait for later. "OK, so you've got a duty to this Sir Bernard. We understand that. But what about Prince Robbert? You're his squire, we heard. Do you have a duty to him?"

"Yes. I…of course I…"

"Then you'd best come with me, Del," Leshie said, thumbing down the nearest alleyway. "We lost him back there somewhere. If you're truly his squire, you'd better help me find him."

Del nodded in agreement, swinging the bow back over his shoulder. "Of course. Yes, I'll come with you…"

Smart, Saska thought. Save knocking him unconscious and carrying him out of here, it seemed the only way to get him moving. *And he'll be safer away from this square.* Not safe, exactly…but safer, she was certain. She stepped to Leshie's side and lowered her voice. "Keep him out of harm's way, Lesh. If you can, try to lead him back to the palace without him knowing."

"Trick him? That's a bit sneaky, Saska."

"Just try. If you can't, fine. But stay with him, OK? Don't leave his side for a second. And if you run into any fighting, you turn the other way."

"So I'm a babysitter now, is that it?"

"It was your idea, Leshie."

"I know, but…" She blew out a breath. "Fine, whatever. If we end up back here, I'll hide him there, behind that same wagon. So you'll know where to find us."

It was the best compromise she was likely to get. There could hardly have been a worse place to reunite with her brother than in the midst of this nightmarish night, but for all that she couldn't complain. He was alive, that was the main thing. And she had to trust Leshie to keep it that way.

The boy was standing patiently aside, glancing away toward the screaming and roaring. Men flashed by, some close enough that Saska could see the colours of their cloaks, the red of the blood on their blades. She listened a moment, trying to detect the heavy stamp and grunt of Rolly, but there was no sign. *Their fight must have taken them across the square.* She would have her work cut out just finding them in all this, but that was a job for her alone. Del's presence would only distract her.

She snatched him into a quick embrace. "Go with Leshie. Protect one another. I'll see you both soon."

She could not give them any more thought.

Turning, she rushed away.

714

63

Robbert

The dagger surged.

Robbert's heart gave a sudden leap and at once he attempted to shift backward, away from the man, but Sir Wenfry Gershan had anticipated it. He moved forward with him, grabbing at the hand Robbert had placed on his shoulder. With a fierce tug, he pulled him closer and in the same movement drove up hard with his dagger, thrusting it with all his might for the prince's exposed face.

Robbert swung up with his spare arm, trying to deflect the blow, but in doing so lost his footing and balance. Sir Wenfry pressed upon him with his weight, driving him down to the ground. Robbert landed on his back with a heavy jolting thud, his attacker sprawling atop him.

"I'm sorry," the man was saying, weeping. "I'm sorry, I didn't want this...I didn't....please forgive me... please forgive me...please forgive me..."

Robbert's right arm was pinned down by hand and knee, his left covering his face, just about holding the knife at bay. He tried to shift, suddenly, and with all his might, but it was no use. Gershan was straddling him, driving his dagger down bit by bit, using his weight, weeping all the while. "It's not my fault...it's not my fault....it's not my fault..."

"Stop...just...just *stop*..." Robbert managed to get out, almost choking on the words. "You don't want to do this...you don't...I know you don't..."

He heaved with his forearm, pushing Gershan back an inch or two, but no more. The dagger came right back down, searching for his eye. A great roar tore from his throat, and he tried to twist again, but nothing. It was no use. A freakish animal strength had commandeered the man.

"I'm sorry...please...forgive me...please forgive me..."

Tears fell, rolling from his eyes and down his cheeks to drop onto Robbert's face. He spat the salty brine away, spraying spittle into Gershan's eyes, but it made no difference.

"I never asked...I never wanted...please...it's not my fault..."

I'm going to die. It was the second time Robbert Lukar had thought it that night, only the second time in his life. All of a sudden he was thinking of his father, watching from the Hall of Green. This was no way to go, stabbed in the face by such as him. The tip of the dagger was right there, right there above his eye, no more than a couple of inches away. He could see his death in it. See it reflecting in the tip. See the mists puffing, swirling up the length of the steel. Robbert Lukar had always thought he would die in battle, but not like this. Not by godsteel. Not by an Emerald Guard. Not by one of his own…

It should have been a dragon, he thought, *not a weasel.*

The thought fuelled him. With a final desperate effort he summoned his might and drove upward, once more, with his forearm, pushing his attacker away a few inches, but with a scream and shriek and shove, Gershan drove straight back down.

"I'm sorry…" the creature wept. "I'm so sorry…I didn't want…"

"Then don't! Don't! *Stop!*" The tears were welling in Robbert's eyes now, of the terror of death approaching. "Stop, Wenfry…stop…stop!"

His pleas went unheeded. The knight only pressed all the harder, to get it done. His face twisted at the sound of Robbert's desperate voice, as though unable to hear it, and he closed his eyes. A grimace filled his face, a grimace of effort and sorrow and fear as he drove the tip of the knife down, closer, closer. Robbert twisted at the hip, jerked, screamed out, but all for nought. He was pinned, trapped, with nowhere to go. The godsteel tip passed his brow, passed his lashes, seemed to kiss the very surface of his eye.

No…no…

Beyond it was a face twisted in agony. "It'll be quick…it'll be quick, my prince…I promise I'll make it quick. Just let go. Let go. Let it happen…let go…"

Robbert shut his eyes, unable to watch any longer. He felt the point of the dagger prick against the skin of his eyelid, piercing through, felt blood beading, spreading, felt the blade go deeper, deeper, cutting into the soft outer flesh of his eye…

His throat tore open in a blood-curdling scream, legs thrashing wildly.

"It's OK…it'll be over soon…just let go…please, *shhhhh, shhhhh*…just let go, my prince…"

He could feel the dagger slicing down, feel the hot blood bubbling up to pool in the socket.

"Shhhh, shhhh, just a moment more. Let go, just let go…you'll see your father again, my prince, let go…."

Something changed.

Suddenly and from nowhere.

It was the man's weight, at first, shifting a little, up and off him. There was a sudden *whooshing* sound as well, and then an instant *pinging*, like the noise an arrow makes as it glances against steel. Gershan gave a dumb grunt of surprise, and Robbert sensed his attacker looking up. Then the dagger slid out of his eye, right out, the cold steel withdrawing, the hot pain remaining.

716

A voice calling. From down the alley. "Hey…you…you…stop…."

Robbert Lukar opened his working right eye. Through blurred vision he saw his Wenfry Gershan staring down the lane, saw the knife hovering, dripping blood. It spattered against his cheek, his nose, his lips. He tasted it, the salt and iron. *My blood*, he thought. *Mine.*

From the depths of him came a primal fury, surging up like molten lava from the ground. Gershan's clamping posture had faltered, his weight shifted back, his attention drawn away. And Robbert seized his chance.

Twisting at the sternum, and with a sudden jerk of strength at the shoulder, he managed to release his pinned arm from beneath Gershans's knee. He closed a fist. The man looked down, mouth agape, eyes stained with craven tears. Dumbly he stared, as Robbert's closed gauntlet swung upward, and struck. The prince felt a sickening crunch of bone, felt the jaw and mouth and nose of Sir Wenfry Gershan crumble. His weight flew off him, right back off him, to land upon the cobbled stone.

"My lord…my lord…"

Robbert knew the voice. He did not look back, but scrambled to his feet, blood gushing from his eye, and leapt upon his foe. Feebly, whimpering, Sir Wenfry attempted to lift his blade to strike, but the prince swung and smashed it away to clatter against the alley wall. Gershan's mouth was full of splintered teeth, his jaw shattered, his face a concave ruin. Some sort of mumbly blubbering sound frothed up through what remained of his lips, as though pleading for mercy.

"Mercy? You want *mercy*?" Robbert roared. A knife was too good for him, lackey though he was. A gauntlet would do much better.

So down his fist came, down and down again, blood spraying, bone crunching. He struck and struck and struck in a maddened frenzy, again and again, until all that remained of Sir Wenfry Gershan's face was a pool of blood and bone and mulched red meat, sloshing inside his helm.

When he was finished, he stood and stumbled back, panting. He felt a hand steady him from behind, and spun. "He's dead, I think. Ten times over, I would say."

The girl, Saska's friend. Del was with her, looking at him in horror, his yew bow clutched in his grasp, shivering. "My lord…your…your eye."

"I have another," Robbert said, in a sharp grunt. He was trembling all over, the adrenaline rushing through his veins. He had to drop back down to one knee to steady himself.

"Del, water," the girl said.

"I…I don't have any."

"We passed a fountain along the way." The girl with the red armour helped lift him, guiding him along down an alley, turning down another. Del hurried to his other flank, bow raised in defence should someone come running, glancing over at Robbert all the while as the blood sept out of his eye to flood down his paling face.

"Who…who was that, my lord? He had a…a green cloak. Was he…"

"Hush now, Del," the girl said. "Now isn't the time for questions."

Robbert could hear the sound of fighting nearby, some way off.

"Bernie," he remembered suddenly. "Bernie…did you find him?" They must have. Del was here. *He must have been with him…*

"We found him," the girl said, though didn't elaborate. "Don't you worry about that just yet. We need to get that eye cleaned up."

Robbert let himself be drawn along, struggling to fully compose his thoughts. After a few more moments the girl spotted a dead man lying to one side against a wall, wearing what looked like an unspoilt brown cloak. Through his blurred vision Robbert could not tell who he was, but he was Tukoran for a certainty, a Huffort man maybe with that shade of brown. She darted quickly over and cut two lengths of it away with her dagger, stashed one strip under her breastplate, keeping the other to hand. A few seconds later she was turning them into a small inner courtyard with a fountain in the middle, tinkling softy. "Here we are."

More men had died here as well. A sunwolf lay sprawled to one side, filled with quarrels and arrows, with a long silver lance sticking out of its neck. Atop it lay his rider, killed by arrows as well. Robbert thought he recognised the man. *One of Krator's Sunriders*, he thought, though the name escaped him. Other Aramatian soldiers under the sunlord's charge had perished as well, in support of that Sunrider perhaps, and here too lay Aram city soldiers and men of House Hasham, their fine white scalemail signifying their worth and rank.

"You just ignore all that," the girl said, leading him over to sit on a stone bench, away from the worst of the death. He'd expected some reprimand about Aramatians killing Aramatians and how it was all partly his fault, but perhaps his blinded eye granted him clemency. "Right, just sit there. I'm going to get you cleaned up, OK?" She rushed over to the fountain, soaked the rag, and returned. "This is going to hurt, but we need to clean that out."

"It was godsteel," Robbert said, beginning to recover his wits. He blinked his good right eye, vision improving. "It won't get infected. Godsteel is too pure."

"I know. I'm worried about other contaminants on the blade. Dirt or blood, from someone else."

Robbert shook his head. "The blade was clean. Just…just wipe the blood away and bandage my head. I'll have it seen to properly later. But right now I need to get back to the fighting."

The girl paused. "You sure that's wise? Fighting with one eye…"

"I'll manage," he said, refusing to dwell on that. "I've seen men fight with one eye before. Good knights."

"As you say." She worked quickly, soaking up the blood such as she could, tossing the bloody rag aside and then taking out the clean strip she'd tucked behind her breastplate to wrap diagonally across his head, tightening and tying it. Robbert tried to ignore the pain, fight the urge to yell out in agony, but several shuddering grunts escaped him all the same. He could feel the blood soaking through the strip of cloth already, but as a temporary fix it would serve. "Right, all done. Hopefully that will help slow the bleeding."

"My thanks," Robbert said, standing. His legs still felt a little wobbly but would firm once he got them moving. She passed him his helm, to place back over his head, keeping his visor up. All the while Del had been watching the street, to give warning should someone come by, but no one had. *Small mercies*, Robbert Lukar thought. "I never got your name," he said to the girl.

"Leshie." She even did a little curtsey, bobbing up and down, armour rustling. "Pleased to meet you, my prince. And don't worry, you're still handsome, even with one eye."

He nodded, and the shadow of a smile passed his lips. Trauma was often best treated with humour, he knew. It was the Tukoran way, the warrior way. This diminutive, red-armoured girl called Leshie was both, that was clear. "You saved my life," he told her. "Both of you." He looked across at Del, and strode to where he stood on guard. "That was your arrow that struck him?"

The boy nodded at his toes. "I missed. If I'd hit him…"

"It wouldn't have made a difference. The damage was already done, and the distraction was enough. You'd only have denied me the pleasure of killing him myself." Robbert reached forward and gripped the boy's armoured arm in gratitude. "I won't forget this, Del. One day as my squire and you've already done more than I could ever have hoped for. Perhaps there was some fate in our meeting?"

"Fate," Leshie echoed, from behind them. "Oh, I could tell you a thing or two about fate. But now might not be the time." She gestured to where the fighting was fiercest, only a few short streets away. "If you want to find your friends still breathing, we'd best be off. Let me tell you, it's chaos out there."

Robbert took just a moment to recompose himself. The world had changed, suddenly and forever. Whatever he might say about one-eyed swordsmen, they were never the same after losing an eye. He'd have to be extra wary of unseen enemies and attacks to his left side now. His depth perception and sense of space would be compromised. A few minutes ago he'd been one of the most gifted fighters in Tukor. Now he was but a middling knight. *I'll never be my father*, came a sour and bitter thought.

He pushed all that side. He was alive, and that was more important. One-eyed, but alive, and more than capable of seeking his vengeance. It did not take much for him to know why Gershan had acted so treacherously. Every puppet had strings, after all, and a master pulling them in the shadows.

He followed the others down the alley, toward the fighting, closing a fist as he went. An unquenchable fury was filling him, driving off his woe, casting aside his pain.

Kill the targets, Sir Wenfry had said.

And all the while, I was one of them.

64

Amron

Amron Daecar put his shoulder to the door and marched inside the bedchamber. "Up," he bellowed. "Get him up and ready, right now!"

Two medics stood either side of Lord Dalton Taynar's bed, peeling off his bloody dressing and preparing to bandage him in a new one. A nurse stood by to aid them and there was another in the room as well, fussing over something beside a table topped with ointments and balms. All looked up when Amron entered, pale-faced and strained. The reason needed no explanation. Through a sliver of a window no wider than an arrow slit the song of battle could be heard outside; the screech of dragons, the whoosh of ballista bolts, the shouts of men upon the walls. King's Point was under siege.

"My lord," one of the physicians said, turning to face him. He was the same one Amron had dealt with before, he of the protuberant eyes and jittery voice. "Forgive me, but…the patient is under a great deal of medication. Roseweed, my lord, in strong quantities so he might sleep through the pain, and drakeshell for the…"

"Healing," Amron said. "And he's healed enough. I need the *patient* up and on his feet at once. Feed him whatever tonic you need to wake him. Death's Denial, if you have any. I need my First Blade, doctor."

"Death's Denial…yes, I believe we have some…" He glanced to the nurse at the table, who nodded in confirmation. "But my lord, please, you must be reasonable…"

"Reasonable? I said I would give you days, and I have."

"A day and change, Lord Daecar. It is not enough. Lord Taynar is in no state to fight."

"Let *him* be the judge of that. Now wake him up and do it quickly. If you haven't damn well noticed, this city is under attack."

He turned on his heels to leave the room, armour clanking, a cloak of House Daecar flowing at his back. Whitebeard stood outside, with Sir Ralf of Rotting Bridge. "Stay here, Ralf," Amron told him. "Make sure they get

Dalton up within the next ten minutes. I want him in his armour and down by the River Gate by the time I get there. With the bloody Sword of Varinar at his hip."

"And if he refuses to fight, my lord?"

"He won't. Say what you will about Dalton Taynar, but he would fight one-legged if he had to. Men take wounds in battle, Ralf, and fight on. The adrenaline will see him through."

The old man nodded. "As you command, my lord."

Amron continued up the steps of the Spear, Rogen Whitebeard at his back, garbed in his dark grey plate and cloak of faded black. After another dozen turns they reached the summit. Amron pushed through the door and out onto the tower battlements. Noise assaulted him at once; shouts of command, the grinding of the ballistas on their turntables, the spring of the mechanisms as they fired out into the night. There were four here, one facing in each direction, the highest defensive weapons in the city. Each of them was covered in a protective shelter, godsteel laced and oiled against fire. The same went for the parapet wall where stood at least a score of archers, firing through the crenels with godsteel-tipped arrows, a protective awning above them.

Sir Torus Stoutman stepped over, the cheeks above his bushy beard flushed red from the sting of the wind, blowing fiercely up so high. "Madness up here, madness, I say." There was a strange joy in this voice, the sort of thrill that fills the hearts of men born for days like this. "Just watched that tower over yonder fall, Amron," he said, pointing with a stubby steel finger. "Seaman's Tower, one of these archers called it. Three dragons took it down. Quite the spectacle it was."

It was a defensive tower in the southwestern corner of the city, a lesser tower than the Spear to be sure, but a stout construction all the same topped with two strong ballistas of its own. Amron peered that way and saw the flames licking up from the tumbled stone, saw the soldiers there dragging men from the rubble as a dragon flew a circle about them, spitting down streams of flame. It was driven off by archers a moment later, but not before setting several men alight.

Elsewhere other fires were raging. Amron scanned the southern walls and towers facing the sea. Red Watch Tower had fires pouring from its windows and the Eye of Amron, the tall spindly lighthouse perched upon a thrust of land within the bay, had been toppled. Though a lighthouse, Amron had placed some bowmen there. It was a suicide mission, in truth, though the men had gone forth to see to their duty willingly all the same. *Brave men,* Amron thought. *Hopefully they surprised a dragon or two before they fell.* That had been the idea.

"The Hangman's is about to come down," Stoutman was going on. "Teetering at the base, that one. Looks like an old drunk swaying down an alley. A few more fiery kisses and it'll fall." He gave a laugh. "The rest are in decent order, though. Forget all their names. The Black Lance. Bowman's Bluff. Another about a maiden or some sort…"

"The Merry Maiden," came a call from one of the men.

"Aye, that's it. Sounds more like a brothel than a tower to me, but I didn't name the bloody things."

"It was named for King Amron the Bold's wife," Amron Daecar told him. "She was a merry woman, the histories say."

"Aye, but not a maiden, leastways not once that big ugly king got through with her." He laughed again, thoroughly enjoying himself, then said, "Oh, we got a dragon as well, my lord. Well, *they* did, not me, these fine ballista men here. Caught it in the head with a five-foot bolt, and sent it spinning off onto the streets. Take a look. You can see its carcass down there now. The bolt's still stuck through its skull."

Amron looked and saw the carcass. It had landed in a sprawl on the steps of the King's Point courthouse, smashing through a balcony on the way down to scatter stone across the street. A host of swordsmen and pikemen had gathered around it, prodding to make sure it was dead. A five-foot bolt to the brain would usually do it, especially for a smaller dragon like this one. Amron observed a saddle on the dragon's back, though could not see a rider down there.

When he asked, Sir Torus said, "He was flung from the beast's back on the way down. Didn't see where he landed, though. No matter, he's dead sure as a whorehouse will have whores."

Amron continued to scan the city fortifications. As expected, the assault had begun under cover of dark, though it had not been as sudden as it might have been, owing to the clear skies and plentiful stars, giving them ample warning to prepare as the bells and horns rang out. From the starry skies the shadows had plunged down, though unlike what Elyon had told them of the Bane, the assault had been less focused, more widespread, targeting every tower and fortified position at once as though to overwhelm them quickly. It had proven a miscalculation. With their strength dispersed, three dragons had been slain almost at once, one felled by the archers at Red Watch, another by a brace of scorpion bolts from Hangman's, a third by a host of men atop the walls when the beast had flown down to scatter them with its talons. The men had been prepared with chains and lances, throwing up the former to tangle it, stabbing it dead with the latter.

After that it was familiar chaos. Amron had spent it marching from place to place, roaring orders, sending men to deliver them to his commanders and his captains. Down by the River Gate, tens of thousands were bustling, the army in camp beyond the walls brought inside in preparation. By night they could do little. By daylight it was different. *If these new Fireborn have any honour at all, they'll meet the challenge when we give it*, Amron thought.

Sir Torus Stoutman completed his updates in his own inimitable way, thrusting his pipe between his lips between each piece of news, smoke swirling to the skies in happy little puffs. Amron had wanted a reliable man up here to give report, and Torus had been that man. He wondered now if he might have chosen someone better. Even now, Stoutman saw a joke in half of what he said.

When the man was done, Amron asked of his son. "Any sightings, Torus? Any signals from the other towers?"

"Think Seaman's was trying to signal us when she fell, though that might have just been the dragonfire." He grinned.

Another man stepped over, a Bladeborn archer with a black tower against an orange sky on his breast, the Brockenhurst colours and arms. "We had a signal from the Eye of Amron before she came down, my lord," he said, in a clear voice, giving Sir Torus a sideward glance to suggest he, too, was weary of his japing. This archer was clearly a captain, by the pin that held his cloak; an arrow piercing a dragon's head. *Most appropriate,* Amron thought. "The fleet is closing," the man went on. "No more than an hour or so away, and that was some half an hour ago. We should see them on the water at any moment."

The sun would rise about then as well; already the light in the east was changing. "Thank you, captain. And my son?"

"Nothing, sire."

Amron nodded. "Back to your post."

The man withdrew, calling orders to the others as he paced back over to the tower battlements. Amron scanned the skies, wondering if Elyon was out there, fighting. He would not put it past him to have returned a while ago, only to get caught up in the battle. He closed a steel fist, eager for the same. Defending a city from aerial attacks was frustrating for a man of terrestrial constraints. This was the dominion of archers and scorpions, not soldiers armed with swords.

Soon, he thought. *When the fleet arrives, they'll storm the shore and rush through the breaches the dragons have made.* Torus had informed him during his report that the fall of Seaman's Tower had broken a section of wall in the southwest corner, and that the dragons had been targeting a particular stretch between Red Watch and the Merry Maiden too, east of the harbour gate. The smoke was too thick down there now to see much of the damage, though according to the stout knight it was considerable. By now it might be a full breach, permitting an easy way into the city.

Amron took his leave, marching back down the steps only to find that Torus Stoutman was right behind him. "Did I say you could leave your post?"

"You didn't say I couldn't. And I'll be damned if I stand up there twiddling my thumbs when there's fighting to be had below. I plan to fight side by side with my sons, Amron. We'll take down a dragon, you'll see."

I probably won't see, Amron thought. No doubt he'd be engaged in battles of his own. *Though I'll most certainly hear about it after.*

He hoped that would be the case, anyway. *After* was never a guarantee, and the fighting was certain to be savage. Of that he could be quite sure. When they reached the room of Lord Dalton Taynar halfway down the tower they found him groggily being filled in by Sir Ralf of Rotting Bridge as he sat on the edge of his bed. "...they're here...al...already?" the man was saying, blinking and rubbing at his forehead. He wore nothing but linen hose, his entire top half exposed, lean to the bone and gristly. Amron had never seen a man so pale. *His skin is as white as that dressing on his gut. This man could be mistaken for a Snowskin.* "I should...I

723

should dress," Lord Dalton went on. "My armour. Where is my armour?"

"It is stored in the next room," Amron said, stepping inside. "Rogen, Torus, please fetch it."

"Amron," Dalton said, looking at him through bleary eyes. "Sir Ralf says…he says…"

"The dragons are here, my lord. Your army is assembled below, awaiting your pleasure."

"My army?" He took a moment to remember that most of the men here were sworn to Taynar banners. "Yes, yes of course." He stood uneasily. Old Sir Ralf reached out to steady him. "I'm OK, Sir Ralf, I'm OK." Dalton Taynar drew a long breath into his lungs, blew it out, and sucked in another. His eyes turned to the slitted window. Through the thick stone of the Spear, the din of the assault reached his ears. He seemed to be noticing it for the first time.

Just how much damn roseweed was he given? Amron thought. He gave the medics a hard look, and saw them dip their eyes. *This is a Bladeborn greatlord, the First Blade of Vandar, not some lily-livered weakling. Minimal medication would have been enough.* He saw no need to reproach them publicly. *What's done is done. We move on.*

Torus and Rogen reappeared with the fine trunk bearing the First Blade's armour and blades. Mist poured out at its opening, and they began withdrawing his plate. "Ought I summon your squire?" Amron asked.

It was a test. So far as he knew, Dalton Taynar had no squire. The man had to think a moment before answering. "Unless one was appointed to me as I slept, I am without a squire, my lord." His faculties were returning, at least. "How long was I out?"

"Less than two days."

Dalton Taynar put a hand to his gut, where he'd been stabbed, prodding gently as though to test the pain. The Death's Denial they'd used to wake him would work against the roseweed in his blood, a matter confirmed when the Lord of House Taynar gave a wince of discomfort. "Two days. I can tell."

"Pain is good," Sir Ralf was quick to tell him. "It'll sharpen your mind during battle, my lord."

Dalton nodded in a way that said he knew the benefits of pain. "I'd sooner be without a gaping hole in my gut," he said, clenching his teeth. He poked once more at the wound, at which point the bug-eyed medic burst forth to say, "My lord, you ought not press so hard. The flesh is still very tender and the sutures could easily break."

Lord Dalton gave him a sour look. "Battle will break them, you can be sure of that. Don't fret over my fingers, doctor." He gave a dour grunt. "Did you catch him?" he asked Amron. "The intruder."

No, he thought. *We have much more pressing matters.* "Inquiries are still being made."

"It was Oloran. Or one of his pets. *Steelheart*," he sneered. "I want his head, Amron. Both of them. I want their heads served to me on a platter."

Amron let him rant, but only for a moment. His face betrayed his lack of interest in indulging the lord his grievances at this time. "Later," he merely said, in a voice that brooked no further discussion on the matter. "For now we have a battle to fight, my lord. I would spend what energy I have on that."

Dalton Taynar assented with a low growl, but assent he did.

"Sir Ralf, help Lord Taynar into his armour. Torus, you as well."

"I can don my own armour."

"It'll be quicker with help. And we need this done quickly. I shall meet you down by the River Gate, Lord Taynar. And remember to bring your blade."

He turned and left, Rogen Strand following him out the door, his silent shadow.

Going up and down the steps of the Spear was busy work, and time consuming. Amron was done with it. The sun was soon to rise and as soon as it did, he would be upon the front lines, doing what he did best. As he reached the main hall at the foot of the tower, he sighted the strong youthful form of Sir Adam Thorley marching in from the open courtyard outside with six men of the Pointed Watch at his heels. As soon as he saw Amron he hurried over. The men converged at the heart of the hall.

"What news, Sir Adam?"

The commander of the watch gave a perfunctory bow, observing the courtesies even now. "Dire news, my lord. The wall is breached, between the Merry Maiden and…"

"Red Watch," Amron cut in. "I know. The dragons have been targeting that section, Sir Torus said."

"They have, my lord. I can't say why; there's no particular weakness there, but it makes no matter. The wall is down. I've ordered men there at once to try you seal the gap, but the dragons will continue to target it. Widen it, even. There are too many of them to fend off forever. We can be sure the enemy will flood through that way when they land ashore."

That and a half dozen others, at this rate. "I'm heading for the River Gate now, Sir Adam. I'll have a strong garrison sent to defend it."

"Very good, my lord. The Black Lance is also under terrible siege, and Hangman's is set to fall. If they both come down, we'll have lost all our defensive towers in the west of the city. Seaman's has fallen already, you may know."

"I saw from the tower battlements. How are our defences faring at the harbour?" He had despatched the man there to take account of things.

The young commander gave a grim shake of the head. "Not well. Our ships at anchor have all been burned and half our catapults destroyed. Lord Florian and the Twins are still standing, however. The dragons are having a hard time getting at them behind the walls."

Lord Florian was not, of course, a reference to the young Lord of King's Point, but a towering trebuchet erected in his name, flanked by a pair of others just behind the harbour wall at intervals and in places of strategic benefit. Their purpose was to fling rocks and barrels of pitch at incoming ships, sinking or burning them before they might land ashore or have time to empty their men into rowboats and skiffs. If even one of them was still standing by the time the fleet came in, Amron Daecar would count himself surprised. *Towers first, then trebuchets*, he thought. The dragons would disable them soon, he did not doubt.

Sir Adam continued his report, updating him on losses of men and siege weapons upon the walls. Amron listened, nodding. It seemed another two dragons had been felled. One had been struck by a lucky shot from a catapult, momentarily disorienting the beast, to send it crashing into the harbour wall. "A dozen crossbowmen and spearmen finished it off," Sir Adam said. The other had been snared by a net of hempen rope fired by a specialised type of ballista, a weapon that tended to work best on smaller dragons. Once the beast had landed in a tangled heap, the spearmen had descended before it might break loose.

"Where they ridden?" Amron asked.

"One. Not the other. The one caught in the net was saddled, my lord."

"And the Fireborn rider?"

"Dead. Took a spear to the throat."

Amron nodded. He wanted to take at least one of them alive for questioning, if possible. "That makes six." That he knew of anyway. More dragons might have fallen elsewhere; King's Point was a large city. "For the loss of less than a thousand men." He had given a speech to the entire army on the eve of battle, only hours ago. "Make them bleed," had been his central point. "I want to see dead dragons falling from the skies."

Six was a fine start, and there were heroes out there already. *Let's make a hundred more*, he thought.

As Sir Adam concluded his report, a commotion sounded from the depths of the hall and Lady Anne Brockenhurst came storming up the steps from the sanctuary forged beneath the castle. She was swatting away the beseeching attentions of Lord Stanley Warton as she went. The Castellan of the Spear was no fighting man and had been ordered below by Amron to keep watch of the women, children, old and infirm who had not yet left the city. Clearly the Pointed Lady had broken through his defences. "….away with you, Stanley, leave me alone," the woman was saying. "I only want to find out what…ah, Lord Daecar!' She bustled right over before he could flee her, in high stiff collar and fox-fur coat. "I'm glad you're here. Please tell me what's happening. I've a hundred weeping women below and they're all desperate for news of their husbands and sons."

Amron had no time for her. "The battle is young, my lady. Go back down and tell them so."

"That's it? That's all you'll give me? The battle is young?"

"There is nothing else to say." He stepped away, nodding for Sir Adam to deal with her. At the same time he gave a gesture for Lord Warton to join him as he strode toward the double doors leading out onto the courtyard. Light was starting to fill the skies now, a predawn glow, red as blood.

"Lord Daecar, I'm so sorry about that…she managed to slip past and

I...I..." He gave a throaty cough, an affliction that simply did not go away. Always was the man coughing. "I had no means to...to stop her..."

"Take her back down, Lord Warton. And make preparations to leave. If the city should fall, every last man, woman and child will be slaughtered. It is important that you make that clear to Lady Anne."

"I...I will, my lord," the old castellan nodded, still coughing. "Is that... likely? The city falling?"

Likely? No. "It is almost certain, my lord."

"C-certain?"

He saw no reason to lie to this man. Amron had always known that the city would fall eventually; Dragon's Bane had proven that. It was just a matter of when, and how much enemy blood they could spill before it did. "We are outnumbered and outmatched, Lord Warton," he said, "and will soon be overwhelmed. We will fight on only until such a time as I see benefit in the defence. But at some point I must make the decision to retreat, or face a rout. If you can rally Lady Anne and the others to leave now, all the better. Take the tunnels, flee upriver, and make at once for Crosswater. The longer you wait, the more of you will die."

The small old man stared up at him, mouth agape. "But the...if we flee, my lord...Lady Anne, she fears that the dragons will hunt us on the river or on the road. These walls are the only thing...the only thing protecting us."

"Nothing can protect you forever, Lord Warton. Not these walls. Not this army. Not me. There is still some darkness remaining, and the dragons will be busy with us for a while yet. If you leave now, you may go unnoticed. But do not delude yourself into thinking that the Agarathi will take you as hostages, should the city fall. They have no need of such. You will burn, my lord, all of you. You'd be better taking your chances on the road."

The man had gone pale as milk, all colour leeching from his skin. Amron put a hand on his shaking shoulder, then turned to walk away.

The blood-red skies were ominous, shadows passing high overhead, screeching. Rumbles sounded across the city as the dragons belched out their flame, strong enough to reduce rock to ruin. Regular buildings crumbled quickly under such an assault, undone by the explosive magic within that unearthly dragonfire. Thicker walls and towers stood much longer, those supported and infused with godsteel in particular, but even those would not stand forever. Already Amron Daecar could hear the booming sounds above as the Spear itself was targeted, see the spouts of flame lighting up the skies as the dragons swept past through the billowing smoke.

Ash was falling from the skies, capering like grey snow against the crimson dawn. Amron marched through the courtyard, bordered by its pillared colonnade, and through the gates of the castle. The guards there held their spears tight, nervously gazing skyward. Several bowed as Amron passed; a few more gave salute. He heard whispers of 'Varin Reborn' as he strode westward down the street in the direction of the River Gate.

Other soldiers were rushing here and there in their squads and units, bearing a variety of colours and sigils on their surcoats, hauberks, capes and cloaks and the various armour they wore; leather, studded and boiled, shirts of mail, rusted and glittering, steel, dinted and damaged or polished to a brand new shine. Much godsteel was in evidence as well, though none wore full suits of it. Those were rare. Only a dozen or so men in the entire city were garbed head to heel in godsteel plate.

Several of those were gathered at the River Gate and up on the battlements above. As soon as Amron entered the square, he saw the giant form of Sir Taegon Cargill standing with the sons of Torus Stoutman, and a number of other knights and men-at-arms sworn to his house. *He'll kill a dragon tonight, that one*, Amron thought. Every time he saw the giant, he said as much, fuelling his confidence, making him believe. By the look on his face, the Varin Knight was ready.

"Lord Daecar," he boomed, bowing. "Have you come to lead the defence?"

"I have, Sir Taegon. The fleet is incoming."

His huge head was housed within a helm extravagantly crested with a warhammer crushing the head of a dragon; his house sigil. It nodded. "We heard the call from the walls, my lord. A thousand ships on the water. Rasalan has failed us."

They had hoped for storms to dash the fleet, but alas no, it hadn't happened. "We cannot rely on the gods, Sir Taegon."

"Says the man bearing a shard of one's heart." The giant was not exactly comely, but there was something endearing about his smile, big and broad and filled with bucket-sized teeth. "I'll rely on that, Lord Daecar. On *you*."

"Better to rely on yourself, Sir Taegon. You know what I want from you tonight?"

He thumped his chest, steel clanging against steel. "Make this house sigil of mine a reality." He bore a greatsword, massive and misting, as well as a warhammer of glowing godsteel, a rare weapon borne by the greatest warrior of his house. "Hasn't been a Cargill dragonslayer for two hundred years. Plan to change that tonight."

"I know you will."

Amron gave the sons of Stoutman a nod in turn, then continued through the crowds. Within the square, enormous rippling pavilions had been thrown up, partly to obscure them, partly to offer protection from dragonfire, the canvas coated and greased with special Rasalanian fireproof oils. Huge numbers of soldiers bustled beneath them, with swords and spears and shields. The men made way for him, saluting and bowing as he passed. About himself Amron Daecar had coated a slim film of frost, melting and misting colourfully as he strode forth. It was Walter Selleck's notion. "Makes you look divine, Amron," he'd said. "Use it to inspire them." He deemed it a reasonable idea.

When he reached the gatehouse, he passed the iron doors and strode up to the wall walk, entering the chaos. Along the battlements, he saw Lythian shouting orders with Sir Storos Pentar alongside him, archers ducking and firing from the crenels, spearmen flinging pikes and lances to the skies. The tower known as Bowman's Bluff stood at the southeast corner of the city walls a hundred metres away, a chunky drumtower almost as wide as it was tall. From its hundred windows and arrow slits bowmen were firing at the dragons that assaulted it, and from the summit ballistas swung about on their turntables flinging thick bolts through the air. Along one side the tower was creaking, the rock smashed and scorched, and there were fires inside as well, some of the windows spitting out flames instead of arrows.

"It'll come down any moment," Amron said to Rogen Whitebeard as they marched along the fortifications.

The ranger looked south, beyond the walls, "The fleet, my lord."

Amron saw it, the enemy armada arrayed along the waters, filling the sea from east to west. Colours of black and red waved at them from great billowing sails, soaring from a forest of masts. The fleet went deep, row after row of warships bobbing toward them on the waves. Already some were approaching the harbour, swift galleys drawn along by oar not sail. Amron could see the soldiers bustling on deck, emptying into smaller rowboats. Some of the larger ships had spotted free jetties where they might land and were making for those with all haste.

Amron grabbed at a passing soldier. "Take a message to the Ironfoot," he commanded. "You'll find him in the square below. There's a breach at Seaman's Tower, in the southwestern corner. Tell him to muster his men to defend it." He'd need a strong man for that charge, and there were few as stout and defiant as Lord Gavron Grave the Ironfoot. "And go to Lord Rosetree as well. There's a hole between the Merry Maiden and Red Watch that needs plugging. That's his. Go. Now." The man nodded, spun, and hurried off.

"Will they listen to you?" Whitebeard asked. "Those are Taynar lords."

I know who they are. "They're Vandarian lords." He continued down the battlements until he reached Lythian, drawing the Frostblade from its sheath as he went, thickening the coat of frozen armour he wore atop his plate. He left his dark blue cloak unfrosted to flap and beat at his back. "Lythian," he roared, over the clamour. The Knight of the Vale turned to him at once. His Varin cloak was badly scorched and his armour was blackened in places too, though it was nothing that a bit of spit and polish wouldn't sort. The man flipped up his visor, golden eyes glittering with a look Amron Daecar hadn't seen in two decades. *He was born for this, as I was.* "Dragons, Lythian. How many?"

"I've seen two fall, Amron. Maybe a third. It was badly injured but flew away, so I'm not sure. As to numbers…dozens, scores. I can't say. Might be a hundred of them out there. Might be more."

"Ridden?" Amron asked.

Lythian opened his mouth to speak, but was cut off as a dragon swept over the walls, screeching, spouting flame, and they ducked away to cover by the parapet. They watched the beast pass, hunted by bolts and arrows and spears as it ascended back into the skies. Then Lythian said, "Most of them, yes. That I've seen anyway. But they're newly bonded, untrained and inexperienced. These aren't like the Fireborn we're used to."

They stood again. A hundred archers were nocking and firing along the wall to left and right as Sir Storos called out commands. In places the crenelations had been blasted apart, merlons missing to widen the embrasures. Bits of rock and stone were scattered everywhere the dead men too, burned and broken.

"Have you seen Elyon?" Amron asked.

"Not yet. But I saw Marak. He flew past on Garlath. I'm sure it was him. He was calling your name."

"My name? In what regard?"

"Challenge," Lythian said. "He knows your death will wound us."

"As his will wound them. I'll meet his challenge." Amron still remembered his father Gideon's blackened body, remembered the stories men said of how Lord Ulrik Marak had laughed as he slew him and King Storris at the Battle of Burning Rock. Lythian claimed otherwise. He'd spent time with Ulrik Marak in the Western Neck and spoke of him in fond terms, but Amron Daecar cared not. Marak was his enemy, his rival, and his death would do a great deal to weaken the Agarathi assault. This was not an opportunity to be missed.

He met his friend's eyes. "The fleet is coming, Lythian. When they come ashore, go out and meet them. You're wasted upon this wall."

Lythian had an uncertain look in his eye. "And you? Where are you to be?"

"Outside, waiting for you. With the corpse of Garlath the Grand at my feet."

65

Lythian

He heard the command go out for the River Gate to open, and alone onto the field strode the greatlord Amron Daecar. Confidently he walked, clad in steel and ice, glistening, gleaming, misting in a hundred hues. Shouts went out from the square below, and from the walls as well, where half the bowmen were watching.

"What's he doing?"

"He's to fight the enemy alone?"

"He cannot defeat them all."

But others were not so pessimistic. "King Amron!" someone suddenly bellowed, an archer not far along the battlements, and "The Crippler of Kings!" roared another, and a moment later a thunderous voice that could only have been Taegon Cargill's echoed from down in the square, booming, "Varin Reborn! Varin Reborn! Varin Reborn! Varin Reborn!" as a hundred voices, a thousand, ten thousand joined him in the chant.

The noise was deafening, defiant and stirring, and as he walked from the gates Amron Daecar raised a fist in salute, and the chanting only grew louder.

"Goodness, what a sight," Sir Storos Pentar exhaled. A smile of wonder lit his eyes. "Varin Reborn indeed."

"He should not fight alone," countered the ranger Whitebeard, watching from Lythian's other flank. "It is lunacy to risk himself like this."

"It is nobility," Storos countered. "It is the honour of the duel, ranger. All Bladeborn knights know this."

"I am not a knight. Your ways are mysterious to me."

This shouldn't be happening at all, was all Lythian Lindar thought. Always had he subscribed to the chivalric rivalry between Fireborn and Bladeborn, the sacred duel between fang and steel, but in this case he saw only woe in the clash. *They should not be fighting. These men should be on the same side.*

For a moment the siege seemed to stop, as Amron Daecar strode out across the coastal plains, roaring out the name of 'Marak!' as he went. To the right of him lay the open sea, filled with ships and sails beyond count; to his left the evacuated encampment where the Taynar army had been housed. In the southeast corner of the high city walls, the massive drum-tower called Bowman's Bluff was burning badly now. Lythian could see more fire through the windows than archers, and one whole wall had completely caved in, yet of dragons there were suddenly none to be seen. The whole world seemed to be holding its breath.

And then, from somewhere nearby, a shout. "Garlath! It's Garlath the Grand!"

And from the skies, he came.

Lythian sensed the collective intake of breath as the massive dragon flapped out through the bloody gold dawn, the biggest that anyone here - save those who had witnessed the mighty Vallath during the war - had ever seen. Garlath had always been hated across Vandar for slaying King Storris Reynar and Gideon Daecar at the Burning Rock, and there was something sacrilegious about the colour of his scales that made him all the more despised. "Blue and bloody silver!" growled a spearmen. "Who does he think he is? Vandarian!"

Others issued similar sentiments, though most of those went unheard as the clamorous chanting resumed, changing now from *Varin Reborn*, to the more simple and truthful 'Daecar! Daecar! Daecar!' as the Champion of Frosts stood confronting his foe.

Lythian's heart was hammering at his ribs. The last he had seen of Lord Marak was at the Nest, the day the Fire Father had come down to take him under his spell, the same as Talasha and Sa'har Nakaan and Sotel Dar as well. *He came upon the back of Garlath,* Lythian thought, remembering that despairing day, when he'd stood rooted to the stone and paralysed, unarmored and unarmed, unable to do anything as the men he had come to admire, as the woman he had come to love, were summoned by the will of their master. For decades Marak had been bonded to Garlath, but after his awakening, Eldur had taken the dragon for his own. "I have broken that tether, Ulrik," Lythian remembered the demigod saying, in that unearthly whispered voice of his. "In time, perhaps I will restore it. But for now, I have need of him."

It seems it has been restored, Lythian thought.

Garlath the Grand was not the only thing that had been returned to Ulrik Marak, however. About his broad and bulky frame was clad the Body of Karagar armour, the very scales of the monstrous beast Karagar, son of Drulgar, slain by Varin at the Battle of Ashmount. That armour was as strong as any godsteel, it was said, ancient and unyielding as the dragons of old had been, and in his grasp Marak held the Fireblade, a weapon so rarely seen it was thought by some to be mythical.

Its reveal brought a nervous murmur to a hundred lips. The singers like to sing of it during their ballads, and everyone had heard the tales. "It can cut clean through godsteel," a man said nearby, in a hushed voice. "I heard it's as strong as the Sword of Varinar," said another, breathing heavily. "Ilith made it," a third put in. "He made it as a gift for the dark demigod.

Forged it by the very Breath of Agarath. Soaked the Fire God's magic in the steel, he did."

I've seen the Breath of Agarath, Lythian might have said. *I've journeyed to the very depths of the mountain where Eldur lay in slumber. I saw Drulgar the Dread made stone, a titan in a tomb, bigger than you'll ever believe.* He might have said a hundred other things, but instead he said nothing at all. It was left to Sir Storos to put them straight.

"The Fireblade is little better than a regular godsteel sword," he told the men. "It's no match for the Frostblade and Marak's no match for Lord Daecar. Just wait. He'll kill the dragonlord and dragon both."

The men continued muttering among themselves, transfixed on the standoff occurring out beyond the walls. "Will he fight him blade to blade, do you think?" one asked. "Frost against Fire, wouldn't that be a thing."

"No," Sir Storos said at once. "That would be folly. His only chance is through the dragon."

"But the Fireblade…"

"Is but a blade, as I said. Lord Daecar would destroy him in a dozen moves if he's fool enough to stand before him."

The men muttered on, exchanging theories, squinting against the rising sun as it crept up and over the horizon, casting a glow upon the Steelrun River where it emptied into the Red Sea. *Silver and red*, Lythian thought. *Steel and blood.* Amron was raising the Frostblade now in challenge; the sword seemed to glow with a light of its own, brilliant colours bursting from its edge. An almighty roar gave out from the men on the battlements, and a mightier one followed as Garlath the Grand spread his enormous silver-blue wings, almost a hundred and fifty feet from tip to tip, and unleashed a thunderous bellow, rolling out across the world.

Beneath all that Lythian heard a low growl to his left. "My lord, I think the impasse is about to end." It was Whitebeard, in his rasping voice. Lythian nodded; it certainly felt that way. But it seemed the approaching duel was not what Rogen was referring to. "No, my lord." He gestured to the southern skies. Several dragons were fast descending upon Bowman's Bluff, wings flapping, chests glowing, the capes of their riders whipping in the wind.

Lythian ripped his eyes from the standoff at once. "Dragons to the south!" he bellowed, his voice piercing through the tumult. "To the south! Prepare to fire! Nock arrows! Nock!" Half the bowmen were still looking down at Amron and Ulrik Marak, unaware of the impending threat. "Nock!" Lythian repeated, louder. "Nock! Dragons incoming! Nock! Prepare to fire!"

He rushed down the wall walk, heading in the direction of the tower, calling the men to action, and slammed his faceplate down. Arrows began spitting out from the windows and loopholes of Bowman's Bluff as the men there saw the beasts coming, and the two remaining ballistas on the roof swung about to take aim. "Ready! Ready on my command!" Lythian shouted. Sir Storos came with him, shouting for the men to take heed. "Ready! Ready! Fire at my order!"

The three approaching dragons separated into a pincer pattern, two arcing around the tower in different directions, one high, one low, the third raining fire over the top. That one took a bolt to the right wing for the trouble, shredding through the webbing, and went veering off and away over the city. The others circled, filling the tower with flame as they went. Lythian heard screams go up from the archers as they were burned to death inside, and then suddenly the walls were crumbling and giving way, the top of the tower collapsing onto the bottom as the buttresses and supports twisted and bent, melted by the heat of the blaze.

"Fire!" Lythian roared, as one of the dragons flew over their position. "Fire!" And a hundred arrows were loosed. Most merely glanced away off the beast's scaly hide, or went pinging into horns and spikes protruding from its shoulders and neck. Others struck at gullet and maw and underbelly, cutting deep. The dragon let out a dreaded shriek and wheeled around, enraged. "Nock!" he shouted. "Nock! On my command!"

The beast descended, its wide maw opening to bathe them all in fire, but Lythian bellowed, "Loose!" and a hundred more arrows flew for its open jaws. Steel and godsteel alike ripped through the soft red flesh of its mouth and the dragon stuttered, screaming, tried to twist away but too fast, and lost its balance. "Fire at will! Fire at will!" Lythian shouted. Shafts plunged deep into the dragon's face, neck, one even striking it dead in the eye. The beast jerked aside and came crashing right down atop them on the battlements, causing men to scatter and leap away. Lythian himself was on it at once, surging forth with his godsteel longsword to grasp, thrusting at its neck. Others drove forth with spears and axes, jabbing and hacking in a frenzy.

It was quick work, and had to be. Even down and disorientated, a dragon was a fearsome foe, and one flick of its tail could send a score of men flying from the walls. This one was of moderate size, a strong lithe beast with scales of blue and brown. They killed it quickly, Lythian cutting it open at the neck as thick blood, almost black in the early dawn light, gushed forth to smear the stone.

Sir Storos gave out a cheer, and his men raised bows and swords aloft in triumph. It was a small victory. Even as the men were cheering, a great grinding and rending of stone filled the air, and Lythian's eyes dashed back to the drumtower as it fell in and collapsed upon itself. Smoke poured up, spewing violently from the wreckage as the bulk of the massive tower teetered and fell away westward, crashing against the city walls, knocking away great chunks of stone, opening a hole to the world outside.

Lythian could see right through the breach. See the dromonds and low-slung longships already driving forward to land upon the shore. See the oars thrashing the waters white. See the rams built into the front of the boats smashing up through the rocks and bollards and sharpened wooden stakes erected along the strand. There was no harbour here in the east of the city, no jetties and wharves, only open coast, and the defences were meagre. At once enemy soldiers began leaping out into the shallow waters, wading through the surf. Others threw rope ladders from the front of the ships and climbed down onto dry land. Arrows and bolts flew out to meet them, fired by the men from the top of the bastions. It wasn't enough. For every man pegged by an arrow, ten more made it ashore, and behind came another hundred as the ships kept rolling in.

Lythian rushed to the parapet. "Breach at Bowman's Bluff!" he called out to the hordes below. "The tower is down! The wall is breached!" There was so much noise that few seemed to hear him, but he caught sight of Sir Quinn Sharp down there and managed to get his attention. "Sir Quinn! Breach at Bowman's! The tower is down!" He pointed, and as he did so a warhorn wailed, and Sir Quinn put it all together and mustered a host for the defence, sprinting off south through the streets.

Lythian spun. More boats were beaching along the bay where the Steelrun ran into the sea, ten of them, thirty, fifty seeming to land at once. Thousands of men poured off, screaming and hollering, giving out their warcries. Not all were Agarathi. Lythian saw some men of the Empire as well, saw ships with sails in silver and gold and bronze, saw moons and stars and suns stitched onto sails, saw glittering copper armour, dazzling in the dawn, and feathered cloaks, and even some riders of sun and star as well, leaping from the decks on their giant cats and wolves.

"Sir Storos," Lythian shouted. "Rogen. On me." He heard Storos mustering his own men, calling Sir Oswin Cole and the others to follow. Lythian marched along the battlements and down the steps behind the wall, through the door of the gatehouse, into the bustle of bodies below. Men in misting steel were awaiting him. Sir Taegon Cargill. Sir Ramsey Stone. Sir Rodmond Taynar. Lords Kindrick and Barrow were here as well, and the three disgraced Greycloaks, Sir Alyn Porter, Sir Nathaniel Oloran and Sir Gerald Strand, Rogen's older, fatter brother. All wore godsteel plate and mail, Bladeborn men of rich blood and breeding, trained from the cradle until this day, where they would likely meet the grave.

Lythian lifted his faceplate and looked every man in the eye. Out through the gate, the duel was raging, and south at the sea, the horde was coming. Behind the lords and knights stood men in their thousands, filling the square and streets beyond. It was not the best and bravest Vandar could offer, but it would do. Only one man was absent. "Where is Lord Taynar?"

He arrived on cue, striding forth with the Sword of Varinar at his hip, the men making way as he came. Sir Torus Stoutman walked with him, and Sir Ralf of Rotting Bridge. The old man's eyes were set. *A warrior's eyes,* Lythian thought. *This man has seen it all.*

"My lord," Lythian said, to Dalton Taynar. "You are right on time."

The man looked pale as milk, but his eyes showed steel. "I'm glad to have you with me, Captain Lythian," he said. He peered out, seeing Amron in the midst of battle out there. "Is that…"

"Garlath," said Torus Stoutman. "Best leave him to Lord Daecar, my lord. That dragon would eat us mere mortals for breakfast."

It seemed to Lythian that the dwarfish knight had said it only to ignite Dalton's pride. The greatlord's eyes hardened yet further, his mouth clamped down in a grimace, and he reached up to shut his visor. Then drawing the Sword of Varinar from its sheath, he raised it aloft, casting a golden glow upon the army, and shouted, "For Vandar! For Vandar! For Vandar!"

As before, the chant rang out.

And from the gates came a storm of steel.

66

Saska

"Stop!" she screamed. "Stop! Stop! We're not enemies. We're *not* enemies! Please, just *stop!*"

The three giant men hardly seemed to hear her, swinging with their enormous blades, parrying, fending, whirling through the fogs. Saska had never stood witness to such a fearsome bout, Sir Bernard, some six and half feet of thick, muscular, godsteel-clad brawn raging about in a mix of Powerform and Rushform, while Sir Lothar, soaring seven feet to the sky, took advantage of his long-armed thrusts and jabs in a swift and elegant Strikeform.

They fought as one, circling and closing, like wolves around a bear, as Sir Ralston swung about with those enormous dual greatswords of his, smashing their strikes aside, roaring inside his flat-topped greathelm, sometimes bursting forward with astonishing speed to shoulder charge one or the other out of the way. The steel giant was almost an army unto himself, but he was tiring, it seemed to her, slowing down just a little, and these others were fearsome fighters as well, just as Leshie had said.

"Stop," Saska called once again, in desperation, trying to make them hear her, hurdling corpses as she went. "Would you just stop, Rolly! Stop! STOP!"

Her pleas still went unheard, her voice gobbled up by the frenzied roar of battle that engulfed the square. Finding the three among the fogs and the fighting had been hard enough. Getting them to hear her appeared even harder.

"You, knight!" a voice cried out in challenge. "Die upon the wings of my spear!"

She whirled. A Sunrider was charging right for her, holding before him a long steel spear, screaming in Aramatian. Feathers fluttered along the spear's long shaft, in silver and black, Nemati colours, and he wore a feathered cloak in the same with glittery scalemail beneath.

"Stop, we're not enemies," Saska yelled, though he didn't hear her either. *Of course he didn't.* She rolled aside, the sooty air billowing. The Sunrider rushed by and wheeled around for another charge.

"Knight! Invader! I send you to your Halls!"

"No, stop! I'm with you! With *you!*" Her voice was muffled by her face-plate, lost among a hundred other sounds. She dove aside once more, beneath his second charge. When she got back to her feet he was coming around again, and lest she kill him he wouldn't stop. There was only one thing for it. She turned and dashed away, disappearing into the fogs.

"Coward!" she heard him say. "Coward! Northern coward!"

She went at least two dozen dashed paces, then stopped and breathed out, looking around. Rolly was nowhere to be seen. *Damnit*, she cursed, trying to listen, but even as she stopped for a moment to focus, a second Sunrider came sweeping through, giving out a maddened war cry, hollering and screaming and swinging a fearsome triple-head flail, with three savage spiked iron heads attached to a club by lengths of chain.

Two of them missed her, but one struck her on the pauldron, clanging so loud her eardrums all but burst. The deadly spikes would have bit deep into regular steel, but against godsteel they left but the faintest scratch.

She dashed away. "Rolly!" she shouted. "Rolly, where are you?"

It was futile. If he could not hear her from a few metres away, how would he now? She could barely see more than a half dozen metres in front of her, and all about her men and mounts were rushing through the mists. There was nothing for her to do but continue going, surging across the battlefield, searching for her guardian. She passed a group of men exhaust-edly hacking at one another with sword and axe and spear; a pair of Star-riders in circling combat, their cats hissing, riders sharing taunts and insults; a huge Tukoran in heavy plate armour doing battle with a mounted paladin knight atop an enormous camel. But of Sir Ralston there was no sign.

Joy prowled close by all the while, protecting her, alerting her to danger. *Find him. Find Rolly*, Saska thought, but even the starcat's senses were muted by this fume and the orchestra of death and dying around them. Smoke filled the air, so dense and noxious in places it made her gag, wafting up her nose, gushing through the eye holes in her helm, ash falling thick from the skies to coat the cobbles grey.

This plaza is vast, she thought. *It's boundless and bloody unending.* For a moment she had to consider the notion that she'd been killed at some point, only she didn't remember, and was wandering through some dreaded version of hell. No matter which way she turned, all she saw was smoke. Smoke and soot and ash, driving down like snow, and bodies in the mist, peppering the pavestones, and shadows surging by.

She turned a full circle again, hopelessly and helplessly lost. *Think, Saska. Think. Find the edge, and go from there.* If she did that, she could at least work her way around the boundary, and return to the lane Leshie and Del had gone down. Leshie had said they'd hide by that wagon if they came back this way. Saska hoped not. She hoped Leshie had found a way to get

Del to the safety of the palace, but could not count on that. *I'll head back,* she decided. *And if I see Rolly along the way, all the better.*

The edge was not difficult to find, though she had to go some way before she reached it, away where the world was quieter. She supposed she had probably gone all the way across to the other side of the square by now, given how far she'd travelled, but in this darkness and smog it was impossible to know for sure. *No matter. I'll circle around.*

She was about to do just that when she sensed a warning from Joy. *Men, coming up behind me.*

Stay back, she thought to the cat. *Stay back. Stay unseen.*

Then she heard a man say, "You, turn around."

She halted, stiffening. *That...that voice...*

"Did you not hear me? Turn around, I said."

Slowly, heart thumping, she turned.

"Yes, that's it. Very good. You understand the northern tongue, at least."

She stared, mute and momentarily immobile. *Him. It's him.*

"All alone out here, are we?" asked Cedrik Kastor. *He* was not alone. Two shadows came with him, clearing as they approached through the shroud. One was an Emerald Guard by his raiment, the other a man in full plate armour, with an orchard of apples embossed onto his breastplate, half seen through soot and grime. All of them had seen battle, and a great deal of it, that was clear, by the blood that spattered their garb.

But all the same, Cedrik Kastor *shone*, his fine sleek suit of fitted armour seeming to gleam despite the foul smoky darkness. At his back was a cape, black and green, emblazoned with the bear paw sigil of his house. A sigil Saska knew so well. One that had flapped upon the banners and flags adorning the walls and towers and halls of Keep Kastor, that dungeon of dread and death.

"Who are you fighting for?" he asked her, calmly. His faceplate was up, unlike the other two, exposing that face, that face of angles and panes and high cheekbones, cruel, handsome, smug. Even here, even now, in the heat of battle, in the midst of failure, he was *smug*. His voice sent a shiver through her. That voice she would never forget. A cold voice that so often issued in heartless laughter, as he sat within her cold damp cell, watching his father whip and beat her, waiting for his turn, legs folded in elegant pose, sipping on a cup of wine. "Well? Can't you speak?"

"My lord," came the voice of the Emerald Guard. "We should not delay. *He* is here, somewhere in this plaza. If we're to take the city..."

"He'll be dealt with soon, Sir Jesse, fear not." Kastor did not take his eyes off her all the while. "So? If you don't say anything, I'm afraid I'm going to have to ask Lord Gullimer here to kill you." Something twinkled in his eyes, as though he knew more than he was letting on, as though it was all a game.

Saska could not summon words. She tried to swallow but that failed her as well.

"My lord," said the one called Gullimer. Saska recognised the name. A middling lord and accomplished swordsman, she'd heard. "I believe Sir Jesse is right. Time is not on our side, and we ought not toy with the girl. We should restrain her at once, if that is still your plan."

The girl, she thought. She had not uttered a word, and in her full plate, how could they know? Unless they knew already. *He knows who I am,* she thought. It was there, right there, in that twinkle in his eye.

Cedrik Kastor smiled. His gaze moved away into the mists, where the din of battle continued to ring out. Yet not here. It felt suddenly like they were in another world entirely, so far away, and so alone. Mist enshrouded them, thick about the edges, yet somehow thinner here, right here where they stood.

"She's gifted," the knight called Sir Jesse said, brandishing his blade. He was watching her closely, and was the only one of them not wearing full armour, but the standard provision of his order; breastplate, gauntlets, greaves, helm. To no surprise, he looked in the worst shape, with blood leaking from a wound on his upper arm. "You can tell, by how she moves."

"She was struck by a *flail,* Sir Jesse," Cedrik Kastor said to that, in mocking tones. "How gifted can she be?"

They've been watching me, she thought. *Following me…*

"Yes, my lord. But elsewise. She moves smoothly, and that's a lot of plate she's wearing. It seems weightless on her."

Lord Cedrik raised a hand to silence him. "Why don't you lift your visor?" he asked her. "Show us that pretty face."

Saska said nothing, did nothing. She could feel Joy nearby, prowling silently. One whispered word, one telepathic command, and the starcat would pounce. *She could get close in these fogs,* Saska thought. *Close enough to strike, maybe.* A set of claws to the face of Cedrik Kastor might be enough to kill him, or blind him at least. *But the risk…*

"Lord Kastor, there really is no time for this," Lord Gullimer said, more firmly. "We came here for a reason, and must see it done. Unless the King's Wall is subdued, any chance we have of winning the city will be greatly hindered."

"You put too much stock in the man, Lord Gullimer. I would have little trouble defeating him in single combat, though why trouble myself, when we can make use of this girl instead?"

"Only if she is who you think she is."

"She is. I am quite sure of it."

Gullimer nodded, though by his tone of voice and manner he did not seem pleased with any of this.

Cedrik Kastor noticed. "Do not tell me you are wavering, Wilson. Where is your sense of daring? Oh, tonight has not gone to plan, far from it, but victory can still be ours. So long as you stick to my plan, the bells of ceasefire will be tolling soon enough. Or would you still prefer to drag this bedraggled corpse of our army back home? To call the retreat, tuck our tails between our legs, and run? Do you consider that the best course, my lord?"

"I would consider it the noble course," said Wilson Gullimer.

The comment sent a shiver of irritation across Cedrik Kastor's face. "Do I need to remind you of Sir Alistair Suffolk?"

Saska did not miss the tension those words provoked. "My lord," Lord Gullimer said, slowly and with great poise. "I feel compelled to tell you that thinly veiled threats will not endear me to your cause. Or to you. I am in two minds over this. A large part of me is drawn to the option of leaving this city, and this land, behind. It has brought us nothing but darkness, doubt, and now death, on calamitous scale."

"Calamitous scale, yes. And if we flee now, all of us will perish. At the very least, we must take the palace, a defensible position from which we can recover and regroup."

"And be surrounded," the apple lord said. "With hordes of angry Aramatians at our doors."

"Peasants," Kastor dismissed, "who will fall to our blades like winter wheat beneath the scythe. We shall become overlords to them, gods from the distant north. In the weeks to come, we can consider our course, but tonight, my lord, tonight we must act."

Lord Gullimer did not seem convinced, though was persuaded enough to give a nod, and say, "The girl, then. If you're certain of her importance, and that she is the key, then it would behove us to waste no further time in delay."

"I quite agree." Cedrik Kastor looked at Sir Jesse, and flicked a wrist in Saska's direction, nonchalant. "Sir Jesse, be a good man and restrain her for us. And make it quick, if you would."

"As you say, my lord."

Saska did not let Sir Jesse make so much as a motion to advance toward her. Even as the two men spoke, she burst forward from a standing start, so quickly the cobbles shattered at her feet, and slashed out at Cedrik Kastor with her blade.

He hadn't expected it. In his hubris he was unprepared. The tip of her sword shaved his face, slicing straight through his cruel perfect nose, splitting it asunder, and continued right across into the neck of the Emerald Guard Sir Jesse who'd never even seen her move. Blood gushed, spurting from his gullet, and the knight jerked back, reaching for his craw.

Lord Gullimer stumbled away in shock, snatching to draw his blade. "My lord!" he shouted, seeing the red rain down the face of Cedrik Kastor, his nose cleaved clean in two. The flow was sudden and violent, pouring past his lips. Sir Jesse went tumbling back, choking on his blood.

On instinct, Cedrik Kastor slapped a gauntlet across his face, drew it away, saw the blood, and screamed out in a terrible bellow, "TAKE HER, GULLIMER! TAKE HER"

Lord Gullimer flew forward to engage. It was Strikeform, given to swift and sudden and often athletic moves. She shot backward, making space, moving into Blockform, its best counter. But that was northern thinking, *knight* thinking. The thinking of men contesting in duels, where each strike won them points. Saska would never likely win a duel against this man, but she might just be able to win a fight.

Use the elements, she thought. *Take advantage of the world around you.* Knights were restricted in their fighting styles, the Butcher had insisted. "Honour traps them," he'd said, with customary barking laughter. "It is like a chain about their wrists and ankles, this honour." He advocated trickery and mischief instead, to kick filth in a man's eye to blind him, or knock a stone beneath their feet to trip him. Such were the sellsword stances, the pit fighter forms. "I pointed over an opponent's shoulder once in the pits," he'd told her. "It was a cheap trick, but it worked. The man turned and I put my axe through the back of his skull. That won me a woman for the night, that trick. I'd take a woman over honour any time."

She was remembering his lessons now.

Gullimer was upon her, striking fast and true. She fended away the first attack, the second and the third, all in Blockform, legs wide, stance steady. When he came at her again, she pirouetted with lightning pace, swivelling in a move the man did not seem to know. Her blade came down hard at his back but he had sensed it, turning to parry.

At once she raised a finger and pointed behind him, leaping back. "Giant! Giant! Giant" she screamed in false fear.

Lord Gullimer turned on impulse, and Saska took her chance, surging up behind him, driving her blade in such a clean thrust that it pierced the plate of his lower left flank, goring through the godsteel a couple of inches before juddering to a halt in his flesh. The apple lord gave out a howl of pain, and pulled away, the tip of Saska's sword showing red.

"I don't want to fight you," she found herself yelling at him. She moved around so that she could see Cedrik Kastor, standing there, enrobed in mist, his hand over his face. Blood leaked out through the steel fingers of his gauntlet, his hand quivering in speechless rage. "This isn't what I want. You're a good man, I have heard, a noble lord. I'm here for him. Not you. *Him.*"

Gullimer stared at her, silent, as though he hadn't expected a Tukoran accent to come pouring from her lips. He paused, dropping his guard, then lifted his visor. A comely face lay behind, square-jawed, kind-eyed, confused, etched in pain. He looked about forty. "Who are you? Show your face."

She hesitated. It was clear that this lord did not know the full story. *But nor does he,* she thought, looking at Cedrik Kastor. *He knows only what Robbert knew.* Somehow they'd put it together - that she was the spy and assassin from Harrowmoor, that she'd escaped from Shellcrest with Sir Ralston, that Safina Nemati was her grandmother - and Kastor had divined in her some importance because of that. *He wants to take me, use me, open the doors of the palace with me.* And it would work, she knew. *They'll give him anything to make sure I'm safe. Anything at all. Even their lives…*

She couldn't let that happen.

"You want to know who I am? You want the truth?" She flipped up her faceplate, and stared right at Cedrik Kastor. "Remember me, my lord? Do you remember *me?*"

He still held his hand over his face, the blood dripping down through

his fingers. Slowly he looked up. His nose was entirely split in half, the carti-
lage cut, an unsightly black chasm between the top half and the bottom.
The black soulless eyes that lurked above were narrowed to the point of
slits. Through them he looked at her, peering past the eddies of smoke. And
then, slowly, recognition dawned.

He knows, she thought. *He remembers.*

For a long moment silence lingered. *Say my name*, she thought. *Go on, say
it, say it.* But he said nothing, just stared at her, a slow and hateful smile
beginning to rise upon his lips. Eventually it got too much.

"Say it," she shouted at him. "Say it! Say my name!"

"Saska," he whispered, drawing the name out, hissing it like a snake.
"Saska, yes. The one with the bright blue eyes. You were always my father's
favourite."

Gullimer looked between them, befuddled. "Your *father*? My lord, I
thought you said this girl was a spy at Harrowmoor. How can your father
have known her?"

"I was a slave, that's why," Saska shouted, entirely unrestrained now, not
caring what she said. "His father abused me, and a hundred other girls in
his castle. At Harrowmoor I wore a disguise so *he* wouldn't know me. I was
there to kill him, to kill him like I did his vile loathsome sire…"

"His sire? I thought Modrik Kastor cracked his head on the hearth?"
He looked over at Cedrik. "Was that not the way of it?"

Saska drank in the look on the man's smug face, supped on it, bathed in
it, gloried in that look. So long had she wanted to tell him, to see the colour
drain from his cheeks, to know that his beloved father, that foul and
monstrous lord, had been slain by the hand of one of his slaves.

"You…*you* killed him?"

She smiled, raised her blade, and pointed it right at his mangled bloody
face. "Yes, *I* killed him. I killed an old drunk man who was trying to rape
me, and when his head hit the hearth, and cracked open like an egg, I
laughed, *Cedrik*, oh how I laughed…"

Her words had the desired effect, and he gave the desired response.
From a standing start, roaring, he surged.

But she was ready for him. As ready as she could be, at least. She did
not turn or run or try to play a trick. She swung her blade in parry, and
shifted sideways and backward in dodge, and thrust and swung and
downcut in attack, and fought him blade to blade.

Cedrik Kastor moved like a man born to dance. There was no Blockform from him, no shift into defence. He came at her in a relentless and
savage assault, swirling in Glideform, darting in Strikeform, swinging from
up to down, down to up, left to right and right to left, straight, diagonal,
thrusting, cutting, slicing, hacking and laughing, she suddenly realised,
laughing a crazed manic laugh all the while as the blood sprayed off his
nose.

"Weak!" he was saying, wrist swishing, his blade moving so quickly it
times it almost seemed to bend. "Weak. Weak. Oh, so weak!" He drove
her backward, too slick and too skilled, bursting forth in a sudden Rush-

form strike to batter her to the ground. "Get up! Get up! Come, Saska, get up!"

He turned and walked away, as though out for a summer stroll. She scrambled to her feet, panting, grimacing. *He's too quick*, she fretted. *Too strong.* Men said that Cedrik Kastor was born to kill, and perhaps they'd been right all along. She turned her eyes to Lord Gullimer, still standing aside, observing. His eyes were knotted and stern, blood trailing down the back of his leg. "Gullimer," Kastor called to him. "How is your back? Can you still fight?"

"The wound is shallow," the apple lord returned.

"Good." Kastor waved a hand, out across the plaza, where the din of battle still sang out. "Go find some friends of ours out there, bring them over. We need to start rallying for our march on the palace."

Gullimer nodded, glanced at Saska and said, "I'll find friends," then turned to stride away.

Something…there was something about that gave her hope.

Cedrik Kastor turned around. "Shall we resume?" He began back toward her, step by menacing step, a cat playing with a mouse. She reached to her dagger and a chuckle slipped through his lips, "What's this now? A dagger? And a fine one, by its look. Now where did you get that, Saska? Did that lumbering buffoon of yours give it to you?"

"King Godrin gave it to me," she said to him. "It belonged to my grandfather, and his father before him, and his before him, and…"

"I think I get the picture." He reached up to touch his nose, pressing at it, inspecting the damage. "A fine strike, I will grant you that. Sir Jesse never even saw it coming."

"I didn't want to kill him. I was trying to get *you*."

"And you did. You got my nose. I may even have a scar after this. It'll be something to remember you by. The fearsome slave who slew my father. Did you know you were Bladeborn back then?" He smiled, licking the blood from his lips; it was smeared across his face now, painting his cheeks and chin red, nightmarish. "No, of course you didn't. You didn't know until Marian Payne saved you from that prison wagon. What a life you have led of late, Saska. I shall look forward to hearing all about it later, at the top of the palace, once I've thrown your grandmother from the terrace. Maybe I'll have that oaf of yours serve me my wine, and make him watch as I whip you as well. My father never did open your legs, did he? No, he was saving you, savouring you, and the night he tried to take what was his, you killed him. Well, I'll not make that same mistake. You're getting a little old now, perhaps, but still, I'll make an exception. Just for you."

He took a pace toward her. She had no words. Only thoughts, memories, the screaming and the whimpering and the echoing in the darkness. The other girls down in those dungeons who'd suffered even worse than she had. Younger girls, smaller girls, who'd never made it out.

"I'll kill you," she whispered, staring at him in blind hate. "I'll kill you… for them."

"What was that? You'll kill me, you say? *How*, exactly? Now I don't doubt that Lady Payne trained you well, and that blundering lump of yours as well, but frankly, Saska, you're just a girl. Eighteen, nineteen, is that right? You've trained for how long? A couple of years?" He tapped a steel finger against his bloodstained chin, enjoying every moment now. There was something utterly deranged glittering in his eyes. "There is no man living who can defeat me, Saska, and if that is the case, and I assure you it is, what hope would you, a southern slave, have?"

A fool's hope, she thought, *a desperate hope*. She put herself into Blockform, as well as she could.

Laughter filled the air. "Well, that's Blockform I suppose. Talent is one thing, technique another." His eyes flashed on her blade once again. "Your grandfather's, did you say? And what of your father, Saska. Who was he?"

"Thalavar,' she said.

He pursed his lips. "Thalavar," he repeated, thoughtful. "I fear I do not know the name. Was he Tukoran, pray tell? Does he have a house name?"

"He was born of Rasalan, from a Vandarian father. His houses were those of Thala, and Varin."

His laughter lapsed away into incredulity for a moment. "Now, I think someone's been telling you fibs, girl. Your grandmother, I suppose. It's said her wits have deserted her."

"My father's father was Lorin, the last of the Varin Kings. His mother was Princess Atia of Rasalan, the fourth child and second daughter of King Astan, and younger sister to King Godrin, who gave me this blade."

A chuckle spat forth once more. "King Lorin perished in the jaws of a kraken, you witless fool. What exactly do they put in the water around here? It has driven you to…"

She cut him off, drawing her dagger. Light spilled off it, casting aside the dark, a beacon glowing bright in silver and blue. "I am the grand-daughter of King Lorin, last of Varin's heirs, a child of the royal and divine House of Thala; Bladeborn, Seaborn, with the Light of Lumo in my veins. I am born of the north and the south, of sea and steel and star and moon. And you, my lord, Cedrik of House Kastor, are completely and utterly *beneath* me."

Black eyes stared at her, black eyes in a cold hard face, painted red in blood from cheek to jowl and pale as milk above. His lips were not parted; he was not laughing anymore. He looked at the blade glowing in her grasp, then he looked at her, and for a long moment he did not speak at all. And then, in a whispered breath, "*I* am beneath *you*?"

Saska looked him dead in the eye. "You are beneath us all."

He nodded, slowly, and to himself, and then inspected the length of his sword. "So this is why you're here. Why Godrin sent his Wall to protect you. The last living heir of Varin…" He mulled on that, then met her eyes. "What is your purpose, I wonder? Something important, for them to go to all this trouble."

Save the world, Saska thought. *Help end the War Eternal*. She said nothing. She'd said far too much already.

"It makes no matter," he told her, when she offered him no response. "A corpse can carry out no duty…other than feeding the worms."

And with those words, he surged.

Saska pulsed backward, dagger still to grasp, broadsword in the other. The fight had changed now, she sensed. *He wants to kill me. Everything else be damned. He's going to have my head.*

In a flash he was upon her, kicking up ash as he came. It billowed and swirled and through it she saw his blade, flashing down from on high. She parried the blow, stabbing at once with her dagger, but his body was no longer there. A whoosh of air sounded behind her. She spun. His blade came arcing. She knocked it aside from in to out, and ducked forward, thrusting again, but he was around her back, swinging, slicing a long thin line up her breastplate.

"Pathetic!" he roared. "The heir of Varin should do better!"

She turned, looking left and right, spinning, but he was gone. She could hear skittering footsteps, but they seemed to come from all around. *How fast is he?* Then a scuttle of feet behind her, and she whirled, swinging hard at once, blade crashing against blade, steel against steel. Mist exploded, filling the air. And through it that red-white face of horror was grinning.

"Good, better. Maybe you've got godblood in you after all."

He set forth into a frenzied assault. She threw her arms left and right, fending, but could not hope to block them all. Eventually one got through, crashing through her guard, a heavy hack that cut right down into her left shoulder pauldron, cleaving into the plate.

She screamed, feeling the steel bite her flesh. He pulled his sword out with a spray of blood, then swung hard in a perfect horizontal sidecut, right for her neck. She backed away just in time, the tip of the blade rasping against the steel of her gorget. Laughter echoed. "Close! So close!" Her left foot landed on something uneven, tripping her, and she stumbled aside, crashing to the floor. It was a body, a trailing leg. Sir Jessie, she saw, lying in a pool of blood. She could see his lifeless eyes rolled over behind his visor. *I'm sorry,* she thought. *It wasn't meant to be you.*

She surged back up, facing her foe, as he rushed back in, swinging. She was given no respite, none at all, sidestepping away, fending with her dagger, stabbing with her sword. She slew a drifting flake of ash, but of Cedrik Kastor she missed entirely. Laughter came again, and calls of "Pathetic! Useless! Weak!" as he mocked and struck, mocked and struck, cutting at her armour, splitting her plate, slicing into the flesh beneath.

She stumbled away, bleeding. *Flesh wounds, shallow,* she knew. Her plate armour was protecting her for now, but each cleave would weaken it, and another strike in the same place could be fatal. He came again, unrelenting, one in every four or five of his strikes now getting through. Some she parried, others she dodged, but the rest crashed into her armour, cutting and cleaving.

"Shall I swap hands?" she heard him chuckle. "You might fare better against my left?" Another series of attacks had her reeling, tripping on something again as she backed away. She crashed to the cobbles, her enemy

746

looming over her. In that moment she was utterly at his mercy, bested and broken, but bully that he was he drew it out. "No, no, I'll not have you die by a random piece of wood. Up, Saska, back on your feet. I'm only just getting warmed up."

They were fighting beside a tavern now, right at the side of the square. The floor was littered with bits of wood, from tables and chairs and broken barrels used in the barriers and blockades. *Use the elements*, she thought. *Take advantage of the world around you.* She began moving away from him, watching his feet, drawing him in. His footwork was delicate and light, dancing in and out between the hazards. She saw a chance and kicked out at a broken chair leg to land beneath his step. His sabaton slid easily aside. "Goodness, is that the best you can do?"

No, she thought.

From the shadows, at last, came Joy, pouncing from behind him. There was nothing for it now; the cat had to engage. She slashed out with her claws, aiming for Kastor's face as he turned, but missed.

"Go," Saska shouted. "Run!"

Joy dashed away, just in time, as their enemy swung out with his blade, all but shaving the fur from her glossy black coat. His eyes narrowed, and he slammed his faceplate down. "The cat," he said. "I knew she was *yours*." He turned to face her, now fully protected. That upturned visor had been Joy's only chance. Her claws and jaws would not be strong enough to puncture his plate. "You are a strange one, aren't you? Godsteel *and* a cat. And what else did you say earlier? Seaborn too?"

Steel and light and sea, she thought.

"My nephew used to keep cats. Griffin, I think you know him. Or *knew* him, I should say. Settle something for me, Saska. Was it you who slew the boy?"

I stabbed him right between the legs, she thought. *And then I put my knife in his throat.* "Yes."

He made a tutting sound. "And you let poor Elyon Daecar suffer for that crime? That wasn't very noble of you, Saska, *heir of Varin*. The boy took ten lashes for that, and savage ones as well. You know, he almost died." He glanced around, as though wary now of Joy. "Those cats of Griffin's, though…I hear not one of them survived. He liked to play with them, you know how boys are, though my nephew did get a little too…*rough*, on occasion. I daresay we Kastors have no real love for cats, Saska. Griffin liked to *play* with little ones, but me…no, I prefer the larger variety. Oh yes, I'll enjoy playing with yours."

Her name is Joy, Saska thought. *Joy!* His goading ignited her hate. She flew at him, screaming, swinging wildly with dagger and sword. He drew back, stepping away, blocking. More laughter wriggled up out of his throat, as he flicked her blows aside. Behind him Saska spotted a broken cartwheel. His foot came down upon it, the weight of his plate crunching through the wood, flattening it, but for a moment he lost his balance. Her eyes lit up as his guard dropped an inch. She swung with her sword. His blade lifted to fend. Her dagger came in behind, thrust forth as though struck by Varin

747

himself, quicker than she could conceive, a flash of light in silver and blue. Its tip bit metal, sinking through steel. One inch, two, three it went, through godsteel and leather, meat and muscle, driving into the flesh of his gut.

He staggered back, his laughter warping into a grunt of shock. Blood issued out from his plate, wending in rivulets down the metal. He swung a hand to the wound and backed away. Saska hunted him, heart alight with sudden hope. The wound would not be fatal, she knew, but he was reeling now, the momentum hers. She surged forward, giving him no room to breathe. A hack of her sword was parried away, and he swung quickly to defend from her dagger. The third strike hit, but it was only a graze, sliding down his flank, scratching his plate. She stabbed with her dagger again, summoning all her might, but he weaved away, rotating at the hip.

And suddenly a hand was reaching out to grab her sword arm, closing about her wrist. He twisted violently, loosening her grip, then drove up hard with the pommel of his sword to crash right into her faceplate. Her head jerked back, rattling in her helm. Spots of light dazzled her vision and she felt her fingers opening, her sword crashing away to the stone.

I got too close. I got too close…

She tried to pull away, tried to thrust with her dagger, but suddenly he was wrestling her to the ground, smashing her onto the cobbles. He grabbed at one of the bladed crab claws that crested her helm and slammed her head down, down, down again, shouting, "Beneath you? *I'm* beneath *you*!" in a wild manic fury. Her head clouded over. She swung with her dagger again, though her strength was gone. "Varin's heir?" he bellowed. "Varin's heir!" He grabbed her arm and cracked it into the stone, then ripped the dagger from her grip, tossing it away.

*Joy…Joy…*Saska could sense the cat coming in behind him. *No, stay back…no, run…*

The starcat leapt at him, clawing at his shoulders, biting at his neck. Kastor roared and stood and lurched back, thrashing, Joy clinging to his back like a limpet. He tried to swung with his sword but could not get to her. Saska heard a horrid rasping and scraping of steel as the cat's fangs and claws raked at his armour, but she had no weapons to hurt him. *He'll kill you…he'll kill you…run,* she thought.

She staggered to her feet, head fogging, and stumbled immediately to the side. A hand came down to steady her balance and she stood again, zeroed in on her foe, and ran to tackle him to the floor. He saw her coming and brushed her aside, somehow getting hold of Joy's tail all the while, squeezing it, swinging. The cat hissed and let go, landing nearly, scrambling straight back to her feet. Cedrik Kastor faced her, crouching, legs splayed wide, sword to grasp. "Come at me!" he roared. "Come play with me, cat!"

"Joy! Her name is Joy!" Saska ran for him, but once more he turned, drove her to the floor, flipping up her faceplate in a single move. He snatched his dagger from its sheath. The steel glinted blue, catching the light of her own dagger, glowing nearby…and stabbed down at once, right for her face. Saska closed her eyes. *This is it,* she thought. She could hear

Joy coming, running for her, but she wouldn't make it, she was too far away...

Something crashed into him, his weight flying off her. *Joy*, she thought, but no, it came from another direction. She opened her eyes, blinked, looked up. *Robbert?* The prince had his uncle beneath him, swinging hard, battering at his helm with his fists, screaming, "You'd have me killed. Me! Your own nephew!" as he swung.

Saska got to a knee, panting, confused, blinking to clear her vision. She managed to stand, unstable, her legs weak as reeds, and almost fell again but someone was there to steady her. A great shadow loomed at her side. She looked up. "R-Rolly?"

"You're safe now," Sir Ralston said. She saw cuts in his armour, blood seeping from a half dozen wounds. "You're safe from him now, my lady."

Tears welled in her eyes. Of shock and fear and unbearable relief. She was shivering all over, her chest heaving up and down. Sir Ralston went down to one knee before her, looking her over, inspecting her wounds. Prince Robbert Lukar was still screaming bloody murder, fists crashing against his uncle's helm, as several figures rushed after him to try to pry him off. She glimpsed Sir Lothar there, and Sir Bernard, both cut and bloody as well, but living, and Lord Gullimer too, calling orders, and others, many others she didn't know, knights and men-at-arms and even lowly soldiers too, all hurrying from the gloom.

"What's...I don't..." Saska managed.

"Lord Gullimer found us," the Whaleheart said. "He told us what was happening." He looked over. "Your dagger, my lady. Varin's dagger. We followed its light to find you. It showed us the way."

A beacon, she thought, looking around at the men. "Leshie, Del, are they..."

"They're safe," he told her. "The Butcher has taken them both back to the palace, my lady, with a strong escort. The fighting is over. The invaders are in retreat."

It was a lot to take in. "You said...you said his name," she murmured, smiling. It was an odd thing to pick up on, but..."The Butcher. You didn't call him the sellsword..."

"He has earned that from me, and a great deal more. The man fought valiantly tonight, and Merinius as well. We must hope that the others have survived. The Butcher's brother. And the Surgeon. All have played their part."

The knights had successfully pried Robbert Lukar away now, kicking and cursing, and were trying to calm him. The prince had a bandage over his left eye, she saw, soaked in blood, with a great deal more of it staining the side of his face. "Strip him!" he was roaring. "Strip him of his armour!"

His men saw to it, as Cedrik Kastor tried to fight them off, but feebly. He seemed as dazed as Saska felt, slurring out, "Ro...Robbert...what... what is this? Why...why..."

"You know why! You know why, Uncle!" Robbert Lukar attempted to

749

surge at him once more, but Lord Gullimer was there to stop him. "A target? *I* was one of your targets? You bastard! You'd steal my crown!"

Distantly, Saska could hear the horns of retreat blasting out through the city. It was over, the battle was over. *But...* "Elio," she remembered suddenly, looking at the Wall. "Is he…"

"We don't know, my lady. His body is being searched for in the square, and near the gate. Some claim that he was caught in the fire, though it's possible he had time to escape…"

"The palace. He hasn't…"

"No. The palace is secure, and your grandmother as well. Lord Hasham is there now, with the Strong Eagle and his men. The sunlord would not dare mount such a charge. We shall discover the truth of his fate soon."

She nodded, blinked, still trying to catch up. Her heart was racing so fast she felt she might just faint. *It's over,* she thought again. *It's…it's really over.* She spotted Robbert Lukar striding over, seeming to take note of her for the first time. "My lady." He gave her a quick and weary bow. "I am sorry we took so long." The hot flush of fury was still on his face, his breathing heavy, yet his voice had somewhat calmed.

"You…you saved my life," she said to him, weakly.

"And your brother saved mine. Without him I'd have lost more than just an eye. I think we can call it even." He managed to smile, though looked utterly exhausted, his skin milk-pale and features drawn out; clearly he'd lost a lot of blood. "I'm loath to give up a good squire, but I feel his place is probably better with you. He'll be safer with you here in Aram."

I'm not staying, she thought, *and nor will Del.* He'd have to come with her now, on her perilous journey, and only worry her all the more. She wondered for a moment if he might be better with Robbert, but the prince would face his perils as well, wherever his path took him. She looked out across the square, hearing the distant blow of the horns. The fogs were thinning now, the fires waning, and in the east, a pale light was dawning. "Where will you go?"

"Back to the camp, for a start," Robbert Lukar told her. "We'll have to piece together what's left of our army, and then…well, I'm not quite sure."

"You could stay," she said, on a whim and without thinking. "If I talk to my grandmother…" But even as she said it, the prince was shaking his head.

"We cannot stay. After what my uncle and Elio Krator have done, we would not be welcome, not even for a day. We have ships at anchor up the coast. If we can reach them, perhaps we can sail home. Or else march north, as we had first intended, into Agarath. We may be able to find a way through the mountains, and across the Bloodmarsh Isles. I am eager now to return home, my lady. There remains a great deal of fighting to be done, I fear."

She nodded, silent, almost wishing for a moment he could come with her, he and his gallant knights. *If only they knew the truth*, she thought. *Might they put all else aside, and help me in my quest?* Having an ally like Robbert Lukar would be more useful than she could say. A northern prince. Even a king…

But she said nothing of it. She only looked over at the prince's uncle and said, "What do you plan to do with him?"

"Kill him." Robbert said, at once, and with complete and utter dispassion. "Right here, and right now. I won't give him a chance to wriggle out of this one. He needs to die, and now."

Saska nodded, hoping he'd say that. She'd said far too much to the man during their duel, and her quest still relied on secrecy. "Will you do it yourself?"

He mulled on it, as though tempted, but shook his head. "I'll not sully myself as a kinkiller. The gods frown upon such, no matter the conditions. No, my lady. It should be *you*. I may have lost an eye to his treacheries, but you…you lost your innocence. What he's done…what he is." He went over to retrieve her dagger, gave it a curious look, then placed it in her palm. "Use this. Stick it in his throat. Be rid of him forever." He paused. "Or don't. It's said that vengeance is an illness without a proper cure, a thirst that can never be properly quenched. If you think it'll help, do it, but if not…" He turned. "I have many a good man who would happily do it instead."

Saska turned her eyes down, thinking. The taking of life had never haunted her, nor given her cause to feel regret. Modrik Kastor. Lord Quintan. Sir Griffin Kastor and that brute of his, Borgin. Balza, Krator's loutish guard, who'd claimed to be the one to kill her father. All of them had deserved to die, and Cedrik Kastor, perhaps, deserved it even more. But somehow the thought had lost its relish. If they were still in the fight she'd have lost an arm for the pleasure, but the fight was done, and she hadn't won, and now it all just felt empty.

No, she thought. *I have a better idea.*

She looked at Prince Robbert Lukar. "I'd like you to meet my bonded starcat," she said to him. "Her name is Joy." He turned, seeing the starcat approach, and drew back on instinct. "It's OK, she won't bite." *Not you.*

He reached a hand out, somewhat tentative, to touch her, and after a moment's wary hesitation, Joy leaned in to let him rub at the top of her head. He smiled as the starcat began purring. "She's beautiful, Saska."

Saska smiled back. *Beautiful, and deadly.* "Your uncle told me that your cousin Griffin kept cats."

Robbert frowned, remembering. "He always seemed to have a different one when we visited. None of us ever liked him, my brother and sister and me. He was wrong in the head, Cousin Griffin. There were always rumours that he killed those cats himself."

She said nothing to that, but it did not take Robbert Lukar long to get her meaning. He considered a moment, then gave a single small nod, withdrew his hand from the top of the starcat's head, and stepped away toward his uncle.

Lord Cedrik Kastor had been stripped of all of his godsteel plate now, the fine armour tossed aside in a misting heap, leaving him in nothing but a set of soiled and sweaty smallclothes. Sir Lothar and Sir Bernard stood to either side of him, holding him in place as he attempted to wriggle free. "Release him," Robbert said to them.

"Oh Robbert...Robbert, dear nephew..." his uncle started. "I...I don't know what you've been told, but whatever it is, we can clear this up. You're my nephew and I love you. I've *always* loved you. We've had our disagreements, I know, but...but..."

"Lord Cedrik of House Kastor," Robbert said, cutting in. "I, Robbert Lukar, Crown Prince and heir to the Kingdom of Tukor, do hereby sentence you to die, for the crime of..."

"Robbert...Robbert, no..." the man blurted. "No...no...you can't..."

"...for the crime of attempted nepoticide, parricide and high treason," the prince went on, "and of the untold atrocities committed during your years of rule and beneath the banners of your house."

"I never...I didn't...no, Robbert, you can't, I'm your *uncle*...your uncle...your mother's beloved brother..." He fell forward onto his knees, blood leaking from the stab wound in his gut and the red rift that split his nose. "Please, please...I beg mercy, please..."

Robbert looked down at him pitilessly. "You brought blood to the parley at Harrowmoor, Uncle. An insult to the gods. Just what did you think would happen?"

"No...I never, that wasn't...please..."

The prince stepped back. "My lady. He is yours."

The horns were still blowing, the smokes receding, the light of dawn rising to brighten the city streets. Saska stepped forward until she was but three paces from the man. *A man*, she thought, looking down at him. *Just a man, weak and brittle, of flesh and blood and bone.*

"Cedrik," she said, coldly, gesturing to her side. "Look, I have brought someone to play with you."

His eyes widened in slow terror as he saw the starcat approach, stalking through shadow, shoulders going up and down. Her lips drew back in a snarl, fangs extended, claws clacking on stone as she came.

"She's called Joy." Saska told him. "Like the joy you and your father stole from me." She gave the starcat a stroke of the head. "Go ahead, Joy. *Play.*"

Soundlessly his lips quivered, and wordlessly he stared. But when the starcat pounced, he was silent no more.

When the starcat pounced, he screamed.

67

Amron

I always knew he was the greater foe, Amron Daecar thought, as the icy armour thickened around his plate, layering up his protection. The earth was churned up where they fought, mud and rock flung out from beneath the beast's great claws. Patches of scorched grass littered the plains; and patches of ice as well, melting in the morning sun.

Amron Daecar cleared his throat. "I understand now how my father fell to you, Lord Marak," he called out over the gusting coastal wind, circling his foe at a distance. "Does it wound you that men say Vallath was the mightier beast? And Dulian the better rider?"

The dragon snorted flame, as though angered by the suggestion, and lashed out with its massive tail, weaponised with savage spikes and horns. Amron leapt above it, casting down a spray of ice as it passed with a flick of the Frostblade. The tail slowed, half-frozen, before bursting free in a glitter of colours.

That isn't going to work. He'd attempted to freeze the tail in place several times, but it was much too big and much too strong. He resumed his circling, studying the dragon and rider as he did so. It was good practice during a duel such as this to be patient, prudent, and precise, watching your enemy's every move and mannerism, searching for chinks in its armour.

This one has few, Amron Daecar had surmised thus far. *Perhaps even none at all.* Prince Dulian had been young, prideful, prone to recklessness. Marak was none of those things. Coldly he sat in his high dark saddle, watching Amron as Amron watched him, more in sync with the dragon beneath him than any pairing of beast and rider Amron had ever known. *This is a truly formidable man,* he thought. *My southern reflection, they say.*

"There's a rumour here in the north," he went on, shouting over the wind once more, and the din of battle nearby, "that says you *laughed* when you killed my father. I've always wondered…is that true?"

Even from here, Amron could see Marak's mouth twist. "Did I laugh?" he repeated, in a deep and reverberating timbre, thick with the accents of his land. His disdain for the notion was clear. "No, Lord Daecar. I did not laugh when I killed your father, no more than I did when I killed your king."

The tail lashed again. Amron ducked it this time, moving between two great bony horns, then stood and swung in a sidecut, spraying a cloud of ice chips from the edge of his blade like a thousand tiny daggers. The dragon reared up, roaring as it spewed forth its flame. Ice met fire, erupting in a cloud of kaleidoscopic mist, and through that mist Amron dashed forward, appearing suddenly before the dragon, thrusting upward from the ground in a powerful surge, the tip of the Frostblade aiming for its gullet...

But beast and rider were wise to it. No sooner had Amron left the ground than the dragon drew back, beating its massive wings in a thunderclap, and from its maw came a river of flame, spraying left and right across the field. The fire poured over him like a flood, thawing his ice-armour, licking at his plate. Amron fled from it, dripping and gleaming. At a thought the ice began to solidify about him again, fogging and coalescing and hardening. When the flame and smoke cleared, billowing upward in a thick black cloud, Garlath had settled some thirty metres away, claws dug deep into the ground. Marak sat atop him, calm and watchful.

He holds back, Amron thought. This was more than just a study of his fighting patterns, he sensed. *He has held back this entire fight. He doubts he should even be here...*

"Are we going to do this dance all day?" he roared out at him. "You were never so wary during the last war, Marak."

"How would you know? We did not fight."

"I heard from other men who did."

"Dead men do not talk, Daecar. I did not suffer your northern knights to live, during our duels. King Tellion asked that I kill, so I killed."

"Tellion," Amron repeated. "A king you served loyally, as you served his son. How has it come to this, my lord... that it is darkness and devilry that now rule you?"

The dragonlord gave no response to that, though the dragon did, great spouts of black smoke pouring from his nostrils. It was an act of intimidation, Amron knew. Certain larger species of dragon could fill the air with fume, to blind a man during a fight, but this was not such an occasion. *No, this is rage, and the fetters of madness. I am fighting slaves*, he thought.

The contest entered an impasse. Amron could sense it, sense Marak's doubt. Away across the plains, the coastlands beyond the city gates were filled with battle. Only a short time ago, Amron had heard the great roar and charge as Lythian and Dalton Taynar led their army out onto the field. He had been glad to see that the First Blade was there, brandishing his great golden sword. *Inspire them*, he had thought. *Lead them*. Even now men were still pouring through the River Gate by the thousand and up from the coast as well, ship after ship emptying out to fill the strand with sword and spear and shield. *They have three times our number*, Amron realised. And that was only here, on the city's eastern front. Hundreds more ships would be plunging into the harbour to send men through the breaches between Red

754

Watch and the Merry Maiden and by the fallen tower of Seaman's as well. *I've sent the Ironfoot to his death. And Lord Rosetree. They'll both be overwhelmed.*

He looked back at the dragonlord. "Lythian told me what you did for him," he called, above the distant clamour of battle. "He considers you a friend for that. Would you say the same?"

The man did not respond; his jaw was clenched hard as rock. *There is a struggle in this one.* It had been clear enough from the start and was growing clearer still. There was a strange red hue to the dragonlord's eyes, as there was to Garlath's as well, a reflection of the tethers that bound them to their master's will. He wondered if those tethers could be cut, the man's freedom restored. *Would that be better than killing him?*

"He says you were not a believer," Amron pressed, twisting the knife. "Prince Tethian was the fanatic. And his tutor, the scholar. But not you. Your intent was to put Tethian on the throne, where he belonged. What changed, my lord?" He waited. No answer. A chuckle leapt from his throat, to stir a reaction. "Has Eldur enslaved your tongue as well as your will? I can see the strings on your back from here, Marak. Are you truly so easily oppressed? All these rich-blooded Fireborn, these strong brave drag-onknights? How many of you dance to his tune? All of you? Is all of Agarath as lost as you are?"

A snarl. An upturned lip. "I serve. I have always served."

"So have I. Peace. It is peace I serve."

A strange look passed over the dragonlord's face. "Peace? You have slain how many hundreds of men? And you call yourself a servant of peace."

"Much blood must be shed in its service. I did not say peace came cheap." He looked at the battle once more, the burning city beyond. "But some costs are more dear than others. Harder to justify. Harder to explain. Men fight out there with sword and spear. Fine. Let them. Let them win honour and die with weapons in their hands and blood in their mouths. That is the way of things. The way of war. But how do you explain the women, and the children, and the infants in their cribs? How do you explain wanton butchery, my lord, and genocide? How do you explain Mudport?"

He paused at that and saw at once that the details had been kept from him. *He does not know. He has not been told how the city fell.*

"My son was there," he went on. "He told me what he saw, what he *heard*. The screaming. The chaos. The savagery. Would you do the same, Lord Marak? Do you consider yourself as bad as Vargo Ven?"

"We are nothing alike," the dragonlord snapped. "Ven hungers only for power and position."

"And what do you hunger for? Honour? Duty?" He flung a hand at the city. "This? Is it this you truly want, Lord Marak? All the world at war?" He turned, looked, saw the dragons descending upon the hordes of men, belching flame in wild assaults, caring not who got caught beneath the fires. Amron had read of such tactics before, if not seen them. When an army's numbers were vastly superior, the more ruthless commanders would happily sacrifice their own men to win the battle. Northern kings and lords had loosed arrows upon clashing hosts in the past, killing both friend and foe in the process, and Agarathi commanders had done the same with their dragons. But something told him this was different. This was not by the command of Ulrik Marak. *It is the will of Agarath*, he knew. Northern, southern, it mattered not. In his ancient primordial world, only the strong survived.

Marak was seeing it too, his neck twisted to observe the battlefield beyond the city. His face betrayed him. Amron saw a measure of shock in it, and outrage, at seeing the dragons killing his own men, though he seemed impotent to act. Beneath the brightening skies, the fleet was still pouring forth to empty men onto the coast, hundreds upon hundreds of ships churning the seas to a wild white froth. Above swirled dragons, small and large, in many colours and many species, many ridden, many not, in a number beyond his count. *Thick like crows above a kill. Like flies upon a corpse.* There was no way they could ever kill them all, not here. They'd need every Bladeborn knight in the north to fend them off, and even then…and then…

Warhorns were blaring all across the city, stirring the air, dragon after dragon diving and swooping, snatching men up with their talons to fling them across the field. Amron saw that some of them were Agarathi, Lumarans, men of the Empire, torn from the earth and snaffled up indiscriminately with all the rest to be crushed and tossed and thrown, dead and dying, to land amidst the sprawl of battle below. He saw a dragonknight in his black armour and red cloak go spinning through the air, saw a man in silver feathers make poor use of them, plummeting back into the carnage from a height of sixty metres. One of the winged beasts had a large sunwolf in its grasp and was flying away east across the river as the Sunrider dangled dead from its saddle, his leg caught in a strap.

It was the tip of the iceberg. A score of other dragons were doing the same. *They're hunting, not fighting*, Amron thought. Some were feasting upon men or mounts on the ground; others were flying free of the battle with prey in their talons to consume them at their leisure elsewhere. He saw three fighting over a massive Piseki camel, ripping it apart, its guts and gore flying everywhere.

This is madness, he thought. He turned to Lord Ulrik Marak, who had seen it all. "Is this what you wanted, Marak? Your dragons killing and *eating* their own?"

The dragonlord had no answer for him. And that was answer enough.

I can't stay here with him, Amron realised suddenly. He was not one to leave a duel undone, but slaying Garlath the Grand and the great armoured lord atop his back might take a good long while, and he did not have that time to spare. *This man will not join the fight*, he knew. *Lythian was right. He is not our true foe.*

He thrust the Frostblade into its sheath. Marak saw. Curiosity swam in his eyes. "I'm not going to fight you, Marak," Amron bellowed at him, over the din. "And you don't want to fight me either, you're making that clear."

"I was bidden to bring him your head."

"Then why aren't you?" Silence followed. "You came here to talk, not take my head. You've made that plain. And the talking is done." Amron stepped away, though warily, watching the dragon from the corner of his eye. His hand clung to the pommel of the Frostblade, just in case, keeping that thick layer of ice around him.

After a dozen paces, he heard Marak say, "Wait."

Amron turned back to face him. He waited.

"Mudport. Is it as you say?"

A single nod. "Genocide, yes. Wanton slaughter."

Marak digested it darkly. There was a struggle in his eyes, as though he was trying to break free, trying to sever the tethers that bound him. It was a battle Amron could understand. *A battle I have faced before. And one I'll face again.* He looked down at the Frostblade, his blessing and his curse, just as the Sword of Varinar had been. He had given up the latter and would give up the former, though knew it would not be easy. Marak appeared to be experiencing something similar. *Break free of him,* he urged. *Sever the tie. Cut the strings...*

A screech snatched at his attention, just south of him toward the sea. He turned in time to see a dragon landing no more than fifty feet away, a small and stunted creature without saddle or rider. Amron tensed at once, fist clutching his blade handle, but the beast seemed not to notice him. He watched, brows tightening. *What's it doing?*

The dragon appeared to be cowering, lowering itself to the ground. Marak took note of it, emerging from his inner struggle. A frown curled upon his brow. Then he raised his broad stubbled chin and looked east, and as he did so, Garlath began lowering himself to the ground as well, his thick long serpentine neck arching like a bow, blue and silver wings spreading, flattening to the earth as though in a posture of reverence and submission.

Bowing. It's...it's like he's bowing, Amron thought.

More shrieking and hissing filled the air, the whoosh of dragons swooping, landing. One, two, five, ten came shooting from the sooty skies, spread out all around him, all adopting the same strange posture, all of them looking east.

Amron squinted that way. A shadow haunted the high horizon, black as death, distant, closing. The Frostblade reacted, thrumming violently in his grasp. A preternatural warning sent cold fingers to climb his spine.

In the skies above the city of King's Point, many other dragons were coming down to perch and bow where they may, atop towers and walls and battlements, and aboard the decks of ships as well, and down on the beach, and beside the river.

But not all. Some of the beasts were screaming, fleeing, flapping wildly away to north and south and west, in fear. Beyond the gates the clash of battle was still raging in places; stilling in others as men looked up, observing the strange spectacle. Some cheered as they saw the dragons flee. Others ran, sensing something, the way animals do before a natural disaster strikes. Starcats were leaping away, sprinting for the bridge that spanned the river to flee into the woods on the far bank, with riders on their backs and without. Sunwolves howled and followed. Camels loped madly in all directions, smashing men out of the way as they ran. Horses threw knights from their saddles as they reared, neighing and bucking.

Hundreds of men, thousands even, were running for the ships. Men in gold and silver and bronze, in copper armour and feathered cloaks. They made for vessels from Lumara and Aramatia and Pisek. The captains and sailors aboard were unfurling their sails, making ready to leave. A few Lightborn Starriders and Sunriders were rushing for the river to cross the bridge, in desperate pursuit of their bonded beasts. Others let them go, fear overwhelming the bond. What cheering there had been from the northmen began to die and sour and curdle into screams. And still the battle continued. Still not all had seen.

But Amron Daecar had. Atop his godsteel plate, he thickened the icy armour about him, another layer, another, another, another. But all the same, it might not matter.

Amron Daecar withdrew the Frostblade from its sheath, and stared east, waiting.

Be Varin Reborn, he thought.

68

Lythian

"Unhand me, Lythian. Damn you, unhand me! I can stand on my own. I do not need your help." Dalton Taynar staggered to his feet, clutching at his gut with a gauntleted hand. Lythian could not see the blood beneath his armour, though knew for a certainty that his wound had opened up.

That strike would have broken every suture they sewed into him, he thought. It had been a lashing tail that did it, knocking the First Blade a full twenty feet through the air to land in a heavy heap. The Sword of Varinar had been dislodged from his grasp during his tumble, planting itself nearby in the mud. Dalton looked around, desperate. "Where is it? Where is it?"

"Right there, my lord." Lythian made a motion toward it…

…and Dalton Taynar sprung at once. "No…no, don't touch it. It's *mine*." The last word was rasped and ugly. He lurched away toward the blade and took it back up in a maddened scramble. "*Never* touch it. You never touch it, do you hear?"

"I hear you, Lord Taynar."

"Good." The golden blade was hoisted aloft, sending a wash of light upon the men nearby, piercing smoke and ash and gloom. Cheers rang out from those who saw, though those were few, and his knights flocked to him, fewer still. "On me! On me! For Vandar!" he roared.

Flanked by Sir Rodmond and Sir Ramsey, the First Blade launched forth into battle, almost stumbling as he went. *He's dazed*, Lythian knew. *That dragon knocked half the sense out of him, and he hasn't much to spare.* Around the beast some seventy or eighty men were attempting to bring it down, some throwing spears, others dashing forward with blades, a few bowmen nocking and firing.

"For Vandar! For Vandar!" Dalton called, speeding right back in. The men gave out a cheer to see their First Blade return, though as he tried to leap into an attack, his foot caught on a dead man's leg and he tripped, face-planting right into the mud. The cheering died.

"Uncle!" Rodmond Taynar rushed to defend him, slashing at the dragon as it whirled, fending it away. Dalton struggled back to his feet, smeared in mud from face to groin, shouted, 'For Vandar!' for the thousandth time, and surged forward to his nephew's side. *He is undeterred, I'll give him that.*

Lythian went to follow, noticing that Sir Ramsey Stone was holding back. "He's your First Blade, Sir Ramsey," he shouted at the Varin Knight. "Get in there and defend him!"

Stone only snorted behind his visor. "Why? We're all going to die here anyway."

"Just get in there, damnit!"

The knight gave a scoff and shook his head. "I'd sooner live a while longer. To hell with Dalton, and to hell with you, Lindar. I'll see you at Varin's Table." He turned and stepped away, pushing his way through the men behind him.

"Sir Ramsey!" Lythian called after him. "Sir Ramsey! Come back here, that's an order!" The man ignored him. "Stone!" he shouted again. "You'll face the gallows for this, Stone! There will be no seat at his Table after *this*!"

Lythian blasted out a breath and turned. *Craven. He was always a feckless craven!* The two Taynars had the dragon's attention away from him. Lythian sighted an immediate chance and sped in behind the beast, thrusting powerfully through the plate of its hindquarters, disabling a leg. The dragon hissed, stumbled, its tail lashing at him; he ducked it, slashing in a fearsome downcut, severing through the tip. Blood gushed at once from its stump and the two Taynars pounced, rushing in, hacking and cutting at its neck and face, as spears and arrows came flinging from the crowds, and a score of men-at-arms descended.

The dragon was shortly overwhelmed, smoke wheezing from several dozen wounds. It was Dalton Taynar who delivered the killing blow, swinging hard with the Sword of Varinar to slice through the beast's skull, just behind the eye. It always amazed Lythian to watch that blade at work. The way it moved so easily through the armour, the scales and horns, with almost no resistance at all. There was something joyously satisfying about that.

The men gave out another cheer. Dripping blood, the Sword of Varinar shot skyward once again, and the man indulged his victory as though he'd slain the beast alone. "For Vandar! For Vandar! For Vandar!" he bellowed. Blood was leaking out through a low seam in his armour now, and after the third roaring repetition, he fell to a knee, heaving for breath. Lythian stepped over. "Take a moment, Lord Taynar. The battle is in its infancy."

"You need attention, Uncle," Sir Rodmond said. He flipped up his visor to get a better look. Sweat dappled his brow, his eyes showing concern. "You're losing a lot of blood."

"I've got plenty to spare." Dalton stood, though shakily, defiantly filling his lungs. "The stitches have come loose, is all. The blood will clot soon enough and seal the wound."

Lythian could not fault the man's determination and courage.

"Where is Sir Ramsey?"

"Fled," Lythian told him.

"Coward," the First Blade spat. "Never liked him."

Few did. Sir Ramsey Stone did not exude characteristics considered likeable.

"The dragons are acting strange," Rodmond pointed out. His eyes scanned the skies, thick with smoke and falling ash. "I saw a pair of them fighting each other. And one came down and snatched a rider from a sunwolf's back. I even saw a *dragonknight* flying through the air. They don't seem to care who they kill."

"They're *dragons*, Rodmond. Wild beasts. They can never be completely tamed." Dalton coughed as he spoke, doubling over in a fit of pain. Lythian heard blood in that cough, spattering against the inside of his faceplate.

"Uncle…I really think you need attention. There are medics, further back. If we…"

"If we what, Rodmond? Remove my breastplate so they can get at the wound? Sew it up again, right here, in the middle of the battle?" He coughed once more. "No. It'll only open up again. I fight on, Nephew." He stepped away, looking increasingly weary, shouting, "For Vandar! For Vandar!" with greatly less volume than before.

"Stay close to him, Rodmond," Lythian said to the young knight, before he might follow. "He could pass out at any moment and will need your protection."

"I'll not leave his side, Captain."

"And don't raise your faceplate again. It only takes one arrow or errant spear."

"Yes, Captain. I understand." Rodmond Taynar slammed his visor back down and rushed off at the heels of his uncle.

Lythian did not join them. *I cannot shadow the man for the entire battle,* he thought. He had his nephew with him, and his knights and men-at-arms and that should suffice. He gave his surroundings a scan and spotted Rogen Strand nearby, putting the finishing touches on a dragonknight kill. The ranger was not a man of the forms, or a knight, and had not been trained to fight in battle, but for all that was a brutal combatant, long-limbed, fast, and unafraid. After killing the knight, he stood, turning slowly, scanning the skies. The fighting churned all about him, but he just stood there like a man enjoying the view.

Lythian hurried to join him. The ranger seemed to sense his presence without so much as giving him a glance. "Some of the dragons are fleeing," he rasped.

Lythian looked up. The ranger wasn't wrong. Several of the beasts appeared to be flapping away north or west, or back out to sea. There was something frantic about the way they flew, something fearful. Lythian could hear their high-pitched screaming below the clatter of bodies, the ring of steel, the growling of wolves and hissing of cats. "Why would they fly away?" he wondered out loud.

"Not all are." Whitebeard was a taller man than Lythian Lindar, though all the same it was hard to see much of anything beyond their immediate vicinity. The ranger stepped onto the corpse of the drag-onknight he had slain to get a better look eastward. He stared for a prolonged moment, still and stable, then said, "They're bowing."

Bowing? That made no sense to the Knight of the Vale. "The dragons? Dragons don't *bow*, Rogen."

"These ones do."

Lythian made no reply. Through the maelstrom of fire and fume he caught a glimpse of the city walls, the broken towers, saw dragons descending to land upon the battlements and blackened ruins, lowering their heads and arching their necks and spreading their wings, facing east. It was a glimpse only, but enough to confirm it. *Bowing. He's right. They're bowing...*

A fist was twisting in his guts. He turned to Whitebeard again, who still stood atop that red-caped corpse, staring east as well. The ranger's eyes were as keen as any in the north, Amron Daecar had told him. Spending long months alone in the Weeping Heights and Icewilds, surrounded by so many dangers, had sharpened his eyesight and hearing beyond the scope of normal Bladeborn knights. "What do you see, Rogen?"

"A shadow in the east. A dragon, approaching fast." He turned his gaze to left and right, searching through the shroud of battle. "Men are fleeing. Making for the woods and the boats. Hundreds of them. Thousands."

"Amron? Where is *Amron*, Rogen?"

"Alone," the ranger said. "He stands alone, my lord."

"On me." Lythian paced forward at once, shoving men aside, stepping over the dead and dying as he went. A dragon passed before him, sending down a river of flame, but he walked straight through it, emerging onto the other side as men rushed beneath the protective shelters of the shield-bearers or dashed away in alarm. Ahead Lythian saw the Giant of Hammerhall standing with his enormous godsteel warhammer in his grasp, holding it aloft, roaring to the skies, bellowing out in taunt to every dragon that flapped overhead. "Sir Taegon!" he shouted.

The steel giant turned, saw him coming through the smoke. "Captain Lythian," he roared back. "These dragons are cowards, every one of them! None will face me! None will dare!"

This one will, Lythian knew. Through the eddies of smoke he could see the black shadow now, growing larger by the moment. *Black and red for Dread,* he thought. *It's as I feared.* "On me, Sir Taegon. Your king stands alone."

"He duels Garlath," Taegon Cargill boomed. "We can't interfere."

"The duel is over, Sir Taegon. A new threat approaches."

Sir Taegon had a better vantage than them all from his towering height. He looked east, then leaned back on instinct, as though struck by a sudden blow. The sudden wash of fear in him was palpable. "That's....thats..."

"Gather your best men," the Knight of the Vale said to him. "We march to join our king."

He paced forward, stepping over the head of a dead camel of monstrous size. Another came charging past him, the paladin knight atop its back trying to wrest control of the loping steed and failing. The camel careened into a clutch of men, knocking several to the ground, trampling a pair more, before a spear came thrusting from the smoke to pierce its neck.

"Sir Storos approaches," Rogen Strand said, gesturing.

Lythian saw the Pentar knight advancing his way, Sir Oswin Cole at his heels, the last of his men-at-arms just behind. "Lythian, the battle goes ill," Sir Storos panted. "The dragons will not engage us in the duel. They're killing without reason, even their own…"

"Look east, Storos," Lythian interrupted. "These dragons are the least of our troubles now."

Sir Storos Pentar looked east. Even from behind his visor, Lythian could see his eyes widen. "Gods, no…it…it can't be…"

"It is, Sir Storos. On me." Lythian Lindar marched on, gathering his host as he went.

The battlefield was opening out before him. Men were rushing away in blind fear now, as they spotted the approach of the titan. Hundreds were already splashing down through the surf, making for their ships. Hundreds more were escaping upriver, or across the bridge that spanned the Steelrun, and into the woods. Huge swathes of soldiers were still engaged in the fighting, but fewer and fewer by the moment. Men were pointing, shouting, panicking, dropping their blades and spears and shields to run. The panic was like a plague, spreading from man to man, voice to voice. Cats and wolves and camels and horses all charged amok, knocking men over, crushing them in their haste to flee.

Only one man stood utterly still, it seemed. Amron Daecar, three hundred metres away toward the river, the Frostblade in his grasp, his gaze on the skies.

Lythian could feel the men gathering at his back, the Bladeborn knights and lords spotting the threat and valiantly marching forth to face it. Sir Taegon stamped beside him, breathing like a bellows, smashing his chest with a steel fist and roaring with each *clang*. Sir Torus Stoutman had joined him, as wide as he was tall, his sons of similar stature following right behind. From the army came too Sir Nathaniel Oloran, the disgraced Greycloak commander, seeking to restore his honour. Lord Kindrick was hurrying out as well, accompanied by his household knights, and Lord Barrow with his and the Varin Knight Sir Quinn Sharp, and Sir Ralf of Rotting Bridge, and others, many others…

But not all. Lythian stopped. "Where is Lord Taynar?" If ever there was a time when they would need the Sword of Varinar, it was now. "Where?" he shouted, to anyone who might answer. He scanned back toward the city, but could not see him. "Someone go back and get him. Sir Quinn. Go fetch the First Blade. Now!"

The broad-faced knight turned and rushed back, shouting for Dalton Taynar as he went. Through the rushing bodies Lythian thought he spotted a golden glow, but couldn't be sure. A voice snatched his attention. "A rider approaches." Sir Storos Pentar was pointing northward, up the river. Amid the hundreds and thousands rushing away in retreat, only one was coming their way. A knight ahorse, wreathed all in godsteel plate, galloping down the banks toward them. On his back billowed a blue cloak, and about the maw of his chestnut stallion was a white frothing lather, as though the destrier had been riding for hours, all night, without so much as stopping for a break.

Lythian knew the horse, as he knew the knight. He raised his blade and shouted, "Sir Vesryn! Vesryn Daecar!"

The man heard him, tugged the reigns, and veered their way, galloping with all haste.

"Vesryn Daecar?" Sir Storos said, confused. "I thought he was imprisoned in Varinar?"

He's meant to be, Lythian thought. This was Elyon's doing, he knew at once. He hurried forward, closing the ground as Sunsilver charged toward him. The destrier was one of the finest in the north, well capable of running a hundred miles in a day without tiring, even with a man in full plate mounted on his back. Lythian had heard Vesryn had sold his steed after he deserted from the siege camp at Harrowmoor, though perhaps that wasn't true. In moments Vesryn was pulling the reins and rearing up before him, leaping at once from the saddle to land upon the muddied earth.

"Lythian," he said, exhaling. "It's good to see you, old friend."

Lythian gripped the man's forearm in a steel embrace, shaking. He had heard of Vesryn's crimes and follies, though he was hardly one to judge. *I've made mistakes of my own.* "You've come at the right time, Vesryn. Elyon set you free?"

"Three nights ago. I've been riding hard ever since." He looked around at the chaos. "I saw the fires from miles away and feared the worst."

"The worst is coming, Vesryn." Lythian Lindar directed the man's gaze east. The shadow was getting larger, the details taking form. The skies seemed to burn in the wake of the Dread, and the demigod on his back.

"Amron," Vesryn said, seeing his older brother. "He's alone out there. We have to help him…" He stepped away.

Lythian detected the voice of Sir Quinn behind him, shouting. He turned back, saw Sir Quinn and Sir Rodmond coming toward them, with Lord Dalton Taynar between the pair. They appeared to be carrying him, *dragging* him almost, as he kept a weak grip on the Sword of Varinar. "Captain Lythian! He is too weak to fight! He's lost too much blood!" Sir Quinn was shouting.

Lythian knew at once what must be done. In two short steps he caught up to Vesryn Daecar, grabbed the godsteel longsword from his grasp, and threw it aside. "What in the blazes are you doing, Lythian?"

"Getting you a better blade."

69

Elyon

I'm too late, was his first thought, as the coast of Vandar appeared before him.

He could see the fire billowing up from the city, see the thousands, the tens of thousands, spreading far and wide across the plains. Hundreds of ships sat beached upon the strand, or bustled shoulder to shoulder in the harbour. Hundreds more were still at sea, galleys, galleons, galleasses, cogs and carracks and caravels, big bulky warships and low-slung oar-ships with skiffs and rowboats beyond his scope to count bobbing between them all.

The city beyond was burning, a hundred fires belching from within the walls of King's Point, sending black and grey fingers to scratch at the hard blue sky. Every tower had been felled but the Spear itself, it looked, the great keep as yet undone by the magic of dragonfire. Seaman's was in ruin, and Hangman's too. Red Watch, the Merry Maiden, the Black Lance, Bowman's bluff. Every tower was a tumble of black and broken stone, coughing fume in great thick puffs. A half dozen breaches had broken open in the walls, each piled high with dead invaders. Bowmen and archers were firing from the bastions and battlements, defending the city even now, but it was futile. The city was lost. That was clear to him at a glance.

He'd never seen so many dragons. Against the rising sun, their numbers were unveiled, swarming the city like ravening locusts. Twoscore of them flew above the fleet, circling, and twoscore more were diving and swooping upon the army. As many as that were flying north and west and even south, toward him, flapping and screaming as they fled the battle. As many more stood still as stone, perched upon the walls of the city or spread out upon the beaches and plains, facing east…

Elyon Daecar looked that way, and took a sharp intake of breath. From down the coast, a dragon that can only have been Drulgar the Dread was approaching, more immense than he could ever have dared believe. A coastal village sank into shadow beneath his bulk, half a forest seemed to darken as he passed. He saw trees ripple and sway, saw them singe and blacken and burn and catch fire as the dragon god flew lower to the ground, leaving a trail of destruction in its wake. Across its shoulders, its neck, even parts of its face, Elyon saw cuts and cleaves, glowing red. Some of them were bleeding, a smoking red lava dripping to the ground to scorch the earth where it landed. *He's seen battle already*, he realised. *But where? Against whom?*

A dozen dragons had landed near the river, where it opened out in a great yawning mouth to empty into the sea. Elyon saw Garlath the Grand there, big and blue and silver, yet an infant next to this titan. Others of various size and shape spread out about him, bowing as they awaited their master. A solitary figure stood down there among them, a figure of silver and white, steel and ice, standing all alone.

Father…

Amron Daecar held the Frostblade aloft, pulsing with a great white light, and atop Drulgar Elyon saw the Fire Father, tiny upon that black mountain of a back, perched amidst a forest of spines in crimson and claret and dark blood red. White hair and scarlet robes billowed, and on the air carried a manic cackling voice, as he lifted above his head a tall black staff, topped with a glowing orb. *The Bondstone…*

The Windblade was thrumming in his grasp; part fear, part frenzy, part thrill. Elyon Daecar accelerated to the upper limits of his speed, casting aside the deep fatigue that had driven down into his bones. He had hoped to rest on his return, but no such gift would be granted him. Drulgar was nearing, descending upon his father. The monster opened its maw and a roar shook the world, and from the Bondstone came a sudden red light, fizzing and blasting down upon Amron Daecar. With it came a strange unearthly screaming, a haunting chorus of tortured souls. Elyon cringed against the sound, turning his head. The beam struck the ground where his father stood, bursting the earth asunder.

"Father!"

Chunks of sandy mud settled, and from the dustcloud, Amron Daecar emerged, standing upright and unharmed. Even from here, Elyon could hear the roar that boomed from his lungs, as he thrust upward with the Frostblade, and from its tip a great spear of ice shot skyward, driving for the neck of the beast. It shattered as it struck the scales, bursting apart like crystal glass. Shards fell to the earth in a radiant glitter, melting in the rising sun, and below, Elyon heard shouts and cheers of 'Varin Reborn' echo thinly on the air as armoured men charged across the plains.

Drulgar the Dread roared again, and in that roar Elyon heard a boundless fury, an inexhaustible hate, as he opened his wings to slow, then furled them all of a sudden like a bat, sending a storm of burning wind to pass across the host. Trees fell flat. Men went flying back the way they'd come. The dragon let his weight drop, feet as large as longships swinging forward to land. The world shuddered beneath him in a thunderous earthquake, sending the waters of the river to rise up in great high waves, washing across the banks. The nearest boats swayed and reeled, masts swinging side

766

to side, and several skiffs were overturned, smashed apart by the churning water.

High on the crest of Drulgar's back, Eldur the Eternal raised his staff, and at once the dragons stirred and shifted, flapping away, descending upon the men who were still charging across the field. Elyon saw Garlath the Grand among them, saw the dragonlord Ulrik Marak saddled on his back, a fiery red blade at his hip.

The Bondstone, Elyon thought. *I must get the Bondstone.* If he could only take the staff and fly it out to sea...*I could drown it, send it down into the abyss where no man could ever find it.* Without his staff Eldur would be vulnerable. *I have to try. I have to try.* Without pausing to think or fret, he descended at a sharp angle, the world rushing past in a blur, the titan rising before him, filling his sight, the demigod on his back, cackling, exulting...

Just a few more seconds...a few seconds more...

Eldur's head snapped toward him, sudden as a thunderclap. Elyon Daecar stuttered in flight. His eyes were two red spots, burning in a bone-white face. Wide they stared, and pupil-less, inhuman. The staff swung about. The Bondstone glowed. A laugh like death and thunder, the laugh of a god, echoed out from him as he crashed the butt of his staff down onto Drulgar's back, and a blasting force Elyon could not describe rushed at once and assaulted him, smashing him off course.

The winds failed him, his power of flight blown out like a candle in a storm, and he went careening into a massive bone horn, dark maroon with veins of lighter red mottling its surface. The impact was violent, his head rattling within his helm, yet somehow he kept hold of the Windblade. Breathing hard, he struggled to his feet, momentarily lost, blinking. Spikes and horns rose up around him as though he'd landed in some infernal forest in the depths of hell. He could feel the dragon's breath beneath his feet, feel the vast pull in and out as the cavernous lungs filled and emptied, feel the heavy deep pounding of its massive heart within, *boom, boom, boom...*

He wondered how far away it was. He wondered how thick were the scales. His blade would barely be long enough to puncture through them, he wagered, yet nearby he saw a cleave, one of the cuts he'd witnessed from afar. It had looked so small from miles away, but he saw now that it was several feet wide, many times as deep...and made by what, he couldn't say. Lava boiled within, steam pouring from the rift. *He is fire incarnate,* Elyon thought. *A volcano in living form.* Yet for all that, the sight gave him hope. *He can bleed,* he told himself, *and that's all that matters. Anything that bleeds can die...*

He turned the point of the Windblade down, and thrust with all his might.

The point cut into the scales, a foot, perhaps a bit more. He pulled the blade out, and thrust again, for the same spot, and again, and again, and again, each time driving it deeper. After the fourth repetition, he felt it slide through the scale armour and into the soft flesh beneath, down into the meat of the monster. The dragon lurched suddenly, roaring, and when Elyon drew the Windblade out he saw steam and smoke pouring up from the puncture, glimpsed that molten blood bubbling up from within. His blade was like a pin-prick to the beast, and he'd need to cut at it a thousand times more to make a difference, but for all that it told him one thing. *He feels pain. And fear.*

The world moved beneath him, and to left and right he saw a pair of huge wings spread out to the edge of his vision, saw them rise high and then beat down in a great flap, felt the world *rush* and move upward, a hundred metres, two hundred, three hundred in a single beat. Elyon stumbled from the motion, tripping aside, reaching out to steady himself against one of those red-veined horns. Ahead, through that forest of spinal scales, he could see Eldur standing between the dragon's shoulder blades, sending beams of screaming red light down upon the world below, cackling.

Go, Elyon told himself. *You might not have a better chance. You have to try…*

He pointed the Windblade forward and flew, driving himself toward the Fire Father's back once more. *Don't turn,* he thought. *Don't turn, don't turn.* He was thirty metres away, twenty, ten…He saw the fiery colours in the Bondstone swirling in a fevered motley, saw the very face of Agarath in the orb, a face of shadow and flame, piercing his very soul, casting his heart in darkness. The screaming grew louder, unbearable. *Eight metres, six, five…*He cringed against that unutterable wailing, sweat pouring from his brow. His heart thrashed as though about to explode; he could feel it pulsing in his temple, his neck. His throat swelled up, choking, and it seemed suddenly as though his eyes were filling with blood, leaking from his tear ducts to wend across his cheeks. But he did not turn away. He *could* not turn away. *Four metres, three…*He reached out with his spare hand to grasp the staff…*Two metres, one…*

The staff shifted away, beyond his reach. Eldur the Eternal's eyes moved, and saw him. A smile twisted upon his ageless grey lips. Elyon surged straight past. Those red eyes followed, and a beam of screaming light was cast in pursuit, closing, closing…

He swung the Windblade down, plunging away. Through the smoke he saw the dragon's head take shape, appearing like a great warship upon a dark foggy sea. A great eye glowed amid the murk, split by a long thin pupil. It saw. The head swung, maw opening, twisting toward him on a neck as thick as a tower. For a moment Elyon Daecar was consumed in shadow, the rising sun blotted out. He saw teeth to either side, the roof of a mouth above, felt searing heat boiling behind him. Then a moment later he was shooting free just as the jaws crashed down, the whole world *cracking*, trembling, firing out through its teeth and into the smog. *Close,* he thought, heart thrashing at his ribs. *Too close. Much too close…*

Below him fires were burning, the earth rent and torn, steam billowing up from fissures. The mouth of the river had been rearranged, a great rift opened up at its heart. Water poured down, sending up great white plumes of mist. To either side the river shallowed to a ford, filled with broken ships and burning sails.

Elyon whipped the Windblade and turned, but the dragon and the demigod were gone. He felt only the great drag and pull of the dragon's wings as he beat them, and saw the colossal shadow flying away toward the city, toward the tens of thousands of men still rushing in chaos across the plains.

He made to follow, then stopped. A voice was bellowing from below.

"Elyon! Elyon!"

He looked down and saw two lights - white and gold - a hundred metres below him. He flew down through the smoke to land beside them, found his father there, bearing the Frostblade, and..."Vesryn?" He remembered his last words to him, when they'd parted outside the gates of Varinar. *Ride hard, and unresting. Ride for war, Uncle...and redemption.* "You came..."

"Just at the right time," Vesryn Daecar said. "Or the wrong time, another might say."

He held the Sword of Varinar in his grasp, misting gold. "How do you..."

"Later," his father cut in. His eyes flashed west. "You have to bring him lower. *Lower*, Elyon. The Sword of Varinar is wasted when the dragon is airborne."

Elyon baulked at those words. "How, exactly? I'm a fly to him, Father."

"A fly. *Exactly*. Buzz about. Be an annoyance. Bring him lower, so Vesryn might have a chance to kill him. If he can get atop the skull, he might be able to reach the brain."

Elyon shook his head. *Not by a long shot*, was his thought, though he only said, "The Sword of Varinar isn't long enough. The armour is thick and the skull will be thicker. The brain is too well protected."

"We have to try," Amron said, unwilling to hear it. "The eyes as well. We must target them, try to blind him if we can. It will make the beast greatly more vulnerable."

The Master of Winds nodded. That made a deal more sense. The eyes were on the surface, at least.

"And forget the Bondstone, Elyon," his father went on. "I've seen you go for it. It's no use. You won't be able to bear the staff."

Elyon sensed that was true. Even being close to it was unendurable. *The face, the voice, the screaming...* He reached up to raise his faceplate, rubbing at his eyes, checking to see if his gauntlets came back smeared in blood. Of sweat there was plenty, but of blood there was none. He breathed out. *It was all in my head.* "I'm trying to sever the link, Father," is all he said. "The Soul of Agarath...it's *controlling* him. If I manage to dislodge it, at least, or..."

Amron Daecar didn't let him finish. "We've heard this before. It is speculation. We don't know for sure that Eldur is being controlled."

"We do. *I* do. I heard it from the very lips of the princess." Elyon saw the confusion on the faces of his father and uncle. Both men had raised their visors for the conference, though all knew it couldn't last long. The Dread was already nearing the city, and when he did the scale of death would be calamitous. "Long story," he said to those looks. "Just...trust me. If we can get the Bondstone off him..."

"Fine. Try, if you must. But bring him back here first." Amron Daecar paused, seeing the satchel on his son's back, the shape of an orb contained within it. "You have it?"

Elyon nodded. In the rush of it he'd half-forgotten. "I'd hoped to get it somewhere safer, but…"

"It's safe enough with you for now."

Away toward the city, a shuddering roar filled the skies. They turned to see Drulgar unleashing fire upon the hordes. Red lightning seemed to wreath him, and dozens of dragons were flying around him as planets about a star, orbiting his great unearthly mass. In that moment all of them seemed to share the same thought, the same despair. *This is a task beyond us*, Elyon thought. He did not utter it. None of them uttered it. "I have to go," he said.

Amron Daecar fixed him with a steely blue gaze. "Bring him back, son. Together we can defeat him."

Elyon raised the Windblade, wreathing himself in swirling air. "Be ready," he told them. Then he gave each man and nod, and soared.

70

Amron

He watched his son depart, flying westward in pursuit of the titan. Silence followed his parting. Silence between brothers, against a backdrop of battle.

"Amron, I…"

"We don't need to talk about it, Vesryn." Amron knew at once by his tone of voice what subject his brother wanted to raise.

"I have to say it."

"You've said it already…"

"I'm sorry. For everything. And for Aleron above all. You know I never intended for him to be hurt. And you…"

"I said *not now*, Vesryn. We can talk after the battle…"

"There may not be an *after*, Amron. I *need* to say this. I *need* you to know…"

"I know. Damnit, I know." He turned to face him, if just to get this done. "You made mistakes. You were envious, resentful, and *young*. Those mistakes have haunted you all your life and they grew into something you never wanted or expected. I understand that. You loved Aleron, I know you did. And Lillia…well, *you* raised her, not me. You and Amara. While I was running from my grief, you were there, taking care of my family. I'll always be grateful for that, Vesryn. And in time…in time I may even be able to forgive you."

Vesryn's eyes changed. "You'll…"

"You heard what I said. Now *enough*," Amron told him, putting an end to it. "They'll be back any moment, and we need to figure out a strategy. How are we going to defeat this titan, Brother? *That* is the only question we need to answer."

Vesryn nodded, considering. A weight seemed to shift from his shoulders at Amron's words. *If it allows him to fight more freely, it was worth it.* "How did they do it before?" his brother asked. "Varin, Elin, Iliva. They bore the same blades as we do, Amron, against the same foe."

No, Amron Daecar thought. *We have it even worse.* According to the histories, Eldur was not there when Drulgar fought Varin and his children three and half thousand years ago, along this very same stretch of coast. The parallels had not been lost on him. *The same blades. The same foe. But we are shadows of what came before…*

He cast those doubts aside. He had to believe the titan could be slain, else all hope would be lost. "Accounts vary," is all he said. "And have probably been mythologised. Which singer do you want to believe? Which telling by which bard? Personally, I don't care for them…I trust what I see with my own two eyes and we've seen the *blood*, Brother. We *know* he can be wounded." He put a steel hand on his shoulder, shaking. "We can do this, Vesryn. You, me, Elyon. For the north. For Vandar. For the glory of House Daecar."

A smile gripped Vesryn's lips, fixed and defiant. "For House Daecar," he echoed, his blue cloak swaying in the breeze.

Amron looked west. The city was no more than a mile away, though still Drulgar looked monstrous. Earlier, as he'd watched him approach, he'd never felt such intense terror and hopelessness, but as with any battle, the waiting was the worst of it. By the time he'd shot that first spear of ice up into the dragon's craw, the thrill of the contest had consumed him and all his fear had fled. "We are dead men," he'd said to Lythian in the audience chamber only days ago. *And dead men do not fear,* he thought now, as he awaited the Dread's return.

The earth about them was scarred and blackened, a wasteland of pits and craters and steaming fissures, as though the land itself was terraformed at Drulgar's passing. *All the north will be the same, lest we defeat him here, and now.* A short distance from where they stood, a dozen duels were taking place between Bladeborn knights and Fireborn dragonriders, minions to their master's will. Through the puffing steam and smoke, Amron caught glimpses of fearsome combat, saw Sir Taegon there, and Nathanial Oloran, and Sir Torus Stoutman and Rogen Whitebeard as well. And Lythian, in his silver and green armour, blade flashing in the dawn. *My friend.* A part of Amron wanted to rush forth and help them, but he could not let himself be distracted. *Their fate is now their own,* he thought. *And we have but one foe to fight.*

Vesryn had planted the Sword of Varinar into the earth before him. He looked up and down its length, then said. "Elyon might be right about the brain, Amron. Striking at it through the skull may not be possible. The dragon is too big. But the neck… If I can cut deep enough to nick the jugular…"

Amron nodded. It was worth a shot. "If you see a chance, take it. Brain, neck, eyes. Just don't waste energy cutting at its toes. Wait until a proper chance arises and then strike." He had a long look into his brother's eyes. "You're tired. Did you not get much rest on the road?"

"Scant little," Vesryn admitted. "Elyon told me to ride hard and unrelenting. I took that to heart, Amron."

Clearly. Varinar was hundreds of miles away, and Elyon must only have released him from his cell three days ago. Not for the first time, Amron Daecar mused on the subject of fate, and providence. His brother's coming could not have come at a more auspicious time, nor the return of Elyon from his long flight south. *The same three blades, the same foe.* That he held the Frostblade put him in the role of Elin, Varin's eldest son...*Yet him,* he thought, looking at Vesryn, at the glowing golden sword planted in the earth at his feet. *He takes on the role of Varin here, not me.* Varin Reborn, they called him. *Perhaps they got the wrong brother,* Amron thought.

The Dread had reached the city. It was hard to make out much from here, though it seemed to Amron that the dragon was attacking the Spear, clamping down upon the great keep with its jaws, tearing out great chunks of stone and snapping godsteel supports as though they were naught but rotten twigs. A shudder climbed his spine to watch the tower reduced so quickly to rubble. *The power...the ferocity...* He spared a thought for the brave men atop it, the bowmen and ballista men who'd been fighting upon its battlements. *I pray they got some shots at him first.* If they were lucky, one of those ballista bolts would blind the beast, but if not every single strike through his armour would help to weaken him. Arrows and quarrels would have no effect, but long, strong godsteel-tipped bolts shot from ballistas and scorpions would be able to penetrate his armour, he hoped. *A thousand good strikes and we'll have a chance...*

Into his great orbit the Dread had taken a score of other dragons now, flying about his wings, beneath him and above him, screeching and screaming as though cheerleaders to their lord. A glint of silver flashed here and there, zipping through and past them, and from between the Great Calamity's shoulders, red beams of light chased after him, bursting from the orb atop the Fire Father's staff. Elyon was too quick and too agile. He avoided each assault, darting through that tempest of wings and fangs and claws, but for all that his luck would not last forever. *I told him to be a fly, and he is. A fly in a swarm of ravens, any one of which could kill him...*

Vesryn seemed similarly concerned. "Drulgar isn't taking the bait," he said. "If Elyon keeps trying to get his attention like that he's going to get himself killed." He took a moment to think, then reached out, suddenly, and drew the Sword of Varinar from the mud. "We have to get his attention ourselves, Amron. We have to draw him back out."

It was easier said than done. "How?"

"With this." Vesryn turned the Sword of Varinar over in his grasp, showing the glowing glyphs and runes that ran the length of the steel, ancient symbols written by Ilith, designating the blade's particular and unique power. "The *Sword that Struck Drulgar*, they call it in Agarath. He will not have forgotten it, Amron. If I show it to him, he'll come."

Amron paused for thought. Vesryn had only just arrived and it was possible Drulgar had not yet seen him, nor Varin's favoured blade. *It might stir his trauma to see a man in misting armour bearing it,* he thought. *His trauma... and his rage.* He looked his brother in the eye. "He'll come after you, Vesryn. You and you alone. He won't stop until you're dead."

"I'm a dead man anyway, Amron. Better in the jaws of the Dread than with my neck in a noose." He gave his brother a firm look. "When he tries to bite down on me, I'll give him a taste of Varin's steel. Let me do this, Brother. Let me die restoring some of that honour I threw away."

A roar bellowed out from the west. Drulgar had brought the Spear down, and was swaying his great head from left to right, gushing flame upon the city. The rest of his minions did the same, filling all of King's Point with a boiling red lake of fire, as a great black fume rose up to fill the sky. For over three thousand years the city had stood watch on the Red Sea, guarding the mouth of the Steelrun River, blocking the way to Varinar. Now it had been reduced to ash and ruin.

A cold fury gripped at the heart of Amron Daecar. He thought of Lord Warton, of Lady Brockenhurst, of the civilians in the sanctuaries and crypts. *Did they get out in time?* Walter Selleck was with them, Amron knew, and if the man still had his luck, now would be the time to use it. *And the rest*, he thought. The thousands of other men upon the battlements and walls and fighting in the city streets. Not just northmen, but soldiers of the south as well. Drulgar and his dragons did not seem to differentiate. Did not seem to care. *They will cover all the land in ash. They will make this world a wasteland…*

Amron Daecar turned to his brother. "Raise the blade, Vesryn," he growled. "Let him see its light."

His brother did not hesitate, not even for a moment. Bravely he thrust the Sword of Varinar at once into the air, and from the steel, light abounded, gold and bold and brilliant, radiating from its edge, casting away the gloom.

Drulgar the Dread turned, and saw.

He paused, as though peering at the blade and bearer, as though remembering the wounds it had inflicted upon him once before. And then, with a roar that shook the very foundations of the world, with a bellow that sent half the dragons about him scattering…he beat his wings and soared their way, a force of unimaginable fury.

"I think we have his attention." Amron studied his brother's eyes. They were steel, he was glad to see, unwilling to wilt, defiant to the last. "Varin is watching," he said. "Show him who you are, Brother."

Drulgar was fast approaching, leaving the rest of the dragons behind. In his wake stirred fire and fume and ash, broken wagon wheels and tents torn from the camp, men and even mounts, all ripped from the earth and dragged along by the vast pull of the dragon's passing.

Ahead, Lythian and Rogen Whitebeard and many others were turning to look, ducking and taking cover as that great wall of fire and fume and burning debris came hurtling at them. Dragons flapped away, ending their duels, screaming. Amron thickened his ice armour, and reaching out to lay a hand on Vesryn's shoulder, clad him in the same. *Vandar protect us*, he thought, in prayer. *Varin, heed us. Heed the might of House Daecar.*

The titan was almost upon them. Amron could see the boundless rage in his eyes. Above, high above, Eldur the Eternal was shouting something. He seemed to be clinging on, and that maddened laughter of his had stopped. *He is trying to calm him*, Amron realised. *Even he cannot control the beast.*

The wall of cloud had washed over the others, devouring all before it. "Brace," Amron said, as it came rushing up to meet them. "Brace, and then move. Drulgar will come right down through it."

He saw Vesryn nod. The air was already rushing past their helms, roaring, growing louder, hotter with each passing heartbeat. Then suddenly the wall consumed them, the world turning black. Fire flashed within the tempest, of burning poles and wheels and planks, and chunks of stone from the city walls came with it, and men as well, screaming as they past. Amron set his feet and leaned forward with all his weight, but even then the storm was near enough to dislodge him. To his side Vesryn was doing the same. "Ready to move!" Amron shouted. "Get ready to move, Brother!"

He glanced up. The shadow of the beast was looming, as he'd thought, the shape of a vast head plunging down through the smog toward them. Amron opened his mouth to shout, "Now!", but as he went to say the word a dead horse came hurtling through the storm, crashing right into his chest, breaking his footing, sending him tumbling back across the field...

He reached down with a hand, dug into the earth with steel fingers. When he came to a stop his feet were submerged in several inches of water, where the banks of the river had broken open, soaking through the plains. Men were still tumbling past, the dead and the dying both, and there were more horses too, and starcats and even camels, great strong Piseki camels rolling to a stop nearby, splashing into the river. Amron looked forward. He could see the shadow of the Dread, the wings spreading out across the world, see the flashes of red lighting, hear the great thunderous grinding and groaning that accompanied his every move.

The world shook beneath his feet. Men were crying out all around him, animals bleating in their own plaintive tongues as they came to a stop, battered and broken. The air was still rushing, bringing a thousand projectiles with it. Amron stamped forward, feet sucking at the sodden earth, ducking bits of broken debris. Above him he saw a glint of silver, as Elyon came diving down into the smog, whipping the Windblade as he went. It was flash only; a moment later he was gone, away behind the great black shadow above. *Son...stay safe, son...*

Amron pushed on. A voice came from his right, weakly, begging. "My lord...help...please..." He turned. It was Hodden Stoutman, Sir Torus's youngest son, barely more than a boy. A wooden stave had pierced right through his stomach, several inches wide and just as thick. He would be dead in moments, Amron knew, and much as it pained him, he could not stop to tend him. He marched on, stopping only to kneel and cup his hand to his cheek and say, "Go in peace, Hodden. You fought well today. You fought *well*."

He hoped it would give him solace in his passing. Hodden Stoutman was no Varin Knight, no knight at all, but would journey as a hero to the Eternal Halls all the same. *How many of us will he meet there? How many of us have died?* This was not like the wars Amron Daecar had fought, not like the battles. This was like nothing they had ever trained for. No one had, not for thousands of years. He looked up at the shadow, tall as a mountain, at the wings that could embrace the world. The body was shifting, as though snapping out at something, and once again Amron saw that silver light, swishing through the shroud, saw his son whipping the Windblade to try to clear the air.

Or maybe he was attacking? Trying to dislodge the staff from Eldur's grip? Amron couldn't know. Nor could he do anything to help from down here. He searched forward, seeking a golden light, and *there*…it was dashing across the field, as the great maw plunged down, snapping, and as it did Vesryn spun and leaped and slashed and cut. *He cut it!* Amron thought, roused by a sudden hope. Blood gushed from the hewn flesh of the dragon's face, boiling and steaming, and suddenly Drulgar was rearing back and roaring, and spraying that lava through the air. Some of it came down atop him, and Amron dashed aside as it spat onto his armour, sizzling at the godsteel plate, leaving scorch marks on the metal.

"Brother!" He burst forward through the veil, found Vesryn there amid the pits and craters, panting. "You *cut* him, Vesryn. You made the Dread bleed."

"Not enough. It was a scratch to him, Amron." Vesryn stared up, searching for that shadow again. "This fume is ungodly. I can barely see a thing."

But they could *hear*, and they could *feel*. Feel the pull of air, hear the beat of wings, know that the beast was rising…rising…and *falling*, suddenly falling toward them, wings furled, weight dropping…

"Run!" Amron bellowed. They sprang away, as the shadow reappeared, the colossus crashing right down where they stood with two enormous, taloned feet. The earth quaked beneath them, tearing, and into the broken world fell the dead and the dying and burning debris, swallowed up by the rents and pits.

The jaws followed once more, crunching down upon that golden light. Vesryn leaped away, as Amron thrust out with the Frostblade, invoking Vandar's will, and sent forth a violent fusillade of ice spears to shatters against the dragon's face. They burst upon his plate armour, melting into magnificent colours, though one…one struck his eye, and the monster lurched away once more, stumbling aside, reeling, falling…

"Now, Vesryn! Now!"

Vesryn rushed forward. Amron followed through the swirling smog. The air cleared, the fume rising. He could see Drulgar standing again, pushing up with one great winged arm, gouging a great rift into the earth. But his head was still low, and his neck…his neck was exposed…

Vesryn Daecar *flew*. The Sword of Varinar flashed, cleaving. Amron saw the meat of the monster's neck open, saw blood flowing out from the wound. His eyes widened in hope. Drulgar continued to rise as Vesryn leaped and swung again, cutting him once more. Amron summoned his might, casting a spear of ice from the tip of the Frostblade. He fired it for the open wound, and saw it drive into the monster's flesh, gouging deeper, hissing and melting and falling in a rain of misting colours.

Another roar, another lurching movement. Drulgar thrashed violently, those massive eyes, blazing red, searching, finding Vesryn, stamping down upon him, but the man dashed away. The dragon continued to stamp, utterly and ferociously enraged, lava spraying from a half dozen wounds. The air pulled and rushed at his motion, the world shaking with every thunderous tread. Amron Daecar rushed to help his brother…

…then spotted Elyon flying down past the dragon, armour catching the sunlight, descending to the ground. He was shouting something as he went. Amron heard his voice clearing through the tumult. "Kill him! Kill him! Kill him!"

Amron spun, and saw. *Gods…*

The Father of Fire had fallen, slipping free of Drulgar's back as he thrashed. Amron could see him now, climbing to his feet, white hair and crimson robes, reaching out to take up his long black staff.

"Stop him! Stop him!" Elyon was shouting. He swung the Windblade, unleashing a spinning vortex of air; it knocked the demigod off balance, and for a moment it looked like he would falter, lose his grip on his staff…

…but no…suddenly he had it in his grasp, and was raising it above his head, and his lips were whispering some ancient incantation, and from the Bondstone a beam of red light was pulsing, fizzing, rushing…

…and striking Elyon in mid-flight. A light flashed; thunder cracked and echoed. His son went tumbling away, end over end, limbs hanging loose, the Windblade flying from his grasp, vanishing into the fume.

"Elyon!" Amron Daecar roared. He rushed at the Fire Father, casting a mist of ice from the Frostblade to bathe him, freeze him, trap him…and from beyond the sorcerer he could see Lythian coming from the other way, and Sir Taegon, and others, closing in, bloody blades to hand, shouting 'For Vandar! For Vandar!' as they ran.

But the ice had no effect. It melted as it neared him, thawed by the great pulsing heat radiating from the Soul of Agarath. Eldur the Eternal raised the orb aloft once more, whispering a spell, and from it erupted a terrible emission of crimson light, flowing and spreading and *screaming*, stopping every man in his tracks. Amron came to a sudden halt, grimacing against the chaos of voices in his head, toppling suddenly forward onto his knees. Spots of light danced against the red haze of his vision. His ears were bleeding, his eyes were burning, it felt like a thousand daggers were stabbing at his mind. He screamed out, crunching his fist around the Frostblade's hilt - *Vandar, be with me* - and suddenly the screams were fading, and his sight was clearing, and he was standing again, and striding forward, sheltered by the spirt of his god.

All others about him were on their knees, stumbling, falling, holding at their heads, pounding at the ground, screaming against the voices. A dragon descended from the skies, drawn by the power of the Bondstone. It landed beside its master, lowering a wing, as Eldur stepped forward to climb atop it. *He is leaving*, Amron realised. *He is weakened…fleeing…*

The thought stirred him. He rushed forward, to Eldur the Eternal, and stood before him, alone."Face me, sorcerer!" he called out in challenge. "Honour the duel, and face me!"

Eldur drew himself onto the dragon's back, turned to look at him with red pupil-less eyes. There was a strange smile on his bloodless lips, part triumph, part regret. "The duel," he said, in that whisper Lythian had described. A strange unearthly voice that seemed to come from all around him, in his right ear and his left and inside his very head. "The duel is between Fireborn, and Bladeborn, Amron Daecar. I am neither. I am *more*."

Amron clenched his teeth against the voice, leaning on the spirit of Vandar to protect him. "Coward. I will not let you leave!"

"Let me? How would you stop me? You cannot, Amron Daecar. No more than you can stop *him*." His red eyes flashed behind him. Amron did not need to glance back to know that Drulgar was taking flight, beating those mighty wings, sending the air rushing in a chaos all about him. He sensed the shadow rising, heading away to the northeast, as his minions stirred and went to follow, flapping and screaming in his wake, a storm of leathern wings.

"Where are you sending him?" Amron demanded. "*Where?* Tell me!"

"I am sending him nowhere, Amron Daecar. Drulgar goes where his own heart wills it. He is driven only by the will of Agarath now. You will get used to living in his shadow."

"Call him back! You bear the Soul of Agarath! Call him back!"

"Why? The Soul of Agarath wills this, child." A cold smile twisted on his lips. "Farewell, son of Varin. You will do well in this new world, I think. It is made for *strong* men like you."

A battlefield, Amron thought. *A world of gods and monsters. A world of eternal war.*

Eldur whispered something, and the dragon beneath him took flight. Amron roared, casting spear after spear in pursuit, but each of them just burst asunder, shattering and melting as they neared. A dozen dragons swept down to fly beside him, escorting their master as he was borne away south, back across the sea to the lands of Agarath, as a blood-red sun rose up in the east.

Silence fell. Amron stood motionless. *We have failed,* he thought. Yet he could not stand there forever, in regret. All around him, men were still weeping and crying in their hands, smashing their fists into the ground, holding their heads and tearing at their hair. Further off, the fire and smoke poured up from the ruin of King's Point, and thousands, tens of thousands of men and mounts lay dead across the field. How many more had fled and scattered Amron could not say. Across the sea, ships were sailing south, but most still remained in the harbour, or beached against the strand, and there he still saw men fighting, Agarathi and Lumarans and northmen all hacking and cutting and killing.

This is the world now, he thought. *This is what he has made it.*

He turned, remembering Elyon, and saw him lying some forty metres away against a bank of churned up earth. He rushed over to him, drawing up his son's visor. Blood trickled from one side of his mouth and his right eyebrow was savagely split in two. He must have smashed his face against his helm as he landed. "Elyon. Elyon, can you hear me?"

Amron gave him a shake. The boy moaned, mumbling something incoherent. His eyes flickered, opening, settling upon the face of his father. "Father? I…did you…did you get him, Father? The…the…"

"Eldur fled, Elyon. He has returned to the south." He looked at the scorch mark the Bondstone had made. It had cut into his armour, though not *through* it, thank the gods. Against lesser plate perhaps it might have, but Elyon had had his armour strengthened and restored at the Steelforge only days ago. It might just have saved his life.

"And…the Dread…is he…" Elyon propped himself up onto an elbow, wincing, looking around. "He's gone…I don't…where…"

"Can you stand, Elyon?"

"Father?"

"Can you stand? I'm worried you may have suffered internal injuries."

"No…I'm fine. I'm sure I'm fine…just dazed, that's all." He stood, with Amron's help, looking as unsteady as a newborn deer on his feet. "I'm OK. I'm fine." Elyon blinked and looked around. The scene of devestation was almost more than Amron could bear, but he had to stay strong. In the new world…in whatever the world became now…he would need to remain a leader. *Hope*, he thought. *So long as we have the Five Blades, we still have hope…*

The Windblade had landed nearby, glowing silver. Elyon went to pick it up, sheathed it, then asked, "Uncle Vesryn. Where…I don't see him, Father."

Amron swallowed. Somehow he knew it, even before he turned and looked and saw…saw the crushed armour, the spoiled earth, the print of the dragon's foot leaving a deep depression in the ground. And the golden blade, glowing in that pit. He'd known it as soon as he saw Drulgar take flight. He had known, then, that his brother was dead.

"Elyon, you need to rest. You're very unsteady on your feet."

"No, no I'm fine. I told you. I just need a moment to catch my…" And then he saw, saw what Amron was trying to spare him. "Uncle? *Uncle*…" He ran, stumbling as he went, regaining his feet, running again. Amron followed more slowly, bracing himself as he approached his brother's body. The armour was badly crushed, shattering the limbs beneath, rending flesh and breaking bones, yet somehow, by some miracle, Vesryn's eyes were open, a smile on his bloodied lips.

"Uncle…" Elyon fell down to kneel beside him, removing his gauntlet, removing Vesryn's, taking his hand, holding it, squeezing. "Uncle…Uncle, can you hear me?"

"Elyon…" His eyes shifted, seeing him. His voice was barely a whisper. "I'm sorry…I'm sorry, I…I failed…"

"You didn't fail…you didn't. You *cut* him, Uncle. You cut him, I saw."

"You did more than anyone could have hoped for, Vesryn," Amron said. He knelt at his other side. "We have a chance now, Brother. You've shown us the way. You've given us hope."

Tears misted in Vesryn's eyes. His skin had gone bone pale, the blood rushing from his body. The light in his eyes was fading. "Amara…will you tell her…"

"We'll tell her you died a hero, Uncle. A hero, for all the north. She'll be so proud of you…so proud…as I am…"

"Proud…" Vesryn whispered. "I don't…deserve…"

"You've restored your honour," Amron told his little brother. He reached out, and took up the Sword of Varinar, wrapping Vesryn's fingers around the hilt, placing it against his armoured chest. "Go to our father now, Vesryn, and to our grandfather. Take your place at Varin's Table, with the other great First Blades of the past."

"Varin saw," Elyon croaked. "He was watching, Uncle. He *saw*…"

"You'll have a place at his side forever now," Amron said. "You and Varin…the only two men to ever drive Drulgar from the field…" He smiled down at him, and Vesryn smiled up, two brothers, two former First Blades, sharing a final look.

"We will see you there, Uncle," Elyon said, squeezing his hand. "We'll all be back together…one day."

Vesryn drew in his final breath, and looking up through the smoke and fume, saw a patch of sunlit sky, calling him forth. And as the sunlight glimmered in his eyes, he uttered his final words.

"Aleron should have been First Blade…" he whispered. "I'll give…my seat…to him…"

71

Jonik

Jonik stood atop the curtain wall looking out over the mountain passes, a frozen white world, gleaming beneath the arc of the sun. "Today," he repeated, breath fogging in the frigid air. "You think we should leave today?"

"Aye," Harden said to him. "Soon as your mother gets here. We just need to pack some provisions up, and get Cabel on a garron. Then we can go. No sense in waiting anymore."

Jonik turned to study the old man, wrapped up warm in his woollen cloak. His voice sounded strained, more urgent than usual. "We have been told repeatedly that we're not allowed to leave until the transference has been completed. What's changed, Harden? Do you know something I don't?"

The man's grey-bristled mouth twitched, as though he wanted to say something, but he only looked away through the mountains. A moment passed. Then another.

"Harden?"

"It's nothing. It's just time to go, is all. Before the storm starts up again. We mightn't have a better chance than now."

The snows had stopped, the fearsome blizzard that had blown across the mountains over the last day and night withering away not long past sunrise. Jonik had awoken to brightening skies and still air, the last few flakes drifting softly down to add the finishing touches to the great white wilderness the Shadowfort had become.

A beautiful day, he had thought, when he'd looked out from the window of his bedchamber. For the first time in a long time his sleep had been uninterrupted, and he'd dozed right through the dawn. He felt fresher and more energised and more optimistic than he had in long months, and the weather had seemed to agree. Even the sad and plaintive whispers of the Nightblade, buried deep within its frozen tomb, were barely audible to him now. *The storm has passed*, he'd thought, smiling. *The fetters at my feet…they're gone.*

He passed his eyes over the trail that led down the mountain. It look badly snowed under in places, though others were protected by the cliffs and overhangs that had borne the brunt of the weather. All the same, there were perils there too. Avalanches and rockslides had been known to kill men of the order in the past, and mostly it was considered prudent to wait in conditions such as these before daring the journey.

He said as much to Harden, who only grunted and replied, "Aye, that's what Gerrin said. Are you all bred wimpy around here?"

"We're bred cautious. And taught to understand the perils of the mountains. I would not expect a man of the Ironmoors to understand. They're rather flat, I have been told."

"As flat as my first wife's chest aye," the man said, with a grunt. It was Harden's version of a laugh. "She wasn't much blessed in the bosom, though a fine woman she was all the same."

Jonik frowned. "I wasn't aware you had a first wife. Or a second." Having a first would suggest a second. "Was there a third?"

"And a fourth," he said. "There's a lot about me you don't know, lad. Didn't take up sellsword work for the fun of it. Women can be expensive. And they seem to die like flies when I'm around too."

This was becoming a darker conversation than Jonik had expected. *Dark words for a bright day.* "You'll have to tell me about them sometime."

"Glad to. Be plenty of time to talk when we're heading down the mountain."

The man was being particularly persistent about this today. *Even more than normal.* "I suppose it would be wise to leave before the weather turns again," Jonik allowed. "If we get any more snow we could be trapped here for weeks. That'd be enough to drive us all insane, I should think."

The Ironmoorer gave a nod. "It's time, Jonik. Long past time, really, but I'll not quibble. I've been patient, you know I have. But my patience has its limits. If we don't leave today…"

"You'll go alone," Jonik said for him. "I know." He'd threatened that several times before, though not once had he followed through. Jonik couldn't be sure what it was that stopped him. *His sense of duty? The regret of leaving us behind? Fear of reprisal from the mages?* It was probably a blend of all three, as well as the fact that he would almost certainly get lost along the way. The heavy snows only made it all the harder to navigate the trails and twisting paths.

All the same, he belligerently refused to admit all that. "Aye, I will. I'll go alone," he insisted. Then he set his jaw and said it again, "I'm *going*, Jonik. You lot can come with me or not, but I'm not staying here another night." He glanced back through the fortress. "Not another bloody night."

Jonik had noticed him do that several times as they'd talked, passing his eyes to the mountains at the back of the fort as though searching for something. *My mother*, he thought. *He's waiting for her to come so he can gather us for a conference and put forth his case.* Half the lanes back there were entirely filled in with snow, and several buildings were scarcely more than white hillocks with the occasional thrust of stone poking out their summits and sides. He'd never known a snowfall like it here. Even in the harshest winters he could not recall the Shadowfort looking like this. He scanned the network of trenches they'd cut through the yard, so they might move more easily between the buildings that bordered it. To the right of the roundtower library, the path his mother took to the refuge had been newly ploughed, it looked.

Huh. He hadn't noticed that yet this morning. "Did she stay here overnight?" he asked.

"Come again, lad?"

"My mother. Was she trapped here because of the blizzard?" It seemed that way, by those tracks. If she'd left last night, the snow would have filled them in. Unless someone else had made them, and neither Harden nor Gerrin were in the habit of visiting the rear of the fort. At least not since Henrik and Hopper had led the pack of boys away down the mountains, leaving the four of them alone.

Harden was looking away from him. "Your mother, did you say?"

"Yes. My mother. The woman who birthed me and abandoned me. Cecilia Blakewood. I think you may be acquainted with her, Harden."

"Ah, yes, your mother. Right." He went silent.

"Well? There are tracks, leading to the back of the fort. Unless you or Gerrin made them…"

"You'd have to ask him. Gerrin knows more than I do about these sorts of things."

He's being evasive. And lying about something. Jonik gave him a searching look. "What aren't you telling me?"

"What was that, lad?"

"You're hiding something. It's obvious." The old man was not a good liar, never had been. *Too honest,* Jonik knew. Rare for a sellsword, but it took all sorts. "What is it?"

"What's what?"

"The thing you're not telling me."

"Loads of things I haven't told you. You just found out I've had four wives. Maybe now you know why I'm so grim all the time. Takes it's toll, all that…"

"Enough," Jonik said. He grabbed him by the shoulder, turned him, and looked directly into his crinkly grey eyes. "I want to know, Harden, and I'm not going to stop until…"

"Fine. Fine, you've twisted my bloody arm." He wrenched away, and gave out a disgruntled sigh. "Promised I wouldn't say, but…well damn it, I don't care anymore. I'm too godsdamn fed up with all these secrets and lies."

"What is it?' Jonik pressed. "Tell me, Harden."

He thrust a black gloved finger over the parapet. "There were footprints earlier, crossing the bridge. Came last night a couple of hours before dawn, we figure. Went right through the postern door, and…"

Jonik's blood froze in his veins. "And *what?* Someone *entered* the fort? Who?"

"We don't know."

"You didn't see? You were on watch last night."

"Aye, I was. Until about two hours before dawn. Then Gerrin came to take over."

"Then he'd have seen." Jonik turned his eyes to the kitchens. A thin trail of smoke was rising from the chimney, like a long skinny finger reaching up to tickle at the belly of the sky. His old master was cooking up a stew for them, keeping himself busy. "What did he say?"

"That he never relieved me. Was one of the mages, we figure. A Shadowcloak or some such foulness, posing as Gerrin so he might unseal the door and let whoever was waiting outside in…"

Jonik was already moving, feet crunching on the snow as he paced away in a hard, fierce stride. He turned back once he'd gone a dozen steps, thinking of something. "Does my mother know? Was she here as well?"

Harden nodded warily. "She…well, she went off to the refuge to find out what happened. Said for us not to tell you, in case…"

In case I take up the Nightblade. The temptation soared in him, sudden as a strike of lightning, and in his weakness a breach opened up, and through it came the whispers, pleading, rasping, whimpering like a lost child. He clamped his jaw down hard and reached into his cloak, clinging to the sword he'd taken from the armoury; a regular longsword, good godsteel, but plain. It braced him, steadied him. He marched on down the steps and along the icy trench through the yard, kicking through the door and into the kitchens. Gerrin looked up from the pot, ladle to hand.

"Why didn't you tell me?" Jonik demanded at once, the door swinging hard to crack against the wall. The man looked befuddled by the sudden intrusion. "The *footprints*, Gerrin. Why didn't you say anything?"

"We didn't want to worry you." Gerrin put the ladle in the pot, leaning the handle against the iron rim. The man was wearing an apron. A bloody *apron*, at a time like this.

"How can you be so calm? Some men have *entered* the fort, Gerrin. A mage mimicked you and let them in and you're standing there in a damn apron!"

"I'm cooking. It stops the sauce from spattering on my clothes."

"It could be the ones who escaped the night we took the fort," Jonik said, thinking. "I've had us all watching the gate for months, Gerrin. *Months.* And the night someone sneaks in, you don't even tell me!"

The old knight stepped away from the pot, removing his apron, hanging it on a hook on the wall. "Your mother told us not to. I offered to go with her, but she refused that as well, Jonik. What was I to do?"

"*Tell me.* Gods, Gerrin, you should have just *told me.*" He paced to the wall and back again, shaking his head all the while. "When did she go? How long ago was it?"

"Around dawn."

Hours, Jonik thought. "And it doesn't worry you that she hasn't come back?"

"A little, yes. But she's always split her time between here and there. She is probably just spending time with Tyrith."

"You don't believe that. I know you don't believe it." Jonik stopped in his pacing and turned to face him. He *was* worried, he could tell. It was evident in the crease between his eyes, the unsure tone of voice, though he was trying to hide it. *For me. He's trying to keep me calm by being calm himself.* Jonik breathed out; the whispers were growing louder and in this state he would be vulnerable. "Damnit, you should have just told me," he said, quieter now. "What if…what if something's happened to her?"

"Nothing will have happened to her, Jonik. You don't need to worry."

"You don't know that. None of us know *anything*." He started toward the door.

"Where are you going?"

"Where do you think? I have to find out if she's OK."

Gerrin rushed to intercept him. He put a hand to his chest. "Not a good idea, Jonik. These mages don't like us meddling in their affairs."

Jonik looked down at the splayed fingers, knuckly and gnarled, spread across his black leather jerkin. "Remove your hand, Gerrin. I'm not going to ask you again." When the old man did nothing, Jonik reached up and yanked his fingers away, twisting, and pushed right past him to the door, stepping outside. Harden had followed him down from the wall. *He's blocking my way to it,* Jonik realised. The grim sellsword was protecting the path toward the Nightblade, that was clear at a glance. "Stand down, Harden. I'm not going to take it back up."

The sellsword made no motion to move. *He doesn't trust me. Even now.* "You got an angry look in your eye, lad. I know where that can lead."

It'll lead me into the refuge, Jonik thought. He heard Gerrin stepping out after him, flexing his fingers and grimacing. "Think you might have cracked a bone, Jonik."

"You'll live. Where's your sword?"

"Hanging on a hook in there." He thumbed back through the door.

"Fetch it. And get some armour on. We might face resistance." He turned back to Harden. "You as well."

Jonik did not wait for the two men to respond. Off he went into the Night Tower, up the stairs to his bedchamber, where he kept the few components of plate armour he'd taken from the stocks Lord Merrymarsh had given them in Calmwater. It was a gift in exchange for the return of his long-lost sister Lady Kathryn, freed from the pits of Pal Palek.

The Moaning Maid, he thought. It was Ranulf Shackton's name for her. *Shackton, who left us in Aram, with that wise-cracking redhead girl.* He wondered what had become of them. As he wondered what had become of the others. *There were many of us once*, he reflected dismally, as he drew on his breastplate, a pair of gauntlets, and shirt of godsteel mail to clink and rustle beneath his black cloak. *Now there are just four…*

The days here had been bleak ever since Borrus Kanabar left with the others, and had grown only worse in the long weeks since when Emeric Manfrey had failed to return. The exiled lord had gone off with the jittery young Varin Knight Sir Lenard Borrington and the mute and menacing Silent Suncoat who's true name he had never known. *They went to fetch Jack and Turner and the others and bring them here. Months. It's been months now and still they haven't come. Unless...*

A thought occurred to him, causing him to tense. Those prints, could they have been made by Emeric and the others? Had they been brought back for some reason? Were they being kept in the refuge, right now, imprisoned against their will? He did not think it likely, but could not discount it either. *I have to find out. One way or another, I have to know...*

He awaited the other two outside, pacing, mulling on all that, glancing at the Nightblade hidden beneath the snow. *I'll not take it up. I promised I wouldn't.* The whispers were growing ugly, violent, demanding, anxious, reflecting his very mood. He could feel the claws on his shoulders, trying to drag him back down, trying to enslave him. *You need me...we need each other,* the voice was hissing. *Free us. Free us. Kill them. Kill them all...*

He wrenched his eyes away, looking steadfastly at the thick wooded door that led into the Night Tower, urging the others to come. Another minute passed, and another, before finally Gerrin emerged, followed shortly after by Harden. Each was garbed in full godsteel plate, or near enough that made no matter, as per their preference, with cloaks on top, and leather boots worn over their sabatons to help mask their tread on stone.

"You ready?" Jonik asked them. His hand was in his cloak, clasped about the hilt of his longsword, the power of his blood-bond bracing him against the temptations and the whispers. In his mind's eye, he knew how he looked; intense of expression, breathing heavily through the nose, the lid of his left eye flickering every once in a while as he fought against the desperate desire to turn and give in and launch himself into the snow, digging and scrambling for the blade. *I need it, I might need it in there. I should take it up, just this once...once we've found my mother and discovered the truth, I'll put it down again, I promise I will...*

It was as though the others were reading all that in his eyes, in the clear and obvious effort he was making *not* to turn around, *not* to lunge for the snow. And there was a slight pleading aspect to his face as well, as though he wanted one of them to suggest just that. "Go ahead, Jonik. We'll be safer if you use it," he wanted them to say. "We trust you to set it down again after. We know you're strong enough to do that."

But they said nothing. They only nodded, tightened their swordbelts and turned, to make for the rear of the fort.

Jonik stood his ground. For a full ten seconds he fought against his wretched longing, even wondering if he might wait for them to turn a corner, and then dive in and dig it out, and hitch it to his waist beneath his cloak, before either of them even noticed. *I could. I could do it. I could let them go ahead, just around a bend or two. Or maybe...maybe I could go with them, now, and then say I forgot something, and run back, run right back here, and then I could get it, dig it out and free it. I could do that, couldn't I? They'd understand that, wouldn't they? That I'm only trying to protect them, and myself, and my mother, and…*

"Jonik." The voice snapped him out of it. He looked up. Gerrin and Harden were both standing and staring at him, just a little way ahead, uneasy and unsure. The voice had been that of his former master. "Are you coming, or aren't you?"

Jonik swallowed, blinked, let out a shuddery breath, and drew in a long, steady, fresh one, to purify his lungs. He opened and closed his fingers about the haft of his sword, severing and re-initiating his blood-bond, feeling the power of Vandar's might and body flowing through him. It was enough. *It's always been enough*, he told himself. He nodded, firming his voice, and said, "I just…needed a moment," as if he had to find some excuse. "But I'm ready now."

"Then lead on, Jonik."

The two men stood aside so he might pass them, putting themselves between him and the misting black blade, hissing beneath the snow. He walked stiffly, as a man thrice his age, forcing his legs to move one after another, left, right, left, right, as he went past them and down the icy trench that led toward the library.

When he reached it, he saw the tracks his mother had made that morning, her prints working deeper into the fortress between the looming black buildings cloaked in white. The whispers were shrieking in a desperate panic now as though sensing this was it, their last chance to ensnare him, but the sight of those prints helped drown them out. *A path*, he thought. *She has made a path for me to follow.* His mother had worked hard to release him from the Nightblade's grip, and somehow, in some strange way, these tracks were a visual symbol of that. *She is leading me away from it…away from it forever.*

"Come," he said, in a loud, strong voice, as though to reassure the men behind him. "My mother has led the way."

They wended through the lanes and training yards and little quadrangles, following the prints, until they intersected with another trail, much fainter and evidently filled in by the storm, though still visible to anyone looking. The tracks here climbed a set of steps, where the snows were thinner, and had spread out to reveal their number, or thereabouts.

"At least half a dozen, then," Harden remarked, looking at them. 'Maybe a couple more."

Gerrin's eyes betrayed a growing concern. "That would line up well enough with the men who escaped that night."

The sellsword scowled and spat aside. "Why'd they come back then? And why'd this skinchanger let them through the door? I said it before… there's some evil work at play here. I can taste it on my tongue."

Let's find out, Jonik thought. "On me," he said, pacing onward up the steps, through a higher ward, onto a wider stair that led toward the refuge door. From here the Shadowfort spread out beneath them, black spires of stone bursting from their thick white cloaks. *It is dead*, he thought. *Dead and buried.* There was no one down there now. No knights, no masters, no boys in training. *Everyone is gone. We are the last. This is the day the order truly dies.*

He strode up the final stairs and onto the high plateau outside the refuge door, the crust of ice atop the snow breaking beneath his boots. The double doors lay open ahead, as though inviting them inside, a film of snow covering the stone within. More prints. More tracks. Some large and some small.

He turned to the others and lowered his voice. "There may be a sentry inside, hidden in shadow by the wall. Look out for misting breath and movement." He'd learned that from his mother, as he had much else besides.

Jonik went first, keeping his blade sheathed for now. It would not serve to march in so armed, or spark conflict where it might be avoided. *Answers*, he thought. *We only want answers.* His eyes shifted to the left and right as he stepped into the wide stone atrium, a great entrance hall that broke off into several different doorways and passages. To either side of the door a pair of massive stone knights rose up, so lifelike that Jonik had once wondered if they had been alive once before, ancient beings frozen in that state to defend the way against intrusion. The stone did not stir. Nor did he see movement by the walls or shifting in the shadows, nor the fog of breath from lips. He stopped as the others stepped in behind him, listening for the sound of a heartbeat, but only three could be heard.

"We're alone," he said. "There's no one else here." His words echoed softly off the walls, spreading out into the vastness of Ilith's ancient sanctuary.

"You're certain?" Harden asked.

"He's right," Gerrin said. The knight's senses were nearly as acute as Jonik's. "It's just the three of us." He looked around at the cavernous hall, at the great high doorways, some wide enough to ride a pair of wagons through two abreast, at the many chambers and rooms that linked one after another after another into darkness. Though a Shadowmaster here for twenty years, Gerrin had never once set foot in this place. "It's even bigger than I imagined." He indulged a moment in wonder, and then said, "Which way, Jonik? Do you know how to reach your mother's room?"

"She drew me a map," Jonik said. "In case I ever needed to come find her. I recall it well enough." He opened his nostrils, breathing deep, trying to detect her scent; there was a faint whiff of it in the air, separate from the others. Everyone had their own distinct smell if you had the nose to find it.

"Do you have it?" Gerrin asked, attempting the same. Harden just stood by, nonplussed.

"It's weak, but there's something. It should get stronger deeper in." Jonik led them on, straight through the interlinking chambers, past the great statues that stood attendance by the walls or cast as the centrepiece of some rooms, beneath the high carved ceilings cut with window shafts through which sunlight poured down, glittering with dust motes, lighting their way.

"So this is Ilith's refuge?" Harden muttered as they stalked along, their leather boots helping to muffle their tread. "What a waste. There's a war going on out there, and there's, what, a handful of rotting mages here? This place could house a million people."

"But not feed them," Gerrin said. "You let people shelter here, and it'll just become their tomb unless it's amply supplied."

"Aye, and feels like a tomb n'all. Wretched place. I'm starting to think I shouldn't have come."

"Feel free to return to the fort." Jonik would not have Harden moaning as they went along; they needed their wits sharp and ears open. "Go and get Cabel on a garron if you want. Pack some provisions, like you said earlier. Get us ready to go. We'll re-join your shortly." *With my mother in tow.*

The old sellsword said nothing for a moment, then grumbled, "I'm here now. Might as well see this through. And if I can put a length of steel into the guts of one of these mages, all the better. I don't even care if they kill me for it. Be worth it to send one of these creatures down the Long Abyss."

They won't be sent down the Long Abyss, Jonik thought. *They'll ascend to the Eternal Halls Above in triumph for their long and dutiful terms of sacrifice and service.* He said nothing of that, though. Harden hated the mages more than anyone, and defending them in his hearing was only likely to stir the sellsword's tongue to yapping in contempt. Right now, that wouldn't do. "Silence now," he merely said. "We don't know who might be listening."

The route took them through at least two dozen chambers of varying size and scope and splendour. They met no one along the way, saw no shadows rippling to suggest a mage was hidden nearby, heard no talking, no footsteps, sensed no movement at all but their own. His mother had made out that the doors were always being watched, but that hadn't been so. *Where are they all?* With these intruders being secretly let through the door overnight, it seemed to him they'd gathered for a reason.

The transference, he had begun to realise. *It can only be the ritual.* The thought set his heart to pacing, as he reflected on the conversation he'd had with his mother in the library the day the boys were released. She'd spoken of a final contract. Of the words she'd translated. Blood. Royal. Divine. She's said that the Steward was waiting for something before the ritual could begin...

Or *someone*...

The thought had him rushing, almost running through the empty passages and halls. Behind him he could hear the others hurrying to keep pace. "What's the sudden rush, Jonik?" asked Harden. "You caught the scent of something?"

Yes, he thought. *Death.*

The light changed down a long dim passage, an orange-red glow fogging out from a wide stone opening. *The heir's forge.* He knew his mother's room was on the same passage, a little down the corridor to the right or so she'd explained it, though which door he didn't know. "It's along here somewhere," he said. "One of these doors. Check them."

They spread out, turning handles, stepping inside, returning to shake their heads and say, "Nothing. She's not here."

"Are you sure you got this right, Jonik?" Gerrin asked him. "She was definitely staying here?"

"Yes. Unless they moved her somewhere else."

"Let's check the forge." Harden was first to it, passing straight inside. Gerrin followed, Jonik right after. The furnaces were burning, fires crackling here and there, the air thick and warm and muggy. There was a great deal of armour on the walls, and weapons as well, stacked and stored, almost all of it godsteel, much of it magnificent. "Look here," said Harden. "This'd suit you well, lad, don't you think?"

The armour was black as jet, slim and thin yet strong, Jonik sensed, more supple than godsteel had any right to be. Set upon a mannequin, it looked about his size, an astonishing suit, with few visible seams and boundaries between the plates of metal. He found himself drawn to it, and wondered for a moment if he might put it on. *The others could as well,* he thought. *We could garb ourselves as gods in here.*

But the thought was fleeting. There was no time. Instead he marched right over to the wall where several dozen blades were lined up, leaning against the stone. Broadswords, longswords, shortswords, bastard swords, greatswords, half-swords, daggers, all were here. Most were of standard northern design, straight and sometimes double-edged and without the curve you often got with southern scimitars, falchions and khopesh blades. *Knight swords,* he thought. *Best for the forms.* He quickly fingered through them, searching for one he liked. They were all brand new, un-dinted, unused, their edges honed and sharpened, the fog of Vandar's soul breathing from them in fine soft mists of silver and grey and even light blended hues in blue and green and gold as well.

It was the heir's work, sure as sunset. The work of the Hammer of Tukor.

"Pick one out," he told the others. "Quickly. You'll find no finer godsteel in the world."

A moment later they were setting aside their current blades and hitching new ones to their belts. Gerrin and Harden favoured shorter basket-hilt broadswords, better for their frames; for Jonik the bastard sword was best. Bigger, longer, with a two-hand grip, it suited his height and extended his range, and as a Bladeborn of rich blood, the blade's weight was inconsequential. *And I'm a bastard too, there's that.*

He replaced his dagger as well with one of superior quality, and fixed beside it a twenty-five inch shortsword for close range combat. The others found daggers and shorter blades to their liking, as Jonik stepped through into an adjoining room to find an even larger armoury, dusty and dimly lit, filled with hundreds upon hundreds of weapons and components of plate armour. Most were old, many gathering dust, untouched for hundreds, even thousands of years. *All for Tyrith to melt down and remake,* Jonik knew. His mother had told him about that as well.

He stepped back through to join the others. "You could equip an entire army in there." Of his mother or the blacksmith, however, there was no sign. His nostrils opened, sifting through the smells of leather and smoke and oil, searching for his mother's scent. *She was here,* he thought. It was faint beneath the rest of all that, but detectable. *And she wasn't alone.*

He hastened outside, turning his eyes up the passage. Torchlight burned occasionally along the walls, leading away into a deeper part of the refuge. "This way." He moved once more into a rush, a sense of dread deepening in his bones. Distantly, weakly, the Nightblade was still haunting him, but so far away it held little sway. "She wasn't alone," he told the others as they went. "I think Tyrith was with her. And Hamlyn as well."

"Then it's happening," Gerrin said, moving quickly at his heels. "Your mother must have been invited to observe. She'd have been there to keep the blacksmith calm."

Jonik gave no reply. *Divine. Royal. Blood.* Something was beginning to twist in his gut. They passed a torch on the wall, throwing warped shadows across the stone. Beyond lay a pool of darkness, and into it they plunged, racing for the next light, the next marker in the distance. His mother's scent was growing stronger, and beneath it he could taste the acrid undertone of iron.

Blood, he knew at once. *Blood has been spilt back here.*

The passage opened into a chamber, huge and featureless, then closed again into another long corridor. Behind him Harden was beginning to puff and pant, his gait growing heavier, his booted feet thumping on the stone. *If there's anyone near, they'll hear,* Jonik thought. He ran on all the same.

The scent of blood thickened. The others began to notice it too. Gerrin first, then Harden shortly after. "*Ritual,*" the latter growled. "Maybe it was the boys…maybe they brought them back to open their veins…" He ran on a little more then spat, "Bastards," loudly, and without a care that someone should hear. The word echoed out down the corridor, *bastards, bastards…* "They've been playing us for fools all along, the foul rotten soulless bast…"

"Quiet," Jonik hissed. He could hear voices ahead now, down the passage, through an arched doorway. They were murmuring in quiet tones, and there was a shuffle of feet as well, the sound of *wiping,* it seemed, cloths moving over stone. He peered through the narrow stone archway; beyond two shards of light shone down from above, illuminating a pair of stone slabs set in the heart of a large open chamber. He thought at once of the bed on which he'd first seen Ilith lying in stasis, but these two were empty. Between them was another, hidden in darkness. Here he saw the murmuring men, standing around it, wiping, mopping up blood he realised, and there between them on the slab, a figure lay, covered in a dark sheet, still…

…silent…

…dead.

Jonik stepped inside. The cloaked men looked up. "Where is my mother?" His voice was choked by a sudden and simmering rage. He knew where she was. He knew…

There were five of them, men or mages he could not tell at a glance. None answered.

"*Where?*"

"Here," came a voice. "I'm right here, son." His *mother's* voice, or a shadow of it. He turned to a side passage, through which she walked, dressed in her large fur cloak, its great hood casting her face in gloom. "You can go, Jonik. It's all over now. You can go," she said, in a soft and persuasive tone.

He stared. Something wasn't right.

"The transference has been completed," his mother went on. "But I'm to stay here now, to stay and help. But you, no, there is no reason for you to remain here any longer. Your duty is done. You may…"

"Show yourself," Jonik demanded. His upper lip skinned back. "*Shadowcloak*."

He saw a twist of amusement in the mouth, saw a pair of eyes flash in the darkness. "That obvious, is it? Guess I needed more time with her. Did a *much* better job mimicking that knight, but oh well, was worth a try." The voice was not his mother's anymore, nor a shadow of it, but the rough old timbre of a man. He gave a shrug, and then in a shimmer and a ripple the disguise melted away to unveil the figure of a mage below.

"Mekynr," Gerrin growled. "You're back."

"Gerrin, fine Shadowmaster, how are you? Not seen you in long years."

"Where is she?" Gerrin asked. "Lady Cecilia. What have you done with her?" His eyes moved to the body beneath the sheet. The men there had their hands in their cloaks. *Blades*, Jonik thought. *Shadowknights*.

"Best you just leave," the mage Mekynr said. "I'll fetch Fhanrir, he'll explain everything to you in due course. You should all be back in the fort. This…you weren't meant to see *this*."

"You killed her?" Gerrin said.

"Me? No, not me. Don't go thinking any of this is *my* doing, Gerrin. Old Talbert's not to blame."

Jonik withdrew his brand new bastard sword and took a step into the chamber.

"Easy now. Easy. All this can be explained." Meknyr drew a step away, back toward the passage he'd come from. "I knew nothing of this, nor did any of us. We brought the princess here as we were tasked to do, and the rest…"

"What princess?" Gerrin's broadsword came scraping from its scabbard, Harden's followed a second later.

"Your one. The Jewel. We needed the last blood of Thala for the ritual. It was all foreseen, all fated to happen." He looked at Jonik again. "Now come, boy, no sense in bringing violence, is there? It's all over now, like I say. Wasn't lying about that. No one else needs to get hurt."

Jonik was done listening. He marched toward the men huddled around the body, saw beneath their hoods features he recognised. *The ones who escaped. They had a final duty to do…*

"Come no closer," one man rasped in a horrid drawl that Jonik knew. *Morken. A Shadowknight.* He stepped away from the others, pulling back his hood. A cleft lip. Half a nose missing from an old battle, years ago. Hair more grey than black, long and lank, falling in patches from a scarred scalp. *A skilled killer, this one.* "You're not meant to be here, boy. None of you are."

"Move or I'll kill you." It was all the warning Jonik was willing to give. He continued forward, refusing to slow in his step.

Morken stood his ground. "Kill one, kill all." He drew his blade.

"So be it." Jonik rushed him, swinging in a vicious sidecut. Steel swung out to meet it, *clanging,* as Morken parried his strike away. The others snatched blades from their cloaks. Jonik heard one of them say, "He's not got the Nightblade. He's given it up," as they all lunged at him, striking and thrusting. He fended one attack, slid past another, too quick for them, and struck. His blade bit through leather and mail and then flesh and bone and one of them was dead, his heart pierced. The man tumbled away, collapsing in a quick death, blood spurting at once from the wound.

"Enough," Meknyr was shouting, across the chamber. "Enough… there's to be no blood here…not here…"

Too late. Jonik kept on going, swinging, scattering them, as the men of the order dashed away. He marched for the stone slab as Gerrin and Harden charged in behind him, blades brandished, entering the fray. The chamber erupted in a clamour, steel ringing out, shouts and grunts filling the air.

Morken was the only one remaining in his way. Behind him the bed lay in shadow, cast between the pair bathed in light. *Death,* Jonik thought, *to buy life.* "Weren't our doing," the half-nosed Shadowknight told him. "Weren't none of our choice, you know that as well as anyone."

"Move aside, Morken."

"Never liked you. You nor Gerrin neither. You two were always thick as thieves round here, thinking you were better than the rest of us. Guess the Nightblade made you think that. Well where is it now, boy? What are you without it?"

"Move," Jonik growled.

"You're one of us," Morken went on. "Never liked you, but you're *still* one of us. This don't need to happen. It's over now, as Meknyr said. He told us all about it on the way. About the contracts, about Ilith, about *everything.* It's over, boy. Give it up."

"Move!" Jonik swung. Morken parried. He swung again and again and again, hammering his foe back and away, driving him from the stone slab, buying space, buying time…then he reached out….reached for the body….reached for the sheet….ripped it away…and saw the woman beneath.

Mother…

Cecilia Blakewood's lifeless face stared up at the shadowed stone ceiling, pale as milk, bloodless, cool green eyes devoid of thought or sentience, empty and open and unfeeling. Her cloak had been removed, and the warm garments she wore beneath, leaving her in linen underclothes only, debased and disused. Both wrists were slashed open, the arteries split along the inner forearm to empty her of her blood. It was smeared across the skin and open flesh of her arms, and the stone, and had dripped to the floor as well.

For a moment he could do nothing but stare. Stare at the woman who'd birthed and abandoned him. The woman who might have been a good mother if given the chance. A spider, they called her, a witch and bastard bitch, selfish and heartless and cruel. *But my mother*, Jonik thought, staring. *My mother, all the same.*

"She asked for it, you should know," Morken said behind him. "She *wanted* it, boy. I heard it with my own ears. The woman wanted to…"

"*Asked* for it?" Jonik turned, eyes dilating in fury. "She *asked* for it?"

"I…I didn't mean it like that. I meant…I only meant…"

He roared, launching himself right at him, beating away his feeble attempts to parry and fend and flee. Within a few moves Jonik had him teetering and tripping backward, his bastard sword cleaving into his shoulder and neck and face, slashing, hacking, cut after cut. Blood splashed with each wild swing, sending gouts to spatter across the room, bright red as they passed the shards of light flowing down from the shafts above.

I am death, Jonik thought, as he had that night in Russet Ridge. *Today. I am death.*

The mage Mekynr was calling for order. "Stop…Jonik…that's enough, *stop.*"

He stopped, turning to face him, chest heaving up and down. Morken's body was a bloody red ruin at his feet, barely recognisable as a man. Across the room, battle rang out, though Jonik did not look over. His eyes were on the mage, and the mage alone. *Ghalto*, he thought, recalling the demon he'd beheaded in the village that night. *The Whisperer.* "Are you a Whisperer too, Meknyr? Like he was? Or do you just imitate and deceive? Is that all you've ever done?"

"I've done my duty, the same as the rest of us. For centuries I have, boy. You don't know the meaning of service." He looked at the mass of black and red on the floor, the wool and leather and meat that was once a man. "You never let him speak," the old mage said angrily. "He was trying to say she wanted this, your mother. She *chose* it, Jonik. That's the truth. She chose it to save your life. And your cousin's…"

Jonik drew his dagger and threw it in a single motion, piercing the creature's neck. Meknyr flew backward from the impact, eyes flaring in shock, cloak fluttering, walking stick spinning from his ancient spindly fingers to rattle on the smooth stone floor. A horrid hissing sound bubbled up out of him as he clutched at the blade, writhing and choking, trying to pull it free.

Jonik stepped over. "I'll not let you speak, *mage*," he said. "I'll not let you get in my head." He took the handle of the blade and twisted, a fountain of black-red blood gushing upward as he pulled it free.

He stood and turned. Another Shadowknight was hurtling toward him, screaming. Jonik shifted stance at once, driving forward in Strikeform, unleashing a terrible diagonal downcut that opened the man up from clavicle to groin. His body peeled apart, showing what lay within, as the man fell sideways in shock, bowels emptying. *I am death. I am death.*

Kill them...kill them all...

The Nightblade was rejoicing in his head, he could hear it. *Yes...rejoice,* he thought. *I'm coming...I'm coming back for you...*

Maddened eyes swept across the chamber, bloodlusted. He saw that another of the enemy was down on his knees, blubbering plaintively for the mother he'd never known as he tried to scoop up his slippery wet guts from the floor. Who had done it Jonik couldn't say, but guessed at Gerrin to see the blood at the edge of his blade. His old master stood side by side with Harden, coralling the last of the cloaked men into a corner. His eyes were darting left and right as though wondering if he could fight them both. When he saw Jonik striding over he threw down his sword at once, seeing no way out. "I yield. Please...please, I yield."

Jonik marched forward, pushing between his men. Gerrin tried to reach for him. "Jonik, he's surrendered. He's thrown down his arms."

"I don't care."

The man saw the dead look in Jonik's eyes, and collapsed to his knees, drawing back his hood. *A young face. Little older than me. I know him. He was a friend to Hopper...*"Please...you don't need to...please, Jonik...I didn't know anything of this..."

Jonik breathed out. "My mother..."

"I didn't know. They said it was all...all fate. That we had no choice... none of us...none of us have a choice..."

"Don't do it, lad," Harden said behind him, in a tone of warning. "That's enough now. Enough butchery. You don't need to kill the boy."

Blood dripped off the edge of his blade, pattering against the stone floor. It made him think of his mother, on the slab, her wrists cut open, blood dripping...His chest went up and down, heaving. A heartbeat passed, two, three. When five became ten he thrust the sword back into its sheath, spun on his heels, and marched away down the passage from which they'd come.

Gerrin sped after him, grabbing his arm, turning him back. "Don't do it, Jonik. I know what you're thinking. *Don't* do it."

"You a mage now, Gerrin? You can read my thoughts?"

"This isn't what you want. You take it up and you'll never be free of it. This is a test, Jonik. It's *your* test."

"A test? A test? My mother's lying dead on a slab, Gerrin! And you're telling me she died because of a test!"

"She chose it. I heard what Meknyr said."

"And you believed him? After everything...all the lies and deceptions... you'd believe a word he said?" He ripped his arm away from him and turned.

Gerrin followed, grabbing him again, and at once Jonik whirled, thrusting his fist into the old man's jaw. He felt a crack, saw a tooth fly free, watched as he tumbled off the side to crash onto the floor. "Don't follow me," he warned Harden. "*Don't.*"

"Don't intend to. You take that blade back up and you're not worth following." The sellsword snorted and shook his head. "What, after everything that's happened here, you've just going to give in? Thought you were stronger than that. *Your father's son*, you said."

"*Don't* speak of my father. Or you'll end up like the rest of these."

Harden looked around at the dead men slumped and heaped across the floor. "Threats? After all I've done for you…." He sighed, thrusting his blade into its scabbard. "Go on then. You go running off to your special little blade and *disappear*. Hide forever for all I care. Seems it's your fate to be a coward."

"*Coward?* I'm going to use it for good, Harden. For *good*. Like my father's done all his life. And my brother now too…"

"That'd be the brother you *didn't* kill?"

Jonik's eye twitched. "I'm warning you…"

"Aye, you said. You'll make me a corpse like this lot. You think I care? After all this, you think I care about anything?"

"You never did. You never cared."

"I cared about *you*. Why else would I have endured all this? Wish I hadn't now. I'd sooner have stayed in the service of Vincent bloody Rose than have watched you fall to madness."

"I'm not mad. I'm…"

"Upset. Aye, I get it. That's your mother over there on a slab, like you said. A mother you pretend not to give two shits about, but you do, you *do*, and all this proves it. Don't sully her memory by failing her, Jonik. You take that blade up and you fail us all."

Jonik didn't want to talk about it anymore, didn't want to think about it, didn't want to be here anymore looking at it, smelling it. *Fate*, he thought. *Thala only saw so far.* That meant what lay ahead had not been seen, so why should he not try to help?

I can do more with the Nightblade, he tried to tell himself. *I can use it to help people, and when the time comes to bring it back, I will, I'll bring it back.* He'd made a promise he wouldn't take it up again, on the lives of Runar and Morris and Lucas. *But maybe I was wrong. Maybe I was meant to come here, meant to see her…* He glanced at the slab, at his mother, his dead mother. *She led me here so I would know the truth. That I'm meant to be its bearer, meant to be its champion. Why leave it sitting here idle? Why…why…why…*

Before he knew it he was running, passing down the long torchlit passage, past the forge, through the high-ceilinged chambers and wide stone corridors they'd taken to get here, seeing the glow of sunlight outside beyond the grand double doors, the sparkling snow, the hard blue skies…

He burst past the exit, the wind rushing through his long black dirty hair. The whispers soared in his mind, screaming in exultation, calling him forth. *I'm coming…I'm coming…we'll be together…together forever…*

The world went by in a blur of black and white, cold stone towers and high drifts of snow. He ploughed through the way they'd come, leaping and bounding down the steps, white waves parting as he went. Flakes sparkled and glittered in the air, magical, and the sun above smiled down upon him, brilliant. *A beautiful day*, he thought, as he had when he'd awoken that morning. *Vandar's Smile. He smiles upon me, as I take a shard of his heart. He wants this, as much as I do. He wants this. It is the way…*

The yard opened out ahead, the Shadowfort empty but for him. The order was dead now, dead and done, but under Jonik it would be restored anew. Jonik, King of the Night, to raise the Shadow Order in its new guise, to revive it in the world below, a force for good, dreaded by dreaded things…

It was his dream, his vision, his fantasy, the one that came to him as he slept, and haunted his waking days. *I tried to fight it, I tried, but I was wrong. This was always meant to be.* He knew that now. *This was always my one true fate…*

He feel to his knees, shovelling the snow aside, wildly, frantically working his arms to left and right, digging, scooping, desperate…cursed…

It is the way, it's my fate, my destiny…

He saw black mist rising through a breach in the snow. He smiled, grinned, laughed out loud. Tears welled in his eyes. He could see the pommel poking out, black on white. His hands swept and scooped, swept and stopped, unearthing and exhuming the only thing he'd ever loved. Nothing else mattered now, nothing…nothing. The hilt was excavated, the crossguard, the scabbard, the snow piled high to either side…

"I'm sorry," he whispered, kneeling before it. "Never again…I'll never leave you again, I promise…"

His fingers reached out to take it up, and in his head he saw it, saw the Nightblade, made manifest, reaching for him too. Like a child, a mother, a father he'd never had. A brother and a sister and a lover and a friend. *Everything*, all he could ever want or need, all at once and forever and evermore…

"Jaycob," said a voice.

He started, fingers drawing back. *Jaycob*, he thought, the name stirring memory. The gallant knight, the *good* knight, the knight who might have been, the antidote to his dream. He frowned. *Mother?* Only his mother had ever called him that, the name of her grandfather, the name she would have given him…in another life.

"Jaycob," the voice said again. It pierced the shroud of darkness about him, soft, *silvery*. "Stand, Jaycob, and look at me."

Jonik stood, and he turned, and he looked at the man behind him. A man mild of face, slim of build, with golden curly hair and emeralds for eyes. He could hear the whispers and the voices calling out to him in a panic. *The blade fears him,* Jonik thought. "Who are you?" he asked.

"You know who I am, Jaycob."

"My name…name is Jonik."

"That is the name they gave you. But that is not who you are."

"Ilith," he whispered. The man was right, he already knew. "Or Tyrith? Which…which is it?"

"Both," the man said. "We are one and the same, Jaycob." He smiled, and the world seemed suddenly brighter. "That blade. I think I know it."

Jonik frowned. "You…*you* forged it, my lord…"

"Oh? Yes, you're right, I did. It was always a troubled one, the Night-blade. I'm amazed that you have fought its lure for so long. Most others would have been reduced to madness long ago. They would not have stayed here, as you have, Jaycob."

"I…I still…I might…" He looked down at the Nightblade again, but suddenly everything felt different. The whispers were weak, and wretched. His desire to bear it had faded, and fled.

"Go ahead, Jaycob. Pick it up. Hand it over." The man reached out a hand, callused and worn by the Hammer of Tukor.

A mortal hand, Jonik thought. *A divine mind.* "I…but what if…"

"You needn't fear, Jaycob. Not anymore. Pick it up. Hand it over."

A test. A real test. He bent down and picked it up…but there was nothing, no urge to keep it, no thirst to bear it, no craving to wield it at all. The whispers had gone out like a torch in a tempest, driven away by this man, this mage, this immortal.

"You see, Jaycob. You're free."

Free…

Jonik extended his hand and passed the blade over, and the demigod gave it a long inspection, studying the symbols and the glyphs. He seemed to be searching his memories, remembering. "It took dark magic to make these blades," he whispered. "Dark magic to break the heart of a god. Is it any wonder the damage they have caused? I wish Varin had never come to me that day. I wish he hadn't asked." He lowered the Nightblade, and raised his eyes. "I'm sorry about your mother. I'm sorry about the things that have happened here. To you, and to others. This place…" He looked back, toward the mountain. "It has sat empty for far too long, shying from its original purpose. I will see these halls filled with light, Jaycob, and warmth, and music. I will see this refuge restored, a haven against the dark-ness beyond."

He stepped closer, dressed in the modest garb of a blacksmith, with a loose brown cloak over the top to help shield him from the cold. "You want to leave, don't you? You never want to return to these halls?"

"I…I just want…" Jonik had to pause, and think. "I want to *help*," he said, after a time. "It's what my mother wanted for me. To help. It's who my father *is*, and my brother. They're out there now, as far as I know, help-ing. I want to be *good*, like they are. Like…like Jaycob," he whispered.

Ilith smiled. "You have always had a good heart, and a righteous will, my child. Together, we can set it to a new purpose, to a brighter path. If you are willing?"

Jonik nodded. The Steward and his mages had always felt wrong to him, embittered by their long existence and foul duty, dehumanised by the things they had done. But this man felt different. From him pulsed an aura of utter probity and virtue. He had not borne witness to the darkness that had enshrouded his refuge, nor been corrupted by it. *I will serve him*, Jonik thought. *I will do whatever he asks of me.* They had made him a tool, a weapon to be swung. *And I have found a hand to wield me…*

But he had one question first. "My friends," he said. "Emeric, Jack…"

"Are alive," Ilith told him.

Jonik breathed out. "How...what happened to them? Why didn't they..."

"Fhanrir sent them away, I am told. He feared their presence would cause problems. Emeric Manfrey reached your friends in the foothills, and joined up with Lord Kanabar and his companions as they passed down the mountain. Your company remain together, Jaycob. In time, you will find them again. Though in what state, I cannot say."

"State? You mean..."

"Death has spread like a shadow across the lands, and the shadow is only growing darker. The days to come will be difficult, Jaycob. The world needs shining lights like you to guide them." He touched Jonik's arm, turning him toward the fort. "Now come, and meet your cousin. Your first duty is a simple one." He smiled, and began walking. "Escort the princess home."

72

Amara

The man had a slimy smile to go with his slimy hair. "The Great One will see you now," he said, in a slimy voice. "Right this way, my lady. I am sorry if we have kept you waiting."

"That's quite all right. I'm used to being kept waiting by kings."

The man liked that, by the look of his greasy little grin. "He prefers Great One, but king will serve."

A blade will serve, right in his giant gut. Amara had caught sight of this so called 'Great One' earlier that morning, and as far as she could tell, the only thing great about him was his girth. Still, she wasn't going to upset him, or this seneschal creature he kept around, if she could avoid it. Clearly, in these parts, he was a power of sorts, a man who ruled a network of islands at the heart of Lake Eshina. The Lords of the Lake, they liked to think of themselves. In truth they were little more than pirates.

The Great One's promised palace proved to a be a disappointment. Amara had spent the last few hours awaiting his summons upon the shore of their secret island haven, hearing from some of the local community of what a wonder she was in for. *A wonder, yes,* she thought now. *It's a wonder they call it a palace at all.*

As they walked down through a corridor of tightly woven trees, she saw it appear, and frowned. It was hardly more than a woodland shack at first glance - much smaller than she had supposed, though she had to admit there was some charm in its natural design. The palace had been *grown*, not built, it seemed to her, fashioned by gardeners rather than stonemasons. Its walls were formed of bark and branch, its roof a natural canopy of thick green leaves. The door was two slender rowan trees, bending inward toward one another to form an arch. Creeping vines entwined the trunks, and hung down to shield the way.

The seneschal smiled. "Well? What do you think?"

"Charming," Amara said. "Is it right through here?"

The man seemed disappointed with her response. "It took many years to grow, my lady. The gardeners who did so worked hard to guide the trees and plants in this particular way. They passed the duty down from son to son, and daughter to daughter, across many generations. Does that not impress you?"

At another time, she thought, *yes it might.* Today she was in no mood for it. "I am in something of a rush, I'm afraid. You will forgive me if I do not gush over the wonders of your sanctuary."

"I understand." The seneschal swept aside the hanging vines, rather blending into the colours of the shack in that 'natural' green and brown garb of him, all leaves and hemp and other earthy materials that looked quite frankly ridiculous. "Right this way then, my lady. He is awaiting you within."

She stepped through the arched rowan door, looked around, and pursed her lips. It was rather larger inside than she'd expected, to be sure, and pleasantly lit by hanging lanterns, burning softly in the air above, and torches grasped in wooden fists along the walls. The furniture was all wood-carved, oak and ash and elm. At the back, draped partitions separated the palace into several rooms, for sleeping, eating, entertaining. The rugs were plentiful, the air was warm, and smelled of earthy spices. Several servants scuttled about, dressed in hempen shifts, their hair tied back in string, belts of the same girding their waists.

"Well, here she is," said a voice.

The Great One sat at the heart of the main room, clasped between the arms of a huge oaken chair. *I'd be swallowed by that thing*, Amara thought, though this pirate lord filled it out with great aplomb. There was something extremely odd about his bodily shape, something whale or seal-like, as though he was born to the waves, with no neck to speak of and soft, sloping shoulders, topped with a bald head with features so grotesquely enveloped in fat they were hard to make out as facial features at all. When she'd seen him earlier, he was being carried on a cushioned litter, heaved across the island by at least a dozen strong men. He had looked big then, from a distance. Now he looked truly colossal.

"I'm told your name is Amara."

"Lady Amara Daecar," she said, still gazing at him in a manner that might have been considered rude. Amara knew it was impolite to stare, but truly, she couldn't help it. "I'm the good sister of the King of Vandar, Amron Daecar. Now surely you've heard of *him*?"

"It rings a distant bell, yes. Though we do not keep your kings out here." His voice was as large as he was, somewhat choked by the rolls of fat about his neck. He wore a cloak that was a sort of blueish-grey, and that only added to his seal-like appearance. *Perhaps it is sealskin, that cloak?* There were many seals on the islands here in the midst of the lake, along with a great host of other creatures. *And this one is the strangest,* Amara thought, staring. She had heard the rumours of mermen living in the lake, but hadn't thought to find a seal-man here as well. "Would you like a drink, my lady?"

"No, thank you. I don't mean to stay long."

"Suit yourself." He waved a hand so corpulent it might have been a flipper, and a serving girl hurried over, setting down a flagon of wine on a table beside his chair. To no surprise, there were great heaps of food there. *Fish, most likely,* she thought. *Seals are very fond of fish.* The Great One wrapped his flipper about the flagon and took a long guzzling drink, wiped his mouth with his sleeve and asked, "So, what is it I can do for you?"

You can not keep me waiting for hours, for a start. She held her tongue, and simply said, "I was informed that my niece had been brought here. Lillia Daecar. She had a Bladeborn knight with her by name of Sir Daryl Blunt."

The Great One indulged another gulp of wine, then set the flagon aside. By the *clunk* it made it sounded almost empty. *Goodness, this creature can drink. He might have even given Sally Scarlet a challenge.* Wine ran down one side of his mouth. A serving girl rushed in with a cloth to wipe it away for him, as though he was some giant ghastly baby, swaddled in his sealskin cloak in that great cot of an oaken throne. He smiled at her lovingly, asked for more wine, picked up a pickled herring, ate it in a single gulp, and finally gave answer.

"What you say is true, my lady," he said. "Your niece was brought here with this knight."

Thank the gods… Amara could have leaped forward and kissed the man, if he wasn't so utterly repulsive. A smile broadened about her lips and she made a sound of profound relief. She and her little band of Bladeborn had been searching high and low for her missing niece for what seemed like forever. Their search had taken them all across the shores and little islets of Lake Eshina, all the way to the northern coast and the ancient city of Elinar, following a trail of rumours and whispers heard on the lips of fishermen, pirates, and other queer folk.

It had been an awakening. Amara had gone boating on the lake more times than she could count, but rarely more than five or so miles from shore. She knew it had many islands, yes, but not so many as this, and these at the heart of the lake especially. It seemed a world of its own, with secret coves and hidden sanctuaries, islands that had huge underground cave systems that led from one to the next beneath the water. Once before, a dozen different pirate lords had fought for supremacy here, but for a decade now this giant grey whale before her had stood supreme over them all. *Or sat supreme,* she corrected herself. She did not imagine the Great One had stood on his own two feet in many a long year. *They probably have to wipe his arse for him too.*

"You seem relieved," the Lord of Seals observed, feasting hungrily on more herring.

Is it that obvious? "I am," she said. "We have been searching for my niece for long days on this lake. To know that she is here…"

"Oh, no, you misunderstand me, my lady. The girl is not *here*."

Her eyes flattened. *What cruelty is this?* "*Not* here? Did I mishear, then? You just said…"

"I said she was *brought* here, with this knight of hers," the pirate king interrupted. "I did not say she remained."

Amara closed a fist. It took a great effort not to scream out in frustration. Her hunt for Lillia had provided far too many of these near-misses already. It seemed that every time she got a sniff of the girl, she was gone again, away to some other place, vanishing like a puff of smoke on the wind. A part of her had come to wonder if she was doing it all on purpose. *Is this just a game to her? Is she doing this all to torture me?* "Pray tell, where did she go?"

"Home. I sent her home, only yesterday." When he smiled, his eyes all but vanished beneath his enormous swollen cheeks.

"Home," she repeated. "To Varinar?"

"Yes. That's it. Var-in-ar." He spelled it out slowly, taking pleasure in pretending that places like Vandar and Varinar were so utterly alien to him. *You live on the lake at the heart of the kingdom, you bloody great sack of lard,* she thought. *You only exist because we allow it.* "Is that how you pronounce it, my lady? Var-in-ar?"

"Yes," she said, not caring to hide her displeasure. She glanced behind her. A pair of burly guardsmen had appeared from the shadows, to block her way out, should she attempt to leave. "And who are your friends?" she asked, all innocence.

"Never mind them, my lady. We need to discuss the tolls."

And there it is. "Tolls," she repeated. "You mean to extort me?"

"All must pay for passage through these islands. Whether prince or pauper, I extract my due, though do not let it be said that the Great One is unfair. I take only what one can afford to give up. A good sister to the King of Vandar, did you say?" His grin was horribly triumphant.

I walked right into that one. "How much?" she asked.

"Well now, let me think…" The Lord of Seals raised one of those flippers of his, counting on his enormously fat fingers. "There is you, and your two knights. And you have the younger lad as well…a serving boy, is he? And the girl with the red hair. Hmmmm…" He thought for a moment, his smile growing increasingly unpleasant. "Maybe you can buy your freedom with *her?* That fiery hair of hers is very appealing to me, oh yes. Leave her here with me, and…"

"No," Amara cut in, sharply. "Unless you want to be made a eunuch, you want no part of Carly."

"Truly? A fierce one, is she?" He gave a little giggle, chins wobbling. "I like them fierce, you know, though would prefer to stay intact. So be it. You may all leave, pending appropriate payment."

"And what is appropriate to you?"

He smiled at her. "We like to be fair here, as I say. Seeing as you are the good sister of a king, I should think you can afford a great deal. We have heard that there is a terrible war unfolding in the south and it is imperative that we gather provisions. For this we need coin. I have many mouths to feed here, my lady."

"Yours alone must cost a fortune." She could hold her tongue no longer.

The whale only chuckled. "Insults. Those cost dearly as well. Another cruel jape and you may not have enough to pay me." He licked his lips.

"My seneschal tells me you do not have coin on your person. Is this true?"

"I have godsteel," she said. "Swords, daggers, armour. Or better yet, I have my word."

"Your word? And what does that buy me?"

"A guarantee. Let me sail home to Varinar and I'll return with whatever toll you require."

He considered a moment. "That is risky, on my part, letting you leave. For this I would require double."

"Double? Do you take me for a fool, pirate?"

"I take you for a lady, and a rich one at that. Rest assured, the price will be a trifling thing to you, but greatly valuable to us. Double of nothing is still nothing, wouldn't you say?"

"It's *double*. How much?" True enough, the toll charge would almost certainly be insignificant to her, but that wasn't the point. This was a matter of pride.

"I have no head for numbers," the Lord of Lard said. "No, I have my seneschal for that. He will take you through the particulars."

The slimy little man was standing aside, smiling his slimy smile. "If I may, Great One?" A flipper gestured him forward. Into the light the seneschal came. "It would be wise, I think, to escort Lady Amara and her companions home, on one of our longships…" He bowed his head, lank black hair dangling past his ears. "*Your* longships, I mean to say. To protect your concerns, and return with the funds, to make sure you are not cheated, my lord."

"*Cheated?*" Amara had to laugh. "A thief is not cheated when he goes away empty handed. In some places he'll get his hand chopped off. *I'm* the only one being cheated here."

The whale ignored her. "It shall be done," he said. "I would not want you to drown, my lady, before you can pay your due. My longships are made for the waters of this lake, and will see you safely home." He waved a flipper, dismissing her. "You may go. My seneschal shall conclude matters with you."

May? The nerve of the man. Amara spun on her heels and left the 'palace' without so much as a word of parting, brushing past the guards behind her. The seneschal scuttled after her like a rat. "He likes amethysts," the slimy little knave told her, as they went. "Lots of amethysts will be good. And rubies too. It's the colours, my lady. The fiery colours, like the hair of this girl. The Great One likes them very much."

"Just write me a bloody list. And don't push your luck. I am not a woman to be taken advantage of, seneschal."

The silly little man with the silly leafy clothes put his hands together and gave a bow. "We hope to be friends, my lady, not enemies. Of course, the price will be appropriate."

Pray that it is. Or I'll return with a bloody armada. "Was my niece given a longship as well?"

"No, I regret to say. This is a special honour afforded only to you. They left on the same vessel we found them on; a good seafaring skiff, reliable on the water. The knight was very sore from all the rowing, I am told. He complained a lot, this knight."

That wasn't like Sir Daryl. He was a man of laughter, not complaints. "They paid a toll as well, I assume?"

"Your niece surrendered a necklace, and the knight surrendered a sword. Gold and godsteel for passage, my lady."

"Give them back," Amara snapped at once. She stopped in the tree-lined tunnel and turned. The guards lumbered to a halt behind.

"Give them back? But they are the toll charges."

"Sir Daryl is a Bladeborn knight. They are most fond of their godsteel blades. And I will not have my niece surrender her necklace for that great sack of suet you call a lord. Give them back. I'll cover the charges myself."

He gave another bow. "It shall be done."

The sunlight struck them when they stepped out of the tunnel, and the shore of the little island sanctuary opened out ahead. It was a fascinating place, she would admit that much, an island-within-an-island, really, as secluded as a place could be. High above her and far to the sides, she could see the grey shimmering walls of the vast watery cavern in which this particular island refuge lay. Ahead, the mouth of the cave opened out into a slow-moving river, which meandered down through a much larger island before emptying into the lake, some way off. In order to keep the precise location of this cave hidden, Amara and her companions had all been blindfolded when the Great One's men had come upon them on the water. It was the very reason why the Lords of the Lake had managed to operate out here for so long, hidden away in their lairs and hideouts.

They met the others down by the beach, under the guard of a dozen of the Great One's men. Sir Connor, Sir Penrose, Jovyn and Carly had all given up their arms, which lay piled to one side, behind the cordon of guardsmen, several of whom were Bladeborn as well. Sir Connor stood at once upon seeing her. "How did it go, my lady? Is there news of Lillia?"

The others looked at her, expectant. After all their false leads, this one had been considered more reliable, and so it had turned out. *Unless the Lord of Seals is lying to me,* she thought. *He will regret it, if so.* "There is news, Sir Connor, yes. It seems that Lillia and Sir Daryl have taken a boat back home to Varinar. They left here only yesterday."

Her words were met by eyes most unamused. "Varinar?" the gloomy knight repeated. "After all this...she's just...back in Varinar? Why did we even bother leaving?"

It was a thoroughly irritating question. "We can't have known how things would turn out, Connor Crawfield," Amara said to him, using his full name as she did when wanting to amply display her annoyance. "The important thing is, she's gone home and has not, I repeat *not*, been taken back in by that dastardly bastard of a grandfather of hers. By tomorrow morning, if luck will have it, we can all be back home as well, with this wearying chase behind us."

The seneschal stepped forward, hand clasped piously at the navel. "The

Great One has decreed you worthy of our aid. A longship will be provided to speed you hence." He clapped his hands. At once voices called out and one of the longships along the shore was pushed into the water, mustered and crewed by a complement of a dozen strong oarsmen. When he clipped his fingers, another man - a scribe, this one - hurried forward to hand him a quill-pen and parchment. The seneschal set about writing his list, then handed it over to Amara. "I hope it is not too bold, my lady."

She scanned, scoffed, and folded the paper in half, stuffing it into a pocket. "If I wasn't so desperate, I'd throw this back in your face. You'll have your gold and jewels, seneschal. But my friendship, no. You've spat on that."

The man made a face like he cared. "A great shame to hear," he said. He did not, however, amend the list. *Clearly my friendship isn't so valuable.* "I will have the sword and necklace returned." He whispered a word to one of his men, and off they went to fetch them.

When the sword and necklace had been brought out, Amara looked them over to make sure of their authenticity, got an assenting nod from Sir Connor that it was, indeed, the blade of Sir Daryl Blunt, handed it to her knight, and put Lillia's necklace into her inner coat pocket. It was one of the few pieces of jewellery that Lillia liked, a piece once worn by her mother Kessia, and the idea that she had to give it up to buy her freedom raised the heckles of Amara Daecar. She had half a mind to command her companions to draw their blades and get them all bloody, but the thought was fleeting.

"Pray we do not meet again," she merely said, to the seneschal.

"We won't," was his reply, delivered with that slimy smile.

Amara climbed aboard, Carly, Jovyn, and her two knights following. Beneath their weight, the longship groaned, though these vessels were deep and strong and designed to bear great loads. It would slow them, though, she knew that much. All of them were blindfolded, as before, their heads wrapped with lengths of thick black cloth. Then the captain gave a shout, the men on the banks gave a push, and the longship lurched into motion.

For a short while no one spoke. There was only the slap of the oars on water, the ringing sound of the oarmaster's voice as he called time. The sounds echoed loudly through the cavern, but when they drifted out through the mouth of the cave, a world of new noises opened out. Birds chirping, bees buzzing, the rush of the river, the sway of the trees. They went straight for a time, or so it seemed, before wending down through a series of different waterways, turning often, as though to intentionally confuse them.

"They're scared we'll find our way back," Sir Connor whispered into her ear. "These pirates have been a plague here for years."

More a minor irritant, Amara thought. She'd heard about these pirate dens in court from time to time, but rarely was it ever a passing issue for the king and greatlords to deal with, quickly set aside and forgotten. So it would be for her, she suspected. There were far more important things happening to the south, and she'd soon forget about these petty pirate lords.

The boat soon levelled out again, and beyond she heard the rush of the open sea. Lake Eshina was not a sea, of course, though it might as well have been, vast as it was. The winds picked up, tugging at her cloak, and she heard the sound of water crashing against the shore.

"Sounds rough out there," she heard Sir Penrose say. "I suppose we should prepare to get wet, my lady."

"Aye," said a voice down the ship. She heard a man stamping down toward them, between the banks of oarsmen. The captain, she knew, a squat man with a shovel beard, brown with a band of grey down the middle. From the brief look she'd had of him, he had crinkly eyes of the sort used to squinting and smiling. His voice had a Rasal twang to it. Most likely he had some Seaborn blood in him. "Hunker down, you lot," he told them. "You'll be dry enough at the front of the boat, but that ain't gonna stop all the spray. Just don't go doing anything stupid like standing up, least-ways not until your blindfolds come off. One of you goes over, we're not fishing you out."

"Your crew must love you," Amara said. "Do you have a name, Captain?"

"I have one, aye, though won't be sharing it. *Captain* will do just fine, if you want to hail me." He stamped away back to the stern.

They entered the lake shortly after, their blindfolds still tied fast about their eyes. Amara knew there were other islands around them, from the way the water crashed against the rocks, though how big or small they were she couldn't say. When they'd sailed through here earlier that morning, the lake had been calm, and covered in mist, and the islands had risen up around them like ghost ships, coming up suddenly and frightening from the shroud. It was then that the Great One's men had found them, three separate boats - a longship and two smaller skiffs - closing in from all sides, before blindfolding them and escorting them to the hidden sanctuary where their master dwelt. That journey had taken at least an hour, though whether they'd sailed five miles in that time, or ten, or simply circled around the same island over and over again, she couldn't hope to say.

It didn't matter, though. They'd gone sailing into those mists because they'd been told by a fisherman that Lillia had gone that way, and all had turned out for the best. *Now we just need to get home*, she thought. *Get home and find her and all will be well…*

The longship cut the waves nicely, though the going was slow as she'd feared. For a while they sailed straight, then turned left it seemed, then right, to suggest they were navigating around an island, or an expanse of dangerous shoals that might gut them from below. That happened several more times, before eventually they straightened out, and the waves grew bigger, swelling as they were prone to do out on the open sea. Amara hailed the captain by calling, "Captain!" and he stamped on down the boat.

"What is it?"

"Was the weather like this yesterday? Rough and stormy." She had to raise her voice over the wind; it had picked up quickly, and was gusting fiercely now.

"No. It was calm yesterday, barely a breath of wind in the air."

"So my niece would have had no trouble?"

"Not from the wind and the waves, no. But a calm sea ain't always a sweet thing, m'lady. Me personally...I prefer a bit o' churn. That eerie calm ain't right. Heard too many stories of sea-serpents and dark-hearted mermen emerging when the water's like that."

Lovely. Don't I feel a lot better.

"I thought sea monsters thrived in rougher weather," Carly said.

"Aye, some do. Not all. Dark mermen like the calm. They whisper beneath the water, and draw you to the edge, and wait just under the surface. When a man looks down, he thinks for a moment he's looking at his reflection, but no...it's one o' *them*. By the time he realises, it's too late. Heard o' a hundred seamen dragged down like that, right down to Daarl's Domain."

"And the sea serpents? They like the calm too, do they?" Carly didn't sound in the least bit afraid.

"Aye. Easier to reach up and snatch a man from the deck when he's all relaxed. Rougher weather keeps us on our toes out here. Makes us wary, harder to catch."

"What other monsters are there?"

"A hundred others, boy," the captain said eagerly, to Jovyn's question. "And much worse than serpents and mermen too." He gave a laugh. "Surprise you, does it? Folk think all the beasties prowl the seas, but that's not so. It's just as dangerous here. Some even think there's a great underwater channel that goes all the way south to the Read Sea, and up north to the Shivering Expanse as well. The monsters use it to come here, sometimes, when the season's right."

Amara sensed the captain was enjoying this a little too much, though had no interest in hearing more. Thankfully, his duties called him away, as he returned to the stern to navigate.

The weather did not improve. For over an hour the longship rocked from side to side and up and down, battling against the swells as the oarmaster called out, "stroke...stroke...stroke..." to keep the men working as one. It was during that period that the captain removed their blindfolds, at which point there was nothing to see but open water, waves and white-caps, churning all around them. The sky was the colour of a corpse, a sort of sickly greyish white, though before too long the sun was setting and there was nothing to see but black.

"Gonna be a long night," the captain warned them. "You should try to get some rest, if you can. Here, this'll help."

He handed her a clay bottle. She pulled the cord, sniffed, smelled whiskey, thanked the man and took a swig, then proceeded to pass it around.

"More where that came from, if you want it," the captain said. "Just don't overdo it. Tonight's not a night to be emptying your guts overboard. You slip in the drink and you're gone. We won't even hear the splash."

Amara settled down against the bulwark, taking her turn to drink whenever the bottle came her way. It did not take long before she had it all to herself, as the others waved it away and settled down to get some sleep, curling up in their cloaks in whatever comfortable nooks they could find. Only Sir Connor remained awake, though he did not touch a drop. "I must remain clear-headed," he proclaimed. "Someone has to stay on watch."

My noble knight. She left him to his solemn duty, swigging on the bottle alone, wondering about a great many things as the longboat rocked and rolled. *The war,* she thought. What was happening in the war? Had the Agarathi crossed the Red Sea yet? What was happening in the east? Tidings had been poor on the lake. It turned out the local fisherfolk knew but little of wider matters, and cared even less, and even when they'd ended up in Elinar, the great city on the northern shore, they'd heard little in the way of reliable reports from the soldiers at the gate, and the traders in the square.

I'll find out soon, Amara told herself. They would be sure to know more in Varinar, and she could always count upon Lady Bradbury, her dear old friend, to fill her in on all the latest gossips she'd heard. *I'll visit with Sir Hank as well.* The Rothwell knight had been left in charge of the city defences along with Sir Bomfrey Sharp and Sir Winslow Bryant. If anyone had word from King's Point and the Twinfort and the cities of East Vandar, it was them. *Maybe Elyon has returned too, to update them,* she thought. That felt likely to her, in the time that she'd been gone. He would want to make sure the capital was kept abreast of important developments, she knew, and only Elyon could be relied upon to deliver messages quickly.

I'll find out soon, she thought again, taking another swig of the captain's strong dark whiskey. There was no sense in dwelling on it, when the answers were so near. *Come tomorrow, I'll know.* What she could do about any of it was another matter, though. *Nothing,* in truth, that was the long and the short of it. It was the curse of women - most women, anyway - to be almost entirely helpless during wartime, relying only on their men to steer their people to victory. That wasn't always so, of course - the Rasalanians had had many queens in the past, and even in Tukor and Vandar there had been occasions when powerful houses had been ruled by greatladies, rather than greatlords - but for the most part women in the north where good for two things; wedding and bedding, so they might make alliances and make children, producing more little lordlings and heroic gallant knights to win the wars like this one.

But I couldn't even do that, Amara Daecar lamented. *I was married off to Vesryn, yes, but never did I bear him a son.* If that was her duty and her purpose, she had failed, and while Vesryn liked to claim that his treachery had cursed them, perhaps that had never been so. *Maybe it was just me,* she thought. *Maybe I was just not fit to be a mother?* The gods had given her some wit, and some cunning, and a tongue to deliver those famous sallies and barbs…but not a womb that worked. *I'd sooner have the working womb than the acid tongue,* she thought bitterly. *Make me a mute, and give me a child, and I'll call that a fair bargain.*

She had another long gulp of whiskey, with half a mind to drink herself into oblivion, as she'd done so often before. Lady Bradbury had told her that she should give up on Vesryn, stop visiting him in his cell, find another man, another lover, another husband to make her happy. The old woman had even suggested that Amara could still bear a child, if she found the right man, but that was missing the point. "That ship has sailed," had been Amara's reply. And as far as she was concerned, Vesryn had always been the right man. No one had ever made her laugh half so hard, and no one had ever made her feel half so loved. That their marriage had been arranged by Janilah Lukar had never made a jot of difference to her. From the seeds of treachery, a great love had grown. That had always been enough for Amara Daecar. *Just enough*, she thought. *Just enough…*

Sleep took her, and the sweetness of dreams. Dreams that were part memory, part fantasy, where she and Vesryn had had children of their own, a tall strong son and a beautiful brilliant daughter, with all the future ahead of them. The daughter looked much like Lillia, of course, and the son a mix of Elyon and Aleron, and sometimes, in the dream, all of them would be there together, in the family feast hall of Keep Daecar, her and Vesryn and their children and Amron and Kessia and theirs. Such a joy it was, such fun, full of laughter and drinking and dancing. A perfect family. A perfect image.

And a lie, she knew, even as she slept. *Nothing but a cold cruel lie…*

The dream changed, shifting. She was on the wide stone terrace of her bedchamber with Vesryn, just she and her husband alone. Beneath them the great unbreachable city of Varinar spread out, with its ten ancient hills ringed by the inner walls, and the many other rises beyond, topped with their towers and forts. Vesryn looked south, careworn and pale. The wind tugged at his cloak, a Daecar cloak, swaying heroically to the side as it caught in a sudden breeze. "Take care of her," he said. "Promise me you will."

Amara did not understand. He was talking about Lillia, he must have been. "I will," she promised him. "Always, and forever."

He nodded, a single dip of the chin. There was something final about that. "The shadow is coming, Amara. You must be strong. You must be strong for them."

I am strong, she thought. She had never doubted that. "I will be," she said. "But do not give up hope, Vesryn. Amron…he may yet change his mind. There is still a chance you'll be pardoned, in time."

Her husband stared out, fixed like stone, and his lips did not part in answer. She clutched his hand, and found it cold as ice. "You're freezing," she whispered, frightened. "Why are you so cold?"

"Be strong for them, Amara," Vesryn merely repeated, in a strange fading voice, as though he was far away. He stared out across the world below, firelight glimmering in his eyes. "The shadow is coming. It comes for us all. The shadow…and the flame."

She awoke with a start. Sir Connor Crawfield was crouching over her, gently shaking her awake. Her heart was hammering at her ribcage. *A dream, just a dream…* She could feel the longship rocking beneath her, though the motion was gentle, and there was no sound of 'stroke', no splash of oars on water. *We've stopped*, she realised. The skies above her were odd, a strange blend of colours and clouds, though the night had passed, and the day had sprung. "What time is it?" she breathed.

"A few hours past dawn." Sir Connor's voice was choked. Beyond him the others were standing, staring, all in the same direction. All the oarsmen, and the oarmaster, and the captain, and Sir Penrose. Only Carly and Jovyn remained asleep. "My lady…you need to see."

See? Cold fingers climbed her spine. Connor Crawfield gave her his hand, and helped her to her feet. There was an ache in her lower back, and a crick in her neck, and her right leg was cramping, but all of that was fast forgotten when she looked across the lake…

…and saw the flames, saw the smoke, saw the swarming leathern wings…saw the towers falling, the keeps crumbling, saw the great red haze burning in the skies, the thick black smog billowing up from a thousand fires. It covered the city, and the bridge, and the Steelforge on its island, and the lands along the lake, and the waters of the lake itself, a roiling mass of toxic fume spreading out across the north.

Gods…

Amara blinked, as though it was all a nightmare. *I'm sleeping. I must be sleeping still. This cannot be happening. It cannot.* "Connor…" she started…and cut herself off. Through the shroud of fume above the city, a shape passed by, a vast winged shadow to dwarf the rest. Sir Connor Crawfield sucked in a breath; the oarsmen behind her did the same. Then suddenly, from nowhere, someone shouted, "We turn back! We *have* to turn back! We have to turn back now! Now!"

"A monster," someone else screamed.

"Dread," a man wailed. "The Dread. We're doomed! Back! Back!"

The men rushed into motion, snatching up oars, desperately pulling at the water. The captain was shouting orders for them to make haste; Sir Connor and Sir Penrose rushed back to confront him. "Take us to shore," she heard Connor Crawfield bellow. "You said you'd take us to shore…"

"The shore's gone," the captain said. "The city's destroyed. To the oars, men! We row back! Back!"

More arguing ensued. Amara had the sense of Sir Connor drawing his blade, making threats and demands, but it all soon became a blur. She could only stand there, staring, trembling as she watched her city burn. Her bowels had gone to water, her eyes were swimming with tears, and all the hope in the world was lost.

She returned only yesterday, she was thinking, heart rending in two. *Only yesterday…my Lillia, my sweet young Lillia…*

For three and a half thousand years men had said the city of Varinar was unbreachable.

For three and a half thousand years…every one of them had been wrong.

EPILOGUE

Ranulf

The *First Tree* loomed before him, five hundred metres tall.

Around its base roots as thick as the biggest northern sequoias Ranulf had ever seen gouged and twisted down into the soil, anchoring the monstrosity to the earth, glowing with luminous mushrooms and mosses, given light by the goddess Aramatia. The trunk was fifty metres across, colossal, so vast a greathall could be carved out into the wood. Above branched out ten thousand limbs and boughs, leaves of light swaying in their millions, glittering with iridescent dust.

The *Second Elder* stood beside him, dressed in his feathered robes; white about the shoulders, dark brown from chest to shin. His feet were bare, dextrous and tough. Thick grey hair flowed across his head like the feathers on an eagle's dome, and around his neck hung a string of talons, clacking softly with each step. *From the eagles he has loved and lost*, Ranulf knew. *He keeps them by his heart, always.* The Elder lifted a hand and gestured toward the tree, looming impossibly before them. "Take the stair, Ranulf Shackton," he said. "The *First Elder* is awaiting you in his eyrie."

Ranulf craned his neck up, swallowing. The stair was comprised of countless wooden steps, spiralling around and around the great trunk of the tree, up and up and up to eternity, lost to the dense canopy above. Each was fixed to the bark by a phosphorescent adhesive sap, a thousand little lights to mark the way.

So many, Ranulf thought, shuddering. *So high.*

So far as he could see, there was no safety rope to cling to, nothing to stop him should he trip and fall. *And the winds are sure to be gusting up there.*

The Second Elder sensed his worry. "Do not be afraid, Ranulf Shackton," he told him, in his calm and reassuring voice. "My eagles will be watching you as you make the ascent. They will steady you if you should wobble or threaten to fall, but truly, you will not need them. You are a great mountaineer, I know, and unafraid of heights. Keep your hand on the bark of the tree at all times; you will find many handholds there to steady you, and give you strength."

Ranulf nodded, saying nothing. He had climbed many mountains, true, and scaled high cliffs as well, but somehow this felt different. Those occasions were for him, personal adventures and selfish endeavours, but this was another matter. He had come here to make a plea of great importance, to ask permission to pass through the woods so that Saska and her companions could reach the northern shores. So far as Ranulf saw it, it was the safest and surest way to Vandar, but without the consent of the First Elder, he'd have to trundle back to Aram empty-handed, in failure.

No, he thought, defiant. *We've come much too far for that.*

"How many steps are there?" he asked the old man. All the Elders here were old, even if they didn't look it. The Second made claim to have lived for a hundred and ninety years, though looked no older than fifty to Ranulf's eyes.

"Many thousands, Ranulf Shackton. But do not let that unman you. Take your time, enjoy the views, stop when you need to rest. But please, do not take *too* long...or you may miss your opportunity."

Another cryptic remark. The Second Elder was full of them. "Opportunity for what, pray tell?"

"To see him, before the rest of us do. That the First Elder has summoned you to his eyrie today, of all days, is a great honour, Ranulf Shackton, and one I hope you are worthy of. To be first to look upon him. To see his light and feel his warmth and bathe beneath his power." His amber eyes glittered. "We have waited a long time, my friend. So very long. But do not let me spoil the surprise. Watch for the second sun, for his light will be as bright as the sudden coming of day. Blinding and brilliant. The First Elder will tell you more. Now go, and no more talking. My eagles will be with you."

Ranulf did not understand much of that, but he'd grown used to the man's mysterious ways and knew not to probe for answers. *I will get them at the top*, he thought, turning again toward the stair, steeling himself for the ascent. And under the spreading blush of dawn, with the sun climbing up to touch the tops of the great trees, he stepped forward to begin the climb.

One by one, step by step, he rose, circling. Around the First Tree, the other eleven of the famous Twelve Trees of Aramatia were spread across a great vast glade, a magical clearing at the heart of the Everwood, full of light and warmth and song. Silver streams twinkled as they crisscrossed between the trunks, and across the glade were magnificent meadows of multicoloured flowers that danced radiant by day, and glowed brilliantly by night. It was a world of wonders beyond anything Ranulf could have imagined. Truly, he had never looked upon a place so grand and beautiful as this.

The Calacania watched him as he went, hundreds of eyes, thousands of them, all peering from their perches. Many of them lived in huts and homes carved from the great Everwood nuts. Many more preferred the open-air living of nests, giant nests akin to those of their eagle brethren made from sticks and leaves and soft woodland grasses. Others still had taken to sleeping in vine hammocks, swinging precariously hundreds of metres above the ground. None slept on the earth, save those enduring punishment for a crime, or suffering a temporary exile. As Ranulf had come to understand it, such matters were rare. "We have not had a crime here in a decade," the Second Elder had proudly told him once.

These communities were not built into the First Tree, however. Here alone the First Elder lived, wandering through the branches, pondering the woes of the world from his high and holy eyric. *And now, finally, I get to join him there…*

It did not take long for Ranulf's thighs to begin to burn, and shortly after that, they were screaming. Each step rose a foot above the one before it, and all were spaced apart as well, some by six inches, others by twelve, a few by twenty or more. Between each was a yawning chasm, a void that grew more terrifying the higher he went. *Don't look down*, was the common advice during such perilous ascents, yet in this case Ranulf had no choice; each time he placed his foot on the next step, he caught a heart-stopping glance to the world below. Yet for all that, the Second Elder had not been wrong. Heights held no fear for a man like Ranulf Shackton. Nay, he had always rather enjoyed them.

At a hundred metres above the ground, the first of the great branches began to appear, so wide they could easily accommodate a half dozen carts lined up side by side. Unlike most sequoias, which were typically fairly narrow, many of these branches spread out broadly, and as soon as Ranulf had passed the first level of them, he was swallowed up in a world of light as the leaves shone out, silver and radiant. The winds moved through them, causing them to hum and murmur in an ethereal melody, as though there was a choir of angels spurring him on.

He needed no such motivation. Ranulf had come for Saska, come for her quest, come for the very saving of the world. If he had to climb up and down this tree a hundred times for that, he would. There was no greater cause on this earth, yet all the same, the sounds were truly beautiful…

At three hundred metres, he began to get glimpses through the branches, to the tops of some of the other Twelve Trees. Almost all the Calacania were down below him, dwelling as they did between a hundred and two hundred metres high. Only the Twelve Elders lived higher, strolling among the branches of their own trees, living within their own private eyries.

Yet none nearly so high as this.

At four hundred metres, the branches were thinning above him. The views had turned spectacular, and the tops of the other trees were now at his eye level, or below. And *beyond…*

Ranulf had to stop and catch his breath, steadying himself against the bark. The *Greater Everwood* was cast below him, the forest spreading out to the edge of his sight. *The lesser sons of grander sires,* someone had called the trees once…for though larger than all other trees in the world, with great looming pines and massive hulking sentinels, they were still dwarfed by the twelve that Aramatia herself had planted.

He indulged the view for a few moments only, knowing it would grow greater still. On he went, step by step, touching glowing leaves as he went, feeling the warmth on the tips of his fingers. Colossal limbs reached out from the trunk, branching into a hundred others, each growing smaller as they spread. Yet even the smaller ones were large. *A twig up here is like a trunk of an oak tree down there*, Ranulf Shackton thought. He smiled, as a soft singing wind moved through his lengthening hair. Grooming had taken a step back on the road, and he was bearded, hirsute, more woolly than he'd been in a while. He wondered for a moment if he should have taken the chance to shave, before meeting with this ancient leader. *Perhaps I ought to pop back down and get Kentu or Tallar Munsoor to cut my hair?* He chuckled out loud, almost giggly, and kept on going, step after step.

Another ten minutes passed; around and around he went. Another five; he did another part-circuit. The trunk was positively skinny up here, only about the size of the biggest redwood he'd ever seen. *Pathetic*, he thought, grinning. *You call yourself a Tree of Aramatia? Branches to the Blackness Above? Pfft. I've seen hillocks more grand than you.*

He giggled like a child; the end was oh-so near. Above him now he could see a place where the top of the trunk seemed to flatten, as though creating a natural platform above, right at the very summit.

The eyrie.

There seemed no way through it at first, but as he got closer he saw an opening in the branches, a sort of ladder that led the way. Above, he could see clear air, bright and unspoilt, hear the wind swirling and singing. The sun had climbed along its morning arc, long past dawn. *I've been climbing for hours*, he realised. It had felt much shorter, somehow, the climb driving a thrill into his bones. His heart was pumping, his legs tingling from the burn in his thighs. *This is it*, he thought. *He's just up there, awaiting me…*

Ranulf Shackton did not delay. He drew a final steadying breath, climbed the branch ladder, and stepped out upon the eyrie, where the First Elder stood alone, waiting.

"You came at last," he said.

His eyes were burnished amber, as deep and dark as bottomless wells, his robes of feathered plumage, mixed gold and bronze and silver, resplendent. From his chin swayed a long white beard, catching in the breeze like a banner. Long unruly eyebrows leapt from his brow, white as snow, making him look more eagle-like than many of his kin. They cast his eyes with a glaring look, though the smile on his lips undid it. "I feared you might have taken a tumble on the way up, Ranulf," he added, with a crinkly smile. "What a relief to see you. Just try not to think of the way back down."

Oh. Ranulf hadn't even considered it, fool that he was. He did not let it dampen his spirits, however, as he staggered up to his feet and righted himself, straightening down his sweaty soiled clothes, and bending his back in a bow. He felt like a pauper standing with a prince, a cobbler with a king. The First Elder was magnificent, and that feathered cloak was the finest he had ever seen, glittering in the colours of Aramatia. Ranulf had been wearing the same cotton and linen clothes for more weeks than he cared to recall. He was suddenly acutely aware of how badly he smelled.

"Do you speak not, Ranulf? I was told you liked to speak."

"Sorry…First Elder. I'm a little…well, I'm a little overwhelmed. The view…" He looked out, taking in the vista for the first time. It was truly astonishing. All-encompassing. Eternal. The Greater Everwood was all around him, the Twelve Trees below, looking smaller than he could have ever thought from up here, so high above them all. The open glade in the forest was almost perfectly square, he realised. He could see pools and streams, fields and meadows, see the Calacania at their work; soil-servers, leaf-gatherers, tree-tenders, nut-carvers, hunters and fishers and teachers and prayer-leaders and men and women of a dozen other duties. Upon the eyrie, at least two dozen eagles were perched here and there, spread out across the great high nest. And great it was, a plateau made of twigs and leaves and grasses, twenty metres by twenty, a perch atop the world.

"You must be thirsty, Ranulf. And weary from the climb. Please, do sit." To one side, the twigs and branches had been worked into a pair of chairs, with a sort of table between them. The First Elder led him over. On the table was a large wooden jug, though no cups from which to drink. The old man put his lips together and gave a whistle, and at once an eagle descended with a pair of cups in its talons, placing them deftly upon the table, flapping away.

The First Elder poured. "The water is most refreshing here, you will find."

He drank deep. Icy tendrils reached in to cool the burning in his chest, and somehow his legs felt revived, the ache in his thighs diminishing.

"The Spring of Aramatia. It has wonderful properties." The old man refilled Ranulf's cup. "Now tell me, Ranulf, how was your journey here?"

Ranulf drank, wiped his mouth, put down his cup and said, "Uneventful, if you would believe it. We had expected resistance on the road, with everything that's been happening. There are many strange creatures climbing from their…"

"I know, Ranulf. I have been watching a great number of them. And you, of course, and your companions. Kentu is a fine guide, and I'm sure that Sunrider Munsoor and his gallant men are stout warriors, capable of battling away any fell beast, but still…I thought it prudent to ease your passing here. It is not typically my duty to interfere, but alas in this case I helped 'clear the road', so to speak."

Ranulf was not entirely understanding. Perhaps his grasp of Aramatian, in which they spoke, was not quite so perfect as he thought, but still… "You mean…*you* made sure we didn't run into trouble?" he asked. "How?"

"My eagles. They can be terribly annoying, you know, when I ask them to be. Have you ever had a fly buzzing about your face, Ranulf? And no matter how many times you swat at it, it simply will not go away? Well, there were one or two occasions when a rather unpleasant creature was nearing your path of travel as you crossed the plains. I thought it wise to… annoy them, and lead them in another direction, so as not to impede you. I wanted you here, you see, *today*. You, Ranulf Shackton, who is one of the chosen, one of the great guides of this world. I thought you deserved the right to be here, when he returned."

Ranulf stared at him. "He? *Who* is returning, my lord?"

"Lord? No, we use no such titles here, Ranulf. Did the Second Elder not tell you?" He grinned and took a sip of sweet spring water, setting his cup aside. "I know you to be a man of wonder, Ranulf, a man of adventure. You have spent your life chasing dreams and hunting mysteries, going to places where most men would not dare to tread. Haunted hills and cursed forests and islands teeming with foul and loathsome things, pirates and cannibals and demons, and creatures even worse than that. You have the courage of a Moonrider, Ranulf Shackton. Even climbing up here today has proven it so, an ascent that so few others would dare to make. Had you been born with the Light of Lumo in your veins, or the Steel of Varin, or the Fire of Eldur, I wonder what you might have been? Would you have bonded a great moonbear, Ranulf? Would you have risen up as a great Bladeborn warrior? Would you be flying atop a dragon, even now, as they assault the north…as they lay siege to its very heart."

"Its *heart*?" Ranulf broke in. If there was a beating heart in the north, few would argue against it being Varinar. But no, he could not believe that was so. "The Agarathi…have they…"

"Varinar is destroyed, Ranulf Shackton. Destroyed by Drulgar the Dread, and the thunder that follows in his wake. This happened only two days ago. Kamcho was there. Kamcho saw it all." An eagle spread its wings and gave a solemn bow.

Ranulf blinked at it. He could not muster words. There had been a rumour of Drulgar's return, but… "You…you saw?"

"Kamcho saw. And thus so did I. Achto was there as well, and Malatan, but both of them perished, I am sad to say." He bowed his head in grief, and all the eagles followed. "Only Kamcho made it back, but even before their deaths, I watched the destruction of Varinar through the eyes of Achto and Malatan as well. Many dragons perished in the fight, but Drulgar…he is unstoppable, Ranulf Shackton, a calamity from an ancient time. Pierced by a hundred bolts, he fought on, and on, and on, in his rage and his wrath, and did not stop until half the city was rubble, and the rest of it was burning. Varinar has always been a thorn in his mind. He wanted to destroy it, no matter the risk, no matter the cost. Now the city has fallen, and the north lies in disarray. Varinar, no more. Varin, dead."

Ranulf sucked a breath. "*Varin*? Do you mean to say…"

"No," the First Elder said, raising a palm. "No, Varin has not arisen, as Eldur has. Would that that were so, but no, we must rely on others to fight this darkness. Yet on the battlefield outside of the city of King's Point, Drulgar fought Varin nonetheless, or a shadow of him, an echo, as he saw it, a man in shining godsteel armour, bearing the Sword of Varinar in his grasp. The Dread slew this man, Ranulf, and he destroyed Varin's city. Now, what drives him, I wonder? Will he bring further chaos to the north, to the world? Will he settle back upon his Nest, to rest, and to sleep?"

But surely you know, Ranulf thought. *You who see all.* He had so many questions. "Was it Amron Daecar?" he asked. "This man. This Varin."

The old Elder shook his head. "His brother. As far as I am aware, Amron Daecar still lives, and his son, who bears the Windblade. But of the other bearers, I do not know. As much as I see, I do not see *everything.* Many of my eagles have perished, Ranulf, by fire and by fang and by claw. It dims my sight, and in the north especially, dangers abound in the skies."

A wound. Each one a wound, Ranulf knew. He could hear the grief in the Elder's voice. "What else have you seen?" he asked, softly.

"Much...and more. I have watched cities fall, and castles burn, and armies clash in storms of steel. These last days, Ranulf...well, I have been kept busy, shall we say. Even if I had wished to summon you sooner, it was not possible, not until today. Yet as fate would allow, today is the perfect day for you to have climbed up here to meet me. Darkness spreads, and the light comes forth to meet it. Today, we shall see a *bright* light, Ranulf. Returning to the world, at last."

The First Elder looked down from his eyrie. Across the glade, the Calacania were stopping in their work, putting down their hoes and nets and tools, gathering into groups. Those still in the trees were gazing up from their platforms and perches. In great nests, prayer groups hummed. Hundreds of eagles, perhaps thousands of them, swarmed the branches, waiting.

"You have come here to ask if you may be granted passage to the north. This is not a request you need to make, Ranulf Shackton. It is by the very will of Lumo, and of Thala, the Far-Seeing Queen, that we are prepared to grant you all the help we can offer."

"She came *here?*" Ranulf asked, reading between the lines. "Thala?"

"Thousands of years ago, yes. When the Twelve Trees were yet young, no more than saplings, and the Greater Everwood had not yet taken seed. She came here together with Lumo, Mother of the Moon, to speak to the very first of us, before we were known as the Calacania, before the eagles came." He looked around at the birds. More were gathering, landing atop his eyrie, their long hooked beaks and amber eyes trained skyward. "You believe, do you not, that those of us here who can bond the eagles derive from an ancient Lightborn line?"

Ranulf nodded. "It's said that one of Lumo's early Lightborn came here, and first learned to bond with the eagles. Some say it was one of Lumo's grandchildren. Others a great-grandchild. Most agree it was a man. From his blood were born the Elders." He met the old man's eyes. "Is that not the truth, First Elder?"

"No, Ranulf, that is not the truth. The truth is rather more tragic, a duty and a sacrifice asked of Lumo herself by the Far-Seeing Queen. When they came here, Lumo's pack numbered two dozen. Eleven starcats, eleven sunwolves, and the famous moonbear twins, Gatosh and Latosh, from whose bloodlines other great bears have been born."

Agarosh, Ranulf thought. It was said he was of the line of Latosh.

"Already at this time, the number of animals that Lumo's lesser kin could bond was dwindling. And Lumo herself was ageing, her light beginning to diminish. Thus did Thala ask of her to make a sacrifice, Ranulf. To pass the last of her light to us. To begin the line of Elders, so we might bond the eagles, and watch the world. She gave up what mattered to her most, her bonds to her beloved pack, the very essence of her life-force. In mere years she had aged rapidly, and when she came to perish, she did so with only a single starcat remaining tethered to her will. Salania, who was her youngest. All the rest left her, to walk the plains and the mountains and the woods alone, in shadow….and in grief."

A tear rolled down the old man's cheek, wending through wrinkles, soaking into his long white beard. "I am called the First Elder, Ranulf, but in truth I am the *Tenth* First, following on from the nine who have come before me. From one to the other is passed a great power, and a great burden; to watch, and to wait. For almost three hundred years I have waited, under the instruction that the Far-Seeing Queen gave to my ancient ancestor. To him she spoke of what she had seen in the Eye of Rasalan. Of this spreading darkness, and the light that *must* meet it. Some of that light shines in *you*, Ranulf Shackton, he who is part of Thala's Puzzle. You carry knowledge, and secrets, and courage, above all. You have guided Varin's heir, taught her, instructed her, and come here for her, so she might travel safely to the north. *Light*, Ranulf. It shines from you, and from her, and from many others across this world. In the north and the south and the east and the west, there are those who are working to drive the darkness away. And from the skies, Ranulf. Light comes from the *skies*, as well."

He looked up. The eagles looked up. The Calacania looked up from their perches and platforms. Atop each of the Twelve Trees, the Elders had taken their places, standing upon their own high eyries, staring into the skies.

Second sun, Ranulf thought, reflecting on the Second Elder's words. *Watch for the second sun, for his light will be as bright as the sudden coming of day. Blinding…and brilliant.*

And there, in the skies above them, suddenly…it *shone*. A bright light, blinding and brilliant, casting a golden sunburst across the world. Ranulf raised a hand to shield his eyes, squinting, and from that great golden glow, a shape appeared, wings outstretched, plumage fluttering, beak opening to emit an echoing screech that sent the very hairs on the back of Ranulf's neck rising.

Open-eyed he stared, as the great eagle flew down, returning to the world at last.

Darkness spreads…and the light shines to meet it…

Calacan, the Eagle of Aramatia, had come.

THE END

The Bladeborn Saga will continue in Book 6 - coming soon!

If you'd be so kind as to leave a review or rating for this book, that would be hugely appreciated. I truly value the support and feedback. Many thanks for reading this far!

Printed in Great Britain
by Amazon

40009696R00463